CLASSIC FICTION

The Classic Works of

JACK

LONDON

Bounty
Books

The Call of the Wild was first published in 1903
The Sea-Wolf was first published in 1904
White Fang was first published in 1906
The Son of the Wild was first published in 1900
The Iron Heel was first published in 1908
The People of the Abyss was first published in 1903

This collected edition was first published in Great Britain in 1983 by
Octopus Books Limited

This edition published in 2014 by Bounty Books
A division of Octopus Publishing Group Ltd
Endeavour House, 189 Shaftesbury Avenue, London WC2H 8JY

www.octopusbooks.co.uk

An Hachette UK Company
www.hachette.co.uk
Design and arrangement © 2014 Octopus Publishing Group Ltd

ISBN: 978-0-753728-17-8

A CIP catalogue record for this title is available at the British Library
Printed in China

CLASSIC FICTION

JACK LONDON

THE CALL
OF THE WILD

INTO THE PRIMITIVE

'Old longings nomadic leap,
Chafing at custom's chain;
Again from its brumal sleep
Wakens the ferine strain.'

Buck did not read the newspapers, or he would have known that trouble was brewing, not alone for himself, but for every tide-water dog, strong of muscle and with warm, long hair, from Puget Sound to San Diego. Because men, groping in the Arctic darkness, had found a yellow metal, and because steamship and transportation companies were booming the find, thousands of men were rushing into the Northland. These men wanted dogs, and the dogs they wanted were heavy dogs, with strong muscles by which to toil, and furry coats to protect them from the frost.

Buck lived at a big house in the sun-kissed Santa Clara Valley. Judge Miller's place, it was called. It stood back from the road, half hidden among the trees, through which glimpses could be caught of the wide cool veranda that ran around its four sides. The house was approached by gravelled driveways which wound about through wide-spreading lawns and under the interlacing boughs of tall poplars. At the rear things were on even a more spacious scale than at the front. There were great stables, where a dozen grooms and boys held forth, rows of vine-clad servants' cottages, an endless and orderly array of outhouses, long grape arbors, green pastures, orchards, and berry patches. Then there was the pumping plant for the artesian well, and the big cement tank where Judge Miller's boys took their morning plunge and kept cool in the hot afternoon.

And over this great demesne Buck ruled. Here he was born, and here he had lived the four years of his life. It was true, there were other dogs, There could not but be other dogs on so vast a place, but they did not count. They came and went, resided in the populous kennels, or lived obscurely in the recesses of the house after the fashion of Toots, the Japanese pug, or Ysabel, the Mexican hairless,—strange creatures that rarely put nose out of doors or set foot to ground. On the other hand, there were the fox terriers, a score of them at least, who yelped fearful promises at Toots and Ysabel looking out of the windows at them and protected by a legion of housemaids armed with brooms and mops.

But Buck was neither house-dog nor kennel-dog. The whole realm was his. He plunged into the swimming tank or went hunting with the Judge's sons; he escorted Mollie and Alice, the Judge's daughters, on long twilight or early morning rambles; on wintry nights he lay at the Judge's feet before the roaring library fire; he carried the Judge's grandsons on his back, or rolled them in the grass, and guarded their footsteps through wild adventures down to the fountain in the stable yard, and even beyond, where the paddocks were, and the berry patches. Among the terriers he stalked imperiously, and Toots and Ysabel he utterly ignored, for he was king,—king over all creeping, crawling, flying things of Judge Miller's place, humans included.

His father, Elmo, a huge St. Bernard, had been the Judge's inseparable companion, and Buck bid fair to follow in the way of his father. He was not so large,—he weighed only one hundred and forty pounds,—for his mother, Shep, had been a Scotch shepherd dog. Nevertheless, one hundred and forty pounds, to which was added the dignity that comes of good living and universal respect, enabled him to carry himself in right royal fashion. During the four years since his puppyhood he had lived the life of a sated aristocrat; he had a fine pride in himself, was even a trifle egotistical, as country gentlemen sometimes become because of their insular situation. But he had saved himself by not becoming a mere pampered house-dog. Hunting and kindred outdoor delights had kept down the fat and hardened his muscles; and to him, as to the cold-tubbing races, the love of water had been a tonic and a health preserver.

And this was the manner of dog Buck was in the fall of 1897, when the Klondike strike dragged men from all the world into the frozen North. But Buck did not read the newspapers, and he did not know that Manuel, one of the gardener's helpers, was an undesirable acquaintance. Manuel had one besetting sin. He loved to play Chinese lottery. Also, in his gambling, he had one besetting weakness—faith in a system; and this made his damnation certain. For to play a system requires money, while the wages of a gardener's helper do not lap over the needs of a wife and numerous progeny.

The Judge was at a meeting of the Raisin Growers' Association, and the boys were busy organizing an athletic club, on the memorable night of Manuel's treachery. No one saw him and Buck go off through the orchard on what Buck imagined was merely a stroll. And with the exception of a solitary man, no one saw them arrive at the little flag station known as College Park. This man talked with Manuel, and money chinked between them.

'You might wrap up the goods before you deliver 'm,' the stranger said gruffly, and Manuel doubled a piece of stout rope around Buck's neck under the collar.

'Twist it, an' you'll choke 'm plentee,' said Manuel, and the stranger grunted a ready affirmative.

Buck had accepted the rope with quiet dignity. To be sure, it was an unwonted performance: but he had learned to trust in men he knew, and to give them credit for a wisdom that outreached his own. But when the ends of the rope were placed in the stranger's hands, he growled menacingly. He had merely intimated his displeasure, in his pride believing that to intimate was to command. But to his surprise the rope tightened around his neck, shutting off his breath. In quick rage he sprang at the man, who met him halfway, grappled him close by the throat, and with a deft twist threw him over on his back. Then the rope tightened mercilessly, while Buck struggled in a fury, his tongue lolling out of his mouth and his great chest panting futilely. Never in all his life had he been so vilely treated, and never in all his life had he been so angry. But his strength ebbed, his eyes glazed, and he knew nothing when the train was flagged and the two men threw him into the baggage car.

The next he knew, he was dimly aware that his tongue was hurting and that he was being jolted along in some kind of a conveyance. The hoarse shriek of a locomotive whistling a crossing told him where he was. He had travelled too often with the Judge not to know the sensation of riding in a baggage car. He opened his eyes, and into them came the unbridled anger of a kidnapped king. The man sprang for his throat, but Buck was too quick for him. His jaws closed on the hand, nor did they relax till his senses were choked out of him once more.

'Yep, has fits,' the man said, hiding his mangled hand from the baggageman, who had been attracted by the sounds of struggle. 'I'm takin' 'm up for the boss to 'Frisco. A crack dog-doctor there thinks that he can cure 'm.'

Concerning that night's ride, the man spoke most eloquently for himself, in a little shed back of a saloon on the San Francisco water front.

'All I get is fifty for it,' he grumbled; 'an' I wouldn't do it over for a thousand, cold cash.'

His hand was wrapped in a bloody handkerchief, and the right trouser leg was ripped from knee to ankle.

'How much did the other mug get?' the saloon-keeper demanded.

'A hundred,' was the reply. 'Wouldn't take a sou less, so help me.'

'That makes a hundred and fifty,' the saloon-keeper calculated; 'and he's worth it, or I'm a squarehead.'

The kidnapper undid the bloody wrappings and looked at his lacerated hand. 'If I don't get the hydrophoby—'

'It'll be because you was born to hang,' laughed the saloon-keeper. 'Here, lend me a hand before you pull your freight,' he added.

Dazed, suffering intolerable pain from throat and tongue, with the life half throttled out of him, Buck attempted to face his tormentors. But he was thrown down and choked repeatedly, till they succeeded in filing the heavy brass collar from off his neck. Then the rope was removed, and he was flung into a cagelike crate.

There he lay for the remainder of the weary night, nursing his wrath and wounded pride. He could not understand what it all meant. What did they want with him, these strange men? Why were they keeping him pent up in this narrow crate? He did not know why, but he felt oppressed by the vague sense of impending calamity. Several times during the night he sprang to his feet when the shed door rattled open, expecting to see the Judge, or the boys at least. But each time it was the bulging face of the saloon-keeper that peered in at him by the sickly light of a tallow candle. And each time the joyful bark that trembled in Buck's throat was twisted into a savage growl.

But the saloon-keeper let him alone, and in the morning four men entered and picked up the crate. More tormentors, Buck decided, for they were evil-looking creatures, ragged and unkempt; and he stormed and raged at them through the bars. They only laughed and poked sticks at him, which he promptly assailed with his teeth till he realized that that was what they wanted. Whereupon he lay down sullenly and allowed the crate to be lifted into a wagon. Then he, and the crate in which he was imprisoned, began a passage through many hands. Clerks in the express office took charge of him; he was carted about in another wagon; a truck carried him, with an assortment of boxes and parcels, upon a ferry steamer; he was trucked off the steamer into a great railway depot, and finally he was deposited in an express car.

For two days and nights this express car was dragged along at the tail of shrieking locomotives; and for two days and nights Buck neither ate nor drank. In his anger he had met the first advances of the express messengers with growls, and they had retaliated by teasing him. When he flung himself against the bars, quivering and frothing, they laughed at him and taunted him. They growled and barked like detestable dogs, mewed, and flapped their arms and crowed. It was all very silly, he knew; but therefore the more outrage to his dignity, and his anger waxed and waxed. He did not mind the hunger so much, but the lack of water caused him severe suffering and fanned his wrath to fever-pitch. For that matter, high-strung and finely sensitive, the ill treatment had flung him into a fever, which was fed by the inflammation of his parched and swollen throat and tongue.

He was glad for one thing: the rope was off his neck. That had given them an unfair advantage; but now that it was off, he would show them. They would never get another rope around his neck. Upon that he was resolved. For two days and nights he neither ate nor drank, and during those two days and nights of torment, he accumulated a fund of wrath that boded ill for whoever first fell foul of him. His eyes turned blood-shot, and he was metamorphosed into a raging fiend. So changed was he that the Judge himself would not have recognized him; and the express messengers breathed with relief when they bundled him off the train at Seattle.

Four men gingerly carried the crate from the wagon into a small, high-walled back yard. A stout man, with a red sweater that sagged generously at the neck, came out and signed the book for the driver. That was the man, Buck divined, the next tormentor, and he hurled himself savagely against the bars. The man smiled grimly, and brought a hatchet and a club.

'You ain't going to take him out now?' the driver asked.

'Sure,' the man replied, driving the hatchet into the crate for a pry.

There was an instantaneous scattering of the four men who had carried it in, and from safe perches on top the wall they prepared to watch the performance.

Buck rushed at the splintering wood, sinking his teeth into it, surging and wrestling with it. Wherever the hatchet fell on the outside, he was there on the inside, snarling and growling, as furiously anxious to get out as the man in the red sweater was calmly intent on getting him out.

'Now, you red-eyed devil,' he said, when he had made an opening sufficient for the passage of Buck's body. At the same time he dropped the hatchet and shifted the club to his right hand.

And Buck was truly a red-eyed devil, as he drew himself together for the spring, hair bristling, mouth foaming, a mad glitter in his blood-shot eyes. Straight at the man he launched his one hundred and forty pounds of fury, surcharged with the pent passion of two days and nights. In mid air, just as his jaws were about to close on the man, he received a shock that checked his body and brought his teeth together with an agonizing clip. He whirled over, fetching the ground on his back and side. He had never been struck by a club in his life, and did not understand. With a snarl that was part bark and more scream he was again on his feet and launched into the air. And again the shock came and he was brought crushingly to the ground. This time he was aware that it was the club, but his madness knew no caution. A dozen times he charged, and as often the club broke the charge and smashed him down.

After a particularly fierce blow, he crawled to his feet, too dazed to rush. He staggered limply about, the blood flowing from nose and mouth and ears, his beautiful coat sprayed and flecked with bloody slaver. Then the man advanced and deliberately dealt him a frightful blow on the nose. All the pain he had endured was as nothing compared with the exquisite agony of this. With a roar that was almost lionlike in its ferocity, he again hurled himself at the man. But the man, shifting the club from right to left, coolly caught him by the under jaw, at the same time wrenching downward and backward. Buck described a complete circle in the air, and half of another, then crashed to the ground on his head and chest.

For the last time he rushed. The man struck the shrewd blow he had purposely withheld for so long, and Buck crumpled up and went down, knocked utterly senseless.

'He's no slouch at dog-breakin', that's wot I say,' one of the men on the wall cried enthusiastically.

'Druther break cayuses any day, and twice on Sundays,' was the reply of the driver, as he climbed on the wagon and started the horses.

Buck's senses came back to him, but not his strength. He lay where he had fallen, and from there he watched the man in the red sweater.

'Answers to the name of Buck,' the man soliloquized, quoting from the saloon-keeper's letter which had announced the consignment of the crate and contents. 'Well, Buck, my boy,' he went on in a genial voice, 'we've had our little ruction, and the best thing we can do is to let it go at that. You've learned your place, and I know mine. Be a good dog and all 'll go well and the goose hang high. Be a bad dog, and I'll whale the stuffin' outa you. Understand?'

As he spoke he fearlessly patted the head he had so mercilessly pounded, and though Buck's hair involuntarily bristled at touch of the hand, he endured it without protest. When the man brought him water he drank eagerly, and later bolted a generous meal of raw meat, chunk by chunk, from the man's hand.

He was beaten (he knew that); but he was not broken. He saw, once for all, that he stood no chance against a man with a club. He had learned the lesson, and in all his after life he never forgot it. That club was a revelation. It was his introduction to the reign of primitive law, and he met the introduction halfway. The facts of life took on a fiercer aspect; and while he faced that aspect uncowed, he faced it with all the latent cunning of his nature aroused. As the days went by, other dogs came, in crates and at the ends of ropes, some docilely, and some raging and roaring as he had come; and, one and all, he watched them pass under the dominion of the man in the red sweater. Again and again, as he looked at each brutal performance, the lesson was driven home to Buck: a man with a club was a lawgiver, a master to be obeyed, though not necessarily conciliated. Of this last Buck was never guilty, though he did see beaten dogs that fawned upon the man, and wagged their tails, and licked his hand. Also he saw one dog, that would neither conciliate nor obey, finally killed in the struggle for mastery.

Now and again men came, strangers, who talked excitedly, wheedlingly, and in all kinds of fashions to the man in the red sweater. And at such times that money passed between them the strangers took one or more of the dogs away with them. Buck wondered where they went, for they never came back; but the fear of the future was strong upon him, and he was glad each time when he was not selected.

Yet his time came, in the end, in the form of a little weazened man who spat broken English and many strange and uncouth exclamations which Buck could not understand.

'Sacredam!' he cried, when his eyes lit upon Buck. 'Dat one dam bully dog! Eh? How moch?'

'Three hundred, and a present at that,' was the prompt reply of the man in the red sweater. 'And seem' it's government money, you ain't got no kick coming, eh, Perrault?'

Perrault grinned. Considering that the price of dogs had been boomed skyward by the unwonted demand, it was not an unfair sum for so fine an animal. The Canadian Government would be no loser, nor would its despatches travel the slower. Perrault knew dogs, and when he looked at Buck he knew that he was one in a thousand— 'One in ten t'ousand,' he commented mentally.

Buck saw money pass between them, and was not surprised when Curly, a good-natured Newfoundland, and he were led away by the little weazened man. That was the last he saw of the man in the red sweater, and as Curly and he looked at receding Seattle from the deck of the Narwhal, it was the last he saw of the warm Southland. Curly and he were taken below by Perrault and turned over to a black-faced giant called Francois. Perrault was a French-Canadian, and swarthy; but Francois was a French-Canadian half-breed, and twice as swarthy. They were a new kind of men to Buck (of which he was destined to see many more), and while he developed no affection for them, he none the less grew honestly to respect them. He speedily learned that Perrault and Francois were fair men, calm and impartial in administering justice, and too wise in the way of dogs to be fooled by dogs.

In the 'tween-decks of the Narwhal, Buck and Curly joined two other dogs. One of them was a big, snow-white fellow from Spitzbergen who had been brought away by a whaling captain, and who had later accompanied a Geological Survey into the Barrens. He was friendly, in a treacherous sort of way, smiling into one's face the while he meditated some underhand trick, as, for instance, when he stole from Buck's food at the first meal. As Buck sprang to punish him, the lash of Francois's whip sang through the air, reaching the culprit first; and nothing remained to Buck but to recover the bone. That was fair of Francois, he decided, and the half-breed began his rise in Buck's estimation.

The other dog made no advances, nor received any; also, he did not attempt to steal from the newcomers. He was a gloomy, morose fellow, and he showed Curly plainly that all he desired was to be left alone, and further, that there would be trouble if he were not left alone. 'Dave' he was called, and he ate and slept, or yawned between times, and took interest in nothing, not even when the Narwhal crossed Queen Charlotte Sound and rolled and pitched and bucked like a thing possessed. When Buck and Curly grew excited, half wild with fear, he raised his head as though annoyed, favored them with an incurious glance, yawned, and went to sleep again.

Day and night the ship throbbed to the tireless pulse of the propeller, and though one day was very like another, it was apparent to Buck that the weather was steadily growing colder. At last, one morning, the propeller was quiet, and the Narwhal was pervaded with an atmosphere of excitement. He felt it, as did the other dogs, and knew that a change was at hand. Francois leashed them and brought them on deck. At the first step upon the cold surface, Buck's feet sank into a white mushy something very like mud. He sprang back with a snort. More of this white stuff was falling through the air. He shook himself, but more of it fell upon him. He sniffed it curiously, then licked some up on his tongue. It bit like fire, and the next instant was gone. This puzzled him. He tried it again, with the same result. The onlookers laughed uproariously, and he felt ashamed, he knew not why, for it was his first snow.

CHAPTER II
THE LAW OF CLUB AND FANG

Buck's first day on the Dyea beach was like a nightmare. Every hour was filled with shock and surprise. He had been suddenly jerked from the heart of civilization and flung into the heart of things primordial. No lazy, sun-kissed life was this, with nothing to do but loaf and be bored. Here was neither peace, nor rest, nor a moment's safety. All was confusion and action, and every moment life and limb were in peril. There was imperative need to be constantly alert; for these dogs and men were not town dogs and men. They were savages, all of them, who knew no law but the law of club and fang.

He had never seen dogs fight as these wolfish creatures fought, and his first experience taught him an unforgetable lesson. It is true, it was a vicarious experience, else he would not have lived to profit by it. Curly was the victim. They were camped near the log store, where she, in her friendly way, made advances to a husky dog the size of a full-grown wolf, though not half so large as she. There was no warning, only a leap in like a flash, a metallic clip of teeth, a leap out equally swift, and Curly's face was ripped open from eye to jaw.

It was the wolf manner of fighting, to strike and leap away; but there was more to it than this. Thirty or forty huskies ran to the spot and surrounded the combatants in an intent and silent circle. Buck did not comprehend that silent intentness, nor the eager way with which they were licking their chops. Curly rushed her antagonist, who struck again and leaped aside. He met her next rush with his chest, in a peculiar fashion that tumbled her off her feet. She never regained them, This was what the onlooking huskies had waited for. They closed in upon her, snarling and yelping, and she was buried, screaming with agony, beneath the bristling mass of bodies.

So sudden was it, and so unexpected, that Buck was taken aback. He saw Spitz run out his scarlet tongue in a way he had of laughing; and he saw Francois, swinging an axe, spring into the mess of dogs. Three men with clubs were helping him to scatter them. It did not take long. Two minutes from the time Curly went down, the last of her assailants were clubbed off. But she lay there limp and lifeless in the bloody, trampled snow, almost literally torn to pieces, the swart half-breed standing over her and cursing horribly. The scene often came back to Buck to trouble him in his sleep. So that was the way. No fair play. Once down, that was the end of you. Well, he would see to it that he never went down. Spitz ran out his tongue and laughed again, and from that moment Buck hated him with a bitter and deathless hatred.

Before he had recovered from the shock caused by the tragic passing of Curly, he received another shock. Francois fastened upon him an arrangement of straps and buckles. It was a harness, such as he had seen the grooms put on the horses at home. And as he had seen horses work, so he was set to work, hauling Francois on a sled to the forest that fringed the valley, and returning with a load of firewood. Though his dignity was sorely hurt by thus being made a draught animal, he was too wise to rebel. He buckled down with a will and did his best, though it was all new and strange. Francois was stern, demanding instant obedience, and by virtue of his whip receiving instant obedience; while Dave, who was an experienced wheeler, nipped Buck's hind quarters whenever he was in error. Spitz was the leader, likewise experienced, and while he could not always get at Buck, he growled sharp reproof now and again, or cunningly threw his weight in the traces to jerk Buck into the way he should go. Buck learned easily, and under the combined tuition of his two mates and Francois made remarkable progress. Ere they returned to camp he knew enough to stop at 'ho,' to go ahead at 'mush,' to swing wide on the bends, and to keep clear of the wheeler when the loaded sled shot downhill at their heels.

'T'ree vair' good dogs,' Francois told Perrault. 'Dat Buck, heem pool lak hell. I tich heem queek as anyt'ing.'

By afternoon, Perrault, who was in a hurry to be on the trail with his despatches, returned with two more dogs. 'Billee' and 'Joe' he called them, two brothers, and true huskies both. Sons of the one mother though they were, they were as different as day and night. Billee's one fault was his excessive good nature, while Joe was the very opposite, sour and introspective, with a perpetual snarl and a malignant eye. Buck received them in comradely fashion, Dave ignored them, while Spitz proceeded to thrash first one and then the other. Billee wagged his tail appeasingly, turned to run when he saw that appeasement was of no avail, and cried (still appeasingly) when Spitz's sharp teeth scored his flank. But no matter how Spitz circled, Joe whirled around on his heels to face him, mane bristling, ears laid back, lips writhing and snarling, jaws clipping together as fast as he could snap, and eyes diabolically gleaming—the incarnation of belligerent fear. So terrible was his appearance that Spitz was forced to forego disciplining him; but to cover his own discomfiture he turned upon the inoffensive and wailing Billee and drove him to the confines of the camp.

By evening Perrault secured another dog, an old husky, long and lean and gaunt, with a battle-scarred face and a single eye which flashed a warning of prowess that commanded respect. He was called Sol-leks, which means the Angry One. Like Dave, he asked nothing, gave nothing, expected nothing; and when he marched slowly and deliberately into their midst, even Spitz left him alone. He had one peculiarity which Buck was unlucky enough to discover. He did not like to be approached on his blind side. Of this offence Buck was unwittingly guilty, and the first knowledge he had of his indiscretion was when Sol-leks whirled upon him and slashed his shoulder to the bone for three inches up and down. Forever after Buck avoided his blind side, and to the last of their comradeship had no more trouble. His only apparent ambition, like Dave's, was to be left alone; though, as Buck was afterward to learn, each of them possessed one other and even more vital ambition.

That night Buck faced the great problem of sleeping. The tent, illumined by a candle, glowed warmly in the midst of the white plain; and when he, as a matter of course, entered it, both Perrault and Francois bombarded him with curses and cooking utensils, till he recovered from his consternation and fled ignominiously into the outer cold. A chill wind was blowing that nipped him sharply and bit with especial venom into his wounded shoulder. He lay down on the snow and attempted to sleep, but the frost soon drove him shivering to his feet. Miserable and disconsolate, he wandered about among the many tents, only to find that one place was as cold as another. Here and there savage dogs rushed upon him, but he bristled his neck-hair and snarled (for he was learning fast), and they let him go his way unmolested.

Finally an idea came to him. He would return and see how his own team-mates were making out. To his astonishment, they had disappeared. Again he wandered about through the great camp, looking for them, and again he returned. Were they in the tent? No, that could not be, else he would not have been driven out. Then where could they possibly be? With drooping tail and shivering body, very forlorn indeed, he aimlessly circled the tent. Suddenly the snow gave way beneath his fore legs and he sank down. Something wriggled under his feet. He sprang back, bristling and snarling, fearful of the unseen and unknown. But a friendly little yelp reassured him, and he went back to investigate. A whiff of warm air ascended to his nostrils, and there, curled up under the snow in a snug ball, lay Billee. He whined placatingly, squirmed and wriggled to show his good will and intentions, and even ventured, as a bribe for peace, to lick Buck's face with his warm wet tongue.

Another lesson. So that was the way they did it, eh? Buck confidently selected a spot, and with much fuss and waste effort proceeded to dig a hole for himself. In a trice the heat from his body filled the confined space and he was asleep. The day had been long and arduous, and he slept soundly and comfortably, though he growled and barked and wrestled with bad dreams.

Nor did he open his eyes till roused by the noises of the waking camp. At first he did not know where he was. It had snowed during the night and he was completely buried. The snow walls pressed him on every side, and a great surge of fear swept through him—the fear of the wild thing for the trap. It was a token that he was harking back through his own life to the lives of his forebears; for he was a civilized dog, an unduly civilized dog, and of his own experience knew no trap and so could not of himself fear it. The muscles of his whole body contracted spasmodically and instinctively, the hair on his neck and shoulders stood on end, and with a ferocious snarl he bounded straight up into the blinding day, the snow flying about him in a flashing cloud. Ere he landed on his feet, he saw the white camp spread out before him and knew where he was and remembered all that had passed from the time he went for a stroll with Manuel to the hole he had dug for himself the night before.

A shout from Francois hailed his appearance. 'Wot I say?' the dog-driver cried to Perrault. 'Dat Buck for sure learn queek as anyt'ing.'

Perrault nodded gravely. As courier for the Canadian Government, bearing important despatches, he was anxious to secure the best dogs, and he was particularly gladdened by the possession of Buck.

Three more huskies were added to the team inside an hour, making a total of nine, and before another quarter of an hour had passed they were in harness and swinging up the trail toward the Dyea Canon. Buck was glad to be gone, and though the work was hard he found he did not particularly despise it. He was surprised at the eagerness which animated the whole team and which was communicated to him; but still more surprising was the change wrought in Dave and Sol-leks. They were new dogs, utterly transformed by the harness. All passiveness and unconcern had dropped from them. They were alert and active, anxious that the work should go well, and fiercely irritable with whatever, by delay or confusion, retarded that work. The toil of the traces seemed the supreme expression of their being, and all that they lived for and the only thing in which they took delight.

Dave was wheeler or sled dog, pulling in front of him was Buck, then came Sol-leks; the rest of the team was strung out ahead, single file, to the leader, which position was filled by Spitz.

Buck had been purposely placed between Dave and Sol-leks so that he might receive instruction. Apt scholar that he was, they were equally apt teachers, never allowing him to linger long in error, and enforcing their teaching with their sharp teeth. Dave was fair and very wise. He never nipped Buck without cause, and he never failed to nip him when he stood in need of it. As Francois's whip backed him up, Buck found it to be cheaper to mend his ways than to retaliate. Once, during a brief halt, when he got tangled in the traces and delayed the start, both Dave and Solleks flew at him and administered a sound trouncing. The resulting tangle was even worse, but Buck took good care to keep the traces clear thereafter; and ere the day was done, so well had he mastered his work, his mates about ceased nagging him. Francois's whip snapped less frequently, and Perrault even honored Buck by lifting up his feet and carefully examining them.

It was a hard day's run, up the Canon, through Sheep Camp, past the Scales and the timber line, across glaciers and snowdrifts hundreds of feet deep, and over the great Chilcoot Divide, which stands between the salt water and the fresh and guards forbiddingly the sad and lonely North. They made good time down the chain of lakes which fills the craters of extinct volcanoes, and late that night pulled into the huge camp at the head of Lake Bennett, where thousands of goldseekers were building boats against the break-up of the ice in the spring. Buck made his hole in the snow and slept the sleep of the exhausted just, but all too early was routed out in the cold darkness and harnessed with his mates to the sled.

That day they made forty miles, the trail being packed; but the next day, and for many days to follow, they broke their own trail, worked harder, and made poorer time. As a rule, Perrault travelled ahead of the team, packing the snow with webbed shoes to make it easier for them. Francois, guiding the sled at the gee-pole, sometimes exchanged places with him, but not often. Perrault was in a hurry, and he prided himself on his knowledge of ice, which knowledge was indispensable, for the fall ice was very thin, and where there was swift water, there was no ice at all.

Day after day, for days unending, Buck toiled in the traces. Always, they broke camp in the dark, and the first gray of dawn found them hitting the trail with fresh miles reeled off behind them. And always they pitched camp after dark, eating their bit of fish, and crawling to sleep into the snow. Buck was ravenous. The pound and a half of sun-dried salmon, which was his ration for each day, seemed to go nowhere. He never had enough, and suffered from perpetual hunger pangs. Yet the other dogs, because they weighed less and were born to the life, received a pound only of the fish and managed to keep in good condition.

He swiftly lost the fastidiousness which had characterized his old life. A dainty eater, he found that his mates, finishing first, robbed him of his unfinished ration.

There was no defending it. While he was fighting off two or three, it was disappearing down the throats of the others. To remedy this, he ate as fast as they; and, so greatly did hunger compel him, he was not above taking what did not belong to him. He watched and learned. When he saw Pike, one of the new dogs, a clever malingerer and thief, slyly steal a slice of bacon when Perrault's back was turned, he duplicated the performance the following day, getting away with the whole chunk. A great uproar was raised, but he was unsuspected; while Dub, an awkward blunderer who was always getting caught, was punished for Buck's misdeed.

This first theft marked Buck as fit to survive in the hostile Northland environment. It marked his adaptability, his capacity to adjust himself to changing conditions, the lack of which would have meant swift and terrible death. It marked, further, the decay or going to pieces of his moral nature, a vain thing and a handicap in the ruthless struggle for existence. It was all well enough in the Southland, under the law of love and fellowship, to respect private property and personal feelings; but in the Northland, under the law of club and fang, whoso took such things into account was a fool, and in so far as he observed them he would fail to prosper.

Not that Buck reasoned it out. He was fit, that was all, and unconsciously he accommodated himself to the new mode of life. All his days, no matter what the odds, he had never run from a fight. But the club of the man in the red sweater had beaten into him a more fundamental and primitive code. Civilized, he could have died for a moral consideration, say the defence of Judge Miller's riding-whip; but the completeness of his decivilization was now evidenced by his ability to flee from the defence of a moral consideration and so save his hide. He did not steal for joy of it, but because of the clamor of his stomach. He did not rob openly, but stole secretly and cunningly, out of respect for club and fang. In short, the things he did were done because it was easier to do them than not to do them.

His development (or retrogression) was rapid. His muscles became hard as iron, and he grew callous to all ordinary pain. He achieved an internal as well as external economy. He could eat anything, no matter how loathsome or indigestible; and, once eaten, the juices of his stomach extracted the last least particle of nutriment; and his blood carried it to the farthest reaches of his body, building it into the toughest and stoutest of tissues. Sight and scent became remarkably keen, while his hearing developed such acuteness that in his sleep he heard the faintest sound and knew whether it heralded peace or peril. He learned to bite the ice out with his teeth when it collected between his toes; and when he was thirsty and there was a thick scum of ice over the water hole, he would break it by rearing and striking it with stiff fore legs. His most conspicuous trait was an ability to scent the wind and forecast it a night in advance. No matter how breathless the air when he dug his nest by tree or bank, the wind that later blew inevitably found him to leeward, sheltered and snug.

And not only did he learn by experience, but instincts long dead became alive again. The domesticated generations fell from him. In vague ways he remembered back to the youth of the breed, to the time the wild dogs ranged in packs through the primeval forest and killed their meat as they ran it down. It was no task for him to learn to fight with cut and slash and the quick wolf snap. In this manner had fought forgotten ancestors. They quickened the old life within him, and the old tricks which they had stamped into the heredity of the breed were his tricks. They came to him without effort or discovery, as though they had been his always. And when, on the still cold nights, he pointed his nose at a star and howled long and wolflike, it was his ancestors, dead and dust, pointing nose at star and howling down through the centuries and through him. And his cadences were their cadences, the cadences which voiced their woe and what to them was the meaning of the stiffness, and the cold, and dark.

Thus, as token of what a puppet thing life is, the ancient song surged through him and he came into his own again; and he came because men had found a yellow metal in the North, and because Manuel was a gardener's helper whose wages did not lap over the needs of his wife and divers small copies of himself.

CHAPTER III
THE DOMINANT PRIMORDIAL BEAST

The dominant primordial beast was strong in Buck, and under the fierce conditions of trail life it grew and grew. Yet it was a secret growth. His newborn cunning gave him poise and control. He was too busy adjusting himself to the new life to feel at ease, and not only did he not pick fights, but he avoided them whenever possible. A certain deliberateness characterized his attitude. He was not prone to rashness and precipitate action; and in the bitter hatred between him and Spitz he betrayed no impatience, shunned all offensive acts.

On the other hand, possibly because he divined in Buck a dangerous rival, Spitz never lost an opportunity of showing his teeth. He even went out of his way to bully Buck, striving constantly to start the fight which could end only in the death of one or the other. Early in the trip this might have taken place had it not been for an unwonted accident. At the end of this day they made a bleak and miserable camp on the shore of Lake Le Barge. Driving snow, a wind that cut like a white-hot knife, and darkness had forced them to grope for a camping place. They could hardly have fared worse. At their backs rose a perpendicular wall of rock, and Perrault and Francois were compelled to make their fire and spread their sleeping robes on the ice of the lake itself. The tent they had discarded at Dyea in order to travel light. A few sticks of driftwood furnished them with a fire that thawed down through the ice and left them to eat supper in the dark.

Close in under the sheltering rock Buck made his nest. So snug and warm was it, that he was loath to leave it when Francois distributed the fish which he had first thawed over the fire. But when Buck finished his ration and returned, he found his nest occupied. A warning snarl told him that the trespasser was Spitz. Till now Buck had avoided trouble with his enemy, but this was too much. The beast in him roared. He sprang upon Spitz with a fury which surprised them both, and Spitz particularly, for his whole experience with Buck had gone to teach him that his rival was an unusually timid dog, who managed to hold his own only because of his great weight and size.

Francois was surprised, too, when they shot out in a tangle from the disrupted nest and he divined the cause of the trouble. 'A-a-ah!' he cried to Buck. 'Gif it to heem, by Gar! Gif it to heem, the dirty t'eef!'

Spitz was equally willing. He was crying with sheer rage and eagerness as he circled back and forth for a chance to spring in. Buck was no less eager, and no less cautious, as he likewise circled back and forth for the advantage. But it was then that the unexpected happened, the thing which projected their struggle for supremacy far into the future, past many a weary mile of trail and toil.

An oath from Perrault, the resounding impact of a club upon a bony frame, and a shrill yelp of pain, heralded the breaking forth of pandemonium. The camp was suddenly discovered to be alive with skulking furry forms,—starving huskies, four or five score of them, who had scented the camp from some Indian village. They had crept in while Buck and Spitz were fighting, and when the two men sprang among them with stout clubs they showed their teeth and fought back. They were crazed by the smell of the food. Perrault found one with head buried in the grub-box. His club landed heavily on the gaunt ribs, and the grub-box was capsized on the ground. On the instant a score of the famished brutes were scrambling for the bread and bacon. The clubs fell upon them unheeded. They yelped and howled under the rain of blows, but struggled none the less madly till the last crumb had been devoured.

In the meantime the astonished team-dogs had burst out of their nests only to be set upon by the fierce invaders. Never had Buck seen such dogs. It seemed as though their bones would burst through their skins. They were mere skeletons, draped loosely in draggled hides, with blazing eyes and slavered fangs. But the hunger-madness made them terrifying, irresistible. There was no opposing them. The team-dogs were swept back against the cliff at the first onset. Buck was beset by three huskies, and in a trice his head and shoulders were ripped and slashed. The din was frightful. Billee was crying as usual. Dave and Sol-leks, dripping blood from a score of wounds, were fighting bravely side by side. Joe was snapping like a demon. Once, his teeth closed on the fore leg of a husky, and he crunched down through the bone. Pike, the malingerer, leaped upon the crippled animal, breaking its neck with a quick flash of teeth and a jerk, Buck got a frothing adversary by the throat, and was sprayed with blood when his teeth sank through the jugular. The warm taste of it in his mouth goaded him to greater fierceness. He flung himself upon another, and at the same time felt teeth sink into his own throat. It was Spitz, treacherously attacking from the side.

Perrault and Francois, having cleaned out their part of the camp, hurried to save their sled-dogs. The wild wave of famished beasts rolled back before them, and Buck shook himself free. But it was only for a moment. The two men were compelled to run back to save the grub, upon which the huskies returned to the attack on the team. Billee, terrified into bravery, sprang through the savage circle and fled away over the ice. Pike and Dub followed on his heels, with the rest of the team behind. As Buck drew himself together to spring after them, out of the tail of his eye he saw Spitz rush upon him with the evident intention of overthrowing him. Once off his feet and under that mass of huskies, there was no hope for him. But he braced himself to the shock of Spitz's charge, then joined the flight out on the lake.

Later, the nine team-dogs gathered together and sought shelter in the forest. Though unpursued, they were in a sorry plight. There was not one who was not wounded in four or five places, while some were wounded grievously. Dub was badly injured in a hind leg; Dolly, the last husky added to the team at Dyea, had a badly torn throat; Joe had lost an eye; while Billee, the good-natured, with an ear chewed and rent to ribbons, cried and whimpered throughout the night. At daybreak they limped warily back to camp, to find the marauders gone and the two men in bad tempers. Fully half their grub supply was gone. The huskies had chewed through the sled lashings and canvas coverings. In fact, nothing, no matter how remotely eatable, had escaped them. They had eaten a pair of Perrault's moose-hide moccasins, chunks out of the leather traces, and even two feet of lash from the end of Francois's whip. He broke from a mournful contemplation of it to look over his wounded dogs.

'Ah, my frien's,' he said softly, 'mebbe it mek you mad dog, dose many bites. Mebbe all mad dog, sacredam! Wot you t'ink, eh, Perrault?'

The courier shook his head dubiously. With four hundred miles of trail still between him and Dawson, he could ill afford to have madness break out among his dogs. Two hours of cursing and exertion got the harnesses into shape, and the wound-stiffened team was under way, struggling painfully over the hardest part of the trail they had yet encountered, and for that matter, the hardest between them and Dawson.

The Thirty Mile River was wide open. Its wild water defied the frost, and it was in the eddies only and in the quiet places that the ice held at all. Six days of exhausting toil were required to cover those thirty terrible miles. And terrible they were, for every foot of them was accomplished at the risk of life to dog and man. A dozen times, Perrault, nosing the way broke through the ice bridges, being saved by the long pole he carried, which he so held that it fell each time across the hole made by his body. But a cold snap was on, the thermometer registering fifty below zero, and each time he broke through he was compelled for very life to build a fire and dry his garments.

Nothing daunted him. It was because nothing daunted him that he had been chosen for government courier. He took all manner of risks, resolutely thrusting his little weazened face into the frost and struggling on from dim dawn to dark. He skirted the frowning shores on rim ice that bent and crackled under foot and upon which they dared not halt. Once, the sled broke through, with Dave and Buck, and they were half-frozen and all but drowned by the time they were dragged out. The usual fire was necessary to save them. They were coated solidly with ice, and the two men kept them on the run around the fire, sweating and thawing, so close that they were singed by the flames.

At another time Spitz went through, dragging the whole team after him up to Buck, who strained backward with all his strength, his fore paws on the slippery edge and the ice quivering and snapping all around. But behind him was Dave, likewise straining backward, and behind the sled was Francois, pulling till his tendons cracked.

Again, the rim ice broke away before and behind, and there was no escape except up the cliff. Perrault scaled it by a miracle, while Francois prayed for just that miracle; and with every thong and sled lashing and the last bit of harness rove into a long rope, the dogs were hoisted, one by one, to the cliff crest. Francois came up last, after the sled and load. Then came the search for a place to descend, which descent was ultimately made by the aid of the rope, and night found them back on the river with a quarter of a mile to the day's credit.

By the time they made the Hootalinqua and good ice, Buck was played out. The rest of the dogs were in like condition; but Perrault, to make up lost time, pushed them late and early. The first day they covered thirty-five miles to the Big Salmon; the next day thirty-five more to the Little Salmon; the third day forty miles, which brought them well up toward the Five Fingers.

Buck's feet were not so compact and hard as the feet of the huskies. His had softened during the many generations since the day his last wild ancestor was tamed by a cave-dweller or river man. All day long he limped in agony, and camp once made, lay down like a dead dog. Hungry as he was, he would not move to receive his ration of fish, which Francois had to bring to him. Also, the dog-driver rubbed Buck's feet for half an hour each night after supper, and sacrificed the tops of his own moccasins to make four moccasins for Buck. This was a great relief, and Buck caused even the weazened face of Perrault to twist itself into a grin one morning, when Francois forgot the moccasins and Buck lay on his back, his four feet waving appealingly in the air, and refused to budge without them. Later his feet grew hard to the trail, and the worn-out foot-gear was thrown away.

At the Pelly one morning, as they were harnessing up, Dolly, who had never been conspicuous for anything, went suddenly mad. She announced her condition by a long, heartbreaking wolf howl that sent every dog bristling with fear, then sprang straight for Buck. He had never seen a dog go mad, nor did he have any reason to fear madness; yet he knew that here was horror, and fled away from it in a panic. Straight away he raced, with Dolly, panting and frothing, one leap behind; nor could she gain on him, so great was his terror, nor could he leave her, so great was her madness. He plunged through the wooded breast of the island, flew down to the lower end, crossed a back channel filled with rough ice to another island, gained a third island, curved back to the main river, and in desperation started to cross it. And all the time, though he did not look, he could hear her snarling just one leap behind. Francois called to him a quarter of a mile away and he doubled back, still one leap ahead, gasping painfully for air and putting all his faith in that Francois would save him. The dog-driver held the axe poised in his hand, and as Buck shot past him the axe crashed down upon mad Dolly's head.

Buck staggered over against the sled, exhausted, sobbing for breath, helpless. This was Spitz's opportunity. He sprang upon Buck, and twice his teeth sank into his unresisting foe and ripped and tore the flesh to the bone. Then Francois's lash descended, and Buck had the satisfaction of watching Spitz receive the worst whipping as yet administered to any of the teams.

'One devil, dat Spitz,' remarked Perrault. 'Some dam day heem keel dat Buck.'

'Dat Buck two devils,' was Francois's rejoinder. 'All de tam I watch dat Buck I know for sure. Lissen: some dam fine day heem get mad lak hell an' den heem chew dat Spitz all up an' spit heem out on de snow. Sure. I know.'

From then on it was war between them. Spitz, as lead-dog and acknowledged master of the team, felt his supremacy threatened by this strange Southland dog. And strange Buck was to him, for of the many Southland dogs he had known, not one had shown up worthily in camp and on trail. They were all too soft, dying under the toil, the frost, and starvation. Buck was the exception. He alone endured and prospered, matching the husky in strength, savagery, and cunning. Then he was a masterful dog, and what made him dangerous was the fact that the club of the man in the red sweater had knocked all blind pluck and rashness out of his desire for mastery. He was preeminently cunning, and could bide his time with a patience that was nothing less than primitive.

It was inevitable that the clash for leadership should come. Buck wanted it. He wanted it because it was his nature, because he had been gripped tight by that nameless, incomprehensible pride of the trail and trace—that pride which holds dogs in the toil to the last gasp, which lures them to die joyfully in the harness, and breaks their hearts if they are cut out of the harness. This was the pride of Dave as wheel-dog, of

Sol-leks as he pulled with all his strength; the pride that laid hold of them at break of camp, transforming them from sour and sullen brutes into straining, eager, ambitious creatures; the pride that spurred them on all day and dropped them at pitch of camp at night, letting them fall back into gloomy unrest and uncontent. This was the pride that bore up Spitz and made him thrash the sled-dogs who blundered and shirked in the traces or hid away at harness-up time in the morning. Likewise it was this pride that made him fear Buck as a possible lead-dog. And this was Buck's pride, too.

He openly threatened the other's leadership. He came between him and the shirks he should have punished. And he did it deliberately. One night there was a heavy snowfall, and in the morning Pike, the malingerer, did not appear. He was securely hidden in his nest under a foot of snow. Francois called him and sought him in vain. Spitz was wild with wrath. He raged through the camp, smelling and digging in every likely place, snarling so frightfully that Pike heard and shivered in his hiding-place.

But when he was at last unearthed, and Spitz flew at him to punish him, Buck flew, with equal rage, in between. So unexpected was it, and so shrewdly managed, that Spitz was hurled backward and off his feet. Pike, who had been trembling abjectly, took heart at this open mutiny, and sprang upon his overthrown leader. Buck, to whom fair play was a forgotten code, likewise sprang upon Spitz. But Francois, chuckling at the incident while unswerving in the administration of justice, brought his lash down upon Buck with all his might. This failed to drive Buck from his prostrate rival, and the butt of the whip was brought into play. Half-stunned by the blow, Buck was knocked backward and the lash laid upon him again and again, while Spitz soundly punished the many times offending Pike.

In the days that followed, as Dawson grew closer and closer, Buck still continued to interfere between Spitz and the culprits; but he did it craftily, when Francois was not around, With the covert mutiny of Buck, a general insubordination sprang up and increased. Dave and Sol-leks were unaffected, but the rest of the team went from bad to worse. Things no longer went right. There was continual bickering and jangling. Trouble was always afoot, and at the bottom of it was Buck. He kept Francois busy, for the dog-driver was in constant apprehension of the life-and-death struggle between the two which he knew must take place sooner or later; and on more than one night the sounds of quarrelling and strife among the other dogs turned him out of his sleeping robe, fearful that Buck and Spitz were at it.

But the opportunity did not present itself, and they pulled into Dawson one dreary afternoon with the great fight still to come. Here were many men, and countless dogs, and Buck found them all at work. It seemed the ordained order of things that dogs should work. All day they swung up and down the main street in long teams, and in the night their jingling bells still went by. They hauled cabin logs and firewood, freighted up to the mines, and did all manner of work that horses did in the Santa Clara Valley. Here and there Buck met Southland dogs, but in the main they were the wild wolf husky breed. Every night, regularly, at nine, at twelve, at three, they lifted a nocturnal song, a weird and eerie chant, in which it was Buck's delight to join.

With the aurora borealis flaming coldly overhead, or the stars leaping in the frost dance, and the land numb and frozen under its pall of snow, this song of the huskies might have been the defiance of life, only it was pitched in minor key, with long-drawn wailings and half-sobs, and was more the pleading of life, the articulate travail of existence. It was an old song, old as the breed itself—one of the first songs of the younger world in a day when songs were sad. It was invested with the woe of unnumbered generations, this plaint by which Buck was so strangely stirred. When he moaned and sobbed, it was with the pain of living that was of old the pain of his wild fathers, and the fear and mystery of the cold and dark that was to them fear and mystery. And that he should be stirred by it marked the completeness with which he harked back through the ages of fire and roof to the raw beginnings of life in the howling ages.

Seven days from the time they pulled into Dawson, they dropped down the steep bank by the Barracks to the Yukon Trail, and pulled for Dyea and Salt Water. Perrault was carrying despatches if anything more urgent than those he had brought in; also, the travel pride had gripped him, and he purposed to make the record trip of the year. Several things favored him in this. The week's rest had recuperated the dogs and put them in thorough trim. The trail they had broken into the country was packed hard by later journeyers. And further, the police had arranged in two or three places deposits of grub for dog and man, and he was travelling light.

They made Sixty Mile, which is a fifty-mile run, on the first day; and the second day saw them booming up the Yukon well on their way to Pelly. But such splendid running was achieved not without great trouble and vexation on the part of Francois. The insidious revolt led by Buck had destroyed the solidarity of the team. It no longer was as one dog leaping in the traces. The encouragement Buck gave the rebels led them into all kinds of petty misdemeanors. No more was Spitz a leader greatly to be feared. The old awe departed, and they grew equal to challenging his authority. Pike robbed him of half a fish one night, and gulped it down under the protection of Buck. Another night Dub and Joe fought Spitz and made him forego the punishment they deserved. And even Billee, the good-natured, was less good-natured, and whined not half so placatingly as in former days. Buck never came near Spitz without snarling and bristling menacingly. In fact, his conduct approached that of a bully, and he was given to swaggering up and down before Spitz's very nose.

The breaking down of discipline likewise affected the dogs in their relations with one another. They quarrelled and bickered more than ever among themselves, till at times the camp was a howling bedlam. Dave and Sol-leks alone were unaltered, though they were made irritable by the unending squabbling. Francois swore strange barbarous oaths, and stamped the snow in futile rage, and tore his hair. His lash was always singing among the dogs, but it was of small avail. Directly his back was turned they were at it again. He backed up Spitz with his whip, while Buck backed up the remainder of the team. Francois knew he was behind all the trouble, and Buck knew he knew; but Buck was too clever ever again to be caught red-handed. He worked faithfully in the harness, for the toil had become a delight to him; yet it was a greater delight slyly to precipitate a fight amongst his mates and tangle the traces.

At the mouth of the Tahkeena, one night after supper, Dub turned up a snowshoe rabbit, blundered it, and missed. In a second the whole team was in full cry. A hundred yards away was a camp of the Northwest Police, with fifty dogs, huskies all, who joined the chase. The rabbit sped down the river, turned off into a small creek, up the frozen bed of which it held steadily. It ran lightly on the surface of the snow, while the dogs ploughed through by main strength. Buck led the pack, sixty strong, around bend after bend, but he could not gain. He lay down low to the race, whining eagerly, his splendid body flashing forward, leap by leap, in the wan white moonlight. And leap by leap, like some pale frost wraith, the snowshoe rabbit flashed on ahead.

All that stirring of old instincts which at stated periods drives men out from the sounding cities to forest and plain to kill things by chemically propelled leaden pellets, the blood lust, the joy to kill—all this was Buck's, only it was infinitely more intimate. He was ranging at the head of the pack, running the wild thing down, the living meat, to kill with his own teeth and wash his muzzle to the eyes in warm blood.

There is an ecstasy that marks the summit of life, and beyond which life cannot rise. And such is the paradox of living, this ecstasy comes when one is most alive, and it comes as a complete forgetfulness that one is alive. This ecstasy, this forgetfulness of living, comes to the artist, caught up and out of himself in a sheet of flame; it comes to the soldier, war-mad on a stricken field and refusing quarter; and it came to Buck, leading the pack, sounding the old wolf-cry, straining after the food that was alive and that fled swiftly before him through the moonlight. He was sounding the deeps of his nature, and of the parts of his nature that were deeper than he, going back into the womb of Time. He was mastered by the sheer surging of life, the tidal wave of being, the perfect joy of each separate muscle, joint, and sinew in that it was everything that was not death, that it was aglow and rampant, expressing itself in movement, flying exultantly under the stars and over the face of dead matter that did not move.

But Spitz, cold and calculating even in his supreme moods, left the pack and cut across a narrow neck of land where the creek made a long bend around. Buck did not know of this, and as he rounded the bend, the frost wraith of a rabbit still flitting before him, he saw another and larger frost wraith leap from the overhanging bank into the immediate path of the rabbit. It was Spitz. The rabbit could not turn, and as the white teeth broke its back in mid air it shrieked as loudly as a stricken man may shriek. At sound of this, the cry of Life plunging down from Life's apex in the grip of Death, the fall pack at Buck's heels raised a hell's chorus of delight.

Buck did not cry out. He did not check himself, but drove in upon Spitz, shoulder to shoulder, so hard that he missed the throat. They rolled over and over in the powdery snow. Spitz gained his feet almost as though he had not been overthrown, slashing Buck down the shoulder and leaping clear. Twice his teeth clipped together, like the steel jaws of a trap, as he backed away for better footing, with lean and lifting lips that writhed and snarled.

In a flash Buck knew it. The time had come. It was to the death. As they circled about, snarling, ears laid back, keenly watchful for the advantage, the scene came to Buck with a sense of familiarity. He seemed to remember it all,—the white woods, and earth, and moonlight, and the thrill of battle. Over the whiteness and silence brooded a ghostly calm. There was not the faintest whisper of air—nothing moved, not a leaf quivered, the visible breaths of the dogs rising slowly and lingering in the frosty air. They had made short work of the snowshoe rabbit, these dogs that were ill-tamed wolves; and they were now drawn up in an expectant circle. They, too, were silent, their eyes only gleaming and their breaths drifting slowly upward. To Buck it was nothing new or strange, this scene of old time. It was as though it had always been, the wonted way of things.

Spitz was a practised fighter. From Spitzbergen through the Arctic, and across Canada and the Barrens, he had held his own with all manner of dogs and achieved to mastery over them. Bitter rage was his, but never blind rage. In passion to rend and destroy, he never forgot that his enemy was in like passion to rend and destroy. He never rushed till he was prepared to receive a rush; never attacked till he had first defended that attack.

In vain Buck strove to sink his teeth in the neck of the big white dog. Wherever his fangs struck for the softer flesh, they were countered by the fangs of Spitz. Fang clashed fang, and lips were cut and bleeding, but Buck could not penetrate his enemy's guard. Then he warmed up and enveloped Spitz in a whirlwind of rushes. Time and time again he tried for the snow-white throat, where life bubbled near to the surface, and each time and every time Spitz slashed him and got away. Then Buck took to rushing, as though for the throat, when, suddenly drawing back his head and curving in from the side, he would drive his shoulder at the shoulder of Spitz, as a ram by which to overthrow him. But instead, Buck's shoulder was slashed down each time as Spitz leaped lightly away.

Spitz was untouched, while Buck was streaming with blood and panting hard. The fight was growing desperate. And all the while the silent and wolfish circle waited to finish off whichever dog went down. As Buck grew winded, Spitz took to rushing, and he kept him staggering for footing. Once Buck went over, and the whole circle of sixty dogs started up; but he recovered himself, almost in mid air, and the circle sank down again and waited.

But Buck possessed a quality that made for greatness—imagination. He fought by instinct, but he could fight by head as well. He rushed, as though attempting the old shoulder trick, but at the last instant swept low to the snow and in. His teeth closed on Spitz's left fore leg. There was a crunch of breaking bone, and the white dog faced him on three legs. Thrice he tried to knock him over, then repeated the trick and broke the right fore leg. Despite the pain and helplessness, Spitz struggled madly to keep up. He saw the silent circle, with gleaming eyes, lolling tongues, and silvery breaths drifting upward, closing in upon him as he had seen similar circles close in upon beaten antagonists in the past. Only this time he was the one who was beaten.

There was no hope for him. Buck was inexorable. Mercy was a thing reserved for gentler climes. He manoeuvred for the final rush. The circle had tightened till he could feel the breaths of the huskies on his flanks. He could see them, beyond Spitz and to either side, half crouching for the spring, their eyes fixed upon him. A pause seemed to fall. Every animal was motionless as though turned to stone. Only Spitz quivered and bristled as he staggered back and forth, snarling with horrible menace, as though to frighten off impending death. Then Buck sprang in and out; but while he was in, shoulder had at last squarely met shoulder. The dark circle became a dot on the moon-flooded snow as Spitz disappeared from view. Buck stood and looked on, the successful champion, the dominant primordial beast who had made his kill and found it good.

CHAPTER IV
WHO HAS WON TO MASTERSHIP

'Eh? Wot I say? I spik true w'en I say dat Buck two devils.' This was Francois's speech next morning when he discovered Spitz missing and Buck covered with wounds. He drew him to the fire and by its light pointed them out.

'Dat Spitz fight lak hell,' said Perrault, as he surveyed the gaping rips and cuts.

'An' dat Buck fight lak two hells,' was Francois's answer. 'An' now we make good time. No more Spitz, no more trouble, sure.'

While Perrault packed the camp outfit and loaded the sled, the dog-driver proceeded to harness the dogs. Buck trotted up to the place Spitz would have occupied as leader; but Francois, not noticing him, brought Sol-leks to the coveted position. In his judgment, Sol-leks was the best lead-dog left. Buck sprang upon Sol-leks in a fury, driving him back and standing in his place.

'Eh? eh?' Francois cried, slapping his thighs gleefully. 'Look at dat Buck. Heem keel dat Spitz, heem t'ink to take de job.'

'Go 'way, Chook!' he cried, but Buck refused to budge.

He took Buck by the scruff of the neck, and though the dog growled threateningly, dragged him to one side and replaced Sol-leks. The old dog did not like it, and showed plainly that he was afraid of Buck. Francois was obdurate, but when he turned his back Buck again displaced Sol-leks, who was not at all unwilling to go.

Francois was angry. 'Now, by Gar, I feex you!' he cried, coming back with a heavy club in his hand.

Buck remembered the man in the red sweater, and retreated slowly; nor did he attempt to charge in when Sol-leks was once more brought forward. But he circled just beyond the range of the club, snarling with bitterness and rage; and while he circled he watched the club so as to dodge it if thrown by Francois, for he was become wise in the way of clubs. The driver went about his work, and he called to Buck when he was ready to put him in his old place in front of Dave. Buck retreated two or three steps. Francois followed him up, whereupon he again retreated. After some time of this, Francois threw down the club, thinking that Buck feared a thrashing. But Buck was in open revolt. He wanted, not to escape a clubbing, but to have the leadership. It was his by right. He had earned it, and he would not be content with less.

Perrault took a hand. Between them they ran him about for the better part of an hour. They threw clubs at him. He dodged. They cursed him, and his fathers and mothers before him, and all his seed to come after him down to the remotest generation, and every hair on his body and drop of blood in his veins; and he answered curse with snarl and kept out of their reach. He did not try to run away, but retreated around and around the camp, advertising plainly that when his desire was met, he would come in and be good.

Francois sat down and scratched his head. Perrault looked at his watch and swore. Time was flying, and they should have been on the trail an hour gone. Francois scratched his head again. He shook it and grinned sheepishly at the courier, who shrugged his shoulders in sign that they were beaten. Then Francois went up to where Sol-leks stood and called to Buck. Buck laughed, as dogs laugh, yet kept his distance. Francois unfastened Sol-leks's traces and put him back in his old place. The team stood harnessed to the sled in an unbroken line, ready for the trail. There was no place for Buck save at the front. Once more Francois called, and once more Buck laughed and kept away.

'T'row down de club,' Perrault commanded.

Francois complied, whereupon Buck trotted in, laughing triumphantly, and swung around into position at the head of the team. His traces were fastened, the sled broken out, and with both men running they dashed out on to the river trail.

Highly as the dog-driver had forevalued Buck, with his two devils, he found, while the day was yet young, that he had undervalued. At a bound Buck took up the duties of leadership; and where judgment was required, and quick thinking and quick acting, he showed himself the superior even of Spitz, of whom Francois had never seen an equal.

But it was in giving the law and making his mates live up to it, that Buck excelled. Dave and Sol-leks did not mind the change in leadership. It was none of their business. Their business was to toil, and toil mightily, in the traces. So long as that were not interfered with, they did not care what happened. Billee, the good-natured, could lead for all they cared, so long as he kept order. The rest of the team, however, had grown unruly during the last days of Spitz, and their surprise was great now that Buck proceeded to lick them into shape.

Pike, who pulled at Buck's heels, and who never put an ounce more of his weight against the breast-band than he was compelled to do, was swiftly and repeatedly shaken for loafing; and ere the first day was done he was pulling more than ever before in his life. The first night in camp, Joe, the sour one, was punished roundly—a thing that Spitz had never succeeded in doing. Buck simply smothered him by virtue of superior weight, and cut him up till he ceased snapping and began to whine for mercy.

The general tone of the team picked up immediately. It recovered its old-time solidarity, and once more the dogs leaped as one dog in the traces. At the Rink Rapids two native huskies, Teek and Koona, were added; and the celerity with which Buck broke them in took away Francois's breath.

'Nevaire such a dog as dat Buck!' he cried. 'No, nevaire! Heem worth one t'ousan' dollair, by Gar! Eh? Wot you say, Perrault?'

And Perrault nodded. He was ahead of the record then, and gaining day by day. The trail was in excellent condition, well packed and hard, and there was no new-fallen snow with which to contend. It was not too cold. The temperature dropped to fifty below zero and remained there the whole trip. The men rode and ran by turn, and the dogs were kept on the jump, with but infrequent stoppages.

The Thirty Mile River was comparatively coated with ice, and they covered in one day going out what had taken them ten days coming in. In one run they made a sixty-mile dash from the foot of Lake Le Barge to the White Horse Rapids. Across Marsh, Tagish, and Bennett (seventy miles of lakes), they flew so fast that the man whose turn it was to run towed behind the sled at the end of a rope. And on the last night of the second week they topped White Pass and dropped down the sea slope with the lights of Skaguay and of the shipping at their feet.

It was a record run. Each day for fourteen days they had averaged forty miles. For three days Perrault and Francois threw chests up and down the main street of Skaguay and were deluged with invitations to drink, while the team was the constant centre of a worshipful crowd of dog-busters and mushers. Then three or four western bad men aspired to clean out the town, were riddled like pepper-boxes for their pains, and public interest turned to other idols. Next came official orders. Francois called Buck to him, threw his arms around him, wept over him. And that was the last of Francois and Perrault. Like other men, they passed out of Buck's life for good.

A Scotch half-breed took charge of him and his mates, and in company with a dozen other dog-teams he started back over the weary trail to Dawson. It was no light running now, nor record time, but heavy toil each day, with a heavy load behind; for this was the mail train, carrying word from the world to the men who sought gold under the shadow of the Pole.

Buck did not like it, but he bore up well to the work, taking pride in it after the manner of Dave and Sol-leks, and seeing that his mates, whether they prided in it or not, did their fair share. It was a monotonous life, operating with machine-like regularity. One day was very like another. At a certain time each morning the cooks turned out, fires were built, and breakfast was eaten. Then, while some broke camp, others harnessed the dogs, and they were under way an hour or so before the darkness fell which gave warning of dawn. At night, camp was made. Some pitched the flies, others cut firewood and pine boughs for the beds, and still others carried water or ice for the cooks. Also, the dogs were fed. To them, this was the one feature of the day, though it was good to loaf around, after the fish was eaten, for an hour or so with the other dogs, of which there were fivescore and odd. There were fierce fighters among them, but three battles with the fiercest brought Buck to mastery, so that when he bristled and showed his teeth they got out of his way.

Best of all, perhaps, he loved to lie near the fire, hind legs crouched under him, fore legs stretched out in front, head raised, and eyes blinking dreamily at the flames. Sometimes he thought of Judge Miller's big house in the sun-kissed Santa Clara Valley, and of the cement swimming-tank, and Ysabel, the Mexican hairless, and Toots, the Japanese pug; but oftener he remembered the man in the red sweater, the death of Curly, the great fight with Spitz, and the good things he had eaten or would like to eat. He was not homesick. The Sunland was very dim and distant, and such memories had no power over him. Far more potent were the memories of his heredity that gave things he had never seen before a seeming familiarity; the instincts (which were but the memories of his ancestors become habits) which had lapsed in later days, and still later, in him, quickened and become alive again.

Sometimes as he crouched there, blinking dreamily at the flames, it seemed that the flames were of another fire, and that as he crouched by this other fire he saw another and different man from the half-breed cook before him. This other man was shorter of leg and longer of arm, with muscles that were stringy and knotty rather than rounded and swelling. The hair of this man was long and matted, and his head slanted back under it from the eyes. He uttered strange sounds, and seemed very much afraid of the darkness, into which he peered continually, clutching in his hand, which hung midway between knee and foot, a stick with a heavy stone made fast to the end. He was all but naked, a ragged and fire-scorched skin hanging part way down his back, but on his body there was much hair. In some places, across the chest and shoulders and down the outside of the arms and thighs, it was matted into almost a thick fur. He did not stand erect, but with trunk inclined forward from the hips, on legs that bent at the knees. About his body there was a peculiar springiness, or resiliency, almost catlike, and a quick alertness as of one who lived in perpetual fear of things seen and unseen.

At other times this hairy man squatted by the fire with head between his legs and slept. On such occasions his elbows were on his knees, his hands clasped above his head as though to shed rain by the hairy arms. And beyond that fire, in the circling darkness, Buck could see many gleaming coals, two by two, always two by two, which he knew to be the eyes of great beasts of prey. And he could hear the crashing of their bodies through the undergrowth, and the noises they made in the night. And dreaming there by the Yukon bank, with lazy eyes blinking at the fire, these sounds and sights of another world would make the hair to rise along his back and stand on end across his shoulders and up his neck, till he whimpered low and suppressedly, or growled softly, and the half-breed cook shouted at him, 'Hey, you Buck, wake up!' Whereupon the other world would vanish and the real world come into his eyes, and he would get up and yawn and stretch as though he had been asleep.

It was a hard trip, with the mail behind them, and the heavy work wore them down. They were short of weight and in poor condition when they made Dawson, and should have had a ten days' or a week's rest at least. But in two days' time they dropped down the Yukon bank from the Barracks, loaded with letters for the outside. The dogs were tired, the drivers grumbling, and to make matters worse, it snowed every day. This meant a soft trail, greater friction on the runners, and heavier pulling for the dogs; yet the drivers were fair through it all, and did their best for the animals.

Each night the dogs were attended to first. They ate before the drivers ate, and no man sought his sleeping-robe till he had seen to the feet of the dogs he drove. Still, their strength went down. Since the beginning of the winter they had travelled eighteen hundred miles, dragging sleds the whole weary distance; and eighteen hundred miles will tell upon life of the toughest. Buck stood it, keeping his mates up to their work and maintaining discipline, though he, too, was very tired. Billee cried and whimpered regularly in his sleep each night. Joe was sourer than ever, and Sol-leks was unapproachable, blind side or other side.

But it was Dave who suffered most of all. Something had gone wrong with him. He became more morose and irritable, and when camp was pitched at once made his nest, where his driver fed him. Once out of the harness and down, he did not get on his feet again till harness-up time in the morning. Sometimes, in the traces, when jerked by a sudden stoppage of the sled, or by straining to start it, he would cry out with pain. The driver examined him, but could find nothing. All the drivers became interested in his case. They talked it over at meal-time, and over their last pipes before going to bed, and one night they held a consultation. He was brought from his nest to the fire and was pressed and prodded till he cried out many times. Something was wrong inside, but they could locate no broken bones, could not make it out.

By the time Cassiar Bar was reached, he was so weak that he was falling repeatedly in the traces. The Scotch half-breed called a halt and took him out of the team, making the next dog, Sol-leks, fast to the sled. His intention was to rest Dave, letting him run free behind the sled. Sick as he was, Dave resented being taken out, grunting and growling while the traces were unfastened, and whimpering broken-heartedly when he saw Sol-leks in the position he had held and served so long. For the pride of trace and trail was his, and, sick unto death, he could not bear that another dog should do his work.

When the sled started, he floundered in the soft snow alongside the beaten trail, attacking Sol-leks with his teeth, rushing against him and trying to thrust him off into the soft snow on the other side, striving to leap inside his traces and get between him and the sled, and all the while whining and yelping and crying with grief and pain. The half-breed tried to drive him away with the whip; but he paid no heed to the stinging lash, and the man had not the heart to strike harder. Dave refused to run quietly on the trail behind the sled, where the going was easy, but continued to flounder alongside in the soft snow, where the going was most difficult, till exhausted. Then he fell, and lay where he fell, howling lugubriously as the long train of sleds churned by.

With the last remnant of his strength he managed to stagger along behind till the train made another stop, when he floundered past the sleds to his own, where he stood alongside Sol-leks. His driver lingered a moment to get a light for his pipe from the man behind. Then he returned and started his dogs. They swung out on the trail with remarkable lack of exertion, turned their heads uneasily, and stopped in surprise. The driver was surprised, too; the sled had not moved. He called his comrades to witness the sight. Dave had bitten through both of Sol-leks's traces, and was standing directly in front of the sled in his proper place.

He pleaded with his eyes to remain there. The driver was perplexed. His comrades talked of how a dog could break its heart through being denied the work that killed it, and recalled instances they had known, where dogs, too old for the toil, or injured, had died because they were cut out of the traces. Also, they held it a mercy, since Dave was to die anyway, that he should die in the traces, heart-easy and content. So he was harnessed in again, and proudly he pulled as of old, though more than once he cried out involuntarily from the bite of his inward hurt. Several times he fell down and was dragged in the traces, and once the sled ran upon him so that he limped thereafter in one of his hind legs.

But he held out till camp was reached, when his driver made a place for him by the fire. Morning found him too weak to travel. At harness-up time he tried to crawl to his driver. By convulsive efforts he got on his feet, staggered, and fell. Then he wormed his way forward slowly toward where the harnesses were being put on his mates. He would advance his fore legs and drag up his body with a sort of hitching movement, when he would advance his fore legs and hitch ahead again for a few more inches. His strength left him, and the last his mates saw of him he lay gasping in the snow and yearning toward them. But they could hear him mournfully howling till they passed out of sight behind a belt of river timber.

Here the train was halted. The Scotch half-breed slowly retraced his steps to the camp they had left. The men ceased talking. A revolver-shot rang out. The man came back hurriedly. The whips snapped, the bells tinkled merrily, the sleds churned along the trail; but Buck knew, and every dog knew, what had taken place behind the belt of river trees.

CHAPTER V

THE TOIL OF TRACE AND TRAIL

Thirty days from the time it left Dawson, the Salt Water Mail, with Buck and his mates at the fore, arrived at Skaguay. They were in a wretched state, worn out and worn down. Buck's one hundred and forty pounds had dwindled to one hundred and fifteen. The rest of his mates, though lighter dogs, had relatively lost more weight than he. Pike, the malingerer, who, in his lifetime of deceit, had often successfully feigned a hurt leg, was now limping in earnest. Sol-leks was limping, and Dub was suffering from a wrenched shoulder-blade.

They were all terribly footsore. No spring or rebound was left in them. Their feet fell heavily on the trail, jarring their bodies and doubling the fatigue of a day's travel. There was nothing the matter with them except that they were dead tired. It was not the dead-tiredness that comes through brief and excessive effort, from which recovery is a matter of hours; but it was the dead-tiredness that comes through the slow and prolonged strength drainage of months of toil. There was no power of recuperation left, no reserve strength to call upon. It had been all used, the last least bit of it. Every muscle, every fibre, every cell, was tired, dead tired. And there was reason for it. In less than five months they had travelled twenty-five hundred miles, during the last eighteen hundred of which they had had but five days' rest. When they arrived at Skaguay they were apparently on their last legs. They could barely keep the traces taut, and on the down grades just managed to keep out of the way of the sled.

'Mush on, poor sore feets,' the driver encouraged them as they tottered down the main street of Skaguay. 'Dis is de las'. Den we get one long res'. Eh? For sure. One bully long res'.'

The drivers confidently expected a long stopover. Themselves, they had covered twelve hundred miles with two days' rest, and in the nature of reason and common justice they deserved an interval of loafing. But so many were the men who had rushed into the Klondike, and so many were the sweethearts, wives, and kin that had not rushed in, that the congested mail was taking on Alpine proportions; also, there were official orders. Fresh batches of Hudson Bay dogs were to take the places of those worthless for the trail. The worthless ones were to be got rid of, and, since dogs count for little against dollars, they were to be sold.

Three days passed, by which time Buck and his mates found how really tired and weak they were. Then, on the morning of the fourth day, two men from the States came along and bought them, harness and all, for a song. The men addressed each other as 'Hal' and 'Charles.' Charles was a middle-aged, lightish-colored man, with weak and watery eyes and a mustache that twisted fiercely and vigorously up, giving the lie to the limply drooping lip it concealed. Hal was a youngster of nineteen or twenty, with a big Colt's revolver and a hunting-knife strapped about him on a belt that fairly bristled with cartridges. This belt was the most salient thing about him. It advertised his callowness—a callowness sheer and unutterable. Both men were manifestly out of place, and why such as they should adventure the North is part of the mystery of things that passes understanding.

Buck heard the chaffering, saw the money pass between the man and the Government agent, and knew that the Scotch half-breed and the mail-train drivers were passing out of his life on the heels of Perrault and Francois and the others who had gone before. When driven with his mates to the new owners' camp, Buck saw a slipshod and slovenly affair, tent half stretched, dishes unwashed, everything in disorder; also, he saw a woman. 'Mercedes' the men called her. She was Charles's wife and Hal's sister—a nice family party.

Buck watched them apprehensively as they proceeded to take down the tent and load the sled. There was a great deal of effort about their manner, but no business-like method. The tent was rolled into an awkward bundle three times as large as it should have been. The tin dishes were packed away unwashed. Mercedes continually fluttered in the way of her men and kept up an unbroken chattering of remonstrance and advice. When they put a clothes-sack on the front of the sled, she suggested it should go on the back; and when they had put it on the back, and covered it over with a couple of other bundles, she discovered overlooked articles which could abide nowhere else but in that very sack, and they unloaded again.

Three men from a neighboring tent came out and looked on, grinning and winking at one another.

'You've got a right smart load as it is,' said one of them; 'and it's not me should tell you your business, but I wouldn't tote that tent along if I was you.'

'Undreamed of!' cried Mercedes, throwing up her hands in dainty dismay. 'However in the world could I manage without a tent?'

'It's springtime, and you won't get any more cold weather,' the man replied.

She shook her head decidedly, and Charles and Hal put the last odds and ends on top the mountainous load.

'Think it'll ride?' one of the men asked.

'Why shouldn't it?' Charles demanded rather shortly.

'Oh, that's all right, that's all right,' the man hastened meekly to say. 'I was just a-wonderin', that is all. It seemed a mite top-heavy.'

Charles turned his back and drew the lashings down as well as he could, which was not in the least well.

'An' of course the dogs can hike along all day with that contraption behind them,' affirmed a second of the men.

'Certainly,' said Hal, with freezing politeness, taking hold of the gee-pole with one hand and swinging his whip from the other. 'Mush!' he shouted. 'Mush on there!'

The dogs sprang against the breast-bands, strained hard for a few moments, then relaxed. They were unable to move the sled.

'The lazy brutes, I'll show them,' he cried, preparing to lash out at them with the whip.

But Mercedes interfered, crying, 'Oh, Hal, you mustn't,' as she caught hold of the whip and wrenched it from him. 'The poor dears! Now you must promise you won't be harsh with them for the rest of the trip, or I won't go a step.'

'Precious lot you know about dogs,' her brother sneered; 'and I wish you'd leave me alone. They're lazy, I tell you, and you've got to whip them to get anything out of them. That's their way. You ask any one. Ask one of those men.'

Mercedes looked at them imploringly, untold repugnance at sight of pain written in her pretty face.

'They're weak as water, if you want to know,' came the reply from one of the men. 'Plum tuckered out, that's what's the matter. They need a rest.'

'Rest be blanked,' said Hal, with his beardless lips; and Mercedes said, 'Oh!' in pain and sorrow at the oath.

But she was a clannish creature, and rushed at once to the defence of her brother. 'Never mind that man,' she said pointedly. 'You're driving our dogs, and you do what you think best with them.'

Again Hal's whip fell upon the dogs. They threw themselves against the breast-bands, dug their feet into the packed snow, got down low to it, and put forth all their strength. The sled held as though it were an anchor. After two efforts, they stood still, panting. The whip was whistling savagely, when once more Mercedes interfered. She dropped on her knees before Buck, with tears in her eyes, and put her arms around his neck.

'You poor, poor dears,' she cried sympathetically, 'why don't you pull hard?—then you wouldn't be whipped.' Buck did not like her, but he was feeling too miserable to resist her, taking it as part of the day's miserable work.

One of the onlookers, who had been clenching his teeth to suppress hot speech, now spoke up:—

'It's not that I care a whoop what becomes of you, but for the dogs' sakes I just want to tell you, you can help them a mighty lot by breaking out that sled. The runners are froze fast. Throw your weight against the gee-pole, right and left, and break it out.'

A third time the attempt was made, but this time, following the advice, Hal broke out the runners which had been frozen to the snow. The overloaded and unwieldy sled forged ahead, Buck and his mates struggling frantically under the rain of blows. A hundred yards ahead the path turned and sloped steeply into the main street. It would have required an experienced man to keep the top-heavy sled upright, and Hal was not such a man. As they swung on the turn the sled went over, spilling half its load through the loose lashings. The dogs never stopped. The lightened sled bounded on its side behind them. They were angry because of the ill treatment they had received and the unjust load. Buck was raging. He broke into a run, the team following his lead. Hal cried 'Whoa! whoa!' but they gave no heed. He tripped and was pulled off his feet. The capsized sled ground over him, and the dogs dashed on up the street, adding to the gayety of Skaguay as they scattered the remainder of the outfit along its chief thoroughfare.

Kind-hearted citizens caught the dogs and gathered up the scattered belongings. Also, they gave advice. Half the load and twice the dogs, if they ever expected to reach Dawson, was what was said. Hal and his sister and brother-in-law listened unwillingly, pitched tent, and overhauled the outfit. Canned goods were turned out that made men laugh, for canned goods on the Long Trail is a thing to dream about. 'Blankets for a hotel' quoth one of the men who laughed and helped. 'Half as many is too much; get rid of them. Throw away that tent, and all those dishes,—who's going to wash them, anyway? Good Lord, do you think you're travelling on a Pullman?'

And so it went, the inexorable elimination of the superfluous. Mercedes cried when her clothes-bags were dumped on the ground and article after article was thrown out. She cried in general, and she cried in particular over each discarded thing. She clasped hands about knees, rocking back and forth broken-heartedly. She averred she would not go an inch, not for a dozen Charleses. She appealed to everybody and to everything, finally wiping her eyes and proceeding to cast out even articles of apparel that were imperative necessaries. And in her zeal, when she had finished with her own, she attacked the belongings of her men and went through them like a tornado.

This accomplished, the outfit, though cut in half, was still a formidable bulk. Charles and Hal went out in the evening and bought six Outside dogs. These, added to the six of the original team, and Teek and Koona, the huskies obtained at the Rink Rapids on the record trip, brought the team up to fourteen. But the Outside dogs, though practically broken in since their landing, did not amount to much. Three were short-haired pointers, one was a Newfoundland, and the other two were mongrels of indeterminate breed. They did not seem to know anything, these newcomers. Buck and his comrades looked upon them with disgust, and though he speedily taught them their places and what not to do, he could not teach them what to do. They did not take kindly to trace and trail. With the exception of the two mongrels, they were bewildered and spirit-broken by the strange savage environment in which they found themselves and by the ill treatment they had received. The two mongrels were without spirit at all; bones were the only things breakable about them.

With the newcomers hopeless and forlorn, and the old team worn out by twenty-five hundred miles of continuous trail, the outlook was anything but bright. The two men, however, were quite cheerful. And they were proud, too. They were doing the thing in style, with fourteen dogs. They had seen other sleds depart over the Pass for Dawson, or come in from Dawson, but never had they seen a sled with so many as fourteen dogs. In the nature of Arctic travel there was a reason why fourteen dogs should not drag one sled, and that was that one sled could not carry the food for fourteen dogs. But Charles and Hal did not know this. They had worked the trip out with a pencil, so much to a dog, so many dogs, so many days, Q.E.D. Mercedes looked over their shoulders and nodded comprehensively, it was all so very simple.

Late next morning Buck led the long team up the street. There was nothing lively about it, no snap or go in him and his fellows. They were starting dead weary. Four times he had covered the distance between Salt Water and Dawson, and the knowledge that, jaded and tired, he was facing the same trail once more, made him bitter. His heart was not in the work, nor was the heart of any dog. The Outsides were timid and frightened, the Insides without confidence in their masters.

Buck felt vaguely that there was no depending upon these two men and the woman. They did not know how to do anything, and as the days went by it became apparent that they could not learn. They were slack in all things, without order or discipline. It took them half the night to pitch a slovenly camp, and half the morning to break that camp and get the sled loaded in fashion so slovenly that for the rest of the day they were occupied in stopping and rearranging the load. Some days they did not make ten miles. On other days they were unable to get started at all. And on no day did they succeed in making more than half the distance used by the men as a basis in their dog-food computation.

It was inevitable that they should go short on dog-food. But they hastened it by overfeeding, bringing the day nearer when underfeeding would commence. The Outside dogs, whose digestions had not been trained by chronic famine to make the most of little, had voracious appetites. And when, in addition to this, the worn-out huskies pulled weakly, Hal decided that the orthodox ration was too small. He doubled it. And to cap it all, when Mercedes, with tears in her pretty eyes and a quaver in her throat, could not cajole him into giving the dogs still more, she stole from the fish-sacks and fed them slyly. But it was not food that Buck and the huskies needed, but rest. And though they were making poor time, the heavy load they dragged sapped their strength severely.

Then came the underfeeding. Hal awoke one day to the fact that his dog-food was half gone and the distance only quarter covered; further, that for love or money no additional dog-food was to be obtained. So he cut down even the orthodox ration and tried to increase the day's travel. His sister and brother-in-law seconded him; but they were frustrated by their heavy outfit and their own incompetence. It was a simple matter to give the dogs less food; but it was impossible to make the dogs travel faster, while their own inability to get under way earlier in the morning prevented them from travelling longer hours. Not only did they not know how to work dogs, but they did not know how to work themselves.

The first to go was Dub. Poor blundering thief that he was, always getting caught and punished, he had none the less been a faithful worker. His wrenched shoulder-blade, untreated and unrested, went from bad to worse, till finally Hal shot him with the big Colt's revolver. It is a saying of the country that an Outside dog starves to death on the ration of the husky, so the six Outside dogs under Buck could do no less than die on half the ration of the husky. The Newfoundland went first, followed by the three short-haired pointers, the two mongrels hanging more grittily on to life, but going in the end.

By this time all the amenities and gentlenesses of the Southland had fallen away from the three people. Shorn of its glamour and romance, Arctic travel became to them a reality too harsh for their manhood and womanhood. Mercedes ceased weeping over the dogs, being too occupied with weeping over herself and with quarrelling with her husband and brother. To quarrel was the one thing they were never too weary to do. Their irritability arose out of their misery, increased with it, doubled upon it, outdistanced it. The wonderful patience of the trail which comes to men who toil hard and suffer sore, and remain sweet of speech and kindly, did not come to these two men and the woman. They had no inkling of such a patience. They were stiff and in pain; their muscles ached, their bones ached, their very hearts ached; and because of this they became sharp of speech, and hard words were first on their lips in the morning and last at night.

Charles and Hal wrangled whenever Mercedes gave them a chance. It was the cherished belief of each that he did more than his share of the work, and neither forbore to speak this belief at every opportunity. Sometimes Mercedes sided with her husband, sometimes with her brother. The result was a beautiful and unending family quarrel. Starting from a dispute as to which should chop a few sticks for the fire (a dispute which concerned only Charles and Hal), presently would be lugged in the rest of the family, fathers, mothers, uncles, cousins, people thousands of miles away, and some of them dead. That Hal's views on art, or the sort of society plays his mother's brother wrote, should have anything to do with the chopping of a few sticks of firewood, passes comprehension; nevertheless the quarrel was as likely to tend in that direction as in the direction of Charles's political prejudices. And that Charles's sister's tale-bearing tongue should be relevant to the building of a Yukon fire, was apparent only to Mercedes, who disburdened herself of copious opinions upon that topic, and incidentally upon a few other traits unpleasantly peculiar to her husband's family. In the meantime the fire remained unbuilt, the camp half pitched, and the dogs unfed.

Mercedes nursed a special grievance—the grievance of sex. She was pretty and soft, and had been chivalrously treated all her days. But the present treatment by her husband and brother was everything save chivalrous. It was her custom to be helpless. They complained. Upon which impeachment of what to her was her most essential sex-prerogative, she made their lives unendurable. She no longer considered the dogs, and because she was sore and tired, she persisted in riding on the sled. She was pretty and soft, but she weighed one hundred and twenty pounds—a lusty last straw to the load dragged by the weak and starving animals. She rode for days, till they fell in the traces and the sled stood still. Charles and Hal begged her to get off and walk, pleaded with her, entreated, the while she wept and importuned Heaven with a recital of their brutality.

On one occasion they took her off the sled by main strength. They never did it again.

She let her legs go limp like a spoiled child, and sat down on the trail. They went on their way, but she did not move. After they had travelled three miles they unloaded the sled, came back for her, and by main strength put her on the sled again.

In the excess of their own misery they were callous to the suffering of their animals. Hal's theory, which he practised on others, was that one must get hardened. He had started out preaching it to his sister and brother-in-law. Failing there, he hammered it into the dogs with a club. At the Five Fingers the dog-food gave out, and a toothless old squaw offered to trade them a few pounds of frozen horse-hide for the Colt's revolver that kept the big hunting-knife company at Hal's hip. A poor substitute for food was this hide, just as it had been stripped from the starved horses of the cattlemen six months back. In its frozen state it was more like strips of galvanized iron, and when a dog wrestled it into his stomach it thawed into thin and innutritious leathery strings and into a mass of short hair, irritating and indigestible.

And through it all Buck staggered along at the head of the team as in a nightmare. He pulled when he could; when he could no longer pull, he fell down and remained down till blows from whip or club drove him to his feet again. All the stiffness and gloss had gone out of his beautiful furry coat. The hair hung down, limp and draggled, or matted with dried blood where Hal's club had bruised him. His muscles had wasted away to knotty strings, and the flesh pads had disappeared, so that each rib and every bone in his frame were outlined cleanly through the loose hide that was wrinkled in folds of emptiness. It was heartbreaking, only Buck's heart was unbreakable. The man in the red sweater had proved that.

As it was with Buck, so was it with his mates. They were perambulating skeletons. There were seven all together, including him. In their very great misery they had become insensible to the bite of the lash or the bruise of the club. The pain of the beating was dull and distant, just as the things their eyes saw and their ears heard seemed dull and distant. They were not half living, or quarter living. They were simply so many bags of bones in which sparks of life fluttered faintly. When a halt was made, they dropped down in the traces like dead dogs, and the spark dimmed and paled and seemed to go out. And when the club or whip fell upon them, the spark fluttered feebly up, and they tottered to their feet and staggered on.

There came a day when Billee, the good-natured, fell and could not rise. Hal had traded off his revolver, so he took the axe and knocked Billee on the head as he lay in the traces, then cut the carcass out of the harness and dragged it to one side. Buck saw, and his mates saw, and they knew that this thing was very close to them. On the next day Koona went, and but five of them remained: Joe, too far gone to be malignant; Pike, crippled and limping, only half conscious and not conscious enough longer to malinger; Sol-leks, the one-eyed, still faithful to the toil of trace and trail, and mournful in that he had so little strength with which to pull; Teek, who had not travelled so far that winter and who was now beaten more than the others because he was fresher; and Buck, still at the head of the team, but no longer enforcing discipline or striving to enforce it, blind with weakness half the time and keeping the trail by the loom of it and by the dim feel of his feet.

It was beautiful spring weather, but neither dogs nor humans were aware of it. Each day the sun rose earlier and set later. It was dawn by three in the morning, and twilight lingered till nine at night. The whole long day was a blaze of sunshine. The ghostly winter silence had given way to the great spring murmur of awakening life.

This murmur arose from all the land, fraught with the joy of living. It came from the things that lived and moved again, things which had been as dead and which had not moved during the long months of frost. The sap was rising in the pines. The willows and aspens were bursting out in young buds. Shrubs and vines were putting on fresh garbs of green. Crickets sang in the nights, and in the days all manner of creeping, crawling things rustled forth into the sun. Partridges and woodpeckers were booming and knocking in the forest. Squirrels were chattering, birds singing, and overhead honked the wild-fowl driving up from the south in cunning wedges that split the air.

From every hill slope came the trickle of running water, the music of unseen fountains. All things were thawing, bending, snapping. The Yukon was straining to break loose the ice that bound it down. It ate away from beneath; the sun ate from above. Air-holes formed, fissures sprang and spread apart, while thin sections of ice fell through bodily into the river. And amid all this bursting, rending, throbbing of awakening life, under the blazing sun and through the soft-sighing breezes, like wayfarers to death, staggered the two men, the woman, and the huskies.

With the dogs falling, Mercedes weeping and riding, Hal swearing innocuously, and Charles's eyes wistfully watering, they staggered into John Thornton's camp at the mouth of White River. When they halted, the dogs dropped down as though they had all been struck dead. Mercedes dried her eyes and looked at John Thornton. Charles sat down on a log to rest. He sat down very slowly and painstakingly what of his great stiffness. Hal did the talking. John Thornton was whittling the last touches on an axe-handle he had made from a stick of birch. He whittled and listened, gave monosyllabic replies, and, when it was asked, terse advice. He knew the breed, and he gave his advice in the certainty that it would not be followed.

'They told us up above that the bottom was dropping out of the trail and that the best thing for us to do was to lay over,' Hal said in response to Thornton's warning to take no more chances on the rotten ice. 'They told us we couldn't make White River, and here we are.' This last with a sneering ring of triumph in it.

'And they told you true,' John Thornton answered. 'The bottom's likely to drop out at any moment. Only fools, with the blind luck of fools, could have made it. I tell you straight, I wouldn't risk my carcass on that ice for all the gold in Alaska.'

'That's because you're not a fool, I suppose,' said Hal. 'All the same, we'll go on to Dawson.' He uncoiled his whip. 'Get up there, Buck! Hi! Get up there! Mush on!'

Thornton went on whittling. It was idle, he knew, to get between a fool and his folly; while two or three fools more or less would not alter the scheme of things.

But the team did not get up at the command. It had long since passed into the stage where blows were required to rouse it. The whip flashed out, here and there, on its merciless errands. John Thornton compressed his lips. Sol-leks was the first to crawl to his feet. Teek followed. Joe came next, yelping with pain. Pike made painful efforts. Twice he fell over, when half up, and on the third attempt managed to rise. Buck made no effort. He lay quietly where he had fallen. The lash bit into him again and again, but he neither whined nor struggled. Several times Thornton started, as though to speak, but changed his mind. A moisture came into his eyes, and, as the whipping continued, he arose and walked irresolutely up and down.

This was the first time Buck had failed, in itself a sufficient reason to drive Hal into a rage. He exchanged the whip for the customary club. Buck refused to move under the rain of heavier blows which now fell upon him. Like his mates, he was barely able to get up, but, unlike them, he had made up his mind not to get up. He had a vague feeling of impending doom. This had been strong upon him when he pulled in to the bank, and it had not departed from him. What of the thin and rotten ice he had felt under his feet all day, it seemed that he sensed disaster close at hand, out there ahead on the ice where his master was trying to drive him. He refused to stir. So greatly had he suffered, and so far gone was he, that the blows did not hurt much. And as they continued to fall upon him, the spark of life within flickered and went down. It was nearly out. He felt strangely numb. As though from a great distance, he was aware that he was being beaten. The last sensations of pain left him. He no longer felt anything, though very faintly he could hear the impact of the club upon his body. But it was no longer his body, it seemed so far away.

And then, suddenly, without warning, uttering a cry that was inarticulate and more like the cry of an animal, John Thornton sprang upon the man who wielded the club. Hal was hurled backward, as though struck by a falling tree. Mercedes screamed. Charles looked on wistfully, wiped his watery eyes, but did not get up because of his stiffness.

John Thornton stood over Buck, struggling to control himself, too convulsed with rage to speak.

'If you strike that dog again, I'll kill you,' he at last managed to say in a choking voice.

'It's my dog,' Hal replied, wiping the blood from his mouth as he came back. 'Get out of my way, or I'll fix you. I'm going to Dawson.'

Thornton stood between him and Buck, and evinced no intention of getting out of the way. Hal drew his long hunting-knife. Mercedes screamed, cried, laughed, and manifested the chaotic abandonment of hysteria. Thornton rapped Hal's knuckles with the axe-handle, knocking the knife to the ground. He rapped his knuckles again as he tried to pick it up. Then he stooped, picked it up himself, and with two strokes cut Buck's traces.

Hal had no fight left in him. Besides, his hands were full with his sister, or his arms, rather; while Buck was too near dead to be of further use in hauling the sled. A few minutes later they pulled out from the bank and down the river. Buck heard them go and raised his head to see, Pike was leading, Sol-leks was at the wheel, and between were Joe and Teek. They were limping and staggering. Mercedes was riding the loaded sled. Hal guided at the gee-pole, and Charles stumbled along in the rear.

As Buck watched them, Thornton knelt beside him and with rough, kindly hands searched for broken bones. By the time his search had disclosed nothing more than many bruises and a state of terrible starvation, the sled was a quarter of a mile away. Dog and man watched it crawling along over the ice. Suddenly, they saw its back end drop down, as into a rut, and the gee-pole, with Hal clinging to it, jerk into the air. Mercedes's scream came to their ears. They saw Charles turn and make one step to run back, and then a whole section of ice give way and dogs and humans disappear. A yawning hole was all that was to be seen. The bottom had dropped out of the trail.

John Thornton and Buck looked at each other.

'You poor devil,' said John Thornton, and Buck licked his hand.

CHAPTER VI
FOR THE LOVE OF A MAN

When John Thornton froze his feet in the previous December his partners had made him comfortable and left him to get well, going on themselves up the river to get out a raft of saw-logs for Dawson. He was still limping slightly at the time he rescued Buck, but with the continued warm weather even the slight limp left him. And here, lying by the river bank through the long spring days, watching the running water, listening lazily to the songs of birds and the hum of nature, Buck slowly won back his strength.

A rest comes very good after one has travelled three thousand miles, and it must be confessed that Buck waxed lazy as his wounds healed, his muscles swelled out, and the flesh came back to cover his bones. For that matter, they were all loafing,—Buck, John Thornton, and Skeet and Nig,—waiting for the raft to come that was to carry them down to Dawson. Skeet was a little Irish setter who early made friends with Buck, who, in a dying condition, was unable to resent her first advances. She had the doctor trait which some dogs possess; and as a mother cat washes her kittens, so she washed and cleansed Buck's wounds. Regularly, each morning after he had finished his breakfast, she performed her self-appointed task, till he came to look for her ministrations as much as he did for Thornton's. Nig, equally friendly, though less demonstrative, was a huge black dog, half bloodhound and half deerhound, with eyes that laughed and a boundless good nature.

To Buck's surprise these dogs manifested no jealousy toward him. They seemed to share the kindliness and largeness of John Thornton. As Buck grew stronger they enticed him into all sorts of ridiculous games, in which Thornton himself could not forbear to join; and in this fashion Buck romped through his convalescence and into a new existence. Love, genuine passionate love, was his for the first time. This he had never experienced at Judge Miller's down in the sun-kissed Santa Clara Valley. With the Judge's sons, hunting and tramping, it had been a working partnership; with the Judge's grandsons, a sort of pompous guardianship; and with the Judge himself, a stately and dignified friendship. But love that was feverish and burning, that was adoration, that was madness, it had taken John Thornton to arouse.

This man had saved his life, which was something; but, further, he was the ideal master. Other men saw to the welfare of their dogs from a sense of duty and business expediency; he saw to the welfare of his as if they were his own children, because he could not help it. And he saw further. He never forgot a kindly greeting or a cheering word, and to sit down for a long talk with them ('gas' he called it) was as much his delight as theirs. He had a way of taking Buck's head roughly between his hands, and resting his own head upon Buck's, of shaking him back and forth, the while calling him ill names that to Buck were love names. Buck knew no greater joy than that rough embrace and the sound of murmured oaths, and at each jerk back and forth it seemed that his heart would be shaken out of his body so great was its ecstasy. And when, released, he sprang to his feet, his mouth laughing, his eyes eloquent, his throat vibrant with unuttered sound, and in that fashion remained without movement, John Thornton would reverently exclaim, 'God! you can all but speak!'

Buck had a trick of love expression that was akin to hurt. He would often seize Thornton's hand in his mouth and close so fiercely that the flesh bore the impress of his teeth for some time afterward. And as Buck understood the oaths to be love words, so the man understood this feigned bite for a caress.

For the most part, however, Buck's love was expressed in adoration. While he went wild with happiness when Thornton touched him or spoke to him, he did not seek these tokens. Unlike Skeet, who was wont to shove her nose under Thornton's hand and nudge and nudge till petted, or Nig, who would stalk up and rest his great head on Thornton's knee, Buck was content to adore at a distance. He would lie by the hour, eager, alert, at Thornton's feet, looking up into his face, dwelling upon it, studying it, following with keenest interest each fleeting expression, every movement or change of feature. Or, as chance might have it, he would lie farther away, to the side or rear, watching the outlines of the man and the occasional movements of his body. And often, such was the communion in which they lived, the strength of Buck's gaze would draw John Thornton's head around, and he would return the gaze, without speech, his heart shining out of his eyes as Buck's heart shone out.

For a long time after his rescue, Buck did not like Thornton to get out of his sight. From the moment he left the tent to when he entered it again, Buck would follow at his heels. His transient masters since he had come into the Northland had bred in him a fear that no master could be permanent. He was afraid that Thornton would pass out of his life as Perrault and Francois and the Scotch half-breed had passed out. Even in the night, in his dreams, he was haunted by this fear. At such times he would shake off sleep and creep through the chill to the flap of the tent, where he would stand and listen to the sound of his master's breathing.

But in spite of this great love he bore John Thornton, which seemed to bespeak the soft civilizing influence, the strain of the primitive, which the Northland had aroused in him, remained alive and active. Faithfulness and devotion, things born of fire and roof, were his; yet he retained his wildness and wiliness. He was a thing of the wild, come in from the wild to sit by John Thornton's fire, rather than a dog of the soft Southland stamped with the marks of generations of civilization. Because of his very great love, he could not steal from this man, but from any other man, in any other camp, he did not hesitate an instant; while the cunning with which he stole enabled him to escape detection.

His face and body were scored by the teeth of many dogs, and he fought as fiercely as ever and more shrewdly. Skeet and Nig were too good-natured for quarrelling,— besides, they belonged to John Thornton; but the strange dog, no matter what the breed or valor, swiftly acknowledged Buck's supremacy or found himself struggling for life with a terrible antagonist. And Buck was merciless. He had learned well the law of club and fang, and he never forewent an advantage or drew back from a foe he had started on the way to Death. He had lessoned from Spitz, and from the chief fighting dogs of the police and mail, and knew there was no middle course. He must master or be mastered; while to show mercy was a weakness. Mercy did not exist in the primordial life. It was misunderstood for fear, and such misunderstandings made for death. Kill or be killed, eat or be eaten, was the law; and this mandate, down out of the depths of Time, he obeyed.

He was older than the days he had seen and the breaths he had drawn. He linked the past with the present, and the eternity behind him throbbed through him in a mighty rhythm to which he swayed as the tides and seasons swayed. He sat by John Thornton's fire, a broad-breasted dog, white-fanged and long-furred; but behind him were the shades of all manner of dogs, half-wolves and wild wolves, urgent and prompting, tasting the savor of the meat he ate, thirsting for the water he drank, scenting the wind with him, listening with him and telling him the sounds made by the wild life in the forest, dictating his moods, directing his actions, lying down to sleep with him when he lay down, and dreaming with him and beyond him and becoming themselves the stuff of his dreams.

So peremptorily did these shades beckon him, that each day mankind and the claims of mankind slipped farther from him. Deep in the forest a call was sounding, and as often as he heard this call, mysteriously thrilling and luring, he felt compelled to turn his back upon the fire and the beaten earth around it, and to plunge into the forest, and on and on, he knew not where or why; nor did he wonder where or why, the call sounding imperiously, deep in the forest. But as often as he gained the soft unbroken earth and the green shade, the love for John Thornton drew him back to the fire again.

Thornton alone held him. The rest of mankind was as nothing. Chance travellers might praise or pet him; but he was cold under it all, and from a too demonstrative man he would get up and walk away. When Thornton's partners, Hans and Pete, arrived on the long-expected raft, Buck refused to notice them till he learned they were close to Thornton; after that he tolerated them in a passive sort of way, accepting favors from them as though he favored them by accepting. They were of the same large type as Thornton, living close to the earth, thinking simply and seeing clearly; and ere they swung the raft into the big eddy by the saw-mill at Dawson, they understood Buck and his ways, and did not insist upon an intimacy such as obtained with Skeet and Nig.

For Thornton, however, his love seemed to grow and grow. He, alone among men, could put a pack upon Buck's back in the summer travelling. Nothing was too great for Buck to do, when Thornton commanded. One day (they had grub-staked themselves from the proceeds of the raft and left Dawson for the head-waters of the Tanana) the men and dogs were sitting on the crest of a cliff which fell away, straight down, to naked bed-rock three hundred feet below. John Thornton was sitting near the edge, Buck at his shoulder. A thoughtless whim seized Thornton, and he drew the attention of Hans and Pete to the experiment he had in mind. 'Jump, Buck!' he commanded, sweeping his arm out and over the chasm. The next instant he was grappling with Buck on the extreme edge, while Hans and Pete were dragging them back into safety.

'It's uncanny,' Pete said, after it was over and they had caught their speech.

Thornton shook his head. 'No, it is splendid, and it is terrible, too. Do you know, it sometimes makes me afraid.'

'I'm not hankering to be the man that lays hands on you while he's around,' Pete announced conclusively, nodding his head toward Buck.

'Py Jingo!' was Hans's contribution. 'Not mineself either.'

It was at Circle City, ere the year was out, that Pete's apprehensions were realized. 'Black' Burton, a man evil-tempered and malicious, had been picking a quarrel with a tenderfoot at the bar, when Thornton stepped good-naturedly between. Buck, as was his custom, was lying in a corner, head on paws, watching his master's every action. Burton struck out, without warning, straight from the shoulder. Thornton was sent spinning, and saved himself from falling only by clutching the rail of the bar.

Those who were looking on heard what was neither bark nor yelp, but a something which is best described as a roar, and they saw Buck's body rise up in the air as he left the floor for Burton's throat. The man saved his life by instinctively throwing out his arm, but was hurled backward to the floor with Buck on top of him. Buck loosed his teeth from the flesh of the arm and drove in again for the throat. This time the man succeeded only in partly blocking, and his throat was torn open. Then the crowd was upon Buck, and he was driven off; but while a surgeon checked the bleeding, he prowled up and down, growling furiously, attempting to rush in, and being forced back by an array of hostile clubs. A 'miners' meeting,' called on the spot, decided that the dog had sufficient provocation, and Buck was discharged. But his reputation was made, and from that day his name spread through every camp in Alaska.

Later on, in the fall of the year, he saved John Thornton's life in quite another fashion. The three partners were lining a long and narrow poling-boat down a bad stretch of rapids on the Forty-Mile Creek. Hans and Pete moved along the bank, snubbing with a thin Manila rope from tree to tree, while Thornton remained in the boat, helping its descent by means of a pole, and shouting directions to the shore. Buck, on the bank, worried and anxious, kept abreast of the boat, his eyes never off his master.

At a particularly bad spot, where a ledge of barely submerged rocks jutted out into the river, Hans cast off the rope, and, while Thornton poled the boat out into the stream, ran down the bank with the end in his hand to snub the boat when it had cleared the ledge. This it did, and was flying down-stream in a current as swift as a mill-race, when Hans checked it with the rope and checked too suddenly. The boat flirted over and snubbed in to the bank bottom up, while Thornton, flung sheer out of it, was carried down-stream toward the worst part of the rapids, a stretch of wild water in which no swimmer could live.

Buck had sprung in on the instant; and at the end of three hundred yards, amid a mad swirl of water, he overhauled Thornton. When he felt him grasp his tail, Buck headed for the bank, swimming with all his splendid strength. But the progress shoreward was slow; the progress down-stream amazingly rapid. From below came the fatal roaring where the wild current went wilder and was rent in shreds and spray by the rocks which thrust through like the teeth of an enormous comb. The suck of the water as it took the beginning of the last steep pitch was frightful, and Thornton knew that the shore was impossible. He scraped furiously over a rock, bruised across a second, and struck a third with crushing force. He clutched its slippery top with both hands, releasing Buck, and above the roar of the churning water shouted: 'Go, Buck! Go!'

Buck could not hold his own, and swept on down-stream, struggling desperately, but unable to win back. When he heard Thornton's command repeated, he partly reared out of the water, throwing his head high, as though for a last look, then turned obediently toward the bank. He swam powerfully and was dragged ashore by Pete and Hans at the very point where swimming ceased to be possible and destruction began.

They knew that the time a man could cling to a slippery rock in the face of that driving current was a matter of minutes, and they ran as fast as they could up the bank to a point far above where Thornton was hanging on. They attached the line with which they had been snubbing the boat to Buck's neck and shoulders, being careful that it should neither strangle him nor impede his swimming, and launched him into the stream. He struck out boldly, but not straight enough into the stream.

He discovered the mistake too late, when Thornton was abreast of him and a bare half-dozen strokes away while he was being carried helplessly past. Hans promptly snubbed with the rope, as though Buck were a boat. The rope thus tightening on him in the sweep of the current, he was jerked under the surface, and under the surface he remained till his body struck against the bank and he was hauled out. He was half drowned, and Hans and Pete threw themselves upon him, pounding the breath into him and the water out of him. He staggered to his feet and fell down. The faint sound of Thornton's voice came to them, and though they could not make out the words of it, they knew that he was in his extremity. His master's voice acted on Buck like an electric shock, He sprang to his feet and ran up the bank ahead of the men to the point of his previous departure.

Again the rope was attached and he was launched, and again he struck out, but this time straight into the stream. He had miscalculated once, but he would not be guilty of it a second time. Hans paid out the rope, permitting no slack, while Pete kept it clear of coils. Buck held on till he was on a line straight above Thornton; then he turned, and with the speed of an express train headed down upon him. Thornton saw him coming, and, as Buck struck him like a battering ram, with the whole force of the current behind him, he reached up and closed with both arms around the shaggy neck. Hans snubbed the rope around the tree, and Buck and Thornton were jerked under the water. Strangling, suffocating, sometimes one uppermost and sometimes the other, dragging over the jagged bottom, smashing against rocks and snags, they veered in to the bank.

Thornton came to, belly downward and being violently propelled back and forth across a drift log by Hans and Pete. His first glance was for Buck, over whose limp and apparently lifeless body Nig was setting up a howl, while Skeet was licking the wet face and closed eyes. Thornton was himself bruised and battered, and he went carefully over Buck's body, when he had been brought around, finding three broken ribs.

'That settles it,' he announced. 'We camp right here.' And camp they did, till Buck's ribs knitted and he was able to travel.

That winter, at Dawson, Buck performed another exploit, not so heroic, perhaps, but one that put his name many notches higher on the totem-pole of Alaskan fame. This exploit was particularly gratifying to the three men; for they stood in need of the outfit which it furnished, and were enabled to make a long-desired trip into the virgin East, where miners had not yet appeared. It was brought about by a conversation in the Eldorado Saloon, in which men waxed boastful of their favorite dogs. Buck, because of his record, was the target for these men, and Thornton was driven stoutly to defend him. At the end of half an hour one man stated that his dog could start a sled with five hundred pounds and walk off with it; a second bragged six hundred for his dog; and a third, seven hundred.

'Pooh! pooh!' said John Thornton; 'Buck can start a thousand pounds.'

'And break it out? and walk off with it for a hundred yards?' demanded Matthewson, a Bonanza King, he of the seven hundred vaunt.

'And break it out, and walk off with it for a hundred yards,' John Thornton said coolly.

'Well,' Matthewson said, slowly and deliberately, so that all could hear, 'I've got a thousand dollars that says he can't. And there it is.' So saying, he slammed a sack of gold dust of the size of a bologna sausage down upon the bar.

Nobody spoke. Thornton's bluff, if bluff it was, had been called. He could feel a flush of warm blood creeping up his face. His tongue had tricked him. He did not know whether Buck could start a thousand pounds. Half a ton! The enormousness of it appalled him. He had great faith in Buck's strength and had often thought him capable of starting such a load; but never, as now, had he faced the possibility of it, the eyes of a dozen men fixed upon him, silent and waiting. Further, he had no thousand dollars; nor had Hans or Pete.

'I've got a sled standing outside now, with twenty fifty-pound sacks of flour on it,' Matthewson went on with brutal directness; 'so don't let that hinder you.'

Thornton did not reply. He did not know what to say. He glanced from face to face in the absent way of a man who has lost the power of thought and is seeking somewhere to find the thing that will start it going again. The face of Jim O'Brien, a Mastodon King and old-time comrade, caught his eyes. It was as a cue to him, seeming to rouse him to do what he would never have dreamed of doing.

'Can you lend me a thousand?' he asked, almost in a whisper.

'Sure,' answered O'Brien, thumping down a plethoric sack by the side of Matthewson's. 'Though it's little faith I'm having, John, that the beast can do the trick.'

The Eldorado emptied its occupants into the street to see the test. The tables were deserted, and the dealers and gamekeepers came forth to see the outcome of the wager and to lay odds. Several hundred men, furred and mittened, banked around the sled within easy distance. Matthewson's sled, loaded with a thousand pounds of flour, had been standing for a couple of hours, and in the intense cold (it was sixty below zero) the runners had frozen fast to the hard-packed snow. Men offered odds of two to one that Buck could not budge the sled. A quibble arose concerning the phrase 'break out.' O'Brien contended it was Thornton's privilege to knock the runners loose, leaving Buck to 'break it out' from a dead standstill. Matthewson insisted that the phrase included breaking the runners from the frozen grip of the snow. A majority of the men who had witnessed the making of the bet decided in his favor, whereat the odds went up to three to one against Buck.

There were no takers. Not a man believed him capable of the feat. Thornton had been hurried into the wager, heavy with doubt; and now that he looked at the sled itself, the concrete fact, with the regular team of ten dogs curled up in the snow before it, the more impossible the task appeared. Matthewson waxed jubilant.

'Three to one!' he proclaimed. 'I'll lay you another thousand at that figure, Thornton. What d'ye say?'

Thornton's doubt was strong in his face, but his fighting spirit was aroused—the fighting spirit that soars above odds, fails to recognize the impossible, and is deaf to all save the clamor for battle. He called Hans and Pete to him. Their sacks were slim, and with his own the three partners could rake together only two hundred dollars. In the ebb of their fortunes, this sum was their total capital; yet they laid it unhesitatingly against Matthewson's six hundred.

The team of ten dogs was unhitched, and Buck, with his own harness, was put into the sled. He had caught the contagion of the excitement, and he felt that in some way he must do a great thing for John Thornton. Murmurs of admiration at his splendid appearance went up. He was in perfect condition, without an ounce of superfluous flesh, and the one hundred and fifty pounds that he weighed were so many pounds of grit and virility. His furry coat shone with the sheen of silk. Down the neck and across the shoulders, his mane, in repose as it was, half bristled and seemed to lift with every movement, as though excess of vigor made each particular hair alive and active. The great breast and heavy fore legs were no more than in proportion with the rest of the body, where the muscles showed in tight rolls underneath the skin. Men felt these muscles and proclaimed them hard as iron, and the odds went down to two to one.

'Gad, sir! Gad, sir!' stuttered a member of the latest dynasty, a king of the Skookum Benches. 'I offer you eight hundred for him, sir, before the test, sir; eight hundred just as he stands.'

Thornton shook his head and stepped to Buck's side.

'You must stand off from him,' Matthewson protested. 'Free play and plenty of room.'

The crowd fell silent; only could be heard the voices of the gamblers vainly offering two to one. Everybody acknowledged Buck a magnificent animal, but twenty fifty-pound sacks of flour bulked too large in their eyes for them to loosen their pouch-strings.

Thornton knelt down by Buck's side. He took his head in his two hands and rested cheek on cheek. He did not playfully shake him, as was his wont, or murmur soft love curses; but he whispered in his ear. 'As you love me, Buck. As you love me,' was what he whispered. Buck whined with suppressed eagerness.

The crowd was watching curiously. The affair was growing mysterious. It seemed like a conjuration. As Thornton got to his feet, Buck seized his mittened hand between his jaws, pressing in with his teeth and releasing slowly, half-reluctantly. It was the answer, in terms, not of speech, but of love. Thornton stepped well back.

'Now, Buck,' he said.

Buck tightened the traces, then slacked them for a matter of several inches. It was the way he had learned.

'Gee!' Thornton's voice rang out, sharp in the tense silence.

Buck swung to the right, ending the movement in a plunge that took up the slack and with a sudden jerk arrested his one hundred and fifty pounds. The load quivered, and from under the runners arose a crisp crackling.

'Haw!' Thornton commanded.

Buck duplicated the manoeuvre, this time to the left. The crackling turned into a snapping, the sled pivoting and the runners slipping and grating several inches to the side. The sled was broken out. Men were holding their breaths, intensely unconscious of the fact.

'Now, MUSH!'

Thornton's command cracked out like a pistol-shot. Buck threw himself forward, tightening the traces with a jarring lunge. His whole body was gathered compactly together in the tremendous effort, the muscles writhing and knotting like live things under the silky fur. His great chest was low to the ground, his head forward and down, while his feet were flying like mad, the claws scarring the hard-packed snow in parallel grooves. The sled swayed and trembled, half-started forward. One of his feet slipped, and one man groaned aloud. Then the sled lurched ahead in what appeared a rapid succession of jerks, though it never really came to a dead stop again...half an inch...an inch... two inches... The jerks perceptibly diminished; as the sled gained momentum, he caught them up, till it was moving steadily along.

Men gasped and began to breathe again, unaware that for a moment they had ceased to breathe. Thornton was running behind, encouraging Buck with short, cheery words. The distance had been measured off, and as he neared the pile of firewood which marked the end of the hundred yards, a cheer began to grow and grow, which burst into a roar as he passed the firewood and halted at command. Every man was tearing himself loose, even Matthewson. Hats and mittens were flying in the air. Men were shaking hands, it did not matter with whom, and bubbling over in a general incoherent babel.

But Thornton fell on his knees beside Buck. Head was against head, and he was shaking him back and forth. Those who hurried up heard him cursing Buck, and he cursed him long and fervently, and softly and lovingly.

'Gad, sir! Gad, sir!' spluttered the Skookum Bench king. 'I'll give you a thousand for him, sir, a thousand, sir—twelve hundred, sir.'

Thornton rose to his feet. His eyes were wet. The tears were streaming frankly down his cheeks. 'Sir,' he said to the Skookum Bench king, 'no, sir. You can go to hell, sir. It's the best I can do for you, sir.'

Buck seized Thornton's hand in his teeth. Thornton shook him back and forth. As though animated by a common impulse, the onlookers drew back to a respectful distance; nor were they again indiscreet enough to interrupt.

CHAPTER VII
THE SOUNDING OF THE CALL

When Buck earned sixteen hundred dollars in five minutes for John Thornton, he made it possible for his master to pay off certain debts and to journey with his partners into the East after a fabled lost mine, the history of which was as old as the history of the country. Many men had sought it; few had found it; and more than a few there were who had never returned from the quest. This lost mine was steeped in tragedy and shrouded in mystery. No one knew of the first man. The oldest tradition stopped before it got back to him. From the beginning there had been an ancient and ramshackle cabin. Dying men had sworn to it, and to the mine the site of which it marked, clinching their testimony with nuggets that were unlike any known grade of gold in the Northland.

But no living man had looted this treasure house, and the dead were dead; wherefore John Thornton and Pete and Hans, with Buck and half a dozen other dogs, faced into the East on an unknown trail to achieve where men and dogs as good as themselves had failed. They sledded seventy miles up the Yukon, swung to the left into the Stewart River, passed the Mayo and the McQuestion, and held on until the Stewart itself became a streamlet, threading the upstanding peaks which marked the backbone of the continent.

John Thornton asked little of man or nature. He was unafraid of the wild. With a handful of salt and a rifle he could plunge into the wilderness and fare wherever he pleased and as long as he pleased. Being in no haste, Indian fashion, he hunted his dinner in the course of the day's travel; and if he failed to find it, like the Indian, he kept on travelling, secure in the knowledge that sooner or later he would come to it. So, on this great journey into the East, straight meat was the bill of fare, ammunition and tools principally made up the load on the sled, and the time-card was drawn upon the limitless future.

To Buck it was boundless delight, this hunting, fishing, and indefinite wandering through strange places. For weeks at a time they would hold on steadily, day after day; and for weeks upon end they would camp, here and there, the dogs loafing and the men burning holes through frozen muck and gravel and washing countless pans of dirt by the heat of the fire. Sometimes they went hungry, sometimes they feasted riotously, all according to the abundance of game and the fortune of hunting. Summer arrived, and dogs and men packed on their backs, rafted across blue mountain lakes, and descended or ascended unknown rivers in slender boats whipsawed from the standing forest.

The months came and went, and back and forth they twisted through the uncharted vastness, where no men were and yet where men had been if the Lost Cabin were true. They went across divides in summer blizzards, shivered under the midnight sun on naked mountains between the timber line and the eternal snows, dropped into summer valleys amid swarming gnats and flies, and in the shadows of glaciers picked strawberries and flowers as ripe and fair as any the Southland could boast. In the fall of the year they penetrated a weird lake country, sad and silent, where wildfowl had been, but where then there was no life nor sign of life—only the blowing of chill winds, the forming of ice in sheltered places, and the melancholy rippling of waves on lonely beaches.

And through another winter they wandered on the obliterated trails of men who had gone before. Once, they came upon a path blazed through the forest, an ancient path, and the Lost Cabin seemed very near. But the path began nowhere and ended nowhere, and it remained mystery, as the man who made it and the reason he made it remained mystery. Another time they chanced upon the time-graven wreckage of a hunting lodge, and amid the shreds of rotted blankets John Thornton found a long-barrelled flint-lock. He knew it for a Hudson Bay Company gun of the young days in the Northwest, when such a gun was worth its height in beaver skins packed flat, And that was all—no hint as to the man who in an early day had reared the lodge and left the gun among the blankets.

Spring came on once more, and at the end of all their wandering they found, not the Lost Cabin, but a shallow placer in a broad valley where the gold showed like yellow butter across the bottom of the washing-pan. They sought no farther. Each day they worked earned them thousands of dollars in clean dust and nuggets, and they worked every day. The gold was sacked in moose-hide bags, fifty pounds to the bag, and piled like so much firewood outside the spruce-bough lodge. Like giants they toiled, days flashing on the heels of days like dreams as they heaped the treasure up.

There was nothing for the dogs to do, save the hauling in of meat now and again that Thornton killed, and Buck spent long hours musing by the fire. The vision of the short-legged hairy man came to him more frequently, now that there was little work to be done; and often, blinking by the fire, Buck wandered with him in that other world which he remembered.

The salient thing of this other world seemed fear. When he watched the hairy man sleeping by the fire, head between his knees and hands clasped above, Buck saw that he slept restlessly, with many starts and awakenings, at which times he would peer fearfully into the darkness and fling more wood upon the fire. Did they walk by the beach of a sea, where the hairy man gathered shellfish and ate them as he gathered, it was with eyes that roved everywhere for hidden danger and with legs prepared to run like the wind at its first appearance. Through the forest they crept noiselessly,

Buck at the hairy man's heels; and they were alert and vigilant, the pair of them, ears twitching and moving and nostrils quivering, for the man heard and smelled as keenly as Buck. The hairy man could spring up into the trees and travel ahead as fast as on the ground, swinging by the arms from limb to limb, sometimes a dozen feet apart, letting go and catching, never falling, never missing his grip. In fact, he seemed as much at home among the trees as on the ground; and Buck had memories of nights of vigil spent beneath trees wherein the hairy man roosted, holding on tightly as he slept.

And closely akin to the visions of the hairy man was the call still sounding in the depths of the forest. It filled him with a great unrest and strange desires. It caused him to feel a vague, sweet gladness, and he was aware of wild yearnings and stirrings for he knew not what. Sometimes he pursued the call into the forest, looking for it as though it were a tangible thing, barking softly or defiantly, as the mood might dictate. He would thrust his nose into the cool wood moss, or into the black soil where long grasses grew, and snort with joy at the fat earth smells; or he would crouch for hours, as if in concealment, behind fungus-covered trunks of fallen trees, wide-eyed and wide-eared to all that moved and sounded about him. It might be, lying thus, that he hoped to surprise this call he could not understand. But he did not know why he did these various things. He was impelled to do them, and did not reason about them at all.

Irresistible impulses seized him. He would be lying in camp, dozing lazily in the heat of the day, when suddenly his head would lift and his ears cock up, intent and listening, and he would spring to his feet and dash away, and on and on, for hours, through the forest aisles and across the open spaces where the niggerheads bunched. He loved to run down dry watercourses, and to creep and spy upon the bird life in the woods. For a day at a time he would lie in the underbrush where he could watch the partridges drumming and strutting up and down. But especially he loved to run in the dim twilight of the summer midnights, listening to the subdued and sleepy murmurs of the forest, reading signs and sounds as man may read a book, and seeking for the mysterious something that called—called, waking or sleeping, at all times, for him to come.

One night he sprang from sleep with a start, eager-eyed, nostrils quivering and scenting, his mane bristling in recurrent waves. From the forest came the call (or one note of it, for the call was many noted), distinct and definite as never before,—a long-drawn howl, like, yet unlike, any noise made by husky dog. And he knew it, in the old familiar way, as a sound heard before. He sprang through the sleeping camp and in swift silence dashed through the woods. As he drew closer to the cry he went more slowly, with caution in every movement, till he came to an open place among the trees, and looking out saw, erect on haunches, with nose pointed to the sky, a long, lean, timber wolf.

He had made no noise, yet it ceased from its howling and tried to sense his presence. Buck stalked into the open, half crouching, body gathered compactly together, tail straight and stiff, feet falling with unwonted care. Every movement advertised commingled threatening and overture of friendliness. It was the menacing truce that marks the meeting of wild beasts that prey. But the wolf fled at sight of him. He followed, with wild leapings, in a frenzy to overtake. He ran him into a blind channel, in the bed of the creek where a timber jam barred the way. The wolf whirled about, pivoting on his hind legs after the fashion of Joe and of all cornered husky dogs, snarling and bristling, clipping his teeth together in a continuous and rapid succession of snaps.

Buck did not attack, but circled him about and hedged him in with friendly advances. The wolf was suspicious and afraid; for Buck made three of him in weight, while his head barely reached Buck's shoulder. Watching his chance, he darted away, and the chase was resumed. Time and again he was cornered, and the thing repeated, though he was in poor condition, or Buck could not so easily have overtaken him. He would run till Buck's head was even with his flank, when he would whirl around at bay, only to dash away again at the first opportunity.

But in the end Buck's pertinacity was rewarded; for the wolf, finding that no harm was intended, finally sniffed noses with him. Then they became friendly, and played about in the nervous, half-coy way with which fierce beasts belie their fierceness. After some time of this the wolf started off at an easy lope in a manner that plainly showed he was going somewhere. He made it clear to Buck that he was to come, and they ran side by side through the sombre twilight, straight up the creek bed, into the gorge from which it issued, and across the bleak divide where it took its rise.

On the opposite slope of the watershed they came down into a level country where were great stretches of forest and many streams, and through these great stretches they ran steadily, hour after hour, the sun rising higher and the day growing warmer. Buck was wildly glad. He knew he was at last answering the call, running by the side of his wood brother toward the place from where the call surely came. Old memories were coming upon him fast, and he was stirring to them as of old he stirred to the realities of which they were the shadows. He had done this thing before, somewhere in that other and dimly remembered world, and he was doing it again, now, running free in the open, the unpacked earth underfoot, the wide sky overhead.

They stopped by a running stream to drink, and, stopping, Buck remembered John Thornton. He sat down. The wolf started on toward the place from where the call surely came, then returned to him, sniffing noses and making actions as though to encourage him. But Buck turned about and started slowly on the back track. For the better part of an hour the wild brother ran by his side, whining softly. Then he sat down, pointed his nose upward, and howled. It was a mournful howl, and as Buck held steadily on his way he heard it grow faint and fainter until it was lost in the distance.

John Thornton was eating dinner when Buck dashed into camp and sprang upon him in a frenzy of affection, overturning him, scrambling upon him, licking his face, biting his hand—'playing the general tom-fool,' as John Thornton characterized it, the while he shook Buck back and forth and cursed him lovingly.

For two days and nights Buck never left camp, never let Thornton out of his sight. He followed him about at his work, watched him while he ate, saw him into his blankets at night and out of them in the morning. But after two days the call in the forest began to sound more imperiously than ever. Buck's restlessness came back on him, and he was haunted by recollections of the wild brother, and of the smiling land beyond the divide and the run side by side through the wide forest stretches. Once again he took to wandering in the woods, but the wild brother came no more; and though he listened through long vigils, the mournful howl was never raised.

He began to sleep out at night, staying away from camp for days at a time; and once he crossed the divide at the head of the creek and went down into the land of timber and streams. There he wandered for a week, seeking vainly for fresh sign of the wild brother, killing his meat as he travelled and travelling with the long, easy lope that seems never to tire. He fished for salmon in a broad stream that emptied somewhere into the sea, and by this stream he killed a large black bear, blinded by the mosquitoes while likewise fishing, and raging through the forest helpless and terrible. Even so, it was a hard fight, and it aroused the last latent remnants of Buck's ferocity. And two days later, when he returned to his kill and found a dozen wolverenes quarrelling over the spoil, he scattered them like chaff; and those that fled left two behind who would quarrel no more.

The blood-longing became stronger than ever before. He was a killer, a thing that preyed, living on the things that lived, unaided, alone, by virtue of his own strength and prowess, surviving triumphantly in a hostile environment where only the strong survived. Because of all this he became possessed of a great pride in himself, which communicated itself like a contagion to his physical being. It advertised itself in all his movements, was apparent in the play of every muscle, spoke plainly as speech in the way he carried himself, and made his glorious furry coat if anything more glorious. But for the stray brown on his muzzle and above his eyes, and for the splash of white hair that ran midmost down his chest, he might well have been mistaken for a gigantic wolf, larger than the largest of the breed. From his St. Bernard father he had inherited size and weight, but it was his shepherd mother who had given shape to that size and weight. His muzzle was the long wolf muzzle, save that it was larger than the muzzle of any wolf; and his head, somewhat broader, was the wolf head on a massive scale.

His cunning was wolf cunning, and wild cunning; his intelligence, shepherd intelligence and St. Bernard intelligence; and all this, plus an experience gained in the fiercest of schools, made him as formidable a creature as any that roamed the wild. A carnivorous animal living on a straight meat diet, he was in full flower, at the high tide of his life, overspilling with vigor and virility. When Thornton passed a caressing hand along his back, a snapping and crackling followed the hand, each hair discharging its pent magnetism at the contact. Every part, brain and body, nerve tissue and fibre, was keyed to the most exquisite pitch; and between all the parts there was a perfect equilibrium or adjustment. To sights and sounds and events which required action, he responded with lightning-like rapidity. Quickly as a husky dog could leap to defend from attack or to attack, he could leap twice as quickly. He saw the movement, or heard sound, and responded in less time than another dog required to compass the mere seeing or hearing. He perceived and determined and responded in the same instant. In point of fact the three actions of perceiving, determining, and responding were sequential; but so infinitesimal were the intervals of time between them that they appeared simultaneous. His muscles were surcharged with vitality, and snapped into play sharply, like steel springs. Life streamed through him in splendid flood, glad and rampant, until it seemed that it would burst him asunder in sheer ecstasy and pour forth generously over the world.

'Never was there such a dog,' said John Thornton one day, as the partners watched Buck marching out of camp.

'When he was made, the mould was broke,' said Pete.

'Py jingo! I t'ink so mineself,' Hans affirmed.

They saw him marching out of camp, but they did not see the instant and terrible transformation which took place as soon as he was within the secrecy of the forest. He no longer marched. At once he became a thing of the wild, stealing along softly, cat-footed, a passing shadow that appeared and disappeared among the shadows. He knew how to take advantage of every cover, to crawl on his belly like a snake, and like a snake to leap and strike. He could take a ptarmigan from its nest, kill a rabbit as it slept, and snap in mid air the little chipmunks fleeing a second too late for the trees. Fish, in open pools, were not too quick for him; nor were beaver, mending their dams, too wary. He killed to eat, not from wantonness; but he preferred to eat what he killed himself. So a lurking humor ran through his deeds, and it was his delight to steal upon the squirrels, and, when he all but had them, to let them go, chattering in mortal fear to the treetops.

As the fall of the year came on, the moose appeared in greater abundance, moving slowly down to meet the winter in the lower and less rigorous valleys. Buck had already dragged down a stray part-grown calf; but he wished strongly for larger and more formidable quarry, and he came upon it one day on the divide at the head of the creek. A band of twenty moose had crossed over from the land of streams and timber, and chief among them was a great bull. He was in a savage temper, and, standing over six feet from the ground, was as formidable an antagonist as even Buck could desire. Back and forth the bull tossed his great palmated antlers, branching to fourteen points and embracing seven feet within the tips. His small eyes burned with a vicious and bitter light, while he roared with fury at sight of Buck.

From the bull's side, just forward of the flank, protruded a feathered arrow-end, which accounted for his savageness. Guided by that instinct which came from the old hunting days of the primordial world, Buck proceeded to cut the bull out from the herd. It was no slight task. He would bark and dance about in front of the bull, just out of reach of the great antlers and of the terrible splay hoofs which could have stamped his life out with a single blow. Unable to turn his back on the fanged danger and go on, the bull would be driven into paroxysms of rage. At such moments he charged Buck, who retreated craftily, luring him on by a simulated inability to escape. But when he was thus separated from his fellows, two or three of the younger bulls would charge back upon Buck and enable the wounded bull to rejoin the herd.

There is a patience of the wild—dogged, tireless, persistent as life itself—that holds motionless for endless hours the spider in its web, the snake in its coils, the panther in its ambuscade; this patience belongs peculiarly to life when it hunts its living food; and it belonged to Buck as he clung to the flank of the herd, retarding its march, irritating the young bulls, worrying the cows with their half-grown calves, and driving the wounded bull mad with helpless rage. For half a day this continued. Buck multiplied himself, attacking from all sides, enveloping the herd in a whirlwind of menace, cutting out his victim as fast as it could rejoin its mates, wearing out the patience of creatures preyed upon, which is a lesser patience than that of creatures preying.

As the day wore along and the sun dropped to its bed in the northwest (the darkness had come back and the fall nights were six hours long), the young bulls retraced their steps more and more reluctantly to the aid of their beset leader. The down-coming winter was harrying them on to the lower levels, and it seemed they could never shake off this tireless creature that held them back. Besides, it was not the life of the herd, or of the young bulls, that was threatened. The life of only one member was demanded, which was a remoter interest than their lives, and in the end they were content to pay the toll.

As twilight fell the old bull stood with lowered head, watching his mates—the cows he had known, the calves he had fathered, the bulls he had mastered—as they shambled on at a rapid pace through the fading light. He could not follow, for before his nose leaped the merciless fanged terror that would not let him go. Three hundredweight more than half a ton he weighed; he had lived a long, strong life, full of fight and struggle, and at the end he faced death at the teeth of a creature whose head did not reach beyond his great knuckled knees.

From then on, night and day, Buck never left his prey, never gave it a moment's rest, never permitted it to browse the leaves of trees or the shoots of young birch and willow. Nor did he give the wounded bull opportunity to slake his burning thirst in the slender trickling streams they crossed. Often, in desperation, he burst into long stretches of flight. At such times Buck did not attempt to stay him, but loped easily at his heels, satisfied with the way the game was played, lying down when the moose stood still, attacking him fiercely when he strove to eat or drink.

The great head drooped more and more under its tree of horns, and the shambling trot grew weak and weaker. He took to standing for long periods, with nose to the ground and dejected ears dropped limply; and Buck found more time in which to get water for himself and in which to rest. At such moments, panting with red lolling tongue and with eyes fixed upon the big bull, it appeared to Buck that a change was coming over the face of things. He could feel a new stir in the land. As the moose were coming into the land, other kinds of life were coming in. Forest and stream and air seemed palpitant with their presence. The news of it was borne in upon him, not by sight, or sound, or smell, but by some other and subtler sense. He heard nothing, saw nothing, yet knew that the land was somehow different; that through it strange things were afoot and ranging; and he resolved to investigate after he had finished the business in hand.

At last, at the end of the fourth day, he pulled the great moose down. For a day and a night he remained by the kill, eating and sleeping, turn and turn about. Then, rested, refreshed and strong, he turned his face toward camp and John Thornton. He broke into the long easy lope, and went on, hour after hour, never at loss for the tangled way, heading straight home through strange country with a certitude of direction that put man and his magnetic needle to shame.

As he held on he became more and more conscious of the new stir in the land. There was life abroad in it different from the life which had been there throughout the summer. No longer was this fact borne in upon him in some subtle, mysterious way. The birds talked of it, the squirrels chattered about it, the very breeze whispered of it. Several times he stopped and drew in the fresh morning air in great sniffs, reading a message which made him leap on with greater speed. He was oppressed with a sense of calamity happening, if it were not calamity already happened; and as he crossed the last watershed and dropped down into the valley toward camp, he proceeded with greater caution.

Three miles away he came upon a fresh trail that sent his neck hair rippling and bristling, It led straight toward camp and John Thornton. Buck hurried on, swiftly and stealthily, every nerve straining and tense, alert to the multitudinous details which told a story—all but the end. His nose gave him a varying description of the passage of the life on the heels of which he was travelling. He remarked the pregnant silence of the forest. The bird life had flitted. The squirrels were in hiding. One only he saw,—a sleek gray fellow, flattened against a gray dead limb so that he seemed a part of it, a woody excrescence upon the wood itself.

As Buck slid along with the obscureness of a gliding shadow, his nose was jerked suddenly to the side as though a positive force had gripped and pulled it. He followed the new scent into a thicket and found Nig. He was lying on his side, dead where he had dragged himself, an arrow protruding, head and feathers, from either side of his body.

A hundred yards farther on, Buck came upon one of the sled-dogs Thornton had bought in Dawson. This dog was thrashing about in a death-struggle, directly on the trail, and Buck passed around him without stopping. From the camp came the faint sound of many voices, rising and falling in a sing-song chant. Bellying forward to the edge of the clearing, he found Hans, lying on his face, feathered with arrows like a porcupine. At the same instant Buck peered out where the spruce-bough lodge had been and saw what made his hair leap straight up on his neck and shoulders. A gust of overpowering rage swept over him. He did not know that he growled, but he growled aloud with a terrible ferocity. For the last time in his life he allowed passion to usurp cunning and reason, and it was because of his great love for John Thornton that he lost his head.

The Yeehats were dancing about the wreckage of the spruce-bough lodge when they heard a fearful roaring and saw rushing upon them an animal the like of which they had never seen before. It was Buck, a live hurricane of fury, hurling himself upon them in a frenzy to destroy. He sprang at the foremost man (it was the chief of the Yeehats), ripping the throat wide open till the rent jugular spouted a fountain of blood. He did not pause to worry the victim, but ripped in passing, with the next bound tearing wide the throat of a second man. There was no withstanding him. He plunged about in their very midst, tearing, rending, destroying, in constant and terrific motion which defied the arrows they discharged at him. In fact, so inconceivably rapid were his movements, and so closely were the Indians tangled together, that they shot one another with the arrows; and one young hunter, hurling a spear at Buck in mid air, drove it through the chest of another hunter with such force that the point broke through the skin of the back and stood out beyond. Then a panic seized the Yeehats, and they fled in terror to the woods, proclaiming as they fled the advent of the Evil Spirit.

And truly Buck was the Fiend incarnate, raging at their heels and dragging them down like deer as they raced through the trees. It was a fateful day for the Yeehats. They scattered far and wide over the country, and it was not till a week later that the last of the survivors gathered together in a lower valley and counted their losses. As for Buck, wearying of the pursuit, he returned to the desolated camp. He found Pete where he had been killed in his blankets in the first moment of surprise. Thornton's desperate struggle was fresh-written on the earth, and Buck scented every detail of it down to the edge of a deep pool. By the edge, head and fore feet in the water, lay Skeet, faithful to the last. The pool itself, muddy and discolored from the sluice boxes, effectually hid what it contained, and it contained John Thornton; for Buck followed his trace into the water, from which no trace led away.

All day Buck brooded by the pool or roamed restlessly about the camp. Death, as a cessation of movement, as a passing out and away from the lives of the living, he knew, and he knew John Thornton was dead. It left a great void in him, somewhat akin to hunger, but a void which ached and ached, and which food could not fill, At times, when he paused to contemplate the carcasses of the Yeehats, he forgot the pain of it; and at such times he was aware of a great pride in himself,—a pride greater than any he had yet experienced. He had killed man, the noblest game of all, and he had killed in the face of the law of club and fang. He sniffed the bodies curiously. They had died so easily. It was harder to kill a husky dog than them. They were no match at all, were it not for their arrows and spears and clubs. Thenceforward he would be unafraid of them except when they bore in their hands their arrows, spears, and clubs.

Night came on, and a full moon rose high over the trees into the sky, lighting the land till it lay bathed in ghostly day. And with the coming of the night, brooding and mourning by the pool, Buck became alive to a stirring of the new life in the forest other than that which the Yeehats had made, He stood up, listening and scenting. From far away drifted a faint, sharp yelp, followed by a chorus of similar sharp yelps. As the moments passed the yelps grew closer and louder. Again Buck knew them as things heard in that other world which persisted in his memory. He walked to the centre of the open space and listened. It was the call, the many-noted call, sounding more luringly and compellingly than ever before. And as never before, he was ready to obey. John Thornton was dead. The last tie was broken. Man and the claims of man no longer bound him.

Hunting their living meat, as the Yeehats were hunting it, on the flanks of the migrating moose, the wolf pack had at last crossed over from the land of streams and timber and invaded Buck's valley. Into the clearing where the moonlight streamed, they poured in a silvery flood; and in the centre of the clearing stood Buck, motionless as a statue, waiting their coming. They were awed, so still and large he stood, and a moment's pause fell, till the boldest one leaped straight for him. Like a flash Buck struck, breaking the neck. Then he stood, without movement, as before, the stricken wolf rolling in agony behind him. Three others tried it in sharp succession; and one after the other they drew back, streaming blood from slashed throats or shoulders.

This was sufficient to fling the whole pack forward, pell-mell, crowded together, blocked and confused by its eagerness to pull down the prey. Buck's marvellous quickness and agility stood him in good stead. Pivoting on his hind legs, and snapping and gashing, he was everywhere at once, presenting a front which was apparently unbroken so swiftly did he whirl and guard from side to side. But to prevent them from getting behind him, he was forced back, down past the pool and into the creek bed, till he brought up against a high gravel bank. He worked along to a right angle in the bank which the men had made in the course of mining, and in this angle he came to bay, protected on three sides and with nothing to do but face the front.

And so well did he face it, that at the end of half an hour the wolves drew back discomfited. The tongues of all were out and lolling, the white fangs showing cruelly white in the moonlight. Some were lying down with heads raised and ears pricked forward; others stood on their feet, watching him; and still others were lapping water from the pool. One wolf, long and lean and gray, advanced cautiously, in a friendly manner, and Buck recognized the wild brother with whom he had run for a night and a day. He was whining softly, and, as Buck whined, they touched noses.

Then an old wolf, gaunt and battle-scarred, came forward. Buck writhed his lips into the preliminary of a snarl, but sniffed noses with him, Whereupon the old wolf sat down, pointed nose at the moon, and broke out the long wolf howl. The others sat down and howled. And now the call came to Buck in unmistakable accents. He, too, sat down and howled. This over, he came out of his angle and the pack crowded around him, sniffing in half-friendly, half-savage manner. The leaders lifted the yelp of the pack and sprang away into the woods. The wolves swung in behind, yelping in chorus. And Buck ran with them, side by side with the wild brother, yelping as he ran.

And here may well end the story of Buck. The years were not many when the Yeehats noted a change in the breed of timber wolves; for some were seen with splashes of brown on head and muzzle, and with a rift of white centring down the chest. But more remarkable than this, the Yeehats tell of a Ghost Dog that runs at the head of the pack. They are afraid of this Ghost Dog, for it has cunning greater than they, stealing from their camps in fierce winters, robbing their traps, slaying their dogs, and defying their bravest hunters.

Nay, the tale grows worse. Hunters there are who fail to return to the camp, and hunters there have been whom their tribesmen found with throats slashed cruelly open and with wolf prints about them in the snow greater than the prints of any wolf. Each fall, when the Yeehats follow the movement of the moose, there is a certain valley which they never enter. And women there are who become sad when the word goes over the fire of how the Evil Spirit came to select that valley for an abiding-place.

In the summers there is one visitor, however, to that valley, of which the Yeehats do not know. It is a great, gloriously coated wolf, like, and yet unlike, all other wolves. He crosses alone from the smiling timber land and comes down into an open space among the trees. Here a yellow stream flows from rotted moose-hide sacks and sinks into the ground, with long grasses growing through it and vegetable mould overrunning it and hiding its yellow from the sun; and here he muses for a time, howling once, long and mournfully, ere he departs.

But he is not always alone. When the long winter nights come on and the wolves follow their meat into the lower valleys, he may be seen running at the head of the pack through the pale moonlight or glimmering borealis, leaping gigantic above his fellows, his great throat a-bellow as he sings a song of the younger world, which is the song of the pack.

THE SEA-WOLF

I scarcely know where to begin, though I sometimes facetiously place the cause of it all to Charley Furuseth's credit. He kept a summer cottage in Mill Valley, under the shadow of Mount Tamalpais, and never occupied it except when he loafed through the winter months and read Nietzsche and Schopenhauer to rest his brain. When summer came on, he elected to sweat out a hot and dusty existence in the city and to toil incessantly. Had it not been my custom to run up to see him every Saturday afternoon and to stop over till Monday morning, this particular January Monday morning would not have found me afloat on San Francisco Bay.

Not but that I was afloat in a safe craft, for the *Martinez* was a new ferry-steamer, making her fourth or fifth trip on the run between Sausalito and San Francisco. The danger lay in the heavy fog which blanketed the bay, and of which, as a landsman, I had little apprehension. In fact, I remember the placid exaltation with which I took up my position on the forward upper deck, directly beneath the pilot-house, and allowed the mystery of the fog to lay hold of my imagination. A fresh breeze was blowing, and for a time I was alone in the moist obscurity—yet not alone, for I was dimly conscious of the presence of the pilot, and of what I took to be the captain, in the glass house above my head.

I remember thinking how comfortable it was, this division of labour which made it unnecessary for me to study fogs, winds, tides, and navigation, in order to visit my friend who lived across an arm of the sea. It was good that men should be specialists, I mused. The peculiar knowledge of the pilot and captain sufficed for many thousands of people who knew no more of the sea and navigation than I knew. On the other hand, instead of having to devote my energy to the learning of a multitude of things, I concentrated it upon a few particular things, such as, for instance, the analysis of Poe's place in American literature—an essay of mine, by the way, in the current *Atlantic*. Coming aboard, as I passed through the cabin, I had noticed with greedy eyes a stout gentleman reading the *Atlantic*, which was open at my very essay. And there it was again, the division of labour, the special knowledge of the pilot and captain which permitted the stout gentleman to read my special knowledge on Poe while they carried him safely from Sausalito to San Francisco.

A red-faced man, slamming the cabin door behind him and stumping out on the deck, interrupted my reflections, though I made a mental note of the topic for use in a projected essay which I had thought of calling 'The Necessity for Freedom: A Plea for the Artist.' The red-faced man shot a glance up at the pilot-house, gazed around at the fog, stumped across the deck and back (he evidently had artificial legs), and stood still by my side, legs wide apart, and with an expression of keen enjoyment on his face. I was not wrong when I decided that his days had been spent on the sea.

'It's nasty weather like this here that turns heads grey before their time,' he said, with a nod toward the pilot-house.

'I had not thought there was any particular strain,' I answered. 'It seems as simple as A, B, C. They know the direction by compass, the distance, and the speed. I should not call it anything more than mathematical certainty.'

'Strain!' he snorted. 'Simple as A, B, C! Mathematical certainty!'

He seemed to brace himself up and lean backward against the air as he stared at me. 'How about this here tide that's rushin' out through the Golden Gate?' he demanded, or bellowed, rather. 'How fast is she ebbin'? What's the drift, eh? Listen to that, will you? A bell-buoy, and we're a-top of it! See 'em alterin' the course!'

From out of the fog came the mournful tolling of a bell, and I could see the pilot turning the wheel with great rapidity. The bell, which had seemed straight ahead, was now sounding from the side. Our own whistle was blowing hoarsely, and from time to time the sound of other whistles came to us from out of the fog.

'That's a ferry-boat of some sort,' the new-comer said, indicating a whistle off to the right. 'And there! D'ye hear that? Blown by mouth. Some scow schooner, most likely. Better watch out, Mr. Schooner-man. Ah, I thought so. Now hell's a-poppin' for somebody!'

The unseen ferry-boat was blowing blast after blast, and the mouth-blown horn was tooting in terror-stricken fashion.

'And now they're payin' their respects to each other and tryin' to get clear,' the red-faced man went on, as the hurried whistling ceased.

His face was shining, his eyes flashing with excitement as he translated into articulate language the speech of the horns and sirens. 'That's a steam-siren a-goin' it over there to the left. And you hear that fellow with a frog in his throat—a steam schooner as near as I can judge, crawlin' in from the Heads against the tide.'

A shrill little whistle, piping as if gone mad, came from directly ahead and from very near at hand. Gongs sounded on the *Martinez*. Our paddle-wheels stopped, their pulsing beat died away, and then they started again. The shrill little whistle, like the chirping of a cricket amid the cries of great beasts, shot through the fog from more to the side and swiftly grew faint and fainter. I looked to my companion for enlightenment.

'One of them dare-devil launches,' he said. 'I almost wish we'd sunk him, the little rip! They're the cause of more trouble. And what good are they? Any jackass gets aboard one and runs it from hell to breakfast, blowin' his whistle to beat the band and tellin' the rest of the world to look out for him, because he's comin' and can't look out for himself! Because he's comin'! And you've got to look out, too! Right of way! Common decency! They don't know the meanin' of it!'

I felt quite amused at his unwarranted choler, and while he stumped indignantly up and down I fell to dwelling upon the romance of the fog. And romantic it certainly was—the fog, like the grey shadow of infinite mystery, brooding over the whirling speck of earth; and men, mere motes of light and sparkle, cursed with an insane relish for work, riding their steeds of wood and steel through the heart of the mystery, groping their way blindly through the Unseen, and clamouring and clanging in confident speech the while their hearts are heavy with incertitude and fear.

The voice of my companion brought me back to myself with a laugh. I too had been groping and floundering, the while I thought I rode clear-eyed through the mystery.

'Hello! somebody comin' our way,' he was saying. 'And d'ye hear that? He's comin' fast. Walking right along. Guess he don't hear us yet. Wind's in wrong direction.'

The fresh breeze was blowing right down upon us, and I could hear the whistle plainly, off to one side and a little ahead.

'Ferry-boat?' I asked.

He nodded, then added, 'Or he wouldn't be keepin' up such a clip.' He gave a short chuckle. 'They're gettin' anxious up there.'

I glanced up. The captain had thrust his head and shoulders out of the pilot-house, and was staring intently into the fog as though by sheer force of will he could penetrate it. His face was anxious, as was the face of my companion, who had stumped over to the rail and was gazing with a like intentness in the direction of the invisible danger.

Then everything happened, and with inconceivable rapidity. The fog seemed to break away as though split by a wedge, and the bow of a steamboat emerged, trailing fog-wreaths on either side like seaweed on the snout of Leviathan. I could see the pilot-house and a white-bearded man leaning partly out of it, on his elbows. He was clad in a blue uniform, and I remember noting how trim and quiet he was. His quietness, under the circumstances, was terrible. He accepted Destiny, marched hand in hand with it, and coolly measured the stroke. As he leaned there, he ran a calm and speculative eye over us, as though to determine the precise point of the collision, and took no notice whatever when our pilot, white with rage, shouted, 'Now you've done it!'

On looking back, I realize that the remark was too obvious to make rejoinder necessary.

'Grab hold of something and hang on,' the red-faced man said to me. All his bluster had gone, and he seemed to have caught the contagion of preternatural calm. 'And listen to the women scream,' he said grimly—almost bitterly, I thought, as though he had been through the experience before.

The vessels came together before I could follow his advice. We must have been struck squarely amidships, for I saw nothing, the strange steamboat having passed beyond my line of vision. The *Martinez* heeled over, sharply, and there was a crashing and rending of timber. I was thrown flat on the wet deck, and before I could scramble to my feet I heard the scream of the women. This it was, I am certain,—the most indescribable of blood-curdling sounds,—that threw me into a panic. I remembered the life-preservers stored in the cabin, but was met at the door and swept backward by a wild rush of men and women. What happened in the next few minutes I do not recollect, though I have a clear remembrance of pulling down life-preservers from the overhead racks, while the red-faced man fastened them about the bodies of an hysterical group of women. This memory is as distinct and sharp as that of any picture I have seen. It is a picture, and I can see it now,—the jagged edges of the hole in the side of the cabin, through which the grey fog swirled and eddied; the empty upholstered seats, littered with all the evidences of sudden flight, such as packages, hand satchels, umbrellas, and wraps; the stout gentleman who had been reading my essay, encased in cork and canvas, the magazine still in his hand, and asking me with monotonous insistence if I thought there was any danger; the red-faced man, stumping gallantly around on his artificial legs and buckling life-preservers on all comers; and finally, the screaming bedlam of women.

This it was, the screaming of the women, that most tried my nerves. It must have tried, too, the nerves of the red-faced man, for I have another picture which will never fade from my mind. The stout gentleman is stuffing the magazine into his overcoat pocket and looking on curiously. A tangled mass of women, with drawn, white faces and open mouths, is shrieking like a chorus of lost souls; and the red-faced man, his face now purplish with wrath, and with arms extended overhead as in the act of hurling thunderbolts, is shouting, 'Shut up! Oh, shut up!'

I remember the scene impelled me to sudden laughter, and in the next instant I realized I was becoming hysterical myself; for these were women of my own kind, like my mother and sisters, with the fear of death upon them and unwilling to die. And I remember that the sounds they made reminded me of the squealing of pigs under the knife of the butcher, and I was struck with horror at the vividness of the analogy. These women, capable of the most sublime emotions, of the tenderest sympathies, were open-mouthed and screaming. They wanted to live, they were helpless, like rats in a trap, and they screamed.

The horror of it drove me out on deck. I was feeling sick and squeamish, and sat down on a bench. In a hazy way I saw and heard men rushing and shouting as they strove to lower the boats. It was just as I had read descriptions of such scenes in books. The tackles jammed. Nothing worked. One boat lowered away with the plugs out, filled with women and children and then with water, and capsized. Another boat had been lowered by one end, and still hung in the tackle by the other end, where it had been abandoned. Nothing was to be seen of the strange steamboat which had caused the disaster, though I heard men saying that she would undoubtedly send boats to our assistance.

I descended to the lower deck. The *Martinez* was sinking fast, for the water was very near. Numbers of the passengers were leaping overboard. Others, in the water, were clamouring to be taken aboard again. No one heeded them. A cry arose that we were sinking. I was seized by the consequent panic, and went over the side in a surge of bodies. How I went over I do not know, though I did know, and instantly, why those in the water were so desirous of getting back on the steamer. The water was cold—so cold that it was painful. The pang, as I plunged into it, was as quick and sharp as that of fire. It bit to the marrow. It was like the grip of death. I gasped with the anguish and shock of it, filling my lungs before the life-preserver popped me to the surface. The taste of the salt was strong in my mouth, and I was strangling with the acrid stuff in my throat and lungs.

But it was the cold that was most distressing. I felt that I could survive but a few minutes. People were struggling and floundering in the water about me. I could hear them crying out to one another. And I heard, also, the sound of oars. Evidently the strange steamboat had lowered its boats. As the time went by I marvelled that I was still alive. I had no sensation whatever in my lower limbs, while a chilling numbness was wrapping about my heart and creeping into it. Small waves, with spiteful foaming crests, continually broke over me and into my mouth, sending me off into more strangling paroxysms.

The noises grew indistinct, though I heard a final and despairing chorus of screams in the distance, and knew that the *Martinez* had gone down. Later,—how much later I have no knowledge,—I came to myself with a start of fear. I was alone. I could hear no calls or cries—only the sound of the waves, made weirdly hollow and reverberant by the fog. A panic in a crowd, which partakes of a sort of community of interest, is not so terrible as a panic when one is by oneself; and such a panic I now suffered. Whither was I drifting? The red-faced man had said that the tide was ebbing through the Golden Gate. Was I, then, being carried out to sea? And the life-preserver in which I floated? Was it not liable to go to pieces at any moment? I had heard of such things being made of paper and hollow rushes which quickly became saturated and lost all buoyancy. And I could not swim a stroke. And I was alone, floating, apparently, in the midst of a grey primordial vastness. I confess that a madness seized me, that I shrieked aloud as the women had shrieked, and beat the water with my numb hands.

How long this lasted I have no conception, for a blankness intervened, of which I remember no more than one remembers of troubled and painful sleep. When I aroused, it was as after centuries of time; and I saw, almost above me and emerging from the fog, the bow of a vessel, and three triangular sails, each shrewdly lapping the other and filled with wind. Where the bow cut the water there was a great foaming and gurgling, and I seemed directly in its path. I tried to cry out, but was too exhausted. The bow plunged down, just missing me and sending a swash of water clear over my head. Then the long, black side of the vessel began slipping past, so near that I could have touched it with my hands. I tried to reach it, in a mad resolve to claw into the wood with my nails, but my arms were heavy and lifeless. Again I strove to call out, but made no sound.

The stern of the vessel shot by, dropping, as it did so, into a hollow between the waves; and I caught a glimpse of a man standing at the wheel, and of another man who seemed to be doing little else than smoke a cigar. I saw the smoke issuing from his lips as he slowly turned his head and glanced out over the water in my direction. It was a careless, unpremeditated glance, one of those haphazard things men do when they have no immediate call to do anything in particular, but act because they are alive and must do something.

But life and death were in that glance. I could see the vessel being swallowed up in the fog; I saw the back of the man at the wheel, and the head of the other man turning, slowly turning, as his gaze struck the water and casually lifted along it toward me. His face wore an absent expression, as of deep thought, and I became afraid that if his eyes did light upon me he would nevertheless not see me. But his eyes did light upon me, and looked squarely into mine; and he did see me, for he sprang to the wheel, thrusting the other man aside, and whirled it round and round, hand over hand, at the same time shouting orders of some sort. The vessel seemed to go off at a tangent to its former course and leapt almost instantly from view into the fog.

I felt myself slipping into unconsciousness, and tried with all the power of my will to fight above the suffocating blankness and darkness that was rising around me. A little later I heard the stroke of oars, growing nearer and nearer, and the calls of a man. When he was very near I heard him crying, in vexed fashion, 'Why in hell don't you sing out?' This meant me, I thought, and then the blankness and darkness rose over me.

CHAPTER II

I seemed swinging in a mighty rhythm through orbit vastness. Sparkling points of light spluttered and shot past me. They were stars, I knew, and flaring comets, that peopled my flight among the suns. As I reached the limit of my swing and prepared to rush back on the counter swing, a great gong struck and thundered. For an immeasurable period, lapped in the rippling of placid centuries, I enjoyed and pondered my tremendous flight.

But a change came over the face of the dream, for a dream I told myself it must be. My rhythm grew shorter and shorter. I was jerked from swing to counter swing with irritating haste. I could scarcely catch my breath, so fiercely was I impelled through the heavens. The gong thundered more frequently and more furiously. I grew to await it with a nameless dread. Then it seemed as though I were being dragged over rasping sands, white and hot in the sun. This gave place to a sense of intolerable anguish. My skin was scorching in the torment of fire. The gong clanged and knelled. The sparkling points of light flashed past me in an interminable stream, as though the whole sidereal system were dropping into the void. I gasped, caught my breath painfully, and opened my eyes. Two men were kneeling beside me, working over me. My mighty rhythm was the lift and forward plunge of a ship on the sea. The terrific gong was a frying-pan, hanging on the wall, that rattled and clattered with each leap of the ship. The rasping, scorching sands were a man's hard hands chafing my naked chest. I squirmed under the pain of it, and half lifted my head. My chest was raw and red, and I could see tiny blood globules starting through the torn and inflamed cuticle.

'That'll do, Yonson,' one of the men said. 'Carn't yer see you've bloomin' well rubbed all the gent's skin orf?'

The man addressed as Yonson, a man of the heavy Scandinavian type, ceased chafing me, and arose awkwardly to his feet. The man who had spoken to him was clearly a Cockney, with the clean lines and weakly pretty, almost effeminate, face of the man who has absorbed the sound of Bow Bells with his mother's milk. A draggled muslin cap on his head and a dirty gunny-sack about his slim hips proclaimed him cook of the decidedly dirty ship's galley in which I found myself.

'An' 'ow yer feelin' now, sir?' he asked, with the subservient smirk which comes only of generations of tip-seeking ancestors.

For reply, I twisted weakly into a sitting posture, and was helped by Yonson to my feet. The rattle and bang of the frying-pan was grating horribly on my nerves. I could not collect my thoughts. Clutching the woodwork of the galley for support,—and I confess the grease with which it was scummed put my teeth on edge,—I reached across a hot cooking-range to the offending utensil, unhooked it, and wedged it securely into the coal-box.

The cook grinned at my exhibition of nerves, and thrust into my hand a steaming mug with an 'Ere, this'll do yer good.' It was a nauseous mess,—ship's coffee,—but the heat of it was reviving. Between gulps of the molten stuff I glanced down at my raw and bleeding chest and turned to the Scandinavian.

'Thank you, Mr. Yonson,' I said; 'but don't you think your measures were rather heroic?'

It was because he understood the reproof of my action, rather than of my words, that he held up his palm for inspection. It was remarkably calloused. I passed my hand over the horny projections, and my teeth went on edge once more from the horrible rasping sensation produced.

'My name is Johnson, not Yonson,' he said, in very good, though slow, English, with no more than a shade of accent to it.

There was mild protest in his pale blue eyes, and withal a timid frankness and manliness that quite won me to him.

'Thank you, Mr. Johnson,' I corrected, and reached out my hand for his.

He hesitated, awkward and bashful, shifted his weight from one leg to the other, then blunderingly gripped my hand in a hearty shake.

'Have you any dry clothes I may put on?' I asked the cook.

'Yes, sir,' he answered, with cheerful alacrity. 'I'll run down an' tyke a look over my kit, sir, if you've no objections, sir, to wearin' my things.'

He dived out of the galley door, or glided rather, with a swiftness and smoothness of gait that struck me as being not so much cat-like as oily. In fact, this oiliness, or greasiness, as I was later to learn, was probably the most salient expression of his personality.

'And where am I?' I asked Johnson, whom I took, and rightly, to be one of the sailors. 'What vessel is this, and where is she bound?'

'Off the Farallones, heading about sou-west,' he answered, slowly and methodically, as though groping for his best English, and rigidly observing the order of my queries. 'The schooner *Ghost*, bound seal-hunting to Japan.'

'And who is the captain? I must see him as soon as I am dressed.'

Johnson looked puzzled and embarrassed. He hesitated while he groped in his vocabulary and framed a complete answer. 'The cap'n is Wolf Larsen, or so men call him. I never heard his other name. But you better speak soft with him. He is mad this morning. The mate—'

But he did not finish. The cook had glided in.

'Better sling yer 'ook out of 'ere, Yonson,' he said. 'The old man'll be wantin' yer on deck, an' this ayn't no d'y to fall foul of 'im.'

Johnson turned obediently to the door, at the same time, over the cook's shoulder, favouring me with an amazingly solemn and portentous wink as though to emphasize his interrupted remark and the need for me to be soft-spoken with the captain.

Hanging over the cook's arm was a loose and crumpled array of evil-looking and sour-smelling garments.

'They was put aw'y wet, sir,' he vouchsafed explanation. 'But you'll 'ave to make them do till I dry yours out by the fire.'

Clinging to the woodwork, staggering with the roll of the ship, and aided by the cook, I managed to slip into a rough woollen undershirt. On the instant my flesh was creeping and crawling from the harsh contact. He noticed my involuntary twitching and grimacing, and smirked:

'I only 'ope yer don't ever 'ave to get used to such as that in this life, 'cos you've got a bloomin' soft skin, that you 'ave, more like a lydy's than any I know of. I was bloomin' well sure you was a gentleman as soon as I set eyes on yer.'

I had taken a dislike to him at first, and as he helped to dress me this dislike increased. There was something repulsive about his touch. I shrank from his hand; my flesh revolted. And between this and the smells arising from various pots boiling and bubbling on the galley fire, I was in haste to get out into the fresh air. Further, there was the need of seeing the captain about what arrangements could be made for getting me ashore.

A cheap cotton shirt, with frayed collar and a bosom discoloured with what I took to be ancient blood-stains, was put on me amid a running and apologetic fire of comment. A pair of workman's brogans encased my feet, and for trousers I was furnished with a pair of pale blue, washed-out overalls, one leg of which was fully ten inches shorter than the other. The abbreviated leg looked as though the devil had there clutched for the Cockney's soul and missed the shadow for the substance.

'And whom have I to thank for this kindness?' I asked, when I stood completely arrayed, a tiny boy's cap on my head, and for coat a dirty, striped cotton jacket which ended at the small of my back and the sleeves of which reached just below my elbows.

The cook drew himself up in a smugly humble fashion, a deprecating smirk on his face. Out of my experience with stewards on the Atlantic liners at the end of the voyage, I could have sworn he was waiting for his tip. From my fuller knowledge of the creature I now know that the posture was unconscious. An hereditary servility, no doubt, was responsible.

'Mugridge, sir,' he fawned, his effeminate features running into a greasy smile. 'Thomas Mugridge, sir, an' at yer service.'

'All right, Thomas,' I said. 'I shall not forget you—when my clothes are dry.'

A soft light suffused his face and his eyes glistened, as though somewhere in the deeps of his being his ancestors had quickened and stirred with dim memories of tips received in former lives.

'Thank you, sir,' he said, very gratefully and very humbly indeed.

Precisely in the way that the door slid back, he slid aside, and I stepped out on deck. I was still weak from my prolonged immersion. A puff of wind caught me,—and I staggered across the moving deck to a corner of the cabin, to which I clung for support. The schooner, heeled over far out from the perpendicular, was bowing and plunging into the long Pacific roll. If she were heading south-west as Johnson had said, the wind, then, I calculated, was blowing nearly from the south. The fog was gone, and in its place the sun sparkled crisply on the surface of the water, I turned to the east, where I knew California must lie, but could see nothing save low-lying fog-banks—the same fog, doubtless, that had brought about the disaster to the *Martinez* and placed me in my present situation. To the north, and not far away, a group of naked rocks thrust above the sea, on one of which I could distinguish a lighthouse. In the south-west, and almost in our course, I saw the pyramidal loom of some vessel's sails.

Having completed my survey of the horizon, I turned to my more immediate surroundings. My first thought was that a man who had come through a collision and rubbed shoulders with death merited more attention than I received. Beyond a sailor at the wheel who stared curiously across the top of the cabin, I attracted no notice whatever.

Everybody seemed interested in what was going on amid ships. There, on a hatch, a large man was lying on his back. He was fully clothed, though his shirt was ripped open in front. Nothing was to be seen of his chest, however, for it was covered with a mass of black hair, in appearance like the furry coat of a dog. His face and neck were hidden beneath a black beard, intershot with grey, which would have been stiff and bushy had it not been limp and draggled and dripping with water. His eyes were closed, and he was apparently unconscious; but his mouth was wide open, his breast, heaving as though from suffocation as he laboured noisily for breath. A sailor, from time to time and quite methodically, as a matter of routine, dropped a canvas bucket into the ocean at the end of a rope, hauled it in hand under hand, and sluiced its contents over the prostrate man.

Pacing back and forth the length of the hatchways and savagely chewing the end of a cigar, was the man whose casual glance had rescued me from the sea. His height was probably five feet ten inches, or ten and a half; but my first impression, or feel of the man, was not of this, but of his strength. And yet, while he was of massive build, with broad shoulders and deep chest, I could not characterize his strength as massive. It was what might be termed a sinewy, knotty strength, of the kind we ascribe to lean and wiry men, but which, in him, because of his heavy build, partook more of the enlarged gorilla order. Not that in appearance he seemed in the least gorilla-like. What I am striving to express is this strength itself, more as a thing apart from his physical semblance. It was a strength we are wont to associate with things primitive, with wild animals, and the creatures we imagine our tree-dwelling prototypes to have been—a strength savage, ferocious, alive in itself, the essence of life in that it is the potency of motion, the elemental stuff itself out of which the many forms of life have been moulded; in short, that which writhes in the body of a snake when the head is cut off, and the snake, as a snake, is dead, or which lingers in the shapeless lump of turtle-meat and recoils and quivers from the prod of a finger.

Such was the impression of strength I gathered from this man who paced up and down. He was firmly planted on his legs; his feet struck the deck squarely and with surety; every movement of a muscle, from the heave of the shoulders to the tightening of the lips about the cigar, was decisive, and seemed to come out of a strength that was excessive and overwhelming. In fact, though this strength pervaded every action of his, it seemed but the advertisement of a greater strength that lurked within, that lay dormant and no more than stirred from time to time, but which might arouse, at any moment, terrible and compelling, like the rage of a lion or the wrath of a storm.

The cook stuck his head out of the galley door and grinned encouragingly at me, at the same time jerking his thumb in the direction of the man who paced up and down by the hatchway. Thus I was given to understand that he was the captain, the 'Old Man,' in the cook's vernacular, the individual whom I must interview and put to the trouble of somehow getting me ashore. I had half started forward, to get over with what I was certain would be a stormy five minutes, when a more violent suffocating paroxysm seized the unfortunate person who was lying on his back. He wrenched and writhed about convulsively. The chin, with the damp black beard, pointed higher in the air as the back muscles stiffened and the chest swelled in an unconscious and instinctive effort to get more air. Under the whiskers, and all unseen, I knew that the skin was taking on a purplish hue.

The captain, or Wolf Larsen, as men called him, ceased pacing and gazed down at the dying man. So fierce had this final struggle become that the sailor paused in the act of flinging more water over him and stared curiously, the canvas bucket partly tilted and dripping its contents to the deck. The dying man beat a tattoo on the hatch with his heels, straightened out his legs, and stiffened in one great tense effort, and rolled his head from side to side. Then the muscles relaxed, the head stopped rolling, and a sigh, as of profound relief, floated upward from his lips. The jaw dropped, the upper lip lifted, and two rows of tobacco-discoloured teeth appeared. It seemed as though his features had frozen into a diabolical grin at the world he had left and outwitted.

Then a most surprising thing occurred. The captain broke loose upon the dead man like a thunderclap. Oaths rolled from his lips in a continuous stream. And they were not namby-pamby oaths, or mere expressions of indecency. Each word was a blasphemy, and there were many words. They crisped and crackled like electric sparks. I had never heard anything like it in my life, nor could I have conceived it possible. With a turn for literary expression myself, and a penchant for forcible figures and phrases, I appreciated, as no other listener, I dare say, the peculiar vividness and strength and absolute blasphemy of his metaphors. The cause of it all, as near as I could make out, was that the man, who was mate, had gone on a debauch before leaving San Francisco, and then had the poor taste to die at the beginning of the voyage and leave Wolf Larsen short-handed.

It should be unnecessary to state, at least to my friends, that I was shocked. Oaths and vile language of any sort had always been repellent to me. I felt a wilting sensation, a sinking at the heart, and, I might just as well say, a giddiness. To me, death had always been invested with solemnity and dignity. It had been peaceful in its occurrence, sacred in its ceremonial. But death in its more sordid and terrible aspects was a thing with which I had been unacquainted till now. As I say, while I appreciated the power of the terrific denunciation that swept out of Wolf Larsen's mouth, I was inexpressibly shocked. The scorching torrent was enough to wither the face of the corpse. I should not have been surprised if the wet black beard had frizzled and curled and flared up in smoke and flame. But the dead man was unconcerned. He continued to grin with a sardonic humour, with a cynical mockery and defiance. He was master of the situation.

CHAPTER III

Wolf Larsen ceased swearing as suddenly as he had begun. He relighted his cigar and glanced around. His eyes chanced upon the cook.

'Well, Cooky?' he began, with a suaveness that was cold and of the temper of steel.

'Yes, sir,' the cook eagerly interpolated, with appeasing and apologetic servility.

'Don't you think you've stretched that neck of yours just about enough? It's unhealthy, you know. The mate's gone, so I can't afford to lose you too. You must be very, very careful of your health, Cooky. Understand?'

His last word, in striking contrast with the smoothness of his previous utterance, snapped like the lash of a whip. The cook quailed under it.

'Yes, sir,' was the meek reply, as the offending head disappeared into the galley.

At this sweeping rebuke, which the cook had only pointed, the rest of the crew became uninterested and fell to work at one task or another. A number of men, however, who were lounging about a companion-way between the galley and hatch, and who did not seem to be sailors, continued talking in low tones with one another. These, I afterward learned, were the hunters, the men who shot the seals, and a very superior breed to common sailor-folk.

'Johansen!' Wolf Larsen called out. A sailor stepped forward obediently. 'Get your palm and needle and sew the beggar up. You'll find some old canvas in the sail-locker. Make it do.'

'What'll I put on his feet, sir?' the man asked, after the customary 'Ay, ay, sir.'

'We'll see to that,' Wolf Larsen answered, and elevated his voice in a call of 'Cooky!'

Thomas Mugridge popped out of his galley like a jack-in-the-box.

'Go below and fill a sack with coal.'

'Any of you fellows got a Bible or Prayer-book?' was the captain's next demand, this time of the hunters lounging about the companion-way.

They shook their heads, and some one made a jocular remark which I did not catch, but which raised a general laugh.

Wolf Larsen made the same demand of the sailors. Bibles and Prayer-books seemed scarce articles, but one of the men volunteered to pursue the quest amongst the watch below, returning in a minute with the information that there was none.

The captain shrugged his shoulders. 'Then we'll drop him over without any palavering, unless our clerical-looking castaway has the burial service at sea by heart.'

By this time he had swung fully around and was facing me. 'You're a preacher, aren't you?' he asked.

The hunters,—there were six of them,—to a man, turned and regarded me. I was painfully aware of my likeness to a scarecrow. A laugh went up at my appearance,—a laugh that was not lessened or softened by the dead man stretched and grinning on the deck before us; a laugh that was as rough and harsh and frank as the sea itself; that arose out of coarse feelings and blunted sensibilities, from natures that knew neither courtesy nor gentleness.

Wolf Larsen did not laugh, though his grey eyes lighted with a slight glint of amusement; and in that moment, having stepped forward quite close to him, I received my first impression of the man himself, of the man as apart from his body, and from the torrent of blasphemy I had heard him spew forth. The face, with large features and strong lines, of the square order, yet well filled out, was apparently massive at first sight; but again, as with the body, the massiveness seemed to vanish, and a conviction to grow of a tremendous and excessive mental or spiritual strength that lay behind, sleeping in the deeps of his being. The jaw, the chin, the brow rising to a goodly height and swelling heavily above the eyes,—these, while strong in themselves, unusually strong, seemed to speak an immense vigour or virility of spirit that lay behind and beyond and out of sight. There was no sounding such a spirit, no measuring, no determining of metes and bounds, nor neatly classifying in some pigeon-hole with others of similar type.

The eyes—and it was my destiny to know them well—were large and handsome, wide apart as the true artist's are wide, sheltering under a heavy brow and arched over by thick black eyebrows. The eyes themselves were of that baffling protean grey which is never twice the same; which runs through many shades and colourings like intershot silk in sunshine; which is grey, dark and light, and greenish-grey, and sometimes of the clear azure of the deep sea. They were eyes that masked the soul with a thousand guises, and that sometimes opened, at rare moments, and allowed it to rush up as though it were about to fare forth nakedly into the world on some wonderful adventure,—eyes that could brood with the hopeless sombreness of leaden skies; that could snap and crackle points of fire like those which sparkle from a whirling sword; that could grow chill as an arctic landscape, and yet again, that could warm and soften and be all a-dance with love-lights, intense and masculine, luring and compelling, which at the same time fascinate and dominate women till they surrender in a gladness of joy and of relief and sacrifice.

But to return. I told him that, unhappily for the burial service, I was not a preacher, when he sharply demanded:

'What do you do for a living?'

I confess I had never had such a question asked me before, nor had I ever canvassed it. I was quite taken aback, and before I could find myself had sillily stammered, 'I—I am a gentleman.'

His lip curled in a swift sneer.

'I have worked, I do work,' I cried impetuously, as though he were my judge and I required vindication, and at the same time very much aware of my arrant idiocy in discussing the subject at all.

'For your living?'

There was something so imperative and masterful about him that I was quite beside myself—'rattled,' as Furuseth would have termed it, like a quaking child before a stern school-master.

'Who feeds you?' was his next question.

'I have an income,' I answered stoutly, and could have bitten my tongue the next instant. 'All of which, you will pardon my observing, has nothing whatsoever to do with what I wish to see you about.'

But he disregarded my protest.

'Who earned it? Eh? I thought so. Your father. You stand on dead men's legs. You've never had any of your own. You couldn't walk alone between two sunrises and hustle the meat for your belly for three meals. Let me see your hand.'

His tremendous, dormant strength must have stirred, swiftly and accurately, or I must have slept a moment, for before I knew it he had stepped two paces forward, gripped my right hand in his, and held it up for inspection. I tried to withdraw it, but his fingers tightened, without visible effort, till I thought mine would be crushed. It is hard to maintain one's dignity under such circumstances. I could not squirm or struggle like a schoolboy. Nor could I attack such a creature who had but to twist my arm to break it. Nothing remained but to stand still and accept the indignity. I had time to notice that the pockets of the dead man had been emptied on the deck, and that his body and his grin had been wrapped from view in canvas, the folds of which the sailor, Johansen, was sewing together with coarse white twine, shoving the needle through with a leather contrivance fitted on the palm of his hand.

Wolf Larsen dropped my hand with a flirt of disdain.

'Dead men's hands have kept it soft. Good for little else than dish-washing and scullion work.'

'I wish to be put ashore,' I said firmly, for I now had myself in control. 'I shall pay you whatever you judge your delay and trouble to be worth.'

He looked at me curiously. Mockery shone in his eyes.

'I have a counter proposition to make, and for the good of your soul. My mate's gone, and there'll be a lot of promotion. A sailor comes aft to take mate's place, cabin-boy goes for'ard to take sailor's place, and you take the cabin-boy's place, sign the articles for the cruise, twenty dollars per month and found. Now what do you say? And mind you, it's for your own soul's sake. It will be the making of you. You might learn in time to stand on your own legs, and perhaps to toddle along a bit.'

But I took no notice. The sails of the vessel I had seen off to the south-west had grown larger and plainer. They were of the same schooner-rig as the *Ghost*, though the hull itself, I could see, was smaller. She was a pretty sight, leaping and flying toward us, and evidently bound to pass at close range. The wind had been momentarily increasing, and the sun, after a few angry gleams, had disappeared. The sea had turned a dull leaden grey and grown rougher, and was now tossing foaming whitecaps to the sky. We were travelling faster, and heeled farther over. Once, in a gust, the rail dipped under the sea, and the decks on that side were for the moment awash with water that made a couple of the hunters hastily lift their feet.

'That vessel will soon be passing us,' I said, after a moment's pause. 'As she is going in the opposite direction, she is very probably bound for San Francisco.'

'Very probably,' was Wolf Larsen's answer, as he turned partly away from me and cried out, 'Cooky! Oh, Cooky!'

The Cockney popped out of the galley.

'Where's that boy? Tell him I want him.'

'Yes, sir;' and Thomas Mugridge fled swiftly aft and disappeared down another companion-way near the wheel. A moment later he emerged, a heavy-set young fellow of eighteen or nineteen, with a glowering, villainous countenance, trailing at his heels.

''Ere 'e is, sir,' the cook said.

But Wolf Larsen ignored that worthy, turning at once to the cabin-boy.

'What's your name, boy?'

'George Leach, sir,' came the sullen answer, and the boy's bearing showed clearly that he divined the reason for which he had been summoned.

'Not an Irish name,' the captain snapped sharply. 'O'Toole or McCarthy would suit your mug a damn sight better. Unless, very likely, there's an Irishman in your mother's woodpile.'

I saw the young fellow's hands clench at the insult, and the blood crawl scarlet up his neck.

'But let that go,' Wolf Larsen continued. 'You may have very good reasons for forgetting your name, and I'll like you none the worse for it as long as you toe the mark. Telegraph Hill, of course, is your port of entry. It sticks out all over your mug. Tough as they make them and twice as nasty. I know the kind. Well, you can make up your mind to have it taken out of you on this craft. Understand? Who shipped you, anyway?'

'McCready and Swanson.'

'Sir!' Wolf Larsen thundered.

'McCready and Swanson, sir,' the boy corrected, his eyes burning with a bitter light.

'Who got the advance money?'

'They did, sir.'

'I thought as much. And damned glad you were to let them have it. Couldn't make yourself scarce too quick, with several gentlemen you may have heard of looking for you.'

The boy metamorphosed into a savage on the instant. His body bunched together as though for a spring, and his face became as an infuriated beast's as he snarled, 'It's a—'

'A what?' Wolf Larsen asked, a peculiar softness in his voice, as though he were overwhelmingly curious to hear the unspoken word.

The boy hesitated, then mastered his temper. 'Nothin', sir. I take it back.'

'And you have shown me I was right.' This with a gratified smile. 'How old are you?'

'Just turned sixteen, sir,'

'A lie. You'll never see eighteen again. Big for your age at that, with muscles like a horse. Pack up your kit and go for'ard into the fo'c'sle. You're a boat-puller now. You're promoted; see?'

Without waiting for the boy's acceptance, the captain turned to the sailor who had just finished the gruesome task of sewing up the corpse. 'Johansen, do you know anything about navigation?'

'No, sir,'

'Well, never mind; you're mate just the same. Get your traps aft into the mate's berth.'

'Ay, ay, sir,' was the cheery response, as Johansen started forward.

In the meantime the erstwhile cabin-boy had not moved. 'What are you waiting for?' Wolf Larsen demanded.

'I didn't sign for boat-puller, sir,' was the reply. 'I signed for cabin-boy. An' I don't want no boat-pullin' in mine.'

'Pack up and go for'ard.'

This time Wolf Larsen's command was thrillingly imperative. The boy glowered sullenly, but refused to move.

Then came another stirring of Wolf Larsen's tremendous strength. It was utterly unexpected, and it was over and done with between the ticks of two seconds. He had sprung fully six feet across the deck and driven his fist into the other's stomach. At the same moment, as though I had been struck myself, I felt a sickening shock in the pit of my stomach. I instance this to show the sensitiveness of my nervous organization at the time, and how unused I was to spectacles of brutality. The cabin-boy—and he weighed one hundred and sixty-five at the very least—crumpled up. His body wrapped limply about the fist like a wet rag about a stick. He lifted into the air, described a short curve, and struck the deck alongside the corpse on his head and shoulders, where he lay and writhed about in agony.

'Well?' Larsen asked of me. 'Have you made up your mind?'

I had glanced occasionally at the approaching schooner, and it was now almost abreast of us and not more than a couple of hundred yards away. It was a very trim and neat little craft. I could see a large, black number on one of its sails, and I had seen pictures of pilot-boats.

'What vessel is that?' I asked.

'The pilot-boat *Lady Mine*,' Wolf Larsen answered grimly. 'Got rid of her pilots and running into San Francisco. She'll be there in five or six hours with this wind.'

'Will you please signal it, then, so that I may be put ashore.'

'Sorry, but I've lost the signal book overboard,' he remarked, and the group of hunters grinned.

I debated a moment, looking him squarely in the eyes. I had seen the frightful treatment of the cabin-boy, and knew that I should very probably receive the same, if not worse. As I say, I debated with myself, and then I did what I consider the bravest act of my life. I ran to the side, waving my arms and shouting:

'*Lady Mine* ahoy! Take me ashore! A thousand dollars if you take me ashore!'

I waited, watching two men who stood by the wheel, one of them steering. The other was lifting a megaphone to his lips. I did not turn my head, though I expected every moment a killing blow from the human brute behind me. At last, after what seemed centuries, unable longer to stand the strain, I looked around. He had not moved. He was standing in the same position, swaying easily to the roll of the ship and lighting a fresh cigar.

'What is the matter? Anything wrong?'

This was the cry from the *Lady Mine.*

'Yes!' I shouted, at the top of my lungs. 'Life or death! One thousand dollars if you take me ashore!'

'Too much 'Frisco tanglefoot for the health of my crew!' Wolf Larsen shouted after. 'This one'—indicating me with his thumb—'fancies sea-serpents and monkeys just now!'

The man on the *Lady Mine* laughed back through the megaphone. The pilot-boat plunged past.

'Give him hell for me!' came a final cry, and the two men waved their arms in farewell.

I leaned despairingly over the rail, watching the trim little schooner swiftly increasing the bleak sweep of ocean between us. And she would probably be in San Francisco in five or six hours! My head seemed bursting. There was an ache in my throat as though my heart were up in it. A curling wave struck the side and splashed salt spray on my lips. The wind puffed strongly, and the *Ghost* heeled far over, burying her lee rail. I could hear the water rushing down upon the deck.

When I turned around, a moment later, I saw the cabin-boy staggering to his feet. His face was ghastly white, twitching with suppressed pain. He looked very sick.

'Well, Leach, are you going for'ard?' Wolf Larsen asked.

'Yes, sir,' came the answer of a spirit cowed.

'And you?' I was asked.

'I'll give you a thousand—' I began, but was interrupted.

'Stow that! Are you going to take up your duties as cabin-boy? Or do I have to take you in hand?'

What was I to do? To be brutally beaten, to be killed perhaps, would not help my case. I looked steadily into the cruel grey eyes. They might have been granite for all the light and warmth of a human soul they contained. One may see the soul stir in some men's eyes, but his were bleak, and cold, and grey as the sea itself.

'Well?'

'Yes,' I said.

'Say 'yes, sir.''

'Yes, sir,' I corrected.

'What is your name?'

'Van Weyden, sir.'

'First name?'

'Humphrey, sir; Humphrey Van Weyden.'

'Age?'

'Thirty-five, sir.'

'That'll do. Go to the cook and learn your duties.'

And thus it was that I passed into a state of involuntary servitude to Wolf Larsen. He was stronger than I, that was all. But it was very unreal at the time. It is no less unreal now that I look back upon it. It will always be to me a monstrous, inconceivable thing, a horrible nightmare.

'Hold on, don't go yet.'

I stopped obediently in my walk toward the galley.

'Johansen, call all hands. Now that we've everything cleaned up, we'll have the funeral and get the decks cleared of useless lumber.'

While Johansen was summoning the watch below, a couple of sailors, under the captain's direction, laid the canvas-swathed corpse upon a hatch-cover. On either side the deck, against the rail and bottoms up, were lashed a number of small boats. Several men picked up the hatch-cover with its ghastly freight, carried it to the lee side, and rested it on the boats, the feet pointing overboard. To the feet was attached the sack of coal which the cook had fetched.

I had always conceived a burial at sea to be a very solemn and awe-inspiring event, but I was quickly disillusioned, by this burial at any rate. One of the hunters, a little dark-eyed man whom his mates called 'Smoke,' was telling stories, liberally inter-sprinkled with oaths and obscenities; and every minute or so the group of hunters gave mouth to a laughter that sounded to me like a wolf-chorus or the barking of hell-hounds. The sailors trooped noisily aft, some of the watch below rubbing the sleep from their eyes, and talked in low tones together. There was an ominous and worried expression on their faces. It was evident that they did not like the outlook of a voyage under such a captain and begun so inauspiciously. From time to time they stole glances at Wolf Larsen, and I could see that they were apprehensive of the man.

He stepped up to the hatch-cover, and all caps came off. I ran my eyes over them— twenty men all told; twenty-two including the man at the wheel and myself. I was pardonably curious in my survey, for it appeared my fate to be pent up with them on this miniature floating world for I knew not how many weeks or months. The sailors, in the main, were English and Scandinavian, and their faces seemed of the heavy, stolid order. The hunters, on the other hand, had stronger and more diversified faces, with hard lines and the marks of the free play of passions. Strange to say, and I noted it all once, Wolf Larsen's features showed no such evil stamp. There seemed nothing vicious in them. True, there were lines, but they were the lines of decision and firmness. It seemed, rather, a frank and open countenance, which frankness or openness was enhanced by the fact that he was smooth-shaven. I could hardly believe—until the next incident occurred—that it was the face of a man who could behave as he had behaved to the cabin-boy.

At this moment, as he opened his mouth to speak, puff after puff struck the schooner and pressed her side under. The wind shrieked a wild song through the rigging. Some of the hunters glanced anxiously aloft. The lee rail, where the dead man lay, was buried in the sea, and as the schooner lifted and righted the water swept across the deck wetting us above our shoe-tops. A shower of rain drove down upon us, each drop stinging like a hailstone. As it passed, Wolf Larsen began to speak, the bare-headed men swaying in unison, to the heave and lunge of the deck.

'I only remember one part of the service,' he said, 'and that is, 'And the body shall be cast into the sea.' So cast it in.'

He ceased speaking. The men holding the hatch-cover seemed perplexed, puzzled no doubt by the briefness of the ceremony. He burst upon them in a fury.

'Lift up that end there, damn you! What the hell's the matter with you?'

They elevated the end of the hatch-cover with pitiful haste, and, like a dog flung overside, the dead man slid feet first into the sea. The coal at his feet dragged him down. He was gone.

'Johansen,' Wolf Larsen said briskly to the new mate, 'keep all hands on deck now they're here. Get in the topsails and jibs and make a good job of it. We're in for a sou'-easter. Better reef the jib and mainsail too, while you're about it.'

In a moment the decks were in commotion, Johansen bellowing orders and the men pulling or letting go ropes of various sorts—all naturally confusing to a landsman such as myself. But it was the heartlessness of it that especially struck me. The dead man was an episode that was past, an incident that was dropped, in a canvas covering with a sack of coal, while the ship sped along and her work went on. Nobody had been affected. The hunters were laughing at a fresh story of Smoke's; the men pulling and hauling, and two of them climbing aloft; Wolf Larsen was studying the clouding sky to windward; and the dead man, dying obscenely, buried sordidly, and sinking down, down—

Then it was that the cruelty of the sea, its relentlessness and awfulness, rushed upon me. Life had become cheap and tawdry, a beastly and inarticulate thing, a soulless stirring of the ooze and slime. I held on to the weather rail, close by the shrouds, and gazed out across the desolate foaming waves to the low-lying fog-banks that hid San Francisco and the California coast. Rain-squalls were driving in between, and I could scarcely see the fog. And this strange vessel, with its terrible men, pressed under by wind and sea and ever leaping up and out, was heading away into the south-west, into the great and lonely Pacific expanse.

CHAPTER IV

What happened to me next on the sealing-schooner *Ghost*, as I strove to fit into my new environment, are matters of humiliation and pain. The cook, who was called 'the doctor' by the crew, 'Tommy' by the hunters, and 'Cooky' by Wolf Larsen, was a changed person. The difference worked in my status brought about a corresponding difference in treatment from him. Servile and fawning as he had been before, he was now as domineering and bellicose. In truth, I was no longer the fine gentleman with a skin soft as a 'lydy's,' but only an ordinary and very worthless cabin-boy.

He absurdly insisted upon my addressing him as Mr. Mugridge, and his behaviour and carriage were insufferable as he showed me my duties. Besides my work in the cabin, with its four small state-rooms, I was supposed to be his assistant in the galley, and my colossal ignorance concerning such things as peeling potatoes or washing greasy pots was a source of unending and sarcastic wonder to him. He refused to take into consideration what I was, or, rather, what my life and the things I was accustomed to had been. This was part of the attitude he chose to adopt toward me; and I confess, ere the day was done, that I hated him with more lively feelings than I had ever hated any one in my life before.

This first day was made more difficult for me from the fact that the *Ghost*, under close reefs (terms such as these I did not learn till later), was plunging through what Mr. Mugridge called an 'owlin' sou'-easter.' At half-past five, under his directions, I set the table in the cabin, with rough-weather trays in place, and then carried the tea and cooked food down from the galley. In this connection I cannot forbear relating my first experience with a boarding sea.

'Look sharp or you'll get doused,' was Mr. Mugridge's parting injunction, as I left the galley with a big tea-pot in one hand, and in the hollow of the other arm several loaves of fresh-baked bread. One of the hunters, a tall, loose-jointed chap named Henderson, was going aft at the time from the steerage (the name the hunters face-tiously gave their midships sleeping quarters) to the cabin. Wolf Larsen was on the poop, smoking his everlasting cigar.

'Ere she comes. Sling yer 'ook!' the cook cried.

I stopped, for I did not know what was coming, and saw the galley door slide shut with a bang. Then I saw Henderson leaping like a madman for the main rigging, up which he shot, on the inside, till he was many feet higher than my head. Also I saw a great wave, curling and foaming, poised far above the rail. I was directly under it. My mind did not work quickly, everything was so new and strange. I grasped that I was in danger, but that was all. I stood still, in trepidation. Then Wolf Larsen shouted from the poop:

'Grab hold something, you—you Hump!'

But it was too late. I sprang toward the rigging, to which I might have clung, and was met by the descending wall of water. What happened after that was very confusing. I was beneath the water, suffocating and drowning. My feet were out from under me, and I was turning over and over and being swept along I knew not where. Several times I collided against hard objects, once striking my right knee a terrible blow. Then the flood seemed suddenly to subside and I was breathing the good air again. I had been swept against the galley and around the steerage companion-way from the weather side into the lee scuppers. The pain from my hurt knee was agonizing. I could not put my weight on it, or, at least, I thought I could not put my weight on it; and I felt sure the leg was broken. But the cook was after me, shouting through the lee galley door:

'Ere, you! Don't tyke all night about it! Where's the pot? Lost overboard? Serve you bloody well right if yer neck was broke!'

I managed to struggle to my feet. The great tea-pot was still in my hand. I limped to the galley and handed it to him. But he was consumed with indignation, real or feigned.

'Gawd blime me if you ayn't a slob. Wot 're you good for anyw'y, I'd like to know? Eh? Wot 're you good for any'wy? Cawn't even carry a bit of tea aft without losin' it. Now I'll 'ave to boil some more.

'An' wot 're you snifflin' about?' he burst out at me, with renewed rage. 'Cos you've 'urt yer pore little leg, pore little mamma's darlin'.'

I was not sniffling, though my face might well have been drawn and twitching from the pain. But I called up all my resolution, set my teeth, and hobbled back and forth from galley to cabin and cabin to galley without further mishap. Two things

I had acquired by my accident: an injured knee-cap that went undressed and from which I suffered for weary months, and the name of 'Hump,' which Wolf Larsen had called me from the poop. Thereafter, fore and aft, I was known by no other name, until the term became a part of my thought-processes and I identified it with myself, thought of myself as Hump, as though Hump were I and had always been I.

It was no easy task, waiting on the cabin table, where sat Wolf Larsen, Johansen, and the six hunters. The cabin was small, to begin with, and to move around, as I was compelled to, was not made easier by the schooner's violent pitching and wallowing. But what struck me most forcibly was the total lack of sympathy on the part of the men whom I served. I could feel my knee through my clothes, swelling, and swelling, and I was sick and faint from the pain of it. I could catch glimpses of my face, white and ghastly, distorted with pain, in the cabin mirror. All the men must have seen my condition, but not one spoke or took notice of me, till I was almost grateful to Wolf Larsen, later on (I was washing the dishes), when he said:

'Don't let a little thing like that bother you. You'll get used to such things in time. It may cripple you some, but all the same you'll be learning to walk.

'That's what you call a paradox, isn't it?' he added.

He seemed pleased when I nodded my head with the customary 'Yes, sir.'

'I suppose you know a bit about literary things? Eh? Good. I'll have some talks with you some time.'

And then, taking no further account of me, he turned his back and went up on deck.

That night, when I had finished an endless amount of work, I was sent to sleep in the steerage, where I made up a spare bunk. I was glad to get out of the detestable presence of the cook and to be off my feet. To my surprise, my clothes had dried on me and there seemed no indications of catching cold, either from the last soaking or from the prolonged soaking from the foundering of the *Martinez*. Under ordinary circumstances, after all that I had undergone, I should have been fit for bed and a trained nurse.

But my knee was bothering me terribly. As well as I could make out, the kneecap seemed turned up on edge in the midst of the swelling. As I sat in my bunk examining it (the six hunters were all in the steerage, smoking and talking in loud voices), Henderson took a passing glance at it.

'Looks nasty,' he commented. 'Tie a rag around it, and it'll be all right.'

That was all; and on the land I would have been lying on the broad of my back, with a surgeon attending on me, and with strict injunctions to do nothing but rest. But I must do these men justice. Callous as they were to my suffering, they were equally callous to their own when anything befell them. And this was due, I believe, first, to habit; and second, to the fact that they were less sensitively organized. I really believe that a finely-organized, high-strung man would suffer twice and thrice as much as they from a like injury.

Tired as I was,—exhausted, in fact,—I was prevented from sleeping by the pain in my knee. It was all I could do to keep from groaning aloud. At home I should undoubtedly have given vent to my anguish; but this new and elemental environment seemed to call for a savage repression. Like the savage, the attitude of these men was stoical in great things, childish in little things. I remember, later in the voyage, seeing Kerfoot, another of the hunters, lose a finger by having it smashed to a jelly; and he did not even murmur or change the expression on his face. Yet I have seen the same man, time and again, fly into the most outrageous passion over a trifle.

He was doing it now, vociferating, bellowing, waving his arms, and cursing like a fiend, and all because of a disagreement with another hunter as to whether a seal pup knew instinctively how to swim. He held that it did, that it could swim the moment it was born. The other hunter, Latimer, a lean, Yankee-looking fellow with shrewd, narrow-slitted eyes, held otherwise, held that the seal pup was born on the land for no other reason than that it could not swim, that its mother was compelled to teach it to swim as birds were compelled to teach their nestlings how to fly.

For the most part, the remaining four hunters leaned on the table or lay in their bunks and left the discussion to the two antagonists. But they were supremely interested, for every little while they ardently took sides, and sometimes all were talking at once, till their voices surged back and forth in waves of sound like mimic thunder-rolls in the confined space. Childish and immaterial as the topic was, the quality of their reasoning was still more childish and immaterial. In truth, there was very little reasoning or none at all. Their method was one of assertion, assumption, and denunciation. They proved that a seal pup could swim or not swim at birth by stating the proposition very bellicosely and then following it up with an attack on the opposing man's judgment, common sense, nationality, or past history. Rebuttal was precisely similar. I have related this in order to show the mental calibre of the men with whom I was thrown in contact. Intellectually they were children, inhabiting the physical forms of men.

And they smoked, incessantly smoked, using a coarse, cheap, and offensive-smelling tobacco. The air was thick and murky with the smoke of it; and this, combined with the violent movement of the ship as she struggled through the storm, would surely have made me sea-sick had I been a victim to that malady. As it was, it made me quite squeamish, though this nausea might have been due to the pain of my leg and exhaustion.

As I lay there thinking, I naturally dwelt upon myself and my situation. It was unparalleled, undreamed-of, that I, Humphrey Van Weyden, a scholar and a dilettante, if you please, in things artistic and literary, should be lying here on a Bering Sea seal-hunting schooner. Cabin-boy! I had never done any hard manual labour, or scullion labour, in my life. I had lived a placid, uneventful, sedentary existence all my days— the life of a scholar and a recluse on an assured and comfortable income. Violent life and athletic sports had never appealed to me. I had always been a book-worm; so my sisters and father had called me during my childhood. I had gone camping but once in my life, and then I left the party almost at its start and returned to the comforts and conveniences of a roof. And here I was, with dreary and endless vistas before me of table-setting, potato-peeling, and dish-washing. And I was not strong. The doctors had always said that I had a remarkable constitution, but I had never developed it or my body through exercise. My muscles were small and soft, like a woman's, or so the doctors had said time and again in the course of their attempts to persuade me to go in for physical-culture fads. But I had preferred to use my head rather than my body; and here I was, in no fit condition for the rough life in prospect.

These are merely a few of the things that went through my mind, and are related for the sake of vindicating myself in advance in the weak and helpless *rôle* I was destined to play. But I thought, also, of my mother and sisters, and pictured their grief.

I was among the missing dead of the *Martinez* disaster, an unrecovered body. I could see the head-lines in the papers; the fellows at the University Club and the Bibelot shaking their heads and saying, 'Poor chap!' And I could see Charley Furuseth, as I had said good-bye to him that morning, lounging in a dressing-gown on the be-pillowed window couch and delivering himself of oracular and pessimistic epigrams.

And all the while, rolling, plunging, climbing the moving mountains and falling and wallowing in the foaming valleys, the schooner *Ghost* was fighting her way farther and farther into the heart of the Pacific—and I was on her. I could hear the wind above. It came to my ears as a muffled roar. Now and again feet stamped overhead. An endless creaking was going on all about me, the woodwork and the fittings groaning and squeaking and complaining in a thousand keys. The hunters were still arguing and roaring like some semi-human amphibious breed. The air was filled with oaths and indecent expressions. I could see their faces, flushed and angry, the brutality distorted and emphasized by the sickly yellow of the sea-lamps which rocked back and forth with the ship. Through the dim smoke-haze the bunks looked like the sleeping dens of animals in a menagerie. Oilskins and sea-boots were hanging from the walls, and here and there rifles and shotguns rested securely in the racks. It was a sea-fitting for the buccaneers and pirates of by-gone years. My imagination ran riot, and still I could not sleep. And it was a long, long night, weary and dreary and long.

CHAPTER V

But my first night in the hunters' steerage was also my last. Next day Johansen, the new mate, was routed from the cabin by Wolf Larsen, and sent into the steerage to sleep thereafter, while I took possession of the tiny cabin state-room, which, on the first day of the voyage, had already had two occupants. The reason for this change was quickly learned by the hunters, and became the cause of a deal of grumbling on their part. It seemed that Johansen, in his sleep, lived over each night the events of the day. His incessant talking and shouting and bellowing of orders had been too much for Wolf Larsen, who had accordingly foisted the nuisance upon his hunters.

After a sleepless night, I arose weak and in agony, to hobble through my second day on the *Ghost*. Thomas Mugridge routed me out at half-past five, much in the fashion that Bill Sykes must have routed out his dog; but Mr. Mugridge's brutality to me was paid back in kind and with interest. The unnecessary noise he made (I had lain wide-eyed the whole night) must have awakened one of the hunters; for a heavy shoe whizzed through the semi-darkness, and Mr. Mugridge, with a sharp howl of pain, humbly begged everybody's pardon. Later on, in the galley, I noticed that his ear was bruised and swollen. It never went entirely back to its normal shape, and was called a 'cauliflower ear' by the sailors.

The day was filled with miserable variety. I had taken my dried clothes down from the galley the night before, and the first thing I did was to exchange the cook's garments for them. I looked for my purse. In addition to some small change (and I have a good memory for such things), it had contained one hundred and eighty-five dollars in gold and paper. The purse I found, but its contents, with the exception of the small silver, had been abstracted. I spoke to the cook about it, when I went on deck to take up my duties in the galley, and though I had looked forward to a surly answer, I had not expected the belligerent harangue that I received.

'Look 'ere, 'Ump,' he began, a malicious light in his eyes and a snarl in his throat; 'd'ye want yer nose punched? If you think I'm a thief, just keep it to yerself, or you'll find 'ow bloody well mistyken you are. Strike me blind if this ayn't gratitude for yer! 'Ere you come, a pore mis'rable specimen of 'uman scum, an' I tykes yer into my galley an' treats yer 'ansom, an' this is wot I get for it. Nex' time you can go to 'ell, say I, an' I've a good mind to give you what-for anyw'y.'

So saying, he put up his fists and started for me. To my shame be it, I cowered away from the blow and ran out the galley door. What else was I to do? Force, nothing but force, obtained on this brute-ship. Moral suasion was a thing unknown. Picture it to yourself: a man of ordinary stature, slender of build, and with weak, undeveloped muscles, who has lived a peaceful, placid life, and is unused to violence of any sort— what could such a man possibly do? There was no more reason that I should stand and face these human beasts than that I should stand and face an infuriated bull.

So I thought it out at the time, feeling the need for vindication and desiring to be at peace with my conscience. But this vindication did not satisfy. Nor, to this day can I permit my manhood to look back upon those events and feel entirely exonerated. The situation was something that really exceeded rational formulas for conduct and demanded more than the cold conclusions of reason. When viewed in the light of formal logic, there is not one thing of which to be ashamed; but nevertheless a shame rises within me at the recollection, and in the pride of my manhood I feel that my manhood has in unaccountable ways been smirched and sullied.

All of which is neither here nor there. The speed with which I ran from the galley caused excruciating pain in my knee, and I sank down helplessly at the break of the poop. But the Cockney had not pursued me.

'Look at 'im run! Look at 'im run!' I could hear him crying. 'An' with a gyme leg at that! Come on back, you pore little mamma's darling. I won't 'it yer; no, I won't.'

I came back and went on with my work; and here the episode ended for the time, though further developments were yet to take place. I set the breakfast-table in the cabin, and at seven o'clock waited on the hunters and officers. The storm had evidently broken during the night, though a huge sea was still running and a stiff wind blowing. Sail had been made in the early watches, so that the *Ghost* was racing along under everything except the two topsails and the flying jib. These three sails, I gathered from the conversation, were to be set immediately after breakfast. I learned, also, that Wolf Larsen was anxious to make the most of the storm, which was driving him to the south-west into that portion of the sea where he expected to pick up with the north-east trades. It was before this steady wind that he hoped to make the major portion of the run to Japan, curving south into the tropics and north again as he approached the coast of Asia.

After breakfast I had another unenviable experience. When I had finished washing the dishes, I cleaned the cabin stove and carried the ashes up on deck to empty them. Wolf Larsen and Henderson were standing near the wheel, deep in conversation. The sailor, Johnson, was steering. As I started toward the weather side I saw him make a sudden motion with his head, which I mistook for a token of recognition and good-morning. In reality, he was attempting to warn me to throw my ashes over the lee side. Unconscious of my blunder, I passed by Wolf Larsen and the hunter and flung the ashes over the side to windward. The wind drove them back, and not only over me, but over Henderson and Wolf Larsen. The next instant the latter kicked me, violently, as a cur is kicked. I had not realized there could be so much pain in a kick. I reeled away from him and leaned against the cabin in a half-fainting condition. Everything was swimming before my eyes, and I turned sick. The nausea overpowered me, and I managed to crawl to the side of the vessel. But Wolf Larsen did not follow me up. Brushing the ashes from his clothes, he had resumed his conversation with Henderson. Johansen, who had seen the affair from the break of the poop, sent a couple of sailors aft to clean up the mess.

Later in the morning I received a surprise of a totally different sort. Following the cook's instructions, I had gone into Wolf Larsen's state-room to put it to rights and make the bed. Against the wall, near the head of the bunk, was a rack filled with books. I glanced over them, noting with astonishment such names as Shakespeare, Tennyson, Poe, and De Quincey. There were scientific works, too, among which were represented men such as Tyndall, Proctor, and Darwin. Astronomy and physics were represented, and I remarked Bulfinch's *Age of Fable*, Shaw's *History of English and American Literature*, and Johnson's *Natural History* in two large volumes. Then there were a number of grammars, such as Metcalf's, and Reed and Kellogg's; and I smiled as I saw a copy of *The Dean's English*.

I could not reconcile these books with the man from what I had seen of him, and I wondered if he could possibly read them. But when I came to make the bed I found, between the blankets, dropped apparently as he had sunk off to sleep, a complete Browning, the Cambridge Edition. It was open at 'In a Balcony,' and I noticed, here and there, passages underlined in pencil. Further, letting drop the volume during a lurch of the ship, a sheet of paper fell out. It was scrawled over with geometrical diagrams and calculations of some sort.

It was patent that this terrible man was no ignorant clod, such as one would inevitably suppose him to be from his exhibitions of brutality. At once he became an enigma. One side or the other of his nature was perfectly comprehensible; but both sides together were bewildering. I had already remarked that his language was excellent, marred with an occasional slight inaccuracy. Of course, in common speech with the sailors and hunters, it sometimes fairly bristled with errors, which was due to the vernacular itself; but in the few words he had held with me it had been clear and correct.

This glimpse I had caught of his other side must have emboldened me, for I resolved to speak to him about the money I had lost.

'I have been robbed,' I said to him, a little later, when I found him pacing up and down the poop alone.

'Sir,' he corrected, not harshly, but sternly.

'I have been robbed, sir,' I amended.

'How did it happen?' he asked.

Then I told him the whole circumstance, how my clothes had been left to dry in the galley, and how, later, I was nearly beaten by the cook when I mentioned the matter.

He smiled at my recital. 'Pickings,' he concluded; 'Cooky's pickings. And don't you think your miserable life worth the price? Besides, consider it a lesson. You'll learn in time how to take care of your money for yourself. I suppose, up to now, your lawyer has done it for you, or your business agent.'

I could feel the quiet sneer through his words, but demanded, 'How can I get it back again?'

'That's your look-out. You haven't any lawyer or business agent now, so you'll have to depend on yourself. When you get a dollar, hang on to it. A man who leaves his money lying around, the way you did, deserves to lose it. Besides, you have sinned. You have no right to put temptation in the way of your fellow-creatures. You tempted Cooky, and he fell. You have placed his immortal soul in jeopardy. By the way, do you believe in the immortal soul?'

His lids lifted lazily as he asked the question, and it seemed that the deeps were opening to me and that I was gazing into his soul. But it was an illusion. Far as it might have seemed, no man has ever seen very far into Wolf Larsen's soul, or seen it at all,—of this I am convinced. It was a very lonely soul, I was to learn, that never unmasked, though at rare moments it played at doing so.

'I read immortality in your eyes,' I answered, dropping the 'sir,'—an experiment, for I thought the intimacy of the conversation warranted it.

He took no notice. 'By that, I take it, you see something that is alive, but that necessarily does not have to live for ever.'

'I read more than that,' I continued boldly.

'Then you read consciousness. You read the consciousness of life that it is alive; but still no further away, no endlessness of life.'

How clearly he thought, and how well he expressed what he thought! From regarding me curiously, he turned his head and glanced out over the leaden sea to windward. A bleakness came into his eyes, and the lines of his mouth grew severe and harsh. He was evidently in a pessimistic mood.

'Then to what end?' he demanded abruptly, turning back to me. 'If I am immortal—why?'

I halted. How could I explain my idealism to this man? How could I put into speech a something felt, a something like the strains of music heard in sleep, a something that convinced yet transcended utterance?

'What do you believe, then?' I countered.

'I believe that life is a mess,' he answered promptly. 'It is like yeast, a ferment, a thing that moves and may move for a minute, an hour, a year, or a hundred years, but that in the end will cease to move. The big eat the little that they may continue to move, the strong eat the weak that they may retain their strength. The lucky eat the most and move the longest, that is all. What do you make of those things?'

He swept his arm in an impatient gesture toward a number of the sailors who were working on some kind of rope stuff amidships.

'They move, so does the jelly-fish move. They move in order to eat in order that they may keep moving. There you have it. They live for their belly's sake, and the belly is for their sake. It's a circle; you get nowhere. Neither do they. In the end they come to a standstill. They move no more. They are dead.'

'They have dreams,' I interrupted, 'radiant, flashing dreams—'

'Of grub,' he concluded sententiously.

'And of more—'

'Grub. Of a larger appetite and more luck in satisfying it.' His voice sounded harsh. There was no levity in it. 'For, look you, they dream of making lucky voyages which will bring them more money, of becoming the mates of ships, of finding fortunes—in short, of being in a better position for preying on their fellows, of having all night in, good grub and somebody else to do the dirty work. You and I are just like them. There is no difference, except that we have eaten more and better. I am eating them now, and you too. But in the past you have eaten more than I have. You have slept in soft beds, and worn fine clothes, and eaten good meals. Who made those beds? and those clothes? and those meals? Not you. You never made anything in your own sweat. You live on an income which your father earned. You are like a frigate bird swooping down upon the boobies and robbing them of the fish they have caught. You are one with a crowd of men who have made what they call a government, who are masters of all the other men, and who eat the food the other men get and would like to eat themselves. You wear the warm clothes. They made the clothes, but they shiver in rags and ask you, the lawyer, or business agent who handles your money, for a job.'

'But that is beside the matter,' I cried.

'Not at all.' He was speaking rapidly now, and his eyes were flashing. 'It is piggishness, and it is life. Of what use or sense is an immortality of piggishness? What is the end? What is it all about? You have made no food. Yet the food you have eaten or wasted might have saved the lives of a score of wretches who made the food but did not eat it. What immortal end did you serve? or did they? Consider yourself and me. What does your boasted immortality amount to when your life runs foul of mine? You would like to go back to the land, which is a favourable place for your kind of piggishness. It is a whim of mine to keep you aboard this ship, where my piggishness flourishes. And keep you I will. I may make or break you. You may die to-day, this week, or next month. I could kill you now, with a blow of my fist, for you are a miserable weakling. But if we are immortal, what is the reason for this? To be piggish as you and I have been all our lives does not seem to be just the thing for immortals to be doing. Again, what's it all about? Why have I kept you here?—'

'Because you are stronger,' I managed to blurt out.

'But why stronger?' he went on at once with his perpetual queries. 'Because I am a bigger bit of the ferment than you? Don't you see? Don't you see?'

'But the hopelessness of it,' I protested.

'I agree with you,' he answered. 'Then why move at all, since moving is living? Without moving and being part of the yeast there would be no hopelessness. But,— and there it is,—we want to live and move, though we have no reason to, because it happens that it is the nature of life to live and move, to want to live and move. If it were not for this, life would be dead. It is because of this life that is in you that you dream of your immortality. The life that is in you is alive and wants to go on being alive for ever. Bah! An eternity of piggishness!'

He abruptly turned on his heel and started forward. He stopped at the break of the poop and called me to him.

'By the way, how much was it that Cooky got away with?' he asked.

'One hundred and eighty-five dollars, sir,' I answered.

He nodded his head. A moment later, as I started down the companion stairs to lay the table for dinner, I heard him loudly cursing some men amidships.

CHAPTER VI

By the following morning the storm had blown itself quite out and the *Ghost* was rolling slightly on a calm sea without a breath of wind. Occasional light airs were felt, however, and Wolf Larsen patrolled the poop constantly, his eyes ever searching the sea to the north-eastward, from which direction the great trade-wind must blow.

The men were all on deck and busy preparing their various boats for the season's hunting. There are seven boats aboard, the captain's dingey, and the six which the hunters will use. Three, a hunter, a boat-puller, and a boat-steerer, compose a boat's crew. On board the schooner the boat-pullers and steerers are the crew. The hunters, too, are supposed to be in command of the watches, subject, always, to the orders of Wolf Larsen.

All this, and more, I have learned. The *Ghost* is considered the fastest schooner in both the San Francisco and Victoria fleets. In fact, she was once a private yacht, and was built for speed. Her lines and fittings—though I know nothing about such things—speak for themselves. Johnson was telling me about her in a short chat I had with him during yesterday's second dog-watch. He spoke enthusiastically, with the love for a fine craft such as some men feel for horses. He is greatly disgusted with the outlook, and I am given to understand that Wolf Larsen bears a very unsavoury reputation among the sealing captains. It was the *Ghost* herself that lured Johnson into signing for the voyage, but he is already beginning to repent.

As he told me, the *Ghost* is an eighty-ton schooner of a remarkably fine model. Her beam, or width, is twenty-three feet, and her length a little over ninety feet. A lead keel of fabulous but unknown weight makes her very stable, while she carries an immense spread of canvas. From the deck to the truck of the maintopmast is something over a hundred feet, while the foremast with its topmast is eight or ten feet shorter. I am giving these details so that the size of this little floating world which holds twenty-two men may be appreciated. It is a very little world, a mote, a speck, and I marvel that men should dare to venture the sea on a contrivance so small and fragile.

Wolf Larsen has, also, a reputation for reckless carrying on of sail. I overheard Henderson and another of the hunters, Standish, a Californian, talking about it. Two years ago he dismasted the *Ghost* in a gale on Bering Sea, whereupon the present masts were put in, which are stronger and heavier in every way. He is said to have remarked, when he put them in, that he preferred turning her over to losing the sticks.

Every man aboard, with the exception of Johansen, who is rather overcome by his promotion, seems to have an excuse for having sailed on the *Ghost*. Half the men forward are deep-water sailors, and their excuse is that they did not know anything about her or her captain. And those who do know, whisper that the hunters, while excellent shots, were so notorious for their quarrelsome and rascally proclivities that they could not sign on any decent schooner.

I have made the acquaintance of another one of the crew,—Louis he is called, a rotund and jovial-faced Nova Scotia Irishman, and a very sociable fellow, prone to talk as long as he can find a listener. In the afternoon, while the cook was below asleep and I was peeling the everlasting potatoes, Louis dropped into the galley for a 'yarn.' His excuse for being aboard was that he was drunk when he signed. He assured me again and again that it was the last thing in the world he would dream of doing in a sober moment. It seems that he has been seal-hunting regularly each season for a dozen years, and is accounted one of the two or three very best boat-steerers in both fleets.

'Ah, my boy,' he shook his head ominously at me, ''tis the worst schooner ye could iv selected, nor were ye drunk at the time as was I. 'Tis sealin' is the sailor's paradise— on other ships than this. The mate was the first, but mark me words, there'll be more dead men before the trip is done with. Hist, now, between you an' meself and the stanchion there, this Wolf Larsen is a regular devil, an' the *Ghost*'ll be a hell-ship like she's always ben since he had hold iv her. Don't I know? Don't I know? Don't I remember him in Hakodate two years gone, when he had a row an' shot four iv his men? Wasn't I a-layin' on the *Emma L.*, not three hundred yards away? An' there was a man the same year he killed with a blow iv his fist. Yes, sir, killed 'im dead-oh. His head must iv smashed like an eggshell. An' wasn't there the Governor of Kura Island, an' the Chief iv Police, Japanese gentlemen, sir, an' didn't they come aboard the *Ghost* as his guests, a-bringin' their wives along—wee an' pretty little bits of things like you see 'em painted on fans. An' as he was a-gettin' under way, didn't the fond husbands get left astern-like in their sampan, as it might be by accident? An' wasn't it a week later that the poor little ladies was put ashore on the other side of the island, with nothin' before 'em but to walk home acrost the mountains on their weeny-teeny little straw sandals which wouldn't hang together a mile? Don't I know? 'Tis the beast he is, this Wolf Larsen—the great big beast mentioned iv in Revelation; an' no good end will he ever come to. But I've said nothin' to ye, mind ye. I've whispered never a word; for old fat Louis'll live the voyage out if the last mother's son of yez go to the fishes.'

'Wolf Larsen!' he snorted a moment later. 'Listen to the word, will ye! Wolf—'tis what he is. He's not black-hearted like some men. 'Tis no heart he has at all. Wolf, just wolf, 'tis what he is. D'ye wonder he's well named?'

'But if he is so well-known for what he is,' I queried, 'how is it that he can get men to ship with him?'

'An' how is it ye can get men to do anything on God's earth an' sea?' Louis demanded with Celtic fire. 'How d'ye find me aboard if 'twasn't that I was drunk as a pig when I put me name down? There's them that can't sail with better men, like the hunters, and them that don't know, like the poor devils of wind-jammers for'ard there. But they'll come to it, they'll come to it, an' be sorry the day they was born. I could weep for the poor creatures, did I but forget poor old fat Louis and the troubles before him. But 'tis not a whisper I've dropped, mind ye, not a whisper.'

'Them hunters is the wicked boys,' he broke forth again, for he suffered from a constitutional plethora of speech. 'But wait till they get to cutting up iv jinks and rowin' 'round. He's the boy'll fix 'em. 'Tis him that'll put the fear of God in their rotten black hearts. Look at that hunter iv mine, Horner. 'Jock' Horner they call him, so quiet-like an' easy-goin', soft-spoken as a girl, till ye'd think butter wouldn't melt in the mouth iv him. Didn't he kill his boat-steerer last year? 'Twas called a sad accident, but I met the boat-puller in Yokohama an' the straight iv it was given me. An' there's Smoke, the black little devil—didn't the Roosians have him for three years in the salt mines of Siberia, for poachin' on Copper Island, which is a Roosian preserve? Shackled he was, hand an' foot, with his mate. An' didn't they have words or a ruction of some kind?—for 'twas the other fellow Smoke sent up in the buckets to the top of the mine; an' a piece at a time he went up, a leg to-day, an' to-morrow an arm, the next day the head, an' so on.'

'But you can't mean it!' I cried out, overcome with the horror of it.

'Mean what!' he demanded, quick as a flash. ''Tis nothin' I've said. Deef I am, and dumb, as ye should be for the sake iv your mother; an' never once have I opened me lips but to say fine things iv them an' him, God curse his soul, an' may he rot in purgatory ten thousand years, and then go down to the last an' deepest hell iv all!'

Johnson, the man who had chafed me raw when I first came aboard, seemed the least equivocal of the men forward or aft. In fact, there was nothing equivocal about him. One was struck at once by his straightforwardness and manliness, which, in turn, were tempered by a modesty which might be mistaken for timidity. But timid he was not. He seemed, rather, to have the courage of his convictions, the certainty of his manhood. It was this that made him protest, at the commencement of our acquaintance, against being called Yonson. And upon this, and him, Louis passed judgment and prophecy.

''Tis a fine chap, that squarehead Johnson we've for'ard with us,' he said. 'The best sailorman in the fo'c'sle. He's my boat-puller. But it's to trouble he'll come with Wolf Larsen, as the sparks fly upward. It's meself that knows. I can see it brewin' an' comin' up like a storm in the sky. I've talked to him like a brother, but it's little he sees in takin' in his lights or flyin' false signals. He grumbles out when things don't go to suit him, and there'll be always some tell-tale carryin' word iv it aft to the Wolf. The Wolf is strong, and it's the way of a wolf to hate strength, an' strength it is he'll see in Johnson—no knucklin' under, and a 'Yes, sir, thank ye kindly, sir,' for a curse or a blow. Oh, she's a-comin'! She's a-comin'! An' God knows where I'll get another boat-puller! What does the fool up an' say, when the old man calls him Yonson, but 'Me name is Johnson, sir,' an' then spells it out, letter for letter. Ye should iv seen the old man's face! I thought he'd let drive at him on the spot. He didn't, but he will, an' he'll break that squarehead's heart, or it's little I know iv the ways iv men on the ships iv the sea.'

Thomas Mugridge is becoming unendurable. I am compelled to Mister him and to Sir him with every speech. One reason for this is that Wolf Larsen seems to have taken a fancy to him. It is an unprecedented thing, I take it, for a captain to be chummy with the cook; but this is certainly what Wolf Larsen is doing. Two or three times he put his head into the galley and chaffed Mugridge good-naturedly, and once, this afternoon, he stood by the break of the poop and chatted with him for fully fifteen minutes. When it was over, and Mugridge was back in the galley, he became greasily radiant, and went about his work, humming coster songs in a nerve-racking and discordant falsetto.

'I always get along with the officers,' he remarked to me in a confidential tone. 'I know the w'y, I do, to myke myself uppreci-yted. There was my last skipper—w'y I thought nothin' of droppin' down in the cabin for a little chat and a friendly glass. 'Mugridge,' sez 'e to me, 'Mugridge,' sez 'e, 'you've missed yer vokytion.' 'An' 'ow's that?' sez I. 'Yer should 'a been born a gentleman, an' never 'ad to work for yer livin'.' God strike me dead, 'Ump, if that ayn't wot 'e sez, an' me a-sittin' there in 'is own cabin, jolly-like an' comfortable, a-smokin' 'is cigars an' drinkin' 'is rum.'

This chitter-chatter drove me to distraction. I never heard a voice I hated so. His oily, insinuating tones, his greasy smile and his monstrous self-conceit grated on my nerves till sometimes I was all in a tremble. Positively, he was the most disgusting and loathsome person I have ever met. The filth of his cooking was indescribable; and, as he cooked everything that was eaten aboard, I was compelled to select what I ate with great circumspection, choosing from the least dirty of his concoctions.

My hands bothered me a great deal, unused as they were to work. The nails were discoloured and black, while the skin was already grained with dirt which even a scrubbing-brush could not remove. Then blisters came, in a painful and never-ending procession, and I had a great burn on my forearm, acquired by losing my balance in a roll of the ship and pitching against the galley stove. Nor was my knee any better. The swelling had not gone down, and the cap was still up on edge. Hobbling about on it from morning till night was not helping it any. What I needed was rest, if it were ever to get well.

Rest! I never before knew the meaning of the word. I had been resting all my life and did not know it. But now, could I sit still for one half-hour and do nothing, not even think, it would be the most pleasurable thing in the world. But it is a revelation, on the other hand. I shall be able to appreciate the lives of the working people hereafter. I did not dream that work was so terrible a thing. From half-past five in the morning till ten o'clock at night I am everybody's slave, with not one moment to myself, except such as I can steal near the end of the second dog-watch. Let me pause for a minute to look out over the sea sparkling in the sun, or to gaze at a sailor going aloft to the gaff-topsails, or running out the bowsprit, and I am sure to hear the hateful voice, 'Ere, you, 'Ump, no sodgerin'. I've got my peepers on yer.'

There are signs of rampant bad temper in the steerage, and the gossip is going around that Smoke and Henderson have had a fight. Henderson seems the best of the hunters, a slow-going fellow, and hard to rouse; but roused he must have been, for Smoke had a bruised and discoloured eye, and looked particularly vicious when he came into the cabin for supper.

A cruel thing happened just before supper, indicative of the callousness and brutishness of these men. There is one green hand in the crew, Harrison by name, a clumsy-looking country boy, mastered, I imagine, by the spirit of adventure, and making his first voyage. In the light baffling airs the schooner had been tacking about a great deal, at which times the sails pass from one side to the other and a man is sent aloft to shift over the fore-gaff-topsail. In some way, when Harrison was aloft, the sheet jammed in the block through which it runs at the end of the gaff. As I understood it, there were two ways of getting it cleared,—first, by lowering the foresail, which was comparatively easy and without danger; and second, by climbing out the peak-halyards to the end of the gaff itself, an exceedingly hazardous performance.

Johansen called out to Harrison to go out the halyards. It was patent to everybody that the boy was afraid. And well he might be, eighty feet above the deck, to trust himself on those thin and jerking ropes. Had there been a steady breeze it would not have been so bad, but the *Ghost* was rolling emptily in a long sea, and with each roll the canvas flapped and boomed and the halyards slacked and jerked taut. They were capable of snapping a man off like a fly from a whip-lash.

Harrison heard the order and understood what was demanded of him, but hesitated. It was probably the first time he had been aloft in his life. Johansen, who had caught the contagion of Wolf Larsen's masterfulness, burst out with a volley of abuse and curses.

'That'll do, Johansen,' Wolf Larsen said brusquely. 'I'll have you know that I do the swearing on this ship. If I need your assistance, I'll call you in.'

'Yes, sir,' the mate acknowledged submissively.

In the meantime Harrison had started out on the halyards. I was looking up from the galley door, and I could see him trembling, as if with ague, in every limb. He proceeded very slowly and cautiously, an inch at a time. Outlined against the clear blue of the sky, he had the appearance of an enormous spider crawling along the tracery of its web.

It was a slight uphill climb, for the foresail peaked high; and the halyards, running through various blocks on the gaff and mast, gave him separate holds for hands and feet. But the trouble lay in that the wind was not strong enough nor steady enough to keep the sail full. When he was half-way out, the *Ghost* took a long roll to windward and back again into the hollow between two seas. Harrison ceased his progress and held on tightly. Eighty feet beneath, I could see the agonized strain of his muscles as he gripped for very life. The sail emptied and the gaff swung amid-ships. The halyards slackened, and, though it all happened very quickly, I could see them sag beneath the weight of his body. Then the gag swung to the side with an abrupt swiftness, the great sail boomed like a cannon, and the three rows of reef-points slatted against the canvas like a volley of rifles. Harrison, clinging on, made the giddy rush through the air. This rush ceased abruptly. The halyards became instantly taut. It was the snap of the whip. His clutch was broken. One hand was torn loose from its hold. The other lingered desperately for a moment, and followed. His body pitched out and down, but in some way he managed to save himself with his legs. He was hanging by them, head downward. A quick effort brought his hands up to the halyards again; but he was a long time regaining his former position, where he hung, a pitiable object.

'I'll bet he has no appetite for supper,' I heard Wolf Larsen's voice, which came to me from around the corner of the galley. 'Stand from under, you, Johansen! Watch out! Here she comes!'

In truth, Harrison was very sick, as a person is sea-sick; and for a long time he clung to his precarious perch without attempting to move. Johansen, however, continued violently to urge him on to the completion of his task.

'It is a shame,' I heard Johnson growling in painfully slow and correct English. He was standing by the main rigging, a few feet away from me. 'The boy is willing enough. He will learn if he has a chance. But this is—' He paused awhile, for the word 'murder' was his final judgment.

'Hist, will ye!' Louis whispered to him, 'For the love iv your mother hold your mouth!'

But Johnson, looking on, still continued his grumbling.

'Look here,' the hunter Standish spoke to Wolf Larsen, 'that's my boat-puller, and I don't want to lose him.'

'That's all right, Standish,' was the reply. 'He's your boat-puller when you've got him in the boat; but he's my sailor when I have him aboard, and I'll do what I damn well please with him.'

'But that's no reason—' Standish began in a torrent of speech.

'That'll do, easy as she goes,' Wolf Larsen counselled back. 'I've told you what's what, and let it stop at that. The man's mine, and I'll make soup of him and eat it if I want to.'

There was an angry gleam in the hunter's eye, but he turned on his heel and entered the steerage companion-way, where he remained, looking upward. All hands were on deck now, and all eyes were aloft, where a human life was at grapples with death. The callousness of these men, to whom industrial organization gave control of the lives of other men, was appalling. I, who had lived out of the whirl of the world, had never dreamed that its work was carried on in such fashion. Life had always seemed a peculiarly sacred thing, but here it counted for nothing, was a cipher in the arithmetic of commerce. I must say, however, that the sailors themselves were sympathetic, as instance the case of Johnson; but the masters (the hunters and the captain) were heartlessly indifferent. Even the protest of Standish arose out of the fact that he did not wish to lose his boat-puller. Had it been some other hunter's boat-puller, he, like them, would have been no more than amused.

But to return to Harrison. It took Johansen, insulting and reviling the poor wretch, fully ten minutes to get him started again. A little later he made the end of the gaff, where, astride the spar itself, he had a better chance for holding on. He cleared the sheet, and was free to return, slightly downhill now, along the halyards to the mast. But he had lost his nerve. Unsafe as was his present position, he was loath to forsake it for the more unsafe position on the halyards.

He looked along the airy path he must traverse, and then down to the deck. His eyes were wide and staring, and he was trembling violently. I had never seen fear so strongly stamped upon a human face. Johansen called vainly for him to come down. At any moment he was liable to be snapped off the gaff, but he was helpless with fright. Wolf Larsen, walking up and down with Smoke and in conversation, took no more notice of him, though he cried sharply, once, to the man at the wheel:

'You're off your course, my man! Be careful, unless you're looking for trouble!'

'Ay, ay, sir,' the helmsman responded, putting a couple of spokes down.

He had been guilty of running the *Ghost* several points off her course in order that what little wind there was should fill the foresail and hold it steady. He had striven to help the unfortunate Harrison at the risk of incurring Wolf Larsen's anger.

The time went by, and the suspense, to me, was terrible. Thomas Mugridge, on the other hand, considered it a laughable affair, and was continually bobbing his head out the galley door to make jocose remarks. How I hated him! And how my hatred for him grew and grew, during that fearful time, to cyclopean dimensions. For the first time in my life I experienced the desire to murder—'saw red,' as some of our picturesque writers phrase it. Life in general might still be sacred, but life in the particular case of Thomas Mugridge had become very profane indeed. I was frightened when I became conscious that I was seeing red, and the thought flashed through my mind: was I, too, becoming tainted by the brutality of my environment?—I, who even in the most flagrant crimes had denied the justice and righteousness of capital punishment?

Fully half-an-hour went by, and then I saw Johnson and Louis in some sort of altercation. It ended with Johnson flinging off Louis's detaining arm and starting forward. He crossed the deck, sprang into the fore rigging, and began to climb. But the quick eye of Wolf Larsen caught him.

'Here, you, what are you up to?' he cried.

Johnson's ascent was arrested. He looked his captain in the eyes and replied slowly: 'I am going to get that boy down.'

'You'll get down out of that rigging, and damn lively about it! D'ye hear? Get down!'

Johnson hesitated, but the long years of obedience to the masters of ships overpowered him, and he dropped sullenly to the deck and went on forward.

At half after five I went below to set the cabin table, but I hardly knew what I did, for my eyes and my brain were filled with the vision of a man, white-faced and trembling, comically like a bug, clinging to the thrashing gaff. At six o'clock, when I served supper, going on deck to get the food from the galley, I saw Harrison, still in the same position. The conversation at the table was of other things. Nobody seemed interested in the wantonly imperilled life. But making an extra trip to the galley a little later, I was gladdened by the sight of Harrison staggering weakly from the rigging to the forecastle scuttle. He had finally summoned the courage to descend.

Before closing this incident, I must give a scrap of conversation I had with Wolf Larsen in the cabin, while I was washing the dishes.

'You were looking squeamish this afternoon,' he began. 'What was the matter?'

I could see that he knew what had made me possibly as sick as Harrison, that he was trying to draw me, and I answered, 'It was because of the brutal treatment of that boy.'

He gave a short laugh. 'Like sea-sickness, I suppose. Some men are subject to it, and others are not.'

'Not so,' I objected.

'Just so,' he went on. 'The earth is as full of brutality as the sea is full of motion. And some men are made sick by the one, and some by the other. That's the only reason.'

'But you, who make a mock of human life, don't you place any value upon it whatever?' I demanded.

'Value? What value?' He looked at me, and though his eyes were steady and motionless, there seemed a cynical smile in them. 'What kind of value? How do you measure it? Who values it?'

'I do,' I made answer.

'Then what is it worth to you? Another man's life, I mean. Come now, what is it worth?'

The value of life? How could I put a tangible value upon it? Somehow, I, who have always had expression, lacked expression when with Wolf Larsen. I have since determined that a part of it was due to the man's personality, but that the greater part was due to his totally different outlook. Unlike other materialists I had met and with whom I had something in common to start on, I had nothing in common with him. Perhaps, also, it was the elemental simplicity of his mind that baffled me. He drove so directly to the core of the matter, divesting a question always of all superfluous details, and with such an air of finality, that I seemed to find myself struggling in deep water, with no footing under me. Value of life? How could I answer the question on the spur of the moment? The sacredness of life I had accepted as axiomatic. That it was intrinsically valuable was a truism I had never questioned. But when he challenged the truism I was speechless.

'We were talking about this yesterday,' he said. 'I held that life was a ferment, a yeasty something which devoured life that it might live, and that living was merely successful piggishness. Why, if there is anything in supply and demand, life is the cheapest thing in the world. There is only so much water, so much earth, so much air; but the life that is demanding to be born is limitless. Nature is a spendthrift. Look at the fish and their millions of eggs. For that matter, look at you and me. In our loins are the possibilities of millions of lives. Could we but find time and opportunity and utilize the last bit and every bit of the unborn life that is in us, we could become the fathers of nations and populate continents. Life? Bah! It has no value. Of cheap things it is the cheapest. Everywhere it goes begging. Nature spills it out with a lavish hand. Where there is room for one life, she sows a thousand lives, and it's life eats life till the strongest and most piggish life is left.'

'You have read Darwin,' I said. 'But you read him misunderstandingly when you conclude that the struggle for existence sanctions your wanton destruction of life.'

He shrugged his shoulders. 'You know you only mean that in relation to human life, for of the flesh and the fowl and the fish you destroy as much as I or any other man. And human life is in no wise different, though you feel it is and think that you reason why it is. Why should I be parsimonious with this life which is cheap and without value? There are more sailors than there are ships on the sea for them, more workers than there are factories or machines for them. Why, you who live on the land know that you house your poor people in the slums of cities and loose famine and pestilence upon them, and that there still remain more poor people, dying for want of a crust of bread and a bit of meat (which is life destroyed), than you know what to do with. Have you ever seen the London dockers fighting like wild beasts for a chance to work?'

He started for the companion stairs, but turned his head for a final word. 'Do you know the only value life has is what life puts upon itself? And it is of course over-estimated since it is of necessity prejudiced in its own favour. Take that man I had aloft. He held on as if he were a precious thing, a treasure beyond diamonds or rubies. To you? No. To me? Not at all. To himself? Yes. But I do not accept his estimate. He sadly overrates himself. There is plenty more life demanding to be born. Had he fallen and dripped his brains upon the deck like honey from the comb, there would have been no loss to the world. He was worth nothing to the world. The supply is too large. To himself only was he of value, and to show how fictitious even this value was, being dead he is unconscious that he has lost himself. He alone rated himself beyond diamonds and rubies. Diamonds and rubies are gone, spread out on the deck to be washed away by a bucket of sea-water, and he does not even know that the diamonds and rubies are gone. He does not lose anything, for with the loss of himself he loses the knowledge of loss. Don't you see? And what have you to say?'

'That you are at least consistent,' was all I could say, and I went on washing the dishes.

CHAPTER VII

At last, after three days of variable winds, we have caught the north-east trades. I came on deck, after a good night's rest in spite of my poor knee, to find the *Ghost* foaming along, wing-and-wing, and every sail drawing except the jibs, with a fresh breeze astern. Oh, the wonder of the great trade-wind! All day we sailed, and all night, and the next day, and the next, day after day, the wind always astern and blowing steadily and strong. The schooner sailed herself. There was no pulling and hauling on sheets and tackles, no shifting of topsails, no work at all for the sailors to do except to steer. At night when the sun went down, the sheets were slackened; in the morning, when they yielded up the damp of the dew and relaxed, they were pulled tight again—and that was all.

Ten knots, twelve knots, eleven knots, varying from time to time, is the speed we are making. And ever out of the north-east the brave wind blows, driving us on our course two hundred and fifty miles between the dawns. It saddens me and gladdens me, the gait with which we are leaving San Francisco behind and with which we are foaming down upon the tropics. Each day grows perceptibly warmer. In the second dog-watch the sailors come on deck, stripped, and heave buckets of water upon one another from overside. Flying-fish are beginning to be seen, and during the night the watch above scrambles over the deck in pursuit of those that fall aboard. In the morning, Thomas Mugridge being duly bribed, the galley is pleasantly areek with the odour of their frying; while dolphin meat is served fore and aft on such occasions as Johnson catches the blazing beauties from the bowsprit end.

Johnson seems to spend all his spare time there or aloft at the crosstrees, watching the *Ghost* cleaving the water under press of sail. There is passion, adoration, in his eyes, and he goes about in a sort of trance, gazing in ecstasy at the swelling sails, the foaming wake, and the heave and the run of her over the liquid mountains that are moving with us in stately procession.

The days and nights are 'all a wonder and a wild delight,' and though I have little time from my dreary work, I steal odd moments to gaze and gaze at the unending glory of what I never dreamed the world possessed. Above, the sky is stainless blue— blue as the sea itself, which under the forefoot is of the colour and sheen of azure satin. All around the horizon are pale, fleecy clouds, never changing, never moving, like a silver setting for the flawless turquoise sky.

I do not forget one night, when I should have been asleep, of lying on the fore-castle-head and gazing down at the spectral ripple of foam thrust aside by the *Ghost's* forefoot. It sounded like the gurgling of a brook over mossy stones in some quiet dell, and the crooning song of it lured me away and out of myself till I was no longer Hump the cabin-boy, nor Van Weyden, the man who had dreamed away thirty-five years among books. But a voice behind me, the unmistakable voice of Wolf Larsen, strong with the invincible certitude of the man and mellow with appreciation of the words he was quoting, aroused me.

> 'O the blazing tropic night, when the wake's a welt of light
>   That holds the hot sky tame,
> And the steady forefoot snores through the planet-powdered floors
>   Where the scared whale flukes in flame.
> Her plates are scarred by the sun, dear lass,
>   And her ropes are taut with the dew,
> For we're booming down on the old trail, our own trail, the out trail,
>   We're sagging south on the Long Trail—the trail that is always new.'

'Eh, Hump? How's it strike you?' he asked, after the due pause which words and setting demanded.

I looked into his face. It was aglow with light, as the sea itself, and the eyes were flashing in the starshine.

'It strikes me as remarkable, to say the least, that you should show enthusiasm,' I answered coldly.

'Why, man, it's living! it's life!' he cried.

'Which is a cheap thing and without value.' I flung his words at him.

He laughed, and it was the first time I had heard honest mirth in his voice.

'Ah, I cannot get you to understand, cannot drive it into your head, what a thing this life is. Of course life is valueless, except to itself. And I can tell you that my life is pretty valuable just now—to myself. It is beyond price, which you will acknowledge is a terrific overrating, but which I cannot help, for it is the life that is in me that makes the rating.'

He appeared waiting for the words with which to express the thought that was in him, and finally went on.

'Do you know, I am filled with a strange uplift; I feel as if all time were echoing through me, as though all powers were mine. I know truth, divine good from evil, right from wrong. My vision is clear and far. I could almost believe in God. But,' and his voice changed and the light went out of his face,—'what is this condition in which I find myself? this joy of living? this exultation of life? this inspiration, I may well call it? It is what comes when there is nothing wrong with one's digestion, when his stomach is in trim and his appetite has an edge, and all goes well. It is the bribe for living, the champagne of the blood, the effervescence of the ferment—that makes some men think holy thoughts, and other men to see God or to create him when they cannot see him. That is all, the drunkenness of life, the stirring and crawling of the yeast, the babbling of the life that is insane with consciousness that it is alive. And— bah! To-morrow I shall pay for it as the drunkard pays. And I shall know that I must die, at sea most likely, cease crawling of myself to be all a-crawl with the corruption of the sea; to be fed upon, to be carrion, to yield up all the strength and movement of my muscles that it may become strength and movement in fin and scale and the guts of fishes. Bah! And bah! again. The champagne is already flat. The sparkle and bubble has gone out and it is a tasteless drink.'

He left me as suddenly as he had come, springing to the deck with the weight and softness of a tiger. The *Ghost* ploughed on her way. I noted the gurgling forefoot was very like a snore, and as I listened to it the effect of Wolf Larsen's swift rush from sublime exultation to despair slowly left me. Then some deep-water sailor, from the waist of the ship, lifted a rich tenor voice in the 'Song of the Trade Wind':

> 'Oh, I am the wind the seamen love—
> I am steady, and strong, and true;
> They follow my track by the clouds above,
> O'er the fathomless tropic blue.

> * * * * *

> Through daylight and dark I follow the bark
> I keep like a hound on her trail;
> I'm strongest at noon, yet under the moon,
> I stiffen the bunt of her sail.'

CHAPTER VIII

Sometimes I think Wolf Larsen mad, or half-mad at least, what of his strange moods and vagaries. At other times I take him for a great man, a genius who has never arrived. And, finally, I am convinced that he is the perfect type of the primitive man, born a thousand years or generations too late and an anachronism in this culminating century of civilization. He is certainly an individualist of the most pronounced type. Not only that, but he is very lonely. There is no congeniality between him and the rest of the men aboard ship. His tremendous virility and mental strength wall him apart. They are more like children to him, even the hunters, and as children he treats them, descending perforce to their level and playing with them as a man plays with puppies. Or else he probes them with the cruel hand of a vivisectionist, groping about in their mental processes and examining their souls as though to see of what soul-stuff is made.

I have seen him a score of times, at table, insulting this hunter or that, with cool and level eyes and, withal, a certain air of interest, pondering their actions or replies or petty rages with a curiosity almost laughable to me who stood onlooker and who understood. Concerning his own rages, I am convinced that they are not real, that they are sometimes experiments, but that in the main they are the habits of a pose or attitude he has seen fit to take toward his fellow-men. I know, with the possible exception of the incident of the dead mate, that I have not seen him really angry; nor do I wish ever to see him in a genuine rage, when all the force of him is called into play.

While on the question of vagaries, I shall tell what befell Thomas Mugridge in the cabin, and at the same time complete an incident upon which I have already touched once or twice. The twelve o'clock dinner was over, one day, and I had just finished putting the cabin in order, when Wolf Larsen and Thomas Mugridge descended the companion stairs. Though the cook had a cubby-hole of a state-room opening off from the cabin, in the cabin itself he had never dared to linger or to be seen, and he flitted to and fro, once or twice a day, a timid spectre.

'So you know how to play 'Nap,' Wolf Larsen was saying in a pleased sort of voice. 'I might have guessed an Englishman would know. I learned it myself in English ships.'

Thomas Mugridge was beside himself, a blithering imbecile, so pleased was he at chumming thus with the captain. The little airs he put on and the painful striving to assume the easy carriage of a man born to a dignified place in life would have been sickening had they not been ludicrous. He quite ignored my presence, though I credited him with being simply unable to see me. His pale, wishy-washy eyes were swimming like lazy summer seas, though what blissful visions they beheld were beyond my imagination.

'Get the cards, Hump,' Wolf Larsen ordered, as they took seats at the table. 'And bring out the cigars and the whisky you'll find in my berth.'

I returned with the articles in time to hear the Cockney hinting broadly that there was a mystery about him, that he might be a gentleman's son gone wrong or something or other; also, that he was a remittance man and was paid to keep away from England—'p'yed 'ansomely, sir,' was the way he put it; 'p'yed 'ansomely to sling my 'ook an' keep slingin' it.'

I had brought the customary liquor glasses, but Wolf Larsen frowned, shook his head, and signalled with his hands for me to bring the tumblers. These he filled two-thirds full with undiluted whisky—'a gentleman's drink?' quoth Thomas Mugridge,—and they clinked their glasses to the glorious game of 'Nap,' lighted cigars, and fell to shuffling and dealing the cards.

They played for money. They increased the amounts of the bets. They drank whisky, they drank it neat, and I fetched more. I do not know whether Wolf Larsen cheated or not,—a thing he was thoroughly capable of doing,—but he won steadily. The cook made repeated journeys to his bunk for money. Each time he performed the journey with greater swagger, but he never brought more than a few dollars at a time. He grew maudlin, familiar, could hardly see the cards or sit upright. As a preliminary to another journey to his bunk, he hooked Wolf Larsen's buttonhole with a greasy forefinger and vacuously proclaimed and reiterated, 'I got money, I got money, I tell yer, an' I'm a gentleman's son.'

Wolf Larsen was unaffected by the drink, yet he drank glass for glass, and if anything his glasses were fuller. There was no change in him. He did not appear even amused at the other's antics.

In the end, with loud protestations that he could lose like a gentleman, the cook's last money was staked on the game—and lost. Whereupon he leaned his head on his hands and wept. Wolf Larsen looked curiously at him, as though about to probe and vivisect him, then changed his mind, as from the foregone conclusion that there was nothing there to probe.

'Hump,' he said to me, elaborately polite, 'kindly take Mr. Mugridge's arm and help him up on deck. He is not feeling very well.'

'And tell Johnson to douse him with a few buckets of salt water,' he added, in a lower tone for my ear alone.

I left Mr. Mugridge on deck, in the hands of a couple of grinning sailors who had been told off for the purpose. Mr. Mugridge was sleepily spluttering that he was a gentleman's son. But as I descended the companion stairs to clear the table I heard him shriek as the first bucket of water struck him.

Wolf Larsen was counting his winnings.

'One hundred and eighty-five dollars even,' he said aloud. 'Just as I thought. The beggar came aboard without a cent.'

'And what you have won is mine, sir,' I said boldly.

He favoured me with a quizzical smile. 'Hump, I have studied some grammar in my time, and I think your tenses are tangled. "Was mine," you should have said, not 'is mine.'

'It is a question, not of grammar, but of ethics,' I answered.

It was possibly a minute before he spoke.

'D'ye know, Hump,' he said, with a slow seriousness which had in it an indefinable strain of sadness, 'that this is the first time I have heard the word 'ethics' in the mouth of a man. You and I are the only men on this ship who know its meaning.'

'At one time in my life,' he continued, after another pause, 'I dreamed that I might some day talk with men who used such language, that I might lift myself out of the place in life in which I had been born, and hold conversation and mingle with men who talked about just such things as ethics. And this is the first time I have ever heard the word pronounced. Which is all by the way, for you are wrong. It is a question neither of grammar nor ethics, but of fact.'

'I understand,' I said. 'The fact is that you have the money.'

His face brightened. He seemed pleased at my perspicacity. 'But it is avoiding the real question,' I continued, 'which is one of right.'

'Ah,' he remarked, with a wry pucker of his mouth, 'I see you still believe in such things as right and wrong.'

'But don't you?—at all?' I demanded.

'Not the least bit. Might is right, and that is all there is to it. Weakness is wrong. Which is a very poor way of saying that it is good for oneself to be strong, and evil for oneself to be weak—or better yet, it is pleasurable to be strong, because of the profits; painful to be weak, because of the penalties. Just now the possession of this money is a pleasurable thing. It is good for one to possess it. Being able to possess it, I wrong myself and the life that is in me if I give it to you and forego the pleasure of possessing it.'

'But you wrong me by withholding it,' I objected.

'Not at all. One man cannot wrong another man. He can only wrong himself. As I see it, I do wrong always when I consider the interests of others. Don't you see? How can two particles of the yeast wrong each other by striving to devour each other? It is their inborn heritage to strive to devour, and to strive not to be devoured. When they depart from this they sin.'

'Then you don't believe in altruism?' I asked.

He received the word as if it had a familiar ring, though he pondered it thoughtfully. 'Let me see, it means something about coöperation, doesn't it?'

'Well, in a way there has come to be a sort of connection,' I answered unsurprised by this time at such gaps in his vocabulary, which, like his knowledge, was the acquirement of a self-read, self-educated man, whom no one had directed in his studies, and who had thought much and talked little or not at all. 'An altruistic act is an act performed for the welfare of others. It is unselfish, as opposed to an act performed for self, which is selfish.'

He nodded his head. 'Oh, yes, I remember it now. I ran across it in Spencer.'

'Spencer!' I cried. 'Have you read him?'

'Not very much,' was his confession. 'I understood quite a good deal of *First Principles*, but his *Biology* took the wind out of my sails, and his *Psychology* left me butting around in the doldrums for many a day. I honestly could not understand what he was driving at. I put it down to mental deficiency on my part, but since then I have decided that it was for want of preparation. I had no proper basis. Only Spencer and myself know how hard I hammered. But I did get something out of his *Data of Ethics*. There's where I ran across 'altruism,' and I remember now how it was used.'

I wondered what this man could have got from such a work. Spencer I remembered enough to know that altruism was imperative to his ideal of highest conduct. Wolf Larsen, evidently, had sifted the great philosopher's teachings, rejecting and selecting according to his needs and desires.

'What else did you run across?' I asked.

His brows drew in slightly with the mental effort of suitably phrasing thoughts which he had never before put into speech. I felt an elation of spirit. I was groping into his soul-stuff as he made a practice of groping in the soul-stuff of others. I was exploring virgin territory. A strange, a terribly strange, region was unrolling itself before my eyes.

'In as few words as possible,' he began, 'Spencer puts it something like this: First, a man must act for his own benefit—to do this is to be moral and good. Next, he must act for the benefit of his children. And third, he must act for the benefit of his race.'

'And the highest, finest, right conduct,' I interjected, 'is that act which benefits at the same time the man, his children, and his race.'

'I wouldn't stand for that,' he replied. 'Couldn't see the necessity for it, nor the common sense. I cut out the race and the children. I would sacrifice nothing for them. It's just so much slush and sentiment, and you must see it yourself, at least for one who does not believe in eternal life. With immortality before me, altruism would be a paying business proposition. I might elevate my soul to all kinds of altitudes. But with nothing eternal before me but death, given for a brief spell this yeasty crawling and squirming which is called life, why, it would be immoral for me to perform any act that was a sacrifice. Any sacrifice that makes me lose one crawl or squirm is foolish,— and not only foolish, for it is a wrong against myself and a wicked thing. I must not lose one crawl or squirm if I am to get the most out of the ferment. Nor will the eternal movelessness that is coming to me be made easier or harder by the sacrifices or selfishnesses of the time when I was yeasty and acrawl.'

'Then you are an individualist, a materialist, and, logically, a hedonist.'

'Big words,' he smiled. 'But what is a hedonist?'

He nodded agreement when I had given the definition. 'And you are also,' I continued, 'a man one could not trust in the least thing where it was possible for a selfish interest to intervene?'

'Now you're beginning to understand,' he said, brightening.

'You are a man utterly without what the world calls morals?'

'That's it.'

'A man of whom to be always afraid—'

'That's the way to put it.'

'As one is afraid of a snake, or a tiger, or a shark?'

'Now you know me,' he said. 'And you know me as I am generally known. Other men call me 'Wolf.'

'You are a sort of monster,' I added audaciously, 'a Caliban who has pondered Setebos, and who acts as you act, in idle moments, by whim and fancy.'

His brow clouded at the allusion. He did not understand, and I quickly learned that he did not know the poem.

'I'm just reading Browning,' he confessed, 'and it's pretty tough. I haven't got very far along, and as it is I've about lost my bearings.'

Not to be tiresome, I shall say that I fetched the book from his state-room and read 'Caliban' aloud. He was delighted. It was a primitive mode of reasoning and of looking at things that he understood thoroughly. He interrupted again and again with comment and criticism. When I finished, he had me read it over a second time, and a third. We fell into discussion—philosophy, science, evolution, religion. He betrayed the inaccuracies of the self-read man, and, it must be granted, the sureness and directness of the primitive mind. The very simplicity of his reasoning was its strength, and his materialism was far more compelling than the subtly complex materialism of Charley Furuseth. Not that I—a confirmed and, as Furuseth phrased it, a temperamental idealist—was to be compelled; but that Wolf Larsen stormed the last strongholds of my faith with a vigour that received respect, while not accorded conviction.

Time passed. Supper was at hand and the table not laid. I became restless and anxious, and when Thomas Mugridge glared down the companion-way, sick and angry of countenance, I prepared to go about my duties. But Wolf Larsen cried out to him:

'Cooky, you've got to hustle to-night. I'm busy with Hump, and you'll do the best you can without him.'

And again the unprecedented was established. That night I sat at table with the captain and the hunters, while Thomas Mugridge waited on us and washed the dishes afterward—a whim, a Caliban-mood of Wolf Larsen's, and one I foresaw would bring me trouble. In the meantime we talked and talked, much to the disgust of the hunters, who could not understand a word.

CHAPTER IX

Three days of rest, three blessed days of rest, are what I had with Wolf Larsen, eating at the cabin table and doing nothing but discuss life, literature, and the universe, the while Thomas Mugridge fumed and raged and did my work as well as his own.

'Watch out for squalls, is all I can say to you,' was Louis's warning, given during a spare half-hour on deck while Wolf Larsen was engaged in straightening out a row among the hunters.

'Ye can't tell what'll be happenin',' Louis went on, in response to my query for more definite information. 'The man's as contrary as air currents or water currents. You can never guess the ways iv him. 'Tis just as you're thinkin' you know him and are makin' a favourable slant along him, that he whirls around, dead ahead and comes howlin' down upon you and a-rippin' all iv your fine-weather sails to rags.'

So I was not altogether surprised when the squall foretold by Louis smote me. We had been having a heated discussion,—upon life, of course,—and, grown over-bold, I was passing stiff strictures upon Wolf Larsen and the life of Wolf Larsen. In fact, I was vivisecting him and turning over his soul-stuff as keenly and thoroughly as it was his custom to do it to others. It may be a weakness of mine that I have an incisive way of speech; but I threw all restraint to the winds and cut and slashed until the whole man of him was snarling. The dark sun-bronze of his face went black with wrath, his eyes were ablaze. There was no clearness or sanity in them—nothing but the terrific rage of a madman. It was the wolf in him that I saw, and a mad wolf at that.

He sprang for me with a half-roar, gripping my arm. I had steeled myself to brazen it out, though I was trembling inwardly; but the enormous strength of the man was too much for my fortitude. He had gripped me by the biceps with his single hand, and when that grip tightened I wilted and shrieked aloud. My feet went out from under me. I simply could not stand upright and endure the agony. The muscles refused their duty. The pain was too great. My biceps was being crushed to a pulp.

He seemed to recover himself, for a lucid gleam came into his eyes, and he relaxed his hold with a short laugh that was more like a growl. I fell to the floor, feeling very faint, while he sat down, lighted a cigar, and watched me as a cat watches a mouse. As I writhed about I could see in his eyes that curiosity I had so often noted, that wonder and perplexity, that questing, that everlasting query of his as to what it was all about.

I finally crawled to my feet and ascended the companion stairs. Fair weather was over, and there was nothing left but to return to the galley. My left arm was numb, as though paralysed, and days passed before I could use it, while weeks went by before the last stiffness and pain went out of it. And he had done nothing but put his hand upon my arm and squeeze. There had been no wrenching or jerking. He had just closed his hand with a steady pressure. What he might have done I did not fully realize till next day, when he put his head into the galley, and, as a sign of renewed friendliness, asked me how my arm was getting on.

'It might have been worse,' he smiled.

I was peeling potatoes. He picked one up from the pan. It was fair-sized, firm, and unpeeled. He closed his hand upon it, squeezed, and the potato squirted out between his fingers in mushy streams. The pulpy remnant he dropped back into the pan and turned away, and I had a sharp vision of how it might have fared with me had the monster put his real strength upon me.

But the three days' rest was good in spite of it all, for it had given my knee the very chance it needed. It felt much better, the swelling had materially decreased, and the cap seemed descending into its proper place. Also, the three days' rest brought the trouble I had foreseen. It was plainly Thomas Mugridge's intention to make me pay for those three days. He treated me vilely, cursed me continually, and heaped his own work upon me. He even ventured to raise his fist to me, but I was becoming animal-like myself, and I snarled in his face so terribly that it must have frightened him back. It is no pleasant picture I can conjure up of myself, Humphrey Van Weyden, in that noisome ship's galley, crouched in a corner over my task, my face raised to the face of the creature about to strike me, my lips lifted and snarling like a dog's, my eyes gleaming with fear and helplessness and the courage that comes of fear and helplessness. I do not like the picture. It reminds me too strongly of a rat in a trap. I do not care to think of it; but it was elective, for the threatened blow did not descend.

Thomas Mugridge backed away, glaring as hatefully and viciously as I glared. A pair of beasts is what we were, penned together and showing our teeth. He was a coward, afraid to strike me because I had not quailed sufficiently in advance; so he chose a new way to intimidate me. There was only one galley knife that, as a knife, amounted to anything. This, through many years of service and wear, had acquired a long, lean blade. It was unusually cruel-looking, and at first I had shuddered every time I used it. The cook borrowed a stone from Johansen and proceeded to sharpen the knife. He did it with great ostentation, glancing significantly at me the while. He whetted it up and down all day long. Every odd moment he could find he had the knife and stone out and was whetting away. The steel acquired a razor edge. He tried it with the ball of his thumb or across the nail. He shaved hairs from the back of his hand, glanced along the edge with microscopic acuteness, and found, or feigned that he found, always, a slight inequality in its edge somewhere. Then he would put it on the stone again and whet, whet, whet, till I could have laughed aloud, it was so very ludicrous.

It was also serious, for I learned that he was capable of using it, that under all his cowardice there was a courage of cowardice, like mine, that would impel him to do the very thing his whole nature protested against doing and was afraid of doing. 'Cooky's sharpening his knife for Hump,' was being whispered about among the sailors, and some of them twitted him about it. This he took in good part, and was really pleased, nodding his head with direful foreknowledge and mystery, until George Leach, the erstwhile cabin-boy, ventured some rough pleasantry on the subject.

Now it happened that Leach was one of the sailors told off to douse Mugridge after his game of cards with the captain. Leach had evidently done his task with a thoroughness that Mugridge had not forgiven, for words followed and evil names involving smirched ancestries. Mugridge menaced with the knife he was sharpening for me. Leach laughed and hurled more of his Telegraph Hill Billingsgate, and before either he or I knew what had happened, his right arm had been ripped open from elbow to wrist by a quick slash of the knife. The cook backed away, a fiendish expression on his face, the knife held before him in a position of defence. But Leach took it quite calmly, though blood was spouting upon the deck as generously as water from a fountain.

'I'm goin' to get you, Cooky,' he said, 'and I'll get you hard. And I won't be in no hurry about it. You'll be without that knife when I come for you.'

So saying, he turned and walked quietly forward. Mugridge's face was livid with fear at what he had done and at what he might expect sooner or later from the man he had stabbed. But his demeanour toward me was more ferocious than ever. In spite of his fear at the reckoning he must expect to pay for what he had done, he could see that it had been an object-lesson to me, and he became more domineering and exultant. Also there was a lust in him, akin to madness, which had come with sight of the blood he had drawn. He was beginning to see red in whatever direction he looked. The psychology of it is sadly tangled, and yet I could read the workings of his mind as clearly as though it were a printed book.

Several days went by, the *Ghost* still foaming down the trades, and I could swear I saw madness growing in Thomas Mugridge's eyes. And I confess that I became afraid, very much afraid. Whet, whet, whet, it went all day long. The look in his eyes as he felt the keen edge and glared at me was positively carnivorous. I was afraid to turn my shoulder to him, and when I left the galley I went out backwards—to the amusement of the sailors and hunters, who made a point of gathering in groups to witness my exit. The strain was too great. I sometimes thought my mind would give way under it—a meet thing on this ship of madmen and brutes. Every hour, every minute of my existence was in jeopardy. I was a human soul in distress, and yet no soul, fore or aft, betrayed sufficient sympathy to come to my aid. At times I thought of throwing myself on the mercy of Wolf Larsen, but the vision of the mocking devil in his eyes that questioned life and sneered at it would come strong upon me and compel me to refrain. At other times I seriously contemplated suicide, and the whole force of my hopeful philosophy was required to keep me from going over the side in the darkness of night.

Several times Wolf Larsen tried to inveigle me into discussion, but I gave him short answers and eluded him. Finally, he commanded me to resume my seat at the cabin table for a time and let the cook do my work. Then I spoke frankly, telling him what I was enduring from Thomas Mugridge because of the three days of favouritism which had been shown me. Wolf Larsen regarded me with smiling eyes.

'So you're afraid, eh?' he sneered.

'Yes,' I said defiantly and honestly, 'I am afraid.'

'That's the way with you fellows,' he cried, half angrily, 'sentimentalizing about your immortal souls and afraid to die. At sight of a sharp knife and a cowardly Cockney the clinging of life to life overcomes all your fond foolishness. Why, my dear fellow, you will live for ever. You are a god, and God cannot be killed. Cooky cannot hurt you. You are sure of your resurrection. What's there to be afraid of?

'You have eternal life before you. You are a millionaire in immortality, and a millionaire whose fortune cannot be lost, whose fortune is less perishable than the stars and as lasting as space or time. It is impossible for you to diminish your principal. Immortality is a thing without beginning or end. Eternity is eternity, and though you die here and now you will go on living somewhere else and hereafter. And it is all very beautiful, this shaking off of the flesh and soaring of the imprisoned spirit. Cooky cannot hurt you. He can only give you a boost on the path you eternally must tread.

'Or, if you do not wish to be boosted just yet, why not boost Cooky? According to your ideas, he, too, must be an immortal millionaire. You cannot bankrupt him. His paper will always circulate at par. You cannot diminish the length of his living by killing him, for he is without beginning or end. He's bound to go on living, somewhere, somehow. Then boost him. Stick a knife in him and let his spirit free. As it is, it's in a nasty prison, and you'll do him only a kindness by breaking down the door. And who knows?—it may be a very beautiful spirit that will go soaring up into the blue from that ugly carcass. Boost him along, and I'll promote you to his place, and he's getting forty-five dollars a month.'

It was plain that I could look for no help or mercy from Wolf Larsen. Whatever was to be done I must do for myself; and out of the courage of fear I evolved the plan of fighting Thomas Mugridge with his own weapons. I borrowed a whetstone from Johansen. Louis, the boat-steerer, had already begged me for condensed milk and sugar. The lazarette, where such delicacies were stored, was situated beneath the cabin floor. Watching my chance, I stole five cans of the milk, and that night, when it was Louis's watch on deck, I traded them with him for a dirk as lean and cruel-looking as Thomas Mugridge's vegetable knife. It was rusty and dull, but I turned the grindstone while Louis gave it an edge. I slept more soundly than usual that night.

Next morning, after breakfast, Thomas Mugridge began his whet, whet, whet. I glanced warily at him, for I was on my knees taking the ashes from the stove. When I returned from throwing them overside, he was talking to Harrison, whose honest yokel's face was filled with fascination and wonder.

'Yes,' Mugridge was saying, 'an' wot does 'is worship do but give me two years in Reading. But blimey if I cared. The other mug was fixed plenty. Should 'a seen 'im. Knife just like this. I stuck it in, like into soft butter, an' the w'y 'e squealed was better'n a tu-penny gaff.' He shot a glance in my direction to see if I was taking it in, and went on. 'I didn't mean it Tommy,' 'e was snifflin'; 'so 'elp me Gawd, I didn't mean it!' 'I'll fix yer bloody well right,' I sez, an' kept right after 'im. I cut 'im in ribbons, that's wot I did, an' 'e a-squealin' all the time. Once 'e got 'is 'and on the knife an' tried to 'old it. 'Ad 'is fingers around it, but I pulled it through, cuttin' to the bone. O, 'e was a sight, I can tell yer.'

A call from the mate interrupted the gory narrative, and Harrison went aft. Mugridge sat down on the raised threshold to the galley and went on with his knife-sharpening. I put the shovel away and calmly sat down on the coal-box facing him. He favoured me with a vicious stare. Still calmly, though my heart was going pitapat, I pulled out Louis's dirk and began to whet it on the stone. I had looked for almost any sort of explosion on the Cockney's part, but to my surprise he did not appear aware of what I was doing. He went on whetting his knife. So did I. And for two hours we sat there, face to face, whet, whet, whet, till the news of it spread abroad and half the ship's company was crowding the galley doors to see the sight.

Encouragement and advice were freely tendered, and Jock Horner, the quiet, self-spoken hunter who looked as though he would not harm a mouse, advised me to leave the ribs alone and to thrust upward for the abdomen, at the same time giving what he called the 'Spanish twist' to the blade. Leach, his bandaged arm prominently to the fore, begged me to leave a few remnants of the cook for him; and Wolf Larsen paused once or twice at the break of the poop to glance curiously at what must have been to him a stirring and crawling of the yeasty thing he knew as life.

And I make free to say that for the time being life assumed the same sordid values to me. There was nothing pretty about it, nothing divine—only two cowardly moving things that sat whetting steel upon stone, and a group of other moving things, cowardly and otherwise, that looked on. Half of them, I am sure, were anxious to see us shedding each other's blood. It would have been entertainment. And I do not think there was one who would have interfered had we closed in a death-struggle.

On the other hand, the whole thing was laughable and childish. Whet, whet, whet,—Humphrey Van Weyden sharpening his knife in a ship's galley and trying its edge with his thumb! Of all situations this was the most inconceivable. I know that my own kind could not have believed it possible. I had not been called 'Sissy' Van Weyden all my days without reason, and that 'Sissy' Van Weyden should be capable of doing this thing was a revelation to Humphrey Van Weyden, who knew not whether to be exultant or ashamed.

But nothing happened. At the end of two hours Thomas Mugridge put away knife and stone and held out his hand.

'Wot's the good of mykin' a 'oly show of ourselves for them mugs?' he demanded. 'They don't love us, an' bloody well glad they'd be a-seein' us cuttin' our throats. Yer not 'arf bad, 'Ump! You've got spunk, as you Yanks s'y, an' I like yer in a w'y. So come on an' shyke.'

Coward that I might be, I was less a coward than he. It was a distinct victory I had gained, and I refused to forego any of it by shaking his detestable hand.

'All right,' he said pridelessly, 'tyke it or leave it, I'll like yer none the less for it.' And to save his face he turned fiercely upon the onlookers. 'Get outa my galley-doors, you bloomin' swabs!'

This command was reinforced by a steaming kettle of water, and at sight of it the sailors scrambled out of the way. This was a sort of victory for Thomas Mugridge, and enabled him to accept more gracefully the defeat I had given him, though, of course, he was too discreet to attempt to drive the hunters away.

'I see Cooky's finish,' I heard Smoke say to Horner.

'You bet,' was the reply. 'Hump runs the galley from now on, and Cooky pulls in his horns.'

Mugridge heard and shot a swift glance at me, but I gave no sign that the conversation had reached me. I had not thought my victory was so far-reaching and complete, but I resolved to let go nothing I had gained. As the days went by, Smoke's prophecy was verified. The Cockney became more humble and slavish to me than even to Wolf Larsen. I mistered him and sirred him no longer, washed no more greasy pots, and peeled no more potatoes. I did my own work, and my own work only, and when and in what fashion I saw fit. Also I carried the dirk in a sheath at my hip, sailor-fashion, and maintained toward Thomas Mugridge a constant attitude which was composed of equal parts of domineering, insult, and contempt.

CHAPTER X

My intimacy with Wolf Larsen increases—if by intimacy may be denoted those relations which exist between master and man, or, better yet, between king and jester. I am to him no more than a toy, and he values me no more than a child values a toy. My function is to amuse, and so long as I amuse all goes well; but let him become bored, or let him have one of his black moods come upon him, and at once I am relegated from cabin table to galley, while, at the same time, I am fortunate to escape with my life and a whole body.

The loneliness of the man is slowly being borne in upon me. There is not a man aboard but hates or fears him, nor is there a man whom he does not despise. He seems consuming with the tremendous power that is in him and that seems never to have found adequate expression in works. He is as Lucifer would be, were that proud spirit banished to a society of soulless, Tomlinsonian ghosts.

This loneliness is bad enough in itself, but, to make it worse, he is oppressed by the primal melancholy of the race. Knowing him, I review the old Scandinavian myths with clearer understanding. The white-skinned, fair-haired savages who created that terrible pantheon were of the same fibre as he. The frivolity of the laughter-loving Latins is no part of him. When he laughs it is from a humour that is nothing else than ferocious. But he laughs rarely; he is too often sad. And it is a sadness as deep-reaching as the roots of the race. It is the race heritage, the sadness which has made the race sober-minded, clean-lived and fanatically moral, and which, in this latter connection, has culminated among the English in the Reformed Church and Mrs. Grundy.

In point of fact, the chief vent to this primal melancholy has been religion in its more agonizing forms. But the compensations of such religion are denied Wolf Larsen. His brutal materialism will not permit it. So, when his blue moods come on, nothing remains for him, but to be devilish. Were he not so terrible a man, I could sometimes feel sorry for him, as instance three mornings ago, when I went into his stateroom to fill his water-bottle and came unexpectedly upon him. He did not see me. His head was buried in his hands, and his shoulders were heaving convulsively as with sobs. He seemed torn by some mighty grief. As I softly withdrew I could hear him groaning, 'God! God! God!' Not that he was calling upon God; it was a mere expletive, but it came from his soul.

At dinner he asked the hunters for a remedy for headache, and by evening, strong man that he was, he was half-blind and reeling about the cabin.

'I've never been sick in my life, Hump,' he said, as I guided him to his room. 'Nor did I ever have a headache except the time my head was healing after having been laid open for six inches by a capstan-bar.'

For three days this blinding headache lasted, and he suffered as wild animals suffer, as it seemed the way on ship to suffer, without plaint, without sympathy, utterly alone.

This morning, however, on entering his state-room to make the bed and put things in order, I found him well and hard at work. Table and bunk were littered with designs and calculations. On a large transparent sheet, compass and square in hand, he was copying what appeared to be a scale of some sort or other.

'Hello, Hump,' he greeted me genially. 'I'm just finishing the finishing touches. Want to see it work?'

'But what is it?' I asked.

'A labour-saving device for mariners, navigation reduced to kindergarten simplicity,' he answered gaily. 'From to-day a child will be able to navigate a ship. No more long-winded calculations. All you need is one star in the sky on a dirty night to know instantly where you are. Look. I place the transparent scale on this star-map, revolving the scale on the North Pole. On the scale I've worked out the circles of altitude and the lines of bearing. All I do is to put it on a star, revolve the scale till it is opposite those figures on the map underneath, and presto! there you are, the ship's precise location!'

There was a ring of triumph in his voice, and his eyes, clear blue this morning as the sea, were sparkling with light.

'You must be well up in mathematics,' I said. 'Where did you go to school?'

'Never saw the inside of one, worse luck,' was the answer. 'I had to dig it out for myself.'

'And why do you think I have made this thing?' he demanded, abruptly. 'Dreaming to leave footprints on the sands of time?' He laughed one of his horrible mocking laughs. 'Not at all. To get it patented, to make money from it, to revel in piggishness with all night in while other men do the work. That's my purpose. Also, I have enjoyed working it out.'

'The creative joy,' I murmured.

'I guess that's what it ought to be called. Which is another way of expressing the joy of life in that it is alive, the triumph of movement over matter, of the quick over the dead, the pride of the yeast because it is yeast and crawls.'

I threw up my hands with helpless disapproval of his inveterate materialism and went about making the bed. He continued copying lines and figures upon the transparent scale. It was a task requiring the utmost nicety and precision, and I could not but admire the way he tempered his strength to the fineness and delicacy of the need.

When I had finished the bed, I caught myself looking at him in a fascinated sort of way. He was certainly a handsome man—beautiful in the masculine sense. And again, with never-failing wonder, I remarked the total lack of viciousness, or wickedness, or sinfulness in his face. It was the face, I am convinced, of a man who did no wrong. And by this I do not wish to be misunderstood. What I mean is that it was the face of a man who either did nothing contrary to the dictates of his conscience, or who had no conscience. I am inclined to the latter way of accounting for it. He was a magnificent atavism, a man so purely primitive that he was of the type that came into the world before the development of the moral nature. He was not immoral, but merely unmoral.

As I have said, in the masculine sense his was a beautiful face. Smooth-shaven, every line was distinct, and it was cut as clear and sharp as a cameo; while sea and sun had tanned the naturally fair skin to a dark bronze which bespoke struggle and battle and added both to his savagery and his beauty. The lips were full, yet possessed of the firmness, almost harshness, which is characteristic of thin lips. The set of his mouth, his chin, his jaw, was likewise firm or harsh, with all the fierceness and indomitableness of the male—the nose also. It was the nose of a being born to conquer and command. It just hinted of the eagle beak. It might have been Grecian, it might have been Roman, only it was a shade too massive for the one, a shade too delicate for the other. And while the whole face was the incarnation of fierceness and strength, the primal melancholy from which he suffered seemed to greaten the lines of mouth and eye and brow, seemed to give a largeness and completeness which otherwise the face would have lacked.

And so I caught myself standing idly and studying him. I cannot say how greatly the man had come to interest me. Who was he? What was he? How had he happened to be? All powers seemed his, all potentialities—why, then, was he no more than the obscure master of a seal-hunting schooner with a reputation for frightful brutality amongst the men who hunted seals?

My curiosity burst from me in a flood of speech.

'Why is it that you have not done great things in this world? With the power that is yours you might have risen to any height. Unpossessed of conscience or moral instinct, you might have mastered the world, broken it to your hand. And yet here you are, at the top of your life, where diminishing and dying begin, living an obscure and sordid existence, hunting sea animals for the satisfaction of woman's vanity and love of decoration, revelling in a piggishness, to use your own words, which is anything and everything except splendid. Why, with all that wonderful strength, have you not done something? There was nothing to stop you, nothing that could stop you. What was wrong? Did you lack ambition? Did you fall under temptation? What was the matter? What was the matter?'

He had lifted his eyes to me at the commencement of my outburst, and followed me complacently until I had done and stood before him breathless and dismayed. He waited a moment, as though seeking where to begin, and then said:

'Hump, do you know the parable of the sower who went forth to sow? If you will remember, some of the seed fell upon stony places, where there was not much earth, and forthwith they sprung up because they had no deepness of earth. And when the sun was up they were scorched, and because they had no root they withered away. And some fell among thorns, and the thorns sprung up and choked them.'

'Well?' I said.

'Well?' he queried, half petulantly. 'It was not well. I was one of those seeds.'

He dropped his head to the scale and resumed the copying. I finished my work and had opened the door to leave, when he spoke to me.

'Hump, if you will look on the west coast of the map of Norway you will see an indentation called Romsdal Fiord. I was born within a hundred miles of that stretch of water. But I was not born Norwegian. I am a Dane. My father and mother were Danes, and how they ever came to that bleak bight of land on the west coast I do not know. I never heard. Outside of that there is nothing mysterious. They were poor people and unlettered. They came of generations of poor unlettered people—peasants of the sea who sowed their sons on the waves as has been their custom since time began. There is no more to tell.'

'But there is,' I objected. 'It is still obscure to me.'

'What can I tell you?' he demanded, with a recrudescence of fierceness. 'Of the meagreness of a child's life? of fish diet and coarse living? of going out with the boats from the time I could crawl? of my brothers, who went away one by one to the deep-sea farming and never came back? of myself, unable to read or write, cabin-boy at the mature age of ten on the coastwise, old-country ships? of the rough fare and rougher usage, where kicks and blows were bed and breakfast and took the place of speech, and fear and hatred and pain were my only soul-experiences? I do not care to remember. A madness comes up in my brain even now as I think of it. But there were coastwise skippers I would have returned and killed when a man's strength came to me, only the lines of my life were cast at the time in other places. I did return, not long ago, but unfortunately the skippers were dead, all but one, a mate in the old days, a skipper when I met him, and when I left him a cripple who would never walk again.'

'But you who read Spencer and Darwin and have never seen the inside of a school, how did you learn to read and write?' I queried.

'In the English merchant service. Cabin-boy at twelve, ship's boy at fourteen, ordinary seamen at sixteen, able seaman at seventeen, and cock of the fo'c'sle, infinite ambition and infinite loneliness, receiving neither help nor sympathy, I did it all for myself—navigation, mathematics, science, literature, and what not. And of what use has it been? Master and owner of a ship at the top of my life, as you say, when I am beginning to diminish and die. Paltry, isn't it? And when the sun was up I was scorched, and because I had no root I withered away.'

'But history tells of slaves who rose to the purple,' I chided.

'And history tells of opportunities that came to the slaves who rose to the purple,' he answered grimly. 'No man makes opportunity. All the great men ever did was to know it when it came to them. The Corsican knew. I have dreamed as greatly as the Corsican. I should have known the opportunity, but it never came. The thorns sprung up and choked me. And, Hump, I can tell you that you know more about me than any living man, except my own brother.'

'And what is he? And where is he?'

'Master of the steamship *Macedonia*, seal-hunter,' was the answer. 'We will meet him most probably on the Japan coast. Men call him 'Death' Larsen.'

'Death Larsen!' I involuntarily cried. 'Is he like you?'

'Hardly. He is a lump of an animal without any head. He has all my—my—'

'Brutishness,' I suggested.

'Yes,—thank you for the word,—all my brutishness, but he can scarcely read or write.'

'And he has never philosophized on life,' I added.

'No,' Wolf Larsen answered, with an indescribable air of sadness. 'And he is all the happier for leaving life alone. He is too busy living it to think about it. My mistake was in ever opening the books.'

CHAPTER XI

The *Ghost* has attained the southernmost point of the arc she is describing across the Pacific, and is already beginning to edge away to the west and north toward some lone island, it is rumoured, where she will fill her water-casks before proceeding to the season's hunt along the coast of Japan. The hunters have experimented and practised with their rifles and shotguns till they are satisfied, and the boat-pullers and steerers have made their spritsails, bound the oars and rowlocks in leather and sennit so that they will make no noise when creeping on the seals, and put their boats in apple-pie order—to use Leach's homely phrase.

His arm, by the way, has healed nicely, though the scar will remain all his life. Thomas Mugridge lives in mortal fear of him, and is afraid to venture on deck after dark. There are two or three standing quarrels in the forecastle. Louis tells me that the gossip of the sailors finds its way aft, and that two of the telltales have been badly beaten by their mates. He shakes his head dubiously over the outlook for the man Johnson, who is boat-puller in the same boat with him. Johnson has been guilty of speaking his mind too freely, and has collided two or three times with Wolf Larsen over the pronunciation of his name. Johansen he thrashed on the amidships deck the other night, since which time the mate has called him by his proper name. But of course it is out of the question that Johnson should thrash Wolf Larsen.

Louis has also given me additional information about Death Larsen, which tallies with the captain's brief description. We may expect to meet Death Larsen on the Japan coast. 'And look out for squalls,' is Louis's prophecy, 'for they hate one another like the wolf whelps they are.' Death Larsen is in command of the only sealing steamer in the fleet, the *Macedonia*, which carries fourteen boats, whereas the rest of the schooners carry only six. There is wild talk of cannon aboard, and of strange raids and expeditions she may make, ranging from opium smuggling into the States and arms smuggling into China, to blackbirding and open piracy. Yet I cannot but believe for I have never yet caught him in a lie, while he has a cyclopædic knowledge of sealing and the men of the sealing fleets.

As it is forward and in the galley, so it is in the steerage and aft, on this veritable hell-ship. Men fight and struggle ferociously for one another's lives. The hunters are looking for a shooting scrape at any moment between Smoke and Henderson, whose old quarrel has not healed, while Wolf Larsen says positively that he will kill the survivor of the affair, if such affair comes off. He frankly states that the position he takes is based on no moral grounds, that all the hunters could kill and eat one another so far as he is concerned, were it not that he needs them alive for the hunting. If they will only hold their hands until the season is over, he promises them a royal carnival, when all grudges can he settled and the survivors may toss the non-survivors overboard and arrange a story as to how the missing men were lost at sea. I think even the hunters are appalled at his cold-bloodedness. Wicked men though they be, they are certainly very much afraid of him.

Thomas Mugridge is cur-like in his subjection to me, while I go about in secret dread of him. His is the courage of fear,—a strange thing I know well of myself,—and at any moment it may master the fear and impel him to the taking of my life. My knee is much better, though it often aches for long periods, and the stiffness is gradually leaving the arm which Wolf Larsen squeezed. Otherwise I am in splendid condition, feel that I am in splendid condition. My muscles are growing harder and increasing in size. My hands, however, are a spectacle for grief. They have a parboiled appearance, are afflicted with hang-nails, while the nails are broken and discoloured, and the edges of the quick seem to be assuming a fungoid sort of growth. Also, I am suffering from boils, due to the diet, most likely, for I was never afflicted in this manner before.

I was amused, a couple of evenings back, by seeing Wolf Larsen reading the Bible, a copy of which, after the futile search for one at the beginning of the voyage, had been found in the dead mate's sea-chest. I wondered what Wolf Larsen could get from it, and he read aloud to me from Ecclesiastes. I could imagine he was speaking the thoughts of his own mind as he read to me, and his voice, reverberating deeply and mournfully in the confined cabin, charmed and held me. He may be uneducated, but he certainly knows how to express the significance of the written word. I can hear him now, as I shall always hear him, the primal melancholy vibrant in his voice as he read:

'I gathered me also silver and gold, and the peculiar treasure of kings and of the provinces; I gat me men singers and women singers, and the delights of the sons of men, as musical instruments, and that of all sorts.

'So I was great, and increased more than all that were before me in Jerusalem; also my wisdom returned with me.

'Then I looked on all the works that my hands had wrought and on the labour that I had laboured to do; and behold, all was vanity and vexation of spirit, and there was no profit under the sun.

'All things come alike to all; there is one event to the righteous and to the wicked; to the good and to the clean, and to the unclean; to him that sacrificeth, and to him that sacrificeth not; as is the good, so is the sinner; and he that sweareth, as he that feareth an oath.

'This is an evil among all things that are done under the sun, that there is one event unto all; yea, also the heart of the sons of men is full of evil, and madness is in their heart while they live, and after that they go to the dead.

'For to him that is joined to all the living there is hope; for a living dog is better than a dead lion.

'For the living know that they shall die; but the dead know not anything, neither have they any more a reward; for the memory of them is forgotten.

'Also their love, and their hatred, and their envy, is now perished; neither have they any more a portion for ever in anything that is done under the sun.'

'There you have it, Hump,' he said, closing the book upon his finger and looking up at me. 'The Preacher who was king over Israel in Jerusalem thought as I think. You call me a pessimist. Is not this pessimism of the blackest?—'All is vanity and vexation of spirit,' 'There is no profit under the sun,' 'There is one event unto all,' to the fool and the wise, the clean and the unclean, the sinner and the saint, and that event is death, and an evil thing, he says. For the Preacher loved life, and did not want to die, saying, 'For a living dog is better than a dead lion.' He preferred the vanity and vexation to the silence and unmovableness of the grave. And so I. To crawl is piggish; but to not crawl, to be as the clod and rock, is loathsome to contemplate. It is loathsome to the life that is in me, the very essence of which is movement, the power of movement, and the consciousness of the power of movement. Life itself is unsatisfaction, but to look ahead to death is greater unsatisfaction.'

'You are worse off than Omar,' I said. 'He, at least, after the customary agonizing of youth, found content and made of his materialism a joyous thing.'

'Who was Omar?' Wolf Larsen asked, and I did no more work that day, nor the next, nor the next.

In his random reading he had never chanced upon the Rubáiyát, and it was to him like a great find of treasure. Much I remembered, possibly two-thirds of the quatrains, and I managed to piece out the remainder without difficulty. We talked for hours over single stanzas, and I found him reading into them a wail of regret and a rebellion which, for the life of me, I could not discover myself. Possibly I recited with a certain joyous lilt which was my own, for—his memory was good, and at a second rendering, very often the first, he made a quatrain his own—he recited the same lines and invested them with an unrest and passionate revolt that was well-nigh convincing.

I was interested as to which quatrain he would like best, and was not surprised when he hit upon the one born of an instant's irritability, and quite at variance with the Persian's complacent philosophy and genial code of life:

'What, without asking, hither hurried *Whence?*
And, without asking, *Whither* hurried hence!
Oh, many a Cup of this forbidden Wine
Must drown the memory of that insolence!'

'Great!' Wolf Larsen cried. 'Great! That's the keynote. Insolence! He could not have used a better word.'

In vain I objected and denied. He deluged me, overwhelmed me with argument.

'It's not the nature of life to be otherwise. Life, when it knows that it must cease living, will always rebel. It cannot help itself. The Preacher found life and the works of life all a vanity and vexation, an evil thing; but death, the ceasing to be able to be vain and vexed, he found an eviler thing. Through chapter after chapter he is worried by the one event that cometh to all alike. So Omar, so I, so you, even you, for you rebelled against dying when Cooky sharpened a knife for you. You were afraid to die; the life that was in you, that composes you, that is greater than you, did not want to die. You have talked of the instinct of immortality. I talk of the instinct of life, which is to live, and which, when death looms near and large, masters the instinct, so called, of immortality. It mastered it in you (you cannot deny it), because a crazy Cockney cook sharpened a knife.

'You are afraid of him now. You are afraid of me. You cannot deny it. If I should catch you by the throat, thus,'—his hand was about my throat and my breath was shut off,—'and began to press the life out of you thus, and thus, your instinct of immortality will go glimmering, and your instinct of life, which is longing for life, will flutter up, and you will struggle to save yourself. Eh? I see the fear of death in your eyes. You beat the air with your arms. You exert all your puny strength to struggle to live. Your hand is clutching my arm, lightly it feels as a butterfly resting there. Your chest is heaving, your tongue protruding, your skin turning dark, your eyes swimming. 'To live! To live! To live!' you are crying; and you are crying to live here and now, not hereafter. You doubt your immortality, eh? Ha! ha! You are not sure of it. You won't chance it. This life only you are certain is real. Ah, it is growing dark and darker. It is the darkness of death, the ceasing to be, the ceasing to feel, the ceasing to move, that is gathering about you, descending upon you, rising around you. Your eyes are becoming set. They are glazing. My voice sounds faint and far. You cannot see my face. And still you struggle in my grip. You kick with your legs. Your body draws itself up in knots like a snake's. Your chest heaves and strains. To live! To live! To live—'

I heard no more. Consciousness was blotted out by the darkness he had so graphically described, and when I came to myself I was lying on the floor and he was smoking a cigar and regarding me thoughtfully with that old familiar light of curiosity in his eyes.

'Well, have I convinced you?' he demanded. 'Here take a drink of this. I want to ask you some questions.'

I rolled my head negatively on the floor. 'Your arguments are too—er—forcible,' I managed to articulate, at cost of great pain to my aching throat.

'You'll be all right in half-an-hour,' he assured me. 'And I promise I won't use any more physical demonstrations. Get up now. You can sit on a chair.'

And, toy that I was of this monster, the discussion of Omar and the Preacher was resumed. And half the night we sat up over it.

CHAPTER XII

The last twenty-four hours have witnessed a carnival of brutality. From cabin to forecastle it seems to have broken out like a contagion. I scarcely know where to begin. Wolf Larsen was really the cause of it. The relations among the men, strained and made tense by feuds, quarrels and grudges, were in a state of unstable equilibrium, and evil passions flared up in flame like prairie-grass.

Thomas Mugridge is a sneak, a spy, an informer. He has been attempting to curry favour and reinstate himself in the good graces of the captain by carrying tales of the men forward. He it was, I know, that carried some of Johnson's hasty talk to Wolf Larsen. Johnson, it seems, bought a suit of oilskins from the slop-chest and found them to be of greatly inferior quality. Nor was he slow in advertising the fact. The slop-chest is a sort of miniature dry-goods store which is carried by all sealing schooners and which is stocked with articles peculiar to the needs of the sailors. Whatever a sailor purchases is taken from his subsequent earnings on the sealing grounds; for, as it is with the hunters so it is with the boat-pullers and steerers—in the place of wages they receive a 'lay,' a rate of so much per skin for every skin captured in their particular boat.

But of Johnson's grumbling at the slop-chest I knew nothing, so that what I witnessed came with a shock of sudden surprise. I had just finished sweeping the cabin, and had been inveigled by Wolf Larsen into a discussion of Hamlet, his favourite Shakespearian character, when Johansen descended the companion stairs followed by Johnson. The latter's cap came off after the custom of the sea, and he stood respectfully in the centre of the cabin, swaying heavily and uneasily to the roll of the schooner and facing the captain.

'Shut the doors and draw the slide,' Wolf Larsen said to me.

As I obeyed I noticed an anxious light come into Johnson's eyes, but I did not dream of its cause. I did not dream of what was to occur until it did occur, but he knew from the very first what was coming and awaited it bravely. And in his action I found complete refutation of all Wolf Larsen's materialism. The sailor Johnson was swayed by idea, by principle, and truth, and sincerity. He was right, he knew he was right, and he was unafraid. He would die for the right if needs be, he would be true to himself, sincere with his soul. And in this was portrayed the victory of the spirit over the flesh, the indomitability and moral grandeur of the soul that knows no restriction and rises above time and space and matter with a surety and invincibleness born of nothing else than eternity and immortality.

But to return. I noticed the anxious light in Johnson's eyes, but mistook it for the native shyness and embarrassment of the man. The mate, Johansen, stood away several feet to the side of him, and fully three yards in front of him sat Wolf Larsen on one of the pivotal cabin chairs. An appreciable pause fell after I had closed the doors and drawn the slide, a pause that must have lasted fully a minute. It was broken by Wolf Larsen.

'Yonson,' he began.

'My name is Johnson, sir,' the sailor boldly corrected.

'Well, Johnson, then, damn you! Can you guess why I have sent for you?'

'Yes, and no, sir,' was the slow reply. 'My work is done well. The mate knows that, and you know it, sir. So there cannot be any complaint.'

'And is that all?' Wolf Larsen queried, his voice soft, and low, and purring.

'I know you have it in for me,' Johnson continued with his unalterable and ponderous slowness. 'You do not like me. You—you—'

'Go on,' Wolf Larsen prompted. 'Don't be afraid of my feelings.'

'I am not afraid,' the sailor retorted, a slight angry flush rising through his sunburn. 'If I speak not fast, it is because I have not been from the old country as long as you. You do not like me because I am too much of a man; that is why, sir.'

'You are too much of a man for ship discipline, if that is what you mean, and if you know what I mean,' was Wolf Larsen's retort.

'I know English, and I know what you mean, sir,' Johnson answered, his flush deepening at the slur on his knowledge of the English language.

'Johnson,' Wolf Larsen said, with an air of dismissing all that had gone before as introductory to the main business in hand, 'I understand you're not quite satisfied with those oilskins?'

'No, I am not. They are no good, sir.'

'And you've been shooting off your mouth about them.'

'I say what I think, sir,' the sailor answered courageously, not failing at the same time in ship courtesy, which demanded that 'sir' be appended to each speech he made.

It was at this moment that I chanced to glance at Johansen. His big fists were clenching and unclenching, and his face was positively fiendish, so malignantly did he look at Johnson. I noticed a black discoloration, still faintly visible, under Johansen's eye, a mark of the thrashing he had received a few nights before from the sailor. For the first time I began to divine that something terrible was about to be enacted,— what, I could not imagine.

'Do you know what happens to men who say what you've said about my slop-chest and me?' Wolf Larsen was demanding.

'I know, sir,' was the answer.

'What?' Wolf Larsen demanded, sharply and imperatively.

'What you and the mate there are going to do to me, sir.'

'Look at him, Hump,' Wolf Larsen said to me, 'look at this bit of animated dust, this aggregation of matter that moves and breathes and defies me and thoroughly believes itself to be compounded of something good; that is impressed with certain human fictions such as righteousness and honesty, and that will live up to them in spite of all personal discomforts and menaces. What do you think of him, Hump? What do you think of him?'

'I think that he is a better man than you are,' I answered, impelled, somehow, with a desire to draw upon myself a portion of the wrath I felt was about to break upon his head. 'His human fictions, as you choose to call them, make for nobility and manhood. You have no fictions, no dreams, no ideals. You are a pauper.'

He nodded his head with a savage pleasantness. 'Quite true, Hump, quite true. I have no fictions that make for nobility and manhood. A living dog is better than a dead lion, say I with the Preacher. My only doctrine is the doctrine of expediency, and it makes for surviving. This bit of the ferment we call 'Johnson,' when he is no longer a bit of the ferment, only dust and ashes, will have no more nobility than any dust and ashes, while I shall still be alive and roaring.'

'Do you know what I am going to do?' he questioned.

I shook my head.

'Well, I am going to exercise my prerogative of roaring and show you how fares nobility. Watch me.'

Three yards away from Johnson he was, and sitting down. Nine feet! And yet he left the chair in full leap, without first gaining a standing position. He left the chair, just as he sat in it, squarely, springing from the sitting posture like a wild animal, a tiger, and like a tiger covered the intervening space. It was an avalanche of fury that Johnson strove vainly to fend off. He threw one arm down to protect the stomach, the other arm up to protect the head; but Wolf Larsen's fist drove midway between, on the chest, with a crushing, resounding impact. Johnson's breath, suddenly expelled, shot from his mouth and as suddenly checked, with the forced, audible expiration of a man wielding an axe. He almost fell backward, and swayed from side to side in an effort to recover his balance.

I cannot give the further particulars of the horrible scene that followed. It was too revolting. It turns me sick even now when I think of it. Johnson fought bravely enough, but he was no match for Wolf Larsen, much less for Wolf Larsen and the mate. It was frightful. I had not imagined a human being could endure so much and still live and struggle on. And struggle on Johnson did. Of course there was no hope for him, not the slightest, and he knew it as well as I, but by the manhood that was in him he could not cease from fighting for that manhood.

It was too much for me to witness. I felt that I should lose my mind, and I ran up the companion stairs to open the doors and escape on deck. But Wolf Larsen, leaving his victim for the moment, and with one of his tremendous springs, gained my side and flung me into the far corner of the cabin.

'The phenomena of life, Hump,' he girded at me. 'Stay and watch it. You may gather data on the immortality of the soul. Besides, you know, we can't hurt Johnson's soul. It's only the fleeting form we may demolish.'

It seemed centuries—possibly it was no more than ten minutes that the beating continued. Wolf Larsen and Johansen were all about the poor fellow. They struck him with their fists, kicked him with their heavy shoes, knocked him down, and dragged him to his feet to knock him down again. His eyes were blinded so that he could not see, and the blood running from ears and nose and mouth turned the cabin into a shambles. And when he could no longer rise they still continued to beat and kick him where he lay.

'Easy, Johansen; easy as she goes,' Wolf Larsen finally said.

But the beast in the mate was up and rampant, and Wolf Larsen was compelled to brush him away with a back-handed sweep of the arm, gentle enough, apparently, but which hurled Johansen back like a cork, driving his head against the wall with a crash. He fell to the floor, half stunned for the moment, breathing heavily and blinking his eyes in a stupid sort of way.

'Jerk open the doors,—Hump,' I was commanded.

I obeyed, and the two brutes picked up the senseless man like a sack of rubbish and hove him clear up the companion stairs, through the narrow doorway, and out on deck. The blood from his nose gushed in a scarlet stream over the feet of the helmsman, who was none other than Louis, his boat-mate. But Louis took and gave a spoke and gazed imperturbably into the binnacle.

Not so was the conduct of George Leach, the erstwhile cabin-boy. Fore and aft there was nothing that could have surprised us more than his consequent behaviour. He it was that came up on the poop without orders and dragged Johnson forward, where he set about dressing his wounds as well as he could and making him comfortable. Johnson, as Johnson, was unrecognizable; and not only that, for his features, as human features at all, were unrecognizable, so discoloured and swollen had they become in the few minutes which had elapsed between the beginning of the beating and the dragging forward of the body.

But of Leach's behaviour—By the time I had finished cleansing the cabin he had taken care of Johnson. I had come up on deck for a breath of fresh air and to try to get some repose for my overwrought nerves. Wolf Larsen was smoking a cigar and examining the patent log which the *Ghost* usually towed astern, but which had been hauled in for some purpose. Suddenly Leach's voice came to my ears. It was tense and hoarse with an overmastering rage. I turned and saw him standing just beneath the break of the poop on the port side of the galley. His face was convulsed and white, his eyes were flashing, his clenched fists raised overhead.

'May God damn your soul to hell, Wolf Larsen, only hell's too good for you, you coward, you murderer, you pig!' was his opening salutation.

I was thunderstruck. I looked for his instant annihilation. But it was not Wolf Larsen's whim to annihilate him. He sauntered slowly forward to the break of the poop, and, leaning his elbow on the corner of the cabin, gazed down thoughtfully and curiously at the excited boy.

And the boy indicted Wolf Larsen as he had never been indicted before. The sailors assembled in a fearful group just outside the forecastle scuttle and watched and listened. The hunters piled pell-mell out of the steerage, but as Leach's tirade continued I saw that there was no levity in their faces. Even they were frightened, not at the boy's terrible words, but at his terrible audacity. It did not seem possible that any living creature could thus beard Wolf Larsen in his teeth. I know for myself that I was shocked into admiration of the boy, and I saw in him the splendid invincibleness of immortality rising above the flesh and the fears of the flesh, as in the prophets of old, to condemn unrighteousness.

And such condemnation! He haled forth Wolf Larsen's soul naked to the scorn of men. He rained upon it curses from God and High Heaven, and withered it with a heat of invective that savoured of a mediæval excommunication of the Catholic Church. He ran the gamut of denunciation, rising to heights of wrath that were sublime and almost Godlike, and from sheer exhaustion sinking to the vilest and most indecent abuse.

His rage was a madness. His lips were flecked with a soapy froth, and sometimes he choked and gurgled and became inarticulate. And through it all, calm and impassive, leaning on his elbow and gazing down, Wolf Larsen seemed lost in a great curiosity.

This wild stirring of yeasty life, this terrific revolt and defiance of matter that moved, perplexed and interested him.

Each moment I looked, and everybody looked, for him to leap upon the boy and destroy him. But it was not his whim. His cigar went out, and he continued to gaze silently and curiously.

Leach had worked himself into an ecstasy of impotent rage.

'Pig! Pig! Pig!' he was reiterating at the top of his lungs. 'Why don't you come down and kill me, you murderer? You can do it! I ain't afraid! There's no one to stop you! Damn sight better dead and outa your reach than alive and in your clutches! Come on, you coward! Kill me! Kill me! Kill me!'

It was at this stage that Thomas Mugridge's erratic soul brought him into the scene. He had been listening at the galley door, but he now came out, ostensibly to fling some scraps over the side, but obviously to see the killing he was certain would take place. He smirked greasily up into the face of Wolf Larsen, who seemed not to see him. But the Cockney was unabashed, though mad, stark mad. He turned to Leach, saying:

'Such langwidge! Shockin'!'

Leach's rage was no longer impotent. Here at last was something ready to hand. And for the first time since the stabbing the Cockney had appeared outside the galley without his knife. The words had barely left his mouth when he was knocked down by Leach. Three times he struggled to his feet, striving to gain the galley, and each time was knocked down.

'Oh, Lord!' he cried. ''Elp! 'Elp! Tyke 'im aw'y, carn't yer? Tyke 'im aw'y!'

The hunters laughed from sheer relief. Tragedy had dwindled, the farce had begun. The sailors now crowded boldly aft, grinning and shuffling, to watch the pummelling of the hated Cockney. And even I felt a great joy surge up within me. I confess that I delighted in this beating Leach was giving to Thomas Mugridge, though it was as terrible, almost, as the one Mugridge had caused to be given to Johnson. But the expression of Wolf Larsen's face never changed. He did not change his position either, but continued to gaze down with a great curiosity. For all his pragmatic certitude, it seemed as if he watched the play and movement of life in the hope of discovering something more about it, of discerning in its maddest writhings a something which had hitherto escaped him,—the key to its mystery, as it were, which would make all clear and plain.

But the beating! It was quite similar to the one I had witnessed in the cabin. The Cockney strove in vain to protect himself from the infuriated boy. And in vain he strove to gain the shelter of the cabin. He rolled toward it, grovelled toward it, fell toward it when he was knocked down. But blow followed blow with bewildering rapidity. He was knocked about like a shuttlecock, until, finally, like Johnson, he was beaten and kicked as he lay helpless on the deck. And no one interfered. Leach could have killed him, but, having evidently filled the measure of his vengeance, he drew away from his prostrate foe, who was whimpering and wailing in a puppyish sort of way, and walked forward.

But these two affairs were only the opening events of the day's programme. In the afternoon Smoke and Henderson fell foul of each other, and a fusillade of shots came up from the steerage, followed by a stampede of the other four hunters for the deck. A column of thick, acrid smoke—the kind always made by black powder—was arising through the open companion-way, and down through it leaped Wolf Larsen. The sound of blows and scuffling came to our ears. Both men were wounded, and he was thrashing them both for having disobeyed his orders and crippled themselves in advance of the hunting season. In fact, they were badly wounded, and, having thrashed them, he proceeded to operate upon them in a rough surgical fashion and to dress their wounds. I served as assistant while he probed and cleansed the passages made by the bullets, and I saw the two men endure his crude surgery without anæsthetics and with no more to uphold them than a stiff tumbler of whisky.

Then, in the first dog-watch, trouble came to a head in the forecastle. It took its rise out of the tittle-tattle and tale-bearing which had been the cause of Johnson's beating, and from the noise we heard, and from the sight of the bruised men next day, it was patent that half the forecastle had soundly drubbed the other half.

The second dog-watch and the day were wound up by a fight between Johansen and the lean, Yankee-looking hunter, Latimer. It was caused by remarks of Latimer's concerning the noises made by the mate in his sleep, and though Johansen was whipped, he kept the steerage awake for the rest of the night while he blissfully slumbered and fought the fight over and over again.

As for myself, I was oppressed with nightmare. The day had been like some horrible dream. Brutality had followed brutality, and flaming passions and cold-blooded cruelty had driven men to seek one another's lives, and to strive to hurt, and maim, and destroy. My nerves were shocked. My mind itself was shocked. All my days had been passed in comparative ignorance of the animality of man. In fact, I had known life only in its intellectual phases. Brutality I had experienced, but it was the brutality of the intellect—the cutting sarcasm of Charley Furuseth, the cruel epigrams and occasional harsh witticisms of the fellows at the Bibelot, and the nasty remarks of some of the professors during my undergraduate days.

That was all. But that men should wreak their anger on others by the bruising of the flesh and the letting of blood was something strangely and fearfully new to me. Not for nothing had I been called 'Sissy' Van Weyden, I thought, as I tossed restlessly on my bunk between one nightmare and another. And it seemed to me that my innocence of the realities of life had been complete indeed. I laughed bitterly to myself, and seemed to find in Wolf Larsen's forbidding philosophy a more adequate explanation of life than I found in my own.

And I was frightened when I became conscious of the trend of my thought. The continual brutality around me was degenerative in its effect. It bid fair to destroy for me all that was best and brightest in life. My reason dictated that the beating Thomas Mugridge had received was an ill thing, and yet for the life of me I could not prevent my soul joying in it. And even while I was oppressed by the enormity of my sin,—for sin it was,—I chuckled with an insane delight. I was no longer Humphrey Van Weyden. I was Hump, cabin-boy on the schooner *Ghost*. Wolf Larsen was my captain, Thomas Mugridge and the rest were my companions, and I was receiving repeated impresses from the die which had stamped them all.

CHAPTER XIII

For three days I did my own work and Thomas Mugridge's too; and I flatter myself that I did his work well. I know that it won Wolf Larsen's approval, while the sailors beamed with satisfaction during the brief time my *régime* lasted.

'The first clean bite since I come aboard,' Harrison said to me at the galley door, as he returned the dinner pots and pans from the forecastle. 'Somehow Tommy's grub always tastes of grease, stale grease, and I reckon he ain't changed his shirt since he left 'Frisco.'

'I know he hasn't,' I answered.

'And I'll bet he sleeps in it,' Harrison added.

'And you won't lose,' I agreed. 'The same shirt, and he hasn't had it off once in all this time.'

But three days was all Wolf Larsen allowed him in which to recover from the effects of the beating. On the fourth day, lame and sore, scarcely able to see, so closed were his eyes, he was haled from his bunk by the nape of the neck and set to his duty. He sniffled and wept, but Wolf Larsen was pitiless.

'And see that you serve no more slops,' was his parting injunction. 'No more grease and dirt, mind, and a clean shirt occasionally, or you'll get a tow over the side. Understand?'

Thomas Mugridge crawled weakly across the galley floor, and a short lurch of the *Ghost* sent him staggering. In attempting to recover himself, he reached for the iron railing which surrounded the stove and kept the pots from sliding off; but he missed the railing, and his hand, with his weight behind it, landed squarely on the hot surface. There was a sizzle and odour of burning flesh, and a sharp cry of pain.

'Oh, Gawd, Gawd, wot 'ave I done?' he wailed; sitting down in the coal-box and nursing his new hurt by rocking back and forth. 'W'y 'as all this come on me? It mykes me fair sick, it does, an' I try so 'ard to go through life 'armless an' 'urtin' nobody.'

The tears were running down his puffed and discoloured cheeks, and his face was drawn with pain. A savage expression flitted across it.

'Oh, 'ow I 'ate 'im! 'Ow I 'ate 'im!' he gritted out.

'Whom?' I asked; but the poor wretch was weeping again over his misfortunes. Less difficult it was to guess whom he hated than whom he did not hate. For I had come to see a malignant devil in him which impelled him to hate all the world. I sometimes thought that he hated even himself, so grotesquely had life dealt with him, and so monstrously. At such moments a great sympathy welled up within me, and I felt shame that I had ever joyed in his discomfiture or pain. Life had been unfair to him. It had played him a scurvy trick when it fashioned him into the thing he was, and it had played him scurvy tricks ever since. What chance had he to be anything else than he was? And as though answering my unspoken thought, he wailed:

'I never 'ad no chance, not 'arf a chance! 'Oo was there to send me to school, or put tommy in my 'ungry belly, or wipe my bloody nose for me, w'en I was a kiddy? 'Oo ever did anything for me, heh? 'Oo, I s'y?'

'Never mind, Tommy,' I said, placing a soothing hand on his shoulder. 'Cheer up. It'll all come right in the end. You've long years before you, and you can make anything you please of yourself.'

'It's a lie! a bloody lie!' he shouted in my face, flinging off the hand. 'It's a lie, and you know it. I'm already myde, an' myde out of leavin's an' scraps. It's all right for you, 'Ump. You was born a gentleman. You never knew wot it was to go 'ungry, to cry yerself asleep with yer little belly gnawin' an' gnawin', like a rat inside yer. It carn't come right. If I was President of the United Stytes to-morrer, 'ow would it fill my belly for one time w'en I was a kiddy and it went empty?

'Ow could it, I s'y? I was born to sufferin' and sorrer. I've had more cruel sufferin' than any ten men, I 'ave. I've been in orspital arf my bleedin' life. I've 'ad the fever in Aspinwall, in 'Avana, in New Orleans. I near died of the scurvy and was rotten with it six months in Barbadoes. Smallpox in 'Onolulu, two broken legs in Shanghai, pnuemonia in Unalaska, three busted ribs an' my insides all twisted in 'Frisco. An' 'ere I am now. Look at me! Look at me! My ribs kicked loose from my back again. I'll be coughin' blood before eyght bells. 'Ow can it be myde up to me, I arsk? 'Oo's goin' to do it? Gawd? 'Ow Gawd must 'ave 'ated me w'en 'e signed me on for a voyage in this bloomin' world of 'is!'

This tirade against destiny went on for an hour or more, and then he buckled to his work, limping and groaning, and in his eyes a great hatred for all created things. His diagnosis was correct, however, for he was seized with occasional sicknesses, during which he vomited blood and suffered great pain. And as he said, it seemed God hated him too much to let him die, for he ultimately grew better and waxed more malignant than ever.

Several days more passed before Johnson crawled on deck and went about his work in a half-hearted way. He was still a sick man, and I more than once observed him creeping painfully aloft to a topsail, or drooping wearily as he stood at the wheel. But, still worse, it seemed that his spirit was broken. He was abject before Wolf Larsen and almost grovelled to Johansen. Not so was the conduct of Leach. He went about the deck like a tiger cub, glaring his hatred openly at Wolf Larsen and Johansen.

'I'll do for you yet, you slab-footed Swede,' I heard him say to Johansen one night on deck.

The mate cursed him in the darkness, and the next moment some missile struck the galley a sharp rap. There was more cursing, and a mocking laugh, and when all was quiet I stole outside and found a heavy knife imbedded over an inch in the solid wood. A few minutes later the mate came fumbling about in search of it, but I returned it privily to Leach next day. He grinned when I handed it over, yet it was a grin that contained more sincere thanks than a multitude of the verbosities of speech common to the members of my own class.

Unlike any one else in the ship's company, I now found myself with no quarrels on my hands and in the good graces of all. The hunters possibly no more than tolerated me, though none of them disliked me; while Smoke and Henderson, convalescent under a deck awning and swinging day and night in their hammocks, assured me that I was better than any hospital nurse, and that they would not forget me at the end of the voyage when they were paid off. (As though I stood in need of their money! I, who could have bought them out, bag and baggage, and the schooner and its equipment, a score of times over!) But upon me had devolved the task of tending their wounds, and pulling them through, and I did my best by them.

Wolf Larsen underwent another bad attack of headache which lasted two days. He must have suffered severely, for he called me in and obeyed my commands like a sick child. But nothing I could do seemed to relieve him. At my suggestion, however, he gave up smoking and drinking; though why such a magnificent animal as he should have headaches at all puzzles me.

'Tis the hand of God, I'm tellin' you,' is the way Louis sees it. 'Tis a visitation for his black-hearted deeds, and there's more behind and comin', or else—'

'Or else,' I prompted.

'God is noddin' and not doin' his duty, though it's me as shouldn't say it.'

I was mistaken when I said that I was in the good graces of all. Not only does Thomas Mugridge continue to hate me, but he has discovered a new reason for hating me. It took me no little while to puzzle it out, but I finally discovered that it was because I was more luckily born than he—'gentleman born,' he put it.

'And still no more dead men,' I twitted Louis, when Smoke and Henderson, side by side, in friendly conversation, took their first exercise on deck.

Louis surveyed me with his shrewd grey eyes, and shook his head portentously. 'She's a-comin', I tell you, and it'll be sheets and halyards, stand by all hands, when she begins to howl. I've had the feel iv it this long time, and I can feel it now as plainly as I feel the rigging iv a dark night. She's close, she's close.'

'Who goes first?' I queried.

'Not fat old Louis, I promise you,' he laughed. 'For 'tis in the bones iv me I know that come this time next year I'll be gazin' in the old mother's eyes, weary with watchin' iv the sea for the five sons she gave to it.'

'Wot's 'e been s'yin' to yer?' Thomas Mugridge demanded a moment later.

'That he's going home some day to see his mother,' I answered diplomatically.

'I never 'ad none,' was the Cockney's comment, as he gazed with lustreless, hopeless eyes into mine.

CHAPTER XIV

It has dawned upon me that I have never placed a proper valuation upon womankind. For that matter, though not amative to any considerable degree so far as I have discovered, I was never outside the atmosphere of women until now. My mother and sisters were always about me, and I was always trying to escape them; for they worried me to distraction with their solicitude for my health and with their periodic inroads on my den, when my orderly confusion, upon which I prided myself, was turned into worse confusion and less order, though it looked neat enough to the eye. I never could find anything when they had departed. But now, alas, how welcome would have been the feel of their presence, the frou-frou and swish-swish of their skirts which I had so cordially detested! I am sure, if I ever get home, that I shall never be irritable with them again. They may dose me and doctor me morning, noon, and night, and dust and sweep and put my den to rights every minute of the day, and I shall only lean back and survey it all and be thankful in that I am possessed of a mother and some several sisters.

All of which has set me wondering. Where are the mothers of these twenty and odd men on the *Ghost*? It strikes me as unnatural and unhealthful that men should be totally separated from women and herd through the world by themselves. Coarseness and savagery are the inevitable results. These men about me should have wives, and sisters, and daughters; then would they be capable of softness, and tenderness, and sympathy. As it is, not one of them is married. In years and years not one of them has been in contact with a good woman, or within the influence, or redemption, which irresistibly radiates from such a creature. There is no balance in their lives. Their masculinity, which in itself is of the brute, has been over-developed. The other and spiritual side of their natures has been dwarfed—atrophied, in fact.

They are a company of celibates, grinding harshly against one another and growing daily more calloused from the grinding. It seems to me impossible sometimes that they ever had mothers. It would appear that they are a half-brute, half-human species, a race apart, wherein there is no such thing as sex; that they are hatched out by the sun like turtle eggs, or receive life in some similar and sordid fashion; and that all their days they fester in brutality and viciousness, and in the end die as unlovely as they have lived.

Rendered curious by this new direction of ideas, I talked with Johansen last night—the first superfluous words with which he has favoured me since the voyage began. He left Sweden when he was eighteen, is now thirty-eight, and in all the intervening time has not been home once. He had met a townsman, a couple of years before, in some sailor boarding-house in Chile, so that he knew his mother to be still alive.

'She must be a pretty old woman now,' he said, staring meditatively into the binnacle and then jerking a sharp glance at Harrison, who was steering a point off the course.

'When did you last write to her?'

He performed his mental arithmetic aloud. 'Eighty-one; no—eighty-two, eh? no—eighty-three? Yes, eighty-three. Ten years ago. From some little port in Madagascar. I was trading.

'You see,' he went on, as though addressing his neglected mother across half the girth of the earth, 'each year I was going home. So what was the good to write? It was only a year. And each year something happened, and I did not go. But I am mate, now, and when I pay off at 'Frisco, maybe with five hundred dollars, I will ship myself on a windjammer round the Horn to Liverpool, which will give me more money; and then I will pay my passage from there home. Then she will not do any more work.'

'But does she work? now? How old is she?'

'About seventy,' he answered. And then, boastingly, 'We work from the time we are born until we die, in my country. That's why we live so long. I will live to a hundred.'

I shall never forget this conversation. The words were the last I ever heard him utter. Perhaps they were the last he did utter, too. For, going down into the cabin to turn in, I decided that it was too stuffy to sleep below. It was a calm night. We were out of the Trades, and the *Ghost* was forging ahead barely a knot an hour. So I tucked a blanket and pillow under my arm and went up on deck.

As I passed between Harrison and the binnacle, which was built into the top of the cabin, I noticed that he was this time fully three points off. Thinking that he was asleep, and wishing him to escape reprimand or worse, I spoke to him. But he was not asleep. His eyes were wide and staring. He seemed greatly perturbed, unable to reply to me.

'What's the matter?' I asked. 'Are you sick?'

He shook his head, and with a deep sign as of awakening, caught his breath.

'You'd better get on your course, then,' I chided.

He put a few spokes over, and I watched the compass-card swing slowly to N.N.W.

and steady itself with slight oscillations.

I took a fresh hold on my bedclothes and was preparing to start on, when some movement caught my eye and I looked astern to the rail. A sinewy hand, dripping with water, was clutching the rail. A second hand took form in the darkness beside it. I watched, fascinated. What visitant from the gloom of the deep was I to behold? Whatever it was, I knew that it was climbing aboard by the log-line. I saw a head, the hair wet and straight, shape itself, and then the unmistakable eyes and face of Wolf Larsen. His right cheek was red with blood, which flowed from some wound in the head.

He drew himself inboard with a quick effort, and arose to his feet, glancing swiftly, as he did so, at the man at the wheel, as though to assure himself of his identity and that there was nothing to fear from him. The sea-water was streaming from him. It made little audible gurgles which distracted me. As he stepped toward me I shrank back instinctively, for I saw that in his eyes which spelled death.

'All right, Hump,' he said in a low voice. 'Where's the mate?'

I shook my head.

'Johansen!' he called softly. 'Johansen!'

'Where is he?' he demanded of Harrison.

The young fellow seemed to have recovered his composure, for he answered steadily enough, 'I don't know, sir. I saw him go for'ard a little while ago.'

'So did I go for'ard. But you will observe that I didn't come back the way I went. Can you explain it?'

'You must have been overboard, sir.'

'Shall I look for him in the steerage, sir?' I asked.

Wolf Larsen shook his head. 'You wouldn't find him, Hump. But you'll do. Come on. Never mind your bedding. Leave it where it is.'

I followed at his heels. There was nothing stirring amidships.

'Those cursed hunters,' was his comment. 'Too damned fat and lazy to stand a four-hour watch.'

But on the forecastle-head we found three sailors asleep. He turned them over and looked at their faces. They composed the watch on deck, and it was the ship's custom, in good weather, to let the watch sleep with the exception of the officer, the helmsman, and the look-out.

'Who's look-out?' he demanded.

'Me, sir,' answered Holyoak, one of the deep-water sailors, a slight tremor in his voice. 'I winked off just this very minute, sir. I'm sorry, sir. It won't happen again.'

'Did you hear or see anything on deck?'

'No, sir, I—'

But Wolf Larsen had turned away with a snort of disgust, leaving the sailor rubbing his eyes with surprise at having been let of so easily.

'Softly, now,' Wolf Larsen warned me in a whisper, as he doubled his body into the forecastle scuttle and prepared to descend.

I followed with a quaking heart. What was to happen I knew no more than did I know what had happened. But blood had been shed, and it was through no whim of Wolf Larsen that he had gone over the side with his scalp laid open. Besides, Johansen was missing.

It was my first descent into the forecastle, and I shall not soon forget my impression of it, caught as I stood on my feet at the bottom of the ladder. Built directly in the eyes of the schooner, it was of the shape of a triangle, along the three sides of which stood the bunks, in double-tier, twelve of them. It was no larger than a hall bedroom in Grub Street, and yet twelve men were herded into it to eat and sleep and carry on all the functions of living. My bedroom at home was not large, yet it could have contained a dozen similar forecastles, and taking into consideration the height of the ceiling, a score at least.

It smelled sour and musty, and by the dim light of the swinging sea-lamp I saw every bit of available wall-space hung deep with sea-boots, oilskins, and garments, clean and dirty, of various sorts. These swung back and forth with every roll of the vessel, giving rise to a brushing sound, as of trees against a roof or wall. Somewhere a boot thumped loudly and at irregular intervals against the wall; and, though it was a mild night on the sea, there was a continual chorus of the creaking timbers and bulkheads and of abysmal noises beneath the flooring.

The sleepers did not mind. There were eight of them,—the two watches below,— and the air was thick with the warmth and odour of their breathing, and the ear was filled with the noise of their snoring and of their sighs and half-groans, tokens plain of the rest of the animal-man. But were they sleeping? all of them? Or had they been sleeping? This was evidently Wolf Larsen's quest—to find the men who appeared to be asleep and who were not asleep or who had not been asleep very recently. And he went about it in a way that reminded me of a story out of Boccaccio.

He took the sea-lamp from its swinging frame and handed it to me. He began at the first bunks forward on the star-board side. In the top one lay Oofty-Oofty, a Kanaka and splendid seaman, so named by his mates. He was asleep on his back and breathing as placidly as a woman. One arm was under his head, the other lay on top of the blankets. Wolf Larsen put thumb and forefinger to the wrist and counted the pulse. In the midst of it the Kanaka roused. He awoke as gently as he slept. There was no movement of the body whatever. The eyes, only, moved. They flashed wide open, big and black, and stared, unblinking, into our faces. Wolf Larsen put his finger to his lips as a sign for silence, and the eyes closed again.

In the lower bunk lay Louis, grossly fat and warm and sweaty, asleep unfeignedly and sleeping laboriously. While Wolf Larsen held his wrist he stirred uneasily, bowing his body so that for a moment it rested on shoulders and heels. His lips moved, and he gave voice to this enigmatic utterance:

'A shilling's worth a quarter; but keep your lamps out for thruppenny-bits, or the publicans 'll shove 'em on you for sixpence.'

Then he rolled over on his side with a heavy, sobbing sigh, saying:

'A sixpence is a tanner, and a shilling a bob; but what a pony is I don't know.'

Satisfied with the honesty of his and the Kanaka's sleep, Wolf Larsen passed on to the next two bunks on the starboard side, occupied top and bottom, as we saw in the light of the sea-lamp, by Leach and Johnson.

As Wolf Larsen bent down to the lower bunk to take Johnson's pulse, I, standing erect and holding the lamp, saw Leach's head rise stealthily as he peered over the side of his bunk to see what was going on. He must have divined Wolf Larsen's trick and the sureness of detection, for the light was at once dashed from my hand and the forecastle was left in darkness. He must have leaped, also, at the same instant, straight down on Wolf Larsen.

The first sounds were those of a conflict between a bull and a wolf. I heard a great infuriated bellow go up from Wolf Larsen, and from Leach a snarling that was desperate and blood-curdling. Johnson must have joined him immediately, so that his abject and grovelling conduct on deck for the past few days had been no more than planned deception.

I was so terror-stricken by this fight in the dark that I leaned against the ladder, trembling and unable to ascend. And upon me was that old sickness at the pit of the stomach, caused always by the spectacle of physical violence. In this instance I could not see, but I could hear the impact of the blows—the soft crushing sound made by flesh striking forcibly against flesh. Then there was the crashing about of the entwined bodies, the laboured breathing, the short quick gasps of sudden pain.

There must have been more men in the conspiracy to murder the captain and mate, for by the sounds I knew that Leach and Johnson had been quickly reinforced by some of their mates.

'Get a knife somebody!' Leach was shouting.

'Pound him on the head! Mash his brains out!' was Johnson's cry.

But after his first bellow, Wolf Larsen made no noise. He was fighting grimly and silently for life. He was sore beset. Down at the very first, he had been unable to gain his feet, and for all of his tremendous strength I felt that there was no hope for him.

The force with which they struggled was vividly impressed on me; for I was knocked down by their surging bodies and badly bruised. But in the confusion I managed to crawl into an empty lower bunk out of the way.

'All hands! We've got him! We've got him!' I could hear Leach crying.

'Who?' demanded those who had been really asleep, and who had wakened to they knew not what.

'It's the bloody mate!' was Leach's crafty answer, strained from him in a smothered sort of way.

This was greeted with whoops of joy, and from then on Wolf Larsen had seven strong men on top of him, Louis, I believe, taking no part in it. The forecastle was like an angry hive of bees aroused by some marauder.

'What ho! below there!' I heard Latimer shout down the scuttle, too cautious to descend into the inferno of passion he could hear raging beneath him in the darkness.

'Won't somebody get a knife? Oh, won't somebody get a knife?' Leach pleaded in the first interval of comparative silence.

The number of the assailants was a cause of confusion. They blocked their own efforts, while Wolf Larsen, with but a single purpose, achieved his. This was to fight his way across the floor to the ladder. Though in total darkness, I followed his progress by its sound. No man less than a giant could have done what he did, once he had gained the foot of the ladder. Step by step, by the might of his arms, the whole pack of men striving to drag him back and down, he drew his body up from the floor till he stood erect. And then, step by step, hand and foot, he slowly struggled up the ladder.

The very last of all, I saw. For Latimer, having finally gone for a lantern, held it so that its light shone down the scuttle. Wolf Larsen was nearly to the top, though I could not see him. All that was visible was the mass of men fastened upon him. It squirmed about, like some huge many-legged spider, and swayed back and forth to the regular roll of the vessel. And still, step by step with long intervals between, the mass ascended. Once it tottered, about to fall back, but the broken hold was regained and it still went up.

'Who is it?' Latimer cried.

In the rays of the lantern I could see his perplexed face peering down.

'Larsen,' I heard a muffled voice from within the mass.

Latimer reached down with his free hand. I saw a hand shoot up to clasp his. Latimer pulled, and the next couple of steps were made with a rush. Then Wolf Larsen's other hand reached up and clutched the edge of the scuttle. The mass swung clear of the ladder, the men still clinging to their escaping foe. They began to drop off, to be brushed off against the sharp edge of the scuttle, to be knocked off by the legs which were now kicking powerfully. Leach was the last to go, falling sheer back from the top of the scuttle and striking on head and shoulders upon his sprawling mates beneath. Wolf Larsen and the lantern disappeared, and we were left in darkness.

CHAPTER XV

There was a deal of cursing and groaning as the men at the bottom of the ladder crawled to their feet.

'Somebody strike a light, my thumb's out of joint,' said one of the men, Parsons, a swarthy, saturnine man, boat-steerer in Standish's boat, in which Harrison was puller.

'You'll find it knockin' about by the bitts,' Leach said, sitting down on the edge of the bunk in which I was concealed.

There was a fumbling and a scratching of matches, and the sea-lamp flared up, dim and smoky, and in its weird light bare-legged men moved about nursing their bruises and caring for their hurts. Oofty-Oofty laid hold of Parsons's thumb, pulling it out stoutly and snapping it back into place. I noticed at the same time that the Kanaka's knuckles were laid open clear across and to the bone. He exhibited them, exposing beautiful white teeth in a grin as he did so, and explaining that the wounds had come from striking Wolf Larsen in the mouth.

'So it was you, was it, you black beggar?' belligerently demanded one Kelly, an Irish-American and a longshoreman, making his first trip to sea, and boat-puller for Kerfoot.

As he made the demand he spat out a mouthful of blood and teeth and shoved his pugnacious face close to Oofty-Oofty. The Kanaka leaped backward to his bunk, to return with a second leap, flourishing a long knife.

'Aw, go lay down, you make me tired,' Leach interfered. He was evidently, for all of his youth and inexperience, cock of the forecastle. 'G'wan, you Kelly. You leave Oofty alone. How in hell did he know it was you in the dark?'

Kelly subsided with some muttering, and the Kanaka flashed his white teeth in a grateful smile. He was a beautiful creature, almost feminine in the pleasing lines of his figure, and there was a softness and dreaminess in his large eyes which seemed to contradict his well-earned reputation for strife and action.

'How did he get away?' Johnson asked.

He was sitting on the side of his bunk, the whole pose of his figure indicating utter dejection and hopelessness. He was still breathing heavily from the exertion he had made. His shirt had been ripped entirely from him in the struggle, and blood from a gash in the cheek was flowing down his naked chest, marking a red path across his white thigh and dripping to the floor.

'Because he is the devil, as I told you before,' was Leach's answer; and thereat he was on his feet and raging his disappointment with tears in his eyes.

'And not one of you to get a knife!' was his unceasing lament.

But the rest of the hands had a lively fear of consequences to come and gave no heed to him.

'How'll he know which was which?' Kelly asked, and as he went on he looked murderously about him—'unless one of us peaches.'

'He'll know as soon as ever he claps eyes on us,' Parsons replied. 'One look at you'd be enough.'

'Tell him the deck flopped up and gouged yer teeth out iv yer jaw,' Louis grinned. He was the only man who was not out of his bunk, and he was jubilant in that he possessed no bruises to advertise that he had had a hand in the night's work. 'Just wait till he gets a glimpse iv yer mugs to-morrow, the gang iv ye,' he chuckled.

'We'll say we thought it was the mate,' said one. And another, 'I know what I'll say—that I heered a row, jumped out of my bunk, got a jolly good crack on the jaw for my pains, and sailed in myself. Couldn't tell who or what it was in the dark and just hit out.'

'An' 'twas me you hit, of course,' Kelly seconded, his face brightening for the moment.

Leach and Johnson took no part in the discussion, and it was plain to see that their mates looked upon them as men for whom the worst was inevitable, who were beyond hope and already dead. Leach stood their fears and reproaches for some time. Then he broke out:

'You make me tired! A nice lot of gazabas you are! If you talked less with yer mouth and did something with yer hands, he'd a-ben done with by now. Why couldn't one of you, just one of you, get me a knife when I sung out? You make me sick! A-beefin' and bellerin' 'round, as though he'd kill you when he gets you! You know damn well he wont. Can't afford to. No shipping masters or beach-combers over here, and he wants yer in his business, and he wants yer bad. Who's to pull or steer or sail ship if he loses yer? It's me and Johnson have to face the music. Get into yer bunks, now, and shut yer faces; I want to get some sleep.'

'That's all right all right,' Parsons spoke up. 'Mebbe he won't do for us, but mark my words, hell 'll be an ice-box to this ship from now on.'

All the while I had been apprehensive concerning my own predicament. What would happen to me when these men discovered my presence? I could never fight my way out as Wolf Larsen had done. And at this moment Latimer called down the scuttles:

'Hump! The old man wants you!'

'He ain't down here!' Parsons called back.

'Yes, he is,' I said, sliding out of the bunk and striving my hardest to keep my voice steady and bold.

The sailors looked at me in consternation. Fear was strong in their faces, and the devilishness which comes of fear.

'I'm coming!' I shouted up to Latimer.

'No you don't!' Kelly cried, stepping between me and the ladder, his right hand shaped into a veritable strangler's clutch. 'You damn little sneak! I'll shut yer mouth!'

'Let him go,' Leach commanded.

'Not on yer life,' was the angry retort.

Leach never changed his position on the edge of the bunk. 'Let him go, I say,' he repeated; but this time his voice was gritty and metallic.

The Irishman wavered. I made to step by him, and he stood aside. When I had gained the ladder, I turned to the circle of brutal and malignant faces peering at me through the semi-darkness. A sudden and deep sympathy welled up in me. I remembered the Cockney's way of putting it. How God must have hated them that they should be tortured so!

'I have seen and heard nothing, believe me,' I said quietly.

'I tell yer, he's all right,' I could hear Leach saying as I went up the ladder. 'He don't like the old man no more nor you or me.'

I found Wolf Larsen in the cabin, stripped and bloody, waiting for me. He greeted me with one of his whimsical smiles.

'Come, get to work, Doctor. The signs are favourable for an extensive practice this voyage. I don't know what the *Ghost* would have been without you, and if I could only cherish such noble sentiments I would tell you her master is deeply grateful.'

I knew the run of the simple medicine-chest the *Ghost* carried, and while I was heating water on the cabin stove and getting the things ready for dressing his wounds, he moved about, laughing and chatting, and examining his hurts with a calculating eye. I had never before seen him stripped, and the sight of his body quite took my breath away. It has never been my weakness to exalt the flesh—far from it; but there is enough of the artist in me to appreciate its wonder.

I must say that I was fascinated by the perfect lines of Wolf Larsen's figure, and by what I may term the terrible beauty of it. I had noted the men in the forecastle. Powerfully muscled though some of them were, there had been something wrong with all of them, an insufficient development here, an undue development there, a twist or a crook that destroyed symmetry, legs too short or too long, or too much sinew or bone exposed, or too little. Oofty-Oofty had been the only one whose lines were at all pleasing, while, in so far as they pleased, that far had they been what I should call feminine.

But Wolf Larsen was the man-type, the masculine, and almost a god in his perfect-ness. As he moved about or raised his arms the great muscles leapt and moved under the satiny skin. I have forgotten to say that the bronze ended with his face. His body, thanks to his Scandinavian stock, was fair as the fairest woman's. I remember his putting his hand up to feel of the wound on his head, and my watching the biceps move like a living thing under its white sheath. It was the biceps that had nearly crushed out my life once, that I had seen strike so many killing blows. I could not take my eyes from him. I stood motionless, a roll of antiseptic cotton in my hand unwinding and spilling itself down to the floor.

He noticed me, and I became conscious that I was staring at him.

'God made you well,' I said.

'Did he?' he answered. 'I have often thought so myself, and wondered why.'

'Purpose—' I began.

'Utility,' he interrupted. 'This body was made for use. These muscles were made to grip, and tear, and destroy living things that get between me and life. But have you thought of the other living things? They, too, have muscles, of one kind and another, made to grip, and tear, and destroy; and when they come between me and life, I out-grip them, out-tear them, out-destroy them. Purpose does not explain that. Utility does.'

'It is not beautiful,' I protested.

'Life isn't, you mean,' he smiled. 'Yet you say I was made well. Do you see this?'

He braced his legs and feet, pressing the cabin floor with his toes in a clutching sort of way. Knots and ridges and mounds of muscles writhed and bunched under the skin.

'Feel them,' he commanded.

They were hard as iron. And I observed, also, that his whole body had unconsciously drawn itself together, tense and alert; that muscles were softly crawling and shaping about the hips, along the back, and across the shoulders; that the arms were slightly lifted, their muscles contracting, the fingers crooking till the hands were like talons; and that even the eyes had changed expression and into them were coming watchfulness and measurement and a light none other than of battle.

'Stability, equilibrium,' he said, relaxing on the instant and sinking his body back into repose. 'Feet with which to clutch the ground, legs to stand on and to help withstand, while with arms and hands, teeth and nails, I struggle to kill and to be not killed. Purpose? Utility is the better word.'

I did not argue. I had seen the mechanism of the primitive fighting beast, and I was as strongly impressed as if I had seen the engines of a great battleship or Atlantic liner.

I was surprised, considering the fierce struggle in the forecastle, at the superficiality of his hurts, and I pride myself that I dressed them dexterously. With the exception of several bad wounds, the rest were merely severe bruises and lacerations. The blow which he had received before going overboard had laid his scalp open several inches. This, under his direction, I cleansed and sewed together, having first shaved the edges of the wound. Then the calf of his leg was badly lacerated and looked as though it had been mangled by a bulldog. Some sailor, he told me, had laid hold of it by his teeth, at the beginning of the fight, and hung on and been dragged to the top of the forecastle ladder, when he was kicked loose.

'By the way, Hump, as I have remarked, you are a handy man,' Wolf Larsen began, when my work was done. 'As you know, we're short a mate. Hereafter you shall stand watches, receive seventy-five dollars per month, and be addressed fore and aft as Mr. Van Weyden.'

'I—I don't understand navigation, you know,' I gasped.

'Not necessary at all.'

'I really do not care to sit in the high places,' I objected. 'I find life precarious enough in my present humble situation. I have no experience. Mediocrity, you see, has its compensations.'

He smiled as though it were all settled.

'I won't be mate on this hell-ship!' I cried defiantly.

I saw his face grow hard and the merciless glitter come into his eyes. He walked to the door of his room, saying:

'And now, Mr. Van Weyden, good-night.'

'Good-night, Mr. Larsen,' I answered weakly.

CHAPTER XVI

I cannot say that the position of mate carried with it anything more joyful than that there were no more dishes to wash. I was ignorant of the simplest duties of mate, and would have fared badly indeed, had the sailors not sympathized with me. I knew nothing of the minutiæ of ropes and rigging, of the trimming and setting of sails; but the sailors took pains to put me to rights,—Louis proving an especially good teacher,—and I had little trouble with those under me.

With the hunters it was otherwise. Familiar in varying degree with the sea, they took me as a sort of joke. In truth, it was a joke to me, that I, the veriest landsman, should be filling the office of mate; but to be taken as a joke by others was a different matter. I made no complaint, but Wolf Larsen demanded the most punctilious sea etiquette in my case,—far more than poor Johansen had ever received; and at the expense of several rows, threats, and much grumbling, he brought the hunters to time. I was 'Mr. Van Weyden' fore and aft, and it was only unofficially that Wolf Larsen himself ever addressed me as 'Hump.'

It was amusing. Perhaps the wind would haul a few points while we were at dinner, and as I left the table he would say, 'Mr. Van Weyden, will you kindly put about on the port tack.' And I would go on deck, beckon Louis to me, and learn from him what was to be done. Then, a few minutes later, having digested his instructions and thoroughly mastered the manœuvre, I would proceed to issue my orders. I remember an early instance of this kind, when Wolf Larsen appeared on the scene just as I had begun to give orders. He smoked his cigar and looked on quietly till the thing was accomplished, and then paced aft by my side along the weather poop.

'Hump,' he said, 'I beg pardon, Mr. Van Weyden, I congratulate you. I think you can now fire your father's legs back into the grave to him. You've discovered your own and learned to stand on them. A little rope-work, sail-making, and experience with storms and such things, and by the end of the voyage you could ship on any coasting schooner.'

It was during this period, between the death of Johansen and the arrival on the sealing grounds, that I passed my pleasantest hours on the *Ghost*. Wolf Larsen was quite considerate, the sailors helped me, and I was no longer in irritating contact with Thomas Mugridge. And I make free to say, as the days went by, that I found I was taking a certain secret pride in myself. Fantastic as the situation was,—a land-lubber second in command,—I was, nevertheless, carrying it off well; and during that brief time I was proud of myself, and I grew to love the heave and roll of the *Ghost* under my feet as she wallowed north and west through the tropic sea to the islet where we filled our water-casks.

But my happiness was not unalloyed. It was comparative, a period of less misery slipped in between a past of great miseries and a future of great miseries. For the *Ghost*, so far as the seamen were concerned, was a hell-ship of the worst description. They never had a moment's rest or peace. Wolf Larsen treasured against them the attempt on his life and the drubbing he had received in the forecastle; and morning, noon, and night, and all night as well, he devoted himself to making life unlivable for them.

He knew well the psychology of the little thing, and it was the little things by which he kept the crew worked up to the verge of madness. I have seen Harrison called from his bunk to put properly away a misplaced paintbrush, and the two watches below haled from their tired sleep to accompany him and see him do it. A little thing, truly, but when multiplied by the thousand ingenious devices of such a mind, the mental state of the men in the forecastle may be slightly comprehended.

Of course much grumbling went on, and little outbursts were continually occurring. Blows were struck, and there were always two or three men nursing injuries at the hands of the human beast who was their master. Concerted action was impossible in face of the heavy arsenal of weapons carried in the steerage and cabin. Leach and Johnson were the two particular victims of Wolf Larsen's diabolic temper, and the look of profound melancholy which had settled on Johnson's face and in his eyes made my heart bleed.

With Leach it was different. There was too much of the fighting beast in him. He seemed possessed by an insatiable fury which gave no time for grief. His lips had become distorted into a permanent snarl, which at mere sight of Wolf Larsen broke out in sound, horrible and menacing and, I do believe, unconsciously. I have seen him follow Wolf Larsen about with his eyes, like an animal its keeper, the while the animal-like snarl sounded deep in his throat and vibrated forth between his teeth.

I remember once, on deck, in bright day, touching him on the shoulder as pre-liminary to giving an order. His back was toward me, and at the first feel of my hand he leaped upright in the air and away from me, snarling and turning his head as he leaped. He had for the moment mistaken me for the man he hated.

Both he and Johnson would have killed Wolf Larsen at the slightest opportunity, but the opportunity never came. Wolf Larsen was too wise for that, and, besides, they had no adequate weapons. With their fists alone they had no chance whatever. Time and again he fought it out with Leach who fought back always, like a wildcat, tooth and nail and fist, until stretched, exhausted or unconscious, on the deck. And he was never averse to another encounter. All the devil that was in him challenged the devil in Wolf Larsen. They had but to appear on deck at the same time, when they would be at it, cursing, snarling, striking; and I have seen Leach fling himself upon Wolf Larsen without warning or provocation. Once he threw his heavy sheath-knife, missing Wolf Larsen's throat by an inch. Another time he dropped a steel marlinspike from the mizzen crosstree. It was a difficult cast to make on a rolling ship, but the sharp point of the spike, whistling seventy-five feet through the air, barely missed Wolf Larsen's head as he emerged from the cabin companion-way and drove its length two inches and over into the solid deck-planking. Still another time, he stole into the steerage, possessed himself of a loaded shot-gun, and was making a rush for the deck with it when caught by Kerfoot and disarmed.

I often wondered why Wolf Larsen did not kill him and make an end of it. But he only laughed and seemed to enjoy it. There seemed a certain spice about it, such as men must feel who take delight in making pets of ferocious animals.

'It gives a thrill to life,' he explained to me, 'when life is carried in one's hand. Man is a natural gambler, and life is the biggest stake he can lay. The greater the odds, the greater the thrill. Why should I deny myself the joy of exciting Leach's soul to fever-pitch? For that matter, I do him a kindness. The greatness of sensation is mutual. He is living more royally than any man for'ard, though he does not know it. For he has what they have not—purpose, something to do and be done, an all-absorbing end to strive to attain, the desire to kill me, the hope that he may kill me. Really, Hump, he is living deep and high. I doubt that he has ever lived so swiftly and keenly before, and I honestly envy him, sometimes, when I see him raging at the summit of passion and sensibility.'

'Ah, but it is cowardly, cowardly!' I cried. 'You have all the advantage.'

'Of the two of us, you and I, who is the greater coward?' he asked seriously. 'If the situation is unpleasing, you compromise with your conscience when you make yourself a party to it. If you were really great, really true to yourself, you would join forces with Leach and Johnson. But you are afraid, you are afraid. You want to live. The life that is in you cries out that it must live, no matter what the cost; so you live ignominiously, untrue to the best you dream of, sinning against your whole pitiful little code, and, if there were a hell, heading your soul straight for it. Bah! I play the braver part. I do no sin, for I am true to the promptings of the life that is in me. I am sincere with my soul at least, and that is what you are not.'

There was a sting in what he said. Perhaps, after all, I was playing a cowardly part. And the more I thought about it the more it appeared that my duty to myself lay in doing what he had advised, lay in joining forces with Johnson and Leach and working for his death. Right here, I think, entered the austere conscience of my Puritan ancestry, impelling me toward lurid deeds and sanctioning even murder as right conduct. I dwelt upon the idea. It would be a most moral act to rid the world of such a monster. Humanity would be better and happier for it, life fairer and sweeter.

I pondered it long, lying sleepless in my bunk and reviewing in endless procession the facts of the situation. I talked with Johnson and Leach, during the night watches when Wolf Larsen was below. Both men had lost hope—Johnson, because of temperamental despondency; Leach, because he had beaten himself out in the vain struggle and was exhausted. But he caught my hand in a passionate grip one night, saying:

'I think yer square, Mr. Van Weyden. But stay where you are and keep yer mouth shut. Say nothin' but saw wood. We're dead men, I know it; but all the same you might be able to do us a favour some time when we need it damn bad.'

It was only next day, when Wainwright Island loomed to windward, close abeam, that Wolf Larsen opened his mouth in prophecy. He had attacked Johnson, been attacked by Leach, and had just finished whipping the pair of them.

'Leach,' he said, 'you know I'm going to kill you some time or other, don't you?'

A snarl was the answer.

'And as for you, Johnson, you'll get so tired of life before I'm through with you that you'll fling yourself over the side. See if you don't.'

'That's a suggestion,' he added, in an aside to me. 'I'll bet you a month's pay he acts upon it.'

I had cherished a hope that his victims would find an opportunity to escape while filling our water-barrels, but Wolf Larsen had selected his spot well. The *Ghost* lay half-a-mile beyond the surf-line of a lonely beach. Here debauched a deep gorge, with precipitous, volcanic walls which no man could scale. And here, under his direct supervision—for he went ashore himself—Leach and Johnson filled the small casks and rolled them down to the beach. They had no chance to make a break for liberty in one of the boats.

Harrison and Kelly, however, made such an attempt. They composed one of the boats' crews, and their task was to ply between the schooner and the shore, carrying a single cask each trip. Just before dinner, starting for the beach with an empty barrel, they altered their course and bore away to the left to round the promontory which jutted into the sea between them and liberty. Beyond its foaming base lay the pretty villages of the Japanese colonists and smiling valleys which penetrated deep into the interior. Once in the fastnesses they promised, and the two men could defy Wolf Larsen.

I had observed Henderson and Smoke loitering about the deck all morning, and I now learned why they were there. Procuring their rifles, they opened fire in a leisurely manner, upon the deserters. It was a cold-blooded exhibition of marksmanship. At first their bullets zipped harmlessly along the surface of the water on either side the boat; but, as the men continued to pull lustily, they struck closer and closer.

'Now, watch me take Kelly's right oar,' Smoke said, drawing a more careful aim.

I was looking through the glasses, and I saw the oar-blade shatter as he shot. Henderson duplicated it, selecting Harrison's right oar. The boat slewed around. The two remaining oars were quickly broken. The men tried to row with the splinters, and had them shot out of their hands. Kelly ripped up a bottom board and began paddling, but dropped it with a cry of pain as its splinters drove into his hands. Then they gave up, letting the boat drift till a second boat, sent from the shore by Wolf Larsen, took them in tow and brought them aboard.

Late that afternoon we hove up anchor and got away. Nothing was before us but the three or four months' hunting on the sealing grounds. The outlook was black indeed, and I went about my work with a heavy heart. An almost funereal gloom seemed to have descended upon the *Ghost*. Wolf Larsen had taken to his bunk with one of his strange, splitting headaches. Harrison stood listlessly at the wheel, half supporting himself by it, as though wearied by the weight of his flesh. The rest of the men were morose and silent. I came upon Kelly crouching to the lee of the forecastle scuttle, his head on his knees, his arms about his head, in an attitude of unutterable despondency.

Johnson I found lying full length on the forecastle head, staring at the troubled churn of the forefoot, and I remembered with horror the suggestion Wolf Larsen had made. It seemed likely to bear fruit. I tried to break in on the man's morbid thoughts by calling him away, but he smiled sadly at me and refused to obey.

Leach approached me as I returned aft.

'I want to ask a favour, Mr. Van Weyden,' he said. 'If it's yer luck to ever make 'Frisco once more, will you hunt up Matt McCarthy? He's my old man. He lives on the Hill, back of the Mayfair bakery, runnin' a cobbler's shop that everybody knows, and you'll have no trouble. Tell him I lived to be sorry for the trouble I brought him and the things I done, and—and just tell him 'God bless him,' for me.'

I nodded my head, but said, 'We'll all win back to San Francisco, Leach, and you'll be with me when I go to see Matt McCarthy.'

'I'd like to believe you,' he answered, shaking my hand, 'but I can't. Wolf Larsen 'll do for me, I know it; and all I can hope is, he'll do it quick.'

And as he left me I was aware of the same desire at my heart. Since it was to be done, let it be done with despatch. The general gloom had gathered me into its folds. The worst appeared inevitable; and as I paced the deck, hour after hour, I found myself afflicted with Wolf Larsen's repulsive ideas. What was it all about? Where was the grandeur of life that it should permit such wanton destruction of human souls? It was a cheap and sordid thing after all, this life, and the sooner over the better. Over and done with! I, too, leaned upon the rail and gazed longingly into the sea, with the certainty that sooner or later I should be sinking down, down, through the cool green depths of its oblivion.

CHAPTER XVII

Strange to say, in spite of the general foreboding, nothing of especial moment happened on the *Ghost*. We ran on to the north and west till we raised the coast of Japan and picked up with the great seal herd. Coming from no man knew where in the illimitable Pacific, it was travelling north on its annual migration to the rookeries of Bering Sea. And north we travelled with it, ravaging and destroying, flinging the naked carcasses to the shark and salting down the skins so that they might later adorn the fair shoulders of the women of the cities.

It was wanton slaughter, and all for woman's sake. No man ate of the seal meat or the oil. After a good day's killing I have seen our decks covered with hides and bodies, slippery with fat and blood, the scuppers running red; masts, ropes, and rails spattered with the sanguinary colour; and the men, like butchers plying their trade, naked and red of arm and hand, hard at work with ripping and flensing-knives, removing the skins from the pretty sea-creatures they had killed.

It was my task to tally the pelts as they came aboard from the boats, to oversee the skinning and afterward the cleansing of the decks and bringing things ship-shape again. It was not pleasant work. My soul and my stomach revolted at it; and yet, in a way, this handling and directing of many men was good for me. It developed what little executive ability I possessed, and I was aware of a toughening or hardening which I was undergoing and which could not be anything but wholesome for 'Sissy' Van Weyden.

One thing I was beginning to feel, and that was that I could never again be quite the same man I had been. While my hope and faith in human life still survived Wolf Larsen's destructive criticism, he had nevertheless been a cause of change in minor matters. He had opened up for me the world of the real, of which I had known practically nothing and from which I had always shrunk. I had learned to look more closely at life as it was lived, to recognize that there were such things as facts in the world, to emerge from the realm of mind and idea and to place certain values on the concrete and objective phases of existence.

I saw more of Wolf Larsen than ever when we had gained the grounds. For when the weather was fair and we were in the midst of the herd, all hands were away in the boats, and left on board were only he and I, and Thomas Mugridge, who did not count. But there was no play about it. The six boats, spreading out fan-wise from the schooner until the first weather boat and the last lee boat were anywhere from ten to twenty miles apart, cruised along a straight course over the sea till nightfall or bad weather drove them in. It was our duty to sail the *Ghost* well to leeward of the last lee boat, so that all the boats should have fair wind to run for us in case of squalls or threatening weather.

It is no slight matter for two men, particularly when a stiff wind has sprung up, to handle a vessel like the *Ghost*, steering, keeping look-out for the boats, and setting or taking in sail; so it devolved upon me to learn, and learn quickly. Steering I picked up easily, but running aloft to the crosstrees and swinging my whole weight by my arms when I left the ratlines and climbed still higher, was more difficult. This, too, I learned, and quickly, for I felt somehow a wild desire to vindicate myself in Wolf Larsen's eyes, to prove my right to live in ways other than of the mind. Nay, the time came when I took joy in the run of the masthead and in the clinging on by my legs at that precarious height while I swept the sea with glasses in search of the boats.

I remember one beautiful day, when the boats left early and the reports of the hunters' guns grew dim and distant and died away as they scattered far and wide over the sea. There was just the faintest wind from the westward; but it breathed its last by the time we managed to get to leeward of the last lee boat. One by one—I was at the masthead and saw—the six boats disappeared over the bulge of the earth as they followed the seal into the west. We lay, scarcely rolling on the placid sea, unable to follow. Wolf Larsen was apprehensive. The barometer was down, and the sky to the east did not please him. He studied it with unceasing vigilance.

'If she comes out of there,' he said, 'hard and snappy, putting us to windward of the boats, it's likely there'll be empty bunks in steerage and fo'c'sle.'

By eleven o'clock the sea had become glass. By midday, though we were well up in the northerly latitudes, the heat was sickening. There was no freshness in the air. It was sultry and oppressive, reminding me of what the old Californians term 'earthquake weather.' There was something ominous about it, and in intangible ways one was made to feel that the worst was about to come. Slowly the whole eastern sky filled with clouds that over-towered us like some black sierra of the infernal regions. So clearly could one see cañon, gorge, and precipice, and the shadows that lie therein, that one looked unconsciously for the white surf-line and bellowing caverns where the sea charges on the land. And still we rocked gently, and there was no wind.

'It's no square' Wolf Larsen said. 'Old Mother Nature's going to get up on her hind legs and howl for all that's in her, and it'll keep us jumping, Hump, to pull through with half our boats. You'd better run up and loosen the topsails.'

'But if it is going to howl, and there are only two of us?' I asked, a note of protest in my voice.

'Why we've got to make the best of the first of it and run down to our boats before our canvas is ripped out of us. After that I don't give a rap what happens. The sticks 'll stand it, and you and I will have to, though we've plenty cut out for us.'

Still the calm continued. We ate dinner, a hurried and anxious meal for me with eighteen men abroad on the sea and beyond the bulge of the earth, and with that heaven-rolling mountain range of clouds moving slowly down upon us. Wolf Larsen did not seem affected, however; though I noticed, when we returned to the deck, a slight twitching of the nostrils, a perceptible quickness of movement. His face was stern, the lines of it had grown hard, and yet in his eyes—blue, clear blue this day— there was a strange brilliancy, a bright scintillating light. It struck me that he was joyous, in a ferocious sort of way; that he was glad there was an impending struggle; that he was thrilled and upborne with knowledge that one of the great moments of living, when the tide of life surges up in flood, was upon him.

Once, and unwitting that he did so or that I saw, he laughed aloud, mockingly and defiantly, at the advancing storm. I see him yet standing there like a pigmy out of the *Arabian Nights* before the huge front of some malignant genie. He was daring destiny, and he was unafraid.

He walked to the galley. 'Cooky, by the time you've finished pots and pans you'll be wanted on deck. Stand ready for a call.'

'Hump,' he said, becoming cognizant of the fascinated gaze I bent upon him, 'this beats whisky and is where your Omar misses. I think he only half lived after all.'

The western half of the sky had by now grown murky. The sun had dimmed and faded out of sight. It was two in the afternoon, and a ghostly twilight, shot through by wandering purplish lights, had descended upon us. In this purplish light Wolf Larsen's face glowed and glowed, and to my excited fancy he appeared encircled by a halo. We lay in the midst of an unearthly quiet, while all about us were signs and omens of oncoming sound and movement. The sultry heat had become unendurable. The sweat was standing on my forehead, and I could feel it trickling down my nose. I felt as though I should faint, and reached out to the rail for support.

And then, just then, the faintest possible whisper of air passed by. It was from the east, and like a whisper it came and went. The drooping canvas was not stirred, and yet my face had felt the air and been cooled.

'Cooky,' Wolf Larsen called in a low voice. Thomas Mugridge turned a pitiable scared face. 'Let go that foreboom tackle and pass it across, and when she's willing let go the sheet and come in snug with the tackle. And if you make a mess of it, it will be the last you ever make. Understand?'

'Mr. Van Weyden, stand by to pass the head-sails over. Then jump for the topsails and spread them quick as God'll let you—the quicker you do it the easier you'll find it. As for Cooky, if he isn't lively bat him between the eyes.'

I was aware of the compliment and pleased, in that no threat had accompanied my instructions. We were lying head to north-west, and it was his intention to jibe over all with the first puff.

'We'll have the breeze on our quarter,' he explained to me. 'By the last guns the boats were bearing away slightly to the south'ard.'

He turned and walked aft to the wheel. I went forward and took my station at the jibs. Another whisper of wind, and another, passed by. The canvas flapped lazily.

'Thank Gawd she's not comin' all of a bunch, Mr. Van Weyden,' was the Cockney's fervent ejaculation.

And I was indeed thankful, for I had by this time learned enough to know, with all our canvas spread, what disaster in such event awaited us. The whispers of wind became puffs, the sails filled, the *Ghost* moved. Wolf Larsen put the wheel hard up, to port, and we began to pay off. The wind was now dead astern, muttering and puffing stronger and stronger, and my head-sails were pounding lustily. I did not see what went on elsewhere, though I felt the sudden surge and heel of the schooner as the wind-pressures changed to the jibing of the fore- and main-sails. My hands were full with the flying-jib, jib, and staysail; and by the time this part of my task was accomplished the *Ghost* was leaping into the south-west, the wind on her quarter and all her sheets to starboard. Without pausing for breath, though my heart was beating like a trip-hammer from my exertions, I sprang to the topsails, and before the wind had become too strong we had them fairly set and were coiling down. Then I went aft for orders.

Wolf Larsen nodded approval and relinquished the wheel to me. The wind was strengthening steadily and the sea rising. For an hour I steered, each moment becoming more difficult. I had not the experience to steer at the gait we were going on a quartering course.

'Now take a run up with the glasses and raise some of the boats. We've made at least ten knots, and we're going twelve or thirteen now. The old girl knows how to walk.'

I contested myself with the fore crosstrees, some seventy feet above the deck. As I searched the vacant stretch of water before me, I comprehended thoroughly the need for haste if we were to recover any of our men. Indeed, as I gazed at the heavy sea through which we were running, I doubted that there was a boat afloat. It did not seem possible that such frail craft could survive such stress of wind and water.

I could not feel the full force of the wind, for we were running with it; but from my lofty perch I looked down as though outside the *Ghost* and apart from her, and saw the shape of her outlined sharply against the foaming sea as she tore along instinct with life. Sometimes she would lift and send across some great wave, burying her starboard-rail from view, and covering her deck to the hatches with the boiling ocean. At such moments, starting from a windward roll, I would go flying through the air with dizzying swiftness, as though I clung to the end of a huge, inverted pendulum, the arc of which, between the greater rolls, must have been seventy feet or more. Once, the terror of this giddy sweep overpowered me, and for a while I clung on, hand and foot, weak and trembling, unable to search the sea for the missing boats or to behold aught of the sea but that which roared beneath and strove to overwhelm the *Ghost.*

But the thought of the men in the midst of it steadied me, and in my quest for them I forgot myself. For an hour I saw nothing but the naked, desolate sea. And then, where a vagrant shaft of sunlight struck the ocean and turned its surface to wrathful silver, I caught a small black speck thrust skyward for an instant and swallowed up. I waited patiently. Again the tiny point of black projected itself through the wrathful blaze a couple of points off our port-bow. I did not attempt to shout, but communicated the news to Wolf Larsen by waving my arm. He changed the course, and I signalled affirmation when the speck showed dead ahead.

It grew larger, and so swiftly that for the first time I fully appreciated the speed of our flight. Wolf Larsen motioned for me to come down, and when I stood beside him at the wheel gave me instructions for heaving to.

'Expect all hell to break loose,' he cautioned me, 'but don't mind it. Yours is to do your own work and to have Cooky stand by the fore-sheet.'

I managed to make my way forward, but there was little choice of sides, for the weather-rail seemed buried as often as the lee. Having instructed Thomas Mugridge as to what he was to do, I clambered into the fore-rigging a few feet. The boat was now very close, and I could make out plainly that it was lying head to wind and sea and dragging on its mast and sail, which had been thrown overboard and made to serve as a sea-anchor. The three men were bailing. Each rolling mountain whelmed them from view, and I would wait with sickening anxiety, fearing that they would never appear again. Then, and with black suddenness, the boat would shoot clear through the foaming crest, bow pointed to the sky, and the whole length of her bottom showing, wet and dark, till she seemed on end. There would be a fleeting glimpse of the three men flinging water in frantic haste, when she would topple over and fall into the yawning valley, bow down and showing her full inside length to the stern upreared almost directly above the bow. Each time that she reappeared was a miracle.

The *Ghost* suddenly changed her course, keeping away, and it came to me with a shock that Wolf Larsen was giving up the rescue as impossible. Then I realized that he was preparing to heave to, and dropped to the deck to be in readiness. We were now dead before the wind, the boat far away and abreast of us. I felt an abrupt easing of the schooner, a loss for the moment of all strain and pressure, coupled with a swift acceleration of speed. She was rushing around on her heel into the wind.

As she arrived at right angles to the sea, the full force of the wind (from which we had hitherto run away) caught us. I was unfortunately and ignorantly facing it. It stood up against me like a wall, filling my lungs with air which I could not expel. And as I choked and strangled, and as the *Ghost* wallowed for an instant, broadside on and rolling straight over and far into the wind, I beheld a huge sea rise far above my head. I turned aside, caught my breath, and looked again. The wave over-topped the *Ghost*, and I gazed sheer up and into it. A shaft of sunlight smote the over-curl, and I caught a glimpse of translucent, rushing green, backed by a milky smother of foam.

Then it descended, pandemonium broke loose, everything happened at once. I was struck a crushing, stunning blow, nowhere in particular and yet everywhere. My hold had been broken loose, I was under water, and the thought passed through my mind that this was the terrible thing of which I had heard, the being swept in the trough of the sea. My body struck and pounded as it was dashed helplessly along and turned over and over, and when I could hold my breath no longer, I breathed the stinging salt water into my lungs. But through it all I clung to the one idea—*I must get the jib backed over to windward.* I had no fear of death. I had no doubt but that I should come through somehow. And as this idea of fulfilling Wolf Larsen's order persisted in my dazed consciousness, I seemed to see him standing at the wheel in the midst of the wild welter, pitting his will against the will of the storm and defying it.

I brought up violently against what I took to be the rail, breathed, and breathed the sweet air again. I tried to rise, but struck my head and was knocked back on hands and knees. By some freak of the waters I had been swept clear under the forecastle-head and into the eyes. As I scrambled out on all fours, I passed over the body of Thomas Mugridge, who lay in a groaning heap. There was no time to investigate. I must get the jib backed over.

When I emerged on deck it seemed that the end of everything had come. On all sides there was a rending and crashing of wood and steel and canvas. The *Ghost* was being wrenched and torn to fragments. The foresail and fore-topsail, emptied of the wind by the manœuvre, and with no one to bring in the sheet in time, were thundering into ribbons, the heavy boom threshing and splintering from rail to rail. The air was thick with flying wreckage, detached ropes and stays were hissing and coiling like snakes, and down through it all crashed the gaff of the foresail.

The spar could not have missed me by many inches, while it spurred me to action. Perhaps the situation was not hopeless. I remembered Wolf Larsen's caution. He had expected all hell to break loose, and here it was. And where was he? I caught sight of him toiling at the main-sheet, heaving it in and flat with his tremendous muscles, the stern of the schooner lifted high in the air and his body outlined against a white surge of sea sweeping past. All this, and more,—a whole world of chaos and wreck,—in possibly fifteen seconds I had seen and heard and grasped.

I did not stop to see what had become of the small boat, but sprang to the jib-sheet. The jib itself was beginning to slap, partially filling and emptying with sharp reports; but with a turn of the sheet and the application of my whole strength each time it slapped, I slowly backed it. This I know: I did my best. I pulled till I burst open the ends of all my fingers; and while I pulled, the flying-jib and staysail split their cloths apart and thundered into nothingness.

Still I pulled, holding what I gained each time with a double turn until the next slap gave me more. Then the sheet gave with greater ease, and Wolf Larsen was beside me, heaving in alone while I was busied taking up the slack.

'Make fast!' he shouted. 'And come on!'

As I followed him, I noted that in spite of rack and ruin a rough order obtained. The *Ghost* was hove to. She was still in working order, and she was still working. Though the rest of her sails were gone, the jib, backed to windward, and the mainsail hauled down flat, were themselves holding, and holding her bow to the furious sea as well.

I looked for the boat, and, while Wolf Larsen cleared the boat-tackles, saw it lift to leeward on a big sea an not a score of feet away. And, so nicely had he made his calculation, we drifted fairly down upon it, so that nothing remained to do but hook the tackles to either end and hoist it aboard. But this was not done so easily as it is written.

In the bow was Kerfoot, Oofty-Oofty in the stern, and Kelly amidships. As we drifted closer the boat would rise on a wave while we sank in the trough, till almost straight above me I could see the heads of the three men craned overside and looking down. Then, the next moment, we would lift and soar upward while they sank far down beneath us. It seemed incredible that the next surge should not crush the *Ghost* down upon the tiny eggshell.

But, at the right moment, I passed the tackle to the Kanaka, while Wolf Larsen did the same thing forward to Kerfoot. Both tackles were hooked in a trice, and the three men, deftly timing the roll, made a simultaneous leap aboard the schooner. As the *Ghost* rolled her side out of water, the boat was lifted snugly against her, and before the return roll came, we had heaved it in over the side and turned it bottom up on the deck. I noticed blood spouting from Kerfoot's left hand. In some way the third finger had been crushed to a pulp. But he gave no sign of pain, and with his single right hand helped us lash the boat in its place.

'Stand by to let that jib over, you Oofty!' Wolf Larsen commanded, the very second we had finished with the boat. 'Kelly, come aft and slack off the main-sheet! You, Kerfoot, go for'ard and see what's become of Cooky! Mr. Van Weyden, run aloft again, and cut away any stray stuff on your way!'

And having commanded, he went aft with his peculiar tigerish leaps to the wheel. While I toiled up the fore-shrouds the *Ghost* slowly paid off. This time, as we went into the trough of the sea and were swept, there were no sails to carry away. And, halfway to the crosstrees and flattened against the rigging by the full force of the wind so that it would have been impossible for me to have fallen, the *Ghost* almost on her beam-ends and the masts parallel with the water, I looked, not down, but at almost right angles from the perpendicular, to the deck of the *Ghost*. But I saw, not the deck, but where the deck should have been, for it was buried beneath a wild tumbling of water. Out of this water I could see the two masts rising, and that was all. The *Ghost*, for the moment, was buried beneath the sea. As she squared off more and more, escaping from the side pressure, she righted herself and broke her deck, like a whale's back, through the ocean surface.

Then we raced, and wildly, across the wild sea, the while I hung like a fly in the crosstrees and searched for the other boats. In half-an-hour I sighted the second one, swamped and bottom up, to which were desperately clinging Jock Horner, fat Louis, and Johnson. This time I remained aloft, and Wolf Larsen succeeded in heaving to without being swept. As before, we drifted down upon it. Tackles were made fast and lines flung to the men, who scrambled aboard like monkeys. The boat itself was crushed and splintered against the schooner's side as it came inboard; but the wreck was securely lashed, for it could be patched and made whole again.

Once more the *Ghost* bore away before the storm, this time so submerging herself that for some seconds I thought she would never reappear. Even the wheel, quite a deal higher than the waist, was covered and swept again and again. At such moments I felt strangely alone with God, alone with him and watching the chaos of his wrath. And then the wheel would reappear, and Wolf Larsen's broad shoulders, his hands gripping the spokes and holding the schooner to the course of his will, himself an earth-god, dominating the storm, flinging its descending waters from him and riding it to his own ends. And oh, the marvel of it! the marvel of it! That tiny men should live and breathe and work, and drive so frail a contrivance of wood and cloth through so tremendous an elemental strife.

As before, the *Ghost* swung out of the trough, lifting her deck again out of the sea, and dashed before the howling blast. It was now half-past five, and half-an-hour later, when the last of the day lost itself in a dim and furious twilight, I sighted a third boat. It was bottom up, and there was no sign of its crew. Wolf Larsen repeated his manœuvre, holding off and then rounding up to windward and drifting down upon it. But this time he missed by forty feet, the boat passing astern.

'Number four boat!' Oofty-Oofty cried, his keen eyes reading its number in the one second when it lifted clear of the foam, and upside down.

It was Henderson's boat and with him had been lost Holyoak and Williams, another of the deep-water crowd. Lost they indubitably were; but the boat remained, and Wolf Larsen made one more reckless effort to recover it. I had come down to the deck, and I saw Horner and Kerfoot vainly protest against the attempt.

'By God, I'll not be robbed of my boat by any storm that ever blew out of hell!' he shouted, and though we four stood with our heads together that we might hear, his voice seemed faint and far, as though removed from us an immense distance.

'Mr. Van Weyden!' he cried, and I heard through the tumult as one might hear a whisper. 'Stand by that jib with Johnson and Oofty! The rest of you tail aft to the mainsheet! Lively now! or I'll sail you all into Kingdom Come! Understand?'

And when he put the wheel hard over and the *Ghost's* bow swung off, there was nothing for the hunters to do but obey and make the best of a risky chance. How great the risk I realized when I was once more buried beneath the pounding seas and clinging for life to the pinrail at the foot of the foremast. My fingers were torn loose, and I swept across to the side and over the side into the sea. I could not swim, but before I could sink I was swept back again. A strong hand gripped me, and when the *Ghost* finally emerged, I found that I owed my life to Johnson. I saw him looking anxiously about him, and noted that Kelly, who had come forward at the last moment, was missing.

This time, having missed the boat, and not being in the same position as in the previous instances, Wolf Larsen was compelled to resort to a different manœuvre. Running off before the wind with everything to starboard, he came about, and returned close-hauled on the port tack.

'Grand!' Johnson shouted in my ear, as we successfully came through the attendant deluge, and I knew he referred, not to Wolf Larsen's seamanship, but to the performance of the *Ghost* herself.

It was now so dark that there was no sign of the boat; but Wolf Larsen held back through the frightful turmoil as if guided by unerring instinct. This time, though we were continually half-buried, there was no trough in which to be swept, and we drifted squarely down upon the upturned boat, badly smashing it as it was heaved inboard.

Two hours of terrible work followed, in which all hands of us—two hunters, three sailors, Wolf Larsen and I—reefed, first one and then the other, the jib and mainsail. Hove to under this short canvas, our decks were comparatively free of water, while the *Ghost* bobbed and ducked amongst the combers like a cork.

I had burst open the ends of my fingers at the very first, and during the reefing I had worked with tears of pain running down my cheeks. And when all was done, I gave up like a woman and rolled upon the deck in the agony of exhaustion.

In the meantime Thomas Mugridge, like a drowned rat, was being dragged out from under the forecastle head where he had cravenly ensconced himself. I saw him pulled aft to the cabin, and noted with a shock of surprise that the galley had disappeared. A clean space of deck showed where it had stood.

In the cabin I found all hands assembled, sailors as well, and while coffee was being cooked over the small stove we drank whisky and crunched hard-tack. Never in my life had food been so welcome. And never had hot coffee tasted so good. So violently did the *Ghost*, pitch and toss and tumble that it was impossible for even the sailors to move about without holding on, and several times, after a cry of 'Now she takes it!' we were heaped upon the wall of the port cabins as though it had been the deck.

'To hell with a look-out,' I heard Wolf Larsen say when we had eaten and drunk our fill. 'There's nothing can be done on deck. If anything's going to run us down we couldn't get out of its way. Turn in, all hands, and get some sleep.'

The sailors slipped forward, setting the side-lights as they went, while the two hunters remained to sleep in the cabin, it not being deemed advisable to open the slide to the steerage companion-way. Wolf Larsen and I, between us, cut off Kerfoot's crushed finger and sewed up the stump. Mugridge, who, during all the time he had been compelled to cook and serve coffee and keep the fire going, had complained of internal pains, now swore that he had a broken rib or two. On examination we found that he had three. But his case was deferred to next day, principally for the reason that I did not know anything about broken ribs and would first have to read it up.

'I don't think it was worth it,' I said to Wolf Larsen, 'a broken boat for Kelly's life.'

'But Kelly didn't amount to much,' was the reply. 'Good-night.'

After all that had passed, suffering intolerable anguish in my finger-ends, and with three boats missing, to say nothing of the wild capers the *Ghost* was cutting, I should have thought it impossible to sleep. But my eyes must have closed the instant my head touched the pillow, and in utter exhaustion I slept throughout the night, the while the *Ghost*, lonely and undirected, fought her way through the storm.

CHAPTER XVIII

The next day, while the storm was blowing itself out, Wolf Larsen and I crammed anatomy and surgery and set Mugridge's ribs. Then, when the storm broke, Wolf Larsen cruised back and forth over that portion of the ocean where we had encountered it, and somewhat more to the westward, while the boats were being repaired and new sails made and bent. Sealing schooner after sealing schooner we sighted and boarded, most of which were in search of lost boats, and most of which were carrying boats and crews they had picked up and which did not belong to them. For the thick of the fleet had been to the westward of us, and the boats, scattered far and wide, had headed in mad flight for the nearest refuge.

Two of our boats, with men all safe, we took off the *Cisco*, and, to Wolf Larsen's huge delight and my own grief, he culled Smoke, with Nilson and Leach, from the *San Diego*. So that, at the end of five days, we found ourselves short but four men— Henderson, Holyoak, Williams, and Kelly,—and were once more hunting on the flanks of the herd.

As we followed it north we began to encounter the dreaded sea-fogs. Day after day the boats lowered and were swallowed up almost ere they touched the water, while we on board pumped the horn at regular intervals and every fifteen minutes fired the bomb gun. Boats were continually being lost and found, it being the custom for a boat to hunt, on lay, with whatever schooner picked it up, until such time it was recovered by its own schooner. But Wolf Larsen, as was to be expected, being a boat short, took possession of the first stray one and compelled its men to hunt with the *Ghost*, not permitting them to return to their own schooner when we sighted it. I remember how he forced the hunter and his two men below, a riffle at their breasts, when their captain passed by at biscuit-toss and hailed us for information.

Thomas Mugridge, so strangely and pertinaciously clinging to life, was soon limping about again and performing his double duties of cook and cabin-boy. Johnson and Leach were bullied and beaten as much as ever, and they looked for their lives to end with the end of the hunting season; while the rest of the crew lived the lives of dogs and were worked like dogs by their pitiless master. As for Wolf Larsen and myself, we got along fairly well; though I could not quite rid myself of the idea that right conduct, for me, lay in killing him. He fascinated me immeasurably, and I feared him immeasurably. And yet, I could not imagine him lying prone in death. There was an endurance, as of perpetual youth, about him, which rose up and forbade the picture. I could see him only as living always, and dominating always, fighting and destroying, himself surviving.

One diversion of his, when we were in the midst of the herd and the sea was too rough to lower the boats, was to lower with two boat-pullers and a steerer and go out himself. He was a good shot, too, and brought many a skin aboard under what the hunters termed impossible hunting conditions. It seemed the breath of his nostrils, this carrying his life in his hands and struggling for it against tremendous odds.

I was learning more and more seamanship; and one clear day—a thing we rarely encountered now—I had the satisfaction of running and handling the *Ghost* and picking up the boats myself. Wolf Larsen had been smitten with one of his headaches, and I stood at the wheel from morning until evening, sailing across the ocean after the last lee boat, and heaving to and picking it and the other five up without command or suggestion from him.

Gales we encountered now and again, for it was a raw and stormy region, and, in the middle of June, a typhoon most memorable to me and most important because of the changes wrought through it upon my future. We must have been caught nearly at the centre of this circular storm, and Wolf Larsen ran out of it and to the southward, first under a double-reefed jib, and finally under bare poles. Never had I imagined so great a sea. The seas previously encountered were as ripples compared with these, which ran a half-mile from crest to crest and which upreared, I am confident, above our masthead. So great was it that Wolf Larsen himself did not dare heave to, though he was being driven far to the southward and out of the seal herd.

We must have been well in the path of the trans-Pacific steamships when the typhoon moderated, and here, to the surprise of the hunters, we found ourselves in the midst of seals—a second herd, or sort of rear-guard, they declared, and a most unusual thing. But it was 'Boats over!' the boom-boom of guns, and the pitiful slaughter through the long day.

It was at this time that I was approached by Leach. I had just finished tallying the skins of the last boat aboard, when he came to my side, in the darkness, and said in a low tone:

'Can you tell me, Mr. Van Weyden, how far we are off the coast, and what the bearings of Yokohama are?'

My heart leaped with gladness, for I knew what he had in mind, and I gave him the bearings—west-north-west, and five hundred miles away.

'Thank you, sir,' was all he said as he slipped back into the darkness.

Next morning No. 3 boat and Johnson and Leach were missing. The water-breakers and grub-boxes from all the other boats were likewise missing, as were the beds and sea bags of the two men. Wolf Larsen was furious. He set sail and bore away into the west-north-west, two hunters constantly at the mastheads and sweeping the sea with glasses, himself pacing the deck like an angry lion. He knew too well my sympathy for the runaways to send me aloft as look-out.

The wind was fair but fitful, and it was like looking for a needle in a haystack to raise that tiny boat out of the blue immensity. But he put the *Ghost* through her best paces so as to get between the deserters and the land. This accomplished, he cruised back and forth across what he knew must be their course.

On the morning of the third day, shortly after eight bells, a cry that the boat was sighted came down from Smoke at the masthead. All hands lined the rail. A snappy breeze was blowing from the west with the promise of more wind behind it; and there, to leeward, in the troubled silver of the rising sun, appeared and disappeared a black speck.

We squared away and ran for it. My heart was as lead. I felt myself turning sick in anticipation; and as I looked at the gleam of triumph in Wolf Larsen's eyes, his form swam before me, and I felt almost irresistibly impelled to fling myself upon him. So unnerved was I by the thought of impending violence to Leach and Johnson that my reason must have left me. I know that I slipped down into the steerage in a daze, and that I was just beginning the ascent to the deck, a loaded shot-gun in my hands, when I heard the startled cry:

'There's five men in that boat!'

I supported myself in the companion-way, weak and trembling, while the observation was being verified by the remarks of the rest of the men. Then my knees gave from under me and I sank down, myself again, but overcome by shock at knowledge of what I had so nearly done. Also, I was very thankful as I put the gun away and slipped back on deck.

No one had remarked my absence. The boat was near enough for us to make out that it was larger than any sealing boat and built on different lines. As we drew closer, the sail was taken in and the mast unstepped. Oars were shipped, and its occupants waited for us to heave to and take them aboard.

Smoke, who had descended to the deck and was now standing by my side, began to chuckle in a significant way. I looked at him inquiringly.

'Talk of a mess!' he giggled.

'What's wrong?' I demanded.

Again he chuckled. 'Don't you see there, in the stern-sheets, on the bottom? May I never shoot a seal again if that ain't a woman!'

I looked closely, but was not sure until exclamations broke out on all sides. The boat contained four men, and its fifth occupant was certainly a woman. We were agog with excitement, all except Wolf Larsen, who was too evidently disappointed in that it was not his own boat with the two victims of his malice.

We ran down the flying jib, hauled the jib-sheets to wind-ward and the main-sheet flat, and came up into the wind. The oars struck the water, and with a few strokes the boat was alongside. I now caught my first fair glimpse of the woman. She was wrapped in a long ulster, for the morning was raw; and I could see nothing but her face and a mass of light brown hair escaping from under the seaman's cap on her head. The eyes were large and brown and lustrous, the mouth sweet and sensitive, and the face itself a delicate oval, though sun and exposure to briny wind had burnt the face scarlet.

She seemed to me like a being from another world. I was aware of a hungry out-reaching for her, as of a starving man for bread. But then, I had not seen a woman for a very long time. I know that I was lost in a great wonder, almost a stupor,—this, then, was a woman?—so that I forgot myself and my mate's duties, and took no part in helping the new-comers aboard. For when one of the sailors lifted her into Wolf Larsen's downstretched arms, she looked up into our curious faces and smiled amusedly and sweetly, as only a woman can smile, and as I had seen no one smile for so long that I had forgotten such smiles existed.

'Mr. Van Weyden!'

Wolf Larsen's voice brought me sharply back to myself.

'Will you take the lady below and see to her comfort? Make up that spare port cabin. Put Cooky to work on it. And see what you can do for that face. It's burned badly.'

He turned brusquely away from us and began to question the new men. The boat was cast adrift, though one of them called it a 'bloody shame' with Yokohama so near.

I found myself strangely afraid of this woman I was escorting aft. Also I was awkward. It seemed to me that I was realizing for the first time what a delicate, fragile creature a woman is; and as I caught her arm to help her down the companion stairs, I was startled by its smallness and softness. Indeed, she was a slender, delicate woman as women go, but to me she was so ethereally slender and delicate that I was quite prepared for her arm to crumble in my grasp. All this, in frankness, to show my first impression, after long denial of women in general and of Maud Brewster in particular.

'No need to go to any great trouble for me,' she protested, when I had seated her in Wolf Larsen's arm-chair, which I had dragged hastily from his cabin. 'The men were looking for land at any moment this morning, and the vessel should be in by night; don't you think so?'

Her simple faith in the immediate future took me aback. How could I explain to her the situation, the strange man who stalked the sea like Destiny, all that it had taken me months to learn? But I answered honestly:

'If it were any other captain except ours, I should say you would be ashore in Yokohama to-morrow. But our captain is a strange man, and I beg of you to be prepared for anything—understand?—for anything.'

'I—I confess I hardly do understand,' she hesitated, a perturbed but not frightened expression in her eyes. 'Or is it a misconception of mine that shipwrecked people are always shown every consideration? This is such a little thing, you know. We are so close to land.'

'Candidly, I do not know,' I strove to reassure her. 'I wished merely to prepare you for the worst, if the worst is to come. This man, this captain, is a brute, a demon, and one can never tell what will be his next fantastic act.'

I was growing excited, but she interrupted me with an 'Oh, I see,' and her voice sounded weary. To think was patently an effort. She was clearly on the verge of physical collapse.

She asked no further questions, and I vouchsafed no remark, devoting myself to Wolf Larsen's command, which was to make her comfortable. I bustled about in quite housewifely fashion, procuring soothing lotions for her sunburn, raiding Wolf Larsen's private stores for a bottle of port I knew to be there, and directing Thomas Mugridge in the preparation of the spare state-room.

The wind was freshening rapidly, the *Ghost* heeling over more and more, and by the time the state-room was ready she was dashing through the water at a lively clip. I had quite forgotten the existence of Leach and Johnson, when suddenly, like a thunderclap, 'Boat ho!' came down the open companion-way. It was Smoke's unmistakable voice, crying from the masthead. I shot a glance at the woman, but she was leaning back in the arm-chair, her eyes closed, unutterably tired. I doubted that she had heard, and I resolved to prevent her seeing the brutality I knew would follow the capture of the deserters. She was tired. Very good. She should sleep.

There were swift commands on deck, a stamping of feet and a slapping of reef-points as the *Ghost* shot into the wind and about on the other tack. As she filled away and heeled, the arm-chair began to slide across the cabin floor, and I sprang for it just in time to prevent the rescued woman from being spilled out.

Her eyes were too heavy to suggest more than a hint of the sleepy surprise that perplexed her as she looked up at me, and she half stumbled, half tottered, as I led her to her cabin. Mugridge grinned insinuatingly in my face as I shoved him out and ordered him back to his galley work; and he won his revenge by spreading glowing reports among the hunters as to what an excellent 'lydy's-myde' I was proving myself to be.

She leaned heavily against me, and I do believe that she had fallen asleep again between the arm-chair and the state-room. This I discovered when she nearly fell into the bunk during a sudden lurch of the schooner. She aroused, smiled drowsily, and was off to sleep again; and asleep I left her, under a heavy pair of sailor's blankets, her head resting on a pillow I had appropriated from Wolf Larsen's bunk.

CHAPTER XIX

I came on deck to find the *Ghost* heading up close on the port tack and cutting in to windward of a familiar spritsail close-hauled on the same tack ahead of us. All hands were on deck, for they knew that something was to happen when Leach and Johnson were dragged aboard.

It was four bells. Louis came aft to relieve the wheel. There was a dampness in the air, and I noticed he had on his oilskins.

'What are we going to have?' I asked him.

'A healthy young slip of a gale from the breath iv it, sir,' he answered, 'with a splatter iv rain just to wet our gills an' no more.'

'Too bad we sighted them,' I said, as the *Ghost's* bow was flung off a point by a large sea and the boat leaped for a moment past the jibs and into our line of vision.

Louis gave a spoke and temporized. 'They'd never iv made the land, sir, I'm thinkin'.'

'Think not?' I queried.

'No, sir. Did you feel that?' (A puff had caught the schooner, and he was forced to put the wheel up rapidly to keep her out of the wind.) ''Tis no egg-shell'll float on this sea an hour come, an' it's a stroke iv luck for them we're here to pick 'em up.'

Wolf Larsen strode aft from amidships, where he had been talking with the rescued men. The cat-like springiness in his tread was a little more pronounced than usual, and his eyes were bright and snappy.

'Three oilers and a fourth engineer,' was his greeting. 'But we'll make sailors out of them, or boat-pullers at any rate. Now, what of the lady?'

I know not why, but I was aware of a twinge or pang like the cut of a knife when he mentioned her. I thought it a certain silly fastidiousness on my part, but it persisted in spite of me, and I merely shrugged my shoulders in answer.

Wolf Larsen pursed his lips in a long, quizzical whistle.

'What's her name, then?' he demanded.

'I don't know,' I replied. 'She is asleep. She was very tired. In fact, I am waiting to hear the news from you. What vessel was it?'

'Mail steamer,' he answered shortly. '*The City of Tokio*, from 'Frisco, bound for Yokohama. Disabled in that typhoon. Old tub. Opened up top and bottom like a sieve. They were adrift four days. And you don't know who or what she is, eh?—maid, wife, or widow? Well, well.'

He shook his head in a bantering way, and regarded me with laughing eyes.

'Are you—' I began. It was on the verge of my tongue to ask if he were going to take the castaways into Yokohama.

'Am I what?' he asked.

'What do you intend doing with Leach and Johnson?'

He shook his head. 'Really, Hump, I don't know. You see, with these additions I've about all the crew I want.'

'And they've about all the escaping they want,' I said. 'Why not give them a change of treatment? Take them aboard, and deal gently with them. Whatever they have done they have been hounded into doing.'

'By me?'

'By you,' I answered steadily. 'And I give you warning, Wolf Larsen, that I may forget love of my own life in the desire to kill you if you go too far in maltreating those poor wretches.'

'Bravo!' he cried. 'You do me proud, Hump! You've found your legs with a vengeance. You're quite an individual. You were unfortunate in having your life cast in easy places, but you're developing, and I like you the better for it.'

His voice and expression changed. His face was serious. 'Do you believe in promises?' he asked. 'Are they sacred things?'

'Of course,' I answered.

'Then here's a compact,' he went on, consummate actor. 'If I promise not to lay my hands upon Leach will you promise, in turn, not to attempt to kill me?'

'Oh, not that I'm afraid of you, not that I'm afraid of you,' he hastened to add.

I could hardly believe my ears. What was coming over the man?

'Is it a go?' he asked impatiently.

'A go,' I answered.

His hand went out to mine, and as I shook it heartily I could have sworn I saw the mocking devil shine up for a moment in his eyes.

We strolled across the poop to the lee side. The boat was close at hand now, and in desperate plight. Johnson was steering, Leach bailing. We overhauled them about two feet to their one. Wolf Larsen motioned Louis to keep off slightly, and we dashed abreast of the boat, not a score of feet to windward. The *Ghost* blanketed it. The spritsail flapped emptily and the boat righted to an even keel, causing the two men swiftly to change position. The boat lost headway, and, as we lifted on a huge surge, toppled and fell into the trough.

It was at this moment that Leach and Johnson looked up into the faces of their shipmates, who lined the rail amidships. There was no greeting. They were as dead men in their comrades' eyes, and between them was the gulf that parts the living and the dead.

The next instant they were opposite the poop, where stood Wolf Larsen and I. We were falling in the trough, they were rising on the surge. Johnson looked at me, and I could see that his face was worn and haggard. I waved my hand to him, and he answered the greeting, but with a wave that was hopeless and despairing. It was as if he were saying farewell. I did not see into the eyes of Leach, for he was looking at Wolf Larsen, the old and implacable snarl of hatred strong as ever on his face.

Then they were gone astern. The spritsail filled with the wind, suddenly, careening the frail open craft till it seemed it would surely capsize. A whitecap foamed above it and broke across in a snow-white smother. Then the boat emerged, half swamped, Leach flinging the water out and Johnson clinging to the steering-oar, his face white and anxious.

Wolf Larsen barked a short laugh in my ear and strode away to the weather side of the poop. I expected him to give orders for the *Ghost* to heave to, but she kept on her course and he made no sign. Louis stood imperturbably at the wheel, but I noticed the grouped sailors forward turning troubled faces in our direction. Still the *Ghost* tore along, till the boat dwindled to a speck, when Wolf Larsen's voice rang out in command and he went about on the starboard tack.

Back we held, two miles and more to windward of the struggling cockle-shell, when the flying jib was run down and the schooner hove to. The sealing boats are not made for windward work. Their hope lies in keeping a weather position so that they may run before the wind for the schooner when it breezes up. But in all that wild waste there was no refuge for Leach and Johnson save on the *Ghost*, and they resolutely began the windward beat. It was slow work in the heavy sea that was running. At any moment they were liable to be overwhelmed by the hissing combers. Time and again and countless times we watched the boat luff into the big whitecaps, lose headway, and be flung back like a cork.

Johnson was a splendid seaman, and he knew as much about small boats as he did about ships. At the end of an hour and a half he was nearly alongside, standing past our stern on the last leg out, aiming to fetch us on the next leg back.

'So you've changed your mind?' I heard Wolf Larsen mutter, half to himself, half to them as though they could hear. 'You want to come aboard, eh? Well, then, just keep a-coming.'

'Hard up with that helm!' he commanded Oofty-Oofty, the Kanaka, who had in the meantime relieved Louis at the wheel.

Command followed command. As the schooner paid off, the fore- and main-sheets were slacked away for fair wind. And before the wind we were, and leaping, when Johnson, easing his sheet at imminent peril, cut across our wake a hundred feet away. Again Wolf Larsen laughed, at the same time beckoning them with his arm to follow. It was evidently his intention to play with them,—a lesson, I took it, in lieu of a beating, though a dangerous lesson, for the frail craft stood in momentary danger of being overwhelmed.

Johnson squared away promptly and ran after us. There was nothing else for him to do. Death stalked everywhere, and it was only a matter of time when some one of those many huge seas would fall upon the boat, roll over it, and pass on.

''Tis the fear iv death at the hearts iv them,' Louis muttered in my ear, as I passed forward to see to taking in the flying jib and staysail.

'Oh, he'll heave to in a little while and pick them up,' I answered cheerfully. 'He's bent upon giving them a lesson, that's all.'

Louis looked at me shrewdly. 'Think so?' he asked.

'Surely,' I answered. 'Don't you?'

'I think nothing but iv my own skin, these days,' was his answer. 'An' 'tis with wonder I'm filled as to the workin' out iv things. A pretty mess that 'Frisco whisky got me into, an' a prettier mess that woman's got you into aft there. Ah, it's myself that knows ye for a blitherin' fool.'

'What do you mean?' I demanded; for, having sped his shaft, he was turning away.

'What do I mean?' he cried. 'And it's you that asks me! 'Tis not what I mean, but what the Wolf 'll mean. The Wolf, I said, the Wolf!'

'If trouble comes, will you stand by?' I asked impulsively, for he had voiced my own fear.

'Stand by? 'Tis old fat Louis I stand by, an' trouble enough it'll be. We're at the beginnin' iv things, I'm tellin' ye, the bare beginnin' iv things.'

'I had not thought you so great a coward,' I sneered.

He favoured me with a contemptuous stare. 'If I raised never a hand for that poor fool,'—pointing astern to the tiny sail,—'d'ye think I'm hungerin' for a broken head for a woman I never laid me eyes upon before this day?'

I turned scornfully away and went aft.

'Better get in those topsails, Mr. Van Weyden,' Wolf Larsen said, as I came on the poop.

137

I felt relief, at least as far as the two men were concerned. It was clear he did not wish to run too far away from them. I picked up hope at the thought and put the order swiftly into execution. I had scarcely opened my mouth to issue the necessary commands, when eager men were springing to halyards and downhauls, and others were racing aloft. This eagerness on their part was noted by Wolf Larsen with a grim smile.

Still we increased our lead, and when the boat had dropped astern several miles we hove to and waited. All eyes watched it coming, even Wolf Larsen's; but he was the only unperturbed man aboard. Louis, gazing fixedly, betrayed a trouble in his face he was not quite able to hide.

The boat drew closer and closer, hurling along through the seething green like a thing alive, lifting and sending and uptossing across the huge-backed breakers, or disappearing behind them only to rush into sight again and shoot skyward. It seemed impossible that it could continue to live, yet with each dizzying sweep it did achieve the impossible. A rain-squall drove past, and out of the flying wet the boat emerged, almost upon us.

'Hard up, there!' Wolf Larsen shouted, himself springing to the wheel and whirling it over.

Again the *Ghost* sprang away and raced before the wind, and for two hours Johnson and Leach pursued us. We hove to and ran away, hove to and ran away, and ever astern the struggling patch of sail tossed skyward and fell into the rushing valleys. It was a quarter of a mile away when a thick squall of rain veiled it from view. It never emerged. The wind blew the air clear again, but no patch of sail broke the troubled surface. I thought I saw, for an instant, the boat's bottom show black in a breaking crest. At the best, that was all. For Johnson and Leach the travail of existence had ceased.

The men remained grouped amidships. No one had gone below, and no one was speaking. Nor were any looks being exchanged. Each man seemed stunned—deeply contemplative, as it were, and, not quite sure, trying to realize just what had taken place. Wolf Larsen gave them little time for thought. He at once put the *Ghost* upon her course—a course which meant the seal herd and not Yokohama harbour. But the men were no longer eager as they pulled and hauled, and I heard curses amongst them, which left their lips smothered and as heavy and lifeless as were they. Not so was it with the hunters. Smoke the irrepressible related a story, and they descended into the steerage, bellowing with laughter.

As I passed to leeward of the galley on my way aft I was approached by the engineer we had rescued. His face was white, his lips were trembling.

'Good God! sir, what kind of a craft is this?' he cried.

'You have eyes, you have seen,' I answered, almost brutally, what of the pain and fear at my own heart.

'Your promise?' I said to Wolf Larsen.

'I was not thinking of taking them aboard when I made that promise,' he answered. 'And anyway, you'll agree I've not laid my hands upon them.'

'Far from it, far from it,' he laughed a moment later.

I made no reply. I was incapable of speaking, my mind was too confused. I must have time to think, I knew. This woman, sleeping even now in the spare cabin, was a responsibility, which I must consider, and the only rational thought that flickered through my mind was that I must do nothing hastily if I were to be any help to her at all.

CHAPTER XX

The remainder of the day passed uneventfully. The young slip of a gale, having wetted our gills, proceeded to moderate. The fourth engineer and the three oilers, after a warm interview with Wolf Larsen, were furnished with outfits from the slop-chests, assigned places under the hunters in the various boats and watches on the vessel, and bundled forward into the forecastle. They went protestingly, but their voices were not loud. They were awed by what they had already seen of Wolf Larsen's character, while the tale of woe they speedily heard in the forecastle took the last bit of rebellion out of them.

Miss Brewster—we had learned her name from the engineer—slept on and on. At supper I requested the hunters to lower their voices, so she was not disturbed; and it was not till next morning that she made her appearance. It had been my intention to have her meals served apart, but Wolf Larsen put down his foot. Who was she that she should be too good for cabin table and cabin society? had been his demand.

But her coming to the table had something amusing in it. The hunters fell silent as clams. Jock Horner and Smoke alone were unabashed, stealing stealthy glances at her now and again, and even taking part in the conversation. The other four men glued their eyes on their plates and chewed steadily and with thoughtful precision, their ears moving and wobbling, in time with their jaws, like the ears of so many animals.

Wolf Larsen had little to say at first, doing no more than reply when he was addressed. Not that he was abashed. Far from it. This woman was a new type to him, a different breed from any he had ever known, and he was curious. He studied her, his eyes rarely leaving her face unless to follow the movements of her hands or shoulders. I studied her myself, and though it was I who maintained the conversation, I know that I was a bit shy, not quite self-possessed. His was the perfect poise, the supreme confidence in self, which nothing could shake; and he was no more timid of a woman than he was of storm and battle.

'And when shall we arrive at Yokohama?' she asked, turning to him and looking him squarely in the eyes.

There it was, the question flat. The jaws stopped working, the ears ceased wobbling, and though eyes remained glued on plates, each man listened greedily for the answer.

'In four months, possibly three if the season closes early,' Wolf Larsen said.

She caught her breath and stammered, 'I—I thought—I was given to understand that Yokohama was only a day's sail away. It—' Here she paused and looked about the table at the circle of unsympathetic faces staring hard at the plates. 'It is not right,' she concluded.

'That is a question you must settle with Mr. Van Weyden there,' he replied, nodding to me with a mischievous twinkle. 'Mr. Van Weyden is what you may call an authority on such things as rights. Now I, who am only a sailor, would look upon the situation somewhat differently. It may possibly be your misfortune that you have to remain with us, but it is certainly our good fortune.'

He regarded her smilingly. Her eyes fell before his gaze, but she lifted them again, and defiantly, to mine. I read the unspoken question there: was it right? But I had decided that the part I was to play must be a neutral one, so I did not answer.

'What do you think?' she demanded.

'That it is unfortunate, especially if you have any engagements falling due in the course of the next several months. But, since you say that you were voyaging to Japan for your health, I can assure you that it will improve no better anywhere than aboard the *Ghost*.'

I saw her eyes flash with indignation, and this time it was I who dropped mine, while I felt my face flushing under her gaze. It was cowardly, but what else could I do?

'Mr. Van Weyden speaks with the voice of authority,' Wolf Larsen laughed.

I nodded my head, and she, having recovered herself, waited expectantly.

'Not that he is much to speak of now,' Wolf Larsen went on, 'but he has improved wonderfully. You should have seen him when he came on board. A more scrawny, pitiful specimen of humanity one could hardly conceive. Isn't that so, Kerfoot?'

Kerfoot, thus directly addressed, was startled into dropping his knife on the floor, though he managed to grunt affirmation.

'Developed himself by peeling potatoes and washing dishes. Eh, Kerfoot?'

Again that worthy grunted.

'Look at him now. True, he is not what you would term muscular, but still he has muscles, which is more than he had when he came aboard. Also, he has legs to stand on. You would not think so to look at him, but he was quite unable to stand alone at first.'

The hunters were snickering, but she looked at me with a sympathy in her eyes which more than compensated for Wolf Larsen's nastiness. In truth, it had been so long since I had received sympathy that I was softened, and I became then, and gladly, her willing slave. But I was angry with Wolf Larsen. He was challenging my manhood with his slurs, challenging the very legs he claimed to be instrumental in getting for me.

'I may have learned to stand on my own legs,' I retorted. 'But I have yet to stamp upon others with them.'

He looked at me insolently. 'Your education is only half completed, then,' he said dryly, and turned to her.

'We are very hospitable upon the *Ghost*. Mr. Van Weyden has discovered that. We do everything to make our guests feel at home, eh, Mr. Van Weyden?'

'Even to the peeling of potatoes and the washing of dishes,' I answered, 'to say nothing to wringing their necks out of very fellowship.'

'I beg of you not to receive false impressions of us from Mr. Van Weyden,' he interposed with mock anxiety. 'You will observe, Miss Brewster, that he carries a dirk in his belt, a—ahem—a most unusual thing for a ship's officer to do. While really very estimable, Mr. Van Weyden is sometimes—how shall I say?—er—quarrelsome, and harsh measures are necessary. He is quite reasonable and fair in his calm moments, and as he is calm now he will not deny that only yesterday he threatened my life.'

I was well-nigh choking, and my eyes were certainly fiery. He drew attention to me.

'Look at him now. He can scarcely control himself in your presence. He is not accustomed to the presence of ladies anyway. I shall have to arm myself before I dare go on deck with him.'

He shook his head sadly, murmuring, 'Too bad, too bad,' while the hunters burst into guffaws of laughter.

The deep-sea voices of these men, rumbling and bellowing in the confined space, produced a wild effect. The whole setting was wild, and for the first time, regarding this strange woman and realizing how incongruous she was in it, I was aware of how much a part of it I was myself. I knew these men and their mental processes, was one of them myself, living the seal-hunting life, eating the seal-hunting fare, thinking, largely, the seal-hunting thoughts. There was for me no strangeness to it, to the rough clothes, the coarse faces, the wild laughter, and the lurching cabin walls and swaying sea-lamps.

As I buttered a piece of bread my eyes chanced to rest upon my hand. The knuckles were skinned and inflamed clear across, the fingers swollen, the nails rimmed with black. I felt the mattress-like growth of beard on my neck, knew that the sleeve of my coat was ripped, that a button was missing from the throat of the blue shirt I wore. The dirk mentioned by Wolf Larsen rested in its sheath on my hip. It was very natural that it should be there,—how natural I had not imagined until now, when I looked upon it with her eyes and knew how strange it and all that went with it must appear to her.

But she divined the mockery in Wolf Larsen's words, and again favoured me with a sympathetic glance. But there was a look of bewilderment also in her eyes. That it was mockery made the situation more puzzling to her.

'I may be taken off by some passing vessel, perhaps,' she suggested.

'There will be no passing vessels, except other sealing-schooners,' Wolf Larsen made answer.

'I have no clothes, nothing,' she objected. 'You hardly realize, sir, that I am not a man, or that I am unaccustomed to the vagrant, careless life which you and your men seem to lead.'

'The sooner you get accustomed to it, the better,' he said.

'I'll furnish you with cloth, needles, and thread,' he added. 'I hope it will not be too dreadful a hardship for you to make yourself a dress or two.'

She made a wry pucker with her mouth, as though to advertise her ignorance of dressmaking. That she was frightened and bewildered, and that she was bravely striving to hide it, was quite plain to me.

'I suppose you're like Mr. Van Weyden there, accustomed to having things done for you. Well, I think doing a few things for yourself will hardly dislocate any joints. By the way, what do you do for a living?'

She regarded him with amazement unconcealed.

'I mean no offence, believe me. People eat, therefore they must procure the wherewithal. These men here shoot seals in order to live; for the same reason I sail this schooner; and Mr. Van Weyden, for the present at any rate, earns his salty grub by assisting me. Now what do you do?'

She shrugged her shoulders.

'Do you feed yourself? Or does some one else feed you?'

'I'm afraid some one else has fed me most of my life,' she laughed, trying bravely to enter into the spirit of his quizzing, though I could see a terror dawning and growing in her eyes as she watched Wolf Larsen.

'And I suppose some one else makes your bed for you?'

'I *have* made beds,' she replied.

'Very often?'

She shook her head with mock ruefulness.

'Do you know what they do to poor men in the States, who, like you, do not work for their living?'

'I am very ignorant,' she pleaded. 'What do they do to the poor men who are like me?'

'They send them to jail. The crime of not earning a living, in their case, is called vagrancy. If I were Mr. Van Weyden, who harps eternally on questions of right and wrong, I'd ask, by what right do you live when you do nothing to deserve living?'

'But as you are not Mr. Van Weyden, I don't have to answer, do I?'

She beamed upon him through her terror-filled eyes, and the pathos of it cut me to the heart. I must in some way break in and lead the conversation into other channels.

'Have you ever earned a dollar by your own labour?' he demanded, certain of her answer, a triumphant vindictiveness in his voice.

'Yes, I have,' she answered slowly, and I could have laughed aloud at his crestfallen visage. 'I remember my father giving me a dollar once, when I was a little girl, for remaining absolutely quiet for five minutes.'

He smiled indulgently.

'But that was long ago,' she continued. 'And you would scarcely demand a little girl of nine to earn her own living.'

'At present, however,' she said, after another slight pause, 'I earn about eighteen hundred dollars a year.'

With one accord, all eyes left the plates and settled on her. A woman who earned eighteen hundred dollars a year was worth looking at. Wolf Larsen was undisguised in his admiration.

'Salary, or piece-work?' he asked.

'Piece-work,' she answered promptly.

'Eighteen hundred,' he calculated. 'That's a hundred and fifty dollars a month. Well, Miss Brewster, there is nothing small about the *Ghost*. Consider yourself on salary during the time you remain with us.'

She made no acknowledgment. She was too unused as yet to the whims of the man to accept them with equanimity.

'I forgot to inquire,' he went on suavely, 'as to the nature of your occupation. What commodities do you turn out? What tools and materials do you require?'

'Paper and ink,' she laughed. 'And, oh! also a typewriter.'

'You are Maud Brewster,' I said slowly and with certainty, almost as though I were charging her with a crime.

Her eyes lifted curiously to mine. 'How do you know?'

'Aren't you?' I demanded.

She acknowledged her identity with a nod. It was Wolf Larsen's turn to be puzzled. The name and its magic signified nothing to him. I was proud that it did mean something to me, and for the first time in a weary while I was convincingly conscious of a superiority over him.

'I remember writing a review of a thin little volume—' I had begun carelessly, when she interrupted me.

'You!' she cried. 'You are—'

She was now staring at me in wide-eyed wonder.

I nodded my identity, in turn.

'Humphrey Van Weyden,' she concluded; then added with a sigh of relief, and unaware that she had glanced that relief at Wolf Larsen, 'I am so glad.'

'I remember the review,' she went on hastily, becoming aware of the awkwardness of her remark; 'that too, too flattering review.'

'Not at all,' I denied valiantly. 'You impeach my sober judgment and make my canons of little worth. Besides, all my brother critics were with me. Didn't Lang include your 'Kiss Endured' among the four supreme sonnets by women in the English language?'

'But you called me the American Mrs. Meynell!'

'Was it not true?' I demanded.

'No, not that,' she answered. 'I was hurt.'

'We can measure the unknown only by the known,' I replied, in my finest academic manner. 'As a critic I was compelled to place you. You have now become a yardstick yourself. Seven of your thin little volumes are on my shelves; and there are two thicker volumes, the essays, which, you will pardon my saying, and I know not which is flattered more, fully equal your verse. The time is not far distant when some unknown will arise in England and the critics will name her the English Maud Brewster.'

'You are very kind, I am sure,' she murmured; and the very conventionality of her tones and words, with the host of associations it aroused of the old life on the other side of the world, gave me a quick thrill—rich with remembrance but stinging sharp with home-sickness.

'And you are Maud Brewster,' I said solemnly, gazing across at her.

'And you are Humphrey Van Weyden,' she said, gazing back at me with equal solemnity and awe. 'How unusual! I don't understand. We surely are not to expect some wildly romantic sea-story from your sober pen.'

'No, I am not gathering material, I assure you,' was my answer. 'I have neither aptitude nor inclination for fiction.'

'Tell me, why have you always buried yourself in California?' she next asked. 'It has not been kind of you. We of the East have seen to very little of you—too little, indeed, of the Dean of American Letters, the Second.'

I bowed to, and disclaimed, the compliment. 'I nearly met you, once, in Philadelphia, some Browning affair or other—you were to lecture, you know. My train was four hours late.'

And then we quite forgot where we were, leaving Wolf Larsen stranded and silent in the midst of our flood of gossip. The hunters left the table and went on deck, and still we talked. Wolf Larsen alone remained. Suddenly I became aware of him, leaning back from the table and listening curiously to our alien speech of a world he did not know.

I broke short off in the middle of a sentence. The present, with all its perils and anxieties, rushed upon me with stunning force. It smote Miss Brewster likewise, a vague and nameless terror rushing into her eyes as she regarded Wolf Larsen.

He rose to his feet and laughed awkwardly. The sound of it was metallic.

'Oh, don't mind me,' he said, with a self-depreciatory wave of his hand. 'I don't count. Go on, go on, I pray you.'

But the gates of speech were closed, and we, too, rose from the table and laughed awkwardly.

CHAPTER XXI

The chagrin Wolf Larsen felt from being ignored by Maud Brewster and me in the conversation at table had to express itself in some fashion, and it fell to Thomas Mugridge to be the victim. He had not mended his ways nor his shirt, though the latter he contended he had changed. The garment itself did not bear out the assertion, nor did the accumulations of grease on stove and pot and pan attest a general cleanliness.

'I've given you warning, Cooky,' Wolf Larsen said, 'and now you've got to take your medicine.'

Mugridge's face turned white under its sooty veneer, and when Wolf Larsen called for a rope and a couple of men, the miserable Cockney fled wildly out of the galley and dodged and ducked about the deck with the grinning crew in pursuit. Few things could have been more to their liking than to give him a tow over the side, for to the forecastle he had sent messes and concoctions of the vilest order. Conditions favoured the undertaking. The *Ghost* was slipping through the water at no more than three miles an hour, and the sea was fairly calm. But Mugridge had little stomach for a dip in it. Possibly he had seen men towed before. Besides, the water was frightfully cold, and his was anything but a rugged constitution.

As usual, the watches below and the hunters turned out for what promised sport. Mugridge seemed to be in rabid fear of the water, and he exhibited a nimbleness and speed we did not dream he possessed. Cornered in the right-angle of the poop and galley, he sprang like a cat to the top of the cabin and ran aft. But his pursuers forestalling him, he doubled back across the cabin, passed over the galley, and gained the deck by means of the steerage-scuttle. Straight forward he raced, the boat-puller Harrison at his heels and gaining on him. But Mugridge, leaping suddenly, caught the jib-boom-lift. It happened in an instant. Holding his weight by his arms, and in mid-air doubling his body at the hips, he let fly with both feet. The oncoming Harrison caught the kick squarely in the pit of the stomach, groaned involuntarily, and doubled up and sank backward to the deck.

Hand-clapping and roars of laughter from the hunters greeted the exploit, while Mugridge, eluding half of his pursuers at the foremast, ran aft and through the remainder like a runner on the football field. Straight aft he held, to the poop and along the poop to the stern. So great was his speed that as he curved past the corner of the cabin he slipped and fell. Nilson was standing at the wheel, and the Cockney's hurtling body struck his legs. Both went down together, but Mugridge alone arose. By some freak of pressures, his frail body had snapped the strong man's leg like a pipe-stem.

Parsons took the wheel, and the pursuit continued. Round and round the decks they went, Mugridge sick with fear, the sailors hallooing and shouting directions to one another, and the hunters bellowing encouragement and laughter. Mugridge went down on the fore-hatch under three men; but he emerged from the mass like an eel, bleeding at the mouth, the offending shirt ripped into tatters, and sprang for the main-rigging. Up he went, clear up, beyond the ratlines, to the very masthead.

Half-a-dozen sailors swarmed to the crosstrees after him, where they clustered and waited while two of their number, Oofty-Oofty and Black (who was Latimer's boat-steerer), continued up the thin steel stays, lifting their bodies higher and higher by means of their arms.

It was a perilous undertaking, for, at a height of over a hundred feet from the deck, holding on by their hands, they were not in the best of positions to protect themselves from Mugridge's feet. And Mugridge kicked savagely, till the Kanaka, hanging on with one hand, seized the Cockney's foot with the other. Black duplicated the performance a moment later with the other foot. Then the three writhed together in a swaying tangle, struggling, sliding, and falling into the arms of their mates on the crosstrees.

The aërial battle was over, and Thomas Mugridge, whining and gibbering, his mouth flecked with bloody foam, was brought down to deck. Wolf Larsen rove a bowline in a piece of rope and slipped it under his shoulders. Then he was carried aft and flung into the sea. Forty,—fifty,—sixty feet of line ran out, when Wolf Larsen cried 'Belay!' Oofty-Oofty took a turn on a bitt, the rope tautened, and the *Ghost*, lunging onward, jerked the cook to the surface.

It was a pitiful spectacle. Though he could not drown, and was nine-lived in addition, he was suffering all the agonies of half-drowning. The *Ghost* was going very slowly, and when her stern lifted on a wave and she slipped forward she pulled the wretch to the surface and gave him a moment in which to breathe; but between each lift the stern fell, and while the bow lazily climbed the next wave the line slacked and he sank beneath.

I had forgotten the existence of Maud Brewster, and I remembered her with a start as she stepped lightly beside me. It was her first time on deck since she had come aboard. A dead silence greeted her appearance.

'What is the cause of the merriment?' she asked.

'Ask Captain Larsen,' I answered composedly and coldly, though inwardly my blood was boiling at the thought that she should be witness to such brutality.

She took my advice and was turning to put it into execution, when her eyes lighted on Oofty-Oofty, immediately before her, his body instinct with alertness and grace as he held the turn of the rope.

'Are you fishing?' she asked him.

He made no reply. His eyes, fixed intently on the sea astern, suddenly flashed.

'Shark ho, sir!' he cried.

'Heave in! Lively! All hands tail on!' Wolf Larsen shouted, springing himself to the rope in advance of the quickest.

Mugridge had heard the Kanaka's warning cry and was screaming madly. I could see a black fin cutting the water and making for him with greater swiftness than he was being pulled aboard. It was an even toss whether the shark or we would get him, and it was a matter of moments. When Mugridge was directly beneath us, the stern descended the slope of a passing wave, thus giving the advantage to the shark. The fin disappeared. The belly flashed white in swift upward rush. Almost equally swift, but not quite, was Wolf Larsen. He threw his strength into one tremendous jerk. The Cockney's body left the water; so did part of the shark's. He drew up his legs, and the man-eater seemed no more than barely to touch one foot, sinking back into the water with a splash. But at the moment of contact Thomas Mugridge cried out. Then he came in like a fresh-caught fish on a line, clearing the rail generously and striking the deck in a heap, on hands and knees, and rolling over.

But a fountain of blood was gushing forth. The right foot was missing, amputated neatly at the ankle. I looked instantly to Maud Brewster. Her face was white, her eyes dilated with horror. She was gazing, not at Thomas Mugridge, but at Wolf Larsen. And he was aware of it, for he said, with one of his short laughs:

'Man-play, Miss Brewster. Somewhat rougher, I warrant, than what you have been used to, but still-man-play. The shark was not in the reckoning. It—'

But at this juncture, Mugridge, who had lifted his head and ascertained the extent of his loss, floundered over on the deck and buried his teeth in Wolf Larsen's leg. Wolf Larsen stooped, coolly, to the Cockney, and pressed with thumb and finger at the rear of the jaws and below the ears. The jaws opened with reluctance, and Wolf Larsen stepped free.

'As I was saying,' he went on, as though nothing unwonted had happened, 'the shark was not in the reckoning. It was—ahem—shall we say Providence?'

She gave no sign that she had heard, though the expression of her eyes changed to one of inexpressible loathing as she started to turn away. She no more than started, for she swayed and tottered, and reached her hand weakly out to mine. I caught her in time to save her from falling, and helped her to a seat on the cabin. I thought she might faint outright, but she controlled herself.

'Will you get a tourniquet, Mr. Van Weyden,' Wolf Larsen called to me.

I hesitated. Her lips moved, and though they formed no words, she commanded me with her eyes, plainly as speech, to go to the help of the unfortunate man. 'Please,' she managed to whisper, and I could but obey.

By now I had developed such skill at surgery that Wolf Larsen, with a few words of advice, left me to my task with a couple of sailors for assistants. For his task he elected a vengeance on the shark. A heavy swivel-hook, baited with fat salt-pork, was dropped overside; and by the time I had compressed the severed veins and arteries, the sailors were singing and heaving in the offending monster. I did not see it myself, but my assistants, first one and then the other, deserted me for a few moments to run amidships and look at what was going on. The shark, a sixteen-footer, was hoisted up against the main-rigging. Its jaws were pried apart to their greatest extension, and a stout stake, sharpened at both ends, was so inserted that when the pries were removed the spread jaws were fixed upon it. This accomplished, the hook was cut out. The shark dropped back into the sea, helpless, yet with its full strength, doomed—to lingering starvation—a living death less meet for it than for the man who devised the punishment.

CHAPTER XXII

I knew what it was as she came toward me. For ten minutes I had watched her talking earnestly with the engineer, and now, with a sign for silence, I drew her out of earshot of the helmsman. Her face was white and set; her large eyes, larger than usual what of the purpose in them, looked penetratingly into mine. I felt rather timid and apprehensive, for she had come to search Humphrey Van Weyden's soul, and Humphrey Van Weyden had nothing of which to be particularly proud since his advent on the *Ghost*.

We walked to the break of the poop, where she turned and faced me. I glanced around to see that no one was within hearing distance.

'What is it?' I asked gently; but the expression of determination on her face did not relax.

'I can readily understand,' she began, 'that this morning's affair was largely an accident; but I have been talking with Mr. Haskins. He tells me that the day we were rescued, even while I was in the cabin, two men were drowned, deliberately drowned—murdered.'

There was a query in her voice, and she faced me accusingly, as though I were guilty of the deed, or at least a party to it.

'The information is quite correct,' I answered. 'The two men were murdered.'

'And you permitted it!' she cried.

'I was unable to prevent it, is a better way of phrasing it,' I replied, still gently.

'But you tried to prevent it?' There was an emphasis on the 'tried,' and a pleading little note in her voice.

'Oh, but you didn't,' she hurried on, divining my answer. 'But why didn't you?'

I shrugged my shoulders. 'You must remember, Miss Brewster, that you are a new inhabitant of this little world, and that you do not yet understand the laws which operate within it. You bring with you certain fine conceptions of humanity, manhood, conduct, and such things; but here you will find them misconceptions. I have found it so,' I added, with an involuntary sigh.

She shook her head incredulously.

'What would you advise, then?' I asked. 'That I should take a knife, or a gun, or an axe, and kill this man?'

She half started back.

'No, not that!'

'Then what should I do? Kill myself?'

'You speak in purely materialistic terms,' she objected. 'There is such a thing as moral courage, and moral courage is never without effect.'

'Ah,' I smiled, 'you advise me to kill neither him nor myself, but to let him kill me.' I held up my hand as she was about to speak. 'For moral courage is a worthless asset on this little floating world. Leach, one of the men who were murdered, had moral courage to an unusual degree. So had the other man, Johnson. Not only did it not stand them in good stead, but it destroyed them. And so with me if I should exercise what little moral courage I may possess.

'You must understand, Miss Brewster, and understand clearly, that this man is a monster. He is without conscience. Nothing is sacred to him, nothing is too terrible for him to do. It was due to his whim that I was detained aboard in the first place. It is due to his whim that I am still alive. I do nothing, can do nothing, because I am a slave to this monster, as you are now a slave to him; because I desire to live, as you will desire to live; because I cannot fight and overcome him, just as you will not be able to fight and overcome him.'

She waited for me to go on.

'What remains? Mine is the role of the weak. I remain silent and suffer ignominy, as you will remain silent and suffer ignominy. And it is well. It is the best we can do if we wish to live. The battle is not always to the strong. We have not the strength with which to fight this man; we must dissimulate, and win, if win we can, by craft. If you will be advised by me, this is what you will do. I know my position is perilous, and I may say frankly that yours is even more perilous. We must stand together, without appearing to do so, in secret alliance. I shall not be able to side with you openly, and, no matter what indignities may be put upon me, you are to remain likewise silent. We must provoke no scenes with this man, nor cross his will. And we must keep smiling faces and be friendly with him no matter how repulsive it may be.'

She brushed her hand across her forehead in a puzzled way, saying, 'Still I do not understand.'

'You must do as I say,' I interrupted authoritatively, for I saw Wolf Larsen's gaze wandering toward us from where he paced up and down with Latimer amidships. 'Do as I say, and ere long you will find I am right.'

'What shall I do, then?' she asked, detecting the anxious glance I had shot at the object of our conversation, and impressed, I flatter myself, with the earnestness of my manner.

'Dispense with all the moral courage you can,' I said briskly. 'Don't arouse this man's animosity. Be quite friendly with him, talk with him, discuss literature and art with him—he is fond of such things. You will find him an interested listener and no fool. And for your own sake try to avoid witnessing, as much as you can, the brutalities of the ship. It will make it easier for you to act your part.'

'I am to lie,' she said in steady, rebellious tones, 'by speech and action to lie.'

Wolf Larsen had separated from Latimer and was coming toward us. I was desperate.

'Please, please understand me,' I said hurriedly, lowering my voice. 'All your experience of men and things is worthless here. You must begin over again. I know,—I can see it—you have, among other ways, been used to managing people with your eyes, letting your moral courage speak out through them, as it were. You have already managed me with your eyes, commanded me with them. But don't try it on Wolf Larsen. You could as easily control a lion, while he would make a mock of you. He would—I have always been proud of the fact that I discovered him,' I said, turning the conversation as Wolf Larsen stepped on the poop and joined us. 'The editors were afraid of him and the publishers would have none of him. But I knew, and his genius and my judgment were vindicated when he made that magnificent hit with his 'Forge.''

'And it was a newspaper poem,' she said glibly.

'It did happen to see the light in a newspaper,' I replied, 'but not because the magazine editors had been denied a glimpse at it.'

'We were talking of Harris,' I said to Wolf Larsen.

'Oh, yes,' he acknowledged. 'I remember the 'Forge.' Filled with pretty sentiments and an almighty faith in human illusions. By the way, Mr. Van Weyden, you'd better look in on Cooky. He's complaining and restless.'

Thus was I bluntly dismissed from the poop, only to find Mugridge sleeping soundly from the morphine I had given him. I made no haste to return on deck, and when I did I was gratified to see Miss Brewster in animated conversation with Wolf Larsen. As I say, the sight gratified me. She was following my advice. And yet I was conscious of a slight shock or hurt in that she was able to do the thing I had begged her to do and which she had notably disliked.

CHAPTER XXIII

Brave winds, blowing fair, swiftly drove the *Ghost* northward into the seal herd. We encountered it well up to the forty-fourth parallel, in a raw and stormy sea across which the wind harried the fog-banks in eternal flight. For days at a time we could never see the sun nor take an observation; then the wind would sweep the face of the ocean clean, the waves would ripple and flash, and we would learn where we were. A day of clear weather might follow, or three days or four, and then the fog would settle down upon us, seemingly thicker than ever.

The hunting was perilous; yet the boats, lowered day after day, were swallowed up in the grey obscurity, and were seen no more till nightfall, and often not till long after, when they would creep in like sea-wraiths, one by one, out of the grey. Wainwright—the hunter whom Wolf Larsen had stolen with boat and men—took advantage of the veiled sea and escaped. He disappeared one morning in the encircling fog with his two men, and we never saw them again, though it was not many days when we learned that they had passed from schooner to schooner until they finally regained their own.

This was the thing I had set my mind upon doing, but the opportunity never offered. It was not in the mate's province to go out in the boats, and though I manœuvred cunningly for it, Wolf Larsen never granted me the privilege. Had he done so, I should have managed somehow to carry Miss Brewster away with me. As it was, the situation was approaching a stage which I was afraid to consider. I involuntarily shunned the thought of it, and yet the thought continually arose in my mind like a haunting spectre.

I had read sea-romances in my time, wherein figured, as a matter of course, the lone woman in the midst of a shipload of men; but I learned, now, that I had never comprehended the deeper significance of such a situation—the thing the writers harped upon and exploited so thoroughly. And here it was, now, and I was face to face with it. That it should be as vital as possible, it required no more than that the woman should be Maud Brewster, who now charmed me in person as she had long charmed me through her work.

No one more out of environment could be imagined. She was a delicate, ethereal creature, swaying and willowy, light and graceful of movement. It never seemed to me that she walked, or, at least, walked after the ordinary manner of mortals. Hers was an extreme lithesomeness, and she moved with a certain indefinable airiness, approaching one as down might float or as a bird on noiseless wings.

She was like a bit of Dresden china, and I was continually impressed with what I may call her fragility. As at the time I caught her arm when helping her below, so at any time I was quite prepared, should stress or rough handling befall her, to see her crumble away. I have never seen body and spirit in such perfect accord. Describe her verse, as the critics have described it, as sublimated and spiritual, and you have described her body. It seemed to partake of her soul, to have analogous attributes, and to link it to life with the slenderest of chains. Indeed, she trod the earth lightly, and in her constitution there was little of the robust clay.

She was in striking contrast to Wolf Larsen. Each was nothing that the other was, everything that the other was not. I noted them walking the deck together one morning, and I likened them to the extreme ends of the human ladder of evolution—the one the culmination of all savagery, the other the finished product of the finest civilization. True, Wolf Larsen possessed intellect to an unusual degree, but it was directed solely to the exercise of his savage instincts and made him but the more formidable a savage. He was splendidly muscled, a heavy man, and though he strode with the certitude and directness of the physical man, there was nothing heavy about his stride. The jungle and the wilderness lurked in the uplift and downput of his feet.

He was cat-footed, and lithe, and strong, always strong. I likened him to some great tiger, a beast of prowess and prey. He looked it, and the piercing glitter that arose at times in his eyes was the same piercing glitter I had observed in the eyes of caged leopards and other preying creatures of the wild.

But this day, as I noted them pacing up and down, I saw that it was she who terminated the walk. They came up to where I was standing by the entrance to the companion-way. Though she betrayed it by no outward sign, I felt, somehow, that she was greatly perturbed. She made some idle remark, looking at me, and laughed lightly enough; but I saw her eyes return to his, involuntarily, as though fascinated; then they fell, but not swiftly enough to veil the rush of terror that filled them.

It was in his eyes that I saw the cause of her perturbation. Ordinarily grey and cold and harsh, they were now warm and soft and golden, and all a-dance with tiny lights that dimmed and faded, or welled up till the full orbs were flooded with a glowing radiance. Perhaps it was to this that the golden colour was due; but golden his eyes were, enticing and masterful, at the same time luring and compelling, and speaking a demand and clamour of the blood which no woman, much less Maud Brewster, could misunderstand.

Her own terror rushed upon me, and in that moment of fear—the most terrible fear a man can experience—I knew that in inexpressible ways she was dear to me. The knowledge that I loved her rushed upon me with the terror, and with both emotions gripping at my heart and causing my blood at the same time to chill and to leap riotously, I felt myself drawn by a power without me and beyond me, and found my eyes returning against my will to gaze into the eyes of Wolf Larsen. But he had recovered himself. The golden colour and the dancing lights were gone. Cold and grey and glittering they were as he bowed brusquely and turned away.

'I am afraid,' she whispered, with a shiver. 'I am so afraid.'

I, too, was afraid, and what of my discovery of how much she meant to me my mind was in a turmoil; but, I succeeded in answering quite calmly:

'All will come right, Miss Brewster. Trust me, it will come right.'

She answered with a grateful little smile that sent my heart pounding, and started to descend the companion-stairs.

For a long while I remained standing where she had left me. There was imperative need to adjust myself, to consider the significance of the changed aspect of things. It had come, at last, love had come, when I least expected it and under the most forbidding conditions. Of course, my philosophy had always recognized the inevitableness of the love-call sooner or later; but long years of bookish silence had made me inattentive and unprepared.

And now it had come! Maud Brewster! My memory flashed back to that first thin little volume on my desk, and I saw before me, as though in the concrete, the row of thin little volumes on my library shelf. How I had welcomed each of them! Each year one had come from the press, and to me each was the advent of the year. They had voiced a kindred intellect and spirit, and as such I had received them into a camaraderie of the mind; but now their place was in my heart.

My heart? A revulsion of feeling came over me. I seemed to stand outside myself and to look at myself incredulously. Maud Brewster! Humphrey Van Weyden, 'the cold-blooded fish,' the 'emotionless monster,' the 'analytical demon,' of Charley Furuseth's christening, in love! And then, without rhyme or reason, all sceptical, my mind flew back to a small biographical note in the red-bound *Who's Who*, and I said to myself, 'She was born in Cambridge, and she is twenty-seven years old.' And then I said, 'Twenty-seven years old and still free and fancy free?' But how did I know she was fancy free? And the pang of new-born jealousy put all incredulity to flight. There was no doubt about it. I was jealous; therefore I loved. And the woman I loved was Maud Brewster.

I, Humphrey Van Weyden, was in love! And again the doubt assailed me. Not that I was afraid of it, however, or reluctant to meet it. On the contrary, idealist that I was to the most pronounced degree, my philosophy had always recognized and guerdoned love as the greatest thing in the world, the aim and the summit of being, the most exquisite pitch of joy and happiness to which life could thrill, the thing of all things to be hailed and welcomed and taken into the heart. But now that it had come I could not believe. I could not be so fortunate. It was too good, too good to be true. Symons's lines came into my head:

> 'I wandered all these years among
> A world of women, seeking you.'

And then I had ceased seeking. It was not for me, this greatest thing in the world, I had decided. Furuseth was right; I was abnormal, an 'emotionless monster,' a strange bookish creature, capable of pleasuring in sensations only of the mind. And though I had been surrounded by women all my days, my appreciation of them had been æsthetic and nothing more. I had actually, at times, considered myself outside the pale, a monkish fellow denied the eternal or the passing passions I saw and understood so well in others. And now it had come! Undreamed of and unheralded, it had come. In what could have been no less than an ecstasy, I left my post at the head of the companion-way and started along the deck, murmuring to myself those beautiful lines of Mrs. Browning:

> 'I lived with visions for my company
> Instead of men and women years ago,
> And found them gentle mates, nor thought to know
> A sweeter music than they played to me.'

But the sweeter music was playing in my ears, and I was blind and oblivious to all about me. The sharp voice of Wolf Larsen aroused me.

'What the hell are you up to?' he was demanding.

I had strayed forward where the sailors were painting, and I came to myself to find my advancing foot on the verge of overturning a paint-pot.

'Sleep-walking, sunstroke,—what?' he barked.

'No; indigestion,' I retorted, and continued my walk as if nothing untoward had occurred.

CHAPTER XXIV

Among the most vivid memories of my life are those of the events on the *Ghost* which occurred during the forty hours succeeding the discovery of my love for Maud Brewster. I, who had lived my life in quiet places, only to enter at the age of thirty-five upon a course of the most irrational adventure I could have imagined, never had more incident and excitement crammed into any forty hours of my experience. Nor can I quite close my ears to a small voice of pride which tells me I did not do so badly, all things considered.

To begin with, at the midday dinner, Wolf Larsen informed the hunters that they were to eat thenceforth in the steerage. It was an unprecedented thing on sealing-schooners, where it is the custom for the hunters to rank, unofficially as officers. He gave no reason, but his motive was obvious enough. Horner and Smoke had been displaying a gallantry toward Maud Brewster, ludicrous in itself and inoffensive to her, but to him evidently distasteful.

The announcement was received with black silence, though the other four hunters glanced significantly at the two who had been the cause of their banishment. Jock Horner, quiet as was his way, gave no sign; but the blood surged darkly across Smoke's forehead, and he half opened his mouth to speak. Wolf Larsen was watching him, waiting for him, the steely glitter in his eyes; but Smoke closed his mouth again without having said anything.

'Anything to say?' the other demanded aggressively.

It was a challenge, but Smoke refused to accept it.

'About what?' he asked, so innocently that Wolf Larsen was disconcerted, while the others smiled.

'Oh, nothing,' Wolf Larsen said lamely. 'I just thought you might want to register a kick.'

'About what?' asked the imperturbable Smoke.

Smoke's mates were now smiling broadly. His captain could have killed him, and I doubt not that blood would have flowed had not Maud Brewster been present. For that matter, it was her presence which enabled. Smoke to act as he did. He was too discreet and cautious a man to incur Wolf Larsen's anger at a time when that anger could be expressed in terms stronger than words. I was in fear that a struggle might take place, but a cry from the helmsman made it easy for the situation to save itself.

'Smoke ho!' the cry came down the open companion-way.

'How's it bear?' Wolf Larsen called up.

'Dead astern, sir.'

'Maybe it's a Russian,' suggested Latimer.

His words brought anxiety into the faces of the other hunters. A Russian could mean but one thing—a cruiser. The hunters, never more than roughly aware of the position of the ship, nevertheless knew that we were close to the boundaries of the forbidden sea, while Wolf Larsen's record as a poacher was notorious. All eyes centred upon him.

'We're dead safe,' he assured them with a laugh. 'No salt mines this time, Smoke. But I'll tell you what—I'll lay odds of five to one it's the *Macedonia*.'

No one accepted his offer, and he went on: 'In which event, I'll lay ten to one there's trouble breezing up.'

'No, thank you,' Latimer spoke up. 'I don't object to losing my money, but I like to get a run for it anyway. There never was a time when there wasn't trouble when you and that brother of yours got together, and I'll lay twenty to one on that.'

A general smile followed, in which Wolf Larsen joined, and the dinner went on smoothly, thanks to me, for he treated me abominably the rest of the meal, sneering at me and patronizing me till I was all a-tremble with suppressed rage. Yet I knew I must control myself for Maud Brewster's sake, and I received my reward when her eyes caught mine for a fleeting second, and they said, as distinctly as if she spoke, 'Be brave, be brave.'

We left the table to go on deck, for a steamer was a welcome break in the monotony of the sea on which we floated, while the conviction that it was Death Larsen and the *Macedonia* added to the excitement. The stiff breeze and heavy sea which had sprung up the previous afternoon had been moderating all morning, so that it was now possible to lower the boats for an afternoon's hunt. The hunting promised to be profitable. We had sailed since daylight across a sea barren of seals, and were now running into the herd.

The smoke was still miles astern, but overhauling us rapidly, when we lowered our boats. They spread out and struck a northerly course across the ocean. Now and again we saw a sail lower, heard the reports of the shot-guns, and saw the sail go up again. The seals were thick, the wind was dying away; everything favoured a big catch. As we ran off to get our leeward position of the last lee boat, we found the ocean fairly carpeted with sleeping seals. They were all about us, thicker than I had ever seen them before, in twos and threes and bunches, stretched full length on the surface and sleeping for all the world like so many lazy young dogs.

Under the approaching smoke the hull and upper-works of a steamer were growing larger. It was the *Macedonia*. I read her name through the glasses as she passed by scarcely a mile to starboard. Wolf Larsen looked savagely at the vessel, while Maud Brewster was curious.

'Where is the trouble you were so sure was breezing up, Captain Larsen?' she asked gaily.

He glanced at her, a moment's amusement softening his features.

'What did you expect? That they'd come aboard and cut our throats?'

'Something like that,' she confessed. 'You understand, seal-hunters are so new and strange to me that I am quite ready to expect anything.'

He nodded his head. 'Quite right, quite right. Your error is that you failed to expect the worst.'

'Why, what can be worse than cutting our throats?' she asked, with pretty naïve surprise.

'Cutting our purses,' he answered. 'Man is so made these days that his capacity for living is determined by the money he possesses.'

'Who steals my purse steals trash,' she quoted.

'Who steals my purse steals my right to live,' was the reply, 'old saws to the contrary. For he steals my bread and meat and bed, and in so doing imperils my life. There are not enough soup-kitchens and bread-lines to go around, you know, and when men have nothing in their purses they usually die, and die miserably—unless they are able to fill their purses pretty speedily.'

'But I fail to see that this steamer has any designs on your purse.'

'Wait and you will see,' he answered grimly.

We did not have long to wait. Having passed several miles beyond our line of boats, the *Macedonia* proceeded to lower her own. We knew she carried fourteen boats to our five (we were one short through the desertion of Wainwright), and she began dropping them far to leeward of our last boat, continued dropping them athwart our course, and finished dropping them far to windward of our first weather boat. The hunting, for us, was spoiled. There were no seals behind us, and ahead of us the line of fourteen boats, like a huge broom, swept the herd before it.

Our boats hunted across the two or three miles of water between them and the point where the *Macedonia's* had been dropped, and then headed for home. The wind had fallen to a whisper, the ocean was growing calmer and calmer, and this, coupled with the presence of the great herd, made a perfect hunting day—one of the two or three days to be encountered in the whole of a lucky season. An angry lot of men, boat-pullers and steerers as well as hunters, swarmed over our side. Each man felt that he had been robbed; and the boats were hoisted in amid curses, which, if curses had power, would have settled Death Larsen for all eternity—'Dead and damned for a dozen iv eternities,' commented Louis, his eyes twinkling up at me as he rested from hauling taut the lashings of his boat.

'Listen to them, and find if it is hard to discover the most vital thing in their souls,' said Wolf Larsen. 'Faith? and love? and high ideals? The good? the beautiful? the true?'

'Their innate sense of right has been violated,' Maud Brewster said, joining the conversation.

She was standing a dozen feet away, one hand resting on the main-shrouds and her body swaying gently to the slight roll of the ship. She had not raised her voice, and yet I was struck by its clear and bell-like tone. Ah, it was sweet in my ears! I scarcely dared look at her just then, for the fear of betraying myself. A boy's cap was perched on her head, and her hair, light brown and arranged in a loose and fluffy order that caught the sun, seemed an aureole about the delicate oval of her face. She was positively bewitching, and, withal, sweetly spirituelle, if not saintly. All my old-time marvel at life returned to me at sight of this splendid incarnation of it, and Wolf Larsen's cold explanation of life and its meaning was truly ridiculous and laughable.

'A sentimentalist,' he sneered, 'like Mr. Van Weyden. Those men are cursing because their desires have been outraged. That is all. What desires? The desires for the good grub and soft beds ashore which a handsome pay-day brings them—the women and the drink, the gorging and the beastliness which so truly expresses them, the best that is in them, their highest aspirations, their ideals, if you please. The exhibition they make of their feelings is not a touching sight, yet it shows how deeply they have been touched, how deeply their purses have been touched, for to lay hands on their purses is to lay hands on their souls.'

'You hardly behave as if your purse had been touched,' she said, smilingly.

'Then it so happens that I am behaving differently, for my purse and my soul have both been touched. At the current price of skins in the London market, and based on a fair estimate of what the afternoon's catch would have been had not the *Macedonia* hogged it, the *Ghost* has lost about fifteen hundred dollars' worth of skins.'

'You speak so calmly—' she began.

'But I do not feel calm; I could kill the man who robbed me,' he interrupted. 'Yes, yes, I know, and that man my brother—more sentiment! Bah!'

His face underwent a sudden change. His voice was less harsh and wholly sincere as he said:

'You must be happy, you sentimentalists, really and truly happy at dreaming and finding things good, and, because you find some of them good, feeling good yourself.

Now, tell me, you two, do you find me good?'

'You are good to look upon—in a way,' I qualified.

'There are in you all powers for good,' was Maud Brewster's answer.

'There you are!' he cried at her, half angrily. 'Your words are empty to me. There is nothing clear and sharp and definite about the thought you have expressed. You cannot pick it up in your two hands and look at it. In point of fact, it is not a thought. It is a feeling, a sentiment, a something based upon illusion and not a product of the intellect at all.'

As he went on his voice again grew soft, and a confiding note came into it. 'Do you know, I sometimes catch myself wishing that I, too, were blind to the facts of life and only knew its fancies and illusions. They're wrong, all wrong, of course, and contrary to reason; but in the face of them my reason tells me, wrong and most wrong, that to dream and live illusions gives greater delight. And after all, delight is the wage for living. Without delight, living is a worthless act. To labour at living and be unpaid is worse than to be dead. He who delights the most lives the most, and your dreams and unrealities are less disturbing to you and more gratifying than are my facts to me.'

He shook his head slowly, pondering.

'I often doubt, I often doubt, the worthwhileness of reason. Dreams must be more substantial and satisfying. Emotional delight is more filling and lasting than intellectual delight; and, besides, you pay for your moments of intellectual delight by having the blues. Emotional delight is followed by no more than jaded senses which speedily recuperate. I envy you, I envy you.'

He stopped abruptly, and then on his lips formed one of his strange quizzical smiles, as he added:

'It's from my brain I envy you, take notice, and not from my heart. My reason dictates it. The envy is an intellectual product. I am like a sober man looking upon drunken men, and, greatly weary, wishing he, too, were drunk.'

'Or like a wise man looking upon fools and wishing he, too, were a fool,' I laughed.

'Quite so,' he said. 'You are a blessed, bankrupt pair of fools. You have no facts in your pocketbook.'

'Yet we spend as freely as you,' was Maud Brewster's contribution.

'More freely, because it costs you nothing.'

'And because we draw upon eternity,' she retorted.

'Whether you do or think you do, it's the same thing. You spend what you haven't got, and in return you get greater value from spending what you haven't got than I get from spending what I have got, and what I have sweated to get.'

'Why don't you change the basis of your coinage, then?' she queried teasingly.

He looked at her quickly, half-hopefully, and then said, all regretfully: 'Too late. I'd like to, perhaps, but I can't. My pocketbook is stuffed with the old coinage, and it's a stubborn thing. I can never bring myself to recognize anything else as valid.'

He ceased speaking, and his gaze wandered absently past her and became lost in the placid sea. The old primal melancholy was strong upon him. He was quivering to it. He had reasoned himself into a spell of the blues, and within few hours one could look for the devil within him to be up and stirring. I remembered Charley Furuseth, and knew this man's sadness as the penalty which the materialist ever pays for his materialism.

CHAPTER XXV

'You've been on deck, Mr. Van Weyden,' Wolf Larsen said, the following morning at the breakfast-table, 'How do things look?'

'Clear enough,' I answered, glancing at the sunshine which streamed down the open companion-way. 'Fair westerly breeze, with a promise of stiffening, if Louis predicts correctly.'

He nodded his head in a pleased way. 'Any signs of fog?'

'Thick banks in the north and north-west.'

He nodded his head again, evincing even greater satisfaction than before.

'What of the *Macedonia?*'

'Not sighted,' I answered.

I could have sworn his face fell at the intelligence, but why he should be disappointed I could not conceive.

I was soon to learn. 'Smoke ho!' came the hail from on deck, and his face brightened.

'Good!' he exclaimed, and left the table at once to go on deck and into the steerage, where the hunters were taking the first breakfast of their exile.

Maud Brewster and I scarcely touched the food before us, gazing, instead, in silent anxiety at each other, and listening to Wolf Larsen's voice, which easily penetrated the cabin through the intervening bulkhead. He spoke at length, and his conclusion was greeted with a wild roar of cheers. The bulkhead was too thick for us to hear what he said; but whatever it was it affected the hunters strongly, for the cheering was followed by loud exclamations and shouts of joy.

From the sounds on deck I knew that the sailors had been routed out and were preparing to lower the boats. Maud Brewster accompanied me on deck, but I left her at the break of the poop, where she might watch the scene and not be in it. The sailors must have learned whatever project was on hand, and the vim and snap they put into their work attested their enthusiasm. The hunters came trooping on deck with shot-guns and ammunition-boxes, and, most unusual, their rifles. The latter were rarely taken in the boats, for a seal shot at long range with a rifle invariably sank before a boat could reach it. But each hunter this day had his rifle and a large supply of cartridges. I noticed they grinned with satisfaction whenever they looked at the *Macedonia's* smoke, which was rising higher and higher as she approached from the west.

The five boats went over the side with a rush, spread out like the ribs of a fan, and set a northerly course, as on the preceding afternoon, for us to follow. I watched for some time, curiously, but there seemed nothing extraordinary about their behaviour. They lowered sails, shot seals, and hoisted sails again, and continued on their way as I had always seen them do. The *Macedonia* repeated her performance of yesterday, 'hogging' the sea by dropping her line of boats in advance of ours and across our course. Fourteen boats require a considerable spread of ocean for comfortable hunting, and when she had completely lapped our line she continued steaming into the north-east, dropping more boats as she went.

'What's up?' I asked Wolf Larsen, unable longer to keep my curiosity in check.

'Never mind what's up,' he answered gruffly. 'You won't be a thousand years in finding out, and in the meantime just pray for plenty of wind.'

'Oh, well, I don't mind telling you,' he said the next moment. 'I'm going to give that brother of mine a taste of his own medicine. In short, I'm going to play the hog myself, and not for one day, but for the rest of the season,—if we're in luck.'

'And if we're not?' I queried.

'Not to be considered,' he laughed. 'We simply must be in luck, or it's all up with us.'

He had the wheel at the time, and I went forward to my hospital in the forecastle, where lay the two crippled men, Nilson and Thomas Mugridge. Nilson was as cheerful as could be expected, for his broken leg was knitting nicely; but the Cockney was desperately melancholy, and I was aware of a great sympathy for the unfortunate creature. And the marvel of it was that still he lived and clung to life. The brutal years had reduced his meagre body to splintered wreckage, and yet the spark of life within burned brightly as ever.

'With an artificial foot—and they make excellent ones—you will be stumping ships' galleys to the end of time,' I assured him jovially.

But his answer was serious, nay, solemn. 'I don't know about wot you s'y, Mr. Van W'yden, but I do know I'll never rest 'appy till I see that 'ell-'ound bloody well dead. 'E cawn't live as long as me. 'E's got no right to live, an' as the Good Word puts it, 'E shall shorely die,' an' I s'y, 'Amen, an' damn soon at that.'

When I returned on deck I found Wolf Larsen steering mainly with one hand, while with the other hand he held the marine glasses and studied the situation of the boats, paying particular attention to the position of the *Macedonia*. The only change noticeable in our boats was that they had hauled close on the wind and were heading several points west of north. Still, I could not see the expediency of the manœuvre, for the free sea was still intercepted by the *Macedonia's* five weather boats, which, in turn, had hauled close on the wind. Thus they slowly diverged toward the west, drawing farther away from the remainder of the boats in their line. Our boats were rowing as well as sailing. Even the hunters were pulling, and with three pairs of oars in the water they rapidly overhauled what I may appropriately term the enemy.

The smoke of the *Macedonia* had dwindled to a dim blot on the north-eastern horizon. Of the steamer herself nothing was to be seen. We had been loafing along, till now, our sails shaking half the time and spilling the wind; and twice, for short periods, we had been hove to. But there was no more loafing. Sheets were trimmed, and Wolf Larsen proceeded to put the *Ghost* through her paces. We ran past our line of boats and bore down upon the first weather boat of the other line.

'Down that flying jib, Mr. Van Weyden,' Wolf Larsen commanded. 'And stand by to back over the jibs.'

I ran forward and had the downhaul of the flying jib all in and fast as we slipped by the boat a hundred feet to leeward. The three men in it gazed at us suspiciously. They had been hogging the sea, and they knew Wolf Larsen, by reputation at any rate. I noted that the hunter, a huge Scandinavian sitting in the bow, held his rifle, ready to hand, across his knees. It should have been in its proper place in the rack. When they came opposite our stern, Wolf Larsen greeted them with a wave of the hand, and cried:

'Come on board and have a 'gam'!'

'To gam,' among the sealing-schooners, is a substitute for the verbs 'to visit,' 'to gossip.' It expresses the garrulity of the sea, and is a pleasant break in the monotony of the life.

The *Ghost* swung around into the wind, and I finished my work forward in time to run aft and lend a hand with the mainsheet.

'You will please stay on deck, Miss Brewster,' Wolf Larsen said, as he started forward to meet his guest. 'And you too, Mr. Van Weyden.'

The boat had lowered its sail and run alongside. The hunter, golden bearded like a sea-king, came over the rail and dropped on deck. But his hugeness could not quite overcome his apprehensiveness. Doubt and distrust showed strongly in his face. It was a transparent face, for all of its hairy shield, and advertised instant relief when he glanced from Wolf Larsen to me, noted that there was only the pair of us, and then glanced over his own two men who had joined him. Surely he had little reason to be afraid. He towered like a Goliath above Wolf Larsen. He must have measured six feet eight or nine inches in stature, and I subsequently learned his weight—240 pounds. And there was no fat about him. It was all bone and muscle.

A return of apprehension was apparent when, at the top of the companion-way, Wolf Larsen invited him below. But he reassured himself with a glance down at his host—a big man himself but dwarfed by the propinquity of the giant. So all hesitancy vanished, and the pair descended into the cabin. In the meantime, his two men, as was the wont of visiting sailors, had gone forward into the forecastle to do some visiting themselves.

Suddenly, from the cabin came a great, choking bellow, followed by all the sounds of a furious struggle. It was the leopard and the lion, and the lion made all the noise. Wolf Larsen was the leopard.

'You see the sacredness of our hospitality,' I said bitterly to Maud Brewster.

She nodded her head that she heard, and I noted in her face the signs of the same sickness at sight or sound of violent struggle from which I had suffered so severely during my first weeks on the *Ghost*.

'Wouldn't it be better if you went forward, say by the steerage companion-way, until it is over?' I suggested.

She shook her head and gazed at me pitifully. She was not frightened, but appalled, rather, at the human animality of it.

'You will understand,' I took advantage of the opportunity to say, 'whatever part I take in what is going on and what is to come, that I am compelled to take it—if you and I are ever to get out of this scrape with our lives.'

'It is not nice—for me,' I added.

'I understand,' she said, in a weak, far-away voice, and her eyes showed me that she did understand.

The sounds from below soon died away. Then Wolf Larsen came alone on deck. There was a slight flush under his bronze, but otherwise he bore no signs of the battle.

'Send those two men aft, Mr. Van Weyden,' he said.

I obeyed, and a minute or two later they stood before him. 'Hoist in your boat,' he said to them. 'Your hunter's decided to stay aboard awhile and doesn't want it pounding alongside.'

'Hoist in your boat, I said,' he repeated, this time in sharper tones as they hesitated to do his bidding.

'Who knows? you may have to sail with me for a time,' he said, quite softly, with a silken threat that belied the softness, as they moved slowly to comply, 'and we might as well start with a friendly understanding. Lively now! Death Larsen makes you jump better than that, and you know it!'

Their movements perceptibly quickened under his coaching, and as the boat swung inboard I was sent forward to let go the jibs. Wolf Larsen, at the wheel, directed the *Ghost* after the *Macedonia's* second weather boat.

Under way, and with nothing for the time being to do, I turned my attention to the situation of the boats. The *Macedonia's* third weather boat was being attacked by two of ours, the fourth by our remaining three; and the fifth, turn about, was taking a hand in the defence of its nearest mate. The fight had opened at long distance, and the rifles were cracking steadily. A quick, snappy sea was being kicked up by the wind, a condition which prevented fine shooting; and now and again, as we drew closer, we could see the bullets zip-zipping from wave to wave.

The boat we were pursuing had squared away and was running before the wind to escape us, and, in the course of its flight, to take part in repulsing our general boat attack.

Attending to sheets and tacks now left me little time to see what was taking place, but I happened to be on the poop when Wolf Larsen ordered the two strange sailors forward and into the forecastle. They went sullenly, but they went. He next ordered Miss Brewster below, and smiled at the instant horror that leapt into her eyes.

'You'll find nothing gruesome down there,' he said, 'only an unhurt man securely made fast to the ring-bolts. Bullets are liable to come aboard, and I don't want you killed, you know.'

Even as he spoke, a bullet was deflected by a brass-capped spoke of the wheel between his hands and screeched off through the air to windward.

'You see,' he said to her; and then to me, 'Mr. Van Weyden, will you take the wheel?'

Maud Brewster had stepped inside the companion-way so that only her head was exposed. Wolf Larsen had procured a rifle and was throwing a cartridge into the barrel. I begged her with my eyes to go below, but she smiled and said:

'We may be feeble land-creatures without legs, but we can show Captain Larsen that we are at least as brave as he.'

He gave her a quick look of admiration.

'I like you a hundred per cent. better for that,' he said. 'Books, and brains, and bravery. You are well-rounded, a blue-stocking fit to be the wife of a pirate chief. Ahem, we'll discuss that later,' he smiled, as a bullet struck solidly into the cabin wall.

I saw his eyes flash golden as he spoke, and I saw the terror mount in her own.

'We are braver,' I hastened to say. 'At least, speaking for myself, I know I am braver than Captain Larsen.'

It was I who was now favoured by a quick look. He was wondering if I were making fun of him. I put three or four spokes over to counteract a sheer toward the wind on the part of the *Ghost*, and then steadied her. Wolf Larsen was still waiting an explanation, and I pointed down to my knees.

'You will observe there,' I said, 'a slight trembling. It is because I am afraid, the flesh is afraid; and I am afraid in my mind because I do not wish to die. But my spirit masters the trembling flesh and the qualms of the mind. I am more than brave. I am courageous. Your flesh is not afraid. You are not afraid. On the one hand, it costs you nothing to encounter danger; on the other hand, it even gives you delight. You enjoy it. You may be unafraid, Mr. Larsen, but you must grant that the bravery is mine.'

'You're right,' he acknowledged at once. 'I never thought of it in that way before.

But is the opposite true? If you are braver than I, am I more cowardly than you?'

We both laughed at the absurdity, and he dropped down to the deck and rested his rifle across the rail. The bullets we had received had travelled nearly a mile, but by now we had cut that distance in half. He fired three careful shots. The first struck fifty feet to windward of the boat, the second alongside; and at the third the boat-steerer let loose his steering-oar and crumpled up in the bottom of the boat.

'I guess that'll fix them,' Wolf Larsen said, rising to his feet. 'I couldn't afford to let the hunter have it, and there is a chance the boat-puller doesn't know how to steer. In which case, the hunter cannot steer and shoot at the same time.'

His reasoning was justified, for the boat rushed at once into the wind and the hunter sprang aft to take the boat-steerer's place. There was no more shooting, though the rifles were still cracking merrily from the other boats.

The hunter had managed to get the boat before the wind again, but we ran down upon it, going at least two feet to its one. A hundred yards away, I saw the boat-puller pass a rifle to the hunter. Wolf Larsen went amidships and took the coil of the throat-halyards from its pin. Then he peered over the rail with levelled rifle. Twice I saw the hunter let go the steering-oar with one hand, reach for his rifle, and hesitate. We were now alongside and foaming past.

'Here, you!' Wolf Larsen cried suddenly to the boat-puller. 'Take a turn!'

At the same time he flung the coil of rope. It struck fairly, nearly knocking the man over, but he did not obey. Instead, he looked to his hunter for orders. The hunter, in turn, was in a quandary. His rifle was between his knees, but if he let go the steering-oar in order to shoot, the boat would sweep around and collide with the schooner. Also he saw Wolf Larsen's rifle bearing upon him and knew he would be shot ere he could get his rifle into play.

'Take a turn,' he said quietly to the man.

The boat-puller obeyed, taking a turn around the little forward thwart and paying the line as it jerked taut. The boat sheered out with a rush, and the hunter steadied it to a parallel course some twenty feet from the side of the *Ghost.*

'Now, get that sail down and come alongside!' Wolf Larsen ordered.

He never let go his rifle, even passing down the tackles with one hand. When they were fast, bow and stern, and the two uninjured men prepared to come aboard, the hunter picked up his rifle as if to place it in a secure position.

'Drop it!' Wolf Larsen cried, and the hunter dropped it as though it were hot and had burned him.

Once aboard, the two prisoners hoisted in the boat and under Wolf Larsen's direction carried the wounded boat-steerer down into the forecastle.

'If our five boats do as well as you and I have done, we'll have a pretty full crew,' Wolf Larsen said to me.

'The man you shot—he is—I hope?' Maud Brewster quavered.

'In the shoulder,' he answered. 'Nothing serious, Mr. Van Weyden will pull him around as good as ever in three or four weeks.'

'But he won't pull those chaps around, from the look of it,' he added, pointing at the *Macedonia's* third boat, for which I had been steering and which was now nearly abreast of us. 'That's Horner's and Smoke's work. I told them we wanted live men, not carcasses. But the joy of shooting to hit is a most compelling thing, when once you've learned how to shoot. Ever experienced it, Mr. Van Weyden?'

I shook my head and regarded their work. It had indeed been bloody, for they had drawn off and joined our other three boats in the attack on the remaining two of the enemy. The deserted boat was in the trough of the sea, rolling drunkenly across each comber, its loose spritsail out at right angles to it and fluttering and flapping in the wind. The hunter and boat-puller were both lying awkwardly in the bottom, but the boat-steerer lay across the gunwale, half in and half out, his arms trailing in the water and his head rolling from side to side.

'Don't look, Miss Brewster, please don't look,' I had begged of her, and I was glad that she had minded me and been spared the sight.

'Head right into the bunch, Mr. Van Weyden,' was Wolf Larsen's command.

As we drew nearer, the firing ceased, and we saw that the fight was over. The remaining two boats had been captured by our five, and the seven were grouped together, waiting to be picked up.

'Look at that!' I cried involuntarily, pointing to the north-east.

The blot of smoke which indicated the *Macedonia's* position had reappeared.

'Yes, I've been watching it,' was Wolf Larsen's calm reply. He measured the distance away to the fog-bank, and for an instant paused to feel the weight of the wind on his cheek. 'We'll make it, I think; but you can depend upon it that blessed brother of mine has twigged our little game and is just a-humping for us. Ah, look at that!'

The blot of smoke had suddenly grown larger, and it was very black.

'I'll beat you out, though, brother mine,' he chuckled. 'I'll beat you out, and I hope you no worse than that you rack your old engines into scrap.'

When we hove to, a hasty though orderly confusion reigned. The boats came aboard from every side at once. As fast as the prisoners came over the rail they were marshalled forward to the forecastle by our hunters, while our sailors hoisted in the boats, pell-mell, dropping them anywhere upon the deck and not stopping to lash them. We were already under way, all sails set and drawing, and the sheets being slacked off for a wind abeam, as the last boat lifted clear of the water and swung in the tackles.

There was need for haste. The *Macedonia*, belching the blackest of smoke from her funnel, was charging down upon us from out of the north-east. Neglecting the boats that remained to her, she had altered her course so as to anticipate ours. She was not running straight for us, but ahead of us. Our courses were converging like the sides of an angle, the vertex of which was at the edge of the fog-bank. It was there, or not at all, that the *Macedonia* could hope to catch us. The hope for the *Ghost* lay in that she should pass that point before the *Macedonia* arrived at it.

Wolf Larsen was steering, his eyes glistening and snapping as they dwelt upon and leaped from detail to detail of the chase. Now he studied the sea to windward for signs of the wind slackening or freshening, now the *Macedonia*; and again, his eyes roved over every sail, and he gave commands to slack a sheet here a trifle, to come in on one there a trifle, till he was drawing out of the *Ghost* the last bit of speed she possessed. All feuds and grudges were forgotten, and I was surprised at the alacrity with which the men who had so long endured his brutality sprang to execute his orders. Strange to say, the unfortunate Johnson came into my mind as we lifted and surged and heeled along, and I was aware of a regret that he was not alive and present; he had so loved the *Ghost* and delighted in her sailing powers.

'Better get your rifles, you fellows,' Wolf Larsen called to our hunters; and the five men lined the lee rail, guns in hand, and waited.

The *Macedonia* was now but a mile away, the black smoke pouring from her funnel at a right angle, so madly she raced, pounding through the sea at a seventeen-knot gait—'Sky-hooting through the brine,' as Wolf Larsen quoted while gazing at her. We were not making more than nine knots, but the fog-bank was very near.

A puff of smoke broke from the *Macedonia's* deck, we heard a heavy report, and a round hole took form in the stretched canvas of our mainsail. They were shooting at us with one of the small cannon which rumour had said they carried on board. Our men, clustering amidships, waved their hats and raised a derisive cheer. Again there was a puff of smoke and a loud report, this time the cannon-ball striking not more than twenty feet astern and glancing twice from sea to sea to windward ere it sank.

But there was no rifle-firing for the reason that all their hunters were out in the boats or our prisoners. When the two vessels were half-a-mile apart, a third shot made another hole in our mainsail. Then we entered the fog. It was about us, veiling and hiding us in its dense wet gauze.

The sudden transition was startling. The moment before we had been leaping through the sunshine, the clear sky above us, the sea breaking and rolling wide to the horizon, and a ship, vomiting smoke and fire and iron missiles, rushing madly upon us. And at once, as in an instant's leap, the sun was blotted out, there was no sky, even our mastheads were lost to view, and our horizon was such as tear-blinded eyes may see. The grey mist drove by us like a rain. Every woollen filament of our garments, every hair of our heads and faces, was jewelled with a crystal globule. The shrouds were wet with moisture; it dripped from our rigging overhead; and on the underside of our booms drops of water took shape in long swaying lines, which were detached and flung to the deck in mimic showers at each surge of the schooner. I was aware of a pent, stifled feeling. As the sounds of the ship thrusting herself through the waves were hurled back upon us by the fog, so were one's thoughts. The mind recoiled from contemplation of a world beyond this wet veil which wrapped us around. This was the world, the universe itself, its bounds so near one felt impelled to reach out both arms and push them back. It was impossible, that the rest could be beyond these walls of grey. The rest was a dream, no more than the memory of a dream.

It was weird, strangely weird. I looked at Maud Brewster and knew that she was similarly affected. Then I looked at Wolf Larsen, but there was nothing subjective about his state of consciousness. His whole concern was with the immediate, objective present. He still held the wheel, and I felt that he was timing Time, reckoning the passage of the minutes with each forward lunge and leeward roll of the *Ghost.*

'Go for'ard and hard alee without any noise,' he said to me in a low voice. 'Clew up the topsails first. Set men at all the sheets. Let there be no rattling of blocks, no sound of voices. No noise, understand, no noise.'

When all was ready, the word 'hard-a-lee' was passed forward to me from man to man; and the *Ghost* heeled about on the port tack with practically no noise at all. And what little there was,—the slapping of a few reef-points and the creaking of a sheave in a block or two,—was ghostly under the hollow echoing pall in which we were swathed.

We had scarcely filled away, it seemed, when the fog thinned abruptly and we were again in the sunshine, the wide-stretching sea breaking before us to the sky-line. But the ocean was bare. No wrathful *Macedonia* broke its surface nor blackened the sky with her smoke.

Wolf Larsen at once squared away and ran down along the rim of the fog-bank. His trick was obvious. He had entered the fog to windward of the steamer, and while the steamer had blindly driven on into the fog in the chance of catching him, he had come about and out of his shelter and was now running down to re-enter to leeward. Successful in this, the old simile of the needle in the haystack would be mild indeed compared with his brother's chance of finding him. He did not run long. Jibing the fore- and main-sails and setting the topsails again, we headed back into the bank. As we entered I could have sworn I saw a vague bulk emerging to windward. I looked quickly at Wolf Larsen. Already we were ourselves buried in the fog, but he nodded his head. He, too, had seen it—the *Macedonia*, guessing his manœuvre and failing by a moment in anticipating it. There was no doubt that we had escaped unseen.

'He can't keep this up,' Wolf Larsen said. 'He'll have to go back for the rest of his boats. Send a man to the wheel, Mr. Van Weyden, keep this course for the present, and you might as well set the watches, for we won't do any lingering to-night.'

'I'd give five hundred dollars, though,' he added, 'just to be aboard the *Macedonia* for five minutes, listening to my brother curse.'

'And now, Mr. Van Weyden,' he said to me when he had been relieved from the wheel, 'we must make these new-comers welcome. Serve out plenty of whisky to the hunters and see that a few bottles slip for'ard. I'll wager every man Jack of them is over the side to-morrow, hunting for Wolf Larsen as contentedly as ever they hunted for Death Larsen.'

'But won't they escape as Wainwright did?' I asked.

He laughed shrewdly. 'Not as long as our old hunters have anything to say about it. I'm dividing amongst them a dollar a skin for all the skins shot by our new hunters. At least half of their enthusiasm to-day was due to that. Oh, no, there won't be any escaping if they have anything to say about it. And now you'd better get for'ard to your hospital duties. There must be a full ward waiting for you.'

CHAPTER XXVI

Wolf Larsen took the distribution of the whisky off my hands, and the bottles began to make their appearance while I worked over the fresh batch of wounded men in the forecastle. I had seen whisky drunk, such as whisky-and-soda by the men of the clubs, but never as these men drank it, from pannikins and mugs, and from the bottles— great brimming drinks, each one of which was in itself a debauch. But they did not stop at one or two. They drank and drank, and ever the bottles slipped forward and they drank more.

Everybody drank; the wounded drank; Oofty-Oofty, who helped me, drank. Only Louis refrained, no more than cautiously wetting his lips with the liquor, though he joined in the revels with an abandon equal to that of most of them. It was a saturnalia. In loud voices they shouted over the day's fighting, wrangled about details, or waxed affectionate and made friends with the men whom they had fought. Prisoners and captors hiccoughed on one another's shoulders, and swore mighty oaths of respect and esteem. They wept over the miseries of the past and over the miseries yet to come under the iron rule of Wolf Larsen. And all cursed him and told terrible tales of his brutality.

It was a strange and frightful spectacle—the small, bunk-lined space, the floor and walls leaping and lurching, the dim light, the swaying shadows lengthening and fore-shortening monstrously, the thick air heavy with smoke and the smell of bodies and iodoform, and the inflamed faces of the men—half-men, I should call them. I noted Oofty-Oofty, holding the end of a bandage and looking upon the scene, his velvety and luminous eyes glistening in the light like a deer's eyes, and yet I knew the barbaric devil that lurked in his breast and belied all the softness and tenderness, almost womanly, of his face and form. And I noticed the boyish face of Harrison,—a good face once, but now a demon's,—convulsed with passion as he told the new-comers of the hell-ship they were in and shrieked curses upon the head of Wolf Larsen.

Wolf Larsen it was, always Wolf Larsen, enslaver and tormentor of men, a male Circe and these his swine, suffering brutes that grovelled before him and revolted only in drunkenness and in secrecy. And was I, too, one of his swine? I thought. And Maud Brewster? No! I ground my teeth in my anger and determination till the man I was attending winced under my hand and Oofty-Oofty looked at me with curiosity. I felt endowed with a sudden strength. What of my new-found love, I was a giant. I feared nothing. I would work my will through it all, in spite of Wolf Larsen and of my own thirty-five bookish years. All would be well. I would make it well. And so, exalted, upborne by a sense of power, I turned my back on the howling inferno and climbed to the deck, where the fog drifted ghostly through the night and the air was sweet and pure and quiet.

The steerage, where were two wounded hunters, was a repetition of the forecastle, except that Wolf Larsen was not being cursed; and it was with a great relief that I again emerged on deck and went aft to the cabin. Supper was ready, and Wolf Larsen and Maud were waiting for me.

While all his ship was getting drunk as fast as it could, he remained sober. Not a drop of liquor passed his lips. He did not dare it under the circumstances, for he had only Louis and me to depend upon, and Louis was even now at the wheel. We were sailing on through the fog without a look-out and without lights. That Wolf Larsen had turned the liquor loose among his men surprised me, but he evidently knew their psychology and the best method of cementing in cordiality, what had begun in bloodshed.

His victory over Death Larsen seemed to have had a remarkable effect upon him. The previous evening he had reasoned himself into the blues, and I had been waiting momentarily for one of his characteristic outbursts. Yet nothing had occurred, and he was now in splendid trim. Possibly his success in capturing so many hunters and boats had counteracted the customary reaction. At any rate, the blues were gone, and the blue devils had not put in an appearance. So I thought at the time; but, ah me, little I knew him or knew that even then, perhaps, he was meditating an outbreak more terrible than any I had seen.

As I say, he discovered himself in splendid trim when I entered the cabin. He had had no headaches for weeks, his eyes were clear blue as the sky, his bronze was beautiful with perfect health; life swelled through his veins in full and magnificent flood. While waiting for me he had engaged Maud in animated discussion. Temptation was the topic they had hit upon, and from the few words I heard I made out that he was contending that temptation was temptation only when a man was seduced by it and fell.

'For look you,' he was saying, 'as I see it, a man does things because of desire. He has many desires. He may desire to escape pain, or to enjoy pleasure. But whatever he does, he does because he desires to do it.'

'But suppose he desires to do two opposite things, neither of which will permit him to do the other?' Maud interrupted.

'The very thing I was coming to,' he said.

'And between these two desires is just where the soul of the man is manifest,' she went on. 'If it is a good soul, it will desire and do the good action, and the contrary if it is a bad soul. It is the soul that decides.'

'Bosh and nonsense!' he exclaimed impatiently. 'It is the desire that decides. Here is a man who wants to, say, get drunk. Also, he doesn't want to get drunk. What does he do? How does he do it? He is a puppet. He is the creature of his desires, and of the two desires he obeys the strongest one, that is all. His soul hasn't anything to do with it. How can he be tempted to get drunk and refuse to get drunk? If the desire to remain sober prevails, it is because it is the strongest desire. Temptation plays no part, unless—' he paused while grasping the new thought which had come into his mind—'unless he is tempted to remain sober.

'Ha! ha!' he laughed. 'What do you think of that, Mr. Van Weyden?'

'That both of you are hair-splitting,' I said. 'The man's soul is his desires. Or, if you will, the sum of his desires is his soul. Therein you are both wrong. You lay the stress upon the desire apart from the soul, Miss Brewster lays the stress on the soul apart from the desire, and in point of fact soul and desire are the same thing.

'However,' I continued, 'Miss Brewster is right in contending that temptation is temptation whether the man yield or overcome. Fire is fanned by the wind until it leaps up fiercely. So is desire like fire. It is fanned, as by a wind, by sight of the thing desired, or by a new and luring description or comprehension of the thing desired. There lies the temptation. It is the wind that fans the desire until it leaps up to mastery. That's temptation. It may not fan sufficiently to make the desire overmastering, but in so far as it fans at all, that far is it temptation. And, as you say, it may tempt for good as well as for evil.'

I felt proud of myself as we sat down to the table. My words had been decisive. At least they had put an end to the discussion.

But Wolf Larsen seemed voluble, prone to speech as I had never seen him before. It was as though he were bursting with pent energy which must find an outlet somehow. Almost immediately he launched into a discussion on love. As usual, his was the sheer materialistic side, and Maud's was the idealistic. For myself, beyond a word or so of suggestion or correction now and again, I took no part.

He was brilliant, but so was Maud, and for some time I lost the thread of the conversation through studying her face as she talked. It was a face that rarely displayed colour, but to-night it was flushed and vivacious. Her wit was playing keenly, and she was enjoying the tilt as much as Wolf Larsen, and he was enjoying it hugely. For some reason, though I know not why in the argument, so utterly had I lost it in the contemplation of one stray brown lock of Maud's hair, he quoted from Iseult at Tintagel, where she says:

'Blessed am I beyond women even herein,
   That beyond all born women is my sin,
   And perfect my transgression.'

As he had read pessimism into Omar, so now he read triumph, stinging triumph and exultation, into Swinburne's lines. And he read rightly, and he read well. He had hardly ceased reading when Louis put his head into the companion-way and whispered down:

'Be easy, will ye? The fog's lifted, an' 'tis the port light iv a steamer that's crossin' our bow this blessed minute.'

Wolf Larsen sprang on deck, and so swiftly that by the time we followed him he had pulled the steerage-slide over the drunken clamour and was on his way forward to close the forecastle-scuttle. The fog, though it remained, had lifted high, where it obscured the stars and made the night quite black. Directly ahead of us I could see a bright red light and a white light, and I could hear the pulsing of a steamer's engines. Beyond a doubt it was the *Macedonia*.

Wolf Larsen had returned to the poop, and we stood in a silent group, watching the lights rapidly cross our bow.

'Lucky for me he doesn't carry a searchlight,' Wolf Larsen said.

'What if I should cry out loudly?' I queried in a whisper.

'It would be all up,' he answered. 'But have you thought upon what would immediately happen?'

Before I had time to express any desire to know, he had me by the throat with his gorilla grip, and by a faint quiver of the muscles—a hint, as it were—he suggested to me the twist that would surely have broken my neck. The next moment he had released me and we were gazing at the *Macedonia's* lights.

'What if I should cry out?' Maud asked.

'I like you too well to hurt you,' he said softly—nay, there was a tenderness and a caress in his voice that made me wince.

'But don't do it, just the same, for I'd promptly break Mr. Van Weyden's neck.'

'Then she has my permission to cry out,' I said defiantly.

'I hardly think you'll care to sacrifice the Dean of American Letters the Second,' he sneered.

We spoke no more, though we had become too used to one another for the silence to be awkward; and when the red light and the white had disappeared we returned to the cabin to finish the interrupted supper.

Again they fell to quoting, and Maud gave Dowson's 'Impenitentia Ultima.' She rendered it beautifully, but I watched not her, but Wolf Larsen. I was fascinated by the fascinated look he bent upon Maud. He was quite out of himself, and I noticed the unconscious movement of his lips as he shaped word for word as fast as she uttered them. He interrupted her when she gave the lines:

'And her eyes should be my light while the sun went out behind me, And the viols in her voice be the last sound in my ear.'

'There are viols in your voice,' he said bluntly, and his eyes flashed their golden light.

I could have shouted with joy at her control. She finished the concluding stanza without faltering and then slowly guided the conversation into less perilous channels. And all the while I sat in a half-daze, the drunken riot of the steerage breaking through the bulkhead, the man I feared and the woman I loved talking on and on. The table was not cleared. The man who had taken Mugridge's place had evidently joined his comrades in the forecastle.

If ever Wolf Larsen attained the summit of living, he attained it then. From time to time I forsook my own thoughts to follow him, and I followed in amaze, mastered for the moment by his remarkable intellect, under the spell of his passion, for he was preaching the passion of revolt. It was inevitable that Milton's Lucifer should be instanced, and the keenness with which Wolf Larsen analysed and depicted the character was a revelation of his stifled genius. It reminded me of Taine, yet I knew the man had never heard of that brilliant though dangerous thinker.

'He led a lost cause, and he was not afraid of God's thunderbolts,' Wolf Larsen was saying. 'Hurled into hell, he was unbeaten. A third of God's angels he had led with him, and straightway he incited man to rebel against God, and gained for himself and hell the major portion of all the generations of man. Why was he beaten out of heaven? Because he was less brave than God? less proud? less aspiring? No! A thousand times no! God was more powerful, as he said, Whom thunder hath made greater. But Lucifer was a free spirit. To serve was to suffocate. He preferred suffering in freedom to all the happiness of a comfortable servility. He did not care to serve God. He cared to serve nothing. He was no figure-head. He stood on his own legs. He was an individual.'

'The first Anarchist,' Maud laughed, rising and preparing to withdraw to her state-room.

'Then it is good to be an anarchist!' he cried. He, too, had risen, and he stood facing her, where she had paused at the door of her room, as he went on:

'Here at least
We shall be free; the Almighty hath not built
Here for his envy; will not drive us hence;
Here we may reign secure; and in my choice
To reign is worth ambition, though in hell:
Better to reign in hell than serve in heaven.'

It was the defiant cry of a mighty spirit. The cabin still rang with his voice, as he stood there, swaying, his bronzed face shining, his head up and dominant, and his eyes, golden and masculine, intensely masculine and insistently soft, flashing upon Maud at the door.

Again that unnamable and unmistakable terror was in her eyes, and she said, almost in a whisper, 'You are Lucifer.'

The door closed and she was gone. He stood staring after her for a minute, then returned to himself and to me.

'I'll relieve Louis at the wheel,' he said shortly, 'and call upon you to relieve at midnight. Better turn in now and get some sleep.'

He pulled on a pair of mittens, put on his cap, and ascended the companion-stairs, while I followed his suggestion by going to bed. For some unknown reason, prompted mysteriously, I did not undress, but lay down fully clothed. For a time I listened to the clamour in the steerage and marvelled upon the love which had come to me; but my sleep on the *Ghost* had become most healthful and natural, and soon the songs and cries died away, my eyes closed, and my consciousness sank down into the half-death of slumber.

I knew not what had aroused me, but I found myself out of my bunk, on my feet, wide awake, my soul vibrating to the warning of danger as it might have thrilled to a trumpet call. I threw open the door. The cabin light was burning low. I saw Maud, my Maud, straining and struggling and crushed in the embrace of Wolf Larsen's arms. I could see the vain beat and flutter of her as she strove, pressing her face against his breast, to escape from him. All this I saw on the very instant of seeing and as I sprang forward.

I struck him with my fist, on the face, as he raised his head, but it was a puny blow. He roared in a ferocious, animal-like way, and gave me a shove with his hand. It was only a shove, a flirt of the wrist, yet so tremendous was his strength that I was hurled backward as from a catapult. I struck the door of the state-room which had formerly been Mugridge's, splintering and smashing the panels with the impact of my body. I struggled to my feet, with difficulty dragging myself clear of the wrecked door, unaware of any hurt whatever. I was conscious only of an overmastering rage. I think I, too, cried aloud, as I drew the knife at my hip and sprang forward a second time.

But something had happened. They were reeling apart. I was close upon him, my knife uplifted, but I withheld the blow. I was puzzled by the strangeness of it. Maud was leaning against the wall, one hand out for support; but he was staggering, his left hand pressed against his forehead and covering his eyes, and with the right he was groping about him in a dazed sort of way. It struck against the wall, and his body seemed to express a muscular and physical relief at the contact, as though he had found his bearings, his location in space as well as something against which to lean.

Then I saw red again. All my wrongs and humiliations flashed upon me with a dazzling brightness, all that I had suffered and others had suffered at his hands, all the enormity of the man's very existence. I sprang upon him, blindly, insanely, and drove the knife into his shoulder. I knew, then, that it was no more than a flesh wound,—I had felt the steel grate on his shoulder-blade,—and I raised the knife to strike at a more vital part.

But Maud had seen my first blow, and she cried, 'Don't! Please don't!'

I dropped my arm for a moment, and a moment only. Again the knife was raised, and Wolf Larsen would have surely died had she not stepped between. Her arms were around me, her hair was brushing my face. My pulse rushed up in an unwonted manner, yet my rage mounted with it. She looked me bravely in the eyes.

'For my sake,' she begged.

'I would kill him for your sake!' I cried, trying to free my arm without hurting her.

'Hush!' she said, and laid her fingers lightly on my lips. I could have kissed them, had I dared, even then, in my rage, the touch of them was so sweet, so very sweet. 'Please, please,' she pleaded, and she disarmed me by the words, as I was to discover they would ever disarm me.

I stepped back, separating from her, and replaced the knife in its sheath. I looked at Wolf Larsen. He still pressed his left hand against his forehead. It covered his eyes. His head was bowed. He seemed to have grown limp. His body was sagging at the hips, his great shoulders were drooping and shrinking forward.

'Van, Weyden!' he called hoarsely, and with a note of fright in his voice. 'Oh, Van Weyden! where are you?'

I looked at Maud. She did not speak, but nodded her head.

'Here I am,' I answered, stepping to his side. 'What is the matter?'

'Help me to a seat,' he said, in the same hoarse, frightened voice.

'I am a sick man; a very sick man, Hump,' he said, as he left my sustaining grip and sank into a chair.

His head dropped forward on the table and was buried in his hands. From time to time it rocked back and forward as with pain. Once, when he half raised it, I saw the sweat standing in heavy drops on his forehead about the roots of his hair.

'I am a sick man, a very sick man,' he repeated again, and yet once again.

'What is the matter?' I asked, resting my hand on his shoulder. 'What can I do for you?'

But he shook my hand off with an irritated movement, and for a long time I stood by his side in silence. Maud was looking on, her face awed and frightened. What had happened to him we could not imagine.

'Hump,' he said at last, 'I must get into my bunk. Lend me a hand. I'll be all right in a little while. It's those damn headaches, I believe. I was afraid of them. I had a feeling—no, I don't know what I'm talking about. Help me into my bunk.'

But when I got him into his bunk he again buried his face in his hands, covering his eyes, and as I turned to go I could hear him murmuring, 'I am a sick man, a very sick man.'

Maud looked at me inquiringly as I emerged. I shook my head, saying:

'Something has happened to him. What, I don't know. He is helpless, and frightened, I imagine, for the first time in his life. It must have occurred before he received the knife-thrust, which made only a superficial wound. You must have seen what happened.'

She shook her head. 'I saw nothing. It is just as mysterious to me. He suddenly released me and staggered away. But what shall we do? What shall I do?'

'If you will wait, please, until I come back,' I answered.

I went on deck. Louis was at the wheel.

'You may go for'ard and turn in,' I said, taking it from him.

He was quick to obey, and I found myself alone on the deck of the *Ghost*. As quietly as was possible, I clewed up the topsails, lowered the flying jib and staysail, backed the jib over, and flattened the mainsail. Then I went below to Maud. I placed my finger on my lips for silence, and entered Wolf Larsen's room. He was in the same position in which I had left him, and his head was rocking—almost writhing—from side to side.

'Anything I can do for you?' I asked.

He made no reply at first, but on my repeating the question he answered, 'No, no; I'm all right. Leave me alone till morning.'

But as I turned to go I noted that his head had resumed its rocking motion. Maud was waiting patiently for me, and I took notice, with a thrill of joy, of the queenly poise of her head and her glorious, calm eyes. Calm and sure they were as her spirit itself.

'Will you trust yourself to me for a journey of six hundred miles or so?' I asked.

'You mean—?' she asked, and I knew she had guessed aright.

'Yes, I mean just that,' I replied. 'There is nothing left for us but the open boat.'

'For me, you mean,' she said. 'You are certainly as safe here as you have been.'

'No, there is nothing left for us but the open boat,' I iterated stoutly. 'Will you please dress as warmly as you can, at once, and make into a bundle whatever you wish to bring with you.'

'And make all haste,' I added, as she turned toward her state-room.

The lazarette was directly beneath the cabin, and, opening the trap-door in the floor and carrying a candle with me, I dropped down and began overhauling the ship's stores. I selected mainly from the canned goods, and by the time I was ready, willing hands were extended from above to receive what I passed up.

We worked in silence. I helped myself also to blankets, mittens, oilskins, caps, and such things, from the slop-chest. It was no light adventure, this trusting ourselves in a small boat to so raw and stormy a sea, and it was imperative that we should guard ourselves against the cold and wet.

We worked feverishly at carrying our plunder on deck and depositing it amidships, so feverishly that Maud, whose strength was hardly a positive quantity, had to give over, exhausted, and sit on the steps at the break of the poop. This did not serve to recover her, and she lay on her back, on the hard deck, arms stretched out, and whole body relaxed. It was a trick I remembered of my sister, and I knew she would soon be herself again. I knew, also, that weapons would not come in amiss, and I re-entered Wolf Larsen's state-room to get his rifle and shot-gun. I spoke to him, but he made no answer, though his head was still rocking from side to side and he was not asleep.

'Good-bye, Lucifer,' I whispered to myself as I softly closed the door.

Next to obtain was a stock of ammunition,—an easy matter, though I had to enter the steerage companion-way to do it. Here the hunters stored the ammunition-boxes they carried in the boats, and here, but a few feet from their noisy revels, I took possession of two boxes.

Next, to lower a boat. Not so simple a task for one man. Having cast off the lashings, I hoisted first on the forward tackle, then on the aft, till the boat cleared the rail, when I lowered away, one tackle and then the other, for a couple of feet, till it hung snugly, above the water, against the schooner's side. I made certain that it contained the proper equipment of oars, rowlocks, and sail. Water was a consideration, and I robbed every boat aboard of its breaker. As there were nine boats all told, it meant that we should have plenty of water, and ballast as well, though there was the chance that the boat would be overloaded, what of the generous supply of other things I was taking.

While Maud was passing me the provisions and I was storing them in the boat, a sailor came on deck from the forecastle. He stood by the weather rail for a time (we were lowering over the lee rail), and then sauntered slowly amidships, where he again paused and stood facing the wind, with his back toward us. I could hear my heart beating as I crouched low in the boat. Maud had sunk down upon the deck and was, I knew, lying motionless, her body in the shadow of the bulwark. But the man never turned, and, after stretching his arms above his head and yawning audibly, he retraced his steps to the forecastle scuttle and disappeared.

A few minutes sufficed to finish the loading, and I lowered the boat into the water. As I helped Maud over the rail and felt her form close to mine, it was all I could do to keep from crying out, 'I love you! I love you!' Truly Humphrey Van Weyden was at last in love, I thought, as her fingers clung to mine while I lowered her down to the boat. I held on to the rail with one hand and supported her weight with the other, and I was proud at the moment of the feat. It was a strength I had not possessed a few months before, on the day I said good-bye to Charley Furuseth and started for San Francisco on the ill-fated *Martinez*.

As the boat ascended on a sea, her feet touched and I released her hands. I cast off the tackles and leaped after her. I had never rowed in my life, but I put out the oars and at the expense of much effort got the boat clear of the *Ghost*. Then I experimented with the sail. I had seen the boat-steerers and hunters set their spritsails many times, yet this was my first attempt. What took them possibly two minutes took me twenty, but in the end I succeeded in setting and trimming it, and with the steering-oar in my hands hauled on the wind.

'There lies Japan,' I remarked, 'straight before us.'

'Humphrey Van Weyden,' she said, 'you are a brave man.'

'Nay,' I answered, 'it is you who are a brave woman.'

We turned our heads, swayed by a common impulse to see the last of the *Ghost*. Her low hull lifted and rolled to windward on a sea; her canvas loomed darkly in the night; her lashed wheel creaked as the rudder kicked; then sight and sound of her faded away, and we were alone on the dark sea.

CHAPTER XXVII

Day broke, grey and chill. The boat was close-hauled on a fresh breeze and the compass indicated that we were just making the course which would bring us to Japan. Though stoutly mittened, my fingers were cold, and they pained from the grip on the steering-oar. My feet were stinging from the bite of the frost, and I hoped fervently that the sun would shine.

Before me, in the bottom of the boat, lay Maud. She, at least, was warm, for under her and over her were thick blankets. The top one I had drawn over her face to shelter it from the night, so I could see nothing but the vague shape of her, and her light-brown hair, escaped from the covering and jewelled with moisture from the air.

Long I looked at her, dwelling upon that one visible bit of her as only a man would who deemed it the most precious thing in the world. So insistent was my gaze that at last she stirred under the blankets, the top fold was thrown back and she smiled out on me, her eyes yet heavy with sleep.

'Good-morning, Mr. Van Weyden,' she said. 'Have you sighted land yet?'

'No,' I answered, 'but we are approaching it at a rate of six miles an hour.'

She made a *mouè* of disappointment.

'But that is equivalent to one hundred and forty-four miles in twenty-four hours,' I added reassuringly.

Her face brightened. 'And how far have we to go?'

'Siberia lies off there,' I said, pointing to the west. 'But to the south-west, some six hundred miles, is Japan. If this wind should hold, we'll make it in five days.'

'And if it storms? The boat could not live?'

She had a way of looking one in the eyes and demanding the truth, and thus she looked at me as she asked the question.

'It would have to storm very hard,' I temporized.

'And if it storms very hard?'

I nodded my head. 'But we may be picked up any moment by a sealing-schooner. They are plentifully distributed over this part of the ocean.'

'Why, you are chilled through!' she cried. 'Look! You are shivering. Don't deny it; you are. And here I have been lying warm as toast.'

'I don't see that it would help matters if you, too, sat up and were chilled,' I laughed.

'It will, though, when I learn to steer, which I certainly shall.'

She sat up and began making her simple toilet. She shook down her hair, and it fell about her in a brown cloud, hiding her face and shoulders. Dear, damp brown hair! I wanted to kiss it, to ripple it through my fingers, to bury my face in it. I gazed entranced, till the boat ran into the wind and the flapping sail warned me I was not attending to my duties. Idealist and romanticist that I was and always had been in spite of my analytical nature, yet I had failed till now in grasping much of the physical characteristics of love. The love of man and woman, I had always held, was a sublimated something related to spirit, a spiritual bond that linked and drew their souls together. The bonds of the flesh had little part in my cosmos of love. But I was learning the sweet lesson for myself that the soul transmuted itself, expressed itself, through the flesh; that the sight and sense and touch of the loved one's hair was as much breath and voice and essence of the spirit as the light that shone from the eyes and the thoughts that fell from the lips. After all, pure spirit was unknowable, a thing to be sensed and divined only; nor could it express itself in terms of itself. Jehovah was anthropomorphic because he could address himself to the Jews only in terms of their understanding; so he was conceived as in their own image, as a cloud, a pillar of fire, a tangible, physical something which the mind of the Israelites could grasp.

And so I gazed upon Maud's light-brown hair, and loved it, and learned more of love than all the poets and singers had taught me with all their songs and sonnets. She flung it back with a sudden adroit movement, and her face emerged, smiling.

'Why don't women wear their hair down always?' I asked. 'It is so much more beautiful.'

'If it didn't tangle so dreadfully,' she laughed. 'There! I've lost one of my precious hair-pins!'

I neglected the boat and had the sail spilling the wind again and again, such was my delight in following her every movement as she searched through the blankets for the pin. I was surprised, and joyfully, that she was so much the woman, and the display of each trait and mannerism that was characteristically feminine gave me keener joy. For I had been elevating her too highly in my concepts of her, removing her too far from the plane of the human, and too far from me. I had been making of her a creature goddess-like and unapproachable. So I hailed with delight the little traits that proclaimed her only woman after all, such as the toss of the head which flung back the cloud of hair, and the search for the pin. She was woman, my kind, on my plane, and the delightful intimacy of kind, of man and woman, was possible, as well as the reverence and awe in which I knew I should always hold her.

She found the pin with an adorable little cry, and I turned my attention more fully to my steering. I proceeded to experiment, lashing and wedging the steering-oar until the boat held on fairly well by the wind without my assistance. Occasionally it came up too close, or fell off too freely; but it always recovered itself and in the main behaved satisfactorily.

'And now we shall have breakfast,' I said. 'But first you must be more warmly clad.'

I got out a heavy shirt, new from the slop-chest and made from blanket goods. I knew the kind, so thick and so close of texture that it could resist the rain and not be soaked through after hours of wetting. When she had slipped this on over her head, I exchanged the boy's cap she wore for a man's cap, large enough to cover her hair, and, when the flap was turned down, to completely cover her neck and ears. The effect was charming. Her face was of the sort that cannot but look well under all circumstances. Nothing could destroy its exquisite oval, its well-nigh classic lines, its delicately stencilled brows, its large brown eyes, clear-seeing and calm, gloriously calm.

A puff, slightly stronger than usual, struck us just then. The boat was caught as it obliquely crossed the crest of a wave. It went over suddenly, burying its gunwale level with the sea and shipping a bucketful or so of water. I was opening a can of tongue at the moment, and I sprang to the sheet and cast it off just in time. The sail flapped and fluttered, and the boat paid off. A few minutes of regulating sufficed to put it on its course again, when I returned to the preparation of breakfast.

'It does very well, it seems, though I am not versed in things nautical,' she said, nodding her head with grave approval at my steering contrivance.

'But it will serve only when we are sailing by the wind,' I explained. 'When running more freely, with the wind astern abeam, or on the quarter, it will be necessary for me to steer.'

'I must say I don't understand your technicalities,' she said, 'but I do your conclusion, and I don't like it. You cannot steer night and day and for ever. So I shall expect, after breakfast, to receive my first lesson. And then you shall lie down and sleep. We'll stand watches just as they do on ships.'

'I don't see how I am to teach you,' I made protest. 'I am just learning for myself. You little thought when you trusted yourself to me that I had had no experience whatever with small boats. This is the first time I have ever been in one.'

'Then we'll learn together, sir. And since you've had a night's start you shall teach me what you have learned. And now, breakfast. My! this air does give one an appetite!'

'No coffee,' I said regretfully, passing her buttered sea-biscuits and a slice of canned tongue. 'And there will be no tea, no soups, nothing hot, till we have made land somewhere, somehow.'

After the simple breakfast, capped with a cup of cold water, Maud took her lesson in steering. In teaching her I learned quite a deal myself, though I was applying the knowledge already acquired by sailing the *Ghost* and by watching the boat-steerers sail the small boats. She was an apt pupil, and soon learned to keep the course, to luff in the puffs and to cast off the sheet in an emergency.

Having grown tired, apparently, of the task, she relinquished the oar to me. I had folded up the blankets, but she now proceeded to spread them out on the bottom. When all was arranged snugly, she said:

'Now, sir, to bed. And you shall sleep until luncheon. Till dinner-time,' she corrected, remembering the arrangement on the *Ghost*.

What could I do? She insisted, and said, 'Please, please,' whereupon I turned the oar over to her and obeyed. I experienced a positive sensuous delight as I crawled into the bed she had made with her hands. The calm and control which were so much a part of her seemed to have been communicated to the blankets, so that I was aware of a soft dreaminess and content, and of an oval face and brown eyes framed in a fisherman's cap and tossing against a background now of grey cloud, now of grey sea, and then I was aware that I had been asleep.

I looked at my watch. It was one o'clock. I had slept seven hours! And she had been steering seven hours! When I took the steering-oar I had first to unbend her cramped fingers. Her modicum of strength had been exhausted, and she was unable even to move from her position. I was compelled to let go the sheet while I helped her to the nest of blankets and chafed her hands and arms.

'I am so tired,' she said, with a quick intake of the breath and a sigh, drooping her head wearily.

But she straightened it the next moment. 'Now don't scold, don't you dare scold,' she cried with mock defiance.

'I hope my face does not appear angry,' I answered seriously; 'for I assure you I am not in the least angry.'

'N-no,' she considered. 'It looks only reproachful.'

'Then it is an honest face, for it looks what I feel. You were not fair to yourself, nor to me. How can I ever trust you again?'

She looked penitent. 'I'll be good,' she said, as a naughty child might say it. 'I promise—'

'To obey as a sailor would obey his captain?'

'Yes,' she answered. 'It was stupid of me, I know.'

'Then you must promise something else,' I ventured.

'Readily.'

'That you will not say, 'Please, please,' too often; for when you do you are sure to override my authority.'

She laughed with amused appreciation. She, too, had noticed the power of the repeated 'please.'

'It is a good word—' I began.

'But I must not overwork it,' she broke in.

But she laughed weakly, and her head drooped again. I left the oar long enough to tuck the blankets about her feet and to pull a single fold across her face. Alas! she was not strong. I looked with misgiving toward the south-west and thought of the six hundred miles of hardship before us—ay, if it were no worse than hardship. On this sea a storm might blow up at any moment and destroy us. And yet I was unafraid. I was without confidence in the future, extremely doubtful, and yet I felt no underlying fear. It must come right, it must come right, I repeated to myself, over and over again.

The wind freshened in the afternoon, raising a stiffer sea and trying the boat and me severely. But the supply of food and the nine breakers of water enabled the boat to stand up to the sea and wind, and I held on as long as I dared. Then I removed the sprit, tightly hauling down the peak of the sail, and we raced along under what sailors call a leg-of-mutton.

Late in the afternoon I sighted a steamer's smoke on the horizon to leeward, and I knew it either for a Russian cruiser, or, more likely, the *Macedonia* still seeking the *Ghost*. The sun had not shone all day, and it had been bitter cold. As night drew on, the clouds darkened and the wind freshened, so that when Maud and I ate supper it was with our mittens on and with me still steering and eating morsels between puffs.

By the time it was dark, wind and sea had become too strong for the boat, and I reluctantly took in the sail and set about making a drag or sea-anchor. I had learned of the device from the talk of the hunters, and it was a simple thing to manufacture. Furling the sail and lashing it securely about the mast, boom, sprit, and two pairs of spare oars, I threw it overboard. A line connected it with the bow, and as it floated low in the water, practically unexposed to the wind, it drifted less rapidly than the boat. In consequence it held the boat bow on to the sea and wind—the safest position in which to escape being swamped when the sea is breaking into whitecaps.

'And now?' Maud asked cheerfully, when the task was accomplished and I pulled on my mittens.

'And now we are no longer travelling toward Japan,' I answered. 'Our drift is to the south-east, or south-south-east, at the rate of at least two miles an hour.'

'That will be only twenty-four miles,' she urged, 'if the wind remains high all night.'

'Yes, and only one hundred and forty miles if it continues for three days and nights.'

'But it won't continue,' she said with easy confidence. 'It will turn around and blow fair.'

'The sea is the great faithless one.'

'But the wind!' she retorted. 'I have heard you grow eloquent over the brave trade-wind.'

'I wish I had thought to bring Wolf Larsen's chronometer and sextant,' I said, still gloomily. 'Sailing one direction, drifting another direction, to say nothing of the set of the current in some third direction, makes a resultant which dead reckoning can never calculate. Before long we won't know where we are by five hundred miles.'

Then I begged her pardon and promised I should not be disheartened any more. At her solicitation I let her take the watch till midnight,—it was then nine o'clock, but I wrapped her in blankets and put an oilskin about her before I lay down. I slept only cat-naps. The boat was leaping and pounding as it fell over the crests, I could hear the seas rushing past, and spray was continually being thrown aboard. And still, it was not a bad night, I mused—nothing to the nights I had been through on the *Ghost*; nothing, perhaps, to the nights we should go through in this cockle-shell. Its planking was three-quarters of an inch thick. Between us and the bottom of the sea was less than an inch of wood.

And yet, I aver it, and I aver it again, I was unafraid. The death which Wolf Larsen and even Thomas Mugridge had made me fear, I no longer feared. The coming of Maud Brewster into my life seemed to have transformed me. After all, I thought, it is better and finer to love than to be loved, if it makes something in life so worth while that one is not loath to die for it. I forget my own life in the love of another life; and yet, such is the paradox, I never wanted so much to live as right now when I place the least value upon my own life. I never had so much reason for living, was my concluding thought; and after that, until I dozed, I contented myself with trying to pierce the darkness to where I knew Maud crouched low in the stern-sheets, watchful of the foaming sea and ready to call me on an instant's notice.

CHAPTER XXVIII

There is no need of going into an extended recital of our suffering in the small boat during the many days we were driven and drifted, here and there, willy-nilly, across the ocean. The high wind blew from the north-west for twenty-four hours, when it fell calm, and in the night sprang up from the south-west. This was dead in our teeth, but I took in the sea-anchor and set sail, hauling a course on the wind which took us in a south-south-easterly direction. It was an even choice between this and the west-north-westerly course which the wind permitted; but the warm airs of the south fanned my desire for a warmer sea and swayed my decision.

In three hours—it was midnight, I well remember, and as dark as I had ever seen it on the sea—the wind, still blowing out of the south-west, rose furiously, and once again I was compelled to set the sea-anchor.

Day broke and found me wan-eyed and the ocean lashed white, the boat pitching, almost on end, to its drag. We were in imminent danger of being swamped by the whitecaps. As it was, spray and spume came aboard in such quantities that I bailed without cessation. The blankets were soaking. Everything was wet except Maud, and she, in oilskins, rubber boots, and sou'wester, was dry, all but her face and hands and a stray wisp of hair. She relieved me at the bailing-hole from time to time, and bravely she threw out the water and faced the storm. All things are relative. It was no more than a stiff blow, but to us, fighting for life in our frail craft, it was indeed a storm.

Cold and cheerless, the wind beating on our faces, the white seas roaring by, we struggled through the day. Night came, but neither of us slept. Day came, and still the wind beat on our faces and the white seas roared past. By the second night Maud was falling asleep from exhaustion. I covered her with oilskins and a tarpaulin. She was comparatively dry, but she was numb with the cold. I feared greatly that she might die in the night; but day broke, cold and cheerless, with the same clouded sky and beating wind and roaring seas.

I had had no sleep for forty-eight hours. I was wet and chilled to the marrow, till I felt more dead than alive. My body was stiff from exertion as well as from cold, and my aching muscles gave me the severest torture whenever I used them, and I used them continually. And all the time we were being driven off into the north-east, directly away from Japan and toward bleak Bering Sea.

And still we lived, and the boat lived, and the wind blew unabated. In fact, toward nightfall of the third day it increased a trifle and something more. The boat's bow plunged under a crest, and we came through quarter-full of water. I bailed like a madman. The liability of shipping another such sea was enormously increased by the water that weighed the boat down and robbed it of its buoyancy. And another such sea meant the end. When I had the boat empty again I was forced to take away the tarpaulin which covered Maud, in order that I might lash it down across the bow. It was well I did, for it covered the boat fully a third of the way aft, and three times, in the next several hours, it flung off the bulk of the down-rushing water when the bow shoved under the seas.

Maud's condition was pitiable. She sat crouched in the bottom of the boat, her lips blue, her face grey and plainly showing the pain she suffered. But ever her eyes looked bravely at me, and ever her lips uttered brave words.

The worst of the storm must have blown that night, though little I noticed it. I had succumbed and slept where I sat in the stern-sheets. The morning of the fourth day found the wind diminished to a gentle whisper, the sea dying down and the sun shining upon us. Oh, the blessed sun! How we bathed our poor bodies in its delicious warmth, reviving like bugs and crawling things after a storm. We smiled again, said amusing things, and waxed optimistic over our situation. Yet it was, if anything, worse than ever. We were farther from Japan than the night we left the *Ghost*. Nor could I more than roughly guess our latitude and longitude. At a calculation of a two-mile drift per hour, during the seventy and odd hours of the storm, we had been driven at least one hundred and fifty miles to the north-east. But was such calculated drift correct? For all I knew, it might have been four miles per hour instead of two. In which case we were another hundred and fifty miles to the bad.

Where we were I did not know, though there was quite a likelihood that we were in the vicinity of the *Ghost*. There were seals about us, and I was prepared to sight a sealing-schooner at any time. We did sight one, in the afternoon, when the north-west breeze had sprung up freshly once more. But the strange schooner lost itself on the sky-line and we alone occupied the circle of the sea.

Came days of fog, when even Maud's spirit drooped and there were no merry words upon her lips; days of calm, when we floated on the lonely immensity of sea, oppressed by its greatness and yet marvelling at the miracle of tiny life, for we still lived and struggled to live; days of sleet and wind and snow-squalls, when nothing could keep us warm; or days of drizzling rain, when we filled our water-breakers from the drip of the wet sail.

And ever I loved Maud with an increasing love. She was so many-sided, so many-mooded—'protean-mooded' I called her. But I called her this, and other and dearer things, in my thoughts only. Though the declaration of my love urged and trembled on my tongue a thousand times, I knew that it was no time for such a declaration. If for no other reason, it was no time, when one was protecting and trying to save a woman, to ask that woman for her love. Delicate as was the situation, not alone in this but in other ways, I flattered myself that I was able to deal delicately with it; and also I flattered myself that by look or sign I gave no advertisement of the love I felt for her. We were like good comrades, and we grew better comrades as the days went by.

One thing about her which surprised me was her lack of timidity and fear. The terrible sea, the frail boat, the storms, the suffering, the strangeness and isolation of the situation,—all that should have frightened a robust woman,—seemed to make no impression upon her who had known life only in its most sheltered and consummately artificial aspects, and who was herself all fire and dew and mist, sublimated spirit, all that was soft and tender and clinging in woman. And yet I am wrong. She *was* timid and afraid, but she possessed courage. The flesh and the qualms of the flesh she was heir to, but the flesh bore heavily only on the flesh. And she was spirit, first and always spirit, etherealized essence of life, calm as her calm eyes, and sure of permanence in the changing order of the universe.

Came days of storm, days and nights of storm, when the ocean menaced us with its roaring whiteness, and the wind smote our struggling boat with a Titan's buffets. And ever we were flung off, farther and farther, to the north-east. It was in such a storm, and the worst that we had experienced, that I cast a weary glance to leeward, not in quest of anything, but more from the weariness of facing the elemental strife, and in mute appeal, almost, to the wrathful powers to cease and let us be. What I saw I could not at first believe. Days and nights of sleeplessness and anxiety had doubtless turned my head. I looked back at Maud, to identify myself, as it were, in time and space. The sight of her dear wet cheeks, her flying hair, and her brave brown eyes convinced me that my vision was still healthy. Again I turned my face to leeward, and again I saw the jutting promontory, black and high and naked, the raging surf that broke about its base and beat its front high up with spouting fountains, the black and forbidden coast-line running toward the south-east and fringed with a tremendous scarf of white.

'Maud,' I said. 'Maud.'

She turned her head and beheld the sight.

'It cannot be Alaska!' she cried.

'Alas, no,' I answered, and asked, 'Can you swim?'

She shook her head.

'Neither can I,' I said. 'So we must get ashore without swimming, in some opening between the rocks through which we can drive the boat and clamber out. But we must be quick, most quick—and sure.'

I spoke with a confidence she knew I did not feel, for she looked at me with that unfaltering gaze of hers and said:

'I have not thanked you yet for all you have done for me but—'

She hesitated, as if in doubt how best to word her gratitude.

'Well?' I said, brutally, for I was not quite pleased with her thanking me.

'You might help me,' she smiled.

'To acknowledge your obligations before you die? Not at all. We are not going to die. We shall land on that island, and we shall be snug and sheltered before the day is done.'

I spoke stoutly, but I did not believe a word. Nor was I prompted to lie through fear. I felt no fear, though I was sure of death in that boiling surge amongst the rocks which was rapidly growing nearer. It was impossible to hoist sail and claw off that shore. The wind would instantly capsize the boat; the seas would swamp it the moment it fell into the trough; and, besides, the sail, lashed to the spare oars, dragged in the sea ahead of us.

As I say, I was not afraid to meet my own death, there, a few hundred yards to leeward; but I was appalled at the thought that Maud must die. My cursed imagination saw her beaten and mangled against the rocks, and it was too terrible. I strove to compel myself to think we would make the landing safely, and so I spoke, not what I believed, but what I preferred to believe.

I recoiled before contemplation of that frightful death, and for a moment I entertained the wild idea of seizing Maud in my arms and leaping overboard. Then I resolved to wait, and at the last moment, when we entered on the final stretch, to take her in my arms and proclaim my love, and, with her in my embrace, to make the desperate struggle and die.

Instinctively we drew closer together in the bottom of the boat. I felt her mittened hand come out to mine. And thus, without speech, we waited the end. We were not far off the line the wind made with the western edge of the promontory, and I watched in the hope that some set of the current or send of the sea would drift us past before we reached the surf.

'We shall go clear,' I said, with a confidence which I knew deceived neither of us.

'By God, we *will* go clear!' I cried, five minutes later.

The oath left my lips in my excitement—the first, I do believe, in my life, unless 'trouble it,' an expletive of my youth, be accounted an oath.

'I beg your pardon,' I said.

'You have convinced me of your sincerity,' she said, with a faint smile. 'I do know, now, that we shall go clear.'

I had seen a distant headland past the extreme edge of the promontory, and as we looked we could see grow the intervening coastline of what was evidently a deep cove. At the same time there broke upon our ears a continuous and mighty bellowing. It partook of the magnitude and volume of distant thunder, and it came to us directly from leeward, rising above the crash of the surf and travelling directly in the teeth of the storm. As we passed the point the whole cove burst upon our view, a half-moon of white sandy beach upon which broke a huge surf, and which was covered with myriads of seals. It was from them that the great bellowing went up.

'A rookery!' I cried. 'Now are we indeed saved. There must be men and cruisers to protect them from the seal-hunters. Possibly there is a station ashore.'

But as I studied the surf which beat upon the beach, I said, 'Still bad, but not so bad. And now, if the gods be truly kind, we shall drift by that next headland and come upon a perfectly sheltered beach, where we may land without wetting our feet.'

And the gods were kind. The first and second headlands were directly in line with the south-west wind; but once around the second,—and we went perilously near,—we picked up the third headland, still in line with the wind and with the other two. But the cove that intervened! It penetrated deep into the land, and the tide, setting in, drifted us under the shelter of the point. Here the sea was calm, save for a heavy but smooth ground-swell, and I took in the sea-anchor and began to row. From the point the shore curved away, more and more to the south and west, until at last it disclosed a cove within the cove, a little land-locked harbour, the water level as a pond, broken only by tiny ripples where vagrant breaths and wisps of the storm hurtled down from over the frowning wall of rock that backed the beach a hundred feet inshore.

Here were no seals whatever. The boat's stern touched the hard shingle. I sprang out, extending my hand to Maud. The next moment she was beside me. As my fingers released hers, she clutched for my arm hastily. At the same moment I swayed, as about to fall to the sand. This was the startling effect of the cessation of motion. We had been so long upon the moving, rocking sea that the stable land was a shock to us. We expected the beach to lift up this way and that, and the rocky walls to swing back and forth like the sides of a ship; and when we braced ourselves, automatically, for these various expected movements, their non-occurrence quite overcame our equilibrium.

'I really must sit down,' Maud said, with a nervous laugh and a dizzy gesture, and forthwith she sat down on the sand.

I attended to making the boat secure and joined her. Thus we landed on Endeavour Island, as we came to it, land-sick from long custom of the sea.

CHAPTER XXIX

'Fool!' I cried aloud in my vexation.

I had unloaded the boat and carried its contents high up on the beach, where I had set about making a camp. There was driftwood, though not much, on the beach, and the sight of a coffee tin I had taken from the *Ghost's* larder had given me the idea of a fire.

'Blithering idiot!' I was continuing.

But Maud said, 'Tut, tut,' in gentle reproval, and then asked why I was a blithering idiot.

'No matches,' I groaned. 'Not a match did I bring. And now we shall have no hot coffee, soup, tea, or anything!'

'Wasn't it—er—Crusoe who rubbed sticks together?' she drawled.

'But I have read the personal narratives of a score of shipwrecked men who tried, and tried in vain,' I answered. 'I remember Winters, a newspaper fellow with an Alaskan and Siberian reputation. Met him at the Bibelot once, and he was telling us how he attempted to make a fire with a couple of sticks. It was most amusing. He told it inimitably, but it was the story of a failure. I remember his conclusion, his black eyes flashing as he said, 'Gentlemen, the South Sea Islander may do it, the Malay may do it, but take my word it's beyond the white man.'

'Oh, well, we've managed so far without it,' she said cheerfully. 'And there's no reason why we cannot still manage without it.'

'But think of the coffee!' I cried. 'It's good coffee, too, I know. I took it from Larsen's private stores. And look at that good wood.'

I confess, I wanted the coffee badly; and I learned, not long afterward, that the berry was likewise a little weakness of Maud's. Besides, we had been so long on a cold diet that we were numb inside as well as out. Anything warm would have been most gratifying. But I complained no more and set about making a tent of the sail for Maud.

I had looked upon it as a simple task, what of the oars, mast, boom, and sprit, to say nothing of plenty of lines. But as I was without experience, and as every detail was an experiment and every successful detail an invention, the day was well gone before her shelter was an accomplished fact. And then, that night, it rained, and she was flooded out and driven back into the boat.

The next morning I dug a shallow ditch around the tent, and, an hour later, a sudden gust of wind, whipping over the rocky wall behind us, picked up the tent and smashed it down on the sand thirty yards away.

Maud laughed at my crestfallen expression, and I said, 'As soon as the wind abates I intend going in the boat to explore the island. There must be a station somewhere, and men. And ships must visit the station. Some Government must protect all these seals. But I wish to have you comfortable before I start.'

'I should like to go with you,' was all she said.

'It would be better if you remained. You have had enough of hardship. It is a miracle that you have survived. And it won't be comfortable in the boat rowing and sailing in this rainy weather. What you need is rest, and I should like you to remain and get it.'

Something suspiciously akin to moistness dimmed her beautiful eyes before she dropped them and partly turned away her head.

'I should prefer going with you,' she said in a low voice, in which there was just a hint of appeal.

'I might be able to help you a—' her voice broke,—'a little. And if anything should happen to you, think of me left here alone.'

'Oh, I intend being very careful,' I answered. 'And I shall not go so far but what I can get back before night. Yes, all said and done, I think it vastly better for you to remain, and sleep, and rest and do nothing.'

She turned and looked me in the eyes. Her gaze was unfaltering, but soft.

'Please, please,' she said, oh, so softly.

I stiffened myself to refuse, and shook my head. Still she waited and looked at me. I tried to word my refusal, but wavered. I saw the glad light spring into her eyes and knew that I had lost. It was impossible to say no after that.

The wind died down in the afternoon, and we were prepared to start the following morning. There was no way of penetrating the island from our cove, for the walls rose perpendicularly from the beach, and, on either side of the cove, rose from the deep water.

Morning broke dull and grey, but calm, and I was awake early and had the boat in readiness.

'Fool! Imbecile! Yahoo!' I shouted, when I thought it was meet to arouse Maud;

but this time I shouted in merriment as I danced about the beach, bareheaded, in mock despair.

Her head appeared under the flap of the sail.

'What now?' she asked sleepily, and, withal, curiously.

'Coffee!' I cried. 'What do you say to a cup of coffee? hot coffee? piping hot?'

'My!' she murmured, 'you startled me, and you are cruel. Here I have been composing my soul to do without it, and here you are vexing me with your vain suggestions.'

'Watch me,' I said.

From under clefts among the rocks I gathered a few dry sticks and chips. These I whittled into shavings or split into kindling. From my note-book I tore out a page, and from the ammunition box took a shot-gun shell. Removing the wads from the latter with my knife, I emptied the powder on a flat rock. Next I pried the primer, or cap, from the shell, and laid it on the rock, in the midst of the scattered powder. All was ready. Maud still watched from the tent. Holding the paper in my left hand, I smashed down upon the cap with a rock held in my right. There was a puff of white smoke, a burst of flame, and the rough edge of the paper was alight.

Maud clapped her hands gleefully. 'Prometheus!' she cried.

But I was too occupied to acknowledge her delight. The feeble flame must be cherished tenderly if it were to gather strength and live. I fed it, shaving by shaving, and sliver by sliver, till at last it was snapping and crackling as it laid hold of the smaller chips and sticks. To be cast away on an island had not entered into my calculations, so we were without a kettle or cooking utensils of any sort; but I made shift with the tin used for bailing the boat, and later, as we consumed our supply of canned goods, we accumulated quite an imposing array of cooking vessels.

I boiled the water, but it was Maud who made the coffee. And how good it was! My contribution was canned beef fried with crumbled sea-biscuit and water. The breakfast was a success, and we sat about the fire much longer than enterprising explorers should have done, sipping the hot black coffee and talking over our situation.

I was confident that we should find a station in some one of the coves, for I knew that the rookeries of Bering Sea were thus guarded; but Maud advanced the theory— to prepare me for disappointment, I do believe, if disappointment were to come— that we had discovered an unknown rookery. She was in very good spirits, however, and made quite merry in accepting our plight as a grave one.

'If you are right,' I said, 'then we must prepare to winter here. Our food will not last, but there are the seals. They go away in the fall, so I must soon begin to lay in a supply of meat. Then there will be huts to build and driftwood to gather. Also we shall try out seal fat for lighting purposes. Altogether, we'll have our hands full if we find the island uninhabited. Which we shall not, I know.'

But she was right. We sailed with a beam wind along the shore, searching the coves with our glasses and landing occasionally, without finding a sign of human life. Yet we learned that we were not the first who had landed on Endeavour Island. High up on the beach of the second cove from ours, we discovered the splintered wreck of a boat—a sealer's boat, for the rowlocks were bound in sennit, a gun-rack was on the starboard side of the bow, and in white letters was faintly visible *Gazelle* No. 2. The boat had lain there for a long time, for it was half filled with sand, and the splintered wood had that weather-worn appearance due to long exposure to the elements. In the stern-sheets I found a rusty ten-gauge shot-gun and a sailor's sheath-knife broken short across and so rusted as to be almost unrecognizable.

'They got away,' I said cheerfully; but I felt a sinking at the heart and seemed to divine the presence of bleached bones somewhere on that beach.

I did not wish Maud's spirits to be dampened by such a find, so I turned seaward again with our boat and skirted the north-eastern point of the island. There were no beaches on the southern shore, and by early afternoon we rounded the black promontory and completed the circumnavigation of the island. I estimated its circumference at twenty-five miles, its width as varying from two to five miles; while my most conservative calculation placed on its beaches two hundred thousand seals. The island was highest at its extreme south-western point, the headlands and backbone diminishing regularly until the north-eastern portion was only a few feet above the sea. With the exception of our little cove, the other beaches sloped gently back for a distance of half-a-mile or so, into what I might call rocky meadows, with here and there patches of moss and tundra grass. Here the seals hauled out, and the old bulls guarded their harems, while the young bulls hauled out by themselves.

This brief description is all that Endeavour Island merits. Damp and soggy where it was not sharp and rocky, buffeted by storm winds and lashed by the sea, with the air continually a-tremble with the bellowing of two hundred thousand amphibians, it was a melancholy and miserable sojourning-place. Maud, who had prepared me for disappointment, and who had been sprightly and vivacious all day, broke down as we landed in our own little cove. She strove bravely to hide it from me, but while I was kindling another fire I knew she was stifling her sobs in the blankets under the sail-tent.

It was my turn to be cheerful, and I played the part to the best of my ability, and with such success that I brought the laughter back into her dear eyes and song on her lips; for she sang to me before she went to an early bed. It was the first time I had heard her sing, and I lay by the fire, listening and transported, for she was nothing if not an artist in everything she did, and her voice, though not strong, was wonderfully sweet and expressive.

I still slept in the boat, and I lay awake long that night, gazing up at the first stars I had seen in many nights and pondering the situation. Responsibility of this sort was a new thing to me. Wolf Larsen had been quite right. I had stood on my father's legs. My lawyers and agents had taken care of my money for me. I had had no responsibilities at all. Then, on the *Ghost* I had learned to be responsible for myself. And now, for the first time in my life, I found myself responsible for some one else. And it was required of me that this should be the gravest of responsibilities, for she was the one woman in the world—the one small woman, as I loved to think of her.

CHAPTER XXX

No wonder we called it Endeavour Island. For two weeks we toiled at building a hut. Maud insisted on helping, and I could have wept over her bruised and bleeding hands. And still, I was proud of her because of it. There was something heroic about this gently-bred woman enduring our terrible hardship and with her pittance of strength bending to the tasks of a peasant woman. She gathered many of the stones which

I built into the walls of the hut; also, she turned a deaf ear to my entreaties when I begged her to desist. She compromised, however, by taking upon herself the lighter labours of cooking and gathering driftwood and moss for our winter's supply.

The hut's walls rose without difficulty, and everything went smoothly until the problem of the roof confronted me. Of what use the four walls without a roof? And of what could a roof be made? There were the spare oars, very true. They would serve as roof-beams; but with what was I to cover them? Moss would never do. Tundra grass was impracticable. We needed the sail for the boat, and the tarpaulin had begun to leak.

'Winters used walrus skins on his hut,' I said.

'There are the seals,' she suggested.

So next day the hunting began. I did not know how to shoot, but I proceeded to learn. And when I had expended some thirty shells for three seals, I decided that the ammunition would be exhausted before I acquired the necessary knowledge. I had used eight shells for lighting fires before I hit upon the device of banking the embers with wet moss, and there remained not over a hundred shells in the box.

'We must club the seals,' I announced, when convinced of my poor marksmanship. 'I have heard the sealers talk about clubbing them.'

'They are so pretty,' she objected. 'I cannot bear to think of it being done. It is so directly brutal, you know; so different from shooting them.'

'That roof must go on,' I answered grimly. 'Winter is almost here. It is our lives against theirs. It is unfortunate we haven't plenty of ammunition, but I think, anyway, that they suffer less from being clubbed than from being all shot up. Besides, I shall do the clubbing.'

'That's just it,' she began eagerly, and broke off in sudden confusion.

'Of course,' I began, 'if you prefer—'

'But what shall I be doing?' she interrupted, with that softness I knew full well to be insistence.

'Gathering firewood and cooking dinner,' I answered lightly.

She shook her head. 'It is too dangerous for you to attempt alone.'

'I know, I know,' she waived my protest. 'I am only a weak woman, but just my small assistance may enable you to escape disaster.'

'But the clubbing?' I suggested.

'Of course, you will do that. I shall probably scream. I'll look away when—'

'The danger is most serious,' I laughed.

'I shall use my judgment when to look and when not to look,' she replied with a grand air.

The upshot of the affair was that she accompanied me next morning. I rowed into the adjoining cove and up to the edge of the beach. There were seals all about us in the water, and the bellowing thousands on the beach compelled us to shout at each other to make ourselves heard.

'I know men club them,' I said, trying to reassure myself, and gazing doubtfully at a large bull, not thirty feet away, upreared on his fore-flippers and regarding me intently. 'But the question is, How do they club them?'

'Let us gather tundra grass and thatch the roof,' Maud said.

She was as frightened as I at the prospect, and we had reason to be gazing at close range at the gleaming teeth and dog-like mouths.

'I always thought they were afraid of men,' I said.

'How do I know they are not afraid?' I queried a moment later, after having rowed a few more strokes along the beach. 'Perhaps, if I were to step boldly ashore, they would cut for it, and I could not catch up with one.' And still I hesitated.

'I heard of a man, once, who invaded the nesting grounds of wild geese,' Maud said. 'They killed him.'

'The geese?'

'Yes, the geese. My brother told me about it when I was a little girl.'

'But I know men club them,' I persisted.

'I think the tundra grass will make just as good a roof,' she said.

Far from her intention, her words were maddening me, driving me on. I could not play the coward before her eyes. 'Here goes,' I said, backing water with one oar and running the bow ashore.

I stepped out and advanced valiantly upon a long-maned bull in the midst of his wives. I was armed with the regular club with which the boat-pullers killed the wounded seals gaffed aboard by the hunters. It was only a foot and a half long, and in my superb ignorance I never dreamed that the club used ashore when raiding the rookeries measured four to five feet. The cows lumbered out of my way, and the distance between me and the bull decreased. He raised himself on his flippers with an angry movement. We were a dozen feet apart. Still I advanced steadily, looking for him to turn tail at any moment and run.

At six feet the panicky thought rushed into my mind, What if he will not run? Why, then I shall club him, came the answer. In my fear I had forgotten that I was there to get the bull instead of to make him run. And just then he gave a snort and a snarl and rushed at me. His eyes were blazing, his mouth was wide open; the teeth gleamed cruelly white. Without shame, I confess that it was I who turned and footed it. He ran awkwardly, but he ran well. He was but two paces behind when I tumbled into the boat, and as I shoved off with an oar his teeth crunched down upon the blade. The stout wood was crushed like an egg-shell. Maud and I were astounded. A moment later he had dived under the boat, seized the keel in his mouth, and was shaking the boat violently.

'My!' said Maud. 'Let's go back.'

I shook my head. 'I can do what other men have done, and I know that other men have clubbed seals. But I think I'll leave the bulls alone next time.'

'I wish you wouldn't,' she said.

'Now don't say, 'Please, please,' I cried, half angrily, I do believe.

She made no reply, and I knew my tone must have hurt her.

'I beg your pardon,' I said, or shouted, rather, in order to make myself heard above the roar of the rookery. 'If you say so, I'll turn and go back; but honestly, I'd rather stay.'

'Now don't say that this is what you get for bringing a woman along,' she said. She smiled at me whimsically, gloriously, and I knew there was no need for forgiveness.

I rowed a couple of hundred feet along the beach so as to recover my nerves, and then stepped ashore again.

'Do be cautious,' she called after me.

I nodded my head and proceeded to make a flank attack on the nearest harem. All went well until I aimed a blow at an outlying cowls head and fell short. She snorted and tried to scramble away. I ran in close and struck another blow, hitting the shoulder instead of the head.

'Watch out!' I heard Maud scream.

In my excitement I had not been taking notice of other things, and I looked up to see the lord of the harem charging down upon me. Again I fled to the boat, hotly pursued; but this time Maud made no suggestion of turning back.

'It would be better, I imagine, if you let harems alone and devoted your attention to lonely and inoffensive-looking seals,' was what she said. 'I think I have read something about them. Dr. Jordan's book, I believe. They are the young bulls, not old enough to have harems of their own. He called them the holluschickie, or something like that. It seems to me if we find where they haul out—'

'It seems to me that your fighting instinct is aroused,' I laughed.

She flushed quickly and prettily. 'I'll admit I don't like defeat any more than you do, or any more than I like the idea of killing such pretty, inoffensive creatures.'

'Pretty!' I sniffed. 'I failed to mark anything pre-eminently pretty about those foamy-mouthed beasts that raced me.'

'Your point of view,' she laughed. 'You lacked perspective. Now if you did not have to get so close to the subject—'

'The very thing!' I cried. 'What I need is a longer club. And there's that broken oar ready to hand.'

'It just comes to me,' she said, 'that Captain Larsen was telling me how the men raided the rookeries. They drive the seals, in small herds, a short distance inland before they kill them.'

'I don't care to undertake the herding of one of those harems,' I objected.

'But there are the holluschickie,' she said. 'The holluschickie haul out by themselves, and Dr. Jordan says that paths are left between the harems, and that as long as the holluschickie keep strictly to the path they are unmolested by the masters of the harem.'

'There's one now,' I said, pointing to a young bull in the water. 'Let's watch him, and follow him if he hauls out.'

He swam directly to the beach and clambered out into a small opening between two harems, the masters of which made warning noises but did not attack him. We watched him travel slowly inward, threading about among the harems along what must have been the path.

'Here goes,' I said, stepping out; but I confess my heart was in my mouth as I thought of going through the heart of that monstrous herd.

'It would be wise to make the boat fast,' Maud said.

She had stepped out beside me, and I regarded her with wonderment.

She nodded her head determinedly. 'Yes, I'm going with you, so you may as well secure the boat and arm me with a club.'

'Let's go back,' I said dejectedly. 'I think tundra grass, will do, after all.'

'You know it won't,' was her reply. 'Shall I lead?'

With a shrug of the shoulders, but with the warmest admiration and pride at heart for this woman, I equipped her with the broken oar and took another for myself. It was with nervous trepidation that we made the first few rods of the journey. Once Maud screamed in terror as a cow thrust an inquisitive nose toward her foot, and several times I quickened my pace for the same reason. But, beyond warning coughs from either side, there were no signs of hostility. It was a rookery which had never been raided by the hunters, and in consequence the seals were mild-tempered and at the same time unafraid.

In the very heart of the herd the din was terrific. It was almost dizzying in its effect. I paused and smiled reassuringly at Maud, for I had recovered my equanimity sooner than she. I could see that she was still badly frightened. She came close to me and shouted:

'I'm dreadfully afraid!'

And I was not. Though the novelty had not yet worn off, the peaceful comportment of the seals had quieted my alarm. Maud was trembling.

'I'm afraid, and I'm not afraid,' she chattered with shaking jaws. 'It's my miserable body, not I.'

'It's all right, it's all right,' I reassured her, my arm passing instinctively and protectingly around her.

I shall never forget, in that moment, how instantly conscious I became of my manhood. The primitive deeps of my nature stirred. I felt myself masculine, the protector of the weak, the fighting male. And, best of all, I felt myself the protector of my loved one. She leaned against me, so light and lily-frail, and as her trembling eased away it seemed as though I became aware of prodigious strength. I felt myself a match for the most ferocious bull in the herd, and I know, had such a bull charged upon me, that I should have met it unflinchingly and quite coolly, and I know that I should have killed it.

'I am all right now,' she said, looking up at me gratefully. 'Let us go on.'

And that the strength in me had quieted her and given her confidence, filled me with an exultant joy. The youth of the race seemed burgeoning in me, over-civilized man that I was, and I lived for myself the old hunting days and forest nights of my remote and forgotten ancestry. I had much for which to thank Wolf Larsen, was my thought as we went along the path between the jostling harems.

A quarter of a mile inland we came upon the holluschickie—sleek young bulls, living out the loneliness of their bachelorhood and gathering strength against the day when they would fight their way into the ranks of the Benedicts.

Everything now went smoothly. I seemed to know just what to do and how to do it. Shouting, making threatening gestures with my club, and even prodding the lazy ones, I quickly cut out a score of the young bachelors from their companions. Whenever one made an attempt to break back toward the water, I headed it off. Maud took an active part in the drive, and with her cries and flourishings of the broken oar was of considerable assistance. I noticed, though, that whenever one looked tired and lagged, she let it slip past. But I noticed, also, whenever one, with a show of fight, tried to break past, that her eyes glinted and showed bright, and she rapped it smartly with her club.

'My, it's exciting!' she cried, pausing from sheer weakness. 'I think I'll sit down.'

I drove the little herd (a dozen strong, now, what of the escapes she had permitted) a hundred yards farther on; and by the time she joined me I had finished the slaughter and was beginning to skin. An hour later we went proudly back along the path between the harems. And twice again we came down the path burdened with skins, till I thought we had enough to roof the hut. I set the sail, laid one tack out of the cove, and on the other tack made our own little inner cove.

'It's just like home-coming,' Maud said, as I ran the boat ashore.

I heard her words with a responsive thrill, it was all so dearly intimate and natural, and I said:

'It seems as though I have lived this life always. The world of books and bookish folk is very vague, more like a dream memory than an actuality. I surely have hunted and forayed and fought all the days of my life. And you, too, seem a part of it. You are—' I was on the verge of saying, 'my woman, my mate,' but glibly changed it to—'standing the hardship well.'

But her ear had caught the flaw. She recognized a flight that midmost broke. She gave me a quick look.

'Not that. You were saying—?'

'That the American Mrs. Meynell was living the life of a savage and living it quite successfully,' I said easily.

'Oh,' was all she replied; but I could have sworn there was a note of disappointment in her voice.

But 'my woman, my mate' kept ringing in my head for the rest of the day and for many days. Yet never did it ring more loudly than that night, as I watched her draw back the blanket of moss from the coals, blow up the fire, and cook the evening meal. It must have been latent savagery stirring in me, for the old words, so bound up with the roots of the race, to grip me and thrill me. And grip and thrill they did, till I fell asleep, murmuring them to myself over and over again.

CHAPTER XXXI

'It will smell,' I said, 'but it will keep in the heat and keep out the rain and snow.'
We were surveying the completed seal-skin roof.

'It is clumsy, but it will serve the purpose, and that is the main thing,' I went on, yearning for her praise.

And she clapped her hands and declared that she was hugely pleased.

'But it is dark in here,' she said the next moment, her shoulders shrinking with a little involuntary shiver.

'You might have suggested a window when the walls were going up,' I said. 'It was for you, and you should have seen the need of a window.'

'But I never do see the obvious, you know,' she laughed back. 'And besides, you can knock a hole in the wall at any time.'

'Quite true; I had not thought of it,' I replied, wagging my head sagely. 'But have you thought of ordering the window-glass? Just call up the firm,—Red, 4451, I think it is,—and tell them what size and kind of glass you wish.'

'That means—' she began.

'No window.'

It was a dark and evil-appearing thing, that hut, not fit for aught better than swine in a civilized land; but for us, who had known the misery of the open boat, it was a snug little habitation. Following the housewarming, which was accomplished by means of seal-oil and a wick made from cotton calking, came the hunting for our winter's meat and the building of the second hut. It was a simple affair, now, to go forth in the morning and return by noon with a boatload of seals. And then, while I worked at building the hut, Maud tried out the oil from the blubber and kept a slow fire under the frames of meat. I had heard of jerking beef on the plains, and our seal-meat, cut in thin strips and hung in the smoke, cured excellently.

The second hut was easier to erect, for I built it against the first, and only three walls were required. But it was work, hard work, all of it. Maud and I worked from dawn till dark, to the limit of our strength, so that when night came we crawled stiffly to bed and slept the animal-like sleep exhaustion. And yet Maud declared that she had never felt better or stronger in her life. I knew this was true of myself, but hers was such a lily strength that I feared she would break down. Often and often, her last-reserve force gone, I have seen her stretched flat on her back on the sand in the way she had of resting and recuperating. And then she would be up on her feet and toiling hard as ever. Where she obtained this strength was the marvel to me.

'Think of the long rest this winter,' was her reply to my remonstrances. 'Why, we'll be clamorous for something to do.'

We held a housewarming in my hut the night it was roofed. It was the end of the third day of a fierce storm which had swung around the compass from the south-east to the north-west, and which was then blowing directly in upon us. The beaches of the outer cove were thundering with the surf, and even in our land-locked inner cove a respectable sea was breaking. No high backbone of island sheltered us from the wind, and it whistled and bellowed about the hut till at times I feared for the strength of the walls. The skin roof, stretched tightly as a drumhead, I had thought, sagged and bellied with every gust; and innumerable interstices in the walls, not so tightly stuffed with moss as Maud had supposed, disclosed themselves. Yet the seal-oil burned brightly and we were warm and comfortable.

It was a pleasant evening indeed, and we voted that as a social function on Endeavour Island it had not yet been eclipsed. Our minds were at ease. Not only had we resigned ourselves to the bitter winter, but we were prepared for it. The seals could depart on their mysterious journey into the south at any time, now, for all we cared; and the storms held no terror for us. Not only were we sure of being dry and warm and sheltered from the wind, but we had the softest and most luxurious mattresses that could be made from moss. This had been Maud's idea, and she had herself jealously gathered all the moss. This was to be my first night on the mattress, and I knew I should sleep the sweeter because she had made it.

As she rose to go she turned to me with the whimsical way she had, and said:

'Something is going to happen—is happening, for that matter. I feel it. Something is coming here, to us. It is coming now. I don't know what, but it is coming.'

'Good or bad?' I asked.

She shook her head. 'I don't know, but it is there, somewhere.'

She pointed in the direction of the sea and wind.

'It's a lee shore,' I laughed, 'and I am sure I'd rather be here than arriving, a night like this.'

'You are not frightened?' I asked, as I stepped to open the door for her.

Her eyes looked bravely into mine.

'And you feel well? perfectly well?'

'Never better,' was her answer.

We talked a little longer before she went.

'Good-night, Maud,' I said.

'Good-night, Humphrey,' she said.

This use of our given names had come about quite as a matter of course, and was as unpremeditated as it was natural. In that moment I could have put my arms around her and drawn her to me. I should certainly have done so out in that world to which we belonged. As it was, the situation stopped there in the only way it could; but I was left alone in my little hut, glowing warmly through and through with a pleasant satisfaction; and I knew that a tie, or a tacit something, existed between us which had not existed before.

CHAPTER XXXII

I awoke, oppressed by a mysterious sensation. There seemed something missing in my environment. But the mystery and oppressiveness vanished after the first few seconds of waking, when I identified the missing something as the wind. I had fallen asleep in that state of nerve tension with which one meets the continuous shock of sound or movement, and I had awakened, still tense, bracing myself to meet the pressure of something which no longer bore upon me.

It was the first night I had spent under cover in several months, and I lay luxuriously for some minutes under my blankets (for once not wet with fog or spray), analysing, first, the effect produced upon me by the cessation of the wind, and next, the joy which was mine from resting on the mattress made by Maud's hands. When I had dressed and opened the door, I heard the waves still lapping on the beach, garrulously attesting the fury of the night. It was a clear day, and the sun was shining. I had slept late, and I stepped outside with sudden energy, bent upon making up lost time as befitted a dweller on Endeavour Island.

And when outside, I stopped short. I believed my eyes without question, and yet I was for the moment stunned by what they disclosed to me. There, on the beach, not fifty feet away, bow on, dismasted, was a black-hulled vessel. Masts and booms, tangled with shrouds, sheets, and rent canvas, were rubbing gently alongside. I could have rubbed my eyes as I looked. There was the home-made galley we had built, the familiar break of the poop, the low yacht-cabin scarcely rising above the rail. It was the *Ghost*.

What freak of fortune had brought it here—here of all spots? what chance of chances? I looked at the bleak, inaccessible wall at my back and know the profundity of despair. Escape was hopeless, out of the question. I thought of Maud, asleep there in the hut we had reared; I remembered her 'Good-night, Humphrey'; 'my woman, my mate,' went ringing through my brain, but now, alas, it was a knell that sounded. Then everything went black before my eyes.

Possibly it was the fraction of a second, but I had no knowledge of how long an interval had lapsed before I was myself again. There lay the *Ghost*, bow on to the beach, her splintered bowsprit projecting over the sand, her tangled spars rubbing against her side to the lift of the crooning waves. Something must be done, must be done.

It came upon me suddenly, as strange, that nothing moved aboard. Wearied from the night of struggle and wreck, all hands were yet asleep, I thought. My next thought was that Maud and I might yet escape. If we could take to the boat and make round the point before any one awoke? I would call her and start. My hand was lifted at her door to knock, when I recollected the smallness of the island. We could never hide ourselves upon it. There was nothing for us but the wide raw ocean. I thought of our snug little huts, our supplies of meat and oil and moss and firewood, and I knew that we could never survive the wintry sea and the great storms which were to come.

So I stood, with hesitant knuckle, without her door. It was impossible, impossible. A wild thought of rushing in and killing her as she slept rose in my mind. And then, in a flash, the better solution came to me. All hands were asleep. Why not creep aboard the *Ghost*,—well I knew the way to Wolf Larsen's bunk,—and kill him in his sleep? After that—well, we would see. But with him dead there was time and space in which to prepare to do other things; and besides, whatever new situation arose, it could not possibly be worse than the present one.

My knife was at my hip. I returned to my hut for the shot-gun, made sure it was loaded, and went down to the *Ghost*. With some difficulty, and at the expense of a wetting to the waist, I climbed aboard. The forecastle scuttle was open. I paused to listen for the breathing of the men, but there was no breathing. I almost gasped as the thought came to me: What if the *Ghost* is deserted? I listened more closely. There was no sound. I cautiously descended the ladder. The place had the empty and musty feel and smell usual to a dwelling no longer inhabited. Everywhere was a thick litter of discarded and ragged garments, old sea-boots, leaky oilskins—all the worthless forecastle dunnage of a long voyage.

Abandoned hastily, was my conclusion, as I ascended to the deck. Hope was alive again in my breast, and I looked about me with greater coolness. I noted that the boats were missing. The steerage told the same tale as the forecastle. The hunters had packed their belongings with similar haste. The *Ghost* was deserted. It was Maud's and mine. I thought of the ship's stores and the lazarette beneath the cabin, and the idea came to me of surprising Maud with something nice for breakfast.

The reaction from my fear, and the knowledge that the terrible deed I had come to do was no longer necessary, made me boyish and eager. I went up the steerage companion-way two steps at a time, with nothing distinct in my mind except joy and the hope that Maud would sleep on until the surprise breakfast was quite ready for her. As I rounded the galley, a new satisfaction was mine at thought of all the splendid cooking utensils inside. I sprang up the break of the poop, and saw—Wolf Larsen. What of my impetus and the stunning surprise, I clattered three or four steps along the deck before I could stop myself. He was standing in the companion-way, only his head and shoulders visible, staring straight at me. His arms were resting on the half-open slide. He made no movement whatever—simply stood there, staring at me.

I began to tremble. The old stomach sickness clutched me. I put one hand on the edge of the house to steady myself. My lips seemed suddenly dry and I moistened them against the need of speech. Nor did I for an instant take my eyes off him. Neither of us spoke. There was something ominous in his silence, his immobility. All my old fear of him returned and by new fear was increased an hundred-fold. And still we stood, the pair of us, staring at each other.

I was aware of the demand for action, and, my old helplessness strong upon me, I was waiting for him to take the initiative. Then, as the moments went by, it came to me that the situation was analogous to the one in which I had approached the long-maned bull, my intention of clubbing obscured by fear until it became a desire to make him run. So it was at last impressed upon me that I was there, not to have Wolf Larsen take the initiative, but to take it myself.

I cocked both barrels and levelled the shot-gun at him. Had he moved, attempted to drop down the companion-way, I know I would have shot him. But he stood motionless and staring as before. And as I faced him, with levelled gun shaking in my hands, I had time to note the worn and haggard appearance of his face. It was as if some strong anxiety had wasted it. The cheeks were sunken, and there was a wearied, puckered expression on the brow. And it seemed to me that his eyes were strange, not only the expression, but the physical seeming, as though the optic nerves and supporting muscles had suffered strain and slightly twisted the eyeballs.

All this I saw, and my brain now working rapidly, I thought a thousand thoughts; and yet I could not pull the triggers. I lowered the gun and stepped to the corner of the cabin, primarily to relieve the tension on my nerves and to make a new start, and incidentally to be closer. Again I raised the gun. He was almost at arm's length. There was no hope for him. I was resolved. There was no possible chance of missing him, no matter how poor my marksmanship. And yet I wrestled with myself and could not pull the triggers.

'Well?' he demanded impatiently.

I strove vainly to force my fingers down on the triggers, and vainly I strove to say something.

'Why don't you shoot?' he asked.

I cleared my throat of a huskiness which prevented speech. 'Hump,' he said slowly, 'you can't do it. You are not exactly afraid. You are impotent. Your conventional morality is stronger than you. You are the slave to the opinions which have credence among the people you have known and have read about. Their code has been drummed into your head from the time you lisped, and in spite of your philosophy, and of what I have taught you, it won't let you kill an unarmed, unresisting man.'

'I know it,' I said hoarsely.

'And you know that I would kill an unarmed man as readily as I would smoke a cigar,' he went on. 'You know me for what I am,—my worth in the world by your standard. You have called me snake, tiger, shark, monster, and Caliban. And yet, you little rag puppet, you little echoing mechanism, you are unable to kill me as you would a snake or a shark, because I have hands, feet, and a body shaped somewhat like yours. Bah! I had hoped better things of you, Hump.'

He stepped out of the companion-way and came up to me.

'Put down that gun. I want to ask you some questions. I haven't had a chance to look around yet. What place is this? How is the *Ghost* lying? How did you get wet? Where's Maud?—I beg your pardon, Miss Brewster—or should I say, "Mrs. Van Weyden"?'

I had backed away from him, almost weeping at my inability to shoot him, but not fool enough to put down the gun. I hoped, desperately, that he might commit some hostile act, attempt to strike me or choke me; for in such way only I knew I could be stirred to shoot.

'This is Endeavour Island,' I said.

'Never heard of it,' he broke in.

'At least, that's our name for it,' I amended.

'Our?' he queried. 'Who's our?'

'Miss Brewster and myself. And the *Ghost* is lying, as you can see for yourself, bow on to the beach.'

'There are seals here,' he said. 'They woke me up with their barking, or I'd be sleeping yet. I heard them when I drove in last night. They were the first warning that I was on a lee shore. It's a rookery, the kind of a thing I've hunted for years. Thanks to my brother Death, I've lighted on a fortune. It's a mint. What's its bearings?'

'Haven't the least idea,' I said. 'But you ought to know quite closely. What were your last observations?'

He smiled inscrutably, but did not answer.

'Well, where's all hands?' I asked. 'How does it come that you are alone?'

I was prepared for him again to set aside my question, and was surprised at the readiness of his reply.

'My brother got me inside forty-eight hours, and through no fault of mine. Boarded me in the night with only the watch on deck. Hunters went back on me. He gave them a bigger lay. Heard him offering it. Did it right before me. Of course the crew gave me the go-by. That was to be expected. All hands went over the side, and there I was, marooned on my own vessel. It was Death's turn, and it's all in the family anyway.'

'But how did you lose the masts?' I asked.

'Walk over and examine those lanyards,' he said, pointing to where the mizzen-rigging should have been.

'They have been cut with a knife!' I exclaimed.

'Not quite,' he laughed. 'It was a neater job. Look again.'

I looked. The lanyards had been almost severed, with just enough left to hold the shrouds till some severe strain should be put upon them.

'Cooky did that,' he laughed again. 'I know, though I didn't spot him at it. Kind of evened up the score a bit.'

'Good for Mugridge!' I cried.

'Yes, that's what I thought when everything went over the side. Only I said it on the other side of my mouth.'

'But what were you doing while all this was going on?' I asked.

'My best, you may be sure, which wasn't much under the circumstances.'

I turned to re-examine Thomas Mugridge's work.

'I guess I'll sit down and take the sunshine,' I heard Wolf Larsen saying.

There was a hint, just a slight hint, of physical feebleness in his voice, and it was so strange that I looked quickly at him. His hand was sweeping nervously across his face, as though he were brushing away cobwebs. I was puzzled. The whole thing was so unlike the Wolf Larsen I had known.

'How are your headaches?' I asked.

'They still trouble me,' was his answer. 'I think I have one coming on now.'

He slipped down from his sitting posture till he lay on the deck. Then he rolled over on his side, his head resting on the biceps of the under arm, the forearm shielding his eyes from the sun. I stood regarding him wonderingly.

'Now's your chance, Hump,' he said.

'I don't understand,' I lied, for I thoroughly understood.

'Oh, nothing,' he added softly, as if he were drowsing; 'only you've got me where you want me.'

'No, I haven't,' I retorted; 'for I want you a few thousand miles away from here.'

He chuckled, and thereafter spoke no more. He did not stir as I passed by him and went down into the cabin. I lifted the trap in the floor, but for some moments gazed dubiously into the darkness of the lazarette beneath. I hesitated to descend. What if his lying down were a ruse? Pretty, indeed, to be caught there like a rat. I crept softly up the companion-way and peeped at him. He was lying as I had left him. Again I went below; but before I dropped into the lazarette I took the precaution of casting down the door in advance. At least there would be no lid to the trap. But it was all needless. I regained the cabin with a store of jams, sea-biscuits, canned meats, and such things,—all I could carry,—and replaced the trap-door.

A peep at Wolf Larsen showed me that he had not moved. A bright thought struck me. I stole into his state-room and possessed myself of his revolvers. There were no other weapons, though I thoroughly ransacked the three remaining state-rooms. To make sure, I returned and went through the steerage and forecastle, and in the galley gathered up all the sharp meat and vegetable knives. Then I bethought me of the great yachtsman's knife he always carried, and I came to him and spoke to him, first softly, then loudly. He did not move. I bent over and took it from his pocket. I breathed more freely. He had no arms with which to attack me from a distance; while I, armed, could always forestall him should he attempt to grapple me with his terrible gorilla arms.

Filling a coffee-pot and frying-pan with part of my plunder, and taking some chinaware from the cabin pantry, I left Wolf Larsen lying in the sun and went ashore.

Maud was still asleep. I blew up the embers (we had not yet arranged a winter kitchen), and quite feverishly cooked the breakfast. Toward the end, I heard her moving about within the hut, making her toilet. Just as all was ready and the coffee poured, the door opened and she came forth.

'It's not fair of you,' was her greeting. 'You are usurping one of my prerogatives. You know you I agreed that the cooking should be mine, and—'

'But just this once,' I pleaded.

'If you promise not to do it again,' she smiled. 'Unless, of course, you have grown tired of my poor efforts.'

To my delight she never once looked toward the beach, and I maintained the banter with such success all unconsciously she sipped coffee from the china cup, ate fried evaporated potatoes, and spread marmalade on her biscuit. But it could not last. I saw the surprise that came over her. She had discovered the china plate from which she was eating. She looked over the breakfast, noting detail after detail. Then she looked at me, and her face turned slowly toward the beach.

'Humphrey!' she said.

The old unnamable terror mounted into her eyes.

'Is—he?' she quavered.

I nodded my head.

CHAPTER XXXIII

We waited all day for Wolf Larsen to come ashore. It was an intolerable period of anxiety. Each moment one or the other of us cast expectant glances toward the *Ghost*. But he did not come. He did not even appear on deck.

'Perhaps it is his headache,' I said. 'I left him lying on the poop. He may lie there all night. I think I'll go and see.'

Maud looked entreaty at me.

'It is all right,' I assured her. 'I shall take the revolvers. You know I collected every weapon on board.'

'But there are his arms, his hands, his terrible, terrible hands!' she objected. And then she cried, 'Oh, Humphrey, I am afraid of him! Don't go—please don't go!'

She rested her hand appealingly on mine, and sent my pulse fluttering. My heart was surely in my eyes for a moment. The dear and lovely woman! And she was so much the woman, clinging and appealing, sunshine and dew to my manhood, rooting it deeper and sending through it the sap of a new strength. I was for putting my arm around her, as when in the midst of the seal herd; but I considered, and refrained.

'I shall not take any risks,' I said. 'I'll merely peep over the bow and see.'

She pressed my hand earnestly and let me go. But the space on deck where I had left him lying was vacant. He had evidently gone below. That night we stood alternate watches, one of us sleeping at a time; for there was no telling what Wolf Larsen might do. He was certainly capable of anything.

The next day we waited, and the next, and still he made no sign.

'These headaches of his, these attacks,' Maud said, on the afternoon of the fourth day; 'Perhaps he is ill, very ill. He may be dead.'

'Or dying,' was her afterthought when she had waited some time for me to speak.

'Better so,' I answered.

'But think, Humphrey, a fellow-creature in his last lonely hour.'

'Perhaps,' I suggested.

'Yes, even perhaps,' she acknowledged. 'But we do not know. It would be terrible if he were. I could never forgive myself. We must do something.'

'Perhaps,' I suggested again.

I waited, smiling inwardly at the woman of her which compelled a solicitude for Wolf Larsen, of all creatures. Where was her solicitude for me, I thought,—for me whom she had been afraid to have merely peep aboard?

She was too subtle not to follow the trend of my silence. And she was as direct as she was subtle.

'You must go aboard, Humphrey, and find out,' she said. 'And if you want to laugh at me, you have my consent and forgiveness.'

I arose obediently and went down the beach.

'Do be careful,' she called after me.

I waved my arm from the forecastle head and dropped down to the deck. Aft I walked to the cabin companion, where I contented myself with hailing below. Wolf Larsen answered, and as he started to ascend the stairs I cocked my revolver. I displayed it openly during our conversation, but he took no notice of it. He appeared the same, physically, as when last I saw him, but he was gloomy and silent. In fact, the few words we spoke could hardly be called a conversation. I did not inquire why he had not been ashore, nor did he ask why I had not come aboard. His head was all right again, he said, and so, without further parley, I left him.

Maud received my report with obvious relief, and the sight of smoke which later rose in the galley put her in a more cheerful mood. The next day, and the next, we saw the galley smoke rising, and sometimes we caught glimpses of him on the poop. But that was all. He made no attempt to come ashore. This we knew, for we still maintained our night-watches. We were waiting for him to do something, to show his hand, so to say, and his inaction puzzled and worried us.

A week of this passed by. We had no other interest than Wolf Larsen, and his presence weighed us down with an apprehension which prevented us from doing any of the little things we had planned.

But at the end of the week the smoke ceased rising from the galley, and he no longer showed himself on the poop. I could see Maud's solicitude again growing, though she timidly—and even proudly, I think—forbore a repetition of her request. After all, what censure could be put upon her? She was divinely altruistic, and she was a woman. Besides, I was myself aware of hurt at thought of this man whom I had tried to kill, dying alone with his fellow-creatures so near. He was right. The code of my group was stronger than I. The fact that he had hands, feet, and a body shaped somewhat like mine, constituted a claim which I could not ignore.

So I did not wait a second time for Maud to send me. I discovered that we stood in need of condensed milk and marmalade, and announced that I was going aboard. I could see that she wavered. She even went so far as to murmur that they were non-essentials and that my trip after them might be inexpedient. And as she had followed the trend of my silence, she now followed the trend of my speech, and she knew that I was going aboard, not because of condensed milk and marmalade, but because of her and of her anxiety, which she knew she had failed to hide.

I took off my shoes when I gained the forecastle head, and went noiselessly aft in my stocking feet. Nor did I call this time from the top of the companion-way. Cautiously descending, I found the cabin deserted. The door to his state-room was closed. At first I thought of knocking, then I remembered my ostensible errand and resolved to carry it out. Carefully avoiding noise, I lifted the trap-door in the floor and set it to one side. The slop-chest, as well as the provisions, was stored in the lazarette, and I took advantage of the opportunity to lay in a stock of underclothing.

As I emerged from the lazarette I heard sounds in Wolf Larsen's state-room. I crouched and listened. The door-knob rattled. Furtively, instinctively, I slunk back behind the table and drew and cocked my revolver. The door swung open and he came forth. Never had I seen so profound a despair as that which I saw on his face,— the face of Wolf Larsen the fighter, the strong man, the indomitable one. For all the world like a woman wringing her hands, he raised his clenched fists and groaned. One fist unclosed, and the open palm swept across his eyes as though brushing away cobwebs.

'God! God!' he groaned, and the clenched fists were raised again to the infinite despair with which his throat vibrated.

It was horrible. I was trembling all over, and I could feel the shivers running up and down my spine and the sweat standing out on my forehead. Surely there can be little in this world more awful than the spectacle of a strong man in the moment when he is utterly weak and broken.

But Wolf Larsen regained control of himself by an exertion of his remarkable will. And it was exertion. His whole frame shook with the struggle. He resembled a man on the verge of a fit. His face strove to compose itself, writhing and twisting in the effort till he broke down again. Once more the clenched fists went upward and he groaned. He caught his breath once or twice and sobbed. Then he was successful. I could have thought him the old Wolf Larsen, and yet there was in his movements a vague suggestion of weakness and indecision. He started for the companion-way, and stepped forward quite as I had been accustomed to see him do; and yet again, in his very walk, there seemed that suggestion of weakness and indecision.

I was now concerned with fear for myself. The open trap lay directly in his path, and his discovery of it would lead instantly to his discovery of me. I was angry with myself for being caught in so cowardly a position, crouching on the floor. There was yet time. I rose swiftly to my feet, and, I know, quite unconsciously assumed a defiant attitude. He took no notice of me. Nor did he notice the open trap. Before I could grasp the situation, or act, he had walked right into the trap. One foot was descending into the opening, while the other foot was just on the verge of beginning the uplift. But when the descending foot missed the solid flooring and felt vacancy beneath, it was the old Wolf Larsen and the tiger muscles that made the falling body spring across the opening, even as it fell, so that he struck on his chest and stomach, with arms outstretched, on the floor of the opposite side. The next instant he had drawn up his legs and rolled clear. But he rolled into my marmalade and underclothes and against the trap-door.

The expression on his face was one of complete comprehension. But before I could guess what he had comprehended, he had dropped the trap-door into place, closing the lazarette. Then I understood. He thought he had me inside. Also, he was blind, blind as a bat. I watched him, breathing carefully so that he should not hear me. He stepped quickly to his state-room. I saw his hand miss the door-knob by an inch, quickly fumble for it, and find it. This was my chance. I tiptoed across the cabin and to the top of the stairs. He came back, dragging a heavy sea-chest, which he deposited on top of the trap. Not content with this he fetched a second chest and placed it on top of the first. Then he gathered up the marmalade and underclothes and put them on the table. When he started up the companion-way, I retreated, silently rolling over on top of the cabin.

He shoved the slide part way back and rested his arms on it, his body still in the companion-way. His attitude was of one looking forward the length of the schooner, or staring, rather, for his eyes were fixed and unblinking. I was only five feet away and directly in what should have been his line of vision. It was uncanny. I felt myself a ghost, what of my invisibility. I waved my hand back and forth, of course without effect; but when the moving shadow fell across his face I saw at once that he was susceptible to the impression. His face became more expectant and tense as he tried to analyze and identify the impression. He knew that he had responded to something from without, that his sensibility had been touched by a changing something in his environment; but what it was he could not discover. I ceased waving my hand, so that the shadow remained stationary. He slowly moved his head back and forth under it and turned from side to side, now in the sunshine, now in the shade, feeling the shadow, as it were, testing it by sensation.

I, too, was busy, trying to reason out how he was aware of the existence of so intangible a thing as a shadow. If it were his eyeballs only that were affected, or if his optic nerve were not wholly destroyed, the explanation was simple. If otherwise, then the only conclusion I could reach was that the sensitive skin recognized the difference of temperature between shade and sunshine. Or, perhaps,—who can tell?—it was that fabled sixth sense which conveyed to him the loom and feel of an object close at hand.

Giving over his attempt to determine the shadow, he stepped on deck and started forward, walking with a swiftness and confidence which surprised me. And still there was that hint of the feebleness of the blind in his walk. I knew it now for what it was.

To my amused chagrin, he discovered my shoes on the forecastle head and brought them back with him into the galley. I watched him build the fire and set about cooking food for himself; then I stole into the cabin for my marmalade and underclothes, slipped back past the galley, and climbed down to the beach to deliver my barefoot report.

CHAPTER XXXIV

'It's too bad the *Ghost* has lost her masts. Why we could sail away in her. Don't you think we could, Humphrey?'

I sprang excitedly to my feet.

'I wonder, I wonder,' I repeated, pacing up and down.

Maud's eyes were shining with anticipation as they followed me. She had such faith in me! And the thought of it was so much added power. I remembered Michelet's 'To man, woman is as the earth was to her legendary son; he has but to fall down and kiss her breast and he is strong again.' For the first time I knew the wonderful truth of his words. Why, I was living them. Maud was all this to me, an unfailing, source of strength and courage. I had but to look at her, or think of her, and be strong again.

'It can be done, it can be done,' I was thinking and asserting aloud. 'What men have done, I can do; and if they have never done this before, still I can do it.'

'What? for goodness' sake,' Maud demanded. 'Do be merciful. What is it you can do?'

'We can do it,' I amended. 'Why, nothing else than put the masts back into the *Ghost* and sail away.'

'Humphrey!' she exclaimed.

And I felt as proud of my conception as if it were already a fact accomplished.

'But how is it possible to be done?' she asked.

'I don't know,' was my answer. 'I know only that I am capable of doing anything these days.'

I smiled proudly at her—too proudly, for she dropped her eyes and was for the moment silent.

'But there is Captain Larsen,' she objected.

'Blind and helpless,' I answered promptly, waving him aside as a straw.

'But those terrible hands of his! You know how he leaped across the opening of the lazarette.'

'And you know also how I crept about and avoided him,' I contended gaily.

'And lost your shoes.'

'You'd hardly expect them to avoid Wolf Larsen without my feet inside of them.'

We both laughed, and then went seriously to work constructing the plan whereby we were to step the masts of the *Ghost* and return to the world. I remembered hazily the physics of my school days, while the last few months had given me practical experience with mechanical purchases. I must say, though, when we walked down to the *Ghost* to inspect more closely the task before us, that the sight of the great masts lying in the water almost disheartened me. Where were we to begin? If there had been one mast standing, something high up to which to fasten blocks and tackles!

But there was nothing. It reminded me of the problem of lifting oneself by one's boot-straps. I understood the mechanics of levers; but where was I to get a fulcrum?

There was the mainmast, fifteen inches in diameter at what was now the butt, still sixty-five feet in length, and weighing, I roughly calculated, at least three thousand pounds. And then came the foremast, larger in diameter, and weighing surely thirty-five hundred pounds. Where was I to begin? Maud stood silently by my side, while I evolved in my mind the contrivance known among sailors as 'shears.' But, though known to sailors, I invented it there on Endeavour Island. By crossing and lashing the ends of two spars, and then elevating them in the air like an inverted 'V,' I could get a point above the deck to which to make fast my hoisting tackle. To this hoisting tackle I could, if necessary, attach a second hoisting tackle. And then there was the windlass!

Maud saw that I had achieved a solution, and her eyes warmed sympathetically.

'What are you going to do?' she asked.

'Clear that raffle,' I answered, pointing to the tangled wreckage overside.

Ah, the decisiveness, the very sound of the words, was good in my ears. 'Clear that raffle!' Imagine so salty a phrase on the lips of the Humphrey Van Weyden of a few months gone!

There must have been a touch of the melodramatic in my pose and voice, for Maud smiled. Her appreciation of the ridiculous was keen, and in all things she unerringly saw and felt, where it existed, the touch of sham, the overshading, the overtone. It was this which had given poise and penetration to her own work and made her of worth to the world. The serious critic, with the sense of humour and the power of expression, must inevitably command the world's ear. And so it was that she had commanded. Her sense of humour was really the artist's instinct for proportion.

'I'm sure I've heard it before, somewhere, in books,' she murmured gleefully.

I had an instinct for proportion myself, and I collapsed forthwith, descending from the dominant pose of a master of matter to a state of humble confusion which was, to say the least, very miserable.

Her hand leapt out at once to mine.

'I'm so sorry,' she said.

'No need to be,' I gulped. 'It does me good. There's too much of the schoolboy in me. All of which is neither here nor there. What we've got to do is actually and literally to clear that raffle. If you'll come with me in the boat, we'll get to work and straighten things out.'

'When the topmen clear the raffle with their clasp-knives in their teeth,' she quoted at me; and for the rest of the afternoon we made merry over our labour.

Her task was to hold the boat in position while I worked at the tangle. And such a tangle—halyards, sheets, guys, down-hauls, shrouds, stays, all washed about and back and forth and through, and twined and knotted by the sea. I cut no more than was necessary, and what with passing the long ropes under and around the booms and masts, of unreeving the halyards and sheets, of coiling down in the boat and uncoiling in order to pass through another knot in the bight, I was soon wet to the skin.

The sails did require some cutting, and the canvas, heavy with water, tried my strength severely; but I succeeded before nightfall in getting it all spread out on the beach to dry. We were both very tired when we knocked off for supper, and we had done good work, too, though to the eye it appeared insignificant.

Next morning, with Maud as able assistant, I went into the hold of the *Ghost* to clear the steps of the mast-butts. We had no more than begun work when the sound of my knocking and hammering brought Wolf Larsen.

'Hello below!' he cried down the open hatch.

The sound of his voice made Maud quickly draw close to me, as for protection, and she rested one hand on my arm while we parleyed.

'Hello on deck,' I replied. 'Good-morning to you.'

'What are you doing down there?' he demanded. 'Trying to scuttle my ship for me?'

'Quite the opposite; I'm repairing her,' was my answer.

'But what in thunder are you repairing?' There was puzzlement in his voice.

'Why, I'm getting everything ready for re-stepping the masts,' I replied easily, as though it were the simplest project imaginable.

'It seems as though you're standing on your own legs at last, Hump,' we heard him say; and then for some time he was silent.

'But I say, Hump,' he called down. 'You can't do it.'

'Oh, yes, I can,' I retorted. 'I'm doing it now.'

'But this is my vessel, my particular property. What if I forbid you?'

'You forget,' I replied. 'You are no longer the biggest bit of the ferment. You were, once, and able to eat me, as you were pleased to phrase it; but there has been a diminishing, and I am now able to eat you. The yeast has grown stale.'

He gave a short, disagreeable laugh. 'I see you're working my philosophy back on me for all it is worth. But don't make the mistake of under-estimating me. For your own good I warn you.'

'Since when have you become a philanthropist?' I queried. 'Confess, now, in warning me for my own good, that you are very consistent.'

He ignored my sarcasm, saying, 'Suppose I clap the hatch on, now? You won't fool me as you did in the lazarette.'

'Wolf Larsen,' I said sternly, for the first time addressing him by this his most familiar name, 'I am unable to shoot a helpless, unresisting man. You have proved that to my satisfaction as well as yours. But I warn you now, and not so much for your own good as for mine, that I shall shoot you the moment you attempt a hostile act. I can shoot you now, as I stand here; and if you are so minded, just go ahead and try to clap on the hatch.'

'Nevertheless, I forbid you, I distinctly forbid your tampering with my ship.'

'But, man!' I expostulated, 'you advance the fact that it is your ship as though it were a moral right. You have never considered moral rights in your dealings with others. You surely do not dream that I'll consider them in dealing with you?'

I had stepped underneath the open hatchway so that I could see him. The lack of expression on his face, so different from when I had watched him unseen, was enhanced by the unblinking, staring eyes. It was not a pleasant face to look upon.

'And none so poor, not even Hump, to do him reverence,' he sneered.

The sneer was wholly in his voice. His face remained expressionless as ever.

'How do you do, Miss Brewster,' he said suddenly, after a pause.

I started. She had made no noise whatever, had not even moved. Could it be that some glimmer of vision remained to him? or that his vision was coming back?

'How do you do, Captain Larsen,' she answered. 'Pray, how did you know I was here?'

'Heard you breathing, of course. I say, Hump's improving, don't you think so?'

'I don't know,' she answered, smiling at me. 'I have never seen him otherwise.'

'You should have seen him before, then.'

'Wolf Larsen, in large doses,' I murmured, 'before and after taking.'

'I want to tell you again, Hump,' he said threateningly, 'that you'd better leave things alone.'

'But don't you care to escape as well as we?' I asked incredulously.

'No,' was his answer. 'I intend dying here.'

'Well, we don't,' I concluded defiantly, beginning again my knocking and hammering.

CHAPTER XXXV

Next day, the mast-steps clear and everything in readiness, we started to get the two topmasts aboard. The maintopmast was over thirty feet in length, the foretopmast nearly thirty, and it was of these that I intended making the shears. It was puzzling work. Fastening one end of a heavy tackle to the windlass, and with the other end fast to the butt of the foretopmast, I began to heave. Maud held the turn on the windlass and coiled down the slack.

We were astonished at the ease with which the spar was lifted. It was an improved crank windlass, and the purchase it gave was enormous. Of course, what it gave us in power we paid for in distance; as many times as it doubled my strength, that many times was doubled the length of rope I heaved in. The tackle dragged heavily across the rail, increasing its drag as the spar arose more and more out of the water, and the exertion on the windlass grew severe.

But when the butt of the topmast was level with the rail, everything came to a standstill.

'I might have known it,' I said impatiently. 'Now we have to do it all over again.'

'Why not fasten the tackle part way down the mast?' Maud suggested.

'It's what I should have done at first,' I answered, hugely disgusted with myself.

Slipping off a turn, I lowered the mast back into the water and fastened the tackle a third of the way down from the butt. In an hour, what of this and of rests between the heaving, I had hoisted it to the point where I could hoist no more. Eight feet of the butt was above the rail, and I was as far away as ever from getting the spar on board. I sat down and pondered the problem. It did not take long. I sprang jubilantly to my feet.

'Now I have it!' I cried. 'I ought to make the tackle fast at the point of balance. And what we learn of this will serve us with everything else we have to hoist aboard.'

Once again I undid all my work by lowering the mast into the water. But I miscalculated the point of balance, so that when I heaved the top of the mast came up instead of the butt. Maud looked despair, but I laughed and said it would do just as well.

Instructing her how to hold the turn and be ready to slack away at command, I laid hold of the mast with my hands and tried to balance it inboard across the rail. When I thought I had it I cried to her to slack away; but the spar righted, despite my efforts, and dropped back toward the water. Again I heaved it up to its old position, for I had now another idea. I remembered the watch-tackle—a small double and single block affair—and fetched it.

While I was rigging it between the top of the spar and the opposite rail, Wolf Larsen came on the scene. We exchanged nothing more than good-mornings, and, though he could not see, he sat on the rail out of the way and followed by the sound all that I did.

Again instructing Maud to slack away at the windlass when I gave the word, I proceeded to heave on the watch-tackle. Slowly the mast swung in until it balanced at right angles across the rail; and then I discovered to my amazement that there was no need for Maud to slack away. In fact, the very opposite was necessary. Making the watch-tackle fast, I hove on the windlass and brought in the mast, inch by inch, till its top tilted down to the deck and finally its whole length lay on the deck.

I looked at my watch. It was twelve o'clock. My back was aching sorely, and I felt extremely tired and hungry. And there on the deck was a single stick of timber to show for a whole morning's work. For the first time I thoroughly realized the extent of the task before us. But I was learning, I was learning. The afternoon would show far more accomplished. And it did; for we returned at one o'clock, rested and strengthened by a hearty dinner.

In less than an hour I had the maintopmast on deck and was constructing the shears. Lashing the two topmasts together, and making allowance for their unequal length, at the point of intersection I attached the double block of the main throat-halyards. This, with the single block and the throat-halyards themselves, gave me a hoisting tackle. To prevent the butts of the masts from slipping on the deck, I nailed down thick cleats. Everything in readiness, I made a line fast to the apex of the shears and carried it directly to the windlass. I was growing to have faith in that windlass, for it gave me power beyond all expectation. As usual, Maud held the turn while I heaved. The shears rose in the air.

Then I discovered I had forgotten guy-ropes. This necessitated my climbing the shears, which I did twice, before I finished guying it fore and aft and to either side. Twilight had set in by the time this was accomplished. Wolf Larsen, who had sat about and listened all afternoon and never opened his mouth, had taken himself off to the galley and started his supper. I felt quite stiff across the small of the back, so much so that I straightened up with an effort and with pain. I looked proudly at my work. It was beginning to show. I was wild with desire, like a child with a new toy, to hoist something with my shears.

'I wish it weren't so late,' I said. 'I'd like to see how it works.'

'Don't be a glutton, Humphrey,' Maud chided me. 'Remember, to-morrow is coming, and you're so tired now that you can hardly stand.'

'And you?' I said, with sudden solicitude. 'You must be very tired. You have worked hard and nobly. I am proud of you, Maud.'

'Not half so proud as I am of you, nor with half the reason,' she answered, looking me straight in the eyes for a moment with an expression in her own and a dancing, tremulous light which I had not seen before and which gave me a pang of quick delight, I know not why, for I did not understand it. Then she dropped her eyes, to lift them again, laughing.

'If our friends could see us now,' she said. 'Look at us. Have you ever paused for a moment to consider our appearance?'

'Yes, I have considered yours, frequently,' I answered, puzzling over what I had seen in her eyes and puzzled by her sudden change of subject.

'Mercy!' she cried. 'And what do I look like, pray?'

'A scarecrow, I'm afraid,' I replied. 'Just glance at your draggled skirts, for instance. Look at those three-cornered tears. And such a waist! It would not require a Sherlock Holmes to deduce that you have been cooking over a camp-fire, to say nothing of trying out seal-blubber. And to cap it all, that cap! And all that is the woman who wrote 'A Kiss Endured.''

She made me an elaborate and stately courtesy, and said, 'As for you, sir—'

And yet, through the five minutes of banter which followed, there was a serious something underneath the fun which I could not but relate to the strange and fleeting expression I had caught in her eyes. What was it? Could it be that our eyes were speaking beyond the will of our speech? My eyes had spoken, I knew, until I had found the culprits out and silenced them. This had occurred several times. But had she seen the clamour in them and understood? And had her eyes so spoken to me? What else could that expression have meant—that dancing, tremulous light, and a something more which words could not describe. And yet it could not be. It was impossible. Besides, I was not skilled in the speech of eyes. I was only Humphrey Van Weyden, a bookish fellow who loved. And to love, and to wait and win love, that surely was glorious enough for me. And thus I thought, even as we chaffed each other's appearance, until we arrived ashore and there were other things to think about.

'It's a shame, after working hard all day, that we cannot have an uninterrupted night's sleep,' I complained, after supper.

'But there can be no danger now? from a blind man?' she queried.

'I shall never be able to trust him,' I averred, 'and far less now that he is blind. The liability is that his part helplessness will make him more malignant than ever. I know what I shall do to-morrow, the first thing—run out a light anchor and kedge the schooner off the beach. And each night when we come ashore in the boat, Mr. Wolf Larsen will be left a prisoner on board. So this will be the last night we have to stand watch, and because of that it will go the easier.'

We were awake early and just finishing breakfast as daylight came.

'Oh, Humphrey!' I heard Maud cry in dismay and suddenly stop.

I looked at her. She was gazing at the *Ghost*. I followed her gaze, but could see nothing unusual. She looked at me, and I looked inquiry back.

'The shears,' she said, and her voice trembled.

I had forgotten their existence. I looked again, but could not see them.

'If he has—' I muttered savagely.

She put her hand sympathetically on mine, and said, 'You will have to begin over again.'

'Oh, believe me, my anger means nothing; I could not hurt a fly,' I smiled back bitterly. 'And the worst of it is, he knows it. You are right. If he has destroyed the shears, I shall do nothing except begin over again.'

'But I'll stand my watch on board hereafter,' I blurted out a moment later. 'And if he interferes—'

'But I dare not stay ashore all night alone,' Maud was saying when I came back to myself. 'It would be so much nicer if he would be friendly with us and help us. We could all live comfortably aboard.'

'We will,' I asserted, still savagely, for the destruction of my beloved shears had hit me hard. 'That is, you and I will live aboard, friendly or not with Wolf Larsen.'

'It's childish,' I laughed later, 'for him to do such things, and for me to grow angry over them, for that matter.'

But my heart smote me when we climbed aboard and looked at the havoc he had done. The shears were gone altogether. The guys had been slashed right and left. The throat-halyards which I had rigged were cut across through every part. And he knew I could not splice. A thought struck me. I ran to the windlass. It would not work. He had broken it. We looked at each other in consternation. Then I ran to the side. The masts, booms, and gaffs I had cleared were gone. He had found the lines which held them, and cast them adrift.

Tears were in Maud's eyes, and I do believe they were for me. I could have wept myself. Where now was our project of remasting the *Ghost*? He had done his work well. I sat down on the hatch-combing and rested my chin on my hands in black despair.

'He deserves to die,' I cried out; 'and God forgive me, I am not man enough to be his executioner.'

But Maud was by my side, passing her hand soothingly through my hair as though I were a child, and saying, 'There, there; it will all come right. We are in the right, and it must come right.'

I remembered Michelet and leaned my head against her; and truly I became strong again. The blessed woman was an unfailing fount of power to me. What did it matter? Only a set-back, a delay. The tide could not have carried the masts far to seaward, and there had been no wind. It meant merely more work to find them and tow them back. And besides, it was a lesson. I knew what to expect. He might have waited and destroyed our work more effectually when we had more accomplished.

'Here he comes now,' she whispered.

I glanced up. He was strolling leisurely along the poop on the port side.

'Take no notice of him,' I whispered. 'He's coming to see how we take it. Don't let him know that we know. We can deny him that satisfaction. Take off your shoes— that's right—and carry them in your hand.'

And then we played hide-and-seek with the blind man. As he came up the port side we slipped past on the starboard; and from the poop we watched him turn and start aft on our track.

He must have known, somehow, that we were on board, for he said 'Good-morning' very confidently, and waited, for the greeting to be returned. Then he strolled aft, and we slipped forward.

'Oh, I know you're aboard,' he called out, and I could see him listen intently after he had spoken.

It reminded me of the great hoot-owl, listening, after its booming cry, for the stir of its frightened prey. But we did not fir, and we moved only when he moved. And so we dodged about the deck, hand in hand, like a couple of children chased by a wicked ogre, till Wolf Larsen, evidently in disgust, left the deck for the cabin. There was glee in our eyes, and suppressed titters in our mouths, as we put on our shoes and clambered over the side into the boat. And as I looked into Maud's clear brown eyes I forgot the evil he had done, and I knew only that I loved her, and that because of her the strength was mine to win our way back to the world.

CHAPTER XXXVI

For two days Maud and I ranged the sea and explored the beaches in search of the missing masts. But it was not till the third day that we found them, all of them, the shears included, and, of all perilous places, in the pounding surf of the grim south-western promontory. And how we worked! At the dark end of the first day we returned, exhausted, to our little cove, towing the mainmast behind us. And we had been compelled to row, in a dead calm, practically every inch of the way.

Another day of heart-breaking and dangerous toil saw us in camp with the two topmasts to the good. The day following I was desperate, and I rafted together the foremast, the fore and main booms, and the fore and main gaffs. The wind was favourable, and I had thought to tow them back under sail, but the wind baffled, then died away, and our progress with the oars was a snail's pace. And it was such dispiriting effort. To throw one's whole strength and weight on the oars and to feel the boat checked in its forward lunge by the heavy drag behind, was not exactly exhilarating.

Night began to fall, and to make matters worse, the wind sprang up ahead. Not only did all forward motion cease, but we began to drift back and out to sea. I struggled at the oars till I was played out. Poor Maud, whom I could never prevent from working to the limit of her strength, lay weakly back in the stern-sheets. I could row no more. My bruised and swollen hands could no longer close on the oar handles. My wrists and arms ached intolerably, and though I had eaten heartily of a twelve-o'clock lunch, I had worked so hard that I was faint from hunger.

I pulled in the oars and bent forward to the line which held the tow. But Maud's hand leaped out restrainingly to mine.

'What are you going to do?' she asked in a strained, tense voice.

'Cast it off,' I answered, slipping a turn of the rope.

But her fingers closed on mine.

'Please don't,' she begged.

'It is useless,' I answered. 'Here is night and the wind blowing us off the land.'

'But think, Humphrey. If we cannot sail away on the *Ghost*, we may remain for years on the island—for life even. If it has never been discovered all these years, it may never be discovered.'

'You forget the boat we found on the beach,' I reminded her.

'It was a seal-hunting boat,' she replied, 'and you know perfectly well that if the men had escaped they would have been back to make their fortunes from the rookery. You know they never escaped.'

I remained silent, undecided.

'Besides,' she added haltingly, 'it's your idea, and I want to see you succeed.'

Now I could harden my heart. As soon as she put it on a flattering personal basis, generosity compelled me to deny her.

'Better years on the island than to die to-night, or to-morrow, or the next day, in the open boat. We are not prepared to brave the sea. We have no food, no water, no blankets, nothing. Why, you'd not survive the night without blankets: I know how strong you are. You are shivering now.'

'It is only nervousness,' she answered. 'I am afraid you will cast off the masts in spite of me.'

'Oh, please, please, Humphrey, don't!' she burst out, a moment later.

And so it ended, with the phrase she knew had all power over me. We shivered miserably throughout the night. Now and again I fitfully slept, but the pain of the cold always aroused me. How Maud could stand it was beyond me. I was too tired to thrash my arms about and warm myself, but I found strength time and again to chafe her hands and feet to restore the circulation. And still she pleaded with me not to cast off the masts. About three in the morning she was caught by a cold cramp, and after I had rubbed her out of that she became quite numb. I was frightened. I got out the oars and made her row, though she was so weak I thought she would faint at every stroke.

Morning broke, and we looked long in the growing light for our island. At last it showed, small and black, on the horizon, fully fifteen miles away. I scanned the sea with my glasses. Far away in the south-west I could see a dark line on the water, which grew even as I looked at it.

'Fair wind!' I cried in a husky voice I did not recognize as my own.

Maud tried to reply, but could not speak. Her lips were blue with cold, and she was hollow-eyed—but oh, how bravely her brown eyes looked at me! How piteously brave!

Again I fell to chafing her hands and to moving her arms up and down and about until she could thrash them herself. Then I compelled her to stand up, and though she would have fallen had I not supported her, I forced her to walk back and forth the several steps between the thwart and the stern-sheets, and finally to spring up and down.

'Oh, you brave, brave woman,' I said, when I saw the life coming back into her face. 'Did you know that you were brave?'

'I never used to be,' she answered. 'I was never brave till I knew you. It is you who have made me brave.'

'Nor I, until I knew you,' I answered.

She gave me a quick look, and again I caught that dancing, tremulous light and something more in her eyes. But it was only for the moment. Then she smiled.

'It must have been the conditions,' she said; but I knew she was wrong, and I wondered if she likewise knew. Then the wind came, fair and fresh, and the boat was soon labouring through a heavy sea toward the island. At half-past three in the afternoon we passed the south-western promontory. Not only were we hungry, but we were now suffering from thirst. Our lips were dry and cracked, nor could we longer moisten them with our tongues. Then the wind slowly died down. By night it was dead calm and I was toiling once more at the oars—but weakly, most weakly. At two in the morning the boat's bow touched the beach of our own inner cove and I staggered out to make the painter fast. Maud could not stand, nor had I strength to carry her. I fell in the sand with her, and, when I had recovered, contented myself with putting my hands under her shoulders and dragging her up the beach to the hut.

The next day we did no work. In fact, we slept till three in the afternoon, or at least I did, for I awoke to find Maud cooking dinner. Her power of recuperation was wonderful. There was something tenacious about that lily-frail body of hers, a clutch on existence which one could not reconcile with its patent weakness.

'You know I was travelling to Japan for my health,' she said, as we lingered at the fire after dinner and delighted in the movelessness of loafing. 'I was not very strong. I never was. The doctors recommended a sea voyage, and I chose the longest.'

'You little knew what you were choosing,' I laughed.

'But I shall be a different women for the experience, as well as a stronger woman,' she answered; 'and, I hope a better woman. At least I shall understand a great deal more life.'

Then, as the short day waned, we fell to discussing Wolf Larsen's blindness. It was inexplicable. And that it was grave, I instanced his statement that he intended to stay and die on Endeavour Island. When he, strong man that he was, loving life as he did, accepted his death, it was plain that he was troubled by something more than mere blindness. There had been his terrific headaches, and we were agreed that it was some sort of brain break-down, and that in his attacks he endured pain beyond our comprehension.

I noticed as we talked over his condition, that Maud's sympathy went out to him more and more; yet I could not but love her for it, so sweetly womanly was it. Besides, there was no false sentiment about her feeling. She was agreed that the most rigorous treatment was necessary if we were to escape, though she recoiled at the suggestion that I might some time be compelled to take his life to save my own—'our own,' she put it.

In the morning we had breakfast and were at work by daylight. I found a light kedge anchor in the fore-hold, where such things were kept; and with a deal of exertion got it on deck and into the boat. With a long running-line coiled down in the stem, I rowed well out into our little cove and dropped the anchor into the water. There was no wind, the tide was high, and the schooner floated. Casting off the shore-lines, I kedged her out by main strength (the windlass being broken), till she rode nearly up and down to the small anchor—too small to hold her in any breeze. So I lowered the big starboard anchor, giving plenty of slack; and by afternoon I was at work on the windlass.

Three days I worked on that windlass. Least of all things was I a mechanic, and in that time I accomplished what an ordinary machinist would have done in as many hours. I had to learn my tools to begin with, and every simple mechanical principle which such a man would have at his finger ends I had likewise to learn. And at the end of three days I had a windlass which worked clumsily. It never gave the satisfaction the old windlass had given, but it worked and made my work possible.

In half a day I got the two topmasts aboard and the shears rigged and guyed as before. And that night I slept on board and on deck beside my work. Maud, who refused to stay alone ashore, slept in the forecastle. Wolf Larsen had sat about, listening to my repairing the windlass and talking with Maud and me upon indifferent subjects. No reference was made on either side to the destruction of the shears; nor did he say anything further about my leaving his ship alone. But still I had feared him, blind and helpless and listening, always listening, and I never let his strong arms get within reach of me while I worked.

On this night, sleeping under my beloved shears, I was aroused by his footsteps on the deck. It was a starlight night, and I could see the bulk of him dimly as he moved about. I rolled out of my blankets and crept noiselessly after him in my stocking feet. He had armed himself with a draw-knife from the tool-locker, and with this he prepared to cut across the throat-halyards I had again rigged to the shears. He felt the halyards with his hands and discovered that I had not made them fast. This would not do for a draw-knife, so he laid hold of the running part, hove taut, and made fast. Then he prepared to saw across with the draw-knife.

'I wouldn't, if I were you,' I said quietly.

He heard the click of my pistol and laughed.

'Hello, Hump,' he said. 'I knew you were here all the time. You can't fool my ears.'

'That's a lie, Wolf Larsen,' I said, just as quietly as before. 'However, I am aching for a chance to kill you, so go ahead and cut.'

'You have the chance always,' he sneered.

'Go ahead and cut,' I threatened ominously.

'I'd rather disappoint you,' he laughed, and turned on his heel and went aft.

'Something must be done, Humphrey,' Maud said, next morning, when I had told her of the night's occurrence. 'If he has liberty, he may do anything. He may sink the vessel, or set fire to it. There is no telling what he may do. We must make him a prisoner.'

'But how?' I asked, with a helpless shrug. 'I dare not come within reach of his arms, and he knows that so long as his resistance is passive I cannot shoot him.'

'There must be some way,' she contended. 'Let me think.'

'There is one way,' I said grimly.

She waited.

I picked up a seal-club.

'It won't kill him,' I said. 'And before he could recover I'd have him bound hard and fast.'

She shook her head with a shudder. 'No, not that. There must be some less brutal way. Let us wait.'

But we did not have to wait long, and the problem solved itself. In the morning, after several trials, I found the point of balance in the foremast and attached my hoisting tackle a few feet above it. Maud held the turn on the windlass and coiled down while I heaved. Had the windlass been in order it would not have been so difficult; as it was, I was compelled to apply all my weight and strength to every inch of the heaving. I had to rest frequently. In truth, my spells of resting were longer than those of working. Maud even contrived, at times when all my efforts could not budge the windlass, to hold the turn with one hand and with the other to throw the weight of her slim body to my assistance.

At the end of an hour the single and double blocks came together at the top of the shears. I could hoist no more. And yet the mast was not swung entirely inboard. The butt rested against the outside of the port rail, while the top of the mast overhung the water far beyond the starboard rail. My shears were too short. All my work had been for nothing. But I no longer despaired in the old way. I was acquiring more confidence in myself and more confidence in the possibilities of windlasses, shears, and hoisting tackles. There was a way in which it could be done, and it remained for me to find that way.

While I was considering the problem, Wolf Larsen came on deck. We noticed something strange about him at once. The indecisiveness, or feebleness, of his movements was more pronounced. His walk was actually tottery as he came down the port side of the cabin. At the break of the poop he reeled, raised one hand to his eyes with the familiar brushing gesture, and fell down the steps—still on his feet—to the main deck, across which he staggered, falling and flinging out his arms for support. He regained his balance by the steerage companion-way and stood there dizzily for a space, when he suddenly crumpled up and collapsed, his legs bending under him as he sank to the deck.

'One of his attacks,' I whispered to Maud.

She nodded her head; and I could see sympathy warm in eyes.

We went up to him, but he seemed unconscious, breathing spasmodically. She took charge of him, lifting his head to keep the blood out of it and despatching me to the cabin for a pillow. I also brought blankets, and we made him comfortable. I took his pulse. It beat steadily and strong, and was quite normal. This puzzled me. I became suspicious.

'What if he should be feigning this?' I asked, still holding his wrist.

Maud shook her head, and there was reproof in her eyes. But just then the wrist I held leaped from my hand, and the hand clasped like a steel trap about my wrist. I cried aloud in awful fear, a wild inarticulate cry; and I caught one glimpse of his face, malignant and triumphant, as his other hand compassed my body and I was drawn down to him in a terrible grip.

My wrist was released, but his other arm, passed around my back, held both my arms so that I could not move. His free hand went to my throat, and in that moment I knew the bitterest foretaste of death earned by one's own idiocy. Why had I trusted myself within reach of those terrible arms? I could feel other hands at my throat. They were Maud's hands, striving vainly to tear loose the hand that was throttling me. She gave it up, and I heard her scream in a way that cut me to the soul, for it was a woman's scream of fear and heart-breaking despair. I had heard it before, during the sinking of the *Martinez*.

My face was against his chest and I could not see, but I heard Maud turn and run swiftly away along the deck. Everything was happening quickly. I had not yet had a glimmering of unconsciousness, and it seemed that an interminable period of time was lapsing before I heard her feet flying back. And just then I felt the whole man sink under me. The breath was leaving his lungs and his chest was collapsing under my weight. Whether it was merely the expelled breath, or his consciousness of his growing impotence, I know not, but his throat vibrated with a deep groan. The hand at my throat relaxed. I breathed. It fluttered and tightened again. But even his tremendous will could not overcome the dissolution that assailed it. That will of his was breaking down. He was fainting.

Maud's footsteps were very near as his hand fluttered for the last time and my throat was released. I rolled off and over to the deck on my back, gasping and blinking in the sunshine. Maud was pale but composed,—my eyes had gone instantly to her face,—and she was looking at me with mingled alarm and relief. A heavy seal-club in her hand caught my eyes, and at that moment she followed my gaze down to it. The club dropped from her hand as though it had suddenly stung her, and at the same moment my heart surged with a great joy. Truly she was my woman, my mate-woman, fighting with me and for me as the mate of a caveman would have fought, all the primitive in her aroused, forgetful of her culture, hard under the softening civilization of the only life she had ever known.

'Dear woman!' I cried, scrambling to my feet.

The next moment she was in my arms, weeping convulsively on my shoulder while I clasped her close. I looked down at the brown glory of her hair, glinting gems in the sunshine far more precious to me than those in the treasure-chests of kings. And I bent my head and kissed her hair softly, so softly that she did not know.

Then sober thought came to me. After all, she was only a woman, crying her relief, now that the danger was past, in the arms of her protector or of the one who had been endangered. Had I been father or brother, the situation would have been in nowise different. Besides, time and place were not meet, and I wished to earn a better right to declare my love. So once again I softly kissed her hair as I felt her receding from my clasp.

'It was a real attack this time,' I said: 'another shock like the one that made him blind. He feigned at first, and in doing so brought it on.'

Maud was already rearranging his pillow.

'No,' I said, 'not yet. Now that I have him helpless, helpless he shall remain. From this day we live in the cabin. Wolf Larsen shall live in the steerage.'

I caught him under the shoulders and dragged him to the companion-way. At my direction Maud fetched a rope. Placing this under his shoulders, I balanced him across the threshold and lowered him down the steps to the floor. I could not lift him directly into a bunk, but with Maud's help I lifted first his shoulders and head, then his body, balanced him across the edge, and rolled him into a lower bunk.

But this was not to be all. I recollected the handcuffs in his state-room, which he preferred to use on sailors instead of the ancient and clumsy ship irons. So, when we left him, he lay handcuffed hand and foot. For the first time in many days I breathed freely. I felt strangely light as I came on deck, as though a weight had been lifted off my shoulders. I felt, also, that Maud and I had drawn more closely together. And I wondered if she, too, felt it, as we walked along the deck side by side to where the stalled foremast hung in the shears.

CHAPTER XXXVII

At once we moved aboard the *Ghost*, occupying our old state-rooms and cooking in the galley. The imprisonment of Wolf Larsen had happened most opportunely, for what must have been the Indian summer of this high latitude was gone and drizzling stormy weather had set in. We were very comfortable, and the inadequate shears, with the foremast suspended from them, gave a business-like air to the schooner and a promise of departure.

And now that we had Wolf Larsen in irons, how little did we need it! Like his first attack, his second had been accompanied by serious disablement. Maud made the discovery in the afternoon while trying to give him nourishment. He had shown signs of consciousness, and she had spoken to him, eliciting no response. He was lying on his left side at the time, and in evident pain. With a restless movement he rolled his head around, clearing his left ear from the pillow against which it had been pressed. At once he heard and answered her, and at once she came to me.

Pressing the pillow against his left ear, I asked him if he heard me, but he gave no sign. Removing the pillow and, repeating the question he answered promptly that he did.

'Do you know you are deaf in the right ear?' I asked.

'Yes,' he answered in a low, strong voice, 'and worse than that. My whole right side is affected. It seems asleep. I cannot move arm or leg.'

'Feigning again?' I demanded angrily.

He shook his head, his stern mouth shaping the strangest, twisted smile. It was indeed a twisted smile, for it was on the left side only, the facial muscles of the right side moving not at all.

'That was the last play of the Wolf,' he said. 'I am paralysed. I shall never walk again. Oh, only on the other side,' he added, as though divining the suspicious glance I flung at his left leg, the knee of which had just then drawn up, and elevated the blankets.

'It's unfortunate,' he continued. 'I'd liked to have done for you first, Hump. And I thought I had that much left in me.'

'But why?' I asked; partly in horror, partly out of curiosity.

Again his stern mouth framed the twisted smile, as he said:

'Oh, just to be alive, to be living and doing, to be the biggest bit of the ferment to the end, to eat you. But to die this way.'

He shrugged his shoulders, or attempted to shrug them, rather, for the left shoulder alone moved. Like the smile, the shrug was twisted.

'But how can you account for it?' I asked. 'Where is the seat of your trouble?'

'The brain,' he said at once. 'It was those cursed headaches brought it on.'

'Symptoms,' I said.

He nodded his head. 'There is no accounting for it. I was never sick in my life. Something's gone wrong with my brain. A cancer, a tumour, or something of that nature,—a thing that devours and destroys. It's attacking my nerve-centres, eating them up, bit by bit, cell by cell—from the pain.'

'The motor-centres, too,' I suggested.

'So it would seem; and the curse of it is that I must lie here, conscious, mentally unimpaired, knowing that the lines are going down, breaking bit by bit communication with the world. I cannot see, hearing and feeling are leaving me, at this rate I shall soon cease to speak; yet all the time I shall be here, alive, active, and powerless.'

'When you say *you* are here, I'd suggest the likelihood of the soul,' I said.

'Bosh!' was his retort. 'It simply means that in the attack on my brain the higher psychical centres are untouched. I can remember, I can think and reason. When that goes, I go. I am not. The soul?'

He broke out in mocking laughter, then turned his left ear to the pillow as a sign that he wished no further conversation.

Maud and I went about our work oppressed by the fearful fate which had overtaken him,—how fearful we were yet fully to realize. There was the awfulness of retribution about it. Our thoughts were deep and solemn, and we spoke to each other scarcely above whispers.

'You might remove the handcuffs,' he said that night, as we stood in consultation over him. 'It's dead safe. I'm a paralytic now. The next thing to watch out for is bed sores.'

He smiled his twisted smile, and Maud, her eyes wide with horror, was compelled to turn away her head.

'Do you know that your smile is crooked?' I asked him; for I knew that she must attend him, and I wished to save her as much as possible.

'Then I shall smile no more,' he said calmly. 'I thought something was wrong. My right cheek has been numb all day. Yes, and I've had warnings of this for the last three days; by spells, my right side seemed going to sleep, sometimes arm or hand, sometimes leg or foot.'

'So my smile is crooked?' he queried a short while after. 'Well, consider henceforth that I smile internally, with my soul, if you please, my soul. Consider that I am smiling now.'

And for the space of several minutes he lay there, quiet, indulging his grotesque fancy. The man of him was not changed. It was the old, indomitable, terrible Wolf Larsen, imprisoned somewhere within that flesh which had once been so invincible and splendid. Now it bound him with insentient fetters, walling his soul in darkness and silence, blocking it from the world which to him had been a riot of action. No more would he conjugate the verb 'to do in every mood and tense.' 'To be' was all that remained to him—to be, as he had defined death, without movement; to will, but not to execute; to think and reason and in the spirit of him to be as alive as ever, but in the flesh to be dead, quite dead.

And yet, though I even removed the handcuffs, we could not adjust ourselves to his condition. Our minds revolted. To us he was full of potentiality. We knew not what to expect of him next, what fearful thing, rising above the flesh, he might break out and do. Our experience warranted this state of mind, and we went about our work with anxiety always upon us.

I had solved the problem which had arisen through the shortness of the shears. By means of the watch-tackle (I had made a new one), I heaved the butt of the foremast across the rail and then lowered it to the deck. Next, by means of the shears, I hoisted the main boom on board. Its forty feet of length would supply the height necessary properly to swing the mast. By means of a secondary tackle I had attached to the shears, I swung the boom to a nearly perpendicular position, then lowered the butt to the deck, where, to prevent slipping, I spiked great cleats around it. The single block of my original shears-tackle I had attached to the end of the boom. Thus, by carrying this tackle to the windlass, I could raise and lower the end of the boom at will, the butt always remaining stationary, and, by means of guys, I could swing the boom from side to side. To the end of the boom I had likewise rigged a hoisting tackle; and when the whole arrangement was completed I could not but be startled by the power and latitude it gave me.

Of course, two days' work was required for the accomplishment of this part of my task, and it was not till the morning of the third day that I swung the foremast from the deck and proceeded to square its butt to fit the step. Here I was especially awkward. I sawed and chopped and chiselled the weathered wood till it had the appearance of having been gnawed by some gigantic mouse. But it fitted.

'It will work, I know it will work,' I cried.

'Do you know Dr. Jordan's final test of truth?' Maud asked.

I shook my head and paused in the act of dislodging the shavings which had drifted down my neck.

'Can we make it work? Can we trust our lives to it? is the test.'

'He is a favourite of yours,' I said.

'When I dismantled my old Pantheon and cast out Napoleon and Cæsar and their fellows, I straightway erected a new Pantheon,' she answered gravely, 'and the first I installed as Dr. Jordan.'

'A modern hero.'

'And a greater because modern,' she added. 'How can the Old World heroes compare with ours?'

I shook my head. We were too much alike in many things for argument. Our points of view and outlook on life at least were very alike.

'For a pair of critics we agree famously,' I laughed.

'And as shipwright and able assistant,' she laughed back.

But there was little time for laughter in those days, what of our heavy work and of the awfulness of Wolf Larsen's living death.

He had received another stroke. He had lost his voice, or he was losing it. He had only intermittent use of it. As he phrased it, the wires were like the stock market, now up, now down. Occasionally the wires were up and he spoke as well as ever, though slowly and heavily. Then speech would suddenly desert him, in the middle of a sentence perhaps, and for hours, sometimes, we would wait for the connection to be re-established. He complained of great pain in his head, and it was during this period that he arranged a system of communication against the time when speech should leave him altogether—one pressure of the hand for 'yes,' two for 'no.' It was well that it was arranged, for by evening his voice had gone from him. By hand pressures, after that, he answered our questions, and when he wished to speak he scrawled his thoughts with his left hand, quite legibly, on a sheet of paper.

The fierce winter had now descended upon us. Gale followed gale, with snow and sleet and rain. The seals had started on their great southern migration, and the rookery was practically deserted. I worked feverishly. In spite of the bad weather, and of the wind which especially hindered me, I was on deck from daylight till dark and making substantial progress.

I profited by my lesson learned through raising the shears and then climbing them to attach the guys. To the top of the foremast, which was just lifted conveniently from the deck, I attached the rigging, stays and throat and peak halyards. As usual, I had underrated the amount of work involved in this portion of the task, and two long days were necessary to complete it. And there was so much yet to be done—the sails, for instance, which practically had to be made over.

While I toiled at rigging the foremast, Maud sewed on canvas, ready always to drop everything and come to my assistance when more hands than two were required. The canvas was heavy and hard, and she sewed with the regular sailor's palm and three-cornered sail-needle. Her hands were soon sadly blistered, but she struggled bravely on, and in addition doing the cooking and taking care of the sick man.

'A fig for superstition,' I said on Friday morning. 'That mast goes in to-day.'

Everything was ready for the attempt. Carrying the boom-tackle to the windlass, I hoisted the mast nearly clear of the deck. Making this tackle fast, I took to the windlass the shears-tackle (which was connected with the end of the boom), and with a few turns had the mast perpendicular and clear.

Maud clapped her hands the instant she was relieved from holding the turn, crying:

'It works! It works! We'll trust our lives to it!'

Then she assumed a rueful expression.

'It's not over the hole,' she add. 'Will you have to begin all over?'

I smiled in superior fashion, and, slacking off on one of the boom-guys and taking in on the other, swung the mast perfectly in the centre of the deck. Still it was not over the hole. Again the rueful expression came on her face, and again I smiled in a superior way. Slacking away on the boom-tackle and hoisting an equivalent amount on the shears-tackle, I brought the butt of the mast into position directly over the hole in the deck. Then I gave Maud careful instructions for lowering away and went into the hold to the step on the schooner's bottom.

I called to her, and the mast moved easily and accurately. Straight toward the square hole of the step the square butt descended; but as it descended it slowly twisted so that square would not fit into square. But I had not even a moment's indecision. Calling to Maud to cease lowering, I went on deck and made the watch-tackle fast to the mast with a rolling hitch. I left Maud to pull on it while I went below. By the light of the lantern I saw the butt twist slowly around till its sides coincided with the sides of the step. Maud made fast and returned to the windlass. Slowly the butt descended the several intervening inches, at the same time slightly twisting again. Again Maud rectified the twist with the watch-tackle, and again she lowered away from the windlass. Square fitted into square. The mast was stepped.

I raised a shout, and she ran down to see. In the yellow lantern light we peered at what we had accomplished. We looked at each other, and our hands felt their way and clasped. The eyes of both of us, I think, were moist with the joy of success.

'It was done so easily after all,' I remarked. 'All the work was in the preparation.'

'And all the wonder in the completion,' Maud added. 'I can scarcely bring myself to realize that that great mast is really up and in; that you have lifted it from the water, swung it through the air, and deposited it here where it belongs. It is a Titan's task.'

'And they made themselves many inventions,' I began merrily, then paused to sniff the air.

I looked hastily at the lantern. It was not smoking. Again I sniffed.

'Something is burning,' Maud said, with sudden conviction.

We sprang together for the ladder, but I raced past her to the deck. A dense volume of smoke was pouring out of the steerage companion-way.

'The Wolf is not yet dead,' I muttered to myself as I sprang down through the smoke.

It was so thick in the confined space that I was compelled to feel my way; and so potent was the spell of Wolf Larsen on my imagination, I was quite prepared for the helpless giant to grip my neck in a strangle hold. I hesitated, the desire to race back and up the steps to the deck almost overpowering me. Then I recollected Maud. The vision of her, as I had last seen her, in the lantern light of the schooner's hold, her brown eyes warm and moist with joy, flashed before me, and I knew that I could not go back.

I was choking and suffocating by the time I reached Wolf Larsen's bunk. I reached my hand and felt for his. He was lying motionless, but moved slightly at the touch of my hand. I felt over and under his blankets. There was no warmth, no sign of fire. Yet that smoke which blinded me and made me cough and gasp must have a source. I lost my head temporarily and dashed frantically about the steerage. A collision with the table partially knocked the wind from my body and brought me to myself. I reasoned that a helpless man could start a fire only near to where he lay.

I returned to Wolf Larsen's bunk. There I encountered Maud. How long she had been there in that suffocating atmosphere I could not guess.

'Go up on deck!' I commanded peremptorily.

'But, Humphrey—' she began to protest in a queer, husky voice.

'Please! please!' I shouted at her harshly.

She drew away obediently, and then I thought, What if she cannot find the steps?

I started after her, to stop at the foot of the companion-way. Perhaps she had gone up. As I stood there, hesitant, I heard her cry softly:

'Oh, Humphrey, I am lost.'

I found her fumbling at the wall of the after bulkhead, and, half leading her, half carrying her, I took her up the companion-way. The pure air was like nectar. Maud was only faint and dizzy, and I left her lying on the deck when I took my second plunge below.

The source of the smoke must be very close to Wolf Larsen—my mind was made up to this, and I went straight to his bunk. As I felt about among his blankets, something hot fell on the back of my hand. It burned me, and I jerked my hand away. Then I understood. Through the cracks in the bottom of the upper bunk he had set fire to the mattress. He still retained sufficient use of his left arm to do this. The damp straw of the mattress, fired from beneath and denied air, had been smouldering all the while.

As I dragged the mattress out of the bunk it seemed to disintegrate in mid-air, at the same time bursting into flames. I beat out the burning remnants of straw in the bunk, then made a dash for the deck for fresh air.

Several buckets of water sufficed to put out the burning mattress in the middle of the steerage floor; and ten minutes later, when the smoke had fairly cleared, I allowed Maud to come below. Wolf Larsen was unconscious, but it was a matter of minutes for the fresh air to restore him. We were working over him, however, when he signed for paper and pencil.

'Pray do not interrupt me,' he wrote. 'I am smiling.'

'I am still a bit of the ferment, you see,' he wrote a little later.

'I am glad you are as small a bit as you are,' I said.

'Thank you,' he wrote. 'But just think of how much smaller I shall be before I die.'

'And yet I am all here, Hump,' he wrote with a final flourish. 'I can think more clearly than ever in my life before. Nothing to disturb me. Concentration is perfect. I am all here and more than here.'

It was like a message from the night of the grave; for this man's body had become his mausoleum. And there, in so strange sepulchre, his spirit fluttered and lived. It would flutter and live till the last line of communication was broken, and after that who was to say how much longer it might continue to flutter and live?

CHAPTER XXXVIII

'I think my left side is going,' Wolf Larsen wrote, the morning after his attempt to fire the ship. 'The numbness is growing. I can hardly move my hand. You will have to speak louder. The last lines are going down.'

'Are you in pain?' I asked.

I was compelled to repeat my question loudly before he answered:

'Not all the time.'

The left hand stumbled slowly and painfully across the paper, and it was with extreme difficulty that we deciphered the scrawl. It was like a 'spirit message,' such as are delivered at séances of spiritualists for a dollar admission.

'But I am still here, all here,' the hand scrawled more slowly and painfully than ever.

The pencil dropped, and we had to replace it in the hand.

'When there is no pain I have perfect peace and quiet. I have never thought so clearly. I can ponder life and death like a Hindoo sage.'

'And immortality?' Maud queried loudly in the ear.

Three times the hand essayed to write but fumbled hopelessly. The pencil fell. In vain we tried to replace it. The fingers could not close on it. Then Maud pressed and held the fingers about the pencil with her own hand and the hand wrote, in large letters, and so slowly that the minutes ticked off to each letter:

'B-O-S-H.'

It was Wolf Larsen's last word, 'bosh,' sceptical and invincible to the end. The arm and hand relaxed. The trunk of the body moved slightly. Then there was no movement. Maud released the hand. The fingers spread slightly, falling apart of their own weight, and the pencil rolled away.

'Do you still hear?' I shouted, holding the fingers and waiting for the single pressure which would signify 'Yes.' There was no response. The hand was dead.

'I noticed the lips slightly move,' Maud said.

I repeated the question. The lips moved. She placed the tips of her fingers on them. Again I repeated the question. 'Yes,' Maud announced. We looked at each other expectantly.

'What good is it?' I asked. 'What can we say now?'

'Oh, ask him—'

She hesitated.

'Ask him something that requires no for an answer,' I suggested. 'Then we will know for certainty.'

'Are you hungry?' she cried.

The lips moved under her fingers, and she answered, 'Yes.'

'Will you have some beef?' was her next query.

'No,' she announced.

'Beef-tea?'

'Yes, he will have some beef-tea,' she said, quietly, looking up at me. 'Until his hearing goes we shall be able to communicate with him. And after that—'

She looked at me queerly. I saw her lips trembling and the tears swimming up in her eyes. She swayed toward me and I caught her in my arms.

'Oh, Humphrey,' she sobbed, 'when will it all end? I am so tired, so tired.'

She buried her head on my shoulder, her frail form shaken with a storm of weeping. She was like a feather in my arms, so slender, so ethereal. 'She has broken down at last,' I thought. 'What can I do without her help?'

But I soothed and comforted her, till she pulled herself bravely together and recuperated mentally as quickly as she was wont to do physically.

'I ought to be ashamed of myself,' she said. Then added, with the whimsical smile I adored, 'but I am only one, small woman.'

That phrase, the 'one small woman,' startled me like an electric shock. It was my own phrase, my pet, secret phrase, my love phrase for her.

'Where did you get that phrase?' I demanded, with an abruptness that in turn startled her.

'What phrase?' she asked.

'One small woman.'

'Is it yours?' she asked.

'Yes,' I answered. 'Mine. I made it.'

'Then you must have talked in your sleep,' she smiled.

The dancing, tremulous light was in her eyes. Mine, I knew, were speaking beyond the will of my speech. I leaned toward her. Without volition I leaned toward her, as a tree is swayed by the wind. Ah, we were very close together in that moment. But she shook her head, as one might shake off sleep or a dream, saying:

'I have known it all my life. It was my father's name for my mother.'

'It is my phrase too,' I said stubbornly.

'For your mother?'

'No,' I answered, and she questioned no further, though I could have sworn her eyes retained for some time a mocking, teasing expression.

With the foremast in, the work now went on apace. Almost before I knew it, and without one serious hitch, I had the mainmast stepped. A derrick-boom, rigged to the foremast, had accomplished this; and several days more found all stays and shrouds in place, and everything set up taut. Topsails would be a nuisance and a danger for a crew of two, so I heaved the topmasts on deck and lashed them fast.

Several more days were consumed in finishing the sails and putting them on. There were only three—the jib, foresail, and mainsail; and, patched, shortened, and distorted, they were a ridiculously ill-fitting suit for so trim a craft as the *Ghost*.

'But they'll work!' Maud cried jubilantly. 'We'll make them work, and trust our lives to them!'

Certainly, among my many new trades, I shone least as a sail-maker. I could sail them better than make them, and I had no doubt of my power to bring the schooner to some northern port of Japan. In fact, I had crammed navigation from text-books aboard; and besides, there was Wolf Larsen's star-scale, so simple a device that a child could work it.

As for its inventor, beyond an increasing deafness and the movement of the lips growing fainter and fainter, there had been little change in his condition for a week. But on the day we finished bending the schooner's sails, he heard his last, and the last movement of his lips died away—but not before I had asked him, 'Are you all there?' and the lips had answered, 'Yes.'

The last line was down. Somewhere within that tomb of the flesh still dwelt the soul of the man. Walled by the living clay, that fierce intelligence we had known burned on; but it burned on in silence and darkness. And it was disembodied. To that intelligence there could be no objective knowledge of a body. It knew no body. The very world was not. It knew only itself and the vastness and profundity of the quiet and the dark.

CHAPTER XXXIX

The day came for our departure. There was no longer anything to detain us on Endeavour Island. The *Ghost's* stumpy masts were in place, her crazy sails bent. All my handiwork was strong, none of it beautiful; but I knew that it would work, and I felt myself a man of power as I looked at it.

'I did it! I did it! With my own hands I did it!' I wanted to cry aloud.

But Maud and I had a way of voicing each other's thoughts, and she said, as we prepared to hoist the mainsail:

'To think, Humphrey, you did it all with your own hands?'

'But there were two other hands,' I answered. 'Two small hands, and don't say that was a phrase, also, of your father.'

She laughed and shook her head, and held her hands up for inspection.

'I can never get them clean again,' she wailed, 'nor soften the weather-beat.'

'Then dirt and weather-beat shall be your guerdon of honour,' I said, holding them in mine; and, spite of my resolutions, I would have kissed the two dear hands had she not swiftly withdrawn them.

Our comradeship was becoming tremulous, I had mastered my love long and well, but now it was mastering me. Wilfully had it disobeyed and won my eyes to speech, and now it was winning my tongue—ay, and my lips, for they were mad this moment to kiss the two small hands which had toiled so faithfully and hard. And I, too, was mad. There was a cry in my being like bugles calling me to her. And there was a wind blowing upon me which I could not resist, swaying the very body of me till I leaned toward her, all unconscious that I leaned. And she knew it. She could not but know it as she swiftly drew away her hands, and yet, could not forbear one quick searching look before she turned away her eyes.

By means of deck-tackles I had arranged to carry the halyards forward to the windlass; and now I hoisted the mainsail, peak and throat, at the same time. It was a clumsy way, but it did not take long, and soon the foresail as well was up and fluttering.

'We can never get that anchor up in this narrow place, once it has left the bottom,' I said. 'We should be on the rocks first.'

'What can you do?' she asked.

'Slip it,' was my answer. 'And when I do, you must do your first work on the windlass. I shall have to run at once to the wheel, and at the same time you must be hoisting the jib.'

This manœuvre of getting under way I had studied and worked out a score of times; and, with the jib-halyard to the windlass, I knew Maud was capable of hoisting that most necessary sail. A brisk wind was blowing into the cove, and though the water was calm, rapid work was required to get us safely out.

When I knocked the shackle-bolt loose, the chain roared out through the hawse-hole and into the sea. I raced aft, putting the wheel up. The *Ghost* seemed to start into life as she heeled to the first fill of her sails. The jib was rising. As it filled, the *Ghost's* bow swung off and I had to put the wheel down a few spokes and steady her.

I had devised an automatic jib-sheet which passed the jib across of itself, so there was no need for Maud to attend to that; but she was still hoisting the jib when I put the wheel hard down. It was a moment of anxiety, for the *Ghost* was rushing directly upon the beach, a stone's throw distant. But she swung obediently on her heel into the wind. There was a great fluttering and flapping of canvas and reef-points, most welcome to my ears, then she filled away on the other tack.

Maud had finished her task and come aft, where she stood beside me, a small cap perched on her wind-blown hair, her cheeks flushed from exertion, her eyes wide and bright with the excitement, her nostrils quivering to the rush and bite of the fresh salt air. Her brown eyes were like a startled deer's. There was a wild, keen look in them

I had never seen before, and her lips parted and her breath suspended as the *Ghost*, charging upon the wall of rock at the entrance to the inner cove, swept into the wind and filled away into safe water.

My first mate's berth on the sealing grounds stood me in good stead, and I cleared the inner cove and laid a long tack along the shore of the outer cove. Once again about, and the *Ghost* headed out to open sea. She had now caught the bosom-breathing of the ocean, and was herself a-breath with the rhythm of it as she smoothly mounted and slipped down each broad-backed wave. The day had been dull and overcast, but the sun now burst through the clouds, a welcome omen, and shone upon the curving beach where together we had dared the lords of the harem and slain the holluschickie. All Endeavour Island brightened under the sun. Even the grim south-western promontory showed less grim, and here and there, where the sea-spray wet its surface, high lights flashed and dazzled in the sun.

'I shall always think of it with pride,' I said to Maud.

She threw her head back in a queenly way but said, 'Dear, dear Endeavour Island! I shall always love it.'

'And I,' I said quickly.

It seemed our eyes must meet in a great understanding, and yet, loath, they struggled away and did not meet.

There was a silence I might almost call awkward, till I broke it, saying:

'See those black clouds to windward. You remember, I told you last night the barometer was falling.'

'And the sun is gone,' she said, her eyes still fixed upon our island, where we had proved our mastery over matter and attained to the truest comradeship that may fall to man and woman.

'And it's slack off the sheets for Japan!' I cried gaily. 'A fair wind and a flowing sheet, you know, or however it goes.'

Lashing the wheel I ran forward, eased the fore and mainsheets, took in on the boom-tackles and trimmed everything for the quartering breeze which was ours. It was a fresh breeze, very fresh, but I resolved to run as long as I dared. Unfortunately, when running free, it is impossible to lash the wheel, so I faced an all-night watch. Maud insisted on relieving me, but proved that she had not the strength to steer in a heavy sea, even if she could have gained the wisdom on such short notice. She appeared quite heart-broken over the discovery, but recovered her spirits by coiling down tackles and halyards and all stray ropes. Then there were meals to be cooked in the galley, beds to make, Wolf Larsen to be attended upon, and she finished the day with a grand house-cleaning attack upon the cabin and steerage.

All night I steered, without relief, the wind slowly and steadily increasing and the sea rising. At five in the morning Maud brought me hot coffee and biscuits she had baked, and at seven a substantial and piping hot breakfast put new lift into me.

Throughout the day, and as slowly and steadily as ever, the wind increased. It impressed one with its sullen determination to blow, and blow harder, and keep on blowing. And still the *Ghost* foamed along, racing off the miles till I was certain she was making at least eleven knots. It was too good to lose, but by nightfall I was exhausted. Though in splendid physical trim, a thirty-six-hour trick at the wheel was the limit of my endurance. Besides, Maud begged me to heave to, and I knew, if the wind and sea increased at the same rate during the night, that it would soon be impossible to heave to. So, as twilight deepened, gladly and at the same time reluctantly, I brought the *Ghost* up on the wind.

But I had not reckoned upon the colossal task the reefing of three sails meant for one man. While running away from the wind I had not appreciated its force, but when we ceased to run I learned to my sorrow, and well-nigh to my despair, how fiercely it was really blowing. The wind balked my every effort, ripping the canvas out of my hands and in an instant undoing what I had gained by ten minutes of severest struggle. At eight o'clock I had succeeded only in putting the second reef into the foresail. At eleven o'clock I was no farther along. Blood dripped from every finger-end, while the nails were broken to the quick. From pain and sheer exhaustion I wept in the darkness, secretly, so that Maud should not know.

Then, in desperation, I abandoned the attempt to reef the mainsail and resolved to try the experiment of heaving to under the close-reefed foresail. Three hours more were required to gasket the mainsail and jib, and at two in the morning, nearly dead, the life almost buffeted and worked out of me, I had barely sufficient consciousness to know the experiment was a success. The close-reefed foresail worked. The *Ghost* clung on close to the wind and betrayed no inclination to fall off broadside to the trough.

I was famished, but Maud tried vainly to get me to eat. I dozed with my mouth full of food. I would fall asleep in the act of carrying food to my mouth and waken in torment to find the act yet uncompleted. So sleepily helpless was I that she was compelled to hold me in my chair to prevent my being flung to the floor by the violent pitching of the schooner.

Of the passage from the galley to the cabin I knew nothing. It was a sleep-walker Maud guided and supported. In fact, I was aware of nothing till I awoke, how long after I could not imagine, in my bunk with my boots off. It was dark. I was stiff and lame, and cried out with pain when the bed-clothes touched my poor finger-ends.

Morning had evidently not come, so I closed my eyes and went to sleep again. I did not know it, but I had slept the clock around and it was night again.

Once more I woke, troubled because I could sleep no better. I struck a match and looked at my watch. It marked midnight. And I had not left the deck until three! I should have been puzzled had I not guessed the solution. No wonder I was sleeping brokenly. I had slept twenty-one hours. I listened for a while to the behaviour of the *Ghost*, to the pounding of the seas and the muffled roar of the wind on deck, and then turned over on my ride and slept peacefully until morning.

When I arose at seven I saw no sign of Maud and concluded she was in the galley preparing breakfast. On deck I found the *Ghost* doing splendidly under her patch of canvas. But in the galley, though a fire was burning and water boiling, I found no Maud.

I discovered her in the steerage, by Wolf Larsen's bunk. I looked at him, the man who had been hurled down from the topmost pitch of life to be buried alive and be worse than dead. There seemed a relaxation of his expressionless face which was new. Maud looked at me and I understood.

'His life flickered out in the storm,' I said.

'But he still lives,' she answered, infinite faith in her voice.

'He had too great strength.'

'Yes,' she said, 'but now it no longer shackles him. He is a free spirit.'

'He is a free spirit surely,' I answered; and, taking her hand, I led her on deck.

The storm broke that night, which is to say that it diminished as slowly as it had arisen. After breakfast next morning, when I had hoisted Wolf Larsen's body on deck ready for burial, it was still blowing heavily and a large sea was running. The deck was continually awash with the sea which came inboard over the rail and through the scuppers. The wind smote the schooner with a sudden gust, and she heeled over till her lee rail was buried, the roar in her rigging rising in pitch to a shriek. We stood in the water to our knees as I bared my head.

'I remember only one part of the service,' I said, 'and that is, 'And the body shall be cast into the sea.''

Maud looked at me, surprised and shocked; but the spirit of something I had seen before was strong upon me, impelling me to give service to Wolf Larsen as Wolf Larsen had once given service to another man. I lifted the end of the hatch cover and the canvas-shrouded body slipped feet first into the sea. The weight of iron dragged it down. It was gone.

'Good-bye, Lucifer, proud spirit,' Maud whispered, so low that it was drowned by the shouting of the wind; but I saw the movement of her lips and knew.

As we clung to the lee rail and worked our way aft, I happened to glance to leeward. The *Ghost*, at the moment, was uptossed on a sea, and I caught a clear view of a small steamship two or three miles away, rolling and pitching, head on to the sea, as it steamed toward us. It was painted black, and from the talk of the hunters of their poaching exploits I recognized it as a United States revenue cutter. I pointed it out to Maud and hurriedly led her aft to the safety of the poop.

I started to rush below to the flag-locker, then remembered that in rigging the *Ghost*. I had forgotten to make provision for a flag-halyard.

'We need no distress signal,' Maud said. 'They have only to see us.'

'We are saved,' I said, soberly and solemnly. And then, in an exuberance of joy, 'I hardly know whether to be glad or not.'

I looked at her. Our eyes were not loath to meet. We leaned toward each other, and before I knew it my arms were about her.

'Need I?' I asked.

And she answered, 'There is no need, though the telling of it would be sweet, so sweet.'

Her lips met the press of mine, and, by what strange trick of the imagination I know not, the scene in the cabin of the *Ghost* flashed upon me, when she had pressed her fingers lightly on my lips and said, 'Hush, hush.'

'My woman, my one small woman,' I said, my free hand petting her shoulder in the way all lovers know though never learn in school.

'My man,' she said, looking at me for an instant with tremulous lids which fluttered down and veiled her eyes as she snuggled her head against my breast with a happy little sigh.

I looked toward the cutter. It was very close. A boat was being lowered.

'One kiss, dear love,' I whispered. 'One kiss more before they come.'

'And rescue us from ourselves,' she completed, with a most adorable smile, whimsical as I had never seen it, for it was whimsical with love.

THE END

WHITE FANG

PART I

CHAPTER I
THE TRAIL OF THE MEAT

Dark spruce forest frowned on either side the frozen waterway. The trees had been stripped by a recent wind of their white covering of frost, and they seemed to lean towards each other, black and ominous, in the fading light. A vast silence reigned over the land. The land itself was a desolation, lifeless, without movement, so lone and cold that the spirit of it was not even that of sadness. There was a hint in it of laughter, but of a laughter more terrible than any sadness—a laughter that was mirthless as the smile of the sphinx, a laughter cold as the frost and partaking of the grimness of infallibility. It was the masterful and incommunicable wisdom of eternity laughing at the futility of life and the effort of life. It was the Wild, the savage, frozen-hearted Northland Wild.

But there *was* life, abroad in the land and defiant. Down the frozen waterway toiled a string of wolfish dogs. Their bristly fur was rimed with frost. Their breath froze in the air as it left their mouths, spouting forth in spumes of vapour that settled upon the hair of their bodies and formed into crystals of frost. Leather harness was on the dogs, and leather traces attached them to a sled which dragged along behind. The sled was without runners. It was made of stout birch-bark, and its full surface rested on the snow. The front end of the sled was turned up, like a scroll, in order to force down and under the bore of soft snow that surged like a wave before it. On the sled, securely lashed, was a long and narrow oblong box. There were other things on the sled—blankets, an axe, and a coffee-pot and frying-pan; but prominent, occupying most of the space, was the long and narrow oblong box.

In advance of the dogs, on wide snowshoes, toiled a man. At the rear of the sled toiled a second man. On the sled, in the box, lay a third man whose toil was over,—a man whom the Wild had conquered and beaten down until he would never move nor struggle again. It is not the way of the Wild to like movement. Life is an offence to it, for life is movement; and the Wild aims always to destroy movement. It freezes

223

the water to prevent it running to the sea; it drives the sap out of the trees till they are frozen to their mighty hearts; and most ferociously and terribly of all does the Wild harry and crush into submission man—man who is the most restless of life, ever in revolt against the dictum that all movement must in the end come to the cessation of movement.

But at front and rear, unawed and indomitable, toiled the two men who were not yet dead. Their bodies were covered with fur and soft-tanned leather. Eyelashes and cheeks and lips were so coated with the crystals from their frozen breath that their faces were not discernible. This gave them the seeming of ghostly masques, undertakers in a spectral world at the funeral of some ghost. But under it all they were men, penetrating the land of desolation and mockery and silence, puny adventurers bent on colossal adventure, pitting themselves against the might of a world as remote and alien and pulseless as the abysses of space.

They travelled on without speech, saving their breath for the work of their bodies. On every side was the silence, pressing upon them with a tangible presence. It affected their minds as the many atmospheres of deep water affect the body of the diver. It crushed them with the weight of unending vastness and unalterable decree. It crushed them into the remotest recesses of their own minds, pressing out of them, like juices from the grape, all the false ardours and exaltations and undue self-values of the human soul, until they perceived themselves finite and small, specks and motes, moving with weak cunning and little wisdom amidst the play and inter-play of the great blind elements and forces.

An hour went by, and a second hour. The pale light of the short sunless day was beginning to fade, when a faint far cry arose on the still air. It soared upward with a swift rush, till it reached its topmost note, where it persisted, palpitant and tense, and then slowly died away. It might have been a lost soul wailing, had it not been invested with a certain sad fierceness and hungry eagerness. The front man turned his head until his eyes met the eyes of the man behind. And then, across the narrow oblong box, each nodded to the other.

A second cry arose, piercing the silence with needle-like shrillness. Both men located the sound. It was to the rear, somewhere in the snow expanse they had just traversed. A third and answering cry arose, also to the rear and to the left of the second cry.

'They're after us, Bill,' said the man at the front.

His voice sounded hoarse and unreal, and he had spoken with apparent effort.

'Meat is scarce,' answered his comrade. 'I ain't seen a rabbit sign for days.'

Thereafter they spoke no more, though their ears were keen for the hunting-cries that continued to rise behind them.

At the fall of darkness they swung the dogs into a cluster of spruce trees on the edge of the waterway and made a camp. The coffin, at the side of the fire, served for seat and table. The wolf-dogs, clustered on the far side of the fire, snarled and bickered among themselves, but evinced no inclination to stray off into the darkness.

'Seems to me, Henry, they're stayin' remarkable close to camp,' Bill commented.

Henry, squatting over the fire and settling the pot of coffee with a piece of ice, nodded. Nor did he speak till he had taken his seat on the coffin and begun to eat.

'They know where their hides is safe,' he said. 'They'd sooner eat grub than be grub. They're pretty wise, them dogs.'

Bill shook his head. 'Oh, I don't know.'

His comrade looked at him curiously. 'First time I ever heard you say anything about their not bein' wise.'

'Henry,' said the other, munching with deliberation the beans he was eating, 'did you happen to notice the way them dogs kicked up when I was a-feedin' 'em?'

'They did cut up more'n usual,' Henry acknowledged.

'How many dogs 've we got, Henry?'

'Six.'

'Well, Henry . . . ' Bill stopped for a moment, in order that his words might gain greater significance. 'As I was sayin', Henry, we've got six dogs. I took six fish out of the bag. I gave one fish to each dog, an', Henry, I was one fish short.'

'You counted wrong.'

'We've got six dogs,' the other reiterated dispassionately. 'I took out six fish. One Ear didn't get no fish. I came back to the bag afterward an' got 'm his fish.'

'We've only got six dogs,' Henry said.

'Henry,' Bill went on. 'I won't say they was all dogs, but there was seven of 'm that got fish.'

Henry stopped eating to glance across the fire and count the dogs.

'There's only six now,' he said.

'I saw the other one run off across the snow,' Bill announced with cool positiveness. 'I saw seven.'

Henry looked at him commiseratingly, and said, 'I'll be almighty glad when this trip's over.'

'What d'ye mean by that?' Bill demanded.

'I mean that this load of ourn is gettin' on your nerves, an' that you're beginnin' to see things.'

'I thought of that,' Bill answered gravely. 'An' so, when I saw it run off across the snow, I looked in the snow an' saw its tracks. Then I counted the dogs an' there was still six of 'em. The tracks is there in the snow now. D'ye want to look at 'em? I'll show 'em to you.'

Henry did not reply, but munched on in silence, until, the meal finished, he topped it with a final cup of coffee. He wiped his mouth with the back of his hand and said:

'Then you're thinkin' as it was—'

A long wailing cry, fiercely sad, from somewhere in the darkness, had interrupted him. He stopped to listen to it, then he finished his sentence with a wave of his hand toward the sound of the cry, '—one of them?'

Bill nodded. 'I'd a blame sight sooner think that than anything else. You noticed yourself the row the dogs made.'

Cry after cry, and answering cries, were turning the silence into a bedlam. From every side the cries arose, and the dogs betrayed their fear by huddling together and so close to the fire that their hair was scorched by the heat. Bill threw on more wood, before lighting his pipe.

'I'm thinking you're down in the mouth some,' Henry said.

'Henry . . . ' He sucked meditatively at his pipe for some time before he went on. 'Henry, I was a-thinkin' what a blame sight luckier he is than you an' me'll ever be.'

He indicated the third person by a downward thrust of the thumb to the box on which they sat.

'You an' me, Henry, when we die, we'll be lucky if we get enough stones over our carcases to keep the dogs off of us.'

'But we ain't got people an' money an' all the rest, like him,' Henry rejoined. 'Long-distance funerals is somethin' you an' me can't exactly afford.'

'What gets me, Henry, is what a chap like this, that's a lord or something in his own country, and that's never had to bother about grub nor blankets; why he comes a-buttin' round the Godforsaken ends of the earth—that's what I can't exactly see.'

'He might have lived to a ripe old age if he'd stayed at home,' Henry agreed.

Bill opened his mouth to speak, but changed his mind. Instead, he pointed towards the wall of darkness that pressed about them from every side. There was no suggestion of form in the utter blackness; only could be seen a pair of eyes gleaming like live coals. Henry indicated with his head a second pair, and a third. A circle of the gleaming eyes had drawn about their camp. Now and again a pair of eyes moved, or disappeared to appear again a moment later.

The unrest of the dogs had been increasing, and they stampeded, in a surge of sudden fear, to the near side of the fire, cringing and crawling about the legs of the men. In the scramble one of the dogs had been overturned on the edge of the fire, and it had yelped with pain and fright as the smell of its singed coat possessed the air. The commotion caused the circle of eyes to shift restlessly for a moment and even to withdraw a bit, but it settled down again as the dogs became quiet.

'Henry, it's a blame misfortune to be out of ammunition.'

Bill had finished his pipe and was helping his companion to spread the bed of fur and blanket upon the spruce boughs which he had laid over the snow before supper. Henry grunted, and began unlacing his moccasins.

'How many cartridges did you say you had left?' he asked.

'Three,' came the answer. 'An' I wisht 'twas three hundred. Then I'd show 'em what for, damn 'em!'

He shook his fist angrily at the gleaming eyes, and began securely to prop his moccasins before the fire.

'An' I wisht this cold snap'd break,' he went on. 'It's ben fifty below for two weeks now. An' I wisht I'd never started on this trip, Henry. I don't like the looks of it. I don't feel right, somehow. An' while I'm wishin', I wisht the trip was over an' done with, an' you an' me a-sittin' by the fire in Fort McGurry just about now an' playing cribbage—that's what I wisht.'

Henry grunted and crawled into bed. As he dozed off he was aroused by his comrade's voice.

'Say, Henry, that other one that come in an' got a fish—why didn't the dogs pitch into it? That's what's botherin' me.'

'You're botherin' too much, Bill,' came the sleepy response. 'You was never like this before. You jes' shut up now, an' go to sleep, an' you'll be all hunkydory in the mornin'. Your stomach's sour, that's what's botherin' you.'

The men slept, breathing heavily, side by side, under the one covering. The fire died down, and the gleaming eyes drew closer the circle they had flung about the camp. The dogs clustered together in fear, now and again snarling menacingly as a pair of eyes drew close. Once their uproar became so loud that Bill woke up. He got out of bed carefully, so as not to disturb the sleep of his comrade, and threw more wood on the fire. As it began to flame up, the circle of eyes drew farther back. He glanced casually at the huddling dogs. He rubbed his eyes and looked at them more sharply. Then he crawled back into the blankets.

'Henry,' he said. 'Oh, Henry.'

Henry groaned as he passed from sleep to waking, and demanded, 'What's wrong now?'

'Nothin',' came the answer; 'only there's seven of 'em again. I just counted.'

Henry acknowledged receipt of the information with a grunt that slid into a snore as he drifted back into sleep.

In the morning it was Henry who awoke first and routed his companion out of bed. Daylight was yet three hours away, though it was already six o'clock; and in the darkness Henry went about preparing breakfast, while Bill rolled the blankets and made the sled ready for lashing.

'Say, Henry,' he asked suddenly, 'how many dogs did you say we had?'

'Six.'

'Wrong,' Bill proclaimed triumphantly.

'Seven again?' Henry queried.

'No, five; one's gone.'

'The hell!' Henry cried in wrath, leaving the cooking to come and count the dogs. 'You're right, Bill,' he concluded. 'Fatty's gone.'

'An' he went like greased lightnin' once he got started. Couldn't 've seen 'm for smoke.'

'No chance at all,' Henry concluded. 'They jes' swallowed 'm alive. I bet he was yelpin' as he went down their throats, damn 'em!'

'He always was a fool dog,' said Bill.

'But no fool dog ought to be fool enough to go off an' commit suicide that way.' He looked over the remainder of the team with a speculative eye that summed up instantly the salient traits of each animal. 'I bet none of the others would do it.'

'Couldn't drive 'em away from the fire with a club,' Bill agreed. 'I always did think there was somethin' wrong with Fatty anyway.'

And this was the epitaph of a dead dog on the Northland trail—less scant than the epitaph of many another dog, of many a man.

CHAPTER II
THE SHE-WOLF

Breakfast eaten and the slim camp-outfit lashed to the sled, the men turned their backs on the cheery fire and launched out into the darkness. At once began to rise the cries that were fiercely sad—cries that called through the darkness and cold to one another and answered back. Conversation ceased. Daylight came at nine o'clock. At midday the sky to the south warmed to rose-colour, and marked where the bulge of the earth intervened between the meridian sun and the northern world. But the rose-colour swiftly faded. The grey light of day that remained lasted until three o'clock, when it, too, faded, and the pall of the Arctic night descended upon the lone and silent land.

As darkness came on, the hunting-cries to right and left and rear drew closer—so close that more than once they sent surges of fear through the toiling dogs, throwing them into short-lived panics.

At the conclusion of one such panic, when he and Henry had got the dogs back in the traces, Bill said:

'I wisht they'd strike game somewheres, an' go away an' leave us alone.'

'They do get on the nerves horrible,' Henry sympathised.

They spoke no more until camp was made.

Henry was bending over and adding ice to the babbling pot of beans when he was startled by the sound of a blow, an exclamation from Bill, and a sharp snarling cry of pain from among the dogs. He straightened up in time to see a dim form disappearing across the snow into the shelter of the dark. Then he saw Bill, standing amid the dogs, half triumphant, half crestfallen, in one hand a stout club, in the other the tail and part of the body of a sun-cured salmon.

'It got half of it,' he announced; 'but I got a whack at it jes' the same. D'ye hear it squeal?'

'What'd it look like?' Henry asked.

'Couldn't see. But it had four legs an' a mouth an' hair an' looked like any dog.'

'Must be a tame wolf, I reckon.'

'It's damned tame, whatever it is, comin' in here at feedin' time an' gettin' its whack of fish.'

That night, when supper was finished and they sat on the oblong box and pulled at their pipes, the circle of gleaming eyes drew in even closer than before.

'I wisht they'd spring up a bunch of moose or something, an' go away an' leave us alone,' Bill said.

Henry grunted with an intonation that was not all sympathy, and for a quarter of an hour they sat on in silence, Henry staring at the fire, and Bill at the circle of eyes that burned in the darkness just beyond the firelight.

'I wisht we was pullin' into McGurry right now,' he began again.

'Shut up your wishin' and your croakin',' Henry burst out angrily. 'Your stomach's sour. That's what's ailin' you. Swallow a spoonful of sody, an' you'll sweeten up wonderful an' be more pleasant company.'

In the morning Henry was aroused by fervid blasphemy that proceeded from the mouth of Bill. Henry propped himself up on an elbow and looked to see his comrade standing among the dogs beside the replenished fire, his arms raised in objurgation, his face distorted with passion.

'Hello!' Henry called. 'What's up now?'

'Frog's gone,' came the answer.

'No.'

'I tell you yes.'

Henry leaped out of the blankets and to the dogs. He counted them with care, and then joined his partner in cursing the power of the Wild that had robbed them of another dog.

'Frog was the strongest dog of the bunch,' Bill pronounced finally.

'An' he was no fool dog neither,' Henry added.

And so was recorded the second epitaph in two days.

A gloomy breakfast was eaten, and the four remaining dogs were harnessed to the sled. The day was a repetition of the days that had gone before. The men toiled without speech across the face of the frozen world. The silence was unbroken save by the cries of their pursuers, that, unseen, hung upon their rear. With the coming of night in the mid-afternoon, the cries sounded closer as the pursuers drew in according to their custom; and the dogs grew excited and frightened, and were guilty of panics that tangled the traces and further depressed the two men.

'There, that'll fix you fool critters,' Bill said with satisfaction that night, standing erect at completion of his task.

Henry left the cooking to come and see. Not only had his partner tied the dogs up, but he had tied them, after the Indian fashion, with sticks. About the neck of each dog he had fastened a leather thong. To this, and so close to the neck that the dog could not get his teeth to it, he had tied a stout stick four or five feet in length. The other end of the stick, in turn, was made fast to a stake in the ground by means of a leather thong. The dog was unable to gnaw through the leather at his own end of the stick. The stick prevented him from getting at the leather that fastened the other end.

Henry nodded his head approvingly.

'It's the only contraption that'll ever hold One Ear,' he said. 'He can gnaw through leather as clean as a knife an' jes' about half as quick. They all'll be here in the mornin' hunkydory.'

'You jes' bet they will,' Bill affirmed. 'If one of em' turns up missin', I'll go without my coffee.'

'They jes' know we ain't loaded to kill,' Henry remarked at bed-time, indicating the gleaming circle that hemmed them in. 'If we could put a couple of shots into 'em, they'd be more respectful. They come closer every night. Get the firelight out of your eyes an' look hard—there! Did you see that one?'

For some time the two men amused themselves with watching the movement of vague forms on the edge of the firelight. By looking closely and steadily at where a pair of eyes burned in the darkness, the form of the animal would slowly take shape. They could even see these forms move at times.

A sound among the dogs attracted the men's attention. One Ear was uttering quick, eager whines, lunging at the length of his stick toward the darkness, and desisting now and again in order to make frantic attacks on the stick with his teeth.

'Look at that, Bill,' Henry whispered.

Full into the firelight, with a stealthy, sidelong movement, glided a doglike animal. It moved with commingled mistrust and daring, cautiously observing the men, its attention fixed on the dogs. One Ear strained the full length of the stick toward the intruder and whined with eagerness.

'That fool One Ear don't seem scairt much,' Bill said in a low tone.

'It's a she-wolf,' Henry whispered back, 'an' that accounts for Fatty an' Frog. She's the decoy for the pack. She draws out the dog an' then all the rest pitches in an' eats 'm up.'

The fire crackled. A log fell apart with a loud spluttering noise. At the sound of it the strange animal leaped back into the darkness.

'Henry, I'm a-thinkin',' Bill announced.

'Thinkin' what?'

'I'm a-thinkin' that was the one I lambasted with the club.'

'Ain't the slightest doubt in the world,' was Henry's response.

'An' right here I want to remark,' Bill went on, 'that that animal's familyarity with campfires is suspicious an' immoral.'

'It knows for certain more'n a self-respectin' wolf ought to know,' Henry agreed. 'A wolf that knows enough to come in with the dogs at feedin' time has had experiences.'

'Ol' Villan had a dog once that run away with the wolves,' Bill cogitates aloud. 'I ought to know. I shot it out of the pack in a moose pasture over 'on Little Stick. An' Ol' Villan cried like a baby. Hadn't seen it for three years, he said. Ben with the wolves all that time.'

'I reckon you've called the turn, Bill. That wolf's a dog, an' it's eaten fish many's the time from the hand of man.'

'An if I get a chance at it, that wolf that's a dog'll be jes' meat,' Bill declared. 'We can't afford to lose no more animals.'

'But you've only got three cartridges,' Henry objected.

'I'll wait for a dead sure shot,' was the reply.

In the morning Henry renewed the fire and cooked breakfast to the accompaniment of his partner's snoring.

'You was sleepin' jes' too comfortable for anything,' Henry told him, as he routed him out for breakfast. 'I hadn't the heart to rouse you.'

Bill began to eat sleepily. He noticed that his cup was empty and started to reach for the pot. But the pot was beyond arm's length and beside Henry.

'Say, Henry,' he chided gently, 'ain't you forgot somethin'?'

Henry looked about with great carefulness and shook his head. Bill held up the empty cup.

'You don't get no coffee,' Henry announced.

'Ain't run out?' Bill asked anxiously.

'Nope.'

'Ain't thinkin' it'll hurt my digestion?'

'Nope.'

A flush of angry blood pervaded Bill's face.

'Then it's jes' warm an' anxious I am to be hearin' you explain yourself,' he said.

'Spanker's gone,' Henry answered.

Without haste, with the air of one resigned to misfortune Bill turned his head, and from where he sat counted the dogs.

'How'd it happen?' he asked apathetically.

Henry shrugged his shoulders. 'Don't know. Unless One Ear gnawed 'm loose. He couldn't a-done it himself, that's sure.'

'The darned cuss.' Bill spoke gravely and slowly, with no hint of the anger that was raging within. 'Jes' because he couldn't chew himself loose, he chews Spanker loose.'

'Well, Spanker's troubles is over anyway; I guess he's digested by this time an' cavortin' over the landscape in the bellies of twenty different wolves,' was Henry's epitaph on this, the latest lost dog. 'Have some coffee, Bill.'

But Bill shook his head.

'Go on,' Henry pleaded, elevating the pot.

Bill shoved his cup aside. 'I'll be ding-dong-danged if I do. I said I wouldn't if ary dog turned up missin', an' I won't.'

'It's darn good coffee,' Henry said enticingly.

But Bill was stubborn, and he ate a dry breakfast washed down with mumbled curses at One Ear for the trick he had played.

'I'll tie 'em up out of reach of each other to-night,' Bill said, as they took the trail.

They had travelled little more than a hundred yards, when Henry, who was in front, bent down and picked up something with which his snowshoe had collided. It was dark, and he could not see it, but he recognised it by the touch. He flung it back, so that it struck the sled and bounced along until it fetched up on Bill's snowshoes.

'Mebbe you'll need that in your business,' Henry said.

Bill uttered an exclamation. It was all that was left of Spanker—the stick with which he had been tied.

'They ate 'm hide an' all,' Bill announced. 'The stick's as clean as a whistle. They've ate the leather offen both ends. They're damn hungry, Henry, an' they'll have you an' me guessin' before this trip's over.'

Henry laughed defiantly. 'I ain't been trailed this way by wolves before, but I've gone through a whole lot worse an' kept my health. Takes more'n a handful of them pesky critters to do for yours truly, Bill, my son.'

'I don't know, I don't know,' Bill muttered ominously.

'Well, you'll know all right when we pull into McGurry.'

'I ain't feelin' special enthusiastic,' Bill persisted.

'You're off colour, that's what's the matter with you,' Henry dogmatised. 'What you need is quinine, an' I'm goin' to dose you up stiff as soon as we make McGurry.'

Bill grunted his disagreement with the diagnosis, and lapsed into silence. The day was like all the days. Light came at nine o'clock. At twelve o'clock the southern horizon was warmed by the unseen sun; and then began the cold grey of afternoon that would merge, three hours later, into night.

It was just after the sun's futile effort to appear, that Bill slipped the rifle from under the sled-lashings and said:

'You keep right on, Henry, I'm goin' to see what I can see.'

'You'd better stick by the sled,' his partner protested. 'You've only got three cartridges, an' there's no tellin' what might happen.'

'Who's croaking now?' Bill demanded triumphantly.

Henry made no reply, and plodded on alone, though often he cast anxious glances back into the grey solitude where his partner had disappeared. An hour later, taking advantage of the cut-offs around which the sled had to go, Bill arrived.

'They're scattered an' rangin' along wide,' he said: 'keeping up with us an' lookin' for game at the same time. You see, they're sure of us, only they know they've got to wait to get us. In the meantime they're willin' to pick up anything eatable that comes handy.'

'You mean they *think* they're sure of us,' Henry objected pointedly.

But Bill ignored him. 'I seen some of them. They're pretty thin. They ain't had a bite in weeks I reckon, outside of Fatty an' Frog an' Spanker; an' there's so many of 'em that that didn't go far. They're remarkable thin. Their ribs is like wash-boards, an' their stomachs is right up against their backbones. They're pretty desperate, I can tell you. They'll be goin' mad, yet, an' then watch out.'

A few minutes later, Henry, who was now travelling behind the sled, emitted a low, warning whistle. Bill turned and looked, then quietly stopped the dogs. To the rear, from around the last bend and plainly into view, on the very trail they had just covered, trotted a furry, slinking form. Its nose was to the trail, and it trotted with a peculiar, sliding, effortless gait. When they halted, it halted, throwing up its head and regarding them steadily with nostrils that twitched as it caught and studied the scent of them.

'It's the she-wolf,' Bill answered.

The dogs had lain down in the snow, and he walked past them to join his partner in the sled. Together they watched the strange animal that had pursued them for days and that had already accomplished the destruction of half their dog-team.

After a searching scrutiny, the animal trotted forward a few steps. This it repeated several times, till it was a short hundred yards away. It paused, head up, close by a clump of spruce trees, and with sight and scent studied the outfit of the watching men. It looked at them in a strangely wistful way, after the manner of a dog; but in its wistfulness there was none of the dog affection. It was a wistfulness bred of hunger, as cruel as its own fangs, as merciless as the frost itself.

It was large for a wolf, its gaunt frame advertising the lines of an animal that was among the largest of its kind.

'Stands pretty close to two feet an' a half at the shoulders,' Henry commented. 'An' I'll bet it ain't far from five feet long.'

'Kind of strange colour for a wolf,' was Bill's criticism. 'I never seen a red wolf before. Looks almost cinnamon to me.'

The animal was certainly not cinnamon-coloured. Its coat was the true wolf-coat. The dominant colour was grey, and yet there was to it a faint reddish hue—a hue that was baffling, that appeared and disappeared, that was more like an illusion of the vision, now grey, distinctly grey, and again giving hints and glints of a vague redness of colour not classifiable in terms of ordinary experience.

'Looks for all the world like a big husky sled-dog,' Bill said. 'I wouldn't be s'prised to see it wag its tail.'

'Hello, you husky!' he called. 'Come here, you whatever-your-name-is.'

'Ain't a bit scairt of you,' Henry laughed.

Bill waved his hand at it threateningly and shouted loudly; but the animal betrayed no fear. The only change in it that they could notice was an accession of alertness. It still regarded them with the merciless wistfulness of hunger. They were meat, and it was hungry; and it would like to go in and eat them if it dared.

'Look here, Henry,' Bill said, unconsciously lowering his voice to a whisper because of what he imitated. 'We've got three cartridges. But it's a dead shot. Couldn't miss it. It's got away with three of our dogs, an' we oughter put a stop to it. What d'ye say?'

Henry nodded his consent. Bill cautiously slipped the gun from under the sled-lashing. The gun was on the way to his shoulder, but it never got there. For in that instant the she-wolf leaped sidewise from the trail into the clump of spruce trees and disappeared.

The two men looked at each other. Henry whistled long and comprehendingly.

'I might have knowed it,' Bill chided himself aloud as he replaced the gun. 'Of course a wolf that knows enough to come in with the dogs at feedin' time, 'd know all about shooting-irons. I tell you right now, Henry, that critter's the cause of all our trouble. We'd have six dogs at the present time, 'stead of three, if it wasn't for her. An' I tell you right now, Henry, I'm goin' to get her. She's too smart to be shot in the open. But I'm goin' to lay for her. I'll bushwhack her as sure as my name is Bill.'

'You needn't stray off too far in doin' it,' his partner admonished. 'If that pack ever starts to jump you, them three cartridges'd be wuth no more'n three whoops in hell. Them animals is damn hungry, an' once they start in, they'll sure get you, Bill.'

They camped early that night. Three dogs could not drag the sled so fast nor for so long hours as could six, and they were showing unmistakable signs of playing out. And the men went early to bed, Bill first seeing to it that the dogs were tied out of gnawing-reach of one another.

But the wolves were growing bolder, and the men were aroused more than once from their sleep. So near did the wolves approach, that the dogs became frantic with terror, and it was necessary to replenish the fire from time to time in order to keep the adventurous marauders at safer distance.

'I've hearn sailors talk of sharks followin' a ship,' Bill remarked, as he crawled back into the blankets after one such replenishing of the fire. 'Well, them wolves is land sharks. They know their business better'n we do, an' they ain't a-holdin' our trail this way for their health. They're goin' to get us. They're sure goin' to get us, Henry.'

'They've half got you a'ready, a-talkin' like that,' Henry retorted sharply. 'A man's half licked when he says he is. An' you're half eaten from the way you're goin' on about it.'

'They've got away with better men than you an' me,' Bill answered.

'Oh, shet up your croakin'. You make me all-fired tired.'

Henry rolled over angrily on his side, but was surprised that Bill made no similar display of temper. This was not Bill's way, for he was easily angered by sharp words. Henry thought long over it before he went to sleep, and as his eyelids fluttered down and he dozed off, the thought in his mind was: 'There's no mistakin' it, Bill's almighty blue. I'll have to cheer him up to-morrow.'

CHAPTER III

THE HUNGER CRY

The day began auspiciously. They had lost no dogs during the night, and they swung out upon the trail and into the silence, the darkness, and the cold with spirits that were fairly light. Bill seemed to have forgotten his forebodings of the previous night, and even waxed facetious with the dogs when, at midday, they overturned the sled on a bad piece of trail.

It was an awkward mix-up. The sled was upside down and jammed between a tree-trunk and a huge rock, and they were forced to unharness the dogs in order to straighten out the tangle. The two men were bent over the sled and trying to right it, when Henry observed One Ear sidling away.

'Here, you, One Ear!' he cried, straightening up and turning around on the dog.

But One Ear broke into a run across the snow, his traces trailing behind him. And there, out in the snow of their back track, was the she-wolf waiting for him. As he neared her, he became suddenly cautious. He slowed down to an alert and mincing walk and then stopped. He regarded her carefully and dubiously, yet desirefully. She seemed to smile at him, showing her teeth in an ingratiating rather than a menacing way. She moved toward him a few steps, playfully, and then halted. One Ear drew near to her, still alert and cautious, his tail and ears in the air, his head held high.

He tried to sniff noses with her, but she retreated playfully and coyly. Every advance on his part was accompanied by a corresponding retreat on her part. Step by step she was luring him away from the security of his human companionship. Once, as though a warning had in vague ways flitted through his intelligence, he turned his head and looked back at the overturned sled, at his team-mates, and at the two men who were calling to him.

But whatever idea was forming in his mind, was dissipated by the she-wolf, who advanced upon him, sniffed noses with him for a fleeting instant, and then resumed her coy retreat before his renewed advances.

In the meantime, Bill had bethought himself of the rifle. But it was jammed beneath the overturned sled, and by the time Henry had helped him to right the load, One Ear and the she-wolf were too close together and the distance too great to risk a shot.

Too late One Ear learned his mistake. Before they saw the cause, the two men saw him turn and start to run back toward them. Then, approaching at right angles to the trail and cutting off his retreat they saw a dozen wolves, lean and grey, bounding across the snow. On the instant, the she-wolf's coyness and playfulness disappeared. With a snarl she sprang upon One Ear. He thrust her off with his shoulder, and, his retreat cut off and still intent on regaining the sled, he altered his course in an attempt to circle around to it. More wolves were appearing every moment and joining in the chase. The she-wolf was one leap behind One Ear and holding her own.

'Where are you goin'?' Henry suddenly demanded, laying his hand on his partner's arm.

Bill shook it off. 'I won't stand it,' he said. 'They ain't a-goin' to get any more of our dogs if I can help it.'

Gun in hand, he plunged into the underbrush that lined the side of the trail. His intention was apparent enough. Taking the sled as the centre of the circle that One Ear was making, Bill planned to tap that circle at a point in advance of the pursuit. With his rifle, in the broad daylight, it might be possible for him to awe the wolves and save the dog.

'Say, Bill!' Henry called after him. 'Be careful! Don't take no chances!'

Henry sat down on the sled and watched. There was nothing else for him to do. Bill had already gone from sight; but now and again, appearing and disappearing amongst the underbrush and the scattered clumps of spruce, could be seen One Ear. Henry judged his case to be hopeless. The dog was thoroughly alive to its danger, but it was running on the outer circle while the wolf-pack was running on the inner and shorter circle. It was vain to think of One Ear so outdistancing his pursuers as to be able to cut across their circle in advance of them and to regain the sled.

The different lines were rapidly approaching a point. Somewhere out there in the snow, screened from his sight by trees and thickets, Henry knew that the wolf-pack, One Ear, and Bill were coming together. All too quickly, far more quickly than he had expected, it happened. He heard a shot, then two shots, in rapid succession, and he knew that Bill's ammunition was gone. Then he heard a great outcry of snarls and yelps. He recognised One Ear's yell of pain and terror, and he heard a wolf-cry that bespoke a stricken animal. And that was all. The snarls ceased. The yelping died away. Silence settled down again over the lonely land.

He sat for a long while upon the sled. There was no need for him to go and see what had happened. He knew it as though it had taken place before his eyes. Once, he roused with a start and hastily got the axe out from underneath the lashings. But for some time longer he sat and brooded, the two remaining dogs crouching and trembling at his feet.

At last he arose in a weary manner, as though all the resilience had gone out of his body, and proceeded to fasten the dogs to the sled. He passed a rope over his shoulder, a man-trace, and pulled with the dogs. He did not go far. At the first hint of darkness he hastened to make a camp, and he saw to it that he had a generous supply of firewood. He fed the dogs, cooked and ate his supper, and made his bed close to the fire.

But he was not destined to enjoy that bed. Before his eyes closed the wolves had drawn too near for safety. It no longer required an effort of the vision to see them. They were all about him and the fire, in a narrow circle, and he could see them plainly in the firelight lying down, sitting up, crawling forward on their bellies, or slinking back and forth. They even slept. Here and there he could see one curled up in the snow like a dog, taking the sleep that was now denied himself.

He kept the fire brightly blazing, for he knew that it alone intervened between the flesh of his body and their hungry fangs. His two dogs stayed close by him, one on either side, leaning against him for protection, crying and whimpering, and at times snarling desperately when a wolf approached a little closer than usual. At such moments, when his dogs snarled, the whole circle would be agitated, the wolves coming to their feet and pressing tentatively forward, a chorus of snarls and eager yelps rising about him. Then the circle would lie down again, and here and there a wolf would resume its broken nap.

But this circle had a continuous tendency to draw in upon him. Bit by bit, an inch at a time, with here a wolf bellying forward, and there a wolf bellying forward, the circle would narrow until the brutes were almost within springing distance. Then he would seize brands from the fire and hurl them into the pack. A hasty drawing back always resulted, accompanied by angry yelps and frightened snarls when a well-aimed brand struck and scorched a too daring animal.

Morning found the man haggard and worn, wide-eyed from want of sleep. He cooked breakfast in the darkness, and at nine o'clock, when, with the coming of daylight, the wolf-pack drew back, he set about the task he had planned through the long hours of the night. Chopping down young saplings, he made them cross-bars of a scaffold by lashing them high up to the trunks of standing trees. Using the sled-lashing for a heaving rope, and with the aid of the dogs, he hoisted the coffin to the top of the scaffold.

'They got Bill, an' they may get me, but they'll sure never get you, young man,' he said, addressing the dead body in its tree-sepulchre.

Then he took the trail, the lightened sled bounding along behind the willing dogs; for they, too, knew that safety lay open in the gaining of Fort McGurry. The wolves were now more open in their pursuit, trotting sedately behind and ranging along on either side, their red tongues lolling out, their lean sides showing the undulating ribs with every movement. They were very lean, mere skin-bags stretched over bony frames, with strings for muscles—so lean that Henry found it in his mind to marvel that they still kept their feet and did not collapse forthright in the snow.

He did not dare travel until dark. At midday, not only did the sun warm the southern horizon, but it even thrust its upper rim, pale and golden, above the sky-line. He received it as a sign. The days were growing longer. The sun was returning. But scarcely had the cheer of its light departed, than he went into camp. There were still several hours of grey daylight and sombre twilight, and he utilised them in chopping an enormous supply of fire-wood.

With night came horror. Not only were the starving wolves growing bolder, but lack of sleep was telling upon Henry. He dozed despite himself, crouching by the fire, the blankets about his shoulders, the axe between his knees, and on either side a dog pressing close against him. He awoke once and saw in front of him, not a dozen feet away, a big grey wolf, one of the largest of the pack. And even as he looked, the brute deliberately stretched himself after the manner of a lazy dog, yawning full in his face and looking upon him with a possessive eye, as if, in truth, he were merely a delayed meal that was soon to be eaten.

This certitude was shown by the whole pack. Fully a score he could count, staring hungrily at him or calmly sleeping in the snow. They reminded him of children gathered about a spread table and awaiting permission to begin to eat. And he was the food they were to eat! He wondered how and when the meal would begin.

As he piled wood on the fire he discovered an appreciation of his own body which he had never felt before. He watched his moving muscles and was interested in the cunning mechanism of his fingers. By the light of the fire he crooked his fingers slowly and repeatedly now one at a time, now all together, spreading them wide or making quick gripping movements. He studied the nail-formation, and prodded the finger-tips, now sharply, and again softly, gauging the while the nerve-sensations produced. It fascinated him, and he grew suddenly fond of this subtle flesh of his that worked so beautifully and smoothly and delicately. Then he would cast a glance of fear at the wolf-circle drawn expectantly about him, and like a blow the realisation would strike him that this wonderful body of his, this living flesh, was no more than so much meat, a quest of ravenous animals, to be torn and slashed by their hungry fangs, to be sustenance to them as the moose and the rabbit had often been sustenance to him.

He came out of a doze that was half nightmare, to see the red-hued she-wolf before him. She was not more than half a dozen feet away sitting in the snow and wistfully regarding him. The two dogs were whimpering and snarling at his feet, but she took no notice of them. She was looking at the man, and for some time he returned her look. There was nothing threatening about her. She looked at him merely with a great wistfulness, but he knew it to be the wistfulness of an equally great hunger. He was the food, and the sight of him excited in her the gustatory sensations. Her mouth opened, the saliva drooled forth, and she licked her chops with the pleasure of anticipation.

A spasm of fear went through him. He reached hastily for a brand to throw at her. But even as he reached, and before his fingers had closed on the missile, she sprang back into safety; and he knew that she was used to having things thrown at her. She had snarled as she sprang away, baring her white fangs to their roots, all her wistfulness vanishing, being replaced by a carnivorous malignity that made him shudder. He glanced at the hand that held the brand, noticing the cunning delicacy of the fingers that gripped it, how they adjusted themselves to all the inequalities of the surface, curling over and under and about the rough wood, and one little finger, too close to the burning portion of the brand, sensitively and automatically writhing back from the hurtful heat to a cooler gripping-place; and in the same instant he seemed to see a vision of those same sensitive and delicate fingers being crushed and torn by the white teeth of the she-wolf. Never had he been so fond of this body of his as now when his tenure of it was so precarious.

All night, with burning brands, he fought off the hungry pack. When he dozed despite himself, the whimpering and snarling of the dogs aroused him. Morning came, but for the first time the light of day failed to scatter the wolves. The man waited in vain for them to go. They remained in a circle about him and his fire, displaying an arrogance of possession that shook his courage born of the morning light.

He made one desperate attempt to pull out on the trail. But the moment he left the protection of the fire, the boldest wolf leaped for him, but leaped short. He saved himself by springing back, the jaws snapping together a scant six inches from his thigh. The rest of the pack was now up and surging upon him, and a throwing of firebrands right and left was necessary to drive them back to a respectful distance.

Even in the daylight he did not dare leave the fire to chop fresh wood. Twenty feet away towered a huge dead spruce. He spent half the day extending his campfire to the tree, at any moment a half dozen burning faggots ready at hand to fling at his enemies. Once at the tree, he studied the surrounding forest in order to fell the tree in the direction of the most firewood.

The night was a repetition of the night before, save that the need for sleep was becoming overpowering. The snarling of his dogs was losing its efficacy. Besides, they were snarling all the time, and his benumbed and drowsy senses no longer took note of changing pitch and intensity. He awoke with a start. The she-wolf was less than a yard from him. Mechanically, at short range, without letting go of it, he thrust a brand full into her open and snarling mouth. She sprang away, yelling with pain, and while he took delight in the smell of burning flesh and hair, he watched her shaking her head and growling wrathfully a score of feet away.

But this time, before he dozed again, he tied a burning pine-knot to his right hand. His eyes were closed but few minutes when the burn of the flame on his flesh awakened him. For several hours he adhered to this programme. Every time he was thus awakened he drove back the wolves with flying brands, replenished the fire, and rearranged the pine-knot on his hand. All worked well, but there came a time when he fastened the pine-knot insecurely. As his eyes closed it fell away from his hand.

He dreamed. It seemed to him that he was in Fort McGurry. It was warm and comfortable, and he was playing cribbage with the Factor. Also, it seemed to him that the fort was besieged by wolves. They were howling at the very gates, and sometimes he and the Factor paused from the game to listen and laugh at the futile efforts of the wolves to get in. And then, so strange was the dream, there was a crash. The door was burst open. He could see the wolves flooding into the big living-room of the fort. They were leaping straight for him and the Factor. With the bursting open of the door, the noise of their howling had increased tremendously. This howling now bothered him. His dream was merging into something else—he knew not what; but through it all, following him, persisted the howling.

And then he awoke to find the howling real. There was a great snarling and yelping. The wolves were rushing him. They were all about him and upon him. The teeth of one had closed upon his arm. Instinctively he leaped into the fire, and as he leaped, he felt the sharp slash of teeth that tore through the flesh of his leg. Then began a fire fight. His stout mittens temporarily protected his hands, and he scooped live coals into the air in all directions, until the campfire took on the semblance of a volcano.

But it could not last long. His face was blistering in the heat, his eyebrows and lashes were singed off, and the heat was becoming unbearable to his feet. With a flaming brand in each hand, he sprang to the edge of the fire. The wolves had been driven back. On every side, wherever the live coals had fallen, the snow was sizzling, and every little while a retiring wolf, with wild leap and snort and snarl, announced that one such live coal had been stepped upon.

Flinging his brands at the nearest of his enemies, the man thrust his smouldering mittens into the snow and stamped about to cool his feet. His two dogs were missing, and he well knew that they had served as a course in the protracted meal which had begun days before with Fatty, the last course of which would likely be himself in the days to follow.

'You ain't got me yet!' he cried, savagely shaking his fist at the hungry beasts; and at the sound of his voice the whole circle was agitated, there was a general snarl, and the she-wolf slid up close to him across the snow and watched him with hungry wistfulness.

He set to work to carry out a new idea that had come to him. He extended the fire into a large circle. Inside this circle he crouched, his sleeping outfit under him as a protection against the melting snow. When he had thus disappeared within his shelter of flame, the whole pack came curiously to the rim of the fire to see what had become of him. Hitherto they had been denied access to the fire, and they now settled down in a close-drawn circle, like so many dogs, blinking and yawning and stretching their lean bodies in the unaccustomed warmth. Then the she-wolf sat down, pointed her nose at a star, and began to howl. One by one the wolves joined her, till the whole pack, on haunches, with noses pointed skyward, was howling its hunger cry.

Dawn came, and daylight. The fire was burning low. The fuel had run out, and there was need to get more. The man attempted to step out of his circle of flame, but the wolves surged to meet him. Burning brands made them spring aside, but they no longer sprang back. In vain he strove to drive them back. As he gave up and stumbled inside his circle, a wolf leaped for him, missed, and landed with all four feet in the coals. It cried out with terror, at the same time snarling, and scrambled back to cool its paws in the snow.

The man sat down on his blankets in a crouching position. His body leaned forward from the hips. His shoulders, relaxed and drooping, and his head on his knees advertised that he had given up the struggle. Now and again he raised his head to note the dying down of the fire. The circle of flame and coals was breaking into segments with openings in between. These openings grew in size, the segments diminished.

'I guess you can come an' get me any time,' he mumbled. 'Anyway, I'm goin' to sleep.'

Once he awakened, and in an opening in the circle, directly in front of him, he saw the she-wolf gazing at him.

Again he awakened, a little later, though it seemed hours to him. A mysterious change had taken place—so mysterious a change that he was shocked wider awake. Something had happened. He could not understand at first. Then he discovered it. The wolves were gone. Remained only the trampled snow to show how closely they had pressed him. Sleep was welling up and gripping him again, his head was sinking down upon his knees, when he roused with a sudden start.

There were cries of men, and churn of sleds, the creaking of harnesses, and the eager whimpering of straining dogs. Four sleds pulled in from the river bed to the camp among the trees. Half a dozen men were about the man who crouched in the centre of the dying fire. They were shaking and prodding him into consciousness. He looked at them like a drunken man and maundered in strange, sleepy speech.

'Red she-wolf. . . . Come in with the dogs at feedin' time. . . . First she ate the dog-food. . . . Then she ate the dogs. . . . An' after that she ate Bill. . . . '

'Where's Lord Alfred?' one of the men bellowed in his ear, shaking him roughly.

He shook his head slowly. 'No, she didn't eat him. . . . He's roostin' in a tree at the last camp.'

'Dead?' the man shouted.

'An' in a box,' Henry answered. He jerked his shoulder petulantly away from the grip of his questioner. 'Say, you lemme alone. . . . I'm jes' plump tuckered out. . . . Goo' night, everybody.'

His eyes fluttered and went shut. His chin fell forward on his chest. And even as they eased him down upon the blankets his snores were rising on the frosty air.

But there was another sound. Far and faint it was, in the remote distance, the cry of the hungry wolf-pack as it took the trail of other meat than the man it had just missed.

PART II

CHAPTER I
THE BATTLE OF THE FANGS

It was the she-wolf who had first caught the sound of men's voices and the whining of the sled-dogs; and it was the she-wolf who was first to spring away from the cornered man in his circle of dying flame. The pack had been loath to forego the kill it had hunted down, and it lingered for several minutes, making sure of the sounds, and then it, too, sprang away on the trail made by the she-wolf.

Running at the forefront of the pack was a large grey wolf—one of its several leaders. It was he who directed the pack's course on the heels of the she-wolf. It was he who snarled warningly at the younger members of the pack or slashed at them with his fangs when they ambitiously tried to pass him. And it was he who increased the pace when he sighted the she-wolf, now trotting slowly across the snow.

She dropped in alongside by him, as though it were her appointed position, and took the pace of the pack. He did not snarl at her, nor show his teeth, when any leap of hers chanced to put her in advance of him. On the contrary, he seemed kindly disposed toward her—too kindly to suit her, for he was prone to run near to her, and when he ran too near it was she who snarled and showed her teeth. Nor was she above slashing his shoulder sharply on occasion. At such times he betrayed no anger. He merely sprang to the side and ran stiffly ahead for several awkward leaps, in carriage and conduct resembling an abashed country swain.

This was his one trouble in the running of the pack; but she had other troubles. On her other side ran a gaunt old wolf, grizzled and marked with the scars of many battles. He ran always on her right side. The fact that he had but one eye, and that the left eye, might account for this. He, also, was addicted to crowding her, to veering toward her till his scarred muzzle touched her body, or shoulder, or neck. As with the running mate on the left, she repelled these attentions with her teeth; but when both bestowed their attentions at the same time she was roughly jostled, being compelled, with quick snaps to either side, to drive both lovers away and at the same time to maintain her forward leap with the pack and see the way of her feet before her. At such times her running mates flashed their teeth and growled threateningly across at each other. They might have fought, but even wooing and its rivalry waited upon the more pressing hunger-need of the pack.

After each repulse, when the old wolf sheered abruptly away from the sharp-toothed object of his desire, he shouldered against a young three-year-old that ran on his blind right side. This young wolf had attained his full size; and, considering the weak and famished condition of the pack, he possessed more than the average vigour and spirit. Nevertheless, he ran with his head even with the shoulder of his one-eyed elder. When he ventured to run abreast of the older wolf (which was seldom), a snarl and a snap sent him back even with the shoulder again. Sometimes, however, he dropped cautiously and slowly behind and edged in between the old leader and the she-wolf. This was doubly resented, even triply resented. When she snarled her displeasure, the old leader would whirl on the three-year-old. Sometimes she whirled with him. And sometimes the young leader on the left whirled, too.

At such times, confronted by three sets of savage teeth, the young wolf stopped precipitately, throwing himself back on his haunches, with fore-legs stiff, mouth menacing, and mane bristling. This confusion in the front of the moving pack always caused confusion in the rear. The wolves behind collided with the young wolf and expressed their displeasure by administering sharp nips on his hind-legs and flanks. He was laying up trouble for himself, for lack of food and short tempers went together; but with the boundless faith of youth he persisted in repeating the manoeuvre every little while, though it never succeeded in gaining anything for him but discomfiture.

Had there been food, love-making and fighting would have gone on apace, and the pack-formation would have been broken up. But the situation of the pack was desperate. It was lean with long-standing hunger. It ran below its ordinary speed. At the rear limped the weak members, the very young and the very old. At the front were the strongest. Yet all were more like skeletons than full-bodied wolves. Nevertheless, with the exception of the ones that limped, the movements of the animals were effortless and tireless. Their stringy muscles seemed founts of inexhaustible energy. Behind every steel-like contraction of a muscle, lay another steel-like contraction, and another, and another, apparently without end.

They ran many miles that day. They ran through the night. And the next day found them still running. They were running over the surface of a world frozen and dead. No life stirred. They alone moved through the vast inertness. They alone were alive, and they sought for other things that were alive in order that they might devour them and continue to live.

They crossed low divides and ranged a dozen small streams in a lower-lying country before their quest was rewarded. Then they came upon moose. It was a big bull they first found. Here was meat and life, and it was guarded by no mysterious fires nor flying missiles of flame. Splay hoofs and palmated antlers they knew, and they flung their customary patience and caution to the wind. It was a brief fight and fierce. The big bull was beset on every side. He ripped them open or split their skulls with shrewdly driven blows of his great hoofs. He crushed them and broke them on his large horns. He stamped them into the snow under him in the wallowing struggle. But he was foredoomed, and he went down with the she-wolf tearing savagely at his throat, and with other teeth fixed everywhere upon him, devouring him alive, before ever his last struggles ceased or his last damage had been wrought.

There was food in plenty. The bull weighed over eight hundred pounds—fully twenty pounds of meat per mouth for the forty-odd wolves of the pack. But if they could fast prodigiously, they could feed prodigiously, and soon a few scattered bones were all that remained of the splendid live brute that had faced the pack a few hours before.

There was now much resting and sleeping. With full stomachs, bickering and quarrelling began among the younger males, and this continued through the few days that followed before the breaking-up of the pack. The famine was over. The wolves were now in the country of game, and though they still hunted in pack, they hunted more cautiously, cutting out heavy cows or crippled old bulls from the small moose-herds they ran across.

There came a day, in this land of plenty, when the wolf-pack split in half and went in different directions. The she-wolf, the young leader on her left, and the one-eyed elder on her right, led their half of the pack down to the Mackenzie River and across into the lake country to the east. Each day this remnant of the pack dwindled. Two by two, male and female, the wolves were deserting. Occasionally a solitary male was driven out by the sharp teeth of his rivals. In the end there remained only four: the she-wolf, the young leader, the one-eyed one, and the ambitious three-year-old.

The she-wolf had by now developed a ferocious temper. Her three suitors all bore the marks of her teeth. Yet they never replied in kind, never defended themselves against her. They turned their shoulders to her most savage slashes, and with wagging tails and mincing steps strove to placate her wrath. But if they were all mildness toward her, they were all fierceness toward one another. The three-year-old grew too ambitious in his fierceness. He caught the one-eyed elder on his blind side and ripped his ear into ribbons. Though the grizzled old fellow could see only on one side, against the youth and vigour of the other he brought into play the wisdom of long years of experience. His lost eye and his scarred muzzle bore evidence to the nature of his experience. He had survived too many battles to be in doubt for a moment about what to do.

The battle began fairly, but it did not end fairly. There was no telling what the outcome would have been, for the third wolf joined the elder, and together, old leader and young leader, they attacked the ambitious three-year-old and proceeded to destroy him. He was beset on either side by the merciless fangs of his erstwhile comrades. Forgotten were the days they had hunted together, the game they had pulled down, the famine they had suffered. That business was a thing of the past. The business of love was at hand—ever a sterner and crueller business than that of food-getting.

And in the meanwhile, the she-wolf, the cause of it all, sat down contentedly on her haunches and watched. She was even pleased. This was her day—and it came not often—when manes bristled, and fang smote fang or ripped and tore the yielding flesh, all for the possession of her.

And in the business of love the three-year-old, who had made this his first adventure upon it, yielded up his life. On either side of his body stood his two rivals. They were gazing at the she-wolf, who sat smiling in the snow. But the elder leader was wise, very wise, in love even as in battle. The younger leader turned his head to lick a wound on his shoulder. The curve of his neck was turned toward his rival. With his one eye the elder saw the opportunity. He darted in low and closed with his fangs. It was a long, ripping slash, and deep as well. His teeth, in passing, burst the wall of the great vein of the throat. Then he leaped clear.

The young leader snarled terribly, but his snarl broke midmost into a tickling cough. Bleeding and coughing, already stricken, he sprang at the elder and fought while life faded from him, his legs going weak beneath him, the light of day dulling on his eyes, his blows and springs falling shorter and shorter.

And all the while the she-wolf sat on her haunches and smiled. She was made glad in vague ways by the battle, for this was the love-making of the Wild, the sex-tragedy of the natural world that was tragedy only to those that died. To those that survived it was not tragedy, but realisation and achievement.

When the young leader lay in the snow and moved no more, One Eye stalked over to the she-wolf. His carriage was one of mingled triumph and caution. He was plainly expectant of a rebuff, and he was just as plainly surprised when her teeth did not flash out at him in anger. For the first time she met him with a kindly manner. She sniffed noses with him, and even condescended to leap about and frisk and play with him in quite puppyish fashion. And he, for all his grey years and sage experience, behaved quite as puppyishly and even a little more foolishly.

Forgotten already were the vanquished rivals and the love-tale red-written on the snow. Forgotten, save once, when old One Eye stopped for a moment to lick his stiffening wounds. Then it was that his lips half writhed into a snarl, and the hair of his neck and shoulders involuntarily bristled, while he half crouched for a spring, his claws spasmodically clutching into the snow-surface for firmer footing. But it was all forgotten the next moment, as he sprang after the she-wolf, who was coyly leading him a chase through the woods.

After that they ran side by side, like good friends who have come to an understanding. The days passed by, and they kept together, hunting their meat and killing and eating it in common. After a time the she-wolf began to grow restless. She seemed to be searching for something that she could not find. The hollows under fallen trees seemed to attract her, and she spent much time nosing about among the larger snow-piled crevices in the rocks and in the caves of overhanging banks. Old One Eye was not interested at all, but he followed her good-naturedly in her quest, and when her investigations in particular places were unusually protracted, he would lie down and wait until she was ready to go on.

They did not remain in one place, but travelled across country until they regained the Mackenzie River, down which they slowly went, leaving it often to hunt game along the small streams that entered it, but always returning to it again. Sometimes they chanced upon other wolves, usually in pairs; but there was no friendliness of intercourse displayed on either side, no gladness at meeting, no desire to return to the pack-formation. Several times they encountered solitary wolves. These were always males, and they were pressingly insistent on joining with One Eye and his mate. This he resented, and when she stood shoulder to shoulder with him, bristling and showing her teeth, the aspiring solitary ones would back off, turn-tail, and continue on their lonely way.

One moonlight night, running through the quiet forest, One Eye suddenly halted. His muzzle went up, his tail stiffened, and his nostrils dilated as he scented the air. One foot also he held up, after the manner of a dog. He was not satisfied, and he continued to smell the air, striving to understand the message borne upon it to him. One careless sniff had satisfied his mate, and she trotted on to reassure him. Though he followed her, he was still dubious, and he could not forbear an occasional halt in order more carefully to study the warning.

She crept out cautiously on the edge of a large open space in the midst of the trees. For some time she stood alone. Then One Eye, creeping and crawling, every sense on the alert, every hair radiating infinite suspicion, joined her. They stood side by side, watching and listening and smelling.

To their ears came the sounds of dogs wrangling and scuffling, the guttural cries of men, the sharper voices of scolding women, and once the shrill and plaintive cry of a child. With the exception of the huge bulks of the skin-lodges, little could be seen save the flames of the fire, broken by the movements of intervening bodies, and the smoke rising slowly on the quiet air. But to their nostrils came the myriad smells of an Indian camp, carrying a story that was largely incomprehensible to One Eye, but every detail of which the she-wolf knew.

She was strangely stirred, and sniffed and sniffed with an increasing delight. But old One Eye was doubtful. He betrayed his apprehension, and started tentatively to go. She turned and touched his neck with her muzzle in a reassuring way, then regarded the camp again. A new wistfulness was in her face, but it was not the wistfulness of hunger. She was thrilling to a desire that urged her to go forward, to be in closer to that fire, to be squabbling with the dogs, and to be avoiding and dodging the stumbling feet of men.

One Eye moved impatiently beside her; her unrest came back upon her, and she knew again her pressing need to find the thing for which she searched. She turned and trotted back into the forest, to the great relief of One Eye, who trotted a little to the fore until they were well within the shelter of the trees.

As they slid along, noiseless as shadows, in the moonlight, they came upon a run-way. Both noses went down to the footprints in the snow. These footprints were very fresh. One Eye ran ahead cautiously, his mate at his heels. The broad pads of their feet were spread wide and in contact with the snow were like velvet. One Eye caught sight of a dim movement of white in the midst of the white. His sliding gait had been deceptively swift, but it was as nothing to the speed at which he now ran. Before him was bounding the faint patch of white he had discovered.

They were running along a narrow alley flanked on either side by a growth of young spruce. Through the trees the mouth of the alley could be seen, opening out on a moonlit glade. Old One Eye was rapidly overhauling the fleeing shape of white. Bound by bound he gained. Now he was upon it. One leap more and his teeth would be sinking into it. But that leap was never made. High in the air, and straight up, soared the shape of white, now a struggling snowshoe rabbit that leaped and bounded, executing a fantastic dance there above him in the air and never once returning to earth.

One Eye sprang back with a snort of sudden fright, then shrank down to the snow and crouched, snarling threats at this thing of fear he did not understand. But the she-wolf coolly thrust past him. She poised for a moment, then sprang for the dancing rabbit. She, too, soared high, but not so high as the quarry, and her teeth clipped emptily together with a metallic snap. She made another leap, and another.

Her mate had slowly relaxed from his crouch and was watching her. He now evinced displeasure at her repeated failures, and himself made a mighty spring upward. His teeth closed upon the rabbit, and he bore it back to earth with him. But at the same time there was a suspicious crackling movement beside him, and his astonished eye saw a young spruce sapling bending down above him to strike him. His jaws let go their grip, and he leaped backward to escape this strange danger, his lips drawn back from his fangs, his throat snarling, every hair bristling with rage and fright. And in that moment the sapling reared its slender length upright and the rabbit soared dancing in the air again.

The she-wolf was angry. She sank her fangs into her mate's shoulder in reproof; and he, frightened, unaware of what constituted this new onslaught, struck back ferociously and in still greater fright, ripping down the side of the she-wolf's muzzle. For him to resent such reproof was equally unexpected to her, and she sprang upon him in snarling indignation. Then he discovered his mistake and tried to placate her. But she proceeded to punish him roundly, until he gave over all attempts at placation, and whirled in a circle, his head away from her, his shoulders receiving the punishment of her teeth.

In the meantime the rabbit danced above them in the air. The she-wolf sat down in the snow, and old One Eye, now more in fear of his mate than of the mysterious sapling, again sprang for the rabbit. As he sank back with it between his teeth, he kept his eye on the sapling. As before, it followed him back to earth. He crouched down under the impending blow, his hair bristling, but his teeth still keeping tight hold of the rabbit. But the blow did not fall. The sapling remained bent above him. When he moved it moved, and he growled at it through his clenched jaws; when he remained still, it remained still, and he concluded it was safer to continue remaining still. Yet the warm blood of the rabbit tasted good in his mouth.

It was his mate who relieved him from the quandary in which he found himself. She took the rabbit from him, and while the sapling swayed and teetered threateningly above her she calmly gnawed off the rabbit's head. At once the sapling shot up, and after that gave no more trouble, remaining in the decorous and perpendicular position in which nature had intended it to grow. Then, between them, the she-wolf and One Eye devoured the game which the mysterious sapling had caught for them.

There were other run-ways and alleys where rabbits were hanging in the air, and the wolf-pair prospected them all, the she-wolf leading the way, old One Eye following and observant, learning the method of robbing snares—a knowledge destined to stand him in good stead in the days to come.

CHAPTER II
THE LAIR

For two days the she-wolf and One Eye hung about the Indian camp. He was worried and apprehensive, yet the camp lured his mate and she was loath to depart. But when, one morning, the air was rent with the report of a rifle close at hand, and a bullet smashed against a tree trunk several inches from One Eye's head, they hesitated no more, but went off on a long, swinging lope that put quick miles between them and the danger.

They did not go far—a couple of days' journey. The she-wolf's need to find the thing for which she searched had now become imperative. She was getting very heavy, and could run but slowly. Once, in the pursuit of a rabbit, which she ordinarily would have caught with ease, she gave over and lay down and rested. One Eye came to her; but when he touched her neck gently with his muzzle she snapped at him with such quick fierceness that he tumbled over backward and cut a ridiculous figure in his effort to escape her teeth. Her temper was now shorter than ever; but he had become more patient than ever and more solicitous.

And then she found the thing for which she sought. It was a few miles up a small stream that in the summer time flowed into the Mackenzie, but that then was frozen over and frozen down to its rocky bottom—a dead stream of solid white from source to mouth. The she-wolf was trotting wearily along, her mate well in advance, when she came upon the overhanging, high clay-bank. She turned aside and trotted over to it. The wear and tear of spring storms and melting snows had underwashed the bank and in one place had made a small cave out of a narrow fissure.

She paused at the mouth of the cave and looked the wall over carefully. Then, on one side and the other, she ran along the base of the wall to where its abrupt bulk merged from the softer-lined landscape. Returning to the cave, she entered its narrow mouth. For a short three feet she was compelled to crouch, then the walls widened and rose higher in a little round chamber nearly six feet in diameter. The roof barely cleared her head. It was dry and cosey. She inspected it with painstaking care, while One Eye, who had returned, stood in the entrance and patiently watched her. She dropped her head, with her nose to the ground and directed toward a point near to her closely bunched feet, and around this point she circled several times; then, with a tired sigh that was almost a grunt, she curled her body in, relaxed her legs, and dropped down, her head toward the entrance. One Eye, with pointed, interested ears, laughed at her, and beyond, outlined against the white light, she could see the brush of his tail waving good-naturedly. Her own ears, with a snuggling movement, laid their sharp points backward and down against the head for a moment, while her mouth opened and her tongue lolled peaceably out, and in this way she expressed that she was pleased and satisfied.

One Eye was hungry. Though he lay down in the entrance and slept, his sleep was fitful. He kept awaking and cocking his ears at the bright world without, where the April sun was blazing across the snow. When he dozed, upon his ears would steal the faint whispers of hidden trickles of running water, and he would rouse and listen intently. The sun had come back, and all the awakening Northland world was calling to him. Life was stirring. The feel of spring was in the air, the feel of growing life under the snow, of sap ascending in the trees, of buds bursting the shackles of the frost.

He cast anxious glances at his mate, but she showed no desire to get up. He looked outside, and half a dozen snow-birds fluttered across his field of vision. He started to get up, then looked back to his mate again, and settled down and dozed. A shrill and minute singing stole upon his hearing. Once, and twice, he sleepily brushed his nose with his paw. Then he woke up. There, buzzing in the air at the tip of his nose, was a lone mosquito. It was a full-grown mosquito, one that had lain frozen in a dry log all winter and that had now been thawed out by the sun. He could resist the call of the world no longer. Besides, he was hungry.

He crawled over to his mate and tried to persuade her to get up. But she only snarled at him, and he walked out alone into the bright sunshine to find the snow-surface soft under foot and the travelling difficult. He went up the frozen bed of the stream, where the snow, shaded by the trees, was yet hard and crystalline. He was gone eight hours, and he came back through the darkness hungrier than when he had started. He had found game, but he had not caught it. He had broken through the melting snow crust, and wallowed, while the snowshoe rabbits had skimmed along on top lightly as ever.

He paused at the mouth of the cave with a sudden shock of suspicion. Faint, strange sounds came from within. They were sounds not made by his mate, and yet they were remotely familiar. He bellied cautiously inside and was met by a warning snarl from the she-wolf. This he received without perturbation, though he obeyed it by keeping his distance; but he remained interested in the other sounds—faint, muffled sobbings and slubberings.

His mate warned him irritably away, and he curled up and slept in the entrance. When morning came and a dim light pervaded the lair, he again sought after the source of the remotely familiar sounds. There was a new note in his mate's warning snarl. It was a jealous note, and he was very careful in keeping a respectful distance. Nevertheless, he made out, sheltering between her legs against the length of her body, five strange little bundles of life, very feeble, very helpless, making tiny whimpering noises, with eyes that did not open to the light. He was surprised. It was not the first time in his long and successful life that this thing had happened. It had happened many times, yet each time it was as fresh a surprise as ever to him.

His mate looked at him anxiously. Every little while she emitted a low growl, and at times, when it seemed to her he approached too near, the growl shot up in her throat to a sharp snarl. Of her own experience she had no memory of the thing happening; but in her instinct, which was the experience of all the mothers of wolves, there lurked a memory of fathers that had eaten their new-born and helpless progeny. It manifested itself as a fear strong within her, that made her prevent One Eye from more closely inspecting the cubs he had fathered.

But there was no danger. Old One Eye was feeling the urge of an impulse, that was, in turn, an instinct that had come down to him from all the fathers of wolves. He did not question it, nor puzzle over it. It was there, in the fibre of his being; and it was the most natural thing in the world that he should obey it by turning his back on his new-born family and by trotting out and away on the meat-trail whereby he lived.

Five or six miles from the lair, the stream divided, its forks going off among the mountains at a right angle. Here, leading up the left fork, he came upon a fresh track. He smelled it and found it so recent that he crouched swiftly, and looked in the direction in which it disappeared. Then he turned deliberately and took the right fork. The footprint was much larger than the one his own feet made, and he knew that in the wake of such a trail there was little meat for him.

Half a mile up the right fork, his quick ears caught the sound of gnawing teeth. He stalked the quarry and found it to be a porcupine, standing upright against a tree and trying his teeth on the bark. One Eye approached carefully but hopelessly. He knew the breed, though he had never met it so far north before; and never in his long life had porcupine served him for a meal. But he had long since learned that there was such a thing as Chance, or Opportunity, and he continued to draw near. There was never any telling what might happen, for with live things events were somehow always happening differently.

The porcupine rolled itself into a ball, radiating long, sharp needles in all directions that defied attack. In his youth One Eye had once sniffed too near a similar, apparently inert ball of quills, and had the tail flick out suddenly in his face. One quill he had carried away in his muzzle, where it had remained for weeks, a rankling flame, until it finally worked out. So he lay down, in a comfortable crouching position, his nose fully a foot away, and out of the line of the tail. Thus he waited, keeping perfectly quiet. There was no telling. Something might happen. The porcupine might unroll. There might be opportunity for a deft and ripping thrust of paw into the tender, unguarded belly.

But at the end of half an hour he arose, growled wrathfully at the motionless ball, and trotted on. He had waited too often and futilely in the past for porcupines to unroll, to waste any more time. He continued up the right fork. The day wore along, and nothing rewarded his hunt.

The urge of his awakened instinct of fatherhood was strong upon him. He must find meat. In the afternoon he blundered upon a ptarmigan. He came out of a thicket and found himself face to face with the slow-witted bird. It was sitting on a log, not a foot beyond the end of his nose. Each saw the other. The bird made a startled rise, but he struck it with his paw, and smashed it down to earth, then pounced upon it, and caught it in his teeth as it scuttled across the snow trying to rise in the air again. As his teeth crunched through the tender flesh and fragile bones, he began naturally to eat. Then he remembered, and, turning on the back-track, started for home, carrying the ptarmigan in his mouth.

A mile above the forks, running velvet-footed as was his custom, a gliding shadow that cautiously prospected each new vista of the trail, he came upon later imprints of the large tracks he had discovered in the early morning. As the track led his way, he followed, prepared to meet the maker of it at every turn of the stream.

He slid his head around a corner of rock, where began an unusually large bend in the stream, and his quick eyes made out something that sent him crouching swiftly down. It was the maker of the track, a large female lynx. She was crouching as he had crouched once that day, in front of her the tight-rolled ball of quills. If he had been a gliding shadow before, he now became the ghost of such a shadow, as he crept and circled around, and came up well to leeward of the silent, motionless pair.

He lay down in the snow, depositing the ptarmigan beside him, and with eyes peering through the needles of a low-growing spruce he watched the play of life before him—the waiting lynx and the waiting porcupine, each intent on life; and, such was the curiousness of the game, the way of life for one lay in the eating of the other, and the way of life for the other lay in being not eaten. While old One Eye, the wolf crouching in the covert, played his part, too, in the game, waiting for some strange freak of Chance, that might help him on the meat-trail which was his way of life.

Half an hour passed, an hour; and nothing happened. The ball of quills might have been a stone for all it moved; the lynx might have been frozen to marble; and old One Eye might have been dead. Yet all three animals were keyed to a tenseness of living that was almost painful, and scarcely ever would it come to them to be more alive than they were then in their seeming petrifaction.

One Eye moved slightly and peered forth with increased eagerness. Something was happening. The porcupine had at last decided that its enemy had gone away. Slowly, cautiously, it was unrolling its ball of impregnable armour. It was agitated by no tremor of anticipation. Slowly, slowly, the bristling ball straightened out and lengthened. One Eye watching, felt a sudden moistness in his mouth and a drooling of saliva, involuntary, excited by the living meat that was spreading itself like a repast before him.

Not quite entirely had the porcupine unrolled when it discovered its enemy. In that instant the lynx struck. The blow was like a flash of light. The paw, with rigid claws curving like talons, shot under the tender belly and came back with a swift ripping movement. Had the porcupine been entirely unrolled, or had it not discovered its enemy a fraction of a second before the blow was struck, the paw would have escaped unscathed; but a side-flick of the tail sank sharp quills into it as it was withdrawn.

Everything had happened at once—the blow, the counter-blow, the squeal of agony from the porcupine, the big cat's squall of sudden hurt and astonishment. One Eye half arose in his excitement, his ears up, his tail straight out and quivering behind him. The lynx's bad temper got the best of her. She sprang savagely at the thing that had hurt her. But the porcupine, squealing and grunting, with disrupted anatomy trying feebly to roll up into its ball-protection, flicked out its tail again, and again the big cat squalled with hurt and astonishment. Then she fell to backing away and sneezing, her nose bristling with quills like a monstrous pin-cushion. She brushed her nose with her paws, trying to dislodge the fiery darts, thrust it into the snow, and rubbed it against twigs and branches, and all the time leaping about, ahead, sidewise, up and down, in a frenzy of pain and fright.

She sneezed continually, and her stub of a tail was doing its best toward lashing about by giving quick, violent jerks. She quit her antics, and quieted down for a long minute. One Eye watched. And even he could not repress a start and an involuntary bristling of hair along his back when she suddenly leaped, without warning, straight up in the air, at the same time emitting a long and most terrible squall. Then she sprang away, up the trail, squalling with every leap she made.

It was not until her racket had faded away in the distance and died out that One Eye ventured forth. He walked as delicately as though all the snow were carpeted with porcupine quills, erect and ready to pierce the soft pads of his feet. The porcupine met his approach with a furious squealing and a clashing of its long teeth. It had managed to roll up in a ball again, but it was not quite the old compact ball; its muscles were too much torn for that. It had been ripped almost in half, and was still bleeding profusely.

One Eye scooped out mouthfuls of the blood-soaked snow, and chewed and tasted and swallowed. This served as a relish, and his hunger increased mightily; but he was too old in the world to forget his caution. He waited. He lay down and waited, while the porcupine grated its teeth and uttered grunts and sobs and occasional sharp little squeals. In a little while, One Eye noticed that the quills were drooping and that a great quivering had set up. The quivering came to an end suddenly. There was a final defiant clash of the long teeth. Then all the quills drooped quite down, and the body relaxed and moved no more.

With a nervous, shrinking paw, One Eye stretched out the porcupine to its full length and turned it over on its back. Nothing had happened. It was surely dead. He studied it intently for a moment, then took a careful grip with his teeth and started off down the stream, partly carrying, partly dragging the porcupine, with head turned to the side so as to avoid stepping on the prickly mass. He recollected something, dropped the burden, and trotted back to where he had left the ptarmigan. He did not hesitate a moment. He knew clearly what was to be done, and this he did by promptly eating the ptarmigan. Then he returned and took up his burden.

When he dragged the result of his day's hunt into the cave, the she-wolf inspected it, turned her muzzle to him, and lightly licked him on the neck. But the next instant she was warning him away from the cubs with a snarl that was less harsh than usual and that was more apologetic than menacing. Her instinctive fear of the father of her progeny was toning down. He was behaving as a wolf-father should, and manifesting no unholy desire to devour the young lives she had brought into the world.

CHAPTER III
THE GREY CUB

He was different from his brothers and sisters. Their hair already betrayed the reddish hue inherited from their mother, the she-wolf; while he alone, in this particular, took after his father. He was the one little grey cub of the litter. He had bred true to the straight wolf-stock—in fact, he had bred true to old One Eye himself, physically, with but a single exception, and that was he had two eyes to his father's one.

The grey cub's eyes had not been open long, yet already he could see with steady clearness. And while his eyes were still closed, he had felt, tasted, and smelled. He knew his two brothers and his two sisters very well. He had begun to romp with them in a feeble, awkward way, and even to squabble, his little throat vibrating with a queer rasping noise (the forerunner of the growl), as he worked himself into a passion. And long before his eyes had opened he had learned by touch, taste, and smell to know his mother—a fount of warmth and liquid food and tenderness. She possessed a gentle, caressing tongue that soothed him when it passed over his soft little body, and that impelled him to snuggle close against her and to doze off to sleep.

Most of the first month of his life had been passed thus in sleeping; but now he could see quite well, and he stayed awake for longer periods of time, and he was coming to learn his world quite well. His world was gloomy; but he did not know that, for he knew no other world. It was dim-lighted; but his eyes had never had to adjust themselves to any other light. His world was very small. Its limits were the walls of the lair; but as he had no knowledge of the wide world outside, he was never oppressed by the narrow confines of his existence.

But he had early discovered that one wall of his world was different from the rest. This was the mouth of the cave and the source of light. He had discovered that it was different from the other walls long before he had any thoughts of his own, any conscious volitions. It had been an irresistible attraction before ever his eyes opened and looked upon it. The light from it had beat upon his sealed lids, and the eyes and the optic nerves had pulsated to little, sparklike flashes, warm-coloured and strangely pleasing. The life of his body, and of every fibre of his body, the life that was the very substance of his body and that was apart from his own personal life, had yearned toward this light and urged his body toward it in the same way that the cunning chemistry of a plant urges it toward the sun.

Always, in the beginning, before his conscious life dawned, he had crawled toward the mouth of the cave. And in this his brothers and sisters were one with him. Never, in that period, did any of them crawl toward the dark corners of the back-wall. The light drew them as if they were plants; the chemistry of the life that composed them demanded the light as a necessity of being; and their little puppet-bodies crawled blindly and chemically, like the tendrils of a vine. Later on, when each developed individuality and became personally conscious of impulsions and desires, the attraction of the light increased. They were always crawling and sprawling toward it, and being driven back from it by their mother.

It was in this way that the grey cub learned other attributes of his mother than the soft, soothing, tongue. In his insistent crawling toward the light, he discovered in her a nose that with a sharp nudge administered rebuke, and later, a paw, that crushed him down and rolled him over and over with swift, calculating stroke. Thus he learned hurt; and on top of it he learned to avoid hurt, first, by not incurring the risk of it; and second, when he had incurred the risk, by dodging and by retreating. These were conscious actions, and were the results of his first generalisations upon the world. Before that he had recoiled automatically from hurt, as he had crawled automatically toward the light. After that he recoiled from hurt because he *knew* that it was hurt.

He was a fierce little cub. So were his brothers and sisters. It was to be expected. He was a carnivorous animal. He came of a breed of meat-killers and meat-eaters. His father and mother lived wholly upon meat. The milk he had sucked with his first flickering life, was milk transformed directly from meat, and now, at a month old, when his eyes had been open for but a week, he was beginning himself to eat meat—meat half-digested by the she-wolf and disgorged for the five growing cubs that already made too great demand upon her breast.

But he was, further, the fiercest of the litter. He could make a louder rasping growl than any of them. His tiny rages were much more terrible than theirs. It was he that first learned the trick of rolling a fellow-cub over with a cunning paw-stroke. And it was he that first gripped another cub by the ear and pulled and tugged and growled through jaws tight-clenched. And certainly it was he that caused the mother the most trouble in keeping her litter from the mouth of the cave.

The fascination of the light for the grey cub increased from day to day. He was perpetually departing on yard-long adventures toward the cave's entrance, and as perpetually being driven back. Only he did not know it for an entrance. He did not know anything about entrances—passages whereby one goes from one place to another place. He did not know any other place, much less of a way to get there. So to him the entrance of the cave was a wall—a wall of light. As the sun was to the outside dweller, this wall was to him the sun of his world. It attracted him as a candle attracts a moth. He was always striving to attain it. The life that was so swiftly expanding within him, urged him continually toward the wall of light. The life that was within him knew that it was the one way out, the way he was predestined to tread. But he himself did not know anything about it. He did not know there was any outside at all.

There was one strange thing about this wall of light. His father (he had already come to recognise his father as the one other dweller in the world, a creature like his mother, who slept near the light and was a bringer of meat)—his father had a way of walking right into the white far wall and disappearing. The grey cub could not understand this. Though never permitted by his mother to approach that wall, he had approached the other walls, and encountered hard obstruction on the end of his tender nose. This hurt. And after several such adventures, he left the walls alone. Without thinking about it, he accepted this disappearing into the wall as a peculiarity of his father, as milk and half-digested meat were peculiarities of his mother.

In fact, the grey cub was not given to thinking—at least, to the kind of thinking customary of men. His brain worked in dim ways. Yet his conclusions were as sharp and distinct as those achieved by men. He had a method of accepting things, without questioning the why and wherefore. In reality, this was the act of classification. He was never disturbed over why a thing happened. How it happened was sufficient for him. Thus, when he had bumped his nose on the back-wall a few times, he accepted that he would not disappear into walls. In the same way he accepted that his father could disappear into walls. But he was not in the least disturbed by desire to find out the reason for the difference between his father and himself. Logic and physics were no part of his mental make-up.

Like most creatures of the Wild, he early experienced famine. There came a time when not only did the meat-supply cease, but the milk no longer came from his mother's breast. At first, the cubs whimpered and cried, but for the most part they slept. It was not long before they were reduced to a coma of hunger. There were no more spats and squabbles, no more tiny rages nor attempts at growling; while the adventures toward the far white wall ceased altogether. The cubs slept, while the life that was in them flickered and died down.

One Eye was desperate. He ranged far and wide, and slept but little in the lair that had now become cheerless and miserable. The she-wolf, too, left her litter and went out in search of meat. In the first days after the birth of the cubs, One Eye had journeyed several times back to the Indian camp and robbed the rabbit snares; but, with the melting of the snow and the opening of the streams, the Indian camp had moved away, and that source of supply was closed to him.

When the grey cub came back to life and again took interest in the far white wall, he found that the population of his world had been reduced. Only one sister remained to him. The rest were gone. As he grew stronger, he found himself compelled to play alone, for the sister no longer lifted her head nor moved about. His little body rounded out with the meat he now ate; but the food had come too late for her. She slept continuously, a tiny skeleton flung round with skin in which the flame flickered lower and lower and at last went out.

Then there came a time when the grey cub no longer saw his father appearing and disappearing in the wall nor lying down asleep in the entrance. This had happened at the end of a second and less severe famine. The she-wolf knew why One Eye never came back, but there was no way by which she could tell what she had seen to the grey cub. Hunting herself for meat, up the left fork of the stream where lived the lynx, she had followed a day-old trail of One Eye. And she had found him, or what remained of him, at the end of the trail. There were many signs of the battle that had been fought, and of the lynx's withdrawal to her lair after having won the victory. Before she went away, the she-wolf had found this lair, but the signs told her that the lynx was inside, and she had not dared to venture in.

After that, the she-wolf in her hunting avoided the left fork. For she knew that in the lynx's lair was a litter of kittens, and she knew the lynx for a fierce, bad-tempered creature and a terrible fighter. It was all very well for half a dozen wolves to drive a lynx, spitting and bristling, up a tree; but it was quite a different matter for a lone wolf to encounter a lynx—especially when the lynx was known to have a litter of hungry kittens at her back.

But the Wild is the Wild, and motherhood is motherhood, at all times fiercely protective whether in the Wild or out of it; and the time was to come when the she-wolf, for her grey cub's sake, would venture the left fork, and the lair in the rocks, and the lynx's wrath.

CHAPTER IV
THE WALL OF THE WORLD

By the time his mother began leaving the cave on hunting expeditions, the cub had learned well the law that forbade his approaching the entrance. Not only had this law been forcibly and many times impressed on him by his mother's nose and paw, but in him the instinct of fear was developing. Never, in his brief cave-life, had he encountered anything of which to be afraid. Yet fear was in him. It had come down to him from a remote ancestry through a thousand thousand lives. It was a heritage he had received directly from One Eye and the she-wolf; but to them, in turn, it had been passed down through all the generations of wolves that had gone before. Fear!—that legacy of the Wild which no animal may escape nor exchange for pottage.

So the grey cub knew fear, though he knew not the stuff of which fear was made. Possibly he accepted it as one of the restrictions of life. For he had already learned that there were such restrictions. Hunger he had known; and when he could not appease his hunger he had felt restriction. The hard obstruction of the cave-wall, the sharp nudge of his mother's nose, the smashing stroke of her paw, the hunger unappeased of several famines, had borne in upon him that all was not freedom in the world, that to life there was limitations and restraints. These limitations and restraints were laws. To be obedient to them was to escape hurt and make for happiness.

He did not reason the question out in this man fashion. He merely classified the things that hurt and the things that did not hurt. And after such classification he avoided the things that hurt, the restrictions and restraints, in order to enjoy the satisfactions and the remunerations of life.

Thus it was that in obedience to the law laid down by his mother, and in obedience to the law of that unknown and nameless thing, fear, he kept away from the mouth of the cave. It remained to him a white wall of light. When his mother was absent, he slept most of the time, while during the intervals that he was awake he kept very quiet, suppressing the whimpering cries that tickled in his throat and strove for noise.

Once, lying awake, he heard a strange sound in the white wall. He did not know that it was a wolverine, standing outside, all a-trembling with its own daring, and cautiously scenting out the contents of the cave. The cub knew only that the sniff was strange, a something unclassified, therefore unknown and terrible—for the unknown was one of the chief elements that went into the making of fear.

The hair bristled upon the grey cub's back, but it bristled silently. How was he to know that this thing that sniffed was a thing at which to bristle? It was not born of any knowledge of his, yet it was the visible expression of the fear that was in him, and for which, in his own life, there was no accounting. But fear was accompanied by another instinct—that of concealment. The cub was in a frenzy of terror, yet he lay without movement or sound, frozen, petrified into immobility, to all appearances dead. His mother, coming home, growled as she smelt the wolverine's track, and bounded into the cave and licked and nozzled him with undue vehemence of affection. And the cub felt that somehow he had escaped a great hurt.

But there were other forces at work in the cub, the greatest of which was growth. Instinct and law demanded of him obedience. But growth demanded disobedience. His mother and fear impelled him to keep away from the white wall. Growth is life, and life is for ever destined to make for light. So there was no damming up the tide of life that was rising within him—rising with every mouthful of meat he swallowed, with every breath he drew. In the end, one day, fear and obedience were swept away by the rush of life, and the cub straddled and sprawled toward the entrance.

Unlike any other wall with which he had had experience, this wall seemed to recede from him as he approached. No hard surface collided with the tender little nose he thrust out tentatively before him. The substance of the wall seemed as permeable and yielding as light. And as condition, in his eyes, had the seeming of form, so he entered into what had been wall to him and bathed in the substance that composed it.

It was bewildering. He was sprawling through solidity. And ever the light grew brighter. Fear urged him to go back, but growth drove him on. Suddenly he found himself at the mouth of the cave. The wall, inside which he had thought himself, as suddenly leaped back before him to an immeasurable distance. The light had become painfully bright. He was dazzled by it. Likewise he was made dizzy by this abrupt and tremendous extension of space. Automatically, his eyes were adjusting themselves to the brightness, focusing themselves to meet the increased distance of objects. At first, the wall had leaped beyond his vision. He now saw it again; but it had taken upon itself a remarkable remoteness. Also, its appearance had changed. It was now a variegated wall, composed of the trees that fringed the stream, the opposing mountain that towered above the trees, and the sky that out-towered the mountain.

A great fear came upon him. This was more of the terrible unknown. He crouched down on the lip of the cave and gazed out on the world. He was very much afraid. Because it was unknown, it was hostile to him. Therefore the hair stood up on end along his back and his lips wrinkled weakly in an attempt at a ferocious and intimidating snarl. Out of his puniness and fright he challenged and menaced the whole wide world.

Nothing happened. He continued to gaze, and in his interest he forgot to snarl. Also, he forgot to be afraid. For the time, fear had been routed by growth, while growth had assumed the guise of curiosity. He began to notice near objects—an open portion of the stream that flashed in the sun, the blasted pine-tree that stood at the base of the slope, and the slope itself, that ran right up to him and ceased two feet beneath the lip of the cave on which he crouched.

Now the grey cub had lived all his days on a level floor. He had never experienced the hurt of a fall. He did not know what a fall was. So he stepped boldly out upon the air. His hind-legs still rested on the cave-lip, so he fell forward head downward. The earth struck him a harsh blow on the nose that made him yelp. Then he began rolling down the slope, over and over. He was in a panic of terror. The unknown had caught him at last. It had gripped savagely hold of him and was about to wreak upon him some terrific hurt. Growth was now routed by fear, and he ki-yi'd like any frightened puppy.

The unknown bore him on he knew not to what frightful hurt, and he yelped and ki-yi'd unceasingly. This was a different proposition from crouching in frozen fear while the unknown lurked just alongside. Now the unknown had caught tight hold of him. Silence would do no good. Besides, it was not fear, but terror, that convulsed him.

But the slope grew more gradual, and its base was grass-covered. Here the cub lost momentum. When at last he came to a stop, he gave one last agonised yell and then a long, whimpering wail. Also, and quite as a matter of course, as though in his life he had already made a thousand toilets, he proceeded to lick away the dry clay that soiled him.

After that he sat up and gazed about him, as might the first man of the earth who landed upon Mars. The cub had broken through the wall of the world, the unknown had let go its hold of him, and here he was without hurt. But the first man on Mars would have experienced less unfamiliarity than did he. Without any antecedent knowledge, without any warning whatever that such existed, he found himself an explorer in a totally new world.

Now that the terrible unknown had let go of him, he forgot that the unknown had any terrors. He was aware only of curiosity in all the things about him. He inspected the grass beneath him, the moss-berry plant just beyond, and the dead trunk of the blasted pine that stood on the edge of an open space among the trees. A squirrel, running around the base of the trunk, came full upon him, and gave him a great fright. He cowered down and snarled. But the squirrel was as badly scared. It ran up the tree, and from a point of safety chattered back savagely.

This helped the cub's courage, and though the woodpecker he next encountered gave him a start, he proceeded confidently on his way. Such was his confidence, that when a moose-bird impudently hopped up to him, he reached out at it with a playful paw. The result was a sharp peck on the end of his nose that made him cower down and ki-yi. The noise he made was too much for the moose-bird, who sought safety in flight.

But the cub was learning. His misty little mind had already made an unconscious classification. There were live things and things not alive. Also, he must watch out for the live things. The things not alive remained always in one place, but the live things moved about, and there was no telling what they might do. The thing to expect of them was the unexpected, and for this he must be prepared.

He travelled very clumsily. He ran into sticks and things. A twig that he thought a long way off, would the next instant hit him on the nose or rake along his ribs. There were inequalities of surface. Sometimes he overstepped and stubbed his nose. Quite as often he understepped and stubbed his feet. Then there were the pebbles and stones that turned under him when he trod upon them; and from them he came to know that the things not alive were not all in the same state of stable equilibrium as was his cave—also, that small things not alive were more liable than large things to fall down or turn over. But with every mishap he was learning. The longer he walked, the better he walked. He was adjusting himself. He was learning to calculate his own muscular movements, to know his physical limitations, to measure distances between objects, and between objects and himself.

His was the luck of the beginner. Born to be a hunter of meat (though he did not know it), he blundered upon meat just outside his own cave-door on his first foray into the world. It was by sheer blundering that he chanced upon the shrewdly hidden ptarmigan nest. He fell into it. He had essayed to walk along the trunk of a fallen pine. The rotten bark gave way under his feet, and with a despairing yelp he pitched down the rounded crescent, smashed through the leafage and stalks of a small bush, and in the heart of the bush, on the ground, fetched up in the midst of seven ptarmigan chicks.

They made noises, and at first he was frightened at them. Then he perceived that they were very little, and he became bolder. They moved. He placed his paw on one, and its movements were accelerated. This was a source of enjoyment to him. He smelled it. He picked it up in his mouth. It struggled and tickled his tongue. At the same time he was made aware of a sensation of hunger. His jaws closed together. There was a crunching of fragile bones, and warm blood ran in his mouth. The taste of it was good. This was meat, the same as his mother gave him, only it was alive between his teeth and therefore better. So he ate the ptarmigan. Nor did he stop till he had devoured the whole brood. Then he licked his chops in quite the same way his mother did, and began to crawl out of the bush.

He encountered a feathered whirlwind. He was confused and blinded by the rush of it and the beat of angry wings. He hid his head between his paws and yelped. The blows increased. The mother ptarmigan was in a fury. Then he became angry. He rose up, snarling, striking out with his paws. He sank his tiny teeth into one of the wings and pulled and tugged sturdily. The ptarmigan struggled against him, showering blows upon him with her free wing. It was his first battle. He was elated. He forgot all about the unknown. He no longer was afraid of anything. He was fighting, tearing at a live thing that was striking at him. Also, this live thing was meat. The lust to kill was on him. He had just destroyed little live things. He would now destroy a big live thing. He was too busy and happy to know that he was happy. He was thrilling and exulting in ways new to him and greater to him than any he had known before.

He held on to the wing and growled between his tight-clenched teeth. The ptarmigan dragged him out of the bush. When she turned and tried to drag him back into the bush's shelter, he pulled her away from it and on into the open. And all the time she was making outcry and striking with her free wing, while feathers were flying like a snow-fall. The pitch to which he was aroused was tremendous. All the fighting blood of his breed was up in him and surging through him. This was living, though he did not know it. He was realising his own meaning in the world; he was doing that for which he was made—killing meat and battling to kill it. He was justifying his existence, than which life can do no greater; for life achieves its summit when it does to the uttermost that which it was equipped to do.

After a time, the ptarmigan ceased her struggling. He still held her by the wing, and they lay on the ground and looked at each other. He tried to growl threateningly, ferociously. She pecked on his nose, which by now, what of previous adventures was sore. He winced but held on. She pecked him again and again. From wincing he went to whimpering. He tried to back away from her, oblivious to the fact that by his hold on her he dragged her after him. A rain of pecks fell on his ill-used nose. The flood of fight ebbed down in him, and, releasing his prey, he turned tail and scampered on across the open in inglorious retreat.

He lay down to rest on the other side of the open, near the edge of the bushes, his tongue lolling out, his chest heaving and panting, his nose still hurting him and causing him to continue his whimper. But as he lay there, suddenly there came to him a feeling as of something terrible impending. The unknown with all its terrors rushed upon him, and he shrank back instinctively into the shelter of the bush. As he did so, a draught of air fanned him, and a large, winged body swept ominously and silently past. A hawk, driving down out of the blue, had barely missed him.

While he lay in the bush, recovering from his fright and peering fearfully out, the mother-ptarmigan on the other side of the open space fluttered out of the ravaged nest. It was because of her loss that she paid no attention to the winged bolt of the sky. But the cub saw, and it was a warning and a lesson to him—the swift downward swoop of the hawk, the short skim of its body just above the ground, the strike of its talons in the body of the ptarmigan, the ptarmigan's squawk of agony and fright, and the hawk's rush upward into the blue, carrying the ptarmigan away with it.

It was a long time before the cub left its shelter. He had learned much. Live things were meat. They were good to eat. Also, live things when they were large enough, could give hurt. It was better to eat small live things like ptarmigan chicks, and to let alone large live things like ptarmigan hens. Nevertheless he felt a little prick of ambition, a sneaking desire to have another battle with that ptarmigan hen—only the hawk had carried her away. May be there were other ptarmigan hens. He would go and see.

He came down a shelving bank to the stream. He had never seen water before. The footing looked good. There were no inequalities of surface. He stepped boldly out on it; and went down, crying with fear, into the embrace of the unknown. It was cold, and he gasped, breathing quickly. The water rushed into his lungs instead of the air that had always accompanied his act of breathing. The suffocation he experienced was like the pang of death. To him it signified death. He had no conscious knowledge of death, but like every animal of the Wild, he possessed the instinct of death. To him it stood as the greatest of hurts. It was the very essence of the unknown; it was the sum of the terrors of the unknown, the one culminating and unthinkable catastrophe that could happen to him, about which he knew nothing and about which he feared everything.

He came to the surface, and the sweet air rushed into his open mouth. He did not go down again. Quite as though it had been a long-established custom of his he struck out with all his legs and began to swim. The near bank was a yard away; but he had come up with his back to it, and the first thing his eyes rested upon was the opposite bank, toward which he immediately began to swim. The stream was a small one, but in the pool it widened out to a score of feet.

Midway in the passage, the current picked up the cub and swept him downstream. He was caught in the miniature rapid at the bottom of the pool. Here was little chance for swimming. The quiet water had become suddenly angry. Sometimes he was under, sometimes on top. At all times he was in violent motion, now being turned over or around, and again, being smashed against a rock. And with every rock he struck, he yelped. His progress was a series of yelps, from which might have been adduced the number of rocks he encountered.

Below the rapid was a second pool, and here, captured by the eddy, he was gently borne to the bank, and as gently deposited on a bed of gravel. He crawled frantically clear of the water and lay down. He had learned some more about the world. Water was not alive. Yet it moved. Also, it looked as solid as the earth, but was without any solidity at all. His conclusion was that things were not always what they appeared to be. The cub's fear of the unknown was an inherited distrust, and it had now been strengthened by experience. Thenceforth, in the nature of things, he would possess an abiding distrust of appearances. He would have to learn the reality of a thing before he could put his faith into it.

One other adventure was destined for him that day. He had recollected that there was such a thing in the world as his mother. And then there came to him a feeling that he wanted her more than all the rest of the things in the world. Not only was his body tired with the adventures it had undergone, but his little brain was equally tired. In all the days he had lived it had not worked so hard as on this one day. Furthermore, he was sleepy. So he started out to look for the cave and his mother, feeling at the same time an overwhelming rush of loneliness and helplessness.

He was sprawling along between some bushes, when he heard a sharp intimidating cry. There was a flash of yellow before his eyes. He saw a weasel leaping swiftly away from him. It was a small live thing, and he had no fear. Then, before him, at his feet, he saw an extremely small live thing, only several inches long, a young weasel, that, like himself, had disobediently gone out adventuring. It tried to retreat before him. He turned it over with his paw. It made a queer, grating noise. The next moment the flash of yellow reappeared before his eyes. He heard again the intimidating cry, and at the same instant received a sharp blow on the side of the neck and felt the sharp teeth of the mother-weasel cut into his flesh.

While he yelped and ki-yi'd and scrambled backward, he saw the mother-weasel leap upon her young one and disappear with it into the neighbouring thicket. The cut of her teeth in his neck still hurt, but his feelings were hurt more grievously, and he sat down and weakly whimpered. This mother-weasel was so small and so savage. He was yet to learn that for size and weight the weasel was the most ferocious, vindictive, and terrible of all the killers of the Wild. But a portion of this knowledge was quickly to be his.

He was still whimpering when the mother-weasel reappeared. She did not rush him, now that her young one was safe. She approached more cautiously, and the cub had full opportunity to observe her lean, snakelike body, and her head, erect, eager, and snake-like itself. Her sharp, menacing cry sent the hair bristling along his back, and he snarled warningly at her. She came closer and closer. There was a leap, swifter than his unpractised sight, and the lean, yellow body disappeared for a moment out of the field of his vision. The next moment she was at his throat, her teeth buried in his hair and flesh.

At first he snarled and tried to fight; but he was very young, and this was only his first day in the world, and his snarl became a whimper, his fight a struggle to escape. The weasel never relaxed her hold. She hung on, striving to press down with her teeth to the great vein where his life-blood bubbled. The weasel was a drinker of blood, and it was ever her preference to drink from the throat of life itself.

The grey cub would have died, and there would have been no story to write about him, had not the she-wolf come bounding through the bushes. The weasel let go the cub and flashed at the she-wolf's throat, missing, but getting a hold on the jaw instead. The she-wolf flirted her head like the snap of a whip, breaking the weasel's hold and flinging it high in the air. And, still in the air, the she-wolf's jaws closed on the lean, yellow body, and the weasel knew death between the crunching teeth.

The cub experienced another access of affection on the part of his mother. Her joy at finding him seemed even greater than his joy at being found. She nozzled him and caressed him and licked the cuts made in him by the weasel's teeth. Then, between them, mother and cub, they ate the blood-drinker, and after that went back to the cave and slept.

CHAPTER V
THE LAW OF MEAT

The cub's development was rapid. He rested for two days, and then ventured forth from the cave again. It was on this adventure that he found the young weasel whose mother he had helped eat, and he saw to it that the young weasel went the way of its mother. But on this trip he did not get lost. When he grew tired, he found his way back to the cave and slept. And every day thereafter found him out and ranging a wider area.

He began to get accurate measurement of his strength and his weakness, and to know when to be bold and when to be cautious. He found it expedient to be cautious all the time, except for the rare moments, when, assured of his own intrepidity, he abandoned himself to petty rages and lusts.

He was always a little demon of fury when he chanced upon a stray ptarmigan. Never did he fail to respond savagely to the chatter of the squirrel he had first met on the blasted pine. While the sight of a moose-bird almost invariably put him into the wildest of rages; for he never forgot the peck on the nose he had received from the first of that ilk he encountered.

But there were times when even a moose-bird failed to affect him, and those were times when he felt himself to be in danger from some other prowling meat hunter. He never forgot the hawk, and its moving shadow always sent him crouching into the nearest thicket. He no longer sprawled and straddled, and already he was developing the gait of his mother, slinking and furtive, apparently without exertion, yet sliding along with a swiftness that was as deceptive as it was imperceptible.

In the matter of meat, his luck had been all in the beginning. The seven ptarmigan chicks and the baby weasel represented the sum of his killings. His desire to kill strengthened with the days, and he cherished hungry ambitions for the squirrel that chattered so volubly and always informed all wild creatures that the wolf-cub was approaching. But as birds flew in the air, squirrels could climb trees, and the cub could only try to crawl unobserved upon the squirrel when it was on the ground.

The cub entertained a great respect for his mother. She could get meat, and she never failed to bring him his share. Further, she was unafraid of things. It did not occur to him that this fearlessness was founded upon experience and knowledge. Its effect on him was that of an impression of power. His mother represented power; and as he grew older he felt this power in the sharper admonishment of her paw; while the reproving nudge of her nose gave place to the slash of her fangs. For this, likewise, he respected his mother. She compelled obedience from him, and the older he grew the shorter grew her temper.

Famine came again, and the cub with clearer consciousness knew once more the bite of hunger. The she-wolf ran herself thin in the quest for meat. She rarely slept any more in the cave, spending most of her time on the meat-trail, and spending it vainly. This famine was not a long one, but it was severe while it lasted. The cub found no more milk in his mother's breast, nor did he get one mouthful of meat for himself.

Before, he had hunted in play, for the sheer joyousness of it; now he hunted in deadly earnestness, and found nothing. Yet the failure of it accelerated his development. He studied the habits of the squirrel with greater carefulness, and strove with greater craft to steal upon it and surprise it. He studied the wood-mice and tried to dig them out of their burrows; and he learned much about the ways of moose-birds and woodpeckers. And there came a day when the hawk's shadow did not drive him crouching into the bushes. He had grown stronger and wiser, and more confident. Also, he was desperate. So he sat on his haunches, conspicuously in an open space, and challenged the hawk down out of the sky. For he knew that there, floating in the blue above him, was meat, the meat his stomach yearned after so insistently. But the hawk refused to come down and give battle, and the cub crawled away into a thicket and whimpered his disappointment and hunger.

The famine broke. The she-wolf brought home meat. It was strange meat, different from any she had ever brought before. It was a lynx kitten, partly grown, like the cub, but not so large. And it was all for him. His mother had satisfied her hunger elsewhere; though he did not know that it was the rest of the lynx litter that had gone to satisfy her. Nor did he know the desperateness of her deed. He knew only that the velvet-furred kitten was meat, and he ate and waxed happier with every mouthful.

A full stomach conduces to inaction, and the cub lay in the cave, sleeping against his mother's side. He was aroused by her snarling. Never had he heard her snarl so terribly. Possibly in her whole life it was the most terrible snarl she ever gave. There was reason for it, and none knew it better than she. A lynx's lair is not despoiled with impunity. In the full glare of the afternoon light, crouching in the entrance of the cave, the cub saw the lynx-mother. The hair rippled up along his back at the sight. Here was fear, and it did not require his instinct to tell him of it. And if sight alone were not sufficient, the cry of rage the intruder gave, beginning with a snarl and rushing abruptly upward into a hoarse screech, was convincing enough in itself.

The cub felt the prod of the life that was in him, and stood up and snarled valiantly by his mother's side. But she thrust him ignominiously away and behind her. Because of the low-roofed entrance the lynx could not leap in, and when she made a crawling rush of it the she-wolf sprang upon her and pinned her down. The cub saw little of the battle. There was a tremendous snarling and spitting and screeching. The two animals threshed about, the lynx ripping and tearing with her claws and using her teeth as well, while the she-wolf used her teeth alone.

Once, the cub sprang in and sank his teeth into the hind leg of the lynx. He clung on, growling savagely. Though he did not know it, by the weight of his body he clogged the action of the leg and thereby saved his mother much damage. A change in the battle crushed him under both their bodies and wrenched loose his hold. The next moment the two mothers separated, and, before they rushed together again, the lynx lashed out at the cub with a huge fore-paw that ripped his shoulder open to the bone and sent him hurtling sidewise against the wall. Then was added to the uproar the cub's shrill yelp of pain and fright. But the fight lasted so long that he had time to cry himself out and to experience a second burst of courage; and the end of the battle found him again clinging to a hind-leg and furiously growling between his teeth.

The lynx was dead. But the she-wolf was very weak and sick. At first she caressed the cub and licked his wounded shoulder; but the blood she had lost had taken with it her strength, and for all of a day and a night she lay by her dead foe's side, without movement, scarcely breathing. For a week she never left the cave, except for water, and then her movements were slow and painful. At the end of that time the lynx was devoured, while the she-wolf's wounds had healed sufficiently to permit her to take the meat-trail again.

The cub's shoulder was stiff and sore, and for some time he limped from the terrible slash he had received. But the world now seemed changed. He went about in it with greater confidence, with a feeling of prowess that had not been his in the days before the battle with the lynx. He had looked upon life in a more ferocious aspect; he had fought; he had buried his teeth in the flesh of a foe; and he had survived. And because of all this, he carried himself more boldly, with a touch of defiance that was new in him. He was no longer afraid of minor things, and much of his timidity had vanished, though the unknown never ceased to press upon him with its mysteries and terrors, intangible and ever-menacing.

He began to accompany his mother on the meat-trail, and he saw much of the killing of meat and began to play his part in it. And in his own dim way he learned the law of meat. There were two kinds of life—his own kind and the other kind. His own kind included his mother and himself. The other kind included all live things that moved. But the other kind was divided. One portion was what his own kind killed and ate. This portion was composed of the non-killers and the small killers. The other portion killed and ate his own kind, or was killed and eaten by his own kind. And out of this classification arose the law. The aim of life was meat. Life itself was meat. Life lived on life. There were the eaters and the eaten. The law was: EAT OR BE EATEN. He did not formulate the law in clear, set terms and moralise about it. He did not even think the law; he merely lived the law without thinking about it at all.

He saw the law operating around him on every side. He had eaten the ptarmigan chicks. The hawk had eaten the ptarmigan-mother. The hawk would also have eaten him. Later, when he had grown more formidable, he wanted to eat the hawk. He had eaten the lynx kitten. The lynx-mother would have eaten him had she not herself been killed and eaten. And so it went. The law was being lived about him by all live things, and he himself was part and parcel of the law. He was a killer. His only food was meat, live meat, that ran away swiftly before him, or flew into the air, or climbed trees, or hid in the ground, or faced him and fought with him, or turned the tables and ran after him.

Had the cub thought in man-fashion, he might have epitomised life as a voracious appetite and the world as a place wherein ranged a multitude of appetites, pursuing and being pursued, hunting and being hunted, eating and being eaten, all in blindness and confusion, with violence and disorder, a chaos of gluttony and slaughter, ruled over by chance, merciless, planless, endless.

But the cub did not think in man-fashion. He did not look at things with wide vision. He was single-purposed, and entertained but one thought or desire at a time.

Besides the law of meat, there were a myriad other and lesser laws for him to learn and obey. The world was filled with surprise. The stir of the life that was in him, the play of his muscles, was an unending happiness. To run down meat was to experience thrills and elations. His rages and battles were pleasures. Terror itself, and the mystery of the unknown, led to his living.

And there were easements and satisfactions. To have a full stomach, to doze lazily in the sunshine—such things were remuneration in full for his ardours and toils, while his ardours and toils were in themselves self-remunerative. They were expressions of life, and life is always happy when it is expressing itself. So the cub had no quarrel with his hostile environment. He was very much alive, very happy, and very proud of himself.

PART III

CHAPTER I
THE MAKERS OF FIRE

The cub came upon it suddenly. It was his own fault. He had been careless. He had left the cave and run down to the stream to drink. It might have been that he took no notice because he was heavy with sleep. (He had been out all night on the meat-trail, and had but just then awakened.) And his carelessness might have been due to the familiarity of the trail to the pool. He had travelled it often, and nothing had ever happened on it.

He went down past the blasted pine, crossed the open space, and trotted in amongst the trees. Then, at the same instant, he saw and smelt. Before him, sitting silently on their haunches, were five live things, the like of which he had never seen before. It was his first glimpse of mankind. But at the sight of him the five men did not spring to their feet, nor show their teeth, nor snarl. They did not move, but sat there, silent and ominous.

Nor did the cub move. Every instinct of his nature would have impelled him to dash wildly away, had there not suddenly and for the first time arisen in him another and counter instinct. A great awe descended upon him. He was beaten down to movelessness by an overwhelming sense of his own weakness and littleness. Here was mastery and power, something far and away beyond him.

The cub had never seen man, yet the instinct concerning man was his. In dim ways he recognised in man the animal that had fought itself to primacy over the other animals of the Wild. Not alone out of his own eyes, but out of the eyes of all his ancestors was the cub now looking upon man—out of eyes that had circled in the darkness around countless winter camp-fires, that had peered from safe distances and from the hearts of thickets at the strange, two-legged animal that was lord over living things. The spell of the cub's heritage was upon him, the fear and the respect born of the centuries of struggle and the accumulated experience of the generations. The heritage was too compelling for a wolf that was only a cub. Had he been full-grown, he would have run away. As it was, he cowered down in a paralysis of fear, already half proffering the submission that his kind had proffered from the first time a wolf came in to sit by man's fire and be made warm.

One of the Indians arose and walked over to him and stooped above him. The cub cowered closer to the ground. It was the unknown, objectified at last, in concrete flesh and blood, bending over him and reaching down to seize hold of him. His hair bristled involuntarily; his lips writhed back and his little fangs were bared. The hand, poised like doom above him, hesitated, and the man spoke laughing, '*Wabam wabisca ip pit tah.*' ('Look! The white fangs!')

The other Indians laughed loudly, and urged the man on to pick up the cub. As the hand descended closer and closer, there raged within the cub a battle of the instincts. He experienced two great impulsions—to yield and to fight. The resulting action was a compromise. He did both. He yielded till the hand almost touched him. Then he fought, his teeth flashing in a snap that sank them into the hand. The next moment he received a clout alongside the head that knocked him over on his side.

Then all fight fled out of him. His puppyhood and the instinct of submission took charge of him. He sat up on his haunches and ki-yi'd. But the man whose hand he had bitten was angry. The cub received a clout on the other side of his head. Whereupon he sat up and ki-yi'd louder than ever.

The four Indians laughed more loudly, while even the man who had been bitten began to laugh. They surrounded the cub and laughed at him, while he wailed out his terror and his hurt. In the midst of it, he heard something. The Indians heard it too. But the cub knew what it was, and with a last, long wail that had in it more of triumph than grief, he ceased his noise and waited for the coming of his mother, of his ferocious and indomitable mother who fought and killed all things and was never afraid. She was snarling as she ran. She had heard the cry of her cub and was dashing to save him.

She bounded in amongst them, her anxious and militant motherhood making her anything but a pretty sight. But to the cub the spectacle of her protective rage was pleasing. He uttered a glad little cry and bounded to meet her, while the man-animals went back hastily several steps. The she-wolf stood over against her cub, facing the men, with bristling hair, a snarl rumbling deep in her throat. Her face was distorted and malignant with menace, even the bridge of the nose wrinkling from tip to eyes so prodigious was her snarl.

Then it was that a cry went up from one of the men. 'Kiche!' was what he uttered. It was an exclamation of surprise. The cub felt his mother wilting at the sound.

'Kiche!' the man cried again, this time with sharpness and authority.

And then the cub saw his mother, the she-wolf, the fearless one, crouching down till her belly touched the ground, whimpering, wagging her tail, making peace signs. The cub could not understand. He was appalled. The awe of man rushed over him again. His instinct had been true. His mother verified it. She, too, rendered submission to the man-animals.

The man who had spoken came over to her. He put his hand upon her head, and she only crouched closer. She did not snap, nor threaten to snap. The other men came up, and surrounded her, and felt her, and pawed her, which actions she made no attempt to resent. They were greatly excited, and made many noises with their mouths. These noises were not indication of danger, the cub decided, as he crouched near his mother still bristling from time to time but doing his best to submit.

'It is not strange,' an Indian was saying. 'Her father was a wolf. It is true, her mother was a dog; but did not my brother tie her out in the woods all of three nights in the mating season? Therefore was the father of Kiche a wolf.'

'It is a year, Grey Beaver, since she ran away,' spoke a second Indian.

'It is not strange, Salmon Tongue,' Grey Beaver answered. 'It was the time of the famine, and there was no meat for the dogs.'

'She has lived with the wolves,' said a third Indian.

'So it would seem, Three Eagles,' Grey Beaver answered, laying his hand on the cub; 'and this be the sign of it.'

The cub snarled a little at the touch of the hand, and the hand flew back to administer a clout. Whereupon the cub covered its fangs, and sank down submissively, while the hand, returning, rubbed behind his ears, and up and down his back.

'This be the sign of it,' Grey Beaver went on. 'It is plain that his mother is Kiche. But his father was a wolf. Wherefore is there in him little dog and much wolf. His fangs be white, and White Fang shall be his name. I have spoken. He is my dog. For was not Kiche my brother's dog? And is not my brother dead?'

The cub, who had thus received a name in the world, lay and watched. For a time the man-animals continued to make their mouth-noises. Then Grey Beaver took a knife from a sheath that hung around his neck, and went into the thicket and cut a stick. White Fang watched him. He notched the stick at each end and in the notches fastened strings of raw-hide. One string he tied around the throat of Kiche. Then he led her to a small pine, around which he tied the other string.

White Fang followed and lay down beside her. Salmon Tongue's hand reached out to him and rolled him over on his back. Kiche looked on anxiously. White Fang felt fear mounting in him again. He could not quite suppress a snarl, but he made no offer to snap. The hand, with fingers crooked and spread apart, rubbed his stomach in a playful way and rolled him from side to side. It was ridiculous and ungainly, lying there on his back with legs sprawling in the air. Besides, it was a position of such utter helplessness that White Fang's whole nature revolted against it. He could do nothing to defend himself. If this man-animal intended harm, White Fang knew that he could not escape it. How could he spring away with his four legs in the air above him? Yet submission made him master his fear, and he only growled softly. This growl he could not suppress; nor did the man-animal resent it by giving him a blow on the head. And furthermore, such was the strangeness of it, White Fang experienced an unaccountable sensation of pleasure as the hand rubbed back and forth. When he was rolled on his side he ceased to growl, when the fingers pressed and prodded at the base of his ears the pleasurable sensation increased; and when, with a final rub and scratch, the man left him alone and went away, all fear had died out of White Fang. He was to know fear many times in his dealing with man; yet it was a token of the fearless companionship with man that was ultimately to be his.

After a time, White Fang heard strange noises approaching. He was quick in his classification, for he knew them at once for man-animal noises. A few minutes later the remainder of the tribe, strung out as it was on the march, trailed in. There were more men and many women and children, forty souls of them, and all heavily burdened with camp equipage and outfit. Also there were many dogs; and these, with the exception of the part-grown puppies, were likewise burdened with camp outfit. On their backs, in bags that fastened tightly around underneath, the dogs carried from twenty to thirty pounds of weight.

White Fang had never seen dogs before, but at sight of them he felt that they were his own kind, only somehow different. But they displayed little difference from the wolf when they discovered the cub and his mother. There was a rush. White Fang bristled and snarled and snapped in the face of the open-mouthed oncoming wave of dogs, and went down and under them, feeling the sharp slash of teeth in his body, himself biting and tearing at the legs and bellies above him. There was a great uproar. He could hear the snarl of Kiche as she fought for him; and he could hear the cries of the man-animals, the sound of clubs striking upon bodies, and the yelps of pain from the dogs so struck.

Only a few seconds elapsed before he was on his feet again. He could now see the man-animals driving back the dogs with clubs and stones, defending him, saving him from the savage teeth of his kind that somehow was not his kind. And though there was no reason in his brain for a clear conception of so abstract a thing as justice, nevertheless, in his own way, he felt the justice of the man-animals, and he knew them for what they were—makers of law and executors of law. Also, he appreciated the power with which they administered the law. Unlike any animals he had ever encountered, they did not bite nor claw. They enforced their live strength with the power of dead things. Dead things did their bidding. Thus, sticks and stones, directed by these strange creatures, leaped through the air like living things, inflicting grievous hurts upon the dogs.

To his mind this was power unusual, power inconceivable and beyond the natural, power that was godlike. White Fang, in the very nature of him, could never know anything about gods; at the best he could know only things that were beyond knowing—but the wonder and awe that he had of these man-animals in ways resembled what would be the wonder and awe of man at sight of some celestial creature, on a mountain top, hurling thunderbolts from either hand at an astonished world.

The last dog had been driven back. The hubbub died down. And White Fang licked his hurts and meditated upon this, his first taste of pack-cruelty and his introduction to the pack. He had never dreamed that his own kind consisted of more than One Eye, his mother, and himself. They had constituted a kind apart, and here, abruptly, he had discovered many more creatures apparently of his own kind. And there was a subconscious resentment that these, his kind, at first sight had pitched upon him and tried to destroy him. In the same way he resented his mother being tied with a stick, even though it was done by the superior man-animals. It savoured of the trap, of bondage. Yet of the trap and of bondage he knew nothing. Freedom to roam and run and lie down at will, had been his heritage; and here it was being infringed upon. His mother's movements were restricted to the length of a stick, and by the length of that same stick was he restricted, for he had not yet got beyond the need of his mother's side.

He did not like it. Nor did he like it when the man-animals arose and went on with their march; for a tiny man-animal took the other end of the stick and led Kiche captive behind him, and behind Kiche followed White Fang, greatly perturbed and worried by this new adventure he had entered upon.

They went down the valley of the stream, far beyond White Fang's widest ranging, until they came to the end of the valley, where the stream ran into the Mackenzie River. Here, where canoes were cached on poles high in the air and where stood fish-racks for the drying of fish, camp was made; and White Fang looked on with wondering eyes. The superiority of these man-animals increased with every moment. There was their mastery over all these sharp-fanged dogs. It breathed of power. But greater than that, to the wolf-cub, was their mastery over things not alive; their capacity to communicate motion to unmoving things; their capacity to change the very face of the world.

It was this last that especially affected him. The elevation of frames of poles caught his eye; yet this in itself was not so remarkable, being done by the same creatures that flung sticks and stones to great distances. But when the frames of poles were made into tepees by being covered with cloth and skins, White Fang was astounded. It was the colossal bulk of them that impressed him. They arose around him, on every side, like some monstrous quick-growing form of life. They occupied nearly the whole circumference of his field of vision. He was afraid of them. They loomed ominously above him; and when the breeze stirred them into huge movements, he cowered down in fear, keeping his eyes warily upon them, and prepared to spring away if they attempted to precipitate themselves upon him.

But in a short while his fear of the tepees passed away. He saw the women and children passing in and out of them without harm, and he saw the dogs trying often to get into them, and being driven away with sharp words and flying stones. After a time, he left Kiche's side and crawled cautiously toward the wall of the nearest tepee. It was the curiosity of growth that urged him on—the necessity of learning and living and doing that brings experience. The last few inches to the wall of the tepee were crawled with painful slowness and precaution. The day's events had prepared him for the unknown to manifest itself in most stupendous and unthinkable ways. At last his nose touched the canvas. He waited. Nothing happened. Then he smelled the strange fabric, saturated with the man-smell. He closed on the canvas with his teeth and gave a gentle tug. Nothing happened, though the adjacent portions of the tepee moved. He tugged harder. There was a greater movement. It was delightful. He tugged still harder, and repeatedly, until the whole tepee was in motion. Then the sharp cry of a squaw inside sent him scampering back to Kiche. But after that he was afraid no more of the looming bulks of the tepees.

A moment later he was straying away again from his mother. Her stick was tied to a peg in the ground and she could not follow him. A part-grown puppy, somewhat larger and older than he, came toward him slowly, with ostentatious and belligerent importance. The puppy's name, as White Fang was afterward to hear him called, was Lip-lip. He had had experience in puppy fights and was already something of a bully.

Lip-lip was White Fang's own kind, and, being only a puppy, did not seem dangerous; so White Fang prepared to meet him in a friendly spirit. But when the strangers walk became stiff-legged and his lips lifted clear of his teeth, White Fang stiffened too, and answered with lifted lips. They half circled about each other, tentatively, snarling and bristling. This lasted several minutes, and White Fang was beginning to enjoy it, as a sort of game. But suddenly, with remarkable swiftness, Lip-lip leaped in, delivering a slashing snap, and leaped away again. The snap had taken effect on the shoulder that had been hurt by the lynx and that was still sore deep down near the bone. The surprise and hurt of it brought a yelp out of White Fang; but the next moment, in a rush of anger, he was upon Lip-lip and snapping viciously.

But Lip-lip had lived his life in camp and had fought many puppy fights. Three times, four times, and half a dozen times, his sharp little teeth scored on the newcomer, until White Fang, yelping shamelessly, fled to the protection of his mother. It was the first of the many fights he was to have with Lip-lip, for they were enemies from the start, born so, with natures destined perpetually to clash.

Kiche licked White Fang soothingly with her tongue, and tried to prevail upon him to remain with her. But his curiosity was rampant, and several minutes later he was venturing forth on a new quest. He came upon one of the man-animals, Grey Beaver, who was squatting on his hams and doing something with sticks and dry moss spread before him on the ground. White Fang came near to him and watched. Grey Beaver made mouth-noises which White Fang interpreted as not hostile, so he came still nearer.

Women and children were carrying more sticks and branches to Grey Beaver. It was evidently an affair of moment. White Fang came in until he touched Grey Beaver's knee, so curious was he, and already forgetful that this was a terrible man-animal. Suddenly he saw a strange thing like mist beginning to arise from the sticks and moss beneath Grey Beaver's hands. Then, amongst the sticks themselves, appeared a live thing, twisting and turning, of a colour like the colour of the sun in the sky. White Fang knew nothing about fire. It drew him as the light, in the mouth of the cave had drawn him in his early puppyhood. He crawled the several steps toward the flame. He heard Grey Beaver chuckle above him, and he knew the sound was not hostile. Then his nose touched the flame, and at the same instant his little tongue went out to it.

For a moment he was paralysed. The unknown, lurking in the midst of the sticks and moss, was savagely clutching him by the nose. He scrambled backward, bursting out in an astonished explosion of ki-yi's. At the sound, Kiche leaped snarling to the end of her stick, and there raged terribly because she could not come to his aid. But Grey Beaver laughed loudly, and slapped his thighs, and told the happening to all the rest of the camp, till everybody was laughing uproariously. But White Fang sat on his haunches and ki-yi'd and ki-yi'd, a forlorn and pitiable little figure in the midst of the man-animals.

It was the worst hurt he had ever known. Both nose and tongue had been scorched by the live thing, sun-coloured, that had grown up under Grey Beaver's hands. He cried and cried interminably, and every fresh wail was greeted by bursts of laughter on the part of the man-animals. He tried to soothe his nose with his tongue, but the tongue was burnt too, and the two hurts coming together produced greater hurt; whereupon he cried more hopelessly and helplessly than ever.

And then shame came to him. He knew laughter and the meaning of it. It is not given us to know how some animals know laughter, and know when they are being laughed at; but it was this same way that White Fang knew it. And he felt shame that the man-animals should be laughing at him. He turned and fled away, not from the hurt of the fire, but from the laughter that sank even deeper, and hurt in the spirit of him. And he fled to Kiche, raging at the end of her stick like an animal gone mad—to Kiche, the one creature in the world who was not laughing at him.

Twilight drew down and night came on, and White Fang lay by his mother's side. His nose and tongue still hurt, but he was perplexed by a greater trouble. He was homesick. He felt a vacancy in him, a need for the hush and quietude of the stream and the cave in the cliff. Life had become too populous. There were so many of the man-animals, men, women, and children, all making noises and irritations. And there were the dogs, ever squabbling and bickering, bursting into uproars and creating confusions. The restful loneliness of the only life he had known was gone. Here the very air was palpitant with life. It hummed and buzzed unceasingly. Continually changing its intensity and abruptly variant in pitch, it impinged on his nerves and senses, made him nervous and restless and worried him with a perpetual imminence of happening.

He watched the man-animals coming and going and moving about the camp. In fashion distantly resembling the way men look upon the gods they create, so looked White Fang upon the man-animals before him. They were superior creatures, of a verity, gods. To his dim comprehension they were as much wonder-workers as gods are to men. They were creatures of mastery, possessing all manner of unknown and impossible potencies, overlords of the alive and the not alive—making obey that which moved, imparting movement to that which did not move, and making life, sun-coloured and biting life, to grow out of dead moss and wood. They were fire-makers! They were gods.

CHAPTER II
THE BONDAGE

The days were thronged with experience for White Fang. During the time that Kiche was tied by the stick, he ran about over all the camp, inquiring, investigating, learning. He quickly came to know much of the ways of the man-animals, but familiarity did not breed contempt. The more he came to know them, the more they vindicated their superiority, the more they displayed their mysterious powers, the greater loomed their god-likeness.

To man has been given the grief, often, of seeing his gods overthrown and his altars crumbling; but to the wolf and the wild dog that have come in to crouch at man's feet, this grief has never come. Unlike man, whose gods are of the unseen and the overguessed, vapours and mists of fancy eluding the garmenture of reality, wandering wraiths of desired goodness and power, intangible out-croppings of self into the realm of spirit—unlike man, the wolf and the wild dog that have come in to the fire find their gods in the living flesh, solid to the touch, occupying earth-space and requiring time for the accomplishment of their ends and their existence. No effort of faith is necessary to believe in such a god; no effort of will can possibly induce disbelief in such a god. There is no getting away from it. There it stands, on its two hind-legs, club in hand, immensely potential, passionate and wrathful and loving, god and mystery and power all wrapped up and around by flesh that bleeds when it is torn and that is good to eat like any flesh.

And so it was with White Fang. The man-animals were gods unmistakable and unescapable. As his mother, Kiche, had rendered her allegiance to them at the first cry of her name, so he was beginning to render his allegiance. He gave them the trail as a privilege indubitably theirs. When they walked, he got out of their way. When they called, he came. When they threatened, he cowered down. When they commanded him to go, he went away hurriedly. For behind any wish of theirs was power to enforce that wish, power that hurt, power that expressed itself in clouts and clubs, in flying stones and stinging lashes of whips.

He belonged to them as all dogs belonged to them. His actions were theirs to command. His body was theirs to maul, to stamp upon, to tolerate. Such was the lesson that was quickly borne in upon him. It came hard, going as it did, counter to much that was strong and dominant in his own nature; and, while he disliked it in the learning of it, unknown to himself he was learning to like it. It was a placing of his destiny in another's hands, a shifting of the responsibilities of existence. This in itself was compensation, for it is always easier to lean upon another than to stand alone.

But it did not all happen in a day, this giving over of himself, body and soul, to the man-animals. He could not immediately forego his wild heritage and his memories of the Wild. There were days when he crept to the edge of the forest and stood and listened to something calling him far and away. And always he returned, restless and uncomfortable, to whimper softly and wistfully at Kiche's side and to lick her face with eager, questioning tongue.

White Fang learned rapidly the ways of the camp. He knew the injustice and greediness of the older dogs when meat or fish was thrown out to be eaten. He came to know that men were more just, children more cruel, and women more kindly and more likely to toss him a bit of meat or bone. And after two or three painful adventures with the mothers of part-grown puppies, he came into the knowledge that it was always good policy to let such mothers alone, to keep away from them as far as possible, and to avoid them when he saw them coming.

But the bane of his life was Lip-lip. Larger, older, and stronger, Lip-lip had selected White Fang for his special object of persecution. White Fang fought willingly enough, but he was outclassed. His enemy was too big. Lip-lip became a nightmare to him. Whenever he ventured away from his mother, the bully was sure to appear, trailing at his heels, snarling at him, picking upon him, and watchful of an opportunity, when no man-animal was near, to spring upon him and force a fight. As Lip-lip invariably won, he enjoyed it hugely. It became his chief delight in life, as it became White Fang's chief torment.

But the effect upon White Fang was not to cow him. Though he suffered most of the damage and was always defeated, his spirit remained unsubdued. Yet a bad effect was produced. He became malignant and morose. His temper had been savage by birth, but it became more savage under this unending persecution. The genial, playful, puppyish side of him found little expression. He never played and gambolled about with the other puppies of the camp. Lip-lip would not permit it. The moment White Fang appeared near them, Lip-lip was upon him, bullying and hectoring him, or fighting with him until he had driven him away.

The effect of all this was to rob White Fang of much of his puppyhood and to make him in his comportment older than his age. Denied the outlet, through play, of his energies, he recoiled upon himself and developed his mental processes. He became cunning; he had idle time in which to devote himself to thoughts of trickery. Prevented from obtaining his share of meat and fish when a general feed was given to the camp-dogs, he became a clever thief. He had to forage for himself, and he foraged well, though he was oft-times a plague to the squaws in consequence. He learned to sneak about camp, to be crafty, to know what was going on everywhere, to see and to hear everything and to reason accordingly, and successfully to devise ways and means of avoiding his implacable persecutor.

It was early in the days of his persecution that he played his first really big crafty game and got there from his first taste of revenge. As Kiche, when with the wolves, had lured out to destruction dogs from the camps of men, so White Fang, in manner somewhat similar, lured Lip-lip into Kiche's avenging jaws. Retreating before Lip-lip, White Fang made an indirect flight that led in and out and around the various tepees of the camp. He was a good runner, swifter than any puppy of his size, and swifter than Lip-lip. But he did not run his best in this chase. He barely held his own, one leap ahead of his pursuer.

Lip-lip, excited by the chase and by the persistent nearness of his victim, forgot caution and locality. When he remembered locality, it was too late. Dashing at top speed around a tepee, he ran full tilt into Kiche lying at the end of her stick. He gave one yelp of consternation, and then her punishing jaws closed upon him. She was tied, but he could not get away from her easily. She rolled him off his legs so that he could not run, while she repeatedly ripped and slashed him with her fangs.

When at last he succeeded in rolling clear of her, he crawled to his feet, badly dishevelled, hurt both in body and in spirit. His hair was standing out all over him in tufts where her teeth had mauled. He stood where he had arisen, opened his mouth, and broke out the long, heart-broken puppy wail. But even this he was not allowed to complete. In the middle of it, White Fang, rushing in, sank his teeth into Lip-lip's hind leg. There was no fight left in Lip-lip, and he ran away shamelessly, his victim hot on his heels and worrying him all the way back to his own tepee. Here the squaws came to his aid, and White Fang, transformed into a raging demon, was finally driven off only by a fusillade of stones.

Came the day when Grey Beaver, deciding that the liability of her running away was past, released Kiche. White Fang was delighted with his mother's freedom. He accompanied her joyfully about the camp; and, so long as he remained close by her side, Lip-lip kept a respectful distance. White-Fang even bristled up to him and walked stiff-legged, but Lip-lip ignored the challenge. He was no fool himself, and whatever vengeance he desired to wreak, he could wait until he caught White Fang alone.

Later on that day, Kiche and White Fang strayed into the edge of the woods next to the camp. He had led his mother there, step by step, and now when she stopped, he tried to inveigle her farther. The stream, the lair, and the quiet woods were calling to him, and he wanted her to come. He ran on a few steps, stopped, and looked back. She had not moved. He whined pleadingly, and scurried playfully in and out of the underbrush. He ran back to her, licked her face, and ran on again. And still she did not move. He stopped and regarded her, all of an intentness and eagerness, physically expressed, that slowly faded out of him as she turned her head and gazed back at the camp.

There was something calling to him out there in the open. His mother heard it too. But she heard also that other and louder call, the call of the fire and of man—the call which has been given alone of all animals to the wolf to answer, to the wolf and the wild-dog, who are brothers.

Kiche turned and slowly trotted back toward camp. Stronger than the physical restraint of the stick was the clutch of the camp upon her. Unseen and occultly, the gods still gripped with their power and would not let her go. White Fang sat down in the shadow of a birch and whimpered softly. There was a strong smell of pine, and subtle wood fragrances filled the air, reminding him of his old life of freedom before the days of his bondage. But he was still only a part-grown puppy, and stronger than the call either of man or of the Wild was the call of his mother. All the hours of his short life he had depended upon her. The time was yet to come for independence. So he arose and trotted forlornly back to camp, pausing once, and twice, to sit down and whimper and to listen to the call that still sounded in the depths of the forest.

In the Wild the time of a mother with her young is short; but under the dominion of man it is sometimes even shorter. Thus it was with White Fang. Grey Beaver was in the debt of Three Eagles. Three Eagles was going away on a trip up the Mackenzie to the Great Slave Lake. A strip of scarlet cloth, a bearskin, twenty cartridges, and Kiche, went to pay the debt. White Fang saw his mother taken aboard Three Eagles' canoe, and tried to follow her. A blow from Three Eagles knocked him backward to the land. The canoe shoved off. He sprang into the water and swam after it, deaf to the sharp cries of Grey Beaver to return. Even a man-animal, a god, White Fang ignored, such was the terror he was in of losing his mother.

But gods are accustomed to being obeyed, and Grey Beaver wrathfully launched a canoe in pursuit. When he overtook White Fang, he reached down and by the nape of the neck lifted him clear of the water. He did not deposit him at once in the bottom of the canoe. Holding him suspended with one hand, with the other hand he proceeded to give him a beating. And it *was* a beating. His hand was heavy. Every blow was shrewd to hurt; and he delivered a multitude of blows.

Impelled by the blows that rained upon him, now from this side, now from that, White Fang swung back and forth like an erratic and jerky pendulum. Varying were the emotions that surged through him. At first, he had known surprise. Then came a momentary fear, when he yelped several times to the impact of the hand. But this was quickly followed by anger. His free nature asserted itself, and he showed his teeth and snarled fearlessly in the face of the wrathful god. This but served to make the god more wrathful. The blows came faster, heavier, more shrewd to hurt.

Grey Beaver continued to beat, White Fang continued to snarl. But this could not last for ever. One or the other must give over, and that one was White Fang. Fear surged through him again. For the first time he was being really man-handled. The occasional blows of sticks and stones he had previously experienced were as caresses compared with this. He broke down and began to cry and yelp. For a time each blow brought a yelp from him; but fear passed into terror, until finally his yelps were voiced in unbroken succession, unconnected with the rhythm of the punishment.

At last Grey Beaver withheld his hand. White Fang, hanging limply, continued to cry. This seemed to satisfy his master, who flung him down roughly in the bottom of the canoe. In the meantime the canoe had drifted down the stream. Grey Beaver picked up the paddle. White Fang was in his way. He spurned him savagely with his foot. In that moment White Fang's free nature flashed forth again, and he sank his teeth into the moccasined foot.

The beating that had gone before was as nothing compared with the beating he now received. Grey Beaver's wrath was terrible; likewise was White Fang's fright. Not only the hand, but the hard wooden paddle was used upon him; and he was bruised and sore in all his small body when he was again flung down in the canoe. Again, and this time with purpose, did Grey Beaver kick him. White Fang did not repeat his attack on the foot. He had learned another lesson of his bondage. Never, no matter what the circumstance, must he dare to bite the god who was lord and master over him; the body of the lord and master was sacred, not to be defiled by the teeth of such as he. That was evidently the crime of crimes, the one offence there was no condoning nor overlooking.

When the canoe touched the shore, White Fang lay whimpering and motionless, waiting the will of Grey Beaver. It was Grey Beaver's will that he should go ashore, for ashore he was flung, striking heavily on his side and hurting his bruises afresh. He crawled tremblingly to his feet and stood whimpering. Lip-lip, who had watched the whole proceeding from the bank, now rushed upon him, knocking him over and sinking his teeth into him. White Fang was too helpless to defend himself, and it would have gone hard with him had not Grey Beaver's foot shot out, lifting Lip-lip into the air with its violence so that he smashed down to earth a dozen feet away. This was the man-animal's justice; and even then, in his own pitiable plight, White Fang experienced a little grateful thrill. At Grey Beaver's heels he limped obediently through the village to the tepee. And so it came that White Fang learned that the right to punish was something the gods reserved for themselves and denied to the lesser creatures under them.

That night, when all was still, White Fang remembered his mother and sorrowed for her. He sorrowed too loudly and woke up Grey Beaver, who beat him. After that he mourned gently when the gods were around. But sometimes, straying off to the edge of the woods by himself, he gave vent to his grief, and cried it out with loud whimperings and wailings.

It was during this period that he might have harkened to the memories of the lair and the stream and run back to the Wild. But the memory of his mother held him. As the hunting man-animals went out and came back, so she would come back to the village some time. So he remained in his bondage waiting for her.

But it was not altogether an unhappy bondage. There was much to interest him. Something was always happening. There was no end to the strange things these gods did, and he was always curious to see. Besides, he was learning how to get along with Grey Beaver. Obedience, rigid, undeviating obedience, was what was exacted of him; and in return he escaped beatings and his existence was tolerated.

Nay, Grey Beaver himself sometimes tossed him a piece of meat, and defended him against the other dogs in the eating of it. And such a piece of meat was of value. It was worth more, in some strange way, then a dozen pieces of meat from the hand of a squaw. Grey Beaver never petted nor caressed. Perhaps it was the weight of his hand, perhaps his justice, perhaps the sheer power of him, and perhaps it was all these things that influenced White Fang; for a certain tie of attachment was forming between him and his surly lord.

Insidiously, and by remote ways, as well as by the power of stick and stone and clout of hand, were the shackles of White Fang's bondage being riveted upon him. The qualities in his kind that in the beginning made it possible for them to come in to the fires of men, were qualities capable of development. They were developing in him, and the camp-life, replete with misery as it was, was secretly endearing itself to him all the time. But White Fang was unaware of it. He knew only grief for the loss of Kiche, hope for her return, and a hungry yearning for the free life that had been his.

CHAPTER III
THE OUTCAST

Lip-lip continued so to darken his days that White Fang became wickeder and more ferocious than it was his natural right to be. Savageness was a part of his make-up, but the savageness thus developed exceeded his make-up. He acquired a reputation for wickedness amongst the man-animals themselves. Wherever there was trouble and uproar in camp, fighting and squabbling or the outcry of a squaw over a bit of stolen meat, they were sure to find White Fang mixed up in it and usually at the bottom of it. They did not bother to look after the causes of his conduct. They saw only the effects, and the effects were bad. He was a sneak and a thief, a mischief-maker, a fomenter of trouble; and irate squaws told him to his face, the while he eyed them alert and ready to dodge any quick-flung missile, that he was a wolf and worthless and bound to come to an evil end.

He found himself an outcast in the midst of the populous camp. All the young dogs followed Lip-lip's lead. There was a difference between White Fang and them. Perhaps they sensed his wild-wood breed, and instinctively felt for him the enmity that the domestic dog feels for the wolf. But be that as it may, they joined with Lip-lip in the persecution. And, once declared against him, they found good reason to continue declared against him. One and all, from time to time, they felt his teeth; and to his credit, he gave more than he received. Many of them he could whip in single fight; but single fight was denied him. The beginning of such a fight was a signal for all the young dogs in camp to come running and pitch upon him.

Out of this pack-persecution he learned two important things: how to take care of himself in a mass-fight against him—and how, on a single dog, to inflict the greatest amount of damage in the briefest space of time. To keep one's feet in the midst of the hostile mass meant life, and this he learnt well. He became cat-like in his ability to stay on his feet. Even grown dogs might hurtle him backward or sideways with the impact of their heavy bodies; and backward or sideways he would go, in the air or sliding on the ground, but always with his legs under him and his feet downward to the mother earth.

When dogs fight, there are usually preliminaries to the actual combat—snarlings and bristlings and stiff-legged struttings. But White Fang learned to omit these preliminaries. Delay meant the coming against him of all the young dogs. He must do his work quickly and get away. So he learnt to give no warning of his intention. He rushed in and snapped and slashed on the instant, without notice, before his foe could prepare to meet him. Thus he learned how to inflict quick and severe damage. Also he learned the value of surprise. A dog, taken off its guard, its shoulder slashed open or its ear ripped in ribbons before it knew what was happening, was a dog half whipped.

Furthermore, it was remarkably easy to overthrow a dog taken by surprise; while a dog, thus overthrown, invariably exposed for a moment the soft underside of its neck—the vulnerable point at which to strike for its life. White Fang knew this point. It was a knowledge bequeathed to him directly from the hunting generation of wolves. So it was that White Fang's method when he took the offensive, was: first to find a young dog alone; second, to surprise it and knock it off its feet; and third, to drive in with his teeth at the soft throat.

Being but partly grown his jaws had not yet become large enough nor strong enough to make his throat-attack deadly; but many a young dog went around camp with a lacerated throat in token of White Fang's intention. And one day, catching one of his enemies alone on the edge of the woods, he managed, by repeatedly overthrowing him and attacking the throat, to cut the great vein and let out the life. There was a great row that night. He had been observed, the news had been carried to the dead dog's master, the squaws remembered all the instances of stolen meat, and Grey Beaver was beset by many angry voices. But he resolutely held the door of his tepee, inside which he had placed the culprit, and refused to permit the vengeance for which his tribespeople clamoured.

White Fang became hated by man and dog. During this period of his development he never knew a moment's security. The tooth of every dog was against him, the hand of every man. He was greeted with snarls by his kind, with curses and stones by his gods. He lived tensely. He was always keyed up, alert for attack, wary of being attacked, with an eye for sudden and unexpected missiles, prepared to act precipitately and coolly, to leap in with a flash of teeth, or to leap away with a menacing snarl.

As for snarling he could snarl more terribly than any dog, young or old, in camp. The intent of the snarl is to warn or frighten, and judgment is required to know when it should be used. White Fang knew how to make it and when to make it. Into his snarl he incorporated all that was vicious, malignant, and horrible. With nose serrulated by continuous spasms, hair bristling in recurrent waves, tongue whipping out like a red snake and whipping back again, ears flattened down, eyes gleaming hatred, lips wrinkled back, and fangs exposed and dripping, he could compel a pause on the part of almost any assailant. A temporary pause, when taken off his guard, gave him the vital moment in which to think and determine his action. But often a pause so gained lengthened out until it evolved into a complete cessation from the attack. And before more than one of the grown dogs White Fang's snarl enabled him to beat an honourable retreat.

An outcast himself from the pack of the part-grown dogs, his sanguinary methods and remarkable efficiency made the pack pay for its persecution of him. Not permitted himself to run with the pack, the curious state of affairs obtained that no member of the pack could run outside the pack. White Fang would not permit it. What of his bushwhacking and waylaying tactics, the young dogs were afraid to run by themselves. With the exception of Lip-lip, they were compelled to hunch together for mutual protection against the terrible enemy they had made. A puppy alone by the river bank meant a puppy dead or a puppy that aroused the camp with its shrill pain and terror as it fled back from the wolf-cub that had waylaid it.

But White Fang's reprisals did not cease, even when the young dogs had learned thoroughly that they must stay together. He attacked them when he caught them alone, and they attacked him when they were bunched. The sight of him was sufficient to start them rushing after him, at which times his swiftness usually carried him into safety. But woe the dog that outran his fellows in such pursuit! White Fang had learned to turn suddenly upon the pursuer that was ahead of the pack and thoroughly to rip him up before the pack could arrive. This occurred with great frequency, for, once in full cry, the dogs were prone to forget themselves in the excitement of the chase, while White Fang never forgot himself. Stealing backward glances as he ran, he was always ready to whirl around and down the overzealous pursuer that outran his fellows.

Young dogs are bound to play, and out of the exigencies of the situation they realised their play in this mimic warfare. Thus it was that the hunt of White Fang became their chief game—a deadly game, withal, and at all times a serious game. He, on the other hand, being the fastest-footed, was unafraid to venture anywhere. During the period that he waited vainly for his mother to come back, he led the pack many a wild chase through the adjacent woods. But the pack invariably lost him. Its noise and outcry warned him of its presence, while he ran alone, velvet-footed, silently, a moving shadow among the trees after the manner of his father and mother before him. Further he was more directly connected with the Wild than they; and he knew more of its secrets and stratagems. A favourite trick of his was to lose his trail in running water and then lie quietly in a near-by thicket while their baffled cries arose around him.

Hated by his kind and by mankind, indomitable, perpetually warred upon and himself waging perpetual war, his development was rapid and one-sided. This was no soil for kindliness and affection to blossom in. Of such things he had not the faintest glimmering. The code he learned was to obey the strong and to oppress the weak. Grey Beaver was a god, and strong. Therefore White Fang obeyed him. But the dog younger or smaller than himself was weak, a thing to be destroyed. His development was in the direction of power. In order to face the constant danger of hurt and even of destruction, his predatory and protective faculties were unduly developed. He became quicker of movement than the other dogs, swifter of foot, craftier, deadlier, more lithe, more lean with ironlike muscle and sinew, more enduring, more cruel, more ferocious, and more intelligent. He had to become all these things, else he would not have held his own nor survive the hostile environment in which he found himself.

CHAPTER IV
THE TRAIL OF THE GODS

In the fall of the year, when the days were shortening and the bite of the frost was coming into the air, White Fang got his chance for liberty. For several days there had been a great hubbub in the village. The summer camp was being dismantled, and the tribe, bag and baggage, was preparing to go off to the fall hunting. White Fang watched it all with eager eyes, and when the tepees began to come down and the canoes were loading at the bank, he understood. Already the canoes were departing, and some had disappeared down the river.

Quite deliberately he determined to stay behind. He waited his opportunity to slink out of camp to the woods. Here, in the running stream where ice was beginning to form, he hid his trail. Then he crawled into the heart of a dense thicket and waited. The time passed by, and he slept intermittently for hours. Then he was aroused by Grey Beaver's voice calling him by name. There were other voices. White Fang could hear Grey Beaver's squaw taking part in the search, and Mit-sah, who was Grey Beaver's son.

White Fang trembled with fear, and though the impulse came to crawl out of his hiding-place, he resisted it. After a time the voices died away, and some time after that he crept out to enjoy the success of his undertaking. Darkness was coming on, and for a while he played about among the trees, pleasuring in his freedom. Then, and quite suddenly, he became aware of loneliness. He sat down to consider, listening to the silence of the forest and perturbed by it. That nothing moved nor sounded, seemed ominous. He felt the lurking of danger, unseen and unguessed. He was suspicious of the looming bulks of the trees and of the dark shadows that might conceal all manner of perilous things.

Then it was cold. Here was no warm side of a tepee against which to snuggle. The frost was in his feet, and he kept lifting first one fore-foot and then the other. He curved his bushy tail around to cover them, and at the same time he saw a vision. There was nothing strange about it. Upon his inward sight was impressed a succession of memory-pictures. He saw the camp again, the tepees, and the blaze of the fires. He heard the shrill voices of the women, the gruff basses of the men, and the snarling of the dogs. He was hungry, and he remembered pieces of meat and fish that had been thrown him. Here was no meat, nothing but a threatening and inedible silence.

His bondage had softened him. Irresponsibility had weakened him. He had forgotten how to shift for himself. The night yawned about him. His senses, accustomed to the hum and bustle of the camp, used to the continuous impact of sights and sounds, were now left idle. There was nothing to do, nothing to see nor hear. They strained to catch some interruption of the silence and immobility of nature. They were appalled by inaction and by the feel of something terrible impending.

He gave a great start of fright. A colossal and formless something was rushing across the field of his vision. It was a tree-shadow flung by the moon, from whose face the clouds had been brushed away. Reassured, he whimpered softly; then he suppressed the whimper for fear that it might attract the attention of the lurking dangers.

A tree, contracting in the cool of the night, made a loud noise. It was directly above him. He yelped in his fright. A panic seized him, and he ran madly toward the village. He knew an overpowering desire for the protection and companionship of man. In his nostrils was the smell of the camp-smoke. In his ears the camp-sounds and cries were ringing loud. He passed out of the forest and into the moonlit open where were no shadows nor darknesses. But no village greeted his eyes. He had forgotten. The village had gone away.

His wild flight ceased abruptly. There was no place to which to flee. He slunk forlornly through the deserted camp, smelling the rubbish-heaps and the discarded rags and tags of the gods. He would have been glad for the rattle of stones about him, flung by an angry squaw, glad for the hand of Grey Beaver descending upon him in wrath; while he would have welcomed with delight Lip-lip and the whole snarling, cowardly pack.

He came to where Grey Beaver's tepee had stood. In the centre of the space it had occupied, he sat down. He pointed his nose at the moon. His throat was afflicted by rigid spasms, his mouth opened, and in a heart-broken cry bubbled up his loneliness and fear, his grief for Kiche, all his past sorrows and miseries as well as his apprehension of sufferings and dangers to come. It was the long wolf-howl, full-throated and mournful, the first howl he had ever uttered.

The coming of daylight dispelled his fears but increased his loneliness. The naked earth, which so shortly before had been so populous; thrust his loneliness more forcibly upon him. It did not take him long to make up his mind. He plunged into the forest and followed the river bank down the stream. All day he ran. He did not rest. He seemed made to run on for ever. His iron-like body ignored fatigue. And even after fatigue came, his heritage of endurance braced him to endless endeavour and enabled him to drive his complaining body onward.

Where the river swung in against precipitous bluffs, he climbed the high mountains behind. Rivers and streams that entered the main river he forded or swam. Often he took to the rim-ice that was beginning to form, and more than once he crashed through and struggled for life in the icy current. Always he was on the lookout for the trail of the gods where it might leave the river and proceed inland.

White Fang was intelligent beyond the average of his kind; yet his mental vision was not wide enough to embrace the other bank of the Mackenzie. What if the trail of the gods led out on that side? It never entered his head. Later on, when he had travelled more and grown older and wiser and come to know more of trails and rivers, it might be that he could grasp and apprehend such a possibility. But that mental power was yet in the future. Just now he ran blindly, his own bank of the Mackenzie alone entering into his calculations.

All night he ran, blundering in the darkness into mishaps and obstacles that delayed but did not daunt. By the middle of the second day he had been running continuously for thirty hours, and the iron of his flesh was giving out. It was the endurance of his mind that kept him going. He had not eaten in forty hours, and he was weak with hunger. The repeated drenchings in the icy water had likewise had their effect on him. His handsome coat was draggled. The broad pads of his feet were bruised and bleeding. He had begun to limp, and this limp increased with the hours. To make it worse, the light of the sky was obscured and snow began to fall—a raw, moist, melting, clinging snow, slippery under foot, that hid from him the landscape he traversed, and that covered over the inequalities of the ground so that the way of his feet was more difficult and painful.

Grey Beaver had intended camping that night on the far bank of the Mackenzie, for it was in that direction that the hunting lay. But on the near bank, shortly before dark, a moose coming down to drink, had been espied by Kloo-kooch, who was Grey Beaver's squaw. Now, had not the moose come down to drink, had not Mit-sah been steering out of the course because of the snow, had not Kloo-kooch sighted the moose, and had not Grey Beaver killed it with a lucky shot from his rifle, all subsequent things would have happened differently. Grey Beaver would not have camped on the near side of the Mackenzie, and White Fang would have passed by and gone on, either to die or to find his way to his wild brothers and become one of them—a wolf to the end of his days.

Night had fallen. The snow was flying more thickly, and White Fang, whimpering softly to himself as he stumbled and limped along, came upon a fresh trail in the snow. So fresh was it that he knew it immediately for what it was. Whining with eagerness, he followed back from the river bank and in among the trees. The camp-sounds came to his ears. He saw the blaze of the fire, Kloo-kooch cooking, and Grey Beaver squatting on his hams and mumbling a chunk of raw tallow. There was fresh meat in camp!

White Fang expected a beating. He crouched and bristled a little at the thought of it. Then he went forward again. He feared and disliked the beating he knew to be waiting for him. But he knew, further, that the comfort of the fire would be his, the protection of the gods, the companionship of the dogs—the last, a companionship of enmity, but none the less a companionship and satisfying to his gregarious needs.

He came cringing and crawling into the firelight. Grey Beaver saw him, and stopped munching the tallow. White Fang crawled slowly, cringing and grovelling in the abjectness of his abasement and submission. He crawled straight toward Grey Beaver, every inch of his progress becoming slower and more painful. At last he lay at the master's feet, into whose possession he now surrendered himself, voluntarily, body and soul. Of his own choice, he came in to sit by man's fire and to be ruled by him. White Fang trembled, waiting for the punishment to fall upon him. There was a movement of the hand above him. He cringed involuntarily under the expected blow. It did not fall. He stole a glance upward. Grey Beaver was breaking the lump of tallow in half! Grey Beaver was offering him one piece of the tallow! Very gently and somewhat suspiciously, he first smelled the tallow and then proceeded to eat it. Grey Beaver ordered meat to be brought to him, and guarded him from the other dogs while he ate. After that, grateful and content, White Fang lay at Grey Beaver's feet, gazing at the fire that warmed him, blinking and dozing, secure in the knowledge that the morrow would find him, not wandering forlorn through bleak forest-stretches, but in the camp of the man-animals, with the gods to whom he had given himself and upon whom he was now dependent.

CHAPTER V
THE COVENANT

When December was well along, Grey Beaver went on a journey up the Mackenzie. Mit-sah and Kloo-kooch went with him. One sled he drove himself, drawn by dogs he had traded for or borrowed. A second and smaller sled was driven by Mit-sah, and to this was harnessed a team of puppies. It was more of a toy affair than anything else, yet it was the delight of Mit-sah, who felt that he was beginning to do a man's work in the world. Also, he was learning to drive dogs and to train dogs; while the puppies themselves were being broken in to the harness. Furthermore, the sled was of some service, for it carried nearly two hundred pounds of outfit and food.

White Fang had seen the camp-dogs toiling in the harness, so that he did not resent overmuch the first placing of the harness upon himself. About his neck was put a moss-stuffed collar, which was connected by two pulling-traces to a strap that passed around his chest and over his back. It was to this that was fastened the long rope by which he pulled at the sled.

There were seven puppies in the team. The others had been born earlier in the year and were nine and ten months old, while White Fang was only eight months old. Each dog was fastened to the sled by a single rope. No two ropes were of the same length, while the difference in length between any two ropes was at least that of a dog's body. Every rope was brought to a ring at the front end of the sled. The sled itself was without runners, being a birch-bark toboggan, with upturned forward end to keep it from ploughing under the snow. This construction enabled the weight of the sled and load to be distributed over the largest snow-surface; for the snow was crystal-powder and very soft. Observing the same principle of widest distribution of weight, the dogs at the ends of their ropes radiated fan-fashion from the nose of the sled, so that no dog trod in another's footsteps.

There was, furthermore, another virtue in the fan-formation. The ropes of varying length prevented the dogs attacking from the rear those that ran in front of them. For a dog to attack another, it would have to turn upon one at a shorter rope. In which case it would find itself face to face with the dog attacked, and also it would find itself facing the whip of the driver. But the most peculiar virtue of all lay in the fact that the dog that strove to attack one in front of him must pull the sled faster, and that the faster the sled travelled, the faster could the dog attacked run away. Thus, the dog behind could never catch up with the one in front. The faster he ran, the faster ran the one he was after, and the faster ran all the dogs. Incidentally, the sled went faster, and thus, by cunning indirection, did man increase his mastery over the beasts.

Mit-sah resembled his father, much of whose grey wisdom he possessed. In the past he had observed Lip-lip's persecution of White Fang; but at that time Lip-lip was another man's dog, and Mit-sah had never dared more than to shy an occasional stone at him. But now Lip-lip was his dog, and he proceeded to wreak his vengeance on him by putting him at the end of the longest rope. This made Lip-lip the leader, and was apparently an honour! but in reality it took away from him all honour, and instead of being bully and master of the pack, he now found himself hated and persecuted by the pack.

Because he ran at the end of the longest rope, the dogs had always the view of him running away before them. All that they saw of him was his bushy tail and fleeing hind legs—a view far less ferocious and intimidating than his bristling mane and gleaming fangs. Also, dogs being so constituted in their mental ways, the sight of him running away gave desire to run after him and a feeling that he ran away from them.

The moment the sled started, the team took after Lip-lip in a chase that extended throughout the day. At first he had been prone to turn upon his pursuers, jealous of his dignity and wrathful; but at such times Mit-sah would throw the stinging lash of the thirty-foot cariboo-gut whip into his face and compel him to turn tail and run on. Lip-lip might face the pack, but he could not face that whip, and all that was left him to do was to keep his long rope taut and his flanks ahead of the teeth of his mates.

But a still greater cunning lurked in the recesses of the Indian mind. To give point to unending pursuit of the leader, Mit-sah favoured him over the other dogs. These favours aroused in them jealousy and hatred. In their presence Mit-sah would give him meat and would give it to him only. This was maddening to them. They would rage around just outside the throwing-distance of the whip, while Lip-lip devoured the meat and Mit-sah protected him. And when there was no meat to give, Mit-sah would keep the team at a distance and make believe to give meat to Lip-lip.

White Fang took kindly to the work. He had travelled a greater distance than the other dogs in the yielding of himself to the rule of the gods, and he had learned more thoroughly the futility of opposing their will. In addition, the persecution he had suffered from the pack had made the pack less to him in the scheme of things, and man more. He had not learned to be dependent on his kind for companionship. Besides, Kiche was well-nigh forgotten; and the chief outlet of expression that remained to him was in the allegiance he tendered the gods he had accepted as masters. So he worked hard, learned discipline, and was obedient. Faithfulness and willingness characterised his toil. These are essential traits of the wolf and the wild-dog when they have become domesticated, and these traits White Fang possessed in unusual measure.

A companionship did exist between White Fang and the other dogs, but it was one of warfare and enmity. He had never learned to play with them. He knew only how to fight, and fight with them he did, returning to them a hundred-fold the snaps and slashes they had given him in the days when Lip-lip was leader of the pack. But Lip-lip was no longer leader—except when he fled away before his mates at the end of his rope, the sled bounding along behind. In camp he kept close to Mit-sah or Grey Beaver or Kloo-kooch. He did not dare venture away from the gods, for now the fangs of all dogs were against him, and he tasted to the dregs the persecution that had been White Fang's.

With the overthrow of Lip-lip, White Fang could have become leader of the pack. But he was too morose and solitary for that. He merely thrashed his team-mates. Otherwise he ignored them. They got out of his way when he came along; nor did the boldest of them ever dare to rob him of his meat. On the contrary, they devoured their own meat hurriedly, for fear that he would take it away from them. White Fang knew the law well: *to oppress the weak and obey the strong*. He ate his share of meat as rapidly as he could. And then woe the dog that had not yet finished! A snarl and a flash of fangs, and that dog would wail his indignation to the uncomforting stars while White Fang finished his portion for him.

Every little while, however, one dog or another would flame up in revolt and be promptly subdued. Thus White Fang was kept in training. He was jealous of the isolation in which he kept himself in the midst of the pack, and he fought often to maintain it. But such fights were of brief duration. He was too quick for the others. They were slashed open and bleeding before they knew what had happened, were whipped almost before they had begun to fight.

As rigid as the sled-discipline of the gods, was the discipline maintained by White Fang amongst his fellows. He never allowed them any latitude. He compelled them to an unremitting respect for him. They might do as they pleased amongst themselves. That was no concern of his. But it *was* his concern that they leave him alone in his isolation, get out of his way when he elected to walk among them, and at all times acknowledge his mastery over them. A hint of stiff-leggedness on their part, a lifted lip or a bristle of hair, and he would be upon them, merciless and cruel, swiftly convincing them of the error of their way.

He was a monstrous tyrant. His mastery was rigid as steel. He oppressed the weak with a vengeance. Not for nothing had he been exposed to the pitiless struggles for life in the day of his cubhood, when his mother and he, alone and unaided, held their own and survived in the ferocious environment of the Wild. And not for nothing had he learned to walk softly when superior strength went by. He oppressed the weak, but he respected the strong. And in the course of the long journey with Grey Beaver he walked softly indeed amongst the full-grown dogs in the camps of the strange man-animals they encountered.

The months passed by. Still continued the journey of Grey Beaver. White Fang's strength was developed by the long hours on trail and the steady toil at the sled; and it would have seemed that his mental development was well-nigh complete. He had come to know quite thoroughly the world in which he lived. His outlook was bleak and materialistic. The world as he saw it was a fierce and brutal world, a world without warmth, a world in which caresses and affection and the bright sweetnesses of the spirit did not exist.

He had no affection for Grey Beaver. True, he was a god, but a most savage god. White Fang was glad to acknowledge his lordship, but it was a lordship based upon superior intelligence and brute strength. There was something in the fibre of White Fang's being that made his lordship a thing to be desired, else he would not have come back from the Wild when he did to tender his allegiance. There were deeps in his nature which had never been sounded. A kind word, a caressing touch of the hand, on the part of Grey Beaver, might have sounded these deeps; but Grey Beaver did not caress, nor speak kind words. It was not his way. His primacy was savage, and savagely he ruled, administering justice with a club, punishing transgression with the pain of a blow, and rewarding merit, not by kindness, but by withholding a blow.

So White Fang knew nothing of the heaven a man's hand might contain for him. Besides, he did not like the hands of the man-animals. He was suspicious of them. It was true that they sometimes gave meat, but more often they gave hurt. Hands were things to keep away from. They hurled stones, wielded sticks and clubs and whips, administered slaps and clouts, and, when they touched him, were cunning to hurt with pinch and twist and wrench. In strange villages he had encountered the hands of the children and learned that they were cruel to hurt. Also, he had once nearly had an eye poked out by a toddling papoose. From these experiences he became suspicious of all children. He could not tolerate them. When they came near with their ominous hands, he got up.

It was in a village at the Great Slave Lake, that, in the course of resenting the evil of the hands of the man-animals, he came to modify the law that he had learned from Grey Beaver: namely, that the unpardonable crime was to bite one of the gods. In this village, after the custom of all dogs in all villages, White Fang went foraging, for food. A boy was chopping frozen moose-meat with an axe, and the chips were flying in the snow. White Fang, sliding by in quest of meat, stopped and began to eat the chips. He observed the boy lay down the axe and take up a stout club. White Fang sprang clear, just in time to escape the descending blow. The boy pursued him, and he, a stranger in the village, fled between two tepees to find himself cornered against a high earth bank.

There was no escape for White Fang. The only way out was between the two tepees, and this the boy guarded. Holding his club prepared to strike, he drew in on his cornered quarry. White Fang was furious. He faced the boy, bristling and snarling, his sense of justice outraged. He knew the law of forage. All the wastage of meat, such as the frozen chips, belonged to the dog that found it. He had done no wrong, broken no law, yet here was this boy preparing to give him a beating. White Fang scarcely knew what happened. He did it in a surge of rage. And he did it so quickly that the boy did not know either. All the boy knew was that he had in some unaccountable way been overturned into the snow, and that his club-hand had been ripped wide open by White Fang's teeth.

But White Fang knew that he had broken the law of the gods. He had driven his teeth into the sacred flesh of one of them, and could expect nothing but a most terrible punishment. He fled away to Grey Beaver, behind whose protecting legs he crouched when the bitten boy and the boy's family came, demanding vengeance. But they went away with vengeance unsatisfied. Grey Beaver defended White Fang. So did Mit-sah and Kloo-kooch. White Fang, listening to the wordy war and watching the angry gestures, knew that his act was justified. And so it came that he learned there were gods and gods. There were his gods, and there were other gods, and between them there was a difference. Justice or injustice, it was all the same, he must take all things from the hands of his own gods. But he was not compelled to take injustice from the other gods. It was his privilege to resent it with his teeth. And this also was a law of the gods.

Before the day was out, White Fang was to learn more about this law. Mit-sah, alone, gathering firewood in the forest, encountered the boy that had been bitten. With him were other boys. Hot words passed. Then all the boys attacked Mit-sah. It was going hard with him. Blows were raining upon him from all sides. White Fang looked on at first. This was an affair of the gods, and no concern of his. Then he realised that this was Mit-sah, one of his own particular gods, who was being maltreated. It was no reasoned impulse that made White Fang do what he then did. A mad rush of anger sent him leaping in amongst the combatants. Five minutes later the landscape was covered with fleeing boys, many of whom dripped blood upon the snow in token that White Fang's teeth had not been idle. When Mit-sah told the story in camp, Grey Beaver ordered meat to be given to White Fang. He ordered much meat to be given, and White Fang, gorged and sleepy by the fire, knew that the law had received its verification.

It was in line with these experiences that White Fang came to learn the law of property and the duty of the defence of property. From the protection of his god's body to the protection of his god's possessions was a step, and this step he made. What was his god's was to be defended against all the world—even to the extent of biting other gods. Not only was such an act sacrilegious in its nature, but it was fraught with peril. The gods were all-powerful, and a dog was no match against them; yet White Fang learned to face them, fiercely belligerent and unafraid. Duty rose above fear, and thieving gods learned to leave Grey Beaver's property alone.

One thing, in this connection, White Fang quickly learnt, and that was that a thieving god was usually a cowardly god and prone to run away at the sounding of the alarm. Also, he learned that but brief time elapsed between his sounding of the alarm and Grey Beaver coming to his aid. He came to know that it was not fear of him that drove the thief away, but fear of Grey Beaver. White Fang did not give the alarm by barking. He never barked. His method was to drive straight at the intruder, and to sink his teeth in if he could. Because he was morose and solitary, having nothing to do with the other dogs, he was unusually fitted to guard his master's property; and in this he was encouraged and trained by Grey Beaver. One result of this was to make White Fang more ferocious and indomitable, and more solitary.

The months went by, binding stronger and stronger the covenant between dog and man. This was the ancient covenant that the first wolf that came in from the Wild entered into with man. And, like all succeeding wolves and wild dogs that had done likewise, White Fang worked the covenant out for himself. The terms were simple. For the possession of a flesh-and-blood god, he exchanged his own liberty. Food and fire, protection and companionship, were some of the things he received from the god. In return, he guarded the god's property, defended his body, worked for him, and obeyed him.

The possession of a god implies service. White Fang's was a service of duty and awe, but not of love. He did not know what love was. He had no experience of love. Kiche was a remote memory. Besides, not only had he abandoned the Wild and his kind when he gave himself up to man, but the terms of the covenant were such that if ever he met Kiche again he would not desert his god to go with her. His allegiance to man seemed somehow a law of his being greater than the love of liberty, of kind and kin.

CHAPTER VI

THE FAMINE

The spring of the year was at hand when Grey Beaver finished his long journey. It was April, and White Fang was a year old when he pulled into the home villages and was loosed from the harness by Mit-sah. Though a long way from his full growth, White Fang, next to Lip-lip, was the largest yearling in the village. Both from his father, the wolf, and from Kiche, he had inherited stature and strength, and already he was measuring up alongside the full-grown dogs. But he had not yet grown compact. His body was slender and rangy, and his strength more stringy than massive, His coat was the true wolf-grey, and to all appearances he was true wolf himself. The quarter-strain of dog he had inherited from Kiche had left no mark on him physically, though it had played its part in his mental make-up.

He wandered through the village, recognising with staid satisfaction the various gods he had known before the long journey. Then there were the dogs, puppies growing up like himself, and grown dogs that did not look so large and formidable as the memory pictures he retained of them. Also, he stood less in fear of them than formerly, stalking among them with a certain careless ease that was as new to him as it was enjoyable.

There was Baseek, a grizzled old fellow that in his younger days had but to uncover his fangs to send White Fang cringing and crouching to the right about. From him White Fang had learned much of his own insignificance; and from him he was now to learn much of the change and development that had taken place in himself. While Baseek had been growing weaker with age, White Fang had been growing stronger with youth.

It was at the cutting-up of a moose, fresh-killed, that White Fang learned of the changed relations in which he stood to the dog-world. He had got for himself a hoof and part of the shin-bone, to which quite a bit of meat was attached. Withdrawn from the immediate scramble of the other dogs—in fact out of sight behind a thicket—he was devouring his prize, when Baseek rushed in upon him. Before he knew what he was doing, he had slashed the intruder twice and sprung clear. Baseek was surprised by the other's temerity and swiftness of attack. He stood, gazing stupidly across at White Fang, the raw, red shin-bone between them.

Baseek was old, and already he had come to know the increasing valour of the dogs it had been his wont to bully. Bitter experiences these, which, perforce, he swallowed, calling upon all his wisdom to cope with them. In the old days he would have sprung upon White Fang in a fury of righteous wrath. But now his waning powers would not permit such a course. He bristled fiercely and looked ominously across the shin-bone at White Fang. And White Fang, resurrecting quite a deal of the old awe, seemed to wilt and to shrink in upon himself and grow small, as he cast about in his mind for a way to beat a retreat not too inglorious.

And right here Baseek erred. Had he contented himself with looking fierce and ominous, all would have been well. White Fang, on the verge of retreat, would have retreated, leaving the meat to him. But Baseek did not wait. He considered the victory already his and stepped forward to the meat. As he bent his head carelessly to smell it, White Fang bristled slightly. Even then it was not too late for Baseek to retrieve the situation. Had he merely stood over the meat, head up and glowering, White Fang would ultimately have slunk away. But the fresh meat was strong in Baseek's nostrils, and greed urged him to take a bite of it.

This was too much for White Fang. Fresh upon his months of mastery over his own team-mates, it was beyond his self-control to stand idly by while another devoured the meat that belonged to him. He struck, after his custom, without warning. With the first slash, Baseek's right ear was ripped into ribbons. He was astounded at the suddenness of it. But more things, and most grievous ones, were happening with equal suddenness. He was knocked off his feet. His throat was bitten. While he was struggling to his feet the young dog sank teeth twice into his shoulder. The swiftness of it was bewildering. He made a futile rush at White Fang, clipping the empty air with an outraged snap. The next moment his nose was laid open, and he was staggering backward away from the meat.

The situation was now reversed. White Fang stood over the shin-bone, bristling and menacing, while Baseek stood a little way off, preparing to retreat. He dared not risk a fight with this young lightning-flash, and again he knew, and more bitterly, the enfeeblement of oncoming age. His attempt to maintain his dignity was heroic. Calmly turning his back upon young dog and shin-bone, as though both were beneath his notice and unworthy of his consideration, he stalked grandly away. Nor, until well out of sight, did he stop to lick his bleeding wounds.

The effect on White Fang was to give him a greater faith in himself, and a greater pride. He walked less softly among the grown dogs; his attitude toward them was less compromising. Not that he went out of his way looking for trouble. Far from it. But upon his way he demanded consideration. He stood upon his right to go his way unmolested and to give trail to no dog. He had to be taken into account, that was all. He was no longer to be disregarded and ignored, as was the lot of puppies, and as continued to be the lot of the puppies that were his team-mates. They got out of the way, gave trail to the grown dogs, and gave up meat to them under compulsion. But White Fang, uncompanionable, solitary, morose, scarcely looking to right or left, redoubtable, forbidding of aspect, remote and alien, was accepted as an equal by his puzzled elders. They quickly learned to leave him alone, neither venturing hostile acts nor making overtures of friendliness. If they left him alone, he left them alone—a state of affairs that they found, after a few encounters, to be pre-eminently desirable.

In midsummer White Fang had an experience. Trotting along in his silent way to investigate a new tepee which had been erected on the edge of the village while he was away with the hunters after moose, he came full upon Kiche. He paused and looked at her. He remembered her vaguely, but he *remembered* her, and that was more than could be said for her. She lifted her lip at him in the old snarl of menace, and his memory became clear. His forgotten cubhood, all that was associated with that familiar snarl, rushed back to him. Before he had known the gods, she had been to him the centre-pin of the universe. The old familiar feelings of that time came back upon him, surged up within him. He bounded towards her joyously, and she met him with shrewd fangs that laid his cheek open to the bone. He did not understand. He backed away, bewildered and puzzled.

But it was not Kiche's fault. A wolf-mother was not made to remember her cubs of a year or so before. So she did not remember White Fang. He was a strange animal, an intruder; and her present litter of puppies gave her the right to resent such intrusion.

One of the puppies sprawled up to White Fang. They were half-brothers, only they did not know it. White Fang sniffed the puppy curiously, whereupon Kiche rushed upon him, gashing his face a second time. He backed farther away. All the old memories and associations died down again and passed into the grave from which they had been resurrected. He looked at Kiche licking her puppy and stopping now and then to snarl at him. She was without value to him. He had learned to get along without her. Her meaning was forgotten. There was no place for her in his scheme of things, as there was no place for him in hers.

He was still standing, stupid and bewildered, the memories forgotten, wondering what it was all about, when Kiche attacked him a third time, intent on driving him away altogether from the vicinity. And White Fang allowed himself to be driven away. This was a female of his kind, and it was a law of his kind that the males must not fight the females. He did not know anything about this law, for it was no generalisation of the mind, not a something acquired by experience of the world. He knew it as a secret prompting, as an urge of instinct—of the same instinct that made him howl at the moon and stars of nights, and that made him fear death and the unknown.

The months went by. White Fang grew stronger, heavier, and more compact, while his character was developing along the lines laid down by his heredity and his environment. His heredity was a life-stuff that may be likened to clay. It possessed many possibilities, was capable of being moulded into many different forms. Environment served to model the clay, to give it a particular form. Thus, had White Fang never come in to the fires of man, the Wild would have moulded him into a true wolf. But the gods had given him a different environment, and he was moulded into a dog that was rather wolfish, but that was a dog and not a wolf.

And so, according to the clay of his nature and the pressure of his surroundings, his character was being moulded into a certain particular shape. There was no escaping it. He was becoming more morose, more uncompanionable, more solitary, more ferocious; while the dogs were learning more and more that it was better to be at peace with him than at war, and Grey Beaver was coming to prize him more greatly with the passage of each day.

White Fang, seeming to sum up strength in all his qualities, nevertheless suffered from one besetting weakness. He could not stand being laughed at. The laughter of men was a hateful thing. They might laugh among themselves about anything they pleased except himself, and he did not mind. But the moment laughter was turned upon him he would fly into a most terrible rage. Grave, dignified, sombre, a laugh made him frantic to ridiculousness. It so outraged him and upset him that for hours he would behave like a demon. And woe to the dog that at such times ran foul of him. He knew the law too well to take it out of Grey Beaver; behind Grey Beaver were a club and godhead. But behind the dogs there was nothing but space, and into this space they flew when White Fang came on the scene, made mad by laughter.

In the third year of his life there came a great famine to the Mackenzie Indians. In the summer the fish failed. In the winter the cariboo forsook their accustomed track. Moose were scarce, the rabbits almost disappeared, hunting and preying animals perished. Denied their usual food-supply, weakened by hunger, they fell upon and devoured one another. Only the strong survived. White Fang's gods were always hunting animals. The old and the weak of them died of hunger. There was wailing in the village, where the women and children went without in order that what little they had might go into the bellies of the lean and hollow-eyed hunters who trod the forest in the vain pursuit of meat.

To such extremity were the gods driven that they ate the soft-tanned leather of their mocassins and mittens, while the dogs ate the harnesses off their backs and the very whip-lashes. Also, the dogs ate one another, and also the gods ate the dogs. The weakest and the more worthless were eaten first. The dogs that still lived, looked on and understood. A few of the boldest and wisest forsook the fires of the gods, which had now become a shambles, and fled into the forest, where, in the end, they starved to death or were eaten by wolves.

In this time of misery, White Fang, too, stole away into the woods. He was better fitted for the life than the other dogs, for he had the training of his cubhood to guide him. Especially adept did he become in stalking small living things. He would lie concealed for hours, following every movement of a cautious tree-squirrel, waiting, with a patience as huge as the hunger he suffered from, until the squirrel ventured out upon the ground. Even then, White Fang was not premature. He waited until he was sure of striking before the squirrel could gain a tree-refuge. Then, and not until then, would he flash from his hiding-place, a grey projectile, incredibly swift, never failing its mark—the fleeing squirrel that fled not fast enough.

Successful as he was with squirrels, there was one difficulty that prevented him from living and growing fat on them. There were not enough squirrels. So he was driven to hunt still smaller things. So acute did his hunger become at times that he was not above rooting out wood-mice from their burrows in the ground. Nor did he scorn to do battle with a weasel as hungry as himself and many times more ferocious.

In the worst pinches of the famine he stole back to the fires of the gods. But he did not go into the fires. He lurked in the forest, avoiding discovery and robbing the snares at the rare intervals when game was caught. He even robbed Grey Beaver's snare of a rabbit at a time when Grey Beaver staggered and tottered through the forest, sitting down often to rest, what of weakness and of shortness of breath.

One day White Fang encountered a young wolf, gaunt and scrawny, loose-jointed with famine. Had he not been hungry himself, White Fang might have gone with him and eventually found his way into the pack amongst his wild brethren. As it was, he ran the young wolf down and killed and ate him.

Fortune seemed to favour him. Always, when hardest pressed for food, he found something to kill. Again, when he was weak, it was his luck that none of the larger preying animals chanced upon him. Thus, he was strong from the two days' eating a lynx had afforded him when the hungry wolf-pack ran full tilt upon him. It was a long, cruel chase, but he was better nourished than they, and in the end outran them. And not only did he outrun them, but, circling widely back on his track, he gathered in one of his exhausted pursuers.

After that he left that part of the country and journeyed over to the valley wherein he had been born. Here, in the old lair, he encountered Kiche. Up to her old tricks, she, too, had fled the inhospitable fires of the gods and gone back to her old refuge to give birth to her young. Of this litter but one remained alive when White Fang came upon the scene, and this one was not destined to live long. Young life had little chance in such a famine.

Kiche's greeting of her grown son was anything but affectionate. But White Fang did not mind. He had outgrown his mother. So he turned tail philosophically and trotted on up the stream. At the forks he took the turning to the left, where he found the lair of the lynx with whom his mother and he had fought long before. Here, in the abandoned lair, he settled down and rested for a day.

During the early summer, in the last days of the famine, he met Lip-lip, who had likewise taken to the woods, where he had eked out a miserable existence.

White Fang came upon him unexpectedly. Trotting in opposite directions along the base of a high bluff, they rounded a corner of rock and found themselves face to face. They paused with instant alarm, and looked at each other suspiciously.

White Fang was in splendid condition. His hunting had been good, and for a week he had eaten his fill. He was even gorged from his latest kill. But in the moment he looked at Lip-lip his hair rose on end all along his back. It was an involuntary bristling on his part, the physical state that in the past had always accompanied the mental state produced in him by Lip-lip's bullying and persecution. As in the past he had bristled and snarled at sight of Lip-lip, so now, and automatically, he bristled and snarled. He did not waste any time. The thing was done thoroughly and with despatch. Lip-lip essayed to back away, but White Fang struck him hard, shoulder to shoulder. Lip-lip was overthrown and rolled upon his back. White Fang's teeth drove into the scrawny throat. There was a death-struggle, during which White Fang walked around, stiff-legged and observant. Then he resumed his course and trotted on along the base of the bluff.

One day, not long after, he came to the edge of the forest, where a narrow stretch of open land sloped down to the Mackenzie. He had been over this ground before, when it was bare, but now a village occupied it. Still hidden amongst the trees, he paused to study the situation. Sights and sounds and scents were familiar to him. It was the old village changed to a new place. But sights and sounds and smells were different from those he had last had when he fled away from it. There was no whimpering nor wailing. Contented sounds saluted his ear, and when he heard the angry voice of a woman he knew it to be the anger that proceeds from a full stomach. And there was a smell in the air of fish. There was food. The famine was gone. He came out boldly from the forest and trotted into camp straight to Grey Beaver's tepee. Grey Beaver was not there; but Kloo-kooch welcomed him with glad cries and the whole of a fresh-caught fish, and he lay down to wait Grey Beaver's coming.

PART IV

CHAPTER I
THE ENEMY OF HIS KIND

Had there been in White Fang's nature any possibility, no matter how remote, of his ever coming to fraternise with his kind, such possibility was irretrievably destroyed when he was made leader of the sled-team. For now the dogs hated him—hated him for the extra meat bestowed upon him by Mit-sah; hated him for all the real and fancied favours he received; hated him for that he fled always at the head of the team, his waving brush of a tail and his perpetually retreating hind-quarters for ever maddening their eyes.

And White Fang just as bitterly hated them back. Being sled-leader was anything but gratifying to him. To be compelled to run away before the yelling pack, every dog of which, for three years, he had thrashed and mastered, was almost more than he could endure. But endure it he must, or perish, and the life that was in him had no desire to perish out. The moment Mit-sah gave his order for the start, that moment the whole team, with eager, savage cries, sprang forward at White Fang.

There was no defence for him. If he turned upon them, Mit-sah would throw the stinging lash of the whip into his face. Only remained to him to run away. He could not encounter that howling horde with his tail and hind-quarters. These were scarcely fit weapons with which to meet the many merciless fangs. So run away he did, violating his own nature and pride with every leap he made, and leaping all day long.

One cannot violate the promptings of one's nature without having that nature recoil upon itself. Such a recoil is like that of a hair, made to grow out from the body, turning unnaturally upon the direction of its growth and growing into the body—a rankling, festering thing of hurt. And so with White Fang. Every urge of his being impelled him to spring upon the pack that cried at his heels, but it was the will of the gods that this should not be; and behind the will, to enforce it, was the whip of cariboo-gut with its biting thirty-foot lash. So White Fang could only eat his heart in bitterness and develop a hatred and malice commensurate with the ferocity and indomitability of his nature.

If ever a creature was the enemy of its kind, White Fang was that creature. He asked no quarter, gave none. He was continually marred and scarred by the teeth of the pack, and as continually he left his own marks upon the pack. Unlike most leaders, who, when camp was made and the dogs were unhitched, huddled near to the gods for protection, White Fang disdained such protection. He walked boldly about the camp, inflicting punishment in the night for what he had suffered in the day. In the time before he was made leader of the team, the pack had learned to get out of his way. But now it was different. Excited by the day-long pursuit of him, swayed subconsciously by the insistent iteration on their brains of the sight of him fleeing away, mastered by the feeling of mastery enjoyed all day, the dogs could not bring themselves to give way to him. When he appeared amongst them, there was always a squabble. His progress was marked by snarl and snap and growl. The very atmosphere he breathed was surcharged with hatred and malice, and this but served to increase the hatred and malice within him.

When Mit-sah cried out his command for the team to stop, White Fang obeyed. At first this caused trouble for the other dogs. All of them would spring upon the hated leader only to find the tables turned. Behind him would be Mit-sah, the great whip singing in his hand. So the dogs came to understand that when the team stopped by order, White Fang was to be let alone. But when White Fang stopped without orders, then it was allowed them to spring upon him and destroy him if they could. After several experiences, White Fang never stopped without orders. He learned quickly. It was in the nature of things, that he must learn quickly if he were to survive the unusually severe conditions under which life was vouchsafed him.

But the dogs could never learn the lesson to leave him alone in camp. Each day, pursuing him and crying defiance at him, the lesson of the previous night was erased, and that night would have to be learned over again, to be as immediately forgotten. Besides, there was a greater consistence in their dislike of him. They sensed between themselves and him a difference of kind—cause sufficient in itself for hostility. Like him, they were domesticated wolves. But they had been domesticated for generations. Much of the Wild had been lost, so that to them the Wild was the unknown, the terrible, the ever-menacing and ever warring. But to him, in appearance and action and impulse, still clung the Wild. He symbolised it, was its personification: so that when they showed their teeth to him they were defending themselves against the powers of destruction that lurked in the shadows of the forest and in the dark beyond the camp-fire.

But there was one lesson the dogs did learn, and that was to keep together. White Fang was too terrible for any of them to face single-handed. They met him with the mass-formation, otherwise he would have killed them, one by one, in a night. As it was, he never had a chance to kill them. He might roll a dog off its feet, but the pack would be upon him before he could follow up and deliver the deadly throat-stroke. At the first hint of conflict, the whole team drew together and faced him. The dogs had quarrels among themselves, but these were forgotten when trouble was brewing with White Fang.

On the other hand, try as they would, they could not kill White Fang. He was too quick for them, too formidable, too wise. He avoided tight places and always backed out of it when they bade fair to surround him. While, as for getting him off his feet, there was no dog among them capable of doing the trick. His feet clung to the earth with the same tenacity that he clung to life. For that matter, life and footing were synonymous in this unending warfare with the pack, and none knew it better than White Fang.

So he became the enemy of his kind, domesticated wolves that they were, softened by the fires of man, weakened in the sheltering shadow of man's strength. White Fang was bitter and implacable. The clay of him was so moulded. He declared a vendetta against all dogs. And so terribly did he live this vendetta that Grey Beaver, fierce savage himself, could not but marvel at White Fang's ferocity. Never, he swore, had there been the like of this animal; and the Indians in strange villages swore likewise when they considered the tale of his killings amongst their dogs.

When White Fang was nearly five years old, Grey Beaver took him on another great journey, and long remembered was the havoc he worked amongst the dogs of the many villages along the Mackenzie, across the Rockies, and down the Porcupine to the Yukon. He revelled in the vengeance he wreaked upon his kind. They were ordinary, unsuspecting dogs. They were not prepared for his swiftness and directness, for his attack without warning. They did not know him for what he was, a lightning-flash of slaughter. They bristled up to him, stiff-legged and challenging, while he, wasting no time on elaborate preliminaries, snapping into action like a steel spring, was at their throats and destroying them before they knew what was happening and while they were yet in the throes of surprise.

He became an adept at fighting. He economised. He never wasted his strength, never tussled. He was in too quickly for that, and, if he missed, was out again too quickly. The dislike of the wolf for close quarters was his to an unusual degree. He could not endure a prolonged contact with another body. It smacked of danger. It made him frantic. He must be away, free, on his own legs, touching no living thing. It was the Wild still clinging to him, asserting itself through him. This feeling had been accentuated by the Ishmaelite life he had led from his puppyhood. Danger lurked in contacts. It was the trap, ever the trap, the fear of it lurking deep in the life of him, woven into the fibre of him.

In consequence, the strange dogs he encountered had no chance against him. He eluded their fangs. He got them, or got away, himself untouched in either event. In the natural course of things there were exceptions to this. There were times when several dogs, pitching on to him, punished him before he could get away; and there were times when a single dog scored deeply on him. But these were accidents. In the main, so efficient a fighter had he become, he went his way unscathed.

Another advantage he possessed was that of correctly judging time and distance. Not that he did this consciously, however. He did not calculate such things. It was all automatic. His eyes saw correctly, and the nerves carried the vision correctly to his brain. The parts of him were better adjusted than those of the average dog. They worked together more smoothly and steadily. His was a better, far better, nervous, mental, and muscular co-ordination. When his eyes conveyed to his brain the moving image of an action, his brain without conscious effort, knew the space that limited that action and the time required for its completion. Thus, he could avoid the leap of another dog, or the drive of its fangs, and at the same moment could seize the infinitesimal fraction of time in which to deliver his own attack. Body and brain, his was a more perfected mechanism. Not that he was to be praised for it. Nature had been more generous to him than to the average animal, that was all.

It was in the summer that White Fang arrived at Fort Yukon. Grey Beaver had crossed the great watershed between Mackenzie and the Yukon in the late winter, and spent the spring in hunting among the western outlying spurs of the Rockies. Then, after the break-up of the ice on the Porcupine, he had built a canoe and paddled down that stream to where it effected its junction with the Yukon just under the Artic circle. Here stood the old Hudson's Bay Company fort; and here were many Indians, much food, and unprecedented excitement. It was the summer of 1898, and thousands of gold-hunters were going up the Yukon to Dawson and the Klondike. Still hundreds of miles from their goal, nevertheless many of them had been on the way for a year, and the least any of them had travelled to get that far was five thousand miles, while some had come from the other side of the world.

Here Grey Beaver stopped. A whisper of the gold-rush had reached his ears, and he had come with several bales of furs, and another of gut-sewn mittens and moccasins. He would not have ventured so long a trip had he not expected generous profits. But what he had expected was nothing to what he realised. His wildest dreams had not exceeded a hundred per cent. profit; he made a thousand per cent. And like a true Indian, he settled down to trade carefully and slowly, even if it took all summer and the rest of the winter to dispose of his goods.

It was at Fort Yukon that White Fang saw his first white men. As compared with the Indians he had known, they were to him another race of beings, a race of superior gods. They impressed him as possessing superior power, and it is on power that godhead rests. White Fang did not reason it out, did not in his mind make the sharp generalisation that the white gods were more powerful. It was a feeling, nothing more, and yet none the less potent. As, in his puppyhood, the looming bulks of the tepees, man-reared, had affected him as manifestations of power, so was he affected now by the houses and the huge fort all of massive logs. Here was power. Those white gods were strong. They possessed greater mastery over matter than the gods he had known, most powerful among which was Grey Beaver. And yet Grey Beaver was as a child-god among these white-skinned ones.

To be sure, White Fang only felt these things. He was not conscious of them. Yet it is upon feeling, more often than thinking, that animals act; and every act White Fang now performed was based upon the feeling that the white men were the superior gods. In the first place he was very suspicious of them. There was no telling what unknown terrors were theirs, what unknown hurts they could administer. He was curious to observe them, fearful of being noticed by them. For the first few hours he was content with slinking around and watching them from a safe distance. Then he saw that no harm befell the dogs that were near to them, and he came in closer.

In turn he was an object of great curiosity to them. His wolfish appearance caught their eyes at once, and they pointed him out to one another. This act of pointing put White Fang on his guard, and when they tried to approach him he showed his teeth and backed away. Not one succeeded in laying a hand on him, and it was well that they did not.

White Fang soon learned that very few of these gods—not more than a dozen—lived at this place. Every two or three days a steamer (another and colossal manifestation of power) came into the bank and stopped for several hours. The white men came from off these steamers and went away on them again. There seemed untold numbers of these white men. In the first day or so, he saw more of them than he had seen Indians in all his life; and as the days went by they continued to come up the river, stop, and then go on up the river out of sight.

But if the white gods were all-powerful, their dogs did not amount to much. This White Fang quickly discovered by mixing with those that came ashore with their masters. They were irregular shapes and sizes. Some were short-legged—too short; others were long-legged—too long. They had hair instead of fur, and a few had very little hair at that. And none of them knew how to fight.

As an enemy of his kind, it was in White Fang's province to fight with them. This he did, and he quickly achieved for them a mighty contempt. They were soft and helpless, made much noise, and floundered around clumsily trying to accomplish by main strength what he accomplished by dexterity and cunning. They rushed bellowing at him. He sprang to the side. They did not know what had become of him; and in that moment he struck them on the shoulder, rolling them off their feet and delivering his stroke at the throat.

Sometimes this stroke was successful, and a stricken dog rolled in the dirt, to be pounced upon and torn to pieces by the pack of Indian dogs that waited. White Fang was wise. He had long since learned that the gods were made angry when their dogs were killed. The white men were no exception to this. So he was content, when he had overthrown and slashed wide the throat of one of their dogs, to drop back and let the pack go in and do the cruel finishing work. It was then that the white men rushed in, visiting their wrath heavily on the pack, while White Fang went free. He would stand off at a little distance and look on, while stones, clubs, axes, and all sorts of weapons fell upon his fellows. White Fang was very wise.

But his fellows grew wise in their own way; and in this White Fang grew wise with them. They learned that it was when a steamer first tied to the bank that they had their fun. After the first two or three strange dogs had been downed and destroyed, the white men hustled their own animals back on board and wrecked savage vengeance on the offenders. One white man, having seen his dog, a setter, torn to pieces before his eyes, drew a revolver. He fired rapidly, six times, and six of the pack lay dead or dying—another manifestation of power that sank deep into White Fang's consciousness.

White Fang enjoyed it all. He did not love his kind, and he was shrewd enough to escape hurt himself. At first, the killing of the white men's dogs had been a diversion. After a time it became his occupation. There was no work for him to do. Grey Beaver was busy trading and getting wealthy. So White Fang hung around the landing with the disreputable gang of Indian dogs, waiting for steamers. With the arrival of a steamer the fun began. After a few minutes, by the time the white men had got over their surprise, the gang scattered. The fun was over until the next steamer should arrive.

But it can scarcely be said that White Fang was a member of the gang. He did not mingle with it, but remained aloof, always himself, and was even feared by it. It is true, he worked with it. He picked the quarrel with the strange dog while the gang waited.

And when he had overthrown the strange dog the gang went in to finish it. But it is equally true that he then withdrew, leaving the gang to receive the punishment of the outraged gods.

It did not require much exertion to pick these quarrels. All he had to do, when the strange dogs came ashore, was to show himself. When they saw him they rushed for him. It was their instinct. He was the Wild—the unknown, the terrible, the ever-menacing, the thing that prowled in the darkness around the fires of the primeval world when they, cowering close to the fires, were reshaping their instincts, learning to fear the Wild out of which they had come, and which they had deserted and betrayed. Generation by generation, down all the generations, had this fear of the Wild been stamped into their natures. For centuries the Wild had stood for terror and destruction. And during all this time free licence had been theirs, from their masters, to kill the things of the Wild. In doing this they had protected both themselves and the gods whose companionship they shared.

And so, fresh from the soft southern world, these dogs, trotting down the gang-plank and out upon the Yukon shore had but to see White Fang to experience the irresistible impulse to rush upon him and destroy him. They might be town-reared dogs, but the instinctive fear of the Wild was theirs just the same. Not alone with their own eyes did they see the wolfish creature in the clear light of day, standing before them. They saw him with the eyes of their ancestors, and by their inherited memory they knew White Fang for the wolf, and they remembered the ancient feud.

All of which served to make White Fang's days enjoyable. If the sight of him drove these strange dogs upon him, so much the better for him, so much the worse for them. They looked upon him as legitimate prey, and as legitimate prey he looked upon them.

Not for nothing had he first seen the light of day in a lonely lair and fought his first fights with the ptarmigan, the weasel, and the lynx. And not for nothing had his puppyhood been made bitter by the persecution of Lip-lip and the whole puppy pack. It might have been otherwise, and he would then have been otherwise. Had Lip-lip not existed, he would have passed his puppyhood with the other puppies and grown up more doglike and with more liking for dogs. Had Grey Beaver possessed the plummet of affection and love, he might have sounded the deeps of White Fang's nature and brought up to the surface all manner of kindly qualities. But these things had not been so. The clay of White Fang had been moulded until he became what he was, morose and lonely, unloving and ferocious, the enemy of all his kind.

CHAPTER II
THE MAD GOD

A small number of white men lived in Fort Yukon. These men had been long in the country. They called themselves Sour-doughs, and took great pride in so classifying themselves. For other men, new in the land, they felt nothing but disdain. The men who came ashore from the steamers were newcomers. They were known as *chechaquos*, and they always wilted at the application of the name. They made their bread with baking-powder. This was the invidious distinction between them and the Sour-doughs, who, forsooth, made their bread from sour-dough because they had no baking-powder.

All of which is neither here nor there. The men in the fort disdained the newcomers and enjoyed seeing them come to grief. Especially did they enjoy the havoc worked amongst the newcomers' dogs by White Fang and his disreputable gang. When a steamer arrived, the men of the fort made it a point always to come down to the bank and see the fun. They looked forward to it with as much anticipation as did the Indian dogs, while they were not slow to appreciate the savage and crafty part played by White Fang.

But there was one man amongst them who particularly enjoyed the sport. He would come running at the first sound of a steamboat's whistle; and when the last fight was over and White Fang and the pack had scattered, he would return slowly to the fort, his face heavy with regret. Sometimes, when a soft southland dog went down, shrieking its death-cry under the fangs of the pack, this man would be unable to contain himself, and would leap into the air and cry out with delight. And always he had a sharp and covetous eye for White Fang.

This man was called 'Beauty' by the other men of the fort. No one knew his first name, and in general he was known in the country as Beauty Smith. But he was anything save a beauty. To antithesis was due his naming. He was pre-eminently unbeautiful. Nature had been niggardly with him. He was a small man to begin with; and upon his meagre frame was deposited an even more strikingly meagre head. Its apex might be likened to a point. In fact, in his boyhood, before he had been named Beauty by his fellows, he had been called 'Pinhead.'

Backward, from the apex, his head slanted down to his neck and forward it slanted uncompromisingly to meet a low and remarkably wide forehead. Beginning here, as though regretting her parsimony, Nature had spread his features with a lavish hand. His eyes were large, and between them was the distance of two eyes. His face, in relation to the rest of him, was prodigious. In order to discover the necessary area, Nature had given him an enormous prognathous jaw. It was wide and heavy, and protruded outward and down until it seemed to rest on his chest. Possibly this appearance was due to the weariness of the slender neck, unable properly to support so great a burden.

This jaw gave the impression of ferocious determination. But something lacked. Perhaps it was from excess. Perhaps the jaw was too large. At any rate, it was a lie. Beauty Smith was known far and wide as the weakest of weak-kneed and snivelling cowards. To complete his description, his teeth were large and yellow, while the two eye-teeth, larger than their fellows, showed under his lean lips like fangs. His eyes were yellow and muddy, as though Nature had run short on pigments and squeezed together the dregs of all her tubes. It was the same with his hair, sparse and irregular of growth, muddy-yellow and dirty-yellow, rising on his head and sprouting out of his face in unexpected tufts and bunches, in appearance like clumped and wind-blown grain.

In short, Beauty Smith was a monstrosity, and the blame of it lay elsewhere. He was not responsible. The clay of him had been so moulded in the making. He did the cooking for the other men in the fort, the dish-washing and the drudgery. They did not despise him. Rather did they tolerate him in a broad human way, as one tolerates any creature evilly treated in the making. Also, they feared him. His cowardly rages made them dread a shot in the back or poison in their coffee. But somebody had to do the cooking, and whatever else his shortcomings, Beauty Smith could cook.

This was the man that looked at White Fang, delighted in his ferocious prowess, and desired to possess him. He made overtures to White Fang from the first. White Fang began by ignoring him. Later on, when the overtures became more insistent, White Fang bristled and bared his teeth and backed away. He did not like the man. The feel of him was bad. He sensed the evil in him, and feared the extended hand and the attempts at soft-spoken speech. Because of all this, he hated the man.

With the simpler creatures, good and bad are things simply understood. The good stands for all things that bring easement and satisfaction and surcease from pain. Therefore, the good is liked. The bad stands for all things that are fraught with discomfort, menace, and hurt, and is hated accordingly. White Fang's feel of Beauty Smith was bad. From the man's distorted body and twisted mind, in occult ways, like mists rising from malarial marshes, came emanations of the unhealth within. Not by reasoning, not by the five senses alone, but by other and remoter and uncharted senses, came the feeling to White Fang that the man was ominous with evil, pregnant with hurtfulness, and therefore a thing bad, and wisely to be hated.

White Fang was in Grey Beaver's camp when Beauty Smith first visited it. At the faint sound of his distant feet, before he came in sight, White Fang knew who was coming and began to bristle. He had been lying down in an abandon of comfort, but he arose quickly, and, as the man arrived, slid away in true wolf-fashion to the edge of the camp. He did not know what they said, but he could see the man and Grey Beaver talking together. Once, the man pointed at him, and White Fang snarled back as though the hand were just descending upon him instead of being, as it was, fifty feet away. The man laughed at this; and White Fang slunk away to the sheltering woods, his head turned to observe as he glided softly over the ground.

Grey Beaver refused to sell the dog. He had grown rich with his trading and stood in need of nothing. Besides, White Fang was a valuable animal, the strongest sled-dog he had ever owned, and the best leader. Furthermore, there was no dog like him on the Mackenzie nor the Yukon. He could fight. He killed other dogs as easily as men killed mosquitoes. (Beauty Smith's eyes lighted up at this, and he licked his thin lips with an eager tongue). No, White Fang was not for sale at any price.

But Beauty Smith knew the ways of Indians. He visited Grey Beaver's camp often, and hidden under his coat was always a black bottle or so. One of the potencies of whisky is the breeding of thirst. Grey Beaver got the thirst. His fevered membranes and burnt stomach began to clamour for more and more of the scorching fluid; while his brain, thrust all awry by the unwonted stimulant, permitted him to go any length to obtain it. The money he had received for his furs and mittens and moccasins began to go. It went faster and faster, and the shorter his money-sack grew, the shorter grew his temper.

In the end his money and goods and temper were all gone. Nothing remained to him but his thirst, a prodigious possession in itself that grew more prodigious with every sober breath he drew. Then it was that Beauty Smith had talk with him again about the sale of White Fang; but this time the price offered was in bottles, not dollars, and Grey Beaver's ears were more eager to hear.

'You ketch um dog you take um all right,' was his last word.

The bottles were delivered, but after two days. 'You ketch um dog,' were Beauty Smith's words to Grey Beaver.

White Fang slunk into camp one evening and dropped down with a sigh of content.

The dreaded white god was not there. For days his manifestations of desire to lay hands on him had been growing more insistent, and during that time White Fang had been compelled to avoid the camp. He did not know what evil was threatened by those insistent hands. He knew only that they did threaten evil of some sort, and that it was best for him to keep out of their reach.

But scarcely had he lain down when Grey Beaver staggered over to him and tied a leather thong around his neck. He sat down beside White Fang, holding the end of the thong in his hand. In the other hand he held a bottle, which, from time to time, was inverted above his head to the accompaniment of gurgling noises.

An hour of this passed, when the vibrations of feet in contact with the ground foreran the one who approached. White Fang heard it first, and he was bristling with recognition while Grey Beaver still nodded stupidly. White Fang tried to draw the thong softly out of his master's hand; but the relaxed fingers closed tightly and Grey Beaver roused himself.

Beauty Smith strode into camp and stood over White Fang. He snarled softly up at the thing of fear, watching keenly the deportment of the hands. One hand extended outward and began to descend upon his head. His soft snarl grew tense and harsh. The hand continued slowly to descend, while he crouched beneath it, eyeing it malignantly, his snarl growing shorter and shorter as, with quickening breath, it approached its culmination. Suddenly he snapped, striking with his fangs like a snake. The hand was jerked back, and the teeth came together emptily with a sharp click. Beauty Smith was frightened and angry. Grey Beaver clouted White Fang alongside the head, so that he cowered down close to the earth in respectful obedience.

White Fang's suspicious eyes followed every movement. He saw Beauty Smith go away and return with a stout club. Then the end of the thong was given over to him by Grey Beaver. Beauty Smith started to walk away. The thong grew taut. White Fang resisted it. Grey Beaver clouted him right and left to make him get up and follow. He obeyed, but with a rush, hurling himself upon the stranger who was dragging him away. Beauty Smith did not jump away. He had been waiting for this. He swung the club smartly, stopping the rush midway and smashing White Fang down upon the ground. Grey Beaver laughed and nodded approval. Beauty Smith tightened the thong again, and White Fang crawled limply and dizzily to his feet.

He did not rush a second time. One smash from the club was sufficient to convince him that the white god knew how to handle it, and he was too wise to fight the inevitable. So he followed morosely at Beauty Smith's heels, his tail between his legs, yet snarling softly under his breath. But Beauty Smith kept a wary eye on him, and the club was held always ready to strike.

At the fort Beauty Smith left him securely tied and went in to bed. White Fang waited an hour. Then he applied his teeth to the thong, and in the space of ten seconds was free. He had wasted no time with his teeth. There had been no useless gnawing. The thong was cut across, diagonally, almost as clean as though done by a knife. White Fang looked up at the fort, at the same time bristling and growling. Then he turned and trotted back to Grey Beaver's camp. He owed no allegiance to this strange and terrible god. He had given himself to Grey Beaver, and to Grey Beaver he considered he still belonged.

But what had occurred before was repeated—with a difference. Grey Beaver again made him fast with a thong, and in the morning turned him over to Beauty Smith.

And here was where the difference came in. Beauty Smith gave him a beating. Tied securely, White Fang could only rage futilely and endure the punishment. Club and whip were both used upon him, and he experienced the worst beating he had ever received in his life. Even the big beating given him in his puppyhood by Grey Beaver was mild compared with this.

Beauty Smith enjoyed the task. He delighted in it. He gloated over his victim, and his eyes flamed dully, as he swung the whip or club and listened to White Fang's cries of pain and to his helpless bellows and snarls. For Beauty Smith was cruel in the way that cowards are cruel. Cringing and snivelling himself before the blows or angry speech of a man, he revenged himself, in turn, upon creatures weaker than he. All life likes power, and Beauty Smith was no exception. Denied the expression of power amongst his own kind, he fell back upon the lesser creatures and there vindicated the life that was in him. But Beauty Smith had not created himself, and no blame was to be attached to him. He had come into the world with a twisted body and a brute intelligence. This had constituted the clay of him, and it had not been kindly moulded by the world.

White Fang knew why he was being beaten. When Grey Beaver tied the thong around his neck, and passed the end of the thong into Beauty Smith's keeping, White Fang knew that it was his god's will for him to go with Beauty Smith. And when Beauty Smith left him tied outside the fort, he knew that it was Beauty Smith's will that he should remain there. Therefore, he had disobeyed the will of both the gods, and earned the consequent punishment. He had seen dogs change owners in the past, and he had seen the runaways beaten as he was being beaten. He was wise, and yet in the nature of him there were forces greater than wisdom. One of these was fidelity. He did not love Grey Beaver, yet, even in the face of his will and his anger, he was faithful to him. He could not help it. This faithfulness was a quality of the clay that composed him. It was the quality that was peculiarly the possession of his kind; the quality that set apart his species from all other species; the quality that has enabled the wolf and the wild dog to come in from the open and be the companions of man.

After the beating, White Fang was dragged back to the fort. But this time Beauty Smith left him tied with a stick. One does not give up a god easily, and so with White Fang. Grey Beaver was his own particular god, and, in spite of Grey Beaver's will, White Fang still clung to him and would not give him up. Grey Beaver had betrayed and forsaken him, but that had no effect upon him. Not for nothing had he surrendered himself body and soul to Grey Beaver. There had been no reservation on White Fang's part, and the bond was not to be broken easily.

So, in the night, when the men in the fort were asleep, White Fang applied his teeth to the stick that held him. The wood was seasoned and dry, and it was tied so closely to his neck that he could scarcely get his teeth to it. It was only by the severest muscular exertion and neck-arching that he succeeded in getting the wood between his teeth, and barely between his teeth at that; and it was only by the exercise of an immense patience, extending through many hours, that he succeeded in gnawing through the stick. This was something that dogs were not supposed to do. It was unprecedented. But White Fang did it, trotting away from the fort in the early morning, with the end of the stick hanging to his neck.

He was wise. But had he been merely wise he would not have gone back to Grey Beaver who had already twice betrayed him. But there was his faithfulness, and he went back to be betrayed yet a third time. Again he yielded to the tying of a thong around his neck by Grey Beaver, and again Beauty Smith came to claim him. And this time he was beaten even more severely than before.

Grey Beaver looked on stolidly while the white man wielded the whip. He gave no protection. It was no longer his dog. When the beating was over White Fang was sick. A soft southland dog would have died under it, but not he. His school of life had been sterner, and he was himself of sterner stuff. He had too great vitality. His clutch on life was too strong. But he was very sick. At first he was unable to drag himself along, and Beauty Smith had to wait half-an-hour for him. And then, blind and reeling, he followed at Beauty Smith's heels back to the fort.

But now he was tied with a chain that defied his teeth, and he strove in vain, by lunging, to draw the staple from the timber into which it was driven. After a few days, sober and bankrupt, Grey Beaver departed up the Porcupine on his long journey to the Mackenzie. White Fang remained on the Yukon, the property of a man more than half mad and all brute. But what is a dog to know in its consciousness of madness? To White Fang, Beauty Smith was a veritable, if terrible, god. He was a mad god at best, but White Fang knew nothing of madness; he knew only that he must submit to the will of this new master, obey his every whim and fancy.

CHAPTER III
THE REIGN OF HATE

Under the tutelage of the mad god, White Fang became a fiend. He was kept chained in a pen at the rear of the fort, and here Beauty Smith teased and irritated and drove him wild with petty torments. The man early discovered White Fang's susceptibility to laughter, and made it a point after painfully tricking him, to laugh at him. This laughter was uproarious and scornful, and at the same time the god pointed his finger derisively at White Fang. At such times reason fled from White Fang, and in his transports of rage he was even more mad than Beauty Smith.

Formerly, White Fang had been merely the enemy of his kind, withal a ferocious enemy. He now became the enemy of all things, and more ferocious than ever. To such an extent was he tormented, that he hated blindly and without the faintest spark of reason. He hated the chain that bound him, the men who peered in at him through the slats of the pen, the dogs that accompanied the men and that snarled malignantly at him in his helplessness. He hated the very wood of the pen that confined him. And, first, last, and most of all, he hated Beauty Smith.

But Beauty Smith had a purpose in all that he did to White Fang. One day a number of men gathered about the pen. Beauty Smith entered, club in hand, and took the chain off from White Fang's neck. When his master had gone out, White Fang turned loose and tore around the pen, trying to get at the men outside. He was magnificently terrible. Fully five feet in length, and standing two and one-half feet at the shoulder, he far outweighed a wolf of corresponding size. From his mother he had inherited the heavier proportions of the dog, so that he weighed, without any fat and without an ounce of superfluous flesh, over ninety pounds. It was all muscle, bone, and sinew-fighting flesh in the finest condition.

The door of the pen was being opened again. White Fang paused. Something unusual was happening. He waited. The door was opened wider. Then a huge dog was thrust inside, and the door was slammed shut behind him. White Fang had never seen such a dog (it was a mastiff); but the size and fierce aspect of the intruder did not deter him. Here was some thing, not wood nor iron, upon which to wreak his hate. He leaped in with a flash of fangs that ripped down the side of the mastiff's neck. The mastiff shook his head, growled hoarsely, and plunged at White Fang. But White Fang was here, there, and everywhere, always evading and eluding, and always leaping in and slashing with his fangs and leaping out again in time to escape punishment.

The men outside shouted and applauded, while Beauty Smith, in an ecstasy of delight, gloated over the ripping and mangling performed by White Fang. There was no hope for the mastiff from the first. He was too ponderous and slow. In the end, while Beauty Smith beat White Fang back with a club, the mastiff was dragged out by its owner. Then there was a payment of bets, and money clinked in Beauty Smith's hand.

White Fang came to look forward eagerly to the gathering of the men around his pen. It meant a fight; and this was the only way that was now vouchsafed him of expressing the life that was in him. Tormented, incited to hate, he was kept a prisoner so that there was no way of satisfying that hate except at the times his master saw fit to put another dog against him. Beauty Smith had estimated his powers well, for he was invariably the victor. One day, three dogs were turned in upon him in succession. Another day a full-grown wolf, fresh-caught from the Wild, was shoved in through the door of the pen. And on still another day two dogs were set against him at the same time. This was his severest fight, and though in the end he killed them both he was himself half killed in doing it.

In the fall of the year, when the first snows were falling and mush-ice was running in the river, Beauty Smith took passage for himself and White Fang on a steamboat bound up the Yukon to Dawson. White Fang had now achieved a reputation in the land. As 'the Fighting Wolf' he was known far and wide, and the cage in which he was kept on the steam-boat's deck was usually surrounded by curious men. He raged and snarled at them, or lay quietly and studied them with cold hatred. Why should he not hate them? He never asked himself the question. He knew only hate and lost himself in the passion of it. Life had become a hell to him. He had not been made for the close confinement wild beasts endure at the hands of men. And yet it was in precisely this way that he was treated. Men stared at him, poked sticks between the bars to make him snarl, and then laughed at him.

They were his environment, these men, and they were moulding the clay of him into a more ferocious thing than had been intended by Nature. Nevertheless, Nature had given him plasticity. Where many another animal would have died or had its spirit broken, he adjusted himself and lived, and at no expense of the spirit. Possibly Beauty Smith, arch-fiend and tormentor, was capable of breaking White Fang's spirit, but as yet there were no signs of his succeeding.

If Beauty Smith had in him a devil, White Fang had another; and the two of them raged against each other unceasingly. In the days before, White Fang had had the wisdom to cower down and submit to a man with a club in his hand; but this wisdom now left him. The mere sight of Beauty Smith was sufficient to send him into transports of fury. And when they came to close quarters, and he had been beaten back by the club, he went on growling and snarling, and showing his fangs. The last growl could never be extracted from him. No matter how terribly he was beaten, he had always another growl; and when Beauty Smith gave up and withdrew, the defiant growl followed after him, or White Fang sprang at the bars of the cage bellowing his hatred.

When the steamboat arrived at Dawson, White Fang went ashore. But he still lived a public life, in a cage, surrounded by curious men. He was exhibited as 'the Fighting Wolf,' and men paid fifty cents in gold dust to see him. He was given no rest. Did he lie down to sleep, he was stirred up by a sharp stick—so that the audience might get its money's worth. In order to make the exhibition interesting, he was kept in a rage most of the time. But worse than all this, was the atmosphere in which he lived. He was regarded as the most fearful of wild beasts, and this was borne in to him through the bars of the cage. Every word, every cautious action, on the part of the men, impressed upon him his own terrible ferocity. It was so much added fuel to the flame of his fierceness. There could be but one result, and that was that his ferocity fed upon itself and increased. It was another instance of the plasticity of his clay, of his capacity for being moulded by the pressure of environment.

In addition to being exhibited he was a professional fighting animal. At irregular intervals, whenever a fight could be arranged, he was taken out of his cage and led off into the woods a few miles from town. Usually this occurred at night, so as to avoid interference from the mounted police of the Territory. After a few hours of waiting, when daylight had come, the audience and the dog with which he was to fight arrived. In this manner it came about that he fought all sizes and breeds of dogs. It was a savage land, the men were savage, and the fights were usually to the death.

Since White Fang continued to fight, it is obvious that it was the other dogs that died. He never knew defeat. His early training, when he fought with Lip-lip and the whole puppy-pack, stood him in good stead. There was the tenacity with which he clung to the earth. No dog could make him lose his footing. This was the favourite trick of the wolf breeds—to rush in upon him, either directly or with an unexpected swerve, in the hope of striking his shoulder and overthrowing him. Mackenzie hounds, Eskimo and Labrador dogs, huskies and Malemutes—all tried it on him, and all failed. He was never known to lose his footing. Men told this to one another, and looked each time to see it happen; but White Fang always disappointed them.

Then there was his lightning quickness. It gave him a tremendous advantage over his antagonists. No matter what their fighting experience, they had never encountered a dog that moved so swiftly as he. Also to be reckoned with, was the immediateness of his attack. The average dog was accustomed to the preliminaries of snarling and bristling and growling, and the average dog was knocked off his feet and finished before he had begun to fight or recovered from his surprise. So often did this happen, that it became the custom to hold White Fang until the other dog went through its preliminaries, was good and ready, and even made the first attack.

But greatest of all the advantages in White Fang's favour, was his experience. He knew more about fighting than did any of the dogs that faced him. He had fought more fights, knew how to meet more tricks and methods, and had more tricks himself, while his own method was scarcely to be improved upon.

As the time went by, he had fewer and fewer fights. Men despaired of matching him with an equal, and Beauty Smith was compelled to pit wolves against him. These were trapped by the Indians for the purpose, and a fight between White Fang and a wolf was always sure to draw a crowd. Once, a full-grown female lynx was secured, and this time White Fang fought for his life. Her quickness matched his; her ferocity equalled his; while he fought with his fangs alone, and she fought with her sharp-clawed feet as well.

But after the lynx, all fighting ceased for White Fang. There were no more animals with which to fight—at least, there was none considered worthy of fighting with him. So he remained on exhibition until spring, when one Tim Keenan, a faro-dealer, arrived in the land. With him came the first bull-dog that had ever entered the Klondike. That this dog and White Fang should come together was inevitable, and for a week the anticipated fight was the mainspring of conversation in certain quarters of the town.

CHAPTER IV
THE CLINGING DEATH

Beauty Smith slipped the chain from his neck and stepped back.

For once White Fang did not make an immediate attack. He stood still, ears pricked forward, alert and curious, surveying the strange animal that faced him. He had never seen such a dog before. Tim Keenan shoved the bull-dog forward with a muttered 'Go to it.' The animal waddled toward the centre of the circle, short and squat and ungainly. He came to a stop and blinked across at White Fang.

There were cries from the crowd of, 'Go to him, Cherokee! Sick 'm, Cherokee! Eat 'm up!'

But Cherokee did not seem anxious to fight. He turned his head and blinked at the men who shouted, at the same time wagging his stump of a tail good-naturedly. He was not afraid, but merely lazy. Besides, it did not seem to him that it was intended he should fight with the dog he saw before him. He was not used to fighting with that kind of dog, and he was waiting for them to bring on the real dog.

Tim Keenan stepped in and bent over Cherokee, fondling him on both sides of the shoulders with hands that rubbed against the grain of the hair and that made slight, pushing-forward movements. These were so many suggestions. Also, their effect was irritating, for Cherokee began to growl, very softly, deep down in his throat. There was a correspondence in rhythm between the growls and the movements of the man's hands. The growl rose in the throat with the culmination of each forward-pushing movement, and ebbed down to start up afresh with the beginning of the next movement. The end of each movement was the accent of the rhythm, the movement ending abruptly and the growling rising with a jerk.

This was not without its effect on White Fang. The hair began to rise on his neck and across the shoulders. Tim Keenan gave a final shove forward and stepped back again. As the impetus that carried Cherokee forward died down, he continued to go forward of his own volition, in a swift, bow-legged run. Then White Fang struck. A cry of startled admiration went up. He had covered the distance and gone in more like a cat than a dog; and with the same cat-like swiftness he had slashed with his fangs and leaped clear.

The bull-dog was bleeding back of one ear from a rip in his thick neck. He gave no sign, did not even snarl, but turned and followed after White Fang. The display on both sides, the quickness of the one and the steadiness of the other, had excited the partisan spirit of the crowd, and the men were making new bets and increasing original bets. Again, and yet again, White Fang sprang in, slashed, and got away untouched, and still his strange foe followed after him, without too great haste, not slowly, but deliberately and determinedly, in a businesslike sort of way. There was purpose in his method—something for him to do that he was intent upon doing and from which nothing could distract him.

His whole demeanour, every action, was stamped with this purpose. It puzzled White Fang. Never had he seen such a dog. It had no hair protection. It was soft, and bled easily. There was no thick mat of fur to baffle White Fang's teeth as they were often baffled by dogs of his own breed. Each time that his teeth struck they sank easily into the yielding flesh, while the animal did not seem able to defend itself. Another disconcerting thing was that it made no outcry, such as he had been accustomed to with the other dogs he had fought. Beyond a growl or a grunt, the dog took its punishment silently. And never did it flag in its pursuit of him.

Not that Cherokee was slow. He could turn and whirl swiftly enough, but White Fang was never there. Cherokee was puzzled, too. He had never fought before with a dog with which he could not close. The desire to close had always been mutual. But here was a dog that kept at a distance, dancing and dodging here and there and all about. And when it did get its teeth into him, it did not hold on but let go instantly and darted away again.

But White Fang could not get at the soft underside of the throat. The bull-dog stood too short, while its massive jaws were an added protection. White Fang darted in and out unscathed, while Cherokee's wounds increased. Both sides of his neck and head were ripped and slashed. He bled freely, but showed no signs of being disconcerted. He continued his plodding pursuit, though once, for the moment baffled, he came to a full stop and blinked at the men who looked on, at the same time wagging his stump of a tail as an expression of his willingness to fight.

In that moment White Fang was in upon him and out, in passing ripping his trimmed remnant of an ear. With a slight manifestation of anger, Cherokee took up the pursuit again, running on the inside of the circle White Fang was making, and striving to fasten his deadly grip on White Fang's throat. The bull-dog missed by a hair's-breadth, and cries of praise went up as White Fang doubled suddenly out of danger in the opposite direction.

The time went by. White Fang still danced on, dodging and doubling, leaping in and out, and ever inflicting damage. And still the bull-dog, with grim certitude, toiled after him. Sooner or later he would accomplish his purpose, get the grip that would win the battle. In the meantime, he accepted all the punishment the other could deal him. His tufts of ears had become tassels, his neck and shoulders were slashed in a score of places, and his very lips were cut and bleeding—all from these lightning snaps that were beyond his foreseeing and guarding.

Time and again White Fang had attempted to knock Cherokee off his feet; but the difference in their height was too great. Cherokee was too squat, too close to the ground. White Fang tried the trick once too often. The chance came in one of his quick doublings and counter-circlings. He caught Cherokee with head turned away as he whirled more slowly. His shoulder was exposed. White Fang drove in upon it: but his own shoulder was high above, while he struck with such force that his momentum carried him on across over the other's body. For the first time in his fighting history, men saw White Fang lose his footing. His body turned a half-somersault in the air, and he would have landed on his back had he not twisted, catlike, still in the air, in the effort to bring his feet to the earth. As it was, he struck heavily on his side. The next instant he was on his feet, but in that instant Cherokee's teeth closed on his throat.

It was not a good grip, being too low down toward the chest; but Cherokee held on. White Fang sprang to his feet and tore wildly around, trying to shake off the bull-dog's body. It made him frantic, this clinging, dragging weight. It bound his movements, restricted his freedom. It was like the trap, and all his instinct resented it and revolted against it. It was a mad revolt. For several minutes he was to all intents insane. The basic life that was in him took charge of him. The will to exist of his body surged over him. He was dominated by this mere flesh-love of life. All intelligence was gone. It was as though he had no brain. His reason was unseated by the blind yearning of the flesh to exist and move, at all hazards to move, to continue to move, for movement was the expression of its existence.

Round and round he went, whirling and turning and reversing, trying to shake off the fifty-pound weight that dragged at his throat. The bull-dog did little but keep his grip. Sometimes, and rarely, he managed to get his feet to the earth and for a moment to brace himself against White Fang. But the next moment his footing would be lost and he would be dragging around in the whirl of one of White Fang's mad gyrations. Cherokee identified himself with his instinct. He knew that he was doing the right thing by holding on, and there came to him certain blissful thrills of satisfaction. At such moments he even closed his eyes and allowed his body to be hurled hither and thither, willy-nilly, careless of any hurt that might thereby come to it. That did not count. The grip was the thing, and the grip he kept.

White Fang ceased only when he had tired himself out. He could do nothing, and he could not understand. Never, in all his fighting, had this thing happened. The dogs he had fought with did not fight that way. With them it was snap and slash and get away, snap and slash and get away. He lay partly on his side, panting for breath. Cherokee still holding his grip, urged against him, trying to get him over entirely on his side. White Fang resisted, and he could feel the jaws shifting their grip, slightly relaxing and coming together again in a chewing movement. Each shift brought the grip closer to his throat. The bull-dog's method was to hold what he had, and when opportunity favoured to work in for more. Opportunity favoured when White Fang remained quiet. When White Fang struggled, Cherokee was content merely to hold on.

The bulging back of Cherokee's neck was the only portion of his body that White Fang's teeth could reach. He got hold toward the base where the neck comes out from the shoulders; but he did not know the chewing method of fighting, nor were his jaws adapted to it. He spasmodically ripped and tore with his fangs for a space. Then a change in their position diverted him. The bull-dog had managed to roll him over on his back, and still hanging on to his throat, was on top of him. Like a cat, White Fang bowed his hind-quarters in, and, with the feet digging into his enemy's abdomen above him, he began to claw with long tearing-strokes. Cherokee might well have been disembowelled had he not quickly pivoted on his grip and got his body off of White Fang's and at right angles to it.

There was no escaping that grip. It was like Fate itself, and as inexorable. Slowly it shifted up along the jugular. All that saved White Fang from death was the loose skin of his neck and the thick fur that covered it. This served to form a large roll in Cherokee's mouth, the fur of which well-nigh defied his teeth. But bit by bit, whenever the chance offered, he was getting more of the loose skin and fur in his mouth. The result was that he was slowly throttling White Fang. The latter's breath was drawn with greater and greater difficulty as the moments went by.

It began to look as though the battle were over. The backers of Cherokee waxed jubilant and offered ridiculous odds. White Fang's backers were correspondingly depressed, and refused bets of ten to one and twenty to one, though one man was rash enough to close a wager of fifty to one. This man was Beauty Smith. He took a step into the ring and pointed his finger at White Fang. Then he began to laugh derisively and scornfully. This produced the desired effect. White Fang went wild with rage. He called up his reserves of strength, and gained his feet. As he struggled around the ring, the fifty pounds of his foe ever dragging on his throat, his anger passed on into panic. The basic life of him dominated him again, and his intelligence fled before the will of his flesh to live. Round and round and back again, stumbling and falling and rising, even uprearing at times on his hind-legs and lifting his foe clear of the earth, he struggled vainly to shake off the clinging death.

At last he fell, toppling backward, exhausted; and the bull-dog promptly shifted his grip, getting in closer, mangling more and more of the fur-folded flesh, throttling White Fang more severely than ever. Shouts of applause went up for the victor, and there were many cries of 'Cherokee!' 'Cherokee!' To this Cherokee responded by vigorous wagging of the stump of his tail. But the clamour of approval did not distract him. There was no sympathetic relation between his tail and his massive jaws. The one might wag, but the others held their terrible grip on White Fang's throat.

It was at this time that a diversion came to the spectators. There was a jingle of bells. Dog-mushers' cries were heard. Everybody, save Beauty Smith, looked apprehensively, the fear of the police strong upon them. But they saw, up the trail, and not down, two men running with sled and dogs. They were evidently coming down the creek from some prospecting trip. At sight of the crowd they stopped their dogs and came over and joined it, curious to see the cause of the excitement. The dog-musher wore a moustache, but the other, a taller and younger man, was smooth-shaven, his skin rosy from the pounding of his blood and the running in the frosty air.

White Fang had practically ceased struggling. Now and again he resisted spasmodically and to no purpose. He could get little air, and that little grew less and less under the merciless grip that ever tightened. In spite of his armour of fur, the great vein of his throat would have long since been torn open, had not the first grip of the bull-dog been so low down as to be practically on the chest. It had taken Cherokee a long time to shift that grip upward, and this had also tended further to clog his jaws with fur and skin-fold.

In the meantime, the abysmal brute in Beauty Smith had been rising into his brain and mastering the small bit of sanity that he possessed at best. When he saw White Fang's eyes beginning to glaze, he knew beyond doubt that the fight was lost. Then he broke loose. He sprang upon White Fang and began savagely to kick him. There were hisses from the crowd and cries of protest, but that was all. While this went on, and Beauty Smith continued to kick White Fang, there was a commotion in the crowd. The tall young newcomer was forcing his way through, shouldering men right and left without ceremony or gentleness. When he broke through into the ring, Beauty Smith was just in the act of delivering another kick. All his weight was on one foot, and he was in a state of unstable equilibrium. At that moment the newcomer's fist landed a smashing blow full in his face. Beauty Smith's remaining leg left the ground, and his whole body seemed to lift into the air as he turned over backward and struck the snow. The newcomer turned upon the crowd.

'You cowards!' he cried. 'You beasts!'

He was in a rage himself—a sane rage. His grey eyes seemed metallic and steel-like as they flashed upon the crowd. Beauty Smith regained his feet and came toward him, sniffling and cowardly. The new-comer did not understand. He did not know how abject a coward the other was, and thought he was coming back intent on fighting. So, with a 'You beast!' he smashed Beauty Smith over backward with a second blow in the face. Beauty Smith decided that the snow was the safest place for him, and lay where he had fallen, making no effort to get up.

'Come on, Matt, lend a hand,' the newcomer called the dog-musher, who had followed him into the ring.

Both men bent over the dogs. Matt took hold of White Fang, ready to pull when Cherokee's jaws should be loosened. This the younger man endeavoured to accomplish by clutching the bulldog's jaws in his hands and trying to spread them. It was a vain undertaking. As he pulled and tugged and wrenched, he kept exclaiming with every expulsion of breath, 'Beasts!'

The crowd began to grow unruly, and some of the men were protesting against the spoiling of the sport; but they were silenced when the newcomer lifted his head from his work for a moment and glared at them.

'You damn beasts!' he finally exploded, and went back to his task.

'It's no use, Mr. Scott, you can't break 'm apart that way,' Matt said at last.

The pair paused and surveyed the locked dogs.

'Ain't bleedin' much,' Matt announced. 'Ain't got all the way in yet.'

'But he's liable to any moment,' Scott answered. 'There, did you see that! He shifted his grip in a bit.'

The younger man's excitement and apprehension for White Fang was growing. He struck Cherokee about the head savagely again and again. But that did not loosen the jaws. Cherokee wagged the stump of his tail in advertisement that he understood the meaning of the blows, but that he knew he was himself in the right and only doing his duty by keeping his grip.

'Won't some of you help?' Scott cried desperately at the crowd.

But no help was offered. Instead, the crowd began sarcastically to cheer him on and showered him with facetious advice.

'You'll have to get a pry,' Matt counselled.

The other reached into the holster at his hip, drew his revolver, and tried to thrust its muzzle between the bull-dog's jaws. He shoved, and shoved hard, till the grating of the steel against the locked teeth could be distinctly heard. Both men were on their knees, bending over the dogs. Tim Keenan strode into the ring. He paused beside Scott and touched him on the shoulder, saying ominously:

'Don't break them teeth, stranger.'

'Then I'll break his neck,' Scott retorted, continuing his shoving and wedging with the revolver muzzle.

'I said don't break them teeth,' the faro-dealer repeated more ominously than before.

But if it was a bluff he intended, it did not work. Scott never desisted from his efforts, though he looked up coolly and asked:

'Your dog?'

The faro-dealer grunted.

'Then get in here and break this grip.'

'Well, stranger,' the other drawled irritatingly, 'I don't mind telling you that's something I ain't worked out for myself. I don't know how to turn the trick.'

'Then get out of the way,' was the reply, 'and don't bother me. I'm busy.'

Tim Keenan continued standing over him, but Scott took no further notice of his presence. He had managed to get the muzzle in between the jaws on one side, and was trying to get it out between the jaws on the other side. This accomplished, he pried gently and carefully, loosening the jaws a bit at a time, while Matt, a bit at a time, extricated White Fang's mangled neck.

'Stand by to receive your dog,' was Scott's peremptory order to Cherokee's owner.

The faro-dealer stooped down obediently and got a firm hold on Cherokee.

'Now!' Scott warned, giving the final pry.

The dogs were drawn apart, the bull-dog struggling vigorously.

'Take him away,' Scott commanded, and Tim Keenan dragged Cherokee back into the crowd.

White Fang made several ineffectual efforts to get up. Once he gained his feet, but his legs were too weak to sustain him, and he slowly wilted and sank back into the snow. His eyes were half closed, and the surface of them was glassy. His jaws were apart, and through them the tongue protruded, draggled and limp. To all appearances he looked like a dog that had been strangled to death. Matt examined him.

'Just about all in,' he announced; 'but he's breathin' all right.'

Beauty Smith had regained his feet and come over to look at White Fang.

'Matt, how much is a good sled-dog worth?' Scott asked.

The dog-musher, still on his knees and stooped over White Fang, calculated for a moment.

'Three hundred dollars,' he answered.

'And how much for one that's all chewed up like this one?' Scott asked, nudging White Fang with his foot.

'Half of that,' was the dog-musher's judgment. Scott turned upon Beauty Smith.

'Did you hear, Mr. Beast? I'm going to take your dog from you, and I'm going to give you a hundred and fifty for him.'

He opened his pocket-book and counted out the bills.

Beauty Smith put his hands behind his back, refusing to touch the proffered money.

'I ain't a-sellin',' he said.

'Oh, yes you are,' the other assured him. 'Because I'm buying. Here's your money. The dog's mine.'

Beauty Smith, his hands still behind him, began to back away.

Scott sprang toward him, drawing his fist back to strike. Beauty Smith cowered down in anticipation of the blow.

'I've got my rights,' he whimpered.

'You've forfeited your rights to own that dog,' was the rejoinder. 'Are you going to take the money? or do I have to hit you again?'

'All right,' Beauty Smith spoke up with the alacrity of fear. 'But I take the money under protest,' he added. 'The dog's a mint. I ain't a-goin' to be robbed. A man's got his rights.'

'Correct,' Scott answered, passing the money over to him. 'A man's got his rights. But you're not a man. You're a beast.'

'Wait till I get back to Dawson,' Beauty Smith threatened. 'I'll have the law on you.'

'If you open your mouth when you get back to Dawson, I'll have you run out of town. Understand?'

Beauty Smith replied with a grunt.

'Understand?' the other thundered with abrupt fierceness.

'Yes,' Beauty Smith grunted, shrinking away.

'Yes what?'

'Yes, sir,' Beauty Smith snarled.

'Look out! He'll bite!' some one shouted, and a guffaw of laughter went up.

Scott turned his back on him, and returned to help the dog-musher, who was working over White Fang.

Some of the men were already departing; others stood in groups, looking on and talking. Tim Keenan joined one of the groups.

'Who's that mug?' he asked.

'Weedon Scott,' some one answered.

'And who in hell is Weedon Scott?' the faro-dealer demanded.

'Oh, one of them crackerjack minin' experts. He's in with all the big bugs. If you want to keep out of trouble, you'll steer clear of him, that's my talk. He's all hunky with the officials. The Gold Commissioner's a special pal of his.'

'I thought he must be somebody,' was the faro-dealer's comment. 'That's why I kept my hands offen him at the start.'

CHAPTER V
THE INDOMITABLE

'It's hopeless,' Weedon Scott confessed.

He sat on the step of his cabin and stared at the dog-musher, who responded with a shrug that was equally hopeless.

Together they looked at White Fang at the end of his stretched chain, bristling, snarling, ferocious, straining to get at the sled-dogs. Having received sundry lessons from Matt, said lessons being imparted by means of a club, the sled-dogs had learned to leave White Fang alone; and even then they were lying down at a distance, apparently oblivious of his existence.

'It's a wolf and there's no taming it,' Weedon Scott announced.

'Oh, I don't know about that,' Matt objected. 'Might be a lot of dog in 'm, for all you can tell. But there's one thing I know sure, an' that there's no gettin' away from.'

The dog-musher paused and nodded his head confidentially at Moosehide Mountain.

'Well, don't be a miser with what you know,' Scott said sharply, after waiting a suitable length of time. 'Spit it out. What is it?'

The dog-musher indicated White Fang with a backward thrust of his thumb. 'Wolf or dog, it's all the same—he's ben tamed 'ready.'

'No!'

'I tell you yes, an' broke to harness. Look close there. D'ye see them marks across the chest?'

'You're right, Matt. He was a sled-dog before Beauty Smith got hold of him.'

'And there's not much reason against his bein' a sled-dog again.'

'What d'ye think?' Scott queried eagerly. Then the hope died down as he added, shaking his head, 'We've had him two weeks now, and if anything he's wilder than ever at the present moment.'

'Give 'm a chance,' Matt counselled. 'Turn 'm loose for a spell.'

The other looked at him incredulously.

'Yes,' Matt went on, 'I know you've tried to, but you didn't take a club.'

'You try it then.'

The dog-musher secured a club and went over to the chained animal. White Fang watched the club after the manner of a caged lion watching the whip of its trainer.

'See 'm keep his eye on that club,' Matt said. 'That's a good sign. He's no fool. Don't dast tackle me so long as I got that club handy. He's not clean crazy, sure.'

As the man's hand approached his neck, White Fang bristled and snarled and crouched down. But while he eyed the approaching hand, he at the same time contrived to keep track of the club in the other hand, suspended threateningly above him. Matt unsnapped the chain from the collar and stepped back.

White Fang could scarcely realise that he was free. Many months had gone by since he passed into the possession of Beauty Smith, and in all that period he had never known a moment of freedom except at the times he had been loosed to fight with other dogs. Immediately after such fights he had always been imprisoned again.

He did not know what to make of it. Perhaps some new devilry of the gods was about to be perpetrated on him. He walked slowly and cautiously, prepared to be assailed at any moment. He did not know what to do, it was all so unprecedented. He took the precaution to sheer off from the two watching gods, and walked carefully to the corner of the cabin. Nothing happened. He was plainly perplexed, and he came back again, pausing a dozen feet away and regarding the two men intently.

'Won't he run away?' his new owner asked.

Matt shrugged his shoulders. 'Got to take a gamble. Only way to find out is to find out.'

'Poor devil,' Scott murmured pityingly. 'What he needs is some show of human kindness,' he added, turning and going into the cabin.

He came out with a piece of meat, which he tossed to White Fang. He sprang away from it, and from a distance studied it suspiciously.

'Hi-yu, Major!' Matt shouted warningly, but too late.

Major had made a spring for the meat. At the instant his jaws closed on it, White Fang struck him. He was overthrown. Matt rushed in, but quicker than he was White Fang. Major staggered to his feet, but the blood spouting from his throat reddened the snow in a widening path.

'It's too bad, but it served him right,' Scott said hastily.

But Matt's foot had already started on its way to kick White Fang. There was a leap, a flash of teeth, a sharp exclamation. White Fang, snarling fiercely, scrambled backward for several yards, while Matt stooped and investigated his leg.

'He got me all right,' he announced, pointing to the torn trousers and under-cloths, and the growing stain of red.

'I told you it was hopeless, Matt,' Scott said in a discouraged voice. 'I've thought about it off and on, while not wanting to think of it. But we've come to it now. It's the only thing to do.'

As he talked, with reluctant movements he drew his revolver, threw open the cylinder, and assured himself of its contents.

'Look here, Mr. Scott,' Matt objected; 'that dog's ben through hell. You can't expect 'm to come out a white an' shinin' angel. Give 'm time.'

'Look at Major,' the other rejoined.

The dog-musher surveyed the stricken dog. He had sunk down on the snow in the circle of his blood and was plainly in the last gasp.

'Served 'm right. You said so yourself, Mr. Scott. He tried to take White Fang's meat, an' he's dead-O. That was to be expected. I wouldn't give two whoops in hell for a dog that wouldn't fight for his own meat.'

'But look at yourself, Matt. It's all right about the dogs, but we must draw the line somewhere.'

'Served me right,' Matt argued stubbornly. 'What'd I want to kick 'm for? You said yourself that he'd done right. Then I had no right to kick 'm.'

'It would be a mercy to kill him,' Scott insisted. 'He's untamable.'

'Now look here, Mr. Scott, give the poor devil a fightin' chance. He ain't had no chance yet. He's just come through hell, an' this is the first time he's ben loose. Give 'm a fair chance, an' if he don't deliver the goods, I'll kill 'm myself. There!'

'God knows I don't want to kill him or have him killed,' Scott answered, putting away the revolver. 'We'll let him run loose and see what kindness can do for him. And here's a try at it.'

He walked over to White Fang and began talking to him gently and soothingly.

'Better have a club handy,' Matt warned.

Scott shook his head and went on trying to win White Fang's confidence.

White Fang was suspicious. Something was impending. He had killed this god's dog, bitten his companion god, and what else was to be expected than some terrible punishment? But in the face of it he was indomitable. He bristled and showed his teeth, his eyes vigilant, his whole body wary and prepared for anything. The god had no club, so he suffered him to approach quite near. The god's hand had come out and was descending upon his head. White Fang shrank together and grew tense as he crouched under it. Here was danger, some treachery or something. He knew the hands of the gods, their proved mastery, their cunning to hurt. Besides, there was his old antipathy to being touched. He snarled more menacingly, crouched still lower, and still the hand descended. He did not want to bite the hand, and he endured the peril of it until his instinct surged up in him, mastering him with its insatiable yearning for life.

Weedon Scott had believed that he was quick enough to avoid any snap or slash. But he had yet to learn the remarkable quickness of White Fang, who struck with the certainty and swiftness of a coiled snake.

Scott cried out sharply with surprise, catching his torn hand and holding it tightly in his other hand. Matt uttered a great oath and sprang to his side. White Fang crouched down, and backed away, bristling, showing his fangs, his eyes malignant with menace. Now he could expect a beating as fearful as any he had received from Beauty Smith.

'Here! What are you doing?' Scott cried suddenly.

Matt had dashed into the cabin and come out with a rifle.

'Nothin',' he said slowly, with a careless calmness that was assumed, 'only goin' to keep that promise I made. I reckon it's up to me to kill 'm as I said I'd do.'

'No you don't!'

'Yes I do. Watch me.'

As Matt had pleaded for White Fang when he had been bitten, it was now Weedon Scott's turn to plead.

'You said to give him a chance. Well, give it to him. We've only just started, and we can't quit at the beginning. It served me right, this time. And—look at him!'

White Fang, near the corner of the cabin and forty feet away, was snarling with blood-curdling viciousness, not at Scott, but at the dog-musher.

'Well, I'll be everlastingly gosh-swoggled!' was the dog-musher's expression of astonishment.

'Look at the intelligence of him,' Scott went on hastily. 'He knows the meaning of firearms as well as you do. He's got intelligence and we've got to give that intelligence a chance. Put up the gun.'

'All right, I'm willin',' Matt agreed, leaning the rifle against the woodpile.

'But will you look at that!' he exclaimed the next moment.

White Fang had quieted down and ceased snarling. 'This is worth investigatin'. Watch.'

Matt, reached for the rifle, and at the same moment White Fang snarled. He stepped away from the rifle, and White Fang's lifted lips descended, covering his teeth.

'Now, just for fun.'

Matt took the rifle and began slowly to raise it to his shoulder. White Fang's snarling began with the movement, and increased as the movement approached its culmination. But the moment before the rifle came to a level on him, he leaped sidewise behind the corner of the cabin. Matt stood staring along the sights at the empty space of snow which had been occupied by White Fang.

The dog-musher put the rifle down solemnly, then turned and looked at his employer.

'I agree with you, Mr. Scott. That dog's too intelligent to kill.'

CHAPTER VI
THE LOVE-MASTER

As White Fang watched Weedon Scott approach, he bristled and snarled to advertise that he would not submit to punishment. Twenty-four hours had passed since he had slashed open the hand that was now bandaged and held up by a sling to keep the blood out of it. In the past White Fang had experienced delayed punishments, and he apprehended that such a one was about to befall him. How could it be otherwise?

He had committed what was to him sacrilege, sunk his fangs into the holy flesh of a god, and of a white-skinned superior god at that. In the nature of things, and of intercourse with gods, something terrible awaited him.

The god sat down several feet away. White Fang could see nothing dangerous in that. When the gods administered punishment they stood on their legs. Besides, this god had no club, no whip, no firearm. And furthermore, he himself was free. No chain nor stick bound him. He could escape into safety while the god was scrambling to his feet. In the meantime he would wait and see.

The god remained quiet, made no movement; and White Fang's snarl slowly dwindled to a growl that ebbed down in his throat and ceased. Then the god spoke, and at the first sound of his voice, the hair rose on White Fang's neck and the growl rushed up in his throat. But the god made no hostile movement, and went on calmly talking. For a time White Fang growled in unison with him, a correspondence of rhythm being established between growl and voice. But the god talked on interminably. He talked to White Fang as White Fang had never been talked to before. He talked softly and soothingly, with a gentleness that somehow, somewhere, touched White Fang. In spite of himself and all the pricking warnings of his instinct, White Fang began to have confidence in this god. He had a feeling of security that was belied by all his experience with men.

After a long time, the god got up and went into the cabin. White Fang scanned him apprehensively when he came out. He had neither whip nor club nor weapon. Nor was his uninjured hand behind his back hiding something. He sat down as before, in the same spot, several feet away. He held out a small piece of meat. White Fang pricked his ears and investigated it suspiciously, managing to look at the same time both at the meat and the god, alert for any overt act, his body tense and ready to spring away at the first sign of hostility.

Still the punishment delayed. The god merely held near to his nose a piece of meat. And about the meat there seemed nothing wrong. Still White Fang suspected; and though the meat was proffered to him with short inviting thrusts of the hand, he refused to touch it. The gods were all-wise, and there was no telling what masterful treachery lurked behind that apparently harmless piece of meat. In past experience, especially in dealing with squaws, meat and punishment had often been disastrously related.

In the end, the god tossed the meat on the snow at White Fang's feet. He smelled the meat carefully; but he did not look at it. While he smelled it he kept his eyes on the god. Nothing happened. He took the meat into his mouth and swallowed it. Still nothing happened. The god was actually offering him another piece of meat. Again he refused to take it from the hand, and again it was tossed to him. This was repeated a number of times. But there came a time when the god refused to toss it. He kept it in his hand and steadfastly proffered it.

The meat was good meat, and White Fang was hungry. Bit by bit, infinitely cautious, he approached the hand. At last the time came that he decided to eat the meat from the hand. He never took his eyes from the god, thrusting his head forward with ears flattened back and hair involuntarily rising and cresting on his neck. Also a low growl rumbled in his throat as warning that he was not to be trifled with. He ate the meat, and nothing happened. Piece by piece, he ate all the meat, and nothing happened. Still the punishment delayed.

He licked his chops and waited. The god went on talking. In his voice was kindness—something of which White Fang had no experience whatever. And within him it aroused feelings which he had likewise never experienced before. He was aware of a certain strange satisfaction, as though some need were being gratified, as though some void in his being were being filled. Then again came the prod of his instinct and the warning of past experience. The gods were ever crafty, and they had unguessed ways of attaining their ends.

Ah, he had thought so! There it came now, the god's hand, cunning to hurt, thrusting out at him, descending upon his head. But the god went on talking. His voice was soft and soothing. In spite of the menacing hand, the voice inspired confidence. And in spite of the assuring voice, the hand inspired distrust. White Fang was torn by conflicting feelings, impulses. It seemed he would fly to pieces, so terrible was the control he was exerting, holding together by an unwonted indecision the counter-forces that struggled within him for mastery.

He compromised. He snarled and bristled and flattened his ears. But he neither snapped nor sprang away. The hand descended. Nearer and nearer it came. It touched the ends of his upstanding hair. He shrank down under it. It followed down after him, pressing more closely against him. Shrinking, almost shivering, he still managed to hold himself together. It was a torment, this hand that touched him and violated his instinct. He could not forget in a day all the evil that had been wrought him at the hands of men. But it was the will of the god, and he strove to submit.

The hand lifted and descended again in a patting, caressing movement. This continued, but every time the hand lifted, the hair lifted under it. And every time the hand descended, the ears flattened down and a cavernous growl surged in his throat. White Fang growled and growled with insistent warning. By this means he announced that he was prepared to retaliate for any hurt he might receive. There was no telling when the god's ulterior motive might be disclosed. At any moment that soft, confidence-inspiring voice might break forth in a roar of wrath, that gentle and caressing hand transform itself into a vice-like grip to hold him helpless and administer punishment.

But the god talked on softly, and ever the hand rose and fell with non-hostile pats. White Fang experienced dual feelings. It was distasteful to his instinct. It restrained him, opposed the will of him toward personal liberty. And yet it was not physically painful. On the contrary, it was even pleasant, in a physical way. The patting movement slowly and carefully changed to a rubbing of the ears about their bases, and the physical pleasure even increased a little. Yet he continued to fear, and he stood on guard, expectant of unguessed evil, alternately suffering and enjoying as one feeling or the other came uppermost and swayed him.

'Well, I'll be gosh-swoggled!'

So spoke Matt, coming out of the cabin, his sleeves rolled up, a pan of dirty dish-water in his hands, arrested in the act of emptying the pan by the sight of Weedon Scott patting White Fang.

At the instant his voice broke the silence, White Fang leaped back, snarling savagely at him.

Matt regarded his employer with grieved disapproval.

'If you don't mind my expressin' my feelin's, Mr. Scott, I'll make free to say you're seventeen kinds of a damn fool an' all of 'em different, an' then some.'

Weedon Scott smiled with a superior air, gained his feet, and walked over to White Fang. He talked soothingly to him, but not for long, then slowly put out his hand, rested it on White Fang's head, and resumed the interrupted patting. White Fang endured it, keeping his eyes fixed suspiciously, not upon the man that patted him, but upon the man that stood in the doorway.

'You may be a number one, tip-top minin' expert, all right all right,' the dog-musher delivered himself oracularly, 'but you missed the chance of your life when you was a boy an' didn't run off an' join a circus.'

White Fang snarled at the sound of his voice, but this time did not leap away from under the hand that was caressing his head and the back of his neck with long, soothing strokes.

It was the beginning of the end for White Fang—the ending of the old life and the reign of hate. A new and incomprehensibly fairer life was dawning. It required much thinking and endless patience on the part of Weedon Scott to accomplish this. And on the part of White Fang it required nothing less than a revolution. He had to ignore the urges and promptings of instinct and reason, defy experience, give the lie to life itself.

Life, as he had known it, not only had had no place in it for much that he now did; but all the currents had gone counter to those to which he now abandoned himself. In short, when all things were considered, he had to achieve an orientation far vaster than the one he had achieved at the time he came voluntarily in from the Wild and accepted Grey Beaver as his lord. At that time he was a mere puppy, soft from the making, without form, ready for the thumb of circumstance to begin its work upon him. But now it was different. The thumb of circumstance had done its work only too well. By it he had been formed and hardened into the Fighting Wolf, fierce and implacable, unloving and unlovable. To accomplish the change was like a reflux of being, and this when the plasticity of youth was no longer his; when the fibre of him had become tough and knotty; when the warp and the woof of him had made of him an adamantine texture, harsh and unyielding; when the face of his spirit had become iron and all his instincts and axioms had crystallised into set rules, cautions, dislikes, and desires.

Yet again, in this new orientation, it was the thumb of circumstance that pressed and prodded him, softening that which had become hard and remoulding it into fairer form. Weedon Scott was in truth this thumb. He had gone to the roots of White Fang's nature, and with kindness touched to life potencies that had languished and well-nigh perished. One such potency was *love*. It took the place of *like*, which latter had been the highest feeling that thrilled him in his intercourse with the gods.

But this love did not come in a day. It began with *like* and out of it slowly developed. White Fang did not run away, though he was allowed to remain loose, because he liked this new god. This was certainly better than the life he had lived in the cage of Beauty Smith, and it was necessary that he should have some god. The lordship of man was a need of his nature. The seal of his dependence on man had been set upon him in that early day when he turned his back on the Wild and crawled to Grey Beaver's feet to receive the expected beating. This seal had been stamped upon him again, and ineradicably, on his second return from the Wild, when the long famine was over and there was fish once more in the village of Grey Beaver.

And so, because he needed a god and because he preferred Weedon Scott to

Beauty Smith, White Fang remained. In acknowledgment of fealty, he proceeded to take upon himself the guardianship of his master's property. He prowled about the cabin while the sled-dogs slept, and the first night-visitor to the cabin fought him off with a club until Weedon Scott came to the rescue. But White Fang soon learned to differentiate between thieves and honest men, to appraise the true value of step and carriage. The man who travelled, loud-stepping, the direct line to the cabin door, he let alone—though he watched him vigilantly until the door opened and he received the endorsement of the master. But the man who went softly, by circuitous ways, peering with caution, seeking after secrecy—that was the man who received no suspension of judgment from White Fang, and who went away abruptly, hurriedly, and without dignity.

Weedon Scott had set himself the task of redeeming White Fang—or rather, of redeeming mankind from the wrong it had done White Fang. It was a matter of principle and conscience. He felt that the ill done White Fang was a debt incurred by man and that it must be paid. So he went out of his way to be especially kind to the Fighting Wolf. Each day he made it a point to caress and pet White Fang, and to do it at length.

At first suspicious and hostile, White Fang grew to like this petting. But there was one thing that he never outgrew—his growling. Growl he would, from the moment the petting began till it ended. But it was a growl with a new note in it. A stranger could not hear this note, and to such a stranger the growling of White Fang was an exhibition of primordial savagery, nerve-racking and blood-curdling. But White Fang's throat had become harsh-fibred from the making of ferocious sounds through the many years since his first little rasp of anger in the lair of his cubhood, and he could not soften the sounds of that throat now to express the gentleness he felt. Nevertheless, Weedon Scott's ear and sympathy were fine enough to catch the new note all but drowned in the fierceness—the note that was the faintest hint of a croon of content and that none but he could hear.

As the days went by, the evolution of *like* into *love* was accelerated. White Fang himself began to grow aware of it, though in his consciousness he knew not what love was. It manifested itself to him as a void in his being—a hungry, aching, yearning void that clamoured to be filled. It was a pain and an unrest; and it received easement only by the touch of the new god's presence. At such times love was joy to him, a wild, keen-thrilling satisfaction. But when away from his god, the pain and the unrest returned; the void in him sprang up and pressed against him with its emptiness, and the hunger gnawed and gnawed unceasingly.

White Fang was in the process of finding himself. In spite of the maturity of his years and of the savage rigidity of the mould that had formed him, his nature was undergoing an expansion. There was a burgeoning within him of strange feelings and unwonted impulses. His old code of conduct was changing. In the past he had liked comfort and surcease from pain, disliked discomfort and pain, and he had adjusted his actions accordingly. But now it was different. Because of this new feeling within him, he ofttimes elected discomfort and pain for the sake of his god. Thus, in the early morning, instead of roaming and foraging, or lying in a sheltered nook, he would wait for hours on the cheerless cabin-stoop for a sight of the god's face. At night, when the god returned home, White Fang would leave the warm sleeping-place he had burrowed in the snow in order to receive the friendly snap of fingers and the word of greeting. Meat, even meat itself, he would forego to be with his god, to receive a caress from him or to accompany him down into the town.

Like had been replaced by *love*. And love was the plummet dropped down into the deeps of him where like had never gone. And responsive out of his deeps had come the new thing—love. That which was given unto him did he return. This was a god indeed, a love-god, a warm and radiant god, in whose light White Fang's nature expanded as a flower expands under the sun.

But White Fang was not demonstrative. He was too old, too firmly moulded, to become adept at expressing himself in new ways. He was too self-possessed, too strongly poised in his own isolation. Too long had he cultivated reticence, aloofness, and moroseness. He had never barked in his life, and he could not now learn to bark a welcome when his god approached. He was never in the way, never extravagant nor foolish in the expression of his love. He never ran to meet his god. He waited at a distance; but he always waited, was always there. His love partook of the nature of worship, dumb, inarticulate, a silent adoration. Only by the steady regard of his eyes did he express his love, and by the unceasing following with his eyes of his god's every movement. Also, at times, when his god looked at him and spoke to him, he betrayed an awkward self-consciousness, caused by the struggle of his love to express itself and his physical inability to express it.

He learned to adjust himself in many ways to his new mode of life. It was borne in upon him that he must let his master's dogs alone. Yet his dominant nature asserted itself, and he had first to thrash them into an acknowledgment of his superiority and leadership. This accomplished, he had little trouble with them. They gave trail to him when he came and went or walked among them, and when he asserted his will they obeyed.

In the same way, he came to tolerate Matt—as a possession of his master. His master rarely fed him. Matt did that, it was his business; yet White Fang divined that it was his master's food he ate and that it was his master who thus fed him vicariously. Matt it was who tried to put him into the harness and make him haul sled with the other dogs. But Matt failed. It was not until Weedon Scott put the harness on White Fang and worked him, that he understood. He took it as his master's will that Matt should drive him and work him just as he drove and worked his master's other dogs.

Different from the Mackenzie toboggans were the Klondike sleds with runners under them. And different was the method of driving the dogs. There was no fan-formation of the team. The dogs worked in single file, one behind another, hauling on double traces. And here, in the Klondike, the leader was indeed the leader. The wisest as well as strongest dog was the leader, and the team obeyed him and feared him. That White Fang should quickly gain this post was inevitable. He could not be satisfied with less, as Matt learned after much inconvenience and trouble. White Fang picked out the post for himself, and Matt backed his judgment with strong language after the experiment had been tried. But, though he worked in the sled in the day, White Fang did not forego the guarding of his master's property in the night. Thus he was on duty all the time, ever vigilant and faithful, the most valuable of all the dogs.

'Makin' free to spit out what's in me,' Matt said one day, 'I beg to state that you was a wise guy all right when you paid the price you did for that dog. You clean swindled Beauty Smith on top of pushin' his face in with your fist.'

A recrudescence of anger glinted in Weedon Scott's grey eyes, and he muttered savagely, 'The beast!'

In the late spring a great trouble came to White Fang. Without warning, the love-master disappeared. There had been warning, but White Fang was unversed in such things and did not understand the packing of a grip. He remembered afterwards that his packing had preceded the master's disappearance; but at the time he suspected nothing. That night he waited for the master to return. At midnight the chill wind that blew drove him to shelter at the rear of the cabin. There he drowsed, only half asleep, his ears keyed for the first sound of the familiar step. But, at two in the morning, his anxiety drove him out to the cold front stoop, where he crouched, and waited.

But no master came. In the morning the door opened and Matt stepped outside. White Fang gazed at him wistfully. There was no common speech by which he might learn what he wanted to know. The days came and went, but never the master. White Fang, who had never known sickness in his life, became sick. He became very sick, so sick that Matt was finally compelled to bring him inside the cabin. Also, in writing to his employer, Matt devoted a postscript to White Fang.

Weedon Scott reading the letter down in Circle City, came upon the following:

'That dam wolf won't work. Won't eat. Aint got no spunk left. All the dogs is licking him. Wants to know what has become of you, and I don't know how to tell him. Mebbe he is going to die.'

It was as Matt had said. White Fang had ceased eating, lost heart, and allowed every dog of the team to thrash him. In the cabin he lay on the floor near the stove, without interest in food, in Matt, nor in life. Matt might talk gently to him or swear at him, it was all the same; he never did more than turn his dull eyes upon the man, then drop his head back to its customary position on his fore-paws.

And then, one night, Matt, reading to himself with moving lips and mumbled sounds, was startled by a low whine from White Fang. He had got upon his feet, his ears cocked towards the door, and he was listening intently. A moment later, Matt heard a footstep. The door opened, and Weedon Scott stepped in. The two men shook hands. Then Scott looked around the room.

'Where's the wolf?' he asked.

Then he discovered him, standing where he had been lying, near to the stove. He had not rushed forward after the manner of other dogs. He stood, watching and waiting.

'Holy smoke!' Matt exclaimed. 'Look at 'm wag his tail!'

Weedon Scott strode half across the room toward him, at the same time calling him. White Fang came to him, not with a great bound, yet quickly. He was awakened from self-consciousness, but as he drew near, his eyes took on a strange expression. Something, an incommunicable vastness of feeling, rose up into his eyes as a light and shone forth.

'He never looked at me that way all the time you was gone!' Matt commented.

Weedon Scott did not hear. He was squatting down on his heels, face to face with White Fang and petting him—rubbing at the roots of the ears, making long caressing strokes down the neck to the shoulders, tapping the spine gently with the balls of his fingers. And White Fang was growling responsively, the crooning note of the growl more pronounced than ever.

But that was not all. What of his joy, the great love in him, ever surging and struggling to express itself, succeeded in finding a new mode of expression. He suddenly thrust his head forward and nudged his way in between the master's arm and body. And here, confined, hidden from view all except his ears, no longer growling, he continued to nudge and snuggle.

The two men looked at each other. Scott's eyes were shining.

'Gosh!' said Matt in an awe-stricken voice.

A moment later, when he had recovered himself, he said, 'I always insisted that wolf was a dog. Look at 'm!'

With the return of the love-master, White Fang's recovery was rapid. Two nights and a day he spent in the cabin. Then he sallied forth. The sled-dogs had forgotten his prowess. They remembered only the latest, which was his weakness and sickness. At the sight of him as he came out of the cabin, they sprang upon him.

'Talk about your rough-houses,' Matt murmured gleefully, standing in the doorway and looking on.

'Give 'm hell, you wolf! Give 'm hell!—an' then some!'

White Fang did not need the encouragement. The return of the love-master was enough. Life was flowing through him again, splendid and indomitable. He fought from sheer joy, finding in it an expression of much that he felt and that otherwise was without speech. There could be but one ending. The team dispersed in ignominious defeat, and it was not until after dark that the dogs came sneaking back, one by one, by meekness and humility signifying their fealty to White Fang.

Having learned to snuggle, White Fang was guilty of it often. It was the final word. He could not go beyond it. The one thing of which he had always been particularly jealous was his head. He had always disliked to have it touched. It was the Wild in him, the fear of hurt and of the trap, that had given rise to the panicky impulses to avoid contacts. It was the mandate of his instinct that that head must be free. And now, with the love-master, his snuggling was the deliberate act of putting himself into a position of hopeless helplessness. It was an expression of perfect confidence, of absolute self-surrender, as though he said: 'I put myself into thy hands. Work thou thy will with me.'

One night, not long after the return, Scott and Matt sat at a game of cribbage preliminary to going to bed. 'Fifteen-two, fifteen-four an' a pair makes six,' Mat was pegging up, when there was an outcry and sound of snarling without. They looked at each other as they started to rise to their feet.

'The wolf's nailed somebody,' Matt said.

A wild scream of fear and anguish hastened them.

'Bring a light!' Scott shouted, as he sprang outside.

Matt followed with the lamp, and by its light they saw a man lying on his back in the snow. His arms were folded, one above the other, across his face and throat. Thus he was trying to shield himself from White Fang's teeth. And there was need for it. White Fang was in a rage, wickedly making his attack on the most vulnerable spot. From shoulder to wrist of the crossed arms, the coat-sleeve, blue flannel shirt and undershirt were ripped in rags, while the arms themselves were terribly slashed and streaming blood.

All this the two men saw in the first instant. The next instant Weedon Scott had White Fang by the throat and was dragging him clear. White Fang struggled and snarled, but made no attempt to bite, while he quickly quieted down at a sharp word from the master.

Matt helped the man to his feet. As he arose he lowered his crossed arms, exposing the bestial face of Beauty Smith. The dog-musher let go of him precipitately, with action similar to that of a man who has picked up live fire. Beauty Smith blinked in the lamplight and looked about him. He caught sight of White Fang and terror rushed into his face.

At the same moment Matt noticed two objects lying in the snow. He held the lamp close to them, indicating them with his toe for his employer's benefit—a steel dog-chain and a stout club.

Weedon Scott saw and nodded. Not a word was spoken. The dog-musher laid his hand on Beauty Smith's shoulder and faced him to the right about. No word needed to be spoken. Beauty Smith started.

In the meantime the love-master was patting White Fang and talking to him.

'Tried to steal you, eh? And you wouldn't have it! Well, well, he made a mistake, didn't he?'

'Must 'a' thought he had hold of seventeen devils,' the dog-musher sniggered.

White Fang, still wrought up and bristling, growled and growled, the hair slowly lying down, the crooning note remote and dim, but growing in his throat.

PART V

THE LONG TRAIL

It was in the air. White Fang sensed the coming calamity, even before there was tangible evidence of it. In vague ways it was borne in upon him that a change was impending. He knew not how nor why, yet he got his feel of the oncoming event from the gods themselves. In ways subtler than they knew, they betrayed their intentions to the wolf-dog that haunted the cabin-stoop, and that, though he never came inside the cabin, knew what went on inside their brains.

'Listen to that, will you!' the dug-musher exclaimed at supper one night.

Weedon Scott listened. Through the door came a low, anxious whine, like a sobbing under the breath that had just grown audible. Then came the long sniff, as White Fang reassured himself that his god was still inside and had not yet taken himself off in mysterious and solitary flight.

'I do believe that wolf's on to you,' the dog-musher said.

Weedon Scott looked across at his companion with eyes that almost pleaded, though this was given the lie by his words.

'What the devil can I do with a wolf in California?' he demanded.

'That's what I say,' Matt answered. 'What the devil can you do with a wolf in California?'

But this did not satisfy Weedon Scott. The other seemed to be judging him in a non-committal sort of way.

'White man's dogs would have no show against him,' Scott went on. 'He'd kill them on sight. If he didn't bankrupt me with damaged suits, the authorities would take him away from me and electrocute him.'

'He's a downright murderer, I know,' was the dog-musher's comment.

Weedon Scott looked at him suspiciously.

'It would never do,' he said decisively.

'It would never do!' Matt concurred. 'Why you'd have to hire a man 'specially to take care of 'm.'

The other suspicion was allayed. He nodded cheerfully. In the silence that followed, the low, half-sobbing whine was heard at the door and then the long, questing sniff.

'There's no denyin' he thinks a hell of a lot of you,' Matt said.

The other glared at him in sudden wrath. 'Damn it all, man! I know my own mind and what's best!'

'I'm agreein' with you, only . . . '

'Only what?' Scott snapped out.

'Only . . . ' the dog-musher began softly, then changed his mind and betrayed a rising anger of his own. 'Well, you needn't get so all-fired het up about it. Judgin' by your actions one'd think you didn't know your own mind.'

Weedon Scott debated with himself for a while, and then said more gently: 'You are right, Matt. I don't know my own mind, and that's what's the trouble.'

'Why, it would be rank ridiculousness for me to take that dog along,' he broke out after another pause.

'I'm agreein' with you,' was Matt's answer, and again his employer was not quite satisfied with him.

'But how in the name of the great Sardanapolis he knows you're goin' is what gets me,' the dog-musher continued innocently.

'It's beyond me, Matt,' Scott answered, with a mournful shake of the head.

Then came the day when, through the open cabin door, White Fang saw the fatal grip on the floor and the love-master packing things into it. Also, there were comings and goings, and the erstwhile placid atmosphere of the cabin was vexed with strange perturbations and unrest. Here was indubitable evidence. White Fang had already scented it. He now reasoned it. His god was preparing for another flight. And since he had not taken him with him before, so, now, he could look to be left behind.

That night he lifted the long wolf-howl. As he had howled, in his puppy days, when he fled back from the Wild to the village to find it vanished and naught but a rubbish-heap to mark the site of Grey Beaver's tepee, so now he pointed his muzzle to the cold stars and told to them his woe.

Inside the cabin the two men had just gone to bed.

'He's gone off his food again,' Matt remarked from his bunk.

There was a grunt from Weedon Scott's bunk, and a stir of blankets.

'From the way he cut up the other time you went away, I wouldn't wonder this time but what he died.'

The blankets in the other bunk stirred irritably.

'Oh, shut up!' Scott cried out through the darkness. 'You nag worse than a woman.'

'I'm agreein' with you,' the dog-musher answered, and Weedon Scott was not quite sure whether or not the other had snickered.

The next day White Fang's anxiety and restlessness were even more pronounced. He dogged his master's heels whenever he left the cabin, and haunted the front stoop when he remained inside. Through the open door he could catch glimpses of the luggage on the floor. The grip had been joined by two large canvas bags and a box. Matt was rolling the master's blankets and fur robe inside a small tarpaulin. White Fang whined as he watched the operation.

Later on two Indians arrived. He watched them closely as they shouldered the luggage and were led off down the hill by Matt, who carried the bedding and the grip. But White Fang did not follow them. The master was still in the cabin. After a time, Matt returned. The master came to the door and called White Fang inside.

'You poor devil,' he said gently, rubbing White Fang's ears and tapping his spine. 'I'm hitting the long trail, old man, where you cannot follow. Now give me a growl— the last, good, good-bye growl.'

But White Fang refused to growl. Instead, and after a wistful, searching look, he snuggled in, burrowing his head out of sight between the master's arm and body.

'There she blows!' Matt cried. From the Yukon arose the hoarse bellowing of a river steamboat. 'You've got to cut it short. Be sure and lock the front door. I'll go out the back. Get a move on!'

The two doors slammed at the same moment, and Weedon Scott waited for Matt to come around to the front. From inside the door came a low whining and sobbing. Then there were long, deep-drawn sniffs.

'You must take good care of him, Matt,' Scott said, as they started down the hill. 'Write and let me know how he gets along.'

'Sure,' the dog-musher answered. 'But listen to that, will you!'

Both men stopped. White Fang was howling as dogs howl when their masters lie dead. He was voicing an utter woe, his cry bursting upward in great heart-breaking rushes, dying down into quavering misery, and bursting upward again with a rush upon rush of grief.

The *Aurora* was the first steamboat of the year for the Outside, and her decks were jammed with prosperous adventurers and broken gold seekers, all equally as mad to get to the Outside as they had been originally to get to the Inside. Near the gang-plank, Scott was shaking hands with Matt, who was preparing to go ashore. But Matt's hand went limp in the other's grasp as his gaze shot past and remained fixed on something behind him. Scott turned to see. Sitting on the deck several feet away and watching wistfully was White Fang.

The dog-musher swore softly, in awe-stricken accents. Scott could only look in wonder.

'Did you lock the front door?' Matt demanded. The other nodded, and asked, 'How about the back?'

'You just bet I did,' was the fervent reply.

White Fang flattened his ears ingratiatingly, but remained where he was, making no attempt to approach.

'I'll have to take 'm ashore with me.'

Matt made a couple of steps toward White Fang, but the latter slid away from him. The dog-musher made a rush of it, and White Fang dodged between the legs of a group of men. Ducking, turning, doubling, he slid about the deck, eluding the other's efforts to capture him.

But when the love-master spoke, White Fang came to him with prompt obedience.

'Won't come to the hand that's fed 'm all these months,' the dog-musher muttered resentfully. 'And you—you ain't never fed 'm after them first days of gettin' acquainted. I'm blamed if I can see how he works it out that you're the boss.'

Scott, who had been patting White Fang, suddenly bent closer and pointed out fresh-made cuts on his muzzle, and a gash between the eyes.

Matt bent over and passed his hand along White Fang's belly.

'We plump forgot the window. He's all cut an' gouged underneath. Must 'a' butted clean through it, b'gosh!'

But Weedon Scott was not listening. He was thinking rapidly. The *Aurora's* whistle hooted a final announcement of departure. Men were scurrying down the gang-plank to the shore. Matt loosened the bandana from his own neck and started to put it around White Fang's. Scott grasped the dog-musher's hand.

'Good-bye, Matt, old man. About the wolf—you needn't write. You see, I've . . . !'

'What!' the dog-musher exploded. 'You don't mean to say . . .?'

'The very thing I mean. Here's your bandana. I'll write to you about him.'

Matt paused halfway down the gang-plank.

'He'll never stand the climate!' he shouted back. 'Unless you clip 'm in warm weather!'

The gang-plank was hauled in, and the *Aurora* swung out from the bank. Weedon Scott waved a last good-bye. Then he turned and bent over White Fang, standing by his side.

'Now growl, damn you, growl,' he said, as he patted the responsive head and rubbed the flattening ears.

CHAPTER II
THE SOUTHLAND

White Fang landed from the steamer in San Francisco. He was appalled. Deep in him, below any reasoning process or act of consciousness, he had associated power with godhead. And never had the white men seemed such marvellous gods as now, when he trod the slimy pavement of San Francisco. The log cabins he had known were replaced by towering buildings. The streets were crowded with perils—waggons, carts, automobiles; great, straining horses pulling huge trucks; and monstrous cable and electric cars hooting and clanging through the midst, screeching their insistent menace after the manner of the lynxes he had known in the northern woods.

All this was the manifestation of power. Through it all, behind it all, was man, governing and controlling, expressing himself, as of old, by his mastery over matter. It was colossal, stunning. White Fang was awed. Fear sat upon him. As in his cubhood he had been made to feel his smallness and puniness on the day he first came in from the Wild to the village of Grey Beaver, so now, in his full-grown stature and pride of strength, he was made to feel small and puny. And there were so many gods! He was made dizzy by the swarming of them. The thunder of the streets smote upon his ears. He was bewildered by the tremendous and endless rush and movement of things. As never before, he felt his dependence on the love-master, close at whose heels he followed, no matter what happened never losing sight of him.

But White Fang was to have no more than a nightmare vision of the city—an experience that was like a bad dream, unreal and terrible, that haunted him for long after in his dreams. He was put into a baggage-car by the master, chained in a corner in the midst of heaped trunks and valises. Here a squat and brawny god held sway, with much noise, hurling trunks and boxes about, dragging them in through the door and tossing them into the piles, or flinging them out of the door, smashing and crashing, to other gods who awaited them.

And here, in this inferno of luggage, was White Fang deserted by the master. Or at least White Fang thought he was deserted, until he smelled out the master's canvas clothes-bags alongside of him, and proceeded to mount guard over them.

'Bout time you come,' growled the god of the car, an hour later, when Weedon Scott appeared at the door. 'That dog of yourn won't let me lay a finger on your stuff.'

White Fang emerged from the car. He was astonished. The nightmare city was gone. The car had been to him no more than a room in a house, and when he had entered it the city had been all around him. In the interval the city had disappeared. The roar of it no longer dinned upon his ears. Before him was smiling country, streaming with sunshine, lazy with quietude. But he had little time to marvel at the transformation. He accepted it as he accepted all the unaccountable doings and manifestations of the gods. It was their way.

There was a carriage waiting. A man and a woman approached the master. The woman's arms went out and clutched the master around the neck—a hostile act! The next moment Weedon Scott had torn loose from the embrace and closed with White Fang, who had become a snarling, raging demon.

'It's all right, mother,' Scott was saying as he kept tight hold of White Fang and placated him. 'He thought you were going to injure me, and he wouldn't stand for it. It's all right. It's all right. He'll learn soon enough.'

'And in the meantime I may be permitted to love my son when his dog is not around,' she laughed, though she was pale and weak from the fright.

She looked at White Fang, who snarled and bristled and glared malevolently.

'He'll have to learn, and he shall, without postponement,' Scott said.

He spoke softly to White Fang until he had quieted him, then his voice became firm.

'Down, sir! Down with you!'

This had been one of the things taught him by the master, and White Fang obeyed, though he lay down reluctantly and sullenly.

'Now, mother.'

Scott opened his arms to her, but kept his eyes on White Fang.

'Down!' he warned. 'Down!'

White Fang, bristling silently, half-crouching as he rose, sank back and watched the hostile act repeated. But no harm came of it, nor of the embrace from the strange man-god that followed. Then the clothes-bags were taken into the carriage, the strange gods and the love-master followed, and White Fang pursued, now running vigilantly behind, now bristling up to the running horses and warning them that he was there to see that no harm befell the god they dragged so swiftly across the earth.

At the end of fifteen minutes, the carriage swung in through a stone gateway and on between a double row of arched and interlacing walnut trees. On either side stretched lawns, their broad sweep broken here and there by great sturdy-limbed oaks. In the near distance, in contrast with the young-green of the tended grass, sunburnt hay-fields showed tan and gold; while beyond were the tawny hills and upland pastures. From the head of the lawn, on the first soft swell from the valley-level, looked down the deep-porched, many-windowed house.

Little opportunity was given White Fang to see all this. Hardly had the carriage entered the grounds, when he was set upon by a sheep-dog, bright-eyed, sharp-muzzled, righteously indignant and angry. It was between him and the master, cutting him off. White Fang snarled no warning, but his hair bristled as he made his silent and deadly rush. This rush was never completed. He halted with awkward abruptness, with stiff fore-legs bracing himself against his momentum, almost sitting down on his haunches, so desirous was he of avoiding contact with the dog he was in the act of attacking. It was a female, and the law of his kind thrust a barrier between. For him to attack her would require nothing less than a violation of his instinct.

But with the sheep-dog it was otherwise. Being a female, she possessed no such instinct. On the other hand, being a sheep-dog, her instinctive fear of the Wild, and especially of the wolf, was unusually keen. White Fang was to her a wolf, the hereditary marauder who had preyed upon her flocks from the time sheep were first herded and guarded by some dim ancestor of hers. And so, as he abandoned his rush at her and braced himself to avoid the contact, she sprang upon him. He snarled involuntarily as he felt her teeth in his shoulder, but beyond this made no offer to hurt her. He backed away, stiff-legged with self-consciousness, and tried to go around her. He dodged this way and that, and curved and turned, but to no purpose. She remained always between him and the way he wanted to go.

'Here, Collie!' called the strange man in the carriage.

Weedon Scott laughed.

'Never mind, father. It is good discipline. White Fang will have to learn many things, and it's just as well that he begins now. He'll adjust himself all right.'

The carriage drove on, and still Collie blocked White Fang's way. He tried to outrun her by leaving the drive and circling across the lawn but she ran on the inner and smaller circle, and was always there, facing him with her two rows of gleaming teeth. Back he circled, across the drive to the other lawn, and again she headed him off.

The carriage was bearing the master away. White Fang caught glimpses of it disappearing amongst the trees. The situation was desperate. He essayed another circle. She followed, running swiftly. And then, suddenly, he turned upon her. It was his old fighting trick. Shoulder to shoulder, he struck her squarely. Not only was she overthrown. So fast had she been running that she rolled along, now on her back, now on her side, as she struggled to stop, clawing gravel with her feet and crying shrilly her hurt pride and indignation.

White Fang did not wait. The way was clear, and that was all he had wanted. She took after him, never ceasing her outcry. It was the straightaway now, and when it came to real running, White Fang could teach her things. She ran frantically, hysterically, straining to the utmost, advertising the effort she was making with every leap: and all the time White Fang slid smoothly away from her silently, without effort, gliding like a ghost over the ground.

As he rounded the house to the *porte-cochère*, he came upon the carriage. It had stopped, and the master was alighting. At this moment, still running at top speed, White Fang became suddenly aware of an attack from the side. It was a deer-hound rushing upon him. White Fang tried to face it. But he was going too fast, and the hound was too close. It struck him on the side; and such was his forward momentum and the unexpectedness of it, White Fang was hurled to the ground and rolled clear over. He came out of the tangle a spectacle of malignancy, ears flattened back, lips writhing, nose wrinkling, his teeth clipping together as the fangs barely missed the hound's soft throat.

The master was running up, but was too far away; and it was Collie that saved the hound's life. Before White Fang could spring in and deliver the fatal stroke, and just as he was in the act of springing in, Collie arrived. She had been out-manoeuvred and out-run, to say nothing of her having been unceremoniously tumbled in the gravel, and her arrival was like that of a tornado—made up of offended dignity, justifiable wrath, and instinctive hatred for this marauder from the Wild. She struck White Fang at right angles in the midst of his spring, and again he was knocked off his feet and rolled over.

The next moment the master arrived, and with one hand held White Fang, while the father called off the dogs.

'I say, this is a pretty warm reception for a poor lone wolf from the Arctic,' the master said, while White Fang calmed down under his caressing hand. 'In all his life he's only been known once to go off his feet, and here he's been rolled twice in thirty seconds.'

The carriage had driven away, and other strange gods had appeared from out the house. Some of these stood respectfully at a distance; but two of them, women, perpetrated the hostile act of clutching the master around the neck. White Fang, however, was beginning to tolerate this act. No harm seemed to come of it, while the noises the gods made were certainly not threatening. These gods also made overtures to White Fang, but he warned them off with a snarl, and the master did likewise with word of mouth. At such times White Fang leaned in close against the master's legs and received reassuring pats on the head.

The hound, under the command, 'Dick! Lie down, sir!' had gone up the steps and lain down to one side of the porch, still growling and keeping a sullen watch on the intruder. Collie had been taken in charge by one of the woman-gods, who held arms around her neck and petted and caressed her; but Collie was very much perplexed and worried, whining and restless, outraged by the permitted presence of this wolf and confident that the gods were making a mistake.

All the gods started up the steps to enter the house. White Fang followed closely at the master's heels. Dick, on the porch, growled, and White Fang, on the steps, bristled and growled back.

'Take Collie inside and leave the two of them to fight it out,' suggested Scott's father. 'After that they'll be friends.'

'Then White Fang, to show his friendship, will have to be chief mourner at the funeral,' laughed the master.

The elder Scott looked incredulously, first at White Fang, then at Dick, and finally at his son.

'You mean . . .?'

Weedon nodded his head. 'I mean just that. You'd have a dead Dick inside one minute—two minutes at the farthest.'

He turned to White Fang. 'Come on, you wolf. It's you that'll have to come inside.'

White Fang walked stiff-legged up the steps and across the porch, with tail rigidly erect, keeping his eyes on Dick to guard against a flank attack, and at the same time prepared for whatever fierce manifestation of the unknown that might pounce out upon him from the interior of the house. But no thing of fear pounced out, and when he had gained the inside he scouted carefully around, looking at it and finding it not. Then he lay down with a contented grunt at the master's feet, observing all that went on, ever ready to spring to his feet and fight for life with the terrors he felt must lurk under the trap-roof of the dwelling.

CHAPTER III
THE GOD'S DOMAIN

Not only was White Fang adaptable by nature, but he had travelled much, and knew the meaning and necessity of adjustment. Here, in Sierra Vista, which was the name of Judge Scott's place, White Fang quickly began to make himself at home. He had no further serious trouble with the dogs. They knew more about the ways of the Southland gods than did he, and in their eyes he had qualified when he accompanied the gods inside the house. Wolf that he was, and unprecedented as it was, the gods had sanctioned his presence, and they, the dogs of the gods, could only recognise this sanction.

Dick, perforce, had to go through a few stiff formalities at first, after which he calmly accepted White Fang as an addition to the premises. Had Dick had his way, they would have been good friends. All but White Fang was averse to friendship. All he asked of other dogs was to be let alone. His whole life he had kept aloof from his kind, and he still desired to keep aloof. Dick's overtures bothered him, so he snarled Dick away. In the north he had learned the lesson that he must let the master's dogs alone, and he did not forget that lesson now. But he insisted on his own privacy and self-seclusion, and so thoroughly ignored Dick that that good-natured creature finally gave him up and scarcely took as much interest in him as in the hitching-post near the stable.

Not so with Collie. While she accepted him because it was the mandate of the gods, that was no reason that she should leave him in peace. Woven into her being was the memory of countless crimes he and his had perpetrated against her ancestry. Not in a day nor a generation were the ravaged sheepfolds to be forgotten. All this was a spur to her, pricking her to retaliation. She could not fly in the face of the gods who permitted him, but that did not prevent her from making life miserable for him in petty ways. A feud, ages old, was between them, and she, for one, would see to it that he was reminded.

So Collie took advantage of her sex to pick upon White Fang and maltreat him. His instinct would not permit him to attack her, while her persistence would not permit him to ignore her. When she rushed at him he turned his fur-protected shoulder to her sharp teeth and walked away stiff-legged and stately. When she forced him too hard, he was compelled to go about in a circle, his shoulder presented to her, his head turned from her, and on his face and in his eyes a patient and bored expression. Sometimes, however, a nip on his hind-quarters hastened his retreat and made it anything but stately. But as a rule he managed to maintain a dignity that was almost solemnity. He ignored her existence whenever it was possible, and made it a point to keep out of her way. When he saw or heard her coming, he got up and walked off.

There was much in other matters for White Fang to learn. Life in the Northland was simplicity itself when compared with the complicated affairs of Sierra Vista. First of all, he had to learn the family of the master. In a way he was prepared to do this. As Mit-sah and Kloo-kooch had belonged to Grey Beaver, sharing his food, his fire, and his blankets, so now, at Sierra Vista, belonged to the love-master all the denizens of the house.

But in this matter there was a difference, and many differences. Sierra Vista was a far vaster affair than the tepee of Grey Beaver. There were many persons to be considered. There was Judge Scott, and there was his wife. There were the master's two sisters, Beth and Mary. There was his wife, Alice, and then there were his children, Weedon and Maud, toddlers of four and six. There was no way for anybody to tell him about all these people, and of blood-ties and relationship he knew nothing whatever and never would be capable of knowing. Yet he quickly worked it out that all of them belonged to the master. Then, by observation, whenever opportunity offered, by study of action, speech, and the very intonations of the voice, he slowly learned the intimacy and the degree of favour they enjoyed with the master. And by this ascertained standard, White Fang treated them accordingly. What was of value to the master he valued; what was dear to the master was to be cherished by White Fang and guarded carefully.

Thus it was with the two children. All his life he had disliked children. He hated and feared their hands. The lessons were not tender that he had learned of their tyranny and cruelty in the days of the Indian villages. When Weedon and Maud had first approached him, he growled warningly and looked malignant. A cuff from the master and a sharp word had then compelled him to permit their caresses, though he growled and growled under their tiny hands, and in the growl there was no crooning note. Later, he observed that the boy and girl were of great value in the master's eyes. Then it was that no cuff nor sharp word was necessary before they could pat him.

Yet White Fang was never effusively affectionate. He yielded to the master's children with an ill but honest grace, and endured their fooling as one would endure a painful operation. When he could no longer endure, he would get up and stalk determinedly away from them. But after a time, he grew even to like the children. Still he was not demonstrative. He would not go up to them. On the other hand, instead of walking away at sight of them, he waited for them to come to him. And still later, it was noticed that a pleased light came into his eyes when he saw them approaching, and that he looked after them with an appearance of curious regret when they left him for other amusements.

All this was a matter of development, and took time. Next in his regard, after the children, was Judge Scott. There were two reasons, possibly, for this. First, he was evidently a valuable possession of the master's, and next, he was undemonstrative. White Fang liked to lie at his feet on the wide porch when he read the newspaper, from time to time favouring White Fang with a look or a word—untroublesome tokens that he recognised White Fang's presence and existence. But this was only when the master was not around. When the master appeared, all other beings ceased to exist so far as White Fang was concerned.

White Fang allowed all the members of the family to pet him and make much of him; but he never gave to them what he gave to the master. No caress of theirs could put the love-croon into his throat, and, try as they would, they could never persuade him into snuggling against them. This expression of abandon and surrender, of absolute trust, he reserved for the master alone. In fact, he never regarded the members of the family in any other light than possessions of the love-master.

Also White Fang had early come to differentiate between the family and the servants of the household. The latter were afraid of him, while he merely refrained from attacking them. This because he considered that they were likewise possessions of the master. Between White Fang and them existed a neutrality and no more. They cooked for the master and washed the dishes and did other things just as Matt had done up in the Klondike. They were, in short, appurtenances of the household.

Outside the household there was even more for White Fang to learn. The master's domain was wide and complex, yet it had its metes and bounds. The land itself ceased at the county road. Outside was the common domain of all gods—the roads and streets. Then inside other fences were the particular domains of other gods. A myriad laws governed all these things and determined conduct; yet he did not know the speech of the gods, nor was there any way for him to learn save by experience. He obeyed his natural impulses until they ran him counter to some law. When this had been done a few times, he learned the law and after that observed it.

But most potent in his education was the cuff of the master's hand, the censure of the master's voice. Because of White Fang's very great love, a cuff from the master hurt him far more than any beating Grey Beaver or Beauty Smith had ever given him. They had hurt only the flesh of him; beneath the flesh the spirit had still raged, splendid and invincible. But with the master the cuff was always too light to hurt the flesh. Yet it went deeper. It was an expression of the master's disapproval, and White Fang's spirit wilted under it.

In point of fact, the cuff was rarely administered. The master's voice was sufficient. By it White Fang knew whether he did right or not. By it he trimmed his conduct and adjusted his actions. It was the compass by which he steered and learned to chart the manners of a new land and life.

In the Northland, the only domesticated animal was the dog. All other animals lived in the Wild, and were, when not too formidable, lawful spoil for any dog. All his days White Fang had foraged among the live things for food. It did not enter his head that in the Southland it was otherwise. But this he was to learn early in his residence in Santa Clara Valley. Sauntering around the corner of the house in the early morning, he came upon a chicken that had escaped from the chicken-yard. White Fang's natural impulse was to eat it. A couple of bounds, a flash of teeth and a frightened squawk, and he had scooped in the adventurous fowl. It was farm-bred and fat and tender; and White Fang licked his chops and decided that such fare was good.

Later in the day, he chanced upon another stray chicken near the stables. One of the grooms ran to the rescue. He did not know White Fang's breed, so for weapon he took a light buggy-whip. At the first cut of the whip, White Fang left the chicken for the man. A club might have stopped White Fang, but not a whip. Silently, without flinching, he took a second cut in his forward rush, and as he leaped for the throat the groom cried out, 'My God!' and staggered backward. He dropped the whip and shielded his throat with his arms. In consequence, his forearm was ripped open to the bone.

The man was badly frightened. It was not so much White Fang's ferocity as it was his silence that unnerved the groom. Still protecting his throat and face with his torn and bleeding arm, he tried to retreat to the barn. And it would have gone hard with him had not Collie appeared on the scene. As she had saved Dick's life, she now saved the groom's. She rushed upon White Fang in frenzied wrath. She had been right. She had known better than the blundering gods. All her suspicions were justified. Here was the ancient marauder up to his old tricks again.

The groom escaped into the stables, and White Fang backed away before Collie's wicked teeth, or presented his shoulder to them and circled round and round. But Collie did not give over, as was her wont, after a decent interval of chastisement. On the contrary, she grew more excited and angry every moment, until, in the end, White Fang flung dignity to the winds and frankly fled away from her across the fields.

'He'll learn to leave chickens alone,' the master said. 'But I can't give him the lesson until I catch him in the act.'

Two nights later came the act, but on a more generous scale than the master had anticipated. White Fang had observed closely the chicken-yards and the habits of the chickens. In the night-time, after they had gone to roost, he climbed to the top of a pile of newly hauled lumber. From there he gained the roof of a chicken-house, passed over the ridgepole and dropped to the ground inside. A moment later he was inside the house, and the slaughter began.

In the morning, when the master came out on to the porch, fifty white Leghorn hens, laid out in a row by the groom, greeted his eyes. He whistled to himself, softly, first with surprise, and then, at the end, with admiration. His eyes were likewise greeted by White Fang, but about the latter there were no signs of shame nor guilt. He carried himself with pride, as though, forsooth, he had achieved a deed praiseworthy and meritorious. There was about him no consciousness of sin. The master's lips tightened as he faced the disagreeable task. Then he talked harshly to the unwitting culprit, and in his voice there was nothing but godlike wrath. Also, he held White Fang's nose down to the slain hens, and at the same time cuffed him soundly.

White Fang never raided a chicken-roost again. It was against the law, and he had learned it. Then the master took him into the chicken-yards. White Fang's natural impulse, when he saw the live food fluttering about him and under his very nose, was to spring upon it. He obeyed the impulse, but was checked by the master's voice. They continued in the yards for half an hour. Time and again the impulse surged over White Fang, and each time, as he yielded to it, he was checked by the master's voice. Thus it was he learned the law, and ere he left the domain of the chickens, he had learned to ignore their existence.

'You can never cure a chicken-killer.' Judge Scott shook his head sadly at luncheon table, when his son narrated the lesson he had given White Fang. 'Once they've got the habit and the taste of blood . . .' Again he shook his head sadly.

But Weedon Scott did not agree with his father. 'I'll tell you what I'll do,' he challenged finally. 'I'll lock White Fang in with the chickens all afternoon.'

'But think of the chickens,' objected the judge.

'And furthermore,' the son went on, 'for every chicken he kills, I'll pay you one dollar gold coin of the realm.'

'But you should penalise father, too,' interpose Beth.

Her sister seconded her, and a chorus of approval arose from around the table. Judge Scott nodded his head in agreement.

'All right.' Weedon Scott pondered for a moment. 'And if, at the end of the afternoon White Fang hasn't harmed a chicken, for every ten minutes of the time he has spent in the yard, you will have to say to him, gravely and with deliberation, just as if you were sitting on the bench and solemnly passing judgment, 'White Fang, you are smarter than I thought.'

From hidden points of vantage the family watched the performance. But it was a fizzle. Locked in the yard and there deserted by the master, White Fang lay down and went to sleep. Once he got up and walked over to the trough for a drink of water. The chickens he calmly ignored. So far as he was concerned they did not exist. At four o'clock he executed a running jump, gained the roof of the chicken-house and leaped to the ground outside, whence he sauntered gravely to the house. He had learned the law. And on the porch, before the delighted family, Judge Scott, face to face with White Fang, said slowly and solemnly, sixteen times, 'White Fang, you are smarter than I thought.'

But it was the multiplicity of laws that befuddled White Fang and often brought him into disgrace. He had to learn that he must not touch the chickens that belonged to other gods. Then there were cats, and rabbits, and turkeys; all these he must let alone. In fact, when he had but partly learned the law, his impression was that he must leave all live things alone. Out in the back-pasture, a quail could flutter up under his nose unharmed. All tense and trembling with eagerness and desire, he mastered his instinct and stood still. He was obeying the will of the gods.

And then, one day, again out in the back-pasture, he saw Dick start a jackrabbit and run it. The master himself was looking on and did not interfere. Nay, he encouraged White Fang to join in the chase. And thus he learned that there was no taboo on jack-rabbits. In the end he worked out the complete law. Between him and all domestic animals there must be no hostilities. If not amity, at least neutrality must obtain. But the other animals—the squirrels, and quail, and cottontails, were creatures of the Wild who had never yielded allegiance to man. They were the lawful prey of any dog. It was only the tame that the gods protected, and between the tame deadly strife was not permitted. The gods held the power of life and death over their subjects, and the gods were jealous of their power.

Life was complex in the Santa Clara Valley after the simplicities of the Northland. And the chief thing demanded by these intricacies of civilisation was control, restraint—a poise of self that was as delicate as the fluttering of gossamer wings and at the same time as rigid as steel. Life had a thousand faces, and White Fang found he must meet them all—thus, when he went to town, in to San Jose, running behind the carriage or loafing about the streets when the carriage stopped. Life flowed past him, deep and wide and varied, continually impinging upon his senses, demanding of him instant and endless adjustments and correspondences, and compelling him, almost always, to suppress his natural impulses.

There were butcher-shops where meat hung within reach. This meat he must not touch. There were cats at the houses the master visited that must be let alone. And there were dogs everywhere that snarled at him and that he must not attack. And then, on the crowded sidewalks there were persons innumerable whose attention he attracted. They would stop and look at him, point him out to one another, examine him, talk of him, and, worst of all, pat him. And these perilous contacts from all these strange hands he must endure. Yet this endurance he achieved. Furthermore, he got over being awkward and self-conscious. In a lofty way he received the attentions of the multitudes of strange gods. With condescension he accepted their condescension. On the other hand, there was something about him that prevented great familiarity. They patted him on the head and passed on, contented and pleased with their own daring.

But it was not all easy for White Fang. Running behind the carriage in the outskirts of San Jose, he encountered certain small boys who made a practice of flinging stones at him. Yet he knew that it was not permitted him to pursue and drag them down. Here he was compelled to violate his instinct of self-preservation, and violate it he did, for he was becoming tame and qualifying himself for civilisation.

Nevertheless, White Fang was not quite satisfied with the arrangement. He had no abstract ideas about justice and fair play. But there is a certain sense of equity that resides in life, and it was this sense in him that resented the unfairness of his being permitted no defence against the stone-throwers. He forgot that in the covenant entered into between him and the gods they were pledged to care for him and defend him. But one day the master sprang from the carriage, whip in hand, and gave the stone-throwers a thrashing. After that they threw stones no more, and White Fang understood and was satisfied.

One other experience of similar nature was his. On the way to town, hanging around the saloon at the cross-roads, were three dogs that made a practice of rushing out upon him when he went by. Knowing his deadly method of fighting, the master had never ceased impressing upon White Fang the law that he must not fight. As a result, having learned the lesson well, White Fang was hard put whenever he passed the cross-roads saloon. After the first rush, each time, his snarl kept the three dogs at a distance but they trailed along behind, yelping and bickering and insulting him. This endured for some time. The men at the saloon even urged the dogs on to attack White Fang. One day they openly sicked the dogs on him. The master stopped the carriage.

'Go to it,' he said to White Fang.

But White Fang could not believe. He looked at the master, and he looked at the dogs. Then he looked back eagerly and questioningly at the master.

The master nodded his head. 'Go to them, old fellow. Eat them up.'

White Fang no longer hesitated. He turned and leaped silently among his enemies. All three faced him. There was a great snarling and growling, a clashing of teeth and a flurry of bodies. The dust of the road arose in a cloud and screened the battle. But at the end of several minutes two dogs were struggling in the dirt and the third was in full flight. He leaped a ditch, went through a rail fence, and fled across a field. White Fang followed, sliding over the ground in wolf fashion and with wolf speed, swiftly and without noise, and in the centre of the field he dragged down and slew the dog.

With this triple killing his main troubles with dogs ceased. The word went up and down the valley, and men saw to it that their dogs did not molest the Fighting Wolf.

CHAPTER IV
THE CALL OF KIND

The months came and went. There was plenty of food and no work in the Southland, and White Fang lived fat and prosperous and happy. Not alone was he in the geographical Southland, for he was in the Southland of life. Human kindness was like a sun shining upon him, and he flourished like a flower planted in good soil.

And yet he remained somehow different from other dogs. He knew the law even better than did the dogs that had known no other life, and he observed the law more punctiliously; but still there was about him a suggestion of lurking ferocity, as though the Wild still lingered in him and the wolf in him merely slept.

He never chummed with other dogs. Lonely he had lived, so far as his kind was concerned, and lonely he would continue to live. In his puppyhood, under the persecution of Lip-lip and the puppy-pack, and in his fighting days with Beauty Smith, he had acquired a fixed aversion for dogs. The natural course of his life had been diverted, and, recoiling from his kind, he had clung to the human.

Besides, all Southland dogs looked upon him with suspicion. He aroused in them their instinctive fear of the Wild, and they greeted him always with snarl and growl and belligerent hatred. He, on the other hand, learned that it was not necessary to use his teeth upon them. His naked fangs and writhing lips were uniformly efficacious, rarely failing to send a bellowing on-rushing dog back on its haunches.

But there was one trial in White Fang's life—Collie. She never gave him a moment's peace. She was not so amenable to the law as he. She defied all efforts of the master to make her become friends with White Fang. Ever in his ears was sounding her sharp and nervous snarl. She had never forgiven him the chicken-killing episode, and persistently held to the belief that his intentions were bad. She found him guilty before the act, and treated him accordingly. She became a pest to him, like a policeman following him around the stable and the hounds, and, if he even so much as glanced curiously at a pigeon or chicken, bursting into an outcry of indignation and wrath. His favourite way of ignoring her was to lie down, with his head on his fore-paws, and pretend sleep. This always dumfounded and silenced her.

With the exception of Collie, all things went well with White Fang. He had learned control and poise, and he knew the law. He achieved a staidness, and calmness, and philosophic tolerance. He no longer lived in a hostile environment. Danger and hurt and death did not lurk everywhere about him. In time, the unknown, as a thing of terror and menace ever impending, faded away. Life was soft and easy. It flowed along smoothly, and neither fear nor foe lurked by the way.

He missed the snow without being aware of it. 'An unduly long summer,' would have been his thought had he thought about it; as it was, he merely missed the snow in a vague, subconscious way. In the same fashion, especially in the heat of summer when he suffered from the sun, he experienced faint longings for the Northland. Their only effect upon him, however, was to make him uneasy and restless without his knowing what was the matter.

White Fang had never been very demonstrative. Beyond his snuggling and the throwing of a crooning note into his love-growl, he had no way of expressing his love. Yet it was given him to discover a third way. He had always been susceptible to the laughter of the gods. Laughter had affected him with madness, made him frantic with rage. But he did not have it in him to be angry with the love-master, and when that god elected to laugh at him in a good-natured, bantering way, he was nonplussed. He could feel the pricking and stinging of the old anger as it strove to rise up in him, but it strove against love. He could not be angry; yet he had to do something. At first he was dignified, and the master laughed the harder. Then he tried to be more dignified, and the master laughed harder than before. In the end, the master laughed him out of his dignity. His jaws slightly parted, his lips lifted a little, and a quizzical expression that was more love than humour came into his eyes. He had learned to laugh.

Likewise he learned to romp with the master, to be tumbled down and rolled over, and be the victim of innumerable rough tricks. In return he feigned anger, bristling and growling ferociously, and clipping his teeth together in snaps that had all the seeming of deadly intention. But he never forgot himself. Those snaps were always delivered on the empty air. At the end of such a romp, when blow and cuff and snap and snarl were last and furious, they would break off suddenly and stand several feet apart, glaring at each other. And then, just as suddenly, like the sun rising on a stormy sea, they would begin to laugh. This would always culminate with the master's arms going around White Fang's neck and shoulders while the latter crooned and growled his love-song.

But nobody else ever romped with White Fang. He did not permit it. He stood on his dignity, and when they attempted it, his warning snarl and bristling mane were anything but playful. That he allowed the master these liberties was no reason that he should be a common dog, loving here and loving there, everybody's property for a romp and good time. He loved with single heart and refused to cheapen himself or his love.

The master went out on horseback a great deal, and to accompany him was one of White Fang's chief duties in life. In the Northland he had evidenced his fealty by toiling in the harness; but there were no sleds in the Southland, nor did dogs pack burdens on their backs. So he rendered fealty in the new way, by running with the master's horse. The longest day never played White Fang out. His was the gait of the wolf, smooth, tireless and effortless, and at the end of fifty miles he would come in jauntily ahead of the horse.

It was in connection with the riding, that White Fang achieved one other mode of expression—remarkable in that he did it but twice in all his life. The first time occurred when the master was trying to teach a spirited thoroughbred the method of opening and closing gates without the rider's dismounting. Time and again and many times he ranged the horse up to the gate in the effort to close it and each time the horse became frightened and backed and plunged away. It grew more nervous and excited every moment. When it reared, the master put the spurs to it and made it drop its fore-legs back to earth, whereupon it would begin kicking with its hind-legs. White Fang watched the performance with increasing anxiety until he could contain himself no longer, when he sprang in front of the horse and barked savagely and warningly.

Though he often tried to bark thereafter, and the master encouraged him, he succeeded only once, and then it was not in the master's presence. A scamper across the pasture, a jackrabbit rising suddenly under the horse's feet, a violent sheer, a stumble, a fall to earth, and a broken leg for the master, was the cause of it. White Fang sprang in a rage at the throat of the offending horse, but was checked by the master's voice.

'Home! Go home!' the master commanded when he had ascertained his injury.

White Fang was disinclined to desert him. The master thought of writing a note, but searched his pockets vainly for pencil and paper. Again he commanded White Fang to go home.

The latter regarded him wistfully, started away, then returned and whined softly. The master talked to him gently but seriously, and he cocked his ears, and listened with painful intentness.

'That's all right, old fellow, you just run along home,' ran the talk. 'Go on home and tell them what's happened to me. Home with you, you wolf. Get along home!'

White Fang knew the meaning of 'home,' and though he did not understand the remainder of the master's language, he knew it was his will that he should go home. He turned and trotted reluctantly away. Then he stopped, undecided, and looked back over his shoulder.

'Go home!' came the sharp command, and this time he obeyed.

The family was on the porch, taking the cool of the afternoon, when White Fang arrived. He came in among them, panting, covered with dust.

'Weedon's back,' Weedon's mother announced.

The children welcomed White Fang with glad cries and ran to meet him. He avoided them and passed down the porch, but they cornered him against a rocking-chair and the railing. He growled and tried to push by them. Their mother looked apprehensively in their direction.

'I confess, he makes me nervous around the children,' she said. 'I have a dread that he will turn upon them unexpectedly some day.'

Growling savagely, White Fang sprang out of the corner, overturning the boy and the girl. The mother called them to her and comforted them, telling them not to bother White Fang.

'A wolf is a wolf!' commented Judge Scott. 'There is no trusting one.'

'But he is not all wolf,' interposed Beth, standing for her brother in his absence.

'You have only Weedon's opinion for that,' rejoined the judge. 'He merely surmises that there is some strain of dog in White Fang; but as he will tell you himself, he knows nothing about it. As for his appearance—'

He did not finish his sentence. White Fang stood before him, growling fiercely.

'Go away! Lie down, sir!' Judge Scott commanded.

White Fang turned to the love-master's wife. She screamed with fright as he seized her dress in his teeth and dragged on it till the frail fabric tore away. By this time he had become the centre of interest.

He had ceased from his growling and stood, head up, looking into their faces. His throat worked spasmodically, but made no sound, while he struggled with all his body, convulsed with the effort to rid himself of the incommunicable something that strained for utterance.

'I hope he is not going mad,' said Weedon's mother. 'I told Weedon that I was afraid the warm climate would not agree with an Arctic animal.'

'He's trying to speak, I do believe,' Beth announced.

At this moment speech came to White Fang, rushing up in a great burst of barking.

'Something has happened to Weedon,' his wife said decisively.

They were all on their feet now, and White Fang ran down the steps, looking back for them to follow. For the second and last time in his life he had barked and made himself understood.

After this event he found a warmer place in the hearts of the Sierra Vista people, and even the groom whose arm he had slashed admitted that he was a wise dog even if he was a wolf. Judge Scott still held to the same opinion, and proved it to everybody's dissatisfaction by measurements and descriptions taken from the encyclopaedia and various works on natural history.

The days came and went, streaming their unbroken sunshine over the Santa Clara Valley. But as they grew shorter and White Fang's second winter in the Southland came on, he made a strange discovery. Collie's teeth were no longer sharp. There was a playfulness about her nips and a gentleness that prevented them from really hurting him. He forgot that she had made life a burden to him, and when she disported herself around him he responded solemnly, striving to be playful and becoming no more than ridiculous.

One day she led him off on a long chase through the back-pasture land into the woods. It was the afternoon that the master was to ride, and White Fang knew it. The horse stood saddled and waiting at the door. White Fang hesitated. But there was that in him deeper than all the law he had learned, than the customs that had moulded him, than his love for the master, than the very will to live of himself; and when, in the moment of his indecision, Collie nipped him and scampered off, he turned and followed after. The master rode alone that day; and in the woods, side by side, White Fang ran with Collie, as his mother, Kiche, and old One Eye had run long years before in the silent Northland forest.

CHAPTER V
THE SLEEPING WOLF

It was about this time that the newspapers were full of the daring escape of a convict from San Quentin prison. He was a ferocious man. He had been ill-made in the making. He had not been born right, and he had not been helped any by the moulding he had received at the hands of society. The hands of society are harsh, and this man was a striking sample of its handiwork. He was a beast—a human beast, it is true, but nevertheless so terrible a beast that he can best be characterised as carnivorous.

In San Quentin prison he had proved incorrigible. Punishment failed to break his spirit. He could die dumb-mad and fighting to the last, but he could not live and be beaten. The more fiercely he fought, the more harshly society handled him, and the only effect of harshness was to make him fiercer. Strait-jackets, starvation, and beatings and clubbings were the wrong treatment for Jim Hall; but it was the treatment he received. It was the treatment he had received from the time he was a little pulpy boy in a San Francisco slum—soft clay in the hands of society and ready to be formed into something.

It was during Jim Hall's third term in prison that he encountered a guard that was almost as great a beast as he. The guard treated him unfairly, lied about him to the warden, lost his credits, persecuted him. The difference between them was that the guard carried a bunch of keys and a revolver. Jim Hall had only his naked hands and his teeth. But he sprang upon the guard one day and used his teeth on the other's throat just like any jungle animal.

After this, Jim Hall went to live in the incorrigible cell. He lived there three years. The cell was of iron, the floor, the walls, the roof. He never left this cell. He never saw the sky nor the sunshine. Day was a twilight and night was a black silence. He was in an iron tomb, buried alive. He saw no human face, spoke to no human thing. When his food was shoved in to him, he growled like a wild animal. He hated all things. For days and nights he bellowed his rage at the universe. For weeks and months he never made a sound, in the black silence eating his very soul. He was a man and a monstrosity, as fearful a thing of fear as ever gibbered in the visions of a maddened brain.

And then, one night, he escaped. The warders said it was impossible, but nevertheless the cell was empty, and half in half out of it lay the body of a dead guard. Two other dead guards marked his trail through the prison to the outer walls, and he had killed with his hands to avoid noise.

He was armed with the weapons of the slain guards—a live arsenal that fled through the hills pursued by the organised might of society. A heavy price of gold was upon his head. Avaricious farmers hunted him with shot-guns. His blood might pay off a mortgage or send a son to college. Public-spirited citizens took down their rifles and went out after him. A pack of bloodhounds followed the way of his bleeding feet. And the sleuth-hounds of the law, the paid fighting animals of society, with telephone, and telegraph, and special train, clung to his trail night and day.

Sometimes they came upon him, and men faced him like heroes, or stampeded through barbed-wire fences to the delight of the commonwealth reading the account at the breakfast table. It was after such encounters that the dead and wounded were carted back to the towns, and their places filled by men eager for the man-hunt.

And then Jim Hall disappeared. The bloodhounds vainly quested on the lost trail. Inoffensive ranchers in remote valleys were held up by armed men and compelled to identify themselves. While the remains of Jim Hall were discovered on a dozen mountain-sides by greedy claimants for blood-money.

In the meantime the newspapers were read at Sierra Vista, not so much with interest as with anxiety. The women were afraid. Judge Scott pooh-poohed and laughed, but not with reason, for it was in his last days on the bench that Jim Hall had stood before him and received sentence. And in open court-room, before all men, Jim Hall had proclaimed that the day would come when he would wreak vengeance on the Judge that sentenced him.

For once, Jim Hall was right. He was innocent of the crime for which he was sentenced. It was a case, in the parlance of thieves and police, of 'rail-roading.' Jim Hall was being 'rail-roaded' to prison for a crime he had not committed. Because of the two prior convictions against him, Judge Scott imposed upon him a sentence of fifty years.

Judge Scott did not know all things, and he did not know that he was party to a police conspiracy, that the evidence was hatched and perjured, that Jim Hall was guiltless of the crime charged. And Jim Hall, on the other hand, did not know that Judge Scott was merely ignorant. Jim Hall believed that the judge knew all about it and was hand in glove with the police in the perpetration of the monstrous injustice. So it was, when the doom of fifty years of living death was uttered by Judge Scott, that Jim Hall, hating all things in the society that misused him, rose up and raged in the court-room until dragged down by half a dozen of his blue-coated enemies. To him, Judge Scott was the keystone in the arch of injustice, and upon Judge Scott he emptied the vials of his wrath and hurled the threats of his revenge yet to come. Then Jim Hall went to his living death . . . and escaped.

Of all this White Fang knew nothing. But between him and Alice, the master's wife, there existed a secret. Each night, after Sierra Vista had gone to bed, she rose and let in White Fang to sleep in the big hall. Now White Fang was not a house-dog, nor was he permitted to sleep in the house; so each morning, early, she slipped down and let him out before the family was awake.

On one such night, while all the house slept, White Fang awoke and lay very quietly. And very quietly he smelled the air and read the message it bore of a strange god's presence. And to his ears came sounds of the strange god's movements. White Fang burst into no furious outcry. It was not his way. The strange god walked softly, but more softly walked White Fang, for he had no clothes to rub against the flesh of his body. He followed silently. In the Wild he had hunted live meat that was infinitely timid, and he knew the advantage of surprise.

The strange god paused at the foot of the great staircase and listened, and White Fang was as dead, so without movement was he as he watched and waited. Up that staircase the way led to the love-master and to the love-master's dearest possessions. White Fang bristled, but waited. The strange god's foot lifted. He was beginning the ascent.

Then it was that White Fang struck. He gave no warning, with no snarl anticipated his own action. Into the air he lifted his body in the spring that landed him on the strange god's back. White Fang clung with his fore-paws to the man's shoulders, at the same time burying his fangs into the back of the man's neck. He clung on for a moment, long enough to drag the god over backward. Together they crashed to the floor. White Fang leaped clear, and, as the man struggled to rise, was in again with the slashing fangs.

Sierra Vista awoke in alarm. The noise from downstairs was as that of a score of battling fiends. There were revolver shots. A man's voice screamed once in horror and anguish. There was a great snarling and growling, and over all arose a smashing and crashing of furniture and glass.

But almost as quickly as it had arisen, the commotion died away. The struggle had not lasted more than three minutes. The frightened household clustered at the top of the stairway. From below, as from out an abyss of blackness, came up a gurgling sound, as of air bubbling through water. Sometimes this gurgle became sibilant, almost a whistle. But this, too, quickly died down and ceased. Then naught came up out of the blackness save a heavy panting of some creature struggling sorely for air.

Weedon Scott pressed a button, and the staircase and downstairs hall were flooded with light. Then he and Judge Scott, revolvers in hand, cautiously descended. There was no need for this caution. White Fang had done his work. In the midst of the wreckage of overthrown and smashed furniture, partly on his side, his face hidden by an arm, lay a man. Weedon Scott bent over, removed the arm and turned the man's face upward. A gaping throat explained the manner of his death.

'Jim Hall,' said Judge Scott, and father and son looked significantly at each other.

Then they turned to White Fang. He, too, was lying on his side. His eyes were closed, but the lids slightly lifted in an effort to look at them as they bent over him, and the tail was perceptibly agitated in a vain effort to wag. Weedon Scott patted him, and his throat rumbled an acknowledging growl. But it was a weak growl at best, and it quickly ceased. His eyelids drooped and went shut, and his whole body seemed to relax and flatten out upon the floor.

'He's all in, poor devil,' muttered the master.

'We'll see about that,' asserted the Judge, as he started for the telephone.

'Frankly, he has one chance in a thousand,' announced the surgeon, after he had worked an hour and a half on White Fang.

Dawn was breaking through the windows and dimming the electric lights. With the exception of the children, the whole family was gathered about the surgeon to hear his verdict.

'One broken hind-leg,' he went on. 'Three broken ribs, one at least of which has pierced the lungs. He has lost nearly all the blood in his body. There is a large likelihood of internal injuries. He must have been jumped upon. To say nothing of three bullet holes clear through him. One chance in a thousand is really optimistic. He hasn't a chance in ten thousand.'

'But he mustn't lose any chance that might be of help to him,' Judge Scott exclaimed. 'Never mind expense. Put him under the X-ray—anything. Weedon, telegraph at once to San Francisco for Doctor Nichols. No reflection on you, doctor, you understand; but he must have the advantage of every chance.'

The surgeon smiled indulgently. 'Of course I understand. He deserves all that can be done for him. He must be nursed as you would nurse a human being, a sick child. And don't forget what I told you about temperature. I'll be back at ten o'clock again.'

White Fang received the nursing. Judge Scott's suggestion of a trained nurse was indignantly clamoured down by the girls, who themselves undertook the task. And White Fang won out on the one chance in ten thousand denied him by the surgeon.

The latter was not to be censured for his misjudgment. All his life he had tended and operated on the soft humans of civilisation, who lived sheltered lives and had descended out of many sheltered generations. Compared with White Fang, they were frail and flabby, and clutched life without any strength in their grip. White Fang had come straight from the Wild, where the weak perish early and shelter is vouchsafed to none. In neither his father nor his mother was there any weakness, nor in the generations before them. A constitution of iron and the vitality of the Wild were White Fang's inheritance, and he clung to life, the whole of him and every part of him, in spirit and in flesh, with the tenacity that of old belonged to all creatures.

Bound down a prisoner, denied even movement by the plaster casts and bandages, White Fang lingered out the weeks. He slept long hours and dreamed much, and through his mind passed an unending pageant of Northland visions. All the ghosts of the past arose and were with him. Once again he lived in the lair with Kiche, crept trembling to the knees of Grey Beaver to tender his allegiance, ran for his life before Lip-lip and all the howling bedlam of the puppy-pack.

He ran again through the silence, hunting his living food through the months of famine; and again he ran at the head of the team, the gut-whips of Mit-sah and Grey Beaver snapping behind, their voices crying 'Ra! Raa!' when they came to a narrow passage and the team closed together like a fan to go through. He lived again all his days with Beauty Smith and the fights he had fought. At such times he whimpered and snarled in his sleep, and they that looked on said that his dreams were bad.

But there was one particular nightmare from which he suffered—the clanking, clanging monsters of electric cars that were to him colossal screaming lynxes. He would lie in a screen of bushes, watching for a squirrel to venture far enough out on the ground from its tree-refuge. Then, when he sprang out upon it, it would transform itself into an electric car, menacing and terrible, towering over him like a mountain, screaming and clanging and spitting fire at him. It was the same when he challenged the hawk down out of the sky. Down out of the blue it would rush, as it dropped upon him changing itself into the ubiquitous electric car. Or again, he would be in the pen of Beauty Smith. Outside the pen, men would be gathering, and he knew that a fight was on. He watched the door for his antagonist to enter. The door would open, and thrust in upon him would come the awful electric car. A thousand times this occurred, and each time the terror it inspired was as vivid and great as ever.

Then came the day when the last bandage and the last plaster cast were taken off. It was a gala day. All Sierra Vista was gathered around. The master rubbed his ears, and he crooned his love-growl. The master's wife called him the 'Blessed Wolf,' which name was taken up with acclaim and all the women called him the Blessed Wolf.

He tried to rise to his feet, and after several attempts fell down from weakness. He had lain so long that his muscles had lost their cunning, and all the strength had gone out of them. He felt a little shame because of his weakness, as though, forsooth, he were failing the gods in the service he owed them. Because of this he made heroic efforts to arise and at last he stood on his four legs, tottering and swaying back and forth.

'The Blessed Wolf!' chorused the women.

Judge Scott surveyed them triumphantly.

'Out of your own mouths be it,' he said. 'Just as I contended right along. No mere dog could have done what he did. He's a wolf.'

'A Blessed Wolf,' amended the Judge's wife.

'Yes, Blessed Wolf,' agreed the Judge. 'And henceforth that shall be my name for him.'

'He'll have to learn to walk again,' said the surgeon; 'so he might as well start in right now. It won't hurt him. Take him outside.'

And outside he went, like a king, with all Sierra Vista about him and tending on him. He was very weak, and when he reached the lawn he lay down and rested for a while.

Then the procession started on, little spurts of strength coming into White Fang's muscles as he used them and the blood began to surge through them. The stables were reached, and there in the doorway, lay Collie, a half-dozen pudgy puppies playing about her in the sun.

White Fang looked on with a wondering eye. Collie snarled warningly at him, and he was careful to keep his distance. The master with his toe helped one sprawling puppy toward him. He bristled suspiciously, but the master warned him that all was well. Collie, clasped in the arms of one of the women, watched him jealously and with a snarl warned him that all was not well.

The puppy sprawled in front of him. He cocked his ears and watched it curiously. Then their noses touched, and he felt the warm little tongue of the puppy on his jowl. White Fang's tongue went out, he knew not why, and he licked the puppy's face.

Hand-clapping and pleased cries from the gods greeted the performance. He was surprised, and looked at them in a puzzled way. Then his weakness asserted itself, and he lay down, his ears cocked, his head on one side, as he watched the puppy. The other puppies came sprawling toward him, to Collie's great disgust; and he gravely permitted them to clamber and tumble over him. At first, amid the applause of the gods, he betrayed a trifle of his old self-consciousness and awkwardness. This passed away as the puppies' antics and mauling continued, and he lay with half-shut patient eyes, drowsing in the sun.

THE SON OF
THE WOLF

1900

THE WHITE SILENCE

'Carmen won't last more than a couple of days.' Mason spat out a chunk of ice and surveyed the poor animal ruefully, then put her foot in his mouth and proceeded to bite out the ice which clustered cruelly between the toes.

'I never saw a dog with a highfalutin' name that ever was worth a rap,' he said, as he concluded his task and shoved her aside. 'They just fade away and die under the responsibility. Did ye ever see one go wrong with a sensible name like Cassiar, Siwash, or Husky? No, sir! Take a look at Shookum here, he's—' Snap! The lean brute flashed up, the white teeth just missing Mason's throat.

'Ye will, will ye?' A shrewd clout behind the ear with the butt of the dog whip stretched the animal in the snow, quivering softly, a yellow slaver dripping from its fangs.

'As I was saying, just look at Shookum here—he's got the spirit. Bet ye he eats Carmen before the week's out.' 'I'll bank another proposition against that,' replied Malemute Kid, reversing the frozen bread placed before the fire to thaw. 'We'll eat Shookum before the trip is over. What d'ye say, Ruth?' The Indian woman settled the coffee with a piece of ice, glanced from Malemute Kid to her husband, then at the dogs, but vouchsafed no reply. It was such a palpable truism that none was necessary. Two hundred miles of unbroken trail in prospect, with a scant six days' grub for themselves and none for the dogs, could admit no other alternative. The two men and the woman grouped about the fire and began their meager meal. The dogs lay in their harnesses for it was a midday halt, and watched each mouthful enviously.

'No more lunches after today,' said Malemute Kid. 'And we've got to keep a close eye on the dogs—they're getting vicious. They'd just as soon pull a fellow down as not, if they get a chance.' 'And I was president of an Epworth once, and taught in the Sunday school.' Having irrelevantly delivered himself of this, Mason fell into a dreamy contemplation of his steaming moccasins, but was aroused by Ruth filling his cup.

'Thank God, we've got slathers of tea! I've seen it growing, down in Tennessee. What wouldn't I give for a hot corn pone just now! Never mind, Ruth; you won't starve much longer, nor wear moccasins either.' The woman threw off her gloom at this, and in her eyes welled up a great love for her white lord—the first white man she had ever seen—the first man whom she had known to treat a woman as something better than a mere animal or beast of burden.

'Yes, Ruth,' continued her husband, having recourse to the macaronic jargon in which it was alone possible for them to understand each other; 'wait till we clean up and pull for the Outside. We'll take the White Man's canoe and go to the Salt Water. Yes, bad water, rough water—great mountains dance up and down all the time. And so big, so far, so far away—you travel ten sleep, twenty sleep, forty sleep'—he graphically enumerated the days on his fingers—'all the time water, bad water. Then you come to great village, plenty people, just the same mosquitoes next summer. Wigwams oh, so high—ten, twenty pines.

'Hi-yu skookum!' He paused impotently, cast an appealing glance at Malemute Kid, then laboriously placed the twenty pines, end on end, by sign language. Malemute Kid smiled with cheery cynicism; but Ruth's eyes were wide with wonder, and with pleasure; for she half believed he was joking, and such condescension pleased her poor woman's heart.

'And then you step into a—a box, and pouf! up you go.' He tossed his empty cup in the air by way of illustration and, as he deftly caught it, cried: 'And biff! down you come. Oh, great medicine men! You go Fort Yukon. I go Arctic City—twenty-five sleep—big string, all the time—I catch him string—I say, 'Hello, Ruth! How are ye?'—and you say, 'Is that my good husband?'—and I say, 'Yes'—and you say, 'No can bake good bread, no more soda'—then I say, 'Look in cache, under flour; good-by.' You look and catch plenty soda. All the time you Fort Yukon, me Arctic City. Hi-yu medicine man!' Ruth smiled so ingenuously at the fairy story that both men burst into laughter. A row among the dogs cut short the wonders of the Outside, and by the time the snarling combatants were separated, she had lashed the sleds and all was ready for the trail.—'Mush! Baldy! Hi! Mush on!' Mason worked his whip smartly and, as the dogs whined low in the traces, broke out the sled with the gee pole. Ruth followed with the second team, leaving Malemute Kid, who had helped her start, to bring up the rear. Strong man, brute that he was, capable of felling an ox at a blow, he could not bear to beat the poor animals, but humored them as a dog driver rarely does—nay, almost wept with them in their misery.

'Come, mush on there, you poor sore-footed brutes!' he murmured, after several ineffectual attempts to start the load. But his patience was at last rewarded, and though whimpering with pain, they hastened to join their fellows.

No more conversation; the toil of the trail will not permit such extravagance. And of all deadening labors, that of the Northland trail is the worst. Happy is the man who can weather a day's travel at the price of silence, and that on a beaten track. And of all heartbreaking labors, that of breaking trail is the worst. At every step the great webbed shoe sinks till the snow is level with the knee. Then up, straight up, the deviation of a fraction of an inch being a certain precursor of disaster, the snowshoe must be lifted till the surface is cleared; then forward, down, and the other foot is raised perpendicularly for the matter of half a yard. He who tries this for the first time, if haply he avoids bringing his shoes in dangerous propinquity and measures not his length on the treacherous footing, will give up exhausted at the end of a hundred yards; he who can keep out of the way of the dogs for a whole day may well crawl into his sleeping bag with a clear conscience and a pride which passeth all understanding; and he who travels twenty sleeps on the Long Trail is a man whom the gods may envy.

The afternoon wore on, and with the awe, born of the White Silence, the voiceless travelers bent to their work. Nature has many tricks wherewith she convinces man of his finity—the ceaseless flow of the tides, the fury of the storm, the shock of the earthquake, the long roll of heaven's artillery—but the most tremendous, the most stupefying of all, is the passive phase of the White Silence. All movement ceases, the sky clears, the heavens are as brass; the slightest whisper seems sacrilege, and man becomes timid, affrighted at the sound of his own voice. Sole speck of life journeying across the ghostly wastes of a dead world, he trembles at his audacity, realizes that his is a maggot's life, nothing more.

Strange thoughts arise unsummoned, and the mystery of all things strives for utterance.

And the fear of death, of God, of the universe, comes over him—the hope of the Resurrection and the Life, the yearning for immortality, the vain striving of the imprisoned essence—it is then, if ever, man walks alone with God.

So wore the day away. The river took a great bend, and Mason headed his team for the cutoff across the narrow neck of land. But the dogs balked at the high bank. Again and again, though Ruth and Malemute Kid were shoving on the sled, they slipped back. Then came the concerted effort. The miserable creatures, weak from hunger, exerted their last strength. Up—up—the sled poised on the top of the bank; but the leader swung the string of dogs behind him to the right, fouling Mason's snowshoes. The result was grievous.

Mason was whipped off his feet; one of the dogs fell in the traces; and the sled toppled back, dragging everything to the bottom again.

Slash! the whip fell among the dogs savagely, especially upon the one which had fallen.

'Don't,—Mason,' entreated Malemute Kid; 'the poor devil's on its last legs. Wait and we'll put my team on.' Mason deliberately withheld the whip till the last word had fallen, then out flashed the long lash, completely curling about the offending creature's body.

Carmen—for it was Carmen—cowered in the snow, cried piteously, then rolled over on her side.

It was a tragic moment, a pitiful incident of the trail—a dying dog, two comrades in anger. Ruth glanced solicitously from man to man. But Malemute Kid restrained himself, though there was a world of reproach in his eyes, and, bending over the dog, cut the traces. No word was spoken. The teams were doublespanned and the difficulty overcome; the sleds were under way again, the dying dog dragging herself along in the rear. As long as an animal can travel, it is not shot, and this last chance is accorded it—the crawling into camp, if it can, in the hope of a moose being killed.

Already penitent for his angry action, but too stubborn to make amends, Mason toiled on at the head of the cavalcade, little dreaming that danger hovered in the air. The timber clustered thick in the sheltered bottom, and through this they threaded their way. Fifty feet or more from the trail towered a lofty pine. For generations it had stood there, and for generations destiny had had this one end in view—perhaps the same had been decreed of Mason.

He stooped to fasten the loosened thong of his moccasin. The sleds came to a halt, and the dogs lay down in the snow without a whimper. The stillness was weird; not a breath rustled the frost-encrusted forest; the cold and silence of outer space had chilled the heart and smote the trembling lips of nature. A sigh pulsed through the air—they did not seem to actually hear it, but rather felt it, like the premonition of movement in a motionless void. Then the great tree, burdened with its weight of years and snow, played its last part in the tragedy of life. He heard the warning crash and attempted to spring up but, almost erect, caught the blow squarely on the shoulder.

The sudden danger, the quick death—how often had Malemute Kid faced it! The pine needles were still quivering as he gave his commands and sprang into action. Nor did the Indian girl faint or raise her voice in idle wailing, as might many of her white sisters. At his order, she threw her weight on the end of a quickly extemporized handspike, easing the pressure and listening to her husband's groans, while Malemute Kid attacked the tree with his ax. The steel rang merrily as it bit into the frozen trunk, each stroke being accompanied by a forced, audible respiration, the 'Huh!' 'Huh!' of the woodsman.

At last the Kid laid the pitiable thing that was once a man in the snow. But worse than his comrade's pain was the dumb anguish in the woman's face, the blended look of hopeful, hopeless query. Little was said; those of the Northland are early taught the futility of words and the inestimable value of deeds. With the temperature at sixty-five below zero, a man cannot lie many minutes in the snow and live. So the sled lashings were cut, and the sufferer, rolled in furs, laid on a couch of boughs. Before him roared a fire, built of the very wood which wrought the mishap. Behind and partially over him was stretched the primitive fly—a piece of canvas, which caught the radiating heat and threw it back and down upon him—a trick which men may know who study physics at the fount.

And men who have shared their bed with death know when the call is sounded. Mason was terribly crushed. The most cursory examination revealed it.

His right arm, leg, and back were broken; his limbs were paralyzed from the hips; and the likelihood of internal injuries was large. An occasional moan was his only sign of life.

No hope; nothing to be done. The pitiless night crept slowly by—Ruth's portion, the despairing stoicism of her race, and Malemute Kid adding new lines to his face of bronze.

In fact, Mason suffered least of all, for he spent his time in eastern Tennessee, in the Great Smoky Mountains, living over the scenes of his childhood. And most pathetic was the melody of his long-forgotten Southern vernacular, as he raved of swimming holes and coon hunts and watermelon raids. It was as Greek to Ruth, but the Kid understood and felt—felt as only one can feel who has been shut out for years from all that civilization means.

Morning brought consciousness to the stricken man, and Malemute Kid bent closer to catch his whispers.

'You remember when we foregathered on the Tanana, four years come next ice run? I didn't care so much for her then. It was more like she was pretty, and there was a smack of excitement about it, I think. But d'ye know, I've come to think a heap of her. She's been a good wife to me, always at my shoulder in the pinch. And when it comes to trading, you know there isn't her equal. D'ye recollect the time she shot the Moosehorn Rapids to pull you and me off that rock, the bullets whipping the water like hailstones?—and the time of the famine at Nuklukyeto?—when she raced the ice run to bring the news?

'Yes, she's been a good wife to me, better'n that other one. Didn't know I'd been there?

'Never told you, eh? Well, I tried it once, down in the States. That's why I'm here. Been raised together, too. I came away to give her a chance for divorce. She got it.

'But that's got nothing to do with Ruth. I had thought of cleaning up and pulling for the Outside next year—her and I—but it's too late. Don't send her back to her people, Kid. It's beastly hard for a woman to go back. Think of it!—nearly four years on our bacon and beans and flour and dried fruit, and then to go back to her fish and caribou. It's not good for her to have tried our ways, to come to know they're better'n her people's, and then return to them. Take care of her, Kid, why don't you—but no, you always fought shy of them—and you never told me why you came to this country. Be kind to her, and send her back to the States as soon as you can. But fix it so she can come back—liable to get homesick, you know.

'And the youngster—it's drawn us closer, Kid. I only hope it is a boy. Think of it!—flesh of my flesh, Kid. He mustn't stop in this country. And if it's a girl, why, she can't. Sell my furs; they'll fetch at least five thousand, and I've got as much more with the company. And handle my interests with yours. I think that bench claim will show up. See that he gets a good schooling; and Kid, above all, don't let him come back. This country was not made for white men.

'I'm a gone man, Kid. Three or four sleeps at the best. You've got to go on. You must go on! Remember, it's my wife, it's my boy—O God! I hope it's a boy! You can't stay by me—and I charge you, a dying man, to pull on.'

'Give me three days,' pleaded Malemute Kid. 'You may change for the better; something may turn up.'

'No.'

'Just three days.'

'You must pull on.'

'Two days.'

'It's my wife and my boy, Kid. You would not ask it.'

'One day.'

'No, no! I charge—'

'Only one day. We can shave it through on the grub, and I might knock over a moose.'

'No—all right; one day, but not a minute more. And, Kid, don't—don't leave me to face it alone. Just a shot, one pull on the trigger. You understand. Think of it! Think of it! Flesh of my flesh, and I'll never live to see him!

'Send Ruth here. I want to say good-by and tell her that she must think of the boy and not wait till I'm dead. She might refuse to go with you if I didn't. Goodby, old man; good-by.

'Kid! I say—a—sink a hole above the pup, next to the slide. I panned out forty cents on my shovel there.

'And, Kid!' He stooped lower to catch the last faint words, the dying man's surrender of his pride. 'I'm sorry—for—you know—Carmen.' Leaving the girl crying softly over her man, Malemute Kid slipped into his parka and snowshoes, tucked his rifle under his arm, and crept away into the forest. He was no tyro in the stern sorrows of the Northland, but never had he faced so stiff a problem as this. In the abstract, it was a plain, mathematical proposition—three possible lives as against one doomed one. But now he hesitated. For five years, shoulder to shoulder, on the rivers and trails, in the camps and mines, facing death by field and flood and famine, had they knitted the bonds of their comradeship. So close was the tie that he had often been conscious of a vague jealousy of Ruth, from the first time she had come between. And now it must be severed by his own hand.

Though he prayed for a moose, just one moose, all game seemed to have deserted the land, and nightfall found the exhausted man crawling into camp, lighthanded, heavyhearted. An uproar from the dogs and shrill cries from Ruth hastened him.

Bursting into the camp, he saw the girl in the midst of the snarling pack, laying about her with an ax. The dogs had broken the iron rule of their masters and were rushing the grub.

He joined the issue with his rifle reversed, and the hoary game of natural selection was played out with all the ruthlessness of its primeval environment. Rifle and ax went up and down, hit or missed with monotonous regularity; lithe bodies flashed, with wild eyes and dripping fangs; and man and beast fought for supremacy to the bitterest conclusion. Then the beaten brutes crept to the edge of the firelight, licking their wounds, voicing their misery to the stars.

The whole stock of dried salmon had been devoured, and perhaps five pounds of flour remained to tide them over two hundred miles of wilderness. Ruth returned to her husband, while Malemute Kid cut up the warm body of one of the dogs, the skull of which had been crushed by the ax. Every portion was carefully put away, save the hide and offal, which were cast to his fellows of the moment before.

Morning brought fresh trouble. The animals were turning on each other. Carmen, who still clung to her slender thread of life, was downed by the pack. The lash fell among them unheeded. They cringed and cried under the blows, but refused to scatter till the last wretched bit had disappeared—bones, hide, hair, everything.

Malemute Kid went about his work, listening to Mason, who was back in Tennessee, delivering tangled discourses and wild exhortations to his brethren of other days.

Taking advantage of neighboring pines, he worked rapidly, and Ruth watched him make a cache similar to those sometimes used by hunters to preserve their meat from the wolverines and dogs. One after the other, he bent the tops of two small pines toward each other and nearly to the ground, making them fast with thongs of moosehide. Then he beat the dogs into submission and harnessed them to two of the sleds, loading the same with everything but the furs which enveloped Mason. These he wrapped and lashed tightly about him, fastening either end of the robes to the bent pines. A single stroke of his hunting knife would release them and send the body high in the air.

Ruth had received her husband's last wishes and made no struggle. Poor girl, she had learned the lesson of obedience well. From a child, she had bowed, and seen all women bow, to the lords of creation, and it did not seem in the nature of things for woman to resist. The Kid permitted her one outburst of grief, as she kissed her husband—her own people had no such custom—then led her to the foremost sled and helped her into her snowshoes. Blindly, instinctively, she took the gee pole and whip, and 'mushed' the dogs out on the trail. Then he returned to Mason, who had fallen into a coma, and long after she was out of sight crouched by the fire, waiting, hoping, praying for his comrade to die.

It is not pleasant to be alone with painful thoughts in the White Silence. The silence of gloom is merciful, shrouding one as with protection and breathing a thousand intangible sympathies; but the bright White Silence, clear and cold, under steely skies, is pitiless.

An hour passed—two hours—but the man would not die. At high noon the sun, without raising its rim above the southern horizon, threw a suggestion of fire athwart the heavens, then quickly drew it back. Malemute Kid roused and dragged himself to his comrade's side. He cast one glance about him. The White Silence seemed to sneer, and a great fear came upon him. There was a sharp report; Mason swung into his aerial sepulcher, and Malemute Kid lashed the dogs into a wild gallop as he fled across the snow.

THE SON OF THE WOLF

Man rarely places a proper valuation upon his womankind, at least not until deprived of them. He has no conception of the subtle atmosphere exhaled by the sex feminine, so long as he bathes in it; but let it be withdrawn, and an ever-growing void begins to manifest itself in his existence, and he becomes hungry, in a vague sort of way, for a something so indefinite that he cannot characterize it. If his comrades have no more experience than himself, they will shake their heads dubiously and dose him with strong physic. But the hunger will continue and become stronger; he will lose interest in the things of his everyday life and wax morbid; and one day, when the emptiness has become unbearable, a revelation will dawn upon him.

In the Yukon country, when this comes to pass, the man usually provisions a poling boat, if it is summer, and if winter, harnesses his dogs, and heads for the Southland. A few months later, supposing him to be possessed of a faith in the country, he returns with a wife to share with him in that faith, and incidentally in his hardships. This but serves to show the innate selfishness of man. It also brings us to the trouble of 'Scruff' Mackenzie, which occurred in the old days, before the country was stampeded and staked by a tidal-wave of the che-cha-quas, and when the Klondike's only claim to notice was its salmon fisheries.

'Scruff' Mackenzie bore the earmarks of a frontier birth and a frontier life.

His face was stamped with twenty-five years of incessant struggle with Nature in her wildest moods,—the last two, the wildest and hardest of all, having been spent in groping for the gold which lies in the shadow of the Arctic Circle. When the yearning sickness came upon him, he was not surprised, for he was a practical man and had seen other men thus stricken. But he showed no sign of his malady, save that he worked harder. All summer he fought mosquitoes and washed the sure-thing bars of the Stuart River for a double grubstake. Then he floated a raft of houselogs down the Yukon to Forty Mile, and put together as comfortable a cabin as any the camp could boast of. In fact, it showed such cozy promise that many men elected to be his partner and to come and live with him. But he crushed their aspirations with rough speech, peculiar for its strength and brevity, and bought a double supply of grub from the trading-post.

As has been noted, 'Scruff' Mackenzie was a practical man. If he wanted a thing he usually got it, but in doing so, went no farther out of his way than was necessary. Though a son of toil and hardship, he was averse to a journey of six hundred miles on the ice, a second of two thousand miles on the ocean, and still a third thousand miles or so to his last stamping-grounds,—all in the mere quest of a wife. Life was too short. So he rounded up his dogs, lashed a curious freight to his sled, and faced across the divide whose westward slopes were drained by the head-reaches of the Tanana.

He was a sturdy traveler, and his wolf-dogs could work harder and travel farther on less grub than any other team in the Yukon. Three weeks later he strode into a hunting-camp of the Upper Tanana Sticks. They marveled at his temerity; for they had a bad name and had been known to kill white men for as trifling a thing as a sharp ax or a broken rifle.

But he went among them single-handed, his bearing being a delicious composite of humility, familiarity, sang-froid, and insolence. It required a deft hand and deep knowledge of the barbaric mind effectually to handle such diverse weapons; but he was a past-master in the art, knowing when to conciliate and when to threaten with Jove-like wrath.

He first made obeisance to the Chief Thling-Tinneh, presenting him with a couple of pounds of black tea and tobacco, and thereby winning his most cordial regard. Then he mingled with the men and maidens, and that night gave a potlach.

The snow was beaten down in the form of an oblong, perhaps a hundred feet in length and quarter as many across. Down the center a long fire was built, while either side was carpeted with spruce boughs. The lodges were forsaken, and the fivescore or so members of the tribe gave tongue to their folk-chants in honor of their guest.

'Scruff' Mackenzie's two years had taught him the not many hundred words of their vocabulary, and he had likewise conquered their deep gutturals, their Japanese idioms, constructions, and honorific and agglutinative particles. So he made oration after their manner, satisfying their instinctive poetry-love with crude flights of eloquence and metaphorical contortions. After Thling-Tinneh and the Shaman had responded in kind, he made trifling presents to the menfolk, joined in their singing, and proved an expert in their fifty-two-stick gambling game.

And they smoked his tobacco and were pleased. But among the younger men there was a defiant attitude, a spirit of braggadocio, easily understood by the raw insinuations of the toothless squaws and the giggling of the maidens. They had known few white men, 'Sons of the Wolf,' but from those few they had learned strange lessons.

Nor had 'Scruff' Mackenzie, for all his seeming carelessness, failed to note these phenomena. In truth, rolled in his sleeping-furs, he thought it all over, thought seriously, and emptied many pipes in mapping out a campaign. One maiden only had caught his fancy,—none other than Zarinska, daughter to the chief. In features, form, and poise, answering more nearly to the white man's type of beauty, she was almost an anomaly among her tribal sisters. He would possess her, make her his wife, and name her—ah, he would name her Gertrude! Having thus decided, he rolled over on his side and dropped off to sleep, a true son of his all-conquering race, a Samson among the Philistines.

It was slow work and a stiff game; but 'Scruff' Mackenzie maneuvered cunningly, with an unconcern which served to puzzle the Sticks. He took great care to impress the men that he was a sure shot and a mighty hunter, and the camp rang with his plaudits when he brought down a moose at six hundred yards. Of a night he visited in Chief Thling-Tinneh's lodge of moose and cariboo skins, talking big and dispensing tobacco with a lavish hand. Nor did he fail to likewise honor the Shaman; for he realized the medicine-man's influence with his people, and was anxious to make of him an ally. But that worthy was high and mighty, refused to be propitiated, and was unerringly marked down as a prospective enemy.

Though no opening presented for an interview with Zarinska, Mackenzie stole many a glance to her, giving fair warning of his intent. And well she knew, yet coquettishly surrounded herself with a ring of women whenever the men were away and he had a chance. But he was in no hurry; besides, he knew she could not help but think of him, and a few days of such thought would only better his suit.

At last, one night, when he deemed the time to be ripe, he abruptly left the chief's smoky dwelling and hastened to a neighboring lodge. As usual, she sat with squaws and maidens about her, all engaged in sewing moccasins and beadwork. They laughed at his entrance, and badinage, which linked Zarinska to him, ran high. But one after the other they were unceremoniously bundled into the outer snow, whence they hurried to spread the tale through all the camp.

His cause was well pleaded, in her tongue, for she did not know his, and at the end of two hours he rose to go.

'So Zarinska will come to the White Man's lodge? Good! I go now to have talk with thy father, for he may not be so minded. And I will give him many tokens; but he must not ask too much. If he say no? Good! Zarinska shall yet come to the White Man's lodge.'

He had already lifted the skin flap to depart, when a low exclamation brought him back to the girl's side. She brought herself to her knees on the bearskin mat, her face aglow with true Eve-light, and shyly unbuckled his heavy belt. He looked down, perplexed, suspicious, his ears alert for the slightest sound without.

But her next move disarmed his doubt, and he smiled with pleasure. She took from her sewing bag a moosehide sheath, brave with bright beadwork, fantastically designed. She drew his great hunting-knife, gazed reverently along the keen edge, half tempted to try it with her thumb, and shot it into place in its new home. Then she slipped the sheath along the belt to its customary resting-place, just above the hip. For all the world, it was like a scene of olden time,—a lady and her knight.

Mackenzie drew her up full height and swept her red lips with his moustache, the, to her, foreign caress of the Wolf. It was a meeting of the stone age and the steel; but she was none the less a woman, as her crimson cheeks and the luminous softness of her eyes attested.

There was a thrill of excitement in the air as 'Scruff' Mackenzie, a bulky bundle under his arm, threw open the flap of Thling-Tinneh's tent. Children were running about in the open, dragging dry wood to the scene of the potlach, a babble of women's voices was growing in intensity, the young men were consulting in sullen

347

groups, while from the Shaman's lodge rose the eerie sounds of an incantation.

The chief was alone with his blear-eyed wife, but a glance sufficed to tell Mackenzie that the news was already told. So he plunged at once into the business, shifting the beaded sheath prominently to the fore as advertisement of the betrothal.

'O Thling-Tinneh, mighty chief of the Sticks And the land of the Tanana, ruler of the salmon and the bear, the moose and the cariboo! The White Man is before thee with a great purpose. Many moons has his lodge been empty, and he is lonely. And his heart has eaten itself in silence, and grown hungry for a woman to sit beside him in his lodge, to meet him from the hunt with warm fire and good food. He has heard strange things, the patter of baby moccasins and the sound of children's voices. And one night a vision came upon him, and he beheld the Raven, who is thy father, the great Raven, who is the father of all the Sticks. And the Raven spake to the lonely White Man, saying: 'Bind thou thy moccasins upon thee, and gird thy snow-shoes on, and lash thy sled with food for many sleeps and fine tokens for the Chief Thling-Tinneh. For thou shalt turn thy face to where the mid-spring sun is wont to sink below the land and journey to this great chief's hunting-grounds. There thou shalt make big presents, and Thling-Tinneh, who is my son, shall become to thee as a father. In his lodge there is a maiden into whom I breathed the breath of life for thee. This maiden shalt thou take to wife.' 'O Chief, thus spake the great Raven; thus do I lay many presents at thy feet; thus am I come to take thy daughter!' The old man drew his furs about him with crude consciousness of royalty, but delayed reply while a youngster crept in, delivered a quick message to appear before the council, and was gone.

'O White Man, whom we have named Moose-Killer, also known as the Wolf, and the Son of the Wolf! We know thou comest of a mighty race; we are proud to have thee our potlach-guest; but the king-salmon does not mate with the dog-salmon, nor the Raven with the Wolf.' 'Not so!' cried Mackenzie. 'The daughters of the Raven have I met in the camps of the Wolf,—the squaw of Mortimer, the squaw of Tregidgo, the squaw of Barnaby, who came two ice-runs back, and I have heard of other squaws, though my eyes beheld them not.' 'Son, your words are true; but it were evil mating, like the water with the sand, like the snow-flake with the sun. But met you one Mason and his squaw' No?

He came ten ice-runs ago,—the first of all the Wolves. And with him there was a mighty man, straight as a willow-shoot, and tall; strong as the bald-faced grizzly, with a heart like the full summer moon; his-' 'Oh!' interrupted Mackenzie, recognizing the well-known Northland figure, 'Malemute Kid!' 'The same,—a mighty man. But saw you aught of the squaw? She was full sister to Zarinska.' 'Nay, Chief; but I have heard. Mason—far, far to the north, a spruce-tree, heavy with years, crushed out his life beneath. But his love was great, and he had much gold. With this, and her boy, she journeyed countless sleeps toward the winter's noonday sun, and there she yet lives,—no biting frost, no snow, no summer's midnight sun, no winter's noonday night.'

A second messenger interrupted with imperative summons from the council.

As Mackenzie threw him into the snow, he caught a glimpse of the swaying forms before the council-fire, heard the deep basses of the men in rhythmic chant, and knew the Shaman was fanning the anger of his people. Time pressed. He turned upon the chief.

'Come! I wish thy child. And now, see! Here are tobacco, tea, many cups of sugar, warm blankets, handkerchiefs, both good and large; and here, a true rifle, with many bullets and much powder.' 'Nay,' replied the old man, struggling against the great wealth spread before him. 'Even now are my people come together. They will not have this marriage.'

'But thou art chief.' 'Yet do my young men rage because the Wolves have taken their maidens so that they may not marry.' 'Listen, O Thling-Tinneh! Ere the night has passed into the day, the Wolf shall face his dogs to the Mountains of the East and fare forth to the Country of the Yukon. And Zarinska shall break trail for his dogs.' 'And ere the night has gained its middle, my young men may fling to the dogs the flesh of the Wolf, and his bones be scattered in the snow till the springtime lay them bare.' It was threat and counter-threat. Mackenzie's bronzed face flushed darkly. He raised his voice. The old squaw, who till now had sat an impassive spectator, made to creep by him for the door.

The song of the men broke suddenly and there was a hubbub of many voices as he whirled the old woman roughly to her couch of skins.

'Again I cry—listen, O Thling-Tinneh! The Wolf dies with teeth fast-locked, and with him there shall sleep ten of thy strongest men,—men who are needed, for the hunting is not begun, and the fishing is not many moons away. And again, of what profit should I die? I know the custom of thy people; thy share of my wealth shall be very small. Grant me thy child, and it shall all be thine. And yet again, my brothers will come, and they are many, and their maws are never filled; and the daughters of the Raven shall bear children in the lodges of the Wolf. My people are greater than thy people. It is destiny. Grant, and all this wealth is thine.' Moccasins were crunching the snow without. Mackenzie threw his rifle to cock, and loosened the twin Colts in his belt.

'Grant, O Chief!' 'And yet will my people say no.' 'Grant, and the wealth is thine. Then shall I deal with thy people after.' 'The Wolf will have it so. I will take his tokens,—but I would warn him.' Mackenzie passed over the goods, taking care to clog the rifle's ejector, and capping the bargain with a kaleidoscopic silk kerchief. The Shaman and half a dozen young braves entered, but he shouldered boldly among them and passed out.

'Pack!' was his laconic greeting to Zarinska as he passed her lodge and hurried to harness his dogs. A few minutes later he swept into the council at the head of the team, the woman by his side. He took his place at the upper end of the oblong, by the side of the chief. To his left, a step to the rear, he stationed Zarinska, her proper place. Besides, the time was ripe for mischief, and there was need to guard his back.

On either side, the men crouched to the fire, their voices lifted in a folk-chant out of the forgotten past. Full of strange, halting cadences and haunting recurrences, it was not beautiful. 'Fearful' may inadequately express it. At the lower end, under the eye of the Shaman, danced half a score of women. Stern were his reproofs of those who did not wholly abandon themselves to the ecstasy of the rite. Half hidden in their heavy masses of raven hair, all dishevelled and falling to their waists, they slowly swayed to and fro, their forms rippling to an ever-changing rhythm.

It was a weird scene; an anachronism. To the south, the nineteenth century was reeling off the few years of its last decade; here flourished man primeval, a shade removed from the prehistoric cave-dweller, forgotten fragment of the Elder World. The tawny wolf-dogs sat between their skin-clad masters or fought for room, the firelight cast backward from their red eyes and dripping fangs. The woods, in ghostly shroud, slept on unheeding.

The White Silence, for the moment driven to the rimming forest, seemed ever crushing inward; the stars danced with great leaps, as is their wont in the time of the Great Cold; while the Spirits of the Pole trailed their robes of glory athwart the heavens.

'Scruff' Mackenzie dimly realized the wild grandeur of the setting as his eyes ranged down the fur-fringed sides in quest of missing faces. They rested for a moment on a newborn babe, suckling at its mother's naked breast. It was forty below,—seven and odd degrees of frost. He thought of the tender women of his own race and smiled grimly. Yet from the loins of some such tender woman had he sprung with a kingly inheritance,—an inheritance which gave to him and his dominance over the land and sea, over the animals and the peoples of all the zones. Single-handed against fivescore, girt by the Arctic winter, far from his own, he felt the prompting of his heritage, the desire to possess, the wild danger—love, the thrill of battle, the power to conquer or to die.

The singing and the dancing ceased, and the Shaman flared up in rude eloquence.

Through the sinuosities of their vast mythology, he worked cunningly upon the credulity of his people. The case was strong. Opposing the creative principles as embodied in the Crow and the Raven, he stigmatized Mackenzie as the Wolf, the fighting and the destructive principle. Not only was the combat of these forces spiritual, but men fought, each to his totem. They were the children of Jelchs, the Raven, the Promethean fire-bringer; Mackenzie was the child of the Wolf, or in other words, the Devil. For them to bring a truce to this perpetual warfare, to marry their daughters to the arch-enemy, were treason and blasphemy of the highest order. No phrase was harsh nor figure vile enough in branding Mackenzie as a sneaking interloper and emissary of Satan. There was a subdued, savage roar in the deep chests of his listeners as he took the swing of his peroration.

'Aye, my brothers, Jelchs is all-powerful! Did he not bring heaven-borne fire that we might be warm? Did he not draw the sun, moon, and stars, from their holes that we might see? Did he not teach us that we might fight the Spirits of Famine and of Frost? But now Jelchs is angry with his children, and they are grown to a handful, and he will not help.

'For they have forgotten him, and done evil things, and trod bad trails, and taken his enemies into their lodges to sit by their fires. And the Raven is sorrowful at the wickedness of his children; but when they shall rise up and show they have come back, he will come out of the darkness to aid them. O brothers! the Fire-Bringer has whispered messages to thy Shaman; the same shall ye hear. Let the young men take the young women to their lodges; let them fly at the throat of the Wolf; let them be undying in their enmity! Then shall their women become fruitful and they shall multiply into a mighty people! And the Raven shall lead great tribes of their fathers and their fathers' fathers from out of the North; and they shall beat back the Wolves till they are as last year's campfires; and they shall again come to rule over all the land! 'Tis the message of Jelchs, the Raven.' This foreshadowing of the Messiah's coming brought a hoarse howl from the Sticks as they leaped to their feet. Mackenzie slipped the thumbs of his mittens and waited. There was a clamor for the 'Fox,' not to be stilled till one of the young men stepped forward to speak.

'Brothers! The Shaman has spoken wisely. The Wolves have taken our women, and our men are childless. We are grown to a handful. The Wolves have taken our warm furs and given for them evil spirits which dwell in bottles, and clothes which come not from the beaver or the lynx, but are made from the grass.

And they are not warm, and our men die of strange sicknesses. I, the Fox, have taken no woman to wife; and why? Twice have the maidens which pleased me gone to the camps of the Wolf. Even now have I laid by skins of the beaver, of the moose, of the cariboo, that I might win favor in the eyes of Thling-Tinneh, that I might marry Zarinska, his daughter. Even now are her snow-shoes bound to her feet, ready to break trail for the dogs of the Wolf. Nor do I speak for myself alone.

As I have done, so has the Bear. He, too, had fain been the father of her children, and many skins has he cured thereto. I speak for all the young men who know not wives. The Wolves are ever hungry. Always do they take the choice meat at the killing. To the Ravens are left the leavings.

'There is Gugkla,' he cried, brutally pointing out one of the women, who was a cripple.

'Her legs are bent like the ribs of a birch canoe. She cannot gather wood nor carry the meat of the hunters. Did the Wolves choose her?' 'Ai! ai!' vociferated his tribesmen.

'There is Moyri, whose eyes are crossed by the Evil Spirit. Even the babes are affrighted when they gaze upon her, and it is said the bald-face gives her the trail.

'Was she chosen?' Again the cruel applause rang out.

'And there sits Pischet. She does not hearken to my words. Never has she heard the cry of the chit-chat, the voice of her husband, the babble of her child.

'She lives in the White Silence. Cared the Wolves aught for her? No! Theirs is the choice of the kill; ours is the leavings.

'Brothers, it shall not be! No more shall the Wolves slink among our campfires. The time is come.' A great streamer of fire, the aurora borealis, purple, green, and yellow, shot across the zenith, bridging horizon to horizon. With head thrown back and arms extended, he swayed to his climax.

'Behold! The spirits of our fathers have arisen and great deeds are afoot this night!' He stepped back, and another young man somewhat diffidently came forward, pushed on by his comrades. He towered a full head above them, his broad chest defiantly bared to the frost. He swung tentatively from one foot to the other.

Words halted upon his tongue, and he was ill at ease. His face was horrible to look upon, for it had at one time been half torn away by some terrific blow. At last he struck his breast with his clenched fist, drawing sound as from a drum, and his voice rumbled forth as does the surf from an ocean cavern.

'I am the Bear,—the Silver-Tip and the Son of the Silver-Tip! When my voice was yet as a girl's, I slew the lynx, the moose, and the cariboo; when it whistled like the wolverines from under a cache, I crossed the Mountains of the South and slew three of the White Rivers; when it became as the roar of the Chinook, I met the bald-faced grizzly, but gave no trail.' At this he paused, his hand significantly sweeping across his hideous scars.

'I am not as the Fox. My tongue is frozen like the river. I cannot make great talk. My words are few. The Fox says great deeds are afoot this night. Good! Talk flows from his tongue like the freshets of the spring, but he is chary of deeds.

'This night shall I do battle with the Wolf. I shall slay him, and Zarinska shall sit by my fire. The Bear has spoken.' Though pandemonium raged about him, 'Scruff' Mackenzie held his ground.

Aware how useless was the rifle at close quarters, he slipped both holsters to the fore, ready for action, and drew his mittens till his hands were barely shielded by the elbow gauntlets. He knew there was no hope in attack en masse, but true to his boast, was prepared to die with teeth fast-locked. But the Bear restrained his comrades, beating back the more impetuous with his terrible fist. As the tumult began to die away, Mackenzie shot a glance in the direction of Zarinska. It was a superb picture. She was leaning forward on her snow-shoes, lips apart and nostrils quivering, like a tigress about to spring. Her great black eyes were fixed upon her tribesmen, in fear and defiance. So extreme the tension, she had forgotten to breathe. With one hand pressed spasmodically against her breast and the other as tightly gripped about the dog-whip, she was as turned to stone. Even as he looked, relief came to her. Her muscles loosened; with a heavy sigh she settled back, giving him a look of more than love—of worship.

Thling-Tinneh was trying to speak, but his people drowned his voice. Then Mackenzie strode forward. The Fox opened his mouth to a piercing yell, but so savagely did Mackenzie whirl upon him that he shrank back, his larynx all agurgle with suppressed sound. His discomfiture was greeted with roars of laughter, and served to soothe his fellows to a listening mood.

'Brothers! The White Man, whom ye have chosen to call the Wolf, came among you with fair words. He was not like the Innuit; he spoke not lies. He came as a friend, as one who would be a brother. But your men have had their say, and the time for soft words is past.

'First, I will tell you that the Shaman has an evil tongue and is a false prophet, that the messages he spake are not those of the Fire-Bringer. His ears are locked to the voice of the Raven, and out of his own head he weaves cunning fancies, and he has made fools of you. He has no power.

'When the dogs were killed and eaten, and your stomachs were heavy with untanned hide and strips of moccasins; when the old men died, and the old women died, and the babes at the dry dugs of the mothers died; when the land was dark, and ye perished as do the salmon in the fall; aye, when the famine was upon you, did the Shaman bring reward to your hunters? did the Shaman put meat in your bellies? Again I say, the Shaman is without power. Thus I spit upon his face!' Though taken aback by the sacrilege, there was no uproar. Some of the women were even frightened, but among the men there was an uplifting, as though in preparation or anticipation of the miracle. All eyes were turned upon the two central figures. The priest realized the crucial moment, felt his power tottering, opened his mouth in denunciation, but fled backward before the truculent advance, upraised fist, and flashing eyes, of Mackenzie. He sneered and resumed.

'Was I stricken dead? Did the lightning burn me? Did the stars fall from the sky and crush me? Pish! I have done with the dog. Now will I tell you of my people, who are the mightiest of all the peoples, who rule in all the lands. At first we hunt as I hunt, alone.

'After that we hunt in packs; and at last, like the cariboo-run, we sweep across all the land.

'Those whom we take into our lodges live; those who will not come die. Zarinska is a comely maiden, full and strong, fit to become the mother of Wolves. Though I die, such shall she become; for my brothers are many, and they will follow the scent of my dogs.

'Listen to the Law of the Wolf: Whoso taketh the life of one Wolf, the forfeit shall ten of his people pay. In many lands has the price been paid; in many lands shall it yet be paid.

'Now will I deal with the Fox and the Bear. It seems they have cast eyes upon the maiden. So? Behold, I have bought her! Thling-Tinneh leans upon the rifle; the goods of purchase are by his fire. Yet will I be fair to the young men. To the Fox, whose tongue is dry with many words, will I give of tobacco five long plugs.

'Thus will his mouth be wetted that he may make much noise in the council. But to the Bear, of whom I am well proud, will I give of blankets two; of flour, twenty cups; of tobacco, double that of the Fox; and if he fare with me over the Mountains of the East, then will I give him a rifle, mate to Thling-Tinneh's. If not? Good! The Wolf is weary of speech. Yet once again will he say the Law: Whoso taketh the life of one Wolf, the forfeit shall ten of his people pay.'

Mackenzie smiled as he stepped back to his old position, but at heart he was full of trouble. The night was yet dark. The girl came to his side, and he listened closely as she told of the Bear's battle-tricks with the knife.

The decision was for war. In a trice, scores of moccasins were widening the space of beaten snow by the fire. There was much chatter about the seeming defeat of the Shaman; some averred he had but withheld his power, while others conned past events and agreed with the Wolf. The Bear came to the center of the battle-ground, a long naked hunting-knife of Russian make in his hand. The Fox called attention to Mackenzie's revolvers; so he stripped his belt, buckling it about Zarinska, into whose hands he also entrusted his rifle. She shook her head that she could not shoot,—small chance had a woman to handle such precious things.

'Then, if danger come by my back, cry aloud, 'My husband!' No; thus, 'My husband!'

He laughed as she repeated it, pinched her cheek, and reentered the circle. Not only in reach and stature had the Bear the advantage of him, but his blade was longer by a good two inches. 'Scruff' Mackenzie had looked into the eyes of men before, and he knew it was a man who stood against him; yet he quickened to the glint of light on the steel, to the dominant pulse of his race.

Time and again he was forced to the edge of the fire or the deep snow, and time and again, with the foot tactics of the pugilist, he worked back to the center. Not a voice was lifted in encouragement, while his antagonist was heartened with applause, suggestions, and warnings. But his teeth only shut the tighter as the knives clashed together, and he thrust or eluded with a coolness born of conscious strength. At first he felt compassion for his enemy; but this fled before the primal instinct of life, which in turn gave way to the lust of slaughter. The ten thousand years of culture fell from him, and he was a cave-dweller, doing battle for his female.

Twice he pricked the Bear, getting away unscathed; but the third time caught, and to save himself, free hands closed on fighting hands, and they came together.

Then did he realize the tremendous strength of his opponent. His muscles were knotted in painful lumps, and cords and tendons threatened to snap with the strain; yet nearer and nearer came the Russian steel. He tried to break away, but only weakened himself. The fur-clad circle closed in, certain of and anxious to see the final stroke. But with wrestler's trick, swinging partly to the side, he struck at his adversary with his head. Involuntarily the Bear leaned back, disturbing his center of gravity. Simultaneous with this, Mackenzie tripped properly and threw his whole weight forward, hurling him clear through the circle into the deep snow. The Bear floundered out and came back full tilt.

'O my husband!' Zarinska's voice rang out, vibrant with danger.

To the twang of a bow-string, Mackenzie swept low to the ground, and a bonebarbed arrow passed over him into the breast of the Bear, whose momentum carried him over his crouching foe. The next instant Mackenzie was up and about. The bear lay motionless, but across the fire was the Shaman, drawing a second arrow. Mackenzie's knife leaped short in the air. He caught the heavy blade by the point. There was a flash of light as it spanned the fire. Then the Shaman, the hilt alone appearing without his throat, swayed and pitched forward into the glowing embers.

Click! Click!—the Fox had possessed himself of Thling-Tinneh's rifle and was vainly trying to throw a shell into place. But he dropped it at the sound of Mackenzie's laughter.

'So the Fox has not learned the way of the plaything? He is yet a woman.

'Come! Bring it, that I may show thee!' The Fox hesitated.

'Come, I say!' He slouched forward like a beaten cur.

'Thus, and thus; so the thing is done.' A shell flew into place and the trigger was at cock as Mackenzie brought it to shoulder.

'The Fox has said great deeds were afoot this night, and he spoke true. There have been great deeds, yet least among them were those of the Fox. Is he still intent to take Zarinska to his lodge? Is he minded to tread the trail already broken by the Shaman and the Bear?

'No? Good!'

Mackenzie turned contemptuously and drew his knife from the priest's throat.

'Are any of the young men so minded? If so, the Wolf will take them by two and three till none are left. No? Good! Thling-Tinneh, I now give thee this rifle a second time. If, in the days to come, thou shouldst journey to the Country of the Yukon, know thou that there shall always be a place and much food by the fire of the Wolf. The night is now passing into the day. I go, but I may come again. And for the last time, remember the Law of the Wolf!' He was supernatural in their sight as he rejoined Zarinska. She took her place at the head of the team, and the dogs swung into motion. A few moments later they were swallowed up by the ghostly forest. Till now Mackenzie had waited; he slipped into his snow-shoes to follow.

'Has the Wolf forgotten the five long plugs?' Mackenzie turned upon the Fox angrily; then the humor of it struck him.

'I will give thee one short plug.' 'As the Wolf sees fit,' meekly responded the Fox, stretching out his hand.

THE MEN OF FORTY MILE

When Big Jim Belden ventured the apparently innocuous proposition that mush-ice was 'rather pecooliar,' he little dreamed of what it would lead to.

Neither did Lon McFane, when he affirmed that anchor-ice was even more so; nor did Bettles, as he instantly disagreed, declaring the very existence of such a form to be a bugaboo.

'An' ye'd be tellin' me this,' cried Lon, 'after the years ye've spint in the land! An' we atin' out the same pot this many's the day!' 'But the thing's agin reasin,' insisted Bettles.

'Look you, water's warmer than ice—' 'An' little the difference, once ye break through.'

'Still it's warmer, because it ain't froze. An' you say it freezes on the bottom?' 'Only the anchor-ice, David, only the anchor-ice. An' have ye niver drifted along, the water clear as glass, whin suddin, belike a cloud over the sun, the mushy-ice comes bubblin' up an' up till from bank to bank an' bind to bind it's drapin' the river like a first snowfall?' 'Unh, hunh! more'n once when I took a doze at the steering-oar. But it allus come out the nighest side-channel, an' not bubblin' up an' up.' 'But with niver a wink at the helm?'

'No; nor you. It's agin reason. I'll leave it to any man!' Bettles appealed to the circle about the stove, but the fight was on between himself and Lon McFane.

'Reason or no reason, it's the truth I'm tellin' ye. Last fall, a year gone, 'twas Sitka Charley and meself saw the sight, droppin' down the riffle ye'll remember below Fort Reliance. An' regular fall weather it was—the glint o' the sun on the golden larch an' the quakin' aspens; an' the glister of light on ivery ripple; an' beyand, the winter an' the blue haze of the North comin' down hand in hand. It's well ye know the same, with a fringe to the river an' the ice formin' thick in the eddies—an' a snap an' sparkle to the air, an' ye a-feelin' it through all yer blood, a-takin' new lease of life with ivery suck of it. 'Tis then, me boy, the world grows small an' the wandtherlust lays ye by the heels.

'But it's meself as wandthers. As I was sayin', we a-paddlin', with niver a sign of ice, barrin' that by the eddies, when the Injun lifts his paddle an' sings out, 'Lon McFane! Look ye below!' So have I heard, but niver thought to see! As ye know, Sitka Charley, like meself, niver drew first breath in the land; so the sight was new. Then we drifted, with a head over ayther side, peerin' down through the sparkly water. For the world like the days I spint with the pearlers, watchin' the coral banks a-growin' the same as so many gardens under the sea. There it was, the anchor-ice, clingin' an' clusterin' to ivery rock, after the manner of the white coral.

'But the best of the sight was to come. Just after clearin' the tail of the riffle, the water turns quick the color of milk, an' the top of it in wee circles, as when the graylin' rise in the spring, or there's a splatter of wet from the sky. 'Twas the anchor-ice comin' up. To the right, to the lift, as far as iver a man cud see, the water was covered with the same.

'An' like so much porridge it was, slickin' along the bark of the canoe, stickin' like glue to the paddles. It's many's the time I shot the self-same riffle before, and it's many's the time after, but niver a wink of the same have I seen. 'Twas the sight of a lifetime.' 'Do tell!' dryly commented Bettles. 'D'ye think I'd b'lieve such a yarn? I'd ruther say the glister of light'd gone to your eyes, and the snap of the air to your tongue.' ''Twas me own eyes that beheld it, an' if Sitka Charley was here, he'd be the lad to back me.' 'But facts is facts, an' they ain't no gettin' round 'em. It ain't in the nature of things for the water furtherest away from the air to freeze first.' 'But me own eyes-' 'Don't git het up over it,' admonished Bettles, as the quick Celtic anger began to mount.

'Then yer not after belavin' me?' 'Sence you're so blamed forehanded about it, no; I'd b'lieve nature first, and facts.'

'Is it the lie ye'd be givin' me?' threatened Lon. 'Ye'd better be askin' that Siwash wife of yours. I'll lave it to her, for the truth I spake.' Bettles flared up in sudden wrath. The Irishman had unwittingly wounded him; for his wife was the half-breed daughter of a Russian fur-trader, married to him in the Greek Mission of Nulato, a thousand miles or so down the Yukon, thus being of much higher caste than the common Siwash, or native, wife. It was a mere Northland nuance, which none but the Northland adventurer may understand.

'I reckon you kin take it that way,' was his deliberate affirmation.

The next instant Lon McFane had stretched him on the floor, the circle was broken up, and half a dozen men had stepped between.

Bettles came to his feet, wiping the blood from his mouth. 'It hain't new, this takin' and payin' of blows, and don't you never think but that this will be squared.' 'An' niver in me life did I take the lie from mortal man,' was the retort courteous. 'An' it's an avil day I'll not be to hand, waitin' an' willin' to help ye lift yer debts, barrin' no manner of way.'

'Still got that 38-55?' Lon nodded.

'But you'd better git a more likely caliber. Mine'll rip holes through you the size of walnuts.'

'Niver fear; it's me own slugs smell their way with soft noses, an' they'll spread like flapjacks against the coming out beyand. An' when'll I have the pleasure of waitin' on ye? The waterhole's a strikin' locality.' 'Tain't bad. Jest be there in an hour, and you won't set long on my coming.' Both men mittened and left the Post, their ears closed to the remonstrances of their comrades. It was such a little thing; yet with such men, little things, nourished by quick tempers and stubborn natures, soon blossomed into big things.

Besides, the art of burning to bedrock still lay in the womb of the future, and the men of Forty-Mile, shut in by the long Arctic winter, grew high-stomached with overeating and enforced idleness, and became as irritable as do the bees in the fall of the year when the hives are overstocked with honey.

There was no law in the land. The mounted police was also a thing of the future. Each man measured an offense, and meted out the punishment inasmuch as it affected himself.

Rarely had combined action been necessary, and never in all the dreary history of the camp had the eighth article of the Decalogue been violated.

Big Jim Belden called an impromptu meeting. Scruff Mackenzie was placed as temporary chairman, and a messenger dispatched to solicit Father Roubeau's good offices. Their position was paradoxical, and they knew it. By the right of might could they interfere to prevent the duel; yet such action, while in direct line with their wishes, went counter to their opinions. While their rough-hewn, obsolete ethics recognized the individual prerogative of wiping out blow with blow, they could not bear to think of two good comrades, such as Bettles and McFane, meeting in deadly battle. Deeming the man who would not fight on provocation a dastard, when brought to the test it seemed wrong that he should fight.

But a scurry of moccasins and loud cries, rounded off with a pistol-shot, interrupted the discussion. Then the storm-doors opened and Malemute Kid entered, a smoking Colt's in his hand, and a merry light in his eye.

'I got him.' He replaced the empty shell, and added, 'Your dog, Scruff.' 'Yellow Fang?'

Mackenzie asked.

'No; the lop-eared one.' 'The devil! Nothing the matter with him.' 'Come out and take a look.' 'That's all right after all. Buess he's got 'em, too. Yellow Fang came back this morning and took a chunk out of him, and came near to making a widower of me. Made a rush for Zarinska, but she whisked her skirts in his face and escaped with the loss of the same and a good roll in the snow. Then he took to the woods again. Hope he don't come back. Lost any yourself?' 'One—the best one of the pack—Shookum. Started amuck this morning, but didn't get very far. Ran foul of Sitka Charley's team, and they scattered him all over the street. And now two of them are loose, and raging mad; so you see he got his work in. The dog census will be small in the spring if we don't do something.'

'And the man census, too.' 'How's that? Who's in trouble now?' 'Oh, Bettles and Lon McFane had an argument, and they'll be down by the waterhole in a few minutes to settle it.' The incident was repeated for his benefit, and Malemute Kid, accustomed to an obedience which his fellow men never failed to render, took charge of the affair. His quickly formulated plan was explained, and they promised to follow his lead implicitly.

'So you see,' he concluded, 'we do not actually take away their privilege of fighting; and yet I don't believe they'll fight when they see the beauty of the scheme. Life's a game and men the gamblers. They'll stake their whole pile on the one chance in a thousand.

'Take away that one chance, and—they won't play.' He turned to the man in charge of the Post. 'Storekeeper, weight out three fathoms of your best half-inch manila.'

'We'll establish a precedent which will last the men of Forty-Mile to the end of time,' he prophesied. Then he coiled the rope about his arm and led his followers out of doors, just in time to meet the principals.

'What danged right'd he to fetch my wife in?' thundered Bettles to the soothing overtures of a friend. 'Twa'n't called for,' he concluded decisively. 'Twa'n't called for,' he reiterated again and again, pacing up and down and waiting for Lon McFane.

And Lon McFane—his face was hot and tongue rapid as he flaunted insurrection in the face of the Church. 'Then, father,' he cried, 'it's with an aisy heart I'll roll in me flamy blankets, the broad of me back on a bed of coals. Niver shall it be said that Lon McFane took a lie 'twixt the teeth without iver liftin' a hand! An' I'll not ask a blessin'. The years have been wild, but it's the heart was in the right place.' 'But it's not the heart, Lon,' interposed Father Roubeau; 'It's pride that bids you forth to slay your fellow man.' 'Yer Frinch,' Lon replied. And then, turning to leave him, 'An' will ye say a mass if the luck is against me?' But the priest smiled, thrust his moccasined feet to the fore, and went out upon the white breast of the silent river. A packed trail, the width of a sixteen-inch sled, led out to the waterhole. On either side lay the deep, soft snow. The men trod in single file, without conversation; and the black-stoled priest in their midst gave to the function the solemn aspect of a funeral. It was a warm winter's day for Forty-Mile—a day in which the sky, filled with heaviness, drew closer to the earth, and the mercury sought the unwonted level of twenty below. But there was no cheer in the warmth. There was little air in the upper strata, and the clouds hung motionless, giving sullen promise of an early snowfall. And the earth, unresponsive, made no preparation, content in its hibernation.

When the waterhole was reached, Bettles, having evidently reviewed the quarrel during the silent walk, burst out in a final 'Twa'n't called for,' while Lon McFane kept grim silence. Indignation so choked him that he could not speak.

Yet deep down, whenever their own wrongs were not uppermost, both men wondered at their comrades. They had expected opposition, and this tacit acquiescence hurt them. It seemed more was due them from the men they had been so close with, and they felt a vague sense of wrong, rebelling at the thought of so many of their brothers coming out, as on a gala occasion, without one word of protest, to see them shoot each other down. It appeared their worth had diminished in the eyes of the community. The proceedings puzzled them.

'Back to back, David. An' will it be fifty paces to the man, or double the quantity?'

'Fifty,' was the sanguinary reply, grunted out, yet sharply cut.

But the new manila, not prominently displayed, but casually coiled about Malemute Kid's arm, caught the quick eye of the Irishman, and thrilled him with a suspicious fear.

'An' what are ye doin' with the rope?' 'Hurry up!' Malemute Kid glanced at his watch.

'I've a batch of bread in the cabin, and I don't want it to fall. Besides, my feet are getting cold.' The rest of the men manifested their impatience in various suggestive ways.

'But the rope, Kid' It's bran' new, an' sure yer bread's not that heavy it needs raisin' with the like of that?' Bettles by this time had faced around. Father Roubeau, the humor of the situation just dawning on him, hid a smile behind his mittened hand.

'No, Lon; this rope was made for a man.' Malemute Kid could be very impressive on occasion.

'What man?' Bettles was becoming aware of a personal interest.

'The other man.' 'An' which is the one ye'd mane by that?' 'Listen, Lon—and you, too, Bettles! We've been talking this little trouble of yours over, and we've come to one conclusion. We know we have no right to stop your fighting-' 'True for ye, me lad!' 'And we're not going to. But this much we can do, and shall do—make this the only duel in the history of Forty-Mile, set an example for every che-cha-qua that comes up or down the Yukon. The man who escapes killing shall be hanged to the nearest tree. Now, go ahead!'

Lon smiled dubiously, then his face lighted up. 'Pace her off, David—fifty paces, wheel, an' niver a cease firin' till a lad's down for good. 'Tis their hearts'll niver let them do the deed, an' it's well ye should know it for a true Yankee bluff.'

He started off with a pleased grin on his face, but Malemute Kid halted him.

'Lon! It's a long while since you first knew me?' 'Many's the day.' 'And you, Bettles?'

'Five year next June high water.' 'And have you once, in all that time, known me to break my word' Or heard of me breaking it?' Both men shook their heads, striving to fathom what lay beyond.

'Well, then, what do you think of a promise made by me?' 'As good as your bond,' from Bettles.

'The thing to safely sling yer hopes of heaven by,' promptly endorsed Lon McFane.

'Listen! I, Malemute Kid, give you my word—and you know what that means that the man who is not shot stretches rope within ten minutes after the shooting.' He stepped back as Pilate might have done after washing his hands.

A pause and a silence came over the men of Forty-Mile. The sky drew still closer, sending down a crystal flight of frost—little geometric designs, perfect, evanescent as a breath, yet destined to exist till the returning sun had covered half its northern journey.

Both men had led forlorn hopes in their time—led with a curse or a jest on their tongues, and in their souls an unswerving faith in the God of Chance. But that merciful deity had been shut out from the present deal. They studied the face of Malemute Kid, but they studied as one might the Sphinx. As the quiet minutes passed, a feeling that speech was incumbent on them began to grow. At last the howl of a wolf-dog cracked the silence from the direction of Forty-Mile. The weird sound swelled with all the pathos of a breaking heart, then died away in a long-drawn sob.

'Well I be danged!' Bettles turned up the collar of his mackinaw jacket and stared about him helplessly.

'It's a gloryus game yer runnin', Kid,' cried Lon McFane. 'All the percentage of the house an' niver a bit to the man that's buckin'. The Devil himself'd niver tackle such a cinch—and damned if I do.' There were chuckles, throttled in gurgling throats, and winks brushed away with the frost which rimed the eyelashes, as the men climbed the ice-notched bank and started across the street to the Post. But the long howl had drawn nearer, invested with a new note of menace. A woman screamed round the corner. There was a cry of, 'Here he comes!' Then an Indian boy, at the head of half a dozen frightened dogs, racing with death, dashed into the crowd. And behind came Yellow Fang, a bristle of hair and a flash of gray. Everybody but the Yankee fled.

The Indian boy had tripped and fallen. Bettles stopped long enough to grip him by the slack of his furs, then headed for a pile of cordwood already occupied by a number of his comrades. Yellow Fang, doubling after one of the dogs, came leaping back. The fleeing animal, free of the rabies, but crazed with fright, whipped Bettles off his feet and flashed on up the street. Malemute Kid took a flying shot at Yellow Fang. The mad dog whirled a half airspring, came down on his back, then, with a single leap, covered half the distance between himself and Bettles.

But the fatal spring was intercepted. Lon McFane leaped from the woodpile, countering him in midair. Over they rolled, Lon holding him by the throat at arm's length, blinking under the fetid slaver which sprayed his face. Then Bettles, revolver in hand and coolly waiting a chance, settled the combat.

'Twas a square game, Kid,' Lon remarked, rising to his feet and shaking the snow from out his sleeves; 'with a fair percentage to meself that bucked it.' That night, while Lon McFane sought the forgiving arms of the Church in the direction of Father Roubeau's cabin, Malemute Kid talked long to little purpose.

'But would you,' persisted Mackenzie, 'supposing they had fought?' 'Have I ever broken my word?' 'No; but that isn't the point. Answer the question. Would you?' Malemute Kid straightened up. 'Scruff, I've been asking myself that question ever since, and—'

'Well?'

'Well, as yet, I haven't found the answer.'

IN A FAR COUNTRY

When a man journeys into a far country, he must be prepared to forget many of the things he has learned, and to acquire such customs as are inherent with existence in the new land; he must abandon the old ideals and the old gods, and oftentimes he must reverse the very codes by which his conduct has hitherto been shaped. To those who have the protean faculty of adaptability, the novelty of such change may even be a source of pleasure; but to those who happen to be hardened to the ruts in which they were created, the pressure of the altered environment is unbearable, and they chafe in body and in spirit under the new restrictions which they do not understand. This chafing is bound to act and react, producing divers evils and leading to various misfortunes. It were better for the man who cannot fit himself to the new groove to return to his own country; if he delay too long, he will surely die.

The man who turns his back upon the comforts of an elder civilization, to face the savage youth, the primordial simplicity of the North, may estimate success at an inverse ratio to the quantity and quality of his hopelessly fixed habits. He will soon discover, if he be a fit candidate, that the material habits are the less important. The exchange of such things as a dainty menu for rough fare, of the stiff leather shoe for the soft, shapeless moccasin, of the feather bed for a couch in the snow, is after all a very easy matter. But his pinch will come in learning properly to shape his mind's attitude toward all things, and especially toward his fellow man. For the courtesies of ordinary life, he must substitute unselfishness, forbearance, and tolerance. Thus, and thus only, can he gain that pearl of great price—true comradeship. He must not say 'thank you'; he must mean it without opening his mouth, and prove it by responding in kind. In short, he must substitute the deed for the word, the spirit for the letter.

When the world rang with the tale of Arctic gold, and the lure of the North gripped the heartstrings of men, Carter Weatherbee threw up his snug clerkship, turned the half of his savings over to his wife, and with the remainder bought an outfit. There was no romance in his nature—the bondage of commerce had crushed all that; he was simply tired of the ceaseless grind, and wished to risk great hazards in view of corresponding returns. Like many another fool, disdaining the old trails used by the Northland pioneers for a score of years, he hurried to Edmonton in the spring of the year; and there, unluckily for his soul's welfare, he allied himself with a party of men.

There was nothing unusual about this party, except its plans. Even its goal, like that of all the other parties, was the Klondike. But the route it had mapped out to attain that goal took away the breath of the hardiest native, born and bred to the vicissitudes of the Northwest. Even Jacques Baptiste, born of a Chippewa woman and a renegade voyageur (having raised his first whimpers in a deerskin lodge north of the sixty-fifth parallel, and had the same hushed by blissful sucks of raw tallow), was surprised. Though he sold his services to them and agreed to travel even to the never-opening ice, he shook his head ominously whenever his advice was asked.

Percy Cuthfert's evil star must have been in the ascendant, for he, too, joined this company of argonauts. He was an ordinary man, with a bank account as deep as his culture, which is saying a good deal. He had no reason to embark on such a venture—no reason in the world save that he suffered from an abnormal development of sentimentality. He mistook this for the true spirit of romance and adventure. Many another man has done the like, and made as fatal a mistake.

The first break-up of spring found the party following the ice-run of Elk River. It was an imposing fleet, for the outfit was large, and they were accompanied by a disreputable contingent of half-breed voyageurs with their women and children. Day in and day out, they labored with the bateaux and canoes, fought mosquitoes and other kindred pests, or sweated and swore at the portages. Severe toil like this lays a man naked to the very roots of his soul, and ere Lake Athabasca was lost in the south, each member of the party had hoisted his true colors.

The two shirks and chronic grumblers were Carter Weatherbee and Percy Cuthfert. The whole party complained less of its aches and pains than did either of them. Not once did they volunteer for the thousand and one petty duties of the camp. A bucket of water to be brought, an extra armful of wood to be chopped, the dishes to be washed and wiped, a search to be made through the outfit for some suddenly indispensable article—and these two effete scions of civilization discovered sprains or blisters requiring instant attention.

They were the first to turn in at night, with score of tasks yet undone; the last to turn out in the morning, when the start should be in readiness before the breakfast was begun.

They were the first to fall to at mealtime, the last to have a hand in the cooking; the first to dive for a slim delicacy, the last to discover they had added to their own another man's share. If they toiled at the oars, they slyly cut the water at each stroke and allowed the boat's momentum to float up the blade. They thought nobody noticed; but their comrades swore under their breaths and grew to hate them, while Jacques Baptiste sneered openly and damned them from morning till night. But Jacques Baptiste was no gentleman.

At the Great Slave, Hudson Bay dogs were purchased, and the fleet sank to the guards with its added burden of dried fish and pemican. Then canoe and bateau answered to the swift current of the Mackenzie, and they plunged into the Great Barren Ground. Every likely-looking 'feeder' was prospected, but the elusive 'pay-dirt' danced ever to the north. At the Great Bear, overcome by the common dread of the Unknown Lands, their voyageurs began to desert, and Fort of Good Hope saw the last and bravest bending to the towlines as they bucked the current down which they had so treacherously glided.

Jacques Baptiste alone remained. Had he not sworn to travel even to the never-opening ice? The lying charts, compiled in main from hearsay, were now constantly consulted.

And they felt the need of hurry, for the sun had already passed its northern solstice and was leading the winter south again. Skirting the shores of the bay, where the Mackenzie disembogues into the Arctic Ocean, they entered the mouth of the Little Peel River. Then began the arduous up-stream toil, and the two Incapables fared worse than ever. Towline and pole, paddle and tumpline, rapids and portages—such tortures served to give the one a deep disgust for great hazards, and printed for the other a fiery text on the true romance of adventure. One day they waxed mutinous, and being vilely cursed by Jacques Baptiste, turned, as worms sometimes will. But the half-breed thrashed the twain, and sent them, bruised and bleeding, about their work. It was the first time either had been manhandled.

Abandoning their river craft at the headwaters of the Little Peel, they consumed the rest of the summer in the great portage over the Mackenzie watershed to the West

Rat. This little stream fed the Porcupine, which in turn joined the Yukon where that mighty highway of the North countermarches on the Arctic Circle.

But they had lost in the race with winter, and one day they tied their rafts to the thick eddy-ice and hurried their goods ashore. That night the river jammed and broke several times; the following morning it had fallen asleep for good. 'We can't be more'n four hundred miles from the Yukon,' concluded Sloper, multiplying his thumb nails by the scale of the map. The council, in which the two Incapables had whined to excellent disadvantage, was drawing to a close.

'Hudson Bay Post, long time ago. No use um now.' Jacques Baptiste's father had made the trip for the Fur Company in the old days, incidentally marking the trail with a couple of frozen toes.

Sufferin' cracky!' cried another of the party. 'No whites?' 'Nary white,' Sloper sententiously affirmed; 'but it's only five hundred more up the Yukon to Dawson. Call it a rough thousand from here.' Weatherbee and Cuthfert groaned in chorus.

'How long'll that take, Baptiste?' The half-breed figured for a moment. 'Workum like hell, no man play out, ten—twenty—forty—fifty days. Um babies come' (designating the Incapables), 'no can tell. Mebbe when hell freeze over; mebbe not then.' The manufacture of snowshoes and moccasins ceased. Somebody called the name of an absent member, who came out of an ancient cabin at the edge of the campfire and joined them. The cabin was one of the many mysteries which lurk in the vast recesses of the North. Built when and by whom, no man could tell.

Two graves in the open, piled high with stones, perhaps contained the secret of those early wanderers. But whose hand had piled the stones? The moment had come. Jacques Baptiste paused in the fitting of a harness and pinned the struggling dog in the snow. The cook made mute protest for delay, threw a handful of bacon into a noisy pot of beans, then came to attention. Sloper rose to his feet. His body was a ludicrous contrast to the healthy physiques of the Incapables. Yellow and weak, fleeing from a South American fever-hole, he had not broken his flight across the zones, and was still able to toil with men. His weight was probably ninety pounds, with the heavy hunting knife thrown in, and his grizzled hair told of a prime which had ceased to be. The fresh young muscles of either Weatherbee or Cuthfert were equal to ten times the endeavor of his; yet he could walk them into the earth in a day's journey. And all this day he had whipped his stronger comrades into venturing a thousand miles of the stiffest hardship man can conceive. He was the incarnation of the unrest of his race, and the old Teutonic stubbornness, dashed with the quick grasp and action of the Yankee, held the flesh in the bondage of the spirit.

'All those in favor of going on with the dogs as soon as the ice sets, say ay.' 'Ay!' rang out eight voices—voices destined to string a trail of oaths along many a hundred miles of pain.

'Contrary minded?' 'No!' For the first time the Incapables were united without some compromise of personal interests.

'And what are you going to do about it?' Weatherbee added belligerently.

'Majority rule! Majority rule!' clamored the rest of the party.

'I know the expedition is liable to fall through if you don't come,' Sloper replied sweetly; 'but I guess, if we try real hard, we can manage to do without you. What do you say, boys?' The sentiment was cheered to the echo.

'But I say, you know,' Cuthfert ventured apprehensively; 'what's a chap like me to do?'

'Ain't you coming with us.' 'No—o.' 'Then do as you damn well please. We won't have nothing to say.' 'Kind o' calkilate yuh might settle it with that canoodlin' pardner of yourn,' suggested a heavy-going Westerner from the Dakotas, at the same time pointing out Weatherbee. 'He'll be shore to ask yuh what yur a-goin' to do when it comes to cookin' an' gatherin' the wood.' 'Then we'll consider it all arranged,' concluded Sloper.

'We'll pull out tomorrow, if we camp within five miles—just to get everything in running order and remember if we've forgotten anything.' The sleds groaned by on their steel-shod runners, and the dogs strained low in the harnesses in which they were born to die.

Jacques Baptiste paused by the side of Sloper to get a last glimpse of the cabin. The smoke curled up pathetically from the Yukon stovepipe. The two Incapables were watching them from the doorway.

Sloper laid his hand on the other's shoulder.

'Jacques Baptiste, did you ever hear of the Kilkenny cats?' The half-breed shook his head.

'Well, my friend and good comrade, the Kilkenny cats fought till neither hide, nor hair, nor yowl, was left. You understand?—till nothing was left. Very good.

Now, these two men don't like work. They'll be all alone in that cabin all winter—a mighty long, dark winter. Kilkenny cats—well?' The Frenchman in Baptiste shrugged his shoulders, but the Indian in him was silent. Nevertheless, it was an eloquent shrug, pregnant with prophecy. Things prospered in the little cabin at first. The rough badinage of their comrades had made Weatherbee and Cuthfert conscious of the mutual responsibility which had devolved upon them; besides, there was not so much work after all for two healthy men. And the removal of the cruel whiphand, or in other words the bulldozing half-breed, had brought with it a joyous reaction. At first, each strove to outdo the other, and they performed petty tasks with an unction which would have opened the eyes of their comrades who were now wearing out bodies and souls on the Long Trail.

All care was banished. The forest, which shouldered in upon them from three sides, was an inexhaustible woodyard. A few yards from their door slept the Porcupine, and a hole through its winter robe formed a bubbling spring of water, crystal clear and painfully cold. But they soon grew to find fault with even that. The hole would persist in freezing up, and thus gave them many a miserable hour of ice-chopping. The unknown builders of the cabin had extended the sidelogs so as to support a cache at the rear. In this was stored the bulk of the party's provisions.

Food there was, without stint, for three times the men who were fated to live upon it. But the most of it was the kind which built up brawn and sinew, but did not tickle the palate.

True, there was sugar in plenty for two ordinary men; but these two were little else than children. They early discovered the virtues of hot water judiciously saturated with sugar, and they prodigally swam their flapjacks and soaked their crusts in the rich, white syrup.

Then coffee and tea, and especially the dried fruits, made disastrous inroads upon it. The first words they had were over the sugar question. And it is a really serious thing when two men, wholly dependent upon each other for company, begin to quarrel.

Weatherbee loved to discourse blatantly on politics, while Cuthfert, who had been prone to clip his coupons and let the commonwealth jog on as best it might, either ignored the subject or delivered himself of startling epigrams. But the clerk was too obtuse to appreciate the clever shaping of thought, and this waste of ammunition irritated Cuthfert.

He had been used to blinding people by his brilliancy, and it worked him quite a hardship, this loss of an audience. He felt personally aggrieved and unconsciously held his muttonhead companion responsible for it.

Save existence, they had nothing in common—came in touch on no single point. Weatherbee was a clerk who had known naught but clerking all his life; Cuthfert was a master of arts, a dabbler in oils, and had written not a little. The one was a lower-class man who considered himself a gentleman, and the other was a gentleman who knew himself to be such. From this it may be remarked that a man can be a gentleman without possessing the first instinct of true comradeship. The clerk was as sensuous as the other was aesthetic, and his love adventures, told at great length and chiefly coined from his imagination, affected the supersensitive master of arts in the same way as so many whiffs of sewer gas. He deemed the clerk a filthy, uncultured brute, whose place was in the muck with the swine, and told him so; and he was reciprocally informed that he was a milk-and-water sissy and a cad. Weatherbee could not have defined 'cad' for his life; but it satisfied its purpose, which after all seems the main point in life.

Weatherbee flatted every third note and sang such songs as 'The Boston Burglar' and 'the Handsome Cabin Boy,' for hours at a time, while Cuthfert wept with rage, till he could stand it no longer and fled into the outer cold. But there was no escape. The intense frost could not be endured for long at a time, and the little cabin crowded them—beds, stove, table, and all—into a space of ten by twelve. The very presence of either became a personal affront to the other, and they lapsed into sullen silences which increased in length and strength as the days went by. Occasionally, the flash of an eye or the curl of a lip got the better of them, though they strove to wholly ignore each other during these mute periods.

And a great wonder sprang up in the breast of each, as to how God had ever come to create the other.

With little to do, time became an intolerable burden to them. This naturally made them still lazier. They sank into a physical lethargy which there was no escaping, and which made them rebel at the performance of the smallest chore. One morning when it was his turn to cook the common breakfast, Weatherbee rolled out of his blankets, and to the snoring of his companion, lighted first the slush lamp and then the fire. The kettles were frozen hard, and there was no water in the cabin with which to wash. But he did not mind that. Waiting for it to thaw, he sliced the bacon and plunged into the hateful task of bread-making. Cuthfert had been slyly watching through his half-closed lids.

Consequently there was a scene, in which they fervently blessed each other, and agreed, henceforth, that each do his own cooking. A week later, Cuthfert neglected his morning ablutions, but none the less complacently ate the meal which he had cooked. Weatherbee grinned. After that the foolish custom of washing passed out of their lives.

As the sugar-pile and other little luxuries dwindled, they began to be afraid they were not getting their proper shares, and in order that they might not be robbed, they fell to gorging themselves. The luxuries suffered in this gluttonous contest, as did also the men.

In the absence of fresh vegetables and exercise, their blood became impoverished, and a loathsome, purplish rash crept over their bodies. Yet they refused to heed the warning.

Next, their muscles and joints began to swell, the flesh turning black, while their mouths, gums, and lips took on the color of rich cream. Instead of being drawn together by their misery, each gloated over the other's symptoms as the scurvy took its course.

They lost all regard for personal appearance, and for that matter, common decency. The cabin became a pigpen, and never once were the beds made or fresh pine boughs laid underneath. Yet they could not keep to their blankets, as they would have wished; for the frost was inexorable, and the fire box consumed much fuel. The hair of their heads and faces grew long and shaggy, while their garments would have disgusted a ragpicker. But they did not care. They were sick, and there was no one to see; besides, it was very painful to move about.

To all this was added a new trouble—the Fear of the North. This Fear was the joint child of the Great Cold and the Great Silence, and was born in the darkness of December, when the sun dipped below the horizon for good. It affected them according to their natures.

Weatherbee fell prey to the grosser superstitions, and did his best to resurrect the spirits which slept in the forgotten graves. It was a fascinating thing, and in his dreams they came to him from out of the cold, and snuggled into his blankets, and told him of their toils and troubles ere they died. He shrank away from the clammy contact as they drew closer and twined their frozen limbs about him, and when they whispered in his ear of things to come, the cabin rang with his frightened shrieks. Cuthfert did not understand—for they no longer spoke—and when thus awakened he invariably grabbed for his revolver. Then he would sit up in bed, shivering nervously, with the weapon trained on the unconscious dreamer. Cuthfert deemed the man going mad, and so came to fear for his life.

His own malady assumed a less concrete form. The mysterious artisan who had laid the cabin, log by log, had pegged a wind-vane to the ridgepole. Cuthfert noticed it always pointed south, and one day, irritated by its steadfastness of purpose, he turned it toward the east. He watched eagerly, but never a breath came by to disturb it. Then he turned the vane to the north, swearing never again to touch it till the wind did blow. But the air frightened him with its unearthly calm, and he often rose in the middle of the night to see if the vane had veered—ten degrees would have satisfied him. But no, it poised above him as unchangeable as fate.

His imagination ran riot, till it became to him a fetish. Sometimes he followed the path it pointed across the dismal dominions, and allowed his soul to become saturated with the Fear. He dwelt upon the unseen and the unknown till the burden of eternity appeared to be crushing him. Everything in the Northland had that crushing effect—the absence of life and motion; the darkness; the infinite peace of the brooding land; the ghastly silence, which made the echo of each heartbeat a sacrilege; the solemn forest which seemed to guard an awful, inexpressible something, which neither word nor thought could compass.

The world he had so recently left, with its busy nations and great enterprises, seemed very far away. Recollections occasionally obtruded—recollections of marts and galleries and crowded thoroughfares, of evening dress and social functions, of good men and dear women he had known—but they were dim memories of a life he had lived long centuries agone, on some other planet. This phantasm was the Reality. Standing beneath the wind-vane, his eyes fixed on the polar skies, he could not bring himself to realize that the Southland really existed, that at that very moment it was a-roar with life and action.

There was no Southland, no men being born of women, no giving and taking in marriage.

Beyond his bleak skyline there stretched vast solitudes, and beyond these still vaster solitudes.

There were no lands of sunshine, heavy with the perfume of flowers. Such things were only old dreams of paradise. The sunlands of the West and the spicelands of the East, the smiling Arcadias and blissful Islands of the Blest—ha! ha! His laughter split the void and shocked him with its unwonted sound. There was no sun.

This was the Universe, dead and cold and dark, and he its only citizen. Weatherbee? At such moments Weatherbee did not count. He was a Caliban, a monstrous phantom, fettered to him for untold ages, the penalty of some forgotten crime.

He lived with Death among the dead, emasculated by the sense of his own insignificance, crushed by the passive mastery of the slumbering ages. The magnitude of all things appalled him. Everything partook of the superlative save himself—the perfect cessation of wind and motion, the immensity of the snow-covered wildness, the height of the sky and the depth of the silence. That wind-vane—if it would only move. If a thunderbolt would fall, or the forest flare up in flame.

The rolling up of the heavens as a scroll, the crash of Doom—anything, anything! But no, nothing moved; the Silence crowded in, and the Fear of the North laid icy fingers on his heart.

Once, like another Crusoe, by the edge of the river he came upon a track—the faint tracery of a snowshoe rabbit on the delicate snow-crust. It was a revelation.

There was life in the Northland. He would follow it, look upon it, gloat over it.

He forgot his swollen muscles, plunging through the deep snow in an ecstasy of anticipation. The forest swallowed him up, and the brief midday twilight vanished; but he pursued his quest till exhausted nature asserted itself and laid him helpless in the snow.

There he groaned and cursed his folly, and knew the track to be the fancy of his brain; and late that night he dragged himself into the cabin on hands and knees, his cheeks frozen and a strange numbness about his feet. Weatherbee grinned malevolently, but made no offer to help him. He thrust needles into his toes and thawed them out by the stove. A week later mortification set in.

But the clerk had his own troubles. The dead men came out of their graves more frequently now, and rarely left him, waking or sleeping. He grew to wait and dread their coming, never passing the twin cairns without a shudder. One night they came to him in his sleep and led him forth to an appointed task. Frightened into inarticulate horror, he awoke between the heaps of stones and fled wildly to the cabin. But he had lain there for some time, for his feet and cheeks were also frozen.

Sometimes he became frantic at their insistent presence, and danced about the cabin, cutting the empty air with an axe, and smashing everything within reach.

During these ghostly encounters, Cuthfert huddled into his blankets and followed the madman about with a cocked revolver, ready to shoot him if he came too near.

But, recovering from one of these spells, the clerk noticed the weapon trained upon him.

His suspicions were aroused, and thenceforth he, too, lived in fear of his life. They watched each other closely after that, and faced about in startled fright whenever either passed behind the other's back. The apprehensiveness became a mania which controlled them even in their sleep. Through mutual fear they tacitly let the slush-lamp burn all night, and saw to a plentiful supply of bacon-grease before retiring. The slightest movement on the part of one was sufficient to arouse the other, and many a still watch their gazes countered as they shook beneath their blankets with fingers on the trigger-guards.

What with the Fear of the North, the mental strain, and the ravages of the disease, they lost all semblance of humanity, taking on the appearance of wild beasts, hunted and desperate. Their cheeks and noses, as an aftermath of the freezing, had turned black.

Their frozen toes had begun to drop away at the first and second joints. Every movement brought pain, but the fire box was insatiable, wringing a ransom of torture from their miserable bodies. Day in, day out, it demanded its food—a veritable pound of flesh—and they dragged themselves into the forest to chop wood on their knees. Once, crawling thus in search of dry sticks, unknown to each other they entered a thicket from opposite sides.

Suddenly, without warning, two peering death's-heads confronted each other. Suffering had so transformed them that recognition was impossible. They sprang to their feet, shrieking with terror, and dashed away on their mangled stumps; and falling at the cabin's door, they clawed and scratched like demons till they discovered their mistake.

Occasionally they lapsed normal, and during one of these sane intervals, the chief bone of contention, the sugar, had been divided equally between them. They guarded their separate sacks, stored up in the cache, with jealous eyes; for there were but a few cupfuls left, and they were totally devoid of faith in each other.

But one day Cuthfert made a mistake. Hardly able to move, sick with pain, with his head swimming and eyes blinded, he crept into the cache, sugar canister in hand, and mistook Weatherbee's sack for his own.

January had been born but a few days when this occurred. The sun had some time since passed its lowest southern declination, and at meridian now threw flaunting streaks of yellow light upon the northern sky. On the day following his mistake with the sugar-bag, Cuthfert found himself feeling better, both in body and in spirit. As noontime drew near and the day brightened, he dragged himself outside to feast on the evanescent glow, which was to him an earnest of the sun's future intentions. Weatherbee was also feeling somewhat better, and crawled out beside him. They propped themselves in the snow beneath the moveless wind-vane, and waited.

The stillness of death was about them. In other climes, when nature falls into such moods, there is a subdued air of expectancy, a waiting for some small voice to take up the broken strain. Not so in the North. The two men had lived seeming eons in this ghostly peace.

They could remember no song of the past; they could conjure no song of the future. This unearthly calm had always been—the tranquil silence of eternity.

Their eyes were fixed upon the north. Unseen, behind their backs, behind the towering mountains to the south, the sun swept toward the zenith of another sky than theirs. Sole spectators of the mighty canvas, they watched the false dawn slowly grow. A faint flame began to glow and smoulder. It deepened in intensity, ringing the changes of reddish-yellow, purple, and saffron. So bright did it become that Cuthfert thought the sun must surely be behind it—a miracle, the sun rising in the north! Suddenly, without warning and without fading, the canvas was swept clean. There was no color in the sky. The light had gone out of the day.

They caught their breaths in half-sobs. But lo! the air was aglint with particles of scintillating frost, and there, to the north, the wind-vane lay in vague outline of the snow.

A shadow! A shadow! It was exactly midday. They jerked their heads hurriedly to the south. A golden rim peeped over the mountain's snowy shoulder, smiled upon them an instant, then dipped from sight again.

There were tears in their eyes as they sought each other. A strange softening came over them. They felt irresistibly drawn toward each other. The sun was coming back again. It would be with them tomorrow, and the next day, and the next.

And it would stay longer every visit, and a time would come when it would ride their heaven day and night, never once dropping below the skyline. There would be no night.

The ice-locked winter would be broken; the winds would blow and the forests answer; the land would bathe in the blessed sunshine, and life renew.

Hand in hand, they would quit this horrid dream and journey back to the Southland. They lurched blindly forward, and their hands met—their poor maimed hands, swollen and distorted beneath their mittens.

But the promise was destined to remain unfulfilled. The Northland is the Northland, and men work out their souls by strange rules, which other men, who have not journeyed into far countries, cannot come to understand.

An hour later, Cuthfert put a pan of bread into the oven, and fell to speculating on what the surgeons could do with his feet when he got back. Home did not seem so very far away now. Weatherbee was rummaging in the cache. Of a sudden, he raised a whirlwind of blasphemy, which in turn ceased with startling abruptness. The other man had robbed his sugar-sack. Still, things might have happened differently, had not the two dead men come out from under the stones and hushed the hot words in his throat. They led him quite gently from the cache, which he forgot to close. That consummation was reached; that something they had whispered to him in his dreams was about to happen. They guided him gently, very gently, to the woodpile, where they put the axe in his hands.

Then they helped him shove open the cabin door, and he felt sure they shut it after him—at least he heard it slam and the latch fall sharply into place. And he knew they were waiting just without, waiting for him to do his task.

'Carter! I say, Carter!' Percy Cuthfert was frightened at the look on the clerk's face, and he made haste to put the table between them.

Carter Weatherbee followed, without haste and without enthusiasm. There was neither pity nor passion in his face, but rather the patient, stolid look of one who has certain work to do and goes about it methodically.

'I say, what's the matter?'

The clerk dodged back, cutting off his retreat to the door, but never opening his mouth.

'I say, Carter, I say; let's talk. There's a good chap.' The master of arts was thinking rapidly, now, shaping a skillful flank movement on the bed where his Smith & Wesson lay. Keeping his eyes on the madman, he rolled backward on the bunk, at the same time clutching the pistol.

'Carter!' The powder flashed full in Weatherbee's face, but he swung his weapon and leaped forward. The axe bit deeply at the base of the spine, and Percy Cuthfert felt all consciousness of his lower limbs leave him. Then the clerk fell heavily upon him, clutching him by the throat with feeble fingers. The sharp bite of the axe had caused Cuthfert to drop the pistol, and as his lungs panted for release, he fumbled aimlessly for it among the blankets. Then he remembered. He slid a hand up the clerk's belt to the sheath-knife; and they drew very close to each other in that last clinch.

Percy Cuthfert felt his strength leave him. The lower portion of his body was useless, The inert weight of Weatherbee crushed him—crushed him and pinned him there like a bear under a trap. The cabin became filled with a familiar odor, and he knew the bread to be burning. Yet what did it matter? He would never need it. And there were all of six cupfuls of sugar in the cache—if he had foreseen this he would not have been so saving the last several days. Would the wind-vane ever move? Why not' Had he not seen the sun today? He would go and see. No; it was impossible to move. He had not thought the clerk so heavy a man.

How quickly the cabin cooled! The fire must be out. The cold was forcing in.

It must be below zero already, and the ice creeping up the inside of the door. He could not see it, but his past experience enabled him to gauge its progress by the cabin's temperature. The lower hinge must be white ere now. Would the tale of this ever reach the world? How would his friends take it? They would read it over their coffee, most likely, and talk it over at the clubs. He could see them very clearly, 'Poor Old Cuthfert,' they murmured; 'not such a bad sort of a chap, after all.' He smiled at their eulogies, and passed on in search of a Turkish bath. It was the same old crowd upon the streets.

Strange, they did not notice his moosehide moccasins and tattered German socks! He would take a cab. And after the bath a shave would not be bad. No; he would eat first.

Steak, and potatoes, and green things how fresh it all was! And what was that? Squares of honey, streaming liquid amber! But why did they bring so much? Ha! ha! he could never eat it all.

Shine! Why certainly. He put his foot on the box. The bootblack looked curiously up at him, and he remembered his moosehide moccasins and went away hastily.

Hark! The wind-vane must be surely spinning. No; a mere singing in his ears.

That was all—a mere singing. The ice must have passed the latch by now. More likely the upper hinge was covered. Between the moss-chinked roof-poles, little points of frost began to appear. How slowly they grew! No; not so slowly. There was a new one, and there another. Two—three—four; they were coming too fast to count. There were two growing together. And there, a third had joined them.

Why, there were no more spots. They had run together and formed a sheet.

Well, he would have company. If Gabriel ever broke the silence of the North, they would stand together, hand in hand, before the great White Throne. And God would judge them, God would judge them!

Then Percy Cuthfert closed his eyes and dropped off to sleep.

TO THE MAN ON THE TRAIL

'Dump it in!' 'But I say, Kid, isn't that going it a little too strong? Whisky and alcohol's bad enough; but when it comes to brandy and pepper sauce and-' 'Dump it in. Who's making this punch, anyway?' And Malemute Kid smiled benignantly through the clouds of steam. 'By the time you've been in this country as long as I have, my son, and lived on rabbit tracks and salmon belly, you'll learn that Christmas comes only once per annum.

And a Christmas without punch is sinking a hole to bedrock with nary a pay streak.'

'Stack up on that fer a high cyard,' approved Big Jim Belden, who had come down from his claim on Mazy May to spend Christmas, and who, as everyone knew, had been living the two months past on straight moose meat. 'Hain't fergot the hooch we-uns made on the Tanana, hey yeh?' 'Well, I guess yes. Boys, it would have done your hearts good to see that whole tribe fighting drunk—and all because of a glorious ferment of sugar and sour dough. That was before your time,' Malemute Kid said as he turned to Stanley Prince, a young mining expert who had been in two years. 'No white women in the country then, and Mason wanted to get married. Ruth's father was chief of the Tananas, and objected, like the rest of the tribe. Stiff? Why, I used my last pound of sugar; finest work in that line I ever did in my life. You should have seen the chase, down the river and across the portage.' 'But the squaw?' asked Louis Savoy, the tall French Canadian, becoming interested; for he had heard of this wild deed when at Forty Mile the preceding winter.

Then Malemute Kid, who was a born raconteur, told the unvarnished tale of the Northland Lochinvar. More than one rough adventurer of the North felt his heart-strings draw closer and experienced vague yearnings for the sunnier pastures of the Southland, where life promised something more than a barren struggle with cold and death.

'We struck the Yukon just behind the first ice run,' he concluded, 'and the tribe only a quarter of an hour behind. But that saved us; for the second run broke the jam above and shut them out. When they finally got into Nuklukyeto, the whole post was ready for them.

'And as to the forgathering, ask Father Roubeau here: he performed the ceremony.' The Jesuit took the pipe from his lips but could only express his gratification with patriarchal smiles, while Protestant and Catholic vigorously applauded.

'By gar!' ejaculated Louis Savoy, who seemed overcome by the romance of it. 'La petite squaw: mon Mason brav. By gar!' Then, as the first tin cups of punch went round, Bettles the Unquenchable sprang to his feet and struck up his favorite drinking song: 'There's Henry Ward Beecher And Sunday-school teachers, All drink of the sassafras root; But you bet all the same, If it had its right name, It's the juice of the forbidden fruit.'

'Oh, the juice of the forbidden fruit,' roared out the bacchanalian chorus, 'Oh, the juice of the forbidden fruit; But you bet all the same, If it had its right name, It's the juice of the forbidden fruit.'

Malemute Kid's frightful concoction did its work; the men of the camps and trails unbent in its genial glow, and jest and song and tales of past adventure went round the board.

Aliens from a dozen lands, they toasted each and all. It was the Englishman, Prince, who pledged 'Uncle Sam, the precocious infant of the New World'; the Yankee, Bettles, who drank to 'The Queen, God bless her'; and together, Savoy and Meyers, the German trader, clanged their cups to Alsace and Lorraine.

Then Malemute Kid arose, cup in hand, and glanced at the greased-paper window, where the frost stood full three inches thick. 'A health to the man on trail this night; may his grub hold out; may his dogs keep their legs; may his matches never miss fire.' Crack!

Crack! heard the familiar music of the dog whip, the whining howl of the Malemutes, and the crunch of a sled as it drew up to the cabin. Conversation languished while they waited the issue.

'An old-timer; cares for his dogs and then himself,' whispered Malemute Kid to Prince as they listened to the snapping jaws and the wolfish snarls and yelps of pain which proclaimed to their practiced ears that the stranger was beating back their dogs while he fed his own.

Then came the expected knock, sharp and confident, and the stranger entered.

Dazzled by the light, he hesitated a moment at the door, giving to all a chance for scrutiny. He was a striking personage, and a most picturesque one, in his Arctic dress of wool and fur. Standing six foot two or three, with proportionate breadth of shoulders and depth of chest, his smooth-shaven face nipped by the cold to a gleaming pink, his long lashes and eyebrows white with ice, and the ear and neck flaps of his great wolfskin cap loosely raised, he seemed, of a verity, the Frost King, just stepped in out of the night.

Clasped outside his Mackinaw jacket, a beaded belt held two large Colt's revolvers and a hunting knife, while he carried, in addition to the inevitable dog whip, a smokeless rifle of the largest bore and latest pattern. As he came forward, for all his step was firm and elastic, they could see that fatigue bore heavily upon him.

An awkward silence had fallen, but his hearty 'What cheer, my lads?' put them quickly at ease, and the next instant Malemute Kid and he had gripped hands. Though they had never met, each had heard of the other, and the recognition was mutual. A sweeping introduction and a mug of punch were forced upon him before he could explain his errand.

How long since that basket sled, with three men and eight dogs, passed?' he asked. 'An even two days ahead. Are you after them?' 'Yes; my team. Run them off under my very nose, the cusses. I've gained two days on them already—pick them up on the next run.' 'Reckon they'll show spunk?' asked Belden, in order to keep up the conversation, for Malemute Kid already had the coffeepot on and was busily frying bacon and moose meat.

The stranger significantly tapped his revolvers.

'When'd yeh leave Dawson?' 'Twelve o'clock.' 'Last night?'—as a matter of course. 'Today.' A murmur of surprise passed round the circle. And well it might; for it was just midnight, and seventy-five miles of rough river trail was not to be sneered at for a twelve hours' run.

The talk soon became impersonal, however, harking back to the trails of childhood. As the young stranger ate of the rude fare Malemute Kid attentively studied his face. Nor was he long in deciding that it was fair, honest, and open, and that he liked it. Still youthful, the lines had been firmly traced by toil and hardship.

Though genial in conversation, and mild when at rest, the blue eyes gave promise of the hard steel-glitter which comes when called into action, especially against odds. The heavy jaw and square-cut chin demonstrated rugged pertinacity and indomitability. Nor, though the attributes of the lion were there, was there wanting the certain softness, the hint of womanliness, which bespoke the emotional nature.

'So thet's how me an' the ol' woman got spliced,' said Belden, concluding the exciting tale of his courtship. 'Here we be, Dad,' sez she. 'An' may yeh be damned,' sez he to her, an' then to me, 'Jim, yeh—yeh git outen them good duds o' yourn; I want a right peart slice o' thet forty acre plowed 'fore dinner.' An' then he sort o' sniffled an' kissed her. An' I was thet happy—but he seen me an' roars out, 'Yeh, Jim!' An' yeh bet I dusted fer the barn.' 'Any kids waiting for you back in the States?' asked the stranger.

'Nope; Sal died 'fore any come. Thet's why I'm here.' Belden abstractedly began to light his pipe, which had failed to go out, and then brightened up with, 'How 'bout yerself, stranger—married man?' For reply, he opened his watch, slipped it from the thong which served for a chain, and passed it over. Belden picked up the slush lamp, surveyed the inside of the case critically, and, swearing admiringly to himself, handed it over to Louis Savoy. With numerous 'By gars!' he finally surrendered it to Prince, and they noticed that his hands trembled and his eyes took on a peculiar softness. And so it passed from horny hand to horny hand—the pasted photograph of a woman, the clinging kind that such men fancy, with a babe at the breast. Those who had not yet seen the wonder were keen with curiosity; those who had became silent and retrospective. They could face the pinch of famine, the grip of scurvy, or the quick death by field or flood; but the pictured semblance of a stranger woman and child made women and children of them all.

'Never have seen the youngster yet—he's a boy, she says, and two years old,' said the stranger as he received the treasure back. A lingering moment he gazed upon it, then snapped the case and turned away, but not quick enough to hide the restrained rush of tears. Malemute Kid led him to a bunk and bade him turn in.

'Call me at four sharp. Don't fail me,' were his last words, and a moment later he was breathing in the heaviness of exhausted sleep.

'By Jove! He's a plucky chap,' commented Prince. 'Three hours' sleep after seventy-five miles with the dogs, and then the trail again. Who is he, Kid?' 'Jack Westondale. Been in going on three years, with nothing but the name of working like a horse, and any amount of bad luck to his credit. I never knew him, but Sitka Charley told me about him.' 'It seems hard that a man with a sweet young wife like his should be putting in his years in this Godforsaken hole, where every year counts two on the outside.' 'The trouble with him is clean grit and stubbornness. He's cleaned up twice with a stake, but lost it both times.' Here the conversation was broken off by an uproar from Bettles, for the effect had begun to wear away. And soon the bleak years of monotonous grub and deadening toil were being forgotten in rough merriment.

Malemute Kid alone seemed unable to lose himself, and cast many an anxious look at his watch. Once he put on his mittens and beaver-skin cap, and, leaving the cabin, fell to rummaging about in the cache.

Nor could he wait the hour designated; for he was fifteen minutes ahead of time in rousing his guest. The young giant had stiffened badly, and brisk rubbing was necessary to bring him to his feet. He tottered painfully out of the cabin, to find his dogs harnessed and everything ready for the start. The company wished him good luck and a short chase, while Father Roubeau, hurriedly blessing him, led the stampede for the cabin; and small wonder, for it is not good to face seventy-four degrees below zero with naked ears and hands.

Malemute Kid saw him to the main trail, and there, gripping his hand heartily, gave him advice.

'You'll find a hundred pounds of salmon eggs on the sled,' he said. 'The dogs will go as far on that as with one hundred and fifty of fish, and you can't get dog food at Pelly, as you probably expected.' The stranger started, and his eyes flashed, but he did not interrupt. 'You can't get an ounce of food for dog or man till you reach Five Fingers, and that's a stiff two hundred miles. Watch out for open water on the Thirty Mile River, and be sure you take the big cutoff above Le Barge.' 'How did you know it? Surely the news can't be ahead of me already?' 'I don't know it; and what's more, I don't want to know it. But you never owned that team you're chasing. Sitka Charley sold it to them last spring. But he sized you up to me as square once, and I believe him. I've seen your face; I like it. And I've seen—why, damn you, hit the high places for salt water and that wife of yours, and—' Here the Kid unmittened and jerked out his sack.

'No; I don't need it,' and the tears froze on his cheeks as he convulsively gripped Malemute Kid's hand.

'Then don't spare the dogs; cut them out of the traces as fast as they drop; buy them, and think they're cheap at ten dollars a pound. You can get them at Five Fingers, Little Salmon, and Hootalinqua. And watch out for wet feet,' was his parting advice. 'Keep a-traveling up to twenty-five, but if it gets below that, build a fire and change your socks.'

Fifteen minutes had barely elapsed when the jingle of bells announced new arrivals. The door opened, and a mounted policeman of the Northwest Territory entered, followed by two half-breed dog drivers. Like Westondale, they were heavily armed and showed signs of fatigue. The half-breeds had been borne to the trail and bore it easily; but the young policeman was badly exhausted. Still, the dogged obstinacy of his race held him to the pace he had set, and would hold him till he dropped in his tracks.

'When did Westondale pull out?' he asked. 'He stopped here, didn't he?' This was supererogatory, for the tracks told their own tale too well.

Malemute Kid had caught Belden's eye, and he, scenting the wind, replied evasively, 'A right peart while back.' 'Come, my man; speak up,' the policeman admonished.

'Yeh seem to want him right smart. Hez he ben gittin' cantankerous down Dawson way?'

'Held up Harry McFarland's for forty thousand; exchanged it at the P.C. store for a check on Seattle; and who's to stop the cashing of it if we don't overtake him? When did he pull out?'

Every eye suppressed its excitement, for Malemute Kid had given the cue, and the young officer encountered wooden faces on every hand.

Striding over to Prince, he put the question to him. Though it hurt him, gazing into the frank, earnest face of his fellow countryman, he replied inconsequentially on the state of the trail.

Then he espied Father Roubeau, who could not lie. 'A quarter of an hour ago,' the priest answered; 'but he had four hours' rest for himself and dogs.' 'Fifteen minutes' start, and he's fresh! My God!' The poor fellow staggered back, half fainting from exhaustion and disappointment, murmuring something about the run from Dawson in ten hours and the dogs being played out.

Malemute Kid forced a mug of punch upon him; then he turned for the door, ordering the dog drivers to follow. But the warmth and promise of rest were too tempting, and they objected strenuously. The Kid was conversant with their French patois, and followed it anxiously.

They swore that the dogs were gone up; that Siwash and Babette would have to be shot before the first mile was covered; that the rest were almost as bad; and that it would be better for all hands to rest up.

'Lend me five dogs?' he asked, turning to Malemute Kid.

But the Kid shook his head.

'I'll sign a check on Captain Constantine for five thousand—here's my papers—I'm authorized to draw at my own discretion.'

Again the silent refusal.

'Then I'll requisition them in the name of the Queen.' Smiling incredulously, the Kid glanced at his well-stocked arsenal, and the Englishman, realizing his impotency, turned for the door. But the dog drivers still objecting, he whirled upon them fiercely, calling them women and curs. The swart face of the older half-breed flushed angrily as he drew himself up and promised in good, round terms that he would travel his leader off his legs, and would then be delighted to plant him in the snow.

The young officer—and it required his whole will—walked steadily to the door, exhibiting a freshness he did not possess. But they all knew and appreciated his proud effort; nor could he veil the twinges of agony that shot across his face. Covered with frost, the dogs were curled up in the snow, and it was almost impossible to get them to their feet. The poor brutes whined under the stinging lash, for the dog drivers were angry and cruel; nor till Babette, the leader, was cut from the traces, could they break out the sled and get under way.

'A dirty scoundrel and a liar!' 'By gar! Him no good!' 'A thief!' 'Worse than an Indian!'

It was evident that they were angry—first at the way they had been deceived; and second at the outraged ethics of the Northland, where honesty, above all, was man's prime jewel.

'An' we gave the cuss a hand, after knowin' what he'd did.' All eyes turned accusingly upon Malemute Kid, who rose from the corner where he had been making Babette comfortable, and silently emptied the bowl for a final round of punch.

'It's a cold night, boys—a bitter cold night,' was the irrelevant commencement of his defense. 'You've all traveled trail, and know what that stands for. Don't jump a dog when he's down. You've only heard one side. A whiter man than Jack Westondale never ate from the same pot nor stretched blanket with you or me.

'Last fall he gave his whole clean-up, forty thousand, to Joe Castrell, to buy in on

Dominion. Today he'd be a millionaire. But, while he stayed behind at Circle City, taking care of his partner with the scurvy, what does Castell do? Goes into McFarland's, jumps the limit, and drops the whole sack. Found him dead in the snow the next day. And poor Jack laying his plans to go out this winter to his wife and the boy he's never seen. You'll notice he took exactly what his partner lost—forty thousand. Well, he's gone out; and what are you going to do about it?' The Kid glanced round the circle of his judges, noted the softening of their faces, then raised his mug aloft. 'So a health to the man on trail this night; may his grub hold out; may his dogs keep their legs; may his matches never miss fire.

'God prosper him; good luck go with him; and—' 'Confusion to the Mounted Police!' cried Bettles, to the crash of the empty cups.

THE PRIESTLY PREROGATIVE

This is the story of a man who did not appreciate his wife; also, of a woman who did him too great an honor when she gave herself to him. Incidentally, it concerns a Jesuit priest who had never been known to lie. He was an appurtenance, and a very necessary one, to the Yukon country; but the presence of the other two was merely accidental. They were specimens of the many strange waifs which ride the breast of a gold rush or come tailing along behind.

Edwin Bentham and Grace Bentham were waifs; they were also tailing along behind, for the Klondike rush of '97 had long since swept down the great river and subsided into the famine-stricken city of Dawson. When the Yukon shut up shop and went to sleep under a three-foot ice-sheet, this peripatetic couple found themselves at the Five Finger Rapids, with the City of Gold still a journey of many sleeps to the north.

Many cattle had been butchered at this place in the fall of the year, and the offal made a goodly heap. The three fellow-voyagers of Edwin Bentham and wife gazed upon this deposit, did a little mental arithmetic, caught a certain glimpse of a bonanza, and decided to remain. And all winter they sold sacks of bones and frozen hides to the famished dog-teams. It was a modest price they asked, a dollar a pound, just as it came. Six months later, when the sun came back and the Yukon awoke, they buckled on their heavy moneybelts and journeyed back to the Southland, where they yet live and lie mightily about the Klondike they never saw.

But Edwin Bentham—he was an indolent fellow, and had he not been possessed of a wife, would have gladly joined issued in the dog-meat speculation. As it was, she played upon his vanity, told him how great and strong he was, how a man such as he certainly was could overcome all obstacles and of a surety obtain the Golden Fleece. So he squared his jaw, sold his share in the bones and hides for a sled and one dog, and turned his snowshoes to the north. Needless to state, Grace Bentham's snowshoes never allowed his tracks to grow cold. Nay, ere their tribulations had seen three days, it was the man who followed in the rear, and the woman who broke trail in advance. Of course, if anybody hove in sight, the position was instantly reversed. Thus did his manhood remain virgin to the travelers who passed like ghosts on the silent trail. There are such men in this world.

How such a man and such a woman came to take each other for better and for worse is unimportant to this narrative. These things are familiar to us all, and those people who do them, or even question them too closely, are apt to lose a beautiful faith which is known as Eternal Fitness.

Edwin Bentham was a boy, thrust by mischance into a man's body,—a boy who could complacently pluck a butterfly, wing from wing, or cower in abject terror before a lean, nervy fellow, not half his size. He was a selfish cry-baby, hidden behind a man's mustache and stature, and glossed over with a skin-deep veneer of culture and conventionality. Yes; he was a clubman and a society man, the sort that grace social functions and utter inanities with a charm and unction which is indescribable; the sort that talk big, and cry over a toothache; the sort that put more hell into a woman's life by marrying her than can the most graceless libertine that ever browsed in forbidden pastures. We meet these men every day, but we rarely know them for what they are. Second to marrying them, the best way to get this knowledge is to eat out of the same pot and crawl under the same blanket with them for—well, say a week; no greater margin is necessary.

To see Grace Bentham, was to see a slender, girlish creature; to know her, was to know a soul which dwarfed your own, yet retained all the elements of the eternal feminine. This was the woman who urged and encouraged her husband in his Northland quest, who broke trail for him when no one was looking, and cried in secret over her weakling woman's body.

So journeyed this strangely assorted couple down to old Fort Selkirk, then through fivescore miles of dismal wilderness to Stuart River. And when the short day left them, and the man lay down in the snow and blubbered, it was the woman who lashed him to the sled, bit her lips with the pain of her aching limbs, and helped the dog haul him to Malemute Kid's cabin. Malemute Kid was not at home, but Meyers, the German trader, cooked great moose-steaks and shook up a bed of fresh pine boughs. Lake, Langham, and Parker, were excited, and not unduly so when the cause was taken into account.

'Oh, Sandy! Say, can you tell a porterhouse from a round? Come out and lend us a hand, anyway!' This appeal emanated from the cache, where Langham was vainly struggling with divers quarters of frozen moose.

'Don't you budge from those dishes!' commanded Parker.

'I say, Sandy; there's a good fellow—just run down to the Missouri Camp and borrow some cinnamon,' begged Lake.

'Oh! oh! hurry up! Why don't—' But the crash of meat and boxes, in the cache, abruptly quenched this peremptory summons.

'Come now, Sandy; it won't take a minute to go down to the Missouri—'

'You leave him alone,' interrupted Parker. 'How am I to mix the biscuits if the table isn't cleared off?'

Sandy paused in indecision, till suddenly the fact that he was Langham's 'man' dawned upon him. Then he apologetically threw down the greasy dishcloth, and went to his master's rescue.

These promising scions of wealthy progenitors had come to the Northland in search of laurels, with much money to burn, and a 'man' apiece. Luckily for their souls, the other two men were up the White River in search of a mythical quartz-ledge; so Sandy had to grin under the responsibility of three healthy masters, each of whom was possessed of peculiar cookery ideas. Twice that morning had a disruption of the whole camp been imminent, only averted by immense concessions from one or the other of these knights of the chafing-dish. But at last their mutual creation, a really dainty dinner, was completed.

Then they sat down to a three-cornered game of 'cut-throat,'—a proceeding which did away with all casus belli for future hostilities, and permitted the victor to depart on a most important mission.

This fortune fell to Parker, who parted his hair in the middle, put on his mittens and bearskin cap, and stepped over to Malemute Kid's cabin. And when he returned, it was in the company of Grace Bentham and Malemute Kid,—the former very sorry her husband could not share with her their hospitality, for he had gone up to look at the Henderson Creek mines, and the latter still a trifle stiff from breaking trail down the Stuart River.

Meyers had been asked, but had declined, being deeply engrossed in an experiment of raising bread from hops.

Well, they could do without the husband; but a woman—why they had not seen one all winter, and the presence of this one promised a new era in their lives.

They were college men and gentlemen, these three young fellows, yearning for the flesh-pots they had been so long denied. Probably Grace Bentham suffered from a similar hunger; at least, it meant much to her, the first bright hour in many weeks of darkness.

But that wonderful first course, which claimed the versatile Lake for its parent, had no sooner been served than there came a loud knock at the door.

'Oh! Ah! Won't you come in, Mr. Bentham?' said Parker, who had stepped to see who the newcomer might be.

'Is my wife here?' gruffly responded that worthy.

'Why, yes. We left word with Mr. Meyers.' Parker was exerting his most dulcet tones, inwardly wondering what the deuce it all meant. 'Won't you come in? Expecting you at any moment, we reserved a place. And just in time for the first course, too.' 'Come in, Edwin, dear,' chirped Grace Bentham from her seat at the table.

Parker naturally stood aside.

'I want my wife,' reiterated Bentham hoarsely, the intonation savoring disagreeably of ownership.

Parker gasped, was within an ace of driving his fist into the face of his boorish visitor, but held himself awkwardly in check. Everybody rose. Lake lost his head and caught himself on the verge of saying, 'Must you go?' Then began the farrago of leave-taking. 'So nice of you—' 'I am awfully sorry' 'By Jove! how things did brighten—' 'Really now, you—'

'Thank you ever so much—' 'Nice trip to Dawson—' etc., etc.

In this wise the lamb was helped into her jacket and led to the slaughter. Then the door slammed, and they gazed woefully upon the deserted table.

'Damn!' Langham had suffered disadvantages in his early training, and his oaths were weak and monotonous. 'Damn!' he repeated, vaguely conscious of the incompleteness and vainly struggling for a more virile term. It is a clever woman who can fill out the many weak places in an inefficient man, by her own indomitability, re-enforce his vacillating nature, infuse her ambitious soul into his, and spur him on to great achievements. And it is indeed a very clever and tactful woman who can do all this, and do it so subtly that the man receives all the credit and believes in his inmost heart that everything is due to him and him alone.

This is what Grace Bentham proceeded to do. Arriving in Dawson with a few pounds of flour and several letters of introduction, she at once applied herself to the task of pushing her big baby to the fore. It was she who melted the stony heart and wrung credit from the rude barbarian who presided over the destiny of the P. C. Company; yet it was Edwin Bentham to whom the concession was ostensibly granted. It was she who dragged her baby up and down creeks, over benches and divides, and on a dozen wild stampedes; yet everybody remarked what an energetic fellow that Bentham was. It was she who studied maps, and catechised miners, and hammered geography and locations into his hollow head, till everybody marveled at his broad grasp of the country and knowledge of its conditions. Of course, they said the wife was a brick, and only a few wise ones appreciated and pitied the brave little woman.

She did the work; he got the credit and reward. In the Northwest Territory a married woman cannot stake or record a creek, bench, or quartz claim; so Edwin Bentham went down to the Gold Commissioner and filed on Bench Claim 23, second tier, of French Hill. And when April came they were washing out a thousand dollars a day, with many, many such days in prospect.

At the base of French Hill lay Eldorado Creek, and on a creek claim stood the cabin of Clyde Wharton. At present he was not washing out a diurnal thousand dollars; but his dumps grew, shift by shift, and there would come a time when those dumps would pass through his sluice-boxes, depositing in the riffles, in the course of half a dozen days, several hundred thousand dollars. He often sat in that cabin, smoked his pipe, and dreamed beautiful little dreams,—dreams in which neither the dumps nor the half-ton of dust in the P. C. Company's big safe, played a part.

And Grace Bentham, as she washed tin dishes in her hillside cabin, often glanced down into Eldorado Creek, and dreamed,—not of dumps nor dust, however. They met frequently, as the trail to the one claim crossed the other, and there is much to talk about in the Northland spring; but never once, by the light of an eye nor the slip of a tongue, did they speak their hearts.

This is as it was at first. But one day Edwin Bentham was brutal. All boys are thus; besides, being a French Hill king now, he began to think a great deal of himself and to forget all he owed to his wife. On this day, Wharton heard of it, and waylaid Grace Bentham, and talked wildly. This made her very happy, though she would not listen, and made him promise to not say such things again. Her hour had not come.

But the sun swept back on its northern journey, the black of midnight changed to the steely color of dawn, the snow slipped away, the water dashed again over the glacial drift, and the wash-up began. Day and night the yellow clay and scraped bedrock hurried through the swift sluices, yielding up its ransom to the strong men from the Southland.

And in that time of tumult came Grace Bentham's hour.

To all of us such hours at some time come,—that is, to us who are not too phlegmatic.

Some people are good, not from inherent love of virtue, but from sheer laziness. But those of us who know weak moments may understand.

Edwin Bentham was weighing dust over the bar of the saloon at the Forks—altogether too much of his dust went over that pine board—when his wife came down the hill and slipped into Clyde Wharton's cabin. Wharton was not expecting her, but that did not alter the case. And much subsequent misery and idle waiting might have been avoided, had not Father Roubeau seen this and turned aside from the main creek trail. 'My child,—' 'Hold on, Father Roubeau! Though I'm not of your faith, I respect you; but you can't come in between this woman and me!' 'You know what you are doing?' 'Know! Were you God Almighty, ready to fling me into eternal fire, I'd bank my will against yours in this matter.' Wharton had placed Grace on a stool and stood belligerently before her.

'You sit down on that chair and keep quiet,' he continued, addressing the Jesuit. 'I'll take my innings now. You can have yours after.'

Father Roubeau bowed courteously and obeyed. He was an easy-going man and had learned to bide his time. Wharton pulled a stool alongside the woman's, smothering her hand in his.

'Then you do care for me, and will take me away?' Her face seemed to reflect the peace of this man, against whom she might draw close for shelter.

'Dear, don't you remember what I said before? Of course I-' 'But how can you?—the wash-up?' 'Do you think that worries? Anyway, I'll give the job to Father Roubeau, here.

'I can trust him to safely bank the dust with the company.' 'To think of it!—I'll never see him again.' 'A blessing!' 'And to go—O, Clyde, I can't! I can't!' 'There, there; of course you can, just let me plan it.—You see, as soon as we get a few traps together, we'll start, and-' 'Suppose he comes back?' 'I'll break every-' 'No, no! No fighting, Clyde! Promise me that.' 'All right! I'll just tell the men to throw him off the claim. They've seen how he's treated you, and haven't much love for him.'

'You mustn't do that. You mustn't hurt him.' 'What then? Let him come right in here and take you away before my eyes?' 'No-o,' she half whispered, stroking his hand softly.

'Then let me run it, and don't worry. I'll see he doesn't get hurt. Precious lot he cared whether you got hurt or not! We won't go back to Dawson. I'll send word down for a couple of the boys to outfit and pole a boat up the Yukon. We'll cross the divide and raft down the Indian River to meet them. Then—' 'And then?' Her head was on his shoulder.

Their voices sank to softer cadences, each word a caress. The Jesuit fidgeted nervously.

'And then?' she repeated.

'Why we'll pole up, and up, and up, and portage the White Horse Rapids and the Box Canon.' 'Yes?' 'And the Sixty-Mile River; then the lakes, Chilcoot, Dyea, and Salt Water.' 'But, dear, I can't pole a boat.' 'You little goose! I'll get Sitka Charley; he knows all the good water and best camps, and he is the best traveler I ever met, if he is an Indian. All you'll have to do, is to sit in the middle of the boat, and sing songs, and play Cleopatra, and fight—no, we're in luck; too early for mosquitoes.'

'And then, O my Antony?' 'And then a steamer, San Francisco, and the world! Never to come back to this cursed hole again. Think of it! The world, and ours to choose from! I'll sell out. Why, we're rich! The Waldworth Syndicate will give me half a million for what's left in the ground, and I've got twice as much in the dumps and with the P. C. Company. We'll go to the Fair in Paris in 1900. We'll go to Jerusalem, if you say so.

'We'll buy an Italian palace, and you can play Cleopatra to your heart's content. No, you shall be Lucretia, Acte, or anybody your little heart sees fit to become. But you mustn't, you really mustn't-' 'The wife of Caesar shall be above reproach.' 'Of course, but—' 'But I won't be your wife, will I, dear?' 'I didn't mean that.' 'But you'll love me just as much, and never even think—oh! I know you'll be like other men; you'll grow tired, and—and-'

'How can you? I—' 'Promise me.' 'Yes, yes; I do promise.' 'You say it so easily, dear; but how do you know?—or I know? I have so little to give, yet it is so much, and all I have. O, Clyde! promise me you won't?'

'There, there! You mustn't begin to doubt already. Till death do us part, you know.'

'Think! I once said that to—to him, and now?' 'And now, little sweetheart, you're not to bother about such things any more.

Of course, I never, never will, and—' And for the first time, lips trembled against lips.

Father Roubeau had been watching the main trail through the window, but could stand the strain no longer.

He cleared his throat and turned around.

'Your turn now, Father!' Wharton's face was flushed with the fire of his first embrace.

There was an exultant ring to his voice as he abdicated in the other's favor. He had no doubt as to the result. Neither had Grace, for a smile played about her mouth as she faced the priest.

'My child,' he began, 'my heart bleeds for you. It is a pretty dream, but it cannot be.'

'And why, Father? I have said yes.' 'You knew not what you did. You did not think of the oath you took, before your God, to that man who is your husband. It remains for me to make you realize the sanctity of such a pledge.' 'And if I do realize, and yet refuse?'

'Then God'

'Which God? My husband has a God which I care not to worship. There must be many such.' 'Child! unsay those words! Ah! you do not mean them. I understand. I, too, have had such moments.' For an instant he was back in his native France, and a wistful, sad-eyed face came as a mist between him and the woman before him.

'Then, Father, has my God forsaken me? I am not wicked above women. My misery with him has been great. Why should it be greater? Why shall I not grasp at happiness? I cannot, will not, go back to him!' 'Rather is your God forsaken. Return. Throw your burden upon Him, and the darkness shall be lifted. O my child,—' 'No; it is useless; I have made my bed and so shall I lie. I will go on. And if God punishes me, I shall bear it somehow. You do not understand. You are not a woman.' 'My mother was a woman.'

'But—' 'And Christ was born of a woman.' She did not answer. A silence fell. Wharton pulled his mustache impatiently and kept an eye on the trail. Grace leaned her elbow on the table, her face set with resolve. The smile had died away. Father Roubeau shifted his ground.

'You have children?'

'At one time I wished—but now—no. And I am thankful.' 'And a mother?' 'Yes.' 'She loves you?' 'Yes.' Her replies were whispers.

'And a brother?—no matter, he is a man. But a sister?' Her head drooped a quavering 'Yes.' 'Younger? Very much?' 'Seven years.' 'And you have thought well about this matter? About them? About your mother? And your sister? She stands on the threshold of her woman's life, and this wildness of yours may mean much to her. Could you go before her, look upon her fresh young face, hold her hand in yours, or touch your cheek to hers?'

To his words, her brain formed vivid images, till she cried out, 'Don't! don't!' and shrank away as do the wolf-dogs from the lash.

'But you must face all this; and better it is to do it now.' In his eyes, which she could not see, there was a great compassion, but his face, tense and quivering, showed no relenting.

She raised her head from the table, forced back the tears, struggled for control.

'I shall go away. They will never see me, and come to forget me. I shall be to them as dead. And—and I will go with Clyde—today.' It seemed final. Wharton stepped forward, but the priest waved him back.

'You have wished for children?' A silent 'Yes.' 'And prayed for them?' 'Often.' 'And have you thought, if you should have children?' Father Roubeau's eyes rested for a moment on the man by the window.

A quick light shot across her face. Then the full import dawned upon her. She raised her hand appealingly, but he went on.

'Can you picture an innocent babe in your arms? A boy? The world is not so hard upon a girl. Why, your very breast would turn to gall! And you could be proud and happy of your boy, as you looked on other children?—' 'O, have pity! Hush!' 'A scapegoat—'

'Don't! don't! I will go back!' She was at his feet.

'A child to grow up with no thought of evil, and one day the world to fling a tender name in his face. A child to look back and curse you from whose loins he sprang!'

'O my God! my God!' She groveled on the floor. The priest sighed and raised her to her feet.

Wharton pressed forward, but she motioned him away.

'Don't come near me, Clyde! I am going back!' The tears were coursing pitifully down her face, but she made no effort to wipe them away.

'After all this? You cannot! I will not let you!' 'Don't touch me!' She shivered and drew back.

'I will! You are mine! Do you hear? You are mine!' Then he whirled upon the priest. 'O what a fool I was to ever let you wag your silly tongue! Thank your God you are not a common man, for I'd—but the priestly prerogative must be exercised, eh? Well, you have exercised it. Now get out of my house, or I'll forget who and what you are!' Father Roubeau bowed, took her hand, and started for the door. But Wharton cut them off.

'Grace! You said you loved me?' 'I did.' 'And you do now?' 'I do.' 'Say it again.'

'I do love you, Clyde; I do.' 'There, you priest!' he cried. 'You have heard it, and with those words on her lips you would send her back to live a lie and a hell with that man?'

But Father Roubeau whisked the woman into the inner room and closed the door. 'No words!' he whispered to Wharton, as he struck a casual posture on a stool. 'Remember, for her sake,' he added.

The room echoed to a rough knock at the door; the latch raised and Edwin Bentham stepped in.

'Seen anything of my wife?' he asked as soon as salutations had been exchanged.

Two heads nodded negatively.

'I saw her tracks down from the cabin,' he continued tentatively, 'and they broke off, just opposite here, on the main trail.' His listeners looked bored.

'And I—I thought—'

'She was here!' thundered Wharton.

The priest silenced him with a look. 'Did you see her tracks leading up to this cabin, my son?' Wily Father Roubeau—he had taken good care to obliterate them as he came up the same path an hour before.

'I didn't stop to look, I—' His eyes rested suspiciously on the door to the other room, then interrogated the priest. The latter shook his head; but the doubt seemed to linger.

Father Roubeau breathed a swift, silent prayer, and rose to his feet. 'If you doubt me, why—' He made as though to open the door.

A priest could not lie. Edwin Bentham had heard this often, and believed it.

'Of course not, Father,' he interposed hurriedly. 'I was only wondering where my wife had gone, and thought maybe—I guess she's up at Mrs. Stanton's on French Gulch. Nice weather, isn't it? Heard the news? Flour's gone down to forty dollars a hundred, and they say the che-cha-quas are flocking down the river in droves.

'But I must be going; so good-by.' The door slammed, and from the window they watched him take his guest up French Gulch. A few weeks later, just after the June high-water, two men shot a canoe into mid-stream and made fast to a derelict pine. This tightened the painter and jerked the frail craft along as would a tow-boat. Father Roubeau had been directed to leave the Upper Country and return to his swarthy children at Minook. The white men had come among them, and they were devoting too little time to fishing, and too much to a certain deity whose transient habitat was in countless black bottles.

Malemute Kid also had business in the Lower Country, so they journeyed together.

But one, in all the Northland, knew the man Paul Roubeau, and that man was Malemute Kid. Before him alone did the priest cast off the sacerdotal garb and stand naked. And why not? These two men knew each other. Had they not shared the last morsel of fish, the last pinch of tobacco, the last and inmost thought, on the barren stretches of Bering Sea, in the heartbreaking mazes of the Great Delta, on the terrible winter journey from Point Barrow to the Porcupine? Father Roubeau puffed heavily at his trail-worn pipe, and gazed on the reddisked sun, poised somberly on the edge of the northern horizon.

Malemute Kid wound up his watch. It was midnight.

'Cheer up, old man!' The Kid was evidently gathering up a broken thread.

'God surely will forgive such a lie. Let me give you the word of a man who strikes a true note: If She have spoken a word, remember thy lips are sealed, And the brand of the Dog is upon him by whom is the secret revealed.

If there be trouble to Herward, and a lie of the blackest can clear, Lie, while thy lips can move or a man is alive to hear.'

Father Roubeau removed his pipe and reflected. 'The man speaks true, but my soul is not vexed with that. The lie and the penance stand with God; but—but—'

'What then? Your hands are clean.' 'Not so. Kid, I have thought much, and yet the thing remains. I knew, and made her go back.' The clear note of a robin rang out from the wooden bank, a partridge drummed the call in the distance, a moose lunged noisily in the eddy; but the twain smoked on in silence.

THE WISDOM OF THE TRAIL

Sitka Charley had achieved the impossible. Other Indians might have known as much of the wisdom of the trail as he did; but he alone knew the white man's wisdom, the honor of the trail, and the law. But these things had not come to him in a day. The aboriginal mind is slow to generalize, and many facts, repeated often, are required to compass an understanding. Sitka Charley, from boyhood, had been thrown continually with white men, and as a man he had elected to cast his fortunes with them, expatriating himself, once and for all, from his own people. Even then, respecting, almost venerating their power, and pondering over it, he had yet to divine its secret essence—the honor and the law. And it was only by the cumulative evidence of years that he had finally come to understand. Being an alien, when he did know, he knew it better than the white man himself; being an Indian, he had achieved the impossible.

And of these things had been bred a certain contempt for his own people—a contempt which he had made it a custom to conceal, but which now burst forth in a polyglot whirlwind of curses upon the heads of Kah-Chucte and Gowhee. They cringed before him like a brace of snarling wolf dogs, too cowardly to spring, too wolfish to cover their fangs. They were not handsome creatures. Neither was Sitka Charley. All three were frightful-looking. There was no flesh to their faces; their cheekbones were massed with hideous scabs which had cracked and frozen alternately under the intense frost; while their eyes burned luridly with the light which is born of desperation and hunger. Men so situated, beyond the pale of the honor and the law, are not to be trusted. Sitka Charley knew this; and this was why he had forced them to abandon their rifles with the rest of the camp outfit ten days before. His rifle and Captain Eppingwell's were the only ones that remained.

'Come, get a fire started,' he commanded, drawing out the precious matchbox with its attendant strips of dry birchbark.

The two Indians fell sullenly to the task of gathering dead branches and underwood. They were weak and paused often, catching themselves, in the act of stooping, with giddy motions, or staggering to the center of operations with their knees shaking like castanets.

After each trip they rested for a moment, as though sick and deadly weary. At times their eyes took on the patient stoicism of dumb suffering; and again the ego seemed almost burst forth with its wild cry, 'I, I, I want to exist!'—the dominant note of the whole living universe.

A light breath of air blew from the south, nipping the exposed portions of their bodies and driving the frost, in needles of fire, through fur and flesh to the bones. So, when the fire had grown lusty and thawed a damp circle in the snow about it, Sitka Charley forced his reluctant comrades to lend a hand in pitching a fly. It was a primitive affair, merely a blanket stretched parallel with the fire and to windward of it, at an angle of perhaps forty-five degrees. This shut out the chill wind and threw the heat backward and down upon those who were to huddle in its shelter. Then a layer of green spruce boughs were spread, that their bodies might not come in contact with the snow. When this task was completed, Kah-Chucte and Gowhee proceeded to take care of their feet. Their icebound moccasins were sadly worn by much travel, and the sharp ice of the river jams had cut them to rags.

Their Siwash socks were similarly conditioned, and when these had been thawed and removed, the dead-white tips of the toes, in the various stages of mortification, told their simple tale of the trail.

Leaving the two to the drying of their footgear, Sitka Charley turned back over the course he had come. He, too, had a mighty longing to sit by the fire and tend his complaining flesh, but the honor and the law forbade. He toiled painfully over the frozen field, each step a protest, every muscle in revolt. Several times, where the open water between the jams had recently crusted, he was forced to miserably accelerate his movements as the fragile footing swayed and threatened beneath him. In such places death was quick and easy; but it was not his desire to endure no more.

His deepening anxiety vanished as two Indians dragged into view round a bend in the river. They staggered and panted like men under heavy burdens; yet the packs on their backs were a matter of but a few pounds. He questioned them eagerly, and their replies seemed to relieve him. He hurried on. Next came two white men, supporting between them a woman. They also behaved as though drunken, and their limbs shook with weakness. But the woman leaned lightly upon them, choosing to carry herself forward with her own strength. At the sight of her a flash of joy cast its fleeting light across Sitka Charley's face. He cherished a very great regard for Mrs. Eppingwell. He had seen many white women, but this was the first to travel the trail with him. When Captain Eppingwell proposed the hazardous undertaking and made him an offer for his services, he had shaken his head gravely; for it was an unknown journey through the dismal vastnesses of the Northland, and he knew it to be of the kind that try to the uttermost the souls of men.

But when he learned that the captain's wife was to accompany them, he had refused flatly to have anything further to do with it. Had it been a woman of his own race he would have harbored no objections; but these women of the Southland—no, no, they were too soft, too tender, for such enterprises.

Sitka Charley did not know this kind of woman. Five minutes before, he did not even dream of taking charge of the expedition; but when she came to him with her wonderful smile and her straight clean English, and talked to the point, without pleading or persuading, he had incontinently yielded. Had there been a softness and appeal to mercy in the eyes, a tremble to the voice, a taking advantage of sex, he would have stiffened to steel; instead her clear-searching eyes and clear-ringing voice, her utter frankness and tacit assumption of equality, had robbed him of his reason. He felt, then, that this was a new breed of woman; and ere they had been trail mates for many days he knew why the sons of such women mastered the land and the sea, and why the sons of his own womankind could not prevail against them. Tender and soft! Day after day he watched her, muscle-weary, exhausted, indomitable, and the words beat in upon him in a perennial refrain. Tender and soft! He knew her feet had been born to easy paths and sunny lands, strangers to the moccasined pain of the North, unkissed by the chill lips of the frost, and he watched and marveled at them twinkling ever through the weary day.

She had always a smile and a word of cheer, from which not even the meanest packer was excluded. As the way grew darker she seemed to stiffen and gather greater strength, and when Kah-Chucte and Gowhee, who had bragged that they knew every landmark of the way as a child did the skin bails of the tepee, acknowledged that they knew not where they were, it was she who raised a forgiving voice amid the curses of the men. She had sung to them that night till they felt the weariness fall from them and were ready to face the future with fresh hope. And when the food failed and each scant stint was measured jealously, she it was who rebelled against the machinations of her husband and Sitka Charley, and demanded and received a share neither greater nor less than that of the others.

Sitka Charley was proud to know this woman. A new richness, a greater breadth, had come into his life with her presence. Hitherto he had been his own mentor, had turned to right or left at no man's beck; he had moulded himself according to his own dictates, nourished his manhood regardless of all save his own opinion. For the first time he had felt a call from without for the best that was in him, just a glance of appreciation from the clear-searching eyes, a word of thanks from the clear-ringing voice, just a slight wreathing of the lips in the wonderful smile, and he walked with the gods for hours to come. It was a new stimulant to his manhood; for the first time he thrilled with a conscious pride in his wisdom of the trail; and between the twain they ever lifted the sinking hearts of their comrades. The faces of the two men and the woman brightened as they saw him, for after all he was the staff they leaned upon. But Sitka Charley, rigid as was his wont, concealing pain and pleasure impartially beneath an iron exterior, asked them the welfare of the rest, told the distance to the fire, and continued on the back-trip.

Next he met a single Indian, unburdened, limping, lips compressed, and eyes set with the pain of a foot in which the quick fought a losing battle with the dead. All possible care had been taken of him, but in the last extremity the weak and unfortunate must perish, and Sitka Charley deemed his days to be few. The man could not keep up for long, so he gave him rough cheering words. After that came two more Indians, to whom he had allotted the task of helping along Joe, the third white man of the party. They had deserted him. Sitka Charley saw at a glance the lurking spring in their bodies, and knew they had at last cast off his mastery. So he was not taken unawares when he ordered them back in quest of their abandoned charge, and saw the gleam of the hunting knives that they drew from the sheaths. A pitiful spectacle, three weak men lifting their puny strength in the face of the mighty vastness; but the two recoiled under the fierce rifle blows of the one and returned like beaten dogs to the leash. Two hours later, with Joe reeling between them and Sitka Charley bringing up the rear, they came to the fire, where the remainder of the expedition crouched in the shelter of the fly.

'A few words, my comrades, before we sleep,' Sitka Charley said after they had devoured their slim rations of unleavened bread. He was speaking to the Indians in their own tongue, having already given the import to the whites. 'A few words, my comrades, for your own good, that ye may yet perchance live. I shall give you the law; on his own head by the death of him that breaks it. We have passed the Hills of Silence, and we now travel the head reaches of the Stuart. It may be one sleep, it may be several, it may be many sleeps, but in time we shall come among the men of the Yukon, who have much grub. It were well that we look to the law. Today Kah-Chucte and Gowhee, whom I commanded to break trail, forgot they were men, and like frightened children ran away.

'True, they forgot; so let us forget. But hereafter, let them remember. If it should happen they do not...' He touched his rifle carelessly, grimly. 'Tomorrow they shall carry the flour and see that the white man Joe lies not down by the trail. The cups of flour are counted; should so much as an ounce be wanting at nightfall... Do ye understand? Today there were others that forgot. Moose Head and Three Salmon left the white man Joe to lie in the snow. Let them forget no more. With the light of day shall they go forth and break trail. Ye have heard the law. Look well, lest ye break it.' Sitka Charley found it beyond him to keep the line close up. From Moose Head and Three Salmon, who broke trail in advance, to Kah-Chucte, Gowhee, and Joe, it straggled out over a mile. Each staggered, fell or rested as he saw fit.

The line of march was a progression through a chain of irregular halts. Each drew upon the last remnant of his strength and stumbled onward till it was expended, but in some miraculous way there was always another last remnant. Each time a man fell it was with the firm belief that he would rise no more; yet he did rise, and again and again. The flesh yielded, the will conquered; but each triumph was a tragedy. The Indian with the frozen foot, no longer erect, crawled forward on hand and knee. He rarely rested, for he knew the penalty exacted by the frost.

Even Mrs. Eppingwell's lips were at last set in a stony smile, and her eyes, seeing, saw not. Often she stopped, pressing a mittened hand to her heart, gasping and dizzy.

Joe, the white man, had passed beyond the stage of suffering. He no longer begged to be let alone, prayed to die; but was soothed and content under the anodyne of delirium. Kah-Chucte and Gowhee dragged him on roughly, venting upon him many a savage glance or blow. To them it was the acme of injustice.

Their hearts were bitter with hate, heavy with fear. Why should they cumber their strength with his weakness? To do so meant death; not to do so—and they remembered the law of Sitka Charley, and the rifle.

Joe fell with greater frequency as the daylight waned, and so hard was he to raise that they dropped farther and farther behind. Sometimes all three pitched into the snow, so weak had the Indians become. Yet on their backs was life, and strength, and warmth.

Within the flour sacks were all the potentialities of existence. They could not but think of this, and it was not strange, that which came to pass. They had fallen by the side of a great timber jam where a thousand cords of firewood waited the match. Near by was an air hole through the ice. Kah-Chucte looked on the wood and the water, as did Gowhee; then they looked at each other.

Never a word was spoken. Gowhee struck a fire; Kah-Chucte filled a tin cup with water and heated it; Joe babbled of things in another land, in a tongue they did not understand.

They mixed flour with the warm water till it was a thin paste, and of this they drank many cups. They did not offer any to Joe; but he did not mind. He did not mind anything, not even his moccasins, which scorched and smoked among the coals.

A crystal mist of snow fell about them, softly, caressingly, wrapping them in clinging robes of white. And their feet would have yet trod many trails had not destiny brushed the clouds aside and cleared the air. Nay, ten minutes' delay would have been salvation.

Sitka Charley, looking back, saw the pillared smoke of their fire, and guessed. And he looked ahead at those who were faithful, and at Mrs. Eppingwell. 'So, my good comrades, ye have again forgotten that you were men? Good! Very good. There will be fewer bellies to feed.' Sitka Charley retied the flour as he spoke, strapping the pack to the one on his own back. He kicked Joe till the pain broke through the poor devil's bliss and brought him doddering to his feet. Then he shoved him out upon the trail and started him on his way. The two Indians attempted to slip off.

'Hold, Gowhee! And thou, too, Kah-Chucte! Hath the flour given such strength to thy legs that they may outrun the swift-winged lead? Think not to cheat the law. Be men for the last time, and be content that ye die full-stomached.

Come, step up, back to the timber, shoulder to shoulder. Come!' The two men obeyed, quietly, without fear; for it is the future which pressed upon the man, not the present.

'Thou, Gowhee, hast a wife and children and a deerskin lodge in the Chipewyan. What is thy will in the matter?' 'Give thou her of the goods which are mine by the word of the captain—the blankets, the beads, the tobacco, the box which makes strange sounds after the manner of the white men. Say that I did die on the trail, but say not how.' 'And thou, Kah-Chucte, who hast nor wife nor child?' 'Mine is a sister, the wife of the factor at Koshim. He beats her, and she is not happy. Give thou her the goods which are mine by the contract, and tell her it were well she go back to her own people. Shouldst thou meet the man, and be so minded, it were a good deed that he should die. He beats her, and she is afraid.' 'Are ye content to die by the law?' 'We are.' 'Then good-bye, my good comrades. May ye sit by the well-filled pot, in warm lodges, ere the day is done.' As he spoke he raised his rifle, and many echoes broke the silence. Hardly had they died away when other rifles spoke in the distance. Sitka Charley started.

There had been more than one shot, yet there was but one other rifle in the party.

He gave a fleeting glance at the men who lay so quietly, smiled viciously at the wisdom of the trail, and hurried on to meet the men of the Yukon.

THE WIFE OF A KING

Once when the northland was very young, the social and civic virtues were remarkably alike for their paucity and their simplicity. When the burden of domestic duties grew grievous, and the fireside mood expanded to a constant protest against its bleak loneliness, the adventurers from the Southland, in lieu of better, paid the stipulated prices and took unto themselves native wives. It was a foretaste of Paradise to the women, for it must be confessed that the white rovers gave far better care and treatment of them than did their Indian copartners. Of course, the white men themselves were satisfied with such deals, as were also the Indian men for that matter. Having sold their daughters and sisters for cotton blankets and obsolete rifles and traded their warm furs for flimsy calico and bad whisky, the sons of the soil promptly and cheerfully succumbed to quick consumption and other swift diseases correlated with the blessings of a superior civilization.

It was in these days of Arcadian simplicity that Cal Galbraith journeyed through the land and fell sick on the Lower River. It was a refreshing advent in the lives of the good Sisters of the Holy Cross, who gave him shelter and medicine; though they little dreamed of the hot elixir infused into his veins by the touch of their soft hands and their gentle ministrations. Cal Galbraith, became troubled with strange thoughts which clamored for attention till he laid eyes on the Mission girl, Madeline. Yet he gave no sign, biding his time patiently. He strengthened with the coming spring, and when the sun rode the heavens in a golden circle, and the joy and throb of life was in all the land, he gathered his still weak body together and departed.

Now, Madeline, the Mission girl, was an orphan. Her white father had failed to give a bald-faced grizzly the trail one day, and had died quickly. Then her Indian mother, having no man to fill the winter cache, had tried the hazardous experiment of waiting till the salmon-run on fifty pounds of flour and half as many of bacon. After that, the baby, Chook-ra, went to live with the good Sisters, and to be thenceforth known by another name.

But Madeline still had kinsfolk, the nearest being a dissolute uncle who outraged his vitals with inordinate quantities of the white man's whisky. He strove daily to walk with the gods, and incidentally, his feet sought shorter trails to the grave. When sober he suffered exquisite torture. He had no conscience. To this ancient vagabond Cal Galbraith duly presented himself, and they consumed many words and much tobacco in the conversation that followed. Promises were also made; and in the end the old heathen took a few pounds of dried salmon and his birch-bark canoe, and paddled away to the Mission of the Holy Cross.

It is not given the world to know what promises he made and what lies he told— the Sisters never gossip; but when he returned, upon his swarthy chest there was a brass crucifix, and in his canoe his niece Madeline. That night there was a grand wedding and a potlach; so that for two days to follow there was no fishing done by the village. But in the morning Madeline shook the dust of the Lower River from her moccasins, and with her husband, in a poling-boat, went to live on the Upper River in a place known as the Lower Country. And in the years which followed she was a good wife, sharing her husband's hardships and cooking his food. And she kept him in straight trails, till he learned to save his dust and to work mightily. In the end, he struck it rich and built a cabin in Circle City; and his happiness was such that men who came to visit him in his home-circle became restless at the sight of it and envied him greatly.

But the Northland began to mature and social amenities to make their appearance.

Hitherto, the Southland had sent forth its sons; but it now belched forth a new exodus—this time of its daughters. Sisters and wives they were not; but they did not fail to put new ideas in the heads of the men, and to elevate the tone of things in ways peculiarly their own. No more did the squaws gather at the dances, go roaring down the center in the good, old Virginia reels, or make merry with jolly 'Dan Tucker.' They fell back on their natural stoicism and uncomplainingly watched the rule of their white sisters from their cabins.

Then another exodus came over the mountains from the prolific Southland.

This time it was of women that became mighty in the land. Their word was law; their law was steel. They frowned upon the Indian wives, while the other women became mild and walked humbly. There were cowards who became ashamed of their ancient covenants with the daughters of the soil, who looked with a new distaste upon their dark-skinned children; but there were also others—men—who remained true and proud of their aboriginal vows. When it became the fashion to divorce the native wives. Cal Galbraith retained his manhood, and in so doing felt the heavy hand of the women who had come last, knew least, but who ruled the land.

One day, the Upper Country, which lies far above Circle City, was pronounced rich. Dog-teams carried the news to Salt Water; golden argosies freighted the lure across the North Pacific; wires and cables sang with the tidings; and the world heard for the first time of the Klondike River and the Yukon Country. Cal Galbraith had lived the years quietly. He had been a good husband to Madeline, and she had blessed him. But somehow discontent fell upon him; he felt vague yearnings for his own kind, for the life he had been shut out from—a general sort of desire, which men sometimes feel, to break out and taste the prime of living. Besides, there drifted down the river wild rumors of the wonderful El Dorado, glowing descriptions of the city of logs and tents, and ludicrous accounts of the che-cha-quas who had rushed in and were stampeding the whole country.

Circle City was dead. The world had moved on up river and become a new and most marvelous world.

Cal Galbraith grew restless on the edge of things, and wished to see with his own eyes.

So, after the wash-up, he weighed in a couple of hundred pounds of dust on the Company's big scales, and took a draft for the same on Dawson. Then he put Tom Dixon in charge of his mines, kissed Madeline good-by, promised to be back before the first mush-ice ran, and took passage on an up-river steamer.

Madeline waited, waited through all the three months of daylight. She fed the dogs, gave much of her time to Young Cal, watched the short summer fade away and the sun begin its long journey to the south. And she prayed much in the manner of the Sisters of the Holy Cross. The fall came, and with it there was mush-ice on the Yukon, and Circle City kings returning to the winter's work at their mines, but no Cal Galbraith. Tom Dixon received a letter, however, for his men sledded up her winter's supply of dry pine. The Company received a letter for its dogteams filled her cache with their best provisions, and she was told that her credit was limitless.

Through all the ages man has been held the chief instigator of the woes of woman; but in this case the men held their tongues and swore harshly at one of their number who was away, while the women failed utterly to emulate them. So, without needless delay, Madeline heard strange tales of Cal Galbraith's doings; also, of a certain Greek dancer who played with men as children did with bubbles. Now Madeline was an Indian woman, and further, she had no woman friend to whom to go for wise counsel. She prayed and planned by turns, and that night, being quick of resolve and action, she harnessed the dogs, and with Young Cal securely lashed to the sled, stole away.

Though the Yukon still ran free, the eddy-ice was growing, and each day saw the river dwindling to a slushy thread. Save him who has done the like, no man may know what she endured in traveling a hundred miles on the rim-ice; nor may they understand the toil and hardship of breaking the two hundred miles of packed ice which remained after the river froze for good. But Madeline was an Indian woman, so she did these things, and one night there came a knock at Malemute Kid's door. Thereat he fed a team of starving dogs, put a healthy youngster to bed, and turned his attention to an exhausted woman. He removed her icebound moccasins while he listened to her tale, and stuck the point of his knife into her feet that he might see how far they were frozen.

Despite his tremendous virility, Malemute Kid was possessed of a softer, womanly element, which could win the confidence of a snarling wolf-dog or draw confessions from the most wintry heart. Nor did he seek them. Hearts opened to him as spontaneously as flowers to the sun. Even the priest, Father Roubeau, had been known to confess to him, while the men and women of the Northland were ever knocking at his door—a door from which the latch-string hung always out. To Madeline, he could do no wrong, make no mistake. She had known him from the time she first cast her lot among the people of her father's race; and to her half-barbaric mind it seemed that in him was centered the wisdom of the ages, that between his vision and the future there could be no intervening veil.

There were false ideals in the land. The social strictures of Dawson were not synonymous with those of the previous era, and the swift maturity of the Northland involved much wrong. Malemute Kid was aware of this, and he had Cal Galbraith's measure accurately.

He knew a hasty word was the father of much evil; besides, he was minded to teach a great lesson and bring shame upon the man. So Stanley Prince, the young mining expert, was called into the conference the following night as was also Lucky Jack Harrington and his violin. That same night, Bettles, who owed a great debt to Malemute Kid, harnessed up Cal Galbraith's dogs, lashed Cal Galbraith, Junior, to the sled, and slipped away in the dark for Stuart River.

II

'So; one—two—three, one—two—three. Now reverse! No, no! Start up again, Jack. See—this way.' Prince executed the movement as one should who has led the cotillion.

'Now; one—two—three, one—two—three. Reverse! Ah! that's better. Try it again. I say, you know, you mustn't look at your feet. One—two—three, one—two—three. Shorter steps! You are not hanging to the gee-pole just now. Try it over.

'There! that's the way. One—two—three, one—two—three.' Round and round went Prince and Madeline in an interminable waltz. The table and stools had been shoved over against the wall to increase the room. Malemute Kid sat on the bunk, chin to knees, greatly interested. Jack Harrington sat beside him, scraping away on his violin and following the dancers.

It was a unique situation, the undertaking of these three men with the woman. The most pathetic part, perhaps, was the businesslike way in which they went about it.

No athlete was ever trained more rigidly for a coming contest, nor wolf-dog for the harness, than was she. But they had good material, for Madeline, unlike most women of her race, in her childhood had escaped the carrying of heavy burdens and the toil of the trail. Besides, she was a clean-limbed, willowy creature, possessed of much grace which had not hitherto been realized. It was this grace which the men strove to bring out and knock into shape.

'Trouble with her she learned to dance all wrong,' Prince remarked to the bunk after having deposited his breathless pupil on the table. 'She's quick at picking up; yet I could do better had she never danced a step. But say, Kid, I can't understand this.' Prince imitated a peculiar movement of the shoulders and head—a weakness Madeline suffered from in walking.

'Lucky for her she was raised in the Mission,' Malemute Kid answered. 'Packing, you know,—the head-strap. Other Indian women have it bad, but she didn't do any packing till after she married, and then only at first. Saw hard lines with that husband of hers. They went through the Forty-Mile famine together.' 'But can we break it?' 'Don't know.

'Perhaps long walks with her trainers will make the riffle. Anyway, they'll take it out some, won't they, Madeline?' The girl nodded assent. If Malemute Kid, who knew all things, said so, why it was so. That was all there was about it.

She had come over to them, anxious to begin again. Harrington surveyed her in quest of her points much in the same manner men usually do horses. It certainly was not disappointing, for he asked with sudden interest, 'What did that beggarly uncle of yours get anyway?' 'One rifle, one blanket, twenty bottles of hooch. Rifle broke.' She said this last scornfully, as though disgusted at how low her maiden-value had been rated.

She spoke fair English, with many peculiarities of her husband's speech, but there was still perceptible the Indian accent, the traditional groping after strange gutturals. Even this her instructors had taken in hand, and with no small success, too.

At the next intermission, Prince discovered a new predicament.

'I say, Kid,' he said, 'we're wrong, all wrong. She can't learn in moccasins.

'Put her feet into slippers, and then onto that waxed floor—phew!' Madeline raised a foot and regarded her shapeless house-moccasins dubiously. In previous winters, both at Circle City and Forty-Mile, she had danced many a night away with similar footgear, and there had been nothing the matter.

But now—well, if there was anything wrong it was for Malemute Kid to know, not her.

But Malemute Kid did know, and he had a good eye for measures; so he put on his cap and mittens and went down the hill to pay Mrs. Eppingwell a call. Her husband, Clove Eppingwell, was prominent in the community as one of the great Government officials.

The Kid had noted her slender little foot one night, at the Governor's Ball. And as he also knew her to be as sensible as she was pretty, it was no task to ask of her a certain small favor.

On his return, Madeline withdrew for a moment to the inner room. When she reappeared Prince was startled.

'By Jove!' he gasped. 'Who'd a' thought it! The little witch! Why my sister—' 'Is an English girl,' interrupted Malemute Kid, 'with an English foot. This girl comes of a small-footed race. Moccasins just broadened her feet healthily, while she did not misshape them by running with the dogs in her childhood.' But this explanation failed utterly to allay Prince's admiration. Harrington's commercial instinct was touched, and as he looked upon the exquisitely turned foot and ankle, there ran through his mind the sordid list—'One rifle, one blanket, twenty bottles of hooch.' Madeline was the wife of a king, a king whose yellow treasure could buy outright a score of fashion's puppets; yet in all her life her feet had known no gear save red-tanned moosehide. At first she had looked in awe at the tiny white-satin slippers; but she had quickly understood the admiration which shone, manlike, in the eyes of the men. Her face flushed with pride. For the moment she was drunken with her woman's loveliness; then she murmured, with increased scorn, 'And one rifle, broke!' So the training went on. Every day Malemute Kid led the girl out on long walks devoted to the correction of her carriage and the shortening of her stride.

There was little likelihood of her identity being discovered, for Cal Galbraith and the rest of the Old-Timers were like lost children among the many strangers who had rushed into the land. Besides, the frost of the North has a bitter tongue, and the tender women of the South, to shield their cheeks from its biting caresses, were prone to the use of canvas masks. With faces obscured and bodies lost in squirrel-skin parkas, a mother and daughter, meeting on trail, would pass as strangers.

The coaching progressed rapidly. At first it had been slow, but later a sudden acceleration had manifested itself. This began from the moment Madeline tried on the white-satin slippers, and in so doing found herself. The pride of her renegade father, apart from any natural self-esteem she might possess, at that instant received its birth. Hitherto, she had deemed herself a woman of an alien breed, of inferior stock, purchased by her lord's favor. Her husband had seemed to her a god, who had lifted her, through no essential virtues on her part, to his own godlike level. But she had never forgotten, even when Young Cal was born, that she was not of his people. As he had been a god, so had his womenkind been goddesses. She might have contrasted herself with them, but she had never compared.

It might have been that familiarity bred contempt; however, be that as it may, she had ultimately come to understand these roving white men, and to weigh them.

True, her mind was dark to deliberate analysis, but she yet possessed her woman's clarity of vision in such matters. On the night of the slippers she had measured the bold, open admiration of her three man-friends; and for the first time comparison had suggested itself. It was only a foot and an ankle, but—but comparison could not, in the nature of things, cease at that point. She judged herself by their standards till the divinity of her white sisters was shattered. After all, they were only women, and why should she not exalt herself to their midst? In doing these things she learned where she lacked and with the knowledge of her weakness came her strength. And so mightily did she strive that her three trainers often marveled late into the night over the eternal mystery of woman.

In this way Thanksgiving Night drew near. At irregular intervals Bettles sent word down from Stuart River regarding the welfare of Young Cal. The time of their return was approaching. More than once a casual caller, hearing dance-music and the rhythmic pulse of feet, entered, only to find Harrington scraping away and the other two beating time or arguing noisily over a mooted step. Madeline was never in evidence, having precipitately fled to the inner room.

On one of these nights Cal Galbraith dropped in. Encouraging news had just come down from Stuart River, and Madeline had surpassed herself—not in walk alone, and carriage and grace, but in womanly roguishness. They had indulged in sharp repartee and she had defended herself brilliantly; and then, yielding to the intoxication of the moment, and of her own power, she had bullied, and mastered, and wheedled, and patronized them with most astonishing success. And instinctively, involuntarily, they had bowed, not to her beauty, her wisdom, her wit, but to that indefinable something in woman to which man yields yet cannot name.

The room was dizzy with sheer delight as she and Prince whirled through the last dance of the evening. Harrington was throwing in inconceivable flourishes, while Malemute Kid, utterly abandoned, had seized the broom and was executing mad gyrations on his own account.

At this instant the door shook with a heavy rap-rap, and their quick glances noted the lifting of the latch. But they had survived similar situations before. Harrington never broke a note. Madeline shot through the waiting door to the inner room. The broom went hurtling under the bunk, and by the time Cal Galbraith and Louis Savoy got their heads in, Malemute Kid and Prince were in each other's arms, wildly schottisching down the room.

As a rule, Indian women do not make a practice of fainting on provocation, but Madeline came as near to it as she ever had in her life. For an hour she crouched on the floor, listening to the heavy voices of the men rumbling up and down in mimic thunder. Like familiar chords of childhood melodies, every intonation, every trick of her husband's voice swept in upon her, fluttering her heart and weakening her knees till she lay half-fainting against the door. It was well she could neither see nor hear when he took his departure.

'When do you expect to go back to Circle City?' Malemute Kid asked simply.

'Haven't thought much about it,' he replied. 'Don't think till after the ice breaks.'

'And Madeline?'

He flushed at the question, and there was a quick droop to his eyes. Malemute Kid could have despised him for that, had he known men less. As it was, his gorge rose against the wives and daughters who had come into the land, and not satisfied with usurping the place of the native women, had put unclean thoughts in the heads of the men and made them ashamed.

'I guess she's all right,' the Circle City King answered hastily, and in an apologetic manner. 'Tom Dixon's got charge of my interests, you know, and he sees to it that she has everything she wants.' Malemute Kid laid hand upon his arm and hushed him suddenly. They had stepped without. Overhead, the aurora, a gorgeous wanton, flaunted miracles of color; beneath lay the sleeping town. Far below, a solitary dog gave tongue.

The King again began to speak, but the Kid pressed his hand for silence. The sound multiplied. Dog after dog took up the strain till the full-throated chorus swayed the night.

To him who hears for the first time this weird song, is told the first and greatest secret of the Northland; to him who has heard it often, it is the solemn knell of lost endeavor. It is the plaint of tortured souls, for in it is invested the heritage of the North, the suffering of countless generations—the warning and the requiem to the world's estrays.

Cal Galbraith shivered slightly as it died away in half-caught sobs. The Kid read his thoughts openly, and wandered back with him through all the weary days of famine and disease; and with him was also the patient Madeline, sharing his pains and perils, never doubting, never complaining. His mind's retina vibrated to a score of pictures, stern, clear-cut, and the hand of the past drew back with heavy fingers on his heart. It was the psychological moment. Malemute Kid was half-tempted to play his reserve card and win the game; but the lesson was too mild as yet, and he let it pass. The next instant they had gripped hands, and the King's beaded moccasins were drawing protests from the outraged snow as he crunched down the hill.

Madeline in collapse was another woman to the mischievous creature of an hour before, whose laughter had been so infectious and whose heightened color and flashing eyes had made her teachers for the while forget. Weak and nerveless, she sat in the chair just as she had been dropped there by Prince and Harrington.

Malemute Kid frowned. This would never do. When the time of meeting her husband came to hand, she must carry things off with high-handed imperiousness. It was very necessary she should do it after the manner of white women, else the victory would be no victory at all. So he talked to her, sternly, without mincing of words, and initiated her into the weaknesses of his own sex, till she came to understand what simpletons men were after all, and why the word of their women was law.

A few days before Thanksgiving Night, Malemute Kid made another call on Mrs. Eppingwell. She promptly overhauled her feminine fripperies, paid a protracted visit to the dry-goods department of the P. C. Company, and returned with the Kid to make Madeline's acquaintance. After that came a period such as the cabin had never seen before, and what with cutting, and fitting, and basting, and stitching, and numerous other wonderful and unknowable things, the male conspirators were more often banished the premises than not. At such times the Opera House opened its double storm-doors to them.

So often did they put their heads together, and so deeply did they drink to curious toasts, that the loungers scented unknown creeks of incalculable richness, and it is known that several checha-quas and at least one Old-Timer kept their stampeding packs stored behind the bar, ready to hit the trail at a moment's notice.

Mrs. Eppingwell was a woman of capacity; so, when she turned Madeline over to her trainers on Thanksgiving Night she was so transformed that they were almost afraid of her. Prince wrapped a Hudson Bay blanket about her with a mock reverence more real than feigned, while Malemute Kid, whose arm she had taken, found it a severe trial to resume his wonted mentorship. Harrington, with the list of purchases still running through his head, dragged along in the rear, nor opened his mouth once all the way down into the town. When they came to the back door of the Opera House they took the blanket from Madeline's shoulders and spread it on the snow. Slipping out of Prince's moccasins, she stepped upon it in new satin slippers. The masquerade was at its height. She hesitated, but they jerked open the door and shoved her in. Then they ran around to come in by the front entrance.

III

'Where is Freda?' the Old-Timers questioned, while the che-cha-quas were equally energetic in asking who Freda was. The ballroom buzzed with her name.

It was on everybody's lips. Grizzled 'sour-dough boys,' day-laborers at the mines but proud of their degree, either patronized the spruce-looking tenderfeet and lied eloquently—the 'sour-dough boys' being specially created to toy with truth—or gave them savage looks of indignation because of their ignorance. Perhaps forty kings of the Upper and Lower Countries were on the floor, each deeming himself hot on the trail and sturdily backing his judgment with the yellow dust of the realm. An assistant was sent to the man at the scales, upon whom had fallen the burden of weighing up the sacks, while several of the gamblers, with the rules of chance at their finger-ends, made up alluring books on the field and favorites.

Which was Freda? Time and again the 'Greek Dancer' was thought to have been discovered, but each discovery brought panic to the betting ring and a frantic registering of new wagers by those who wished to hedge. Malemute Kid took an interest in the hunt, his advent being hailed uproariously by the revelers, who knew him to a man.

The Kid had a good eye for the trick of a step, and ear for the lilt of a voice, and his private choice was a marvelous creature who scintillated as the 'Aurora Borealis.' But the Greek dancer was too subtle for even his penetration. The majority of the gold-hunters seemed to have centered their verdict on the 'Russian Princess,' who was the most graceful in the room, and hence could be no other than Freda Moloof.

During a quadrille a roar of satisfaction went up. She was discovered. At previous balls, in the figure, 'all hands round,' Freda had displayed an inimitable step and variation peculiarly her own. As the figure was called, the 'Russian Princess' gave the unique rhythm to limb and body. A chorus of I-told-you-so's shook the squared roof-beams, when lo! it was noticed that 'Aurora Borealis' and another masque, the 'Spirit of the Pole,' were performing the same trick equally well. And when two twin 'Sun-Dogs' and a 'Frost Queen' followed suit, a second assistant was dispatched to the aid of the man at the scales.

Bettles came off trail in the midst of the excitement, descending upon them in a hurricane of frost. His rimed brows turned to cataracts as he whirled about; his mustache, still frozen, seemed gemmed with diamonds and turned the light in vari-colored rays; while the flying feet slipped on the chunks of ice which rattled from his moccasins and German socks. A Northland dance is quite an informal affair, the men of the creeks and trails having lost whatever fastidiousness they might have at one time possessed; and only in the high official circles are conventions at all observed. Here, caste carried no significance. Millionaires and paupers, dog-drivers and mounted policemen joined hands with 'ladies in the center,' and swept around the circle performing most remarkable capers. Primitive in their pleasure, boisterous and rough, they displayed no rudeness, but rather a crude chivalry more genuine than the most polished courtesy.

In his quest for the 'Greek Dancer,' Cal Galbraith managed to get into the same set with the 'Russian Princess,' toward whom popular suspicion had turned.

But by the time he had guided her through one dance, he was willing not only to stake his millions that she was not Freda, but that he had had his arm about her waist before. When or where he could not tell, but the puzzling sense of familiarity so wrought upon him that he turned his attention to the discovery of her identity. Malemute Kid might have aided him instead of occasionally taking the Princess for a few turns and talking earnestly to her in low tones. But it was Jack Harrington who paid the 'Russian Princess' the most assiduous court. Once he drew Cal Galbraith aside and hazarded wild guesses as to who she was, and explained to him that he was going in to win. That rankled the Circle City King, for man is not by nature monogamic, and he forgot both Madeline and Freda in the new quest.

It was soon noised about that the 'Russian Princess' was not Freda Moloof. Interest deepened. Here was a fresh enigma. They knew Freda though they could not find her, but here was somebody they had found and did not know. Even the women could not place her, and they knew every good dancer in the camp. Many took her for one of the official clique, indulging in a silly escapade. Not a few asserted she would disappear before the unmasking. Others were equally positive that she was the woman-reporter of the Kansas City Star, come to write them up at ninety dollars per column. And the men at the scales worked busily.

At one o'clock every couple took to the floor. The unmasking began amid laughter and delight, like that of carefree children. There was no end of Oh's and

Ah's as mask after mask was lifted. The scintillating 'Aurora Borealis' became the brawny negress whose income from washing the community's clothes ran at about five hundred a month. The twin 'Sun-Dogs' discovered mustaches on their upper lips, and were recognized as brother Fraction-Kings of El Dorado. In one of the most prominent sets, and the slowest in uncovering, was Cal Galbraith with the 'Spirit of the Pole.' Opposite him was Jack Harrington and the 'Russian Princess.' The rest had discovered themselves, yet the 'Greek Dancer' was still missing. All eyes were upon the group. Cal Galbraith, in response to their cries, lifted his partner's mask. Freda's wonderful face and brilliant eyes flashed out upon them. A roar went up, to be squelched suddenly in the new and absorbing mystery of the 'Russian Princess.' Her face was still hidden, and Jack Harrington was struggling with her. The dancers tittered on the tiptoes of expectancy. He crushed her dainty costume roughly, and then—and then the revelers exploded. The joke was on them. They had danced all night with a tabooed native woman.

But those that knew, and they were many, ceased abruptly, and a hush fell upon the room.

Cal Galbraith crossed over with great strides, angrily, and spoke to Madeline in polyglot Chinook. But she retained her composure, apparently oblivious to the fact that she was the cynosure of all eyes, and answered him in English. She showed neither fright nor anger, and Malemute Kid chuckled at her well-bred equanimity. The King felt baffled, defeated; his common Siwash wife had passed beyond him.

'Come!' he said finally. 'Come on home.' 'I beg pardon,' she replied; 'I have agreed to go to supper with Mr. Harrington. Besides, there's no end of dances promised.'

Harrington extended his arm to lead her away. He evinced not the slightest disinclination toward showing his back, but Malemute Kid had by this time edged in closer. The Circle City King was stunned. Twice his hand dropped to his belt, and twice the Kid gathered himself to spring; but the retreating couple passed through the supper-room door where canned oysters were spread at five dollars the plate.

The crowd sighed audibly, broke up into couples, and followed them. Freda pouted and went in with Cal Galbraith; but she had a good heart and a sure tongue, and she spoiled his oysters for him. What she said is of no importance, but his face went red and white at intervals, and he swore repeatedly and savagely at himself.

The supper-room was filled with a pandemonium of voices, which ceased suddenly as Cal Galbraith stepped over to his wife's table. Since the unmasking considerable weights of dust had been placed as to the outcome. Everybody watched with breathless interest.

Harrington's blue eyes were steady, but under the overhanging tablecloth a Smith & Wesson balanced on his knee. Madeline looked up, casually, with little interest.

'May—may I have the next round dance with you?' the King stuttered.

The wife of the King glanced at her card and inclined her head.

AN ODYSSEY OF THE NORTH

The sleds were singing their eternal lament to the creaking of the harness and the tinkling bells of the leaders; but the men and dogs were tired and made no sound. The trail was heavy with new-fallen snow, and they had come far, and the runners, burdened with flint-like quarters of frozen moose, clung tenaciously to the unpacked surface and held back with a stubbornness almost human.

Darkness was coming on, but there was no camp to pitch that night. The snow fell gently through the pulseless air, not in flakes, but in tiny frost crystals of delicate design. It was very warm—barely ten below zero—and the men did not mind. Meyers and Bettles had raised their ear flaps, while Malemute Kid had even taken off his mittens.

The dogs had been fagged out early in the after noon, but they now began to show new vigor. Among the more astute there was a certain restlessness—an impatience at the restraint of the traces, an indecisive quickness of movement, a sniffing of snouts and pricking of ears. These became incensed at their more phlegmatic brothers, urging them on with numerous sly nips on their hinder quarters. Those, thus chidden, also contracted and helped spread the contagion. At last the leader of the foremost sled uttered a sharp whine of satisfaction, crouching lower in the snow and throwing himself against the collar. The rest followed suit.

There was an ingathering of back hands, a tightening of traces; the sleds leaped forward, and the men clung to the gee poles, violently accelerating the uplift of their feet that they might escape going under the runners. The weariness of the day fell from them, and they whooped encouragement to the dogs. The animals responded with joyous yelps. They were swinging through the gathering darkness at a rattling gallop.

'Gee! Gee!' the men cried, each in turn, as their sleds abruptly left the main trail, heeling over on single runners like luggers on the wind.

Then came a hundred yards' dash to the lighted parchment window, which told its own story of the home cabin, the roaring Yukon stove, and the steaming pots of tea. But the home cabin had been invaded. Threescore huskies chorused defiance, and as many furry forms precipitated themselves upon the dogs which drew the first sled. The door was flung open, and a man, clad in the scarlet tunic of the Northwest Police, waded knee-deep among the furious brutes, calmly and impartially dispensing soothing justice with the butt end of a dog whip. After that the men shook hands; and in this wise was Malemute Kid welcomed to his own cabin by a stranger.

Stanley Prince, who should have welcomed him, and who was responsible for the Yukon stove and hot tea aforementioned, was busy with his guests. There were a dozen or so of them, as nondescript a crowd as ever served the Queen in the enforcement of her laws or the delivery of her mails. They were of many breeds, but their common life had formed of them a certain type—a lean and wiry type, with trail-hardened muscles, and sun-browned faces, and untroubled souls which gazed frankly forth, clear-eyed and steady.

They drove the dogs of the Queen, wrought fear in the hearts of her enemies, ate of her meager fare, and were happy. They had seen life, and done deeds, and lived romances; but they did not know it.

And they were very much at home. Two of them were sprawled upon Malemute Kid's bunk, singing chansons which their French forebears sang in the days when first they entered the Northwest land and mated with its Indian women. Bettles' bunk had suffered a similar invasion, and three or four lusty voyageurs worked their toes among its blankets as they listened to the tale of one who had served on the boat brigade with Wolseley when he fought his way to Khartoum.

397

And when he tired, a cowboy told of courts and kings and lords and ladies he had seen when Buffalo Bill toured the capitals of Europe. In a corner two half-breeds, ancient comrades in a lost campaign, mended harnesses and talked of the days when the Northwest flamed with insurrection and Louis Riel was king.

Rough jests and rougher jokes went up and down, and great hazards by trail and river were spoken of in the light of commonplaces, only to be recalled by virtue of some grain of humor or ludicrous happening. Prince was led away by these uncrowned heroes who had seen history made, who regarded the great and the romantic as but the ordinary and the incidental in the routine of life. He passed his precious tobacco among them with lavish disregard, and rusty chains of reminiscence were loosened, and forgotten odysseys resurrected for his especial benefit.

When conversation dropped and the travelers filled the last pipes and lashed their tight-rolled sleeping furs. Prince fell back upon his comrade for further information.

'Well, you know what the cowboy is,' Malemute Kid answered, beginning to unlace his moccasins; 'and it's not hard to guess the British blood in his bed partner. As for the rest, they're all children of the coureurs du bois, mingled with God knows how many other bloods. The two turning in by the door are the regulation 'breeds' or Boisbrules. That lad with the worsted breech scarf—notice his eyebrows and the turn of his jaw—shows a Scotchman wept in his mother's smoky tepee. And that handsome looking fellow putting the capote under his head is a French half-breed—you heard him talking; he doesn't like the two Indians turning in next to him. You see, when the 'breeds' rose under the Riel the full-bloods kept the peace, and they've not lost much love for one another since.' 'But I say, what's that glum-looking fellow by the stove? I'll swear he can't talk English. He hasn't opened his mouth all night.' 'You're wrong. He knows English well enough. Did you follow his eyes when he listened? I did. But he's neither kith nor kin to the others. When they talked their own patois you could see he didn't understand. I've been wondering myself what he is. Let's find out.' 'Fire a couple of sticks into the stove!'

Malemute Kid commanded, raising his voice and looking squarely at the man in question.

He obeyed at once.

'Had discipline knocked into him somewhere.' Prince commented in a low tone.

Malemute Kid nodded, took off his socks, and picked his way among recumbent men to the stove. There he hung his damp footgear among a score or so of mates.

'When do you expect to get to Dawson?' he asked tentatively.

The man studied him a moment before replying. 'They say seventy-five mile. So? Maybe two days.' The very slightest accent was perceptible, while there was no awkward hesitancy or groping for words.

'Been in the country before?' 'No.' 'Northwest Territory?' 'Yes.' 'Born there?' 'No.'

'Well, where the devil were you born? You're none of these.' Malemute Kid swept his hand over the dog drivers, even including the two policemen who had turned into Prince's bunk. 'Where did you come from? I've seen faces like yours before, though I can't remember just where.' 'I know you,' he irrelevantly replied, at once turning the drift of Malemute Kid's questions.

'Where? Ever see me?' 'No; your partner, him priest, Pastilik, long time ago. Him ask me if I see you, Malemute Kid. Him give me grub. I no stop long. You hear him speak 'bout me?' 'Oh! you're the fellow that traded the otter skins for the dogs?' The man nodded, knocked out his pipe, and signified his disinclination for conversation by rolling up in his furs. Malemute Kid blew out the slush lamp and crawled under the blankets with Prince.

'Well, what is he?' 'Don't know—turned me off, somehow, and then shut up like a clam.

'But he's a fellow to whet your curiosity. I've heard of him. All the coast wondered about him eight years ago. Sort of mysterious, you know. He came down out of the North in the dead of winter, many a thousand miles from here, skirting Bering Sea and traveling as though the devil were after him. No one ever learned where he came from, but he must have come far. He was badly travel-worn when he got food from the Swedish missionary on Golovin Bay and asked the way south. We heard of all this afterward. Then he abandoned the shore line, heading right across Norton Sound. Terrible weather, snowstorms and high winds, but he pulled through where a thousand other men would have died, missing St. Michaels and making the land at Pastilik. He'd lost all but two dogs, and was nearly gone with starvation.

'He was so anxious to go on that Father Roubeau fitted him out with grub; but he couldn't let him have any dogs, for he was only waiting my arrival, to go on a trip himself. Mr. Ulysses knew too much to start on without animals, and fretted around for several days. He had on his sled a bunch of beautifully cured otter skins, sea otters, you know, worth their weight in gold. There was also at Pastilik an old Shylock of a Russian trader, who had dogs to kill. Well, they didn't dicker very long, but when the Strange One headed south again, it was in the rear of a spanking dog team. Mr. Shylock, by the way, had the otter skins. I saw them, and they were magnificent. We figured it up and found the dogs brought him at least five hundred apiece. And it wasn't as if the Strange One didn't know the value of sea otter; he was an Indian of some sort, and what little he talked showed he'd been among white men.

'After the ice passed out of the sea, word came up from Nunivak Island that he'd gone in there for grub. Then he dropped from sight, and this is the first heard of him in eight years. Now where did he come from? and what was he doing there? and why did he come from there? He's Indian, he's been nobody knows where, and he's had discipline, which is unusual for an Indian. Another mystery of the North for you to solve, Prince.' 'Thanks awfully, but I've got too many on hand as it is,' he replied.

Malemute Kid was already breathing heavily; but the young mining engineer gazed straight up through the thick darkness, waiting for the strange orgasm which stirred his blood to die away. And when he did sleep, his brain worked on, and for the nonce he, too, wandered through the white unknown, struggled with the dogs on endless trails, and saw men live, and toil, and die like men. The next morning, hours before daylight, the dog drivers and policemen pulled out for Dawson. But the powers that saw to Her Majesty's interests and ruled the destinies of her lesser creatures gave the mailmen little rest, for a week later they appeared at Stuart River, heavily burdened with letters for Salt Water.

However, their dogs had been replaced by fresh ones; but, then, they were dogs.

The men had expected some sort of a layover in which to rest up; besides, this Klondike was a new section of the Northland, and they had wished to see a little something of the Golden City where dust flowed like water and dance halls rang with never-ending revelry. But they dried their socks and smoked their evening pipes with much the same gusto as on their former visit, though one or two bold spirits speculated on desertion and the possibility of crossing the unexplored Rockies to the east, and thence, by the Mackenzie Valley, of gaining their old stamping grounds in the Chippewyan country.

Two or three even decided to return to their homes by that route when their terms of service had expired, and they began to lay plans forthwith, looking forward to the hazardous undertaking in much the same way a city-bred man would to a day's holiday in the woods.

He of the Otter Skins seemed very restless, though he took little interest in the discussion, and at last he drew Malemute Kid to one side and talked for some time in low tones.

Prince cast curious eyes in their direction, and the mystery deepened when they put on caps and mittens and went outside. When they returned, Malemute Kid placed his gold scales on the table, weighed out the matter of sixty ounces, and transferred them to the Strange One's sack. Then the chief of the dog drivers joined the conclave, and certain business was transacted with him.

The next day the gang went on upriver, but He of the Otter Skins took several pounds of grub and turned his steps back toward Dawson.

'Didn't know what to make of it,' said Malemute Kid in response to Prince's queries; 'but the poor beggar wanted to be quit of the service for some reason or other—at least it seemed a most important one to him, though he wouldn't let on what. You see, it's just like the army: he signed for two years, and the only way to get free was to buy himself out. He couldn't desert and then stay here, and he was just wild to remain in the country.

'Made up his mind when he got to Dawson, he said; but no one knew him, hadn't a cent, and I was the only one he'd spoken two words with. So he talked it over with the lieutenant-governor, and made arrangements in case he could get the money from me—loan, you know. Said he'd pay back in the year, and, if I wanted, would put me onto something rich. Never'd seen it, but he knew it was rich.

'And talk! why, when he got me outside he was ready to weep. Begged and pleaded; got down in the snow to me till I hauled him out of it. Palavered around like a crazy man.

'Swore he's worked to this very end for years and years, and couldn't bear to be disappointed now. Asked him what end, but he wouldn't say.

'Said they might keep him on the other half of the trail and he wouldn't get to Dawson in two years, and then it would be too late. Never saw a man take on so in my life. And when I said I'd let him have it, had to yank him out of the snow again. Told him to consider it in the light of a grubstake. Think he'd have it? No sir! Swore he'd give me all he found, make me rich beyond the dreams of avarice, and all such stuff. Now a man who puts his life and time against a grubstake ordinarily finds it hard enough to turn over half of what he finds. Something behind all this, Prince; just you make a note of it. We'll hear of him if he stays in the country—' 'And if he doesn't?' 'Then my good nature gets a shock, and I'm sixty some odd ounces out.' The cold weather had come on with the long nights, and the sun had begun to play his ancient game of peekaboo along the southern snow line ere aught was heard of Malemute Kid's grubstake. And then, one bleak morning in early January, a heavily laden dog train pulled into his cabin below Stuart River. He of the Otter Skins was there, and with him walked a man such as the gods have almost forgotten how to fashion. Men never talked of luck and pluck and five-hundred-dollar dirt without bringing in the name of Axel Gunderson; nor could tales of nerve or strength or daring pass up and down the campfire without the summoning of his presence. And when the conversation flagged, it blazed anew at mention of the woman who shared his fortunes.

As has been noted, in the making of Axel Gunderson the gods had remembered their old-time cunning and cast him after the manner of men who were born when the world was young. Full seven feet he towered in his picturesque costume which marked a king of Eldorado. His chest, neck, and limbs were those of a giant. To bear his three hundred pounds of bone and muscle, his snowshoes were greater by a generous yard than those of other men. Rough-hewn, with rugged brow and massive jaw and unflinching eyes of palest blue, his face told the tale of one who knew but the law of might. Of the yellow of ripe corn silk, his frost-incrusted hair swept like day across the night and fell far down his coat of bearskin.

A vague tradition of the sea seemed to cling about him as he swung down the narrow trail in advance of the dogs; and he brought the butt of his dog whip against Malemute Kid's door as a Norse sea rover, on southern foray, might thunder for admittance at the castle gate.

Prince bared his womanly arms and kneaded sour-dough bread, casting, as he did so, many a glance at the three guests—three guests the like of which might never come under a man's roof in a lifetime. The Strange One, whom Malemute Kid had surnamed Ulysses, still fascinated him; but his interest chiefly gravitated between Axel Gunderson and Axel Gunderson's wife. She felt the day's journey, for she had softened in comfortable cabins during the many days since her husband mastered the wealth of frozen pay streaks, and she was tired. She rested against his great breast like a slender flower against a wall, replying lazily to Malemute Kid's good-natured banter, and stirring Prince's blood strangely with an occasional sweep of her deep, dark eyes. For Prince was a man, and healthy, and had seen few women in many months. And she was older than he, and an Indian besides. But she was different from all native wives he had met: she had traveled—had been in his country among others, he gathered from the conversation; and she knew most of the things the women of his own race knew, and much more that it was not in the nature of things for them to know. She could make a meal of sun-dried fish or a bed in the snow; yet she teased them with tantalizing details of many-course dinners, and caused strange internal dissensions to arise at the mention of various quondam dishes which they had well-nigh forgotten. She knew the ways of the moose, the bear, and the little blue fox, and of the wild amphibians of the Northern seas; she was skilled in the lore of the woods, and the streams, and the tale writ by man and bird and beast upon the delicate snow crust was to her an open book; yet Prince caught the appreciative twinkle in her eye as she read the Rules of the Camp. These rules had been fathered by the Unquenchable Bettles at a time when his blood ran high, and were remarkable for the terse simplicity of their humor.

Prince always turned them to the wall before the arrival of ladies; but who could suspect that this native wife—Well, it was too late now.

This, then, was the wife of Axel Gunderson, a woman whose name and fame had traveled with her husband's, hand in hand, through all the Northland. At table, Malemute Kid baited her with the assurance of an old friend, and Prince shook off the shyness of first acquaintance and joined in. But she held her own in the unequal contest, while her husband, slower in wit, ventured naught but applause. And he was very proud of her; his every look and action revealed the magnitude of the place she occupied in his life. He of the Otter Skins ate in silence, forgotten in the merry battle; and long ere the others were done he pushed back from the table and went out among the dogs. Yet all too soon his fellow travelers drew on their mittens and parkas and followed him.

There had been no snow for many days, and the sleds slipped along the hardpacked Yukon trail as easily as if it had been glare ice. Ulysses led the first sled; with the second came Prince and Axel Gunderson's wife; while Malemute Kid and the yellow-haired giant brought up the third.

'It's only a hunch, Kid,' he said, 'but I think it's straight. He's never been there, but he tells a good story, and shows a map I heard of when I was in the Kootenay country years ago. I'd like to have you go along; but he's a strange one, and swore point-blank to throw it up if anyone was brought in. But when I come back you'll get first tip, and I'll stake you next to me, and give you a half share in the town site besides.' 'No! no!' he cried, as the other strove to interrupt. 'I'm running this, and before I'm done it'll need two heads.

'If it's all right, why, it'll be a second Cripple Creek, man; do you hear?—a second Cripple Creek! It's quartz, you know, not placer; and if we work it right we'll corral the whole thing—millions upon millions. I've heard of the place before, and so have you. We'll build a town—thousands of workmen—good waterways—steamship lines—big carrying trade—light-draught steamers for head reaches—survey a railroad, perhaps—sawmills—electric-light plant—do our own banking—commercial company—syndicate—Say! Just you hold your hush till I get back!' The sleds came to a halt where the trail crossed the mouth of Stuart River. An unbroken sea of frost, its wide expanse stretched away into the unknown east.

The snowshoes were withdrawn from the lashings of the sleds. Axel Gunderson shook hands and stepped to the fore, his great webbed shoes sinking a fair half yard into the feathery surface and packing the snow so the dogs should not wallow. His wife fell in behind the last sled, betraying long practice in the art of handling the awkward footgear, The stillness was broken with cheery farewells; the dogs whined; and He of the Otter Skins talked with his whip to a recalcitrant wheeler.

An hour later the train had taken on the likeness of a black pencil crawling in a long, straight line across a mighty sheet of foolscap.

II

One night, many weeks later, Malemute Kid and Prince fell to solving chess problems from the torn page of an ancient magazine. The Kid had just returned from his Bonanza properties and was resting up preparatory to a long moose hunt.

Prince, too, had been on creek and trail nearly all winter, and had grown hungry for a blissful week of cabin life.

'Interpose the black knight, and force the king. No, that won't do. See, the next move-'

'Why advance the pawn two squares? Bound to take it in transit, and with the bishop out of the way-' 'But hold on! That leaves a hole, and-' 'No; it's protected. Go ahead! You'll see it works.' It was very interesting. Somebody knocked at the door a second time before Malemute Kid said, 'Come in.' The door swung open. Something staggered in.

Prince caught one square look and sprang to his feet. The horror in his eyes caused Malemute Kid to whirl about; and he, too, was startled, though he had seen bad things before. The thing tottered blindly toward them. Prince edged away till he reached the nail from which hung his Smith & Wesson.

'My God! what is it?' he whispered to Malemute Kid.

'Don't know. Looks like a case of freezing and no grub,' replied the Kid, sliding away in the opposite direction. 'Watch out! It may be mad,' he warned, coming back from closing the door.

The thing advanced to the table. The bright flame of the slush lamp caught its eye. It was amused, and gave voice to eldritch cackles which betokened mirth.

Then, suddenly, he—for it was a man—swayed back, with a hitch to his skin trousers, and began to sing a chantey, such as men lift when they swing around the capstan circle and the sea snorts in their ears:

Yan-kee ship come down de ri-ib-er, Pull! my bully boys! Pull! D'yeh
    want—to know de captain ru-uns her? Pull! my bully boys! Pull!
Jon-a-than Jones ob South Caho-li-in-a, Pull! my bully.

He broke off abruptly, tottered with a wolfish snarl to the meat shelf, and before they could intercept was tearing with his teeth at a chunk of raw bacon. The struggle was fierce between him and Malemute Kid; but his mad strength left him as suddenly as it had come, and he weakly surrendered the spoil. Between them they got him upon a stool, where he sprawled with half his body across the table.

A small dose of whiskey strengthened him, so that he could dip a spoon into the sugar caddy which Malemute Kid placed before him. After his appetite had been somewhat cloyed, Prince, shuddering as he did so, passed him a mug of weak beef tea.

The creature's eyes were alight with a somber frenzy, which blazed and waned with every mouthful. There was very little skin to the face. The face, for that matter, sunken and emaciated, bore little likeness to human countenance.

Frost after frost had bitten deeply, each depositing its stratum of scab upon the half-healed scar that went before. This dry, hard surface was of a bloody-black color, serrated by grievous cracks wherein the raw red flesh peeped forth. His skin garments were dirty and in tatters, and the fur of one side was singed and burned away, showing where he had lain upon his fire.

Malemute Kid pointed to where the sun-tanned hide had been cut away, strip by strip—the grim signature of famine.

'Who—are—you?' slowly and distinctly enunciated the Kid.

The man paid no heed.

'Where do you come from?' 'Yan-kee ship come down de ri-ib-er,' was the quavering response.

'Don't doubt the beggar came down the river,' the Kid said, shaking him in an endeavor to start a more lucid flow of talk.

But the man shrieked at the contact, clapping a hand to his side in evident pain. He rose slowly to his feet, half leaning on the table.

'She laughed at me—so—with the hate in her eye; and she—would—not—come.'
His voice died away, and he was sinking back when Malemute Kid gripped him by the

wrist and shouted, 'Who? Who would not come?' 'She, Unga. She laughed, and struck at me, so, and so. And then-' 'Yes?'

'And then—' 'And then what?' 'And then he lay very still in the snow a long time. He is-still in—the—snow.' The two men looked at each other helplessly.

'Who is in the snow?' 'She, Unga. She looked at me with the hate in her eye, and then—'

'Yes, yes.' 'And then she took the knife, so; and once, twice—she was weak. I traveled very slow. And there is much gold in that place, very much gold.' 'Where is Unga?' For all Malemute Kid knew, she might be dying a mile away. He shook the man savagely, repeating again and again, 'Where is Unga? Who is Unga?' 'She—is—in—the—snow.' 'Go on!' The Kid was pressing his wrist cruelly.

'So—I—would—be—in—the snow—but—I—had—a—debt—to—pay. It—was—heavy—I—had—a-debt—to—pay—a—debt—to—pay I—had-' The faltering mono-syllables ceased as he fumbled in his pouch and drew forth a buckskin sack. 'A—debt—to—pay—five—pounds—of—gold-grub— stake—Mal—e—mute—Kid—I—y—' The exhausted head dropped upon the table; nor could Malemute Kid rouse it again.

'It's Ulysses,' he said quietly, tossing the bag of dust on the table. 'Guess it's all day with Axel Gunderson and the woman. Come on, let's get him between the blankets. He's Indian; he'll pull through and tell a tale besides.' As they cut his garments from him, near his right breast could be seen two unhealed, hard-lipped knife thrusts.

III

'I will talk of the things which were in my own way; but you will understand. I will begin at the beginning, and tell of myself and the woman, and, after that, of the man.' He of the Otter Skins drew over to the stove as do men who have been deprived of fire and are afraid the Promethean gift may vanish at any moment. Malemute Kid picked up the slush lamp and placed it so its light might fall upon the face of the narrator. Prince slid his body over the edge of the bunk and joined them.

'I am Naass, a chief, and the son of a chief, born between a sunset and a rising, on the dark seas, in my father's oomiak. All of a night the men toiled at the paddles, and the women cast out the waves which threw in upon us, and we fought with the storm. The salt spray froze upon my mother's breast till her breath passed with the passing of the tide. But I—I raised my voice with the wind and the storm, and lived.

'We dwelt in Akatan—' 'Where?' asked Malemute Kid.

'Akatan, which is in the Aleutians; Akatan, beyond Chignik, beyond Kardalak, beyond Unimak. As I say, we dwelt in Akatan, which lies in the midst of the sea on the edge of the world. We farmed the salt seas for the fish, the seal, and the otter; and our homes shouldered about one another on the rocky strip between the rim of the forest and the yellow beach where our kayaks lay. We were not many, and the world was very small. There were strange lands to the east—islands like Akatan; so we thought all the world was islands and did not mind.

'I was different from my people. In the sands of the beach were the crooked timbers and wave-warped planks of a boat such as my people never built; and I remember on the point of the island which overlooked the ocean three ways there stood a pine tree which never grew there, smooth and straight and tall. It is said the two men came to that spot, turn about, through many days, and watched with the passing of the light. These two men came from out of the sea in the boat which lay in pieces on the beach. And they were white like you, and weak as the little children when the seal have gone away and the hunters come home empty. I know of these things from the old men and the old women, who got them from their fathers and mothers before them. These strange white men did not take kindly to our ways at first, but they grew strong, what of the fish and the oil, and fierce. And they built them each his own house, and took the pick of our women, and in time children came. Thus he was born who was to become the father of my father's father.

'As I said, I was different from my people, for I carried the strong, strange blood of this white man who came out of the sea. It is said we had other laws in the days before these men; but they were fierce and quarrelsome, and fought with our men till there were no more left who dared to fight. Then they made themselves chiefs, and took away our old laws, and gave us new ones, insomuch that the man was the son of his father, and not his mother, as our way had been. They also ruled that the son, first-born, should have all things which were his father's before him, and that the brothers and sisters should shift for themselves. And they gave us other laws. They showed us new ways in the catching of fish and the killing of bear which were thick in the woods; and they taught us to lay by bigger stores for the time of famine. And these things were good.

'But when they had become chiefs, and there were no more men to face their anger, they fought, these strange white men, each with the other. And the one whose blood I carry drove his seal spear the length of an arm through the other's body. Their children took up the fight, and their children's children; and there was great hatred between them, and black doings, even to my time, so that in each family but one lived to pass down the blood of them that went before. Of my blood I was alone; of the other man's there was but a girl, Unga, who lived with her mother. Her father and my father did not come back from the fishing one night; but afterward they washed up to the beach on the big tides, and they held very close to each other.

'The people wondered, because of the hatred between the houses, and the old men shook their heads and said the fight would go on when children were born to her and children to me. They told me this as a boy, till I came to believe, and to look upon Unga as a foe, who was to be the mother of children which were to fight with mine. I thought of these things day by day, and when I grew to a stripling I came to ask why this should be so.

'And they answered, 'We do not know, but that in such way your fathers did.' And I marveled that those which were to come should fight the battles of those that were gone, and in it I could see no right. But the people said it must be, and I was only a stripling.

'And they said I must hurry, that my blood might be the older and grow strong before hers. This was easy, for I was head man, and the people looked up to me because of the deeds and the laws of my fathers, and the wealth which was mine. Any maiden would come to me, but I found none to my liking. And the old men and the mothers of maidens told me to hurry, for even then were the hunters bidding high to the mother of Unga; and should her children grow strong before mine, mine would surely die.

'Nor did I find a maiden till one night coming back from the fishing. The sunlight was lying, so, low and full in the eyes, the wind free, and the kayacks racing with the white seas. Of a sudden the kayak of Unga came driving past me, and she looked upon me, so, with her black hair flying like a cloud of night and the spray wet on her cheek. As I say, the sunlight was full in the eyes, and I was a stripling; but somehow it was all clear, and I knew it to be the call of kind to kind.

'As she whipped ahead she looked back within the space of two strokes—looked as only the woman Unga could look—and again I knew it as the call of kind. The people shouted as we ripped past the lazy oomiaks and left them far behind. But she was quick at the paddle, and my heart was like the belly of a sail, and I did not gain. The wind freshened, the sea whitened, and, leaping like the seals on the windward breech, we roared down the golden pathway of the sun.' Naass was crouched half out of his stool, in the attitude of one driving a paddle, as he ran the race anew. Somewhere across the stove he beheld the tossing kayak and the flying hair of Unga. The voice of the wind was in his ears, and its salt beat fresh upon his nostrils.

'But she made the shore, and ran up the sand, laughing, to the house of her mother. And a great thought came to me that night—a thought worthy of him that was chief over all the people of Akatan. So, when the moon was up, I went down to the house of her mother, and looked upon the goods of Yash-Noosh, which were piled by the door—the goods of Yash-Noosh, a strong hunter who had it in mind to be the father of the children of Unga. Other young men had piled their goods there and taken them away again; and each young man had made a pile greater than the one before.

'And I laughed to the moon and the stars, and went to my own house where my wealth was stored. And many trips I made, till my pile was greater by the fingers of one hand than the pile of Yash-Noosh. There were fish, dried in the sun and smoked; and forty hides of the hair seal, and half as many of the fur, and each hide was tied at the mouth and big bellied with oil; and ten skins of bear which I killed in the woods when they came out in the spring. And there were beads and blankets and scarlet cloths, such as I got in trade from the people who lived to the east, and who got them in trade from the people who lived still beyond in the east.

'And I looked upon the pile of Yash-Noosh and laughed, for I was head man in Akatan, and my wealth was greater than the wealth of all my young men, and my fathers had done deeds, and given laws, and put their names for all time in the mouths of the people.

'So, when the morning came, I went down to the beach, casting out of the corner of my eye at the house of the mother of Unga. My offer yet stood untouched.

'And the women smiled, and said sly things one to the other. I wondered, for never had such a price been offered; and that night I added more to the pile, and put beside it a kayak of well-tanned skins which never yet had swam in the sea. But in the day it was yet there, open to the laughter of all men. The mother of Unga was crafty, and I grew angry at the shame in which I stood before my people. So that night I added till it became a great pile, and I hauled up my oomiak, which was of the value of twenty kayaks. And in the morning there was no pile.

'Then made I preparation for the wedding, and the people that lived even to the east came for the food of the feast and the potlatch token. Unga was older than I by the age of four suns in the way we reckoned the years. I was only a stripling; but then I was a chief, and the son of a chief, and it did not matter.

'But a ship shoved her sails above the floor of the ocean, and grew larger with the breath of the wind. From her scuppers she ran clear water, and the men were in haste and worked hard at the pumps. On the bow stood a mighty man, watching the depth of the water and giving commands with a voice of thunder. His eyes were of the pale blue of the deep waters, and his head was maned like that of a sea lion. And his hair was yellow, like the straw of a southern harvest or the manila rope yarns which sailormen plait.

'Of late years we had seen ships from afar, but this was the first to come to the beach of Akatan. The feast was broken, and the women and children fled to the houses, while we men strung our bows and waited with spears in hand. But when the ship's forefoot smelled the beach the strange men took no notice of us, being busy with their own work. With the falling of the tide they careened the schooner and patched a great hole in her bottom. So the women crept back, and the feast went on.

'When the tide rose, the sea wanderers kedged the schooner to deep water and then came among us. They bore presents and were friendly; so I made room for them, and out of the largeness of my heart gave them tokens such as I gave all the guests, for it was my wedding day, and I was head man in Akatan. And he with the mane of the sea lion was there, so tall and strong that one looked to see the earth shake with the fall of his feet. He looked much and straight at Unga, with his arms folded, so, and stayed till the sun went away and the stars came out. Then he went down to his ship. After that I took Unga by the hand and led her to my own house. And there was singing and great laughter, and the women said sly things, after the manner of women at such times. But we did not care. Then the people left us alone and went home.

'The last noise had not died away when the chief of the sea wanderers came in by the door. And he had with him black bottles, from which we drank and made merry. You see, I was only a stripling, and had lived all my days on the edge of the world. So my blood became as fire, and my heart as light as the froth that flies from the surf to the cliff. Unga sat silent among the skins in the corner, her eyes wide, for she seemed to fear. And he with the mane of the sea lion looked upon her straight and long. Then his men came in with bundles of goods, and he piled before me wealth such as was not in all Akatan. There were guns, both large and small, and powder and shot and shell, and bright axes and knives of steel, and cunning tools, and strange things the like of which I had never seen. When he showed me by sign that it was all mine, I thought him a great man to be so free; but he showed me also that Unga was to go away with him in his ship.

'Do you understand?—that Unga was to go away with him in his ship. The blood of my fathers flamed hot on the sudden, and I made to drive him through with my spear. But the spirit of the bottles had stolen the life from my arm, and he took me by the neck, so, and knocked my head against the wall of the house. And I was made weak like a newborn child, and my legs would no more stand under me.

'Unga screamed, and she laid hold of the things of the house with her hands, till they fell all about us as he dragged her to the door. Then he took her in his great arms, and when she tore at his yellow hair laughed with a sound like that of the big bull seal in the rut.

'I crawled to the beach and called upon my people, but they were afraid. Only Yash-Noosh was a man, and they struck him on the head with an oar, till he lay with his face in the sand and did not move. And they raised the sails to the sound of their songs, and the ship went away on the wind.

'The people said it was good, for there would be no more war of the bloods in Akatan; but I said never a word, waiting till the time of the full moon, when I put fish and oil in my kayak and went away to the east. I saw many islands and many people, and I, who had lived on the edge, saw that the world was very large. I talked by signs; but they had not seen a schooner nor a man with the mane of a sea lion, and they pointed always to the east. And I slept in queer places, and ate odd things, and met strange faces. Many laughed, for they thought me light of head; but sometimes old men turned my face to the light and blessed me, and the eyes of the young women grew soft as they asked me of the strange ship, and Unga, and the men of the sea.

'And in this manner, through rough seas and great storms, I came to Unalaska. There were two schooners there, but neither was the one I sought. So I passed on to the east, with the world growing ever larger, and in the island of Unamok there was no word of the ship, nor in Kadiak, nor in Atognak. And so I came one day to a rocky land, where men dug great holes in the mountain. And there was a schooner, but not my schooner, and men loaded upon it the rocks which they dug. This I thought childish, for all the world was made of rocks; but they gave me food and set me to work. When the schooner was deep in the water, the captain gave me money and told me to go; but I asked which way he went, and he pointed south. I made signs that I would go with him, and he laughed at first, but then, being short of men, took me to help work the ship. So I came to talk after their manner, and to heave on ropes, and to reef the stiff sails in sudden squalls, and to take my turn at the wheel. But it was not strange, for the blood of my fathers was the blood of the men of the sea.

'I had thought it an easy task to find him I sought, once I got among his own people; and when we raised the land one day, and passed between a gateway of the sea to a port, I looked for perhaps as many schooners as there were fingers to my hands. But the ships lay against the wharves for miles, packed like so many little fish; and when I went among them to ask for a man with the mane of a sea lion, they laughed, and answered me in the tongues of many peoples. And I found that they hailed from the uttermost parts of the earth.

'And I went into the city to look upon the face of every man. But they were like the cod when they run thick on the banks, and I could not count them. And the noise smote upon me till I could not hear, and my head was dizzy with much movement. So I went on and on, through the lands which sang in the warm sunshine; where the harvests lay rich on the plains; and where great cities were fat with men that lived like women, with false words in their mouths and their hearts black with the lust of gold. And all the while my people of Akatan hunted and fished, and were happy in the thought that the world was small.

'But the look in the eyes of Unga coming home from the fishing was with me always, and I knew I would find her when the time was met. She walked down quiet lanes in the dusk of the evening, or led me chases across the thick fields wet with the morning dew, and there was a promise in her eyes such as only the woman Unga could give.

'So I wandered through a thousand cities. Some were gentle and gave me food, and others laughed, and still others cursed; but I kept my tongue between my teeth, and went strange ways and saw strange sights. Sometimes I, who was a chief and the son of a chief, toiled for men—men rough of speech and hard as iron, who wrung gold from the sweat and sorrow of their fellow men. Yet no word did I get of my quest till I came back to the sea like a homing seal to the rookeries.

'But this was at another port, in another country which lay to the north. And there I heard dim tales of the yellow-haired sea wanderer, and I learned that he was a hunter of seals, and that even then he was abroad on the ocean.

'So I shipped on a seal schooner with the lazy Siwashes, and followed his trackless trail to the north where the hunt was then warm. And we were away weary months, and spoke many of the fleet, and heard much of the wild doings of him I sought; but never once did we raise him above the sea. We went north, even to the Pribilofs, and killed the seals in herds on the beach, and brought their warm bodies aboard till our scuppers ran grease and blood and no man could stand upon the deck. Then were we chased by a ship of slow steam, which fired upon us with great guns. But we put sail till the sea was over our decks and washed them clean, and lost ourselves in a fog.

'It is said, at this time, while we fled with fear at our hearts, that the yellow-haired sea wanderer put in to the Pribilofs, right to the factory, and while the part of his men held the servants of the company, the rest loaded ten thousand green skins from the salt houses. I say it is said, but I believe; for in the voyages I made on the coast with never a meeting the northern seas rang with his wildness and daring, till the three nations which have lands there sought him with their ships.

'And I heard of Unga, for the captains sang loud in her praise, and she was always with him. She had learned the ways of his people, they said, and was happy. But I knew better—knew that her heart harked back to her own people by the yellow beach of Akatan.

'So, after a long time, I went back to the port which is by a gateway of the sea, and there I learned that he had gone across the girth of the great ocean to hunt for the seal to the east of the warm land which runs south from the Russian seas.

'And I, who was become a sailorman, shipped with men of his own race, and went after him in the hunt of the seal. And there were few ships off that new land; but we hung on the flank of the seal pack and harried it north through all the spring of the year. And when the cows were heavy with pup and crossed the Russian line, our men grumbled and were afraid. For there was much fog, and every day men were lost in the boats. They would not work, so the captain turned the ship back toward the way it came. But I knew the yellow-haired sea wanderer was unafraid, and would hang by the pack, even to the Russian Isles, where few men go. So I took a boat, in the black of night, when the lookout dozed on the fo'c'slehead, and went alone to the warm, long land. And I journeyed south to meet the men by Yeddo Bay, who are wild and unafraid. And the Yoshiwara girls were small, and bright like steel, and good to look upon; but I could not stop, for I knew that Unga rolled on the tossing floor by the rookeries of the north.

'The men by Yeddo Bay had met from the ends of the earth, and had neither gods nor homes, sailing under the flag of the Japanese. And with them I went to the rich beaches of Copper Island, where our salt piles became high with skins.

'And in that silent sea we saw no man till we were ready to come away. Then one day the fog lifted on the edge of a heavy wind, and there jammed down upon us a schooner, with close in her wake the cloudy funnels of a Russian man-of-war. We fled away on the beam of the wind, with the schooner jamming still closer and plunging ahead three feet to our two. And upon her poop was the man with the mane of the sea lion, pressing the rails under with the canvas and laughing in his strength of life. And Unga was there—I knew her on the moment—but he sent her below when the cannons began to talk across the sea.

As I say, with three feet to our two, till we saw the rudder lift green at every jump—and I swinging on to the wheel and cursing, with my back to the Russian shot. For we knew he had it in mind to run before us, that he might get away while we were caught. And they knocked our masts out of us till we dragged into the wind like a wounded gull; but he went on over the edge of the sky line—he and Unga.

'What could we? The fresh hides spoke for themselves. So they took us to a Russian port, and after that to a lone country, where they set us to work in the mines to dig salt. And some died, and—and some did not die.' Naass swept the blanket from his shoulders, disclosing the gnarled and twisted flesh, marked with the unmistakable striations of the knout. Prince hastily covered him, for it was not nice to look upon.

'We were there a weary time and sometimes men got away to the south, but they always came back. So, when we who hailed from Yeddo Bay rose in the night and took the guns from the guards, we went to the north. And the land was very large, with plains, soggy with water, and great forests. And the cold came, with much snow on the ground, and no man knew the way. Weary months we journeyed through the endless forest—I do not remember, now, for there was little food and often we lay down to die. But at last we came to the cold sea, and but three were left to look upon it. One had shipped from Yeddo as captain, and he knew in his head the lay of the great lands, and of the place where men may cross from one to the other on the ice. And he led us—I do not know, it was so long—till there were but two. When we came to that place we found five of the strange people which live in that country, and they had dogs and skins, and we were very poor. We fought in the snow till they died, and the captain died, and the dogs and skins were mine. Then I crossed on the ice, which was broken, and once I drifted till a gale from the west put me upon the shore. And after that, Golovin Bay, Pastilik, and the priest. Then south, south, to the warm sunlands where first I wandered.

'But the sea was no longer fruitful, and those who went upon it after the seal went to little profit and great risk. The fleets scattered, and the captains and the men had no word of those I sought. So I turned away from the ocean which never rests, and went among the lands, where the trees, the houses, and the mountains sit always in one place and do not move. I journeyed far, and came to learn many things, even to the way of reading and writing from books. It was well I should do this, for it came upon me that Unga must know these things, and that someday, when the time was met—we—you understand, when the time was met.

'So I drifted, like those little fish which raise a sail to the wind but cannot steer. But my eyes and my ears were open always, and I went among men who traveled much, for I knew they had but to see those I sought to remember. At last there came a man, fresh from the mountains, with pieces of rock in which the free gold stood to the size of peas, and he had heard, he had met, he knew them. They were rich, he said, and lived in the place where they drew the gold from the ground.

'It was in a wild country, and very far away; but in time I came to the camp, hidden between the mountains, where men worked night and day, out of the sight of the sun. Yet the time was not come. I listened to the talk of the people. He had gone away—they had gone away—to England, it was said, in the matter of bringing men with much money together to form companies. I saw the house they had lived in; more like a palace, such as one sees in the old countries. In the nighttime I crept in through a window that I might see in what manner he treated her. I went from room to room, and in such way thought kings and queens must live, it was all so very good. And they all said he treated her like a queen, and many marveled as to what breed of woman she was for there was other blood in her veins, and she was different from the women of Akatan, and no one knew her for what she was. Aye, she was a queen; but I was a chief, and the son of a chief, and I had paid for her an untold price of skin and boat and bead.

'But why so many words? I was a sailorman, and knew the way of the ships on the seas. I followed to England, and then to other countries. Sometimes I heard of them by word of mouth, sometimes I read of them in the papers; yet never once could I come by them, for they had much money, and traveled fast, while I was a poor man. Then came trouble upon them, and their wealth slipped away one day like a curl of smoke. The papers were full of it at the time; but after that nothing was said, and I knew they had gone back where more gold could be got from the ground.

'They had dropped out of the world, being now poor, and so I wandered from camp to camp, even north to the Kootenay country, where I picked up the cold scent. They had come and gone, some said this way, and some that, and still others that they had gone to the country of the Yukon. And I went this way, and I went that, ever journeying from place to place, till it seemed I must grow weary of the world which was so large. But in the Kootenay I traveled a bad trail, and a long trail, with a breed of the Northwest, who saw fit to die when the famine pinched. He had been to the Yukon by an unknown way over the mountains, and when he knew his time was near gave me the map and the secret of a place where he swore by his gods there was much gold.

'After that all the world began to flock into the north. I was a poor man; I sold myself to be a driver of dogs. The rest you know. I met him and her in Dawson.

'She did not know me, for I was only a stripling, and her life had been large, so she had no time to remember the one who had paid for her an untold price.

'So? You bought me from my term of service. I went back to bring things about in my own way, for I had waited long, and now that I had my hand upon him was in no hurry.

'As I say, I had it in mind to do my own way, for I read back in my life, through all I had seen and suffered, and remembered the cold and hunger of the endless forest by the Russian seas. As you know, I led him into the east—him and Unga—into the east where many have gone and few returned. I led them to the spot where the bones and the curses of men lie with the gold which they may not have.

'The way was long and the trail unpacked. Our dogs were many and ate much; nor could our sleds carry till the break of spring. We must come back before the river ran free. So here and there we cached grub, that our sleds might be lightened and there be no chance of famine on the back trip. At the McQuestion there were three men, and near them we built a cache, as also did we at the Mayo, where was a hunting camp of a dozen Pellys which had crossed the divide from the south.

'After that, as we went on into the east, we saw no men; only the sleeping river, the moveless forest, and the White Silence of the North. As I say, the way was long and the trail unpacked. Sometimes, in a day's toil, we made no more than eight miles, or ten, and at night we slept like dead men. And never once did they dream that I was Naass, head man of Akatan, the righter of wrongs.

'We now made smaller caches, and in the nighttime it was a small matter to go back on the trail we had broken and change them in such way that one might deem the wolverines the thieves. Again there be places where there is a fall to the river, and the water is unruly, and the ice makes above and is eaten away beneath.

'In such a spot the sled I drove broke through, and the dogs; and to him and Unga it was ill luck, but no more. And there was much grub on that sled, and the dogs the strongest.

'But he laughed, for he was strong of life, and gave the dogs that were left little grub till we cut them from the harnesses one by one and fed them to their mates. We would go home light, he said, traveling and eating from cache to cache, with neither dogs nor sleds; which was true, for our grub was very short, and the last dog died in the traces the night we came to the gold and the bones and the curses of men.

'To reach that place—and the map spoke true—in the heart of the great mountains, we cut ice steps against the wall of a divide. One looked for a valley beyond, but there was no valley; the snow spread away, level as the great harvest plains, and here and there about us mighty mountains shoved their white heads among the stars. And midway on that strange plain which should have been a valley the earth and the snow fell away, straight down toward the heart of the world.

'Had we not been sailormen our heads would have swung round with the sight, but we stood on the dizzy edge that we might see a way to get down. And on one side, and one side only, the wall had fallen away till it was like the slope of the decks in a topsail breeze. I do not know why this thing should be so, but it was so. 'It is the mouth of hell,' he said; 'let us go down.' And we went down.

'And on the bottom there was a cabin, built by some man, of logs which he had cast down from above. It was a very old cabin, for men had died there alone at different times, and on pieces of birch bark which were there we read their last words and their curses.

'One had died of scurvy; another's partner had robbed him of his last grub and powder and stolen away; a third had been mauled by a baldface grizzly; a fourth had hunted for game and starved—and so it went, and they had been loath to leave the gold, and had died by the side of it in one way or another. And the worthless gold they had gathered yellowed the floor of the cabin like in a dream.

'But his soul was steady, and his head clear, this man I had led thus far. 'We have nothing to eat,' he said, 'and we will only look upon this gold, and see whence it comes and how much there be. Then we will go away quick, before it gets into our eyes and steals away our judgment. And in this way we may return in the end, with more grub, and possess it all.' So we looked upon the great vein, which cut the wall of the pit as a true vein should, and we measured it, and traced it from above and below, and drove the stakes of the claims and blazed the trees in token of our rights. Then, our knees shaking with lack of food, and a sickness in our bellies, and our hearts chugging close to our mouths, we climbed the mighty wall for the last time and turned our faces to the back trip.

'The last stretch we dragged Unga between us, and we fell often, but in the end we made the cache. And lo, there was no grub. It was well done, for he thought it the wolverines, and damned them and his gods in one breath. But Unga was brave, and smiled, and put her hand in his, till I turned away that I might hold myself. 'We will rest by the fire,' she said, 'till morning, and we will gather strength from our moccasins.' So we cut the tops of our moccasins in strips, and boiled them half of the night, that we might chew them and swallow them. And in the morning we talked of our chance. The next cache was five days' journey; we could not make it. We must find game.

'We will go forth and hunt,' he said.

'Yes,' said I, 'we will go forth and hunt.' 'And he ruled that Unga stay by the fire and save her strength. And we went forth, he in quest of the moose and I to the cache I had changed. But I ate little, so they might not see in me much strength. And in the night he fell many times as he drew into camp. And I, too, made to suffer great weakness, stumbling over my snowshoes as though each step might be my last. And we gathered strength from our moccasins.

'He was a great man. His soul lifted his body to the last; nor did he cry aloud, save for the sake of Unga. On the second day I followed him, that I might not miss the end. And he lay down to rest often. That night he was near gone; but in the morning he swore weakly and went forth again. He was like a drunken man, and I looked many times for him to give up, but his was the strength of the strong, and his soul the soul of a giant, for he lifted his body through all the weary day. And he shot two ptarmigan, but would not eat them. He needed no fire; they meant life; but his thought was for Unga, and he turned toward camp. 'He no longer walked, but crawled on hand and knee through the snow. I came to him, and read death in his eyes. Even then it was not too late to eat of the ptarmigan. He cast away his rifle and carried the birds in his mouth like a dog. I walked by his side, upright. And he looked at me during the moments he rested, and wondered that I was so strong. I could see it, though he no longer spoke; and when his lips moved, they moved without sound.

'As I say, he was a great man, and my heart spoke for softness; but I read back in my life, and remembered the cold and hunger of the endless forest by the Russian seas. Besides, Unga was mine, and I had paid for her an untold price of skin and boat and bead.

'And in this manner we came through the white forest, with the silence heavy upon us like a damp sea mist. And the ghosts of the past were in the air and all about us; and I saw the yellow beach of Akatan, and the kayaks racing home from the fishing, and the houses on the rim of the forest. And the men who had made themselves chiefs were there, the lawgivers whose blood I bore and whose blood I had wedded in Unga. Aye, and Yash-Noosh walked with me, the wet sand in his hair, and his war spear, broken as he fell upon it, still in his hand. And I knew the time was meet, and saw in the eyes of Unga the promise.

'As I say, we came thus through the forest, till the smell of the camp smoke was in our nostrils. And I bent above him, and tore the ptarmigan from his teeth.

'He turned on his side and rested, the wonder mounting in his eyes, and the hand which was under slipping slow toward the knife at his hip. But I took it from him, smiling close in his face. Even then he did not understand. So I made to drink from black bottles, and to build high upon the snow a pile—of goods, and to live again the things which had happened on the night of my marriage. I spoke no word, but he understood. Yet was he unafraid. There was a sneer to his lips, and cold anger, and he gathered new strength with the knowledge. It was not far, but the snow was deep, and he dragged himself very slow.

'Once he lay so long I turned him over and gazed into his eyes. And sometimes he looked forth, and sometimes death. And when I loosed him he struggled on again. In this way we came to the fire. Unga was at his side on the instant. His lips moved without sound; then he pointed at me, that Unga might understand. And after that he lay in the snow, very still, for a long while. Even now is he there in the snow.

'I said no word till I had cooked the ptarmigan. Then I spoke to her, in her own tongue, which she had not heard in many years. She straightened herself, so, and her eyes were wonder-wide, and she asked who I was, and where I had learned that speech.

'I am Naass,' I said.

'You?' she said. 'You?' And she crept close that she might look upon me.

'Yes,' I answered; 'I am Naass, head man of Akatan, the last of the blood, as you are the last of the blood.' 'And she laughed. By all the things I have seen and the deeds I have done may I never hear such a laugh again. It put the chill to my soul, sitting there in the White Silence, alone with death and this woman who laughed.

'Come!' I said, for I thought she wandered. 'Eat of the food and let us be gone. It is a far fetch from here to Akatan.' 'But she shoved her face in his yellow mane, and laughed till it seemed the heavens must fall about our ears. I had thought she would be overjoyed at the sight of me, and eager to go back to the memory of old times, but this seemed a strange form to take.

'Come!' I cried, taking her strong by the hand. 'The way is long and dark. Let us hurry!' 'Where?' she asked, sitting up, and ceasing from her strange mirth.

'To Akatan,' I answered, intent on the light to grow on her face at the thought. But it became like his, with a sneer to the lips, and cold anger.

'Yes,' she said; 'we will go, hand in hand, to Akatan, you and I. And we will live in the dirty huts, and eat of the fish and oil, and bring forth a spawn—a spawn to be proud of all the days of our life. We will forget the world and be happy, very happy. It is good, most good. Come! Let us hurry. Let us go back to Akatan.' And she ran her hand through his yellow hair, and smiled in a way which was not good. And there was no promise in her eyes.

'I sat silent, and marveled at the strangeness of woman. I went back to the night when he dragged her from me and she screamed and tore at his hair—at his hair which now she played with and would not leave. Then I remembered the price and the long years of waiting; and I gripped her close, and dragged her away as he had done. And she held back, even as on that night, and fought like a she-cat for its whelp. And when the fire was between us and the man. I loosed her, and she sat and listened. And I told her of all that lay between, of all that had happened to me on strange seas, of all that I had done in strange lands; of my weary quest, and the hungry years, and the promise which had been mine from the first. Aye, I told all, even to what had passed that day between the man and me, and in the days yet young. And as I spoke I saw the promise grow in her eyes, full and large like the break of dawn. And I read pity there, the tenderness of woman, the love, the heart and the soul of Unga. And I was a stripling again, for the look was the look of Unga as she ran up the beach, laughing, to the home of her mother. The stern unrest was gone, and the hunger, and the weary waiting.

'The time was met. I felt the call of her breast, and it seemed there I must pillow my head and forget. She opened her arms to me, and I came against her. Then, sudden, the hate flamed in her eye, her hand was at my hip. And once, twice, she passed the knife.

'Dog!' she sneered, as she flung me into the snow. 'Swine!' And then she laughed till the silence cracked, and went back to her dead.

'As I say, once she passed the knife, and twice; but she was weak with hunger, and it was not meant that I should die. Yet was I minded to stay in that place, and to close my eyes in the last long sleep with those whose lives had crossed with mine and led my feet on unknown trails. But there lay a debt upon me which would not let me rest.

'And the way was long, the cold bitter, and there was little grub. The Pellys had found no moose, and had robbed my cache. And so had the three white men, but they lay thin and dead in their cabins as I passed. After that I do not remember, till I came here, and found food and fire—much fire.' As he finished, he crouched closely, even jealously, over the stove. For a long while the slush-lamp shadows played tragedies upon the wall.

'But Unga!' cried Prince, the vision still strong upon him.

'Unga? She would not eat of the ptarmigan. She lay with her arms about his neck, her face deep in his yellow hair. I drew the fire close, that she might not feel the frost, but she crept to the other side. And I built a fire there; yet it was little good, for she would not eat. And in this manner they still lie up there in the snow.'

'And you?' asked Malemute Kid.

'I do not know; but Akatan is small, and I have little wish to go back and live on the edge of the world. Yet is there small use in life. I can go to Constantine, and he will put irons upon me, and one day they will tie a piece of rope, so, and I will sleep good. Yet—no; I do not know.' 'But, Kid,' protested Prince, 'this is murder!' 'Hush!' commanded Malemute Kid. 'There be things greater than our wisdom, beyond our justice. The right and the wrong of this we cannot say, and it is not for us to judge.' Naass drew yet closer to the fire. There was a great silence, and in each man's eyes many pictures came and went.

THE END

415

THE IRON HEEL

FOREWORD

It cannot be said that the Everhard Manuscript is an important historical document. To the historian it bristles with errors—not errors of fact, but errors of interpretation. Looking back across the seven centuries that have lapsed since Avis Everhard completed her manuscript, events, and the bearings of events, that were confused and veiled to her, are clear to us. She lacked perspective. She was too close to the events she writes about. Nay, she was merged in the events she has described.

Nevertheless, as a personal document, the Everhard Manuscript is of inestimable value. But here again enter error of perspective, and vitiation due to the bias of love. Yet we smile, indeed, and forgive Avis Everhard for the heroic lines upon which she modelled her husband. We know to-day that he was not so colossal, and that he loomed among the events of his times less largely than the Manuscript would lead us to believe.

We know that Ernest Everhard was an exceptionally strong man, but not so exceptional as his wife thought him to be. He was, after all, but one of a large number of heroes who, throughout the world, devoted their lives to the Revolution; though it must be conceded that he did unusual work, especially in his elaboration and interpretation of working-class philosophy. 'Proletarian science' and 'proletarian philosophy' were his phrases for it, and therein he shows the provincialism of his mind—a defect, however, that was due to the times and that none in that day could escape.

But to return to the Manuscript. Especially valuable is it in communicating to us the FEEL of those terrible times. Nowhere do we find more vividly portrayed the psychology of the persons that lived in that turbulent period embraced between the years 1912 and 1932—their mistakes and ignorance, their doubts and fears and misapprehensions, their ethical delusions, their violent passions, their inconceivable sordidness and selfishness. These are the things that are so hard for us of this enlightened age to understand. History tells us that these things were, and biology and psychology tell us why they were; but history and biology and psychology do not make these things alive. We accept them as facts, but we are left without sympathetic comprehension of them.

This sympathy comes to us, however, as we peruse the Everhard Manuscript. We enter into the minds of the actors in that long-ago world-drama, and for the time being their mental processes are our mental processes. Not alone do we understand Avis Everhard's love for her hero-husband, but we feel, as he felt, in those first days, the vague and terrible loom of the Oligarchy. The Iron Heel (well named) we feel descending upon and crushing mankind.

And in passing we note that that historic phrase, the Iron Heel, originated in Ernest Everhard's mind. This, we may say, is the one moot question that this new-found document clears up. Previous to this, the earliest-known use of the phrase occurred in the pamphlet, 'Ye Slaves,' written by George Milford and published in December, 1912. This George Milford was an obscure agitator about whom nothing is known, save the one additional bit of information gained from the Manuscript, which mentions that he was shot in the Chicago Commune. Evidently he had heard Ernest Everhard make use of the phrase in some public speech, most probably when he was running for Congress in the fall of 1912. From the Manuscript we learn that Everhard used the phrase at a private dinner in the spring of 1912. This is, without discussion, the earliest-known occasion on which the Oligarchy was so designated.

The rise of the Oligarchy will always remain a cause of secret wonder to the historian and the philosopher. Other great historical events have their place in social evolution. They were inevitable. Their coming could have been predicted with the same certitude that astronomers to-day predict the outcome of the movements of stars. Without these other great historical events, social evolution could not have proceeded. Primitive communism, chattel slavery, serf slavery, and wage slavery were necessary stepping-stones in the evolution of society. But it were ridiculous to assert that the Iron Heel was a necessary stepping-stone. Rather, to-day, is it adjudged a step aside, or a step backward, to the social tyrannies that made the early world a hell, but that were as necessary as the Iron Heel was unnecessary.

Black as Feudalism was, yet the coming of it was inevitable. What else than Feudalism could have followed upon the breakdown of that great centralized governmental machine known as the Roman Empire? Not so, however, with the Iron Heel. In the orderly procedure of social evolution there was no place for it. It was not necessary, and it was not inevitable. It must always remain the great curiosity of history—a whim, a fantasy, an apparition, a thing unexpected and undreamed; and it should serve as a warning to those rash political theorists of to-day who speak with certitude of social processes.

Capitalism was adjudged by the sociologists of the time to be the culmination of bourgeois rule, the ripened fruit of the bourgeois revolution. And we of to-day can but applaud that judgment. Following upon Capitalism, it was held, even by such intellectual and antagonistic giants as Herbert Spencer, that Socialism would come. Out of the decay of self-seeking capitalism, it was held, would arise that flower of the ages, the Brotherhood of Man. Instead of which, appalling alike to us who look back and to those that lived at the time, capitalism, rotten-ripe, sent forth that monstrous offshoot, the Oligarchy.

Too late did the socialist movement of the early twentieth century divine the coming of the Oligarchy. Even as it was divined, the Oligarchy was there—a fact established in blood, a stupendous and awful reality. Nor even then, as the Everhard Manuscript well shows, was any permanence attributed to the Iron Heel. Its overthrow was a matter of a few short years, was the judgment of the revolutionists. It is true, they realized that the Peasant Revolt was unplanned, and that the First Revolt was premature; but they little realized that the Second Revolt, planned and mature, was doomed to equal futility and more terrible punishment.

It is apparent that Avis Everhard completed the Manuscript during the last days of preparation for the Second Revolt; hence the fact that there is no mention of the disastrous outcome of the Second Revolt. It is quite clear that she intended the Manuscript for immediate publication, as soon as the Iron Heel was overthrown, so that her husband, so recently dead, should receive full credit for all that he had ventured and accomplished. Then came the frightful crushing of the Second Revolt, and it is probable that in the moment of danger, ere she fled or was captured by the Mercenaries, she hid the Manuscript in the hollow oak at Wake Robin Lodge.

Of Avis Everhard there is no further record. Undoubtedly she was executed by the Mercenaries; and, as is well known, no record of such executions was kept by the Iron Heel. But little did she realize, even then, as she hid the Manuscript and prepared to flee, how terrible had been the breakdown of the Second Revolt. Little did she realize that the tortuous and distorted evolution of the next three centuries would compel a Third Revolt and a Fourth Revolt, and many Revolts, all drowned in seas of blood, ere the world-movement of labor should come into its own. And little did she dream that for seven long centuries the tribute of her love to Ernest Everhard would repose undisturbed in the heart of the ancient oak of Wake Robin Lodge.

ANTHONY MEREDITH
Ardis,
November 27, 419 B.O.M.

CHAPTER I
MY EAGLE

The soft summer wind stirs the redwoods, and Wild-Water ripples sweet cadences over its mossy stones. There are butterflies in the sunshine, and from everywhere arises the drowsy hum of bees. It is so quiet and peaceful, and I sit here, and ponder, and am restless. It is the quiet that makes me restless. It seems unreal. All the world is quiet, but it is the quiet before the storm. I strain my ears, and all my senses, for some betrayal of that impending storm. Oh, that it may not be premature! That it may not be premature!*

Small wonder that I am restless. I think, and think, and I cannot cease from thinking. I have been in the thick of life so long that I am oppressed by the peace and quiet, and I cannot forbear from dwelling upon that mad maelstrom of death and destruction so soon to burst forth. In my ears are the cries of the stricken; and I can see, as I have seen in the past,** all the marring and mangling of the sweet, beautiful flesh, and the souls torn with violence from proud bodies and hurled to God. Thus do we poor humans attain our ends, striving through carnage and destruction to bring lasting peace and happiness upon the earth.

And then I am lonely. When I do not think of what is to come, I think of what has been and is no more—my Eagle, beating with tireless wings the void, soaring toward what was ever his sun, the flaming ideal of human freedom. I cannot sit idly by and wait the great event that is his making, though he is not here to see. He devoted all the years of his manhood to it, and for it he gave his life. It is his handiwork. He made it.***

And so it is, in this anxious time of waiting, that I shall write of my husband. There is much light that I alone of all persons living can throw upon his character, and so noble a character cannot be blazoned forth too brightly. His was a great soul, and, when my love grows unselfish, my chiefest regret is that he is not here to witness to-morrow's dawn. We cannot fail. He has built too stoutly and too surely for that. Woe to the Iron Heel! Soon shall it be thrust back from off prostrate humanity. When the word goes forth, the labor hosts of all the world shall rise. There has been nothing like it in the history of the world. The solidarity of labor is assured, and for the first time will there be an international revolution wide as the world is wide.****

---

* The Second Revolt was largely the work of Ernest Everhard, though he cooperated, of course, with the European leaders. The capture and secret execution of Everhard was the great event of the spring of 1932 A.D. Yet so thoroughly had he prepared for the revolt, that his fellow-conspirators were able, with little confusion or delay, to carry out his plans. It was after Everhard's execution that his wife went to Wake Robin Lodge, a small bungalow in the Sonoma Hills of California.

** Without doubt she here refers to the Chicago Commune.

*** With all respect to Avis Everhard, it must be pointed out that Everhard was but one of many able leaders who planned the Second Revolt. And we to-day, looking back across the centuries, can safely say that even had he lived, the Second Revolt would not have been less calamitous in its outcome than it was.

**** The Second Revolt was truly international. It was a colossal plan—too colossal to be wrought by the genius of one man alone. Labor, in all the oligarchies of the world, was prepared to rise at the signal. Germany, Italy, France, and all Australasia were labor countries—socialist states. They were ready to lend aid to the revolution. Gallantly they did; and it was for this reason, when the Second Revolt was crushed, that they, too, were crushed by the united oligarchies of the world, their socialist governments being replaced by oligarchical governments.

You see, I am full of what is impending. I have lived it day and night utterly and for so long that it is ever present in my mind. For that matter, I cannot think of my husband without thinking of it. He was the soul of it, and how can I possibly separate the two in thought?

As I have said, there is much light that I alone can throw upon his character. It is well known that he toiled hard for liberty and suffered sore. How hard he toiled and how greatly he suffered, I well know; for I have been with him during these twenty anxious years and I know his patience, his untiring effort, his infinite devotion to the Cause for which, only two months gone, he laid down his life.

I shall try to write simply and to tell here how Ernest Everhard entered my life— how I first met him, how he grew until I became a part of him, and the tremendous changes he wrought in my life. In this way may you look at him through my eyes and learn him as I learned him—in all save the things too secret and sweet for me to tell.

It was in February, 1912, that I first met him, when, as a guest of my father's[*] at dinner, he came to our house in Berkeley. I cannot say that my very first impression of him was favorable. He was one of many at dinner, and in the drawing-room where we gathered and waited for all to arrive, he made a rather incongruous appearance. It was 'preacher's night,' as my father privately called it, and Ernest was certainly out of place in the midst of the churchmen.

In the first place, his clothes did not fit him. He wore a ready-made suit of dark cloth that was ill adjusted to his body. In fact, no ready-made suit of clothes ever could fit his body. And on this night, as always, the cloth bulged with his muscles, while the coat between the shoulders, what of the heavy shoulder-development, was a maze of wrinkles. His neck was the neck of a prize-fighter,[**] thick and strong. So this was the social philosopher and ex-horseshoer my father had discovered, was my thought. And he certainly looked it with those bulging muscles and that bull-throat. Immediately I classified him—a sort of prodigy, I thought, a Blind Tom[***] of the working class.

And then, when he shook hands with me! His handshake was firm and strong, but he looked at me boldly with his black eyes—too boldly, I thought. You see, I was a creature of environment, and at that time had strong class instincts. Such boldness on the part of a man of my own class would have been almost unforgivable. I know that I could not avoid dropping my eyes, and I was quite relieved when I passed him on and turned to greet Bishop Morehouse—a favorite of mine, a sweet and serious man of middle age, Christ-like in appearance and goodness, and a scholar as well.

But this boldness that I took to be presumption was a vital clew to the nature of Ernest Everhard. He was simple, direct, afraid of nothing, and he refused to waste time on conventional mannerisms. 'You pleased me,' he explained long afterward;

---

[*] John Cunningham, Avis Everhard's father, was a professor at the State University at Berkeley, California. His chosen field was physics, and in addition he did much original research and was greatly distinguished as a scientist. His chief contribution to science was his studies of the electron and his monumental work on the 'Identification of Matter and Energy,' wherein he established, beyond cavil and for all time, that the ultimate unit of matter and the ultimate unit of force were identical. This idea had been earlier advanced, but not demonstrated, by Sir Oliver Lodge and other students in the new field of radio-activity.

[**] In that day it was the custom of men to compete for purses of money. They fought with their hands. When one was beaten into insensibility or killed, the survivor took the money.

[***] This obscure reference applies to a blind negro musician who took the world by storm in the latter half of the nineteenth century of the Christian Era.

'and why should I not fill my eyes with that which pleases me?' I have said that he was afraid of nothing. He was a natural aristocrat—and this in spite of the fact that he was in the camp of the non-aristocrats. He was a superman, a blond beast such as Nietzsche* has described, and in addition he was aflame with democracy.

In the interest of meeting the other guests, and what of my unfavorable impression, I forgot all about the working-class philosopher, though once or twice at table I noticed him—especially the twinkle in his eye as he listened to the talk first of one minister and then of another. He has humor, I thought, and I almost forgave him his clothes. But the time went by, and the dinner went by, and he never opened his mouth to speak, while the ministers talked interminably about the working class and its relation to the church, and what the church had done and was doing for it. I noticed that my father was annoyed because Ernest did not talk. Once father took advantage of a lull and asked him to say something; but Ernest shrugged his shoulders and with an 'I have nothing to say' went on eating salted almonds.

But father was not to be denied. After a while he said:

'We have with us a member of the working class. I am sure that he can present things from a new point of view that will be interesting and refreshing. I refer to Mr. Everhard.'

The others betrayed a well-mannered interest, and urged Ernest for a statement of his views. Their attitude toward him was so broadly tolerant and kindly that it was really patronizing. And I saw that Ernest noted it and was amused. He looked slowly about him, and I saw the glint of laughter in his eyes.

'I am not versed in the courtesies of ecclesiastical controversy,' he began, and then hesitated with modesty and indecision.

'Go on,' they urged, and Dr. Hammerfield said: 'We do not mind the truth that is in any man. If it is sincere,' he amended.

'Then you separate sincerity from truth?' Ernest laughed quickly.

Dr. Hammerfield gasped, and managed to answer, 'The best of us may be mistaken, young man, the best of us.'

Ernest's manner changed on the instant. He became another man.

'All right, then,' he answered; 'and let me begin by saying that you are all mistaken. You know nothing, and worse than nothing, about the working class. Your sociology is as vicious and worthless as is your method of thinking.'

It was not so much what he said as how he said it. I roused at the first sound of his voice. It was as bold as his eyes. It was a clarion-call that thrilled me. And the whole table was aroused, shaken alive from monotony and drowsiness.

'What is so dreadfully vicious and worthless in our method of thinking, young man?' Dr. Hammerfield demanded, and already there was something unpleasant in his voice and manner of utterance.

'You are metaphysicians. You can prove anything by metaphysics; and having done so, every metaphysician can prove every other metaphysician wrong—to his own satisfaction. You are anarchists in the realm of thought. And you are mad cosmos-makers. Each of you dwells in a cosmos of his own making, created out of his own fancies and desires. You do not know the real world in which you live, and your thinking has no place in the real world except in so far as it is phenomena of mental aberration.

---

* Friederich Nietzsche, the mad philosopher of the nineteenth century of the Christian Era, who caught wild glimpses of truth, but who, before he was done, reasoned himself around the great circle of human thought and off into madness.

'Do you know what I was reminded of as I sat at table and listened to you talk and talk? You reminded me for all the world of the scholastics of the Middle Ages who gravely and learnedly debated the absorbing question of how many angels could dance on the point of a needle. Why, my dear sirs, you are as remote from the intellectual life of the twentieth century as an Indian medicine-man making incantation in the primeval forest ten thousand years ago.'

As Ernest talked he seemed in a fine passion; his face glowed, his eyes snapped and flashed, and his chin and jaw were eloquent with aggressiveness. But it was only a way he had. It always aroused people. His smashing, sledge-hammer manner of attack invariably made them forget themselves. And they were forgetting themselves now. Bishop Morehouse was leaning forward and listening intently. Exasperation and anger were flushing the face of Dr. Hammerfield. And others were exasperated, too, and some were smiling in an amused and superior way. As for myself, I found it most enjoyable. I glanced at father, and I was afraid he was going to giggle at the effect of this human bombshell he had been guilty of launching amongst us.

'Your terms are rather vague,' Dr. Hammerfield interrupted. 'Just precisely what do you mean when you call us metaphysicians?'

'I call you metaphysicians because you reason metaphysically,' Ernest went on. 'Your method of reasoning is the opposite to that of science. There is no validity to your conclusions. You can prove everything and nothing, and no two of you can agree upon anything. Each of you goes into his own consciousness to explain himself and the universe. As well may you lift yourselves by your own bootstraps as to explain consciousness by consciousness.'

'I do not understand,' Bishop Morehouse said. 'It seems to me that all things of the mind are metaphysical. That most exact and convincing of all sciences, mathematics, is sheerly metaphysical. Each and every thought-process of the scientific reasoner is metaphysical. Surely you will agree with me?'

'As you say, you do not understand,' Ernest replied. 'The metaphysician reasons deductively out of his own subjectivity. The scientist reasons inductively from the facts of experience. The metaphysician reasons from theory to facts, the scientist reasons from facts to theory. The metaphysician explains the universe by himself, the scientist explains himself by the universe.'

'Thank God we are not scientists,' Dr. Hammerfield murmured complacently.

'What are you then?' Ernest demanded.

'Philosophers.'

'There you go,' Ernest laughed. 'You have left the real and solid earth and are up in the air with a word for a flying machine. Pray come down to earth and tell me precisely what you do mean by philosophy.'

'Philosophy is—' (Dr. Hammerfield paused and cleared his throat)—'something that cannot be defined comprehensively except to such minds and temperaments as are philosophical. The narrow scientist with his nose in a test-tube cannot understand philosophy.'

Ernest ignored the thrust. It was always his way to turn the point back upon an opponent, and he did it now, with a beaming brotherliness of face and utterance.

'Then you will undoubtedly understand the definition I shall now make of philosophy. But before I make it, I shall challenge you to point out error in it or to remain a silent metaphysician. Philosophy is merely the widest science of all. Its reasoning method is the same as that of any particular science and of all particular sciences. And by that same method of reasoning, the inductive method, philosophy fuses all particular sciences into one great science. As Spencer says, the data of any particular science are partially unified knowledge. Philosophy unifies the knowledge that is contributed by all the sciences. Philosophy is the science of science, the master science, if you please. How do you like my definition?'

'Very creditable, very creditable,' Dr. Hammerfield muttered lamely.

But Ernest was merciless.

'Remember,' he warned, 'my definition is fatal to metaphysics. If you do not now point out a flaw in my definition, you are disqualified later on from advancing metaphysical arguments. You must go through life seeking that flaw and remaining metaphysically silent until you have found it.'

Ernest waited. The silence was painful. Dr. Hammerfield was pained. He was also puzzled. Ernest's sledge-hammer attack disconcerted him. He was not used to the simple and direct method of controversy. He looked appealingly around the table, but no one answered for him. I caught father grinning into his napkin.

'There is another way of disqualifying the metaphysicians,' Ernest said, when he had rendered Dr. Hammerfield's discomfiture complete. 'Judge them by their works. What have they done for mankind beyond the spinning of airy fancies and the mistaking of their own shadows for gods? They have added to the gayety of mankind, I grant; but what tangible good have they wrought for mankind? They philosophized, if you will pardon my misuse of the word, about the heart as the seat of the emotions, while the scientists were formulating the circulation of the blood. They declaimed about famine and pestilence as being scourges of God, while the scientists were building granaries and draining cities. They builded gods in their own shapes and out of their own desires, while the scientists were building roads and bridges. They were describing the earth as the centre of the universe, while the scientists were discovering America and probing space for the stars and the laws of the stars. In short, the metaphysicians have done nothing, absolutely nothing, for mankind. Step by step, before the advance of science, they have been driven back. As fast as the ascertained facts of science have overthrown their subjective explanations of things, they have made new subjective explanations of things, including explanations of the latest ascertained facts. And this, I doubt not, they will go on doing to the end of time. Gentlemen, a metaphysician is a medicine man. The difference between you and the Eskimo who makes a fur-clad blubber-eating god is merely a difference of several thousand years of ascertained facts. That is all.'

'Yet the thought of Aristotle ruled Europe for twelve centuries,' Dr. Ballingford announced pompously. 'And Aristotle was a metaphysician.'

Dr. Ballingford glanced around the table and was rewarded by nods and smiles of approval.

'Your illustration is most unfortunate,' Ernest replied. 'You refer to a very dark period in human history. In fact, we call that period the Dark Ages. A period wherein science was raped by the metaphysicians, wherein physics became a search for the Philosopher's Stone, wherein chemistry became alchemy, and astronomy became astrology. Sorry the domination of Aristotle's thought!'

Dr. Ballingford looked pained, then he brightened up and said:

'Granted this horrible picture you have drawn, yet you must confess that metaphysics was inherently potent in so far as it drew humanity out of this dark period and on into the illumination of the succeeding centuries.'

'Metaphysics had nothing to do with it,' Ernest retorted.

'What?' Dr. Hammerfield cried. 'It was not the thinking and the speculation that led to the voyages of discovery?'

'Ah, my dear sir,' Ernest smiled, 'I thought you were disqualified. You have not yet picked out the flaw in my definition of philosophy. You are now on an unsubstantial basis. But it is the way of the metaphysicians, and I forgive you. No, I repeat, metaphysics had nothing to do with it. Bread and butter, silks and jewels, dollars and cents, and, incidentally, the closing up of the overland trade-routes to India, were the things that caused the voyages of discovery. With the fall of Constantinople, in 1453, the Turks blocked the way of the caravans to India. The traders of Europe had to find another route. Here was the original cause for the voyages of discovery. Columbus sailed to find a new route to the Indies. It is so stated in all the history books. Incidentally, new facts were learned about the nature, size, and form of the earth, and the Ptolemaic system went glimmering.'

Dr. Hammerfield snorted.

'You do not agree with me?' Ernest queried. 'Then wherein am I wrong?'

'I can only reaffirm my position,' Dr. Hammerfield retorted tartly. 'It is too long a story to enter into now.'

'No story is too long for the scientist,' Ernest said sweetly. 'That is why the scientist gets to places. That is why he got to America.'

I shall not describe the whole evening, though it is a joy to me to recall every moment, every detail, of those first hours of my coming to know Ernest Everhard.

Battle royal raged, and the ministers grew red-faced and excited, especially at the moments when Ernest called them romantic philosophers, shadow-projectors, and similar things. And always he checked them back to facts. 'The fact, man, the irrefragable fact!' he would proclaim triumphantly, when he had brought one of them a cropper. He bristled with facts. He tripped them up with facts, ambuscaded them with facts, bombarded them with broadsides of facts.

'You seem to worship at the shrine of fact,' Dr. Hammerfield taunted him.

'There is no God but Fact, and Mr. Everhard is its prophet,' Dr. Ballingford paraphrased.

Ernest smilingly acquiesced.

'I'm like the man from Texas,' he said. And, on being solicited, he explained. 'You see, the man from Missouri always says, 'You've got to show me.' But the man from Texas says, 'You've got to put it in my hand.' From which it is apparent that he is no metaphysician.'

Another time, when Ernest had just said that the metaphysical philosophers could never stand the test of truth, Dr. Hammerfield suddenly demanded:

'What is the test of truth, young man? Will you kindly explain what has so long puzzled wiser heads than yours?'

'Certainly,' Ernest answered. His cocksureness irritated them. 'The wise heads have puzzled so sorely over truth because they went up into the air after it. Had they remained on the solid earth, they would have found it easily enough—ay, they would have found that they themselves were precisely testing truth with every practical act and thought of their lives.'

'The test, the test,' Dr. Hammerfield repeated impatiently. 'Never mind the preamble. Give us that which we have sought so long—the test of truth. Give it us, and we will be as gods.'

There was an impolite and sneering scepticism in his words and manner that secretly pleased most of them at the table, though it seemed to bother Bishop Morehouse.

'Dr. Jordan* has stated it very clearly,' Ernest said. 'His test of truth is: 'Will it work? Will you trust your life to it?''

'Pish!' Dr. Hammerfield sneered. 'You have not taken Bishop Berkeley** into account. He has never been answered.'

'The noblest metaphysician of them all,' Ernest laughed. 'But your example is unfortunate. As Berkeley himself attested, his metaphysics didn't work.'

Dr. Hammerfield was angry, righteously angry. It was as though he had caught Ernest in a theft or a lie.

'Young man,' he trumpeted, 'that statement is on a par with all you have uttered to-night. It is a base and unwarranted assumption.'

'I am quite crushed,' Ernest murmured meekly. 'Only I don't know what hit me. You'll have to put it in my hand, Doctor.'

'I will, I will,' Dr. Hammerfield spluttered. 'How do you know? You do not know that Bishop Berkeley attested that his metaphysics did not work. You have no proof. Young man, they have always worked.'

'I take it as proof that Berkeley's metaphysics did not work, because—' Ernest paused calmly for a moment. 'Because Berkeley made an invariable practice of going through doors instead of walls. Because he trusted his life to solid bread and butter and roast beef. Because he shaved himself with a razor that worked when it removed the hair from his face.'

'But those are actual things!' Dr. Hammerfield cried. 'Metaphysics is of the mind.'

'And they work—in the mind?' Ernest queried softly.

The other nodded.

'And even a multitude of angels can dance on the point of a needle—in the mind,' Ernest went on reflectively. 'And a blubber-eating, fur-clad god can exist and work—in the mind; and there are no proofs to the contrary—in the mind. I suppose, Doctor, you live in the mind?'

'My mind to me a kingdom is,' was the answer.

'That's another way of saying that you live up in the air. But you come back to earth at meal-time, I am sure, or when an earthquake happens along. Or, tell me, Doctor, do you have no apprehension in an earthquake that that incorporeal body of yours will be hit by an immaterial brick?'

Instantly, and quite unconsciously, Dr. Hammerfield's hand shot up to his head, where a scar disappeared under the hair. It happened that Ernest had blundered on an apposite illustration. Dr. Hammerfield had been nearly killed in the Great Earthquake*** by a falling chimney. Everybody broke out into roars of laughter.

* A noted educator of the late nineteenth and early twentieth centuries of the Christian Era. He was president of the Stanford University, a private benefaction of the times.
** An idealistic monist who long puzzled the philosophers of that time with his denial of the existence of matter, but whose clever argument was finally demolished when the new empiric facts of science were philosophically generalized.
*** The Great Earthquake of 1906 A.D. that destroyed San Francisco.

'Well?' Ernest asked, when the merriment had subsided. 'Proofs to the contrary?'

And in the silence he asked again, 'Well?' Then he added, 'Still well, but not so well, that argument of yours.'

But Dr. Hammerfield was temporarily crushed, and the battle raged on in new directions. On point after point, Ernest challenged the ministers. When they affirmed that they knew the working class, he told them fundamental truths about the working class that they did not know, and challenged them for disproofs. He gave them facts, always facts, checked their excursions into the air, and brought them back to the solid earth and its facts.

How the scene comes back to me! I can hear him now, with that war-note in his voice, flaying them with his facts, each fact a lash that stung and stung again. And he was merciless. He took no quarter,[*] and gave none. I can never forget the flaying he gave them at the end:

'You have repeatedly confessed to-night, by direct avowal or ignorant statement, that you do not know the working class. But you are not to be blamed for this. How can you know anything about the working class? You do not live in the same locality with the working class. You herd with the capitalist class in another locality. And why not? It is the capitalist class that pays you, that feeds you, that puts the very clothes on your backs that you are wearing to-night. And in return you preach to your employers the brands of metaphysics that are especially acceptable to them; and the especially acceptable brands are acceptable because they do not menace the established order of society.'

Here there was a stir of dissent around the table.

'Oh, I am not challenging your sincerity,' Ernest continued. 'You are sincere. You preach what you believe. There lies your strength and your value—to the capitalist class. But should you change your belief to something that menaces the established order, your preaching would be unacceptable to your employers, and you would be discharged. Every little while some one or another of you is so discharged.[**] Am I not right?'

This time there was no dissent. They sat dumbly acquiescent, with the exception of Dr. Hammerfield, who said:

'It is when their thinking is wrong that they are asked to resign.'

'Which is another way of saying when their thinking is unacceptable,' Ernest answered, and then went on. 'So I say to you, go ahead and preach and earn your pay, but for goodness' sake leave the working class alone. You belong in the enemy's camp. You have nothing in common with the working class. Your hands are soft with the work others have performed for you. Your stomachs are round with the plenitude of eating.' (Here Dr. Ballingford winced, and every eye glanced at his prodigious girth. It was said he had not seen his own feet in years.) 'And your minds are filled with doctrines that are buttresses of the established order. You are as much mercenaries (sincere mercenaries, I grant) as were the men of the Swiss Guard.[***] Be true to your

---

* This figure arises from the customs of the times. When, among men fighting to the death in their wild-animal way, a beaten man threw down his weapons, it was at the option of the victor to slay him or spare him.

** During this period there were many ministers cast out of the church for preaching unacceptable doctrine. Especially were they cast out when their preaching became tainted with socialism.

*** The hired foreign palace guards of Louis XVI, a king of France that was beheaded by his people.

salt and your hire; guard, with your preaching, the interests of your employers; but do not come down to the working class and serve as false leaders. You cannot honestly be in the two camps at once. The working class has done without you. Believe me, the working class will continue to do without you. And, furthermore, the working class can do better without you than with you.'

CHAPTER II
CHALLENGES.

After the guests had gone, father threw himself into a chair and gave vent to roars of Gargantuan laughter. Not since the death of my mother had I known him to laugh so heartily.

'I'll wager Dr. Hammerfield was never up against anything like it in his life,' he laughed. 'The courtesies of ecclesiastical controversy!' Did you notice how he began like a lamb—Everhard, I mean, and how quickly he became a roaring lion? He has a splendidly disciplined mind. He would have made a good scientist if his energies had been directed that way.'

I need scarcely say that I was deeply interested in Ernest Everhard. It was not alone what he had said and how he had said it, but it was the man himself. I had never met a man like him. I suppose that was why, in spite of my twenty-four years, I had not married. I liked him; I had to confess it to myself. And my like for him was founded on things beyond intellect and argument. Regardless of his bulging muscles and prize-fighter's throat, he impressed me as an ingenuous boy. I felt that under the guise of an intellectual swashbuckler was a delicate and sensitive spirit. I sensed this, in ways I knew not, save that they were my woman's intuitions.

There was something in that clarion-call of his that went to my heart. It still rang in my ears, and I felt that I should like to hear it again—and to see again that glint of laughter in his eyes that belied the impassioned seriousness of his face. And there were further reaches of vague and indeterminate feelings that stirred in me. I almost loved him then, though I am confident, had I never seen him again, that the vague feelings would have passed away and that I should easily have forgotten him.

But I was not destined never to see him again. My father's new-born interest in sociology and the dinner parties he gave would not permit. Father was not a sociologist. His marriage with my mother had been very happy, and in the researches of his own science, physics, he had been very happy. But when mother died, his own work could not fill the emptiness. At first, in a mild way, he had dabbled in philosophy; then, becoming interested, he had drifted on into economics and sociology. He had a strong sense of justice, and he soon became fired with a passion to redress wrong. It was with gratitude that I hailed these signs of a new interest in life, though I little dreamed what the outcome would be. With the enthusiasm of a boy he plunged excitedly into these new pursuits, regardless of whither they led him.

He had been used always to the laboratory, and so it was that he turned the dining room into a sociological laboratory. Here came to dinner all sorts and conditions of men,—scientists, politicians, bankers, merchants, professors, labor leaders, socialists, and anarchists. He stirred them to discussion, and analyzed their thoughts of life and society.

He had met Ernest shortly prior to the 'preacher's night.' And after the guests were gone, I learned how he had met him, passing down a street at night and stopping to listen to a man on a soap-box who was addressing a crowd of workingmen. The man on the box was Ernest. Not that he was a mere soap-box orator. He stood high in the councils of the socialist party, was one of the leaders, and was the acknowledged leader in the philosophy of socialism. But he had a certain clear way of stating the abstruse in simple language, was a born expositor and teacher, and was not above the soap-box as a means of interpreting economics to the workingmen.

My father stopped to listen, became interested, effected a meeting, and, after quite an acquaintance, invited him to the ministers' dinner. It was after the dinner that father told me what little he knew about him. He had been born in the working class, though he was a descendant of the old line of Everhards that for over two hundred years had lived in America.* At ten years of age he had gone to work in the mills, and later he served his apprenticeship and became a horseshoer. He was self-educated, had taught himself German and French, and at that time was earning a meagre living by translating scientific and philosophical works for a struggling socialist publishing house in Chicago. Also, his earnings were added to by the royalties from the small sales of his own economic and philosophic works.

This much I learned of him before I went to bed, and I lay long awake, listening in memory to the sound of his voice. I grew frightened at my thoughts. He was so unlike the men of my own class, so alien and so strong. His masterfulness delighted me and terrified me, for my fancies wantonly roved until I found myself considering him as a lover, as a husband. I had always heard that the strength of men was an irresistible attraction to women; but he was too strong. 'No! no!' I cried out. 'It is impossible, absurd!' And on the morrow I awoke to find in myself a longing to see him again. I wanted to see him mastering men in discussion, the war-note in his voice; to see him, in all his certitude and strength, shattering their complacency, shaking them out of their ruts of thinking. What if he did swashbuckle? To use his own phrase, 'it worked,' it produced effects. And, besides, his swashbuckling was a fine thing to see. It stirred one like the onset of battle.

Several days passed during which I read Ernest's books, borrowed from my father. His written word was as his spoken word, clear and convincing. It was its absolute simplicity that convinced even while one continued to doubt. He had the gift of lucidity. He was the perfect expositor. Yet, in spite of his style, there was much that I did not like. He laid too great stress on what he called the class struggle, the antagonism between labor and capital, the conflict of interest.

Father reported with glee Dr. Hammerfield's judgment of Ernest, which was to the effect that he was 'an insolent young puppy, made bumptious by a little and very inadequate learning.' Also, Dr. Hammerfield declined to meet Ernest again.

But Bishop Morehouse turned out to have become interested in Ernest, and was anxious for another meeting. 'A strong young man,' he said; 'and very much alive, very much alive. But he is too sure, too sure.'

Ernest came one afternoon with father. The Bishop had already arrived, and we were having tea on the veranda. Ernest's continued presence in Berkeley, by the way, was accounted for by the fact that he was taking special courses in biology at the

---

* The distinction between being native born and foreign born was sharp and invidious in those days.

university, and also that he was hard at work on a new book entitled 'Philosophy and Revolution.'*

The veranda seemed suddenly to have become small when Ernest arrived. Not that he was so very large—he stood only five feet nine inches; but that he seemed to radiate an atmosphere of largeness. As he stopped to meet me, he betrayed a certain slight awkwardness that was strangely at variance with his bold-looking eyes and his firm, sure hand that clasped for a moment in greeting. And in that moment his eyes were just as steady and sure. There seemed a question in them this time, and as before he looked at me over long.

'I have been reading your 'Working-class Philosophy,'' I said, and his eyes lighted in a pleased way.

'Of course,' he answered, 'you took into consideration the audience to which it was addressed.'

'I did, and it is because I did that I have a quarrel with you,' I challenged.

'I, too, have a quarrel with you, Mr. Everhard,' Bishop Morehouse said.

Ernest shrugged his shoulders whimsically and accepted a cup of tea.

The Bishop bowed and gave me precedence.

'You foment class hatred,' I said. 'I consider it wrong and criminal to appeal to all that is narrow and brutal in the working class. Class hatred is anti-social, and, it seems to me, anti-socialistic.'

'Not guilty,' he answered. 'Class hatred is neither in the text nor in the spirit of anything I have every written.'

'Oh!' I cried reproachfully, and reached for his book and opened it.

He sipped his tea and smiled at me while I ran over the pages.

'Page one hundred and thirty-two,' I read aloud: 'The class struggle, therefore, presents itself in the present stage of social development between the wage-paying and the wage-paid classes.'

I looked at him triumphantly.

'No mention there of class hatred,' he smiled back.

'But,' I answered, 'you say 'class struggle.'

'A different thing from class hatred,' he replied. 'And, believe me, we foment no hatred. We say that the class struggle is a law of social development. We are not responsible for it. We do not make the class struggle. We merely explain it, as Newton explained gravitation. We explain the nature of the conflict of interest that produces the class struggle.'

'But there should be no conflict of interest!' I cried.

'I agree with you heartily,' he answered. 'That is what we socialists are trying to bring about,—the abolition of the conflict of interest. Pardon me. Let me read an extract.' He took his book and turned back several pages. 'Page one hundred and twenty-six: 'The cycle of class struggles which began with the dissolution of rude, tribal communism and the rise of private property will end with the passing of private property in the means of social existence.'

'But I disagree with you,' the Bishop interposed, his pale, ascetic face betraying by a faint glow the intensity of his feelings. 'Your premise is wrong. There is no such thing as a conflict of interest between labor and capital—or, rather, there ought not to be.'

---

* This book continued to be secretly printed throughout the three centuries of the Iron Heel. There are several copies of various editions in the National Library of Ardis.

'Thank you,' Ernest said gravely. 'By that last statement you have given me back my premise.'

'But why should there be a conflict?' the Bishop demanded warmly.

Ernest shrugged his shoulders. 'Because we are so made, I guess.'

'But we are not so made!' cried the other.

'Are you discussing the ideal man?' Ernest asked, '—unselfish and godlike, and so few in numbers as to be practically non-existent, or are you discussing the common and ordinary average man?'

'The common and ordinary man,' was the answer.

'Who is weak and fallible, prone to error?'

Bishop Morehouse nodded.

'And petty and selfish?'

Again he nodded.

'Watch out!' Ernest warned. 'I said 'selfish.'

'The average man IS selfish,' the Bishop affirmed valiantly.

'Wants all he can get?'

'Wants all he can get—true but deplorable.'

'Then I've got you.' Ernest's jaw snapped like a trap. 'Let me show you. Here is a man who works on the street railways.'

'He couldn't work if it weren't for capital,' the Bishop interrupted.

'True, and you will grant that capital would perish if there were no labor to earn the dividends.'

The Bishop was silent.

'Won't you?' Ernest insisted.

The Bishop nodded.

'Then our statements cancel each other,' Ernest said in a matter-of-fact tone, 'and we are where we were. Now to begin again. The workingmen on the street railway furnish the labor. The stockholders furnish the capital. By the joint effort of the workingmen and the capital, money is earned.* They divide between them this money that is earned. Capital's share is called 'dividends.' Labor's share is called 'wages.'

'Very good,' the Bishop interposed. 'And there is no reason that the division should not be amicable.'

'You have already forgotten what we had agreed upon,' Ernest replied. 'We agreed that the average man is selfish. He is the man that is. You have gone up in the air and are arranging a division between the kind of men that ought to be but are not. But to return to the earth, the workingman, being selfish, wants all he can get in the division. The capitalist, being selfish, wants all he can get in the division. When there is only so much of the same thing, and when two men want all they can get of the same thing, there is a conflict of interest between labor and capital. And it is an irreconcilable conflict. As long as workingmen and capitalists exist, they will continue to quarrel over the division. If you were in San Francisco this afternoon, you'd have to walk. There isn't a street car running.'

'Another strike?'** the Bishop queried with alarm.

---

* In those days, groups of predatory individuals controlled all the means of transportation, and for the use of same levied toll upon the public.

** These quarrels were very common in those irrational and anarchic times. Sometimes the laborers refused to work. Sometimes the capitalists refused to let the laborers work. In the

'Yes, they're quarrelling over the division of the earnings of the street railways.'
Bishop Morehouse became excited.

'It is wrong!' he cried. 'It is so short-sighted on the part of the workingmen. How can they hope to keep our sympathy—'

'When we are compelled to walk,' Ernest said slyly.

But Bishop Morehouse ignored him and went on:

'Their outlook is too narrow. Men should be men, not brutes. There will be violence and murder now, and sorrowing widows and orphans. Capital and labor should be friends. They should work hand in hand and to their mutual benefit.'

'Ah, now you are up in the air again,' Ernest remarked dryly. 'Come back to earth. Remember, we agreed that the average man is selfish.'

'But he ought not to be!' the Bishop cried.

'And there I agree with you,' was Ernest's rejoinder. 'He ought not to be selfish, but he will continue to be selfish as long as he lives in a social system that is based on pig-ethics.'

The Bishop was aghast, and my father chuckled.

'Yes, pig-ethics,' Ernest went on remorselessly. 'That is the meaning of the capitalist system. And that is what your church is standing for, what you are preaching for every time you get up in the pulpit. Pig-ethics! There is no other name for it.'

Bishop Morehouse turned appealingly to my father, but he laughed and nodded his head.

'I'm afraid Mr. Everhard is right,' he said. 'LAISSEZ-FAIRE, the let-alone policy of each for himself and devil take the hindmost. As Mr. Everhard said the other night, the function you churchmen perform is to maintain the established order of society, and society is established on that foundation.'

'But that is not the teaching of Christ!' cried the Bishop.

'The Church is not teaching Christ these days,' Ernest put in quickly. 'That is why the workingmen will have nothing to do with the Church. The Church condones the frightful brutality and savagery with which the capitalist class treats the working class.'

'The Church does not condone it,' the Bishop objected.

'The Church does not protest against it,' Ernest replied. 'And in so far as the Church does not protest, it condones, for remember the Church is supported by the capitalist class.'

'I had not looked at it in that light,' the Bishop said naively. 'You must be wrong. I know that there is much that is sad and wicked in this world. I know that the Church has lost the—what you call the proletariat.'*

'You never had the proletariat,' Ernest cried. 'The proletariat has grown up outside the Church and without the Church.'

'I do not follow you,' the Bishop said faintly.

'Then let me explain. With the introduction of machinery and the factory

violence and turbulence of such disagreements much property was destroyed and many lives lost. All this is inconceivable to us—as inconceivable as another custom of that time, namely, the habit the men of the lower classes had of breaking the furniture when they quarrelled with their wives.

* Proletariat: Derived originally from the Latin PROLETARII, the name given in the census of Servius Tullius to those who were of value to the state only as the rearers of offspring (PROLES); in other words, they were of no importance either for wealth, or position, or exceptional ability.

system in the latter part of the eighteenth century, the great mass of the working people was separated from the land. The old system of labor was broken down. The working people were driven from their villages and herded in factory towns. The mothers and children were put to work at the new machines. Family life ceased. The conditions were frightful. It is a tale of blood.'

'I know, I know,' Bishop Morehouse interrupted with an agonized expression on his face. 'It was terrible. But it occurred a century and a half ago.'

'And there, a century and a half ago, originated the modern proletariat,' Ernest continued. 'And the Church ignored it. While a slaughter-house was made of the nation by the capitalist, the Church was dumb. It did not protest, as to-day it does not protest. As Austin Lewis* says, speaking of that time, those to whom the command 'Feed my lambs' had been given, saw those lambs sold into slavery and worked to death without a protest.** The Church was dumb, then, and before I go on I want you either flatly to agree with me or flatly to disagree with me. Was the Church dumb then?'

Bishop Morehouse hesitated. Like Dr. Hammerfield, he was unused to this fierce 'infighting,' as Ernest called it.

'The history of the eighteenth century is written,' Ernest prompted. 'If the Church was not dumb, it will be found not dumb in the books.'

'I am afraid the Church was dumb,' the Bishop confessed.

'And the Church is dumb to-day.'

'There I disagree,' said the Bishop.

Ernest paused, looked at him searchingly, and accepted the challenge.

'All right,' he said. 'Let us see. In Chicago there are women who toil all the week for ninety cents. Has the Church protested?'

'This is news to me,' was the answer. 'Ninety cents per week! It is horrible!'

'Has the Church protested?' Ernest insisted.

'The Church does not know.' The Bishop was struggling hard.

'Yet the command to the Church was, 'Feed my lambs,' Ernest sneered. And then, the next moment, 'Pardon my sneer, Bishop. But can you wonder that we lose patience with you? When have you protested to your capitalistic congregations at the working of children in the Southern cotton mills?*** Children, six and

---

* Candidate for Governor of California on the Socialist ticket in the fall election of 1906 Christian Era. An Englishman by birth, a writer of many books on political economy and philosophy, and one of the Socialist leaders of the times

** There is no more horrible page in history than the treatment of the child and women slaves in the English factories in the latter half of the eighteenth century of the Christian Era. In such industrial hells arose some of the proudest fortunes of that day.

*** Everhard might have drawn a better illustration from the Southern Church's outspoken defence of chattel slavery prior to what is known as the 'War of the Rebellion.' Several such illustrations, culled from the documents of the times, are here appended. In 1835 A.D., the General Assembly of the Presbyterian Church resolved that: 'slavery is recognized in both the Old and the New Testaments, and is not condemned by the authority of God.' The Charleston Baptist Association issued the following, in an address, in 1835 A.D.: 'The right of masters to dispose of the time of their slaves has been distinctly recognized by the Creator of all things, who is surely at liberty to vest the right of property over any object whomsoever He pleases.' The Rev. E. D. Simon, Doctor of Divinity and professor in the Randolph-Macon Methodist College of Virginia, wrote: 'Extracts from Holy Writ unequivocally assert the right of property in slaves, together with the usual incidents to that right. The right to buy and sell is clearly

seven years of age, working every night at twelve-hour shifts? They never see the blessed sunshine. They die like flies. The dividends are paid out of their blood. And out of the dividends magnificent churches are builded in New England, wherein your kind preaches pleasant platitudes to the sleek, full-bellied recipients of those dividends.'

'I did not know,' the Bishop murmured faintly. His face was pale, and he seemed suffering from nausea.

'Then you have not protested?'

The Bishop shook his head.

'Then the Church is dumb to-day, as it was in the eighteenth century?'

The Bishop was silent, and for once Ernest forbore to press the point.

'And do not forget, whenever a churchman does protest, that he is discharged.'

'I hardly think that is fair,' was the objection.

'Will you protest?' Ernest demanded.

'Show me evils, such as you mention, in our own community, and I will protest.'

'I'll show you,' Ernest said quietly. 'I am at your disposal. I will take you on a journey through hell.'

'And I shall protest.' The Bishop straightened himself in his chair, and over his gentle face spread the harshness of the warrior. 'The Church shall not be dumb!'

'You will be discharged,' was the warning.

'I shall prove the contrary,' was the retort. 'I shall prove, if what you say is so, that the Church has erred through ignorance. And, furthermore, I hold that whatever is horrible in industrial society is due to the ignorance of the capitalist class. It will mend all that is wrong as soon as it receives the message. And this message it shall be the duty of the Church to deliver.'

Ernest laughed. He laughed brutally, and I was driven to the Bishop's defence.

'Remember,' I said, 'you see but one side of the shield. There is much good in us, though you give us credit for no good at all. Bishop Morehouse is right. The industrial wrong, terrible as you say it is, is due to ignorance. The divisions of society have become too widely separated.'

'The wild Indian is not so brutal and savage as the capitalist class,' he answered; and in that moment I hated him.

'You do not know us,' I answered. 'We are not brutal and savage.'

'Prove it,' he challenged.

'How can I prove it . . . to you?' I was growing angry.

stated. Upon the whole, then, whether we consult the Jewish policy instituted by God himself, or the uniform opinion and practice of mankind in all ages, or the injunctions of the New Testament and the moral law, we are brought to the conclusion that slavery is not immoral. Having established the point that the first African slaves were legally brought into bondage, the right to detain their children in bondage follows as an indispensable consequence. Thus we see that the slavery that exists in America was founded in right.' It is not at all remarkable that this same note should have been struck by the Church a generation or so later in relation to the defence of capitalistic property. In the great museum at Asgard there is a book entitled 'Essays in Application,' written by Henry van Dyke. The book was published in 1905 of the Christian Era. From what we can make out, Van Dyke must have been a churchman. The book is a good example of what Everhard would have called bourgeois thinking. Note the similarity between the utterance of the Charleston Baptist Association quoted above, and the following utterance of Van Dyke seventy years later: 'The Bible teaches that God owns the world. He distributes to every man according to His own good pleasure, conformably to general laws.

He shook his head. 'I do not ask you to prove it to me. I ask you to prove it to yourself.'

'I know,' I said.

'You know nothing,' was his rude reply.

'There, there, children,' father said soothingly.

'I don't care—' I began indignantly, but Ernest interrupted.

'I understand you have money, or your father has, which is the same thing—money invested in the Sierra Mills.'

'What has that to do with it?' I cried.

'Nothing much,' he began slowly, 'except that the gown you wear is stained with blood. The food you eat is a bloody stew. The blood of little children and of strong men is dripping from your very roof-beams. I can close my eyes, now, and hear it drip, drop, drip, drop, all about me.'

And suiting the action to the words, he closed his eyes and leaned back in his chair. I burst into tears of mortification and hurt vanity. I had never been so brutally treated in my life. Both the Bishop and my father were embarrassed and perturbed. They tried to lead the conversation away into easier channels; but Ernest opened his eyes, looked at me, and waved them aside. His mouth was stern, and his eyes too; and in the latter there was no glint of laughter. What he was about to say, what terrible castigation he was going to give me, I never knew; for at that moment a man, passing along the sidewalk, stopped and glanced in at us. He was a large man, poorly dressed, and on his back was a great load of rattan and bamboo stands, chairs, and screens. He looked at the house as if debating whether or not he should come in and try to sell some of his wares.

'That man's name is Jackson,' Ernest said.

'With that strong body of his he should be at work, and not peddling,'* I answered curtly.

'Notice the sleeve of his left arm,' Ernest said gently.

I looked, and saw that the sleeve was empty.

'It was some of the blood from that arm that I heard dripping from your roof-beams,' Ernest said with continued gentleness. 'He lost his arm in the Sierra Mills, and like a broken-down horse you turned him out on the highway to die. When I say 'you,' I mean the superintendent and the officials that you and the other stockholders pay to manage the mills for you. It was an accident. It was caused by his trying to save the company a few dollars. The toothed drum of the picker caught his arm. He might have let the small flint that he saw in the teeth go through. It would have smashed out a double row of spikes. But he reached for the flint, and his arm was picked and clawed to shreds from the finger tips to the shoulder. It was at night. The mills were working overtime. They paid a fat dividend that quarter. Jackson had been working many hours, and his muscles had lost their resiliency and snap. They made his movements a bit slow. That was why the machine caught him. He had a wife and three children.'

'And what did the company do for him?' I asked.

'Nothing. Oh, yes, they did do something. They successfully fought the damage

---

* In that day there were many thousands of these poor merchants called PEDLERS. They carried their whole stock in trade from door to door. It was a most wasteful expenditure of energy. Distribution was as confused and irrational as the whole general system of society.

suit he brought when he came out of hospital. The company employs very efficient lawyers, you know.'

'You have not told the whole story,' I said with conviction. 'Or else you do not know the whole story. Maybe the man was insolent.'

'Insolent! Ha! ha!' His laughter was Mephistophelian. 'Great God! Insolent! And with his arm chewed off! Nevertheless he was a meek and lowly servant, and there is no record of his having been insolent.'

'But the courts,' I urged. 'The case would not have been decided against him had there been no more to the affair than you have mentioned.'

'Colonel Ingram is leading counsel for the company. He is a shrewd lawyer.' Ernest looked at me intently for a moment, then went on. 'I'll tell you what you do, Miss Cunningham. You investigate Jackson's case.'

'I had already determined to,' I said coldly.

'All right,' he beamed good-naturedly, 'and I'll tell you where to find him. But I tremble for you when I think of all you are to prove by Jackson's arm.'

And so it came about that both the Bishop and I accepted Ernest's challenges. They went away together, leaving me smarting with a sense of injustice that had been done me and my class. The man was a beast. I hated him, then, and consoled myself with the thought that his behavior was what was to be expected from a man of the working class.

CHAPTER III
JACKSON'S ARM.

Little did I dream the fateful part Jackson's arm was to play in my life. Jackson himself did not impress me when I hunted him out. I found him in a crazy, ramshackle* house down near the bay on the edge of the marsh. Pools of stagnant water stood around the house, their surfaces covered with a green and putrid-looking scum, while the stench that arose from them was intolerable.

I found Jackson the meek and lowly man he had been described. He was making some sort of rattan-work, and he toiled on stolidly while I talked with him. But in spite of his meekness and lowliness, I fancied I caught the first note of a nascent bitterness in him when he said:

'They might a-given me a job as watchman,** anyway.'

I got little out of him. He struck me as stupid, and yet the deftness with which he worked with his one hand seemed to belie his stupidity. This suggested an idea to me.

'How did you happen to get your arm caught in the machine?' I asked.

---

* An adjective descriptive of ruined and dilapidated houses in which great numbers of the working people found shelter in those days. They invariably paid rent, and, considering the value of such houses, enormous rent, to the landlords.

** In those days thievery was incredibly prevalent. Everybody stole property from everybody else. The lords of society stole legally or else legalized their stealing, while the poorer classes stole illegally. Nothing was safe unless guarded. Enormous numbers of men were employed as watchmen to protect property. The houses of the well-to-do were a combination of safe deposit vault and fortress. The appropriation of the personal belongings of others by our own children of to-day is looked upon as a rudimentary survival of the theft-characteristic that in those early times was universal.

He looked at me in a slow and pondering way, and shook his head. 'I don't know. It just happened.'

'Carelessness?' I prompted.

'No,' he answered, 'I ain't for callin' it that. I was workin' overtime, an' I guess I was tired out some. I worked seventeen years in them mills, an' I've took notice that most of the accidents happens just before whistle-blow.* I'm willin' to bet that more accidents happens in the hour before whistle-blow than in all the rest of the day. A man ain't so quick after workin' steady for hours. I've seen too many of 'em cut up an' gouged an' chawed not to know.'

'Many of them?' I queried.

'Hundreds an' hundreds, an' children, too.'

With the exception of the terrible details, Jackson's story of his accident was the same as that I had already heard. When I asked him if he had broken some rule of working the machinery, he shook his head.

'I chucked off the belt with my right hand,' he said, 'an' made a reach for the flint with my left. I didn't stop to see if the belt was off. I thought my right hand had done it—only it didn't. I reached quick, and the belt wasn't all the way off. And then my arm was chewed off.'

'It must have been painful,' I said sympathetically.

'The crunchin' of the bones wasn't nice,' was his answer.

His mind was rather hazy concerning the damage suit. Only one thing was clear to him, and that was that he had not got any damages. He had a feeling that the testimony of the foremen and the superintendent had brought about the adverse decision of the court. Their testimony, as he put it, 'wasn't what it ought to have ben.' And to them I resolved to go.

One thing was plain, Jackson's situation was wretched. His wife was in ill health, and he was unable to earn, by his rattan-work and peddling, sufficient food for the family. He was back in his rent, and the oldest boy, a lad of eleven, had started to work in the mills.

'They might a-given me that watchman's job,' were his last words as I went away.

By the time I had seen the lawyer who had handled Jackson's case, and the two foremen and the superintendent at the mills who had testified, I began to feel that there was something after all in Ernest's contention.

He was a weak and inefficient-looking man, the lawyer, and at sight of him I did not wonder that Jackson's case had been lost. My first thought was that it had served Jackson right for getting such a lawyer. But the next moment two of Ernest's statements came flashing into my consciousness: 'The company employs very efficient lawyers' and 'Colonel Ingram is a shrewd lawyer.' I did some rapid thinking. It dawned upon me that of course the company could afford finer legal talent than could a workingman like Jackson. But this was merely a minor detail. There was some very good reason, I was sure, why Jackson's case had gone against him.

'Why did you lose the case?' I asked.

The lawyer was perplexed and worried for a moment, and I found it in my heart to pity the wretched little creature. Then he began to whine. I do believe his whine was congenital. He was a man beaten at birth. He whined about the testimony. The witnesses had given only the evidence that helped the other side. Not one word could

---

* The laborers were called to work and dismissed by savage, screaming, nerve-racking steam-whistles.

he get out of them that would have helped Jackson. They knew which side their bread was buttered on. Jackson was a fool. He had been brow-beaten and confused by Colonel Ingram. Colonel Ingram was brilliant at cross-examination. He had made Jackson answer damaging questions.

'How could his answers be damaging if he had the right on his side?' I demanded.

'What's right got to do with it?' he demanded back. 'You see all those books.' He moved his hand over the array of volumes on the walls of his tiny office. 'All my reading and studying of them has taught me that law is one thing and right is another thing. Ask any lawyer. You go to Sunday-school to learn what is right. But you go to those books to learn . . . law.'

'Do you mean to tell me that Jackson had the right on his side and yet was beaten?' I queried tentatively. 'Do you mean to tell me that there is no justice in Judge Caldwell's court?'

The little lawyer glared at me a moment, and then the belligerence faded out of his face.

'I hadn't a fair chance,' he began whining again. 'They made a fool out of Jackson and out of me, too. What chance had I? Colonel Ingram is a great lawyer. If he wasn't great, would he have charge of the law business of the Sierra Mills, of the Erston Land Syndicate, of the Berkeley Consolidated, of the Oakland, San Leandro, and Pleasanton Electric? He's a corporation lawyer, and corporation lawyers are not paid for being fools.* What do you think the Sierra Mills alone give him twenty thousand dollars a year for? Because he's worth twenty thousand dollars a year to them, that's what for. I'm not worth that much. If I was, I wouldn't be on the outside, starving and taking cases like Jackson's. What do you think I'd have got if I'd won Jackson's case?'

'You'd have robbed him, most probably,' I answered.

'Of course I would,' he cried angrily. 'I've got to live, haven't I?'**

'He has a wife and children,' I chided.

'So have I a wife and children,' he retorted. 'And there's not a soul in this world except myself that cares whether they starve or not.'

His face suddenly softened, and he opened his watch and showed me a small photograph of a woman and two little girls pasted inside the case.

'There they are. Look at them. We've had a hard time, a hard time. I had hoped to send them away to the country if I'd won Jackson's case. They're not healthy here, but I can't afford to send them away.'

When I started to leave, he dropped back into his whine.

'I hadn't the ghost of a chance. Colonel Ingram and Judge Caldwell are pretty friendly. I'm not saying that if I'd got the right kind of testimony out of their witnesses

---

* The function of the corporation lawyer was to serve, by corrupt methods, the money-grabbing propensities of the corporations. It is on record that Theodore Roosevelt, at that time President of the United States, said in 1905 A.D., in his address at Harvard Commencement: 'We all know that, as things actually are, many of the most influential and most highly remunerated members of the Bar in every centre of wealth, make it their special task to work out bold and ingenious schemes by which their wealthy clients, individual or corporate, can evade the laws which were made to regulate, in the interests of the public, the uses of great wealth.'

** A typical illustration of the internecine strife that permeated all society. Men preyed upon one another like ravening wolves. The big wolves ate the little wolves, and in the social pack Jackson was one of the least of the little wolves.

on cross-examination, that friendship would have decided the case. And yet I must say that Judge Caldwell did a whole lot to prevent my getting that very testimony. Why, Judge Caldwell and Colonel Ingram belong to the same lodge and the same club. They live in the same neighborhood—one I can't afford. And their wives are always in and out of each other's houses. They're always having whist parties and such things back and forth.'

'And yet you think Jackson had the right of it?' I asked, pausing for the moment on the threshold.

'I don't think; I know it,' was his answer. 'And at first I thought he had some show, too. But I didn't tell my wife. I didn't want to disappoint her. She had her heart set on a trip to the country hard enough as it was.'

'Why did you not call attention to the fact that Jackson was trying to save the machinery from being injured?' I asked Peter Donnelly, one of the foremen who had testified at the trial.

He pondered a long time before replying. Then he cast an anxious look about him and said:

'Because I've a good wife an' three of the sweetest children ye ever laid eyes on, that's why.'

'I do not understand,' I said.

'In other words, because it wouldn't a-ben healthy,' he answered.

'You mean—' I began.

But he interrupted passionately.

'I mean what I said. It's long years I've worked in the mills. I began as a little lad on the spindles. I worked up ever since. It's by hard work I got to my present exalted position. I'm a foreman, if you please. An' I doubt me if there's a man in the mills that'd put out a hand to drag me from drownin'. I used to belong to the union. But I've stayed by the company through two strikes. They called me 'scab.' There's not a man among 'em to-day to take a drink with me if I asked him. D'ye see the scars on me head where I was struck with flying bricks? There ain't a child at the spindles but what would curse me name. Me only friend is the company. It's not me duty, but me bread an' butter an' the life of me children to stand by the mills. That's why.'

'Was Jackson to blame?' I asked.

'He should a-got the damages. He was a good worker an' never made trouble.'

'Then you were not at liberty to tell the whole truth, as you had sworn to do?'

He shook his head.

'The truth, the whole truth, and nothing but the truth?' I said solemnly.

Again his face became impassioned, and he lifted it, not to me, but to heaven.

'I'd let me soul an' body burn in everlastin' hell for them children of mine,' was his answer.

Henry Dallas, the superintendent, was a vulpine-faced creature who regarded me insolently and refused to talk. Not a word could I get from him concerning the trial and his testimony. But with the other foreman I had better luck. James Smith was a hard-faced man, and my heart sank as I encountered him. He, too, gave me the impression that he was not a free agent, as we talked I began to see that he was mentally superior to the average of his kind. He agreed with Peter Donnelly that Jackson should have got damages, and he went farther and called the action heartless and cold-blooded that had turned the worker adrift after he had been made helpless by the accident. Also, he explained that there were many accidents in the mills, and that the company's policy was to fight to the bitter end all consequent damage suits.

'It means hundreds of thousands a year to the stockholders,' he said; and as he spoke I remembered the last dividend that had been paid my father, and the pretty gown for me and the books for him that had been bought out of that dividend. I remembered Ernest's charge that my gown was stained with blood, and my flesh began to crawl underneath my garments.

'When you testified at the trial, you didn't point out that Jackson received his accident through trying to save the machinery from damage?' I said.

'No, I did not,' was the answer, and his mouth set bitterly. 'I testified to the effect that Jackson injured himself by neglect and carelessness, and that the company was not in any way to blame or liable.'

'Was it carelessness?' I asked.

'Call it that, or anything you want to call it. The fact is, a man gets tired after he's been working for hours.'

I was becoming interested in the man. He certainly was of a superior kind.

'You are better educated than most workingmen,' I said.

'I went through high school,' he replied. 'I worked my way through doing janitor-work. I wanted to go through the university. But my father died, and I came to work in the mills.

'I wanted to become a naturalist,' he explained shyly, as though confessing a weakness. 'I love animals. But I came to work in the mills. When I was promoted to foreman I got married, then the family came, and . . . well, I wasn't my own boss any more.'

'What do you mean by that?' I asked.

'I was explaining why I testified at the trial the way I did—why I followed instructions.'

'Whose instructions?'

'Colonel Ingram. He outlined the evidence I was to give.'

'And it lost Jackson's case for him.'

He nodded, and the blood began to rise darkly in his face.

'And Jackson had a wife and two children dependent on him.'

'I know,' he said quietly, though his face was growing darker.

'Tell me,' I went on, 'was it easy to make yourself over from what you were, say in high school, to the man you must have become to do such a thing at the trial?'

The suddenness of his outburst startled and frightened me. He ripped* out a savage oath, and clenched his fist as though about to strike me.

'I beg your pardon,' he said the next moment. 'No, it was not easy. And now I guess you can go away. You've got all you wanted out of me. But let me tell you this before you go. It won't do you any good to repeat anything I've said. I'll deny it, and there are no witnesses. I'll deny every word of it; and if I have to, I'll do it under oath on the witness stand.'

After my interview with Smith I went to my father's office in the Chemistry Building and there encountered Ernest. It was quite unexpected, but he met me with

---

* It is interesting to note the virilities of language that were common speech in that day, as indicative of the life, 'red of claw and fang,' that was then lived. Reference is here made, of course, not to the oath of Smith, but to the verb ripped used by Avis Everhard.

his bold eyes and firm hand-clasp, and with that curious blend of his awkwardness and ease. It was as though our last stormy meeting was forgotten; but I was not in the mood to have it forgotten.

'I have been looking up Jackson's case,' I said abruptly.

He was all interested attention, and waited for me to go on, though I could see in his eyes the certitude that my convictions had been shaken.

'He seems to have been badly treated,' I confessed. 'I—I—think some of his blood is dripping from our roof-beams.'

'Of course,' he answered. 'If Jackson and all his fellows were treated mercifully, the dividends would not be so large.'

'I shall never be able to take pleasure in pretty gowns again,' I added.

I felt humble and contrite, and was aware of a sweet feeling that Ernest was a sort of father confessor. Then, as ever after, his strength appealed to me. It seemed to radiate a promise of peace and protection.

'Nor will you be able to take pleasure in sackcloth,' he said gravely. 'There are the jute mills, you know, and the same thing goes on there. It goes on everywhere. Our boasted civilization is based upon blood, soaked in blood, and neither you nor I nor any of us can escape the scarlet stain. The men you talked with—who were they?'

I told him all that had taken place.

'And not one of them was a free agent,' he said. 'They were all tied to the merciless industrial machine. And the pathos of it and the tragedy is that they are tied by their heartstrings. Their children—always the young life that it is their instinct to protect. This instinct is stronger than any ethic they possess. My father! He lied, he stole, he did all sorts of dishonorable things to put bread into my mouth and into the mouths of my brothers and sisters. He was a slave to the industrial machine, and it stamped his life out, worked him to death.'

'But you,' I interjected. 'You are surely a free agent.'

'Not wholly,' he replied. 'I am not tied by my heartstrings. I am often thankful that I have no children, and I dearly love children. Yet if I married I should not dare to have any.'

'That surely is bad doctrine,' I cried.

'I know it is,' he said sadly. 'But it is expedient doctrine. I am a revolutionist, and it is a perilous vocation.'

I laughed incredulously.

'If I tried to enter your father's house at night to steal his dividends from the Sierra Mills, what would he do?'

'He sleeps with a revolver on the stand by the bed,' I answered. 'He would most probably shoot you.'

'And if I and a few others should lead a million and a half of men[*] into the houses of all the well-to-do, there would be a great deal of shooting, wouldn't there?'

'Yes, but you are not doing that,' I objected.

'It is precisely what I am doing. And we intend to take, not the mere wealth in the houses, but all the sources of that wealth, all the mines, and railroads, and factories,

---

[*] This reference is to the socialist vote cast in the United States in 1910. The rise of this vote clearly indicates the swift growth of the party of revolution. Its voting strength in the United States in 1888 was 2068; in 1902, 127,713; in 1904, 435,040; in 1908, 1,108,427; and in 1910, 1,688,211.

and banks, and stores. That is the revolution. It is truly perilous. There will be more shooting, I am afraid, than even I dream of. But as I was saying, no one to-day is a free agent. We are all caught up in the wheels and cogs of the industrial machine. You found that you were, and that the men you talked with were. Talk with more of them. Go and see Colonel Ingram. Look up the reporters that kept Jackson's case out of the papers, and the editors that run the papers. You will find them all slaves of the machine.'

A little later in our conversation I asked him a simple little question about the liability of workingmen to accidents, and received a statistical lecture in return.

'It is all in the books,' he said. 'The figures have been gathered, and it has been proved conclusively that accidents rarely occur in the first hours of the morning work, but that they increase rapidly in the succeeding hours as the workers grow tired and slower in both their muscular and mental processes.

'Why, do you know that your father has three times as many chances for safety of life and limb than has a working-man? He has. The insurance* companies know. They will charge him four dollars and twenty cents a year on a thousand-dollar accident policy, and for the same policy they will charge a laborer fifteen dollars.'

'And you?' I asked; and in the moment of asking I was aware of a solicitude that was something more than slight.

'Oh, as a revolutionist, I have about eight chances to the workingman's one of being injured or killed,' he answered carelessly. 'The insurance companies charge the highly trained chemists that handle explosives eight times what they charge the workingmen. I don't think they'd insure me at all. Why did you ask?'

My eyes fluttered, and I could feel the blood warm in my face. It was not that he had caught me in my solicitude, but that I had caught myself, and in his presence.

Just then my father came in and began making preparations to depart with me. Ernest returned some books he had borrowed, and went away first. But just as he was going, he turned and said:

'Oh, by the way, while you are ruining your own peace of mind and I am ruining the Bishop's, you'd better look up Mrs. Wickson and Mrs. Pertonwaithe. Their husbands, you know, are the two principal stockholders in the Mills. Like all the rest of humanity, those two women are tied to the machine, but they are so tied that they sit on top of it.'

CHAPTER IV
SLAVES OF THE MACHINE

The more I thought of Jackson's arm, the more shaken I was. I was confronted by the concrete. For the first time I was seeing life. My university life, and study and culture, had not been real. I had learned nothing but theories of life and society that looked all very well on the printed page, but now I had seen life itself. Jackson's arm was a fact of life. 'The fact, man, the irrefragable fact!' of Ernest's was ringing in my consciousness.

* In the terrible wolf-struggle of those centuries, no man was permanently safe, no matter how much wealth he amassed. Out of fear for the welfare of their families, men devised the scheme of insurance. To us, in this intelligent age, such a device is laughably absurd and primitive. But in that age insurance was a very serious matter. The amusing part of it is that the funds of the insurance companies were frequently plundered and wasted by the very officials who were intrusted with the management of them.

It seemed monstrous, impossible, that our whole society was based upon blood. And yet there was Jackson. I could not get away from him. Constantly my thought swung back to him as the compass to the Pole. He had been monstrously treated. His blood had not been paid for in order that a larger dividend might be paid. And I knew a score of happy complacent families that had received those dividends and by that much had profited by Jackson's blood. If one man could be so monstrously treated and society move on its way unheeding, might not many men be so monstrously treated? I remembered Ernest's women of Chicago who toiled for ninety cents a week, and the child slaves of the Southern cotton mills he had described. And I could see their wan white hands, from which the blood had been pressed, at work upon the cloth out of which had been made my gown. And then I thought of the Sierra Mills and the dividends that had been paid, and I saw the blood of Jackson upon my gown as well. Jackson I could not escape. Always my meditations led me back to him.

Down in the depths of me I had a feeling that I stood on the edge of a precipice. It was as though I were about to see a new and awful revelation of life. And not I alone. My whole world was turning over. There was my father. I could see the effect Ernest was beginning to have on him. And then there was the Bishop. When I had last seen him he had looked a sick man. He was at high nervous tension, and in his eyes there was unspeakable horror. From the little I learned I knew that Ernest had been keeping his promise of taking him through hell. But what scenes of hell the Bishop's eyes had seen, I knew not, for he seemed too stunned to speak about them.

Once, the feeling strong upon me that my little world and all the world was turning over, I thought of Ernest as the cause of it; and also I thought, 'We were so happy and peaceful before he came!' And the next moment I was aware that the thought was a treason against truth, and Ernest rose before me transfigured, the apostle of truth, with shining brows and the fearlessness of one of Gods own angels, battling for the truth and the right, and battling for the succor of the poor and lonely and oppressed. And then there arose before me another figure, the Christ! He, too, had taken the part of the lowly and oppressed, and against all the established power of priest and pharisee. And I remembered his end upon the cross, and my heart contracted with a pang as I thought of Ernest. Was he, too, destined for a cross?—he, with his clarion call and war-noted voice, and all the fine man's vigor of him!

And in that moment I knew that I loved him, and that I was melting with desire to comfort him. I thought of his life. A sordid, harsh, and meagre life it must have been. And I thought of his father, who had lied and stolen for him and been worked to death. And he himself had gone into the mills when he was ten! All my heart seemed bursting with desire to fold my arms around him, and to rest his head on my breast—his head that must be weary with so many thoughts; and to give him rest—just rest—and easement and forgetfulness for a tender space.

I met Colonel Ingram at a church reception. Him I knew well and had known well for many years. I trapped him behind large palms and rubber plants, though he did not know he was trapped. He met me with the conventional gayety and gallantry. He was ever a graceful man, diplomatic, tactful, and considerate. And as for appearance, he was the most distinguished-looking man in our society. Beside him even the venerable head of the university looked tawdry and small.

And yet I found Colonel Ingram situated the same as the unlettered mechanics. He was not a free agent. He, too, was bound upon the wheel. I shall never forget the change in him when I mentioned Jackson's case. His smiling good nature vanished like a ghost. A sudden, frightful expression distorted his well-bred face. I felt the same alarm that I had felt when James Smith broke out. But Colonel Ingram did not curse. That was the slight difference that was left between the workingman and him. He was famed as a wit, but he had no wit now. And, unconsciously, this way and that he glanced for avenues of escape. But he was trapped amid the palms and rubber trees.

Oh, he was sick of the sound of Jackson's name. Why had I brought the matter up? He did not relish my joke. It was poor taste on my part, and very inconsiderate. Did I not know that in his profession personal feelings did not count? He left his personal feelings at home when he went down to the office. At the office he had only professional feelings.

'Should Jackson have received damages?' I asked.

'Certainly,' he answered. 'That is, personally, I have a feeling that he should. But that has nothing to do with the legal aspects of the case.'

He was getting his scattered wits slightly in hand.

'Tell me, has right anything to do with the law?' I asked.

'You have used the wrong initial consonant,' he smiled in answer.

'Might?' I queried; and he nodded his head. 'And yet we are supposed to get justice by means of the law?'

'That is the paradox of it,' he countered. 'We do get justice.'

'You are speaking professionally now, are you not?' I asked.

Colonel Ingram blushed, actually blushed, and again he looked anxiously about him for a way of escape. But I blocked his path and did not offer to move.

'Tell me,' I said, 'when one surrenders his personal feelings to his professional feelings, may not the action be defined as a sort of spiritual mayhem?'

I did not get an answer. Colonel Ingram had ingloriously bolted, overturning a palm in his flight.

Next I tried the newspapers. I wrote a quiet, restrained, dispassionate account of Jackson's case. I made no charges against the men with whom I had talked, nor, for that matter, did I even mention them. I gave the actual facts of the case, the long years Jackson had worked in the mills, his effort to save the machinery from damage and the consequent accident, and his own present wretched and starving condition. The three local newspapers rejected my communication, likewise did the two weeklies.

I got hold of Percy Layton. He was a graduate of the university, had gone in for journalism, and was then serving his apprenticeship as reporter on the most influential of the three newspapers. He smiled when I asked him the reason the newspapers suppressed all mention of Jackson or his case.

'Editorial policy,' he said. 'We have nothing to do with that. It's up to the editors.'

'But why is it policy?' I asked.

'We're all solid with the corporations,' he answered. 'If you paid advertising rates, you couldn't get any such matter into the papers. A man who tried to smuggle it in would lose his job. You couldn't get it in if you paid ten times the regular advertising rates.'

'How about your own policy?' I questioned. 'It would seem your function is to twist truth at the command of your employers, who, in turn, obey the behests of the corporations.'

'I haven't anything to do with that.' He looked uncomfortable for the moment, then brightened as he saw his way out. 'I, myself, do not write untruthful things. I keep square all right with my own conscience. Of course, there's lots that's repugnant in the course of the day's work. But then, you see, that's all part of the day's work,' he wound up boyishly.

'Yet you expect to sit at an editor's desk some day and conduct a policy.'

'I'll be case-hardened by that time,' was his reply.

'Since you are not yet case-hardened, tell me what you think right now about the general editorial policy.'

'I don't think,' he answered quickly. 'One can't kick over the ropes if he's going to succeed in journalism. I've learned that much, at any rate.'

And he nodded his young head sagely.

'But the right?' I persisted.

'You don't understand the game. Of course it's all right, because it comes out all right, don't you see?'

'Delightfully vague,' I murmured; but my heart was aching for the youth of him, and I felt that I must either scream or burst into tears.

I was beginning to see through the appearances of the society in which I had always lived, and to find the frightful realities that were beneath. There seemed a tacit conspiracy against Jackson, and I was aware of a thrill of sympathy for the whining lawyer who had ingloriously fought his case. But this tacit conspiracy grew large. Not alone was it aimed against Jackson. It was aimed against every workingman who was maimed in the mills. And if against every man in the mills, why not against every man in all the other mills and factories? In fact, was it not true of all the industries?

And if this was so, then society was a lie. I shrank back from my own conclusions. It was too terrible and awful to be true. But there was Jackson, and Jackson's arm, and the blood that stained my gown and dripped from my own roof-beams. And there were many Jacksons—hundreds of them in the mills alone, as Jackson himself had said. Jackson I could not escape.

I saw Mr. Wickson and Mr. Pertonwaithe, the two men who held most of the stock in the Sierra Mills. But I could not shake them as I had shaken the mechanics in their employ. I discovered that they had an ethic superior to that of the rest of society. It was what I may call the aristocratic ethic or the master ethic.* They talked in large ways of policy, and they identified policy and right. And to me they talked in fatherly ways, patronizing my youth and inexperience. They were the most hopeless of all I had encountered in my quest. They believed absolutely that their conduct was right. There was no question about it, no discussion. They were convinced that they were the saviours of society, and that it was they who made happiness for the many. And they drew pathetic pictures of what would be the sufferings of the working class were it not for the employment that they, and they alone, by their wisdom, provided for it.

Fresh from these two masters, I met Ernest and related my experience. He looked at me with a pleased expression, and said:

'Really, this is fine. You are beginning to dig truth for yourself. It is your own empirical generalization, and it is correct. No man in the industrial machine is a

---

* Before Avis Everhard was born, John Stuart Mill, in his essay, ON LIBERTY, wrote: 'Wherever there is an ascendant class, a large portion of the morality emanates from its class interests and its class feelings of superiority.'

free-will agent, except the large capitalist, and he isn't, if you'll pardon the Irishism.*
You see, the masters are quite sure that they are right in what they are doing. That is
the crowning absurdity of the whole situation. They are so tied by their human nature
that they can't do a thing unless they think it is right. They must have a sanction for
their acts.

'When they want to do a thing, in business of course, they must wait till there arises
in their brains, somehow, a religious, or ethical, or scientific, or philosophic, concept
that the thing is right. And then they go ahead and do it, unwitting that one of the
weaknesses of the human mind is that the wish is parent to the thought. No matter
what they want to do, the sanction always comes. They are superficial casuists. They
are Jesuitical. They even see their way to doing wrong that right may come of it. One
of the pleasant and axiomatic fictions they have created is that they are superior to the
rest of mankind in wisdom and efficiency. Therefrom comes their sanction to manage
the bread and butter of the rest of mankind. They have even resurrected the theory
of the divine right of kings—commercial kings in their case.**

'The weakness in their position lies in that they are merely business men. They are
not philosophers. They are not biologists nor sociologists. If they were, of course all
would be well. A business man who was also a biologist and a sociologist would know,
approximately, the right thing to do for humanity. But, outside the realm of business,
these men are stupid. They know only business. They do not know mankind nor
society, and yet they set themselves up as arbiters of the fates of the hungry millions
and all the other millions thrown in. History, some day, will have an excruciating
laugh at their expense.'

I was not surprised when I had my talk out with Mrs. Wickson and Mrs.
Pertonwaithe. They were society women.*** Their homes were palaces. They had many
homes scattered over the country, in the mountains, on lakes, and by the sea. They
were tended by armies of servants, and their social activities were bewildering. They
patronized the university and the churches, and the pastors especially bowed at their
knees in meek subservience.**** They were powers, these two women, what of the money
that was theirs. The power of subsidization of thought was theirs to a remarkable
degree, as I was soon to learn under Ernest's tuition.

They aped their husbands, and talked in the same large ways about policy, and
the duties and responsibilities of the rich. They were swayed by the same ethic that
dominated their husbands—the ethic of their class; and they uttered glib phrases that
their own ears did not understand.

Also, they grew irritated when I told them of the deplorable condition of Jackson's
family, and when I wondered that they had made no voluntary provision for the man.

---

* Verbal contradictions, called BULLS, were long an amiable weakness of the ancient Irish.
** The newspapers, in 1902 of that era, credited the president of the Anthracite Coal Trust,
George F. Baer, with the enunciation of the following principle: 'The rights and interests of the
laboring man will be protected by the Christian men to whom God in His infinite wisdom has
given the property interests of the country.'
*** SOCIETY is here used in a restricted sense, a common usage of the times to denote the
gilded drones that did no labor, but only glutted themselves at the honey-vats of the workers.
Neither the business men nor the laborers had time or opportunity for SOCIETY. SOCIETY
was the creation of the idle rich who toiled not and who in this way played.
**** 'Bring on your tainted money,' was the expressed sentiment of the Church during this
period.

I was told that they thanked no one for instructing them in their social duties. When I asked them flatly to assist Jackson, they as flatly refused. The astounding thing about it was that they refused in almost identically the same language, and this in face of the fact that I interviewed them separately and that one did not know that I had seen or was going to see the other. Their common reply was that they were glad of the opportunity to make it perfectly plain that no premium would ever be put on carelessness by them; nor would they, by paying for accident, tempt the poor to hurt themselves in the machinery.*

And they were sincere, these two women. They were drunk with conviction of the superiority of their class and of themselves. They had a sanction, in their own class-ethic, for every act they performed. As I drove away from Mrs. Pertonwaithe's great house, I looked back at it, and I remembered Ernest's expression that they were bound to the machine, but that they were so bound that they sat on top of it.

CHAPTER V
THE PHILOMATHS

Ernest was often at the house. Nor was it my father, merely, nor the controversial dinners, that drew him there. Even at that time I flattered myself that I played some part in causing his visits, and it was not long before I learned the correctness of my surmise. For never was there such a lover as Ernest Everhard. His gaze and his hand-clasp grew firmer and steadier, if that were possible; and the question that had grown from the first in his eyes, grew only the more imperative.

My impression of him, the first time I saw him, had been unfavorable. Then I had found myself attracted toward him. Next came my repulsion, when he so savagely attacked my class and me. After that, as I saw that he had not maligned my class, and that the harsh and bitter things he said about it were justified, I had drawn closer to him again. He became my oracle. For me he tore the sham from the face of society and gave me glimpses of reality that were as unpleasant as they were undeniably true.

As I have said, there was never such a lover as he. No girl could live in a university town till she was twenty-four and not have love experiences. I had been made love to by beardless sophomores and gray professors, and by the athletes and the football giants. But not one of them made love to me as Ernest did. His arms were around me before I knew. His lips were on mine before I could protest or resist. Before his earnestness conventional maiden dignity was ridiculous. He swept me off my feet by the splendid invincible rush of him. He did not propose. He put his arms around me and kissed me and took it for granted that we should be married. There was no discussion about it. The only discussion—and that arose afterward—was when we should be married.

It was unprecedented. It was unreal. Yet, in accordance with Ernest's test of truth, it worked. I trusted my life to it. And fortunate was the trust. Yet during those first days of our love, fear of the future came often to me when I thought of the violence and

---

* In the files of the OUTLOOK, a critical weekly of the period, in the number dated August 18, 1906, is related the circumstance of a workingman losing his arm, the details of which are quite similar to those of Jackson's case as related by Avis Everhard.

impetuosity of his love-making. Yet such fears were groundless. No woman was ever blessed with a gentler, tenderer husband. This gentleness and violence on his part was a curious blend similar to the one in his carriage of awkwardness and ease. That slight awkwardness! He never got over it, and it was delicious. His behavior in our drawing-room reminded me of a careful bull in a china shop.[*]

It was at this time that vanished my last doubt of the completeness of my love for him (a subconscious doubt, at most). It was at the Philomath Club—a wonderful night of battle, wherein Ernest bearded the masters in their lair. Now the Philomath Club was the most select on the Pacific Coast. It was the creation of Miss Brentwood, an enormously wealthy old maid; and it was her husband, and family, and toy. Its members were the wealthiest in the community, and the strongest-minded of the wealthy, with, of course, a sprinkling of scholars to give it intellectual tone.

The Philomath had no club house. It was not that kind of a club. Once a month its members gathered at some one of their private houses to listen to a lecture. The lecturers were usually, though not always, hired. If a chemist in New York made a new discovery in say radium, all his expenses across the continent were paid, and as well he received a princely fee for his time. The same with a returning explorer from the polar regions, or the latest literary or artistic success. No visitors were allowed, while it was the Philomath's policy to permit none of its discussions to get into the papers. Thus great statesmen—and there had been such occasions—were able fully to speak their minds.

I spread before me a wrinkled letter, written to me by Ernest twenty years ago, and from it I copy the following:

'Your father is a member of the Philomath, so you are able to come. Therefore come next Tuesday night. I promise you that you will have the time of your life. In your recent encounters, you failed to shake the masters. If you come, I'll shake them for you. I'll make them snarl like wolves. You merely questioned their morality. When their morality is questioned, they grow only the more complacent and superior. But I shall menace their money-bags. That will shake them to the roots of their primitive natures. If you can come, you will see the cave-man, in evening dress, snarling and snapping over a bone. I promise you a great caterwauling and an illuminating insight into the nature of the beast.

'They've invited me in order to tear me to pieces. This is the idea of Miss Brentwood. She clumsily hinted as much when she invited me. She's given them that kind of fun before. They delight in getting trustful-souled gentle reformers before them. Miss Brentwood thinks I am as mild as a kitten and as good-natured and stolid as the family cow. I'll not deny that I helped to give her that impression. She was very tentative at first, until she divined my harmlessness. I am to receive a handsome fee—two hundred and fifty dollars—as befits the man who, though a radical, once ran for governor. Also, I am to wear evening dress. This is compulsory. I never was so apparelled in my life. I suppose I'll have to hire one somewhere. But I'd do more than that to get a chance at the Philomaths.'

Of all places, the Club gathered that night at the Pertonwaithe house. Extra chairs

---

[*] In those days it was still the custom to fill the living rooms with bric-a-brac. They had not discovered simplicity of living. Such rooms were museums, entailing endless labor to keep clean. The dust-demon was the lord of the household. There were a myriad devices for catching dust, and only a few devices for getting rid of it.

had been brought into the great drawing-room, and in all there must have been two hundred Philomaths that sat down to hear Ernest. They were truly lords of society. I amused myself with running over in my mind the sum of the fortunes represented, and it ran well into the hundreds of millions. And the possessors were not of the idle rich. They were men of affairs who took most active parts in industrial and political life.

We were all seated when Miss Brentwood brought Ernest in. They moved at once to the head of the room, from where he was to speak. He was in evening dress, and, what of his broad shoulders and kingly head, he looked magnificent. And then there was that faint and unmistakable touch of awkwardness in his movements. I almost think I could have loved him for that alone. And as I looked at him I was aware of a great joy. I felt again the pulse of his palm on mine, the touch of his lips; and such pride was mine that I felt I must rise up and cry out to the assembled company: 'He is mine! He has held me in his arms, and I, mere I, have filled that mind of his to the exclusion of all his multitudinous and kingly thoughts!'

At the head of the room, Miss Brentwood introduced him to Colonel Van Gilbert, and I knew that the latter was to preside. Colonel Van Gilbert was a great corporation lawyer. In addition, he was immensely wealthy. The smallest fee he would deign to notice was a hundred thousand dollars. He was a master of law. The law was a puppet with which he played. He moulded it like clay, twisted and distorted it like a Chinese puzzle into any design he chose. In appearance and rhetoric he was old-fashioned, but in imagination and knowledge and resource he was as young as the latest statute. His first prominence had come when he broke the Shardwell will.* His fee for this one act was five hundred thousand dollars. From then on he had risen like a rocket. He was often called the greatest lawyer in the country—corporation lawyer, of course; and no classification of the three greatest lawyers in the United States could have excluded him.

He arose and began, in a few well-chosen phrases that carried an undertone of faint irony, to introduce Ernest. Colonel Van Gilbert was subtly facetious in his introduction of the social reformer and member of the working class, and the audience smiled. It made me angry, and I glanced at Ernest. The sight of him made me doubly angry. He did not seem to resent the delicate slurs. Worse than that, he did not seem to be aware of them. There he sat, gentle, and stolid, and somnolent. He really looked stupid. And for a moment the thought rose in my mind, What if he were overawed by this imposing array of power and brains? Then I smiled. He couldn't fool me. But he fooled the others, just as he had fooled Miss Brentwood. She occupied a chair right up to the front, and several times she turned her head toward one or another of her CONFRERES and smiled her appreciation of the remarks.

Colonel Van Gilbert done, Ernest arose and began to speak. He began in a low voice, haltingly and modestly, and with an air of evident embarrassment. He spoke

---

* This breaking of wills was a peculiar feature of the period. With the accumulation of vast fortunes, the problem of disposing of these fortunes after death was a vexing one to the accumulators. Will-making and will-breaking became complementary trades, like armor-making and gun-making. The shrewdest will-making lawyers were called in to make wills that could not be broken. But these wills were always broken, and very often by the very lawyers that had drawn them up. Nevertheless the delusion persisted in the wealthy class that an absolutely unbreakable will could be cast; and so, through the generations, clients and lawyers pursued the illusion. It was a pursuit like unto that of the Universal Solvent of the mediaeval alchemists.

of his birth in the working class, and of the sordidness and wretchedness of his environment, where flesh and spirit were alike starved and tormented. He described his ambitions and ideals, and his conception of the paradise wherein lived the people of the upper classes. As he said:

'Up above me, I knew, were unselfishnesses of the spirit, clean and noble thinking, keen intellectual living. I knew all this because I read 'Seaside Library'* novels, in which, with the exception of the villains and adventuresses, all men and women thought beautiful thoughts, spoke a beautiful tongue, and performed glorious deeds. In short, as I accepted the rising of the sun, I accepted that up above me was all that was fine and noble and gracious, all that gave decency and dignity to life, all that made life worth living and that remunerated one for his travail and misery.'

He went on and traced his life in the mills, the learning of the horseshoeing trade, and his meeting with the socialists. Among them, he said, he had found keen intellects and brilliant wits, ministers of the Gospel who had been broken because their Christianity was too wide for any congregation of mammon-worshippers, and professors who had been broken on the wheel of university subservience to the ruling class. The socialists were revolutionists, he said, struggling to overthrow the irrational society of the present and out of the material to build the rational society of the future. Much more he said that would take too long to write, but I shall never forget how he described the life among the revolutionists. All halting utterance vanished. His voice grew strong and confident, and it glowed as he glowed, and as the thoughts glowed that poured out from him. He said:

'Amongst the revolutionists I found, also, warm faith in the human, ardent idealism, sweetnesses of unselfishness, renunciation, and martyrdom—all the splendid, stinging things of the spirit. Here life was clean, noble, and alive. I was in touch with great souls who exalted flesh and spirit over dollars and cents, and to whom the thin wail of the starved slum child meant more than all the pomp and circumstance of commercial expansion and world empire. All about me were nobleness of purpose and heroism of effort, and my days and nights were sunshine and starshine, all fire and dew, with before my eyes, ever burning and blazing, the Holy Grail, Christ's own Grail, the warm human, long-suffering and maltreated but to be rescued and saved at the last.'

As before I had seen him transfigured, so now he stood transfigured before me. His brows were bright with the divine that was in him, and brighter yet shone his eyes from the midst of the radiance that seemed to envelop him as a mantle. But the others did not see this radiance, and I assumed that it was due to the tears of joy and love that dimmed my vision. At any rate, Mr. Wickson, who sat behind me, was unaffected, for I heard him sneer aloud, 'Utopian.'**

Ernest went on to his rise in society, till at last he came in touch with members of

---

* A curious and amazing literature that served to make the working class utterly misapprehend the nature of the leisure class.

** The people of that age were phrase slaves. The abjectness of their servitude is incomprehensible to us. There was a magic in words greater than the conjurer's art. So befuddled and chaotic were their minds that the utterance of a single word could negative the generalizations of a lifetime of serious research and thought. Such a word was the adjective UTOPIAN. The mere utterance of it could damn any scheme, no matter how sanely conceived, of economic amelioration or regeneration. Vast populations grew frenzied over such phrases as 'an honest dollar' and 'a full dinner pail.' The coinage of such phrases was considered strokes of genius.

the upper classes, and rubbed shoulders with the men who sat in the high places. Then came his disillusionment, and this disillusionment he described in terms that did not flatter his audience. He was surprised at the commonness of the clay. Life proved not to be fine and gracious. He was appalled by the selfishness he encountered, and what had surprised him even more than that was the absence of intellectual life. Fresh from his revolutionists, he was shocked by the intellectual stupidity of the master class. And then, in spite of their magnificent churches and well-paid preachers, he had found the masters, men and women, grossly material. It was true that they prattled sweet little ideals and dear little moralities, but in spite of their prattle the dominant key of the life they lived was materialistic. And they were without real morality—for instance, that which Christ had preached but which was no longer preached.

'I met men,' he said, 'who invoked the name of the Prince of Peace in their diatribes against war, and who put rifles in the hands of Pinkertons* with which to shoot down strikers in their own factories. I met men incoherent with indignation at the brutality of prize-fighting, and who, at the same time, were parties to the adulteration of food that killed each year more babes than even red-handed Herod had killed.

'This delicate, aristocratic-featured gentleman was a dummy director and a tool of corporations that secretly robbed widows and orphans. This gentleman, who collected fine editions and was a patron of literature, paid blackmail to a heavy-jowled, black-browed boss of a municipal machine. This editor, who published patent medicine advertisements, called me a scoundrelly demagogue because I dared him to print in his paper the truth about patent medicines.** This man, talking soberly and earnestly about the beauties of idealism and the goodness of God, had just betrayed his comrades in a business deal. This man, a pillar of the church and heavy contributor to foreign missions, worked his shop girls ten hours a day on a starvation wage and thereby directly encouraged prostitution. This man, who endowed chairs in universities and erected magnificent chapels, perjured himself in courts of law over dollars and cents. This railroad magnate broke his word as a citizen, as a gentleman, and as a Christian, when he granted a secret rebate, and he granted many secret rebates. This senator was the tool and the slave, the little puppet, of a brutal uneducated machine boss;*** so was this governor and this supreme court judge; and all three rode on railroad passes; and, also, this sleek capitalist owned the machine, the machine boss, and the railroads that issued the passes.

'And so it was, instead of in paradise, that I found myself in the arid desert of commercialism. I found nothing but stupidity, except for business. I found none clean, noble, and alive, though I found many who were alive—with rottenness. What I did find was monstrous selfishness and heartlessness, and a gross, gluttonous, practised, and practical materialism.'

---

* Originally, they were private detectives; but they quickly became hired fighting men of the capitalists, and ultimately developed into the Mercenaries of the Oligarchy.

** PATENT MEDICINES were patent lies, but, like the charms and indulgences of the Middle Ages, they deceived the people. The only difference lay in that the patent medicines were more harmful and more costly.

*** Even as late as 1912, A.D., the great mass of the people still persisted in the belief that they ruled the country by virtue of their ballots. In reality, the country was ruled by what were called POLITICAL MACHINES. At first the machine bosses charged the master capitalists extortionate tolls for legislation; but in a short time the master capitalists found it cheaper to own the political machines themselves and to hire the machine bosses.

Much more Ernest told them of themselves and of his disillusionment. Intellectually they had bored him; morally and spiritually they had sickened him; so that he was glad to go back to his revolutionists, who were clean, noble, and alive, and all that the capitalists were not.

'And now,' he said, 'let me tell you about that revolution.'

But first I must say that his terrible diatribe had not touched them. I looked about me at their faces and saw that they remained complacently superior to what he had charged. And I remembered what he had told me: that no indictment of their morality could shake them. However, I could see that the boldness of his language had affected Miss Brentwood. She was looking worried and apprehensive.

Ernest began by describing the army of revolution, and as he gave the figures of its strength (the votes cast in the various countries), the assemblage began to grow restless. Concern showed in their faces, and I noticed a tightening of lips. At last the gage of battle had been thrown down. He described the international organization of the socialists that united the million and a half in the United States with the twenty-three millions and a half in the rest of the world.

'Such an army of revolution,' he said, 'twenty-five millions strong, is a thing to make rulers and ruling classes pause and consider. The cry of this army is: 'No quarter! We want all that you possess. We will be content with nothing less than all that you possess. We want in our hands the reins of power and the destiny of mankind. Here are our hands. They are strong hands. We are going to take your governments, your palaces, and all your purpled ease away from you, and in that day you shall work for your bread even as the peasant in the field or the starved and runty clerk in your metropolises. Here are our hands. They are strong hands!'

And as he spoke he extended from his splendid shoulders his two great arms, and the horseshoer's hands were clutching the air like eagle's talons. He was the spirit of regnant labor as he stood there, his hands outreaching to rend and crush his audience. I was aware of a faintly perceptible shrinking on the part of the listeners before this figure of revolution, concrete, potential, and menacing. That is, the women shrank, and fear was in their faces. Not so with the men. They were of the active rich, and not the idle, and they were fighters. A low, throaty rumble arose, lingered on the air a moment, and ceased. It was the forerunner of the snarl, and I was to hear it many times that night—the token of the brute in man, the earnest of his primitive passions. And they were unconscious that they had made this sound. It was the growl of the pack, mouthed by the pack, and mouthed in all unconsciousness. And in that moment, as I saw the harshness form in their faces and saw the fight-light flashing in their eyes, I realized that not easily would they let their lordship of the world be wrested from them.

Ernest proceeded with his attack. He accounted for the existence of the million and a half of revolutionists in the United States by charging the capitalist class with having mismanaged society. He sketched the economic condition of the cave-man and of the savage peoples of to-day, pointing out that they possessed neither tools nor machines, and possessed only a natural efficiency of one in producing power. Then he traced the development of machinery and social organization so that to-day the producing power of civilized man was a thousand times greater than that of the savage.

'Five men,' he said, 'can produce bread for a thousand. One man can produce cotton cloth for two hundred and fifty people, woollens for three hundred, and boots and shoes for a thousand. One would conclude from this that under a capable management of society modern civilized man would be a great deal better off than the cave-man. But is he? Let us see. In the United States to-day there are fifteen million[*] people living in poverty; and by poverty is meant that condition in life in which, through lack of food and adequate shelter, the mere standard of working efficiency cannot be maintained. In the United States to-day, in spite of all your so-called labor legislation, there are three millions of child laborers.[**] In twelve years their numbers have been doubled. And in passing I will ask you managers of society why you did not make public the census figures of 1910? And I will answer for you, that you were afraid. The figures of misery would have precipitated the revolution that even now is gathering.

'But to return to my indictment. If modern man's producing power is a thousand times greater than that of the cave-man, why then, in the United States to-day, are there fifteen million people who are not properly sheltered and properly fed? Why then, in the United States to-day, are there three million child laborers? It is a true indictment. The capitalist class has mismanaged. In face of the facts that modern man lives more wretchedly than the cave-man, and that his producing power is a thousand times greater than that of the cave-man, no other conclusion is possible than that the capitalist class has mismanaged, that you have mismanaged, my masters, that you have criminally and selfishly mismanaged. And on this count you cannot answer me here to-night, face to face, any more than can your whole class answer the million and a half of revolutionists in the United States. You cannot answer. I challenge you to answer. And furthermore, I dare to say to you now that when I have finished you will not answer. On that point you will be tongue-tied, though you will talk wordily enough about other things.

'You have failed in your management. You have made a shambles of civilization. You have been blind and greedy. You have risen up (as you to-day rise up), shamelessly, in our legislative halls, and declared that profits were impossible without the toil of children and babes. Don't take my word for it. It is all in the records against you. You have lulled your conscience to sleep with prattle of sweet ideals and dear moralities. You are fat with power and possession, drunken with success; and you have no more hope against us than have the drones, clustered about the honey-vats, when the worker-bees spring upon them to end their rotund existence. You have failed in your management of society, and your management is to be taken away from you. A million and a half of the men of the working class say that they are going to get the rest of the working class to join with them and take the management away from you. This is the revolution, my masters. Stop it if you can.'

For an appreciable lapse of time Ernest's voice continued to ring through the great room. Then arose the throaty rumble I had heard before, and a dozen men were on their feet clamoring for recognition from Colonel Van Gilbert. I noticed Miss Brentwood's shoulders moving convulsively, and for the moment I was angry, for I thought that she was laughing at Ernest. And then I discovered that it was not laughter,

---

[*] Robert Hunter, in 1906, in a book entitled 'Poverty,' pointed out that at that time there were ten millions in the United States living in poverty.
[**] In the United States Census of 1900 (the last census the figures of which were made public), the number of child laborers was placed at 1,752,187.

but hysteria. She was appalled by what she had done in bringing this firebrand before her blessed Philomath Club.

Colonel Van Gilbert did not notice the dozen men, with passion-wrought faces, who strove to get permission from him to speak. His own face was passion-wrought. He sprang to his feet, waving his arms, and for a moment could utter only incoherent sounds. Then speech poured from him. But it was not the speech of a one-hundred-thousand-dollar lawyer, nor was the rhetoric old-fashioned.

'Fallacy upon fallacy!' he cried. 'Never in all my life have I heard so many fallacies uttered in one short hour. And besides, young man, I must tell you that you have said nothing new. I learned all that at college before you were born. Jean Jacques Rousseau enunciated your socialistic theory nearly two centuries ago. A return to the soil, forsooth! Reversion! Our biology teaches the absurdity of it. It has been truly said that a little learning is a dangerous thing, and you have exemplified it to-night with your madcap theories. Fallacy upon fallacy! I was never so nauseated in my life with overplus of fallacy. That for your immature generalizations and childish reasonings!'

He snapped his fingers contemptuously and proceeded to sit down. There were lip-exclamations of approval on the part of the women, and hoarser notes of confirmation came from the men. As for the dozen men who were clamoring for the floor, half of them began speaking at once. The confusion and babel was indescribable. Never had Mrs. Pertonwaithe's spacious walls beheld such a spectacle. These, then, were the cool captains of industry and lords of society, these snarling, growling savages in evening clothes. Truly Ernest had shaken them when he stretched out his hands for their moneybags, his hands that had appeared in their eyes as the hands of the fifteen hundred thousand revolutionists.

But Ernest never lost his head in a situation. Before Colonel Van Gilbert had succeeded in sitting down, Ernest was on his feet and had sprung forward.

'One at a time!' he roared at them.

The sound arose from his great lungs and dominated the human tempest. By sheer compulsion of personality he commanded silence.

'One at a time,' he repeated softly. 'Let me answer Colonel Van Gilbert. After that the rest of you can come at me—but one at a time, remember. No mass-plays here. This is not a football field.

'As for you,' he went on, turning toward Colonel Van Gilbert, 'you have replied to nothing I have said. You have merely made a few excited and dogmatic assertions about my mental caliber. That may serve you in your business, but you can't talk to me like that. I am not a workingman, cap in hand, asking you to increase my wages or to protect me from the machine at which I work. You cannot be dogmatic with truth when you deal with me. Save that for dealing with your wage-slaves. They will not dare reply to you because you hold their bread and butter, their lives, in your hands.

'As for this return to nature that you say you learned at college before I was born, permit me to point out that on the face of it you cannot have learned anything since. Socialism has no more to do with the state of nature than has differential calculus with a Bible class. I have called your class stupid when outside the realm of business. You, sir, have brilliantly exemplified my statement.'

This terrible castigation of her hundred-thousand-dollar lawyer was too much for Miss Brentwood's nerves. Her hysteria became violent, and she was helped, weeping and laughing, out of the room. It was just as well, for there was worse to follow.

'Don't take my word for it,' Ernest continued, when the interruption had been led away. 'Your own authorities with one unanimous voice will prove you stupid. Your own hired purveyors of knowledge will tell you that you are wrong. Go to your meekest little assistant instructor of sociology and ask him what is the difference between Rousseau's theory of the return to nature and the theory of socialism; ask your greatest orthodox bourgeois political economists and sociologists; question through the pages of every text-book written on the subject and stored on the shelves of your subsidized libraries; and from one and all the answer will be that there is nothing congruous between the return to nature and socialism. On the other hand, the unanimous affirmative answer will be that the return to nature and socialism are diametrically opposed to each other. As I say, don't take my word for it. The record of your stupidity is there in the books, your own books that you never read. And so far as your stupidity is concerned, you are but the exemplar of your class.

'You know law and business, Colonel Van Gilbert. You know how to serve corporations and increase dividends by twisting the law. Very good. Stick to it. You are quite a figure. You are a very good lawyer, but you are a poor historian, you know nothing of sociology, and your biology is contemporaneous with Pliny.'

Here Colonel Van Gilbert writhed in his chair. There was perfect quiet in the room. Everybody sat fascinated—paralyzed, I may say. Such fearful treatment of the great Colonel Van Gilbert was unheard of, undreamed of, impossible to believe—the great Colonel Van Gilbert before whom judges trembled when he arose in court. But Ernest never gave quarter to an enemy.

'This is, of course, no reflection on you,' Ernest said. 'Every man to his trade. Only you stick to your trade, and I'll stick to mine. You have specialized. When it comes to a knowledge of the law, of how best to evade the law or make new law for the benefit of thieving corporations, I am down in the dirt at your feet. But when it comes to sociology—my trade—you are down in the dirt at my feet. Remember that. Remember, also, that your law is the stuff of a day, and that you are not versatile in the stuff of more than a day. Therefore your dogmatic assertions and rash generalizations on things historical and sociological are not worth the breath you waste on them.'

Ernest paused for a moment and regarded him thoughtfully, noting his face dark and twisted with anger, his panting chest, his writhing body, and his slim white hands nervously clenching and unclenching.

'But it seems you have breath to use, and I'll give you a chance to use it. I indicted your class. Show me that my indictment is wrong. I pointed out to you the wretchedness of modern man—three million child slaves in the United States, without whose labor profits would not be possible, and fifteen million under-fed, ill-clothed, and worse-housed people. I pointed out that modern man's producing power through social organization and the use of machinery was a thousand times greater than that of the cave-man. And I stated that from these two facts no other conclusion was possible than that the capitalist class had mismanaged. This was my indictment, and I specifically and at length challenged you to answer it. Nay, I did more. I prophesied that you would not answer. It remains for your breath to smash my prophecy. You called my speech fallacy. Show the fallacy, Colonel Van Gilbert. Answer the indictment that I and my fifteen hundred thousand comrades have brought against your class and you.'

Colonel Van Gilbert quite forgot that he was presiding, and that in courtesy he should permit the other clamorers to speak. He was on his feet, flinging his arms, his rhetoric, and his control to the winds, alternately abusing Ernest for his youth and demagoguery, and savagely attacking the working class, elaborating its inefficiency and worthlessness.

'For a lawyer, you are the hardest man to keep to a point I ever saw,' Ernest began his answer to the tirade. 'My youth has nothing to do with what I have enunciated. Nor has the worthlessness of the working class. I charged the capitalist class with having mismanaged society. You have not answered. You have made no attempt to answer. Why? Is it because you have no answer? You are the champion of this whole audience. Every one here, except me, is hanging on your lips for that answer. They are hanging on your lips for that answer because they have no answer themselves. As for me, as I said before, I know that you not only cannot answer, but that you will not attempt an answer.'

'This is intolerable!' Colonel Van Gilbert cried out. 'This is insult!'

'That you should not answer is intolerable,' Ernest replied gravely. 'No man can be intellectually insulted. Insult, in its very nature, is emotional. Recover yourself. Give me an intellectual answer to my intellectual charge that the capitalist class has mismanaged society.'

Colonel Van Gilbert remained silent, a sullen, superior expression on his face, such as will appear on the face of a man who will not bandy words with a ruffian.

'Do not be downcast,' Ernest said. 'Take consolation in the fact that no member of your class has ever yet answered that charge.' He turned to the other men who were anxious to speak. 'And now it's your chance. Fire away, and do not forget that I here challenge you to give the answer that Colonel Van Gilbert has failed to give.'

It would be impossible for me to write all that was said in the discussion. I never realized before how many words could be spoken in three short hours. At any rate, it was glorious. The more his opponents grew excited, the more Ernest deliberately excited them. He had an encyclopaedic command of the field of knowledge, and by a word or a phrase, by delicate rapier thrusts, he punctured them. He named the points of their illogic. This was a false syllogism, that conclusion had no connection with the premise, while that next premise was an impostor because it had cunningly hidden in it the conclusion that was being attempted to be proved. This was an error, that was an assumption, and the next was an assertion contrary to ascertained truth as printed in all the text-books.

And so it went. Sometimes he exchanged the rapier for the club and went smashing amongst their thoughts right and left. And always he demanded facts and refused to discuss theories. And his facts made for them a Waterloo. When they attacked the working class, he always retorted, 'The pot calling the kettle black; that is no answer to the charge that your own face is dirty.' And to one and all he said: 'Why have you not answered the charge that your class has mismanaged? You have talked about other things and things concerning other things, but you have not answered. Is it because you have no answer?'

It was at the end of the discussion that Mr. Wickson spoke. He was the only one that was cool, and Ernest treated him with a respect he had not accorded the others.

'No answer is necessary,' Mr. Wickson said with slow deliberation. 'I have followed the whole discussion with amazement and disgust. I am disgusted with you gentlemen, members of my class. You have behaved like foolish little schoolboys, what with intruding ethics and the thunder of the common politician into such a discussion. You have been outgeneralled and outclassed. You have been very wordy, and all you have done is buzz. You have buzzed like gnats about a bear. Gentlemen, there stands the bear' (he pointed at Ernest), 'and your buzzing has only tickled his ears.

'Believe me, the situation is serious. That bear reached out his paws tonight to crush us. He has said there are a million and a half of revolutionists in the United States. That is a fact. He has said that it is their intention to take away from us our governments, our palaces, and all our purpled ease. That, also, is a fact. A change, a great change, is coming in society; but, haply, it may not be the change the bear anticipates. The bear has said that he will crush us. What if we crush the bear?'

The throat-rumble arose in the great room, and man nodded to man with indorsement and certitude. Their faces were set hard. They were fighters, that was certain.

'But not by buzzing will we crush the bear,' Mr. Wickson went on coldly and dispassionately. 'We will hunt the bear. We will not reply to the bear in words. Our reply shall be couched in terms of lead. We are in power. Nobody will deny it. By virtue of that power we shall remain in power.'

He turned suddenly upon Ernest. The moment was dramatic.

'This, then, is our answer. We have no words to waste on you. When you reach out your vaunted strong hands for our palaces and purpled ease, we will show you what strength is. In roar of shell and shrapnel and in whine of machine-guns will our answer be couched.* We will grind you revolutionists down under our heel, and we shall walk upon your faces. The world is ours, we are its lords, and ours it shall remain. As for the host of labor, it has been in the dirt since history began, and I read history aright. And in the dirt it shall remain so long as I and mine and those that come after us have the power. There is the word. It is the king of words—Power. Not God, not Mammon, but Power. Pour it over your tongue till it tingles with it. Power.'

'I am answered,' Ernest said quietly. 'It is the only answer that could be given. Power. It is what we of the working class preach. We know, and well we know by bitter experience, that no appeal for the right, for justice, for humanity, can ever touch you. Your hearts are hard as your heels with which you tread upon the faces of the poor. So we have preached power. By the power of our ballots on election day will we take your government away from you—'

'What if you do get a majority, a sweeping majority, on election day?' Mr. Wickson broke in to demand. 'Suppose we refuse to turn the government over to you after you have captured it at the ballot-box?'

'That, also, have we considered,' Ernest replied. 'And we shall give you an answer in terms of lead. Power you have proclaimed the king of words. Very good. Power it shall be. And in the day that we sweep to victory at the ballot-box, and you refuse to turn over to us the government we have constitutionally and peacefully captured, and you demand what we are going to do about it—in that day, I say, we shall answer you; and in roar of shell and shrapnel and in whine of machine-guns shall our answer be couched.

'You cannot escape us. It is true that you have read history aright. It is true that labor has from the beginning of history been in the dirt. And it is equally true that

---

* To show the tenor of thought, the following definition is quoted from 'The Cynic's Word Book' (1906 A.D.), written by one Ambrose Bierce, an avowed and confirmed misanthrope of the period: 'Grapeshot, n. An argument which the future is preparing in answer to the demands of American Socialism.'

so long as you and yours and those that come after you have power, that labor shall remain in the dirt. I agree with you. I agree with all that you have said. Power will be the arbiter, as it always has been the arbiter. It is a struggle of classes. Just as your class dragged down the old feudal nobility, so shall it be dragged down by my class, the working class. If you will read your biology and your sociology as clearly as you do your history, you will see that this end I have described is inevitable. It does not matter whether it is in one year, ten, or a thousand—your class shall be dragged down. And it shall be done by power. We of the labor hosts have conned that word over till our minds are all a-tingle with it. Power. It is a kingly word.'

And so ended the night with the Philomaths.

CHAPTER VI
ADUMBRATIONS

It was about this time that the warnings of coming events began to fall about us thick and fast. Ernest had already questioned father's policy of having socialists and labor leaders at his house, and of openly attending socialist meetings; and father had only laughed at him for his pains. As for myself, I was learning much from this contact with the working-class leaders and thinkers. I was seeing the other side of the shield. I was delighted with the unselfishness and high idealism I encountered, though I was appalled by the vast philosophic and scientific literature of socialism that was opened up to me. I was learning fast, but I learned not fast enough to realize then the peril of our position.

There were warnings, but I did not heed them. For instance, Mrs. Pertonwaithe and Mrs. Wickson exercised tremendous social power in the university town, and from them emanated the sentiment that I was a too-forward and self-assertive young woman with a mischievous penchant for officiousness and interference in other persons' affairs. This I thought no more than natural, considering the part I had played in investigating the case of Jackson's arm. But the effect of such a sentiment, enunciated by two such powerful social arbiters, I underestimated.

True, I noticed a certain aloofness on the part of my general friends, but this I ascribed to the disapproval that was prevalent in my circles of my intended marriage with Ernest. It was not till some time afterward that Ernest pointed out to me clearly that this general attitude of my class was something more than spontaneous, that behind it were the hidden springs of an organized conduct. 'You have given shelter to an enemy of your class,' he said. 'And not alone shelter, for you have given your love, yourself. This is treason to your class. Think not that you will escape being penalized.'

But it was before this that father returned one afternoon. Ernest was with me, and we could see that father was angry—philosophically angry. He was rarely really angry; but a certain measure of controlled anger he allowed himself. He called it a tonic. And we could see that he was tonic-angry when he entered the room.

'What do you think?' he demanded. 'I had luncheon with Wilcox.'

Wilcox was the superannuated president of the university, whose withered mind was stored with generalizations that were young in 1870, and which he had since failed to revise.

'I was invited,' father announced. 'I was sent for.'

He paused, and we waited.

'Oh, it was done very nicely, I'll allow; but I was reprimanded. I! And by that old fossil!'

'I'll wager I know what you were reprimanded for,' Ernest said.

'Not in three guesses,' father laughed.

'One guess will do,' Ernest retorted. 'And it won't be a guess. It will be a deduction. You were reprimanded for your private life.'

'The very thing!' father cried. 'How did you guess?'

'I knew it was coming. I warned you before about it.'

'Yes, you did,' father meditated. 'But I couldn't believe it. At any rate, it is only so much more clinching evidence for my book.'

'It is nothing to what will come,' Ernest went on, 'if you persist in your policy of having these socialists and radicals of all sorts at your house, myself included.'

'Just what old Wilcox said. And of all unwarranted things! He said it was in poor taste, utterly profitless, anyway, and not in harmony with university traditions and policy. He said much more of the same vague sort, and I couldn't pin him down to anything specific. I made it pretty awkward for him, and he could only go on repeating himself and telling me how much he honored me, and all the world honored me, as a scientist. It wasn't an agreeable task for him. I could see he didn't like it.'

'He was not a free agent,' Ernest said. 'The leg-bar* is not always worn graciously.'

'Yes. I got that much out of him. He said the university needed ever so much more money this year than the state was willing to furnish; and that it must come from wealthy personages who could not but be offended by the swerving of the university from its high ideal of the passionless pursuit of passionless intelligence. When I tried to pin him down to what my home life had to do with swerving the university from its high ideal, he offered me a two years' vacation, on full pay, in Europe, for recreation and research. Of course I couldn't accept it under the circumstances.'

'It would have been far better if you had,' Ernest said gravely.

'It was a bribe,' father protested; and Ernest nodded.

'Also, the beggar said that there was talk, tea-table gossip and so forth, about my daughter being seen in public with so notorious a character as you, and that it was not in keeping with university tone and dignity. Not that he personally objected—oh, no; but that there was talk and that I would understand.'

Ernest considered this announcement for a moment, and then said, and his face was very grave, withal there was a sombre wrath in it:

'There is more behind this than a mere university ideal. Somebody has put pressure on President Wilcox.'

'Do you think so?' father asked, and his face showed that he was interested rather than frightened.

'I wish I could convey to you the conception that is dimly forming in my own mind,' Ernest said. 'Never in the history of the world was society in so terrific flux as it is right now. The swift changes in our industrial system are causing equally swift changes in our religious, political, and social structures. An unseen and fearful revolution is taking place in the fibre and structure of society. One can only dimly feel these things. But they are in the air, now, to-day. One can feel the loom of them—things vast, vague,

* LEG-BAR—the African slaves were so manacled; also criminals. It was not until the coming of the Brotherhood of Man that the leg-bar passed out of use.

459

and terrible. My mind recoils from contemplation of what they may crystallize into. You heard Wickson talk the other night. Behind what he said were the same nameless, formless things that I feel. He spoke out of a superconscious apprehension of them.'

'You mean . . . ?' father began, then paused.

'I mean that there is a shadow of something colossal and menacing that even now is beginning to fall across the land. Call it the shadow of an oligarchy, if you will; it is the nearest I dare approximate it. What its nature may be I refuse to imagine.* But what I wanted to say was this: You are in a perilous position—a peril that my own fear enhances because I am not able even to measure it. Take my advice and accept the vacation.'

'But it would be cowardly,' was the protest.

'Not at all. You are an old man. You have done your work in the world, and a great work. Leave the present battle to youth and strength. We young fellows have our work yet to do. Avis will stand by my side in what is to come. She will be your representative in the battle-front.'

'But they can't hurt me,' father objected. 'Thank God I am independent. Oh, I assure you, I know the frightful persecution they can wage on a professor who is economically dependent on his university. But I am independent. I have not been a professor for the sake of my salary. I can get along very comfortably on my own income, and the salary is all they can take away from me.'

'But you do not realize,' Ernest answered. 'If all that I fear be so, your private income, your principal itself, can be taken from you just as easily as your salary.'

Father was silent for a few minutes. He was thinking deeply, and I could see the lines of decision forming in his face. At last he spoke.

'I shall not take the vacation.' He paused again. 'I shall go on with my book.** You may be wrong, but whether you are wrong or right, I shall stand by my guns.'

'All right,' Ernest said. 'You are travelling the same path that Bishop Morehouse is, and toward a similar smash-up. You'll both be proletarians before you're done with it.'

The conversation turned upon the Bishop, and we got Ernest to explain what he had been doing with him.

'He is soul-sick from the journey through hell I have given him. I took him through the homes of a few of our factory workers. I showed him the human wrecks cast aside

---

* Though, like Everhard, they did not dream of the nature of it, there were men, even before his time, who caught glimpses of the shadow. John C. Calhoun said: 'A power has risen up in the government greater than the people themselves, consisting of many and various and powerful interests, combined into one mass, and held together by the cohesive power of the vast surplus in the banks.' And that great humanist, Abraham Lincoln, said, just before his assassination: 'I see in the near future a crisis approaching that unnerves me and causes me to tremble for the safety of my country. . . . Corporations have been enthroned, an era of corruption in high places will follow, and the money-power of the country will endeavor to prolong its reign by working upon the prejudices of the people until the wealth is aggregated in a few hands and the Republic is destroyed.'

** This book, 'Economics and Education,' was published in that year. Three copies of it are extant; two at Ardis, and one at Asgard. It dealt, in elaborate detail, with one factor in the persistence of the established, namely, the capitalistic bias of the universities and common schools. It was a logical and crushing indictment of the whole system of education that developed in the minds of the students only such ideas as were favorable to the capitalistic regime, to the exclusion of all ideas that were inimical and subversive. The book created a furor, and was promptly suppressed by the Oligarchy.

by the industrial machine, and he listened to their life stories. I took him through the slums of San Francisco, and in drunkenness, prostitution, and criminality he learned a deeper cause than innate depravity. He is very sick, and, worse than that, he has got out of hand. He is too ethical. He has been too severely touched. And, as usual, he is unpractical. He is up in the air with all kinds of ethical delusions and plans for mission work among the cultured. He feels it is his bounden duty to resurrect the ancient spirit of the Church and to deliver its message to the masters. He is over-wrought. Sooner or later he is going to break out, and then there's going to be a smash-up. What form it will take I can't even guess. He is a pure, exalted soul, but he is so unpractical. He's beyond me. I can't keep his feet on the earth. And through the air he is rushing on to his Gethsemane. And after this his crucifixion. Such high souls are made for crucifixion.'

'And you?' I asked; and beneath my smile was the seriousness of the anxiety of love.

'Not I,' he laughed back. 'I may be executed, or assassinated, but I shall never be crucified. I am planted too solidly and stolidly upon the earth.'

'But why should you bring about the crucifixion of the Bishop?' I asked. 'You will not deny that you are the cause of it.'

'Why should I leave one comfortable soul in comfort when there are millions in travail and misery?' he demanded back.

'Then why did you advise father to accept the vacation?'

'Because I am not a pure, exalted soul,' was the answer. 'Because I am solid and stolid and selfish. Because I love you and, like Ruth of old, thy people are my people. As for the Bishop, he has no daughter. Besides, no matter how small the good, nevertheless his little inadequate wail will be productive of some good in the revolution, and every little bit counts.'

I could not agree with Ernest. I knew well the noble nature of Bishop Morehouse, and I could not conceive that his voice raised for righteousness would be no more than a little inadequate wail. But I did not yet have the harsh facts of life at my fingers' ends as Ernest had. He saw clearly the futility of the Bishop's great soul, as coming events were soon to show as clearly to me.

It was shortly after this day that Ernest told me, as a good story, the offer he had received from the government, namely, an appointment as United States Commissioner of Labor. I was overjoyed. The salary was comparatively large, and would make safe our marriage. And then it surely was congenial work for Ernest, and, furthermore, my jealous pride in him made me hail the proffered appointment as a recognition of his abilities.

Then I noticed the twinkle in his eyes. He was laughing at me.

'You are not going to . . . to decline?' I quavered.

'It is a bribe,' he said. 'Behind it is the fine hand of Wickson, and behind him the hands of greater men than he. It is an old trick, old as the class struggle is old—stealing the captains from the army of labor. Poor betrayed labor! If you but knew how many of its leaders have been bought out in similar ways in the past. It is cheaper, so much cheaper, to buy a general than to fight him and his whole army. There was—but I'll not call any names. I'm bitter enough over it as it is. Dear heart, I am a captain of labor. I could not sell out. If for no other reason, the memory of my poor old father and the way he was worked to death would prevent.'

The tears were in his eyes, this great, strong hero of mine. He never could forgive the way his father had been malformed—the sordid lies and the petty thefts he had been compelled to, in order to put food in his children's mouths.

'My father was a good man,' Ernest once said to me. 'The soul of him was good, and yet it was twisted, and maimed, and blunted by the savagery of his life. He was made into a broken-down beast by his masters, the arch-beasts. He should be alive to-day, like your father. He had a strong constitution. But he was caught in the machine and worked to death—for profit. Think of it. For profit—his life blood transmuted into a wine-supper, or a jewelled gewgaw, or some similar sense-orgy of the parasitic and idle rich, his masters, the arch-beasts.'

CHAPTER VII

THE BISHOP'S VISION

'The Bishop is out of hand,' Ernest wrote me. 'He is clear up in the air. Tonight he is going to begin putting to rights this very miserable world of ours. He is going to deliver his message. He has told me so, and I cannot dissuade him. To-night he is chairman of the I.P.H.,* and he will embody his message in his introductory remarks.

'May I bring you to hear him? Of course, he is foredoomed to futility. It will break your heart—it will break his; but for you it will be an excellent object lesson. You know, dear heart, how proud I am because you love me. And because of that I want you to know my fullest value, I want to redeem, in your eyes, some small measure of my unworthiness. And so it is that my pride desires that you shall know my thinking is correct and right. My views are harsh; the futility of so noble a soul as the Bishop will show you the compulsion for such harshness. So come to-night. Sad though this night's happening will be, I feel that it will but draw you more closely to me.'

The I.P.H. held its convention that night in San Francisco.** This convention had been called to consider public immorality and the remedy for it. Bishop Morehouse presided. He was very nervous as he sat on the platform, and I could see the high tension he was under. By his side were Bishop Dickinson; H. H. Jones, the head of the ethical department in the University of California; Mrs. W. W. Hurd, the great charity organizer; Philip Ward, the equally great philanthropist; and several lesser luminaries in the field of morality and charity. Bishop Morehouse arose and abruptly began:

'I was in my brougham, driving through the streets. It was night-time. Now and then I looked through the carriage windows, and suddenly my eyes seemed to be opened, and I saw things as they really are. At first I covered my eyes with my hands to shut out the awful sight, and then, in the darkness, the question came to me: What is to be done? What is to be done? A little later the question came to me in another way: What would the Master do? And with the question a great light seemed to fill the place, and I saw my duty sun-clear, as Saul saw his on the way to Damascus.

'I stopped the carriage, got out, and, after a few minutes' conversation, persuaded two of the public women to get into the brougham with me. If Jesus was right, then these two unfortunates were my sisters, and the only hope of their purification was in my affection and tenderness.

---

* There is no clew to the name of the organization for which these initials stand.
** It took but a few minutes to cross by ferry from Berkeley to San Francisco. These, and the other bay cities, practically composed one community.

462

'I live in one of the loveliest localities of San Francisco. The house in which I live cost a hundred thousand dollars, and its furnishings, books, and works of art cost as much more. The house is a mansion. No, it is a palace, wherein there are many servants. I never knew what palaces were good for. I had thought they were to live in. But now I know. I took the two women of the street to my palace, and they are going to stay with me. I hope to fill every room in my palace with such sisters as they.'

The audience had been growing more and more restless and unsettled, and the faces of those that sat on the platform had been betraying greater and greater dismay and consternation. And at this point Bishop Dickinson arose, and with an expression of disgust on his face, fled from the platform and the hall. But Bishop Morehouse, oblivious to all, his eyes filled with his vision, continued:

'Oh, sisters and brothers, in this act of mine I find the solution of all my difficulties. I didn't know what broughams were made for, but now I know. They are made to carry the weak, the sick, and the aged; they are made to show honor to those who have lost the sense even of shame.

'I did not know what palaces were made for, but now I have found a use for them. The palaces of the Church should be hospitals and nurseries for those who have fallen by the wayside and are perishing.'

He made a long pause, plainly overcome by the thought that was in him, and nervous how best to express it.

'I am not fit, dear brethren, to tell you anything about morality. I have lived in shame and hypocrisies too long to be able to help others; but my action with those women, sisters of mine, shows me that the better way is easy to find. To those who believe in Jesus and his gospel there can be no other relation between man and man than the relation of affection. Love alone is stronger than sin—stronger than death. I therefore say to the rich among you that it is their duty to do what I have done and am doing. Let each one of you who is prosperous take into his house some thief and treat him as his brother, some unfortunate and treat her as his sister, and San Francisco will need no police force and no magistrates; the prisons will be turned into hospitals, and the criminal will disappear with his crime.

'We must give ourselves and not our money alone. We must do as Christ did; that is the message of the Church today. We have wandered far from the Master's teaching. We are consumed in our own flesh-pots. We have put mammon in the place of Christ. I have here a poem that tells the whole story. I should like to read it to you. It was written by an erring soul who yet saw clearly.[*] It must not be mistaken for an attack upon the Catholic Church. It is an attack upon all churches, upon the pomp and splendor of all churches that have wandered from the Master's path and hedged themselves in from his lambs. Here it is:

'The silver trumpets rang across the Dome;
The people knelt upon the ground with awe;
And borne upon the necks of men I saw,
Like some great God, the Holy Lord of Rome.
'Priest-like, he wore a robe more white than foam,
And, king-like, swathed himself in royal red,
Three crowns of gold rose high upon his head;

* Oscar Wilde, one of the lords of language of the nineteenth century of the Christian Era.

In splendor and in light the Pope passed home.
'My heart stole back across wide wastes of years
To One who wandered by a lonely sea;
And sought in vain for any place of rest:
'Foxes have holes, and every bird its nest,
I, only I, must wander wearily,
And bruise my feet, and drink wine salt with tears.'

The audience was agitated, but unresponsive. Yet Bishop Morehouse was not aware of it. He held steadily on his way.

'And so I say to the rich among you, and to all the rich, that bitterly you oppress the Master's lambs. You have hardened your hearts. You have closed your ears to the voices that are crying in the land—the voices of pain and sorrow that you will not hear but that some day will be heard. And so I say—'

But at this point H. H. Jones and Philip Ward, who had already risen from their chairs, led the Bishop off the platform, while the audience sat breathless and shocked.

Ernest laughed harshly and savagely when he had gained the street. His laughter jarred upon me. My heart seemed ready to burst with suppressed tears.

'He has delivered his message,' Ernest cried. 'The manhood and the deep-hidden, tender nature of their Bishop burst out, and his Christian audience, that loved him, concluded that he was crazy! Did you see them leading him so solicitously from the platform? There must have been laughter in hell at the spectacle.'

'Nevertheless, it will make a great impression, what the Bishop did and said to-night,' I said.

'Think so?' Ernest queried mockingly.

'It will make a sensation,' I asserted. 'Didn't you see the reporters scribbling like mad while he was speaking?'

'Not a line of which will appear in to-morrow's papers.'

'I can't believe it,' I cried.

'Just wait and see,' was the answer. 'Not a line, not a thought that he uttered. The daily press? The daily suppressage!'

'But the reporters,' I objected. 'I saw them.'

'Not a word that he uttered will see print. You have forgotten the editors. They draw their salaries for the policy they maintain. Their policy is to print nothing that is a vital menace to the established. The Bishop's utterance was a violent assault upon the established morality. It was heresy. They led him from the platform to prevent him from uttering more heresy. The newspapers will purge his heresy in the oblivion of silence. The press of the United States? It is a parasitic growth that battens on the capitalist class. Its function is to serve the established by moulding public opinion, and right well it serves it.

'Let me prophesy. To-morrow's papers will merely mention that the Bishop is in poor health, that he has been working too hard, and that he broke down last night. The next mention, some days hence, will be to the effect that he is suffering from nervous prostration and has been given a vacation by his grateful flock. After that, one of two things will happen: either the Bishop will see the error of his way and return from his vacation a well man in whose eyes there are no more visions, or else he will persist in his madness, and then you may expect to see in the papers, couched pathetically and tenderly, the announcement of his insanity. After that he will be left to gibber his visions to padded walls.'

'Now there you go too far!' I cried out.

'In the eyes of society it will truly be insanity,' he replied. 'What honest man, who is not insane, would take lost women and thieves into his house to dwell with him sisterly and brotherly? True, Christ died between two thieves, but that is another story. Insanity? The mental processes of the man with whom one disagrees, are always wrong. Therefore the mind of the man is wrong. Where is the line between wrong mind and insane mind? It is inconceivable that any sane man can radically disagree with one's most sane conclusions.

'There is a good example of it in this evening's paper. Mary McKenna lives south of Market Street. She is a poor but honest woman. She is also patriotic. But she has erroneous ideas concerning the American flag and the protection it is supposed to symbolize. And here's what happened to her. Her husband had an accident and was laid up in hospital three months. In spite of taking in washing, she got behind in her rent. Yesterday they evicted her. But first, she hoisted an American flag, and from under its folds she announced that by virtue of its protection they could not turn her out on to the cold street. What was done? She was arrested and arraigned for insanity. To-day she was examined by the regular insanity experts. She was found insane. She was consigned to the Napa Asylum.'

'But that is far-fetched,' I objected. 'Suppose I should disagree with everybody about the literary style of a book. They wouldn't send me to an asylum for that.'

'Very true,' he replied. 'But such divergence of opinion would constitute no menace to society. Therein lies the difference. The divergence of opinion on the parts of Mary McKenna and the Bishop do menace society. What if all the poor people should refuse to pay rent and shelter themselves under the American flag? Landlordism would go crumbling. The Bishop's views are just as perilous to society. Ergo, to the asylum with him.'

But still I refused to believe.

'Wait and see,' Ernest said, and I waited.

Next morning I sent out for all the papers. So far Ernest was right. Not a word that Bishop Morehouse had uttered was in print. Mention was made in one or two of the papers that he had been overcome by his feelings. Yet the platitudes of the speakers that followed him were reported at length.

Several days later the brief announcement was made that he had gone away on a vacation to recover from the effects of overwork. So far so good, but there had been no hint of insanity, nor even of nervous collapse. Little did I dream the terrible road the Bishop was destined to travel—the Gethsemane and crucifixion that Ernest had pondered about.

CHAPTER VIII

THE MACHINE BREAKERS

It was just before Ernest ran for Congress, on the socialist ticket, that father gave what he privately called his 'Profit and Loss' dinner. Ernest called it the dinner of the Machine Breakers. In point of fact, it was merely a dinner for business men—small business men, of course. I doubt if one of them was interested in any business the total capitalization of which exceeded a couple of hundred thousand dollars. They were truly representative middle-class business men.

There was Owen, of Silverberg, Owen & Company—a large grocery firm with several branch stores. We bought our groceries from them. There were both partners of the big drug firm of Kowalt & Washburn, and Mr. Asmunsen, the owner of a large granite quarry in Contra Costa County. And there were many similar men, owners or part-owners in small factories, small businesses and small industries—small capitalists, in short.

They were shrewd-faced, interesting men, and they talked with simplicity and clearness. Their unanimous complaint was against the corporations and trusts. Their creed was, 'Bust the Trusts.' All oppression originated in the trusts, and one and all told the same tale of woe. They advocated government ownership of such trusts as the railroads and telegraphs, and excessive income taxes, graduated with ferocity, to destroy large accumulations. Likewise they advocated, as a cure for local ills, municipal ownership of such public utilities as water, gas, telephones, and street railways.

Especially interesting was Mr. Asmunsen's narrative of his tribulations as a quarry owner. He confessed that he never made any profits out of his quarry, and this, in spite of the enormous volume of business that had been caused by the destruction of San Francisco by the big earthquake. For six years the rebuilding of San Francisco had been going on, and his business had quadrupled and octupled, and yet he was no better off.

'The railroad knows my business just a little bit better than I do,' he said. 'It knows my operating expenses to a cent, and it knows the terms of my contracts. How it knows these things I can only guess. It must have spies in my employ, and it must have access to the parties to all my contracts. For look you, when I place a big contract, the terms of which favor me a goodly profit, the freight rate from my quarry to market is promptly raised. No explanation is made. The railroad gets my profit. Under such circumstances I have never succeeded in getting the railroad to reconsider its raise. On the other hand, when there have been accidents, increased expenses of operating, or contracts with less profitable terms, I have always succeeded in getting the railroad to lower its rate. What is the result? Large or small, the railroad always gets my profits.'

'What remains to you over and above,' Ernest interrupted to ask, 'would roughly be the equivalent of your salary as a manager did the railroad own the quarry.'

'The very thing,' Mr. Asmunsen replied. 'Only a short time ago I had my books gone through for the past ten years. I discovered that for those ten years my gain was just equivalent to a manager's salary. The railroad might just as well have owned my quarry and hired me to run it.'

'But with this difference,' Ernest laughed; 'the railroad would have had to assume all the risk which you so obligingly assumed for it.'

'Very true,' Mr. Asmunsen answered sadly.

Having let them have they say, Ernest began asking questions right and left. He began with Mr. Owen.

'You started a branch store here in Berkeley about six months ago?'

'Yes,' Mr. Owen answered.

'And since then I've noticed that three little corner groceries have gone out of business. Was your branch store the cause of it?'

Mr. Owen affirmed with a complacent smile. 'They had no chance against us.'

'Why not?'

'We had greater capital. With a large business there is always less waste and greater efficiency.'

'And your branch store absorbed the profits of the three small ones. I see. But tell me, what became of the owners of the three stores?'

'One is driving a delivery wagon for us. I don't know what happened to the other two.'

Ernest turned abruptly on Mr. Kowalt.

'You sell a great deal at cut-rates.* What have become of the owners of the small drug stores that you forced to the wall?'

'One of them, Mr. Haasfurther, has charge now of our prescription department,' was the answer.

'And you absorbed the profits they had been making?'

'Surely. That is what we are in business for.'

'And you?' Ernest said suddenly to Mr. Asmunsen. 'You are disgusted because the railroad has absorbed your profits?'

Mr. Asmunsen nodded.

'What you want is to make profits yourself?'

Again Mr. Asmunsen nodded.

'Out of others?'

There was no answer.

'Out of others?' Ernest insisted.

'That is the way profits are made,' Mr. Asmunsen replied curtly.

'Then the business game is to make profits out of others, and to prevent others from making profits out of you. That's it, isn't it?'

Ernest had to repeat his question before Mr. Asmunsen gave an answer, and then he said:

'Yes, that's it, except that we do not object to the others making profits so long as they are not extortionate.'

'By extortionate you mean large; yet you do not object to making large profits yourself? . . . Surely not?'

And Mr. Asmunsen amiably confessed to the weakness. There was one other man who was quizzed by Ernest at this juncture, a Mr. Calvin, who had once been a great dairy-owner.

'Some time ago you were fighting the Milk Trust,' Ernest said to him; 'and now you are in Grange politics.** How did it happen?'

'Oh, I haven't quit the fight,' Mr. Calvin answered, and he looked belligerent enough. 'I'm fighting the Trust on the only field where it is possible to fight—the political field. Let me show you. A few years ago we dairymen had everything our own way.'

'But you competed among yourselves?' Ernest interrupted.

'Yes, that was what kept the profits down. We did try to organize, but independent

* A lowering of selling price to cost, and even to less than cost. Thus, a large company could sell at a loss for a longer period than a small company, and so drive the small company out of business. A common device of competition.

** Many efforts were made during this period to organize the perishing farmer class into a political party, the aim of which was destroy the trusts and corporations by drastic legislation. All such attempts ended in failure.

dairymen always broke through us. Then came the Milk Trust.'

'Financed by surplus capital from Standard Oil,'* Ernest said.

'Yes,' Mr. Calvin acknowledged. 'But we did not know it at the time. Its agents approached us with a club. 'Come in and be fat,' was their proposition, 'or stay out and starve.' Most of us came in. Those that didn't, starved. Oh, it paid us . . . at first. Milk was raised a cent a quart. One-quarter of this cent came to us. Three-quarters of it went to the Trust. Then milk was raised another cent, only we didn't get any of that cent. Our complaints were useless. The Trust was in control. We discovered that we were pawns. Finally, the additional quarter of a cent was denied us. Then the Trust began to squeeze us out. What could we do? We were squeezed out. There were no dairymen, only a Milk Trust.'

'But with milk two cents higher, I should think you could have competed,' Ernest suggested slyly.

'So we thought. We tried it.' Mr. Calvin paused a moment. 'It broke us. The Trust could put milk upon the market more cheaply than we. It could sell still at a slight profit when we were selling at actual loss. I dropped fifty thousand dollars in that venture. Most of us went bankrupt.** The dairymen were wiped out of existence.'

'So the Trust took your profits away from you,' Ernest said, 'and you've gone into politics in order to legislate the Trust out of existence and get the profits back?'

Mr. Calvin's face lighted up. 'That is precisely what I say in my speeches to the farmers. That's our whole idea in a nutshell.'

'And yet the Trust produces milk more cheaply than could the independent dairymen?' Ernest queried.

'Why shouldn't it, with the splendid organization and new machinery its large capital makes possible?'

'There is no discussion,' Ernest answered. 'It certainly should, and, furthermore, it does.'

Mr. Calvin here launched out into a political speech in exposition of his views. He was warmly followed by a number of the others, and the cry of all was to destroy the trusts.

'Poor simple folk,' Ernest said to me in an undertone. 'They see clearly as far as they see, but they see only to the ends of their noses.'

A little later he got the floor again, and in his characteristic way controlled it for the rest of the evening.

'I have listened carefully to all of you,' he began, 'and I see plainly that you play the business game in the orthodox fashion. Life sums itself up to you in profits. You have a firm and abiding belief that you were created for the sole purpose of making profits. Only there is a hitch. In the midst of your own profit-making along comes the trust and takes your profits away from you. This is a dilemma that interferes somehow with the aim of creation, and the only way out, as it seems to you, is to destroy that which takes from you your profits.

'I have listened carefully, and there is only one name that will epitomize you. I shall call you that name. You are machine-breakers. Do you know what a machine-breaker

* The first successful great trust—almost a generation in advance of the rest.
** Bankruptcy—a peculiar institution that enabled an individual, who had failed in competitive industry, to forego paying his debts. The effect was to ameliorate the too savage conditions of the fang-and-claw social struggle.

is? Let me tell you. In the eighteenth century, in England, men and women wove cloth on hand-looms in their own cottages. It was a slow, clumsy, and costly way of weaving cloth, this cottage system of manufacture. Along came the steam-engine and labor-saving machinery. A thousand looms assembled in a large factory, and driven by a central engine wove cloth vastly more cheaply than could the cottage weavers on their hand-looms. Here in the factory was combination, and before it competition faded away. The men and women who had worked the hand-looms for themselves now went into the factories and worked the machine-looms, not for themselves, but for the capitalist owners. Furthermore, little children went to work on the machine-looms, at lower wages, and displaced the men. This made hard times for the men. Their standard of living fell. They starved. And they said it was all the fault of the machines. Therefore, they proceeded to break the machines. They did not succeed, and they were very stupid.

'Yet you have not learned their lesson. Here are you, a century and a half later, trying to break machines. By your own confession the trust machines do the work more efficiently and more cheaply than you can. That is why you cannot compete with them. And yet you would break those machines. You are even more stupid than the stupid workmen of England. And while you maunder about restoring competition, the trusts go on destroying you.

'One and all you tell the same story,—the passing away of competition and the coming on of combination. You, Mr. Owen, destroyed competition here in Berkeley when your branch store drove the three small groceries out of business. Your combination was more effective. Yet you feel the pressure of other combinations on you, the trust combinations, and you cry out. It is because you are not a trust. If you were a grocery trust for the whole United States, you would be singing another song. And the song would be, 'Blessed are the trusts.' And yet again, not only is your small combination not a trust, but you are aware yourself of its lack of strength. You are beginning to divine your own end. You feel yourself and your branch stores a pawn in the game. You see the powerful interests rising and growing more powerful day by day; you feel their mailed hands descending upon your profits and taking a pinch here and a pinch there—the railroad trust, the oil trust, the steel trust, the coal trust; and you know that in the end they will destroy you, take away from you the last per cent of your little profits.

'You, sir, are a poor gamester. When you squeezed out the three small groceries here in Berkeley by virtue of your superior combination, you swelled out your chest, talked about efficiency and enterprise, and sent your wife to Europe on the profits you had gained by eating up the three small groceries. It is dog eat dog, and you ate them up. But, on the other hand, you are being eaten up in turn by the bigger dogs, wherefore you squeal. And what I say to you is true of all of you at this table. You are all squealing. You are all playing the losing game, and you are all squealing about it.

'But when you squeal you don't state the situation flatly, as I have stated it. You don't say that you like to squeeze profits out of others, and that you are making all the row because others are squeezing your profits out of you. No, you are too cunning for that. You say something else. You make small-capitalist political speeches such as Mr. Calvin made. What did he say? Here are a few of his phrases I caught: 'Our original principles are all right,' 'What this country requires is a return to fundamental American methods—free opportunity for all,' 'The spirit of liberty in which this nation was born,' 'Let us return to the principles of our forefathers.'

'When he says 'free opportunity for all,' he means free opportunity to squeeze profits, which freedom of opportunity is now denied him by the great trusts. And the absurd thing about it is that you have repeated these phrases so often that you believe them. You want opportunity to plunder your fellow-men in your own small way, but you hypnotize yourselves into thinking you want freedom. You are piggish and acquisitive, but the magic of your phrases leads you to believe that you are patriotic. Your desire for profits, which is sheer selfishness, you metamorphose into altruistic solicitude for suffering humanity. Come on now, right here amongst ourselves, and be honest for once. Look the matter in the face and state it in direct terms.'

There were flushed and angry faces at the table, and withal a measure of awe. They were a little frightened at this smooth-faced young fellow, and the swing and smash of his words, and his dreadful trait of calling a spade a spade. Mr. Calvin promptly replied.

'And why not?' he demanded. 'Why can we not return to ways of our fathers when this republic was founded? You have spoken much truth, Mr. Everhard, unpalatable though it has been. But here amongst ourselves let us speak out. Let us throw off all disguise and accept the truth as Mr. Everhard has flatly stated it. It is true that we smaller capitalists are after profits, and that the trusts are taking our profits away from us. It is true that we want to destroy the trusts in order that our profits may remain to us. And why can we not do it? Why not? I say, why not?'

'Ah, now we come to the gist of the matter,' Ernest said with a pleased expression. 'I'll try to tell you why not, though the telling will be rather hard. You see, you fellows have studied business, in a small way, but you have not studied social evolution at all. You are in the midst of a transition stage now in economic evolution, but you do not understand it, and that's what causes all the confusion. Why cannot you return? Because you can't. You can no more make water run up hill than can you cause the tide of economic evolution to flow back in its channel along the way it came. Joshua made the sun stand still upon Gibeon, but you would outdo Joshua. You would make the sun go backward in the sky. You would have time retrace its steps from noon to morning.

'In the face of labor-saving machinery, of organized production, of the increased efficiency of combination, you would set the economic sun back a whole generation or so to the time when there were no great capitalists, no great machinery, no railroads—a time when a host of little capitalists warred with each other in economic anarchy, and when production was primitive, wasteful, unorganized, and costly. Believe me, Joshua's task was easier, and he had Jehovah to help him. But God has forsaken you small capitalists. The sun of the small capitalists is setting. It will never rise again. Nor is it in your power even to make it stand still. You are perishing, and you are doomed to perish utterly from the face of society.

'This is the fiat of evolution. It is the word of God. Combination is stronger than competition. Primitive man was a puny creature hiding in the crevices of the rocks. He combined and made war upon his carnivorous enemies. They were competitive beasts. Primitive man was a combinative beast, and because of it he rose to primacy over all the animals. And man has been achieving greater and greater combinations ever since. It is combination versus competition, a thousand centuries long struggle, in which competition has always been worsted. Whoso enlists on the side of competition perishes.'

'But the trusts themselves arose out of competition,' Mr. Calvin interrupted.

'Very true,' Ernest answered. 'And the trusts themselves destroyed competition. That, by your own word, is why you are no longer in the dairy business.'

The first laughter of the evening went around the table, and even Mr. Calvin joined in the laugh against himself.

'And now, while we are on the trusts,' Ernest went on, 'let us settle a few things. I shall make certain statements, and if you disagree with them, speak up. Silence will mean agreement. Is it not true that a machine-loom will weave more cloth and weave more cheaply than a hand-loom?' He paused, but nobody spoke up. 'Is it not then highly irrational to break the machine-loom and go back to the clumsy and more costly hand-loom method of weaving?' Heads nodded in acquiescence. 'Is it not true that that known as a trust produces more efficiently and cheaply than can a thousand competing small concerns?' Still no one objected. 'Then is it not irrational to destroy that cheap and efficient combination?'

No one answered for a long time. Then Mr. Kowalt spoke.

'What are we to do, then?' he demanded. 'To destroy the trusts is the only way we can see to escape their domination.'

Ernest was all fire and aliveness on the instant.

'I'll show you another way!' he cried. 'Let us not destroy those wonderful machines that produce efficiently and cheaply. Let us control them. Let us profit by their efficiency and cheapness. Let us run them for ourselves. Let us oust the present owners of the wonderful machines, and let us own the wonderful machines ourselves. That, gentlemen, is socialism, a greater combination than the trusts, a greater economic and social combination than any that has as yet appeared on the planet. It is in line with evolution. We meet combination with greater combination. It is the winning side. Come on over with us socialists and play on the winning side.'

Here arose dissent. There was a shaking of heads, and mutterings arose.

'All right, then, you prefer to be anachronisms,' Ernest laughed. 'You prefer to play atavistic roles. You are doomed to perish as all atavisms perish. Have you ever asked what will happen to you when greater combinations than even the present trusts arise? Have you ever considered where you will stand when the great trusts themselves combine into the combination of combinations—into the social, economic, and political trust?'

He turned abruptly and irrelevantly upon Mr. Calvin.

'Tell me,' Ernest said, 'if this is not true. You are compelled to form a new political party because the old parties are in the hands of the trusts. The chief obstacle to your Grange propaganda is the trusts. Behind every obstacle you encounter, every blow that smites you, every defeat that you receive, is the hand of the trusts. Is this not so? Tell me.'

Mr. Calvin sat in uncomfortable silence.

'Go ahead,' Ernest encouraged.

'It is true,' Mr. Calvin confessed. 'We captured the state legislature of Oregon and put through splendid protective legislation, and it was vetoed by the governor, who was a creature of the trusts. We elected a governor of Colorado, and the legislature refused to permit him to take office. Twice we have passed a national income tax, and each time the supreme court smashed it as unconstitutional. The courts are in the hands of the trusts. We, the people, do not pay our judges sufficiently. But there will come a time—'

'When the combination of the trusts will control all legislation, when the combination of the trusts will itself be the government,' Ernest interrupted.

'Never! never!' were the cries that arose. Everybody was excited and belligerent.

'Tell me,' Ernest demanded, 'what will you do when such a time comes?'

'We will rise in our strength!' Mr. Asmunsen cried, and many voices backed his decision.

'That will be civil war,' Ernest warned them.

'So be it, civil war,' was Mr. Asmunsen's answer, with the cries of all the men at the table behind him. 'We have not forgotten the deeds of our forefathers. For our liberties we are ready to fight and die.'

Ernest smiled.

'Do not forget,' he said, 'that we had tacitly agreed that liberty in your case, gentlemen, means liberty to squeeze profits out of others.'

The table was angry, now, fighting angry; but Ernest controlled the tumult and made himself heard.

'One more question. When you rise in your strength, remember, the reason for your rising will be that the government is in the hands of the trusts. Therefore, against your strength the government will turn the regular army, the navy, the militia, the police—in short, the whole organized war machinery of the United States. Where will your strength be then?'

Dismay sat on their faces, and before they could recover, Ernest struck again.

'Do you remember, not so long ago, when our regular army was only fifty thousand? Year by year it has been increased until to-day it is three hundred thousand.'

Again he struck.

'Nor is that all. While you diligently pursued that favorite phantom of yours, called profits, and moralized about that favorite fetich of yours, called competition, even greater and more direful things have been accomplished by combination. There is the militia.'

'It is our strength!' cried Mr. Kowalt. 'With it we would repel the invasion of the regular army.'

'You would go into the militia yourself,' was Ernest's retort, 'and be sent to Maine, or Florida, or the Philippines, or anywhere else, to drown in blood your own comrades civil-warring for their liberties. While from Kansas, or Wisconsin, or any other state, your own comrades would go into the militia and come here to California to drown in blood your own civil-warring.'

Now they were really shocked, and they sat wordless, until Mr. Owen murmured:

'We would not go into the militia. That would settle it. We would not be so foolish.'

Ernest laughed outright.

'You do not understand the combination that has been effected. You could not help yourself. You would be drafted into the militia.'

'There is such a thing as civil law,' Mr. Owen insisted.

'Not when the government suspends civil law. In that day when you speak of rising in your strength, your strength would be turned against yourself. Into the militia you would go, willy-nilly. Habeas corpus, I heard some one mutter just now. Instead of habeas corpus you would get post mortems. If you refused to go into the militia, or to obey after you were in, you would be tried by drumhead court martial and shot down like dogs. It is the law.'

'It is not the law!' Mr. Calvin asserted positively. 'There is no such law. Young man, you have dreamed all this. Why, you spoke of sending the militia to the Philippines. That is unconstitutional. The Constitution especially states that the militia cannot be sent out of the country.'

'What's the Constitution got to do with it?' Ernest demanded. 'The courts interpret the Constitution, and the courts, as Mr. Asmunsen agreed, are the creatures of the trusts. Besides, it is as I have said, the law. It has been the law for years, for nine years, gentlemen.'

'That we can be drafted into the militia?' Mr. Calvin asked incredulously. 'That they can shoot us by drumhead court martial if we refuse?'

'Yes,' Ernest answered, 'precisely that.'

'How is it that we have never heard of this law?' my father asked, and I could see that it was likewise new to him.

'For two reasons,' Ernest said. 'First, there has been no need to enforce it. If there had, you'd have heard of it soon enough. And secondly, the law was rushed through Congress and the Senate secretly, with practically no discussion. Of course, the newspapers made no mention of it. But we socialists knew about it. We published it in our papers. But you never read our papers.'

'I still insist you are dreaming,' Mr. Calvin said stubbornly. 'The country would never have permitted it.'

'But the country did permit it,' Ernest replied. 'And as for my dreaming—' he put his hand in his pocket and drew out a small pamphlet—'tell me if this looks like dream-stuff.'

He opened it and began to read:

'Section One, be it enacted, and so forth and so forth, that the militia shall consist of every able-bodied male citizen of the respective states, territories, and District of Columbia, who is more than eighteen and less than forty-five years of age.'

'Section Seven, that any officer or enlisted man'—remember Section One, gentlemen, you are all enlisted men—'that any enlisted man of the militia who shall refuse or neglect to present himself to such mustering officer upon being called forth as herein prescribed, shall be subject to trial by court martial, and shall be punished as such court martial shall direct.'

'Section Eight, that courts martial, for the trial of officers or men of the militia, shall be composed of militia officers only.'

'Section Nine, that the militia, when called into the actual service of the United States, shall be subject to the same rules and articles of war as the regular troops of the United States.'

'There you are gentlemen, American citizens, and fellow-militiamen. Nine years ago we socialists thought that law was aimed against labor. But it would seem that it was aimed against you, too. Congressman Wiley, in the brief discussion that was permitted, said that the bill 'provided for a reserve force to take the mob by the throat'—you're the mob, gentlemen—'and protect at all hazards life, liberty, and property.' And in the time to come, when you rise in your strength, remember that you will be rising against the property of the trusts, and the liberty of the trusts, according to the law, to squeeze you. Your teeth are pulled, gentlemen. Your claws are trimmed. In the day you rise in your strength, toothless and clawless, you will be as harmless as any army of clams.'

'I don't believe it!' Kowalt cried. 'There is no such law. It is a canard got up by you socialists.'

'This bill was introduced in the House of Representatives on July 30, 1902,' was the reply. 'It was introduced by Representative Dick of Ohio. It was rushed through. It was passed unanimously by the Senate on January 14, 1903. And just seven days afterward was approved by the President of the United States.'[*]

CHAPTER IX
THE MATHEMATICS OF A DREAM

In the midst of the consternation his revelation had produced, Ernest began again to speak.

'You have said, a dozen of you to-night, that socialism is impossible. You have asserted the impossible, now let me demonstrate the inevitable. Not only is it inevitable that you small capitalists shall pass away, but it is inevitable that the large capitalists, and the trusts also, shall pass away. Remember, the tide of evolution never flows backward. It flows on and on, and it flows from competition to combination, and from little combination to large combination, and from large combination to colossal combination, and it flows on to socialism, which is the most colossal combination of all.

'You tell me that I dream. Very good. I'll give you the mathematics of my dream; and here, in advance, I challenge you to show that my mathematics are wrong. I shall develop the inevitability of the breakdown of the capitalist system, and I shall demonstrate mathematically why it must break down. Here goes, and bear with me if at first I seem irrelevant.

'Let us, first of all, investigate a particular industrial process, and whenever I state something with which you disagree, please interrupt me. Here is a shoe factory. This factory takes leather and makes it into shoes. Here is one hundred dollars' worth of leather. It goes through the factory and comes out in the form of shoes, worth, let us say, two hundred dollars. What has happened? One hundred dollars has been added to the value of the leather. How was it added? Let us see.

'Capital and labor added this value of one hundred dollars. Capital furnished the factory, the machines, and paid all the expenses. Labor furnished labor. By the joint effort of capital and labor one hundred dollars of value was added. Are you all agreed so far?'

Heads nodded around the table in affirmation.

'Labor and capital having produced this one hundred dollars, now proceed to divide it. The statistics of this division are fractional; so let us, for the sake of conven-

---

[*] Everhard was right in the essential particulars, though his date of the introduction of the bill is in error. The bill was introduced on June 30, and not on July 30. The Congressional Record is here in Ardis, and a reference to it shows mention of the bill on the following dates: June 30, December 9, 15, 16, and 17, 1902, and January 7 and 14, 1903. The ignorance evidenced by the business men at the dinner was nothing unusual. Very few people knew of the existence of this law. E. Untermann, a revolutionist, in July, 1903, published a pamphlet at Girard, Kansas, on the 'Militia Bill.' This pamphlet had a small circulation among workingmen; but already had the segregation of classes proceeded so far, that the members of the middle class never heard of the pamphlet at all, and so remained in ignorance of the law.

ience, make them roughly approximate. Capital takes fifty dollars as its share, and labor gets in wages fifty dollars as its share. We will not enter into the squabbling over the division.* No matter how much squabbling takes place, in one percentage or another the division is arranged. And take notice here, that what is true of this particular industrial process is true of all industrial processes. Am I right?'

Again the whole table agreed with Ernest.

'Now, suppose labor, having received its fifty dollars, wanted to buy back shoes. It could only buy back fifty dollars' worth. That's clear, isn't it?

'And now we shift from this particular process to the sum total of all industrial processes in the United States, which includes the leather itself, raw material, transportation, selling, everything. We will say, for the sake of round figures, that the total production of wealth in the United States is one year is four billion dollars. Then labor has received in wages, during the same period, two billion dollars. Four billion dollars has been produced. How much of this can labor buy back? Two billions. There is no discussion of this, I am sure. For that matter, my percentages are mild. Because of a thousand capitalistic devices, labor cannot buy back even half of the total product.

'But to return. We will say labor buys back two billions. Then it stands to reason that labor can consume only two billions. There are still two billions to be accounted for, which labor cannot buy back and consume.'

'Labor does not consume its two billions, even,' Mr. Kowalt spoke up. 'If it did, it would not have any deposits in the savings banks.'

'Labor's deposits in the savings banks are only a sort of reserve fund that is consumed as fast as it accumulates. These deposits are saved for old age, for sickness and accident, and for funeral expenses. The savings bank deposit is simply a piece of the loaf put back on the shelf to be eaten next day. No, labor consumes all of the total product that its wages will buy back.

'Two billions are left to capital. After it has paid its expenses, does it consume the remainder? Does capital consume all of its two billions?'

Ernest stopped and put the question point blank to a number of the men. They shook their heads.

'I don't know,' one of them frankly said.

'Of course you do,' Ernest went on. 'Stop and think a moment. If capital consumed its share, the sum total of capital could not increase. It would remain constant. If you will look at the economic history of the United States, you will see that the sum total of capital has continually increased. Therefore capital does not consume its share. Do you remember when England owned so much of our railroad bonds? As the years went by, we bought back those bonds. What does that mean? That part of capital's unconsumed share bought back the bonds. What is the meaning of the fact that to-day the capitalists of the United States own hundreds and hundreds of millions of dollars of Mexican bonds, Russian bonds, Italian bonds, Grecian bonds? The meaning is that those hundreds and hundreds of millions were part of capital's share which capital did not consume. Furthermore, from the very beginning of the

---

* Everhard here clearly develops the cause of all the labor troubles of that time. In the division of the joint-product, capital wanted all it could get, and labor wanted all it could get. This quarrel over the division was irreconcilable. So long as the system of capitalistic production existed, labor and capital continued to quarrel over the division of the joint-product. It is a ludicrous spectacle to us, but we must not forget that we have seven centuries' advantage over those that lived in that time.

capitalist system, capital has never consumed all of its share.

'And now we come to the point. Four billion dollars of wealth is produced in one year in the United States. Labor buys back and consumes two billions. Capital does not consume the remaining two billions. There is a large balance left over unconsumed. What is done with this balance? What can be done with it? Labor cannot consume any of it, for labor has already spent all its wages. Capital will not consume this balance, because, already, according to its nature, it has consumed all it can. And still remains the balance. What can be done with it? What is done with it?'

'It is sold abroad,' Mr. Kowalt volunteered.

'The very thing,' Ernest agreed. 'Because of this balance arises our need for a foreign market. This is sold abroad. It has to be sold abroad. There is no other way of getting rid of it. And that unconsumed surplus, sold abroad, becomes what we call our favorable balance of trade. Are we all agreed so far?'

'Surely it is a waste of time to elaborate these A B C's of commerce,' Mr. Calvin said tartly. 'We all understand them.'

'And it is by these A B C's I have so carefully elaborated that I shall confound you,' Ernest retorted. 'There's the beauty of it. And I'm going to confound you with them right now. Here goes.

'The United States is a capitalist country that has developed its resources. According to its capitalist system of industry, it has an unconsumed surplus that must be got rid of, and that must be got rid of abroad.[*] What is true of the United States is true of every other capitalist country with developed resources. Every one of such countries has an unconsumed surplus. Don't forget that they have already traded with one another, and that these surpluses yet remain. Labor in all these countries has spent it wages, and cannot buy any of the surpluses. Capital in all these countries has already consumed all it is able according to its nature. And still remain the surpluses. They cannot dispose of these surpluses to one another. How are they going to get rid of them?'

'Sell them to countries with undeveloped resources,' Mr. Kowalt suggested.

'The very thing. You see, my argument is so clear and simple that in your own minds you carry it on for me. And now for the next step. Suppose the United States disposes of its surplus to a country with undeveloped resources like, say, Brazil. Remember this surplus is over and above trade, which articles of trade have been consumed. What, then, does the United States get in return from Brazil?'

'Gold,' said Mr. Kowalt.

'But there is only so much gold, and not much of it, in the world,' Ernest objected.

'Gold in the form of securities and bonds and so forth,' Mr. Kowalt amended.

'Now you've struck it,' Ernest said. 'From Brazil the United States, in return for her surplus, gets bonds and securities. And what does that mean? It means that the United States is coming to own railroads in Brazil, factories, mines, and lands in Brazil.

---

[*] Theodore Roosevelt, President of the United States a few years prior to this time, made the following public declaration: 'A more liberal and extensive reciprocity in the purchase and sale of commodities is necessary, so that the overproduction of the United States can be satisfactorily disposed of to foreign countries.' Of course, this overproduction he mentions was the profits of the capitalist system over and beyond the consuming power of the capitalists. It was at this time that Senator Mark Hanna said: 'The production of wealth in the United States is one-third larger annually than its consumption.' Also a fellow-Senator, Chauncey Depew, said: 'The American people produce annually two billions more wealth than they consume.'

And what is the meaning of that in turn?'

Mr. Kowalt pondered and shook his head.

'I'll tell you,' Ernest continued. 'It means that the resources of Brazil are being developed. And now, the next point. When Brazil, under the capitalist system, has developed her resources, she will herself have an unconsumed surplus. Can she get rid of this surplus to the United States? No, because the United States has herself a surplus. Can the United States do what she previously did—get rid of her surplus to Brazil? No, for Brazil now has a surplus, too.

'What happens? The United States and Brazil must both seek out other countries with undeveloped resources, in order to unload the surpluses on them. But by the very process of unloading the surpluses, the resources of those countries are in turn developed. Soon they have surpluses, and are seeking other countries on which to unload. Now, gentlemen, follow me. The planet is only so large. There are only so many countries in the world. What will happen when every country in the world, down to the smallest and last, with a surplus in its hands, stands confronting every other country with surpluses in their hands?'

He paused and regarded his listeners. The bepuzzlement in their faces was delicious. Also, there was awe in their faces. Out of abstractions Ernest had conjured a vision and made them see it. They were seeing it then, as they sat there, and they were frightened by it.

'We started with A B C, Mr. Calvin,' Ernest said slyly. 'I have now given you the rest of the alphabet. It is very simple. That is the beauty of it. You surely have the answer forthcoming. What, then, when every country in the world has an unconsumed surplus? Where will your capitalist system be then?'

But Mr. Calvin shook a troubled head. He was obviously questing back through Ernest's reasoning in search of an error.

'Let me briefly go over the ground with you again,' Ernest said. 'We began with a particular industrial process, the shoe factory. We found that the division of the joint product that took place there was similar to the division that took place in the sum total of all industrial processes. We found that labor could buy back with its wages only so much of the product, and that capital did not consume all of the remainder of the product. We found that when labor had consumed to the full extent of its wages, and when capital had consumed all it wanted, there was still left an unconsumed surplus. We agreed that this surplus could only be disposed of abroad. We agreed, also, that the effect of unloading this surplus on another country would be to develop the resources of that country, and that in a short time that country would have an unconsumed surplus. We extended this process to all the countries on the planet, till every country was producing every year, and every day, an unconsumed surplus, which it could dispose of to no other country. And now I ask you again, what are we going to do with those surpluses?'

Still no one answered.

'Mr. Calvin?' Ernest queried.

'It beats me,' Mr. Calvin confessed.

'I never dreamed of such a thing,' Mr. Asmunsen said. 'And yet it does seem clear as print.'

It was the first time I had ever heard Karl Marx's[*] doctrine of surplus value

---

[*] Karl Marx—the great intellectual hero of Socialism. A German Jew of the nineteenth

elaborated, and Ernest had done it so simply that I, too, sat puzzled and dumbfounded.

'I'll tell you a way to get rid of the surplus,' Ernest said. 'Throw it into the sea. Throw every year hundreds of millions of dollars' worth of shoes and wheat and clothing and all the commodities of commerce into the sea. Won't that fix it?'

'It will certainly fix it,' Mr. Calvin answered. 'But it is absurd for you to talk that way.'

Ernest was upon him like a flash.

'Is it a bit more absurd than what you advocate, you machine-breaker, returning to the antediluvian ways of your forefathers? What do you propose in order to get rid of the surplus? You would escape the problem of the surplus by not producing any surplus. And how do you propose to avoid producing a surplus? By returning to a primitive method of production, so confused and disorderly and irrational, so wasteful and costly, that it will be impossible to produce a surplus.'

Mr. Calvin swallowed. The point had been driven home. He swallowed again and cleared his throat.

'You are right,' he said. 'I stand convicted. It is absurd. But we've got to do something. It is a case of life and death for us of the middle class. We refuse to perish. We elect to be absurd and to return to the truly crude and wasteful methods of our forefathers. We will put back industry to its pre-trust stage. We will break the machines. And what are you going to do about it?'

'But you can't break the machines,' Ernest replied. 'You cannot make the tide of evolution flow backward. Opposed to you are two great forces, each of which is more powerful than you of the middle class. The large capitalists, the trusts, in short, will not let you turn back. They don't want the machines destroyed. And greater than the trusts, and more powerful, is labor. It will not let you destroy the machines. The ownership of the world, along with the machines, lies between the trusts and labor. That is the battle alignment. Neither side wants the destruction of the machines. But each side wants to possess the machines. In this battle the middle class has no place. The middle class is a pygmy between two giants. Don't you see, you poor perishing middle class, you are caught between the upper and nether millstones, and even now has the grinding begun.

'I have demonstrated to you mathematically the inevitable breakdown of the capitalist system. When every country stands with an unconsumed and unsalable surplus on its hands, the capitalist system will break down under the terrific structure of profits that it itself has reared. And in that day there won't be any destruction of the machines. The struggle then will be for the ownership of the machines. If labor wins, your way will be easy. The United States, and the whole world for that matter, will enter upon a new and tremendous era. Instead of being crushed by the machines, life will be made fairer, and happier, and nobler by them. You of the destroyed middle class, along with labor—there will be nothing but labor then; so you, and all the rest of labor, will participate in the equitable distribution of the products of the wonderful machines. And we, all of us, will make new and more wonderful machines. And there won't be any unconsumed surplus, because there won't be any profits.'

'But suppose the trusts win in this battle over the ownership of the machines and

---

century. A contemporary of John Stuart Mill. It seems incredible to us that whole generations should have elapsed after the enunciation of Marx's economic discoveries, in which time he was sneered at by the world's accepted thinkers and scholars. Because of his discoveries he was banished from his native country, and he died an exile in England.

the world?' Mr. Kowalt asked.

'Then,' Ernest answered, 'you, and labor, and all of us, will be crushed under the iron heel of a despotism as relentless and terrible as any despotism that has blackened the pages of the history of man. That will be a good name for that despotism, the Iron Heel.'[*]

There was a long pause, and every man at the table meditated in ways unwonted and profound.

'But this socialism of yours is a dream,' Mr. Calvin said; and repeated, 'a dream.'

'I'll show you something that isn't a dream, then,' Ernest answered. 'And that something I shall call the Oligarchy. You call it the Plutocracy. We both mean the same thing, the large capitalists or the trusts. Let us see where the power lies today. And in order to do so, let us apportion society into its class divisions.

'There are three big classes in society. First comes the Plutocracy, which is composed of wealthy bankers, railway magnates, corporation directors, and trust magnates. Second, is the middle class, your class, gentlemen, which is composed of farmers, merchants, small manufacturers, and professional men. And third and last comes my class, the proletariat, which is composed of the wage-workers.[**]

'You cannot but grant that the ownership of wealth constitutes essential power in the United States to-day. How is this wealth owned by these three classes? Here are the figures. The Plutocracy owns sixty-seven billions of wealth. Of the total number of persons engaged in occupations in the United States, only nine-tenths of one per cent are from the Plutocracy, yet the Plutocracy owns seventy per cent of the total wealth. The middle class owns twenty-four billions. Twenty-nine per cent of those in occupations are from the middle class, and they own twenty-five per cent of the total wealth. Remains the proletariat. It owns four billions. Of all persons in occupations, seventy per cent come from the proletariat; and the proletariat owns four per cent of the total wealth. Where does the power lie, gentlemen?'

'From your own figures, we of the middle class are more powerful than labor,' Mr. Asmunsen remarked.

'Calling us weak does not make you stronger in the face of the strength of the Plutocracy,' Ernest retorted. 'And furthermore, I'm not done with you. There is a greater strength than wealth, and it is greater because it cannot be taken away. Our strength, the strength of the proletariat, is in our muscles, in our hands to cast ballots, in our fingers to pull triggers. This strength we cannot be stripped of. It is the primitive strength, it is the strength that is to life germane, it is the strength that is stronger than wealth, and that wealth cannot take away.

'But your strength is detachable. It can be taken away from you. Even now the Plutocracy is taking it away from you. In the end it will take it all away from you. And then you will cease to be the middle class. You will descend to us. You will become proletarians. And the beauty of it is that you will then add to our strength. We will hail you brothers, and we will fight shoulder to shoulder in the cause of humanity.

'You see, labor has nothing concrete of which to be despoiled. Its share of the

---

[*] The earliest known use of that name to designate the Oligarchy.

[**] This division of society made by Everhard is in accordance with that made by Lucien Sanial, one of the statistical authorities of that time. His calculation of the membership of these divisions by occupation, from the United States Census of 1900, is as follows: Plutocratic class, 250,251; Middle class, 8,429,845; and Proletariat class, 20,393,137.

wealth of the country consists of clothes and household furniture, with here and there, in very rare cases, an unencumbered home. But you have the concrete wealth, twenty-four billions of it, and the Plutocracy will take it away from you. Of course, there is the large likelihood that the proletariat will take it away first. Don't you see your position, gentlemen? The middle class is a wobbly little lamb between a lion and a tiger. If one doesn't get you, the other will. And if the Plutocracy gets you first, why it's only a matter of time when the Proletariat gets the Plutocracy.

'Even your present wealth is not a true measure of your power. The strength of your wealth at this moment is only an empty shell. That is why you are crying out your feeble little battle-cry, 'Return to the ways of our fathers.' You are aware of your impotency. You know that your strength is an empty shell. And I'll show you the emptiness of it.

'What power have the farmers? Over fifty per cent are thralls by virtue of the fact that they are merely tenants or are mortgaged. And all of them are thralls by virtue of the fact that the trusts already own or control (which is the same thing only better)— own and control all the means of marketing the crops, such as cold storage, railroads, elevators, and steamship lines. And, furthermore, the trusts control the markets. In all this the farmers are without power. As regards their political and governmental power, I'll take that up later, along with the political and governmental power of the whole middle class.

'Day by day the trusts squeeze out the farmers as they squeezed out Mr. Calvin and the rest of the dairymen. And day by day are the merchants squeezed out in the same way. Do you remember how, in six months, the Tobacco Trust squeezed out over four hundred cigar stores in New York City alone? Where are the old-time owners of the coal fields? You know today, without my telling you, that the Railroad Trust owns or controls the entire anthracite and bituminous coal fields. Doesn't the Standard Oil Trust* own a score of the ocean lines? And does it not also control copper, to say nothing of running a smelter trust as a little side enterprise? There are ten thousand cities in the United States to-night lighted by the companies owned or controlled by Standard Oil, and in as many cities all the electric transportation,—urban, suburban, and interurban,—is in the hands of Standard Oil. The small capitalists who were in these thousands of enterprises are gone. You know that. It's the same way that you are going.

'The small manufacturer is like the farmer; and small manufacturers and farmers to-day are reduced, to all intents and purposes, to feudal tenure. For that matter, the professional men and the artists are at this present moment villeins in everything but name, while the politicians are henchmen. Why do you, Mr. Calvin, work all your nights and days to organize the farmers, along with the rest of the middle class, into a new political party? Because the politicians of the old parties will have nothing to do with your atavistic ideas; and with your atavistic ideas, they will have nothing to do because they are what I said they are, henchmen, retainers of the Plutocracy.

'I spoke of the professional men and the artists as villeins. What else are they? One and all, the professors, the preachers, and the editors, hold their jobs by serving the Plutocracy, and their service consists of propagating only such ideas as are either harmless to or commendatory of the Plutocracy. Whenever they propagate ideas that menace the Plutocracy, they lose their jobs, in which case, if they have not provided

---

* Standard Oil and Rockefeller—see upcoming footnote: 'Rockefeller began as a member.'

for the rainy day, they descend into the proletariat and either perish or become working-class agitators. And don't forget that it is the press, the pulpit, and the university that mould public opinion, set the thought-pace of the nation. As for the artists, they merely pander to the little less than ignoble tastes of the Plutocracy.

'But after all, wealth in itself is not the real power; it is the means to power, and power is governmental. Who controls the government to-day? The proletariat with its twenty millions engaged in occupations? Even you laugh at the idea. Does the middle class, with its eight million occupied members? No more than the proletariat. Who, then, controls the government? The Plutocracy, with its paltry quarter of a million of occupied members. But this quarter of a million does not control the government, though it renders yeoman service. It is the brain of the Plutocracy that controls the government, and this brain consists of seven* small and powerful groups of men. And do not forget that these groups are working to-day practically in unison.

'Let me point out the power of but one of them, the railroad group. It employs forty thousand lawyers to defeat the people in the courts. It issues countless thousands of free passes to judges, bankers, editors, ministers, university men, members of state legislatures, and of Congress. It maintains luxurious lobbies** at every state capital, and at the national capital; and in all the cities and towns of the land it employs an immense army of pettifoggers and small politicians whose business is to attend primaries, pack conventions, get on juries, bribe judges, and in every way to work for its interests.***

'Gentlemen, I have merely sketched the power of one of the seven groups that constitute the brain of the Plutocracy.**** Your twenty-four billions of wealth does not

---

* Even as late as 1907, it was considered that eleven groups dominated the country, but this number was reduced by the amalgamation of the five railroad groups into a supreme combination of all the railroads. These five groups so amalgamated, along with their financial and political allies, were (1) James J. Hill with his control of the Northwest; (2) the Pennsylvania railway group, Schiff financial manager, with big banking firms of Philadelphia and New York; (3) Harriman, with Frick for counsel and Odell as political lieutenant, controlling the central continental, Southwestern and Southern Pacific Coast lines of transportation; (4) the Gould family railway interests; and (5) Moore, Reid, and Leeds, known as the 'Rock Island crowd.' These strong oligarchs arose out of the conflict of competition and travelled the inevitable road toward combination.
** Lobby—a peculiar institution for bribing, bulldozing, and corrupting the legislators who were supposed to represent the people's interests.
*** A decade before this speech of Everhard's, the New York Board of Trade issued a report from which the following is quoted: 'The railroads control absolutely the legislatures of a majority of the states of the Union; they make and unmake United States Senators, congressmen, and governors, and are practically dictators of the governmental policy of the United States.'
**** Rockefeller began as a member of the proletariat, and through thrift and cunning succeeded in developing the first perfect trust, namely that known as Standard Oil. We cannot forbear giving the following remarkable page from the history of the times, to show how the need for reinvestment of the Standard Oil surplus crushed out small capitalists and hastened the breakdown of the capitalist system. David Graham Phillips was a radical writer of the period, and the quotation, by him, is taken from a copy of the Saturday Evening Post, dated October 4, 1902 A.D. This is the only copy of this publication that has come down to us, and yet, from its appearance and content, we cannot but conclude that it was one of the popular periodicals with a large circulation. The quotation here follows: 'About ten years ago Rockefeller's income was given as thirty millions by an excellent authority. He had reached the

limit of profitable investment of profits in the oil industry. Here, then, were these enormous sums in cash pouring in—more than $2,000,000 a month for John Davison Rockefeller alone. The problem of reinvestment became more serious. It became a nightmare. The oil income was swelling, swelling, and the number of sound investments limited, even more limited than it is now. It was through no special eagerness for more gains that the Rockefellers began to branch out from oil into other things. They were forced, swept on by this inrolling tide of wealth which their monopoly magnet irresistibly attracted. They developed a staff of investment seekers and investigators. It is said that the chief of this staff has a salary of $125,000 a year. 'The first conspicuous excursion and incursion of the Rockefellers was into the railway field. By 1895 they controlled one-fifth of the railway mileage of the country. What do they own or, through dominant ownership, control to-day? They are powerful in all the great railways of New York, north, east, and west, except one, where their share is only a few millions. They are in most of the great railways radiating from Chicago. They dominate in several of the systems that extend to the Pacific. It is their votes that make Mr. Morgan so potent, though, it may be added, they need his brains more than he needs their votes— at present, and the combination of the two constitutes in large measure the 'community of interest.' 'But railways could not alone absorb rapidly enough those mighty floods of gold. Presently John D. Rockefeller's $2,500,000 a month had increased to four, to five, to six millions a month, to $75,000,000 a year. Illuminating oil was becoming all profit. The reinvestments of income were adding their mite of many annual millions. 'The Rockefellers went into gas and electricity when those industries had developed to the safe investment stage. And now a large part of the American people must begin to enrich the Rockefellers as soon as the sun goes down, no matter what form of illuminant they use. They went into farm mortgages. It is said that when prosperity a few years ago enabled the farmers to rid themselves of their mortgages, John D. Rockefeller was moved almost to tears; eight millions which he had thought taken care of for years to come at a good interest were suddenly dumped upon his doorstep and there set up a-squawking for a new home. This unexpected addition to his worriments in finding places for the progeny of his petroleum and their progeny and their progeny's progeny was too much for the equanimity of a man without a digestion. . . . 'The Rockefellers went into mines—iron and coal and copper and lead; into other industrial companies; into street railways, into national, state, and municipal bonds; into steamships and steamboats and telegraphy; into real estate, into skyscrapers and residences and hotels and business blocks; into life insurance, into banking. There was soon literally no field of industry where their millions were not at work. . . . 'The Rockefeller bank—the National City Bank—is by itself far and away the biggest bank in the United States. It is exceeded in the world only by the Bank of England and the Bank of France. The deposits average more than one hundred millions a day; and it dominates the call loan market on Wall Street and the stock market. But it is not alone; it is the head of the Rockefeller chain of banks, which includes fourteen banks and trust companies in New York City, and banks of great strength and influence in every large money center in the country. 'John D. Rockefeller owns Standard Oil stock worth between four and five hundred millions at the market quotations. He has a hundred millions in the steel trust, almost as much in a single western railway system, half as much in a second, and so on and on and on until the mind wearies of the cataloguing. His income last year was about $100,000,000— it is doubtful if the incomes of all the Rothschilds together make a greater sum. And it is going up by leaps and bounds.'

Little discussion took place after this, and the dinner soon broke up. All were quiet and subdued, and leave-taking was done with low voices. It seemed almost that they were scared by the vision of the times they had seen. 'The situation is, indeed, serious,' Mr. Calvin said to Ernest. 'I have little quarrel with the way you have depicted it. Only I disagree with you about the doom of the middle class. We shall survive, and we shall overthrow the trusts.' 'And return to the ways of your fathers,' Ernest finished for him. 'Even so,' Mr. Calvin answered gravely. 'I know it's a sort of machine-breaking, and that it is absurd. But then life seems absurd to-day, what of the machinations of the Plutocracy. And at any rate, our sort of machine-breaking is

give you twenty-five cents' worth of governmental power. It is an empty shell, and soon even the empty shell will be taken away from you. The Plutocracy has all power in its hands to-day. It to-day makes the laws, for it owns the Senate, Congress, the courts, and the state legislatures. And not only that. Behind law must be force to execute the law. To-day the Plutocracy makes the law, and to enforce the law it has at its beck and call the, police, the army, the navy, and, lastly, the militia, which is you, and me, and all of us.'

CHAPTER X
THE VORTEX

Following like thunder claps upon the Business Men's dinner, occurred event after event of terrifying moment; and I, little I, who had lived so placidly all my days in the quiet university town, found myself and my personal affairs drawn into the vortex of the great world-affairs. Whether it was my love for Ernest, or the clear sight he had given me of the society in which I lived, that made me a revolutionist, I know not; but a revolutionist I became, and I was plunged into a whirl of happenings that would have been inconceivable three short months before.

The crisis in my own fortunes came simultaneously with great crises in society. First of all, father was discharged from the university. Oh, he was not technically discharged. His resignation was demanded, that was all. This, in itself, did not amount to much. Father, in fact, was delighted. He was especially delighted because his discharge had been precipitated by the publication of his book, 'Economics and Education.' It clinched his argument, he contended. What better evidence could be advanced to prove that education was dominated by the capitalist class?

But this proof never got anywhere. Nobody knew he had been forced to resign from the university. He was so eminent a scientist that such an announcement, coupled with the reason for his enforced resignation, would have created somewhat of a furor all over the world. The newspapers showered him with praise and honor, and commended him for having given up the drudgery of the lecture room in order to devote his whole time to scientific research.

At first father laughed. Then he became angry—tonic angry. Then came the suppression of his book. This suppression was performed secretly, so secretly that at first we could not comprehend. The publication of the book had immediately caused a bit of excitement in the country. Father had been politely abused in the capitalist press, the tone of the abuse being to the effect that it was a pity so great a scientist should leave his field and invade the realm of sociology, about which he knew nothing and wherein he had promptly become lost. This lasted for a week, while father chuckled and said the book had touched a sore spot on capitalism. And then, abruptly, the newspapers and the critical magazines ceased saying anything about the book at all. Also, and with equal suddenness, the book disappeared from the market. Not a copy was obtainable from any bookseller. Father wrote to the publishers and was informed

---

at least practical and possible, which your dream is not. Your socialistic dream is . . . well, a dream. We cannot follow you.' 'I only wish you fellows knew a little something about evolution and sociology,' Ernest said wistfully, as they shook hands. 'We would be saved so much trouble if you did.'

that the plates had been accidentally injured. An unsatisfactory correspondence followed. Driven finally to an unequivocal stand, the publishers stated that they could not see their way to putting the book into type again, but that they were willing to relinquish their rights in it.

'And you won't find another publishing house in the country to touch it,' Ernest said. 'And if I were you, I'd hunt cover right now. You've merely got a foretaste of the Iron Heel.'

But father was nothing if not a scientist. He never believed in jumping to conclusions. A laboratory experiment was no experiment if it were not carried through in all its details. So he patiently went the round of the publishing houses. They gave a multitude of excuses, but not one house would consider the book.

When father became convinced that the book had actually been suppressed, he tried to get the fact into the newspapers; but his communications were ignored. At a political meeting of the socialists, where many reporters were present, father saw his chance. He arose and related the history of the suppression of the book. He laughed next day when he read the newspapers, and then he grew angry to a degree that eliminated all tonic qualities. The papers made no mention of the book, but they misreported him beautifully. They twisted his words and phrases away from the context, and turned his subdued and controlled remarks into a howling anarchistic speech. It was done artfully. One instance, in particular, I remember. He had used the phrase 'social revolution.' The reporter merely dropped out 'social.' This was sent out all over the country in an Associated Press despatch, and from all over the country arose a cry of alarm. Father was branded as a nihilist and an anarchist, and in one cartoon that was copied widely he was portrayed waving a red flag at the head of a mob of long-haired, wild-eyed men who bore in their hands torches, knives, and dynamite bombs.

He was assailed terribly in the press, in long and abusive editorials, for his anarchy, and hints were made of mental breakdown on his part. This behavior, on the part of the capitalist press, was nothing new, Ernest told us. It was the custom, he said, to send reporters to all the socialist meetings for the express purpose of misreporting and distorting what was said, in order to frighten the middle class away from any possible affiliation with the proletariat. And repeatedly Ernest warned father to cease fighting and to take to cover.

The socialist press of the country took up the fight, however, and throughout the reading portion of the working class it was known that the book had been suppressed. But this knowledge stopped with the working class. Next, the 'Appeal to Reason,' a big socialist publishing house, arranged with father to bring out the book. Father was jubilant, but Ernest was alarmed.

'I tell you we are on the verge of the unknown,' he insisted. 'Big things are happening secretly all around us. We can feel them. We do not know what they are, but they are there. The whole fabric of society is a-tremble with them. Don't ask me. I don't know myself. But out of this flux of society something is about to crystallize. It is crystallizing now. The suppression of the book is a precipitation. How many books have been suppressed? We haven't the least idea. We are in the dark. We have no way of learning. Watch out next for the suppression of the socialist press and socialist publishing houses. I'm afraid it's coming. We are going to be throttled.'

Ernest had his hand on the pulse of events even more closely than the rest of the socialists, and within two days the first blow was struck. The Appeal to Reason was a weekly, and its regular circulation amongst the proletariat was seven hundred and fifty thousand. Also, it very frequently got out special editions of from two to five millions. These great editions were paid for and distributed by the small army of voluntary workers who had marshalled around the Appeal. The first blow was aimed at these special editions, and it was a crushing one. By an arbitrary ruling of the Post Office, these editions were decided to be not the regular circulation of the paper, and for that reason were denied admission to the mails.

A week later the Post Office Department ruled that the paper was seditious, and barred it entirely from the mails. This was a fearful blow to the socialist propaganda. The Appeal was desperate. It devised a plan of reaching its subscribers through the express companies, but they declined to handle it. This was the end of the Appeal. But not quite. It prepared to go on with its book publishing. Twenty thousand copies of father's book were in the bindery, and the presses were turning off more. And then, without warning, a mob arose one night, and, under a waving American flag, singing patriotic songs, set fire to the great plant of the Appeal and totally destroyed it.

Now Girard, Kansas, was a quiet, peaceable town. There had never been any labor troubles there. The Appeal paid union wages; and, in fact, was the backbone of the town, giving employment to hundreds of men and women. It was not the citizens of Girard that composed the mob. This mob had risen up out of the earth apparently, and to all intents and purposes, its work done, it had gone back into the earth. Ernest saw in the affair the most sinister import.

'The Black Hundreds* are being organized in the United States,' he said. 'This is the beginning. There will be more of it. The Iron Heel is getting bold.'

And so perished father's book. We were to see much of the Black Hundreds as the days went by. Week by week more of the socialist papers were barred from the mails, and in a number of instances the Black Hundreds destroyed the socialist presses. Of course, the newspapers of the land lived up to the reactionary policy of the ruling class, and the destroyed socialist press was misrepresented and vilified, while the Black Hundreds were represented as true patriots and saviours of society. So convincing was all this misrepresentation that even sincere ministers in the pulpit praised the Black Hundreds while regretting the necessity of violence.

History was making fast. The fall elections were soon to occur, and Ernest was nominated by the socialist party to run for Congress. His chance for election was most favorable. The street-car strike in San Francisco had been broken. And following upon it the teamsters' strike had been broken. These two defeats had been very disastrous to organized labor. The whole Water Front Federation, along with its allies in the structural trades, had backed up the teamsters, and all had smashed down ingloriously. It had been a bloody strike. The police had broken countless heads with their riot clubs; and the death list had been augmented by the turning loose of a machine-gun on the strikers from the barns of the Marsden Special Delivery Company.

In consequence, the men were sullen and vindictive. They wanted blood, and revenge. Beaten on their chosen field, they were ripe to seek revenge by means of political action. They still maintained their labor organization, and this gave them

---

* The Black Hundreds were reactionary mobs organized by the perishing Autocracy in the Russian Revolution. These reactionary groups attacked the revolutionary groups, and also, at needed moments, rioted and destroyed property so as to afford the Autocracy the pretext of calling out the Cossacks.

strength in the political struggle that was on. Ernest's chance for election grew stronger and stronger. Day by day unions and more unions voted their support to the socialists, until even Ernest laughed when the Undertakers' Assistants and the Chicken Pickers fell into line. Labor became mulish. While it packed the socialist meetings with mad enthusiasm, it was impervious to the wiles of the old-party politicians. The old-party orators were usually greeted with empty halls, though occasionally they encountered full halls where they were so roughly handled that more than once it was necessary to call out the police reserves.

History was making fast. The air was vibrant with things happening and impending. The country was on the verge of hard times,* caused by a series of prosperous years wherein the difficulty of disposing abroad of the unconsumed surplus had become increasingly difficult. Industries were working short time; many great factories were standing idle against the time when the surplus should be gone; and wages were being cut right and left.

Also, the great machinist strike had been broken. Two hundred thousand machinists, along with their five hundred thousand allies in the metalworking trades, had been defeated in as bloody a strike as had ever marred the United States. Pitched battles had been fought with the small armies of armed strike-breakers** put in the field by the employers' associations; the Black Hundreds, appearing in scores of wide-scattered places, had destroyed property; and, in consequence, a hundred thousand regular soldiers of the United States has been called out to put a frightful end to the whole affair. A number of the labor leaders had been executed; many others had been sentenced to prison, while thousands of the rank and file of the strikers had been herded into bull-pens*** and abominably treated by the soldiers.

The years of prosperity were now to be paid for. All markets were glutted; all markets were falling; and amidst the general crumble of prices the price of labor crumbled fastest of all. The land was convulsed with industrial dissensions. Labor was striking here, there, and everywhere; and where it was not striking, it was being turned out by the capitalists. The papers were filled with tales of violence and blood. And through it all the Black Hundreds played their part. Riot, arson, and wanton destruction of property was their function, and well they performed it. The whole regular army was in the field, called there by the actions of the Black Hundreds.**** All

---

* Under the capitalist regime these periods of hard times were as inevitable as they were absurd. Prosperity always brought calamity. This, of course, was due to the excess of unconsumed profits that was piled up.

** Strike-breakers—these were, in purpose and practice and everything except name, the private soldiers of the capitalists. They were thoroughly organized and well armed, and they were held in readiness to be hurled in special trains to any part of the country where labor went on strike or was locked out by the employers. Only those curious times could have given rise to the amazing spectacle of one, Farley, a notorious commander of strike-breakers, who, in 1906, swept across the United States in special trains from New York to San Francisco with an army of twenty-five hundred men, fully armed and equipped, to break a strike of the San Francisco street-car men. Such an act was in direct violation of the laws of the land. The fact that this act, and thousands of similar acts, went unpunished, goes to show how completely the judiciary was the creature of the Plutocracy.

*** Bull-pen—in a miners' strike in Idaho, in the latter part of the nineteenth century, it happened that many of the strikers were confined in a bull-pen by the troops. The practice and the name continued in the twentieth century.

**** The name only, and not the idea, was imported from Russia. The Black Hundreds were

cities and towns were like armed camps, and laborers were shot down like dogs. Out of the vast army of the unemployed the strike-breakers were recruited; and when the strike-breakers were worsted by the labor unions, the troops always appeared and crushed the unions. Then there was the militia. As yet, it was not necessary to have recourse to the secret militia law. Only the regularly organized militia was out, and it was out everywhere. And in this time of terror, the regular army was increased an additional hundred thousand by the government.

Never had labor received such an all-around beating. The great captains of industry, the oligarchs, had for the first time thrown their full weight into the breach the struggling employers' associations had made. These associations were practically middle-class affairs, and now, compelled by hard times and crashing markets, and aided by the great captains of industry, they gave organized labor an awful and decisive defeat. It was an all-powerful alliance, but it was an alliance of the lion and the lamb, as the middle class was soon to learn.

Labor was bloody and sullen, but crushed. Yet its defeat did not put an end to the hard times. The banks, themselves constituting one of the most important forces of the Oligarchy, continued to call in credits. The Wall Street[*] group turned the stock market into a maelstrom where the values of all the land crumbled away almost to nothingness. And out of all the rack and ruin rose the form of the nascent Oligarchy, imperturbable, indifferent, and sure. Its serenity and certitude was terrifying. Not only did it use its own vast power, but it used all the power of the United States Treasury to carry out its plans.

The captains of industry had turned upon the middle class. The employers' associations, that had helped the captains of industry to tear and rend labor, were now torn and rent by their quondam allies. Amidst the crashing of the middle men, the small business men and manufacturers, the trusts stood firm. Nay, the trusts did more than stand firm. They were active. They sowed wind, and wind, and ever more wind; for they alone knew how to reap the whirlwind and make a profit out of it. And such profits! Colossal profits! Strong enough themselves to weather the storm that was largely their own brewing, they turned loose and plundered the wrecks that floated about them. Values were pitifully and inconceivably shrunken, and the trusts added hugely to their holdings, even extending their enterprises into many new fields—and always at the expense of the middle class.

Thus the summer of 1912 witnessed the virtual death-thrust to the middle class. Even Ernest was astounded at the quickness with which it had been done. He shook

---

a development out of the secret agents of the capitalists, and their use arose in the labor struggles of the nineteenth century. There is no discussion of this. No less an authority of the times than Carroll D. Wright, United States Commissioner of Labor, is responsible for the statement. From his book, entitled 'The Battles of Labor,' is quoted the declaration that 'in some of the great historic strikes the employers themselves have instigated acts of violence;' that manufacturers have deliberately provoked strikes in order to get rid of surplus stock; and that freight cars have been burned by employers' agents during railroad strikes in order to increase disorder. It was out of these secret agents of the employers that the Black Hundreds arose; and it was they, in turn, that later became that terrible weapon of the Oligarchy, the agents- provocateurs.

* Wall Street—so named from a street in ancient New York, where was situated the stock exchange, and where the irrational organization of society permitted underhanded manipulation of all the industries of the country.

his head ominously and looked forward without hope to the fall elections.

'It's no use,' he said. 'We are beaten. The Iron Heel is here. I had hoped for a peaceable victory at the ballot-box. I was wrong. Wickson was right. We shall be robbed of our few remaining liberties; the Iron Heel will walk upon our faces; nothing remains but a bloody revolution of the working class. Of course we will win, but I shudder to think of it.'

And from then on Ernest pinned his faith in revolution. In this he was in advance of his party. His fellow-socialists could not agree with him. They still insisted that victory could be gained through the elections. It was not that they were stunned. They were too cool-headed and courageous for that. They were merely incredulous, that was all. Ernest could not get them seriously to fear the coming of the Oligarchy. They were stirred by him, but they were too sure of their own strength. There was no room in their theoretical social evolution for an oligarchy, therefore the Oligarchy could not be.

'We'll send you to Congress and it will be all right,' they told him at one of our secret meetings.

'And when they take me out of Congress,' Ernest replied coldly, 'and put me against a wall, and blow my brains out—what then?'

'Then we'll rise in our might,' a dozen voices answered at once.

'Then you'll welter in your gore,' was his retort. 'I've heard that song sung by the middle class, and where is it now in its might?'

CHAPTER XI
THE GREAT ADVENTURE

Mr. Wickson did not send for father. They met by chance on the ferry-boat to San Francisco, so that the warning he gave father was not premeditated. Had they not met accidentally, there would not have been any warning. Not that the outcome would have been different, however. Father came of stout old Mayflower* stock, and the blood was imperative in him.

'Ernest was right,' he told me, as soon as he had returned home. 'Ernest is a very remarkable young man, and I'd rather see you his wife than the wife of Rockefeller himself or the King of England.'

'What's the matter?' I asked in alarm.

'The Oligarchy is about to tread upon our faces—yours and mine. Wickson as much as told me so. He was very kind—for an oligarch. He offered to reinstate me in the university. What do you think of that? He, Wickson, a sordid money-grabber, has the power to determine whether I shall or shall not teach in the university of the state. But he offered me even better than that—offered to make me president of some great college of physical sciences that is being planned—the Oligarchy must get rid of its surplus somehow, you see.

'Do you remember what I told that socialist lover of your daughter's?' he said. 'I told him that we would walk upon the faces of the working class. And so we shall. As

---

* One of the first ships that carried colonies to America, after the discovery of the New World. Descendants of these original colonists were for a while inordinately proud of their genealogy; but in time the blood became so widely diffused that it ran in the veins practically of all Americans.

for you, I have for you a deep respect as a scientist; but if you throw your fortunes in with the working class—well, watch out for your face, that is all.' And then he turned and left me.'

'It means we'll have to marry earlier than you planned,' was Ernest's comment when we told him.

I could not follow his reasoning, but I was soon to learn it. It was at this time that the quarterly dividend of the Sierra Mills was paid—or, rather, should have been paid, for father did not receive his. After waiting several days, father wrote to the secretary. Promptly came the reply that there was no record on the books of father's owning any stock, and a polite request for more explicit information.

'I'll make it explicit enough, confound him,' father declared, and departed for the bank to get the stock in question from his safe-deposit box.

'Ernest is a very remarkable man,' he said when he got back and while I was helping him off with his overcoat. 'I repeat, my daughter, that young man of yours is a very remarkable young man.'

I had learned, whenever he praised Ernest in such fashion, to expect disaster.

'They have already walked upon my face,' father explained. 'There was no stock. The box was empty. You and Ernest will have to get married pretty quickly.'

Father insisted on laboratory methods. He brought the Sierra Mills into court, but he could not bring the books of the Sierra Mills into court. He did not control the courts, and the Sierra Mills did. That explained it all. He was thoroughly beaten by the law, and the bare-faced robbery held good.

It is almost laughable now, when I look back on it, the way father was beaten. He met Wickson accidentally on the street in San Francisco, and he told Wickson that he was a damned scoundrel. And then father was arrested for attempted assault, fined in the police court, and bound over to keep the peace. It was all so ridiculous that when he got home he had to laugh himself. But what a furor was raised in the local papers! There was grave talk about the bacillus of violence that infected all men who embraced socialism; and father, with his long and peaceful life, was instanced as a shining example of how the bacillus of violence worked. Also, it was asserted by more than one paper that father's mind had weakened under the strain of scientific study, and confinement in a state asylum for the insane was suggested. Nor was this merely talk. It was an imminent peril. But father was wise enough to see it. He had the Bishop's experience to lesson from, and he lessoned well. He kept quiet no matter what injustice was perpetrated on him, and really, I think, surprised his enemies.

There was the matter of the house—our home. A mortgage was foreclosed on it, and we had to give up possession. Of course there wasn't any mortgage, and never had been any mortgage. The ground had been bought outright, and the house had been paid for when it was built. And house and lot had always been free and unencumbered. Nevertheless there was the mortgage, properly and legally drawn up and signed, with a record of the payments of interest through a number of years. Father made no outcry. As he had been robbed of his money, so was he now robbed of his home. And he had no recourse. The machinery of society was in the hands of those who were bent on breaking him. He was a philosopher at heart, and he was no longer even angry.

'I am doomed to be broken,' he said to me; 'but that is no reason that I should not try to be shattered as little as possible. These old bones of mine are fragile, and I've learned my lesson. God knows I don't want to spend my last days in an insane asylum.'

Which reminds me of Bishop Morehouse, whom I have neglected for many pages. But first let me tell of my marriage. In the play of events, my marriage sinks into insignificance, I know, so I shall barely mention it.

'Now we shall become real proletarians,' father said, when we were driven from our home. 'I have often envied that young man of yours for his actual knowledge of the proletariat. Now I shall see and learn for myself.'

Father must have had strong in him the blood of adventure. He looked upon our catastrophe in the light of an adventure. No anger nor bitterness possessed him. He was too philosophic and simple to be vindictive, and he lived too much in the world of mind to miss the creature comforts we were giving up. So it was, when we moved to San Francisco into four wretched rooms in the slum south of Market Street, that he embarked upon the adventure with the joy and enthusiasm of a child—combined with the clear sight and mental grasp of an extraordinary intellect. He really never crystallized mentally. He had no false sense of values. Conventional or habitual values meant nothing to him. The only values he recognized were mathematical and scientific facts. My father was a great man. He had the mind and the soul that only great men have. In ways he was even greater than Ernest, than whom I have known none greater.

Even I found some relief in our change of living. If nothing else, I was escaping from the organized ostracism that had been our increasing portion in the university town ever since the enmity of the nascent Oligarchy had been incurred. And the change was to me likewise adventure, and the greatest of all, for it was love-adventure. The change in our fortunes had hastened my marriage, and it was as a wife that I came to live in the four rooms on Pell Street, in the San Francisco slum.

And this out of all remains: I made Ernest happy. I came into his stormy life, not as a new perturbing force, but as one that made toward peace and repose. I gave him rest. It was the guerdon of my love for him. It was the one infallible token that I had not failed. To bring forgetfulness, or the light of gladness, into those poor tired eyes of his—what greater joy could have blessed me than that?

Those dear tired eyes. He toiled as few men ever toiled, and all his lifetime he toiled for others. That was the measure of his manhood. He was a humanist and a lover. And he, with his incarnate spirit of battle, his gladiator body and his eagle spirit—he was as gentle and tender to me as a poet. He was a poet. A singer in deeds. And all his life he sang the song of man. And he did it out of sheer love of man, and for man he gave his life and was crucified.

And all this he did with no hope of future reward. In his conception of things there was no future life. He, who fairly burnt with immortality, denied himself immortality—such was the paradox of him. He, so warm in spirit, was dominated by that cold and forbidding philosophy, materialistic monism. I used to refute him by telling him that I measured his immortality by the wings of his soul, and that I should have to live endless aeons in order to achieve the full measurement. Whereat he would laugh, and his arms would leap out to me, and he would call me his sweet metaphysician; and the tiredness would pass out of his eyes, and into them would flood the happy love-light that was in itself a new and sufficient advertisement of his immortality.

Also, he used to call me his dualist, and he would explain how Kant, by means of pure reason, had abolished reason, in order to worship God. And he drew the parallel and included me guilty of a similar act. And when I pleaded guilty, but defended the act as highly rational, he but pressed me closer and laughed as only one of God's own lovers could laugh. I was wont to deny that heredity and environment could explain his own originality and genius, any more than could the cold groping finger of science catch and analyze and classify that elusive essence that lurked in the constitution of life itself.

I held that space was an apparition of God, and that soul was a projection of the character of God; and when he called me his sweet metaphysician, I called him my immortal materialist. And so we loved and were happy; and I forgave him his materialism because of his tremendous work in the world, performed without thought of soul-gain thereby, and because of his so exceeding modesty of spirit that prevented him from having pride and regal consciousness of himself and his soul.

But he had pride. How could he have been an eagle and not have pride? His contention was that it was finer for a finite mortal speck of life to feel Godlike, than for a god to feel godlike; and so it was that he exalted what he deemed his mortality. He was fond of quoting a fragment from a certain poem. He had never seen the whole poem, and he had tried vainly to learn its authorship. I here give the fragment, not alone because he loved it, but because it epitomized the paradox that he was in the spirit of him, and his conception of his spirit. For how can a man, with thrilling, and burning, and exaltation, recite the following and still be mere mortal earth, a bit of fugitive force, an evanescent form? Here it is:

'Joy upon joy and gain upon gain
Are the destined rights of my birth,
And I shout the praise of my endless days
To the echoing edge of the earth.
Though I suffer all deaths that a man can die
To the uttermost end of time,
I have deep-drained this, my cup of bliss,
In every age and clime—
'The froth of Pride, the tang of Power,
The sweet of Womanhood!
I drain the lees upon my knees,
For oh, the draught is good;
I drink to Life, I drink to Death,
And smack my lips with song,
For when I die, another 'I' shall pass the cup along.
'The man you drove from Eden's grove
Was I, my Lord, was I,
And I shall be there when the earth and the air
Are rent from sea to sky;
For it is my world, my gorgeous world,
The world of my dearest woes,
From the first faint cry of the newborn
To the rack of the woman's throes.
'Packed with the pulse of an unborn race,
Torn with a world's desire,
The surging flood of my wild young blood

491

Would quench the judgment fire.
I am Man, Man, Man, from the tingling flesh
To the dust of my earthly goal,
From the nestling gloom of the pregnant womb
To the sheen of my naked soul.
Bone of my bone and flesh of my flesh
The whole world leaps to my will,
And the unslaked thirst of an Eden cursed
Shall harrow the earth for its fill.
Almighty God, when I drain life's glass
Of all its rainbow gleams,
The hapless plight of eternal night
Shall be none too long for my dreams.
'The man you drove from Eden's grove
Was I, my Lord, was I,
And I shall be there when the earth and the air
Are rent from sea to sky;
For it is my world, my gorgeous world,
The world of my dear delight,
From the brightest gleam of the Arctic stream
To the dusk of my own love-night.'

Ernest always overworked. His wonderful constitution kept him up; but even that constitution could not keep the tired look out of his eyes. His dear, tired eyes! He never slept more than four and one-half hours a night; yet he never found time to do all the work he wanted to do. He never ceased from his activities as a propagandist, and was always scheduled long in advance for lectures to workingmen's organizations. Then there was the campaign. He did a man's full work in that alone. With the suppression of the socialist publishing houses, his meagre royalties ceased, and he was hard-put to make a living; for he had to make a living in addition to all his other labor. He did a great deal of translating for the magazines on scientific and philosophic subjects; and, coming home late at night, worn out from the strain of the campaign, he would plunge into his translating and toil on well into the morning hours. And in addition to everything, there was his studying. To the day of his death he kept up his studies, and he studied prodigiously.

And yet he found time in which to love me and make me happy. But this was accomplished only through my merging my life completely into his. I learned shorthand and typewriting, and became his secretary. He insisted that I succeeded in cutting his work in half; and so it was that I schooled myself to understand his work. Our interests became mutual, and we worked together and played together.

And then there were our sweet stolen moments in the midst of our work—just a word, or caress, or flash of love-light; and our moments were sweeter for being stolen. For we lived on the heights, where the air was keen and sparkling, where the toil was for humanity, and where sordidness and selfishness never entered. We loved love, and our love was never smirched by anything less than the best. And this out of all remains: I did not fail. I gave him rest—he who worked so hard for others, my dear, tired-eyed mortalist.

CHAPTER XII
THE BISHOP

It was after my marriage that I chanced upon Bishop Morehouse. But I must give the events in their proper sequence. After his outbreak at the I. P. H. Convention, the Bishop, being a gentle soul, had yielded to the friendly pressure brought to bear upon him, and had gone away on a vacation. But he returned more fixed than ever in his determination to preach the message of the Church. To the consternation of his congregation, his first sermon was quite similar to the address he had given before the Convention. Again he said, and at length and with distressing detail, that the Church had wandered away from the Master's teaching, and that Mammon had been instated in the place of Christ.

And the result was, willy-nilly, that he was led away to a private sanitarium for mental disease, while in the newspapers appeared pathetic accounts of his mental breakdown and of the saintliness of his character. He was held a prisoner in the sanitarium. I called repeatedly, but was denied access to him; and I was terribly impressed by the tragedy of a sane, normal, saintly man being crushed by the brutal will of society. For the Bishop was sane, and pure, and noble. As Ernest said, all that was the matter with him was that he had incorrect notions of biology and sociology, and because of his incorrect notions he had not gone about it in the right way to rectify matters.

What terrified me was the Bishop's helplessness. If he persisted in the truth as he saw it, he was doomed to an insane ward. And he could do nothing. His money, his position, his culture, could not save him. His views were perilous to society, and society could not conceive that such perilous views could be the product of a sane mind. Or, at least, it seems to me that such was society's attitude.

But the Bishop, in spite of the gentleness and purity of his spirit, was possessed of guile. He apprehended clearly his danger. He saw himself caught in the web, and he tried to escape from it. Denied help from his friends, such as father and Ernest and I could have given, he was left to battle for himself alone. And in the enforced solitude of the sanitarium he recovered. He became again sane. His eyes ceased to see visions; his brain was purged of the fancy that it was the duty of society to feed the Master's lambs.

As I say, he became well, quite well, and the newspapers and the church people hailed his return with joy. I went once to his church. The sermon was of the same order as the ones he had preached long before his eyes had seen visions. I was disappointed, shocked. Had society then beaten him into submission? Was he a coward? Had he been bulldozed into recanting? Or had the strain been too great for him, and had he meekly surrendered to the juggernaut of the established?

I called upon him in his beautiful home. He was woefully changed. He was thinner, and there were lines on his face which I had never seen before. He was manifestly distressed by my coming. He plucked nervously at his sleeve as we talked; and his eyes were restless, fluttering here, there, and everywhere, and refusing to meet mine. His mind seemed preoccupied, and there were strange pauses in his conversation, abrupt changes of topic, and an inconsecutiveness that was bewildering. Could this, then, be the firm-poised, Christ-like man I had known, with pure, limpid eyes and a gaze steady and unfaltering as his soul? He had been man-handled; he had been cowed into subjection. His spirit was too gentle. It had not been mighty enough to face the organized wolf-pack of society.

I felt sad, unutterably sad. He talked ambiguously, and was so apprehensive of what I might say that I had not the heart to catechise him. He spoke in a far-away manner of his illness, and we talked disjointedly about the church, the alterations in the organ, and about petty charities; and he saw me depart with such evident relief that I should have laughed had not my heart been so full of tears.

The poor little hero! If I had only known! He was battling like a giant, and I did not guess it. Alone, all alone, in the midst of millions of his fellow-men, he was fighting his fight. Torn by his horror of the asylum and his fidelity to truth and the right, he clung steadfastly to truth and the right; but so alone was he that he did not dare to trust even me. He had learned his lesson well—too well.

But I was soon to know. One day the Bishop disappeared. He had told nobody that he was going away; and as the days went by and he did not reappear, there was much gossip to the effect that he had committed suicide while temporarily deranged. But this idea was dispelled when it was learned that he had sold all his possessions,—his city mansion, his country house at Menlo Park, his paintings, and collections, and even his cherished library. It was patent that he had made a clean and secret sweep of everything before he disappeared.

This happened during the time when calamity had overtaken us in our own affairs; and it was not till we were well settled in our new home that we had opportunity really to wonder and speculate about the Bishop's doings. And then, everything was suddenly made clear. Early one evening, while it was yet twilight, I had run across the street and into the butcher-shop to get some chops for Ernest's supper. We called the last meal of the day 'supper' in our new environment.

Just at the moment I came out of the butcher-shop, a man emerged from the corner grocery that stood alongside. A queer sense familiarity made me look again. But the man had turned and was walking rapidly away. There was something about the slope of the shoulders and the fringe of silver hair between coat collar and slouch hat that aroused vague memories. Instead of crossing the street, I hurried after the man. I quickened my pace, trying not to think the thoughts that formed unbidden in my brain. No, it was impossible. It could not be—not in those faded overalls, too long in the legs and frayed at the bottoms.

I paused, laughed at myself, and almost abandoned the chase. But the haunting familiarity of those shoulders and that silver hair! Again I hurried on. As I passed him, I shot a keen look at his face; then I whirled around abruptly and confronted—the Bishop.

He halted with equal abruptness, and gasped. A large paper bag in his right hand fell to the sidewalk. It burst, and about his feet and mine bounced and rolled a flood of potatoes. He looked at me with surprise and alarm, then he seemed to wilt away; the shoulders drooped with dejection, and he uttered a deep sigh.

I held out my hand. He shook it, but his hand felt clammy. He cleared his throat in embarrassment, and I could see the sweat starting out on his forehead. It was evident that he was badly frightened.

'The potatoes,' he murmured faintly. 'They are precious.'

Between us we picked them up and replaced them in the broken bag, which he now held carefully in the hollow of his arm. I tried to tell him my gladness at meeting him and that he must come right home with me.

'Father will be rejoiced to see you,' I said. 'We live only a stone's throw away.'

'I can't,' he said, 'I must be going. Good-by.'

He looked apprehensively about him, as though dreading discovery, and made an attempt to walk on.

'Tell me where you live, and I shall call later,' he said, when he saw that I walked beside him and that it was my intention to stick to him now that he was found.

'No,' I answered firmly. 'You must come now.'

He looked at the potatoes spilling on his arm, and at the small parcels on his other arm.

'Really, it is impossible,' he said. 'Forgive me for my rudeness. If you only knew.'

He looked as if he were going to break down, but the next moment he had himself in control.

'Besides, this food,' he went on. 'It is a sad case. It is terrible. She is an old woman. I must take it to her at once. She is suffering from want of it. I must go at once. You understand. Then I will return. I promise you.'

'Let me go with you,' I volunteered. 'Is it far?'

He sighed again, and surrendered.

'Only two blocks,' he said. 'Let us hasten.'

Under the Bishop's guidance I learned something of my own neighborhood. I had not dreamed such wretchedness and misery existed in it. Of course, this was because I did not concern myself with charity. I had become convinced that Ernest was right when he sneered at charity as a poulticing of an ulcer. Remove the ulcer, was his remedy; give to the worker his product; pension as soldiers those who grow honorably old in their toil, and there will be no need for charity. Convinced of this, I toiled with him at the revolution, and did not exhaust my energy in alleviating the social ills that continuously arose from the injustice of the system.

I followed the Bishop into a small room, ten by twelve, in a rear tenement. And there we found a little old German woman—sixty-four years old, the Bishop said. She was surprised at seeing me, but she nodded a pleasant greeting and went on sewing on the pair of men's trousers in her lap. Beside her, on the floor, was a pile of trousers. The Bishop discovered there was neither coal nor kindling, and went out to buy some.

I took up a pair of trousers and examined her work.

'Six cents, lady,' she said, nodding her head gently while she went on stitching. She stitched slowly, but never did she cease from stitching. She seemed mastered by the verb 'to stitch.'

'For all that work?' I asked. 'Is that what they pay? How long does it take you?'

'Yes,' she answered, 'that is what they pay. Six cents for finishing. Two hours' sewing on each pair.'

'But the boss doesn't know that,' she added quickly, betraying a fear of getting him into trouble. 'I'm slow. I've got the rheumatism in my hands. Girls work much faster. They finish in half that time. The boss is kind. He lets me take the work home, now that I am old and the noise of the machine bothers my head. If it wasn't for his kindness, I'd starve.

'Yes, those who work in the shop get eight cents. But what can you do? There is not enough work for the young. The old have no chance. Often one pair is all I can get. Sometimes, like to-day, I am given eight pair to finish before night.'

I asked her the hours she worked, and she said it depended on the season.

'In the summer, when there is a rush order, I work from five in the morning to nine at night. But in the winter it is too cold. The hands do not early get over the stiffness. Then you must work later—till after midnight sometimes.

'Yes, it has been a bad summer. The hard times. God must be angry. This is the first work the boss has given me in a week. It is true, one cannot eat much when there is no work. I am used to it. I have sewed all my life, in the old country and here in San Francisco—thirty-three years.

'If you are sure of the rent, it is all right. The houseman is very kind, but he must have his rent. It is fair. He only charges three dollars for this room. That is cheap. But it is not easy for you to find all of three dollars every month.'

She ceased talking, and, nodding her head, went on stitching.

'You have to be very careful as to how you spend your earnings,' I suggested.

She nodded emphatically.

'After the rent it's not so bad. Of course you can't buy meat. And there is no milk for the coffee. But always there is one meal a day, and often two.'

She said this last proudly. There was a smack of success in her words. But as she stitched on in silence, I noticed the sadness in her pleasant eyes and the droop of her mouth. The look in her eyes became far away. She rubbed the dimness hastily out of them; it interfered with her stitching.

'No, it is not the hunger that makes the heart ache,' she explained. 'You get used to being hungry. It is for my child that I cry. It was the machine that killed her. It is true she worked hard, but I cannot understand. She was strong. And she was young—only forty; and she worked only thirty years. She began young, it is true; but my man died. The boiler exploded down at the works. And what were we to do? She was ten, but she was very strong. But the machine killed her. Yes, it did. It killed her, and she was the fastest worker in the shop. I have thought about it often, and I know. That is why I cannot work in the shop. The machine bothers my head. Always I hear it saying, 'I did it, I did it.' And it says that all day long. And then I think of my daughter, and I cannot work.'

The moistness was in her old eyes again, and she had to wipe it away before she could go on stitching.

I heard the Bishop stumbling up the stairs, and I opened the door. What a spectacle he was. On his back he carried half a sack of coal, with kindling on top. Some of the coal dust had coated his face, and the sweat from his exertions was running in streaks. He dropped his burden in the corner by the stove and wiped his face on a coarse bandana handkerchief. I could scarcely accept the verdict of my senses. The Bishop, black as a coal-heaver, in a workingman's cheap cotton shirt (one button was missing from the throat), and in overalls! That was the most incongruous of all—the overalls, frayed at the bottoms, dragged down at the heels, and held up by a narrow leather belt around the hips such as laborers wear.

Though the Bishop was warm, the poor swollen hands of the old woman were already cramping with the cold; and before we left her, the Bishop had built the fire, while I had peeled the potatoes and put them on to boil. I was to learn, as time went by, that there were many cases similar to hers, and many worse, hidden away in the monstrous depths of the tenements in my neighborhood.

We got back to find Ernest alarmed by my absence. After the first surprise of greeting was over, the Bishop leaned back in his chair, stretched out his overall-covered legs, and actually sighed a comfortable sigh. We were the first of his old friends he had met since his disappearance, he told us; and during the intervening weeks he must have suffered greatly from loneliness. He told us much, though he told us more of the joy he had experienced in doing the Master's bidding.

'For truly now,' he said, 'I am feeding his lambs. And I have learned a great lesson. The soul cannot be ministered to till the stomach is appeased. His lambs must be fed bread and butter and potatoes and meat; after that, and only after that, are their spirits ready for more refined nourishment.'

He ate heartily of the supper I cooked. Never had he had such an appetite at our table in the old days. We spoke of it, and he said that he had never been so healthy in his life.

'I walk always now,' he said, and a blush was on his cheek at the thought of the time when he rode in his carriage, as though it were a sin not lightly to be laid.

'My health is better for it,' he added hastily. 'And I am very happy—indeed, most happy. At last I am a consecrated spirit.'

And yet there was in his face a permanent pain, the pain of the world that he was now taking to himself. He was seeing life in the raw, and it was a different life from what he had known within the printed books of his library.

'And you are responsible for all this, young man,' he said directly to Ernest.

Ernest was embarrassed and awkward.

'I—I warned you,' he faltered.

'No, you misunderstand,' the Bishop answered. 'I speak not in reproach, but in gratitude. I have you to thank for showing me my path. You led me from theories about life to life itself. You pulled aside the veils from the social shams. You were light in my darkness, but now I, too, see the light. And I am very happy, only . . .' he hesitated painfully, and in his eyes fear leaped large. 'Only the persecution. I harm no one. Why will they not let me alone? But it is not that. It is the nature of the persecution. I shouldn't mind if they cut my flesh with stripes, or burned me at the stake, or crucified me head—downward. But it is the asylum that frightens me. Think of it! Of me—in an asylum for the insane! It is revolting. I saw some of the cases at the sanitarium. They were violent. My blood chills when I think of it. And to be imprisoned for the rest of my life amid scenes of screaming madness! No! no! Not that! Not that!'

It was pitiful. His hands shook, his whole body quivered and shrank away from the picture he had conjured. But the next moment he was calm.

'Forgive me,' he said simply. 'It is my wretched nerves. And if the Master's work leads there, so be it. Who am I to complain?'

I felt like crying aloud as I looked at him: 'Great Bishop! O hero! God's hero!'

As the evening wore on we learned more of his doings.

'I sold my house—my houses, rather,' he said, 'all my other possessions. I knew I must do it secretly, else they would have taken everything away from me. That would have been terrible. I often marvel these days at the immense quantity of potatoes two or three hundred thousand dollars will buy, or bread, or meat, or coal and kindling.' He turned to Ernest. 'You are right, young man. Labor is dreadfully underpaid. I never did a bit of work in my life, except to appeal aesthetically to Pharisees—I thought I was preaching the message—and yet I was worth half a million dollars. I never knew what half a million dollars meant until I realized how much potatoes and bread and butter and meat it could buy. And then I realized something more. I realized that all those potatoes and that bread and butter and meat were mine, and that I had not worked to make them. Then it was clear to me, some one else had worked and made them and been robbed of them. And when I came down amongst the poor I found those who had been robbed and who were hungry and wretched because they had been robbed.'

We drew him back to his narrative.

'The money? I have it deposited in many different banks under different names. It can never be taken away from me, because it can never be found. And it is so good, that money. It buys so much food. I never knew before what money was good for.'

'I wish we could get some of it for the propaganda,' Ernest said wistfully. 'It would do immense good.'

'Do you think so?' the Bishop said. 'I do not have much faith in politics. In fact, I am afraid I do not understand politics.'

Ernest was delicate in such matters. He did not repeat his suggestion, though he knew only too well the sore straits the Socialist Party was in through lack of money.

'I sleep in cheap lodging houses,' the Bishop went on. 'But I am afraid, and never stay long in one place. Also, I rent two rooms in workingmen's houses in different quarters of the city. It is a great extravagance, I know, but it is necessary. I make up for it in part by doing my own cooking, though sometimes I get something to eat in cheap coffee-houses. And I have made a discovery. Tamales* are very good when the air grows chilly late at night. Only they are so expensive. But I have discovered a place where I can get three for ten cents. They are not so good as the others, but they are very warming.

'And so I have at last found my work in the world, thanks to you, young man. It is the Master's work.' He looked at me, and his eyes twinkled. 'You caught me feeding his lambs, you know. And of course you will all keep my secret.'

He spoke carelessly enough, but there was real fear behind the speech. He promised to call upon us again. But a week later we read in the newspaper of the sad case of Bishop Morehouse, who had been committed to the Napa Asylum and for whom there were still hopes held out. In vain we tried to see him, to have his case reconsidered or investigated. Nor could we learn anything about him except the reiterated statements that slight hopes were still held for his recovery.

'Christ told the rich young man to sell all he had,' Ernest said bitterly. 'The Bishop obeyed Christ's injunction and got locked up in a madhouse. Times have changed since Christ's day. A rich man to-day who gives all he has to the poor is crazy. There is no discussion. Society has spoken.'

---

* A Mexican dish, referred to occasionally in the literature of the times. It is supposed that it was warmly seasoned. No recipe of it has come down to us.

CHAPTER XIII
THE GENERAL STRIKE

Of course Ernest was elected to Congress in the great socialist landslide that took place in the fall of 1912. One great factor that helped to swell the socialist vote was the destruction of Hearst.* This the Plutocracy found an easy task. It cost Hearst eighteen million dollars a year to run his various papers, and this sum, and more, he got back from the middle class in payment for advertising. The source of his financial strength lay wholly in the middle class. The trusts did not advertise.** To destroy Hearst, all that was necessary was to take away from him his advertising.

The whole middle class had not yet been exterminated. The sturdy skeleton of it remained; but it was without power. The small manufacturers and small business men who still survived were at the complete mercy of the Plutocracy. They had no economic nor political souls of their own. When the fiat of the Plutocracy went forth, they withdrew their advertisements from the Hearst papers.

Hearst made a gallant fight. He brought his papers out at a loss of a million and a half each month. He continued to publish the advertisements for which he no longer received pay. Again the fiat of the Plutocracy went forth, and the small business men and manufacturers swamped him with a flood of notices that he must discontinue running their old advertisements. Hearst persisted. Injunctions were served on him. Still he persisted. He received six months' imprisonment for contempt of court in disobeying the injunctions, while he was bankrupted by countless damage suits. He had no chance. The Plutocracy had passed sentence on him. The courts were in the hands of the Plutocracy to carry the sentence out. And with Hearst crashed also to destruction the Democratic Party that he had so recently captured.

With the destruction of Hearst and the Democratic Party, there were only two paths for his following to take. One was into the Socialist Party; the other was into the Republican Party. Then it was that we socialists reaped the fruit of Hearst's pseudo-socialistic preaching; for the great Majority of his followers came over to us.

The expropriation of the farmers that took place at this time would also have swelled our vote had it not been for the brief and futile rise of the Grange Party. Ernest and the socialist leaders fought fiercely to capture the farmers; but the destruction of the socialist press and publishing houses constituted too great a handicap, while the mouth-to-mouth propaganda had not yet been perfected. So it was that politicians like Mr. Calvin, who were themselves farmers long since expropriated, captured the farmers and threw their political strength away in a vain campaign.

'The poor farmers,' Ernest once laughed savagely; 'the trusts have them both coming and going.'

---

* William Randolph Hearst—a young California millionaire who became the most powerful newspaper owner in the country. His newspapers were published in all the large cities, and they appealed to the perishing middle class and to the proletariat. So large was his following that he managed to take possession of the empty shell of the old Democratic Party. He occupied an anomalous position, preaching an emasculated socialism combined with a nondescript sort of petty bourgeois capitalism. It was oil and water, and there was no hope for him, though for a short period he was a source of serious apprehension to the Plutocrats.
** The cost of advertising was amazing in those helter-skelter times. Only the small capitalists competed, and therefore they did the advertising. There being no competition where there was a trust, there was no need for the trusts to advertise.

And that was really the situation. The seven great trusts, working together, had pooled their enormous surpluses and made a farm trust. The railroads, controlling rates, and the bankers and stock exchange gamesters, controlling prices, had long since bled the farmers into indebtedness. The bankers, and all the trusts for that matter, had likewise long since loaned colossal amounts of money to the farmers. The farmers were in the net. All that remained to be done was the drawing in of the net. This the farm trust proceeded to do.

The hard times of 1912 had already caused a frightful slump in the farm markets. Prices were now deliberately pressed down to bankruptcy, while the railroads, with extortionate rates, broke the back of the farmer-camel. Thus the farmers were compelled to borrow more and more, while they were prevented from paying back old loans. Then ensued the great foreclosing of mortgages and enforced collection of notes. The farmers simply surrendered the land to the farm trust. There was nothing else for them to do. And having surrendered the land, the farmers next went to work for the farm trust, becoming managers, superintendents, foremen, and common laborers. They worked for wages. They became villeins, in short—serfs bound to the soil by a living wage. They could not leave their masters, for their masters composed the Plutocracy. They could not go to the cities, for there, also, the Plutocracy was in control. They had but one alternative,—to leave the soil and become vagrants, in brief, to starve. And even there they were frustrated, for stringent vagrancy laws were passed and rigidly enforced.

Of course, here and there, farmers, and even whole communities of farmers, escaped expropriation by virtue of exceptional conditions. But they were merely strays and did not count, and they were gathered in anyway during the following year.*

Thus it was that in the fall of 1912 the socialist leaders, with the exception of Ernest, decided that the end of capitalism had come. What of the hard times and the consequent vast army of the unemployed; what of the destruction of the farmers and the middle class; and what of the decisive defeat administered all along the line to the labor unions; the socialists were really justified in believing that the end of capitalism had come and in themselves throwing down the gauntlet to the Plutocracy.

Alas, how we underestimated the strength of the enemy! Everywhere the socialists proclaimed their coming victory at the ballot-box, while, in unmistakable terms, they stated the situation. The Plutocracy accepted the challenge. It was the Plutocracy, weighing and balancing, that defeated us by dividing our strength. It was the Plutocracy, through its secret agents, that raised the cry that socialism was sacrilegious and atheistic; it was the Plutocracy that whipped the churches, and especially the Catholic Church, into line, and robbed us of a portion of the labor vote. And it was the Plutocracy, through its secret agents of course, that encouraged the Grange Party

---

* The destruction of the Roman yeomanry proceeded far less rapidly than the destruction of the American farmers and small capitalists. There was momentum in the twentieth century, while there was practically none in ancient Rome. Numbers of the farmers, impelled by an insane lust for the soil, and willing to show what beasts they could become, tried to escape expropriation by withdrawing from any and all market-dealing. They sold nothing. They bought nothing. Among themselves a primitive barter began to spring up. Their privation and hardships were terrible, but they persisted. It became quite a movement, in fact. The manner in which they were beaten was unique and logical and simple. The Plutocracy, by virtue of its possession of the government, raised their taxes. It was the weak joint in their armor. Neither buying nor selling, they had no money, and in the end their land was sold to pay the taxes.

and even spread it to the cities into the ranks of the dying middle class.

Nevertheless the socialist landslide occurred. But, instead of a sweeping victory with chief executive officers and majorities in all legislative bodies, we found ourselves in the minority. It is true, we elected fifty Congressmen; but when they took their seats in the spring of 1913, they found themselves without power of any sort. Yet they were more fortunate than the Grangers, who captured a dozen state governments, and who, in the spring, were not permitted to take possession of the captured offices. The incumbents refused to retire, and the courts were in the hands of the Oligarchy. But this is too far in advance of events. I have yet to tell of the stirring times of the winter of 1912.

The hard times at home had caused an immense decrease in consumption. Labor, out of work, had no wages with which to buy. The result was that the Plutocracy found a greater surplus than ever on its hands. This surplus it was compelled to dispose of abroad, and, what of its colossal plans, it needed money. Because of its strenuous efforts to dispose of the surplus in the world market, the Plutocracy clashed with Germany. Economic clashes were usually succeeded by wars, and this particular clash was no exception. The great German war-lord prepared, and so did the United States prepare.

The war-cloud hovered dark and ominous. The stage was set for a world-catastrophe, for in all the world were hard times, labor troubles, perishing middle classes, armies of unemployed, clashes of economic interests in the world-market, and mutterings and rumblings of the socialist revolution.*

The Oligarchy wanted the war with Germany. And it wanted the war for a dozen reasons. In the juggling of events such a war would cause, in the reshuffling of the international cards and the making of new treaties and alliances, the Oligarchy had much to gain. And, furthermore, the war would consume many national surpluses, reduce the armies of unemployed that menaced all countries, and give the Oligarchy a breathing space in which to perfect its plans and carry them out. Such a war would virtually put the Oligarchy in possession of the world-market. Also, such a war would create a large standing army that need never be disbanded, while in the minds of the people would be substituted the issue, 'America versus Germany,' in place of 'Socialism versus Oligarchy.'

And truly the war would have done all these things had it not been for the socialists.

---

* For a long time these mutterings and rumblings had been heard. As far back as 1906 A.D., Lord Avebury, an Englishman, uttered the following in the House of Lords: 'The unrest in Europe, the spread of socialism, and the ominous rise of Anarchism, are warnings to the governments and the ruling classes that the condition of the working classes in Europe is becoming intolerable, and that if a revolution is to be avoided some steps must be taken to increase wages, reduce the hours of labor, and lower the prices of the necessaries of life.' The Wall Street Journal, a stock gamesters' publication, in commenting upon Lord Avebury's speech, said: 'These words were spoken by an aristocrat and a member of the most conservative body in all Europe. That gives them all the more significance. They contain more valuable political economy than is to be found in most of the books. They sound a note of warning. Take heed, gentlemen of the war and navy departments!' At the same time, Sydney Brooks, writing in America, in Harper's Weekly, said: 'You will not hear the socialists mentioned in Washington. Why should you? The politicians are always the last people in this country to see what is going on under their noses. They will jeer at me when I prophesy, and prophesy with the utmost confidence, that at the next presidential election the socialists will poll over a million votes.'

A secret meeting of the Western leaders was held in our four tiny rooms in Pell Street. Here was first considered the stand the socialists were to take. It was not the first time we had put our foot down upon war,* but it was the first time we had done so in the United States. After our secret meeting we got in touch with the national organization, and soon our code cables were passing back and forth across the Atlantic between us and the International Bureau.

The German socialists were ready to act with us. There were over five million of them, many of them in the standing army, and, in addition, they were on friendly terms with the labor unions. In both countries the socialists came out in bold declaration against the war and threatened the general strike. And in the meantime they made preparation for the general strike. Furthermore, the revolutionary parties in all countries gave public utterance to the socialist principle of international peace that must be preserved at all hazards, even to the extent of revolt and revolution at home.

The general strike was the one great victory we American socialists won. On the 4th of December the American minister was withdrawn from the German capital. That night a German fleet made a dash on Honolulu, sinking three American cruisers and a revenue cutter, and bombarding the city. Next day both Germany and the United States declared war, and within an hour the socialists called the general strike in both countries.

For the first time the German war-lord faced the men of his empire who made his empire go. Without them he could not run his empire. The novelty of the situation lay in that their revolt was passive. They did not fight. They did nothing. And by doing nothing they tied their war-lord's hands. He would have asked for nothing better than an opportunity to loose his war-dogs on his rebellious proletariat. But this was denied him. He could not loose his war-dogs. Neither could he mobilize his army to go forth to war, nor could he punish his recalcitrant subjects. Not a wheel moved in his empire. Not a train ran, not a telegraphic message went over the wires, for the telegraphers and railroad men had ceased work along with the rest of the population.

And as it was in Germany, so it was in the United States. At last organized labor had learned its lesson. Beaten decisively on its own chosen field, it had abandoned that field and come over to the political field of the socialists; for the general strike was a political strike. Besides, organized labor had been so badly beaten that it did not care. It joined in the general strike out of sheer desperation. The workers threw down their tools and left their tasks by the millions. Especially notable were the machinists. Their heads were bloody, their organization had apparently been destroyed, yet out they came, along with their allies in the metal-working trades.

Even the common laborers and all unorganized labor ceased work. The strike had tied everything up so that nobody could work. Besides, the women proved to be the strongest promoters of the strike. They set their faces against the war. They did not want their men to go forth to die. Then, also, the idea of the general strike caught

* It was at the very beginning of the twentieth century A.D., that the international organization of the socialists finally formulated their long-maturing policy on war. Epitomized their doctrine was: 'Why should the workingmen of one country fight with the workingmen of another country for the benefit of their capitalist masters?' On May 21, 1905 A.D., when war threatened between Austria and Italy, the socialists of Italy, Austria, and Hungary held a conference at Trieste, and threatened a general strike of the workingmen of both countries in case war was declared. This was repeated the following year, when the 'Morocco Affair' threatened to involve France, Germany, and England.

the mood of the people. It struck their sense of humor. The idea was infectious. The children struck in all the schools, and such teachers as came, went home again from deserted class rooms. The general strike took the form of a great national picnic. And the idea of the solidarity of labor, so evidenced, appealed to the imagination of all. And, finally, there was no danger to be incurred by the colossal frolic. When everybody was guilty, how was anybody to be punished?

The United States was paralyzed. No one knew what was happening. There were no newspapers, no letters, no despatches. Every community was as completely isolated as though ten thousand miles of primeval wilderness stretched between it and the rest of the world. For that matter, the world had ceased to exist. And for a week this state of affairs was maintained.

In San Francisco we did not know what was happening even across the bay in Oakland or Berkeley. The effect on one's sensibilities was weird, depressing. It seemed as though some great cosmic thing lay dead. The pulse of the land had ceased to beat. Of a truth the nation had died. There were no wagons rumbling on the streets, no factory whistles, no hum of electricity in the air, no passing of street cars, no cries of news-boys—nothing but persons who at rare intervals went by like furtive ghosts, themselves oppressed and made unreal by the silence.

And during that week of silence the Oligarchy was taught its lesson. And well it learned the lesson. The general strike was a warning. It should never occur again. The Oligarchy would see to that.

At the end of the week, as had been prearranged, the telegraphers of Germany and the United States returned to their posts. Through them the socialist leaders of both countries presented their ultimatum to the rulers. The war should be called off, or the general strike would continue. It did not take long to come to an understanding. The war was declared off, and the populations of both countries returned to their tasks.

It was this renewal of peace that brought about the alliance between Germany and the United States. In reality, this was an alliance between the Emperor and the Oligarchy, for the purpose of meeting their common foe, the revolutionary proletariat of both countries. And it was this alliance that the Oligarchy afterward so treacherously broke when the German socialists rose and drove the war-lord from his throne. It was the very thing the Oligarchy had played for—the destruction of its great rival in the world-market. With the German Emperor out of the way, Germany would have no surplus to sell abroad. By the very nature of the socialist state, the German population would consume all that it produced. Of course, it would trade abroad certain things it produced for things it did not produce; but this would be quite different from an unconsumable surplus.

'I'll wager the Oligarchy finds justification,' Ernest said, when its treachery to the German Emperor became known. 'As usual, the Oligarchy will believe it has done right.'

And sure enough. The Oligarchy's public defence for the act was that it had done it for the sake of the American people whose interests it was looking out for. It had flung its hated rival out of the world-market and enabled us to dispose of our surplus in that market.

'And the howling folly of it is that we are so helpless that such idiots really are managing our interests,' was Ernest's comment. 'They have enabled us to sell more abroad, which means that we'll be compelled to consume less at home.'

CHAPTER XIV

THE BEGINNING OF THE END

As early as January, 1913, Ernest saw the true trend of affairs, but he could not get his brother leaders to see the vision of the Iron Heel that had arisen in his brain. They were too confident. Events were rushing too rapidly to culmination. A crisis had come in world affairs. The American Oligarchy was practically in possession of the world-market, and scores of countries were flung out of that market with unconsumable and unsalable surpluses on their hands. For such countries nothing remained but reorganization. They could not continue their method of producing surpluses. The capitalistic system, so far as they were concerned, had hopelessly broken down.

The reorganization of these countries took the form of revolution. It was a time of confusion and violence. Everywhere institutions and governments were crashing. Everywhere, with the exception of two or three countries, the erstwhile capitalist masters fought bitterly for their possessions. But the governments were taken away from them by the militant proletariat. At last was being realized Karl Marx's classic: 'The knell of private capitalist property sounds. The expropriators are expropriated.' And as fast as capitalistic governments crashed, cooperative commonwealths arose in their place.

'Why does the United States lag behind?'; 'Get busy, you American revolutionists!'; 'What's the matter with America?'—were the messages sent to us by our successful comrades in other lands. But we could not keep up. The Oligarchy stood in the way. Its bulk, like that of some huge monster, blocked our path.

'Wait till we take office in the spring,' we answered. 'Then you'll see.'

Behind this lay our secret. We had won over the Grangers, and in the spring a dozen states would pass into their hands by virtue of the elections of the preceding fall. At once would be instituted a dozen cooperative commonwealth states. After that, the rest would be easy.

'But what if the Grangers fail to get possession?' Ernest demanded. And his comrades called him a calamity howler.

But this failure to get possession was not the chief danger that Ernest had in mind. What he foresaw was the defection of the great labor unions and the rise of the castes.

'Ghent has taught the oligarchs how to do it,' Ernest said. 'I'll wager they've made a text-book out of his 'Benevolent Feudalism.'*

Never shall I forget the night when, after a hot discussion with half a dozen labor leaders, Ernest turned to me and said quietly: 'That settles it. The Iron Heel has won. The end is in sight.'

This little conference in our home was unofficial; but Ernest, like the rest of his comrades, was working for assurances from the labor leaders that they would call out their men in the next general strike. O'Connor, the president of the Association of Machinists, had been foremost of the six leaders present in refusing to give such assurance.

---

* 'Our Benevolent Feudalism,' a book published in 1902 A.D., by W. J. Ghent. It has always been insisted that Ghent put the idea of the Oligarchy into the minds of the great capitalists. This belief persists throughout the literature of the three centuries of the Iron Heel, and even in the literature of the first century of the Brotherhood of Man. To-day we know better, but our knowledge does not overcome the fact that Ghent remains the most abused innocent man in all history.

'You have seen that you were beaten soundly at your old tactics of strike and boycott,' Ernest urged.

O'Connor and the others nodded their heads.

'And you saw what a general strike would do,' Ernest went on. 'We stopped the war with Germany. Never was there so fine a display of the solidarity and the power of labor. Labor can and will rule the world. If you continue to stand with us, we'll put an end to the reign of capitalism. It is your only hope. And what is more, you know it. There is no other way out. No matter what you do under your old tactics, you are doomed to defeat, if for no other reason because the masters control the courts.'*

'You run ahead too fast,' O'Connor answered. 'You don't know all the ways out. There is another way out. We know what we're about. We're sick of strikes. They've got us beaten that way to a frazzle. But I don't think we'll ever need to call our men out again.'

'What is your way out?' Ernest demanded bluntly.

O'Connor laughed and shook his head. 'I can tell you this much: We've not been asleep. And we're not dreaming now.'

'There's nothing to be afraid of, or ashamed of, I hope,' Ernest challenged.

'I guess we know our business best,' was the retort.

'It's a dark business, from the way you hide it,' Ernest said with growing anger.

'We've paid for our experience in sweat and blood, and we've earned all that's coming to us,' was the reply. 'Charity begins at home.'

'If you're afraid to tell me your way out, I'll tell it to you.' Ernest's blood was up. 'You're going in for grab-sharing. You've made terms with the enemy, that's what you've done. You've sold out the cause of labor, of all labor. You are leaving the battle-field like cowards.'

'I'm not saying anything,' O'Connor answered sullenly. 'Only I guess we know what's best for us a little bit better than you do.'

'And you don't care a cent for what is best for the rest of labor. You kick it into the ditch.'

'I'm not saying anything,' O'Connor replied, 'except that I'm president of the Machinists' Association, and it's my business to consider the interests of the men I represent, that's all.'

And then, when the labor leaders had left, Ernest, with the calmness of defeat, outlined to me the course of events to come.

---

* As a sample of the decisions of the courts adverse to labor, the following instances are given. In the coal- mining regions the employment of children was notorious. In 1905 A.D., labor succeeded in getting a law passed in Pennsylvania providing that proof of the age of the child and of certain educational qualifications must accompany the oath of the parent. This was promptly declared unconstitutional by the Luzerne County Court, on the ground that it violated the Fourteenth Amendment in that it discriminated between individuals of the same class—namely, children above fourteen years of age and children below. The state court sustained the decision. The New York Court of Special Sessions, in 1905 A.D., declared unconstitutional the law prohibiting minors and women from working in factories after nine o'clock at night, the ground taken being that such a law was 'class legislation.' Again, the bakers of that time were terribly overworked. The New York Legislature passed a law restricting work in bakeries to ten hours a day. In 1906 A.D., the Supreme Court of the United States declared this law to be unconstitutional. In part the decision read: 'There is no reasonable ground for interfering with the liberty of persons or the right of free contract by determining the hours of labor in the occupation of a baker.'

'The socialists used to foretell with joy,' he said, 'the coming of the day when organized labor, defeated on the industrial field, would come over on to the political field. Well, the Iron Heel has defeated the labor unions on the industrial field and driven them over to the political field; and instead of this being joyful for us, it will be a source of grief. The Iron Heel learned its lesson. We showed it our power in the general strike. It has taken steps to prevent another general strike.'

'But how?' I asked.

'Simply by subsidizing the great unions. They won't join in the next general strike. Therefore it won't be a general strike.'

'But the Iron Heel can't maintain so costly a programme forever,' I objected.

'Oh, it hasn't subsidized all of the unions. That's not necessary. Here is what is going to happen. Wages are going to be advanced and hours shortened in the railroad unions, the iron and steel workers unions, and the engineer and machinist unions. In these unions more favorable conditions will continue to prevail. Membership in these unions will become like seats in Paradise.'

'Still I don't see,' I objected. 'What is to become of the other unions? There are far more unions outside of this combination than in it.'

'The other unions will be ground out of existence—all of them. For, don't you see, the railway men, machinists and engineers, iron and steel workers, do all of the vitally essential work in our machine civilization. Assured of their faithfulness, the Iron Heel can snap its fingers at all the rest of labor. Iron, steel, coal, machinery, and transportation constitute the backbone of the whole industrial fabric.'

'But coal?' I queried. 'There are nearly a million coal miners.'

They are practically unskilled labor. They will not count. Their wages will go down and their hours will increase. They will be slaves like all the rest of us, and they will become about the most bestial of all of us. They will be compelled to work, just as the farmers are compelled to work now for the masters who robbed them of their land. And the same with all the other unions outside the combination. Watch them wobble and go to pieces, and their members become slaves driven to toil by empty stomachs and the law of the land.

'Do you know what will happen to Farley[*] and his strike-breakers? I'll tell you. Strike-breaking as an occupation will cease. There won't be any more strikes. In place of strikes will be slave revolts. Farley and his gang will be promoted to slave-driving. Oh, it won't be called that; it will be called enforcing the law of the land that compels the laborers to work. It simply prolongs the fight, this treachery of the big unions. Heaven only knows now where and when the Revolution will triumph.'

'But with such a powerful combination as the Oligarchy and the big unions, is there any reason to believe that the Revolution will ever triumph?' I queried. 'May not the combination endure forever?'

He shook his head. 'One of our generalizations is that every system founded upon class and caste contains within itself the germs of its own decay. When a system is founded upon class, how can caste be prevented? The Iron Heel will not be able to prevent it, and in the end caste will destroy the Iron Heel. The oligarchs have already

---

[*] James Farley—a notorious strike-breaker of the period. A man more courageous than ethical, and of undeniable ability. He rose high under the rule of the Iron Heel and finally was translated into the oligarch class. He was assassinated in 1932 by Sarah Jenkins, whose husband, thirty years before, had been killed by Farley's strike-breakers.

developed caste among themselves; but wait until the favored unions develop caste. The Iron Heel will use all its power to prevent it, but it will fail.

'In the favored unions are the flower of the American workingmen. They are strong, efficient men. They have become members of those unions through competition for place. Every fit workman in the United States will be possessed by the ambition to become a member of the favored unions. The Oligarchy will encourage such ambition and the consequent competition. Thus will the strong men, who might else be revolutionists, be won away and their strength used to bolster the Oligarchy.

'On the other hand, the labor castes, the members of the favored unions, will strive to make their organizations into close corporations. And they will succeed. Membership in the labor castes will become hereditary. Sons will succeed fathers, and there will be no inflow of new strength from that eternal reservoir of strength, the common people. This will mean deterioration of the labor castes, and in the end they will become weaker and weaker. At the same time, as an institution, they will become temporarily all-powerful. They will be like the guards of the palace in old Rome, and there will be palace revolutions whereby the labor castes will seize the reins of power. And there will be counter-palace revolutions of the oligarchs, and sometimes the one, and sometimes the other, will be in power. And through it all the inevitable caste-weakening will go on, so that in the end the common people will come into their own.'

This foreshadowing of a slow social evolution was made when Ernest was first depressed by the defection of the great unions. I never agreed with him in it, and I disagree now, as I write these lines, more heartily than ever; for even now, though Ernest is gone, we are on the verge of the revolt that will sweep all oligarchies away. Yet I have here given Ernest's prophecy because it was his prophecy. In spite of his belief in it, he worked like a giant against it, and he, more than any man, has made possible the revolt that even now waits the signal to burst forth.*

'But if the Oligarchy persists,' I asked him that evening, 'what will become of the great surpluses that will fall to its share every year?'

'The surpluses will have to be expended somehow,' he answered; 'and trust the oligarchs to find a way. Magnificent roads will be built. There will be great achievements in science, and especially in art. When the oligarchs have completely mastered the people, they will have time to spare for other things. They will become worshippers of beauty. They will become art-lovers. And under their direction and generously rewarded, will toil the artists. The result will be great art; for no longer, as up to yesterday, will the artists pander to the bourgeois taste of the middle class. It will be great art, I tell you, and wonder cities will arise that will make tawdry and cheap the cities of old time. And in these cities will the oligarchs dwell and worship beauty.**

'Thus will the surplus be constantly expended while labor does the work. The building of these great works and cities will give a starvation ration to millions of common laborers, for the enormous bulk of the surplus will compel an equally enormous expenditure, and the oligarchs will build for a thousand years—ay, for ten

---

* Everhard's social foresight was remarkable. As clearly as in the light of past events, he saw the defection of the favored unions, the rise and the slow decay of the labor castes, and the struggle between the decaying oligarchs and labor castes for control of the great governmental machine.

** We cannot but marvel at Everhard's foresight. Before ever the thought of wonder cities like Ardis and Asgard entered the minds of the oligarchs, Everhard saw those cities and the inevitable necessity for their creation.

thousand years. They will build as the Egyptians and the Babylonians never dreamed of building; and when the oligarchs have passed away, their great roads and their wonder cities will remain for the brotherhood of labor to tread upon and dwell within.*

'These things the oligarchs will do because they cannot help doing them. These great works will be the form their expenditure of the surplus will take, and in the same way that the ruling classes of Egypt of long ago expended the surplus they robbed from the people by the building of temples and pyramids. Under the oligarchs will flourish, not a priest class, but an artist class. And in place of the merchant class of bourgeoisie will be the labor castes. And beneath will be the abyss, wherein will fester and starve and rot, and ever renew itself, the common people, the great bulk of the population. And in the end, who knows in what day, the common people will rise up out of the abyss; the labor castes and the Oligarchy will crumble away; and then, at last, after the travail of the centuries, will it be the day of the common man. I had thought to see that day; but now I know that I shall never see it.'

He paused and looked at me, and added:

'Social evolution is exasperatingly slow, isn't it, sweetheart?'

My arms were about him, and his head was on my breast.

'Sing me to sleep,' he murmured whimsically. 'I have had a visioning, and I wish to forget.'

CHAPTER XV
LAST DAYS

It was near the end of January, 1913, that the changed attitude of the Oligarchy toward the favored unions was made public. The newspapers published information of an unprecedented rise in wages and shortening of hours for the railroad employees, the iron and steel workers, and the engineers and machinists. But the whole truth was not told. The oligarchs did not dare permit the telling of the whole truth. In reality, the wages had been raised much higher, and the privileges were correspondingly greater. All this was secret, but secrets will out. Members of the favored unions told their wives, and the wives gossiped, and soon all the labor world knew what had happened.

It was merely the logical development of what in the nineteenth century had been known as grab-sharing. In the industrial warfare of that time, profit-sharing had been tried. That is, the capitalists had striven to placate the workers by interesting them financially in their work. But profit-sharing, as a system, was ridiculous and impossible. Profit-sharing could be successful only in isolated cases in the midst of a system of industrial strife; for if all labor and all capital shared profits, the same conditions would obtain as did obtain when there was no profit-sharing.

So, out of the unpractical idea of profit-sharing, arose the practical idea of grab-sharing. 'Give us more pay and charge it to the public,' was the slogan of the strong

---

* And since that day of prophecy, have passed away the three centuries of the Iron Heel and the four centuries of the Brotherhood of Man, and to-day we tread the roads and dwell in the cities that the oligarchs built. It is true, we are even now building still more wonderful wonder cities, but the wonder cities of the oligarchs endure, and I write these lines in Ardis, one of the most wonderful of them all.

unions.* And here and there this selfish policy worked successfully. In charging it to the public, it was charged to the great mass of unorganized labor and of weakly organized labor. These workers actually paid the increased wages of their stronger brothers who were members of unions that were labor monopolies. This idea, as I say, was merely carried to its logical conclusion, on a large scale, by the combination of the oligarchs and the favored unions.

As soon as the secret of the defection of the favored unions leaked out, there were rumblings and mutterings in the labor world. Next, the favored unions withdrew from the international organizations and broke off all affiliations. Then came trouble and violence. The members of the favored unions were branded as traitors, and in saloons and brothels, on the streets and at work, and, in fact, everywhere, they were assaulted by the comrades they had so treacherously deserted.

Countless heads were broken, and there were many killed. No member of the favored unions was safe. They gathered together in bands in order to go to work or to return from work. They walked always in the middle of the street. On the sidewalk they were liable to have their skulls crushed by bricks and cobblestones thrown from windows and house-tops. They were permitted to carry weapons, and the authorities aided them in every way. Their persecutors were sentenced to long terms in prison, where they were harshly treated; while no man, not a member of the favored unions, was permitted to carry weapons. Violation of this law was made a high misdemeanor and punished accordingly.

Outraged labor continued to wreak vengeance on the traitors. Caste lines formed automatically. The children of the traitors were persecuted by the children of the workers who had been betrayed, until it was impossible for the former to play on the streets or to attend the public schools. Also, the wives and families of the traitors were ostracized, while the corner groceryman who sold provisions to them was boycotted.

As a result, driven back upon themselves from every side, the traitors and their families became clannish. Finding it impossible to dwell in safety in the midst of the betrayed proletariat, they moved into new localities inhabited by themselves alone. In this they were favored by the oligarchs. Good dwellings, modern and sanitary, were built for them, surrounded by spacious yards, and separated here and there by parks and playgrounds. Their children attended schools especially built for them, and in these schools manual training and applied science were specialized upon. Thus, and unavoidably, at the very beginning, out of this segregation arose caste. The members of the favored unions became the aristocracy of labor. They were set apart from the rest of labor. They were better housed, better clothed, better fed, better treated. They were grab-sharing with a vengeance.

In the meantime, the rest of the working class was more harshly treated. Many

---

* All the railroad unions entered into this combination with the oligarchs, and it is of interest to note that the first definite application of the policy of profit-grabbing was made by a railroad union in the nineteenth century A.D., namely, the Brotherhood of Locomotive Engineers. P. M. Arthur was for twenty years Grand Chief of the Brotherhood. After the strike on the Pennsylvania Railroad in 1877, he broached a scheme to have the Locomotive Engineers make terms with the railroads and to 'go it alone' so far as the rest of the labor unions were concerned. This scheme was eminently successful. It was as successful as it was selfish, and out of it was coined the word 'arthurization,' to denote grab-sharing on the part of labor unions. This word 'arthurization' has long puzzled the etymologists, but its derivation, I hope, is now made clear.

little privileges were taken away from it, while its wages and its standard of living steadily sank down. Incidentally, its public schools deteriorated, and education slowly ceased to be compulsory. The increase in the younger generation of children who could not read nor write was perilous.

The capture of the world-market by the United States had disrupted the rest of the world. Institutions and governments were everywhere crashing or transforming. Germany, Italy, France, Australia, and New Zealand were busy forming cooperative commonwealths. The British Empire was falling apart. England's hands were full. In India revolt was in full swing. The cry in all Asia was, 'Asia for the Asiatics!' And behind this cry was Japan, ever urging and aiding the yellow and brown races against the white. And while Japan dreamed of continental empire and strove to realize the dream, she suppressed her own proletarian revolution. It was a simple war of the castes, Coolie versus Samurai, and the coolie socialists were executed by tens of thousands. Forty thousand were killed in the street-fighting of Tokio and in the futile assault on the Mikado's palace. Kobe was a shambles; the slaughter of the cotton operatives by machine-guns became classic as the most terrific execution ever achieved by modern war machines. Most savage of all was the Japanese Oligarchy that arose. Japan dominated the East, and took to herself the whole Asiatic portion of the world-market, with the exception of India.

England managed to crush her own proletarian revolution and to hold on to India, though she was brought to the verge of exhaustion. Also, she was compelled to let her great colonies slip away from her. So it was that the socialists succeeded in making Australia and New Zealand into cooperative commonwealths. And it was for the same reason that Canada was lost to the mother country. But Canada crushed her own socialist revolution, being aided in this by the Iron Heel. At the same time, the Iron Heel helped Mexico and Cuba to put down revolt. The result was that the Iron Heel was firmly established in the New World. It had welded into one compact political mass the whole of North America from the Panama Canal to the Arctic Ocean.

And England, at the sacrifice of her great colonies, had succeeded only in retaining India. But this was no more than temporary. The struggle with Japan and the rest of Asia for India was merely delayed. England was destined shortly to lose India, while behind that event loomed the struggle between a united Asia and the world.

And while all the world was torn with conflict, we of the United States were not placid and peaceful. The defection of the great unions had prevented our prole-tarian revolt, but violence was everywhere. In addition to the labor troubles, and the discontent of the farmers and of the remnant of the middle class, a religious revival had blazed up. An offshoot of the Seventh Day Adventists sprang into sudden prominence, proclaiming the end of the world.

'Confusion thrice confounded!' Ernest cried. 'How can we hope for solidarity with all these cross purposes and conflicts?'

And truly the religious revival assumed formidable proportions. The people, what of their wretchedness, and of their disappointment in all things earthly, were ripe and eager for a heaven where industrial tyrants entered no more than camels passed through needle-eyes. Wild-eyed itinerant preachers swarmed over the land; and despite the prohibition of the civil authorities, and the persecution for disobedience, the flames of religious frenzy were fanned by countless camp-meetings.

It was the last days, they claimed, the beginning of the end of the world. The four winds had been loosed. God had stirred the nations to strife. It was a time of visions and miracles, while seers and prophetesses were legion. The people ceased work by hundreds of thousands and fled to the mountains, there to await the imminent coming of God and the rising of the hundred and forty and four thousand to heaven. But in the meantime God did not come, and they starved to death in great numbers. In their desperation they ravaged the farms for food, and the consequent tumult and anarchy in the country districts but increased the woes of the poor expropriated farmers.

Also, the farms and warehouses were the property of the Iron Heel. Armies of troops were put into the field, and the fanatics were herded back at the bayonet point to their tasks in the cities. There they broke out in ever recurring mobs and riots. Their leaders were executed for sedition or confined in madhouses. Those who were executed went to their deaths with all the gladness of martyrs. It was a time of madness. The unrest spread. In the swamps and deserts and waste places, from Florida to Alaska, the small groups of Indians that survived were dancing ghost dances and waiting the coming of a Messiah of their own.

And through it all, with a serenity and certitude that was terrifying, continued to rise the form of that monster of the ages, the Oligarchy. With iron hand and iron heel it mastered the surging millions, out of confusion brought order, out of the very chaos wrought its own foundation and structure.

'Just wait till we get in,' the Grangers said—Calvin said it to us in our Pell Street quarters. 'Look at the states we've captured. With you socialists to back us, we'll make them sing another song when we take office.'

'The millions of the discontented and the impoverished are ours,' the socialists said. 'The Grangers have come over to us, the farmers, the middle class, and the laborers. The capitalist system will fall to pieces. In another month we send fifty men to Congress. Two years hence every office will be ours, from the President down to the local dog-catcher.'

To all of which Ernest would shake his head and say:

'How many rifles have you got? Do you know where you can get plenty of lead? When it comes to powder, chemical mixtures are better than mechanical mixtures, you take my word.'

CHAPTER XVI
THE END

When it came time for Ernest and me to go to Washington, father did not accompany us. He had become enamoured of proletarian life. He looked upon our slum neighborhood as a great sociological laboratory, and he had embarked upon an apparently endless orgy of investigation. He chummed with the laborers, and was an intimate in scores of homes. Also, he worked at odd jobs, and the work was play as well as learned investigation, for he delighted in it and was always returning home with copious notes and bubbling over with new adventures. He was the perfect scientist.

There was no need for his working at all, because Ernest managed to earn enough from his translating to take care of the three of us. But father insisted on pursuing his favorite phantom, and a protean phantom it was, judging from the jobs he worked at. I shall never forget the evening he brought home his street pedler's outfit of shoe-laces and suspenders, nor the time I went into the little corner grocery to make some purchase and had him wait on me. After that I was not surprised when he tended bar for a week in the saloon across the street. He worked as a night watchman, hawked potatoes on the street, pasted labels in a cannery warehouse, was utility man in a paper-box factory, and water-carrier for a street railway construction gang, and even joined the Dishwashers' Union just before it fell to pieces.

I think the Bishop's example, so far as wearing apparel was concerned, must have fascinated father, for he wore the cheap cotton shirt of the laborer and the overalls with the narrow strap about the hips. Yet one habit remained to him from the old life; he always dressed for dinner, or supper, rather.

I could be happy anywhere with Ernest; and father's happiness in our changed circumstances rounded out my own happiness.

'When I was a boy,' father said, 'I was very curious. I wanted to know why things were and how they came to pass. That was why I became a physicist. The life in me to-day is just as curious as it was in my boyhood, and it's the being curious that makes life worth living.'

Sometimes he ventured north of Market Street into the shopping and theatre district, where he sold papers, ran errands, and opened cabs. There, one day, closing a cab, he encountered Mr. Wickson. In high glee father described the incident to us that evening.

'Wickson looked at me sharply when I closed the door on him, and muttered, 'Well, I'll be damned.' Just like that he said it, 'Well, I'll be damned.' His face turned red and he was so confused that he forgot to tip me. But he must have recovered himself quickly, for the cab hadn't gone fifty feet before it turned around and came back. He leaned out of the door.

'Look here, Professor,' he said, 'this is too much. What can I do for you?'

'I closed the cab door for you,' I answered. 'According to common custom you might give me a dime.'

'Bother that!' he snorted. 'I mean something substantial.'

'He was certainly serious—a twinge of ossified conscience or something; and so I considered with grave deliberation for a moment.

'His face was quite expectant when I began my answer, but you should have seen it when I finished.

'You might give me back my home,' I said, 'and my stock in the Sierra Mills.'

Father paused.

'What did he say?' I questioned eagerly.

'What could he say? He said nothing. But I said. 'I hope you are happy.' He looked at me curiously. 'Tell me, are you happy?' I asked.

'He ordered the cabman to drive on, and went away swearing horribly. And he didn't give me the dime, much less the home and stock; so you see, my dear, your father's street-arab career is beset with disappointments.'

And so it was that father kept on at our Pell Street quarters, while Ernest and I went to Washington. Except for the final consummation, the old order had passed away, and the final consummation was nearer than I dreamed. Contrary to our expectation, no obstacles were raised to prevent the socialist Congressmen from taking their seats. Everything went smoothly, and I laughed at Ernest when he looked upon the very smoothness as something ominous.

We found our socialist comrades confident, optimistic of their strength and of the things they would accomplish. A few Grangers who had been elected to Congress increased our strength, and an elaborate programme of what was to be done was prepared by the united forces. In all of which Ernest joined loyally and energetically, though he could not forbear, now and again, from saying, apropos of nothing in particular, 'When it comes to powder, chemical mixtures are better than mechanical mixtures, you take my word.'

The trouble arose first with the Grangers in the various states they had captured at the last election. There were a dozen of these states, but the Grangers who had been elected were not permitted to take office. The incumbents refused to get out. It was very simple. They merely charged illegality in the elections and wrapped up the whole situation in the interminable red tape of the law. The Grangers were powerless. The courts were in the hands of their enemies.

This was the moment of danger. If the cheated Grangers became violent, all was lost. How we socialists worked to hold them back! There were days and nights when Ernest never closed his eyes in sleep. The big leaders of the Grangers saw the peril and were with us to a man. But it was all of no avail. The Oligarchy wanted violence, and it set its agents-provocateurs to work. Without discussion, it was the agents-provocateurs who caused the Peasant Revolt.

In a dozen states the revolt flared up. The expropriated farmers took forcible possession of the state governments. Of course this was unconstitutional, and of course the United States put its soldiers into the field. Everywhere the agents-provocateurs urged the people on. These emissaries of the Iron Heel disguised themselves as artisans, farmers, and farm laborers. In Sacramento, the capital of California, the Grangers had succeeded in maintaining order. Thousands of secret agents were rushed to the devoted city. In mobs composed wholly of themselves, they fired and looted buildings and factories. They worked the people up until they joined them in the pillage. Liquor in large quantities was distributed among the slum classes further to inflame their minds. And then, when all was ready, appeared upon the scene the soldiers of the United States, who were, in reality, the soldiers of the Iron Heel. Eleven thousand men, women, and children were shot down on the streets of Sacramento or murdered in their houses. The national government took possession of the state government, and all was over for California.

And as with California, so elsewhere. Every Granger state was ravaged with violence and washed in blood. First, disorder was precipitated by the secret agents and the Black Hundreds, then the troops were called out. Rioting and mob-rule reigned throughout the rural districts. Day and night the smoke of burning farms, warehouses, villages, and cities filled the sky. Dynamite appeared. Railroad bridges and tunnels were blown up and trains were wrecked. The poor farmers were shot and hanged in great numbers. Reprisals were bitter, and many plutocrats and army officers were murdered. Blood and vengeance were in men's hearts. The regular troops fought the farmers as savagely as had they been Indians. And the regular troops had cause. Twenty-eight hundred of them had been annihilated in a tremendous series of dynamite explosions in Oregon, and in a similar manner, a number of train loads, at different times and places, had been destroyed. So it was that the regular troops fought for their lives as well as did the farmers.

As for the militia, the militia law of 1903 was put into effect, and the workers of one state were compelled, under pain of death, to shoot down their comrade-workers in other states. Of course, the militia law did not work smoothly at first. Many militia officers were murdered, and many militiamen were executed by drumhead court martial. Ernest's prophecy was strikingly fulfilled in the cases of Mr. Kowalt and Mr. Asmunsen. Both were eligible for the militia, and both were drafted to serve in the punitive expedition that was despatched from California against the farmers of Missouri. Mr. Kowalt and Mr. Asmunsen refused to serve. They were given short shrift. Drumhead court martial was their portion, and military execution their end. They were shot with their backs to the firing squad.

Many young men fled into the mountains to escape serving in the militia. There they became outlaws, and it was not until more peaceful times that they received their punishment. It was drastic. The government issued a proclamation for all law-abiding citizens to come in from the mountains for a period of three months. When the proclaimed date arrived, half a million soldiers were sent into the mountainous districts everywhere. There was no investigation, no trial. Wherever a man was encountered, he was shot down on the spot. The troops operated on the basis that no man not an outlaw remained in the mountains. Some bands, in strong positions, fought gallantly, but in the end every deserter from the militia met death.

A more immediate lesson, however, was impressed on the minds of the people by the punishment meted out to the Kansas militia. The great Kansas Mutiny occurred at the very beginning of military operations against the Grangers. Six thousand of the militia mutinied. They had been for several weeks very turbulent and sullen, and for that reason had been kept in camp. Their open mutiny, however, was without doubt precipitated by the agents-provocateurs.

On the night of the 22d of April they arose and murdered their officers, only a small remnant of the latter escaping. This was beyond the scheme of the Iron Heel, for the agents-provocateurs had done their work too well. But everything was grist to the Iron Heel. It had prepared for the outbreak, and the killing of so many officers gave it justification for what followed. As by magic, forty thousand soldiers of the regular army surrounded the malcontents. It was a trap. The wretched militiamen found that their machine-guns had been tampered with, and that the cartridges from the captured magazines did not fit their rifles. They hoisted the white flag of surrender, but it was ignored. There were no survivors. The entire six thousand were annihilated. Common shell and shrapnel were thrown in upon them from a distance, and, when, in their desperation, they charged the encircling lines, they were mowed down by the machine-guns. I talked with an eye-witness, and he said that the nearest any militiaman approached the machine-guns was a hundred and fifty yards. The earth was carpeted with the slain, and a final charge of cavalry, with trampling of horses' hoofs, revolvers, and sabres, crushed the wounded into the ground.

Simultaneously with the destruction of the Grangers came the revolt of the coal miners. It was the expiring effort of organized labor. Three-quarters of a million of miners went out on strike. But they were too widely scattered over the country to advantage from their own strength. They were segregated in their own districts and beaten into submission. This was the first great slave-drive. Pocock* won his spurs as

---

* Albert Pocock, another of the notorious strike-breakers of earlier years, who, to the day of his death, successfully held all the coal-miners of the country to their task. He was succeeded

a slave-driver and earned the undying hatred of the proletariat. Countless attempts were made upon his life, but he seemed to bear a charmed existence. It was he who was responsible for the introduction of the Russian passport system among the miners, and the denial of their right of removal from one part of the country to another.

In the meantime, the socialists held firm. While the Grangers expired in flame and blood, and organized labor was disrupted, the socialists held their peace and perfected their secret organization. In vain the Grangers pleaded with us. We rightly contended that any revolt on our part was virtually suicide for the whole Revolution. The Iron Heel, at first dubious about dealing with the entire proletariat at one time, had found the work easier than it had expected, and would have asked nothing better than an uprising on our part. But we avoided the issue, in spite of the fact that agents-provocateurs swarmed in our midst. In those early days, the agents of the Iron Heel were clumsy in their methods. They had much to learn and in the meantime our Fighting Groups weeded them out. It was bitter, bloody work, but we were fighting for life and for the Revolution, and we had to fight the enemy with its own weapons. Yet we were fair. No agent of the Iron Heel was executed without a trial. We may have made mistakes, but if so, very rarely. The bravest, and the most combative and self-sacrificing of our comrades went into the Fighting Groups. Once, after ten years had passed, Ernest made a calculation from figures furnished by the chiefs of the Fighting Groups, and his conclusion was that the average life of a man or woman after becoming a member was five years. The comrades of the Fighting Groups were heroes all, and the peculiar thing about it was that they were opposed to the taking of life. They violated their own natures, yet they loved liberty and knew of no sacrifice too great to make for the Cause.*

---

by his son, Lewis Pocock, and for five generations this remarkable line of slave-drivers handled the coal mines. The elder Pocock, known as Pocock I., has been described as follows: 'A long, lean head, semicircled by a fringe of brown and gray hair, with big cheek-bones and a heavy chin, . . . a pale face, lustreless gray eyes, a metallic voice, and a languid manner.' He was born of humble parents, and began his career as a bartender. He next became a private detective for a street railway corporation, and by successive steps developed into a professional strikebreaker. Pocock V., the last of the line, was blown up in a pump-house by a bomb during a petty revolt of the miners in the Indian Territory. This occurred in 2073 A.D.

* These Fighting groups were modelled somewhat after the Fighting Organization of the Russian Revolution, and, despite the unceasing efforts of the Iron Heel, these groups persisted throughout the three centuries of its existence. Composed of men and women actuated by lofty purpose and unafraid to die, the Fighting Groups exercised tremendous influence and tempered the savage brutality of the rulers. Not alone was their work confined to unseen warfare with the secret agents of the Oligarchy. The oligarchs themselves were compelled to listen to the decrees of the Groups, and often, when they disobeyed, were punished by death—and likewise with the subordinates of the oligarchs, with the officers of the army and the leaders of the labor castes. Stern justice was meted out by these organized avengers, but most remarkable was their passionless and judicial procedure. There were no snap judgments. When a man was captured he was given fair trial and opportunity for defence. Of necessity, many men were tried and condemned by proxy, as in the case of General Lampton. This occurred in 2138 A.D. Possibly the most bloodthirsty and malignant of all the mercenaries that ever served the Iron Heel, he was informed by the Fighting Groups that they had tried him, found him guilty, and condemned him to death—and this, after three warnings for him to cease from his ferocious treatment of the proletariat. After his condemnation he surrounded himself with a myriad protective devices. Years passed, and in vain the Fighting Groups strove to execute their decree. Comrade after comrade, men and women, failed in

The task we set ourselves was threefold. First, the weeding out from our circles of the secret agents of the Oligarchy. Second, the organizing of the Fighting Groups, and outside of them, of the general secret organization of the Revolution. And third, the introduction of our own secret agents into every branch of the Oligarchy—into the labor castes and especially among the telegraphers and secretaries and clerks, into the army, the agents-provocateurs, and the slave-drivers. It was slow work, and perilous, and often were our efforts rewarded with costly failures.

The Iron Heel had triumphed in open warfare, but we held our own in the new warfare, strange and awful and subterranean, that we instituted. All was unseen, much was unguessed; the blind fought the blind; and yet through it all was order, purpose, control. We permeated the entire organization of the Iron Heel with our agents, while our own organization was permeated with the agents of the Iron Heel. It was warfare dark and devious, replete with intrigue and conspiracy, plot and counterplot. And behind all, ever menacing, was death, violent and terrible. Men and women disappeared, our nearest and dearest comrades. We saw them to-day. To-morrow they were gone; we never saw them again, and we knew that they had died.

There was no trust, no confidence anywhere. The man who plotted beside us, for all we knew, might be an agent of the Iron Heel. We mined the organization of the Iron Heel with our secret agents, and the Iron Heel countermined with its secret agents inside its own organization. And it was the same with our organization. And despite the absence of confidence and trust we were compelled to base our every effort on confidence and trust. Often were we betrayed. Men were weak. The Iron Heel could offer money, leisure, the joys and pleasures that waited in the repose of the wonder cities. We could offer nothing but the satisfaction of being faithful to a noble ideal. As for the rest, the wages of those who were loyal were unceasing peril, torture, and death.

Men were weak, I say, and because of their weakness we were compelled to make the only other reward that was within our power. It was the reward of death. Out of necessity we had to punish our traitors. For every man who betrayed us, from one to a dozen faithful avengers were loosed upon his heels. We might fail to carry out our decrees against our enemies, such as the Pococks, for instance; but the one thing we could not afford to fail in was the punishment of our own traitors. Comrades

---

their attempts, and were cruelly executed by the Oligarchy. It was the case of General Lampton that revived crucifixion as a legal method of execution. But in the end the condemned man found his executioner in the form of a slender girl of seventeen, Madeline Provence, who, to accomplish her purpose, served two years in his palace as a seamstress to the household. She died in solitary confinement after horrible and prolonged torture; but to-day she stands in imperishable bronze in the Pantheon of Brotherhood in the wonder city of Serles. We, who by personal experience know nothing of bloodshed, must not judge harshly the heroes of the Fighting Groups. They gave up their lives for humanity, no sacrifice was too great for them to accomplish, while inexorable necessity compelled them to bloody expression in an age of blood. The Fighting Groups constituted the one thorn in the side of the Iron Heel that the Iron Heel could never remove. Everhard was the father of this curious army, and its accomplishments and successful persistence for three hundred years bear witness to the wisdom with which he organized and the solid foundation he laid for the succeeding generations to build upon. In some respects, despite his great economic and sociological contributions, and his work as a general leader in the Revolution, his organization of the Fighting Groups must be regarded as his greatest achievement.

turned traitor by permission, in order to win to the wonder cities and there execute our sentences on the real traitors. In fact, so terrible did we make ourselves, that it became a greater peril to betray us than to remain loyal to us.

The Revolution took on largely the character of religion. We worshipped at the shrine of the Revolution, which was the shrine of liberty. It was the divine flashing through us. Men and women devoted their lives to the Cause, and new-born babes were sealed to it as of old they had been sealed to the service of God. We were lovers of Humanity.

CHAPTER XVII
THE SCARLET LIVERY

With the destruction of the Granger states, the Grangers in Congress disappeared. They were being tried for high treason, and their places were taken by the creatures of the Iron Heel. The socialists were in a pitiful minority, and they knew that their end was near. Congress and the Senate were empty pretences, farces. Public questions were gravely debated and passed upon according to the old forms, while in reality all that was done was to give the stamp of constitutional procedure to the mandates of the Oligarchy.

Ernest was in the thick of the fight when the end came. It was in the debate on the bill to assist the unemployed. The hard times of the preceding year had thrust great masses of the proletariat beneath the starvation line, and the continued and wide-reaching disorder had but sunk them deeper. Millions of people were starving, while the oligarchs and their supporters were surfeiting on the surplus.* We called these wretched people the people of the abyss,** and it was to alleviate their awful suffering that the socialists had introduced the unemployed bill. But this was not to the fancy of the Iron Heel. In its own way it was preparing to set these millions to work, but the way was not our way, wherefore it had issued its orders that our bill should be voted down. Ernest and his fellows knew that their effort was futile, but they were tired of the suspense. They wanted something to happen. They were accomplishing nothing, and the best they hoped for was the putting of an end to the legislative farce in which they were unwilling players. They knew not what end would come, but they never anticipated a more disastrous end than the one that did come.

I sat in the gallery that day. We all knew that something terrible was imminent.

---

* The same conditions obtained in the nineteenth century A.D. under British rule in India. The natives died of starvation by the million, while their rulers robbed them of the fruits of their toil and expended it on magnificent pageants and mumbo-jumbo fooleries. Perforce, in this enlightened age, we have much to blush for in the acts of our ancestors. Our only consolation is philosophic. We must accept the capitalistic stage in social evolution as about on a par with the earlier monkey stage. The human had to pass through those stages in its rise from the mire and slime of low organic life. It was inevitable that much of the mire and slime should cling and be not easily shaken off.

** The people of the abyss—this phrase was struck out by the genius of H. G. Wells in the late nineteenth century A.D. Wells was a sociological seer, sane and normal as well as warm human. Many fragments of his work have come down to us, while two of his greatest achievements, 'Anticipations' and 'Mankind in the Making,' have come down intact. Before the oligarchs, and before Everhard, Wells speculated upon the building of the wonder cities, though in his writings they are referred to as 'pleasure cities.'

It was in the air, and its presence was made visible by the armed soldiers drawn up in lines in the corridors, and by the officers grouped in the entrances to the House itself. The Oligarchy was about to strike. Ernest was speaking. He was describing the sufferings of the unemployed, as if with the wild idea of in some way touching their hearts and consciences; but the Republican and Democratic members sneered and jeered at him, and there was uproar and confusion. Ernest abruptly changed front.

'I know nothing that I may say can influence you,' he said. 'You have no souls to be influenced. You are spineless, flaccid things. You pompously call yourselves Republicans and Democrats. There is no Republican Party. There is no Democratic Party. There are no Republicans nor Democrats in this House. You are lick-spittlers and panderers, the creatures of the Plutocracy. You talk verbosely in antiquated terminology of your love of liberty, and all the while you wear the scarlet livery of the Iron Heel.'

Here the shouting and the cries of 'Order! order!' drowned his voice, and he stood disdainfully till the din had somewhat subsided. He waved his hand to include all of them, turned to his own comrades, and said:

'Listen to the bellowing of the well-fed beasts.'

Pandemonium broke out again. The Speaker rapped for order and glanced expectantly at the officers in the doorways. There were cries of 'Sedition!' and a great, rotund New York member began shouting 'Anarchist!' at Ernest. And Ernest was not pleasant to look at. Every fighting fibre of him was quivering, and his face was the face of a fighting animal, withal he was cool and collected.

'Remember,' he said, in a voice that made itself heard above the din, 'that as you show mercy now to the proletariat, some day will that same proletariat show mercy to you.'

The cries of 'Sedition!' and 'Anarchist!' redoubled.

'I know that you will not vote for this bill,' Ernest went on. 'You have received the command from your masters to vote against it. And yet you call me anarchist. You, who have destroyed the government of the people, and who shamelessly flaunt your scarlet shame in public places, call me anarchist. I do not believe in hell-fire and brimstone; but in moments like this I regret my unbelief. Nay, in moments like this I almost do believe. Surely there must be a hell, for in no less place could it be possible for you to receive punishment adequate to your crimes. So long as you exist, there is a vital need for hell-fire in the Cosmos.'

There was movement in the doorways. Ernest, the Speaker, all the members turned to see.

'Why do you not call your soldiers in, Mr. Speaker, and bid them do their work?' Ernest demanded. 'They should carry out your plan with expedition.'

'There are other plans afoot,' was the retort. 'That is why the soldiers are present.'

'Our plans, I suppose,' Ernest sneered. 'Assassination or something kindred.'

But at the word 'assassination' the uproar broke out again. Ernest could not make himself heard, but he remained on his feet waiting for a lull. And then it happened. From my place in the gallery I saw nothing except the flash of the explosion. The roar of it filled my ears and I saw Ernest reeling and falling in a swirl of smoke, and the soldiers rushing up all the aisles. His comrades were on their feet, wild with anger, capable of any violence. But Ernest steadied himself for a moment, and waved his arms for silence.

'It is a plot!' his voice rang out in warning to his comrades. 'Do nothing, or you will be destroyed.'

Then he slowly sank down, and the soldiers reached him. The next moment soldiers were clearing the galleries and I saw no more.

Though he was my husband, I was not permitted to get to him. When I announced who I was, I was promptly placed under arrest. And at the same time were arrested all socialist Congressmen in Washington, including the unfortunate Simpson, who lay ill with typhoid fever in his hotel.

The trial was prompt and brief. The men were foredoomed. The wonder was that Ernest was not executed. This was a blunder on the part of the Oligarchy, and a costly one. But the Oligarchy was too confident in those days. It was drunk with success, and little did it dream that that small handful of heroes had within them the power to rock it to its foundations. To-morrow, when the Great Revolt breaks out and all the world resounds with the tramp, tramp of the millions, the Oligarchy, will realize, and too late, how mightily that band of heroes has grown.[*]

As a revolutionist myself, as one on the inside who knew the hopes and fears and secret plans of the revolutionists, I am fitted to answer, as very few are, the charge that they were guilty of exploding the bomb in Congress. And I can say flatly, without qualification or doubt of any sort, that the socialists, in Congress and out, had no hand in the affair. Who threw the bomb we do not know, but the one thing we are absolutely sure of is that we did not throw it.

On the other hand, there is evidence to show that the Iron Heel was responsible for the act. Of course, we cannot prove this. Our conclusion is merely presumptive. But here are such facts as we do know. It had been reported to the Speaker of the House, by secret-service agents of the government, that the Socialist Congressmen were about to resort to terroristic tactics, and that they had decided upon the day when their tactics would go into effect. This day was the very day of the explosion. Wherefore the Capitol had been packed with troops in anticipation. Since we knew nothing about the bomb, and since a bomb actually was exploded, and since the authorities had prepared in advance for the explosion, it is only fair to conclude that the Iron Heel did know. Furthermore, we charge that the Iron Heel was guilty of the outrage, and that the Iron Heel planned and perpetrated the outrage for the purpose of foisting the guilt on our shoulders and so bringing about our destruction.

From the Speaker the warning leaked out to all the creatures in the House that

---

[*] Avis Everhard took for granted that her narrative would be read in her own day, and so omits to mention the outcome of the trial for high treason. Many other similar disconcerting omissions will be noticed in the Manuscript. Fifty-two socialist Congressmen were tried, and all were found guilty. Strange to relate, not one received the death sentence. Everhard and eleven others, among whom were Theodore Donnelson and Matthew Kent, received life imprisonment. The remaining forty received sentences varying from thirty to forty-five years; while Arthur Simpson, referred to in the Manuscript as being ill of typhoid fever at the time of the explosion, received only fifteen years. It is the tradition that he died of starvation in solitary confinement, and this harsh treatment is explained as having been caused by his uncompromising stubbornness and his fiery and tactless hatred for all men that served the despotism. He died in Cabanas in Cuba, where three of his comrades were also confined. The fifty- two socialist Congressmen were confined in military fortresses scattered all over the United States. Thus, Du Bois and Woods were held in Porto Rico, while Everhard and Merryweather were placed in Alcatraz, an island in San Francisco Bay that had already seen long service as a military prison.

wore the scarlet livery. They knew, while Ernest was speaking, that some violent act was to be committed. And to do them justice, they honestly believed that the act was to be committed by the socialists. At the trial, and still with honest belief, several testified to having seen Ernest prepare to throw the bomb, and that it exploded prematurely. Of course they saw nothing of the sort. In the fevered imagination of fear they thought they saw, that was all.

As Ernest said at the trial: 'Does it stand to reason, if I were going to throw a bomb, that I should elect to throw a feeble little squib like the one that was thrown? There wasn't enough powder in it. It made a lot of smoke, but hurt no one except me. It exploded right at my feet, and yet it did not kill me. Believe me, when I get to throwing bombs, I'll do damage. There'll be more than smoke in my petards.'

In return it was argued by the prosecution that the weakness of the bomb was a blunder on the part of the socialists, just as its premature explosion, caused by Ernest's losing his nerve and dropping it, was a blunder. And to clinch the argument, there were the several Congressmen who testified to having seen Ernest fumble and drop the bomb.

As for ourselves, not one of us knew how the bomb was thrown. Ernest told me that the fraction of an instant before it exploded he both heard and saw it strike at his feet. He testified to this at the trial, but no one believed him. Besides, the whole thing, in popular slang, was 'cooked up.' The Iron Heel had made up its mind to destroy us, and there was no withstanding it.

There is a saying that truth will out. I have come to doubt that saying. Nineteen years have elapsed, and despite our untiring efforts, we have failed to find the man who really did throw the bomb. Undoubtedly he was some emissary of the Iron Heel, but he has escaped detection. We have never got the slightest clew to his identity. And now, at this late date, nothing remains but for the affair to take its place among the mysteries of history.*

---

* Avis Everhard would have had to live for many generations ere she could have seen the clearing up of this particular mystery. A little less than a hundred years ago, and a little more than six hundred years after the death, the confession of Pervaise was discovered in the secret archives of the Vatican. It is perhaps well to tell a little something about this obscure document, which, in the main, is of interest to the historian only. Pervaise was an American, of French descent, who in 1913 A.D., was lying in the Tombs Prison, New York City, awaiting trial for murder. From his confession we learn that he was not a criminal. He was warm-blooded, passionate, emotional. In an insane fit of jealousy he killed his wife—a very common act in those times. Pervaise was mastered by the fear of death, all of which is recounted at length in his confession. To escape death he would have done anything, and the police agents prepared him by assuring him that he could not possibly escape conviction of murder in the first degree when his trial came off. In those days, murder in the first degree was a capital offense. The guilty man or woman was placed in a specially constructed death-chair, and, under the supervision of competent physicians, was destroyed by a current of electricity. This was called electrocution, and it was very popular during that period. Anaesthesia, as a mode of compulsory death, was not introduced until later. This man, good at heart but with a ferocious animalism close at the surface of his being, lying in jail and expectant of nothing less than death, was prevailed upon by the agents of the Iron Heel to throw the bomb in the House of Representatives. In his confession he states explicitly that he was informed that the bomb was to be a feeble thing and that no lives would be lost. This is directly in line with the fact that the bomb was lightly charged, and that its explosion at Everhard's feet was not deadly. Pervaise was smuggled into one of the galleries ostensibly closed for repairs. He was to select the moment for the throwing of the bomb, and he naively confesses that in his interest in Everhard's

CHAPTER XVIII
IN THE SHADOW OF SONOMA

Of myself, during this period, there is not much to say. For six months I was kept in prison, though charged with no crime. I was a suspect—a word of fear that all revolutionists were soon to come to know. But our own nascent secret service was beginning to work. By the end of my second month in prison, one of the jailers made himself known as a revolutionist in touch with the organization. Several weeks later, Joseph Parkhurst, the prison doctor who had just been appointed, proved himself to be a member of one of the Fighting Groups.

---

tirade and the general commotion raised thereby, he nearly forgot his mission. Not only was he released from prison in reward for his deed, but he was granted an income for life. This he did not long enjoy. In 1914 A.D., in September, he was stricken with rheumatism of the heart and lived for three days. It was then that he sent for the Catholic priest, Father Peter Durban, and to him made confession. So important did it seem to the priest, that he had the confession taken down in writing and sworn to. What happened after this we can only surmise. The document was certainly important enough to find its way to Rome. Powerful influences must have been brought to bear, hence its suppression. For centuries no hint of its existence reached the world. It was not until in the last century that Lorbia, the brilliant Italian scholar, stumbled upon it quite by chance during his researches in the Vatican. There is to-day no doubt whatever that the Iron Heel was responsible for the bomb that exploded in the House of Representatives in 1913 A.D. Even though the Pervaise confession had never come to light, no reasonable doubt could obtain; for the act in question, that sent fifty-two Congressmen to prison, was on a par with countless other acts committed by the oligarchs, and, before them, by the capitalists. There is the classic instance of the ferocious and wanton judicial murder of the innocent and so-called Haymarket Anarchists in Chicago in the penultimate decade of the nineteenth century A.D. In a category by itself is the deliberate burning and destruction of capitalist property by the capitalists themselves. For such destruction of property innocent men were frequently punished—'railroaded' in the parlance of the times. In the labor troubles of the first decade of the twentieth century A.D., between the capitalists and the Western Federation of Miners, similar but more bloody tactics were employed. The railroad station at Independence was blown up by the agents of the capitalists. Thirteen men were killed, and many more were wounded. And then the capitalists, controlling the legislative and judicial machinery of the state of Colorado, charged the miners with the crime and came very near to convicting them. Romaines, one of the tools in this affair, like Pervaise, was lying in jail in another state, Kansas, awaiting trial, when he was approached by the agents of the capitalists. But, unlike Pervaise the confession of Romaines was made public in his own time. Then, during this same period, there was the case of Moyer and Haywood, two strong, fearless leaders of labor. One was president and the other was secretary of the Western Federation of Miners. The ex-governor of Idaho had been mysteriously murdered. The crime, at the time, was openly charged to the mine owners by the socialists and miners. Nevertheless, in violation of the national and state constitutions, and by means of conspiracy on the parts of the governors of Idaho and Colorado, Moyer and Haywood were kidnapped, thrown into jail, and charged with the murder. It was this instance that provoked from Eugene V. Debs, national leader of the American socialists at the time, the following words: 'The labor leaders that cannot be bribed nor bullied, must be ambushed and murdered. The only crime of Moyer and Haywood is that they have been unswervingly true to the working class. The capitalists have stolen our country, debauched our politics, defiled our judiciary, and ridden over us rough-shod, and now they propose to murder those who will not abjectly surrender to their brutal dominion. The governors of Colorado and Idaho are but executing the mandates of their masters, the Plutocracy. The issue is the Workers versus the Plutocracy. If they strike the first violent blow, we will strike the last.'

Thus, throughout the organization of the Oligarchy, our own organization, weblike and spidery, was insinuating itself. And so I was kept in touch with all that was happening in the world without. And furthermore, every one of our imprisoned leaders was in contact with brave comrades who masqueraded in the livery of the Iron Heel. Though Ernest lay in prison three thousand miles away, on the Pacific Coast, I was in unbroken communication with him, and our letters passed regularly back and forth.

The leaders, in prison and out, were able to discuss and direct the campaign. It would have been possible, within a few months, to have effected the escape of some of them; but since imprisonment proved no bar to our activities, it was decided to avoid anything premature. Fifty-two Congressmen were in prison, and fully three hundred more of our leaders. It was planned that they should be delivered simultaneously. If part of them escaped, the vigilance of the oligarchs might be aroused so as to prevent the escape of the remainder. On the other hand, it was held that a simultaneous jail-delivery all over the land would have immense psychological influence on the proletariat. It would show our strength and give confidence.

So it was arranged, when I was released at the end of six months, that I was to disappear and prepare a secure hiding-place for Ernest. To disappear was in itself no easy thing. No sooner did I get my freedom than my footsteps began to be dogged by the spies of the Iron Heel. It was necessary that they should be thrown off the track, and that I should win to California. It is laughable, the way this was accomplished.

Already the passport system, modelled on the Russian, was developing. I dared not cross the continent in my own character. It was necessary that I should be completely lost if ever I was to see Ernest again, for by trailing me after he escaped, he would be caught once more. Again, I could not disguise myself as a proletarian and travel. There remained the disguise of a member of the Oligarchy. While the arch-oligarchs were no more than a handful, there were myriads of lesser ones of the type, say, of Mr. Wickson—men, worth a few millions, who were adherents of the arch-oligarchs. The wives and daughters of these lesser oligarchs were legion, and it was decided that I should assume the disguise of such a one. A few years later this would have been impossible, because the passport system was to become so perfect that no man, woman, nor child in all the land was unregistered and unaccounted for in his or her movements.

When the time was ripe, the spies were thrown off my track. An hour later Avis Everhard was no more. At that time one Felice Van Verdighan, accompanied by two maids and a lap-dog, with another maid for the lap-dog,[*] entered a drawing-room on a Pullman,[**] and a few minutes later was speeding west.

The three maids who accompanied me were revolutionists. Two were members of the Fighting Groups, and the third, Grace Holbrook, entered a group the following year, and six months later was executed by the Iron Heel. She it was who waited upon the dog. Of the other two, Bertha Stole disappeared twelve years later, while Anna

---

[*] This ridiculous picture well illustrates the heartless conduct of the masters. While people starved, lap-dogs were waited upon by maids. This was a serious masquerade on the part of Avis Everhard. Life and death and the Cause were in the issue; therefore the picture must be accepted as a true picture. It affords a striking commentary of the times.

[**] Pullman—the designation of the more luxurious railway cars of the period and so named from the inventor.

Roylston still lives and plays an increasingly important part in the Revolution.[*]

Without adventure we crossed the United States to California. When the train stopped at Sixteenth Street Station, in Oakland, we alighted, and there Felice Van Verdighan, with her two maids, her lap-dog, and her lap-dog's maid, disappeared forever. The maids, guided by trusty comrades, were led away. Other comrades took charge of me. Within half an hour after leaving the train I was on board a small fishing boat and out on the waters of San Francisco Bay. The winds baffled, and we drifted aimlessly the greater part of the night. But I saw the lights of Alcatraz where Ernest lay, and found comfort in the thought of nearness to him. By dawn, what with the rowing of the fishermen, we made the Marin Islands. Here we lay in hiding all day, and on the following night, swept on by a flood tide and a fresh wind, we crossed San Pablo Bay in two hours and ran up Petaluma Creek.

Here horses were ready and another comrade, and without delay we were away through the starlight. To the north I could see the loom of Sonoma Mountain, toward which we rode. We left the old town of Sonoma to the right and rode up a canyon that lay between outlying buttresses of the mountain. The wagon-road became a wood-road, the wood-road became a cow-path, and the cow-path dwindled away and ceased among the upland pastures. Straight over Sonoma Mountain we rode. It was the safest route. There was no one to mark our passing.

Dawn caught us on the northern brow, and in the gray light we dropped down through chaparral into redwood canyons deep and warm with the breath of passing summer. It was old country to me that I knew and loved, and soon I became the guide. The hiding-place was mine. I had selected it. We let down the bars and crossed an upland meadow. Next, we went over a low, oak-covered ridge and descended into a smaller meadow. Again we climbed a ridge, this time riding under red-limbed madronos and manzanitas of deeper red. The first rays of the sun streamed upon our backs as we climbed. A flight of quail thrummed off through the thickets. A big jackrabbit crossed our path, leaping swiftly and silently like a deer. And then a deer, a many-pronged buck, the sun flashing red-gold from neck and shoulders, cleared the crest of the ridge before us and was gone.

We followed in his wake a space, then dropped down a zigzag trail that he disdained into a group of noble redwoods that stood about a pool of water murky with minerals from the mountain side. I knew every inch of the way. Once a writer friend of mine had owned the ranch; but he, too, had become a revolutionist, though more disastrously than I, for he was already dead and gone, and none knew where nor how. He alone, in the days he had lived, knew the secret of the hiding-place for which I was bound. He had bought the ranch for beauty, and paid a round price for it, much to the disgust of the local farmers. He used to tell with great glee how they were wont to shake their heads mournfully at the price, to accomplish ponderously a bit of mental arithmetic, and then to say, 'But you can't make six per cent on it.'

---

* Despite continual and almost inconceivable hazards, Anna Roylston lived to the royal age of ninety-one. As the Pococks defied the executioners of the Fighting Groups, so she defied the executioners of the Iron Heel. She bore a charmed life and prospered amid dangers and alarms. She herself was an executioner for the Fighting Groups, and, known as the Red Virgin, she became one of the inspired figures of the Revolution. When she was an old woman of sixty-nine she shot 'Bloody' Halcliffe down in the midst of his armed escort and got away unscathed. In the end she died peacefully of old age in a secret refuge of the revolutionists in the Ozark mountains.

But he was dead now, nor did the ranch descend to his children. Of all men, it was now the property of Mr. Wickson, who owned the whole eastern and northern slopes of Sonoma Mountain, running from the Spreckels estate to the divide of Bennett Valley. Out of it he had made a magnificent deer-park, where, over thousands of acres of sweet slopes and glades and canyons, the deer ran almost in primitive wildness. The people who had owned the soil had been driven away. A state home for the feeble-minded had also been demolished to make room for the deer.

To cap it all, Wickson's hunting lodge was a quarter of a mile from my hiding-place. This, instead of being a danger, was an added security. We were sheltered under the very aegis of one of the minor oligarchs. Suspicion, by the nature of the situation, was turned aside. The last place in the world the spies of the Iron Heel would dream of looking for me, and for Ernest when he joined me, was Wickson's deer-park.

We tied our horses among the redwoods at the pool. From a cache behind a hollow rotting log my companion brought out a variety of things,—a fifty-pound sack of flour, tinned foods of all sorts, cooking utensils, blankets, a canvas tarpaulin, books and writing material, a great bundle of letters, a five-gallon can of kerosene, an oil stove, and, last and most important, a large coil of stout rope. So large was the supply of things that a number of trips would be necessary to carry them to the refuge.

But the refuge was very near. Taking the rope and leading the way, I passed through a glade of tangled vines and bushes that ran between two wooded knolls. The glade ended abruptly at the steep bank of a stream. It was a little stream, rising from springs, and the hottest summer never dried it up. On every hand were tall wooded knolls, a group of them, with all the seeming of having been flung there from some careless Titan's hand. There was no bed-rock in them. They rose from their bases hundreds of feet, and they were composed of red volcanic earth, the famous wine-soil of Sonoma. Through these the tiny stream had cut its deep and precipitous channel.

It was quite a scramble down to the stream bed, and, once on the bed, we went down stream perhaps for a hundred feet. And then we came to the great hole. There was no warning of the existence of the hole, nor was it a hole in the common sense of the word. One crawled through tight-locked briers and branches, and found oneself on the very edge, peering out and down through a green screen. A couple of hundred feet in length and width, it was half of that in depth. Possibly because of some fault that had occurred when the knolls were flung together, and certainly helped by freakish erosion, the hole had been scooped out in the course of centuries by the wash of water. Nowhere did the raw earth appear. All was garmented by vegetation, from tiny maiden-hair and gold-back ferns to mighty redwood and Douglas spruces. These great trees even sprang out from the walls of the hole. Some leaned over at angles as great as forty-five degrees, though the majority towered straight up from the soft and almost perpendicular earth walls.

It was a perfect hiding-place. No one ever came there, not even the village boys of Glen Ellen. Had this hole existed in the bed of a canyon a mile long, or several miles long, it would have been well known. But this was no canyon. From beginning to end the length of the stream was no more than five hundred yards. Three hundred yards above the hole the stream took its rise in a spring at the foot of a flat meadow. A hundred yards below the hole the stream ran out into open country, joining the main stream and flowing across rolling and grass-covered land.

My companion took a turn of the rope around a tree, and with me fast on the other end lowered away. In no time I was on the bottom. And in but a short while he had carried all the articles from the cache and lowered them down to me. He hauled the rope up and hid it, and before he went away called down to me a cheerful parting.

Before I go on I want to say a word for this comrade, John Carlson, a humble figure of the Revolution, one of the countless faithful ones in the ranks. He worked for Wickson, in the stables near the hunting lodge. In fact, it was on Wickson's horses that we had ridden over Sonoma Mountain. For nearly twenty years now John Carlson has been custodian of the refuge. No thought of disloyalty, I am sure, has ever entered his mind during all that time. To betray his trust would have been in his mind a thing undreamed. He was phlegmatic, stolid to such a degree that one could not but wonder how the Revolution had any meaning to him at all. And yet love of freedom glowed sombrely and steadily in his dim soul. In ways it was indeed good that he was not flighty and imaginative. He never lost his head. He could obey orders, and he was neither curious nor garrulous. Once I asked how it was that he was a revolutionist.

'When I was a young man I was a soldier,' was his answer. 'It was in Germany. There all young men must be in the army. So I was in the army. There was another soldier there, a young man, too. His father was what you call an agitator, and his father was in jail for lese majesty—what you call speaking the truth about the Emperor. And the young man, the son, talked with me much about people, and work, and the robbery of the people by the capitalists. He made me see things in new ways, and I became a socialist. His talk was very true and good, and I have never forgotten. When I came to the United States I hunted up the socialists. I became a member of a section—that was in the day of the S. L. P. Then later, when the split came, I joined the local of the S. P. I was working in a livery stable in San Francisco then. That was before the Earthquake. I have paid my dues for twenty-two years. I am yet a member, and I yet pay my dues, though it is very secret now. I will always pay my dues, and when the cooperative commonwealth comes, I will be glad.'

Left to myself, I proceeded to cook breakfast on the oil stove and to prepare my home. Often, in the early morning, or in the evening after dark, Carlson would steal down to the refuge and work for a couple of hours. At first my home was the tarpaulin. Later, a small tent was put up. And still later, when we became assured of the perfect security of the place, a small house was erected. This house was completely hidden from any chance eye that might peer down from the edge of the hole. The lush vegetation of that sheltered spot make a natural shield. Also, the house was built against the perpendicular wall; and in the wall itself, shored by strong timbers, well drained and ventilated, we excavated two small rooms. Oh, believe me, we had many comforts. When Biedenbach, the German terrorist, hid with us some time later, he installed a smoke-consuming device that enabled us to sit by crackling wood fires on winter nights.

And here I must say a word for that gentle-souled terrorist, than whom there is no comrade in the Revolution more fearfully misunderstood. Comrade Biedenbach did not betray the Cause. Nor was he executed by the comrades as is commonly supposed. This canard was circulated by the creatures of the Oligarchy. Comrade Biedenbach was absent-minded, forgetful. He was shot by one of our lookouts at the cave-refuge at Carmel, through failure on his part to remember the secret signals. It was all a sad mistake. And that he betrayed his Fighting Group is an absolute lie. No truer, more loyal man ever labored for the Cause.[*]

---

[*] Search as we may through all the material of those times that has come down to us, we can find no clew to the Biedenbach here referred to. No mention is made of him anywhere save in the Everhard Manuscript.

For nineteen years now the refuge that I selected had been almost continuously occupied, and in all that time, with one exception, it has never been discovered by an outsider. And yet it was only a quarter of a mile from Wickson's hunting-lodge, and a short mile from the village of Glen Ellen. I was able, always, to hear the morning and evening trains arrive and depart, and I used to set my watch by the whistle at the brickyards.*

CHAPTER XIX
TRANSFORMATION

'You must make yourself over again,' Ernest wrote to me. 'You must cease to be. You must become another woman—and not merely in the clothes you wear, but inside your skin under the clothes. You must make yourself over again so that even I would not know you—your voice, your gestures, your mannerisms, your carriage, your walk, everything.'

This command I obeyed. Every day I practised for hours in burying forever the old Avis Everhard beneath the skin of another woman whom I may call my other self. It was only by long practice that such results could be obtained. In the mere detail of voice intonation I practised almost perpetually till the voice of my new self became fixed, automatic. It was this automatic assumption of a role that was considered imperative. One must become so adept as to deceive oneself. It was like learning a new language, say the French. At first speech in French is self-conscious, a matter of the will. The student thinks in English and then transmutes into French, or reads in French but transmutes into English before he can understand. Then later, becoming firmly grounded, automatic, the student reads, writes, and THINKS in French, without any recourse to English at all.

And so with our disguises. It was necessary for us to practise until our assumed roles became real; until to be our original selves would require a watchful and strong

---

* If the curious traveller will turn south from Glen Ellen, he will find himself on a boulevard that is identical with the old country road seven centuries ago. A quarter of a mile from Glen Ellen, after the second bridge is passed, to the right will be noticed a barranca that runs like a scar across the rolling land toward a group of wooded knolls. The barranca is the site of the ancient right of way that in the time of private property in land ran across the holding of one Chauvet, a French pioneer of California who came from his native country in the fabled days of gold. The wooded knolls are the same knolls referred to by Avis Everhard. The Great Earthquake of 2368 A.D. broke off the side of one of these knolls and toppled it into the hole where the Everhards made their refuge. Since the finding of the Manuscript excavations have been made, and the house, the two cave rooms, and all the accumulated rubbish of long occupancy have been brought to light. Many valuable relics have been found, among which, curious to relate, is the smoke-consuming device of Biedenbach's mentioned in the narrative. Students interested in such matters should read the brochure of Arnold Bentham soon to be published. A mile northwest from the wooded knolls brings one to the site of Wake Robin Lodge at the junction of Wild-Water and Sonoma Creeks. It may be noticed, in passing, that Wild-Water was originally called Graham Creek and was so named on the early local maps. But the later name sticks. It was at Wake Robin Lodge that Avis Everhard later lived for short periods, when, disguised as an agent-provocateur of the Iron Heel, she was enabled to play with impunity her part among men and events. The official permission to occupy Wake Robin Lodge is still on the records, signed by no less a man than Wickson, the minor oligarch of the Manuscript.

exercise of will. Of course, at first, much was mere blundering experiment. We were creating a new art, and we had much to discover. But the work was going on everywhere; masters in the art were developing, and a fund of tricks and expedients was being accumulated. This fund became a sort of text-book that was passed on, a part of the curriculum, as it were, of the school of Revolution.[*]

It was at this time that my father disappeared. His letters, which had come to me regularly, ceased. He no longer appeared at our Pell Street quarters. Our comrades sought him everywhere. Through our secret service we ransacked every prison in the land. But he was lost as completely as if the earth had swallowed him up, and to this day no clew to his end has been discovered.[**]

Six lonely months I spent in the refuge, but they were not idle months. Our organization went on apace, and there were mountains of work always waiting to be done. Ernest and his fellow-leaders, from their prisons, decided what should be done; and it remained for us on the outside to do it. There was the organization of the mouth-to-mouth propaganda; the organization, with all its ramifications, of our spy system; the establishment of our secret printing-presses; and the establishment of our underground railways, which meant the knitting together of all our myriads of places of refuge, and the formation of new refuges where links were missing in the chains we ran over all the land.

So I say, the work was never done. At the end of six months my loneliness was broken by the arrival of two comrades. They were young girls, brave souls and passionate lovers of liberty: Lora Peterson, who disappeared in 1922, and Kate Bierce, who later married Du Bois,[***] and who is still with us with eyes lifted to to-morrow's sun, that heralds in the new age.

The two girls arrived in a flurry of excitement, danger, and sudden death. In the crew of the fishing boat that conveyed them across San Pablo Bay was a spy. A creature of the Iron Heel, he had successfully masqueraded as a revolutionist and penetrated deep into the secrets of our organization. Without doubt he was on my trail, for we had long since learned that my disappearance had been cause of deep concern to the secret service of the Oligarchy. Luckily, as the outcome proved, he had not divulged his discoveries to any one. He had evidently delayed reporting, preferring to wait until he had brought things to a successful conclusion by discovering my hiding-place and capturing me. His information died with him. Under some pretext, after the girls had landed at Petaluma Creek and taken to the horses, he managed to get away from the boat.

---

[*] Disguise did become a veritable art during that period. The revolutionists maintained schools of acting in all their refuges. They scorned accessories, such as wigs and beards, false eyebrows, and such aids of the theatrical actors. The game of revolution was a game of life and death, and mere accessories were traps. Disguise had to be fundamental, intrinsic, part and parcel of one's being, second nature. The Red Virgin is reported to have been one of the most adept in the art, to which must be ascribed her long and successful career.

[**] Disappearance was one of the horrors of the time. As a motif, in song and story, it constantly crops up. It was an inevitable concomitant of the subterranean warfare that raged through those three centuries. This phenomenon was almost as common in the oligarch class and the labor castes, as it was in the ranks of the revolutionists. Without warning, without trace, men and women, and even children, disappeared and were seen no more, their end shrouded in mystery.

[***] Du Bois, the present librarian of Ardis, is a lineal descendant of this revolutionary pair.

Part way up Sonoma Mountain, John Carlson let the girls go on, leading his horse, while he went back on foot. His suspicions had been aroused. He captured the spy, and as to what then happened, Carlson gave us a fair idea.

'I fixed him,' was Carlson's unimaginative way of describing the affair. 'I fixed him,' he repeated, while a sombre light burnt in his eyes, and his huge, toil-distorted hands opened and closed eloquently. 'He made no noise. I hid him, and tonight I will go back and bury him deep.'

During that period I used to marvel at my own metamorphosis. At times it seemed impossible, either that I had ever lived a placid, peaceful life in a college town, or else that I had become a revolutionist inured to scenes of violence and death. One or the other could not be. One was real, the other was a dream, but which was which? Was this present life of a revolutionist, hiding in a hole, a nightmare? or was I a revolutionist who had somewhere, somehow, dreamed that in some former existence I have lived in Berkeley and never known of life more violent than teas and dances, debating societies, and lectures rooms? But then I suppose this was a common experience of all of us who had rallied under the red banner of the brotherhood of man.

I often remembered figures from that other life, and, curiously enough, they appeared and disappeared, now and again, in my new life. There was Bishop Morehouse. In vain we searched for him after our organization had developed. He had been transferred from asylum to asylum. We traced him from the state hospital for the insane at Napa to the one in Stockton, and from there to the one in the Santa Clara Valley called Agnews, and there the trail ceased. There was no record of his death. In some way he must have escaped. Little did I dream of the awful manner in which I was to see him once again—the fleeting glimpse of him in the whirlwind carnage of the Chicago Commune.

Jackson, who had lost his arm in the Sierra Mills and who had been the cause of my own conversion into a revolutionist, I never saw again; but we all knew what he did before he died. He never joined the revolutionists. Embittered by his fate, brooding over his wrongs, he became an anarchist—not a philosophic anarchist, but a mere animal, mad with hate and lust for revenge. And well he revenged himself. Evading the guards, in the nighttime while all were asleep, he blew the Pertonwaithe palace into atoms. Not a soul escaped, not even the guards. And in prison, while awaiting trial, he suffocated himself under his blankets.

Dr. Hammerfield and Dr. Ballingford achieved quite different fates from that of Jackson. They have been faithful to their salt, and they have been correspondingly rewarded with ecclesiastical palaces wherein they dwell at peace with the world. Both are apologists for the Oligarchy. Both have grown very fat. 'Dr. Hammerfield,' as Ernest once said, 'has succeeded in modifying his metaphysics so as to give God's sanction to the Iron Heel, and also to include much worship of beauty and to reduce to an invisible wraith the gaseous vertebrate described by Haeckel—the difference between Dr. Hammerfield and Dr. Ballingford being that the latter has made the God of the oligarchs a little more gaseous and a little less vertebrate.'

Peter Donnelly, the scab foreman at the Sierra Mills whom I encountered while investigating the case of Jackson, was a surprise to all of us. In 1918 I was present at a meeting of the 'Frisco Reds. Of all our Fighting Groups this one was the most formidable, ferocious, and merciless. It was really not a part of our organization. Its members were fanatics, madmen. We dared not encourage such a spirit. On the other hand, though they did not belong to us, we remained on friendly terms with them. It was a matter of vital importance that brought me there that night. I, alone in the midst of a score of men, was the only person unmasked. After the business that brought me there was transacted, I was led away by one of them. In a dark passage this guide struck a match, and, holding it close to his face, slipped back his mask. For a moment I gazed upon the passion-wrought features of Peter Donnelly. Then the match went out.

'I just wanted you to know it was me,' he said in the darkness. 'D'you remember Dallas, the superintendent?'

I nodded at recollection of the vulpine-face superintendent of the Sierra Mills.

'Well, I got him first,' Donnelly said with pride. ''Twas after that I joined the Reds.'

'But how comes it that you are here?' I queried. 'Your wife and children?'

'Dead,' he answered. 'That's why. No,' he went on hastily, ''tis not revenge for them. They died easily in their beds—sickness, you see, one time and another. They tied my arms while they lived. And now that they're gone, 'tis revenge for my blasted manhood I'm after. I was once Peter Donnelly, the scab foreman. But to-night I'm Number 27 of the 'Frisco Reds. Come on now, and I'll get you out of this.'

More I heard of him afterward. In his own way he had told the truth when he said all were dead. But one lived, Timothy, and him his father considered dead because he had taken service with the Iron Heel in the Mercenaries.* A member of the 'Frisco Reds pledged himself to twelve annual executions. The penalty for failure was death. A member who failed to complete his number committed suicide. These executions were not haphazard. This group of madmen met frequently and passed wholesale judgments upon offending members and servitors of the Oligarchy. The executions were afterward apportioned by lot.

In fact, the business that brought me there the night of my visit was such a trial. One of our own comrades, who for years had successfully maintained himself in a clerical position in the local bureau of the secret service of the Iron Heel, had fallen under the ban of the 'Frisco Reds and was being tried. Of course he was not present, and of course his judges did not know that he was one of our men. My mission had been to testify to his identity and loyalty. It may be wondered how we came to know of the affair at all. The explanation is simple. One of our secret agents was a member of the 'Frisco Reds. It was necessary for us to keep an eye on friend as well as foe, and this group of madmen was not too unimportant to escape our surveillance.

But to return to Peter Donnelly and his son. All went well with Donnelly until, in the following year, he found among the sheaf of executions that fell to him the name of Timothy Donnelly. Then it was that that clannishness, which was his to so extraordinary a degree, asserted itself. To save his son, he betrayed his comrades. In this he was partially blocked, but a dozen of the 'Frisco Reds were executed, and the group was well-nigh destroyed. In retaliation, the survivors meted out to Donnelly the death he had earned by his treason.

Nor did Timothy Donnelly long survive. The 'Frisco Reds pledged themselves to

---

* In addition to the labor castes, there arose another caste, the military. A standing army of professional soldiers was created, officered by members of the Oligarchy and known as the Mercenaries. This institution took the place of the militia, which had proved impracticable under the new regime. Outside the regular secret service of the Iron Heel, there was further established a secret service of the Mercenaries, this latter forming a connecting link between the police and the military.

his execution. Every effort was made by the Oligarchy to save him. He was transferred from one part of the country to another. Three of the Reds lost their lives in vain efforts to get him. The Group was composed only of men. In the end they fell back on a woman, one of our comrades, and none other than Anna Roylston. Our Inner Circle forbade her, but she had ever a will of her own and disdained discipline. Furthermore, she was a genius and lovable, and we could never discipline her anyway. She is in a class by herself and not amenable to the ordinary standards of the revolutionists.

Despite our refusal to grant permission to do the deed, she went on with it. Now Anna Roylston was a fascinating woman. All she had to do was to beckon a man to her. She broke the hearts of scores of our young comrades, and scores of others she captured, and by their heart-strings led into our organization. Yet she steadfastly refused to marry. She dearly loved children, but she held that a child of her own would claim her from the Cause, and that it was the Cause to which her life was devoted.

It was an easy task for Anna Roylston to win Timothy Donnelly. Her conscience did not trouble her, for at that very time occurred the Nashville Massacre, when the Mercenaries, Donnelly in command, literally murdered eight hundred weavers of that city. But she did not kill Donnelly. She turned him over, a prisoner, to the 'Frisco Reds. This happened only last year, and now she had been renamed. The revolutionists everywhere are calling her the 'Red Virgin.'*

Colonel Ingram and Colonel Van Gilbert are two more familiar figures that I was later to encounter. Colonel Ingram rose high in the Oligarchy and became Minister to Germany. He was cordially detested by the proletariat of both countries. It was in Berlin that I met him, where, as an accredited international spy of the Iron Heel, I was received by him and afforded much assistance. Incidentally, I may state that in my dual role I managed a few important things for the Revolution.

Colonel Van Gilbert became known as 'Snarling' Van Gilbert. His important part was played in drafting the new code after the Chicago Commune. But before that, as trial judge, he had earned sentence of death by his fiendish malignancy. I was one of those that tried him and passed sentence upon him. Anna Roylston carried out the execution.

Still another figure arises out of the old life—Jackson's lawyer. Least of all would I have expected again to meet this man, Joseph Hurd. It was a strange meeting. Late at night, two years after the Chicago Commune, Ernest and I arrived together at the Benton Harbor refuge. This was in Michigan, across the lake from Chicago. We arrived just at the conclusion of the trial of a spy. Sentence of death had been passed, and he was being led away. Such was the scene as we came upon it. The next moment the wretched man had wrenched free from his captors and flung himself at my feet, his arms clutching me about the knees in a vicelike grip as he prayed in a frenzy for mercy. As he turned his agonized face up to me, I recognized him as Joseph Hurd. Of all the terrible things I have witnessed, never have I been so unnerved as by this frantic creature's pleading for life. He was mad for life. It was pitiable. He refused to let go of me, despite

---

* It was not until the Second Revolt was crushed, that the 'Frisco Reds flourished again. And for two generations the Group flourished. Then an agent of the Iron Heel managed to become a member, penetrated all its secrets, and brought about its total annihilation. This occurred in 2002 A.D. The members were executed one at a time, at intervals of three weeks, and their bodies exposed in the labor-ghetto of San Francisco.

the hands of a dozen comrades. And when at last he was dragged shrieking away, I sank down fainting upon the floor. It is far easier to see brave men die than to hear a coward beg for life*

CHAPTER XX
A LOST OLIGARCH

But in remembering the old life I have run ahead of my story into the new life. The wholesale jail delivery did not occur until well along into 1915. Complicated as it was, it was carried through without a hitch, and as a very creditable achievement it cheered us on in our work. From Cuba to California, out of scores of jails, military prisons, and fortresses, in a single night, we delivered fifty-one of our fifty-two Congressmen, and in addition over three hundred other leaders. There was not a single instance of miscarriage. Not only did they escape, but every one of them won to the refuges as planned. The one comrade Congressman we did not get was Arthur Simpson, and he had already died in Cabanas after cruel tortures.

The eighteen months that followed was perhaps the happiest of my life with Ernest. During that time we were never apart. Later, when we went back into the world, we were separated much. Not more impatiently do I await the flame of to-morrow's revolt than did I that night await the coming of Ernest. I had not seen him for so long, and the thought of a possible hitch or error in our plans that would keep him still in his island prison almost drove me mad. The hours passed like ages. I was all alone. Biedenbach, and three young men who had been living in the refuge, were out and over the mountain, heavily armed and prepared for anything. The refuges all over the land were quite empty, I imagine, of comrades that night.

Just as the sky paled with the first warning of dawn, I heard the signal from above and gave the answer. In the darkness I almost embraced Biedenbach, who came down first; but the next moment I was in Ernest's arms. And in that moment, so complete had been my transformation, I discovered it was only by an effort of will that I could be the old Avis Everhard, with the old mannerisms and smiles, phrases and intonations of voice. It was by strong effort only that I was able to maintain my old identity; I could not allow myself to forget for an instant, so automatically imperative had become the new personality I had created.

Once inside the little cabin, I saw Ernest's face in the light. With the exception of the prison pallor, there was no change in him—at least, not much. He was my same lover-husband and hero. And yet there was a certain ascetic lengthening of the lines of his face. But he could well stand it, for it seemed to add a certain nobility of refinement to the riotous excess of life that had always marked his features. He might have been a trifle graver than of yore, but the glint of laughter still was in his eyes. He was twenty pounds lighter, but in splendid physical condition. He had kept

---

* The Benton Harbor refuge was a catacomb, the entrance of which was cunningly contrived by way of a well. It has been maintained in a fair state of preservation, and the curious visitor may to-day tread its labyrinths to the assembly hall, where, without doubt, occurred the scene described by Avis Everhard. Farther on are the cells where the prisoners were confined, and the death chamber where the executions took place. Beyond is the cemetery—long, winding galleries hewn out of the solid rock, with recesses on either hand, wherein, tier above tier, lie the revolutionists just as they were laid away by their comrades long years agone.

up exercise during the whole period of confinement, and his muscles were like iron. In truth, he was in better condition than when he had entered prison. Hours passed before his head touched pillow and I had soothed him off to sleep. But there was no sleep for me. I was too happy, and the fatigue of jail-breaking and riding horseback had not been mine.

While Ernest slept, I changed my dress, arranged my hair differently, and came back to my new automatic self. Then, when Biedenbach and the other comrades awoke, with their aid I concocted a little conspiracy. All was ready, and we were in the cave-room that served for kitchen and dining room when Ernest opened the door and entered. At that moment Biedenbach addressed me as Mary, and I turned and answered him. Then I glanced at Ernest with curious interest, such as any young comrade might betray on seeing for the first time so noted a hero of the Revolution. But Ernest's glance took me in and questioned impatiently past and around the room. The next moment I was being introduced to him as Mary Holmes.

To complete the deception, an extra plate was laid, and when we sat down to table one chair was not occupied. I could have cried with joy as I noted Ernest's increasing uneasiness and impatience. Finally he could stand it no longer.

'Where's my wife?' he demanded bluntly.

'She is still asleep,' I answered.

It was the crucial moment. But my voice was a strange voice, and in it he recognized nothing familiar. The meal went on. I talked a great deal, and enthusiastically, as a hero-worshipper might talk, and it was obvious that he was my hero. I rose to a climax of enthusiasm and worship, and, before he could guess my intention, threw my arms around his neck and kissed him on the lips. He held me from him at arm's length and stared about in annoyance and perplexity. The four men greeted him with roars of laughter, and explanations were made. At first he was sceptical. He scrutinized me keenly and was half convinced, then shook his head and would not believe. It was not until I became the old Avis Everhard and whispered secrets in his ear that none knew but he and Avis Everhard, that he accepted me as his really, truly wife.

It was later in the day that he took me in his arms, manifesting great embarrassment and claiming polygamous emotions.

'You are my Avis,' he said, 'and you are also some one else. You are two women, and therefore you are my harem. At any rate, we are safe now. If the United States becomes too hot for us, why I have qualified for citizenship in Turkey.'*

Life became for me very happy in the refuge. It is true, we worked hard and for long hours; but we worked together. We had each other for eighteen precious months, and we were not lonely, for there was always a coming and going of leaders and comrades—strange voices from the under-world of intrigue and revolution, bringing stranger tales of strife and war from all our battle-line. And there was much fun and delight. We were not mere gloomy conspirators. We toiled hard and suffered greatly, filled the gaps in our ranks and went on, and through all the labour and the play and interplay of life and death we found time to laugh and love. There were artists, scientists, scholars, musicians, and poets among us; and in that hole in the ground culture was higher and finer than in the palaces of wonder-cities of the oligarchs. In truth, many of our comrades toiled at making beautiful those same palaces and wonder-cities.**

---

* At that time polygamy was still practised in Turkey.
** This is not braggadocio on the part of Avis Everhard. The flower of the artistic and

Nor were we confined to the refuge itself. Often at night we rode over the mountains for exercise, and we rode on Wickson's horses. If only he knew how many revolutionists his horses have carried! We even went on picnics to isolated spots we knew, where we remained all day, going before daylight and returning after dark. Also, we used Wickson's cream and butter,* and Ernest was not above shooting Wickson's quail and rabbits, and, on occasion, his young bucks.

Indeed, it was a safe refuge. I have said that it was discovered only once, and this brings me to the clearing up of the mystery of the disappearance of young Wickson. Now that he is dead, I am free to speak. There was a nook on the bottom of the great hole where the sun shone for several hours and which was hidden from above. Here we had carried many loads of gravel from the creek-bed, so that it was dry and warm, a pleasant basking place; and here, one afternoon, I was drowsing, half asleep, over a volume of Mendenhall.** I was so comfortable and secure that even his flaming lyrics failed to stir me.

I was aroused by a clod of earth striking at my feet. Then from above, I heard a sound of scrambling. The next moment a young man, with a final slide down the crumbling wall, alighted at my feet. It was Philip Wickson, though I did not know him at the time. He looked at me coolly and uttered a low whistle of surprise.

'Well,' he said; and the next moment, cap in hand, he was saying, 'I beg your pardon. I did not expect to find any one here.'

I was not so cool. I was still a tyro so far as concerned knowing how to behave in desperate circumstances. Later on, when I was an international spy, I should have been less clumsy, I am sure. As it was, I scrambled to my feet and cried out the danger call.

'Why did you do that?' he asked, looking at me searchingly.

It was evident that he had no suspicion of our presence when making the descent. I recognized this with relief.

'For what purpose do you think I did it?' I countered. I was indeed clumsy in those days.

'I don't know,' he answered, shaking his head. 'Unless you've got friends about. Anyway, you've got some explanations to make. I don't like the look of it. You are trespassing. This is my father's land, and—'

But at that moment, Biedenbach, every polite and gentle, said from behind him in a low voice, 'Hands up, my young sir.'

Young Wickson put his hands up first, then turned to confront Biedenbach, who held a thirty-thirty automatic rifle on him. Wickson was imperturbable.

'Oh, ho,' he said, 'a nest of revolutionists—and quite a hornet's nest it would seem. Well, you won't abide here long, I can tell you.'

---

intellectual world were revolutionists. With the exception of a few of the musicians and singers, and of a few of the oligarchs, all the great creators of the period whose names have come down to us, were revolutionists.

* Even as late as that period, cream and butter were still crudely extracted from cow's milk. The laboratory preparation of foods had not yet begun.

** In all the extant literature and documents of that period, continual reference is made to the poems of Rudolph Mendenhall. By his comrades he was called 'The Flame.' He was undoubtedly a great genius; yet, beyond weird and haunting fragments of his verse, quoted in the writings of others, nothing of his has come down to us. He was executed by the Iron Heel in 1928 A.D.

'Maybe you'll abide here long enough to reconsider that statement,' Biedenbach said quietly. 'And in the meanwhile I must ask you to come inside with me.'

'Inside?' The young man was genuinely astonished. 'Have you a catacomb here? I have heard of such things.'

'Come and see,' Biedenbach answered with his adorable accent.

'But it is unlawful,' was the protest.

'Yes, by your law,' the terrorist replied significantly. 'But by our law, believe me, it is quite lawful. You must accustom yourself to the fact that you are in another world than the one of oppression and brutality in which you have lived.'

'There is room for argument there,' Wickson muttered.

'Then stay with us and discuss it.'

The young fellow laughed and followed his captor into the house. He was led into the inner cave-room, and one of the young comrades left to guard him, while we discussed the situation in the kitchen.

Biedenbach, with tears in his eyes, held that Wickson must die, and was quite relieved when we outvoted him and his horrible proposition. On the other hand, we could not dream of allowing the young oligarch to depart.

'I'll tell you what to do,' Ernest said. 'We'll keep him and give him an education.'

'I bespeak the privilege, then, of enlightening him in jurisprudence,' Biedenbach cried.

And so a decision was laughingly reached. We would keep Philip Wickson a prisoner and educate him in our ethics and sociology. But in the meantime there was work to be done. All trace of the young oligarch must be obliterated. There were the marks he had left when descending the crumbling wall of the hole. This task fell to Biedenbach, and, slung on a rope from above, he toiled cunningly for the rest of the day till no sign remained. Back up the canyon from the lip of the hole all marks were likewise removed. Then, at twilight, came John Carlson, who demanded Wickson's shoes.

The young man did not want to give up his shoes, and even offered to fight for them, till he felt the horseshoer's strength in Ernest's hands. Carlson afterward reported several blisters and much grievous loss of skin due to the smallness of the shoes, but he succeeded in doing gallant work with them. Back from the lip of the hole, where ended the young man's obliterated trial, Carlson put on the shoes and walked away to the left. He walked for miles, around knolls, over ridges and through canyons, and finally covered the trail in the running water of a creek-bed. Here he removed the shoes and, still hiding trail for a distance, at last put on his own shoes. A week later Wickson got back his shoes.

That night the hounds were out, and there was little sleep in the refuge. Next day, time and again, the baying hounds came down the canyon, plunged off to the left on the trail Carlson had made for them, and were lost to ear in the farther canyons high up the mountain. And all the time our men waited in the refuge, weapons in hand—automatic revolvers and rifles, to say nothing of half a dozen infernal machines of Biedenbach's manufacture. A more surprised party of rescuers could not be imagined, had they ventured down into our hiding-place.

I have now given the true disappearance of Philip Wickson, one-time oligarch, and, later, comrade in the Revolution. For we converted him in the end. His mind was fresh and plastic, and by nature he was very ethical. Several months later we rode him, on one of his father's horses, over Sonoma Mountains to Petaluma Creek and embarked him in a small fishing-launch. By easy stages we smuggled him along our underground railway to the Carmel refuge.

There he remained eight months, at the end of which time, for two reasons, he was loath to leave us. One reason was that he had fallen in love with Anna Roylston, and the other was that he had become one of us. It was not until he became convinced of the hopelessness of his love affair that he acceded to our wishes and went back to his father. Ostensibly an oligarch until his death, he was in reality one of the most valuable of our agents. Often and often has the Iron Heel been dumbfounded by the miscarriage of its plans and operations against us. If it but knew the number of its own members who are our agents, it would understand. Young Wickson never wavered in his loyalty to the Cause. In truth, his very death was incurred by his devotion to duty. In the great storm of 1927, while attending a meeting of our leaders, he contracted the pneumonia of which he died.*

CHAPTER XXI
THE ROARING ABYSMAL BEAST

During the long period of our stay in the refuge, we were kept closely in touch with what was happening in the world without, and we were learning thoroughly the strength of the Oligarchy with which we were at war. Out of the flux of transition the new institutions were forming more definitely and taking on the appearance and attributes of permanence. The oligarchs had succeeded in devising a governmental machine, as intricate as it was vast, that worked—and this despite all our efforts to clog and hamper.

This was a surprise to many of the revolutionists. They had not conceived it possible. Nevertheless the work of the country went on. The men toiled in the mines and fields—perforce they were no more than slaves. As for the vital industries, everything prospered. The members of the great labor castes were contented and worked on merrily. For the first time in their lives they knew industrial peace. No more were they worried by slack times, strike and lockout, and the union label. They lived in more comfortable homes and in delightful cities of their own—delightful compared with the slums and ghettos in which they had formerly dwelt. They had better food to eat, less hours of labor, more holidays, and a greater amount and variety of interests and pleasures. And for their less fortunate brothers and sisters, the unfavored laborers, the driven people of the abyss, they cared nothing. An age of selfishness was dawning upon mankind. And yet this is not altogether true. The labor castes were honeycombed by our agents—men whose eyes saw, beyond the belly-need, the radiant figure of liberty and brotherhood.

Another great institution that had taken form and was working smoothly was the Mercenaries. This body of soldiers had been evolved out of the old regular army and was now a million strong, to say nothing of the colonial forces. The Mercenaries

---

* The case of this young man was not unusual. Many young men of the Oligarchy, impelled by sense of right conduct, or their imaginations captured by the glory of the Revolution, ethically or romantically devoted their lives to it. In similar way, many sons of the Russian nobility played their parts in the earlier and protracted revolution in that country.

constituted a race apart. They dwelt in cities of their own which were practically self-governed, and they were granted many privileges. By them a large portion of the perplexing surplus was consumed. They were losing all touch and sympathy with the rest of the people, and, in fact, were developing their own class morality and consciousness. And yet we had thousands of our agents among them.[*]

The oligarchs themselves were going through a remarkable and, it must be confessed, unexpected development. As a class, they disciplined themselves. Every member had his work to do in the world, and this work he was compelled to do. There were no more idle-rich young men. Their strength was used to give united strength to the Oligarchy. They served as leaders of troops and as lieutenants and captains of industry. They found careers in applied science, and many of them became great engineers. They went into the multitudinous divisions of the government, took service in the colonial possessions, and by tens of thousands went into the various secret services. They were, I may say, apprenticed to education, to art, to the church, to science, to literature; and in those fields they served the important function of moulding the thought-processes of the nation in the direction of the perpetuity of the Oligarchy.

They were taught, and later they in turn taught, that what they were doing was right. They assimilated the aristocratic idea from the moment they began, as children, to receive impressions of the world. The aristocratic idea was woven into the making of them until it became bone of them and flesh of them. They looked upon themselves as wild-animal trainers, rulers of beasts. From beneath their feet rose always the subterranean rumbles of revolt. Violent death ever stalked in their midst; bomb and knife and bullet were looked upon as so many fangs of the roaring abysmal beast they must dominate if humanity were to persist. They were the saviours of humanity, and they regarded themselves as heroic and sacrificing laborers for the highest good.

They, as a class, believed that they alone maintained civilization. It was their belief that if ever they weakened, the great beast would ingulf them and everything of beauty and wonder and joy and good in its cavernous and slime-dripping maw. Without them, anarchy would reign and humanity would drop backward into the primitive night out of which it had so painfully emerged. The horrid picture of anarchy was held always before their child's eyes until they, in turn, obsessed by this cultivated fear, held the picture of anarchy before the eyes of the children that followed them. This was the beast to be stamped upon, and the highest duty of the aristocrat was to stamp upon it. In short, they alone, by their unremitting toil and sacrifice, stood between weak humanity and the all-devouring beast; and they believed it, firmly believed it.

I cannot lay too great stress upon this high ethical righteousness of the whole oligarch class. This has been the strength of the Iron Heel, and too many of the comrades have been slow or loath to realize it. Many of them have ascribed the strength of the Iron Heel to its system of reward and punishment. This is a mistake. Heaven and hell may be the prime factors of zeal in the religion of a fanatic; but for the great majority of the religious, heaven and hell are incidental to right and wrong. Love of the right, desire for the right, unhappiness with anything less than the right—

---

[*] The Mercenaries, in the last days of the Iron Heel, played an important role. They constituted the balance of power in the struggles between the labor castes and the oligarchs, and now to one side and now to the other, threw their strength according to the play of intrigue and conspiracy.

in short, right conduct, is the prime factor of religion. And so with the Oligarchy. Prisons, banishment and degradation, honors and palaces and wonder-cities, are all incidental. The great driving force of the oligarchs is the belief that they are doing right. Never mind the exceptions, and never mind the oppression and injustice in which the Iron Heel was conceived. All is granted. The point is that the strength of the Oligarchy today lies in its satisfied conception of its own righteousness.*

For that matter, the strength of the Revolution, during these frightful twenty years, has resided in nothing else than the sense of righteousness. In no other way can be explained our sacrifices and martyrdoms. For no other reason did Rudolph Mendenhall flame out his soul for the Cause and sing his wild swan-song that last night of life. For no other reason did Hurlbert die under torture, refusing to the last to betray his comrades. For no other reason has Anna Roylston refused blessed motherhood. For no other reason has John Carlson been the faithful and unrewarded custodian of the Glen Ellen Refuge. It does not matter, young or old, man or woman, high or low, genius or clod, go where one will among the comrades of the Revolution, the motor-force will be found to be a great and abiding desire for the right.

But I have run away from my narrative. Ernest and I well understood, before we left the refuge, how the strength of the Iron Heel was developing. The labor castes, the Mercenaries, and the great hordes of secret agents and police of various sorts were all pledged to the Oligarchy. In the main, and ignoring the loss of liberty, they were better off than they had been. On the other hand, the great helpless mass of the population, the people of the abyss, was sinking into a brutish apathy of content with misery. Whenever strong proletarians asserted their strength in the midst of the mass, they were drawn away from the mass by the oligarchs and given better conditions by being made members of the labor castes or of the Mercenaries. Thus discontent was lulled and the proletariat robbed of its natural leaders.

The condition of the people of the abyss was pitiable. Common school education, so far as they were concerned, had ceased. They lived like beasts in great squalid labor-ghettos, festering in misery and degradation. All their old liberties were gone. They were labor-slaves. Choice of work was denied them. Likewise was denied them the right to move from place to place, or the right to bear or possess arms. They were not land serfs like the farmers. They were machine-serfs and labor-serfs. When unusual needs arose for them, such as the building of the great highways and air-lines, of canals, tunnels, subways, and fortifications, levies were made on the labor-ghettos, and tens of thousands of serfs, willy-nilly, were transported to the scene of operations. Great armies of them are toiling now at the building of Ardis, housed in wretched barracks where family life cannot exist, and where decency is displaced by dull bestiality. In all truth, there in the labor-ghettos is the roaring abysmal beast the oligarchs fear so dreadfully—but it is the beast of their own making. In it they will not let the ape and tiger die.

And just now the word has gone forth that new levies are being imposed for the

---

* Out of the ethical incoherency and inconsistency of capitalism, the oligarchs emerged with a new ethics, coherent and definite, sharp and severe as steel, the most absurd and unscientific and at the same time the most potent ever possessed by any tyrant class. The oligarchs believed their ethics, in spite of the fact that biology and evolution gave them the lie; and, because of their faith, for three centuries they were able to hold back the mighty tide of human progress—a spectacle, profound, tremendous, puzzling to the metaphysical moralist, and one that to the materialist is the cause of many doubts and reconsiderations.

building of Asgard, the projected wonder-city that will far exceed Ardis when the latter is completed.* We of the Revolution will go on with that great work, but it will not be done by the miserable serfs. The walls and towers and shafts of that fair city will arise to the sound of singing, and into its beauty and wonder will be woven, not sighs and groans, but music and laughter.

Ernest was madly impatient to be out in the world and doing, for our ill-fated First Revolt, that had miscarried in the Chicago Commune, was ripening fast. Yet he possessed his soul with patience, and during this time of his torment, when Hadly, who had been brought for the purpose from Illinois, made him over into another man** he revolved great plans in his head for the organization of the learned proletariat, and for the maintenance of at least the rudiments of education amongst the people of the abyss—all this of course in the event of the First Revolt being a failure.

It was not until January, 1917, that we left the refuge. All had been arranged. We took our place at once as agents-provocateurs in the scheme of the Iron Heel. I was supposed to be Ernest's sister. By oligarchs and comrades on the inside who were high in authority, place had been made for us, we were in possession of all necessary documents, and our pasts were accounted for. With help on the inside, this was not difficult, for in that shadow-world of secret service identity was nebulous. Like ghosts the agents came and went, obeying commands, fulfilling duties, following clews, making their reports often to officers they never saw or cooperating with other agents they had never seen before and would never see again.

CHAPTER XXII
THE CHICAGO COMMUNE

As agents-provocateurs, not alone were we able to travel a great deal, but our very work threw us in contact with the proletariat and with our comrades, the revolutionists. Thus we were in both camps at the same time, ostensibly serving the Iron Heel and secretly working with all our might for the Cause. There were many of us in the various secret services of the Oligarchy, and despite the shakings-up and reorganizations the secret services have undergone, they have never been able to weed all of us out.

---

* Ardis was completed in 1942 A.D., Asgard was not completed until 1984 A.D. It was fifty-two years in the building, during which time a permanent army of half a million serfs was employed. At times these numbers swelled to over a million—without any account being taken of the hundreds of thousands of the labor castes and the artists.

** Among the Revolutionists were many surgeons, and in vivisection they attained marvellous proficiency. In Avis Everhard's words, they could literally make a man over. To them the elimination of scars and disfigurements was a trivial detail. They changed the features with such microscopic care that no traces were left of their handiwork. The nose was a favorite organ to work upon. Skin-grafting and hair-transplanting were among their commonest devices. The changes in expression they accomplished were wizard-like. Eyes and eyebrows, lips, mouths, and ears, were radically altered. By cunning operations on tongue, throat, larynx, and nasal cavities a man's whole enunciation and manner of speech could be changed. Desperate times give need for desperate remedies, and the surgeons of the Revolution rose to the need. Among other things, they could increase an adult's stature by as much as four or five inches and decrease it by one or two inches. What they did is to-day a lost art. We have no need for it.

Ernest had largely planned the First Revolt, and the date set had been somewhere early in the spring of 1918. In the fall of 1917 we were not ready; much remained to be done, and when the Revolt was precipitated, of course it was doomed to failure. The plot of necessity was frightfully intricate, and anything premature was sure to destroy it. This the Iron Heel foresaw and laid its schemes accordingly.

We had planned to strike our first blow at the nervous system of the Oligarchy. The latter had remembered the general strike, and had guarded against the defection of the telegraphers by installing wireless stations, in the control of the Mercenaries. We, in turn, had countered this move. When the signal was given, from every refuge, all over the land, and from the cities, and towns, and barracks, devoted comrades were to go forth and blow up the wireless stations. Thus at the first shock would the Iron Heel be brought to earth and lie practically dismembered.

At the same moment, other comrades were to blow up the bridges and tunnels and disrupt the whole network of railroads. Still further, other groups of comrades, at the signal, were to seize the officers of the Mercenaries and the police, as well as all Oligarchs of unusual ability or who held executive positions. Thus would the leaders of the enemy be removed from the field of the local battles that would inevitably be fought all over the land.

Many things were to occur simultaneously when the signal went forth. The Canadian and Mexican patriots, who were far stronger than the Iron Heel dreamed, were to duplicate our tactics. Then there were comrades (these were the women, for the men would be busy elsewhere) who were to post the proclamations from our secret presses. Those of us in the higher employ of the Iron Heel were to proceed immediately to make confusion and anarchy in all our departments. Inside the Mercenaries were thousands of our comrades. Their work was to blow up the magazines and to destroy the delicate mechanism of all the war machinery. In the cities of the Mercenaries and of the labor castes similar programmes of disruption were to be carried out.

In short, a sudden, colossal, stunning blow was to be struck. Before the paralyzed Oligarchy could recover itself, its end would have come. It would have meant terrible times and great loss of life, but no revolutionist hesitates at such things. Why, we even depended much, in our plan, on the unorganized people of the abyss. They were to be loosed on the palaces and cities of the masters. Never mind the destruction of life and property. Let the abysmal brute roar and the police and Mercenaries slay. The abysmal brute would roar anyway, and the police and Mercenaries would slay anyway. It would merely mean that various dangers to us were harmlessly destroying one another. In the meantime we would be doing our own work, largely unhampered, and gaining control of all the machinery of society.

Such was our plan, every detail of which had to be worked out in secret, and, as the day drew near, communicated to more and more comrades. This was the danger point, the stretching of the conspiracy. But that danger-point was never reached. Through its spy-system the Iron Heel got wind of the Revolt and prepared to teach us another of its bloody lessons. Chicago was the devoted city selected for the instruction, and well were we instructed.

Chicago* was the ripest of all—Chicago which of old time was the city of blood

---

* Chicago was the industrial inferno of the nineteenth century A.D. A curious anecdote has come down to us of John Burns, a great English labor leader and one time member of the

and which was to earn anew its name. There the revolutionary spirit was strong. Too many bitter strikes had been curbed there in the days of capitalism for the workers to forget and forgive. Even the labor castes of the city were alive with revolt. Too many heads had been broken in the early strikes. Despite their changed and favorable conditions, their hatred for the master class had not died. This spirit had infected the Mercenaries, of which three regiments in particular were ready to come over to us en masse.

Chicago had always been the storm-centre of the conflict between labor and capital, a city of street-battles and violent death, with a class-conscious capitalist organization and a class-conscious workman organization, where, in the old days, the very school-teachers were formed into labor unions and affiliated with the hod-carriers and brick-layers in the American Federation of Labor. And Chicago became the storm-centre of the premature First Revolt.

The trouble was precipitated by the Iron Heel. It was cleverly done. The whole population, including the favored labor castes, was given a course of outrageous treatment. Promises and agreements were broken, and most drastic punishments visited upon even petty offenders. The people of the abyss were tormented out of their apathy. In fact, the Iron Heel was preparing to make the abysmal beast roar. And hand in hand with this, in all precautionary measures in Chicago, the Iron Heel was inconceivably careless. Discipline was relaxed among the Mercenaries that remained, while many regiments had been withdrawn and sent to various parts of the country.

It did not take long to carry out this programme—only several weeks. We of the Revolution caught vague rumors of the state of affairs, but had nothing definite enough for an understanding. In fact, we thought it was a spontaneous spirit of revolt that would require careful curbing on our part, and never dreamed that it was deliberately manufactured—and it had been manufactured so secretly, from the very innermost circle of the Iron Heel, that we had got no inkling. The counter-plot was an able achievement, and ably carried out.

I was in New York when I received the order to proceed immediately to Chicago. The man who gave me the order was one of the oligarchs, I could tell that by his speech, though I did not know his name nor see his face. His instructions were too clear for me to make a mistake. Plainly I read between the lines that our plot had been discovered, that we had been countermined. The explosion was ready for the flash of powder, and countless agents of the Iron Heel, including me, either on the ground or being sent there, were to supply that flash. I flatter myself that I maintained my composure under the keen eye of the oligarch, but my heart was beating madly. I could almost have shrieked and flown at his throat with my naked hands before his final, cold-blooded instructions were given.

Once out of his presence, I calculated the time. I had just the moments to spare, if I were lucky, to get in touch with some local leader before catching my train. Guarding against being trailed, I made a rush of it for the Emergency Hospital. Luck was with me, and I gained access at once to comrade Galvin, the surgeon-in-chief. I started to

---

British Cabinet. In Chicago, while on a visit to the United States, he was asked by a newspaper reporter for his opinion of that city. 'Chicago,' he answered, 'is a pocket edition of hell.' Some time later, as he was going aboard his steamer to sail to England, he was approached by another reporter, who wanted to know if he had changed his opinion of Chicago. 'Yes, I have,' was his reply. 'My present opinion is that hell is a pocket edition of Chicago.'

gasp out my information, but he stopped me.

'I already know,' he said quietly, though his Irish eyes were flashing. 'I knew what you had come for. I got the word fifteen minutes ago, and I have already passed it along. Everything shall be done here to keep the comrades quiet. Chicago is to be sacrificed, but it shall be Chicago alone.'

'Have you tried to get word to Chicago?' I asked.

He shook his head. 'No telegraphic communication. Chicago is shut off. It's going to be hell there.'

He paused a moment, and I saw his white hands clinch. Then he burst out:

'By God! I wish I were going to be there!'

'There is yet a chance to stop it,' I said, 'if nothing happens to the train and I can get there in time. Or if some of the other secret-service comrades who have learned the truth can get there in time.'

'You on the inside were caught napping this time,' he said.

I nodded my head humbly.

'It was very secret,' I answered. 'Only the inner chiefs could have known up to to-day. We haven't yet penetrated that far, so we couldn't escape being kept in the dark. If only Ernest were here. Maybe he is in Chicago now, and all is well.'

Dr. Galvin shook his head. 'The last news I heard of him was that he had been sent to Boston or New Haven. This secret service for the enemy must hamper him a lot, but it's better than lying in a refuge.'

I started to go, and Galvin wrung my hand.

'Keep a stout heart,' were his parting words. 'What if the First Revolt is lost? There will be a second, and we will be wiser then. Good-by and good luck. I don't know whether I'll ever see you again. It's going to be hell there, but I'd give ten years of my life for your chance to be in it.'

The Twentieth Century* left New York at six in the evening, and was supposed to arrive at Chicago at seven next morning. But it lost time that night. We were running behind another train. Among the travellers in my Pullman was comrade Hartman, like myself in the secret service of the Iron Heel. He it was who told me of the train that immediately preceded us. It was an exact duplicate of our train, though it contained no passengers. The idea was that the empty train should receive the disaster were an attempt made to blow up the Twentieth Century. For that matter there were very few people on the train—only a baker's dozen in our car.

'There must be some big men on board,' Hartman concluded. 'I noticed a private car on the rear.'

Night had fallen when we made our first change of engine, and I walked down the platform for a breath of fresh air and to see what I could see. Through the windows of the private car I caught a glimpse of three men whom I recognized. Hartman was right. One of the men was General Altendorff; and the other two were Mason and Vanderbold, the brains of the inner circle of the Oligarchy's secret service.

It was a quiet moonlight night, but I tossed restlessly and could not sleep. At five in the morning I dressed and abandoned my bed.

I asked the maid in the dressing-room how late the train was, and she told me two hours. She was a mulatto woman, and I noticed that her face was haggard, with great circles under the eyes, while the eyes themselves were wide with some haunting fear.

---

* This was reputed to be the fastest train in the world then. It was quite a famous train.

'What is the matter?' I asked.

'Nothing, miss; I didn't sleep well, I guess,' was her reply.

I looked at her closely, and tried her with one of our signals. She responded, and I made sure of her.

'Something terrible is going to happen in Chicago,' she said. 'There's that fake[*] train in front of us. That and the troop-trains have made us late.'

'Troop-trains?' I queried.

She nodded her head. 'The line is thick with them. We've been passing them all night. And they're all heading for Chicago. And bringing them over the air-line—that means business.

'I've a lover in Chicago,' she added apologetically. 'He's one of us, and he's in the Mercenaries, and I'm afraid for him.'

Poor girl. Her lover was in one of the three disloyal regiments.

Hartman and I had breakfast together in the dining car, and I forced myself to eat. The sky had clouded, and the train rushed on like a sullen thunderbolt through the gray pall of advancing day. The very negroes that waited on us knew that something terrible was impending. Oppression sat heavily upon them; the lightness of their natures had ebbed out of them; they were slack and absent-minded in their service, and they whispered gloomily to one another in the far end of the car next to the kitchen. Hartman was hopeless over the situation.

'What can we do?' he demanded for the twentieth time, with a helpless shrug of the shoulders.

He pointed out of the window. 'See, all is ready. You can depend upon it that they're holding them like this, thirty or forty miles outside the city, on every road.'

He had reference to troop-trains on the side-track. The soldiers were cooking their breakfasts over fires built on the ground beside the track, and they looked up curiously at us as we thundered past without slackening our terrific speed.

All was quiet as we entered Chicago. It was evident nothing had happened yet. In the suburbs the morning papers came on board the train. There was nothing in them, and yet there was much in them for those skilled in reading between the lines that it was intended the ordinary reader should read into the text. The fine hand of the Iron Heel was apparent in every column. Glimmerings of weakness in the armor of the Oligarchy were given. Of course, there was nothing definite. It was intended that the reader should feel his way to these glimmerings. It was cleverly done. As fiction, those morning papers of October 27th were masterpieces.

The local news was missing. This in itself was a masterstroke. It shrouded Chicago in mystery, and it suggested to the average Chicago reader that the Oligarchy did not dare give the local news. Hints that were untrue, of course, were given of insubordination all over the land, crudely disguised with complacent references to punitive measures to be taken. There were reports of numerous wireless stations that had been blown up, with heavy rewards offered for the detection of the perpetrators. Of course no wireless stations had been blown up. Many similar outrages, that dovetailed with the plot of the revolutionists, were given. The impression to be made on the minds of the Chicago comrades was that the general Revolt was beginning, albeit with a confusing miscarriage in many details. It was impossible for one uninformed to escape the vague yet certain feeling that all the land was ripe for the revolt that had

---

[*] False.

already begun to break out.

It was reported that the defection of the Mercenaries in California had become so serious that half a dozen regiments had been disbanded and broken, and that their members with their families had been driven from their own city and on into the labor-ghettos. And the California Mercenaries were in reality the most faithful of all to their salt! But how was Chicago, shut off from the rest of the world, to know? Then there was a ragged telegram describing an outbreak of the populace in New York City, in which the labor castes were joining, concluding with the statement (intended to be accepted as a bluff[*]) that the troops had the situation in hand.

And as the oligarchs had done with the morning papers, so had they done in a thousand other ways. These we learned afterward, as, for example, the secret messages of the oligarchs, sent with the express purpose of leaking to the ears of the revolutionists, that had come over the wires, now and again, during the first part of the night.

'I guess the Iron Heel won't need our services,' Hartman remarked, putting down the paper he had been reading, when the train pulled into the central depot. 'They wasted their time sending us here. Their plans have evidently prospered better than they expected. Hell will break loose any second now.'

He turned and looked down the train as we alighted.

'I thought so,' he muttered. 'They dropped that private car when the papers came aboard.'

Hartman was hopelessly depressed. I tried to cheer him up, but he ignored my effort and suddenly began talking very hurriedly, in a low voice, as we passed through the station. At first I could not understand.

'I have not been sure,' he was saying, 'and I have told no one. I have been working on it for weeks, and I cannot make sure. Watch out for Knowlton. I suspect him. He knows the secrets of a score of our refuges. He carries the lives of hundreds of us in his hands, and I think he is a traitor. It's more a feeling on my part than anything else. But I thought I marked a change in him a short while back. There is the danger that he has sold us out, or is going to sell us out. I am almost sure of it. I wouldn't whisper my suspicions to a soul, but, somehow, I don't think I'll leave Chicago alive. Keep your eye on Knowlton. Trap him. Find out. I don't know anything more. It is only an intuition, and so far I have failed to find the slightest clew.' We were just stepping out upon the sidewalk. 'Remember,' Hartman concluded earnestly. 'Keep your eyes upon Knowlton.'

And Hartman was right. Before a month went by Knowlton paid for his treason with his life. He was formally executed by the comrades in Milwaukee.

All was quiet on the streets—too quiet. Chicago lay dead. There was no roar and rumble of traffic. There were not even cabs on the streets. The surface cars and the elevated were not running. Only occasionally, on the sidewalks, were there stray pedestrians, and these pedestrians did not loiter. They went their ways with great haste and definiteness, withal there was a curious indecision in their movements, as though they expected the buildings to topple over on them or the sidewalks to sink under their feet or fly up in the air. A few gamins, however, were around, in their eyes a suppressed eagerness in anticipation of wonderful and exciting things to happen.

From somewhere, far to the south, the dull sound of an explosion came to our ears. That was all. Then quiet again, though the gamins had startled and listened, like

---

* A lie.

young deer, at the sound. The doorways to all the buildings were closed; the shutters to the shops were up. But there were many police and watchmen in evidence, and now and again automobile patrols of the Mercenaries slipped swiftly past.

Hartman and I agreed that it was useless to report ourselves to the local chiefs of the secret service. Our failure so to report would be excused, we knew, in the light of subsequent events. So we headed for the great labor-ghetto on the South Side in the hope of getting in contact with some of the comrades. Too late! We knew it. But we could not stand still and do nothing in those ghastly, silent streets. Where was Ernest? I was wondering. What was happening in the cities of the labor castes and Mercenaries? In the fortresses?

As if in answer, a great screaming roar went up, dim with distance, punctuated with detonation after detonation.

'It's the fortresses,' Hartman said. 'God pity those three regiments!'

At a crossing we noticed, in the direction of the stockyards, a gigantic pillar of smoke. At the next crossing several similar smoke pillars were rising skyward in the direction of the West Side. Over the city of the Mercenaries we saw a great captive war-balloon that burst even as we looked at it, and fell in flaming wreckage toward the earth. There was no clew to that tragedy of the air. We could not determine whether the balloon had been manned by comrades or enemies. A vague sound came to our ears, like the bubbling of a gigantic caldron a long way off, and Hartman said it was machine-guns and automatic rifles.

And still we walked in immediate quietude. Nothing was happening where we were. The police and the automobile patrols went by, and once half a dozen fire-engines, returning evidently from some conflagration. A question was called to the fireman by an officer in an automobile, and we heard one shout in reply: 'No water! They've blown up the mains!'

'We've smashed the water supply,' Hartman cried excitedly to me. 'If we can do all this in a premature, isolated, abortive attempt, what can't we do in a concerted, ripened effort all over the land?'

The automobile containing the officer who had asked the question darted on. Suddenly there was a deafening roar. The machine, with its human freight, lifted in an upburst of smoke, and sank down a mass of wreckage and death.

Hartman was jubilant. 'Well done! well done!' he was repeating, over and over, in a whisper. 'The proletariat gets its lesson to-day, but it gives one, too.'

Police were running for the spot. Also, another patrol machine had halted. As for myself, I was in a daze. The suddenness of it was stunning. How had it happened? I knew not how, and yet I had been looking directly at it. So dazed was I for the moment that I was scarcely aware of the fact that we were being held up by the police. I abruptly saw that a policeman was in the act of shooting Hartman. But Hartman was cool and was giving the proper passwords. I saw the levelled revolver hesitate, then sink down, and heard the disgusted grunt of the policeman. He was very angry, and was cursing the whole secret service. It was always in the way, he was averring, while Hartman was talking back to him and with fitting secret-service pride explaining to him the clumsiness of the police.

The next moment I knew how it had happened. There was quite a group about the wreck, and two men were just lifting up the wounded officer to carry him to the other machine. A panic seized all of them, and they scattered in every direction, running in blind terror, the wounded officer, roughly dropped, being left behind. The cursing policeman alongside of me also ran, and Hartman and I ran, too, we knew not why, obsessed with the same blind terror to get away from that particular spot.

Nothing really happened then, but everything was explained. The flying men were sheepishly coming back, but all the while their eyes were raised apprehensively to the many-windowed, lofty buildings that towered like the sheer walls of a canyon on each side of the street. From one of those countless windows the bomb had been thrown, but which window? There had been no second bomb, only a fear of one.

Thereafter we looked with speculative comprehension at the windows. Any of them contained possible death. Each building was a possible ambuscade. This was warfare in that modern jungle, a great city. Every street was a canyon, every building a mountain. We had not changed much from primitive man, despite the war automobiles that were sliding by.

Turning a corner, we came upon a woman. She was lying on the pavement, in a pool of blood. Hartman bent over and examined her. As for myself, I turned deathly sick. I was to see many dead that day, but the total carnage was not to affect me as did this first forlorn body lying there at my feet abandoned on the pavement. 'Shot in the breast,' was Hartman's report. Clasped in the hollow of her arm, as a child might be clasped, was a bundle of printed matter. Even in death she seemed loath to part with that which had caused her death; for when Hartman had succeeded in withdrawing the bundle, we found that it consisted of large printed sheets, the proclamations of the revolutionists.

'A comrade,' I said.

But Hartman only cursed the Iron Heel, and we passed on. Often we were halted by the police and patrols, but our passwords enabled us to proceed. No more bombs fell from the windows, the last pedestrians seemed to have vanished from the streets, and our immediate quietude grew more profound; though the gigantic caldron continued to bubble in the distance, dull roars of explosions came to us from all directions, and the smoke-pillars were towering more ominously in the heavens.

CHAPTER XXIII
THE PEOPLE OF THE ABYSS

Suddenly a change came over the face of things. A tingle of excitement ran along the air. Automobiles fled past, two, three, a dozen, and from them warnings were shouted to us. One of the machines swerved wildly at high speed half a block down, and the next moment, already left well behind it, the pavement was torn into a great hole by a bursting bomb. We saw the police disappearing down the cross-streets on the run, and knew that something terrible was coming. We could hear the rising roar of it.

'Our brave comrades are coming,' Hartman said.

We could see the front of their column filling the street from gutter to gutter, as the last war-automobile fled past. The machine stopped for a moment just abreast of us. A soldier leaped from it, carrying something carefully in his hands. This, with the same care, he deposited in the gutter. Then he leaped back to his seat and the machine dashed on, took the turn at the corner, and was gone from sight. Hartman ran to the gutter and stooped over the object.

'Keep back,' he warned me.

I could see he was working rapidly with his hands. When he returned to me the sweat was heavy on his forehead.

'I disconnected it,' he said, 'and just in the nick of time. The soldier was clumsy. He intended it for our comrades, but he didn't give it enough time. It would have exploded prematurely. Now it won't explode at all.'

Everything was happening rapidly now. Across the street and half a block down, high up in a building, I could see heads peering out. I had just pointed them out to Hartman, when a sheet of flame and smoke ran along that portion of the face of the building where the heads had appeared, and the air was shaken by the explosion. In places the stone facing of the building was torn away, exposing the iron construction beneath. The next moment similar sheets of flame and smoke smote the front of the building across the street opposite it. Between the explosions we could hear the rattle of the automatic pistols and rifles. For several minutes this mid-air battle continued, then died out. It was patent that our comrades were in one building, that Mercenaries were in the other, and that they were fighting across the street. But we could not tell which was which—which building contained our comrades and which the Mercenaries.

By this time the column on the street was almost on us. As the front of it passed under the warring buildings, both went into action again—one building dropping bombs into the street, being attacked from across the street, and in return replying to that attack. Thus we learned which building was held by our comrades, and they did good work, saving those in the street from the bombs of the enemy.

Hartman gripped my arm and dragged me into a wide entrance.

'They're not our comrades,' he shouted in my ear.

The inner doors to the entrance were locked and bolted. We could not escape. The next moment the front of the column went by. It was not a column, but a mob, an awful river that filled the street, the people of the abyss, mad with drink and wrong, up at last and roaring for the blood of their masters. I had seen the people of the abyss before, gone through its ghettos, and thought I knew it; but I found that I was now looking on it for the first time. Dumb apathy had vanished. It was now dynamic—a fascinating spectacle of dread. It surged past my vision in concrete waves of wrath, snarling and growling, carnivorous, drunk with whiskey from pillaged warehouses, drunk with hatred, drunk with lust for blood—men, women, and children, in rags and tatters, dim ferocious intelligences with all the godlike blotted from their features and all the fiendlike stamped in, apes and tigers, anaemic consumptives and great hairy beasts of burden, wan faces from which vampire society had sucked the juice of life, bloated forms swollen with physical grossness and corruption, withered hags and death's-heads bearded like patriarchs, festering youth and festering age, faces of fiends, crooked, twisted, misshapen monsters blasted with the ravages of disease and all the horrors of chronic innutrition—the refuse and the scum of life, a raging, screaming, screeching, demoniacal horde.

And why not? The people of the abyss had nothing to lose but the misery and pain of living. And to gain?—nothing, save one final, awful glut of vengeance. And as I looked the thought came to me that in that rushing stream of human lava were men, comrades and heroes, whose mission had been to rouse the abysmal beast and to keep the enemy occupied in coping with it.

And now a strange thing happened to me. A transformation came over me. The fear of death, for myself and for others, left me. I was strangely exalted, another being in another life. Nothing mattered. The Cause for this one time was lost, but the Cause would be here to-morrow, the same Cause, ever fresh and ever burning. And thereafter, in the orgy of horror that raged through the succeeding hours, I was able to take a calm interest. Death meant nothing, life meant nothing. I was an interested spectator of events, and, sometimes swept on by the rush, was myself a curious participant. For my mind had leaped to a star-cool altitude and grasped a passionless transvaluation of values. Had it not done this, I know that I should have died.

Half a mile of the mob had swept by when we were discovered. A woman in fantastic rags, with cheeks cavernously hollow and with narrow black eyes like burning gimlets, caught a glimpse of Hartman and me. She let out a shrill shriek and bore in upon us. A section of the mob tore itself loose and surged in after her. I can see her now, as I write these lines, a leap in advance, her gray hair flying in thin tangled strings, the blood dripping down her forehead from some wound in the scalp, in her right hand a hatchet, her left hand, lean and wrinkled, a yellow talon, gripping the air convulsively. Hartman sprang in front of me. This was no time for explanations. We were well dressed, and that was enough. His fist shot out, striking the woman between her burning eyes. The impact of the blow drove her backward, but she struck the wall of her on-coming fellows and bounced forward again, dazed and helpless, the brandished hatchet falling feebly on Hartman's shoulder.

The next moment I knew not what was happening. I was overborne by the crowd. The confined space was filled with shrieks and yells and curses. Blows were falling on me. Hands were ripping and tearing at my flesh and garments. I felt that I was being torn to pieces. I was being borne down, suffocated. Some strong hand gripped my shoulder in the thick of the press and was dragging fiercely at me. Between pain and pressure I fainted. Hartman never came out of that entrance. He had shielded me and received the first brunt of the attack. This had saved me, for the jam had quickly become too dense for anything more than the mad gripping and tearing of hands.

I came to in the midst of wild movement. All about me was the same movement. I had been caught up in a monstrous flood that was sweeping me I knew not whither. Fresh air was on my cheek and biting sweetly in my lungs. Faint and dizzy, I was vaguely aware of a strong arm around my body under the arms, and half-lifting me and dragging me along. Feebly my own limbs were helping me. In front of me I could see the moving back of a man's coat. It had been slit from top to bottom along the centre seam, and it pulsed rhythmically, the slit opening and closing regularly with every leap of the wearer. This phenomenon fascinated me for a time, while my senses were coming back to me. Next I became aware of stinging cheeks and nose, and could feel blood dripping on my face. My hat was gone. My hair was down and flying, and from the stinging of the scalp I managed to recollect a hand in the press of the entrance that had torn at my hair. My chest and arms were bruised and aching in a score of places.

My brain grew clearer, and I turned as I ran and looked at the man who was holding me up. He it was who had dragged me out and saved me. He noticed my movement.

'It's all right!' he shouted hoarsely. 'I knew you on the instant.'

I failed to recognize him, but before I could speak I trod upon something that was alive and that squirmed under my foot. I was swept on by those behind and could not look down and see, and yet I knew that it was a woman who had fallen and who was being trampled into the pavement by thousands of successive feet.

'It's all right,' he repeated. 'I'm Garthwaite.'

He was bearded and gaunt and dirty, but I succeeded in remembering him as the stalwart youth that had spent several months in our Glen Ellen refuge three years before. He passed me the signals of the Iron Heel's secret service, in token that he, too, was in its employ.

'I'll get you out of this as soon as I can get a chance,' he assured me. 'But watch your footing. On your life don't stumble and go down.'

All things happened abruptly on that day, and with an abruptness that was sickening the mob checked itself. I came in violent collision with a large woman in front of me (the man with the split coat had vanished), while those behind collided against me. A devilish pandemonium reigned,—shrieks, curses, and cries of death, while above all rose the churning rattle of machine-guns and the put-a-put, put-a-put of rifles. At first I could make out nothing. People were falling about me right and left. The woman in front doubled up and went down, her hands on her abdomen in a frenzied clutch. A man was quivering against my legs in a death-struggle.

It came to me that we were at the head of the column. Half a mile of it had disappeared—where or how I never learned. To this day I do not know what became of that half-mile of humanity—whether it was blotted out by some frightful bolt of war, whether it was scattered and destroyed piecemeal, or whether it escaped. But there we were, at the head of the column instead of in its middle, and we were being swept out of life by a torrent of shrieking lead.

As soon as death had thinned the jam, Garthwaite, still grasping my arm, led a rush of survivors into the wide entrance of an office building. Here, at the rear, against the doors, we were pressed by a panting, gasping mass of creatures. For some time we remained in this position without a change in the situation.

'I did it beautifully,' Garthwaite was lamenting to me. 'Ran you right into a trap. We had a gambler's chance in the street, but in here there is no chance at all. It's all over but the shouting. Vive la Revolution!'

Then, what he expected, began. The Mercenaries were killing without quarter. At first, the surge back upon us was crushing, but as the killing continued the pressure was eased. The dead and dying went down and made room. Garthwaite put his mouth to my ear and shouted, but in the frightful din I could not catch what he said. He did not wait. He seized me and threw me down. Next he dragged a dying woman over on top of me, and, with much squeezing and shoving, crawled in beside me and partly over me. A mound of dead and dying began to pile up over us, and over this mound, pawing and moaning, crept those that still survived. But these, too, soon ceased, and a semi-silence settled down, broken by groans and sobs and sounds of strangulation.

I should have been crushed had it not been for Garthwaite. As it was, it seemed inconceivable that I could bear the weight I did and live. And yet, outside of pain, the only feeling I possessed was one of curiosity. How was it going to end? What would death be like? Thus did I receive my red baptism in that Chicago shambles. Prior to that, death to me had been a theory; but ever afterward death has been a simple fact that does not matter, it is so easy.

But the Mercenaries were not content with what they had done. They invaded the entrance, killing the wounded and searching out the unhurt that, like ourselves, were playing dead. I remember one man they dragged out of a heap, who pleaded abjectly until a revolver shot cut him short. Then there was a woman who charged from a heap, snarling and shooting. She fired six shots before they got her, though what damage she did we could not know. We could follow these tragedies only by the sound. Every little while flurries like this occurred, each flurry culminating in the revolver shot that put an end to it. In the intervals we could hear the soldiers talking and swearing as they rummaged among the carcasses, urged on by their officers to hurry up.

At last they went to work on our heap, and we could feel the pressure diminish as they dragged away the dead and wounded. Garthwaite began uttering aloud the signals. At first he was not heard. Then he raised his voice.

'Listen to that,' we heard a soldier say. And next the sharp voice of an officer. 'Hold on there! Careful as you go!'

Oh, that first breath of air as we were dragged out! Garthwaite did the talking at first, but I was compelled to undergo a brief examination to prove service with the Iron Heel.

'Agents-provocateurs all right,' was the officer's conclusion. He was a beardless young fellow, a cadet, evidently, of some great oligarch family.

'It's a hell of a job,' Garthwaite grumbled. 'I'm going to try and resign and get into the army. You fellows have a snap.'

'You've earned it,' was the young officer's answer. 'I've got some pull, and I'll see if it can be managed. I can tell them how I found you.'

He took Garthwaite's name and number, then turned to me.

'And you?'

'Oh, I'm going to be married,' I answered lightly, 'and then I'll be out of it all.'

And so we talked, while the killing of the wounded went on. It is all a dream, now, as I look back on it; but at the time it was the most natural thing in the world. Garthwaite and the young officer fell into an animated conversation over the difference between so-called modern warfare and the present street-fighting and sky-scraper fighting that was taking place all over the city. I followed them intently, fixing up my hair at the same time and pinning together my torn skirts. And all the time the killing of the wounded went on. Sometimes the revolver shots drowned the voices of Garthwaite and the officer, and they were compelled to repeat what they had been saying.

I lived through three days of the Chicago Commune, and the vastness of it and of the slaughter may be imagined when I say that in all that time I saw practically nothing outside the killing of the people of the abyss and the mid-air fighting between sky-scrapers. I really saw nothing of the heroic work done by the comrades. I could hear the explosions of their mines and bombs, and see the smoke of their conflagrations, and that was all. The mid-air part of one great deed I saw, however, and that was the balloon attacks made by our comrades on the fortresses. That was on the second day. The three disloyal regiments had been destroyed in the fortresses to the last man. The fortresses were crowded with Mercenaries, the wind blew in the right direction, and up went our balloons from one of the office buildings in the city.

Now Biedenbach, after he left Glen Ellen, had invented a most powerful explosive—'expedite' he called it. This was the weapon the balloons used. They were only hot-air balloons, clumsily and hastily made, but they did the work. I saw it all from the top of an office building. The first balloon missed the fortresses completely and disappeared into the country; but we learned about it afterward. Burton and O'Sullivan were in it. As they were descending they swept across a railroad directly over a troop-train that was heading at full speed for Chicago. They dropped their whole supply of expedite upon the locomotive. The resulting wreck tied the line up for days. And the best of it was that, released from the weight of expedite, the balloon shot up into the air and did not come down for half a dozen miles, both heroes escaping unharmed.

The second balloon was a failure. Its flight was lame. It floated too low and was shot full of holes before it could reach the fortresses. Herford and Guinness were in it, and they were blown to pieces along with the field into which they fell. Biedenbach was in despair—we heard all about it afterward—and he went up alone in the third balloon. He, too, made a low flight, but he was in luck, for they failed seriously to puncture his balloon. I can see it now as I did then, from the lofty top of the building—that inflated bag drifting along the air, and that tiny speck of a man clinging on beneath. I could not see the fortress, but those on the roof with me said he was directly over it. I did not see the expedite fall when he cut it loose. But I did see the balloon suddenly leap up into the sky. An appreciable time after that the great column of the explosion towered in the air, and after that, in turn, I heard the roar of it. Biedenbach the gentle had destroyed a fortress. Two other balloons followed at the same time. One was blown to pieces in the air, the expedite exploding, and the shock of it disrupted the second balloon, which fell prettily into the remaining fortress. It couldn't have been better planned, though the two comrades in it sacrificed their lives.

But to return to the people of the abyss. My experiences were confined to them. They raged and slaughtered and destroyed all over the city proper, and were in turn destroyed; but never once did they succeed in reaching the city of the oligarchs over on the west side. The oligarchs had protected themselves well. No matter what destruction was wreaked in the heart of the city, they, and their womenkind and children, were to escape hurt. I am told that their children played in the parks during those terrible days and that their favorite game was an imitation of their elders stamping upon the proletariat.

But the Mercenaries found it no easy task to cope with the people of the abyss and at the same time fight with the comrades. Chicago was true to her traditions, and though a generation of revolutionists was wiped out, it took along with it pretty close to a generation of its enemies. Of course, the Iron Heel kept the figures secret, but, at a very conservative estimate, at least one hundred and thirty thousand Mercenaries were slain. But the comrades had no chance. Instead of the whole country being hand in hand in revolt, they were all alone, and the total strength of the Oligarchy could have been directed against them if necessary. As it was, hour after hour, day after day, in endless train-loads, by hundreds of thousands, the Mercenaries were hurled into Chicago.

And there were so many of the people of the abyss! Tiring of the slaughter, a great herding movement was begun by the soldiers, the intent of which was to drive the street mobs, like cattle, into Lake Michigan. It was at the beginning of this movement that Garthwaite and I had encountered the young officer. This herding movement was practically a failure, thanks to the splendid work of the comrades. Instead of the great host the Mercenaries had hoped to gather together, they succeeded in driving no more than forty thousand of the wretches into the lake. Time and again, when a mob of them was well in hand and being driven along the streets to the water, the comrades would create a diversion, and the mob would escape through the consequent hole torn in the encircling net.

Garthwaite and I saw an example of this shortly after meeting with the young officer. The mob of which we had been a part, and which had been put in retreat, was prevented from escaping to the south and east by strong bodies of troops. The troops we had fallen in with had held it back on the west. The only outlet was north, and north it went toward the lake, driven on from east and west and south by machine-gun fire and automatics. Whether it divined that it was being driven toward the lake, or whether it was merely a blind squirm of the monster, I do not know; but at any rate the mob took a cross street to the west, turned down the next street, and came back upon its track, heading south toward the great ghetto.

Garthwaite and I at that time were trying to make our way westward to get out of the territory of street-fighting, and we were caught right in the thick of it again. As we came to the corner we saw the howling mob bearing down upon us. Garthwaite seized my arm and we were just starting to run, when he dragged me back from in front of the wheels of half a dozen war automobiles, equipped with machine-guns, that were rushing for the spot. Behind them came the soldiers with their automatic rifles. By the time they took position, the mob was upon them, and it looked as though they would be overwhelmed before they could get into action.

Here and there a soldier was discharging his rifle, but this scattered fire had no effect in checking the mob. On it came, bellowing with brute rage. It seemed the machine-guns could not get started. The automobiles on which they were mounted blocked the street, compelling the soldiers to find positions in, between, and on the sidewalks. More and more soldiers were arriving, and in the jam we were unable to get away. Garthwaite held me by the arm, and we pressed close against the front of a building.

The mob was no more than twenty-five feet away when the machine-guns opened up; but before that flaming sheet of death nothing could live. The mob came on, but it could not advance. It piled up in a heap, a mound, a huge and growing wave of dead and dying. Those behind urged on, and the column, from gutter to gutter, telescoped upon itself. Wounded creatures, men and women, were vomited over the top of that awful wave and fell squirming down the face of it till they threshed about under the automobiles and against the legs of the soldiers. The latter bayoneted the struggling wretches, though one I saw who gained his feet and flew at a soldier's throat with his teeth. Together they went down, soldier and slave, into the welter.

The firing ceased. The work was done. The mob had been stopped in its wild attempt to break through. Orders were being given to clear the wheels of the war-machines. They could not advance over that wave of dead, and the idea was to run them down the cross street. The soldiers were dragging the bodies away from the wheels when it happened. We learned afterward how it happened. A block distant a hundred of our comrades had been holding a building. Across roofs and through buildings they made their way, till they found themselves looking down upon the close-packed soldiers. Then it was counter-massacre.

Without warning, a shower of bombs fell from the top of the building. The automobiles were blown to fragments, along with many soldiers. We, with the survivors, swept back in mad retreat. Half a block down another building opened fire on us. As the soldiers had carpeted the street with dead slaves, so, in turn, did they themselves become carpet. Garthwaite and I bore charmed lives. As we had done before, so again we sought shelter in an entrance. But he was not to be caught napping this time. As the roar of the bombs died away, he began peering out.

'The mob's coming back!' he called to me. 'We've got to get out of this!'

We fled, hand in hand, down the bloody pavement, slipping and sliding, and making for the corner. Down the cross street we could see a few soldiers still running. Nothing was happening to them. The way was clear. So we paused a moment and looked back. The mob came on slowly. It was busy arming itself with the rifles of the slain and killing the wounded. We saw the end of the young officer who had rescued us. He painfully lifted himself on his elbow and turned loose with his automatic pistol.

'There goes my chance of promotion,' Garthwaite laughed, as a woman bore down on the wounded man, brandishing a butcher's cleaver. 'Come on. It's the wrong direction, but we'll get out somehow.'

And we fled eastward through the quiet streets, prepared at every cross street for anything to happen. To the south a monster conflagration was filling the sky, and we knew that the great ghetto was burning. At last I sank down on the sidewalk. I was exhausted and could go no farther. I was bruised and sore and aching in every limb; yet I could not escape smiling at Garthwaite, who was rolling a cigarette and saying:

'I know I'm making a mess of rescuing you, but I can't get head nor tail of the situation. It's all a mess. Every time we try to break out, something happens and we're turned back. We're only a couple of blocks now from where I got you out of that entrance. Friend and foe are all mixed up. It's chaos. You can't tell who is in those darned buildings. Try to find out, and you get a bomb on your head. Try to go peaceably on your way, and you run into a mob and are killed by machine-guns, or you run into the Mercenaries and are killed by your own comrades from a roof. And on the top of it all the mob comes along and kills you, too.'

He shook his head dolefully, lighted his cigarette, and sat down beside me.

'And I'm that hungry,' he added, 'I could eat cobblestones.'

The next moment he was on his feet again and out in the street prying up a cobblestone. He came back with it and assaulted the window of a store behind us.

'It's ground floor and no good,' he explained as he helped me through the hole he had made; 'but it's the best we can do. You get a nap and I'll reconnoitre. I'll finish this rescue all right, but I want time, time, lots of it—and something to eat.'

It was a harness store we found ourselves in, and he fixed me up a couch of horse blankets in the private office well to the rear. To add to my wretchedness a splitting headache was coming on, and I was only too glad to close my eyes and try to sleep.

'I'll be back,' were his parting words. 'I don't hope to get an auto, but I'll surely bring some grub,* anyway.'

And that was the last I saw of Garthwaite for three years. Instead of coming back, he was carried away to a hospital with a bullet through his lungs and another through the fleshy part of his neck.

---

* Food.

CHAPTER XXIV

NIGHTMARE

I had not closed my eyes the night before on the Twentieth Century, and what of that and of my exhaustion I slept soundly. When I first awoke, it was night. Garthwaite had not returned. I had lost my watch and had no idea of the time. As I lay with my eyes closed, I heard the same dull sound of distant explosions. The inferno was still raging. I crept through the store to the front. The reflection from the sky of vast conflagrations made the street almost as light as day. One could have read the finest print with ease. From several blocks away came the crackle of small hand-bombs and the churning of machine-guns, and from a long way off came a long series of heavy explosions. I crept back to my horse blankets and slept again.

When next I awoke, a sickly yellow light was filtering in on me. It was dawn of the second day. I crept to the front of the store. A smoke pall, shot through with lurid gleams, filled the sky. Down the opposite side of the street tottered a wretched slave. One hand he held tightly against his side, and behind him he left a bloody trail. His eyes roved everywhere, and they were filled with apprehension and dread. Once he looked straight across at me, and in his face was all the dumb pathos of the wounded and hunted animal. He saw me, but there was no kinship between us, and with him, at least, no sympathy of understanding; for he cowered perceptibly and dragged himself on. He could expect no aid in all God's world. He was a helot in the great hunt of helots that the masters were making. All he could hope for, all he sought, was some hole to crawl away in and hide like any animal. The sharp clang of a passing ambulance at the corner gave him a start. Ambulances were not for such as he. With a groan of pain he threw himself into a doorway. A minute later he was out again and desperately hobbling on.

I went back to my horse blankets and waited an hour for Garthwaite. My headache had not gone away. On the contrary, it was increasing. It was by an effort of will only that I was able to open my eyes and look at objects. And with the opening of my eyes and the looking came intolerable torment. Also, a great pulse was beating in my brain. Weak and reeling, I went out through the broken window and down the street, seeking to escape, instinctively and gropingly, from the awful shambles. And thereafter I lived nightmare. My memory of what happened in the succeeding hours is the memory one would have of nightmare. Many events are focussed sharply on my brain, but between these indelible pictures I retain are intervals of unconsciousness. What occurred in those intervals I know not, and never shall know.

I remember stumbling at the corner over the legs of a man. It was the poor hunted wretch that had dragged himself past my hiding-place. How distinctly do I remember his poor, pitiful, gnarled hands as he lay there on the pavement—hands that were more hoof and claw than hands, all twisted and distorted by the toil of all his days, with on the palms a horny growth of callous a half inch thick. And as I picked myself up and started on, I looked into the face of the thing and saw that it still lived; for the eyes, dimly intelligent, were looking at me and seeing me.

After that came a kindly blank. I knew nothing, saw nothing, merely tottered on in my quest for safety. My next nightmare vision was a quiet street of the dead. I came upon it abruptly, as a wanderer in the country would come upon a flowing stream. Only this stream I gazed upon did not flow. It was congealed in death. From pavement to pavement, and covering the sidewalks, it lay there, spread out quite evenly, with only here and there a lump or mound of bodies to break the surface. Poor driven people of the abyss, hunted helots—they lay there as the rabbits in California after a drive.* Up the street and down I looked. There was no movement, no sound. The quiet buildings looked down upon the scene from their many windows. And once, and once only, I saw an arm that moved in that dead stream. I swear I saw it move, with a strange writhing gesture of agony, and with it lifted a head, gory with nameless horror, that gibbered at me and then lay down again and moved no more.

I remember another street, with quiet buildings on either side, and the panic that smote me into consciousness as again I saw the people of the abyss, but this time in a stream that flowed and came on. And then I saw there was nothing to fear. The stream moved slowly, while from it arose groans and lamentations, cursings, babblings of senility, hysteria, and insanity; for these were the very young and the very old, the feeble and the sick, the helpless and the hopeless, all the wreckage of the ghetto. The burning of the great ghetto on the South Side had driven them forth into the inferno of the street-fighting, and whither they wended and whatever became of them I did not know and never learned.**

I have faint memories of breaking a window and hiding in some shop to escape a street mob that was pursued by soldiers. Also, a bomb burst near me, once, in some still street, where, look as I would, up and down, I could see no human being. But my next sharp recollection begins with the crack of a rifle and an abrupt becoming aware that I am being fired at by a soldier in an automobile. The shot missed, and the next moment I was screaming and motioning the signals. My memory of riding in the automobile is very hazy, though this ride, in turn, is broken by one vivid picture. The crack of the rifle of the soldier sitting beside me made me open my eyes, and I saw George Milford, whom I had known in the Pell Street days, sinking slowly down to the sidewalk. Even as he sank the soldier fired again, and Milford doubled in, then flung his body out, and fell sprawling. The soldier chuckled, and the automobile sped on.

The next I knew after that I was awakened out of a sound sleep by a man who walked up and down close beside me. His face was drawn and strained, and the sweat rolled down his nose from his forehead. One hand was clutched tightly against his chest by the other hand, and blood dripped down upon the floor as he walked. He wore the uniform of the Mercenaries. From without, as through thick walls, came the muffled roar of bursting bombs. I was in some building that was locked in combat with some other building.

A surgeon came in to dress the wounded soldier, and I learned that it was two in the afternoon. My headache was no better, and the surgeon paused from his work long enough to give me a powerful drug that would depress the heart and bring relief. I slept again, and the next I knew I was on top of the building. The immediate fighting had ceased, and I was watching the balloon attack on the fortresses. Some one had an arm around me and I was leaning close against him. It came to me quite as a matter

---

* In those days, so sparsely populated was the land that wild animals often became pests. In California the custom of rabbit-driving obtained. On a given day all the farmers in a locality would assemble and sweep across the country in converging lines, driving the rabbits by scores of thousands into a prepared enclosure, where they were clubbed to death by men and boys.
** It was long a question of debate, whether the burning of the South Side ghetto was accidental, or whether it was done by the Mercenaries; but it is definitely settled now that the ghetto was fired by the Mercenaries under orders from their chiefs.

of course that this was Ernest, and I found myself wondering how he had got his hair and eyebrows so badly singed.

It was by the merest chance that we had found each other in that terrible city. He had had no idea that I had left New York, and, coming through the room where I lay asleep, could not at first believe that it was I. Little more I saw of the Chicago Commune. After watching the balloon attack, Ernest took me down into the heart of the building, where I slept the afternoon out and the night. The third day we spent in the building, and on the fourth, Ernest having got permission and an automobile from the authorities, we left Chicago.

My headache was gone, but, body and soul, I was very tired. I lay back against Ernest in the automobile, and with apathetic eyes watched the soldiers trying to get the machine out of the city. Fighting was still going on, but only in isolated localities. Here and there whole districts were still in possession of the comrades, but such districts were surrounded and guarded by heavy bodies of troops. In a hundred segregated traps were the comrades thus held while the work of subjugating them went on. Subjugation meant death, for no quarter was given, and they fought heroically to the last man.[*]

Whenever we approached such localities, the guards turned us back and sent us around. Once, the only way past two strong positions of the comrades was through a burnt section that lay between. From either side we could hear the rattle and roar of war, while the automobile picked its way through smoking ruins and tottering walls. Often the streets were blocked by mountains of debris that compelled us to go around. We were in a labyrinth of ruin, and our progress was slow.

The stockyards (ghetto, plant, and everything) were smouldering ruins. Far off to the right a wide smoke haze dimmed the sky,—the town of Pullman, the soldier chauffeur told us, or what had been the town of Pullman, for it was utterly destroyed. He had driven the machine out there, with despatches, on the afternoon of the third day. Some of the heaviest fighting had occurred there, he said, many of the streets being rendered impassable by the heaps of the dead.

Swinging around the shattered walls of a building, in the stockyards district, the automobile was stopped by a wave of dead. It was for all the world like a wave tossed up by the sea. It was patent to us what had happened. As the mob charged past the corner, it had been swept, at right angles and point-blank range, by the machine-guns drawn up on the cross street. But disaster had come to the soldiers. A chance bomb must have exploded among them, for the mob, checked until its dead and dying formed the wave, had white-capped and flung forward its foam of living, fighting slaves. Soldiers and slaves lay together, torn and mangled, around and over the wreckage of the automobiles and guns.

Ernest sprang out. A familiar pair of shoulders in a cotton shirt and a familiar fringe of white hair had caught his eye. I did not watch him, and it was not until he was back beside me and we were speeding on that he said:

'It was Bishop Morehouse.'

---

[*] Numbers of the buildings held out over a week, while one held out eleven days. Each building had to be stormed like a fort, and the Mercenaries fought their way upward floor by floor. It was deadly fighting. Quarter was neither given nor taken, and in the fighting the revolutionists had the advantage of being above. While the revolutionists were wiped out, the loss was not one-sided. The proud Chicago proletariat lived up to its ancient boast. For as many of itself as were killed, it killed that many of the enemy.

Soon we were in the green country, and I took one last glance back at the smoke-filled sky. Faint and far came the low thud of an explosion. Then I turned my face against Ernest's breast and wept softly for the Cause that was lost. Ernest's arm about me was eloquent with love.

'For this time lost, dear heart,' he said, 'but not forever. We have learned. To-morrow the Cause will rise again, strong with wisdom and discipline.'

The automobile drew up at a railroad station. Here we would catch a train to New York. As we waited on the platform, three trains thundered past, bound west to Chicago. They were crowded with ragged, unskilled laborers, people of the abyss.

'Slave-levies for the rebuilding of Chicago,' Ernest said. 'You see, the Chicago slaves are all killed.'

CHAPTER XXV
THE TERRORISTS

It was not until Ernest and I were back in New York, and after weeks had elapsed, that we were able to comprehend thoroughly the full sweep of the disaster that had befallen the Cause. The situation was bitter and bloody. In many places, scattered over the country, slave revolts and massacres had occurred. The roll of the martyrs increased mightily. Countless executions took place everywhere. The mountains and waste regions were filled with outlaws and refugees who were being hunted down mercilessly. Our own refuges were packed with comrades who had prices on their heads. Through information furnished by its spies, scores of our refuges were raided by the soldiers of the Iron Heel.

Many of the comrades were disheartened, and they retaliated with terroristic tactics. The set-back to their hopes made them despairing and desperate. Many terrorist organizations unaffiliated with us sprang into existence and caused us much trouble.* These misguided people sacrificed their own lives wantonly, very often made our own plans go astray, and retarded our organization.

And through it all moved the Iron Heel, impassive and deliberate, shaking up the whole fabric of the social structure in its search for the comrades, combing out the Mercenaries, the labor castes, and all its secret services, punishing without mercy

---

* The annals of this short-lived era of despair make bloody reading. Revenge was the ruling motive, and the members of the terroristic organizations were careless of their own lives and hopeless about the future. The Danites, taking their name from the avenging angels of the Mormon mythology, sprang up in the mountains of the Great West and spread over the Pacific Coast from Panama to Alaska. The Valkyries were women. They were the most terrible of all. No woman was eligible for membership who had not lost near relatives at the hands of the Oligarchy. They were guilty of torturing their prisoners to death. Another famous organization of women was The Widows of War. A companion organization to the Valkyries was the Berserkers. These men placed no value whatever upon their own lives, and it was they who totally destroyed the great Mercenary city of Bellona along with its population of over a hundred thousand souls. The Bedlamites and the Helldamites were twin slave organizations, while a new religious sect that did not flourish long was called The Wrath of God. Among others, to show the whimsicality of their deadly seriousness, may be mentioned the following: The Bleeding Hearts, Sons of the Morning, the Morning Stars, The Flamingoes, The Triple Triangles, The Three Bars, The Rubonics, The Vindicators, The Comanches, and the Erebusites.

and without malice, suffering in silence all retaliations that were made upon it, and filling the gaps in its fighting line as fast as they appeared. And hand in hand with this, Ernest and the other leaders were hard at work reorganizing the forces of the Revolution. The magnitude of the task may be understood when it is taken into[*]

---

[*] This is the end of the Everhard Manuscript. It breaks off abruptly in the middle of a sentence. She must have received warning of the coming of the Mercenaries, for she had time safely to hide the Manuscript before she fled or was captured. It is to be regretted that she did not live to complete her narrative, for then, undoubtedly, would have been cleared away the mystery that has shrouded for seven centuries the execution of Ernest Everhard.

THE PEOPLE
OF THE ABYSS

PREFACE

The experiences related in this volume fell to me in the summer of 1902. I went down into the under-world of London with an attitude of mind which I may best liken to that of the explorer. I was open to be convinced by the evidence of my eyes, rather than by the teachings of those who had not seen, or by the words of those who had seen and gone before. Further, I took with me certain simple criteria with which to measure the life of the under-world. That which made for more life, for physical and spiritual health, was good; that which made for less life, which hurt, and dwarfed, and distorted life, was bad.

It will be readily apparent to the reader that I saw much that was bad. Yet it must not be forgotten that the time of which I write was considered 'good times' in England. The starvation and lack of shelter I encountered constituted a chronic condition of misery which is never wiped out, even in the periods of greatest prosperity.

Following the summer in question came a hard winter. Great numbers of the unemployed formed into processions, as many as a dozen at a time, and daily marched through the streets of London crying for bread. Mr. Justin McCarthy, writing in the month of January 1903, to the New York *Independent*, briefly epitomises the situation as follows:-

> 'The workhouses have no space left in which to pack the starving crowds who are craving every day and night at their doors for food and shelter. All the charitable institutions have exhausted their means in trying to raise supplies of food for the famishing residents of the garrets and cellars of London lanes and alleys. The quarters of the Salvation Army in various parts of London are nightly besieged by hosts of the unemployed and the hungry for whom neither shelter nor the means of sustenance can be provided.'

It has been urged that the criticism I have passed on things as they are in England is too pessimistic. I must say, in extenuation, that of optimists I am the most optimistic. But I measure manhood less by political aggregations than by individuals. Society grows, while political machines rack to pieces and become 'scrap.' For the English, so far as manhood and womanhood and health and happiness go, I see a broad and smiling future. But for a great deal of the political machinery, which at present mismanages for them, I see nothing else than the scrap heap.

JACK LONDON.
PIEDMONT, CALIFORNIA.

CHAPTER I
THE DESCENT

Christ look upon us in this city,
and keep our sympathy and pity
fresh, and our faces heavenward,
lest we grow hard.

THOMAS ASHE

'But you can't do it, you know,' friends said, to whom I applied for assistance in the matter of sinking myself down into the East End of London. 'You had better see the police for a guide,' they added, on second thought, painfully endeavouring to adjust themselves to the psychological processes of a madman who had come to them with better credentials than brains.

'But I don't want to see the police,' I protested. 'What I wish to do is to go down into the East End and see things for myself. I wish to know how those people are living there, and why they are living there, and what they are living for. In short, I am going to live there myself.'

'You don't want to *live* down there!' everybody said, with disapprobation writ large upon their faces. 'Why, it is said there are places where a man's life isn't worth tu'pence.'

'The very places I wish to see,' I broke in.

'But you can't, you know,' was the unfailing rejoinder.

'Which is not what I came to see you about,' I answered brusquely, somewhat nettled by their incomprehension. 'I am a stranger here, and I want you to tell me what you know of the East End, in order that I may have something to start on.'

'But we know nothing of the East End. It is over there, somewhere.' And they waved their hands vaguely in the direction where the sun on rare occasions may be seen to rise.

'Then I shall go to Cook's,' I announced.

'Oh yes,' they said, with relief. 'Cook's will be sure to know.'

But O Cook, O Thomas Cook & Son, path-finders and trail-clearers, living sign-posts to all the world, and bestowers of first aid to bewildered travellers—unhesitatingly and instantly, with ease and celerity, could you send me to Darkest Africa or

Innermost Thibet, but to the East End of London, barely a stone's throw distant from Ludgate Circus, you know not the way!

'You can't do it, you know,' said the human emporium of routes and fares at Cook's Cheapside branch. 'It is so—hem—so unusual.'

'Consult the police,' he concluded authoritatively, when I had persisted. 'We are not accustomed to taking travellers to the East End; we receive no call to take them there, and we know nothing whatsoever about the place at all.'

'Never mind that,' I interposed, to save myself from being swept out of the office by his flood of negations. 'Here's something you can do for me. I wish you to understand in advance what I intend doing, so that in case of trouble you may be able to identify me.'

'Ah, I see! should you be murdered, we would be in position to identify the corpse.'

He said it so cheerfully and cold-bloodedly that on the instant I saw my stark and mutilated cadaver stretched upon a slab where cool waters trickle ceaselessly, and him I saw bending over and sadly and patiently identifying it as the body of the insane American who *would* see the East End.

'No, no,' I answered; 'merely to identify me in case I get into a scrape with the 'bobbies.' This last I said with a thrill; truly, I was gripping hold of the vernacular.

'That,' he said, 'is a matter for the consideration of the Chief Office.'

'It is so unprecedented, you know,' he added apologetically.

The man at the Chief Office hemmed and hawed. 'We make it a rule,' he explained, 'to give no information concerning our clients.'

'But in this case,' I urged, 'it is the client who requests you to give the information concerning himself.'

Again he hemmed and hawed.

'Of course,' I hastily anticipated, 'I know it is unprecedented, but—'

'As I was about to remark,' he went on steadily, 'it is unprecedented, and I don't think we can do anything for you.'

However, I departed with the address of a detective who lived in the East End, and took my way to the American consul-general. And here, at last, I found a man with whom I could 'do business.' There was no hemming and hawing, no lifted brows, open incredulity, or blank amazement. In one minute I explained myself and my project, which he accepted as a matter of course. In the second minute he asked my age, height, and weight, and looked me over. And in the third minute, as we shook hands at parting, he said: 'All right, Jack. I'll remember you and keep track.'

I breathed a sigh of relief. Having burnt my ships behind me, I was now free to plunge into that human wilderness of which nobody seemed to know anything. But at once I encountered a new difficulty in the shape of my cabby, a grey-whiskered and eminently decorous personage who had imperturbably driven me for several hours about the 'City.'

'Drive me down to the East End,' I ordered, taking my seat.

'Where, sir?' he demanded with frank surprise.

'To the East End, anywhere. Go on.'

The hansom pursued an aimless way for several minutes, then came to a puzzled stop. The aperture above my head was uncovered, and the cabman peered down perplexedly at me.

'I say,' he said, 'wot plyce yer wanter go?'

'East End,' I repeated. 'Nowhere in particular. Just drive me around anywhere.'

'But wot's the haddress, sir?'

'See here!' I thundered. 'Drive me down to the East End, and at once!'

It was evident that he did not understand, but he withdrew his head, and grumblingly started his horse.

Nowhere in the streets of London may one escape the sight of abject poverty, while five minutes' walk from almost any point will bring one to a slum; but the region my hansom was now penetrating was one unending slum. The streets were filled with a new and different race of people, short of stature, and of wretched or beer-sodden appearance. We rolled along through miles of bricks and squalor, and from each cross street and alley flashed long vistas of bricks and misery. Here and there lurched a drunken man or woman, and the air was obscene with sounds of jangling and squabbling. At a market, tottery old men and women were searching in the garbage thrown in the mud for rotten potatoes, beans, and vegetables, while little children clustered like flies around a festering mass of fruit, thrusting their arms to the shoulders into the liquid corruption, and drawing forth morsels but partially decayed, which they devoured on the spot.

Not a hansom did I meet with in all my drive, while mine was like an apparition from another and better world, the way the children ran after it and alongside. And as far as I could see were the solid walls of brick, the slimy pavements, and the screaming streets; and for the first time in my life the fear of the crowd smote me. It was like the fear of the sea; and the miserable multitudes, street upon street, seemed so many waves of a vast and malodorous sea, lapping about me and threatening to well up and over me.

'Stepney, sir; Stepney Station,' the cabby called down.

I looked about. It was really a railroad station, and he had driven desperately to it as the one familiar spot he had ever heard of in all that wilderness.

'Well,' I said.

He spluttered unintelligibly, shook his head, and looked very miserable. 'I'm a strynger 'ere,' he managed to articulate. 'An' if yer don't want Stepney Station, I'm blessed if I know wotcher do want.'

'I'll tell you what I want,' I said. 'You drive along and keep your eye out for a shop where old clothes are sold. Now, when you see such a shop, drive right on till you turn the corner, then stop and let me out.'

I could see that he was growing dubious of his fare, but not long afterwards he pulled up to the curb and informed me that an old-clothes shop was to be found a bit of the way back.

'Won'tcher py me?' he pleaded. 'There's seven an' six owin' me.'

'Yes,' I laughed, 'and it would be the last I'd see of you.'

'Lord lumme, but it'll be the last I see of you if yer don't py me,' he retorted.

But a crowd of ragged onlookers had already gathered around the cab, and I laughed again and walked back to the old-clothes shop.

Here the chief difficulty was in making the shopman understand that I really and truly wanted old clothes. But after fruitless attempts to press upon me new and impossible coats and trousers, he began to bring to light heaps of old ones, looking mysterious the while and hinting darkly. This he did with the palpable intention of letting me know that he had 'piped my lay,' in order to bulldose me, through fear of exposure, into paying heavily for my purchases. A man in trouble, or a high-class criminal from across the water, was what he took my measure for—in either case, a person anxious to avoid the police.

But I disputed with him over the outrageous difference between prices and values, till I quite disabused him of the notion, and he settled down to drive a hard bargain with a hard customer. In the end I selected a pair of stout though well-worn trousers, a frayed jacket with one remaining button, a pair of brogans which had plainly seen service where coal was shovelled, a thin leather belt, and a very dirty cloth cap. My underclothing and socks, however, were new and warm, but of the sort that any American waif, down in his luck, could acquire in the ordinary course of events.

'I must sy yer a sharp 'un,' he said, with counterfeit admiration, as I handed over the ten shillings finally agreed upon for the outfit. 'Blimey, if you ain't ben up an' down Petticut Lane afore now. Yer trouseys is wuth five bob to hany man, an' a docker 'ud give two an' six for the shoes, to sy nothin' of the coat an' cap an' new stoker's singlet an' hother things.'

'How much will you give me for them?' I demanded suddenly. 'I paid you ten bob for the lot, and I'll sell them back to you, right now, for eight! Come, it's a go!'

But he grinned and shook his head, and though I had made a good bargain, I was unpleasantly aware that he had made a better one.

I found the cabby and a policeman with their heads together, but the latter, after looking me over sharply, and particularly scrutinizing the bundle under my arm, turned away and left the cabby to wax mutinous by himself. And not a step would he budge till I paid him the seven shillings and sixpence owing him. Whereupon he was willing to drive me to the ends of the earth, apologising profusely for his insistence, and explaining that one ran across queer customers in London Town.

But he drove me only to Highbury Vale, in North London, where my luggage was waiting for me. Here, next day, I took off my shoes (not without regret for their lightness and comfort), and my soft, grey travelling suit, and, in fact, all my clothing; and proceeded to array myself in the clothes of the other and unimaginable men, who must have been indeed unfortunate to have had to part with such rags for the pitiable sums obtainable from a dealer.

Inside my stoker's singlet, in the armpit, I sewed a gold sovereign (an emergency sum certainly of modest proportions); and inside my stoker's singlet I put myself. And then I sat down and moralised upon the fair years and fat, which had made my skin soft and brought the nerves close to the surface; for the singlet was rough and raspy as a hair shirt, and I am confident that the most rigorous of ascetics suffer no more than I did in the ensuing twenty-four hours.

The remainder of my costume was fairly easy to put on, though the brogans, or brogues, were quite a problem. As stiff and hard as if made of wood, it was only after a prolonged pounding of the uppers with my fists that I was able to get my feet into them at all. Then, with a few shillings, a knife, a handkerchief, and some brown papers and flake tobacco stowed away in my pockets, I thumped down the stairs and said good-bye to my foreboding friends. As I paused out of the door, the 'help,' a comely middle-aged woman, could not conquer a grin that twisted her lips and separated them till the throat, out of involuntary sympathy, made the uncouth animal noises we are wont to designate as 'laughter.'

No sooner was I out on the streets than I was impressed by the difference in status effected by my clothes. All servility vanished from the demeanour of the common people with whom I came in contact. Presto! in the twinkling of an eye, so to say, I had become one of them. My frayed and out-at-elbows jacket was the badge and advertisement of my class, which was their class. It made me of like kind, and in place of the fawning and too respectful attention I had hitherto received, I now shared with them a comradeship. The man in corduroy and dirty neckerchief no longer addressed me as 'sir' or 'governor.' It was 'mate' now—and a fine and hearty word, with a tingle to it, and a warmth and gladness, which the other term does not possess. Governor! It smacks of mastery, and power, and high authority—the tribute of the man who is under to the man on top, delivered in the hope that he will let up a bit and ease his weight, which is another way of saying that it is an appeal for alms.

This brings me to a delight I experienced in my rags and tatters which is denied the average American abroad. The European traveller from the States, who is not a Croesus, speedily finds himself reduced to a chronic state of self-conscious sordidness by the hordes of cringing robbers who clutter his steps from dawn till dark, and deplete his pocket-book in a way that puts compound interest to the blush.

In my rags and tatters I escaped the pestilence of tipping, and encountered men on a basis of equality. Nay, before the day was out I turned the tables, and said, most gratefully, 'Thank you, sir,' to a gentleman whose horse I held, and who dropped a penny into my eager palm.

Other changes I discovered were wrought in my condition by my new garb. In crossing crowded thoroughfares I found I had to be, if anything, more lively in avoiding vehicles, and it was strikingly impressed upon me that my life had cheapened in direct ratio with my clothes. When before I inquired the way of a policeman, I was usually asked, 'Bus or 'ansom, sir?' But now the query became, 'Walk or ride?' Also, at the railway stations, a third-class ticket was now shoved out to me as a matter of course.

But there was compensation for it all. For the first time I met the English lower classes face to face, and knew them for what they were. When loungers and workmen, at street corners and in public-houses, talked with me, they talked as one man to another, and they talked as natural men should talk, without the least idea of getting anything out of me for what they talked or the way they talked.

And when at last I made into the East End, I was gratified to find that the fear of the crowd no longer haunted me. I had become a part of it. The vast and malodorous sea had welled up and over me, or I had slipped gently into it, and there was nothing fearsome about it—with the one exception of the stoker's singlet.

CHAPTER II
JOHNNY UPRIGHT

The people live in squalid dens, where there can be no health and no hope, but dogged discontent at their own lot, and futile discontent at the wealth which they see possessed by others.

THOROLD ROGERS

I shall not give you the address of Johnny Upright. Let it suffice that he lives in the most respectable street in the East End—a street that would be considered very mean in America, but a veritable oasis in the desert of East London. It is surrounded on every side by close-packed squalor and streets jammed by a young and vile and dirty generation; but its own pavements are comparatively bare of the children who have no other place to play, while it has an air of desertion, so few are the people that come and go.

Each house in this street, as in all the streets, is shoulder to shoulder with its neighbours. To each house there is but one entrance, the front door; and each house is about eighteen feet wide, with a bit of a brick-walled yard behind, where, when it is not raining, one may look at a slate-coloured sky. But it must be understood that this is East End opulence we are now considering. Some of the people in this street are even so well-to-do as to keep a 'slavey.' Johnny Upright keeps one, as I well know, she being my first acquaintance in this particular portion of the world.

To Johnny Upright's house I came, and to the door came the 'slavey.' Now, mark you, her position in life was pitiable and contemptible, but it was with pity and contempt that she looked at me. She evinced a plain desire that our conversation should be short. It was Sunday, and Johnny Upright was not at home, and that was all there was to it. But I lingered, discussing whether or not it was all there was to it, till Mrs. Johnny Upright was attracted to the door, where she scolded the girl for not having closed it before turning her attention to me.

No, Mr. Johnny Upright was not at home, and further, he saw nobody on Sunday. It is too bad, said I. Was I looking for work? No, quite the contrary; in fact, I had come to see Johnny Upright on business which might be profitable to him.

A change came over the face of things at once. The gentleman in question was at church, but would be home in an hour or thereabouts, when no doubt he could be seen.

Would I kindly step in?—no, the lady did not ask me, though I fished for an invitation by stating that I would go down to the corner and wait in a public-house. And down to the corner I went, but, it being church time, the 'pub' was closed. A miserable drizzle was falling, and, in lieu of better, I took a seat on a neighbourly doorstep and waited.

And here to the doorstep came the 'slavey,' very frowzy and very perplexed, to tell me that the missus would let me come back and wait in the kitchen.

'So many people come 'ere lookin' for work,' Mrs. Johnny Upright apologetically explained. 'So I 'ope you won't feel bad the way I spoke.'

'Not at all, not at all,' I replied in my grandest manner, for the nonce investing my rags with dignity. 'I quite understand, I assure you. I suppose people looking for work almost worry you to death?'

'That they do,' she answered, with an eloquent and expressive glance; and thereupon ushered me into, not the kitchen, but the dining room—a favour, I took it, in recompense for my grand manner.

This dining-room, on the same floor as the kitchen, was about four feet below the level of the ground, and so dark (it was midday) that I had to wait a space for my eyes to adjust themselves to the gloom. Dirty light filtered in through a window, the top of which was on a level with a sidewalk, and in this light I found that I was able to read newspaper print.

And here, while waiting the coming of Johnny Upright, let me explain my errand. While living, eating, and sleeping with the people of the East End, it was my intention to have a port of refuge, not too far distant, into which could run now and again to assure myself that good clothes and cleanliness still existed. Also in such port I could receive my mail, work up my notes, and sally forth occasionally in changed garb to civilisation.

But this involved a dilemma. A lodging where my property would be safe implied a landlady apt to be suspicious of a gentleman leading a double life; while a landlady who would not bother her head over the double life of her lodgers would imply lodgings where property was unsafe. To avoid the dilemma was what had brought me to Johnny Upright. A detective of thirty-odd years' continuous service in the East End, known far and wide by a name given him by a convicted felon in the dock, he was just the man to find me an honest landlady, and make her rest easy concerning the strange comings and goings of which I might be guilty.

His two daughters beat him home from church—and pretty girls they were in their Sunday dresses; withal it was the certain weak and delicate prettiness which characterises the Cockney lasses, a prettiness which is no more than a promise with no grip on time, and doomed to fade quickly away like the colour from a sunset sky.

They looked me over with frank curiosity, as though I were some sort of a strange animal, and then ignored me utterly for the rest of my wait. Then Johnny Upright himself arrived, and I was summoned upstairs to confer with him.

'Speak loud,' he interrupted my opening words. 'I've got a bad cold, and I can't hear well.'

Shades of Old Sleuth and Sherlock Holmes! I wondered as to where the assistant was located whose duty it was to take down whatever information I might loudly vouchsafe. And to this day, much as I have seen of Johnny Upright and much as I have puzzled over the incident, I have never been quite able to make up my mind as to whether or not he had a cold, or had an assistant planted in the other room. But of one thing I am sure: though I gave Johnny Upright the facts concerning myself and project, he withheld judgment till next day, when I dodged into his street conventionally garbed and in a hansom. Then his greeting was cordial enough, and I went down into the dining-room to join the family at tea.

'We are humble here,' he said, 'not given to the flesh, and you must take us for what we are, in our humble way.'

The girls were flushed and embarrassed at greeting me, while he did not make it any the easier for them.

'Ha! ha!' he roared heartily, slapping the table with his open hand till the dishes rang. 'The girls thought yesterday you had come to ask for a piece of bread! Ha! ha! ho! ho! ho!'

This they indignantly denied, with snapping eyes and guilty red cheeks, as though it were an essential of true refinement to be able to discern under his rags a man who had no need to go ragged.

And then, while I ate bread and marmalade, proceeded a play at cross purposes, the daughters deeming it an insult to me that I should have been mistaken for a beggar, and the father considering it as the highest compliment to my cleverness to succeed in being so mistaken. All of which I enjoyed, and the bread, the marmalade, and the tea, till the time came for Johnny Upright to find me a lodging, which he did, not half-a-dozen doors away, in his own respectable and opulent street, in a house as like to his own as a pea to its mate.

CHAPTER III
MY LODGING AND SOME OTHERS

The poor, the poor, the poor, they stand,
Wedged by the pressing of Trade's hand,
Against an inward-opening door
That pressure tightens evermore;
They sigh a monstrous, foul-air sigh
For the outside leagues of liberty,
Where art, sweet lark, translates the sky
Into a heavenly melody.

SIDNEY LANIER

From an East London standpoint, the room I rented for six shillings, or a dollar and a half, per week, was a most comfortable affair. From the American standpoint, on the other hand, it was rudely furnished, uncomfortable, and small. By the time I had added an ordinary typewriter table to its scanty furnishing, I was hard put to turn around; at the best, I managed to navigate it by a sort of vermicular progression requiring great dexterity and presence of mind.

Having settled myself, or my property rather, I put on my knockabout clothes and went out for a walk. Lodgings being fresh in my mind, I began to look them up, bearing in mind the hypothesis that I was a poor young man with a wife and large family.

My first discovery was that empty houses were few and far between—so far between, in fact, that though I walked miles in irregular circles over a large area, I still remained between. Not one empty house could I find—a conclusive proof that the district was 'saturated.'

It being plain that as a poor young man with a family I could rent no houses at all in this most undesirable region, I next looked for rooms, unfurnished rooms, in which I could store my wife and babies and chattels. There were not many, but I found them, usually in the singular, for one appears to be considered sufficient for a poor man's family in which to cook and eat and sleep. When I asked for two rooms, the sublettees looked at me very much in the manner, I imagine, that a certain personage looked at Oliver Twist when he asked for more.

Not only was one room deemed sufficient for a poor man and his family, but I learned that many families, occupying single rooms, had so much space to spare as to be able to take in a lodger or two. When such rooms can be rented for from three to six shillings per week, it is a fair conclusion that a lodger with references should obtain floor space for, say, from eightpence to a shilling. He may even be able to board with the sublettees for a few shillings more. This, however, I failed to inquire into—a reprehensible error on my part, considering that I was working on the basis of a hypothetical family.

Not only did the houses I investigated have no bath-tubs, but I learned that there were no bath-tubs in all the thousands of houses I had seen. Under the circumstances, with my wife and babies and a couple of lodgers suffering from the too great spaciousness of one room, taking a bath in a tin wash-basin would be an unfeasible undertaking. But, it seems, the compensation comes in with the saving of soap, so all's well, and God's still in heaven.

However, I rented no rooms, but returned to my own Johnny Upright's street. What with my wife, and babies, and lodgers, and the various cubby-holes into which I had fitted them, my mind's eye had become narrow-angled, and I could not quite take in all of my own room at once. The immensity of it was awe-inspiring. Could this be the room I had rented for six shillings a week? Impossible! But my landlady, knocking at the door to learn if I were comfortable, dispelled my doubts.

'Oh yes, sir,' she said, in reply to a question. 'This street is the very last. All the other streets were like this eight or ten years ago, and all the people were very respectable. But the others have driven our kind out. Those in this street are the only ones left. It's shocking, sir!'

And then she explained the process of saturation, by which the rental value of a neighbourhood went up, while its tone went down.

'You see, sir, our kind are not used to crowding in the way the others do. We need more room. The others, the foreigners and lower-class people, can get five and six families into this house, where we only get one. So they can pay more rent for the house than we can afford. It *is* shocking, sir; and just to think, only a few years ago all this neighbourhood was just as nice as it could be.'

I looked at her. Here was a woman, of the finest grade of the English working-class, with numerous evidences of refinement, being slowly engulfed by that noisome and rotten tide of humanity which the powers that be are pouring eastward out of London Town. Bank, factory, hotel, and office building must go up, and the city poor folk are a nomadic breed; so they migrate eastward, wave upon wave, saturating and degrading neighbourhood by neighbourhood, driving the better class of workers before them to pioneer, on the rim of the city, or dragging them down, if not in the first generation, surely in the second and third.

It is only a question of months when Johnny Upright's street must go. He realises it himself.

'In a couple of years,' he says, 'my lease expires. My landlord is one of our kind. He has not put up the rent on any of his houses here, and this has enabled us to stay. But any day he may sell, or any day he may die, which is the same thing so far as we are concerned. The house is bought by a money breeder, who builds a sweat shop on the patch of ground at the rear where my grapevine is, adds to the house, and rents it a room to a family. There you are, and Johnny Upright's gone!'

And truly I saw Johnny Upright, and his good wife and fair daughters, and frowzy slavey, like so many ghosts flitting eastward through the gloom, the monster city roaring at their heels.

But Johnny Upright is not alone in his flitting. Far, far out, on the fringe of the city, live the small business men, little managers, and successful clerks. They dwell in cottages and semi-detached villas, with bits of flower garden, and elbow room, and breathing space. They inflate themselves with pride, and throw out their chests when they contemplate the Abyss from which they have escaped, and they thank God that they are not as other men. And lo! down upon them comes Johnny Upright and the monster city at his heels. Tenements spring up like magic, gardens are built upon, villas are divided and subdivided into many dwellings, and the black night of London settles down in a greasy pall.

CHAPTER IV
A MAN AND THE ABYSS

After a momentary silence spake
Some vessel of a more ungainly make;
They sneer at me for leaning all awry:
What! did the hand then of the Potter shake?

OMAR KHAYYAM

'I say, can you let a lodging?'

These words I discharged carelessly over my shoulder at a stout and elderly woman, of whose fare I was partaking in a greasy coffee-house down near the Pool and not very far from Limehouse.

'Oh yus,' she answered shortly, my appearance possibly not approximating the standard of affluence required by her house.

I said no more, consuming my rasher of bacon and pint of sickly tea in silence. Nor did she take further interest in me till I came to pay my reckoning (fourpence), when I pulled all of ten shillings out of my pocket. The expected result was produced.

'Yus, sir,' she at once volunteered; 'I 'ave nice lodgin's you'd likely tyke a fancy to. Back from a voyage, sir?'

'How much for a room?' I inquired, ignoring her curiosity.

She looked me up and down with frank surprise. 'I don't let rooms, not to my reg'lar lodgers, much less casuals.'

'Then I'll have to look along a bit,' I said, with marked disappointment.

But the sight of my ten shillings had made her keen. 'I can let you have a nice bed in with two hother men,' she urged. 'Good, respectable men, an' steady.'

'But I don't want to sleep with two other men,' I objected.

'You don't 'ave to. There's three beds in the room, an' hit's not a very small room.'

'How much?' I demanded.

'Arf a crown a week, two an' six, to a regular lodger. You'll fancy the men, I'm sure. One works in the ware'ouse, an' 'e's been with me two years now. An' the hother's bin with me six—six years, sir, an' two months comin' nex' Saturday. 'E's a scene-shifter,' she went on. 'A steady, respectable man, never missin' a night's work in the time 'e's bin with me. An' 'e likes the 'ouse; 'e says as it's the best 'e can do in the w'y of lodgin's. I board 'im, an' the hother lodgers too.'

'I suppose he's saving money right along,' I insinuated innocently.

'Bless you, no! Nor can 'e do as well helsewhere with 'is money.'

And I thought of my own spacious West, with room under its sky and unlimited air for a thousand Londons; and here was this man, a steady and reliable man, never missing a night's work, frugal and honest, lodging in one room with two other men, paying two dollars and a half per month for it, and out of his experience adjudging it to be the best he could do! And here was I, on the strength of the ten shillings in my pocket, able to enter in with my rags and take up my bed with him. The human soul is a lonely thing, but it must be very lonely sometimes when there are three beds to a room, and casuals with ten shillings are admitted.

'How long have you been here?' I asked.

'Thirteen years, sir; an' don't you think you'll fancy the lodgin'?'

The while she talked she was shuffling ponderously about the small kitchen in which she cooked the food for her lodgers who were also boarders. When I first entered, she had been hard at work, nor had she let up once throughout the conversation. Undoubtedly she was a busy woman. 'Up at half-past five,' 'to bed the last thing at night,' 'workin' fit ter drop,' thirteen years of it, and for reward, grey hairs, frowzy clothes, stooped shoulders, slatternly figure, unending toil in a foul and noisome coffee-house that faced on an alley ten feet between the walls, and a waterside environment that was ugly and sickening, to say the least.

'You'll be hin hagain to 'ave a look?' she questioned wistfully, as I went out of the door.

And as I turned and looked at her, I realized to the full the deeper truth underlying that very wise old maxim: 'Virtue is its own reward.'

I went back to her. 'Have you ever taken a vacation?' I asked.

'Vycytion!'

'A trip to the country for a couple of days, fresh air, a day off, you know, a rest.'

'Lor' lumme!' she laughed, for the first time stopping from her work. 'A vycytion, eh? for the likes o' me? Just fancy, now!—Mind yer feet!'—this last sharply, and to me, as I stumbled over the rotten threshold.

Down near the West India Dock I came upon a young fellow staring disconsolately at the muddy water. A fireman's cap was pulled down across his eyes, and the fit and sag of his clothes whispered unmistakably of the sea.

'Hello, mate,' I greeted him, sparring for a beginning. 'Can you tell me the way to Wapping?'

'Worked yer way over on a cattle boat?' he countered, fixing my nationality on the instant.

And thereupon we entered upon a talk that extended itself to a public-house and a couple of pints of 'arf an' arf.' This led to closer intimacy, so that when I brought to light all of a shilling's worth of coppers (ostensibly my all), and put aside sixpence for a bed, and sixpence for more arf an' arf, he generously proposed that we drink up the whole shilling.

'My mate, 'e cut up rough las' night,' he explained. 'An' the bobbies got 'm, so you can bunk in wi' me. Wotcher say?'

I said yes, and by the time we had soaked ourselves in a whole shilling's worth of beer, and slept the night on a miserable bed in a miserable den, I knew him pretty fairly for what he was. And that in one respect he was representative of a large body of the lower-class London workman, my later experience substantiates.

He was London-born, his father a fireman and a drinker before him. As a child, his home was the streets and the docks. He had never learned to read, and had never felt the need for it—a vain and useless accomplishment, he held, at least for a man of his station in life.

He had had a mother and numerous squalling brothers and sisters, all crammed into a couple of rooms and living on poorer and less regular food than he could ordinarily rustle for himself. In fact, he never went home except at periods when he was unfortunate in procuring his own food. Petty pilfering and begging along the streets and docks, a trip or two to sea as mess-boy, a few trips more as coal-trimmer, and then a full-fledged fireman, he had reached the top of his life.

And in the course of this he had also hammered out a philosophy of life, an ugly and repulsive philosophy, but withal a very logical and sensible one from his point of view. When I asked him what he lived for, he immediately answered, 'Booze.' A voyage to sea (for a man must live and get the wherewithal), and then the paying off and the big drunk at the end. After that, haphazard little drunks, sponged in the 'pubs' from mates with a few coppers left, like myself, and when sponging was played out another trip to sea and a repetition of the beastly cycle.

'But women,' I suggested, when he had finished proclaiming booze the sole end of existence.

'Wimmen!' He thumped his pot upon the bar and orated eloquently. 'Wimmen is a thing my edication 'as learnt me t' let alone. It don't pay, matey; it don't pay. Wot's a man like me want o' wimmen, eh? jest you tell me. There was my mar, she was enough, a-bangin' the kids about an' makin' the ole man mis'rable when 'e come 'ome, w'ich was seldom, I grant. An' fer w'y? Becos o' mar! She didn't make 'is 'ome 'appy, that was w'y. Then, there's the other wimmen, 'ow do they treat a pore stoker with a few shillin's in 'is trouseys? A good drunk is wot 'e's got in 'is pockits, a good long drunk, an' the wimmen skin 'im out of his money so quick 'e ain't 'ad 'ardly a glass. I know. I've 'ad my fling, an' I know wot's wot. An' I tell you, where's wimmen is trouble— screechin' an' carryin' on, fightin', cuttin', bobbies, magistrates, an' a month's 'ard labour back of it all, an' no pay-day when you come out.'

'But a wife and children,' I insisted. 'A home of your own, and all that. Think of it, back from a voyage, little children climbing on your knee, and the wife happy and smiling, and a kiss for you when she lays the table, and a kiss all round from the babies when they go to bed, and the kettle singing and the long talk afterwards of where you've been and what you've seen, and of her and all the little happenings at home while you've been away, and—'

'Garn!' he cried, with a playful shove of his fist on my shoulder. 'Wot's yer game, eh? A missus kissin' an' kids clim'in', an' kettle singin', all on four poun' ten a month w'en you 'ave a ship, an' four nothin' w'en you 'aven't. I'll tell you wot I'd get on four poun' ten—a missus rowin', kids squallin', no coal t' make the kettle sing, an' the kettle up the spout, that's wot I'd get. Enough t' make a bloke bloomin' well glad to be back t' sea. A missus! Wot for? T' make you mis'rable? Kids? Jest take my counsel, matey, an' don't 'ave 'em. Look at me! I can 'ave my beer w'en I like, an' no blessed missus an' kids a-crying for bread. I'm 'appy, I am, with my beer an' mates like you, an' a good ship comin', an' another trip to sea. So I say, let's 'ave another pint. Arf an' arf's good enough for me.'

Without going further with the speech of this young fellow of two-and-twenty, I think I have sufficiently indicated his philosophy of life and the underlying economic reason for it. Home life he had never known. The word 'home' aroused nothing but unpleasant associations. In the low wages of his father, and of other men in the same walk in life, he found sufficient reason for branding wife and children as encumbrances and causes of masculine misery. An unconscious hedonist, utterly unmoral and materialistic, he sought the greatest possible happiness for himself, and found it in drink.

A young sot; a premature wreck; physical inability to do a stoker's work; the gutter or the workhouse; and the end—he saw it all as clearly as I, but it held no terrors for him. From the moment of his birth, all the forces of his environment had tended to harden him, and he viewed his wretched, inevitable future with a callousness and unconcern I could not shake.

And yet he was not a bad man. He was not inherently vicious and brutal. He had normal mentality, and a more than average physique. His eyes were blue and round, shaded by long lashes, and wide apart. And there was a laugh in them, and a fund of humour behind. The brow and general features were good, the mouth and lips sweet, though already developing a harsh twist. The chin was weak, but not too weak; I have seen men sitting in the high places with weaker.

His head was shapely, and so gracefully was it poised upon a perfect neck that I was not surprised by his body that night when he stripped for bed. I have seen many men strip, in gymnasium and training quarters, men of good blood and upbringing, but I have never seen one who stripped to better advantage than this young sot of two-and-twenty, this young god doomed to rack and ruin in four or five short years, and to pass hence without posterity to receive the splendid heritage it was his to bequeath.

It seemed sacrilege to waste such life, and yet I was forced to confess that he was right in not marrying on four pounds ten in London Town. Just as the scene-shifter was happier in making both ends meet in a room shared with two other men, than he would have been had he packed a feeble family along with a couple of men into a cheaper room, and failed in making both ends meet.

And day by day I became convinced that not only is it unwise, but it is criminal for the people of the Abyss to marry. They are the stones by the builder rejected. There is no place for them, in the social fabric, while all the forces of society drive them downward till they perish. At the bottom of the Abyss they are feeble, besotted, and imbecile. If they reproduce, the life is so cheap that perforce it perishes of itself. The work of the world goes on above them, and they do not care to take part in it, nor are they able. Moreover, the work of the world does not need them. There are plenty, far fitter than they, clinging to the steep slope above, and struggling frantically to slide no more.

In short, the London Abyss is a vast shambles. Year by year, and decade after decade, rural England pours in a flood of vigorous strong life, that not only does not renew itself, but perishes by the third generation. Competent authorities aver that the London workman whose parents and grand-parents were born in London is so remarkable a specimen that he is rarely found.

Mr. A. C. Pigou has said that the aged poor, and the residuum which compose the 'submerged tenth,' constitute 71 per cent, of the population of London. Which is to say that last year, and yesterday, and to-day, at this very moment, 450,000 of these creatures are dying miserably at the bottom of the social pit called 'London.' As to how they die, I shall take an instance from this morning's paper.

SELF-NEGLECT

Yesterday Dr. Wynn Westcott held an inquest at Shoreditch, respecting the death of Elizabeth Crews, aged 77 years, of 32 East Street, Holborn, who died on Wednesday last. Alice Mathieson stated that she was landlady of the house where deceased lived. Witness last saw her alive on the previous Monday. She lived quite alone. Mr. Francis Birch, relieving officer for the Holborn district, stated that deceased had occupied the room in question for thirty-five years. When witness was called, on the 1st, he found the old woman in a terrible state, and the ambulance and coachman had to be disinfected after the removal. Dr. Chase Fennell said death was due to blood-poisoning from bed-sores, due to self-neglect and filthy surroundings, and the jury returned a verdict to that effect.

The most startling thing about this little incident of a woman's death is the smug complacency with which the officials looked upon it and rendered judgment. That an old woman of seventy-seven years of age should die of SELF-NEGLECT is the most optimistic way possible of looking at it. It was the old dead woman's fault that she died, and having located the responsibility, society goes contentedly on about its own affairs.

Of the 'submerged tenth' Mr. Pigou has said: 'Either through lack of bodily strength, or of intelligence, or of fibre, or of all three, they are inefficient or unwilling workers, and consequently unable to support themselves . . . They are often so degraded in intellect as to be incapable of distinguishing their right from their left hand, or of recognising the numbers of their own houses; their bodies are feeble and without stamina, their affections are warped, and they scarcely know what family life means.'

Four hundred and fifty thousand is a whole lot of people. The young fireman was only one, and it took him some time to say his little say. I should not like to hear them all talk at once. I wonder if God hears them?

CHAPTER V

THOSE ON THE EDGE

I assure you I found nothing worse, nothing more degrading, nothing so hopeless, nothing nearly so intolerably dull and miserable as the life I left behind me in the East End of London.

HUXLEY

My first impression of East London was naturally a general one. Later the details began to appear, and here and there in the chaos of misery I found little spots where a fair measure of happiness reigned—sometimes whole rows of houses in little out-of-the-way streets, where artisans dwell and where a rude sort of family life obtains. In the evenings the men can be seen at the doors, pipes in their mouths and children on their knees, wives gossiping, and laughter and fun going on. The content of these people is manifestly great, for, relative to the wretchedness that encompasses them, they are well off.

But at the best, it is a dull, animal happiness, the content of the full belly. The dominant note of their lives is materialistic. They are stupid and heavy, without imagination. The Abyss seems to exude a stupefying atmosphere of torpor, which wraps about them and deadens them. Religion passes them by. The Unseen holds for them neither terror nor delight. They are unaware of the Unseen; and the full belly and the evening pipe, with their regular 'arf an' arf,' is all they demand, or dream of demanding, from existence.

This would not be so bad if it were all; but it is not all. The satisfied torpor in which they are sunk is the deadly inertia that precedes dissolution. There is no progress, and with them not to progress is to fall back and into the Abyss. In their own lives they may only start to fall, leaving the fall to be completed by their children and their children's children. Man always gets less than he demands from life; and so little do they demand, that the less than little they get cannot save them.

At the best, city life is an unnatural life for the human; but the city life of London is so utterly unnatural that the average workman or workwoman cannot stand it. Mind and body are sapped by the undermining influences ceaselessly at work. Moral and physical stamina are broken, and the good workman, fresh from the soil, becomes in the first city generation a poor workman; and by the second city generation, devoid of push and go and initiative, and actually unable physically to perform the labour his father did, he is well on the way to the shambles at the bottom of the Abyss.

If nothing else, the air he breathes, and from which he never escapes, is sufficient to weaken him mentally and physically, so that he becomes unable to compete with the fresh virile life from the country hastening on to London Town to destroy and be destroyed.

Leaving out the disease germs that fill the air of the East End, consider but the one item of smoke. Sir William Thiselton-Dyer, curator of Kew Gardens, has been studying smoke deposits on vegetation, and, according to his calculations, no less than six tons of solid matter, consisting of soot and tarry hydrocarbons, are deposited every week on every quarter of a square mile in and about London. This is equivalent to twenty-four tons per week to the square mile, or 1248 tons per year to the square

574

mile. From the cornice below the dome of St. Paul's Cathedral was recently taken a solid deposit of crystallised sulphate of lime. This deposit had been formed by the action of the sulphuric acid in the atmosphere upon the carbonate of lime in the stone. And this sulphuric acid in the atmosphere is constantly being breathed by the London workmen through all the days and nights of their lives.

It is incontrovertible that the children grow up into rotten adults, without virility or stamina, a weak-kneed, narrow-chested, listless breed, that crumples up and goes down in the brute struggle for life with the invading hordes from the country. The railway men, carriers, omnibus drivers, corn and timber porters, and all those who require physical stamina, are largely drawn from the country; while in the Metropolitan Police there are, roughly, 12,000 country-born as against 3000 London-born.

So one is forced to conclude that the Abyss is literally a huge man-killing machine, and when I pass along the little out-of-the-way streets with the full-bellied artisans at the doors, I am aware of a greater sorrow for them than for the 450,000 lost and hopeless wretches dying at the bottom of the pit. They, at least, are dying, that is the point; while these have yet to go through the slow and preliminary pangs extending through two and even three generations.

And yet the quality of the life is good. All human potentialities are in it. Given proper conditions, it could live through the centuries, and great men, heroes and masters, spring from it and make the world better by having lived.

I talked with a woman who was representative of that type which has been jerked out of its little out-of-the-way streets and has started on the fatal fall to the bottom. Her husband was a fitter and a member of the Engineers' Union. That he was a poor engineer was evidenced by his inability to get regular employment. He did not have the energy and enterprise necessary to obtain or hold a steady position.

The pair had two daughters, and the four of them lived in a couple of holes, called 'rooms' by courtesy, for which they paid seven shillings per week. They possessed no stove, managing their cooking on a single gas-ring in the fireplace. Not being persons of property, they were unable to obtain an unlimited supply of gas; but a clever machine had been installed for their benefit. By dropping a penny in the slot, the gas was forthcoming, and when a penny's worth had forthcome the supply was automatically shut off. 'A penny gawn in no time,' she explained, 'an' the cookin' not arf done!'

Incipient starvation had been their portion for years. Month in and month out, they had arisen from the table able and willing to eat more. And when once on the downward slope, chronic innutrition is an important factor in sapping vitality and hastening the descent.

Yet this woman was a hard worker. From 4.30 in the morning till the last light at night, she said, she had toiled at making cloth dress-skirts, lined up and with two flounces, for seven shillings a dozen. Cloth dress-skirts, mark you, lined up with two flounces, for seven shillings a dozen! This is equal to $1.75 per dozen, or 14.75 cents per skirt.

The husband, in order to obtain employment, had to belong to the union, which collected one shilling and sixpence from him each week. Also, when strikes were afoot and he chanced to be working, he had at times been compelled to pay as high as seventeen shillings into the union's coffers for the relief fund.

One daughter, the elder, had worked as green hand for a dressmaker, for one shilling and sixpence per week—37.5 cents per week, or a fraction over 5 cents per day. However, when the slack season came she was discharged, though she had been taken on at such low pay with the understanding that she was to learn the trade and work up. After that she had been employed in a bicycle store for three years, for which she received five shillings per week, walking two miles to her work, and two back, and being fined for tardiness.

As far as the man and woman were concerned, the game was played. They had lost handhold and foothold, and were falling into the pit. But what of the daughters? Living like swine, enfeebled by chronic innutrition, being sapped mentally, morally, and physically, what chance have they to crawl up and out of the Abyss into which they were born falling?

As I write this, and for an hour past, the air has been made hideous by a free-for-all, rough-and-tumble fight going on in the yard that is back to back with my yard. When the first sounds reached me I took it for the barking and snarling of dogs, and some minutes were required to convince me that human beings, and women at that, could produce such a fearful clamour.

Drunken women fighting! It is not nice to think of; it is far worse to listen to. Something like this it runs—

Incoherent babble, shrieked at the top of the lungs of several women; a lull, in which is heard a child crying and a young girl's voice pleading tearfully; a woman's voice rises, harsh and grating, 'You 'it me! Jest you 'it me!' then, swat! challenge accepted and fight rages afresh.

The back windows of the houses commanding the scene are lined with enthusiastic spectators, and the sound of blows, and of oaths that make one's blood run cold, are borne to my ears. Happily, I cannot see the combatants.

A lull; 'You let that child alone!' child, evidently of few years, screaming in downright terror. 'Awright,' repeated insistently and at top pitch twenty times straight running; 'you'll git this rock on the 'ead!' and then rock evidently on the head from the shriek that goes up.

A lull; apparently one combatant temporarily disabled and being resuscitated; child's voice audible again, but now sunk to a lower note of terror and growing exhaustion.

Voices begin to go up the scale, something like this:-

'Yes?'

'Yes!'

'Yes?'

'Yes!'

'Yes?'

'Yes!'

'Yes?'

'Yes!'

Sufficient affirmation on both sides, conflict again precipitated. One combatant gets overwhelming advantage, and follows it up from the way the other combatant screams bloody murder. Bloody murder gurgles and dies out, undoubtedly throttled by a strangle hold.

Entrance of new voices; a flank attack; strangle hold suddenly broken from the way bloody murder goes up half an octave higher than before; general hullaballoo, everybody fighting.

Lull; new voice, young girl's, 'I'm goin' ter tyke my mother's part;' dialogue, repeated about five times, 'I'll do as I like, blankety, blank, blank!' 'I'd like ter see yer, blankety, blank, blank!' renewed conflict, mothers, daughters, everybody, during which my landlady calls her young daughter in from the back steps, while I wonder what will be the effect of all that she has heard upon her moral fibre.

CHAPTER VI
FRYING-PAN ALLEY AND A GLIMPSE OF INFERNO

The beasts they hunger, and eat, and die,
And so do we, and the world's a sty.
'Swinehood hath no remedy,'
Say many men, and hasten by.

SIDNEY LANIER

Three of us walked down Mile End Road, and one was a hero. He was a slender lad of nineteen, so slight and frail, in fact, that, like Fra Lippo Lippi, a puff of wind might double him up and turn him over. He was a burning young socialist, in the first throes of enthusiasm and ripe for martyrdom. As platform speaker or chairman he had taken an active and dangerous part in the many indoor and outdoor pro-Boer meetings which have vexed the serenity of Merry England these several years back. Little items he had been imparting to me as he walked along; of being mobbed in parks and on tram-cars; of climbing on the platform to lead the forlorn hope, when brother speaker after brother speaker had been dragged down by the angry crowd and cruelly beaten; of a siege in a church, where he and three others had taken sanctuary, and where, amid flying missiles and the crashing of stained glass, they had fought off the mob till rescued by platoons of constables; of pitched and giddy battles on stairways, galleries, and balconies; of smashed windows, collapsed stairways, wrecked lecture halls, and broken heads and bones—and then, with a regretful sigh, he looked at me and said: 'How I envy you big, strong men! I'm such a little mite I can't do much when it comes to fighting.'

And I, walking head and shoulders above my two companions, remembered my own husky West, and the stalwart men it had been my custom, in turn, to envy there. Also, as I looked at the mite of a youth with the heart of a lion, I thought, this is the type that on occasion rears barricades and shows the world that men have not forgotten how to die.

But up spoke my other companion, a man of twenty-eight, who eked out a precarious existence in a sweating den.

'I'm a 'earty man, I am,' he announced. 'Not like the other chaps at my shop, I ain't. They consider me a fine specimen of manhood. W'y, d' ye know, I weigh ten stone!'

I was ashamed to tell him that I weighed one hundred and seventy pounds, or over twelve stone, so I contented myself with taking his measure. Poor, misshapen little man! His skin an unhealthy colour, body gnarled and twisted out of all decency, contracted chest, shoulders bent prodigiously from long hours of toil, and head hanging heavily forward and out of place! A 'earty man,' 'e was!'

'How tall are you?'

'Five foot two,' he answered proudly; 'an' the chaps at the shop . . . '

'Let me see that shop,' I said.

The shop was idle just then, but I still desired to see it. Passing Leman Street, we cut off to the left into Spitalfields, and dived into Frying-pan Alley. A spawn of children cluttered the slimy pavement, for all the world like tadpoles just turned frogs on the bottom of a dry pond. In a narrow doorway, so narrow that perforce we stepped over her, sat a woman with a young babe, nursing at breasts grossly naked and libelling all the sacredness of motherhood. In the black and narrow hall behind her we waded through a mess of young life, and essayed an even narrower and fouler stairway. Up we went, three flights, each landing two feet by three in area, and heaped with filth and refuse.

There were seven rooms in this abomination called a house. In six of the rooms, twenty-odd people, of both sexes and all ages, cooked, ate, slept, and worked. In size the rooms averaged eight feet by eight, or possibly nine. The seventh room we entered. It was the den in which five men 'sweated.' It was seven feet wide by eight long, and the table at which the work was performed took up the major portion of the space. On this table were five lasts, and there was barely room for the men to stand to their work, for the rest of the space was heaped with cardboard, leather, bundles of shoe uppers, and a miscellaneous assortment of materials used in attaching the uppers of shoes to their soles.

In the adjoining room lived a woman and six children. In another vile hole lived a widow, with an only son of sixteen who was dying of consumption. The woman hawked sweetmeats on the street, I was told, and more often failed than not to supply her son with the three quarts of milk he daily required. Further, this son, weak and dying, did not taste meat oftener than once a week; and the kind and quality of this meat cannot possibly be imagined by people who have never watched human swine eat.

'The w'y 'e coughs is somethin' terrible,' volunteered my sweated friend, referring to the dying boy. 'We 'ear 'im 'ere, w'ile we're workin', an' it's terrible, I say, terrible!'

And, what of the coughing and the sweetmeats, I found another menace added to the hostile environment of the children of the slum.

My sweated friend, when work was to be had, toiled with four other men in his eight-by-seven room. In the winter a lamp burned nearly all the day and added its fumes to the over-loaded air, which was breathed, and breathed, and breathed again.

In good times, when there was a rush of work, this man told me that he could earn as high as 'thirty bob a week.'—Thirty shillings! Seven dollars and a half!

'But it's only the best of us can do it,' he qualified. 'An' then we work twelve, thirteen, and fourteen hours a day, just as fast as we can. An' you should see us sweat! Just running from us! If you could see us, it'd dazzle your eyes—tacks flyin' out of mouth like from a machine. Look at my mouth.'

I looked. The teeth were worn down by the constant friction of the metallic brads, while they were coal-black and rotten.

'I clean my teeth,' he added, 'else they'd be worse.'

After he had told me that the workers had to furnish their own tools, brads, 'grindery,' cardboard, rent, light, and what not, it was plain that his thirty bob was a diminishing quantity.

'But how long does the rush season last, in which you receive this high wage of thirty bob?' I asked.

'Four months,' was the answer; and for the rest of the year, he informed me, they average from 'half a quid' to a 'quid' a week, which is equivalent to from two dollars and a half to five dollars. The present week was half gone, and he had earned four bob, or one dollar. And yet I was given to understand that this was one of the better grades of sweating.

I looked out of the window, which should have commanded the back yards of the neighbouring buildings. But there were no back yards, or, rather, they were covered with one-storey hovels, cowsheds, in which people lived. The roofs of these hovels were covered with deposits of filth, in some places a couple of feet deep—the contributions from the back windows of the second and third storeys. I could make out fish and meat bones, garbage, pestilential rags, old boots, broken earthenware, and all the general refuse of a human sty.

'This is the last year of this trade; they're getting machines to do away with us,' said the sweated one mournfully, as we stepped over the woman with the breasts grossly naked and waded anew through the cheap young life.

We next visited the municipal dwellings erected by the London County Council on the site of the slums where lived Arthur Morrison's 'Child of the Jago.' While the buildings housed more people than before, it was much healthier. But the dwellings were inhabited by the better-class workmen and artisans. The slum people had simply drifted on to crowd other slums or to form new slums.

'An' now,' said the sweated one, the 'earty man who worked so fast as to dazzle one's eyes, 'I'll show you one of London's lungs. This is Spitalfields Garden.' And he mouthed the word 'garden' with scorn.

The shadow of Christ's Church falls across Spitalfields Garden, and in the shadow of Christ's Church, at three o'clock in the afternoon, I saw a sight I never wish to see again. There are no flowers in this garden, which is smaller than my own rose garden at home. Grass only grows here, and it is surrounded by a sharp-spiked iron fencing, as are all the parks of London Town, so that homeless men and women may not come in at night and sleep upon it.

As we entered the garden, an old woman, between fifty and sixty, passed us, striding with sturdy intention if somewhat rickety action, with two bulky bundles, covered with sacking, slung fore and aft upon her. She was a woman tramp, a houseless soul, too independent to drag her failing carcass through the workhouse door. Like the snail, she carried her home with her. In the two sacking-covered bundles were her household goods, her wardrobe, linen, and dear feminine possessions.

We went up the narrow gravelled walk. On the benches on either side arrayed a mass of miserable and distorted humanity, the sight of which would have impelled Doré to more diabolical flights of fancy than he ever succeeded in achieving. It was a welter of rags and filth, of all manner of loathsome skin diseases, open sores, bruises, grossness, indecency, leering monstrosities, and bestial faces. A chill, raw wind was blowing, and these creatures huddled there in their rags, sleeping for the most part, or trying to sleep. Here were a dozen women, ranging in age from twenty years to seventy. Next a babe, possibly of nine months, lying asleep, flat on the hard bench, with neither pillow nor covering, nor with any one looking after it. Next half-a-dozen men, sleeping bolt upright or leaning against one another in their sleep. In one place a family group, a child asleep in its sleeping mother's arms, and the husband (or male mate) clumsily mending a dilapidated shoe. On another bench a woman trimming the frayed strips of her rags with a knife, and another woman, with thread and needle, sewing up rents. Adjoining, a man holding a sleeping woman in his arms. Farther on, a man, his clothing caked with gutter mud, asleep, with head in the lap of a woman, not more than twenty-five years old, and also asleep.

It was this sleeping that puzzled me. Why were nine out of ten of them asleep or trying to sleep? But it was not till afterwards that I learned. *It is a law of the powers that be that the homeless shall not sleep by night.* On the pavement, by the portico of Christ's Church, where the stone pillars rise toward the sky in a stately row, were whole rows of men lying asleep or drowsing, and all too deep sunk in torpor to rouse or be made curious by our intrusion.

'A lung of London,' I said; 'nay, an abscess, a great putrescent sore.'

'Oh, why did you bring me here?' demanded the burning young socialist, his delicate face white with sickness of soul and stomach sickness.

'Those women there,' said our guide, 'will sell themselves for thru'pence, or tu'pence, or a loaf of stale bread.'

He said it with a cheerful sneer.

But what more he might have said I do not know, for the sick man cried, 'For heaven's sake let us get out of this.'

CHAPTER VII
A WINNER OF THE VICTORIA CROSS

From out of the populous city men groan, and the soul of the wounded crieth out.

JOB

I have found that it is not easy to get into the casual ward of the workhouse. I have made two attempts now, and I shall shortly make a third. The first time I started out at seven o'clock in the evening with four shillings in my pocket. Herein I committed two errors. In the first place, the applicant for admission to the casual ward must be destitute, and as he is subjected to a rigorous search, he must really be destitute; and fourpence, much less four shillings, is sufficient affluence to disqualify him. In the second place, I made the mistake of tardiness. Seven o'clock in the evening is too late in the day for a pauper to get a pauper's bed.

For the benefit of gently nurtured and innocent folk, let me explain what a ward is. It is a building where the homeless, bedless, penniless man, if he be lucky, may *casually* rest his weary bones, and then work like a navvy next day to pay for it.

My second attempt to break into the casual ward began more auspiciously. I started in the middle of the afternoon, accompanied by the burning young socialist and another friend, and all I had in my pocket was thru'pence. They piloted me to the Whitechapel Workhouse, at which I peered from around a friendly corner. It was a few minutes past five in the afternoon but already a long and melancholy line was formed, which strung out around the corner of the building and out of sight.

It was a most woeful picture, men and women waiting in the cold grey end of the day for a pauper's shelter from the night, and I confess it almost unnerved me. Like the boy before the dentist's door, I suddenly discovered a multitude of reasons for being elsewhere. Some hints of the struggle going on within must have shown in my face, for one of my companions said, 'Don't funk; you can do it.'

Of course I could do it, but I became aware that even thru'pence in my pocket was too lordly a treasure for such a throng; and, in order that all invidious distinctions might be removed, I emptied out the coppers. Then I bade good-bye to my friends, and with my heart going pit-a-pat, slouched down the street and took my place at the end of the line. Woeful it looked, this line of poor folk tottering on the steep pitch to death; how woeful it was I did not dream.

Next to me stood a short, stout man. Hale and hearty, though aged, strong-featured, with the tough and leathery skin produced by long years of sunbeat and weatherbeat, his was the unmistakable sea face and eyes; and at once there came to me a bit of Kipling's 'Galley Slave':-

> 'By the brand upon my shoulder, by the gall of clinging steel;
> By the welt the whips have left me, by the scars that never heal;
> By eyes grown old with staring through the sun-wash on the brine,
> I am paid in full for service . . . '

How correct I was in my surmise, and how peculiarly appropriate the verse was, you shall learn.

'I won't stand it much longer, I won't,' he was complaining to the man on the other side of him. 'I'll smash a windy, a big 'un, an' get run in for fourteen days. Then I'll have a good place to sleep, never fear, an' better grub than you get here. Though I'd miss my bit of bacey'—this as an after-thought, and said regretfully and resignedly.

'I've been out two nights now,' he went on; 'wet to the skin night before last, an' I can't stand it much longer. I'm gettin' old, an' some mornin' they'll pick me up dead.'

He whirled with fierce passion on me: 'Don't you ever let yourself grow old, lad. Die when you're young, or you'll come to this. I'm tellin' you sure. Seven an' eighty years am I, an' served my country like a man. Three good-conduct stripes and the Victoria Cross, an' this is what I get for it. I wish I was dead, I wish I was dead. Can't come any too quick for me, I tell you.'

The moisture rushed into his eyes, but, before the other man could comfort him, he began to hum a lilting sea song as though there was no such thing as heartbreak in the world.

Given encouragement, this is the story he told while waiting in line at the workhouse after two nights of exposure in the streets.

As a boy he had enlisted in the British navy, and for two score years and more served faithfully and well. Names, dates, commanders, ports, ships, engagements, and battles, rolled from his lips in a steady stream, but it is beyond me to remember them all, for it is not quite in keeping to take notes at the poorhouse door. He had been through the 'First War in China,' as he termed it; had enlisted with the East India Company and served ten years in India; was back in India again, in the English navy, at the time of the Mutiny; had served in the Burmese War and in the Crimea; and all this in addition to having fought and toiled for the English flag pretty well over the rest of the globe.

Then the thing happened. A little thing, it could only be traced back to first causes: perhaps the lieutenant's breakfast had not agreed with him; or he had been up late the night before; or his debts were pressing; or the commander had spoken brusquely to him. The point is, that on this particular day the lieutenant was irritable. The sailor, with others, was 'setting up' the fore rigging.

Now, mark you, the sailor had been over forty years in the navy, had three good-conduct stripes, and possessed the Victoria Cross for distinguished service in battle; so he could not have been such an altogether bad sort of a sailorman. The lieutenant was irritable; the lieutenant called him a name—well, not a nice sort of name. It referred to his mother. When I was a boy it was our boys' code to fight like little demons should such an insult be given our mothers; and many men have died in my part of the world for calling other men this name.

However, the lieutenant called the sailor this name. At that moment it chanced the sailor had an iron lever or bar in his hands. He promptly struck the lieutenant over the head with it, knocking him out of the rigging and overboard.

And then, in the man's own words: 'I saw what I had done. I knew the Regulations, and I said to myself, 'It's all up with you, Jack, my boy; so here goes.' An' I jumped over after him, my mind made up to drown us both. An' I'd ha' done it, too, only the pinnace from the flagship was just comin' alongside. Up we came to the top, me a hold of him an' punchin' him. This was what settled for me. If I hadn't ben strikin' him, I could have claimed that, seein' what I had done, I jumped over to save him.'

Then came the court-martial, or whatever name a sea trial goes by. He recited his sentence, word for word, as though memorised and gone over in bitterness many times. And here it is, for the sake of discipline and respect to officers not always gentlemen, the punishment of a man who was guilty of manhood. To be reduced to the rank of ordinary seaman; to be debarred all prize-money due him; to forfeit all rights to pension; to resign the Victoria Cross; to be discharged from the navy with a good character (this being his first offence); to receive fifty lashes; and to serve two years in prison.

'I wish I had drowned that day, I wish to God I had,' he concluded, as the line moved up and we passed around the corner.

At last the door came in sight, through which the paupers were being admitted in bunches. And here I learned a surprising thing: *this being Wednesday, none of us would be released till Friday morning.* Furthermore, and oh, you tobacco users, take heed: *we would not be permitted to take in any tobacco.* This we would have to surrender as we entered. Sometimes, I was told, it was returned on leaving and sometimes it was destroyed.

The old man-of-war's man gave me a lesson. Opening his pouch, he emptied the tobacco (a pitiful quantity) into a piece of paper. This, snugly and flatly wrapped, went down his sock inside his shoe. Down went my piece of tobacco inside my sock, for forty hours without tobacco is a hardship all tobacco users will understand.

Again and again the line moved up, and we were slowly but surely approaching the wicket. At the moment we happened to be standing on an iron grating, and a man appearing underneath, the old sailor called down to him,—

'How many more do they want?'

'Twenty-four,' came the answer.

We looked ahead anxiously and counted. Thirty-four were ahead of us. Disappointment and consternation dawned upon the faces about me. It is not a nice thing, hungry and penniless, to face a sleepless night in the streets. But we hoped against hope, till, when ten stood outside the wicket, the porter turned us away.

'Full up,' was what he said, as he banged the door.

Like a flash, for all his eighty-seven years, the old sailor was speeding away on the desperate chance of finding shelter elsewhere. I stood and debated with two other men, wise in the knowledge of casual wards, as to where we should go. They decided on the Poplar Workhouse, three miles away, and we started off.

As we rounded the corner, one of them said, 'I could a' got in 'ere to-day. I come by at one o'clock, an' the line was beginnin' to form then—pets, that's what they are. They let 'm in, the same ones, night upon night.'

CHAPTER VIII

THE CARTER AND THE CARPENTER

It is not to die, nor even to die of hunger, that makes a man wretched. Many men have died; all men must die. But it is to live miserable, we know not why; to work sore, and yet gain nothing; to be heart-worn, weary, yet isolated, unrelated, girt in with a cold universal Laissez-faire.

CARLYLE

The Carter, with his clean-cut face, chin beard, and shaved upper lip, I should have taken in the United States for anything from a master workman to a well-to-do farmer. The Carpenter—well, I should have taken him for a carpenter. He looked it, lean and wiry, with shrewd, observant eyes, and hands that had grown twisted to the handles of tools through forty-seven years' work at the trade. The chief difficulty with these men was that they were old, and that their children, instead of growing up to take care of them, had died. Their years had told on them, and they had been forced out of the whirl of industry by the younger and stronger competitors who had taken their places.

These two men, turned away from the casual ward of Whitechapel Workhouse, were bound with me for Poplar Workhouse. Not much of a show, they thought, but to chance it was all that remained to us. It was Poplar, or the streets and night. Both men were anxious for a bed, for they were 'about gone,' as they phrased it. The Carter, fifty-eight years of age, had spent the last three nights without shelter or sleep, while the Carpenter, sixty-five years of age, had been out five nights.

But, O dear, soft people, full of meat and blood, with white beds and airy rooms waiting you each night, how can I make you know what it is to suffer as you would suffer if you spent a weary night on London's streets! Believe me, you would think a thousand centuries had come and gone before the east paled into dawn; you would shiver till you were ready to cry aloud with the pain of each aching muscle; and you would marvel that you could endure so much and live. Should you rest upon a bench, and your tired eyes close, depend upon it the policeman would rouse you and gruffly order you to 'move on.' You may rest upon the bench, and benches are few and far between; but if rest means sleep, on you must go, dragging your tired body through the endless streets. Should you, in desperate slyness, seek some forlorn alley or dark passageway and lie down, the omnipresent policeman will rout you out just the same. It is his business to rout you out. It is a law of the powers that be that you shall be routed out.

But when the dawn came, the nightmare over, you would hale you home to refresh yourself, and until you died you would tell the story of your adventure to groups of admiring friends. It would grow into a mighty story. Your little eight-hour night would become an Odyssey and you a Homer.

Not so with these homeless ones who walked to Poplar Workhouse with me. And there are thirty-five thousand of them, men and women, in London Town this night. Please don't remember it as you go to bed; if you are as soft as you ought to be you may not rest so well as usual. But for old men of sixty, seventy, and eighty, ill-fed, with neither meat nor blood, to greet the dawn unrefreshed, and to stagger through the day in mad search for crusts, with relentless night rushing down upon them again, and to do this five nights and days—O dear, soft people, full of meat and blood, how can you ever understand?

I walked up Mile End Road between the Carter and the Carpenter. Mile End Road is a wide thoroughfare, cutting the heart of East London, and there were tens of thousands of people abroad on it. I tell you this so that you may fully appreciate what I shall describe in the next paragraph. As I say, we walked along, and when they grew bitter and cursed the land, I cursed with them, cursed as an American waif would curse, stranded in a strange and terrible land. And, as I tried to lead them to believe, and succeeded in making them believe, they took me for a 'seafaring man,' who had spent his money in riotous living, lost his clothes (no unusual occurrence with seafaring men ashore), and was temporarily broke while looking for a ship. This accounted for my ignorance of English ways in general and casual wards in particular, and my curiosity concerning the same.

The Carter was hard put to keep the pace at which we walked (he told me that he had eaten nothing that day), but the Carpenter, lean and hungry, his grey and ragged overcoat flapping mournfully in the breeze, swung on in a long and tireless stride which reminded me strongly of the plains wolf or coyote. Both kept their eyes upon the pavement as they walked and talked, and every now and then one or the other would stoop and pick something up, never missing the stride the while. I thought it was cigar and cigarette stumps they were collecting, and for some time took no notice. Then I did notice.

From the slimy, spittle-drenched, sidewalk, they were picking up bits of orange peel, apple skin, and grape stems, and, they were eating them. The pits of greengage plums they cracked between their teeth for the kernels inside. They picked up stray bits of bread the size of peas, apple cores so black and dirty one would not take them to be apple cores, and these things these two men took into their mouths, and chewed them, and swallowed them; and this, between six and seven o'clock in the evening of August 20, year of our Lord 1902, in the heart of the greatest, wealthiest, and most powerful empire the world has ever seen.

These two men talked. They were not fools, they were merely old. And, naturally, their guts a-reek with pavement offal, they talked of bloody revolution. They talked as anarchists, fanatics, and madmen would talk. And who shall blame them? In spite of my three good meals that day, and the snug bed I could occupy if I wished, and my social philosophy, and my evolutionary belief in the slow development and metamorphosis of things—in spite of all this, I say, I felt impelled to talk rot with them or hold my tongue. Poor fools! Not of their sort are revolutions bred. And when they are dead and dust, which will be shortly, other fools will talk bloody revolution as they gather offal from the spittle-drenched sidewalk along Mile End Road to Poplar Workhouse.

Being a foreigner, and a young man, the Carter and the Carpenter explained things to me and advised me. Their advice, by the way, was brief, and to the point; it was to get out of the country. 'As fast as God'll let me,' I assured them; 'I'll hit only the high places, till you won't be able to see my trail for smoke.' They felt the force of my figures, rather than understood them, and they nodded their heads approvingly.

'Actually make a man a criminal against 'is will,' said the Carpenter. 'Ere I am, old, younger men takin' my place, my clothes gettin' shabbier an' shabbier, an' makin' it 'arder every day to get a job. I go to the casual ward for a bed. Must be there by two or three in the afternoon or I won't get in. You saw what happened to-day. What chance does that give me to look for work? S'pose I do get into the casual ward? Keep me in all day to-morrow, let me out mornin' o' next day. What then? The law sez I can't get in another casual ward that night less'n ten miles distant. Have to hurry an' walk to be there in time that day. What chance does that give me to look for a job? S'pose I don't walk. S'pose I look for a job? In no time there's night come, an' no bed. No sleep all night, nothin' to eat, what shape am I in the mornin' to look for work? Got to make up my sleep in the park somehow' (the vision of Christ's Church, Spitalfield, was strong on me) 'an' get something to eat. An' there I am! Old, down, an' no chance to get up.'

'Used to be a toll-gate 'ere,' said the Carter. 'Many's the time I've paid my toll 'ere in my cartin' days.'

'I've 'ad three 'a'penny rolls in two days,' the Carpenter announced, after a long pause in the conversation. 'Two of them I ate yesterday, an' the third to-day,' he concluded, after another long pause.

'I ain't 'ad anything to-day,' said the Carter. 'An' I'm fagged out. My legs is hurtin' me something fearful.'

'The roll you get in the 'spike' is that 'ard you can't eat it nicely with less'n a pint of water,' said the Carpenter, for my benefit. And, on asking him what the 'spike' was, he answered, 'The casual ward. It's a cant word, you know.'

But what surprised me was that he should have the word 'cant' in his vocabulary, a vocabulary that I found was no mean one before we parted.

I asked them what I might expect in the way of treatment, if we succeeded in getting into the Poplar Workhouse, and between them I was supplied with much information. Having taken a cold bath on entering, I would be given for supper six ounces of bread and 'three parts of skilly.' 'Three parts' means three-quarters of a pint, and 'skilly' is a fluid concoction of three quarts of oatmeal stirred into three buckets and a half of hot water.

'Milk and sugar, I suppose, and a silver spoon?' I queried.

'No fear. Salt's what you'll get, an' I've seen some places where you'd not get any spoon. 'Old 'er up an' let 'er run down, that's 'ow they do it.'

'You do get good skilly at 'Ackney,' said the Carter.

'Oh, wonderful skilly, that,' praised the Carpenter, and each looked eloquently at the other.

'Flour an' water at St. George's in the East,' said the Carter.

The Carpenter nodded. He had tried them all.

'Then what?' I demanded

And I was informed that I was sent directly to bed. 'Call you at half after five in the mornin', an' you get up an' take a 'sluice'—if there's any soap. Then breakfast, same as supper, three parts o' skilly an' a six-ounce loaf.'

'Tisn't always six ounces,' corrected the Carter.

'Tisn't, no; an' often that sour you can 'ardly eat it. When first I started I couldn't eat the skilly nor the bread, but now I can eat my own an' another man's portion.'

'I could eat three other men's portions,' said the Carter. 'I 'aven't 'ad a bit this blessed day.'

'Then what?'

'Then you've got to do your task, pick four pounds of oakum, or clean an' scrub, or break ten to eleven hundredweight o' stones. I don't 'ave to break stones; I'm past sixty, you see. They'll make you do it, though. You're young an' strong.'

'What I don't like,' grumbled the Carter, 'is to be locked up in a cell to pick oakum. It's too much like prison.'

'But suppose, after you've had your night's sleep, you refuse to pick oakum, or break stones, or do any work at all?' I asked.

'No fear you'll refuse the second time; they'll run you in,' answered the Carpenter. 'Wouldn't advise you to try it on, my lad.'

'Then comes dinner,' he went on. 'Eight ounces of bread, one and a arf ounces of cheese, an' cold water. Then you finish your task an' 'ave supper, same as before, three parts o' skilly any six ounces o' bread. Then to bed, six o'clock, an' next mornin' you're turned loose, provided you've finished your task.'

We had long since left Mile End Road, and after traversing a gloomy maze of narrow, winding streets, we came to Poplar Workhouse. On a low stone wall we spread our handkerchiefs, and each in his handkerchief put all his worldly possessions, with the exception of the 'bit o' baccy' down his sock. And then, as the last light was fading from the drab-coloured sky, the wind blowing cheerless and cold, we stood, with our pitiful little bundles in our hands, a forlorn group at the workhouse door.

Three working girls came along, and one looked pityingly at me; as she passed I followed her with my eyes, and she still looked pityingly back at me. The old men she did not notice. Dear Christ, she pitied me, young and vigorous and strong, but she had no pity for the two old men who stood by my side! She was a young woman, and I was a young man, and what vague sex promptings impelled her to pity me put her sentiment on the lowest plane. Pity for old men is an altruistic feeling, and besides, the workhouse door is the accustomed place for old men. So she showed no pity for them, only for me, who deserved it least or not at all. Not in honour do grey hairs go down to the grave in London Town.

On one side the door was a bell handle, on the other side a press button.

'Ring the bell,' said the Carter to me.

And just as I ordinarily would at anybody's door, I pulled out the handle and rang a peal.

'Oh! Oh!' they cried in one terrified voice. 'Not so 'ard!'

I let go, and they looked reproachfully at me, as though I had imperilled their chance for a bed and three parts of skilly. Nobody came. Luckily it was the wrong bell, and I felt better.

'Press the button,' I said to the Carpenter.

'No, no, wait a bit,' the Carter hurriedly interposed.

From all of which I drew the conclusion that a poorhouse porter, who commonly draws a yearly salary of from seven to nine pounds, is a very finicky and important personage, and cannot be treated too fastidiously by—paupers.

So we waited, ten times a decent interval, when the Carter stealthily advanced a timid forefinger to the button, and gave it the faintest, shortest possible push. I have looked at waiting men where life or death was in the issue; but anxious suspense showed less plainly on their faces than it showed on the faces of these two men as they waited on the coming of the porter.

He came. He barely looked at us. 'Full up,' he said and shut the door.

'Another night of it,' groaned the Carpenter. In the dim light the Carter looked wan and grey.

Indiscriminate charity is vicious, say the professional philanthropists. Well, I resolved to be vicious.

'Come on; get your knife out and come here,' I said to the Carter, drawing him into a dark alley.

He glared at me in a frightened manner, and tried to draw back. Possibly he took me for a latter-day Jack-the-Ripper, with a penchant for elderly male paupers. Or he may have thought I was inveigling him into the commission of some desperate crime. Anyway, he was frightened.

It will be remembered, at the outset, that I sewed a pound inside my stoker's singlet under the armpit. This was my emergency fund, and I was now called upon to use it for the first time.

Not until I had gone through the acts of a contortionist, and shown the round coin sewed in, did I succeed in getting the Carter's help. Even then his hand was trembling so that I was afraid he would cut me instead of the stitches, and I was forced to take the knife away and do it myself. Out rolled the gold piece, a fortune in their hungry eyes; and away we stampeded for the nearest coffee-house.

Of course I had to explain to them that I was merely an investigator, a social student, seeking to find out how the other half lived. And at once they shut up like clams. I was not of their kind; my speech had changed, the tones of my voice were different, in short, I was a superior, and they were superbly class conscious.

'What will you have?' I asked, as the waiter came for the order.

'Two slices an' a cup of tea,' meekly said the Carter.

'Two slices an' a cup of tea,' meekly said the Carpenter.

Stop a moment, and consider the situation. Here were two men, invited by me into the coffee-house. They had seen my gold piece, and they could understand that I was no pauper. One had eaten a ha'penny roll that day, the other had eaten nothing. And they called for 'two slices an' a cup of tea!' Each man had given a tu'penny order. 'Two slices,' by the way, means two slices of bread and butter.

This was the same degraded humility that had characterised their attitude toward the poorhouse porter. But I wouldn't have it. Step by step I increased their order—

eggs, rashers of bacon, more eggs, more bacon, more tea, more slices and so forth—they denying wistfully all the while that they cared for anything more, and devouring it ravenously as fast as it arrived.

'First cup o' tea I've 'ad in a fortnight,' said the Carter.

'Wonderful tea, that,' said the Carpenter.

They each drank two pints of it, and I assure you that it was slops. It resembled tea less than lager beer resembles champagne. Nay, it was 'water-bewitched,' and did not resemble tea at all.

It was curious, after the first shock, to notice the effect the food had on them. At first they were melancholy, and talked of the divers times they had contemplated suicide. The Carter, not a week before, had stood on the bridge and looked at the water, and pondered the question. Water, the Carpenter insisted with heat, was a bad route. He, for one, he knew, would struggle. A bullet was 'andier,' but how under the sun was he to get hold of a revolver? That was the rub.

They grew more cheerful as the hot 'tea' soaked in, and talked more about themselves. The Carter had buried his wife and children, with the exception of one son, who grew to manhood and helped him in his little business. Then the thing happened. The son, a man of thirty-one, died of the smallpox. No sooner was this over than the father came down with fever and went to the hospital for three months. Then he was done for. He came out weak, debilitated, no strong young son to stand by him, his little business gone glimmering, and not a farthing. The thing had happened, and the game was up. No chance for an old man to start again. Friends all poor and unable to help. He had tried for work when they were putting up the stands for the first Coronation parade. 'An' I got fair sick of the answer: 'No! no! no!' It rang in my ears at night when I tried to sleep, always the same, 'No! no! no!' Only the past week he had answered an advertisement in Hackney, and on giving his age was told, 'Oh, too old, too old by far.'

The Carpenter had been born in the army, where his father had served twenty-two years. Likewise, his two brothers had gone into the army; one, troop sergeant-major of the Seventh Hussars, dying in India after the Mutiny; the other, after nine years under Roberts in the East, had been lost in Egypt. The Carpenter had not gone into the army, so here he was, still on the planet.

'But 'ere, give me your 'and,' he said, ripping open his ragged shirt. 'I'm fit for the anatomist, that's all. I'm wastin' away, sir, actually wastin' away for want of food. Feel my ribs an' you'll see.'

I put my hand under his shirt and felt. The skin was stretched like parchment over the bones, and the sensation produced was for all the world like running one's hand over a washboard.

'Seven years o' bliss I 'ad,' he said. 'A good missus and three bonnie lassies. But they all died. Scarlet fever took the girls inside a fortnight.'

'After this, sir,' said the Carter, indicating the spread, and desiring to turn the conversation into more cheerful channels; 'after this, I wouldn't be able to eat a workhouse breakfast in the morning.'

'Nor I,' agreed the Carpenter, and they fell to discussing belly delights and the fine dishes their respective wives had cooked in the old days.

'I've gone three days and never broke my fast,' said the Carter.

'And I, five,' his companion added, turning gloomy with the memory of it. 'Five days once, with nothing on my stomach but a bit of orange peel, an' outraged nature wouldn't stand it, sir, an' I near died. Sometimes, walkin' the streets at night, I've ben that desperate I've made up my mind to win the horse or lose the saddle. You know what I mean, sir—to commit some big robbery. But when mornin' come, there was I, too weak from 'unger an' cold to 'arm a mouse.'

As their poor vitals warmed to the food, they began to expand and wax boastful, and to talk politics. I can only say that they talked politics as well as the average middle-class man, and a great deal better than some of the middle-class men I have heard. What surprised me was the hold they had on the world, its geography and peoples, and on recent and contemporaneous history. As I say, they were not fools, these two men. They were merely old, and their children had undutifully failed to grow up and give them a place by the fire.

One last incident, as I bade them good-bye on the corner, happy with a couple of shillings in their pockets and the certain prospect of a bed for the night. Lighting a cigarette, I was about to throw away the burning match when the Carter reached for it. I proffered him the box, but he said, 'Never mind, won't waste it, sir.' And while he lighted the cigarette I had given him, the Carpenter hurried with the filling of his pipe in order to have a go at the same match.

'It's wrong to waste,' said he.

'Yes,' I said, but I was thinking of the wash-board ribs over which I had run my hand.

CHAPTER IX
THE SPIKE

The old Spartans had a wiser method; and went out and hunted down their Helots, and speared and spitted them, when they grew too numerous. With our improved fashions of hunting, now after the invention of firearms and standing armies, how much easier were such a hunt! Perhaps in the most thickly peopled country, some three days annually might suffice to shoot all the able-bodied paupers that had accumulated within the year.

CARLYLE

First of all, I must beg forgiveness of my body for the vileness through which I have dragged it, and forgiveness of my stomach for the vileness which I have thrust into it. I have been to the spike, and slept in the spike, and eaten in the spike; also, I have run away from the spike.

After my two unsuccessful attempts to penetrate the Whitechapel casual ward, I started early, and joined the desolate line before three o'clock in the afternoon. They did not 'let in' till six, but at that early hour I was number twenty, while the news had gone forth that only twenty-two were to be admitted. By four o'clock there were thirty-four in line, the last ten hanging on in the slender hope of getting in by some kind of a miracle. Many more came, looked at the line, and went away, wise to the bitter fact that the spike would be 'full up.'

Conversation was slack at first, standing there, till the man on one side of me and the man on the other side of me discovered that they had been in the smallpox hospital at the same time, though a full house of sixteen hundred patients had prevented their becoming acquainted. But they made up for it, discussing and comparing the more loathsome features of their disease in the most cold-blooded, matter-of-fact way. I learned that the average mortality was one in six, that one of them had been in three months and the other three months and a half, and that they had been 'rotten wi' it.' Whereat my flesh began to creep and crawl, and I asked them how long they had been out. One had been out two weeks, and the other three weeks. Their faces were badly pitted (though each assured the other that this was not so), and further, they showed me in their hands and under the nails the smallpox 'seeds' still working out. Nay, one of them worked a seed out for my edification, and pop it went, right out of his flesh into the air. I tried to shrink up smaller inside my clothes, and I registered a fervent though silent hope that it had not popped on me.

In both instances, I found that the smallpox was the cause of their being 'on the doss,' which means on the tramp. Both had been working when smitten by the disease, and both had emerged from the hospital 'broke,' with the gloomy task before them of hunting for work. So far, they had not found any, and they had come to the spike for a 'rest up' after three days and nights on the street.

It seems that not only the man who becomes old is punished for his involuntary misfortune, but likewise the man who is struck by disease or accident. Later on, I talked with another man—'Ginger' we called him—who stood at the head of the line—a sure indication that he had been waiting since one o'clock. A year before, one day, while in the employ of a fish dealer, he was carrying a heavy box of fish which was too much for him. Result: 'something broke,' and there was the box on the ground, and he on the ground beside it.

At the first hospital, whither he was immediately carried, they said it was a rupture, reduced the swelling, gave him some vaseline to rub on it, kept him four hours, and told him to get along. But he was not on the streets more than two or three hours when he was down on his back again. This time he went to another hospital and was patched up. But the point is, the employer did nothing, positively nothing, for the man injured in his employment, and even refused him 'a light job now and again,' when he came out. As far as Ginger is concerned, he is a broken man. His only chance to earn a living was by heavy work. He is now incapable of performing heavy work, and from now until he dies, the spike, the peg, and the streets are all he can look forward to in the way of food and shelter. The thing happened—that is all. He put his back under too great a load of fish, and his chance for happiness in life was crossed off the books.

Several men in the line had been to the United States, and they were wishing that they had remained there, and were cursing themselves for their folly in ever having left. England had become a prison to them, a prison from which there was no hope of escape. It was impossible for them to get away. They could neither scrape together the passage money, nor get a chance to work their passage. The country was too overrun by poor devils on that 'lay.'

I was on the seafaring-man-who-had-lost-his-clothes-and-money tack, and they all condoled with me and gave me much sound advice. To sum it up, the advice was something like this: To keep out of all places like the spike. There was nothing good in it for me. To head for the coast and bend every effort to get away on a ship. To go to work, if possible, and scrape together a pound or so, with which I might bribe some steward or underling to give me chance to work my passage. They envied me my youth and strength, which would sooner or later get me out of the country. These they no longer possessed. Age and English hardship had broken them, and for them the game was played and up.

There was one, however, who was still young, and who, I am sure, will in the end make it out. He had gone to the United States as a young fellow, and in fourteen years' residence the longest period he had been out of work was twelve hours. He had saved his money, grown too prosperous, and returned to the mother-country. Now he was standing in line at the spike.

For the past two years, he told me, he had been working as a cook. His hours had been from 7 a.m. to 10.30 p.m., and on Saturday to 12.30 p.m.—ninety-five hours per week, for which he had received twenty shillings, or five dollars.

'But the work and the long hours was killing me,' he said, 'and I had to chuck the job. I had a little money saved, but I spent it living and looking for another place.'

This was his first night in the spike, and he had come in only to get rested. As soon as he emerged, he intended to start for Bristol, a one-hundred-and-ten-mile walk, where he thought he would eventually get a ship for the States.

But the men in the line were not all of this calibre. Some were poor, wretched beasts, inarticulate and callous, but for all of that, in many ways very human. I remember a carter, evidently returning home after the day's work, stopping his cart before us so that his young hopeful, who had run to meet him, could climb in. But the cart was big, the young hopeful little, and he failed in his several attempts to swarm up. Whereupon one of the most degraded-looking men stepped out of the line and hoisted him in. Now the virtue and the joy of this act lies in that it was service of love, not hire. The carter was poor, and the man knew it; and the man was standing in the spike line, and the carter knew it; and the man had done the little act, and the carter had thanked him, even as you and I would have done and thanked.

Another beautiful touch was that displayed by the 'Hopper' and his 'ole woman.' He had been in line about half-an-hour when the 'ole woman' (his mate) came up to him. She was fairly clad, for her class, with a weather-worn bonnet on her grey head and a sacking-covered bundle in her arms. As she talked to him, he reached forward, caught the one stray wisp of the white hair that was flying wild, deftly twirled it between his fingers, and tucked it back properly behind her ear. From all of which one may conclude many things. He certainly liked her well enough to wish her to be neat and tidy. He was proud of her, standing there in the spike line, and it was his desire that she should look well in the eyes of the other unfortunates who stood in the spike line. But last and best, and underlying all these motives, it was a sturdy affection he bore her; for man is not prone to bother his head over neatness and tidiness in a woman for whom he does not care, nor is he likely to be proud of such a woman.

And I found myself questioning why this man and his mate, hard workers I knew from their talk, should have to seek a pauper lodging. He had pride, pride in his old woman and pride in himself. When I asked him what he thought I, a greenhorn, might expect to earn at 'hopping,' he sized me up, and said that it all depended. Plenty of people were too slow to pick hops and made a failure of it. A man, to succeed, must use his head and be quick with his fingers, must be exceeding quick with his fingers. Now he and his old woman could do very well at it, working the one bin between them and not going to sleep over it; but then, they had been at it for years.

'I 'ad a mate as went down last year,' spoke up a man. 'It was 'is fust time, but 'e come back wi' two poun' ten in 'is pockit, an' 'e was only gone a month.'

'There you are,' said the Hopper, a wealth of admiration in his voice. ''E was quick. 'E was jest nat'rally born to it, 'e was.'

Two pound ten—twelve dollars and a half—for a month's work when one is 'jest nat'rally born to it!' And in addition, sleeping out without blankets and living the Lord knows how. There are moments when I am thankful that I was not 'jest nat'rally born' a genius for anything, not even hop-picking,

In the matter of getting an outfit for 'the hops,' the Hopper gave me some sterling advice, to which same give heed, you soft and tender people, in case you should ever be stranded in London Town.

'If you ain't got tins an' cookin' things, all as you can get'll be bread and cheese. No bloomin' good that! You must 'ave 'ot tea, an' wegetables, an' a bit o' meat, now an' again, if you're goin' to do work as is work. Cawn't do it on cold wittles. Tell you wot you do, lad. Run around in the mornin' an' look in the dust pans. You'll find plenty o' tins to cook in. Fine tins, wonderful good some o' them. Me an' the ole woman got ours that way.' (He pointed at the bundle she held, while she nodded proudly, beaming on me with good-nature and consciousness of success and prosperity.) 'This overcoat is as good as a blanket,' he went on, advancing the skirt of it that I might feel its thickness. 'An' 'oo knows, I may find a blanket before long.'

Again the old woman nodded and beamed, this time with the dead certainty that he *would* find a blanket before long.

'I call it a 'oliday, 'oppin',' he concluded rapturously. 'A tidy way o' gettin' two or three pounds together an' fixin' up for winter. The only thing I don't like'—and here was the rift within the lute—'is paddin' the 'oof down there.'

It was plain the years were telling on this energetic pair, and while they enjoyed the quick work with the fingers, 'paddin' the 'oof,' which is walking, was beginning to bear heavily upon them. And I looked at their grey hairs, and ahead into the future ten years, and wondered how it would be with them.

I noticed another man and his old woman join the line, both of them past fifty. The woman, because she was a woman, was admitted into the spike; but he was too late, and, separated from his mate, was turned away to tramp the streets all night.

The street on which we stood, from wall to wall, was barely twenty feet wide. The sidewalks were three feet wide. It was a residence street. At least workmen and their families existed in some sort of fashion in the houses across from us. And each day and every day, from one in the afternoon till six, our ragged spike line is the principal feature of the view commanded by their front doors and windows. One workman sat in his door directly opposite us, taking his rest and a breath of air after the toil of the day. His wife came to chat with him. The doorway was too small for two, so she stood up. Their babes sprawled before them. And here was the spike line, less than a score of feet away—neither privacy for the workman, nor privacy for the pauper. About our feet played the children of the neighbourhood. To them our presence was nothing unusual. We were not an intrusion. We were as natural and ordinary as the brick walls and stone curbs of their environment. They had been born to the sight of the spike line, and all their brief days they had seen it.

At six o'clock the line moved up, and we were admitted in groups of three. Name, age, occupation, place of birth, condition of destitution, and the previous night's 'doss,' were taken with lightning-like rapidity by the superintendent; and as I turned I was startled by a man's thrusting into my hand something that felt like a brick, and shouting into my ear, 'any knives, matches, or tobacco?' 'No, sir,' I lied, as lied every man who entered. As I passed downstairs to the cellar, I looked at the brick in my hand, and saw that by doing violence to the language it might be called 'bread.' By its weight and hardness it certainly must have been unleavened.

The light was very dim down in the cellar, and before I knew it some other man had thrust a pannikin into my other hand. Then I stumbled on to a still darker room, where were benches and tables and men. The place smelled vilely, and the sombre gloom, and the mumble of voices from out of the obscurity, made it seem more like some anteroom to the infernal regions.

Most of the men were suffering from tired feet, and they prefaced the meal by removing their shoes and unbinding the filthy rags with which their feet were wrapped. This added to the general noisomeness, while it took away from my appetite.

In fact, I found that I had made a mistake. I had eaten a hearty dinner five hours before, and to have done justice to the fare before me I should have fasted for a couple of days. The pannikin contained skilly, three-quarters of a pint, a mixture of Indian corn and hot water. The men were dipping their bread into heaps of salt scattered over the dirty tables. I attempted the same, but the bread seemed to stick in my mouth, and I remembered the words of the Carpenter, 'You need a pint of water to eat the bread nicely.'

I went over into a dark corner where I had observed other men going and found the water. Then I returned and attacked the skilly. It was coarse of texture, unseasoned, gross, and bitter. This bitterness which lingered persistently in the mouth after the skilly had passed on, I found especially repulsive. I struggled manfully, but was mastered by my qualms, and half-a-dozen mouthfuls of skilly and bread was the measure of my success. The man beside me ate his own share, and mine to boot, scraped the pannikins, and looked hungrily for more.

'I met a 'towny,' and he stood me too good a dinner,' I explained.

'An' I 'aven't 'ad a bite since yesterday mornin',' he replied.

'How about tobacco?' I asked. 'Will the bloke bother with a fellow now?'

'Oh no,' he answered me. 'No bloomin' fear. This is the easiest spike goin'. Y'oughto see some of them. Search you to the skin.'

The pannikins scraped clean, conversation began to spring up. 'This super'tendent 'ere is always writin' to the papers 'bout us mugs,' said the man on the other side of me.

'What does he say?' I asked.

'Oh, 'e sez we're no good, a lot o' blackguards an' scoundrels as won't work. Tells all the ole tricks I've bin 'earin' for twenty years an' w'ich I never seen a mug ever do. Las' thing of 'is I see, 'e was tellin' 'ow a mug gets out o' the spike, wi' a crust in 'is pockit. An' w'en 'e sees a nice ole gentleman comin' along the street 'e chucks the crust into the drain, an' borrows the old gent's stick to poke it out. An' then the ole gent gi'es 'im a tanner.'

A roar of applause greeted the time-honoured yarn, and from somewhere over in the deeper darkness came another voice, orating angrily:

'Talk o' the country bein' good for tommy [food]; I'd like to see it. I jest came up from Dover, an' blessed little tommy I got. They won't gi' ye a drink o' water, they won't, much less tommy.'

'There's mugs never go out of Kent,' spoke a second voice, 'they live bloomin' fat all along.'

'I come through Kent,' went on the first voice, still more angrily, 'an' Gawd blimey if I see any tommy. An' I always notices as the blokes as talks about 'ow much they can get, w'en they're in the spike can eat my share o' skilly as well as their bleedin' own.'

'There's chaps in London,' said a man across the table from me, 'that get all the tommy they want, an' they never think o' goin' to the country. Stay in London the year 'round. Nor do they think of lookin' for a kip [place to sleep], till nine or ten o'clock at night.'

A general chorus verified this statement

'But they're bloomin' clever, them chaps,' said an admiring voice.

'Course they are,' said another voice. 'But it's not the likes of me an' you can do it. You got to be born to it, I say. Them chaps 'ave ben openin' cabs an' sellin' papers since the day they was born, an' their fathers an' mothers before 'em. It's all in the trainin', I say, an' the likes of me an' you 'ud starve at it.'

This also was verified by the general chorus, and likewise the statement that there were 'mugs as lives the twelvemonth 'round in the spike an' never get a blessed bit o' tommy other than spike skilly an' bread.'

'I once got arf a crown in the Stratford spike,' said a new voice. Silence fell on the instant, and all listened to the wonderful tale. 'There was three of us breakin' stones. Winter-time, an' the cold was cruel. T'other two said they'd be blessed if they do it, an' they didn't; but I kept wearin' into mine to warm up, you know. An' then the guardians come, an' t'other chaps got run in for fourteen days, an' the guardians, w'en they see wot I'd been doin', gives me a tanner each, five o' them, an' turns me up.'

The majority of these men, nay, all of them, I found, do not like the spike, and only come to it when driven in. After the 'rest up' they are good for two or three days and nights on the streets, when they are driven in again for another rest. Of course, this continuous hardship quickly breaks their constitutions, and they realise it, though only in a vague way; while it is so much the common run of things that they do not worry about it.

'On the doss,' they call vagabondage here, which corresponds to 'on the road' in the United States. The agreement is that kipping, or dossing, or sleeping, is the hardest problem they have to face, harder even than that of food. The inclement weather and the harsh laws are mainly responsible for this, while the men themselves ascribe their homelessness to foreign immigration, especially of Polish and Russian Jews, who take their places at lower wages and establish the sweating system.

By seven o'clock we were called away to bathe and go to bed. We stripped our clothes, wrapping them up in our coats and buckling our belts about them, and deposited them in a heaped rack and on the floor—a beautiful scheme for the spread of vermin. Then, two by two, we entered the bathroom. There were two ordinary tubs, and this I know: the two men preceding had washed in that water, we washed in the same water, and it was not changed for the two men that followed us. This I know; but I am also certain that the twenty-two of us washed in the same water.

I did no more than make a show of splashing some of this dubious liquid at myself, while I hastily brushed it off with a towel wet from the bodies of other men. My equanimity was not restored by seeing the back of one poor wretch a mass of blood from attacks of vermin and retaliatory scratching.

A shirt was handed me—which I could not help but wonder how many other men had worn; and with a couple of blankets under my arm I trudged off to the sleeping apartment. This was a long, narrow room, traversed by two low iron rails. Between these rails were stretched, not hammocks, but pieces of canvas, six feet long and less than two feet wide. These were the beds, and they were six inches apart and about eight inches above the floor. The chief difficulty was that the head was somewhat higher than the feet, which caused the body constantly to slip down. Being slung to the same rails, when one man moved, no matter how slightly, the rest were set rocking; and whenever I dozed somebody was sure to struggle back to the position from which he had slipped, and arouse me again.

Many hours passed before I won to sleep. It was only seven in the evening, and the voices of children, in shrill outcry, playing in the street, continued till nearly midnight. The smell was frightful and sickening, while my imagination broke loose, and my skin crept and crawled till I was nearly frantic. Grunting, groaning, and snoring arose like the sounds emitted by some sea monster, and several times, afflicted by nightmare, one or another, by his shrieks and yells, aroused the lot of us. Toward morning I was awakened by a rat or some similar animal on my breast. In the quick transition from sleep to waking, before I was completely myself, I raised a shout to wake the dead. At any rate, I woke the living, and they cursed me roundly for my lack of manners.

But morning came, with a six o'clock breakfast of bread and skilly, which I gave away, and we were told off to our various tasks. Some were set to scrubbing and cleaning, others to picking oakum, and eight of us were convoyed across the street to the Whitechapel Infirmary where we were set at scavenger work. This was the method by which we paid for our skilly and canvas, and I, for one, know that I paid in full many times over.

Though we had most revolting tasks to perform, our allotment was considered the best and the other men deemed themselves lucky in being chosen to perform it.

'Don't touch it, mate, the nurse sez it's deadly,' warned my working partner, as I held open a sack into which he was emptying a garbage can.

It came from the sick wards, and I told him that I purposed neither to touch it, nor to allow it to touch me. Nevertheless, I had to carry the sack, and other sacks, down five flights of stairs and empty them in a receptacle where the corruption was speedily sprinkled with strong disinfectant.

Perhaps there is a wise mercy in all this. These men of the spike, the peg, and the street, are encumbrances. They are of no good or use to any one, nor to themselves. They clutter the earth with their presence, and are better out of the way. Broken by hardship, ill fed, and worse nourished, they are always the first to be struck down by disease, as they are likewise the quickest to die.

They feel, themselves, that the forces of society tend to hurl them out of existence. We were sprinkling disinfectant by the mortuary, when the dead waggon drove up and five bodies were packed into it. The conversation turned to the 'white potion' and 'black jack,' and I found they were all agreed that the poor person, man or woman, who in the Infirmary gave too much trouble or was in a bad way, was 'polished off.' That is to say, the incurables and the obstreperous were given a dose of 'black jack' or the 'white potion,' and sent over the divide. It does not matter in the least whether this be actually so or not. The point is, they have the feeling that it is so, and they have created the language with which to express that feeling—'black jack' 'white potion,' 'polishing off.'

At eight o'clock we went down into a cellar under the infirmary, where tea was brought to us, and the hospital scraps. These were heaped high on a huge platter in an indescribable mess—pieces of bread, chunks of grease and fat pork, the burnt skin from the outside of roasted joints, bones, in short, all the leavings from the fingers and mouths of the sick ones suffering from all manner of diseases. Into this mess the men plunged their hands, digging, pawing, turning over, examining, rejecting, and scrambling for. It wasn't pretty. Pigs couldn't have done worse. But the poor devils were hungry, and they ate ravenously of the swill, and when they could eat no more they bundled what was left into their handkerchiefs and thrust it inside their shirts.

'Once, w'en I was 'ere before, wot did I find out there but a 'ole lot of pork-ribs,' said Ginger to me. By 'out there' he meant the place where the corruption was dumped and sprinkled with strong disinfectant. 'They was a prime lot, no end o' meat on 'em, an' I 'ad 'em into my arms an' was out the gate an' down the street, a-lookin' for some 'un to gi' 'em to. Couldn't see a soul, an' I was runnin' 'round clean crazy, the bloke runnin' after me an' thinkin' I was 'slingin' my 'ook' [running away]. But jest before 'e got me, I got a ole woman an' poked 'em into 'er apron.'

O Charity, O Philanthropy, descend to the spike and take a lesson from Ginger. At the bottom of the Abyss he performed as purely an altruistic act as was ever performed outside the Abyss. It was fine of Ginger, and if the old woman caught some contagion from the 'no end o' meat' on the pork-ribs, it was still fine, though not so fine. But the most salient thing in this incident, it seems to me, is poor Ginger, 'clean crazy' at sight of so much food going to waste.

It is the rule of the casual ward that a man who enters must stay two nights and a day; but I had seen sufficient for my purpose, had paid for my skilly and canvas, and was preparing to run for it.

'Come on, let's sling it,' I said to one of my mates, pointing toward the open gate through which the dead waggon had come.

'An' get fourteen days?'

'No; get away.'

'Aw, I come 'ere for a rest,' he said complacently. 'An' another night's kip won't 'urt me none.'

They were all of this opinion, so I was forced to 'sling it' alone.

'You cawn't ever come back 'ere again for a doss,' they warned me.

'No fear,' said I, with an enthusiasm they could not comprehend; and, dodging out the gate, I sped down the street.

Straight to my room I hurried, changed my clothes, and less than an hour from my escape, in a Turkish bath, I was sweating out whatever germs and other things had penetrated my epidermis, and wishing that I could stand a temperature of three hundred and twenty rather than two hundred and twenty.

CHAPTER X
CARRYING THE BANNER

I would not have the laborer sacrificed to the result. I would not have
the laborer sacrificed to my convenience and pride, nor to that of a
great class of such as me. Let there be worse cotton and better men.
The weaver should not be bereaved of his superiority to his work.

EMERSON

'To carry the banner' means to walk the streets all night; and I, with the figurative emblem hoisted, went out to see what I could see. Men and women walk the streets at night all over this great city, but I selected the West End, making Leicester Square my base, and scouting about from the Thames Embankment to Hyde Park.

The rain was falling heavily when the theatres let out, and the brilliant throng which poured from the places of amusement was hard put to find cabs. The streets were so many wild rivers of cabs, most of which were engaged, however; and here I saw the desperate attempts of ragged men and boys to get a shelter from the night by procuring cabs for the cabless ladies and gentlemen. I use the word 'desperate' advisedly, for these wretched, homeless ones were gambling a soaking against a bed; and most of them, I took notice, got the soaking and missed the bed. Now, to go through a stormy night with wet clothes, and, in addition, to be ill nourished and not to have tasted meat for a week or a month, is about as severe a hardship as a man can undergo. Well fed and well clad, I have travelled all day with the spirit thermometer down to seventy-four degrees below zero—one hundred and six degrees of frost {1}; and though I suffered, it was a mere nothing compared with carrying the banner for a night, ill fed, ill clad, and soaking wet.

The streets grew very quiet and lonely after the theatre crowd had gone home. Only were to be seen the ubiquitous policemen, flashing their dark lanterns into doorways and alleys, and men and women and boys taking shelter in the lee of buildings from the wind and rain. Piccadilly, however, was not quite so deserted. Its pavements were brightened by well-dressed women without escort, and there was more life and action there than elsewhere, due to the process of finding escort. But by three o'clock the last of them had vanished, and it was then indeed lonely.

At half-past one the steady downpour ceased, and only showers fell thereafter. The homeless folk came away from the protection of the buildings, and slouched up and down and everywhere, in order to rush up the circulation and keep warm.

One old woman, between fifty and sixty, a sheer wreck, I had noticed earlier in the night standing in Piccadilly, not far from Leicester Square. She seemed to have neither the sense nor the strength to get out of the rain or keep walking, but stood stupidly, whenever she got the chance, meditating on past days, I imagine, when life was young and blood was warm. But she did not get the chance often. She was moved on by every policeman, and it required an average of six moves to send her doddering off one man's beat and on to another's. By three o'clock, she had progressed as far as St. James Street, and as the clocks were striking four I saw her sleeping soundly against the iron railings of Green Park. A brisk shower was falling at the time, and she must have been drenched to the skin.

Now, said I, at one o'clock, to myself; consider that you are a poor young man, penniless, in London Town, and that to-morrow you must look for work. It is necessary, therefore, that you get some sleep in order that you may have strength to look for work and to do work in case you find it.

So I sat down on the stone steps of a building. Five minutes later a policeman was looking at me. My eyes were wide open, so he only grunted and passed on. Ten minutes later my head was on my knees, I was dozing, and the same policeman was saying gruffly, 'Ere, you, get outa that!'

I got. And, like the old woman, I continued to get; for every time I dozed, a policeman was there to rout me along again. Not long after, when I had given this up, I was walking with a young Londoner (who had been out to the colonies and wished he were out to them again), when I noticed an open passage leading under a building and disappearing in darkness. A low iron gate barred the entrance.

'Come on,' I said. 'Let's climb over and get a good sleep.'

'Wot?' he answered, recoiling from me. 'An' get run in fer three months! Blimey if I do!'

Later on I was passing Hyde Park with a young boy of fourteen or fifteen, a most wretched-looking youth, gaunt and hollow-eyed and sick.

'Let's go over the fence,' I proposed, 'and crawl into the shrubbery for a sleep. The bobbies couldn't find us there.'

'No fear,' he answered. 'There's the park guardians, and they'd run you in for six months.'

Times have changed, alas! When I was a youngster I used to read of homeless boys sleeping in doorways. Already the thing has become a tradition. As a stock situation it will doubtless linger in literature for a century to come, but as a cold fact it has ceased to be. Here are the doorways, and here are the boys, but happy conjunctions are no longer effected. The doorways remain empty, and the boys keep awake and carry the banner.

'I was down under the arches,' grumbled another young fellow. By 'arches' he meant the shore arches where begin the bridges that span the Thames. 'I was down under the arches wen it was ryning its 'ardest, an' a bobby comes in an' chyses me out. But I come back, an' 'e come too. 'Ere,' sez 'e, 'wot you doin' 'ere?' An' out I goes, but I sez, 'Think I want ter pinch [steal] the bleedin' bridge?'

Among those who carry the banner, Green Park has the reputation of opening its gates earlier than the other parks, and at quarter-past four in the morning, I, and many more, entered Green Park. It was raining again, but they were worn out with the night's walking, and they were down on the benches and asleep at once. Many of the men stretched out full length on the dripping wet grass, and, with the rain falling steadily upon them, were sleeping the sleep of exhaustion.

And now I wish to criticise the powers that be. They *are* the powers, therefore they may decree whatever they please; so I make bold only to criticise the ridiculousness of their decrees. All night long they make the homeless ones walk up and down. They drive them out of doors and passages, and lock them out of the parks. The evident intention of all this is to deprive them of sleep. Well and good, the powers have the power to deprive them of sleep, or of anything else for that matter; but why under the sun do they open the gates of the parks at five o'clock in the morning and let the homeless ones go inside and sleep? If it is their intention to deprive them of sleep, why do they let them sleep after five in the morning? And if it is not their intention to deprive them of sleep, why don't they let them sleep earlier in the night?

In this connection, I will say that I came by Green Park that same day, at one in the afternoon, and that I counted scores of the ragged wretches asleep in the grass. It was Sunday afternoon, the sun was fitfully appearing, and the well-dressed West Enders, with their wives and progeny, were out by thousands, taking the air. It was not a pleasant sight for them, those horrible, unkempt, sleeping vagabonds; while the vagabonds themselves, I know, would rather have done their sleeping the night before.

And so, dear soft people, should you ever visit London Town, and see these men asleep on the benches and in the grass, please do not think they are lazy creatures, preferring sleep to work. Know that the powers that be have kept them walking all the night long, and that in the day they have nowhere else to sleep.

CHAPTER XI
THE PEG

And I believe that this claim for a healthy body for all of us carries
with it all other due claims; for who knows where the seeds of disease,
which even rich people suffer from, were first sown? From the luxury
of an ancestor, perhaps; yet often, I suspect, from his poverty.

WILLIAM MORRIS

But, after carrying the banner all night, I did not sleep in Green Park when morning dawned. I was wet to the skin, it is true, and I had had no sleep for twenty-four hours; but, still adventuring as a penniless man looking for work, I had to look about me, first for a breakfast, and next for the work.

During the night I had heard of a place over on the Surrey side of the Thames, where the Salvation Army every Sunday morning gave away a breakfast to the unwashed. (And, by the way, the men who carry the banner are unwashed in the morning, and unless it is raining they do not have much show for a wash, either.) This, thought I, is the very thing—breakfast in the morning, and then the whole day in which to look for work.

It was a weary walk. Down St. James Street I dragged my tired legs, along Pall Mall, past Trafalgar Square, to the Strand. I crossed the Waterloo Bridge to the Surrey side, cut across to Blackfriars Road, coming out near the Surrey Theatre, and arrived at the Salvation Army barracks before seven o'clock. This was 'the peg.' And by 'the peg,' in the argot, is meant the place where a free meal may be obtained.

Here was a motley crowd of woebegone wretches who had spent the night in the rain. Such prodigious misery! and so much of it! Old men, young men, all manner of men, and boys to boot, and all manner of boys. Some were drowsing standing up; half a score of them were stretched out on the stone steps in most painful postures, all of them sound asleep, the skin of their bodies showing red through the holes, and rents in their rags. And up and down the street and across the street for a block either way, each doorstep had from two to three occupants, all asleep, their heads bent forward on their knees. And, it must be remembered, these are not hard times in England. Things are going on very much as they ordinarily do, and times are neither hard nor easy.

And then came the policeman. 'Get outa that, you bloomin' swine! Eigh! eigh! Get out now!' And like swine he drove them from the doorways and scattered them to the four winds of Surrey. But when he encountered the crowd asleep on the steps he was astounded. 'Shocking!' he exclaimed. 'Shocking! And of a Sunday morning! A pretty sight! Eigh! eigh! Get outa that, you bleeding nuisances!'

Of course it was a shocking sight, I was shocked myself. And I should not care to have my own daughter pollute her eyes with such a sight, or come within half a mile of it; but—and there we were, and there you are, and 'but' is all that can be said.

The policeman passed on, and back we clustered, like flies around a honey jar. For was there not that wonderful thing, a breakfast, awaiting us? We could not have clustered more persistently and desperately had they been giving away million-dollar bank-notes. Some were already off to sleep, when back came the policeman and away we scattered only to return again as soon as the coast was clear.

At half-past seven a little door opened, and a Salvation Army soldier stuck out his head. 'Ayn't no sense blockin' the wy up that wy,' he said. 'Those as 'as tickets cawn come hin now, an' those as 'asn't cawn't come hin till nine.'

Oh, that breakfast! Nine o'clock! An hour and a half longer! The men who held tickets were greatly envied. They were permitted to go inside, have a wash, and sit down and rest until breakfast, while we waited for the same breakfast on the street. The tickets had been distributed the previous night on the streets and along the Embankment, and the possession of them was not a matter of merit, but of chance.

At eight-thirty, more men with tickets were admitted, and by nine the little gate was opened to us. We crushed through somehow, and found ourselves packed in a courtyard like sardines. On more occasions than one, as a Yankee tramp in Yankeeland, I have had to work for my breakfast; but for no breakfast did I ever work so hard as for this one. For over two hours I had waited outside, and for over another hour I waited in this packed courtyard. I had had nothing to eat all night, and I was weak and faint, while the smell of the soiled clothes and unwashed bodies, steaming from pent animal heat, and blocked solidly about me, nearly turned my stomach. So tightly were we packed, that a number of the men took advantage of the opportunity and went soundly asleep standing up.

Now, about the Salvation Army in general I know nothing, and whatever criticism I shall make here is of that particular portion of the Salvation Army which does business on Blackfriars Road near the Surrey Theatre. In the first place, this forcing of men who have been up all night to stand on their feet for hours longer, is as cruel as it is needless. We were weak, famished, and exhausted from our night's hardship and lack of sleep, and yet there we stood, and stood, and stood, without rhyme or reason.

Sailors were very plentiful in this crowd. It seemed to me that one man in four was looking for a ship, and I found at least a dozen of them to be American sailors. In accounting for their being 'on the beach,' I received the same story from each and all, and from my knowledge of sea affairs this story rang true. English ships sign their sailors for the voyage, which means the round trip, sometimes lasting as long as three years; and they cannot sign off and receive their discharges until they reach the home port, which is England. Their wages are low, their food is bad, and their treatment worse. Very often they are really forced by their captains to desert in the New World or the colonies, leaving a handsome sum of wages behind them—a distinct gain, either to the captain or the owners, or to both. But whether for this reason alone or not, it is a fact that large numbers of them desert. Then, for the home voyage, the ship engages whatever sailors it can find on the beach. These men are engaged at the somewhat higher wages that obtain in other portions of the world, under the agreement that they shall sign off on reaching England. The reason for this is obvious; for it would be poor business policy to sign them for any longer time, since seamen's wages are low in England, and England is always crowded with sailormen on the beach. So this fully accounted for the American seamen at the Salvation Army barracks. To get off the beach in other outlandish places they had come to England, and gone on the beach in the most outlandish place of all.

There were fully a score of Americans in the crowd, the non-sailors being 'tramps royal,' the men whose 'mate is the wind that tramps the world.' They were all cheerful, facing things with the pluck which is their chief characteristic and which seems never to desert them, withal they were cursing the country with lurid metaphors quite refreshing after a month of unimaginative, monotonous Cockney swearing. The Cockney has one oath, and one oath only, the most indecent in the language, which he uses on any and every occasion. Far different is the luminous and varied Western swearing, which runs to blasphemy rather than indecency. And after all, since men will swear, I think I prefer blasphemy to indecency; there is an audacity about it, an adventurousness and defiance that is better than sheer filthiness.

There was one American tramp royal whom I found particularly enjoyable. I first noticed him on the street, asleep in a doorway, his head on his knees, but a hat on his head that one does not meet this side of the Western Ocean. When the policeman routed him out, he got up slowly and deliberately, looked at the policeman, yawned and stretched himself, looked at the policeman again as much as to say he didn't know whether he would or wouldn't, and then sauntered leisurely down the sidewalk. At the outset I was sure of the hat, but this made me sure of the wearer of the hat.

In the jam inside I found myself alongside of him, and we had quite a chat. He had been through Spain, Italy, Switzerland, and France, and had accomplished the practically impossible feat of beating his way three hundred miles on a French railway without being caught at the finish. Where was I hanging out? he asked. And how did I manage for 'kipping'?—which means sleeping. Did I know the rounds yet? He was getting on, though the country was 'horstyl' and the cities were 'bum.' Fierce, wasn't it? Couldn't 'batter' (beg) anywhere without being 'pinched.' But he wasn't going to quit it. Buffalo Bill's Show was coming over soon, and a man who could drive eight horses was sure of a job any time. These mugs over here didn't know beans about driving anything more than a span. What was the matter with me hanging on and waiting for Buffalo Bill? He was sure I could ring in somehow.

And so, after all, blood is thicker than water. We were fellow-countrymen and strangers in a strange land. I had warmed to his battered old hat at sight of it, and he was as solicitous for my welfare as if we were blood brothers. We swapped all manner of useful information concerning the country and the ways of its people, methods by which to obtain food and shelter and what not, and we parted genuinely sorry at having to say good-bye.

One thing particularly conspicuous in this crowd was the shortness of stature. I, who am but of medium height, looked over the heads of nine out of ten. The natives were all short, as were the foreign sailors. There were only five or six in the crowd who could be called fairly tall, and they were Scandinavians and Americans. The tallest man there, however, was an exception. He was an Englishman, though not a Londoner. 'Candidate for the Life Guards,' I remarked to him. 'You've hit it, mate,' was his reply; 'I've served my bit in that same, and the way things are I'll be back at it before long.'

For an hour we stood quietly in this packed courtyard. Then the men began to grow restless. There was pushing and shoving forward, and a mild hubbub of voices. Nothing rough, however, nor violent; merely the restlessness of weary and hungry men. At this juncture forth came the adjutant. I did not like him. His eyes were not good. There was nothing of the lowly Galilean about him, but a great deal of the centurion who said: 'For I am a man in authority, having soldiers under me; and I say to this man, Go, and he goeth; and to another, Come, and he cometh; and to my servant, Do this, and he doeth it.'

Well, he looked at us in just that way, and those nearest to him quailed. Then he lifted his voice.

'Stop this 'ere, now, or I'll turn you the other wy an' march you out, an' you'll get no breakfast.'

I cannot convey by printed speech the insufferable way in which he said this. He seemed to me to revel in that he was a man in authority, able to say to half a thousand ragged wretches, 'you may eat or go hungry, as I elect.'

To deny us our breakfast after standing for hours! It was an awful threat, and the pitiful, abject silence which instantly fell attested its awfulness. And it was a cowardly threat. We could not strike back, for we were starving; and it is the way of the world that when one man feeds another he is that man's master. But the centurion—I mean the adjutant—was not satisfied. In the dead silence he raised his voice again, and repeated the threat, and amplified it.

At last we were permitted to enter the feasting hall, where we found the 'ticket men' washed but unfed. All told, there must have been nearly seven hundred of us who sat down—not to meat or bread, but to speech, song, and prayer. From all of which I am convinced that Tantalus suffers in many guises this side of the infernal regions. The adjutant made the prayer, but I did not take note of it, being too engrossed with the massed picture of misery before me. But the speech ran something like this: 'You will feast in Paradise. No matter how you starve and suffer here, you will feast in Paradise, that is, if you will follow the directions.' And so forth and so forth. A clever bit of propaganda, I took it, but rendered of no avail for two reasons. First, the men who received it were unimaginative and materialistic, unaware of the existence of any Unseen, and too inured to hell on earth to be frightened by hell to come. And second, weary and exhausted from the night's sleeplessness and hardship, suffering from the long wait upon their feet, and faint from hunger, they were yearning, not for salvation, but for grub. The 'soul-snatchers' (as these men call all religious propagandists), should study the physiological basis of psychology a little, if they wish to make their efforts more effective.

All in good time, about eleven o'clock, breakfast arrived. It arrived, not on plates, but in paper parcels. I did not have all I wanted, and I am sure that no man there had all he wanted, or half of what he wanted or needed. I gave part of my bread to the tramp royal who was waiting for Buffalo Bill, and he was as ravenous at the end as he was in the beginning. This is the breakfast: two slices of bread, one small piece of bread with raisins in it and called 'cake,' a wafer of cheese, and a mug of 'water bewitched.' Numbers of the men had been waiting since five o'clock for it, while all of us had waited at least four hours; and in addition, we had been herded like swine, packed like sardines, and treated like curs, and been preached at, and sung to, and prayed for. Nor was that all.

No sooner was breakfast over (and it was over almost as quickly as it takes to tell), than the tired heads began to nod and droop, and in five minutes half of us were sound asleep. There were no signs of our being dismissed, while there were unmistakable signs of preparation for a meeting. I looked at a small clock hanging on the wall. It indicated twenty-five minutes to twelve. Heigh-ho, thought I, time is flying, and I have yet to look for work.

'I want to go,' I said to a couple of waking men near me.

'Got ter sty fer the service,' was the answer.

'Do you want to stay?' I asked.

They shook their heads.

'Then let us go and tell them we want to get out,' I continued. 'Come on.'

But the poor creatures were aghast. So I left them to their fate, and went up to the nearest Salvation Army man.

'I want to go,' I said. 'I came here for breakfast in order that I might be in shape to look for work. I didn't think it would take so long to get breakfast. I think I have a chance for work in Stepney, and the sooner I start, the better chance I'll have of getting it.'

He was really a good fellow, though he was startled by my request. 'Wy,' he said, 'we're goin' to 'old services, and you'd better sty.'

'But that will spoil my chances for work,' I urged. 'And work is the most important thing for me just now.'

As he was only a private, he referred me to the adjutant, and to the adjutant I repeated my reasons for wishing to go, and politely requested that he let me go.

'But it cawn't be done,' he said, waxing virtuously indignant at such ingratitude. 'The idea!' he snorted. 'The idea!'

'Do you mean to say that I can't get out of here?' I demanded. 'That you will keep me here against my will?'

'Yes,' he snorted.

I do not know what might have happened, for I was waxing indignant myself; but the 'congregation' had 'piped' the situation, and he drew me over to a corner of the room, and then into another room. Here he again demanded my reasons for wishing to go.

'I want to go,' I said, 'because I wish to look for work over in Stepney, and every hour lessens my chance of finding work. It is now twenty-five minutes to twelve. I did not think when I came in that it would take so long to get a breakfast.'

'You 'ave business, eh?' he sneered. 'A man of business you are, eh? Then wot did you come 'ere for?'

'I was out all night, and I needed a breakfast in order to strengthen me to find work. That is why I came here.'

'A nice thing to do,' he went on in the same sneering manner. 'A man with business shouldn't come 'ere. You've tyken some poor man's breakfast 'ere this morning, that's wot you've done.'

Which was a lie, for every mother's son of us had come in.

Now I submit, was this Christian-like, or even honest?—after I had plainly stated that I was homeless and hungry, and that I wished to look for work, for him to call my looking for work 'business,' to call me therefore a business man, and to draw the corollary that a man of business, and well off, did not require a charity breakfast, and that by taking a charity breakfast I had robbed some hungry waif who was not a man of business.

I kept my temper, but I went over the facts again, and clearly and concisely demonstrated to him how unjust he was and how he had perverted the facts. As I manifested no signs of backing down (and I am sure my eyes were beginning to snap), he led me to the rear of the building where, in an open court, stood a tent. In the same sneering tone he informed a couple of privates standing there that 'ere is a fellow that 'as business an' 'e wants to go before services.'

They were duly shocked, of course, and they looked unutterable horror while he went into the tent and brought out the major. Still in the same sneering manner, laying particular stress on the 'business,' he brought my case before the commanding officer. The major was of a different stamp of man. I liked him as soon as I saw him, and to him I stated my case in the same fashion as before.

'Didn't you know you had to stay for services?' he asked.

'Certainly not,' I answered, 'or I should have gone without my breakfast. You have no placards posted to that effect, nor was I so informed when I entered the place.'

He meditated a moment. 'You can go,' he said.

It was twelve o'clock when I gained the street, and I couldn't quite make up my mind whether I had been in the army or in prison. The day was half gone, and it was a far fetch to Stepney. And besides, it was Sunday, and why should even a starving man look for work on Sunday? Furthermore, it was my judgment that I had done a hard night's work walking the streets, and a hard day's work getting my breakfast; so I disconnected myself from my working hypothesis of a starving young man in search of employment, hailed a bus, and climbed aboard.

After a shave and a bath, with my clothes all off, I got in between clean white sheets and went to sleep. It was six in the evening when I closed my eyes. When they opened again, the clocks were striking nine next morning. I had slept fifteen straight hours. And as I lay there drowsily, my mind went back to the seven hundred unfortunates I had left waiting for services. No bath, no shave for them, no clean white sheets and all clothes off, and fifteen hours' straight sleep. Services over, it was the weary streets again, the problem of a crust of bread ere night, and the long sleepless night in the streets, and the pondering of the problem of how to obtain a crust at dawn.

CHAPTER XII
CORONATION DAY

O thou that sea-walls sever
From lands unwalled by seas!
Wilt thou endure forever,
O Milton's England, these?
Thou that wast his Republic,
Wilt thou clasp their knees?
These royalties rust-eaten,
These worm-corroded lies
That keep thy head storm-beaten,
And sun-like strength of eyes
From the open air and heaven
Of intercepted skies!

SWINBURNE

Vivat Rex Eduardus! They crowned a king this day, and there has been great rejoicing and elaborate tomfoolery, and I am perplexed and saddened. I never saw anything to compare with the pageant, except Yankee circuses and Alhambra ballets; nor did I ever see anything so hopeless and so tragic.

To have enjoyed the Coronation procession, I should have come straight from America to the Hotel Cecil, and straight from the Hotel Cecil to a five-guinea seat among the washed. My mistake was in coming from the unwashed of the East End. There were not many who came from that quarter. The East End, as a whole, remained in the East End and got drunk. The Socialists, Democrats, and Republicans went off to the country for a breath of fresh air, quite unaffected by the fact that four hundred millions of people were taking to themselves a crowned and anointed ruler. Six thousand five hundred prelates, priests, statesmen, princes, and warriors beheld the crowning and anointing, and the rest of us the pageant as it passed.

I saw it at Trafalgar Square, 'the most splendid site in Europe,' and the very innermost heart of the empire. There were many thousands of us, all checked and held in order by a superb display of armed power. The line of march was double-walled with soldiers. The base of the Nelson Column was triple-fringed with bluejackets. Eastward, at the entrance to the square, stood the Royal Marine Artillery. In the triangle of Pall Mall and Cockspur Street, the statue of George III. was buttressed on either side by the Lancers and Hussars. To the west were the red-coats of the Royal Marines, and from the Union Club to the embouchure of Whitehall swept the glittering, massive curve of the 1st Life Guards—gigantic men mounted on gigantic chargers, steel-breastplated, steel-helmeted, steel-caparisoned, a great war-sword of steel ready to the hand of the powers that be. And further, throughout the crowd, were flung long lines of the Metropolitan Constabulary, while in the rear were the reserves—tall, well-fed men, with weapons to wield and muscles to wield them in ease of need.

And as it was thus at Trafalgar Square, so was it along the whole line of march—force, overpowering force; myriads of men, splendid men, the pick of the people, whose sole function in life is blindly to obey, and blindly to kill and destroy and stamp out life. And that they should be well fed, well clothed, and well armed, and have ships to hurl them to the ends of the earth, the East End of London, and the 'East End' of all England, toils and rots and dies.

There is a Chinese proverb that if one man lives in laziness another will die of hunger; and Montesquieu has said, 'The fact that many men are occupied in making clothes for one individual is the cause of there being many people without clothes.' So one explains the other. We cannot understand the starved and runty toiler of the East End (living with his family in a one-room den, and letting out the floor space for lodgings to other starved and runty toilers) till we look at the strapping Life Guardsmen of the West End, and come to know that the one must feed and clothe and groom the other.

And while in Westminster Abbey the people were taking unto themselves a king, I, jammed between the Life Guards and Constabulary of Trafalgar Square, was dwelling upon the time when the people of Israel first took unto themselves a king. You all know how it runs. The elders came to the prophet Samuel, and said: 'Make us a king to judge us like all the nations.'

And the Lord said unto Samuel: Now therefore hearken unto their voice; howbeit thou shalt show them the manner of the king that shall reign over them.

And Samuel told all the words of the Lord unto the people that asked of him a king, and he said:

This will be the manner of the king that shall reign over you; he will take your sons, and appoint them unto him, for his chariots, and to be his horsemen, and they shall run before his chariots.

And he will appoint them unto him for captains of thousands, and captains of fifties; and he will set some to plough his ground, and to reap his harvest, and to make his instruments of war, and the instruments of his chariots.

And he will take your daughters to be confectionaries, and to be cooks, and to be bakers.

And he will take your fields and your vineyards, and your oliveyards, even the best of them, and give them to his servants.

And he will take a tenth of your seed, and of your vineyards, and give to his officers, and to his servants.

And he will take your menservants, and your maidservants, and your goodliest young men, and your asses, and put them to his work.

He will take a tenth of your flocks; and ye shall be his servants.

And ye shall call out in that day because of your king which ye shall have chosen you; and the Lord will not answer you in that day.

All of which came to pass in that ancient day, and they did cry out to Samuel, saying: 'Pray for thy servants unto the Lord thy God, that we die not; for we have added unto all our sins this evil, to ask us a king.' And after Saul, David, and Solomon, came Rehoboam, who 'answered the people roughly, saying: My father made your yoke heavy, but I will add to your yoke; my father chastised you with whips, but I will chastise you with scorpions.'

And in these latter days, five hundred hereditary peers own one-fifth of England; and they, and the officers and servants under the King, and those who go to compose the powers that be, yearly spend in wasteful luxury $1,850,000,000, or £370,000,000, which is thirty-two per cent. of the total wealth produced by all the toilers of the country.

At the Abbey, clad in wonderful golden raiment, amid fanfare of trumpets and throbbing of music, surrounded by a brilliant throng of masters, lords, and rulers, the King was being invested with the insignia of his sovereignty. The spurs were placed to his heels by the Lord Great Chamberlain, and a sword of state, in purple scabbard, was presented him by the Archbishop of Canterbury, with these words:-

> Receive this kingly sword brought now from the altar of God, and delivered to you by the hands of the bishops and servants of God, though unworthy.

Whereupon, being girded, he gave heed to the Archbishop's exhortation:-

> With this sword do justice, stop the growth of iniquity, protect the Holy Church of God, help and defend widows and orphans, restore the things that are gone to decay, maintain the things that are restored, punish and reform what is amiss, and confirm what is in good order.

But hark! There is cheering down Whitehall; the crowd sways, the double walls of soldiers come to attention, and into view swing the King's watermen, in fantastic mediaeval garbs of red, for all the world like the van of a circus parade. Then a royal carriage, filled with ladies and gentlemen of the household, with powdered footmen and coachmen most gorgeously arrayed. More carriages, lords, and chamberlains, viscounts, mistresses of the robes—lackeys all. Then the warriors, a kingly escort, generals, bronzed and worn, from the ends of the earth come up to London Town, volunteer officers, officers of the militia and regular forces; Spens and Plumer, Broadwood and Cooper who relieved Ookiep, Mathias of Dargai, Dixon of Vlakfontein; General Gaselee and Admiral Seymour of China; Kitchener of Khartoum; Lord Roberts of India and all the world—the fighting men of England, masters of destruction, engineers of death! Another race of men from those of the shops and slums, a totally different race of men.

But here they come, in all the pomp and certitude of power, and still they come, these men of steel, these war lords and world harnessers. Pell-mell, peers and commoners, princes and maharajahs, Equerries to the King and Yeomen of the Guard. And here the colonials, lithe and hardy men; and here all the breeds of all the world-soldiers from Canada, Australia, New Zealand; from Bermuda, Borneo, Fiji, and the Gold Coast; from Rhodesia, Cape Colony, Natal, Sierra Leone and Gambia, Nigeria, and Uganda; from Ceylon, Cyprus, Hong-Kong, Jamaica, and Wei-Hai-Wei; from Lagos, Malta, St. Lucia, Singapore, Trinidad. And here the conquered men of Ind, swarthy horsemen and sword wielders, fiercely barbaric, blazing in crimson and scarlet, Sikhs, Rajputs, Burmese, province by province, and caste by caste.

And now the Horse Guards, a glimpse of beautiful cream ponies, and a golden panoply, a hurricane of cheers, the crashing of bands—'The King! the King! God save the King!' Everybody has gone mad. The contagion is sweeping me off my feet—I, too, want to shout, 'The King! God save the King!' Ragged men about me, tears in their eyes, are tossing up their hats and crying ecstatically, 'Bless 'em! Bless 'em! Bless 'em!' See, there he is, in that wondrous golden coach, the great crown flashing on his head, the woman in white beside him likewise crowned.

And I check myself with a rush, striving to convince myself that it is all real and rational, and not some glimpse of fairyland. This I cannot succeed in doing, and it is better so. I much prefer to believe that all this pomp, and vanity, and show, and mumbo-jumbo foolery has come from fairyland, than to believe it the performance of sane and sensible people who have mastered matter and solved the secrets of the stars.

Princes and princelings, dukes, duchesses, and all manner of coroneted folk of the royal train are flashing past; more warriors, and lackeys, and conquered peoples, and the pagent is over. I drift with the crowd out of the square into a tangle of narrow streets, where the public-houses are a-roar with drunkenness, men, women, and children mixed together in colossal debauch. And on every side is rising the favourite song of the Coronation:-

'Oh! on Coronation Day, on Coronation Day,
We'll have a spree, a jubilee, and shout, Hip, hip, hooray,
For we'll all be marry, drinking whisky, wine, and sherry,
We'll all be merry on Coronation Day.'

The rain is pouring down. Up the street come troops of the auxiliaries, black Africans and yellow Asiatics, beturbaned and befezed, and coolies swinging along with machine guns and mountain batteries on their heads, and the bare feet of all, in quick rhythm, going *slish, slish, slish* through the pavement mud. The public-houses empty by magic, and the swarthy allegiants are cheered by their British brothers, who return at once to the carouse.

'And how did you like the procession, mate?' I asked an old man on a bench in Green Park.

'Ow did I like it? A bloomin' good chawnce, sez I to myself, for a sleep, wi' all the coppers aw'y, so I turned into the corner there, along wi' fifty others. But I couldn't sleep, a-lyin' there an' thinkin' 'ow I'd worked all the years o' my life an' now 'ad no plyce to rest my 'ead; an' the music comin' to me, an' the cheers an' cannon, till I got almost a hanarchist an' wanted to blow out the brains o' the Lord Chamberlain.'

Why the Lord Chamberlain I could not precisely see, nor could he, but that was the way he felt, he said conclusively, and them was no more discussion.

As night drew on, the city became a blaze of light. Splashes of colour, green, amber, and ruby, caught the eye at every point, and 'E. R.,' in great crystal letters and backed by flaming gas, was everywhere. The crowds in the streets increased by hundreds of thousands, and though the police sternly put down mafficking, drunkenness and rough play abounded. The tired workers seemed to have gone mad with the relaxation and excitement, and they surged and danced down the streets, men and women, old and young, with linked arms and in long rows, singing, 'I may be crazy, but I love you,' 'Dolly Gray,' and 'The Honeysuckle and the Bee'—the last rendered something like this:-

'Yew aw the enny, ennyseckle, Oi em ther bee,
Oi'd like ter sip ther enny from those red lips, yew see.'

I sat on a bench on the Thames Embankment, looking across the illuminated water. It was approaching midnight, and before me poured the better class of merrymakers, shunning the more riotous streets and returning home. On the bench beside me sat two ragged creatures, a man and a woman, nodding and dozing. The woman sat with her arms clasped across the breast, holding tightly, her body in constant play—now dropping forward till it seemed its balance would be overcome and she would fall to the pavement; now inclining to the left, sideways, till her head rested on the man's shoulder; and now to the right, stretched and strained, till the pain of it awoke her and she sat bolt upright. Whereupon the dropping forward would begin again and go through its cycle till she was aroused by the strain and stretch.

Every little while boys and young men stopped long enough to go behind the bench and give vent to sudden and fiendish shouts. This always jerked the man and woman abruptly from their sleep; and at sight of the startled woe upon their faces the crowd would roar with laughter as it flooded past.

This was the most striking thing, the general heartlessness exhibited on every hand. It is a commonplace, the homeless on the benches, the poor miserable folk who may be teased and are harmless. Fifty thousand people must have passed the bench while I sat upon it, and not one, on such a jubilee occasion as the crowning of the King, felt his heart-strings touched sufficiently to come up and say to the woman: 'Here's sixpence; go and get a bed.' But the women, especially the young women, made witty remarks upon the woman nodding, and invariably set their companions laughing.

To use a Briticism, it was 'cruel'; the corresponding Americanism was more appropriate—it was 'fierce.' I confess I began to grow incensed at this happy crowd streaming by, and to extract a sort of satisfaction from the London statistics which demonstrate that one in every four adults is destined to die on public charity, either in the workhouse, the infirmary, or the asylum.

I talked with the man. He was fifty-four and a broken-down docker. He could only find odd work when there was a large demand for labour, for the younger and stronger men were preferred when times were slack. He had spent a week, now, on the benches of the Embankment; but things looked brighter for next week, and he might possibly get in a few days' work and have a bed in some doss-house. He had lived all his life in London, save for five years, when, in 1878, he saw foreign service in India.

Of course he would eat; so would the girl. Days like this were uncommon hard on such as they, though the coppers were so busy poor folk could get in more sleep. I awoke the girl, or woman, rather, for she was 'Eyght an' twenty, sir,' and we started for a coffee-house.

'Wot a lot o' work puttin' up the lights,' said the man at sight of some building superbly illuminated. This was the keynote of his being. All his life he had worked, and the whole objective universe, as well as his own soul, he could express in terms only of work. 'Coronations is some good,' he went on. 'They give work to men.'

'But your belly is empty,' I said.

'Yes,' he answered. 'I tried, but there wasn't any chawnce. My age is against me. Wot do you work at? Seafarin' chap, eh? I knew it from yer clothes.'

'I know wot you are,' said the girl, 'an Eyetalian.'

'No 'e ayn't,' the man cried heatedly. ''E's a Yank, that's wot 'e is. I know.'

'Lord lumne, look a' that,' she exclaimed, as we debauched upon the Strand, choked with the roaring, reeling Coronation crowd, the men bellowing and the girls singing in high throaty notes:-

> 'Oh! on Coronation D'y, on Coronation D'y,
> We'll 'ave a spree, a jubilee, an' shout 'Ip, 'ip, 'ooray;

> For we'll all be merry, drinkin' whisky, wine, and sherry,
> We'll all be merry on Coronation D'y.'

'Ow dirty I am, bein' around the w'y I 'ave,' the woman said, as she sat down in a coffee-house, wiping the sleep and grime from the corners of her eyes. 'An' the sights I 'ave seen this d'y, an' I enjoyed it, though it was lonesome by myself. An' the duchesses an' the lydies 'ad sich gran' w'ite dresses. They was jest bu'ful, bu'ful.'

'I'm Irish,' she said, in answer to a question. 'My nyme's Eyethorne.'

'What?' I asked.

'Eyethorne, sir; Eyethorne.'

'Spell it.'

'H-a-y-t-h-o-r-n-e, Eyethorne.'

'Oh,' I said, 'Irish Cockney.'

'Yes, sir, London-born.'

She had lived happily at home till her father died, killed in an accident, when she had found herself on the world. One brother was in the army, and the other brother, engaged in keeping a wife and eight children on twenty shillings a week and unsteady employment, could do nothing for her. She had been out of London once in her life, to a place in Essex, twelve miles away, where she had picked fruit for three weeks: 'An' I was as brown as a berry w'en I come back. You won't b'lieve it, but I was.'

The last place in which she had worked was a coffee-house, hours from seven in the morning till eleven at night, and for which she had received five shillings a week and her food. Then she had fallen sick, and since emerging from the hospital had been unable to find anything to do. She wasn't feeling up to much, and the last two nights had been spent in the street.

Between them they stowed away a prodigious amount of food, this man and woman, and it was not till I had duplicated and triplicated their original orders that they showed signs of easing down.

Once she reached across and felt the texture of my coat and shirt, and remarked upon the good clothes the Yanks wore. My rags good clothes! It put me to the blush; but, on inspecting them more closely and on examining the clothes worn by the man and woman, I began to feel quite well dressed and respectable.

'What do you expect to do in the end?' I asked them. 'You know you're growing older every day.'

'Work'ouse,' said he.

'Gawd blimey if I do,' said she. 'There's no 'ope for me, I know, but I'll die on the streets. No work'ouse for me, thank you. No, indeed,' she sniffed in the silence that fell.

'After you have been out all night in the streets,' I asked, 'what do you do in the morning for something to eat?'

'Try to get a penny, if you 'aven't one saved over,' the man explained. 'Then go to a coffee-'ouse an' get a mug o' tea.'

'But I don't see how that is to feed you,' I objected.

The pair smiled knowingly.

'You drink your tea in little sips,' he went on, 'making it last its longest. An' you look sharp, an' there's some as leaves a bit be'ind 'em.'

'It's s'prisin', the food wot some people leaves,' the woman broke in.

'The thing,' said the man judicially, as the trick dawned upon me, 'is to get 'old o' the penny.'

As we started to leave, Miss Haythorne gathered up a couple of crusts from the neighbouring tables and thrust them somewhere into her rags.

'Cawn't wyste 'em, you know,' said she; to which the docker nodded, tucking away a couple of crusts himself.

At three in the morning I strolled up the Embankment. It was a gala night for the homeless, for the police were elsewhere; and each bench was jammed with sleeping occupants. There were as many women as men, and the great majority of them, male and female, were old. Occasionally a boy was to be seen. On one bench I noticed a family, a man sitting upright with a sleeping babe in his arms, his wife asleep, her head on his shoulder, and in her lap the head of a sleeping youngster. The man's eyes were wide open. He was staring out over the water and thinking, which is not a good thing for a shelterless man with a family to do. It would not be a pleasant thing to speculate upon his thoughts; but this I know, and all London knows, that the cases of out-of-works killing their wives and babies is not an uncommon happening.

One cannot walk along the Thames Embankment, in the small hours of morning, from the Houses of Parliament, past Cleopatra's Needle, to Waterloo Bridge, without being reminded of the sufferings, seven and twenty centuries old, recited by the author of 'Job':-

> There are that remove the landmarks; they violently take away flocks
> and feed them.
> They drive away the ass of the fatherless, they take the widow's ox for a
> pledge.
> They turn the needy out of the way; the poor of the earth hide
> themselves together.
> Behold, as wild asses in the desert they go forth to their work, seeking
> diligently for meat; the wilderness yieldeth them food for their
> children.
> They cut their provender in the field, and they glean the vintage of the
> wicked.
> They lie all night naked without clothing, and have no covering in the
> cold.
> They are wet with the showers of the mountains, and embrace the rock
> for want of a shelter.
> There are that pluck the fatherless from the breast, and take a pledge
> of the poor.
> So that they go about naked without clothing, and being an hungered
> they carry the sheaves.—Job xxiv. 2-10.

Seven and twenty centuries agone! And it is all as true and apposite to-day in the innermost centre of this Christian civilisation whereof Edward VII. is king.

CHAPTER XIII
DAN CULLEN, DOCKER

Life scarce can tread majestically
Foul court and fever-stricken alley.

THOMAS ASHE

I stood, yesterday, in a room in one of the 'Municipal Dwellings,' not far from Leman Street. If I looked into a dreary future and saw that I would have to live in such a room until I died, I should immediately go down, plump into the Thames, and cut the tenancy short.

It was not a room. Courtesy to the language will no more permit it to be called a room than it will permit a hovel to be called a mansion. It was a den, a lair. Seven feet by eight were its dimensions, and the ceiling was so low as not to give the cubic air space required by a British soldier in barracks. A crazy couch, with ragged coverlets, occupied nearly half the room. A rickety table, a chair, and a couple of boxes left little space in which to turn around. Five dollars would have purchased everything in sight. The floor was bare, while the walls and ceiling were literally covered with blood marks and splotches. Each mark represented a violent death—of an insect, for the place swarmed with vermin, a plague with which no person could cope single-handed.

The man who had occupied this hole, one Dan Cullen, docker, was dying in hospital. Yet he had impressed his personality on his miserable surroundings sufficiently to give an inkling as to what sort of man he was. On the walls were cheap pictures of Garibaldi, Engels, Dan Burns, and other labour leaders, while on the table lay one of Walter Besant's novels. He knew his Shakespeare, I was told, and had read history, sociology, and economics. And he was self-educated.

On the table, amidst a wonderful disarray, lay a sheet of paper on which was scrawled: *Mr. Cullen, please return the large white jug and corkscrew I lent you*—articles loaned, during the first stages of his sickness, by a woman neighbour, and demanded back in anticipation of his death. A large white jug and a corkscrew are far too valuable to a creature of the Abyss to permit another creature to die in peace. To the last, Dan Cullen's soul must be harrowed by the sordidness out of which it strove vainly to rise.

It is a brief little story, the story of Dan Cullen, but there is much to read between the lines. He was born lowly, in a city and land where the lines of caste are tightly drawn. All his days he toiled hard with his body; and because he had opened the books, and been caught up by the fires of the spirit, and could 'write a letter like a lawyer,' he had been selected by his fellows to toil hard for them with his brain. He became a leader of the fruit-porters, represented the dockers on the London Trades Council, and wrote trenchant articles for the labour journals.

He did not cringe to other men, even though they were his economic masters, and controlled the means whereby he lived, and he spoke his mind freely, and fought the good fight. In the 'Great Dock Strike' he was guilty of taking a leading part. And that was the end of Dan Cullen. From that day he was a marked man, and every day, for ten years and more, he was 'paid off' for what he had done.

A docker is a casual labourer. Work ebbs and flows, and he works or does not work according to the amount of goods on hand to be moved. Dan Cullen was discriminated against. While he was not absolutely turned away (which would have caused trouble, and which would certainly have been more merciful), he was called in by the foreman to do not more than two or three days' work per week. This is what is called being 'disciplined,' or 'drilled.' It means being starved. There is no politer word. Ten years of it broke his heart, and broken-hearted men cannot live.

He took to his bed in his terrible den, which grew more terrible with his helplessness. He was without kith or kin, a lonely old man, embittered and pessimistic, fighting vermin the while and looking at Garibaldi, Engels, and Dan Burns gazing down at him from the blood-bespattered walls. No one came to see him in that crowded municipal barracks (he had made friends with none of them), and he was left to rot.

But from the far reaches of the East End came a cobbler and his son, his sole friends. They cleansed his room, brought fresh linen from home, and took from off his limbs the sheets, greyish-black with dirt. And they brought to him one of the Queen's Bounty nurses from Aldgate.

She washed his face, shook up his conch, and talked with him. It was interesting to talk with him—until he learned her name. Oh, yes, Blank was her name, she replied innocently, and Sir George Blank was her brother. Sir George Blank, eh? thundered old Dan Cullen on his death-bed; Sir George Blank, solicitor to the docks at Cardiff, who, more than any other man, had broken up the Dockers' Union of Cardiff, and was knighted? And she was his sister? Thereupon Dan Cullen sat up on his crazy couch and pronounced anathema upon her and all her breed; and she fled, to return no more, strongly impressed with the ungratefulness of the poor.

Dan Cullen's feet became swollen with dropsy. He sat up all day on the side of the bed (to keep the water out of his body), no mat on the floor, a thin blanket on his legs, and an old coat around his shoulders. A missionary brought him a pair of paper slippers, worth fourpence (I saw them), and proceeded to offer up fifty prayers or so for the good of Dan Cullen's soul. But Dan Cullen was the sort of man that wanted his soul left alone. He did not care to have Tom, Dick, or Harry, on the strength of fourpenny slippers, tampering with it. He asked the missionary kindly to open the window, so that he might toss the slippers out. And the missionary went away, to return no more, likewise impressed with the ungratefulness of the poor.

The cobbler, a brave old hero himself, though unaneled and unsung, went privily to the head office of the big fruit brokers for whom Dan Cullen had worked as a casual labourer for thirty years. Their system was such that the work was almost entirely done by casual hands. The cobbler told them the man's desperate plight, old, broken, dying, without help or money, reminded them that he had worked for them thirty years, and asked them to do something for him.

'Oh,' said the manager, remembering Dan Cullen without having to refer to the books, 'you see, we make it a rule never to help casuals, and we can do nothing.'

Nor did they do anything, not even sign a letter asking for Dan Cullen's admission to a hospital. And it is not so easy to get into a hospital in London Town. At Hampstead, if he passed the doctors, at least four months would elapse before he could get in, there were so many on the books ahead of him. The cobbler finally got him into the Whitechapel Infirmary, where he visited him frequently. Here he found that Dan Cullen had succumbed to the prevalent feeling, that, being hopeless, they were hurrying him out of the way. A fair and logical conclusion, one must agree, for an old and broken man to arrive at, who has been resolutely 'disciplined' and 'drilled' for ten years. When they sweated him for Bright's disease to remove the fat from the kidneys, Dan Cullen contended that the sweating was hastening his death; while Bright's disease, being a wasting away of the kidneys, there was therefore no fat to remove, and the doctor's excuse was a palpable lie. Whereupon the doctor became wroth, and did not come near him for nine days.

Then his bed was tilted up so that his feet and legs were elevated. At once dropsy appeared in the body, and Dan Cullen contended that the thing was done in order to run the water down into his body from his legs and kill him more quickly. He demanded his discharge, though they told him he would die on the stairs, and dragged himself, more dead than alive, to the cobbler's shop. At the moment of writing this, he is dying at the Temperance Hospital, into which place his staunch friend, the cobbler, moved heaven and earth to have him admitted.

Poor Dan Cullen! A Jude the Obscure, who reached out after knowledge; who toiled with his body in the day and studied in the watches of the night; who dreamed his dream and struck valiantly for the Cause; a patriot, a lover of human freedom, and a fighter unafraid; and in the end, not gigantic enough to beat down the conditions which baffled and stifled him, a cynic and a pessimist, gasping his final agony on a pauper's couch in a charity ward,—'For a man to die who might have been wise and was not, this I call a tragedy.'

CHAPTER XIV
HOPS AND HOPPERS

Ill fares the land, to hastening ills a prey,
Where wealth accumulates and men decay:
Princes and lords may flourish, or may fade,
A breath can make them, as a breath is made;
But a bold peasantry, their country's pride,
When once destroyed, can never be supplied.

GOLDSMITH

So far has the divorcement of the worker from the soil proceeded, that the farming districts, the civilised world over, are dependent upon the cities for the gathering of the harvests. Then it is, when the land is spilling its ripe wealth to waste, that the street folk, who have been driven away from the soil, are called back to it again. But in England they return, not as prodigals, but as outcasts still, as vagrants and pariahs, to be doubted and flouted by their country brethren, to sleep in jails and casual wards, or under the hedges, and to live the Lord knows how.

It is estimated that Kent alone requires eighty thousand of the street people to pick her hops. And out they come, obedient to the call, which is the call of their bellies and of the lingering dregs of adventure-lust still in them. Slum, stews, and ghetto pour them forth, and the festering contents of slum, stews, and ghetto are undiminished. Yet they overrun the country like an army of ghouls, and the country does not want them. They are out of place. As they drag their squat, misshapen bodies along the highways and byways, they resemble some vile spawn from underground.

Their very presence, the fact of their existence, is an outrage to the fresh, bright sun and the green and growing things. The clean, upstanding trees cry shame upon them and their withered crookedness, and their rottenness is a slimy desecration of the sweetness and purity of nature.

Is the picture overdrawn? It all depends. For one who sees and thinks life in terms of shares and coupons, it is certainly overdrawn. But for one who sees and thinks life in terms of manhood and womanhood, it cannot be overdrawn. Such hordes of beastly wretchedness and inarticulate misery are no compensation for a millionaire brewer who lives in a West End palace, sates himself with the sensuous delights of London's golden theatres, hobnobs with lordlings and princelings, and is knighted by the king. Wins his spurs—God forbid! In old time the great blonde beasts rode in the battle's van and won their spurs by cleaving men from pate to chine. And, after all, it is finer to kill a strong man with a clean-slicing blow of singing steel than to make a beast of him, and of his seed through the generations, by the artful and spidery manipulation of industry and politics.

But to return to the hops. Here the divorcement from the soil is as apparent as in every other agricultural line in England. While the manufacture of beer steadily increases, the growth of hops steadily decreases. In 1835 the acreage under hops was 71,327. To-day it stands at 48,024, a decrease of 3103 from the acreage of last year.

Small as the acreage is this year, a poor summer and terrible storms reduced the yield. This misfortune is divided between the people who own hops and the people who pick hops. The owners perforce must put up with less of the nicer things of life, the pickers with less grub, of which, in the best of times, they never get enough. For weary weeks headlines like the following have appeared in the London papers.-

TRAMPS PLENTIFUL, BUT THE HOPS ARE FEW AND NOT YET READY.

Then there have been numberless paragraphs like this:-

From the neighbourhood of the hop fields comes news of a distressing nature. The bright outburst of the last two days has sent many hundreds of hoppers into Kent, who will have to wait till the fields are ready for them. At Dover the number of vagrants in the workhouse is treble the number there last year at this time, and in other towns the lateness of the season is responsible for a large increase in the number of casuals.

To cap their wretchedness, when at last the picking had begun, hops and hoppers were well-nigh swept away by a frightful storm of wind, rain, and hail. The hops were stripped clean from the poles and pounded into the earth, while the hoppers, seeking shelter from the stinging hail, were close to drowning in their huts and camps on the low-lying ground. Their condition after the storm was pitiable, their state of vagrancy more pronounced than ever; for, poor crop that it was, its destruction had taken away the chance of earning a few pennies, and nothing remained for thousands of them but to 'pad the hoof' back to London.

'We ayn't crossin'-sweepers,' they said, turning away from the ground, carpeted ankle-deep with hops.

Those that remained grumbled savagely among the half-stripped poles at the seven bushels for a shilling—a rate paid in good seasons when the hops are in prime condition, and a rate likewise paid in bad seasons by the growers because they cannot afford more.

I passed through Teston and East and West Farleigh shortly after the storm, and listened to the grumbling of the hoppers and saw the hops rotting on the ground. At the hothouses of Barham Court, thirty thousand panes of glass had been broken by the hail, while peaches, plums, pears, apples, rhubarb, cabbages, mangolds, everything, had been pounded to pieces and torn to shreds.

All of which was too bad for the owners, certainly; but at the worst, not one of them, for one meal, would have to go short of food or drink. Yet it was to them that the newspapers devoted columns of sympathy, their pecuniary losses being detailed at harrowing length. 'Mr. Herbert L— calculates his loss at £8000;' 'Mr. F—, of brewery fame, who rents all the land in this parish, loses £10,000;' and 'Mr. L—, the Wateringbury brewer, brother to Mr. Herbert L—, is another heavy loser.' As for the hoppers, they did not count. Yet I venture to assert that the several almost-square meals lost by underfed William Buggles, and underfed Mrs. Buggles, and the underfed Buggles kiddies, was a greater tragedy than the £10,000 lost by Mr. F—. And in addition, underfed William Buggles' tragedy might be multiplied by thousands where Mr. F—'s could not be multiplied by five.

To see how William Buggles and his kind fared, I donned my seafaring togs and started out to get a job. With me was a young East London cobbler, Bert, who had yielded to the lure of adventure and joined me for the trip. Acting on my advice, he had brought his 'worst rags,' and as we hiked up the London road out of Maidstone he was worrying greatly for fear we had come too ill-dressed for the business.

Nor was he to be blamed. When we stopped in a tavern the publican eyed us gingerly, nor did his demeanour brighten till we showed him the colour of our cash. The natives along the coast were all dubious; and 'bean-feasters' from London, dashing past in coaches, cheered and jeered and shouted insulting things after us. But before we were done with the Maidstone district my friend found that we were as well clad, if not better, than the average hopper. Some of the bunches of rags we chanced upon were marvellous.

'The tide is out,' called a gypsy-looking woman to her mates, as we came up a long row of bins into which the pickers were stripping the hops.

'Do you twig?' Bert whispered. 'She's on to you.'

I twigged. And it must be confessed the figure was an apt one. When the tide is out boats are left on the beach and do not sail, and a sailor, when the tide is out, does not sail either. My seafaring togs and my presence in the hop field proclaimed that I was a seaman without a ship, a man on the beach, and very like a craft at low water.

'Can yer give us a job, governor?' Bert asked the bailiff, a kindly faced and elderly man who was very busy.

His 'No' was decisively uttered; but Bert clung on and followed him about, and I followed after, pretty well all over the field. Whether our persistency struck the bailiff as anxiety to work, or whether he was affected by our hard-luck appearance and tale, neither Bert nor I succeeded in making out; but in the end he softened his heart and found us the one unoccupied bin in the place—a bin deserted by two other men, from what I could learn, because of inability to make living wages.

'No bad conduct, mind ye,' warned the bailiff, as he left us at work in the midst of the women.

It was Saturday afternoon, and we knew quitting time would come early; so we applied ourselves earnestly to the task, desiring to learn if we could at least make our salt. It was simple work, woman's work, in fact, and not man's. We sat on the edge of the bin, between the standing hops, while a pole-puller supplied us with great fragrant branches. In an hour's time we became as expert as it is possible to become. As soon as the fingers became accustomed automatically to differentiate between hops and leaves and to strip half-a-dozen blossoms at a time there was no more to learn.

We worked nimbly, and as fast as the women themselves, though their bins filled more rapidly because of their swarming children, each of which picked with two hands almost as fast as we picked.

'Don'tcher pick too clean, it's against the rules,' one of the women informed us; and we took the tip and were grateful.

As the afternoon wore along, we realised that living wages could not be made—by men. Women could pick as much as men, and children could do almost as well as women; so it was impossible for a man to compete with a woman and half-a-dozen children. For it is the woman and the half-dozen children who count as a unit, and by their combined capacity determine the unit's pay.

'I say, matey, I'm beastly hungry,' said I to Bert. We had not had any dinner.

'Blimey, but I could eat the 'ops,' he replied.

Whereupon we both lamented our negligence in not rearing up a numerous progeny to help us in this day of need. And in such fashion we whiled away the time and talked for the edification of our neighbours. We quite won the sympathy of the pole-puller, a young country yokel, who now and again emptied a few picked blossoms into our bin, it being part of his business to gather up the stray clusters torn off in the process of pulling.

With him we discussed how much we could 'sub,' and were informed that while we were being paid a shilling for seven bushels, we could only 'sub,' or have advanced to us, a shilling for every twelve bushels. Which is to say that the pay for five out of every twelve bushels was withheld—a method of the grower to hold the hopper to his work whether the crop runs good or bad, and especially if it runs bad.

After all, it was pleasant sitting there in the bright sunshine, the golden pollen showering from our hands, the pungent aromatic odour of the hops biting our nostrils, and the while remembering dimly the sounding cities whence these people came. Poor street people! Poor gutter folk! Even they grow earth-hungry, and yearn vaguely for the soil from which they have been driven, and for the free life in the open, and the wind and rain and sun all undefiled by city smirches. As the sea calls to the sailor, so calls the land to them; and, deep down in their aborted and decaying carcasses, they are stirred strangely by the peasant memories of their forbears who lived before cities were. And in incomprehensible ways they are made glad by the earth smells and sights and sounds which their blood has not forgotten though unremembered by them.

'No more 'ops, matey,' Bert complained.

It was five o'clock, and the pole-pullers had knocked off, so that everything could be cleaned up, there being no work on Sunday. For an hour we were forced idly to wait the coming of the measurers, our feet tingling with the frost which came on the heels of the setting sun. In the adjoining bin, two women and half-a-dozen children had picked nine bushels: so that the five bushels the measurers found in our bin demonstrated that we had done equally well, for the half-dozen children had ranged from nine to fourteen years of age.

Five bushels! We worked it out to eight-pence ha'penny, or seventeen cents, for two men working three hours and a half. Fourpence farthing apiece! a little over a penny an hour! But we were allowed only to 'sub' fivepence of the total sum, though the tally-keeper, short of change, gave us sixpence. Entreaty was in vain. A hard-luck story could not move him. He proclaimed loudly that we had received a penny more than our due, and went his way.

Granting, for the sake of the argument, that we were what we represented ourselves to be—namely, poor men and broke—then here was out position: night was coming on; we had had no supper, much less dinner; and we possessed sixpence between us. I was hungry enough to eat three sixpenn'orths of food, and so was Bert. One thing was patent. By doing 16.3 per cent. justice to our stomachs, we would expend the sixpence, and our stomachs would still be gnawing under 83.3 per cent. injustice. Being broke again, we could sleep under a hedge, which was not so bad, though the cold would sap an undue portion of what we had eaten. But the morrow was Sunday, on which we could do no work, though our silly stomachs would not knock off on that account. Here, then, was the problem: how to get three meals on Sunday, and two on Monday (for we could not make another 'sub' till Monday evening).

We knew that the casual wards were overcrowded; also, that if we begged from farmer or villager, there was a large likelihood of our going to jail for fourteen days. What was to be done? We looked at each other in despair—

—Not a bit of it. We joyfully thanked God that we were not as other men, especially hoppers, and went down the road to Maidstone, jingling in our pockets the half-crowns and florins we had brought from London.

CHAPTER XV
THE SEA WIFE

*These stupid peasants, who, throughout the world, hold potentates on
their thrones, make statesmen illustrious, provide generals with lasting
victories, all with ignorance, indifference, or half-witted hatred, moving
the world with the strength of their arms, and getting their heads
knocked together in the name of God, the king, or the stock exchange
– immortal, dreaming, hopeless asses, who surrender their reason to the
care of a shining puppet, and persuade some toy to carry their lives in
his purse.*

STEPHEN CRANE

You might not expect to find the Sea Wife in the heart of Kent, but that is where I
found her, in a mean street, in the poor quarter of Maidstone. In her window she
had no sign of lodgings to let, and persuasion was necessary before she could bring
herself to let me sleep in her front room. In the evening I descended to the semi-subterranean kitchen, and talked with her and her old man, Thomas Mugridge by name.

And as I talked to them, all the subtleties and complexities of this tremendous
machine civilisation vanished away. It seemed that I went down through the skin
and the flesh to the naked soul of it, and in Thomas Mugridge and his old woman
gripped hold of the essence of this remarkable English breed. I found there the spirit
of the wanderlust which has lured Albion's sons across the zones; and I found there
the colossal unreckoning which has tricked the English into foolish squabblings
and preposterous fights, and the doggedness and stubbornness which have brought
them blindly through to empire and greatness; and likewise I found that vast, incomprehensible patience which has enabled the home population to endure under the
burden of it all, to toil without complaint through the weary years, and docilely to
yield the best of its sons to fight and colonise to the ends of the earth.

Thomas Mugridge was seventy-one years old and a little man. It was because he
was little that he had not gone for a soldier. He had remained at home and worked.
His first recollections were connected with work. He knew nothing else but work. He
had worked all his days, and at seventy-one he still worked. Each morning saw him up
with the lark and afield, a day labourer, for as such he had been born. Mrs. Mugridge
was seventy-three. From seven years of age she had worked in the fields, doing a boy's
work at first, and later a man's. She still worked, keeping the house shining, washing,
boiling, and baking, and, with my advent, cooking for me and shaming me by making
my bed. At the end of threescore years and more of work they possessed nothing, had
nothing to look forward to save more work. And they were contented. They expected
nothing else, desired nothing else.

They lived simply. Their wants were few—a pint of beer at the end of the day,
sipped in the semi-subterranean kitchen, a weekly paper to pore over for seven
nights hand-running, and conversation as meditative and vacant as the chewing of a
heifer's cud. From a wood engraving on the wall a slender, angelic girl looked down
upon them, and underneath was the legend: 'Our Future Queen.' And from a highly
coloured lithograph alongside looked down a stout and elderly lady, with underneath:

'Our Queen—Diamond Jubilee.'

'What you earn is sweetest,' quoth Mrs. Mugridge, when I suggested that it was about time they took a rest.

'No, an' we don't want help,' said Thomas Mugridge, in reply to my question as to whether the children lent them a hand.

'We'll work till we dry up and blow away, mother an' me,' he added; and Mrs. Mugridge nodded her head in vigorous indorsement.

Fifteen children she had borne, and all were away and gone, or dead. The 'baby,' however, lived in Maidstone, and she was twenty-seven. When the children married they had their hands full with their own families and troubles, like their fathers and mothers before them.

Where were the children? Ah, where were they not? Lizzie was in Australia; Mary was in Buenos Ayres; Poll was in New York; Joe had died in India—and so they called them up, the living and the dead, soldier and sailor, and colonist's wife, for the traveller's sake who sat in their kitchen.

They passed me a photograph. A trim young fellow, in soldier's garb looked out at me. 'And which son is this?' I asked.

They laughed a hearty chorus. Son! Nay, grandson, just back from Indian service and a soldier-trumpeter to the King. His brother was in the same regiment with him. And so it ran, sons and daughters, and grand sons and daughters, world-wanderers and empire-builders, all of them, while the old folks stayed at home and worked at building empire too.

> 'There dwells a wife by the Northern Gate,
>   And a wealthy wife is she;
> She breeds a breed o' rovin' men
>   And casts them over sea.
> 'And some are drowned in deep water,
>   And some in sight of shore;
> And word goes back to the weary wife,
>   And ever she sends more.'

But the Sea Wife's child-bearing is about done. The stock is running out, and the planet is filling up. The wives of her sons may carry on the breed, but her work is past. The erstwhile men of England are now the men of Australia, of Africa, of America. England has sent forth 'the best she breeds' for so long, and has destroyed those that remained so fiercely, that little remains for her to do but to sit down through the long nights and gaze at royalty on the wall.

The true British merchant seaman has passed away. The merchant service is no longer a recruiting ground for such sea dogs as fought with Nelson at Trafalgar and the Nile. Foreigners largely man the merchant ships, though Englishmen still continue to officer them and to prefer foreigners for'ard. In South Africa the colonial teaches the islander how to shoot, and the officers muddle and blunder; while at home the street people play hysterically at mafficking, and the War Office lowers the stature for enlistment.

It could not be otherwise. The most complacent Britisher cannot hope to draw off the life-blood, and underfeed, and keep it up forever. The average Mrs. Thomas Mugridge has been driven into the city, and she is not breeding very much of anything save an anaemic and sickly progeny which cannot find enough to eat. The strength of the English-speaking race to-day is not in the tight little island, but in the New World overseas, where are the sons and daughters of Mrs. Thomas Mugridge. The Sea Wife by the Northern Gate has just about done her work in the world, though she does not realize it. She must sit down and rest her tired loins for a space; and if the casual ward and the workhouse do not await her, it is because of the sons and daughters she has reared up against the day of her feebleness and decay.

CHAPTER XVI
PROPERTY VERSUS PERSON

The rights of property have been so much extended that the rights of the community have almost altogether disappeared, and it is hardly too much to say that the prosperity and the comfort and the liberties of a great proportion of the population has been laid at the feet of a small number of proprietors, who neither toil nor spin.

JOSEPH CHAMBERLAIN

In a civilisation frankly materialistic and based upon property, not soul, it is inevitable that property shall be exalted over soul, that crimes against property shall be considered far more serious than crimes against the person. To pound one's wife to a jelly and break a few of her ribs is a trivial offence compared with sleeping out under the naked stars because one has not the price of a doss. The lad who steals a few pears from a wealthy railway corporation is a greater menace to society than the young brute who commits an unprovoked assault upon an old man over seventy years of age. While the young girl who takes a lodging under the pretence that she has work commits so dangerous an offence, that, were she not severely punished, she and her kind might bring the whole fabric of property clattering to the ground. Had she unholily tramped Piccadilly and the Strand after midnight, the police would not have interfered with her, and she would have been able to pay for her lodging.

The following illustrative cases are culled from the police-court reports for a single week:-

Widnes Police Court. Before Aldermen Gossage and Neil. Thomas Lynch, charged with being drunk and disorderly and with assaulting a constable. Defendant rescued a woman from custody, kicked the constable, and threw stones at him. Fined 3s. 6d. for the first offence, and 10s. and costs for the assault.

Glasgow Queen's Park Police Court. Before Baillie Norman Thompson. John Kane pleaded guilty to assaulting his wife. There were five previous convictions. Fined £2, 2s.

Taunton County Petty Sessions. John Painter, a big, burly fellow, described as a labourer, charged with assaulting his wife. The woman received two severe black eyes, and her face was badly swollen. Fined £1, 8s., including costs, and bound over to keep the peace.

Widnes Police Court. Richard Bestwick and George Hunt, charged with trespassing in search of game. Hunt fined £1 and costs, Bestwick £2 and costs; in default, one month.

Shaftesbury Police Court. Before the Mayor (Mr. A. T. Carpenter). Thomas Baker, charged with sleeping out. Fourteen days.

Glasgow Central Police Court. Before Bailie Dunlop. Edward Morrison, a lad, convicted of stealing fifteen pears from a lorry at the railroad station. Seven days.

Doncaster Borough Police Court. Before Alderman Clark and other magistrates. James M'Gowan, charged under the Poaching Prevention Act with being found in possession of poaching implements and a number of rabbits. Fined £2 and costs, or one month.

Dunfermline Sheriff Court. Before Sheriff Gillespie. John Young, a pit-head worker, pleaded guilty to assaulting Alexander Storrar by beating him about the head and body with his fists, throwing him on the ground, and also striking him with a pit prop. Fined £1.

Kirkcaldy Police Court. Before Bailie Dishart. Simon Walker pleaded guilty to assaulting a man by striking and knocking him down. It was an unprovoked assault, and the magistrate described the accused as a perfect danger to the community. Fined 30s.

Mansfield Police Court. Before the Mayor, Messrs. F. J. Turner, J. Whitaker, F. Tidsbury, E. Holmes, and Dr. R. Nesbitt. Joseph Jackson, charged with assaulting Charles Nunn. Without any provocation, defendant struck the complainant a violent blow in the face, knocking him down, and then kicked him on the side of the head. He was rendered unconscious, and he remained under medical treatment for a fortnight. Fined 21s.

Perth Sheriff Court. Before Sheriff Sym. David Mitchell, charged with poaching. There were two previous convictions, the last being three years ago. The sheriff was asked to deal leniently with Mitchell, who was sixty-two years of age, and who offered no resistance to the gamekeeper. Four months.

Dundee Sheriff Court. Before Hon. Sheriff-Substitute R. C. Walker. John Murray, Donald Craig, and James Parkes, charged with poaching. Craig and Parkes fined £1 each or fourteen days; Murray, £5 or one month.

Reading Borough Police Court. Before Messrs. W. B. Monck, F. B. Parfitt, H. M. Wallis, and G. Gillagan. Alfred Masters, aged sixteen, charged with sleeping out on a waste piece of ground and having no visible means of subsistence. Seven days.

Salisbury City Petty Sessions. Before the Mayor, Messrs. C. Hoskins, G. Fullford, E. Alexander, and W. Marlow. James Moore, charged with stealing a pair of boots from outside a shop. Twenty-one days.

Horncastle Police Court. Before the Rev. W. F. Massingberd, the Rev. J. Graham, and Mr. N. Lucas Calcraft. George Brackenbury, a young labourer, convicted of what the magistrates characterised as an altogether unprovoked and brutal assault upon James Sargeant Foster, a man over seventy years of age. Fined £1 and 5s. 6d. costs.

Worksop Petty Sessions. Before Messrs. F. J. S. Foljambe, R. Eddison, and S. Smith. John Priestley, charged with assaulting the Rev. Leslie Graham. Defendant, who was drunk, was wheeling a perambulator and pushed it in front of a lorry, with the result that the perambulator was overturned and the baby in it thrown out. The lorry passed over the perambulator, but the baby was uninjured. Defendant then attacked the driver of the lorry, and afterwards assaulted the complainant, who remonstrated with him upon his conduct. In consequence of the injuries defendant inflicted, complainant had to consult a doctor. Fined 40s. and costs.

Rotherham West Riding Police Court. Before Messrs. C. Wright and G. Pugh and Colonel Stoddart. Benjamin Storey, Thomas Brammer, and Samuel Wilcock, charged with poaching. One month each.

Southampton County Police Court. Before Admiral J. C. Rowley, Mr. H. H. Culme-Seymour, and other magistrates. Henry Thorrington, charged with sleeping out. Seven days.

Eckington Police Court. Before Major L. B. Bowden, Messrs. R. Eyre, and H. A. Fowler, and Dr. Court. Joseph Watts, charged with stealing nine ferns from a garden. One month.

Ripley Petty Sessions. Before Messrs. J. B. Wheeler, W. D. Bembridge, and M. Hooper. Vincent Allen and George Hall, charged under the Poaching Prevention Act with being found in possession of a number of rabbits, and John Sparham, charged with aiding and abetting them. Hall and Sparham fined £1, 17s. 4d., and Allen £2, 17s. 4d., including costs; the former committed for fourteen days and the latter for one month in default of payment.

South-western Police Court, London. Before Mr. Rose. John Probyn, charged with doing grievous bodily harm to a constable. Prisoner had been kicking his wife, and also assaulting another woman who protested against his brutality. The constable tried to persuade him to go inside his house, but prisoner suddenly turned upon him, knocking him down by a blow on the face, kicking him as he lay on the ground, and attempting to strangle him. Finally the prisoner deliberately kicked the officer in a dangerous part, inflicting an injury which will keep him off duty for a long time to come. Six weeks.

Lambeth Police Court, London. Before Mr. Hopkins. 'Baby' Stuart, aged nineteen, described as a chorus girl, charged with obtaining food and lodging to the value of 5s. by false pretences, and with intent to defraud Emma Brasier. Emma Brasier, complainant, lodging-house keeper of Atwell Road. Prisoner took apartments at her house on the representation that she was employed at the Crown Theatre. After prisoner had been in her house two or three days, Mrs. Brasier made inquiries, and, finding the girl's story untrue, gave her into custody. Prisoner told the magistrate that she would have worked had she not had such bad health. Six weeks' hard labour.

CHAPTER XVII
INEFFICIENCY

I'd rather die on the high road under the open blue. I'd rather starve to death in the sweet air, or drown in the brave, salt sea, or have one fierce glad hour of battle, and then a bullet, than lead the life of a brute in a stinking hell, and gasp out my broken breath at last on a pauper's pallet.

ROBERT BLATCHFORD

I stopped a moment to listen to an argument on the Mile End Waste. It was night-time, and they were all workmen of the better class. They had surrounded one of their number, a pleasant-faced man of thirty, and were giving it to him rather heatedly.

'But 'ow about this 'ere cheap immigration?' one of them demanded. 'The Jews of Whitechapel, say, a-cutting our throats right along?'

'You can't blame them,' was the answer. 'They're just like us, and they've got to live. Don't blame the man who offers to work cheaper than you and gets your job.'

'But 'ow about the wife an' kiddies?' his interlocutor demanded.

'There you are,' came the answer. 'How about the wife and kiddies of the man who works cheaper than you and gets your job? Eh? How about his wife and kiddies? He's more interested in them than in yours, and he can't see them starve. So he cuts the price of labour and out you go. But you mustn't blame him, poor devil. He can't help it. Wages always come down when two men are after the same job. That's the fault of competition, not of the man who cuts the price.'

'But wyges don't come down where there's a union,' the objection was made.

'And there you are again, right on the head. The union cheeks competition among the labourers, but makes it harder where there are no unions. There's where your cheap labour of Whitechapel comes in. They're unskilled, and have no unions, and cut each other's throats, and ours in the bargain, if we don't belong to a strong union.'

Without going further into the argument, this man on the Mile End Waste pointed the moral that when two men were after the one job wages were bound to fall. Had he gone deeper into the matter, he would have found that even the union, say twenty thousand strong, could not hold up wages if twenty thousand idle men were trying to displace the union men. This is admirably instanced, just now, by the return and disbandment of the soldiers from South Africa. They find themselves, by tens of thousands, in desperate straits in the army of the unemployed. There is a general decline in wages throughout the land, which, giving rise to labour disputes and strikes, is taken advantage of by the unemployed, who gladly pick up the tools thrown down by the strikers.

Sweating, starvation wages, armies of unemployed, and great numbers of the homeless and shelterless are inevitable when there are more men to do work than there is work for men to do. The men and women I have met upon the streets, and in the spikes and pegs, are not there because as a mode of life it may be considered a 'soft snap.' I have sufficiently outlined the hardships they undergo to demonstrate that their existence is anything but 'soft.'

It is a matter of sober calculation, here in England, that it is softer to work for twenty shillings a week, and have regular food, and a bed at night, than it is to walk the streets. The man who walks the streets suffers more, and works harder, for far less return. I have depicted the nights they spend, and how, driven in by physical exhaustion, they go to the casual ward for a 'rest up.' Nor is the casual ward a soft snap. To pick four pounds of oakum, break twelve hundredweight of stones, or perform the most revolting tasks, in return for the miserable food and shelter they receive, is an unqualified extravagance on the part of the men who are guilty of it. On the part of the authorities it is sheer robbery. They give the men far less for their labour than do the capitalistic employers. The wage for the same amount of labour, performed for a private employer, would buy them better beds, better food, more good cheer, and, above all, greater freedom.

As I say, it is an extravagance for a man to patronise a casual ward. And that they know it themselves is shown by the way these men shun it till driven in by physical exhaustion. Then why do they do it? Not because they are discouraged workers. The very opposite is true; they are discouraged vagabonds. In the United States the tramp is almost invariably a discouraged worker. He finds tramping a softer mode of life than working. But this is not true in England. Here the powers that be do their utmost to discourage the tramp and vagabond, and he is, in all truth, a mightily discouraged creature. He knows that two shillings a day, which is only fifty cents, will buy him three fair meals, a bed at night, and leave him a couple of pennies for pocket money. He would rather work for those two shillings than for the charity of the casual ward; for he knows that he would not have to work so hard, and that he would not be so abominably treated. He does not do so, however, because there are more men to do work than there is work for men to do.

When there are more men than there is work to be done, a sifting-out process must obtain. In every branch of industry the less efficient are crowded out. Being crowded out because of inefficiency, they cannot go up, but must descend, and continue to descend, until they reach their proper level, a place in the industrial fabric where they are efficient. It follows, therefore, and it is inexorable, that the least efficient must descend to the very bottom, which is the shambles wherein they perish miserably.

A glance at the confirmed inefficients at the bottom demonstrates that they are, as a rule, mental, physical, and moral wrecks. The exceptions to the rule are the late arrivals, who are merely very inefficient, and upon whom the wrecking process is just beginning to operate. All the forces here, it must be remembered, are destructive. The good body (which is there because its brain is not quick and capable) is speedily wrenched and twisted out of shape; the clean mind (which is there because of its weak body) is speedily fouled and contaminated.

The mortality is excessive, but, even then, they die far too lingering deaths.

Here, then, we have the construction of the Abyss and the shambles. Throughout the whole industrial fabric a constant elimination is going on. The inefficient are weeded out and flung downward. Various things constitute inefficiency. The engineer who is irregular or irresponsible will sink down until he finds his place, say as a casual labourer, an occupation irregular in its very nature and in which there is little or no responsibility. Those who are slow and clumsy, who suffer from weakness of body or mind, or who lack nervous, mental, and physical stamina, must sink down, sometimes rapidly, sometimes step by step, to the bottom. Accident, by disabling an efficient worker, will make him inefficient, and down he must go. And the worker who becomes aged, with failing energy and numbing brain, must begin the frightful descent which knows no stopping-place short of the bottom and death.

In this last instance, the statistics of London tell a terrible tale. The population of London is one-seventh of the total population of the United Kingdom, and in London, year in and year out, one adult in every four dies on public charity, either in the workhouse, the hospital, or the asylum. When the fact that the well-to-do do not end thus is taken into consideration, it becomes manifest that it is the fate of at least one in every three adult workers to die on public charity.

As an illustration of how a good worker may suddenly become inefficient, and what then happens to him, I am tempted to give the case of M'Garry, a man thirty-two years of age, and an inmate of the workhouse. The extracts are quoted from the annual report of the trade union.

I worked at Sullivan's place in Widnes, better known as the British Alkali Chemical Works. I was working in a shed, and I had to cross the yard. It was ten o'clock at night, and there was no light about. While crossing the yard I felt something take hold of my leg and screw it off. I became unconscious; I didn't know what became of me for a day or two. On the following Sunday night I came to my senses, and found myself in the hospital. I asked the nurse what was to do with my legs, and she told me both legs were off.

There was a stationary crank in the yard, let into the ground; the hole was 18 inches long, 15 inches deep, and 15 inches wide. The crank revolved in the hole three revolutions a minute. There was no fence or covering over the hole. Since my accident they have stopped it altogether, and have covered the hole up with a piece of sheet iron. . . . They gave me £25. They didn't reckon that as compensation; they said it was only for charity's sake. Out of that I paid £9 for a machine by which to wheel myself about.

I was labouring at the time I got my legs off. I got twenty-four shillings a week, rather better pay than the other men, because I used to take shifts. When there was heavy work to be done I used to be picked out to do it. Mr. Manton, the manager, visited me at the hospital several times. When I was getting better, I asked him if he would be able to find me a job. He told me not to trouble myself, as the firm was not cold-hearted. I would be right enough in any case . . . Mr. Manton stopped coming to see me; and the last time, he said he thought of asking the directors to give me a fifty-pound note, so I could go home to my friends in Ireland.

Poor M'Garry! He received rather better pay than the other men because he was ambitious and took shifts, and when heavy work was to be done he was the man picked out to do it. And then the thing happened, and he went into the workhouse. The alternative to the workhouse is to go home to Ireland and burden his friends for the rest of his life. Comment is superfluous.

It must be understood that efficiency is not determined by the workers themselves, but is determined by the demand for labour. If three men seek one position, the most efficient man will get it. The other two, no matter how capable they may be, will none the less be inefficients. If Germany, Japan, and the United States should capture the entire world market for iron, coal, and textiles, at once the English workers would be thrown idle by hundreds of thousands. Some would emigrate, but the rest would rush their labour into the remaining industries. A general shaking up of the workers from top to bottom would result; and when equilibrium had been restored, the number of the inefficients at the bottom of the Abyss would have been increased by hundreds of thousands. On the other hand, conditions remaining constant and all the workers doubling their efficiency, there would still be as many inefficients, though each inefficient were twice as capable as he had been and more capable than many of the efficients had previously been.

When there are more men to work than there is work for men to do, just as many men as are in excess of work will be inefficients, and as inefficients they are doomed to lingering and painful destruction. It shall be the aim of future chapters to show, by their work and manner of living, not only how the inefficients are weeded out and destroyed, but to show how inefficients are being constantly and wantonly created by the forces of industrial society as it exists to-day.

CHAPTER XVIII
WAGES

Some sell their lives for bread;
Some sell their souls for gold;
Some seek the river bed;
Some seek the workhouse mold.

Such is proud England's sway,
Where wealth may work its will;
White flesh is cheap to-day,
White souls are cheaper still.

FANTASIAS

When I learned that in Lesser London there were 1,292,737 people who received twenty-one shillings or less a week per family, I became interested as to how the wages could best be spent in order to maintain the physical efficiency of such families. Families of six, seven, eight or ten being beyond consideration, I have based the following table upon a family of five—a father, mother, and three children; while I have made twenty-one shillings equivalent to $5.25, though actually, twenty-one shillings are equivalent to about $5.11.

Rent	$1.50	or 6/0	Bread	1.00	' 4/0	Meat	0.87.5	'	3/6
Vegetables	0.62.5	' 2/6	Coals	0.25	' 1/0	Tea	0.18	'	0/9
Oil	0.16	' 0/8	Sugar	0.18	' 0/9	Milk	0.12	'	0/6
Soap	0.08	' 0/4	Butter	0.20	' 0/10	Firewood	0.08	'	0/4
						Total	$5.25	21/2	

An analysis of one item alone will show how little room there is for waste. *Bread*, $1: for a family of five, for seven days, one dollar's worth of bread will give each a daily ration of 2.8 cents; and if they eat three meals a day, each may consume per meal 9.5 mills' worth of bread, a little less than one halfpennyworth. Now bread is the heaviest item. They will get less of meat per mouth each meal, and still less of vegetates; while the smaller items become too microscopic for consideration. On the other hand, these food articles are all bought at small retail, the most expensive and wasteful method of purchasing.

While the table given above will permit no extravagance, no overloading of stomachs, it will be noticed that there is no surplus. The whole guinea is spent for food and rent. There is no pocket-money left over. Does the man buy a glass of beer, the family must eat that much less; and in so far as it eats less, just that far will it impair its physical efficiency. The members of this family cannot ride in busses or trams, cannot write letters, take outings, go to a 'tu'penny gaff' for cheap vaudeville, join social or benefit clubs, nor can they buy sweetmeats, tobacco, books, or newspapers.

And further, should one child (and there are three) require a pair of shoes, the family must strike meat for a week from its bill of fare. And since there are five pairs of feet requiring shoes, and five heads requiring hats, and five bodies requiring clothes, and since there are laws regulating indecency, the family must constantly impair its physical efficiency in order to keep warm and out of jail. For notice, when rent, coals, oil, soap, and firewood are extracted from the weekly income, there remains a daily allowance for food of 4.5d. to each person; and that 4.5d. cannot be lessened by buying clothes without impairing the physical efficiency.

All of which is hard enough. But the thing happens; the husband and father breaks his leg or his neck. No 4.5d. a day per mouth for food is coming in; no halfpennyworth of bread per meal; and, at the end of the week, no six shillings for rent. So out they must go, to the streets or the workhouse, or to a miserable den, somewhere, in which the mother will desperately endeavour to hold the family together on the ten shillings she may possibly be able to earn.

While in London there are 1,292,737 people who receive twenty-one shillings or less a week per family, it must be remembered that we have investigated a family of five living on a twenty-one shilling basis. There are larger families, there are many families that live on less than twenty-one shillings, and there is much irregular employment. The question naturally arises, How do *they* live? The answer is that they do not live. They do not know what life is. They drag out a subterbestial existence until mercifully released by death.

Before descending to the fouler depths, let the case of the telephone girls be cited. Here are clean, fresh English maids, for whom a higher standard of living than that of the beasts is absolutely necessary. Otherwise they cannot remain clean, fresh English maids. On entering the service, a telephone girl receives a weekly wage of eleven shillings. If she be quick and clever, she may, at the end of five years, attain a minimum wage of one pound. Recently a table of such a girl's weekly expenditure was furnished to Lord Londonderry. Here it is:-

	s.	d.		s.	d.		s.	d.
Rent, fire, and light	7	6	Board at home	3	6	Board at the office	4	6
Street car fare	1	6	Laundry	1	0	Total	18	0

This leaves nothing for clothes, recreation, or sickness. And yet many of the girls are receiving, not eighteen shillings, but eleven shillings, twelve shillings, and fourteen shillings per week. They must have clothes and recreation, and—

> Man to Man so oft unjust,
> Is always so to Woman.

At the Trades Union Congress now being held in London, the Gasworkers' Union moved that instructions be given the Parliamentary Committee to introduce a Bill to prohibit the employment of children under fifteen years of age. Mr. Shackleton, Member of Parliament and a representative of the Northern Counties Weavers, opposed the resolution on behalf of the textile workers, who, he said, could not dispense with the earnings of their children and live on the scale of wages which obtained. The representatives of 514,000 workers voted against the resolution, while the representatives of 535,000 workers voted in favour of it. When 514,000 workers oppose a resolution prohibiting child-labour under fifteen, it is evident that a less-than-living wage is being paid to an immense number of the adult workers of the country.

I have spoken with women in Whitechapel who receive right along less than one shilling for a twelve-hour day in the coat-making sweat shops; and with women trousers finishers who receive an average princely and weekly wage of three to four shillings.

A case recently cropped up of men, in the employ of a wealthy business house, receiving their board and six shillings per week for six working days of sixteen hours each. The sandwich men get fourteenpence per day and find themselves. The average weekly earnings of the hawkers and costermongers are not more than ten to twelve shillings. The average of all common labourers, outside the dockers, is less than sixteen shillings per week, while the dockers average from eight to nine shillings. These figures are taken from a royal commission report and are authentic.

Conceive of an old woman, broken and dying, supporting herself and four children, and paying three shillings per week rent, by making match boxes at 2.25d. per gross. Twelve dozen boxes for 2.25d., and, in addition, finding her own paste and thread! She never knew a day off, either for sickness, rest, or recreation. Each day and every day, Sundays as well, she toiled fourteen hours. Her day's stint was seven gross, for which she received 1s. 3.75d. In the week of ninety-eight hours' work, she made 7066 match boxes, and earned 4s. 10.25d., less per paste and thread.

Last year, Mr. Thomas Holmes, a police-court missionary of note, after writing about the condition of the women workers, received the following letter, dated April 18, 1901:-

> Sir,—Pardon the liberty I am taking, but, having read what you said about poor women working fourteen hours a day for ten shillings per week, I beg to state my case. I am a tie-maker, who, after working all the week, cannot earn more than five shillings, and I have a poor afflicted husband to keep who hasn't earned a penny for more than ten years.

Imagine a woman, capable of writing such a clear, sensible, grammatical letter, supporting her husband and self on five shillings per week! Mr. Holmes visited her. He had to squeeze to get into the room. There lay her sick husband; there she worked all day long; there she cooked, ate, washed, and slept; and there her husband and she performed all the functions of living and dying. There was no space for the missionary to sit down, save on the bed, which was partially covered with ties and silk. The sick man's lungs were in the last stages of decay. He coughed and expectorated constantly, the woman ceasing from her work to assist him in his paroxysms. The silken fluff from the ties was not good for his sickness; nor was his sickness good for the ties, and the handlers and wearers of the ties yet to come.

Another case Mr. Holmes visited was that of a young girl, twelve years of age, charged in the police court with stealing food. He found her the deputy mother of a boy of nine, a crippled boy of seven, and a younger child. Her mother was a widow and a blouse-maker. She paid five shillings a week rent. Here are the last items in her housekeeping account: Tea. 0.5d.; sugar, 0.5d.; bread, 0.25d.; margarine, 1d.; oil, 1.5d.; and firewood, 1d. Good housewives of the soft and tender folk, imagine yourselves marketing and keeping house on such a scale, setting a table for five, and keeping an eye on your deputy mother of twelve to see that she did not steal food for her little brothers and sisters, the while you stitched, stitched, stitched at a nightmare line of blouses, which stretched away into the gloom and down to the pauper's coffin a-yawn for you.

CHAPTER XIX
THE GHETTO

Is it well that while we range with Science, glorying in the time,
City children soak and blacken soul and sense in city slime?
There among the gloomy alleys Progress halts on palsied feet;
Crime and hunger cast out maidens by the thousand on the street;

There the master scrimps his haggard seamstress of her daily bread;
There the single sordid attic holds the living and the dead;
There the smouldering fire of fever creeps across the rotted floor,
And the crowded couch of incest, in the warrens of the poor.

TENNYSON

At one time the nations of Europe confined the undesirable Jews in city ghettos. But to-day the dominant economic class, by less arbitrary but none the less rigorous methods, has confined the undesirable yet necessary workers into ghettos of remarkable meanness and vastness. East London is such a ghetto, where the rich and the powerful do not dwell, and the traveller cometh not, and where two million workers swarm, procreate, and die.

It must not be supposed that all the workers of London are crowded into the East End, but the tide is setting strongly in that direction. The poor quarters of the city proper are constantly being destroyed, and the main stream of the unhoused is toward the east. In the last twelve years, one district, 'London over the Border,' as it is called, which lies well beyond Aldgate, Whitechapel, and Mile End, has increased 260,000, or over sixty per cent. The churches in this district, by the way, can seat but one in every thirty-seven of the added population.

The City of Dreadful Monotony, the East End is often called, especially by well-fed, optimistic sightseers, who look over the surface of things and are merely shocked by the intolerable sameness and meanness of it all. If the East End is worthy of no worse title than The City of Dreadful Monotony, and if working people are unworthy of variety and beauty and surprise, it would not be such a bad place in which to live. But the East End does merit a worse title. It should be called The City of Degradation. While it is not a city of slums, as some people imagine, it may well be said to be one gigantic slum. From the standpoint of simple decency and clean manhood and womanhood, any mean street, of all its mean streets, is a slum. Where sights and sounds abound which neither you nor I would care to have our children see and hear is a place where no man's children should live, and see, and hear. Where you and I would not care to have our wives pass their lives is a place where no other man's wife should have to pass her life. For here, in the East End, the obscenities and brute vulgarities of life are rampant. There is no privacy. The bad corrupts the good, and all fester together. Innocent childhood is sweet and beautiful: but in East London innocence is a fleeting thing, and you must catch them before they crawl out of the cradle, or you will find the very babes as unholily wise as you.

The application of the Golden Rule determines that East London is an unfit place in which to live. Where you would not have your own babe live, and develop, and gather to itself knowledge of life and the things of life, is not a fit place for the babes of other men to live, and develop, and gather to themselves knowledge of life and the things of life. It is a simple thing, this Golden Rule, and all that is required. Political economy and the survival of the fittest can go hang if they say otherwise. What is not good enough for you is not good enough for other men, and there's no more to be said.

There are 300,000 people in London, divided into families, that live in one-room tenements. Far, far more live in two and three rooms and are as badly crowded, regardless of sex, as those that live in one room. The law demands 400 cubic feet of space for each person. In army barracks each soldier is allowed 600 cubic feet. Professor Huxley, at one time himself a medical officer in East London, always held that each person should have 800 cubic feet of space, and that it should be well ventilated with pure air. Yet in London there are 900,000 people living in less than the 400 cubic feet prescribed by the law.

Mr. Charles Booth, who engaged in a systematic work of years in charting and classifying the toiling city population, estimates that there are 1,800,000 people in London who are *poor* and *very poor*. It is of interest to mark what he terms poor. By *poor* he means families which have a total weekly income of from eighteen to twenty-one shillings. The *very poor* fall greatly below this standard.

The workers, as a class, are being more and more segregated by their economic masters; and this process, with its jamming and overcrowding, tends not so much toward immorality as unmorality. Here is an extract from a recent meeting of the London County Council, terse and bald, but with a wealth of horror to be read between the lines:-

Mr. Bruce asked the Chairman of the Public Health Committee whether his attention had been called to a number of cases of serious overcrowding in the East End. In St. Georges-in-the-East a man and his wife and their family of eight occupied one small room. This family consisted of five daughters, aged twenty, seventeen, eight, four, and an infant; and three sons, aged fifteen, thirteen, and twelve. In Whitechapel a man and his wife and their three daughters, aged sixteen, eight, and four, and two sons, aged ten and twelve years, occupied a smaller room. In Bethnal Green a man and his wife, with four sons, aged twenty-three, twenty-one, nineteen, and sixteen, and two daughters, aged fourteen and seven, were also found in one room. He asked whether it was not the duty of the various local authorities to prevent such serious overcrowding.

But with 900,000 people actually living under illegal conditions, the authorities have their hands full. When the overcrowded folk are ejected they stray off into some other hole; and, as they move their belongings by night, on hand-barrows (one hand-barrow accommodating the entire household goods and the sleeping children), it is next to impossible to keep track of them. If the Public Health Act of 1891 were suddenly and completely enforced, 900,000 people would receive notice to clear out of their houses and go on to the streets, and 500,000 rooms would have to be built before they were all legally housed again.

The mean streets merely look mean from the outside, but inside the walls are to be found squalor, misery, and tragedy. While the following tragedy may be revolting to read, it must not be forgotten that the existence of it is far more revolting.

In Devonshire Place, Lisson Grove, a short while back died an old woman of seventy-five years of age. At the inquest the coroner's officer stated that 'all he found in the room was a lot of old rags covered with vermin. He had got himself smothered with the vermin. The room was in a shocking condition, and he had never seen anything like it. Everything was absolutely covered with vermin.'

The doctor said: 'He found deceased lying across the fender on her back. She had one garment and her stockings on. The body was quite alive with vermin, and all the clothes in the room were absolutely grey with insects. Deceased was very badly nourished and was very emaciated. She had extensive sores on her legs, and her stockings were adherent to those sores. The sores were the result of vermin.'

A man present at the inquest wrote: 'I had the evil fortune to see the body of the unfortunate woman as it lay in the mortuary; and even now the memory of that gruesome sight makes me shudder. There she lay in the mortuary shell, so starved and emaciated that she was a mere bundle of skin and bones. Her hair, which was matted with filth, was simply a nest of vermin. Over her bony chest leaped and rolled hundreds, thousands, myriads of vermin!'

If it is not good for your mother and my mother so to die, then it is not good for this woman, whosoever's mother she might be, so to die.

Bishop Wilkinson, who has lived in Zululand, recently said, 'No human of an African village would allow such a promiscuous mixing of young men and women, boys and girls.' He had reference to the children of the overcrowded folk, who at five have nothing to learn and much to unlearn which they will never unlearn.

It is notorious that here in the Ghetto the houses of the poor are greater profit earners than the mansions of the rich. Not only does the poor worker have to live like a beast, but he pays proportionately more for it than does the rich man for his spacious comfort. A class of house-sweaters has been made possible by the competition of the poor for houses. There are more people than there is room, and numbers are in the workhouse because they cannot find shelter elsewhere. Not only are houses let, but they are sublet, and sub-sublet down to the very rooms.

'A part of a room to let.' This notice was posted a short while ago in a window not five minutes' walk from St. James's Hall. The Rev. Hugh Price Hughes is authority for the statement that beds are let on the three-relay system—that is, three tenants to a bed, each occupying it eight hours, so that it never grows cold; while the floor space underneath the bed is likewise let on the three-relay system. Health officers are not at all unused to finding such cases as the following: in one room having a cubic capacity of 1000 feet, three adult females in the bed, and two adult females under the bed; and in one room of 1650 cubic feet, one adult male and two children in the bed, and two adult females under the bed.

Here is a typical example of a room on the more respectable two-relay system. It is occupied in the daytime by a young woman employed all night in a hotel. At seven o'clock in the evening she vacates the room, and a bricklayer's labourer comes in. At seven in the morning he vacates, and goes to his work, at which time she returns from hers.

The Rev. W. N. Davies, rector of Spitalfields, took a census of some of the alleys in his parish. He says:-

In one alley there are ten houses—fifty-one rooms, nearly all about 8 feet by 9 feet—and 254 people. In six instances only do 2 people occupy one room; and in others the number varied from 3 to 9. In another court with six houses and twenty-two rooms were 84 people—again 6, 7, 8, and 9 being the number living in one room, in several instances. In one house with eight rooms are 45 people—one room containing 9 persons, one 8, two 7, and another 6.

This Ghetto crowding is not through inclination, but compulsion. Nearly fifty per cent. of the workers pay from one-fourth to one-half of their earnings for rent. The average rent in the larger part of the East End is from four to six shillings per week for one room, while skilled mechanics, earning thirty-five shillings per week, are forced to part with fifteen shillings of it for two or three pokey little dens, in which they strive desperately to obtain some semblance of home life. And rents are going up all the time. In one street in Stepney the increase in only two years has been from thirteen to eighteen shillings; in another street from eleven to sixteen shillings; and in another street, from eleven to fifteen shillings; while in Whitechapel, two-room houses that recently rented for ten shillings are now costing twenty-one shillings. East, west, north, and south the rents are going up. When land is worth from £20,000 to £30,000 an acre, some one must pay the landlord.

Mr. W. C. Steadman, in the House of Commons, in a speech concerning his constituency in Stepney, related the following:-

This morning, not a hundred yards from where I am myself living, a widow stopped me. She has six children to support, and the rent of her house was fourteen shillings per week. She gets her living by letting the house to lodgers and doing a day's washing or charring. That woman, with tears in her eyes, told me that the landlord had increased the rent from fourteen shillings to eighteen shillings. What could the woman do? There is no accommodation in Stepney. Every place is taken up and overcrowded.

Class supremacy can rest only on class degradation; and when the workers are segregated in the Ghetto, they cannot escape the consequent degradation. A short and stunted people is created—a breed strikingly differentiated from their masters' breed, a pavement folk, as it were lacking stamina and strength. The men become caricatures of what physical men ought to be, and their women and children are pale and anaemic, with eyes ringed darkly, who stoop and slouch, and are early twisted out of all shapeliness and beauty.

To make matters worse, the men of the Ghetto are the men who are left—a deteriorated stock, left to undergo still further deterioration. For a hundred and fifty years, at least, they have been drained of their best. The strong men, the men of pluck, initiative, and ambition, have been faring forth to the fresher and freer portions of the globe, to make new lands and nations. Those who are lacking, the weak of heart and head and hand, as well as the rotten and hopeless, have remained to carry on the breed. And year by year, in turn, the best they breed are taken from them. Wherever a man of vigour and stature manages to grow up, he is haled forthwith into the army. A soldier, as Bernard Shaw has said, 'ostensibly a heroic and patriotic defender of his country, is really an unfortunate man driven by destitution to offer himself as food for powder for the sake of regular rations, shelter, and clothing.'

This constant selection of the best from the workers has impoverished those who are left, a sadly degraded remainder, for the great part, which, in the Ghetto, sinks to the deepest depths. The wine of life has been drawn off to spill itself in blood and progeny over the rest of the earth. Those that remain are the lees, and they are segregated and steeped in themselves. They become indecent and bestial. When they kill, they kill with their hands, and then stupidly surrender themselves to the executioners. There is no splendid audacity about their transgressions. They gouge a mate with a dull knife, or beat his head in with an iron pot, and then sit down and wait for the police. Wife-beating is the masculine prerogative of matrimony. They wear remarkable boots of brass and iron, and when they have polished off the mother of their children with a black eye or so, they knock her down and proceed to trample her very much as a Western stallion tramples a rattlesnake.

A woman of the lower Ghetto classes is as much the slave of her husband as is the Indian squaw. And I, for one, were I a woman and had but the two choices, should prefer being a squaw. The men are economically dependent on their masters, and the women are economically dependent on the men. The result is, the woman gets the beating the man should give his master, and she can do nothing. There are the kiddies, and he is the bread-winner, and she dare not send him to jail and leave herself and children to starve. Evidence to convict can rarely be obtained when such cases come into the courts; as a rule, the trampled wife and mother is weeping and hysterically beseeching the magistrate to let her husband off for the kiddies' sakes.

The wives become screaming harridans or, broken-spirited and doglike, lose what little decency and self-respect they have remaining over from their maiden days, and all sink together, unheeding, in their degradation and dirt.

Sometimes I become afraid of my own generalizations upon the massed misery of this Ghetto life, and feel that my impressions are exaggerated, that I am too close to the picture and lack perspective. At such moments I find it well to turn to the testimony of other men to prove to myself that I am not becoming over-wrought and addle-pated. Frederick Harrison has always struck me as being a level-headed, well-controlled man, and he says:-

> To me, at least, it would be enough to condemn modern society as hardly an advance on slavery or serfdom, if the permanent condition of industry were to be that which we behold, that ninety per cent. of the actual producers of wealth have no home that they can call their own beyond the end of the week; have no bit of soil, or so much as a room that belongs to them; have nothing

of value of any kind, except as much old furniture as will go into a cart; have the precarious chance of weekly wages, which barely suffice to keep them in health; are housed, for the most part, in places that no man thinks fit for his horse; are separated by so narrow a margin from destitution that a month of bad trade, sickness, or unexpected loss brings them face to face with hunger and pauperism . . . But below this normal state of the average workman in town and country, there is found the great band of destitute outcasts—the camp followers of the army of industry—at least one-tenth the whole proletarian population, whose normal condition is one of sickening wretchedness. If this is to be the permanent arrangement of modern society, civilization must be held to bring a curse on the great majority of mankind.

Ninety per cent.! The figures are appalling, yet Mr. Stopford Brooke, after drawing a frightful London picture, finds himself compelled to multiply it by half a million. Here it is:-

I often used to meet, when I was curate at Kensington, families drifting into London along the Hammersmith Road. One day there came along a labourer and his wife, his son and two daughters. Their family had lived for a long time on an estate in the country, and managed, with the help of the common-land and their labour, to get on. But the time came when the common was encroached upon, and their labour was not needed on the estate, and they were quietly turned out of their cottage. Where should they go? Of course to London, where work was thought to be plentiful. They had a little savings, and they thought they could get two decent rooms to live in. But the inexorable land question met them in London. They tried the decent courts for lodgings, and found that two rooms would cost ten shillings a week. Food was dear and bad, water was bad, and in a short time their health suffered. Work was hard to get, and its wage was so low that they were soon in debt. They became more ill and more despairing with the poisonous surroundings, the darkness, and the long hours of work; and they were driven forth to seek a cheaper lodging. They found it in a court I knew well—a hotbed of crime and nameless horrors. In this they got a single room at a cruel rent, and work was more difficult for them to get now, as they came from a place of such bad repute, and they fell into the hands of those who sweat the last drop out of man and woman and child, for wages which are the food only of despair. And the darkness and the dirt, the bad food and the sickness, and the want of water was worse than before; and the crowd and the companionship of the court robbed them of the last shreds of self-respect. The drink demon seized upon them. Of course there was a public-house at both ends of the court. There they fled, one and all, for shelter, and warmth, and society, and forgetfulness. And they came out in deeper debt, with inflamed senses and burning brains, and an unsatisfied craving for drink they would do anything to satiate. And in a few months the father was in prison, the wife dying, the son a criminal, and the daughters on the street. *Multiply this by half a million, and you will be beneath the truth.*

No more dreary spectacle can be found on this earth than the whole of the 'awful East,' with its Whitechapel, Hoxton, Spitalfields, Bethnal Green, and Wapping to the East India Docks. The colour of life is grey and drab. Everything is helpless, hopeless, unrelieved, and dirty. Bath tubs are a thing totally unknown, as mythical as the ambrosia of the gods. The people themselves are dirty, while any attempt at cleanliness becomes howling farce, when it is not pitiful and tragic. Strange, vagrant odours come drifting along the greasy wind, and the rain, when it falls, is more like grease than water from heaven. The very cobblestones are scummed with grease.

Here lives a population as dull and unimaginative as its long grey miles of dingy brick. Religion has virtually passed it by, and a gross and stupid materialism reigns, fatal alike to the things of the spirit and the finer instincts of life.

It used to be the proud boast that every Englishman's home was his castle. But to-day it is an anachronism. The Ghetto folk have no homes. They do not know the significance and the sacredness of home life. Even the municipal dwellings, where live the better-class workers, are overcrowded barracks. They have no home life. The very language proves it. The father returning from work asks his child in the street where her mother is; and back the answer comes, 'In the buildings.'

A new race has sprung up, a street people. They pass their lives at work and in the streets. They have dens and lairs into which to crawl for sleeping purposes, and that is all. One cannot travesty the word by calling such dens and lairs 'homes.' The traditional silent and reserved Englishman has passed away. The pavement folk are noisy, voluble, high-strung, excitable—when they are yet young. As they grow older they become steeped and stupefied in beer. When they have nothing else to do, they ruminate as a cow ruminates. They are to be met with everywhere, standing on curbs and corners, and staring into vacancy. Watch one of them. He will stand there, motionless, for hours, and when you go away you will leave him still staring into vacancy. It is most absorbing. He has no money for beer, and his lair is only for sleeping purposes, so what else remains for him to do? He has already solved the mysteries of girl's love, and wife's love, and child's love, and found them delusions and shams, vain and fleeting as dew-drops, quick-vanishing before the ferocious facts of life.

As I say, the young are high-strung, nervous, excitable; the middle-aged are empty-headed, stolid, and stupid. It is absurd to think for an instant that they can compete with the workers of the New World. Brutalised, degraded, and dull, the Ghetto folk will be unable to render efficient service to England in the world struggle for industrial supremacy which economists declare has already begun. Neither as workers nor as soldiers can they come up to the mark when England, in her need, calls upon them, her forgotten ones; and if England be flung out of the world's industrial orbit, they will perish like flies at the end of summer. Or, with England critically situated, and with them made desperate as wild beasts are made desperate, they may become a menace and go 'swelling' down to the West End to return the 'slumming' the West End has done in the East. In which case, before rapid-fire guns and the modern machinery of warfare, they will perish the more swiftly and easily.

CHAPTER XX
COFFEE-HOUSES AND DOSS-HOUSES

Why should we be packed, head and tail, like canned sardines?

ROBERT BLATCHFORD

Another phrase gone glimmering, shorn of romance and tradition and all that goes to make phrases worth keeping! For me, henceforth, 'coffee-house' will possess anything but an agreeable connotation. Over on the other side of the world, the mere mention of the word was sufficient to conjure up whole crowds of its historic frequenters, and to send trooping through my imagination endless groups of wits and dandies, pamphleteers and bravos, and bohemians of Grub Street.

But here, on this side of the world, alas and alack, the very name is a misnomer. Coffee-house: a place where people drink coffee. Not at all. You cannot obtain coffee in such a place for love or money. True, you may call for coffee, and you will have brought you something in a cup purporting to be coffee, and you will taste it and be disillusioned, for coffee it certainly is not.

And what is true of the coffee is true of the coffee-house. Working-men, in the main, frequent these places, and greasy, dirty places they are, without one thing about them to cherish decency in a man or put self-respect into him. Table-cloths and napkins are unknown. A man eats in the midst of the débris left by his predecessor, and dribbles his own scraps about him and on the floor. In rush times, in such places, I have positively waded through the muck and mess that covered the floor, and I have managed to eat because I was abominably hungry and capable of eating anything.

This seems to be the normal condition of the working-man, from the zest with which he addresses himself to the board. Eating is a necessity, and there are no frills about it. He brings in with him a primitive voraciousness, and, I am confident, carries away with him a fairly healthy appetite. When you see such a man, on his way to work in the morning, order a pint of tea, which is no more tea than it is ambrosia, pull a hunk of dry bread from his pocket, and wash the one down with the other, depend upon it, that man has not the right sort of stuff in his belly, nor enough of the wrong sort of stuff, to fit him for big day's work. And further, depend upon it, he and a thousand of his kind will not turn out the quantity or quality of work that a thousand men will who have eaten heartily of meat and potatoes, and drunk coffee that is coffee.

As a vagrant in the 'Hobo' of a California jail, I have been served better food and drink than the London workman receives in his coffee-houses; while as an American labourer I have eaten a breakfast for twelvepence such as the British labourer would not dream of eating. Of course, he will pay only three or four pence for his; which is, however, as much as I paid, for I would be earning six shillings to his two or two and a half. On the other hand, though, and in return, I would turn out an amount of work in the course of the day that would put to shame the amount he turned out. So there are two sides to it. The man with the high standard of living will always do more work and better than the man with the low standard of living.

There is a comparison which sailormen make between the English and American merchant services. In an English ship, they say, it is poor grub, poor pay, and easy work; in an American ship, good grub, good pay, and hard work. And this is applicable to the working populations of both countries. The ocean greyhounds have to pay for speed and steam, and so does the workman. But if the workman is not able to pay for it, he will not have the speed and steam, that is all. The proof of it is when the English workman comes to America. He will lay more bricks in New York than he will in London, still more bricks in St. Louis, and still more bricks when he gets to San Francisco. {3} His standard of living has been rising all the time.

Early in the morning, along the streets frequented by workmen on the way to work, many women sit on the sidewalk with sacks of bread beside them. No end of workmen purchase these, and eat them as they walk along. They do not even wash the dry bread down with the tea to be obtained for a penny in the coffee-houses. It is incontestable that a man is not fit to begin his day's work on a meal like that; and it is equally incontestable that the loss will fall upon his employer and upon the nation. For some time, now, statesmen have been crying, 'Wake up, England!' It would show more hard-headed common sense if they changed the tune to 'Feed up, England!'

Not only is the worker poorly fed, but he is filthily fed. I have stood outside a butcher-shop and watched a horde of speculative housewives turning over the trimmings and scraps and shreds of beef and mutton—dog-meat in the States. I would not vouch for the clean fingers of these housewives, no more than I would vouch for the cleanliness of the single rooms in which many of them and their families lived; yet they raked, and pawed, and scraped the mess about in their anxiety to get the worth of their coppers. I kept my eye on one particularly offensive-looking bit of meat, and followed it through the clutches of over twenty women, till it fell to the lot of a timid-appearing little woman whom the butcher bluffed into taking it. All day long this heap of scraps was added to and taken away from, the dust and dirt of the street falling upon it, flies settling on it, and the dirty fingers turning it over and over.

The costers wheel loads of specked and decaying fruit around in the barrows all day, and very often store it in their one living and sleeping room for the night. There it is exposed to the sickness and disease, the effluvia and vile exhalations of over-crowded and rotten life, and next day it is carted about again to be sold.

The poor worker of the East End never knows what it is to eat good, wholesome meat or fruit—in fact, he rarely eats meat or fruit at all; while the skilled workman has nothing to boast of in the way of what he eats. Judging from the coffee-houses, which is a fair criterion, they never know in all their lives what tea, coffee, or cocoa tastes like. The slops and water-witcheries of the coffee-houses, varying only in sloppiness and witchery, never even approximate or suggest what you and I are accustomed to drink as tea and coffee.

A little incident comes to me, connected with a coffee-house not far from Jubilee Street on the Mile End Road.

'Cawn yer let me 'ave somethin' for this, daughter? Anythin', Hi don't mind. Hi 'aven't 'ad a bite the blessed dy, an' Hi'm that fynt . . . '

She was an old woman, clad in decent black rags, and in her hand she held a penny. The one she had addressed as 'daughter' was a careworn woman of forty, pro-prietress and waitress of the house.

I waited, possibly as anxiously as the old woman, to see how the appeal would be received. It was four in the afternoon, and she looked faint and sick. The woman hesitated an instant, then brought a large plate of 'stewed lamb and young peas.' I was eating a plate of it myself, and it is my judgment that the lamb was mutton and that the peas might have been younger without being youthful. However, the point is, the dish was sold at sixpence, and the proprietress gave it for a penny, demonstrating anew the old truth that the poor are the most charitable.

The old woman, profuse in her gratitude, took a seat on the other side of the narrow table and ravenously attacked the smoking stew. We ate steadily and silently, the pair of us, when suddenly, explosively and most gleefully, she cried out to me,—

'Hi sold a box o' matches! Yus,' she confirmed, if anything with greater and more explosive glee. 'Hi sold a box o' matches! That's 'ow Hi got the penny.'

'You must be getting along in years,' I suggested.

'Seventy-four yesterday,' she replied, and returned with gusto to her plate.

'Blimey, I'd like to do something for the old girl, that I would, but this is the first I've 'ad to-dy,' the young fellow alongside volunteered to me. 'An' I only 'ave this because I 'appened to make an odd shilling washin' out, Lord lumme! I don't know 'ow many pots.'

'No work at my own tryde for six weeks,' he said further, in reply to my questions; 'nothin' but odd jobs a blessed long wy between.'

* * * * *

One meets with all sorts of adventures in coffee-house, and I shall not soon forget a Cockney Amazon in a place near Trafalgar Square, to whom I tendered a sovereign when paying my score. (By the way, one is supposed to pay before he begins to eat, and if he be poorly dressed he is compelled to pay before he eats).

The girl bit the gold piece between her teeth, rang it on the counter, and then looked me and my rags witheringly up and down.

'Where'd you find it?' she at length demanded.

'Some mug left it on the table when he went out, eh, don't you think?' I retorted.

'Wot's yer gyme?' she queried, looking me calmly in the eyes.

'I makes 'em,' quoth I.

She sniffed superciliously and gave me the change in small silver, and I had my revenge by biting and ringing every piece of it.

'I'll give you a ha'penny for another lump of sugar in the tea,' I said.

'I'll see you in 'ell first,' came the retort courteous. Also, she amplified the retort courteous in divers vivid and unprintable ways.

I never had much talent for repartee, but she knocked silly what little I had, and I gulped down my tea a beaten man, while she gloated after me even as I passed out to the street.

While 300,000 people of London live in one-room tenements, and 900,000 are illegally and viciously housed, 38,000 more are registered as living in common lodging-houses—known in the vernacular as 'doss-houses.' There are many kinds of doss-houses, but in one thing they are all alike, from the filthy little ones to the monster big ones paying five per cent. and blatantly lauded by smug middle-class men who know but one thing about them, and that one thing is their uninhabitableness. By this I do not mean that the roofs leak or the walls are draughty; but what I do mean is that life in them is degrading and unwholesome.

'The poor man's hotel,' they are often called, but the phrase is caricature. Not to possess a room to one's self, in which sometimes to sit alone; to be forced out of bed willy-nilly, the first thing in the morning; to engage and pay anew for a bed each night;

and never to have any privacy, surely is a mode of existence quite different from that of hotel life.

This must not be considered a sweeping condemnation of the big private and municipal lodging-houses and working-men's homes. Far from it. They have remedied many of the atrocities attendant upon the irresponsible small doss-houses, and they give the workman more for his money than he ever received before; but that does not make them as habitable or wholesome as the dwelling-place of a man should be who does his work in the world.

The little private doss-houses, as a rule, are unmitigated horrors. I have slept in them, and I know; but let me pass them by and confine myself to the bigger and better ones. Not far from Middlesex Street, Whitechapel, I entered such a house, a place inhabited almost entirely by working men. The entrance was by way of a flight of steps descending from the sidewalk to what was properly the cellar of the building. Here were two large and gloomily lighted rooms, in which men cooked and ate. I had intended to do some cooking myself, but the smell of the place stole away my appetite, or, rather, wrested it from me; so I contented myself with watching other men cook and eat.

One workman, home from work, sat down opposite me at the rough wooden table, and began his meal. A handful of salt on the not over-clean table constituted his butter. Into it he dipped his bread, mouthful by mouthful, and washed it down with tea from a big mug. A piece of fish completed his bill of fare. He ate silently, looking neither to right nor left nor across at me. Here and there, at the various tables, other men were eating, just as silently. In the whole room there was hardly a note of conversation. A feeling of gloom pervaded the ill-lighted place. Many of them sat and brooded over the crumbs of their repast, and made me wonder, as Childe Roland wondered, what evil they had done that they should be punished so.

From the kitchen came the sounds of more genial life, and I ventured into the range where the men were cooking. But the smell I had noticed on entering was stronger here, and a rising nausea drove me into the street for fresh air.

On my return I paid fivepence for a 'cabin,' took my receipt for the same in the form of a huge brass check, and went upstairs to the smoking-room. Here, a couple of small billiard tables and several checkerboards were being used by young working-men, who waited in relays for their turn at the games, while many men were sitting around, smoking, reading, and mending their clothes. The young men were hilarious, the old men were gloomy. In fact, there were two types of men, the cheerful and the sodden or blue, and age seemed to determine the classification.

But no more than the two cellar rooms did this room convey the remotest suggestion of home. Certainly there could be nothing home-like about it to you and me, who know what home really is. On the walls were the most preposterous and insulting notices regulating the conduct of the guests, and at ten o'clock the lights were put out, and nothing remained but bed. This was gained by descending again to the cellar, by surrendering the brass check to a burly doorkeeper, and by climbing a long flight of stairs into the upper regions. I went to the top of the building and down again, passing several floors filled with sleeping men. The 'cabins' were the best accommodation, each cabin allowing space for a tiny bed and room alongside of it in which to undress. The bedding was clean, and with neither it nor the bed do I find any fault. But there was no privacy about it, no being alone.

To get an adequate idea of a floor filled with cabins, you have merely to magnify a layer of the pasteboard pigeon-holes of an egg-crate till each pigeon-hole is seven feet in height and otherwise properly dimensioned, then place the magnified layer on the floor of a large, barnlike room, and there you have it. There are no ceilings to the pigeon-holes, the walls are thin, and the snores from all the sleepers and every move and turn of your nearer neighbours come plainly to your ears. And this cabin is yours only for a little while. In the morning out you go. You cannot put your trunk in it, or come and go when you like, or lock the door behind you, or anything of the sort. In fact, there is no door at all, only a doorway. If you care to remain a guest in this poor man's hotel, you must put up with all this, and with prison regulations which impress upon you constantly that you are nobody, with little soul of your own and less to say about it.

Now I contend that the least a man who does his day's work should have is a room to himself, where he can lock the door and be safe in his possessions; where he can sit down and read by a window or look out; where he can come and go whenever he wishes; where he can accumulate a few personal belongings other than those he carries about with him on his back and in his pockets; where he can hang up pictures of his mother, sister, sweet-heart, ballet dancers, or bulldogs, as his heart listeth—in short, one place of his own on the earth of which he can say: 'This is mine, my castle; the world stops at the threshold; here am I lord and master.' He will be a better citizen, this man; and he will do a better day's work.

I stood on one floor of the poor man's hotel and listened. I went from bed to bed and looked at the sleepers. They were young men, from twenty to forty, most of them. Old men cannot afford the working-man's home. They go to the workhouse. But I looked at the young men, scores of them, and they were not bad-looking fellows. Their faces were made for women's kisses, their necks for women's arms. They were lovable, as men are lovable. They were capable of love. A woman's touch redeems and softens, and they needed such redemption and softening instead of each day growing harsh and harsher. And I wondered where these women were, and heard a 'harlot's ginny laugh.' Leman Street, Waterloo Road, Piccadilly, The Strand, answered me, and I knew where they were.

CHAPTER XXI
THE PRECARIOUSNESS OF LIFE

What do you work at? You look ill.
It's me lungs. I make sulphuric acid.

You are a salt-cake man?
Yes.
Is it hard work?
It is damned hard work.

Why do you work at such a slavish trade?
I am married. I have children. Am I to starve and let them?

Why do you lead this life?
I am married. There's a terrible lot of men out of work in St. Helen's.

What do you call hard work?
My work. You come and heave them three-hundred-weight lumps with
a fifty-pound bar, in that heat at the furnace door, and try it.
I will not. I am a philosopher.
Oh! Well, thee stick to t' job. Ours is t' vary devil.

From interviews with workmen by ROBERT BLATCHFORD.

I was talking with a very vindictive man. In his opinion, his wife had wronged him and the law had wronged him. The merits and morals of the case are immaterial. The meat of the matter is that she had obtained a separation, and he was compelled to pay ten shillings each week for the support of her and the five children. 'But look you,' said he to me, 'wot'll 'appen to 'er if I don't py up the ten shillings? S'posin', now, just s'posin' a accident 'appens to me, so I cawn't work. S'posin' I get a rupture, or the rheumatics, or the cholera. Wot's she goin' to do, eh? Wot's she goin' to do?'

He shook his head sadly. 'No 'ope for 'er. The best she cawn do is the work'ouse, an' that's 'ell. An' if she don't go to the work'ouse, it'll be a worse 'ell. Come along 'ith me an' I'll show you women sleepin' in a passage, a dozen of 'em. An' I'll show you worse, wot she'll come to if anythin' 'appens to me and the ten shillings.'

The certitude of this man's forecast is worthy of consideration. He knew conditions sufficiently to know the precariousness of his wife's grasp on food and shelter. For her game was up when his working capacity was impaired or destroyed. And when this state of affairs is looked at in its larger aspect, the same will be found true of hundreds of thousands and even millions of men and women living amicably together and co-operating in the pursuit of food and shelter.

The figures are appalling: 1,800,000 people in London live on the poverty line and below it, and 1,000,000 live with one week's wages between them and pauperism. In all England and Wales, eighteen per cent. of the whole population are driven to the parish for relief, and in London, according to the statistics of the London County Council, twenty-one per cent. of the whole population are driven to the parish for relief. Between being driven to the parish for relief and being an out-and-out pauper there is a great difference, yet London supports 123,000 paupers, quite a city of folk in themselves. One in every four in London dies on public charity, while 939 out of every 1000 in the United Kingdom die in poverty; 8,000,000 simply struggle on the ragged edge of starvation, and 20,000,000 more are not comfortable in the simple and clean sense of the word.

It is interesting to go more into detail concerning the London people who die on charity.

In 1886, and up to 1893, the percentage of pauperism to population was less in London than in all England; but since 1893, and for every succeeding year, the percentage of pauperism to population has been greater in London than in all England. Yet, from the Registrar-General's Report for 1886, the following figures are taken:-

Out of 81,951 deaths in London (1884):-

| In workhouses | 9,909 | In hospitals | 6,559 | In lunatic asylums | 278 |
| | | | | Total in public refuges | 16,746 |

Commenting on these figures, a Fabian writer says: 'Considering that comparatively few of these are children, it is probable that one in every three London adults will be driven into one of these refuges to die, and the proportion in the case of the manual labour class must of course be still larger.'

These figures serve somewhat to indicate the proximity of the average worker to pauperism. Various things make pauperism. An advertisement, for instance, such as this, appearing in yesterday morning's paper:-

'Clerk wanted, with knowledge of shorthand, typewriting, and invoicing: wages ten shillings ($2.50) a week. Apply by letter,' &c.

And in to-day's paper I read of a clerk, thirty-five years of age and an inmate of a London workhouse, brought before a magistrate for non-performance of task. He claimed that he had done his various tasks since he had been an inmate; but when the master set him to breaking stones, his hands blistered, and he could not finish the task. He had never been used to an implement heavier than a pen, he said. The magistrate sentenced him and his blistered hands to seven days' hard labour.

Old age, of course, makes pauperism. And then there is the accident, the thing happening, the death or disablement of the husband, father, and bread-winner. Here is a man, with a wife and three children, living on the ticklish security of twenty shillings per week—and there are hundreds of thousands of such families in London. Perforce, to even half exist, they must live up to the last penny of it, so that a week's wages (one pound) is all that stands between this family and pauperism or starvation. The thing happens, the father is struck down, and what then? A mother with three children can do little or nothing. Either she must hand her children over to society as juvenile paupers, in order to be free to do something adequate for herself, or she must go to the sweat-shops for work which she can perform in the vile den possible to her reduced income. But with the sweat-shops, married women who eke out their husband's earnings, and single women who have but themselves miserably to support, determine the scale of wages. And this scale of wages, so determined, is so low that the mother and her three children can live only in positive beastliness and semi-starvation, till decay and death end their suffering.

To show that this mother, with her three children to support, cannot compete in the sweating industries, I instance from the current newspapers the two following cases:-

A father indignantly writes that his daughter and a girl companion receive 8.5d. per gross for making boxes. They made each day four gross. Their expenses were 8d. for car fare, 2d. for stamps, 2.5d. for glue, and 1d. for string, so that all they earned between them was 1s. 9d., or a daily wage each of 10.5d.

In the second ewe, before the Luton Guardians a few days ago, an old woman of seventy-two appeared, asking for relief. 'She was a straw-hat maker, but had been compelled to give up the work owing to the price she obtained for them— namely, 2.25d. each. For that price she had to provide plait trimmings and make and finish the hats.'

Yet this mother and her three children we are considering have done no wrong that they should be so punished. They have not sinned. The thing happened, that is all; the husband, father and bread-winner, was struck down. There is no guarding against it. It is fortuitous. A family stands so many chances of escaping the bottom of the Abyss, and so many chances of falling plump down to it. The chance is reducible to cold, pitiless figures, and a few of these figures will not be out of place.

Sir A. Forwood calculates that—

1 of every 1400 workmen is killed annually.
1 of every 2500 workmen is totally disabled.
1 of every 300 workmen is permanently partially disabled.
1 of every 8 workmen is temporarily disabled 3 or 4 weeks.

But these are only the accidents of industry. The high mortality of the people who live in the Ghetto plays a terrible part. The average age at death among the people of the West End is fifty-five years; the average age at death among the people of the East End is thirty years. That is to say, the person in the West End has twice the chance for life that the person has in the East End. Talk of war! The mortality in South Africa and the Philippines fades away to insignificance. Here, in the heart of peace, is where the blood is being shed; and here not even the civilised rules of warfare obtain, for the women and children and babes in the arms are killed just as ferociously as the men are killed. War! In England, every year, 500,000 men, women, and children, engaged in the various industries, are killed and disabled, or are injured to disablement by disease.

In the West End eighteen per cent. of the children die before five years of age; in the East End fifty-five per cent. of the children die before five years of age. And there are streets in London where out of every one hundred children born in a year, fifty die during the next year; and of the fifty that remain, twenty-five die before they are five years old. Slaughter! Herod did not do quite so badly.

That industry causes greater havoc with human life than battle does no better substantiation can be given than the following extract from a recent report of the Liverpool Medical Officer, which is not applicable to Liverpool alone:-

In many instances little if any sunlight could get to the courts, and the atmosphere within the dwellings was always foul, owing largely to the saturated condition of the walls and ceilings, which for so many years had absorbed the exhalations of the occupants into their porous material. Singular testimony to the absence of sunlight in these courts was furnished by the action of the Parks and Gardens Committee, who desired to brighten the homes of the poorest class by gifts of growing flowers and window-boxes; but these gifts could not be made in courts such as these, *as flowers and plants were susceptible to the unwholesome surroundings, and would not live.*

Mr. George Haw has compiled the following table on the three St. George's parishes (London parishes):-

	Percentage of Population Overcrowded	Death-rate per 1000
St. George's West	10	13.2
St. George's South	35	23.7
St. George's East	40	26.4

Then there are the 'dangerous trades,' in which countless workers are employed. Their hold on life is indeed precarious—far, far more precarious than the hold of the twentieth-century soldier on life. In the linen trade, in the preparation of the flax, wet feet and wet clothes cause an unusual amount of bronchitis, pneumonia, and severe rheumatism; while in the carding and spinning departments the fine dust produces lung disease in the majority of cases, and the woman who starts carding at seventeen or eighteen begins to break up and go to pieces at thirty. The chemical labourers, picked from the strongest and most splendidly-built men to be found, live, on an average, less than forty-eight years.

Says Dr. Arlidge, of the potter's trade: 'Potter's dust does not kill suddenly, but settles, year after year, a little more firmly into the lungs, until at length a case of plaster is formed. Breathing becomes more and more difficult and depressed, and finally ceases.'

Steel dust, stone dust, clay dust, alkali dust, fluff dust, fibre dust—all these things kill, and they are more deadly than machine-guns and pom-poms. Worst of all is the lead dust in the white-lead trades. Here is a description of the typical dissolution of a young, healthy, well-developed girl who goes to work in a white-lead factory:-

Here, after a varying degree of exposure, she becomes anaemic. It may be that her gums show a very faint blue line, or perchance her teeth and gums are perfectly sound, and no blue line is discernible. Coincidently with the anaemia she has been getting thinner, but so gradually as scarcely to impress itself upon her or her friends. Sickness, however, ensues, and headaches, growing in intensity, are developed. These are frequently attended by obscuration of vision or temporary blindness. Such a girl passes into what appears to her friends and medical adviser as ordinary hysteria. This gradually deepens without warning, until she is suddenly seized with a convulsion, beginning in one half of the face, then involving the arm, next the leg of the same side of the body, until the convulsion, violent and purely epileptic form in character, becomes universal. This is attended by loss of consciousness, out of which she passes into a series of convulsions, gradually increasing in severity, in one of which she dies—or consciousness, partial or perfect, is regained, either, it may be, for a few minutes, a few hours, or days, during which violent headache is complained of, or she is delirious and excited, as in acute mania, or dull and sullen as in melancholia, and requires to be roused, when she is found wandering, and her speech is somewhat imperfect. Without further warning, save that the pulse, which has become soft, with nearly the normal number of beats, all at once becomes low and hard; she is suddenly seized with another convulsion, in which she dies, or passes into a state of coma from which she never rallies. In another case the convulsions will gradually subside, the headache disappears and the patient recovers, only to find that she has completely lost her eyesight, a loss that may be temporary or permanent.

And here are a few specific cases of white-lead poisoning:-

Charlotte Rafferty, a fine, well-grown young woman with a splendid constitution—who had never had a day's illness in her life—became a white-lead worker. Convulsions seized her at the foot of the ladder in the works. Dr. Oliver examined her, found the blue line along her gums, which shows that the system is under the influence of the lead. He knew that the convulsions would shortly return. They did so, and she died.

Mary Ann Toler—a girl of seventeen, who had never had a fit in her life—three times became ill, and had to leave off work in the factory. Before she was nineteen she showed symptoms of lead poisoning—had fits, frothed at the mouth, and died.

Mary A., an unusually vigorous woman, was able to work in the lead factory for *twenty years*, having colic once only during that time. Her eight children all died in early infancy from convulsions. One morning, whilst brushing her hair, this woman suddenly lost all power in both her wrists.

Eliza H., aged twenty-five, *after five months* at lead works, was seized with colic. She entered another factory (after being refused by the first one) and worked on uninterruptedly for two years. Then the former symptoms returned, she was seized with convulsions, and died in two days of acute lead poisoning.

Mr. Vaughan Nash, speaking of the unborn generation, says: 'The children of the white-lead worker enter the world, as a rule, only to die from the convulsions of lead poisoning—they are either born prematurely, or die within the first year.'

And, finally, let me instance the case of Harriet A. Walker, a young girl of seventeen, killed while leading a forlorn hope on the industrial battlefield. She was employed as an enamelled ware brusher, wherein lead poisoning is encountered. Her father and brother were both out of employment. She concealed her illness, walked six miles a day to and from work, earned her seven or eight shillings per week, and died, at seventeen.

Depression in trade also plays an important part in hurling the workers into the Abyss. With a week's wages between a family and pauperism, a month's enforced idleness means hardship and misery almost indescribable, and from the ravages of which the victims do not always recover when work is to be had again. Just now the daily papers contain the report of a meeting of the Carlisle branch of the Dockers' Union, wherein it is stated that many of the men, for months past, have not averaged a weekly income of more than from four to five shillings. The stagnated state of the shipping industry in the port of London is held accountable for this condition of affairs.

To the young working-man or working-woman, or married couple, there is no assurance of happy or healthy middle life, nor of solvent old age. Work as they will, they cannot make their future secure. It is all a matter of chance. Everything depends upon the thing happening, the thing with which they have nothing to do. Precaution cannot fend it off, nor can wiles evade it. If they remain on the industrial battlefield they must face it and take their chance against heavy odds. Of course, if they are favourably made and are not tied by kinship duties, they may run away from the industrial battlefield. In which event the safest thing the man can do is to join the army; and for the woman, possibly, to become a Red Cross nurse or go into a nunnery. In either case they must forego home and children and all that makes life worth living and old age other than a nightmare.

CHAPTER XXII
SUICIDE

England is the paradise of the rich, the purgatory of the wise, and the hell of the poor.

THEODORE PARKER

With life so precarious, and opportunity for the happiness of life so remote, it is inevitable that life shall be cheap and suicide common. So common is it, that one cannot pick up a daily paper without running across it; while an attempt-at-suicide case in a police court excites no more interest than an ordinary 'drunk,' and is handled with the same rapidity and unconcern.

I remember such a case in the Thames Police Court. I pride myself that I have good eyes and ears, and a fair working knowledge of men and things; but I confess, as I stood in that court-room, that I was half bewildered by the amazing despatch with which drunks, disorderlies, vagrants, brawlers, wife-beaters, thieves, fences, gamblers, and women of the street went through the machine of justice. The dock stood in the centre of the court (where the light is best), and into it and out again stepped men, women, and children, in a stream as steady as the stream of sentences which fell from the magistrate's lips.

I was still pondering over a consumptive 'fence' who had pleaded inability to work and necessity for supporting wife and children, and who had received a year at hard labour, when a young boy of about twenty appeared in the dock. 'Alfred Freeman,' I caught his name, but failed to catch the charge. A stout and motherly-looking woman bobbed up in the witness-box and began her testimony. Wife of the Britannia lock-keeper, I learned she was. Time, night; a splash; she ran to the lock and found the prisoner in the water.

I flashed my gaze from her to him. So that was the charge, self-murder. He stood there dazed and unheeding, his bonny brown hair rumpled down his forehead, his face haggard and careworn and boyish still.

'Yes, sir,' the lock-keeper's wife was saying. 'As fast as I pulled to get 'im out, 'e crawled back. Then I called for 'elp, and some workmen 'appened along, and we got 'im out and turned 'im over to the constable.'

The magistrate complimented the woman on her muscular powers, and the court-room laughed; but all I could see was a boy on the threshold of life, passionately crawling to muddy death, and there was no laughter in it.

A man was now in the witness-box, testifying to the boy's good character and giving extenuating evidence. He was the boy's foreman, or had been. Alfred was a good boy, but he had had lots of trouble at home, money matters. And then his mother was sick. He was given to worrying, and he worried over it till he laid himself out and wasn't fit for work. He (the foreman), for the sake of his own reputation, the boy's work being bad, had been forced to ask him to resign.

'Anything to say?' the magistrate demanded abruptly.

The boy in the dock mumbled something indistinctly. He was still dazed.

'What does he say, constable?' the magistrate asked impatiently.

The stalwart man in blue bent his ear to the prisoner's lips, and then replied loudly, 'He says he's very sorry, your Worship.'

'Remanded,' said his Worship; and the next case was under way, the first witness already engaged in taking the oath. The boy, dazed and unheeding, passed out with the jailer. That was all, five minutes from start to finish; and two hulking brutes in the dock were trying strenuously to shift the responsibility of the possession of a stolen fishing-pole, worth probably ten cents.

The chief trouble with these poor folk is that they do not know how to commit suicide, and usually have to make two or three attempts before they succeed. This, very naturally, is a horrid nuisance to the constables and magistrates, and gives them no end of trouble. Sometimes, however, the magistrates are frankly outspoken about the matter, and censure the prisoners for the slackness of their attempts. For instance Mr. R. S—, chairman of the S— B— magistrates, in the case the other day of Ann Wood, who tried to make away with herself in the canal: 'If you wanted to do it, why didn't you do it and get it done with?' demanded the indignant Mr. R. S—. 'Why did you not get under the water and make an end of it, instead of giving us all this trouble and bother?'

Poverty, misery, and fear of the workhouse, are the principal causes of suicide among the working classes. 'I'll drown myself before I go into the workhouse,' said Ellen Hughes Hunt, aged fifty-two. Last Wednesday they held an inquest on her body at Shoreditch. Her husband came from the Islington Workhouse to testify. He had been a cheesemonger, but failure in business and poverty had driven him into the workhouse, whither his wife had refused to accompany him.

She was last seen at one in the morning. Three hours later her hat and jacket were found on the towing path by the Regent's Canal, and later her body was fished from the water. *Verdict: Suicide during temporary insanity.*

Such verdicts are crimes against truth. The Law is a lie, and through it men lie most shamelessly. For instance, a disgraced woman, forsaken and spat upon by kith and kin, doses herself and her baby with laudanum. The baby dies; but she pulls through after a few weeks in hospital, is charged with murder, convicted, and sentenced to ten years' penal servitude. Recovering, the Law holds her responsible for her actions; yet, had she died, the same Law would have rendered a verdict of temporary insanity.

Now, considering the case of Ellen Hughes Hunt, it is as fair and logical to say that her husband was suffering from temporary insanity when he went into the Islington

Workhouse, as it is to say that she was suffering from temporary insanity when she went into the Regent's Canal. As to which is the preferable sojourning place is a matter of opinion, of intellectual judgment. I, for one, from what I know of canals and workhouses, should choose the canal, were I in a similar position. And I make bold to contend that I am no more insane than Ellen Hughes Hunt, her husband, and the rest of the human herd.

Man no longer follows instinct with the old natural fidelity. He has developed into a reasoning creature, and can intellectually cling to life or discard life just as life happens to promise great pleasure or pain. I dare to assert that Ellen Hughes Hunt, defrauded and bilked of all the joys of life which fifty-two years' service in the world has earned, with nothing but the horrors of the workhouse before her, was very rational and level-headed when she elected to jump into the canal. And I dare to assert, further, that the jury had done a wiser thing to bring in a verdict charging society with temporary insanity for allowing Ellen Hughes Hunt to be defrauded and bilked of all the joys of life which fifty-two years' service in the world had earned.

Temporary insanity! Oh, these cursed phrases, these lies of language, under which people with meat in their bellies and whole shirts on their backs shelter themselves, and evade the responsibility of their brothers and sisters, empty of belly and without whole shirts on their backs.

From one issue of the *Observer*, an East End paper, I quote the following commonplace events:-

A ship's fireman, named Johnny King, was charged with attempting to commit suicide. On Wednesday defendant went to Bow Police Station and stated that he had swallowed a quantity of phosphor paste, as he was hard up and unable to obtain work. King was taken inside and an emetic administered, when he vomited up a quantity of the poison. Defendant now said he was very sorry. Although he had sixteen years' good character, he was unable to obtain work of any kind. Mr. Dickinson had defendant put back for the court missionary to see him.

Timothy Warner, thirty-two, was remanded for a similar offence. He jumped off Limehouse Pier, and when rescued, said, 'I intended to do it.'
A decent-looking young woman, named Ellen Gray, was remanded on a charge of attempting to commit suicide. About half-past eight on Sunday morning Constable 834 K found defendant lying in a doorway in Benworth Street, and she was in a very drowsy condition. She was holding an empty bottle in one hand, and stated that some two or three hours previously she had swallowed a quantity of laudanum. As she was evidently very ill, the divisional surgeon was sent for, and having administered some coffee, ordered that she was to be kept awake. When defendant was charged, she stated that the reason why she attempted to take her life was she had neither home nor friends.

I do not say that all people who commit suicide are sane, no more than I say that all people who do not commit suicide are sane. Insecurity of food and shelter, by the way, is a great cause of insanity among the living. Costermongers, hawkers, and pedlars, a class of workers who live from hand to mouth more than those of any other class, form the highest percentage of those in the lunatic asylums. Among the males each year, 26.9 per 10,000 go insane, and among the women, 36.9. On the other hand, of soldiers, who are at least sure of food and shelter, 13 per 10,000 go insane; and of farmers and graziers, only 5.1. So a coster is twice as likely to lose his reason as a soldier, and five times as likely as a farmer.

Misfortune and misery are very potent in turning people's heads, and drive one person to the lunatic asylum, and another to the morgue or the gallows. When the thing happens, and the father and husband, for all of his love for wife and children and his willingness to work, can get no work to do, it is a simple matter for his reason to totter and the light within his brain go out. And it is especially simple when it is taken into consideration that his body is ravaged by innutrition and disease, in addition to his soul being torn by the sight of his suffering wife and little ones.

'He is a good-looking man, with a mass of black hair, dark, expressive eyes, delicately chiselled nose and chin, and wavy, fair moustache.' This is the reporter's description of Frank Cavilla as he stood in court, this dreary month of September, 'dressed in a much worn grey suit, and wearing no collar.'

Frank Cavilla lived and worked as a house decorator in London. He is described as a good workman, a steady fellow, and not given to drink, while all his neighbours unite in testifying that he was a gentle and affectionate husband and father.

His wife, Hannah Cavilla, was a big, handsome, light-hearted woman. She saw to it that his children were sent neat and clean (the neighbours all remarked the fact) to the Childeric Road Board School. And so, with such a man, so blessed, working steadily and living temperately, all went well, and the goose hung high.

Then the thing happened. He worked for a Mr. Beck, builder, and lived in one of his master's houses in Trundley Road. Mr. Beck was thrown from his trap and killed. The thing was an unruly horse, and, as I say, it happened. Cavilla had to seek fresh employment and find another house.

This occurred eighteen months ago. For eighteen months he fought the big fight. He got rooms in a little house in Batavia Road, but could not make both ends meet. Steady work could not be obtained. He struggled manfully at casual employment of all sorts, his wife and four children starving before his eyes. He starved himself, and grew weak, and fell ill. This was three months ago, and then there was absolutely no food at all. They made no complaint, spoke no word; but poor folk know. The housewives of Batavia Road sent them food, but so respectable were the Cavillas that the food was sent anonymously, mysteriously, so as not to hurt their pride.

The thing had happened. He had fought, and starved, and suffered for eighteen months. He got up one September morning, early. He opened his pocket-knife. He cut the throat of his wife, Hannah Cavilla, aged thirty-three. He cut the throat of his first-born, Frank, aged twelve. He cut the throat of his son, Walter, aged eight. He cut the throat of his daughter, Nellie, aged four. He cut the throat of his youngest-born, Ernest, aged sixteen months. Then he watched beside the dead all day until the evening, when the police came, and he told them to put a penny in the slot of the gas-meter in order that they might have light to see.

Frank Cavilla stood in court, dressed in a much worn grey suit, and wearing no collar. He was a good-looking man, with a mass of black hair, dark, expressive eyes, delicately chiselled nose and chin, and wavy, fair moustache.

CHAPTER XXIII

THE CHILDREN

'Where home is a hovel, and dull we grovel,
Forgetting the world is fair.'

There is one beautiful sight in the East End, and only one, and it is the children dancing in the street when the organ-grinder goes his round. It is fascinating to watch them, the new-born, the next generation, swaying and stepping, with pretty little mimicries and graceful inventions all their own, with muscles that move swiftly and easily, and bodies that leap airily, weaving rhythms never taught in dancing school.

I have talked with these children, here, there, and everywhere, and they struck me as being bright as other children, and in many ways even brighter. They have most active little imaginations. Their capacity for projecting themselves into the realm of romance and fantasy is remarkable. A joyous life is romping in their blood. They delight in music, and motion, and colour, and very often they betray a startling beauty of face and form under their filth and rags.

But there is a Pied Piper of London Town who steals them all away. They disappear. One never sees them again, or anything that suggests them. You may look for them in vain amongst the generation of grown-ups. Here you will find stunted forms, ugly faces, and blunt and stolid minds. Grace, beauty, imagination, all the resiliency of mind and muscle, are gone. Sometimes, however, you may see a woman, not necessarily old, but twisted and deformed out of all womanhood, bloated and drunken, lift her draggled skirts and execute a few grotesque and lumbering steps upon the pavement. It is a hint that she was once one of those children who danced to the organ-grinder. Those grotesque and lumbering steps are all that is left of the promise of childhood. In the befogged recesses of her brain has arisen a fleeting memory that she was once a girl. The crowd closes in. Little girls are dancing beside her, about her, with all the pretty graces she dimly recollects, but can no more than parody with her body. Then she pants for breath, exhausted, and stumbles out through the circle. But the little girls dance on.

The children of the Ghetto possess all the qualities which make for noble manhood and womanhood; but the Ghetto itself, like an infuriated tigress turning on its young, turns upon and destroys all these qualities, blots out the light and laughter, and moulds those it does not kill into sodden and forlorn creatures, uncouth, degraded, and wretched below the beasts of the field.

As to the manner in which this is done, I have in previous chapters described it at length; here let Professor Huxley describe it in brief:-

'Any one who is acquainted with the state of the population of all great industrial centres, whether in this or other countries, is aware that amidst a large and increasing body of that population there reigns supreme . . . that condition which the French call *la misère*, a word for which I do not think there is any exact English equivalent. It is a condition in which the food, warmth, and clothing which are necessary for the mere maintenance of the functions of the body in their normal state cannot be obtained; in which men, women, and children are forced to crowd into dens wherein decency is abolished, and the most ordinary conditions of healthful existence are impossible of attainment;

in which the pleasures within reach are reduced to brutality and drunkenness; in which the pains accumulate at compound interest in the shape of starvation, disease, stunted development, and moral degradation; in which the prospect of even steady and honest industry is a life of unsuccessful battling with hunger, rounded by a pauper's grave.'

In such conditions, the outlook for children is hopeless. They die like flies, and those that survive, survive because they possess excessive vitality and a capacity of adaptation to the degradation with which they are surrounded. They have no home life. In the dens and lairs in which they live they are exposed to all that is obscene and indecent. And as their minds are made rotten, so are their bodies made rotten by bad sanitation, overcrowding, and underfeeding. When a father and mother live with three or four children in a room where the children take turn about in sitting up to drive the rats away from the sleepers, when those children never have enough to eat and are preyed upon and made miserable and weak by swarming vermin, the sort of men and women the survivors will make can readily be imagined.

> 'Dull despair and misery
> Lie about them from their birth;
> Ugly curses, uglier mirth,
> Are their earliest lullaby.'

A man and a woman marry and set up housekeeping in one room. Their income does not increase with the years, though their family does, and the man is exceedingly lucky if he can keep his health and his job. A baby comes, and then another. This means that more room should be obtained; but these little mouths and bodies mean additional expense and make it absolutely impossible to get more spacious quarters. More babies come. There is not room in which to turn around. The youngsters run the streets, and by the time they are twelve or fourteen the room-issue comes to a head, and out they go on the streets for good. The boy, if he be lucky, can manage to make the common lodging-houses, and he may have any one of several ends. But the girl of fourteen or fifteen, forced in this manner to leave the one room called home, and able to earn at the best a paltry five or six shillings per week, can have but one end. And the bitter end of that one end is such as that of the woman whose body the police found this morning in a doorway in Dorset Street, Whitechapel. Homeless, shelterless, sick, with no one with her in her last hour, she had died in the night of exposure. She was sixty-two years old and a match vendor. She died as a wild animal dies.

Fresh in my mind is the picture of a boy in the dock of an East End police court. His head was barely visible above the railing. He was being proved guilty of stealing two shillings from a woman, which he had spent, not for candy and cakes and a good time, but for food.

'Why didn't you ask the woman for food?' the magistrate demanded, in a hurt sort of tone. 'She would surely have given you something to eat.'

'If I 'ad arsked 'er, I'd got locked up for beggin',' was the boy's reply.

The magistrate knitted his brows and accepted the rebuke. Nobody knew the boy, nor his father or mother. He was without beginning or antecedent, a waif, a stray, a young cub seeking his food in the jungle of empire, preying upon the weak and being preyed upon by the strong.

The people who try to help, who gather up the Ghetto children and send them away on a day's outing to the country, believe that not very many children reach the age of ten without having had at least one day there. Of this, a writer says: 'The mental change caused by one day so spent must not be undervalued. Whatever the circumstances, the children learn the meaning of fields and woods, so that descriptions of country scenery in the books they read, which before conveyed no impression, become now intelligible.'

One day in the fields and woods, if they are lucky enough to be picked up by the people who try to help! And they are being born faster every day than they can be carted off to the fields and woods for the one day in their lives. One day! In all their lives, one day! And for the rest of the days, as the boy told a certain bishop, 'At ten we 'ops the wag; at thirteen we nicks things; an' at sixteen we bashes the copper.' Which is to say, at ten they play truant, at thirteen steal, and at sixteen are sufficiently developed hooligans to smash the policemen.

The Rev. J. Cartmel Robinson tells of a boy and girl of his parish who set out to walk to the forest. They walked and walked through the never-ending streets, expecting always to see it by-and-by; until they sat down at last, faint and despairing, and were rescued by a kind woman who brought them back. Evidently they had been overlooked by the people who try to help.

The same gentleman is authority for the statement that in a street in Hoxton (a district of the vast East End), over seven hundred children, between five and thirteen years, live in eighty small houses. And he adds: 'It is because London has largely shut her children in a maze of streets and houses and robbed them of their rightful inheritance in sky and field and brook, that they grow up to be men and women physically unfit.'

He tells of a member of his congregation who let a basement room to a married couple. 'They said they had two children; when they got possession it turned out that they had four. After a while a fifth appeared, and the landlord gave them notice to quit. They paid no attention to it. Then the sanitary inspector who has to wink at the law so often, came in and threatened my friend with legal proceedings. He pleaded that he could not get them out. They pleaded that nobody would have them with so many children at a rental within their means, which is one of the commonest complaints of the poor, by-the-bye. What was to be done? The landlord was between two millstones. Finally he applied to the magistrate, who sent up an officer to inquire into the case. Since that time about twenty days have elapsed, and nothing has yet been done. Is this a singular case? By no means; it is quite common.'

Last week the police raided a disorderly house. In one room were found two young children. They were arrested and charged with being inmates the same as the women had been. Their father appeared at the trial. He stated that himself and wife and two older children, besides the two in the dock, occupied that room; he stated also that he occupied it because he could get no other room for the half-crown a week he paid for it. The magistrate discharged the two juvenile offenders and warned the father that he was bringing his children up unhealthily.

But there is no need further to multiply instances. In London the slaughter of the innocents goes on on a scale more stupendous than any before in the history of the world. And equally stupendous is the callousness of the people who believe in Christ, acknowledge God, and go to church regularly on Sunday. For the rest of the week they riot about on the rents and profits which come to them from the East End stained with the blood of the children. Also, at times, so peculiarly are they made, they will take half a million of these rents and profits and send it away to educate the black boys of the Soudan.

CHAPTER XXIV
A VISION OF THE NIGHT

All these were years ago little red-coloured, pulpy infants, capable of being kneaded, baked, into any social form you chose.

CARLYLE.

Late last night I walked along Commercial Street from Spitalfields to Whitechapel, and still continuing south, down Leman Street to the docks. And as I walked I smiled at the East End papers, which, filled with civic pride, boastfully proclaim that there is nothing the matter with the East End as a living place for men and women.

It is rather hard to tell a tithe of what I saw. Much of it is untenable. But in a general way I may say that I saw a nightmare, a fearful slime that quickened the pavement with life, a mess of unmentionable obscenity that put into eclipse the 'nightly horror' of Piccadilly and the Strand. It *was* a menagerie of garmented bipeds that looked something like humans and more like beasts, and to complete the picture, brass-buttoned keepers kept order among them when they snarled too fiercely.

I was glad the keepers were there, for I did not have on my 'seafaring' clothes, and I was what is called a 'mark' for the creatures of prey that prowled up and down. At times, between keepers, these males looked at me sharply, hungrily, gutter-wolves that they were, and I was afraid of their hands, of their naked hands, as one may be afraid of the paws of a gorilla. They reminded me of gorillas. Their bodies were small, ill-shaped, and squat. There were no swelling muscles, no abundant thews and wide-spreading shoulders. They exhibited, rather, an elemental economy of nature, such as the cave-men must have exhibited. But there was strength in those meagre bodies, the ferocious, primordial strength to clutch and gripe and tear and rend. When they spring upon their human prey they are known even to bend the victim backward and double its body till the back is broken. They possess neither conscience nor sentiment, and they will kill for a half-sovereign, without fear or favour, if they are given but half a chance. They are a new species, a breed of city savages. The streets and houses, alleys and courts, are their hunting grounds. As valley and mountain are to the natural savage, street and building are valley and mountain to them. The slum is their jungle, and they live and prey in the jungle.

The dear soft people of the golden theatres and wonder-mansions of the West End do not see these creatures, do not dream that they exist. But they are here, alive, very much alive in their jungle. And woe the day, when England is fighting in her last trench, and her able-bodied men are on the firing line! For on that day they will crawl out of their dens and lairs, and the people of the West End will see them, as the dear soft aristocrats of Feudal France saw them and asked one another, 'Whence came they?' 'Are they men?'

But they were not the only beasts that ranged the menagerie. They were only here and there, lurking in dark courts and passing like grey shadows along the walls; but the women from whose rotten loins they spring were everywhere. They whined insolently, and in maudlin tones begged me for pennies, and worse. They held carouse in every boozing ken, slatternly, unkempt, bleary-eyed, and towsled, leering and gibbering, overspilling with foulness and corruption, and, gone in debauch, sprawling across benches and bars, unspeakably repulsive, fearful to look upon.

And there were others, strange, weird faces and forms and twisted monstrosities that shouldered me on every side, inconceivable types of sodden ugliness, the wrecks of society, the perambulating carcasses, the living deaths—women, blasted by disease and drink till their shame brought not tuppence in the open mart; and men, in fantastic rags, wrenched by hardship and exposure out of all semblance of men, their faces in a perpetual writhe of pain, grinning idiotically, shambling like apes, dying with every step they took and each breath they drew. And there were young girls, of eighteen and twenty, with trim bodies and faces yet untouched with twist and bloat, who had fetched the bottom of the Abyss plump, in one swift fall. And I remember a lad of fourteen, and one of six or seven, white-faced and sickly, homeless, the pair of them, who sat upon the pavement with their backs against a railing and watched it all.

The unfit and the unneeded! Industry does not clamour for them. There are no jobs going begging through lack of men and women. The dockers crowd at the entrance gate, and curse and turn away when the foreman does not give them a call. The engineers who have work pay six shillings a week to their brother engineers who can find nothing to do; 514,000 textile workers oppose a resolution condemning the employment of children under fifteen. Women, and plenty to spare, are found to toil under the sweat-shop masters for tenpence a day of fourteen hours. Alfred Freeman crawls to muddy death because he loses his job. Ellen Hughes Hunt prefers Regent's Canal to Islington Workhouse. Frank Cavilla cuts the throats of his wife and children because he cannot find work enough to give them food and shelter.

The unfit and the unneeded! The miserable and despised and forgotten, dying in the social shambles. The progeny of prostitution—of the prostitution of men and women and children, of flesh and blood, and sparkle and spirit; in brief, the prostitution of labour. If this is the best that civilisation can do for the human, then give us howling and naked savagery. Far better to be a people of the wilderness and desert, of the cave and the squatting-place, than to be a people of the machine and the Abyss.

CHAPTER XXV
THE HUNGER WAIL

*I hold, if the Almighty had ever made a set of men to do all of the
eating and none of the work, he would have made them with mouths
only, and no hands; and if he had ever made another set that he had
intended should do all the work and none of the eating, he would
have made them without mouths and with all hands.*

ABRAHAM LINCOLN

'My father has more stamina than I, for he is country-born.'

The speaker, a bright young East Ender, was lamenting his poor physical development.

'Look at my scrawny arm, will you.' He pulled up his sleeve. 'Not enough to eat, that's what's the matter with it. Oh, not now. I have what I want to eat these days. But it's too late. It can't make up for what I didn't have to eat when I was a kiddy. Dad came up to London from the Fen Country. Mother died, and there were six of us kiddies and dad living in two small rooms.

'He had hard times, dad did. He might have chucked us, but he didn't. He slaved all day, and at night he came home and cooked and cared for us. He was father and mother, both. He did his best, but we didn't have enough to eat. We rarely saw meat, and then of the worst. And it is not good for growing kiddies to sit down to a dinner of bread and a bit of cheese, and not enough of it.

'And what's the result? I am undersized, and I haven't the stamina of my dad. It was starved out of me. In a couple of generations there'll be no more of me here in London. Yet there's my younger brother; he's bigger and better developed. You see, dad and we children held together, and that accounts for it.'

'But I don't see,' I objected. 'I should think, under such conditions, that the vitality should decrease and the younger children be born weaker and weaker.'

'Not when they hold together,' he replied. 'Whenever you come along in the East End and see a child of from eight to twelve, good-sized, well-developed, and healthy-looking, just you ask and you will find that it is the youngest in the family, or at least is one of the younger. The way of it is this: the older children starve more than the younger ones. By the time the younger ones come along, the older ones are starting to work, and there is more money coming in, and more food to go around.'

He pulled down his sleeve, a concrete instance of where chronic semi-starvation kills not, but stunts. His voice was but one among the myriads that raise the cry of the hunger wail in the greatest empire in the world. On any one day, over 1,000,000 people are in receipt of poor-law relief in the United Kingdom. One in eleven of the whole working-class receive poor-law relief in the course of the year; 37,500,000 people receive less than £12 per month, per family; and a constant army of 8,000,000 lives on the border of starvation.

A committee of the London County school board makes this declaration: 'At times, *when there is no special distress*, 55,000 children in a state of hunger, which makes it useless to attempt to teach them, are in the schools of London alone.' The italics are mine. 'When there is no special distress' means good times in England; for the people of England have come to look upon starvation and suffering, which they call 'distress,' as part of the social order. Chronic starvation is looked upon as a matter of course. It is only when acute starvation makes its appearance on a large scale that they think something is unusual

I shall never forget the bitter wail of a blind man in a little East End shop at the close of a murky day. He had been the eldest of five children, with a mother and no father. Being the eldest, he had starved and worked as a child to put bread into the mouths of his little brothers and sisters. Not once in three months did he ever taste meat. He never knew what it was to have his hunger thoroughly appeased. And he claimed that this chronic starvation of his childhood had robbed him of his sight. To support the claim, he quoted from the report of the Royal Commission on the Blind, 'Blindness is more prevalent in poor districts, and poverty accelerates this dreadful affliction.'

But he went further, this blind man, and in his voice was the bitterness of an afflicted man to whom society did not give enough to eat. He was one of an enormous army of blind in London, and he said that in the blind homes they did not receive half enough to eat. He gave the diet for a day:-

Breakfast— 0.75 pint of skilly and dry bread.
Dinner   — 3 oz. meat. 1 slice of bread. 0.5 lb. potatoes.
Supper   — 0.75 pint of skilly and dry bread.

Oscar Wilde, God rest his soul, voices the cry of the prison child, which, in varying degree, is the cry of the prison man and woman:-

'The second thing from which a child suffers in prison is hunger. The food that is given to it consists of a piece of usually bad-baked prison bread and a tin of water for breakfast at half-past seven. At twelve o'clock it gets dinner, composed of a tin of coarse Indian meal stirabout (skilly), and at half-past five it gets a piece of dry bread and a tin of water for its supper. This diet in the case of a strong grown man is always productive of illness of some kind, chiefly of course diarrhoea, with its attendant weakness. In fact, in a big prison astringent medicines are served out regularly by the warders as a matter of course. In the case of a child, the child is, as a rule, incapable of eating the food at all. Any one who knows anything about children knows how easily a child's digestion is upset by a fit of crying, or trouble and mental distress of any kind. A child who has been crying all day long, and perhaps half the night, in a lonely dim-lit cell, and is preyed upon by terror, simply cannot eat food of this coarse, horrible kind. In the case of the little child to whom Warder Martin gave the biscuits, the child was crying with hunger on Tuesday morning, and utterly unable to eat the bread and water served to it for its breakfast. Martin went out after the breakfasts had been served and bought the few sweet biscuits for the child rather than see it starving. It was a beautiful action on his part, and was so recognised by the child, who, utterly unconscious of the regulations of the Prison Board, told one of the senior wardens how kind this junior warden had been to him. The result was, of course, a report and a dismissal.'

Robert Blatchford compares the workhouse pauper's daily diet with the soldier's, which, when he was a soldier, was not considered liberal enough, and yet is twice as liberal as the pauper's.

PAUPER	DIET	SOLDIER
3.25 oz.	Meat	12 oz.
15.5 oz.	Bread	24 oz.
6 oz.	Vegetables	8 oz.

The adult male pauper gets meat (outside of soup) but once a week, and the paupers 'have nearly all that pallid, pasty complexion which is the sure mark of starvation.'

Here is a table, comparing the workhouse officer's weekly allowance:-

OFFICER	DIET	PAUPER
7 lb.	Bread	6.75 lb.
5 lb.	Meat	1 lb. 2 oz.
12 oz.	Bacon	2.5 oz.
8 oz.	Cheese	2 oz.
7 lb.	Potatoes	1.5 lb.
6 lb.	Vegetables	none.
1 lb.	Flour	none.
2 oz.	Lard	none.
12 oz.	Butter	7 oz.
none.	Rice Pudding	1 lb.

And as the same writer remarks: 'The officer's diet is still more liberal than the pauper's; but evidently it is not considered liberal enough, for a footnote is added to the officer's table saying that 'a cash payment of two shillings and sixpence a week is also made to each resident officer and servant.' If the pauper has ample food, why does the officer have more? And if the officer has not too much, can the pauper be properly fed on less than half the amount?'

But it is not alone the Ghetto-dweller, the prisoner, and the pauper that starve. Hodge, of the country, does not know what it is always to have a full belly. In truth, it is his empty belly which has driven him to the city in such great numbers. Let us investigate the way of living of a labourer from a parish in the Bradfield Poor Law Union, Berks. Supposing him to have two children, steady work, a rent-free cottage, and an average weekly wage of thirteen shillings, which is equivalent to $3.25, then here is his weekly budget:-

	s.	d.
Bread (5 quarterns)	1	10
Flour (0.5 gallon)	0	4
Tea (0.25 lb.)	0	6
Butter (1 lb.)	1	3
Lard (1 lb.)	0	6
Sugar (6 lb.)	1	0
Bacon or other meat (about 0.25 lb.)	2	8
Cheese (1 lb.)	0	8
Milk (half-tin condensed)	0	3.25
Coal	1	6
Beer		none
Tobacco		none
Insurance ('Prudential')	0	3
Labourers' Union	0	1
Wood, tools, dispensary, &c.	0	6
Insurance ('Foresters') and margin	1	1.75
for clothes Total	13	0

The guardians of the workhouse in the above Union pride themselves on their rigid economy. It costs per pauper per week:-

	s.	d.
Men	6	1.5
Women	5	6.5
Children	5	1.25

If the labourer whose budget has been described should quit his toil and go into the workhouse, he would cost the guardians for

	s.	d.
Himself	6	1.5
Wife	5	6.5
Two children	10	2.5
Total	21	10.5
Or roughly,	$5.46	

It would require more than a guinea for the workhouse to care for him and his family, which he, somehow, manages to do on thirteen shillings. And in addition, it is an understood fact that it is cheaper to cater for a large number of people—buying, cooking, and serving wholesale—than it is to cater for a small number of people, say a family.

Nevertheless, at the time this budget was compiled, there was in that parish another family, not of four, but eleven persons, who had to live on an income, not of thirteen shillings, but of twelve shillings per week (eleven shillings in winter), and which had, not a rent-free cottage, but a cottage for which it paid three shillings per week.

This must be understood, and understood clearly: *Whatever is true of London in the way of poverty and degradation, is true of all England.* While Paris is not by any means France, the city of London is England. The frightful conditions which mark London an inferno likewise mark the United Kingdom an inferno. The argument that the decentralisation of London would ameliorate conditions is a vain thing and false. If the 6,000,000 people of London were separated into one hundred cities each with a population of 60,000, misery would be decentralised but not diminished. The sum of it would remain as large.

In this instance, Mr. B. S. Rowntree, by an exhaustive analysis, has proved for the country town what Mr. Charles Booth has proved for the metropolis, that fully one-fourth of the dwellers are condemned to a poverty which destroys them physically and spiritually; that fully one-fourth of the dwellers do not have enough to eat, are inadequately clothed, sheltered, and warmed in a rigorous climate, and are doomed to a moral degeneracy which puts them lower than the savage in cleanliness and decency.

After listening to the wail of an old Irish peasant in Kerry, Robert Blatchford asked him what he wanted. 'The old man leaned upon his spade and looked out across the black peat fields at the lowering skies. 'What is it that I'm wantun?' he said; then in a deep plaintive tone he continued, more to himself than to me, 'All our brave bhoys and dear gurrls is away an' over the says, an' the agent has taken the pig off me, an' the wet has spiled the praties, an' I'm an owld man, *an' I want the Day av Judgment.*'

The Day of Judgment! More than he want it. From all the land rises the hunger wail, from Ghetto and countryside, from prison and casual ward, from asylum and workhouse—the cry of the people who have not enough to eat. Millions of people, men, women, children, little babes, the blind, the deaf, the halt, the sick, vagabonds and toilers, prisoners and paupers, the people of Ireland, England, Scotland, Wales, who have not enough to eat. And this, in face of the fact that five men can produce bread for a thousand; that one workman can produce cotton cloth for 250 people, woollens for 300, and boots and shoes for 1000. It would seem that 40,000,000 people are keeping a big house, and that they are keeping it badly. The income is all right, but there is something criminally wrong with the management. And who dares to say that it is not criminally mismanaged, this big house, when five men can produce bread for a thousand, and yet millions have not enough to eat?

CHAPTER XXVI

DRINK, TEMPERANCE, AND THRIFT

Sometimes the poor are praised for being thrifty. But to recommend thrift to the poor is both grotesque and insulting. It is like advising a man who is starving to eat less. For a town or country laborer to practice thrift would be absolutely immoral. Man should not be ready to show that he can live like a badly-fed animal.

OSCAR WILDE

The English working classes may be said to be soaked in beer. They are made dull and sodden by it. Their efficiency is sadly impaired, and they lose whatever imagination, invention, and quickness may be theirs by right of race. It may hardly be called an acquired habit, for they are accustomed to it from their earliest infancy. Children are begotten in drunkenness, saturated in drink before they draw their first breath, born to the smell and taste of it, and brought up in the midst of it.

The public-house is ubiquitous. It flourishes on every corner and between corners, and it is frequented almost as much by women as by men. Children are to be found in it as well, waiting till their fathers and mothers are ready to go home, sipping from the glasses of their elders, listening to the coarse language and degrading conversation, catching the contagion of it, familiarising themselves with licentiousness and debauchery.

Mrs. Grundy rules as supremely over the workers as she does over the bourgeoisie; but in the case of the workers, the one thing she does not frown upon is the public-house. No disgrace or shame attaches to it, nor to the young woman or girl who makes a practice of entering it.

I remember a girl in a coffee-house saying, 'I never drink spirits when in a pub-lic-'ouse.' She was a young and pretty waitress, and she was laying down to another waitress her pre-eminent respectability and discretion. Mrs. Grundy drew the line at spirits, but allowed that it was quite proper for a clean young girl to drink beer, and to go into a public-house to drink it.

Not only is this beer unfit for the people to drink, but too often the men and women are unfit to drink it. On the other hand, it is their very unfitness that drives them to drink it. Ill-fed, suffering from innutrition and the evil effects of overcrowding and squalor, their constitutions develop a morbid craving for the drink, just as the sickly stomach of the overstrung Manchester factory operative hankers after excessive quantities of pickles and similar weird foods. Unhealthy working and living engenders unhealthy appetites and desires. Man cannot be worked worse than a horse is worked, and be housed and fed as a pig is housed and fed, and at the same time have clean and wholesome ideals and aspirations.

As home-life vanishes, the public-house appears. Not only do men and women abnormally crave drink, who are overworked, exhausted, suffering from deranged stomachs and bad sanitation, and deadened by the ugliness and monotony of existence, but the gregarious men and women who have no home-life flee to the bright and clattering public-house in a vain attempt to express their gregariousness. And when a family is housed in one small room, home-life is impossible.

A brief examination of such a dwelling will serve to bring to light one important cause of drunkenness. Here the family arises in the morning, dresses, and makes its toilet, father, mother, sons, and daughters, and in the same room, shoulder to shoulder (for the room is small), the wife and mother cooks the breakfast. And in the same room, heavy and sickening with the exhalations of their packed bodies throughout the night, that breakfast is eaten. The father goes to work, the elder children go to school or into the street, and the mother remains with her crawling, toddling youngsters to do her housework—still in the same room. Here she washes the clothes, filling the pent space with soapsuds and the smell of dirty clothes, and overhead she hangs the wet linen to dry.

Here, in the evening, amid the manifold smells of the day, the family goes to its virtuous couch. That is to say, as many as possible pile into the one bed (if bed they have), and the surplus turns in on the floor. And this is the round of their existence, month after month, year after year, for they never get a vacation save when they are evicted. When a child dies, and some are always bound to die, since fifty-five per cent. of the East End children die before they are five years old, the body is laid out in the same room. And if they are very poor, it is kept for some time until they can bury it. During the day it lies on the bed; during the night, when the living take the bed, the dead occupies the table, from which, in the morning, when the dead is put back into the bed, they eat their breakfast. Sometimes the body is placed on the shelf which serves as a pantry for their food. Only a couple of weeks ago, an East End woman was in trouble, because, in this fashion, being unable to bury it, she had kept her dead child three weeks.

Now such a room as I have described is not home but horror; and the men and women who flee away from it to the public-house are to be pitied, not blamed. There are 300,000 people, in London, divided into families that live in single rooms, while there are 900,000 who are illegally housed according to the Public Health Act of 1891—a respectable recruiting-ground for the drink traffic.

Then there are the insecurity of happiness, the precariousness of existence, the well-founded fear of the future—potent factors in driving people to drink. Wretchedness squirms for alleviation, and in the public-house its pain is eased and forgetfulness is obtained. It is unhealthy. Certainly it is, but everything else about their lives is unhealthy, while this brings the oblivion that nothing else in their lives can bring. It even exalts them, and makes them feel that they are finer and better, though at the same time it drags them down and makes them more beastly than ever. For the unfortunate man or woman, it is a race between miseries that ends with death.

It is of no avail to preach temperance and teetotalism to these people. The drink habit may be the cause of many miseries; but it is, in turn, the effect of other and prior miseries. The temperance advocates may preach their hearts out over the evils of drink, but until the evils that cause people to drink are abolished, drink and its evils will remain.

Until the people who try to help realise this, their well-intentioned efforts will be futile, and they will present a spectacle fit only to set Olympus laughing. I have gone through an exhibition of Japanese art, got up for the poor of Whitechapel with the idea of elevating them, of begetting in them yearnings for the Beautiful and True and Good. Granting (what is not so) that the poor folk are thus taught to know and yearn after the Beautiful and True and Good, the foul facts of their existence and the social law that dooms one in three to a public-charity death, demonstrate that this knowledge and yearning will be only so much of an added curse to them. They will have so much more to forget than if they had never known and yearned. Did Destiny to-day bind me down to the life of an East End slave for the rest of my years, and did Destiny grant me but one wish, I should ask that I might forget all about the Beautiful and True and Good; that I might forget all I had learned from the open books, and forget the people I had known, the things I had heard, and the lands I had seen. And if Destiny didn't grant it, I am pretty confident that I should get drunk and forget it as often as possible.

These people who try to help! Their college settlements, missions, charities, and what not, are failures. In the nature of things they cannot but be failures. They are wrongly, though sincerely, conceived. They approach life through a misunderstanding of life, these good folk. They do not understand the West End, yet they come down to the East End as teachers and savants. They do not understand the simple sociology of Christ, yet they come to the miserable and the despised with the pomp of social redeemers. They have worked faithfully, but beyond relieving an infinitesimal fraction of misery and collecting a certain amount of data which might otherwise have been more scientifically and less expensively collected, they have achieved nothing.

As some one has said, they do everything for the poor except get off their backs. The very money they dribble out in their child's schemes has been wrung from the poor. They come from a race of successful and predatory bipeds who stand between the worker and his wages, and they try to tell the worker what he shall do with the pitiful balance left to him. Of what use, in the name of God, is it to establish nurseries for women workers, in which, for instance, a child is taken while the mother makes violets in Islington at three farthings a gross, when more children and violet-makers than they can cope with are being born right along? This violet-maker handles each flower four times, 576 handlings for three farthings, and in the day she handles the flowers 6912 times for a wage of ninepence. She is being robbed. Somebody is on her back, and a yearning for the Beautiful and True and Good will not lighten her burden. They do nothing for her, these dabblers; and what they do not do for the mother, undoes at night, when the child comes home, all that they have done for the child in the day.

And one and all, they join in teaching a fundamental lie. They do not know it is a lie, but their ignorance does not make it more of a truth. And the lie they preach is 'thrift.' An instant will demonstrate it. In overcrowded London, the struggle for a chance to work is keen, and because of this struggle wages sink to the lowest means of subsistence. To be thrifty means for a worker to spend less than his income—in other words, to live on less. This is equivalent to a lowering of the standard of living. In the competition for a chance to work, the man with a lower standard of living will underbid the man with a higher standard. And a small group of such thrifty workers in any overcrowded industry will permanently lower the wages of that industry. And the thrifty ones will no longer be thrifty, for their income will have been reduced till it balances their expenditure.

In short, thrift negates thrift. If every worker in England should heed the preachers of thrift and cut expenditure in half, the condition of there being more men to work than there is work to do would swiftly cut wages in half. And then none of the workers of England would be thrifty, for they would be living up to their diminished incomes. The short-sighted thrift-preachers would naturally be astounded at the outcome. The measure of their failure would be precisely the measure of the success of their propaganda. And, anyway, it is sheer bosh and nonsense to preach thrift to the 1,800,000 London workers who are divided into families which have a total income of less than 21s. per week, one quarter to one half of which must be paid for rent.

Concerning the futility of the people who try to help, I wish to make one notable, noble exception, namely, the Dr. Barnardo Homes. Dr. Barnardo is a child-catcher. First, he catches them when they are young, before they are set, hardened, in the vicious social mould; and then he sends them away to grow up and be formed in another and better social mould. Up to date he has sent out of the country 13,340 boys, most of them to Canada, and not one in fifty has failed. A splendid record, when it is considered that these lads are waifs and strays, homeless and parentless, jerked out from the very bottom of the Abyss, and forty-nine out of fifty of them made into men.

Every twenty-four hours in the year Dr. Barnardo snatches nine waifs from the streets; so the enormous field he has to work in may be comprehended. The people who try to help have something to learn from him. He does not play with palliatives. He traces social viciousness and misery to their sources. He removes the progeny of the gutter-folk from their pestilential environment, and gives them a healthy, wholesome environment in which to be pressed and prodded and moulded into men.

When the people who try to help cease their playing and dabbling with day nurseries and Japanese art exhibits and go back and learn their West End and the sociology of Christ, they will be in better shape to buckle down to the work they ought to be doing in the world. And if they do buckle down to the work, they will follow Dr. Barnardo's lead, only on a scale as large as the nation is large. They won't cram yearnings for the Beautiful, and True, and Good down the throat of the woman making violets for three farthings a gross, but they will make somebody get off her back and quit cramming himself till, like the Romans, he must go to a bath and sweat it out. And to their consternation, they will find that they will have to get off that woman's back themselves, as well as the backs of a few other women and children they did not dream they were riding upon.

CHAPTER XXVII
THE MANAGEMENT

*Seven men working sixteen hours could produce food by best improved
machinery to support one thousand men.*

EDWARD ATKINSON

In this final chapter it were well to look at the Social Abyss in its widest aspect, and
to put certain questions to Civilisation, by the answers to which Civilisation must
stand or fall. For instance, has Civilisation bettered the lot of man? 'Man,' I use in
its democratic sense, meaning the average man. So the question re-shapes itself: *Has
Civilisation bettered the lot of the average man?*

Let us see. In Alaska, along the banks of the Yukon River, near its mouth, live
the Innuit folk. They are a very primitive people, manifesting but mere glimmering
adumbrations of that tremendous artifice, Civilisation. Their capital amounts possibly
to £2 per head. They hunt and fish for their food with bone-headed spews and arrows.
They never suffer from lack of shelter. Their clothes, largely made from the skins
of animals, are warm. They always have fuel for their fires, likewise timber for their
houses, which they build partly underground, and in which they lie snugly during the
periods of intense cold. In the summer they live in tents, open to every breeze and
cool. They are healthy, and strong, and happy. Their one problem is food. They have
their times of plenty and times of famine. In good times they feast; in bad times they
die of starvation. But starvation, as a chronic condition, present with a large number
of them all the time, is a thing unknown. Further, they have no debts.

In the United Kingdom, on the rim of the Western Ocean, live the English folk.
They are a consummately civilised people. Their capital amounts to at least £300 per
head. They gain their food, not by hunting and fishing, but by toil at colossal artifices.
For the most part, they suffer from lack of shelter. The greater number of them are
vilely housed, do not have enough fuel to keep them warm, and are insufficiently
clothed. A constant number never have any houses at all, and sleep shelterless under
the stars. Many are to be found, winter and summer, shivering on the streets in their
rags. They have good times and bad. In good times most of them manage to get
enough to eat, in bad times they die of starvation. They are dying now, they were
dying yesterday and last year, they will die to-morrow and next year, of starvation;
for they, unlike the Innuit, suffer from a chronic condition of starvation. There are
40,000,000 of the English folk, and 939 out of every 1000 of them die in poverty, while
a constant army of 8,000,000 struggles on the ragged edge of starvation. Further, each
babe that is born, is born in debt to the sum of £22. This is because of an artifice
called the National Debt.

In a fair comparison of the average Innuit and the average Englishman, it will be
seen that life is less rigorous for the Innuit; that while the Innuit suffers only during
bad times from starvation, the Englishman suffers during good times as well; that no
Innuit lacks fuel, clothing, or housing, while the Englishman is in perpetual lack of
these three essentials. In this connection it is well to instance the judgment of a man
such as Huxley. From the knowledge gained as a medical officer in the East End of
London, and as a scientist pursuing investigations among the most elemental savages,

he concludes, 'Were the alternative presented to me, I would deliberately prefer the life of the savage to that of those people of Christian London.'

The creature comforts man enjoys are the products of man's labour. Since Civilisation has failed to give the average Englishman food and shelter equal to that enjoyed by the Innuit, the question arises: *Has Civilisation increased the producing power of the average man?* If it has not increased man's producing power, then Civilisation cannot stand.

But, it will be instantly admitted, Civilisation has increased man's producing power. Five men can produce bread for a thousand. One man can produce cotton cloth for 250 people, woollens for 300, and boots and shoes for 1000. Yet it has been shown throughout the pages of this book that English folk by the millions do not receive enough food, clothes, and boots. Then arises the third and inexorable question: *If Civilisation has increased the producing power of the average man, why has it not bettered the lot of the average man?*

There can be one answer only—MISMANAGEMENT. Civilisation has made possible all manner of creature comforts and heart's delights. In these the average Englishman does not participate. If he shall be forever unable to participate, then Civilisation falls. There is no reason for the continued existence of an artifice so avowed a failure. But it is impossible that men should have reared this tremendous artifice in vain. It stuns the intellect. To acknowledge so crushing a defeat is to give the death-blow to striving and progress.

One other alternative, and one other only, presents itself. *Civilisation must be compelled to better the lot of the average men.* This accepted, it becomes at once a question of business management. Things profitable must be continued; things unprofitable must be eliminated. Either the Empire is a profit to England, or it is a loss. If it is a loss, it must be done away with. If it is a profit, it must be managed so that the average man comes in for a share of the profit.

If the struggle for commercial supremacy is profitable, continue it. If it is not, if it hurts the worker and makes his lot worse than the lot of a savage, then fling foreign markets and industrial empire overboard. For it is a patent fact that if 40,000,000 people, aided by Civilisation, possess a greater individual producing power than the Innuit, then those 40,000,000 people should enjoy more creature comforts and heart's delights than the Innuits enjoy.

If the 400,000 English gentlemen, 'of no occupation,' according to their own statement in the Census of 1881, are unprofitable, do away with them. Set them to work ploughing game preserves and planting potatoes. If they are profitable, continue them by all means, but let it be seen to that the average Englishman shares somewhat in the profits they produce by working at no occupation.

In short, society must be reorganised, and a capable management put at the head. That the present management is incapable, there can be no discussion. It has drained the United Kingdom of its life-blood. It has enfeebled the stay-at-home folk till they are unable longer to struggle in the van of the competing nations. It has built up a West End and an East End as large as the Kingdom is large, in which one end is riotous and rotten, the other end sickly and underfed.

A vast empire is foundering on the hands of this incapable management. And by empire is meant the political machinery which holds together the English-speaking people of the world outside of the United States. Nor is this charged in a pessimistic spirit. Blood empire is greater than political empire, and the English of the New World and the Antipodes are strong and vigorous as ever. But the political empire under which they are nominally assembled is perishing. The political machine known as the British Empire is running down. In the hands of its management it is losing momentum every day.

It is inevitable that this management, which has grossly and criminally mismanaged, shall be swept away. Not only has it been wasteful and inefficient, but it has misappropriated the funds. Every worn-out, pasty-faced pauper, every blind man, every prison babe, every man, woman, and child whose belly is gnawing with hunger pangs, is hungry because the funds have been misappropriated by the management.

Nor can one member of this managing class plead not guilty before the judgment bar of Man. 'The living in their houses, and in their graves the dead,' are challenged by every babe that dies of innutrition, by every girl that flees the sweater's den to the nightly promenade of Piccadilly, by every worked-out toiler that plunges into the canal. The food this managing class eats, the wine it drinks, the shows it makes, and the fine clothes it wears, are challenged by eight million mouths which have never had enough to fill them, and by twice eight million bodies which have never been sufficiently clothed and housed.

There can be no mistake. Civilisation has increased man's producing power an hundred-fold, and through mismanagement the men of Civilisation live worse than the beasts, and have less to eat and wear and protect them from the elements than the savage Innuit in a frigid climate who lives to-day as he lived in the stone age ten thousand years ago.